PRAISE FOR *THE SUN SWORD* SERIES:

THE RIVEN SHIELD:
"Far superior work . . . The saga doesn't end with this one either, and it appears that great armies will have to resolve matters in the old-fashioned way. Intricately plotted, featuring several skillfully developed characters, this is one of the longest and best fantasies of the year." —*SF Chronicle*

THE SHINING COURT:
"The climactic fireworks are spectacular, and the revelations enticing . . . a fantastic finale." —*Locus*

THE UNCROWNED KING:
"A fine example of epic fantasy, showing the development of intense characters in a setting rich in conflict and intrigue."—*SF Site*

THE BROKEN CROWN:
". . . this compelling tale builds up a tremendous momentum that will keep you reading far into the night." —*Romantic Times*

"As expected from a writer of Michelle West's talent and depth . . . complex characters and an even more complex plot. Alliances and plots amongst the noble families of Tor Leonne and Averalaan Aramarelas keep the reader thoroughly engrossed . . . this is going to be another great series, one well worth the wait between books." —*SF Site*

THE SUN SWORD

The Sun Sword: Book Six

Michelle West

DAW BOOKS, INC.

DONALD A. WOLLHEIM, FOUNDER
375 Hudson Street, New York, NY 10014

ELIZABETH R. WOLLHEIM
SHEILA E. GILBERT
PUBLISHERS
http://www.dawbooks.com

First Printing, January 2004
9 8 7 6 5 4 3 2 1

This is for John Rose.

He owned Bakka for twenty years, and saw it through all kinds of difficulties without losing his particular brand of humor and his unflagging patience—much of which was tested during the writing of the many books that comprise this, or any of my other, series.

I miss the quiet of the back room, in which much of my early work was done.

Thank you for everything. Except maybe the caricatures.

ACKNOWLEDGMENTS

This series is some 7800 manuscript pages in length, and of necessity, it required an enormous amount of patience on the part of many people, some whose names I don't even know. The production department is probably owed a debt of gratitude that words alone couldn't pay—but words are what I have. Thanks.

Jody Lee painted wonderful covers for my novels, capturing some essential part of their mood and tone, for which I'm eternally grateful.

Debra Euler saw me through a number of bumps and roadblocks with unfailing, but ever pragmatic, patience—I'm sure she'd say she's not a saint, but the facts pretty much speak for themselves. Betsy Wollheim, whose responsibility I'm not, was also very encouraging when I was at a particularly stressful point.

My parents, as always, did double duty, giving me time to sleep and write; my husband and my children were about as patient as one could expect, and John and Kristen smoothed out the edges of impatience when I was mentally absent from the fray, as did my brother Gary and his wife Ayami; my sister Kelly, I'm certain, made sure that the book was available on the West Coast. The entire West Coast.

My memory is not what it should be; I'm certain that I'm forgetting to thank people who deserve a great deal of thanks. Chris Szego was particularly patient when working with me at the store. Terry Pearson kept me amused when my spirits were flagging, and the denizens of the Michelle West Yahoo group, Lisa Campos chief among them, provided encouragement and obvious interest in a similar situation.

And Sheila Gilbert saw this through from beginning to end, with an unflagging faith in my sense of the story's imperative; she allowed me room to expand—and offered advice when I was uncertain. She saw the series go from two books to six without blinking an eye. She has always shown a remarkable faith in my writing, the more so because she sees the book through all of its many stages, and these books would not have been possible without her.

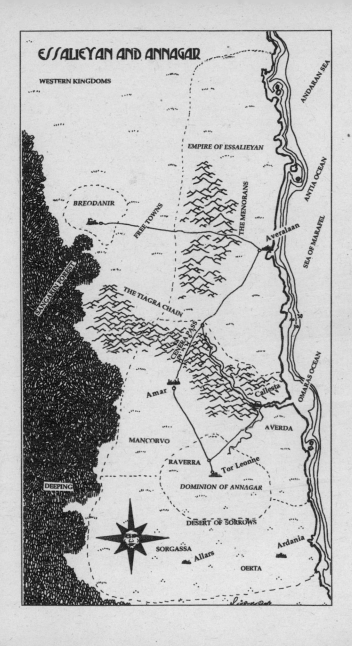

Annagarian Ranks

Tyr'agar	Ruler of the Dominion
Tyr'agnate	Ruler of one of the five Terreans of the Dominion
Tyr	The *Tyr'agar* or one of the four *Tyr'agnate*
Tyran	Personal bodyguard (oathguard) of a *Tyr*
Tor'agar	A noble in service to a *Tyr*
Tor'agnate	A noble in service to a *Tor'agar;* least of noble ranks
Tor	A *Tor'agar* or *Tor'agnate*
Toran	Personal bodyguard (oathguard) of a *Tor*
Ser	A clansman
Serra	The primary wife and legitimate daughters of a clansman
kai	The holder or first in line to the clan title
par	The brother of the first in line; the direct son of the title holder

Dramatis Personae

ESSALIEYAN

AVANTARI (The Palace)

The Royals
King Reymalyn: The Justice-born King
King Cormalyn: The Wisdom-born King
Princess Mirialyn ACormaris: Daughter of Queen Marieyan & King Cormalyn

The Astari
Duvari: The Lord of the Compact; leader of the Astari, the protectors of the Kings
Devon ATerafin: Member of the Astari and of House Terafin
Gregori ATerafin: The second of the Astari to take the Terafin oath

The Hostages
Serra Marlena en'Leonne: Valedan's mother; born a slave but granted honorific "Serra" because her son has been recognized and claimed as legitimate
Ser Kyro di'Lorenza (Sorgassa): The oldest of the hostages

Imperial Army
The Eagle: **Commander Bruce Allen**—commands the First army
Verrus Simonson: Commander Allen's adjutant
The Hawk: **Commander Berriliya**—commands the Second army; leads House Berriliya
Verrus Sedgewick: Commander Berriliya's adjutant
The Kestrel: **Commander Kalakar**—commands the Third army and the Ospreys; leads House Kalakar
Verrus Korama: Commander Kalakar's adjutant

THE TEN

KALAKAR
Ellora: The Kalakar
Verrus Korama: Her closest friend and adjutant
Verrus Vernon Loris: Friend and counselor

The Ospreys
Primus Duarte: Leader
Alexis: (Sentrus or Decarus)
Auralis: (Sentrus or Decarus)
Fiara: (Sentrus)
Cook: (Sentrus)
Sanderton: (Decarus)
Kiriel di'Ashaf

BERRILIYA
Devran: The Berriliya

TERAFIN
Amarais Handernesse ATerafin: The Terafin
Morretz: her domicis
Jewel Markess ATerafin: Part of her House Council; also seer-born; her den are:
> *Finch*: Member in full standing of the House Council
> *Teller*: Member in full standing of the House Council
> *Angel*: He is not ATerafin but is a House Guard
> *Carver*: Part of the Terafin House Guards
> *Arann*: Member of the Chosen
> *Jester*: Adjutant to Finch and Teller upon the Council
> *Daine*: Healer-born
> *Adam of Arkosa*: Healer-born
> *Ellerson*: Serves the den as domicis
Avandar Gallais: Also known as Viandaran, or the Warlord; he is Jewel's domicis
The Winter King: Great stag, taken from the Stone Deepings
Lord Celleriant of the Green Deepings: Compelled by Arianne to serve Jewel for his failure, he is Arianni
Ariel: Young child given Jewel by Lord Isladar for her protection
Rymark ATerafin: Member of the House Council
Gabriel ATerafin: Right-kin to Amarais; father of Rymark
Haerrad ATerafin: Member of the House Council

Elonne ATerafin: Member of the House Council

Marrick Tremblant ATerafin: Member of the House Council

Torvan ATerafin: Captain of the Chosen

Arrendas ATerafin: Captain of the Chosen

Gregori ATerafin: House Guard, specifically serving the den; also Astari

Devon ATerafin: Serves the Astari, as well as the House

Lucille ATerafin: Serves Terafin in the Merchant Authority

Merry ATerafin: Carver's girlfriend, and a maid in the House

Alowan Rowanson: Not formally a member of Terafin, he nonetheless serves in the healerie at The Terafin's command

Lila ATerafin: The youngest of his assistants; a girl, new to the House

Fiona ATerafin: An older woman, married with two children, who also serves in the healerie

THE HOUSES OF HEALING
Levec: Master of the House of Healing upon the Isle

THE GOD-BORN
Micah: Young man, Judgment-born; aids Allister APorphan in his investigations

THE ORDER OF KNOWLEDGE
Meralonne APhaniel: Member of the Council of the Magi; First Circle magi

Sigurne Mellifas: Member of the Council of the Magi; First Circle magi

Gyrrick: One of Meralonne's warrior magi; seconded by the army

Allister APorphan: Magi who serves the Magisterium in murder investigations

Member Gervano: Investigative branch of the Magi

Member Timman: Investigative branch of the Magi

Member Tipurne: One of the few women to serve Meralonne upon the field, her specialty is illusion

SENNIEL COLLEGE
Solran Marten: Bardmaster of Senniel College

Sioban Glassen: Former bardmaster of Senniel College

Kallandras: Master bard of Senniel College

ANNAGAR

THE CLANS

LEONNE: Ruling clan of the Dominion of Annagar
Ser Valedan kai di'Leonne (Raverra) : The heir to the Dominion
Markaso kai di'Leonne: The assassinated Tyr'agar, Valedan's father
Serra Diora en'Leonne: Also Serra Diora di'Marano

Serra Diora's harem wives
Faida en'Leonne: Oathwife to Diora; dead
Ruatha en'Leonne: Oathwife to Diora; dead
Dierdre en'Leonne: Oathwife to Diora; dead
Serra Selena: Oldest of Ser Illara's wives; dead
Teyla en'Leonne

In Service to Leonne
Ser Baredan di'Navarre: Former General of the Third army, under Valedan's father
Ser Halvero: Served under Baredan in the Third army, and serves him still
Ser Anton di'Guivera: Foremost swordmaster of the Dominion; twice winner of the Kings' Crown
Ser Andaro di'Corsarro: Tyran; the only Tyran who serves Valedan kai di'Leonne
Ser Laonis di'Caveras: Healer-born; he has left his home in the North to travel with Valedan
Aidan a'Cooper: Standard-bearer or mascot; a young boy
The Ospreys

In Service to the Kings' Army
Merilee of the Mother: God-born, but hiding it, she is in charge of the field infirmary
Frederik: From the Houses of Healing on the Isle, he serves under Merilee
Edmond: From the Houses of Healing, younger; he serves under Merilee

CALLESTA: Ruling clan of the Terrean of Averda
Ser Ramiro kai di'Callesta: The Tyr
Serra Amara en'Callesta: Wife to the Tyr
Eliana en'Callesta: Concubine to the Tyr

Aliane en'Callesta: Concubine to the Tyr

Maria en'Callesta: Concubine to the Tyr

Sara en'Callesta: Concubine to the Tyr

Deana en'Callesta: Concubine to the Tyr

Ser Fillipo par di'Callesta: Brother to the Tyr'agnate of Averda, Captain of his Tyran

Ser Carelo kai di'Callesta: The heir to Callesta, Ramiro's oldest son; dead

Ser Alfredo par di'Callesta: Youngest son of Ramiro, and now his heir

Ser Karro di Callesta: Tyran; half brother (concubine's son); the oldest of the Tyran

Ser Miko di'Callesta: Tyran; half brother (concubine's son)

Valente

Ser Danello kai di'Valente: Ashaf's lord and a son of the harem in which she resided

Ser Daro di'Valente: Village overseer in Russo during Ashaf's time and after

Serra Nora en'Valente: Ser Daro's wife

Valla kep'Valente: Ashaf's friend

Arrego kep'Valente: Valla's husband

GARRARDI: Ruling clan of the Terrean of Oerta

Eduardo kai di'Garrardi: The Tyr'agnate of the Terrean of Oerta

LAMBERTO: Ruling clan of the Terrean of Mancorvo

Ser Mareo kai di'Lamberto: The Tyr'agnate of Mancorvo

Ser Fredero par di'Lamberto: Younger brother to the Tyr'agnate; left the clan in order to become the kai el'Sol, the leader of the Radann

Serra Alina di'Lamberto: Once given as hostage to the Imperial Court in Essalieyan, she now advises *Ser Valedan kai di'Leonne*, and travels with his forces

Serra Donna en'Lamberto: Mareo's Serra

Ser Galen kai di'Lamberto: The kai (former par)

Ser Andreas kai di'Lamberto: The dead kai

Marano

Ser Adano kai di'Marano: Tor'agar to Mareo kai di'Lamberto

Ser Sendari par di'Marano: His brother; Widan; also called Ser Sendari di'Sendari, the founding name of a new clan

Serra Fiona en'Marano: Sendari's wife
Ser Artano: Sendari's oldest son
Serra Diora di'Marano: Sendari's only child by his first wife
Serra Teresa di'Marano: Sister to Adano and Sendari; companion to Yollana of the Havalla Voyani, aunt to the Serra Diora

Clemente
Ser Alessandro kai di'Clemente: The Tor'agar; his Tyr is Ser Mareo

LORENZA: Ruling clan of the Terrean of Sorgassa
Ser Jarrani kai di'Lorenza: The Tyr'agnate of Sorgassa
Ser Hectore kai di'Lorenza: The kai, heir to Sorgassa
Ser Alef par di'Lorenza: Hectore's younger brother
Serra Maria en'Lorenza: Ser Hectore's wife

THE SWORD OF KNOWLEDGE
Ser Cortano di'Alexes: The Sword's Edge; the ruler of the Widan
Ser Sendari di'Marano: Widan; Alesso di'Marente's closest adviser and friend
Ser Mikalis di'Arretta: Widan

THE RADANN
Radann Fredero kai el'Sol: The former leader of the Radann; died in the Lake of the Tor Leonne, drawing the Sun Sword
Jevri el'Sol: His loyal servitor; he also serves Lamberto after the death of the kai el'Sol
Radann Peder kai el'Sol: The man who now leads the Radann
Radann Samiel par el'Sol: Youngest of the Hand of God
Radann Marakas par el'Sol: Contemporary of Fredero; healer-born
Radann Samadar par el'Sol: Oldest of the Hand of God

THE VOYANI

Arkosa
Evallen of the Arkosa Voyani: The former Matriarch
Margret of the Arkosa Voyani: The current Matriarch
Elena Tamaraan: Margret's heir, Daughter to Arkosa

Havalla
Yollana of the Havalla Voyani: Ruler of the Havallans

Nadia: Her oldest daughter, and Daughter to the Havallans
Varya: Her younger daughter

THE SHINING COURT

The Lord of the Shining Court: *Allasakar*

THE LORD'S FIST
Lord Assarak
Lord Alcrax
Lord Ishavriel
Lord Etridian
Lord Nugratz

THE COURT
The Kialli:
Lord Isladar
Lord Telakar
Anduvin the Smith: Forged the sword that Kiriel now wields

The Humans:
Anya a'Cooper: Powerful mage, serves Ishavriel—sometimes;
she's not sane

CHAPTER ONE

24th of Corvil, 427 AA
Terafin Manse, Averalaan Aramarelas

THE Terafin was ill.

In the quiet rise of sweeping halls, beneath the two-story height that gave even the most jaded of visitors pause, servants toiled in silence, spreading rumors behind the backs of carefully positioned hands.

In a manse such as House Terafin upon the Isle, those servants were as educated in their way as new merchants—but they were expected to be a great deal more publicly restrained. The Mistress of the Household staff had been forced to remind them of decorum on more than one occasion, and her perfect demeanor was beginning to fray.

Still, rumor traveled between the boys and girls that ran from the great, open halls to the hidden, secret ones, exchanging the width and breadth of wealth and power for the cramped turns and small windows of narrow stoneways in which servants were meant to move, unseen and unrecognized.

In those stone halls, words were louder, and whispers could easily be heard at a remove. But in those stone halls, none of the ATerafin proper journeyed, save those who had earned their name by literal service to the manse itself. They were not few in number.

And they were worried.

The boys and the girls, as they were often called, did their best both to avoid that worry and to mine it; they were curious, and if that curiosity was a morbid one, it was still theirs.

They were too young to have lived through the last House War. But not too young to need to make a living; not too young to understand that a House War—if there was one—would leave many of the powerful and notable dead.

"Merry, why don't you ask Carver if it's true?" one such girl said to another, her hair peeking between the fringes of the starched cap they all wore.

Merry blushed, looking decidedly unsuited to her name. "What makes you think he'd tell me?"

The girl laughed. "He tells you other things," she said with a broad wink. "And I know he's come down to the servants' hall at all hours when you're off duty."

"Well, he shouldn't be here. Not now. He's adviser to a member of the *House Council*." She spoke in a quiet voice that was one part awkward pride and two parts fear. Because he was important now, and important people didn't come here.

"He's always done as he pleases," her companion shot back. "And he's not here for the scenery. Well, not *this* scenery anyway. I don't think The Terafin herself could stop him; Jewel ATerafin couldn't even do that."

Merry looked down at her hands; they'd balled into fists. She wasn't a plain girl, but she wasn't a raving beauty; she had very few illusions. But like many people who had few, she held dear the ones that she did have. Lila touched her arm gently. "Don't you worry," she said, relenting a little. "He's not much one for fancy ladies."

"I don't want to get him in trouble." It was both true and untrue. A little more of her fear showed, changing the round and generous lines of her face. She pushed strands of dark hair up and into her cap, turning to look over her shoulder. The grand and expensive clocks that needed so much care and cleaning weren't wasted on the servants; time was a matter of instinct, and hers, here, was drawing to a close.

"It's not like he cares about trouble," Lila added, and this time she frowned at the other two girls. "He's going to keep coming here. He's more at home in these halls than he is in the grand ones."

"He should," Merry said at last. "He should care."

"Just ask him, 'kay? We're all dying to know!" the youngest of the girls said, dipping her face forward until her nose was almost touching Merry's.

One of the boys slid between them in the narrow hall; Merry shrieked as he pinched her backside. He laughed; they all did.

And if it was nervous laughter, they were giddy enough not to recognize it.

Finch ATerafin stared at hands that were shaking with exhaustion; they lay against the kitchen table, pale palms hidden from the sun's light. She had thrown the windows wide to let in the sea air; a faint tang of salt dusted lips that were a little too dry.

Morretz had taken the seat opposite her, and it creaked with the full force of his weight. His sleeves spread across the table like her hands, but they were turned out like flightless wings. Gone was the grace and effortless elegance that marked him; he was exhausted.

No, he was more than exhausted, but he had always been such a private, such a distant, man that his expression denied her any open display of concern.

And concern was there. He looked older.

"When did this happen?" Finch asked at last.

He looked up.

Before he could answer—if he intended to—the door slid open with a creak. Ellerson rose in an instant, moving with careful grace to catch the handle before it flew wide.

Teller slipped into the room as Ellerson closed the door. His eyes were dark, and beneath them, pale as bruises, the semicircles that told of sleep's lack. He glanced at Morretz and then took a seat beside Finch. They huddled at one end of the table as if they were still children.

Ellerson cleared his throat, reminding them tactfully that they were not, in fact, any such thing.

Council members, Finch thought bitterly, did *not* huddle. She drew herself up to her full height.

But she didn't let go of Teller's hand.

"Three days ago," Morretz said quietly. "She was . . . difficult to wake. Pale. Her pupils were distended."

"Poison?"

Morretz smiled wearily. "If it were poison," he said quietly, "we would know. She would not now be confined to her quarters. Understand, ATerafin, that she is *not* ill to the rest of the House."

Finch decided, wisely, to let that one pass. She had heard rumors, of course; Carver brought them. But she'd listened carefully to these, because they were shorn of his usual cocky glee. She didn't want to get the serving girls in trouble, and she also didn't want to destroy one of the best sources of information the den had. "What does the rest of the House think?" she asked, buying time.

"They believe she has retreated to her library to better study the intricacies of sea law."

"Sea law?"

Teller heaved a sigh that was altogether too much of a criticism. "Finch, have you been sleeping?"

"Not much," she shot back, and then, looking at his face, added meekly, "but probably more than you have. You look awful."

His annoyance lapsed into a sheepish little smile. "Sorry. You've been studying the Menoran trade. *I've* been studying the sea trade.

We do some business with the South via the Omaran, and there are—apparently—whole islands in the oceans to the east that have actual cities on them. We take things from the Empire and they give us . . . stuff."

Ellerson cleared his throat again.

"Pearls," Teller said grudgingly. "And herbs of some sort. Birds. Really odd things. Not many of our ships go there; there's apparently some difficulty if you land on the wrong beach."

Finch frowned. "What kind of difficulty?"

"Losing whole ships without any explanation kind of difficulty." He shrugged. "We're not the only House to send expeditions to the East. We're one of three that have been successful. Where successful means someone has come back."

Something about the sentence jogged her sluggish memory. "Weren't there some sort of piracy accusations leveled against the House?"

He nodded grimly. "We're still not sure what that's all about. But we've certainly had our difficulties. If it were up to me—"

Morretz raised a hand; light played quirkily along the closed line of his lips, lending his expression the patina of a smile.

"Uh, right. Sorry, Morretz." He exhaled. "Besides the accusations—House Fennesar, I think, but it also involved Morriset—there have been really strange weather patterns fifty miles from the sea wall. Maybe a hundred."

"Odd?"

"Storms, unseasonal storms. One of the Darias merchants said his ship—and it's one of the great merchant boats that shouldn't even be able to float by all accounts—was *beached* eight miles from our port."

"Beached?"

He nodded.

"I don't understand."

"No one does. But he claims to have hit a sandbar. A great, wide, sandbar."

"But . . ."

"Yes," Teller said. "It's in the middle of the ocean. There's nothing there. No reefs, no *nothing*. Well, except for sand."

She frowned.

"And that's another thing: There were no dolphins. No whales. Almost no fish. Just the sand." He shrugged. "It's gone now. It lasted long enough to get the Magi there and back, so we know the captain wasn't heavily into his cups."

Morretz nodded. "There is some lively argument in the Council of The Ten in *Avantari*; it appears that the cost of the magi's efforts, in this case, is not one that the Council wishes to underwrite."

Finch snorted. "Is there *any* situation in which The Ten won't chip away at Terafin?"

Ellerson raised a white brow.

"I guess not."

"Terafin has long enjoyed the position of first among the Houses," the domicis said stiffly. "And if the Kings are not subject to the whims of ambition and greed, the same cannot be said of those that rise to rule The Ten. Not even The Terafin herself is above using such ruses in order to maintain the prominence of her House."

"Indeed," Morretz added, unruffled by the rough manners of the two youngest members of the House Council. "And it is therefore entirely believable that she be unavailable at this time."

"Has Alowan been to see her?"

A bronze brow rose. Finch flushed. "Sorry," she muttered.

"He has been three times, Finch. It is difficult; to bring him to the library without the notice of the rest of the House requires much subtlety and the use of magic."

Yours, she thought, but didn't say it.

"And he hasn't healed her?"

"Yes," Morretz said quietly. "He *has*. Each of the three days. But he deals, he says, with the physical damage caused."

"And the disease?"

"There is no disease."

Silence again, uncomfortable now. Sharp.

"Ellerson," Finch said, without looking up. "Go and get Daine."

Ellerson bowed. "ATerafin," he said quietly. She listened as he left her. But he left her in Morretz' care, and Morretz was a man she trusted almost as much.

"How can there be *no* disease if she's ill?"

"We don't know."

"But you ruled out poison. And anyway Alowan would know poison."

"Over a hundred of them," Morretz agreed genially. His eyes were black. She wondered at that; they were normally a much paler color.

Is this it? she thought, and something tight pinched her stomach. *Is this how she dies? Is this how she deserts us?* And she hated herself for the pettiness, the fear, of that thought.

"Is it magic?" she asked quietly.

"You must ask Sigurne Mellifas that question," he said quietly.

"But you—"

"I am trained, and I have some small gift, but magic was not my calling. It was simply my talent." The words were bitter. She heard the "if only" in them, and she reached out across the table to touch his hand.

He did not withdraw.

Teller said, "There is a plague that has taken hold of some ten of the hundred holdings."

Morretz nodded.

"Is it—is it like this?"

"We are waiting upon that information now." Calm reply. Finch didn't ask who "we" was.

Instead she rose, almost blindly. Fear was thickening her tongue. "I'll go," she told him quietly.

Morretz raised a brow. "Go?"

"Out," she said, waving a hand toward the open window. "I have . . . duties in the Common."

"You have duties at the Merchant Authority?"

She nodded grimly. "A desk's worth of duties, and about ten pounds' worth of red and blue wax. I'll go."

He nodded. "Thank you, ATerafin." He knew, as well as she, that the visit to the Merchant Authority would hide many a destination. All roads in Averalaan, even those that led from the Isle, met in the Common.

It took some time to get ready. In the old days—pre-House Council—it had taken scant minutes, and most of those hovering in indecision about whether or not to take an umbrella or a hat. But as a member of the House Council, Finch was entitled to an escort. And when Ellerson used the word entitled in that particular tone of voice, it robbed the word of any sense of volition.

Today, however, it suited her just fine.

"Teller?"

"I'll stay," he told her quietly. "I have a meeting with The Terafin."

She didn't ask him how that had been arranged; she'd left the kitchen before Morretz had, and she could guess.

"Won't that raise a few brows?"

"More than a few. Do you care?"

"Yes," she said, but not convincingly. It was hard to care about a misstep when The Terafin was in trouble. And it was trouble: they both knew it. Morretz would have said nothing, otherwise.

Daine flew into the hall, and stopped, skidding across the carpet. Months in House Terafin had added weight and heft to the line of his shoulders, and it surprised her to realize that he was not a small man.

"It's okay," she said, lifting both hands, palms out, before his face. "Everyone's okay. No one's hurt."

He drew breath. Rather a lot of them, actually. His eyes were narrowed with accusation; no one liked to worry.

"I'm sorry," she added quietly, "but I want your company."

"My company?" He frowned. His eyes, she thought, had been touched by the same shadows that clung to Teller's. Was no one in this House getting sleep?

"Is the healerie that bad?" she asked him softly.

He forced his muscles to prop up his smile. All in all, it was about as convincing as a merchant's first offering price.

"Never mind," she told him. Not even she could stand to look at something so patently false. "We're going to the Merchant Authority."

"Us?"

"We're taking a guard."

"Three guards," Angel said.

She snorted. "Three, then. I still don't count the two of you as House Guards. Do you think that *either* of you could stop the nocturnal visits to the kitchen maids?"

His smile was sharp and pleasant, as genuine a smile as she'd seen all day. She almost forgave him his indiscretion right there.

"I can't," Carver said, peering around. "Merry will have my, uh, head." His smile was broader than Angel's. His hair had flopped back into its careless position over one eye; only when he was on official House Council watch was it pulled back, and she was certain that the first thing he did when he came off that particular shift was to douse it with water and soap until it became the usual unruly black she so loved.

"If Merry hasn't killed you yet, she's probably not about to start any time soon. Have you ever thought about just *marrying* her?"

His one exposed brow disappeared up his hair line.

"Never mind. Don't even try to answer." She glanced at the fall of sunlight in the only window the den's hall boasted; it was too slender to grant easy access to thieves. As if thieves were something she had to fear, here.

"We waiting for Arann?"

"No," she said quietly.

"Then who?"

"Gregori."

Carver and Angel glanced at each other, and the joviality of their exploits fell away from their faces. Gregori wasn't one of them. He was Devon's gift: a member of the Astari, a man who served the Kings. But he had been given the House name, as Devon had; he balanced on the edge of the same loyalties.

Gregori ATerafin knew how to make an entrance; she often wondered if he listened for the sound of his name before he walked into a room. If he did, he took pains to conceal the eavesdropping.

He bowed to Finch. "ATerafin."

"ATerafin," she replied, struggling for formality. It wasn't as much of a struggle as it had been when he'd first arrived. Proof that a person could get used to *anything*. Even living in the manse. Perhaps especially that. "You are to form part of my escort; I have business at the Merchant Authority that will not wait."

He brought his fist to his chest in a sharp salute, and after a moment, Angel and Carver did the same. She wished they hadn't; the difference between the nature of their gestures was the difference between a puddle and the ocean.

"Ellerson," she said quietly, "we'll return when we've concluded our business."

"Will you take late dinner, then?"

She nodded, twisting the heavy gold ring that bound her finger.

Averalaan Aramarelas had become her home. She had never expected it to happen, even when she had been given the House name. The buildings and the gates that girded the manse were so fine, so sparse, and so damn *clean*, it had taken her years to get used to their forbidding appearance. They had a character that the cramped tenements of the twenty-fifth holding could never even aspire to; they spoke of money, of power, of the certainty of both.

And the streets were wide enough that it had taken some time to become accustomed to the feeling of exposure they gave her; no four-story shadows here, no garbage, no beggars hiding their crippled limbs—or worse, their whole ones—beneath tattered cloth and blankets. No drunks, no would-be bards singing off-key and playing battered instruments, no merchants on the side roads, avoiding the taxes that came with respectability.

And no thieves, no obvious ones at least, dogging their every step. Most of the thieves of her acquaintance couldn't afford the tolls across the bridges that led to the Isle.

She stopped, examining the bridge from the wrong side. Or rather, from the right one.

"ATerafin?" Gregori said sharply.

Started again. "Sorry," she murmured. "Sometimes it's hard to remember where I am."

His dark brow rose, but he did not speak. Which was just as well. Since Devon had introduced them, she had called upon his services for every meeting of import in the House, and those were without number: Elonne invited her for dinner—early dinner—at least twice a week; she lunched with Rymark on Selday; she took drinks—carefully—with Haerrad; she visited Marrick at whatever time she could.

The last was a bit of a danger. He was charming in a way that appealed to Finch, and she struggled to remember that he was a threat every time she crossed his threshold. Had to struggle; he was so friendly, his speech so common, that she could almost treat him as an equal.

And he wasn't; he was far and above her. He had been born to Tremblant, a noble House that was just shy of The Ten in wealth, and although he had disavowed his kin—as all members of Terafin must who chose to take her name—he met with them frequently. The only glance he might have given her, had he met her in any other circumstance, would have been one of justifiably cold suspicion.

She shook her head to clear it.

"Come on," she said quietly.

The guards along the bridge were Kings' men. They bore the rod and the swords across a gray background, and they numbered four. Although their shifts were long, they somehow managed to avoid the look of boredom she was certain made up the whole of their day. She did not pay them their toll; she lifted the signet ring and they nodded her through, pausing a moment to note the number of her party. Terafin would receive a bill for it sometime, and someone else would have the trouble of accounting for it.

The bridge itself was wide, and like the Isle, clean and empty. She paused a moment, steadying herself upon stone rails. The wind blew sea salt across her lips, her cheeks, her hair; she felt its sting and smiled. The sun was high; the day itself was bright. She took a deep, deep breath, held it, and then shook herself.

Gregori ATerafin said nothing; Carver pretended to snore. She really *really* had to do something about him, one of these days.

But not this one; she kicked him as she passed by and he laughed. The guards on the other side of the bridge bowed as she lifted her ring again. One of them smiled broadly; she recognized his face because he'd held his post for years. She'd never asked his name, although she knew the name of his wife and his four children. She would have asked after them on another day, and his smile dimmed slightly as she closed her lips on the words.

But the look that he offered was one of concern, and she shook her head, to put him at ease. Was aware that she hadn't by the darkening of his expression. *Yes,* she thought, *I'm at home here.*

And at home, as well, in the streets of the upper holdings—the ones lucky enough to border the bridge that led to *Averalaan Aramarelas*. At home on the stone roads, and at home on the cobbled ones; at home in the wide streets that began, with crowds and older buildings, to narrow as they moved toward the Common at the heart of the Old City.

She paused a moment beneath the great trees that could be seen at almost any distance—by land or sea; they were the pride of Averalaan, and if their roots caused difficulty to those who lived near them, the complaints they made were couched in grudging respect. Even Gregori looked up toward their heights and offered a rare smile.

It was the only time he took his eyes off her back.

Wagons and horses now joined them in the causeways; the languages of the Old City grew louder and more varied. People gestured over the din that had grown with every step taken, and some of those gestures would have curdled Ellerson's blood. They made her smile.

If she felt at home on the Isle, she could take comfort from the fact that she also felt at home on the mainland; she was part of both worlds.

But she could not fail to notice the respect given her clothing—it was her clothing; neither height nor presence demanded much—and her guards. *Terafin,* she heard, to either side. She looked ahead.

She led them through the crowded streets of the Common until they came at last to the imposing stone structure known as the Merchant Authority, and when she placed foot upon the first of its broad steps she turned to glance at Gregori. His smile was thin, devoid of warmth. But he nodded.

"Yes," he told her quietly. "We've been followed."

"How many?"

"Two."

"Whose?"

His eyes narrowed slightly. "Haerrad's," he said, after a pause. "Or Rymark's."

She cursed, her smile sweet and demure around the shocking words. His brows did not so much as rise.

"Can we lose them here?"

"There are many ways into the Merchant Authority at this time of day," he replied. "If they choose to speak with the guards who watch those routes, they'll know that you've left by an alternate one; your position, sadly, has been noted."

"Don't worry about it," she said, with unfeigned confidence. As reward, she saw his open curiosity. She shouldn't have been pleased, but she was; Gregori, like Devon, was almost unflappable. Still, it had been a lot easier to lose pursuit in the old days. Neither she nor her pursuers were forced to be subtle, and dignity did have its cost.

She took the steps one at a time; Angel and Carver flanked her, and Dalne preceded her. A man met them at the door, as he always did; Gregori's words were true.

"ATerafin!" he said, in his oily voice.

"Jelnick," she replied, in her sweetest.

"You've been absent from the floor for far too long." His laugh was loud and annoying. He ran a hand through hair that was flat with scented oil, and then extended it; she tried not to look at it as if it were a dead fish.

Ellerson would have been proud.

Especially as she prevented herself from flinching when he lifted her hand to lips and kissed it. Southern customs, she thought, in annoyance. She waited only as long as politeness decreed before she retrieved her hand.

"Forgive me, Lady," he said, grin broadening over perfect teeth—the only part of him that *was* perfect. "We so seldom have people of note who are not fat, fifty, and dour."

She could not understand how he could speak so loudly and still have a job. But her smile was now firmly fixed on her face. He offered to escort her, and Gregori at last chose to rescue her, interposing his slender body between hers and the merchant warden's girth.

Beyond his bulk, the Merchant Authority crawled with people, each going about their business. Some were voluble; their raised voices could be heard over the gaudy din and jangle of money and jewelry. She was familiar with only two of the languages, but as was so often the case, she had learned all the curse words first; she grimaced, shook her head, and began to move, drifting between the shoulders of men and women who were inches taller.

They made their way across the floor, and her hands dropped defensively to her purse. Not that there were thieves here, but crowds of this nature always made her nervous. Angel and Carver were no better; Daine, on the other hand, didn't seem to notice.

So it was Daine who led them to the offices that were permanently occupied by Terafin representatives. They were not large, these offices; space in the Merchant Authority was costly, and permanent space afforded to the few who could comfortably hold it.

And among those, of course, was House Terafin.

Finch was grateful when she saw the woman seated behind the broad desk in the outer room; Lucille ATerafin. This place was much like a gatehouse, Finch thought, although it looked nothing like one. The carpets on the floor were a dark, deep burgundy, and the walls were of rose and gold; there were paintings in gilded frames which bore signatures that she almost recognized, and given her ignorance of fine art, this said much; there were chairs that were wide and inviting, tables that habitually bore more silver than she could comfortably carry; crystal vases and crystal goblets beside stoppered decanters that were clearly not meant for decoration. It was a stately, perfect room.

But only those with legitimate business—and Lucille could be very, *very* picky about what was considered legitimate—were allowed to bypass this room. Many were the members of House Terafin who were made to cool their heels at her pleasure—or displeasure—because many, many of said members came from the Terafin Manse.

And having quarters in the Terafin Manse was considered by many members of the House—all of them born to the patriciate— to be the thing that separated them from those who merely had the *name*. Terafin owned many Houses throughout the Empire, after all, and only men and women of *value* were given rooms upon the Isle.

Lucille could not stand *attitude,* as she called it. Funny, that she could then exude so much of it.

But Jay had made some sort of peace with the old dragon who guarded the hoard, and that peace extended to all of the den. Well, to Teller and Finch at least.

Her snort made it clear she'd seen Angel and Carver.

Lucille rose at once, and circumnavigated the imposing desk behind which other doors—all closed—lay. She was not a small woman; Finch wondered if she had *ever* been small. And to be honest, she would not have been out of place behind the bar of a particularly boisterous tavern, club in hand a punctuation to her loud words.

But she wasn't in a bar; she was in the Merchant Authority, and if she was in theory subordinate to the men and women who labored over contracts and royal commissions behind her broad back, it was a very tenuous theory.

"Finch!" She wrapped her arms around the younger woman, and then pushed her away and frowned. "You've *lost weight*," she said, as if the losing were an almost unspeakable crime.

"It's the paperwork," Finch said meekly.

"Paperwork?" Lucille's eyes were a deep blue-green, an astonishing color. "We've got all kinds of useless Terafin members here—why don't you leave it to them?"

"Jay's not here to check their work," she offered.

Lucille's eyes narrowed. "And I'm not watchful enough, is that it?"

Lucille's bark, as the members of the Terafin merchant arm were wont to say, was worse than her bite. But Finch had seen her bite, and she wasn't so certain.

"I brought a few documents that have to be looked at and drawn up properly," she said, making her voice a shade meeker—which shouldn't have been possible.

"Well, let me see them." Taking her seat again, Lucille pointed at the surface of her gleaming desk.

I'm too good at following orders, Finch thought guiltily. She heaved the large, flat bag up onto the desk and opened its leather ties.

"You two!" Lucille barked.

Carver and Angel flinched.

"You're big, strong men—what were you thinking, making her carry that all this way? It weighs as much as she does!"

"Aw, Lucille," Carver muttered. "We're supposed to be on duty."

"And there are now so many assassins in the streets that you had to hold on to those swords the entire way?" She snorted. "It's not as if you know how to *use* them."

Carver wisely chose to offer no other defense, and Angel had actually moved to stand *behind* him. Finch was suddenly very glad they'd left Ellerson behind.

Lucille began to look through the unsigned, unsealed contracts. She frowned, and the frown brought out the map of lines that made her face so interesting. Smiles, Finch thought, and the fiercest of frowns, resided in the crinkles around her eyes and mouth, and one never knew which you would find if you followed the creases to their natural end.

A gray brow—iron gray, not the delicate white of real age— rose. She set down the papers. "Is that Daine I see with you?"

"Yes, ma'am," Daine said, striving for the same meekness of tone that seemed to afford Finch so much protection.

"Don't mumble, boy. At your age, it's a discourtesy to the elderly."

No one pointed out that Lucille was not, and would *never* be, elderly.

"You've come all the way to the Authority for *these?*" Her voice had dropped; she wasn't exactly whispering, but the quiet in her tone was as close as a booming voice could get.

Finch swallowed. "Not exactly," she said at last.

"Are those jumped-up nobles on the House Council giving you trouble, girl?"

"Not more than usual."

The frown deepened. Not for the first time, Finch was grateful for her size.

"I'm thinking that young Daine isn't here to keep you company."

Daine looked confused.

"You'll want to leave by the back, yes?"

Finch, on the other hand, looked grateful. She was.

"You'll want to leave by an exit the ATerafin don't normally use either."

"Lucille, I don't want to be trouble—"

"Nonsense. You do want to be trouble, just not to me." Her grin was wide. "You leave these complicated things with me and I'll see that those layabouts do something with them. Cormaris knows they're slow as slugs; they'll take hours. Or should that be days?"

"Hours," Finch said promptly.

"Hours, then. Come with me, Finch." She paused. "And you two lackwits, you follow as well."

Angel rolled his eyes, but only when her back was entirely turned.

Unfortunately for him, she turned again, spinning so quickly it was hard to believe she was a big woman. She casually smacked him upside the head; it was loud, but it wasn't—Finch hoped—too painful. "I've had sons," she said grimly. "Don't you give me attitude."

"Yes, ma'am."

She snorted, and then paused. "And who's this?"

Gregori ATerafin brought his hand to his chest.

"New here, I see," she said, giving him the thorough once over. "You must be a real House Guard."

"Lucille!" Carver squeaked.

"I have that honor, ATerafin," Gregori replied.

"Hmmph. Well, see that you mind her," Lucille said, nodding to Finch. "And see that no harm befalls her. I promised young Jay I'd keep an eye out. And I don't like to break my promises."

"ATerafin."

She snorted again. "You should have brought Arann," she told Finch.

"He's kind of busy at home."

"Well, maybe he is; you know best, dear. Come on; I'll see you out."

She did. She also told the two guards at the base of the set of small stairs that she'd box their ears—and worse—if they wagged their tongues at the wrong people, and by that she clearly meant *anyone but me*. They smiled genially, used to her threats, and stepped aside to allow Finch and her companions to pass.

"They'll be coming back this way, mind," Lucille said. "In a few hours."

"But, ma'am," one of the hapless guards said, "we'll be off duty by then."

"Or not," the other guard said, before she could speak.

Although it was hard to think of the Merchant Authority as a quiet place, the noise of the Common assaulted the ears the moment the doors slid shut at their backs. They were upwind of the food stalls, and the pleasant scent of baking bread mingled with the far less pleasant reek of dead fish.

Neither seemed to bother the thousands of people who walked these roads.

"You know," Finch said, as they exited into the High Market streets, "I have no idea why Lucille isn't living at the House."

Angel and Carver exchanged a broad glance. It was Angel who answered. "Because almost anyone *else* who lived there would be dead?"

Her laughter was brief and high, a bird cry. Her name. "She's not so bad," she said, when it had trailed off. "And she likes *us*."

"Speak for yourself," Angel replied, rubbing the side of his head.

Gregori offered them all a rare smile. "You have heard the Northern saying, haven't you?"

"Which one? I've probably heard a dozen, and eleven of them can't be repeated in company."

The smile deepened. "Something about two heads and one crown. That woman rules her own domain; I can't imagine that she wouldn't take charge and clean up if she were allowed to live at the manse."

Finch wrinkled her nose, trying to imagine Lucille and The Terafin in the same room. Her imagination, usually quite vivid, was in no way up to the task. "You're probably right."

"Besides which, she seems a formidable ally where she is." The smile had gone from his face; what was left was an expression that was at once thoughtful and cautious. His usual expression.

Finch nodded. Her hair was flat with the humidity, but the day was otherwise cool. The storms that haunted the ocean failed to hover above the city itself. "Daine?"

He nodded, turning to glance over his shoulder as if looking for sight of Lucille.

"She's a dragon," Carver told him. "She doesn't leave her den unless some moron with a sword tries to make her."

"That happens often?"

He shrugged. "Don't know. She probably eats the corpses."

"Carver!"

He grinned and sidestepped Finch's halfhearted slap.

Angel turned right. "Houses of healing?"

She nodded quietly. "We need to speak with Levec."

Daine's eyes widened as understanding *finally* dawned. "You don't just walk in and speak with Levec," he began. But something in her expression dampened the rest of the energetic warning.

"He'll see us," she said quietly.

"I hope so. We're going to feel like idiots if he has us thrown out."

She nodded in the direction of Carver and Angel. "We probably look like idiots anyway," she said cheerfully.

Was surprised to find that she *was* cheerful.

The city walls rose and fell to either side, fronted by gardens that could be glimpsed through the lattice of fancy gates. Men with horses rode by; carriages clattered against the dips in cobbled stone. Some stretch of Averalaan had been given to flat, smooth roads— but those roads led to the Isle, and not to the houses of healing.

She knew them all, now. Knew them better than she knew the twenty-fifth holding. Had the circumstances been different, she would have found the walk peaceful.

But her mission was oppressive, and the farther away she moved from the Merchant Authority, the more oppressive it became. She had spoken with confidence, but confidence was like the tide. It ebbed as time passed.

Gregori informed her that they were no longer being followed and she nodded quietly. Just as Jay might've, had she been here.

Better not to think about that. Better not to think that Jay would have told them what was making The Terafin ill. Jay had made her choice, and from the sound of her voice the last time they'd heard it, it hadn't been much of a choice.

Then again, neither was sitting on the House Council.

She twisted the ring on her hand, forcing the face of the heavy gold crest up toward the light. Most days, she kept it turned palm-in; she disliked the attention it garnered. Old habit, that; attention was something to be avoided at all costs.

But not today.

Not today, please Kalliaris. She thought she'd never needed the goddess of luck to smile more than she did today.

The gates of the House of Healing were better guarded than the storefronts of the most expensive of the jewelers in the High Market. The house itself was not fenced in; it was *walled*. From the height of the wall, metal tines extruded, ending in barbed points. Someone had taken the time to polish them; they shone in sunlight as if they were golden.

But Levec would have died before he wasted money on gold.

Stopping at the gates, she held out her hand; her arm shook slightly, as if the weight of the ring was too great. But shaking or no, the Terafin House Council crest was recognized. The guards were no fools.

"Please wait in the gatehouse," the man in charge said. He barked other orders, and she noted them idly, turning to run her fingers along the carved words that adorned the gatehouse walls. They were not in a language she could read, although she recognized the stylized curves and runes: Old Weston.

Old Weston was better than Weston; if Levec had had any hand in the words, they would have been succinct and to the point: *Go away*.

As if Daine could hear her, he smiled. "He's really not that bad," he told her quietly.

"I know." She did. Sort of. But Levec's single thick brow seemed etched across his face like thundercloud in a storm without end; his voice was harsher than Lucille's at her worst, and his hands, thick and blunt, seemed as likely to strangle a man as to offer him succor.

Gregori ATerafin waited with the perfect ease and grace that made most people look clumsy and incompetent. She envied him his composure, although she wasn't certain she wanted to live the life that led to it. He had been with the House—and with the den—for weeks now, and she had no better idea of who he was, what he wanted, what he feared, than she had the first night she'd met him.

Devon hadn't been helpful either. *Ask, if you must*, he said, *but accept the answer he gives*.

Which, of course, was none at all.

Still, she'd come to understand the nuance of his external expression, the subtle shift in his posture, the almost unnoticeable narrowing—or widening—of eyes.

And because of this, she turned as a man in robes, flanked on either side by two guards, approached the gatehouse.

She didn't recognize him, although she thought he was a foreigner; his skin was a shade too dark, his eyes a shade too wide, for Averalaan.

But Daine, apparently, did. "Andaru!"

The older man smiled. "Daine." He turned to the guards at his right. "Why wasn't I informed that Healer Daine was present?"

The guard brought his hand smartly to his chest and bowed his head, the universal apology that the dignified offered.

"Don't be too hard on them, Master Andaru," Daine said, apologetically.

"Master, is it?"

"I'm not wearing the medallion."

Gray brows drew down in a frown over a straight, narrow nose. "And why would that be?"

"It's my choice," he said, a little too quickly.

Great, Finch thought, as the iron gaze shifted and landed on her face. She squared her slender shoulders and lifted her chin.

"Alowan thought it best." Her voice came out too thin, but at least she didn't stammer.

They were, or appeared to be, the right words; the frown eased slightly. "Politics and healers make poor bedfellows," he told Daine. "But this is not the place for a lecture. Follow me."

He led them to the House of Healing, but he did not choose to dismiss the guards. Angel and Carver struggled with dignity, and for the most part—given who they were—they won. Gregori, of course, fell into step with the House guards; were it not for his crest, he might have been one of them.

It was a way of hiding, Finch realized. Belonging was a way of hiding. Master Andaru failed to notice. Or appeared to fail; she wasn't certain. She wondered if she should have sent Teller instead. He was far, far better at reading people than she had ever been, and while she'd improved over the years, so had he.

The guards left them at the doors.

Master Andaru turned to Carver, Angel, and Gregori. "If you will not surrender your weapons," he said, "you will be required to remain here."

"Finch?"

"Leave them."

Angel was already unbuckling his sword. He had no intention of being left behind. Carver joined him. Gregori did likewise, divesting himself of the daggers he carried. After an awkward pause, Carver and Angel did the same.

Finch surrendered hers with less reluctance; it had never been her job to fight. Daine carried no weapon.

"I should warn you, Daine, that Master Levec is not in the best of moods."

So what else is new? Finch was wise enough not to say the words out loud.

"The plague?" Daine asked.

"The same. Have you heard of it in Terafin?"

Daine nodded quietly. He started to speak, thought better of it, and fell silent.

This time, Healer Andaru did notice. "So," he said softly.

Daine reddened. He seemed to have shed years in the archway that defined inside from outside.

"Best of moods or no, he'll see you."

Daine nodded.

The older healer turned to leave, and then turned back. His expression was unreadable. "Do you understand Alowan's choice, Daine?"

"Better than I did when I was a student here," was the quiet reply.

"And when you see the cost, will you remember what you understand now?"

"I . . . don't know. But I can't come back."

"No," the old man said quietly.

"I miss the House."

"The House misses you," Master Andaru replied gently. "And we will never cease to regret our failure. We are better protected now than we have been since the founding," he added. "Too little, for your sake."

"I'm not the only healer to be lost. I'm one of the few to be recovered." Daine straightened his shoulders. "Master Andaru, I'm not unhappy."

"They treat you well?"

"They hardly notice me at all," was the sheepish reply. He glanced at Finch. "But yes, the people who matter treat me well."

"They had better."

Finch held her breath as the doors to Levec's offices opened wide.

They were not like the Terafin offices. Instead of fine desks, finer chairs, tables that looked like they were made by the maker-born at the dawn of time, it boasted beds, long, narrow cots, and cupboards that would do a kitchen proud on every conceivable inch of wall.

"ATerafin," Master Levec said, and she jumped.

A man that large should *not* be able to move so damn silently.

"Master Levec."

"Have you come to visit Adam?"

Her smile was rueful. "Yes," she told him, and then, when his frown deepened—and it never left his face—she added, "but not just for that."

"Did someone call me?"

Adam appeared from behind Levec's broad chest. He was almost spider thin; he seemed to have grown three inches, and his hair was a shocking disarray of loose curls. But his eyes were the same: haunted. Isolated.

She smiled at him. Up at him; he seemed so young that she often glanced down instinctively. "Adam," she said in Torra.

"Healer Levec has said that you're almost ready to—to leave the house of healing."

The boy's eyes brightened; his smile was unfettered by suspicion, by wariness, by any of the things that had hemmed the den in when they were his age. "He says I'm to live with you."

She nodded, smiling in spite of herself. "We're not as grouchy as he is, that's for sure."

"May I remind you," the healer said, in rough and accented Torra, "that speaking about me as if I were not present is considered unwise, not to mention rude?"

"Yes, sir," she said.

He rolled his eyes. But he grabbed Adam's shoulder and dragged him around. Finch noticed that he did not immediately release him. Adam had come that far.

Far enough that he didn't reach out to grab her hand or her arm. He wanted to; she could see that. But he held his ground.

Master Levec had claimed that this boy was powerful. Finch wondered what the word meant; she had had her fill of the powerful, and none of them had the life, the bright joy and the open vulnerability of Adam.

"You didn't come to see me," he said, and his chest seemed to shrink by the three inches he'd grown. The word crestfallen did not do him justice.

"I didn't come *just* to see you." She reached out and offered him her hand; he took it. His grip was still tight enough to turn her fingers white. "But I knew you'd be here."

He nodded, content. She drew him almost unconsciously to her side, away from Levec's broad shadow. Straightening her shoulders, she slid her free arm around him in a ferocious hug. When it relaxed, he still held her waist.

She didn't know why, but Adam seemed most comfortable around women.

"Master Levec." She slid into Weston. "I don't know if you've heard from Alowan—"

"I've heard," he replied grimly. He turned and shoved his hands into a silver pail; they came up glistening with water. A towel absorbed it, and became tangled in his knuckles; he held it as he spoke. "You can speak freely here, ATerafin. In this room, and in the tower room, if you're ever invited back."

This was the Levec she was accustomed to.

"The Terafin," she said quietly.

"Yes. Alowan has described the symptoms as clearly as possible. He has not traveled to the Houses of Healing; I believe he is afraid to leave the healerie."

"Not the healerie," Finch replied quietly. "The House."

"To Alowan, they are one and the same."

"They were."

"Ah. And now?"

She shook her head. "Alowan wrote to you?"

"No."

"But you said—"

"I said he told me what he believed I needed to hear. And you, youngling, know better than to ask *me* how. I will not be questioned by children in the healerie."

"Yes, Healer Levec."

He set the thoroughly wet towel down on the counterpane of the nearest bed, and followed it with his bulk. Even seated, he was a giant. She wondered idly what the beds were made of; they seemed far too slight to bear his weight.

"My Torra is . . . not good," Levec said, after a long and thoughtful pause. "And for reasons that should be clear to a young woman in your position," he glared at the House ring before he continued, "you will understand why I have not sought the services of a native translator."

She nodded again, willing to wait until he was ready to speak his mind; it usually didn't take all that long.

"Adam," he said. "Tell her."

"But you said—" Unlike Levec's Torra, Adam's Weston had improved considerably.

"I know what I said, boy. Tell her anyway."

It was clear to Finch that Adam's caution had nothing to do with her and everything to do with Levec. But he didn't smile when he turned to her; his face was awkward. Pale.

"In the hundred holdings," he said dropping his voice and sliding into his exotic Torra, "many have fallen ill." His glance flickered off Levec's impassive face. "I went there with Master Levec. And Healer Dantallon went as well."

Aie. Dantallon was one of the royal healers. He never left *Avantari*, the palace of Kings. Almost never.

"Just the three of you?"

"And about a hundred Kings' Swords."

Her lips twitched.

"Also, the Princess Royale."

She closed her eyes. "Levec," she said quietly.

"Yes," he replied. Just that. "But it is subtle, this illness."

The way he said the last word made her hair rise. Gregori ATerafin came to stand beside her. Levec's frown grew edges. "Gregori," he said coolly.

"Master Levec."

"You two know each other?" Finch asked, curiosity bright and shining.

"In passing," Levec answered. "He's your guard now, is he?"

She nodded quietly. "He's really observant."

"He's that." He clearly had more to say—and just as clearly, wouldn't. But he didn't much care for Gregori ATerafin.

Finch glanced around the room to avoid the sudden chill. "Angel," she said severely, "don't touch anything."

Angel shrugged, sliding his hands back to his sides. Old habits.

Levec looked like he was about to say something worse, and Finch lifted a small hand. "It's not a normal illness."

"Very good, ATerafin. No, it's not."

"Not poison, not the water?"

"Not, as you must suspect, poison."

"Then . . . what is it?"

Again, Levec's glance turned to Adam. Adam shifted restlessly on his feet. After a moment, he said, "I think it has something to do with dreaming."

"Dreaming?"

"Adam," Levec said.

He cringed. "I don't know *why*," he told her softly. "But some of the . . . ill . . . are dreaming."

"They're asleep?"

"They're unconscious. They can swallow. They can't eat." He swallowed, his throat bobbing. "I—" Again his glance went to Levec. Levec nodded.

"I can see some of what they see."

"When you heal them, you mean?" She had heard of this.

He looked pained. "We *can't* heal them. Not really. We can . . . fix the things that have gone wrong because they can't eat. But we can't . . . heal them."

"*Adam.*"

"I . . . can wake them up."

Levec snorted. "What he won't say, ATerafin, is that he is the *only* one who can wake them."

"They don't stay awake," Adam added, defensive. "But I can

wake them, for a little while." His frown deepened. "My mother—" he began, and then after a moment, corrected himself. "My sister might understand what's happening."

"Your sister?"

"She's—the Matriarch of Arkosa."

This was supposed to mean something to Finch, but it was clear to Adam that it didn't; his brows bunched together in frustration.

"There are four . . . families . . . in the Dominion."

"There are a lot more than four."

"There are four that wander," Levec continued. "And Adam's sister appears to be the leader of one of them."

"And she would know something about this?"

Adam shrugged again. "If anyone would, a Matriarch would. Maybe Yollana. Of Havalla," he added, hopefully.

"I'm sorry," she told him, "but I don't recognize that one either." She would have squeezed his hand, but her fingers had gone numb. "Levec, do you think this is the same thing that The Terafin suffers from?"

"Almost certainly," he replied grimly.

"But The Terafin isn't sleeping."

"No, ATerafin," Levec said quietly. "Not yet."

Not yet. "This is magic, isn't it?"

"We don't know." Levec's heavy hands slid behind his broad back. His eyes narrowed. "The magi have been summoned, and as they can, they assist us. If magic is at work here, it is not a magic that most understand."

Jay, Finch thought. "Do any?"

"Some branches of magic are old," was his careful reply.

"And some," Gregori added, "are forbidden."

The day, she thought, couldn't be any darker. "You think this is forbidden magery?"

"We are not certain *what* it is, ATerafin. If we were, we would be more open. We don't need witch hunts; a plague brings its own demons in its wake."

She didn't like the use of the word demon. At all.

"Do they have anything in common?"

"The victims? Not that we can trace. And we have been working these three weeks on *nothing* else."

She asked the only question left to ask. "How many have died?"

"A dozen. But if we cannot work our way through this puzzle, many more will follow."

"No one has recovered?"

"None. But the people that Adam have treated seem to gain strength for a few days before they lapse into sleep again."

She turned her gaze upon the young healer. "You need him here," she said, testing the words.

"Yes. But not so much as you will, if our understanding of the illness is any indication. He is to go with you, ATerafin, when you leave."

"But—"

"The Kings may second him. We have made it clear that he owes service to the Healing Houses, and not to the Crowns, but our relationship with the Crowns has always been one of cooperation in the case of epidemics."

She swallowed; her throat was dry. "Adam?"

"I'd like to go with you," he said.

"Good."

But Gregori ATerafin seemed far less pleased, although he did not say a word.

CHAPTER TWO

25th of Corvil, 427 AA
Terafin Manse, Averalaan Aramarelas

NIGHT over Terafin.

Adam was past gaping at the size of the Terafin Manse, although Finch had gone and left him in the den's foyer because he'd forgotten to keep walking. She had ordered—well, as much of an order as anyone ever gave Ellerson—rooms to be opened for his use, and Ellerson had gravely complied.

It was the first time, since they had arrived in Terafin and been given the wing, that new rooms had been opened; Daine, technically part of the den, was often confined to menial tasks—and quarters—in the healerie.

"Shouldn't I be with Daine?" Adam asked, watching the older healer vanish down the hall.

"Only if you want Levec to murder me," Finch replied, with a wry smile. "Don't worry about Daine," she added, when she realized that he was worried. *How much do you know, Adam? How much do you see?* "Daine isn't allowed to heal."

"W—what?"

"In the healerie, all healing is done by Alowan. Daine is . . . like any of his other aides. He cuts bandages. He binds wounds that Alowan considers too minor to expend power healing. He sets bones. Things like that."

"But—but—"

She shook her head. "Most of the House doesn't know Daine's a healer."

"Why do they think he's here, then?"

"They *think* he's here as another one of our flotsam and jetsam crew. House Terafin is one of The Ten, but Jay is a bit unusual."

He smiled and nodded. "She's strong, though."

"Always has been." Her smile faded; she looked to the South. "And she's impossible to kill. Mostly." Praying, as she said it, that it was still true.

"I want to see the healerie."

"Not at this time of night, you don't."

He raised a brow.

"Alowan is an *old* man. Levec just pretends. You can meet Alowan in the morning."

But the morning—that morning—never came.

Instead, the night fell, loud and fast. The footsteps that had padded away down the long hall came back in a thunderous roar. She heard them through closed doors; saw them in Adam's sudden stiffness.

Ellerson appeared, cutting through the dining room and swinging the gabled doors wide. "ATerafin!" he cried, his voice as loud as she had ever heard it.

"Ellerson?"

His eyes were wide; they seemed almost silver, a trick of the lights that never went out. Teller's door swung open, and it was followed in quick succession by everyone else's. Even Arann's.

"Master Daine has . . . returned from the healerie," he said. Just that.

"Oh, gods," she whispered, or thought she whispered. She was in motion. She felt her feet move, her knees bend, her stride lengthen; she cursed her skirts, the daywear that the title of House Council member demanded.

Her hands pushed the doors wide; she collided with the nearest chair, bruised her ribs, swore, and kept moving.

Not this, she thought, as the small foyer loomed in view. *Not this, too.*

She heard swords being drawn. She heard voices being raised. She heard something like her heartbeat, but it was too loud to be that.

Daine was standing in the frame of the double doors that kept the rest of Terafin out of the den's hideout. His hair was wild. His face was glistening. Sweat, she thought. It was hot. Humid.

Sweat.

But his hands were turned toward her, his palms exposed, and she knew that sweat wasn't that color.

Red. Not yet sticky, not yet the impersonal brown of something that could no longer be healed because it no longer bled.

His eyes were wide; his eyes were dark. She no longer knew what color they were. But she knew that his expression was sliding into something cold and dangerous, something that, dark and cruel, lay dormant within him. *Needed* to lay dormant.

She crossed the distance between them, put her arms out, caught his, stiff as the dead, and held him close. He was taller than she was. Everyone was taller than she was. But he was younger. She tried to remember that.

"Daine," she said, not speaking his name so much as calling it with all the force she could muster. "*Daine.*"

And when he didn't answer, she leaned up on toe tips, and whispered a different name into his pale ears. "Jay."

His expression stiffened; he tried to push her away. But she knew this game; she knew the price of losing it. She held him fast.

Called him again. Called Jay from within him. He had healed Jay. He had called her back from the dead. Some part of her lay over him, like a guardian. Like a shroud.

It was a better shroud than the older one.

The man he had been forced to heal.

The man that no one named.

He fought her for just a second longer, and then she felt the stiffness leave him. When it did, she allowed herself to be pushed away.

Because that gesture was different; familiar enough to someone who had lived life in the twenty-fifth holding. Jay *hated* to be touched.

"He never hurt anyone," Daine said, his eyes filmed now, the rage dissolving into an entirely different anger. Reaching up, he shoved his hair out of his eyes—which was unfortunate, because it wasn't in his eyes—and said again, "He never hurt *anyone*."

She shook her head. Her own vision wasn't entirely free from the wavering that water caused. Her palm touched her lips. His, wet, had stained the front of her dress.

She didn't want to ask him what had happened.

And she didn't have to.

Torvan ATerafin and Arrendas ATerafin, Chosen both, appeared on either side of him. She thought she glimpsed the play of light off other armor, but the door would only hold three men comfortably. She was fiercely glad that the other two were The Terafin's.

She looked to Torvan; his face was white, his lips compressed into a thin line.

She knew that Alowan was dead. If he hadn't been, Daine wouldn't be here; he would be by the old man's side. He would be beyond them, in the land that the dead—and the healer-born—walked.

She didn't want to know how.

"ATerafin," Torvan said.

The word steadied her.

And made her ashamed. Because she knew that only ATerafin could have done this.

"ATerafin," he said again, his gaze shifting from her tear-stained face.

Teller came to stand beside her. Beside Daine.

He bowed briefly to the Captains of the Chosen. "ATerafin," he said, taking refuge in formality. "ATerafin."

"The House has not yet been informed."

"The House knows," Finch said woodenly. "Only the deaf could avoid knowing. You—"

"And The Terafin has not yet been informed. ATerafin," he said again, to Teller.

Teller closed his eyes. Nodded.

Finch would not allow him to go alone. Torvan was grim-faced, shuttered; what warmth was left him was something a little too hot to invoke. "Daine," she said quietly, "stay with Angel and Carver. Speak to *no one* until we return, is that understood?"

His eyes flashed. Some of Jay in him, she thought. She hoped. But he nodded, his rough compliance the only compliance she was likely to get.

"Jester," she said, her eyes on Torvan, "get Gregori. Tell him—"

"I'm already here, ATerafin."

"Belay that, then. Gregori, attend."

He had drawn sword.

"Sheathe it," she snapped. "We've got The Chosen as escort; we don't need anyone else."

He was well-trained. He obeyed without pause.

"Ellerson?"

"ATerafin."

"I think . . . you should come with us."

"Are you certain that's wise?"

"What the hell is wise, right now?" Jay's voice. Jay's voice in hers. She struggled to find her own. "Morretz will be there," she said at last.

He bowed.

Last, she turned to Adam.

His eyes were wide, his face pale beneath the sun-dark skin. "Finch?" he said. Torra, Weston, a name was a name.

"I'm sorry," she told him quietly. "But I think . . . I think you should come, too."

Torra. "Should I be there? The Terafin is—Levec said—"

"I don't think this would have happened," she said, and unhappily, "if The Terafin were . . ." she couldn't say it. She *could not* say it.

But he heard it anyway; his hand was on her arm. When had that happened?

"I'll come."

They walked quickly. The night halls were alive with far too many people; there were whispers that devolved into sharp questions, sharper orders, as the Chosen walked by. Finch, Teller, Adam were sequestered within their ranks; Ellerson chose to walk behind them, dignity his shield. It worked, for him. She'd have to ask him to teach her that, later.

If there was a later.

Snap out of it, Finch, she thought, angry with herself. Angry, truth be told, with Jay, with House Terafin, even with the Chosen. Too much anger. She prayed that she would see no sign of the rest of the House Council; that would have been more than she could bear in silence.

And in this, at least, Kalliaris smiled. Servants, guards, members of the House and the Household staff, lined the halls, fluttering like wounded birds, as they formed a macabre procession line.

She tried not to look at them, and she found it easy; she concentrated on Torvan's broad back. Let him be what she was too weak to be, this eve; she would be better tomorrow.

The stairs had never been steeper. She mounted them one at a time, as if her feet grew heavy with each forced step. Her knees ached. Her breath was ragged.

She felt Adam's concern; his hand was warm. She wanted to shunt it aside; she no more liked being touched than Jay did, and for the same reasons.

But she needed that touch. She needed the comfort it gave her. Despised herself for needing it; he was a *boy*. He was a child.

We were children, too, when we first came to the House. And we saved it.

Yes, think that. Think of past glories. Better that than the present, without Jay. She wanted to rip down the tapestries, to turn the paintings toward the walls, to deface the silvered mirrors. *Wealth,* she thought bitterly. *Power. What good were they?*

Another hand touched hers; she stumbled as she took it.

Teller met her gaze and held it a moment. He didn't ask her if she was all right. He knew she wasn't.

But he helped. He had held her hand a hundred times before; a thousand. In the streets of the twenty-fifth, when they were the two weakest members of Jay's den; the two smallest, the two most easily moved to fear or silence. Thinking of that brought her some peace.

Bitter peace, but it was better than nothing.

They cleared the stairs. The hall opened up before them and it was blessedly empty of anyone who *wasn't* Chosen. Even so, they were stopped three times; form was followed precisely.

Torvan and Arrendas answered each challenge as if they expected to receive it; the men and women who offered the challenges recognized their ranks only after they had received the necessary responses.

Morretz was the last guardian.

Finch had never though of him quite that way until this moment, but he stood in front of the doors of the library that was the gateway to The Terafin's private universe.

"The Terafin sleeps," he said quietly. "She is not to be disturbed."

Torvan ATerafin fell to one knee at the domicis' feet; Arrendas did likewise. As they dropped, they exposed the den, although Finch's head barely cleared their helms.

Morretz' eyes narrowed. "ATerafin," he said coolly. "ATerafin." When his gaze fell upon Adam, he said nothing.

Finch cleared her throat. Which is to say, she tried to speak, croaked, and cleared her throat. "I'll explain," she told him. "I'll explain when we—when we can talk."

His eyes widened briefly, and then he said, "You can speak now." He hadn't moved an inch.

"He's from—from the houses of healing. I went, today. I—" He lifted a hand.

But she'd started to talk, and the words suddenly bunched up behind her lips and expelled themselves in a rush. "Alowan's dead, Morretz. Alowan's dead. They killed him. And—and Adam is here because he can do what Alowan *couldn't*. We need to see her. We need to see her *now*."

She wasn't certain how much of what she'd said was heard. "Alowan?" Morretz turned to Arrendas. "Captain?"

Arrendas dropped his head.

Morretz bowed his. The resignation in the gesture was perhaps the worst thing that she had seen this eve. It hollowed her; it removed the last of the shaky ground from beneath her feet.

Because she thought she saw a glimmer of tears in his eyes before he chose to hide them in formality. Or in something else.

At that moment, Ellerson of the Guild of the Domicis stepped forward, coming around them all, unmindful of sword points, of armor, of protocol.

He did not touch Morretz. But he did speak; she heard the muted syllables as if they were spoken at great distance; the words themselves were lost to witnesses.

Finch said, "Adam can wake her." Just that.

And Morretz lifted his head.

"Enter," he said, struggling visibly with the single word. "But, ATerafin—*all of* you—you are forbidden upon pain of death to speak of what you see."

He had never threatened her before.

But she nodded grimly.

* * *

He led the way. The Chosen did not flank him; they stayed behind, forming a wall between Morretz, Ellerson, and the rest of the den. Morretz did not send Ellerson away, although he hardly appeared to be aware of the older man's presence. He moved forward, as Finch had done, as if every step was weighted with consequence.

The library was empty; darkness robbed the shelves that Finch secretly envied of life. The skylight was open to night, and moon's silver provided the only light they could see by.

He led them past the stacks and the shelves, past the gliding brass ladders, past the great tables that were heavier than horses. But he did not lead them into any of the chambers that Finch had seen before; he passed them by, their closed doors a part of the walls.

Wooden floors gave way to carpets, and the tread of heavy soles were silenced by pile that seemed gray or black in the nightscape.

But the journey itself came to an end. Morretz stopped in front of closed doors, and touched them with the flats of his palms. They opened silently inward.

Here, too, he led. He spoke a word only when the doors had shut at their backs, and light—pale, luminous, much like the moon— filled the chamber.

A sitting room. A room with an empty desk, an armoire, twin sets of rising dressers. There was a mirror here, but it was cloaked with a fine silk meant to keep dust at bay; there was a chandelier that was almost invisible.

All this she saw in a glance; she would have seen more if Morretz had chosen to pause. It was easier than seeing the domicis. But he continued to walk. Another door. A large one, with Old Weston runes carved across its heart. He said, "Only the Chosen may bear weapons into this chamber. The Chosen and the right-kin. If you have weapons, ATerafin, divest yourselves of them; they will be untouched."

Before he had finished, Angel and Carver were doing just that. Finch removed her dagger; Teller removed his. Gregori ATerafin bowed and said, "I will wait here."

Morretz nodded as if he expected no less. His brass hair was streaked with a pale white that might have been reflected light.

But she caught no more than a glimpse of this suggestion of age, of shock; he had turned to the door. He began to speak, his voice quiet. Each syllable burned in the air—burned literally, a thing of moving fire. He spoke without intonation, without urgency; the words that came forth were curiously flat.

Curiously exact.

Only when he fell silent again did he reach out to touch the door. It vanished.

Beyond it, Finch saw the largest bed she had ever seen. It was canopied, and a great swathe of silk ran from its height to the floor behind the headboard. It trailed round the poles, a feminine touch that seemed incongruous with the woman who ruled House Terafin.

More than that, she didn't see: her gaze, following silk's fall, had fallen, and she saw the woman who lay beneath thin covers.

Not even moonlight could explain the color of her skin.

Panic took her then. A fear that was so sudden, and so terrible, she could not move past it. Teller, hand in hers, was frozen by the same emotion; they were young again, and the labyrinth had just divested itself of demons.

But Adam of Arkosa was not likewise bound.

If Morretz was sentinel and wall, Adam was a thief who could slide past him in shadows, and he did just that, letting go of Finch without thought.

She felt the sudden cold of his hand's absence, and reached up to massage her arm; Teller's hand brought her up short. If Adam had found the strength to leave her, Teller had not, and she endured cold, watching the back of the youngest member of the den—and the only one not chosen by Jay.

Morretz followed him only when he walked past, unseeing.

"You mustn't touch him," Finch found the strength to say to the domicis. "Whatever else you do, you mustn't touch him."

Morretz did not acknowledge the warning.

Instead, he came to stand on the side of the bed opposite young Adam. She could not see his face; he had lifted his hood.

Until then, she didn't know that his robes had a hood.

Adam reached out and lifted The Terafin's limp hands. His eyes closed, and the light seemed to leech out of the room, curling a moment beneath the frayed edge of his perfect lashes.

No one spoke.

The moment stretched out, the silence a burden that no one should have had to bear. And then he lifted his face, his wild hair curled in a way reminiscent of Jay's. "Finch."

No fear in that word; no hesitance.

She stepped forward, dragging Teller with her. Morretz did not demur.

"Adam?"

"What I . . . must do . . . will tell me much about this woman. Is she like a Matriarch?"

The question made no sense.

And he knew it; he frowned. Nervousness was there, masked by the intensity of his vocation. He hesitated, glancing at Morretz.

"If you can't trust him," Finch said quietly, "You will *never* find a person in Terafin that you *can* trust."

"The Matriarchs are almost never healed," he said quietly.

"But—"

"Oh, they get injured enough," he added grimly. "And in desperation, they can make exceptions. But . . ."

"Adam, we *don't have time*."

"We have time," he said softly, "or I wouldn't ask."

She swallowed.

"It's . . . rare . . . for help to be accepted from outsiders. I'm not her kin," he added, as if he now realized that this wouldn't somehow be obvious to Finch. "And in the South it's not safe for even kin to . . . know things . . . that the Matriarchs know. Men have died."

Morretz said, in flawless Torra, "The laws of the Empire are not the laws of the South. What you know, you may not speak of. But this will not be the first time that a healer has been called for The Terafin; not the first time that she has . . . shared . . . some part of who she is.

"If you require permission, you have it."

Still Adam looked to Finch, and she realized, belatedly, that it was because she was the only conscious woman in the room. "Do what you can, Adam."

He nodded. Arranging himself on the bed, he touched first The Terafin's hands, slack and limp, and then her face. Although she was almost a room's length away, Finch could feel the gentleness in the movements.

He frowned. "There is . . ."

"Yes? What?" Too eager. She strove for calm.

"This is like the plague in the maze," he told her quietly, "and unlike."

"Unlike how?"

"I don't know. Maybe Levec—"

"No," she said curtly. "Not yet. Not him."

He swallowed. "There's something else here."

Morretz had shed fear and resignation. He leaned across the bed until his face was inches away from Adam's.

"Adam," he said quietly.

The boy looked up. The frown had not eased itself from his features, and it aged him. He looked like a man, Finch thought. A gangly, slender man.

"I am not very good at this," he told Morretz. "I'm new. I don't understand everything I should."

"You understand more than Alowan does."

Does, Finch thought. The past had not yet resolved itself into word and thought.

Adam frowned. Softly, hesitantly, he said, "Magic."

Morretz's expression did not change at all. "I am familiar with magic," he said quietly. "It is not magic."

Adam nodded.

But Finch said, "Send for Sigurne."

Morretz started, as if he had forgotten that anyone else was in the room. "Sigurne, I assure you, *has* been consulted."

"Then. This is now. Now might be different. Morretz—please."

The domicis stood. He was taller, and prouder; he had shed the subtlety of his rank. She wasn't sure what he was, now. But he reached over to the beside table, and he placed his hand upon the circle occupied by the lamp.

The lamp blazed suddenly, blinding them all with the intensity of its light. Even Adam flinched.

Trapped in blown glass, the light roiled and moved, turning in upon itself as if it were storm cloud.

And at the heart of the storm was a face that Finch recognized. Sigurne Mellifas.

"Member Mellifas," Morretz said, in perfectly modulated tones. She nodded.

"Forgive me for this intrusion. You are needed in House Terafin."

"How urgently?"

"Use the gateway," he said softly.

She nodded.

Fifteen minutes later, Sigurne Mellifas entered the bedchamber. The Chosen parted before her, and Arrendas ATerafin offered her his arm. She was frail with age; delicate with it.

But Finch sensed only her power. Finch stopped herself from falling to her knees only because she had become used to seeing Member Mellifas in the closed meetings of the House Council.

"ATerafin," Sigurne said quietly, acknowledging Finch. "ATerafin."

Teller bowed.

"Morretz—" She stopped. Looked at the unconscious form of The Terafin with a practiced eye that could not mistake her repose for sleep. She closed her eyes. Drew herself up to her full height. "So," she said softly. Wearily.

"Alowan is dead," Morretz told her.

"When?"

He turned to Torvan.

Torvan said, "Not an hour."

"How?"

"He was beheaded."

"The healerie?"

"The two girls are also dead. We have no witnesses."

"We'll see," she said, voice cold, fragility denied. She closed her eyes, and her lids, veined like opals, flickered.

Morretz did not stop her.

"Two hours," she told him quietly.

He bowed.

"The Terafin," she said.

"She is not dead."

"Good. When did she fall unconscious?"

"I attempted to wake her two hours ago," he replied. "She habitually seeks the Terafin Shrine in the evenings. This evening, she did not wake."

She nodded again, as if she had expected the news, as if it was no news at all.

"The boy," Morretz continued, "is not here."

"Understood."

But Adam had turned to her, and he was staring, slack-jawed, at her face. When she met his gaze, he almost prostrated himself; would have, if it didn't mean he'd be lying on top of The Terafin.

"Boy," she said quietly.

"He's from Levec," Finch said, finding words.

"I . . . have heard . . . of him." Sigurne's smile was gentle; tinged with sadness. "But I did not expect to find him here so soon."

"She's not like the others," he said quietly.

"Oh?"

"She sleeps like the others."

"But?"

"There's something else with her. Within her. I can't explain it." For the first time, he looked genuinely frightened at the inability.

"You think it is magical."

"*I don't know.* I don't know what magic feels like. I only know—"

"Adam," Sigurne Mellifas said quietly. She walked over to where he sat and put her arm around his shoulder. Finch did not warn her not to touch him; it was too late.

"Touch me," she continued.

When he hesitated, she caught his hands and drew them to her face. "Morretz?"

"I have no blade," he said quietly. "The room will not allow them."

She grimaced. "It can't be helped," she said quietly. "Can I use magic?"

He shook his head. "Not here."

Sigurne nodded. "I would deride your caution if I could not see for myself why it so necessary. Very well. Adam, I am old. My body is not what it was, and I have seldom given myself over to the ministration of healers.

"Heal me."

"But—" Wide-eyed now. Afraid.

"Sigurne—" Finch began.

But Sigurne shook her head.

"Heal me," she said, "and look *carefully* while you do."

"But I'll—"

"I know," she told him grimly. "But there is no other way to teach you what you need to know. I cannot touch The Terafin as you do. I have been here. I have looked for the signs of magery, and I have found nothing."

"Finch thought tonight might be different."

"Finch is a talented and wise young woman, but she is sadly optimistic. I *have* looked," she added. "As I entered the room. I see what the others see, and only what the others see." She smiled. "I have lived a long life, and I am afraid of very little of it. My past is my past, but it *is* past.

"And House Terafin is one of the most important Houses in the Empire. Heal me." She made of these quiet words a command.

Adam closed his eyes; his hands relaxed.

Finch's did not; they were balled into fists, and they'd taken poor Teller's fingers with them. But she looked. She watched.

Adam's expression became fluid; he was like parchment, she thought, as words were scrawled across it. No, not that, but perhaps like a harp in the hands of a master bard. He was taller than Sigurne, but he bent slowly over her until their faces were on a level; his eyes were still closed.

Sigurne's closed as well. She was careful; her face gave nothing away. If Adam could have been as careful, Finch would have seen nothing. But he had spent very little time with Levec. Enough to learn some part of his craft. Enough to use it, and still be sane.

He bit his lip. It bled. It stopped bleeding.

Time moved only around the two of them; it had ceased to pass in the room. Not even breathing measured its pace; they were silent, who bore witness.

But Adam was not. He cried out in shock; Sigurne reached out and caught his hands before he could withdraw them.

"Yes," she said, her voice strange to Finch's ears. "Even that. Especially that. I am sorry, Adam."

He struggled a moment, and then he stilled.

A minute later, she let him go.

It was hard to say which of the two was more exhausted by the ordeal. Sigurne had once again cloaked herself with her age; Adam had no such refuge. He was shaking.

But he did not try to touch her again.

That wasn't how it was supposed to work, Finch thought. Levec's dire warnings had made clear what the cost to Adam might be, and none of those warnings were useful. She drew a deep breath and then walked toward Adam.

Her, he reached for. Her, he clutched. He was shaking.

She was afraid of Sigurne Mellifas for the first time in her life. Not intimidated—that happened every time they met. Fear was worse.

But he must have sensed some of this, for he looked up at her, and he said, "No, it's not like that. She's not like that."

She flushed.

"It's what she's *seen*," he said softly. "It's what she had to bear. It's—"

"Adam," Sigurne said gently.

He retreated into silence.

"I have nothing else to teach you," she told him. "And I am weary. I ask you not to speak of what you have learned, but I do no more than *ask*."

He swallowed and nodded.

She met his gaze and said, "Levec underestimated your value. I will take Captain Arrendas, if he can be spared; my magi will arrive soon, and the healerie must be prepared."

Arrendas bowed instantly. "Member Mellifas," he said, touching his chest with his mailed fist.

She held out her arm, and he offered his; it was not, strictly speaking, correct etiquette; this type of escort made the drawing of blade difficult. Then again, there weren't many people who were stupid enough to attack Sigurne Mellifas; she was of the First Circle, and the head of the magi.

They left the bedchamber; Arrendas retrieved his swords and his daggers, and, sheathing them, offered Sigurne his arm again. Finch watched them go.

When she looked back, Adam had once again resumed his place by The Terafin's side. His lashes closed; they were lovely, a dark fringe to egg-shell lids. The moon hid all blemishes, all scars, all imperfections; he sat in repose like an earnest statue, like the best of the maker-born artifacts.

It was peaceful, to watch him.

But peace was something earned, and obviously she wasn't meant to hold it long. Morretz broke her watchful silence, and she could not turn away from him.

"Finch," he said quietly, discarding the formality that was his life. "Who is that boy?"

"He came from the South," she said quietly. "He brought us word of Jay."

"You've already mentioned his name." It was an accusation.

"I'm sorry. He's not ATerafin. He's not even adult. I wanted to—"

"Protect him?"

She nodded.

"From us?"

"From everyone. But he's here now. I guess I'm really not good at protecting anything." She looked up at his jaw, at the stiff lines of his face. "Is it worth it?" she asked him softly.

"What?"

"If he wakes her, we'll have to tell her about Alowan. And she won't stay awake. She'll . . . just lapse . . . back into *this*. That's what Levec told us. That's what Adam says. Maybe we do her no kindness."

"She is not a woman who receives kindness with gratitude," he said, and a faint smile pierced the mask, surfacing across his lips. "Tell me about this Adam."

"He's healer-born." She turned to fully face him, and after a moment, she reached out to touch his face. As if he were den-kin, he started and drew back. Her fingers were sensitive, had always been sensitive; they told her a story. "But he's more than that. I don't understand the healer-born," she added. "But Levec says that Adam is—might be—the most powerful healer that we'll ever see."

"And Sigurne said that Levec had underestimated his value." Morretz shook his head. "Do you believe in fate?"

"I don't know."

"I did once. When I was young. I lost that belief as I grew older." His fingers curved inward, protecting his palms. "I found it, briefly, when I found Amarais. When I lose her—"

She waited for the rest of the words, although she suspected he wouldn't give them. He surprised her.

"I have made her life *my* life. I am her domicis. I will never be good for anything else again. But in Adam, tonight, I see fate's hand. I had forgotten."

He lapsed into silence, and she turned again; Adam had not moved.

She could not say how long he sat thus; could not say how long they stood in their loose formation, waiting for some sign, some word, that might release them. But her legs began to ache, and her back, and beyond this room, the shade of night began to lift its veil.

Morretz stirred first. He frowned. "Your pardon, ATerafin," he said, bowing slightly. "But there is a . . . visitor . . . outside of the library doors."

"A visitor?"

"The Chosen have detained him, but I believe that detention will not hold House Terafin in good stead. I must leave you for a moment. Watch her."

Finch nodded. She would have said, *with my life,* but she had come to understand that her life wasn't the weight that would sway the balance. Beside her, Teller stirred. When Morretz drifted out of the room, he disentangled his hand from Finch's.

"I'll go with him," he said.

"Send Ellerson."

"No. I'll go."

She shrugged. Teller understood people in a way that she didn't—in a way that no one did, not even Jay. He disappeared from the corner of her eye; she did not turn to follow his progress. The Terafin held her fast.

And without Morretz or Teller to anchor her, she drifted toward the bed, circumnavigating its width and length until she stood opposite Adam, as Morretz had done.

This woman had given them their lives.

Jay, she thought. *Come home. Come home now.*

She heard voices before she saw the people they belonged to, but she had come to recognize all of them. Morretz's modulated, respectful tones, Teller's brief sentences. These, she expected. But louder than either—and a good deal more irritable, was Master Levec. Healer Levec.

His words would have done sailors proud, and if she had had any way of ignoring them, she would have—but something about these rooms took sound and magnified it; no one could *sneak* into The Terafin's personal chambers.

Luckily, life in the twenty-fifth holding at least ensured that none of the words he spoke were new to her. She grimaced.

The door to the bedchamber was apparently not entirely as it seemed, for Levec cursed it roundly, and it was clear that he could see nothing that passed within.

Morretz, apologizing, began his monotonous incantation; it took about three times longer than it had when he had allowed the den entrance, and that hadn't been short. But Levec was not patient, this eve.

She saw his beard, the edges of it shaking with the rest of his broad face. Saw the pursed, generous form of his lips. But his eyes contained all of his fire, and had she not had previous experience of him, she would have automatically sought a hiding place. A big man. An angry man. Not a good combination.

She knew the moment when the door vanished—for him—because his eyes widened as they met hers and traveled to Adam, falling a moment to skirt The Terafin's unconscious body.

Then he pushed his way past Morretz, and his stride carried him through Torvan and Carver. They did not seek to stop him, which was just as well; he had momentum in his favor, and one did not raise hand or sword against a healer. Not if one was attached to the House name.

She rose at once, ready to surrender the place she had chosen to occupy, but he grabbed her shoulder and shoved her back down.

And she felt his hands trembling; they were cold.

She started to speak, and her voice caught on the words that she couldn't force out.

Then, for the first time that night, she lost control of her face, her eyes, and she began to cry. She didn't weep; she was afraid to disturb Adam.

Levec caught her chin in his other hand. "Finch."

She shook her head, shoving her palms across her eyes. The tears didn't stop. "Alowan's *dead.*"

"I know," he said, gruff now. It was as close to gentle as he could come. He put his arm around her shoulder, engulfing her, and after a moment she surrendered, collapsing against him. "Sigurne told me."

"S–Sigurne?"

"She sent for me."

"B–but—"

"Hush. She sent for me, and it appears I owe her at least two apologies. I . . . sleep seldom, and I dislike to be awakened."

"But you can't *do* anything!"

She couldn't see his face, but she felt his words as if they were the rumbling of elemental earth. They traveled the length of her slender arms, her right cheek, her forehead.

"I can," he said quietly. Had he spoken any other way, she might have found the strength to pull free. "I can wake The Terafin."

"But Adam said—"

"Yes. But what Adam said is not known, unless you repeated it. When I leave, she will be awake. Thus Daine will be free from suspicion."

"Daine's not even here."

"No. But he has worked in the healerie. And had he been in it, he would be dead now."

"And Adam?"

"Adam will be beneath suspicion for some time, ATerafin."

"But—"

"You do not understand the patriciate. And I like you better for the lack of understanding. He is a *boy*, and he is Annagarian; he cannot even speak Weston respectably. Until they are given reason to suspect him, the House will ignore him as just another one of . . ."

"Of the thieves and urchins that came in off the street," Angel offered.

"Of your den, yes."

She hadn't even thought of it. She wanted Adam to be safe, and *she hadn't even thought.* Her hands flew to her mouth, and she pulled as far back as Levec would let her—which wasn't far at all, all things considered. "Levec—I'm so sorry. I—"

"Hush," he said again.

This time, she obeyed him wholeheartedly. She was tired. Worse than tired. The world she knew had shifted so completely beneath her feet she no longer knew where home was. Levec did. And she let him.

Sunlight brought color to Adam. But motion was denied him. She studied the dirt beneath his fingernails, the half circles that had formed beneath his closed lashes. She watched him as if watching were sustenance. Levec allowed her that; he picked her up, turned her around, and caught her from behind. His beard spilled over her forehead; his chin braced her skull. He was stale with the scent of old sweat, and she inhaled deeply.

It reminded her of the living, that smell. It reminded her that there existed men like Levec, who worked, and continued to work, when a life of idle wealth was theirs for the taking; it reminded her that there were people to whom the House and its political fate was of little import in the grand scheme of things. She hated herself for needing the reminder, but she clung to it anyway, until The Terafin moved.

She did not stir; she did not come to wakefulness as a sleeper did; she did not, in fact, wake at all. But her body was racked by sudden convulsions.

Morretz cried out, wordless.

Levec's arms tightened a moment, and then he let Finch go, as if she were her namesake and could simply fly for cover. She did, leaping out of his way.

Adam spoke. His motions were entirely reactions; his hands followed the jerking rise and fall of The Terafin's face. "Master Levec," he said, all pretense at Weston annunciation lost.

Finch was shocked that he realized Levec was present at all. He had never once opened his eyes.

But Levec accepted what seemed impossible. He bracketed The Terafin. Made her seem small and frail. "I'm here," he said, his Torra as atrocious as Adam's Weston pronunciation.

"I need your help."

"What?"

"He says he needs your help," Finch told him.

Levec hesitated.

"*Levec.*" Adam's eyes flew open. "*I need your help now!*"

The larger man's hands reached out. They pushed The Terafin's bed-dress aside, exposing ivory flesh. He took a deep breath, and then brought both of his palms into contact with her skin.

Morretz did not utter a word.

"What must I do?" the master healer whispered.

Finch translated, flying at Torra as if it were the cage in which she might at last be safe.

"Heal her," Adam snapped. "Do what I cannot do."

Levec's brow—his single dark brow—rose. He did not argue with Adam, but had they been alone, Finch had no doubt he would have.

Where Adam had been beautiful in his healing repose, Levec was not, but there was about the older healer a sense of solidity, a reality, that Adam failed to invoke. Levec's brow lowered; his lids followed. She saw sweat bead his forehead, glistening in the creases decades of habitual frown had etched there.

Warriors, she thought them, shorn of sword and armor, but no less committed for the lack.

The Terafin *screamed*.

Adam joined her.

Levec's lip bled.

Finch started to move, and Ellerson snapped a single sharp syllable into the blended cries.

Her name.

She jumped back from the bed, and hit Teller's slender chest. His hand caught her shoulder, steadying her.

And then The Terafin's scream stopped. As abruptly as it started, the terrible song left her voice; only Adam and Levec were left to their twinned expression of pain, and Finch thought it was because they were no longer aware of the noises they made.

She had seen healings before. She had seen death denied. Nothing in that experience prepared her for this one.

The Terafin's eyes opened. They were silver-gray, and they shone like polished metal.

"Morretz," she said, her teeth chattering.

"I'm here." And he was. Although he was not a small man, he managed to find room for himself by her side; his hand reached out, and then withdrew. The effort was costly.

"What day is it?"

"It is dawn on the twenty-fifth day of Corvil."

She nodded, her body spasming. She could not force herself to speak loudly, but she was The Terafin; she understood the art of making her will known above the din of swords and the screams of the dying. The cries of two healers presented her with little difficulty.

"Terafin." Morretz spoke the word as if he had never expected to have it acknowledged again.

Finch looked away. She had once walked in on Carver and a guest, and she had been embarrassed; that was nothing compared to this involuntary intrusion.

"They will . . . stop . . . soon."

"Terafin—"

"No. Send for Sigurne."

"Sigurne is within the manse."

"I know. Summon her to my chambers. Now."

"I'll go," Finch said.

"No," The Terafin replied, terse, the word laced with suppressed pain. "Send Torvan."

Torvan was gone before anyone could argue.

When he returned, the room was silent.

Levec withdrew his hands first, and brought them to his chest; sweat smeared the broad, cotton cloth before it was absorbed. He was shaking. Finch tried not to notice.

Adam did not withdraw.

Not until The Terafin reached up and gently removed his hands. His eyes snapped open as he lost contact with her face.

Finch could see the marks his hands had left there.

"I am in your debt, Adam of Arkosa," she said, speaking Torra as flawlessly as Morretz had.

He shook his head, wordless.

"Adam."

No one ignored Levec. Not even when they were trying very hard. But that was because he refused to *be* ignored. He called Adam's name again, and when Adam failed to turn to him, failed to acknowledge the command inherent in the two syllables, he slid off the bed, walked over to Adam, and bodily removed him.

Adam's body struggled. His limbs flailed awkwardly, as if in seizure. But Levec held him, and held him tight.

"It would seem," he said, his voice cracked and dry, "that I was wrong."

Finch offered him confusion and silence.

He smiled grimly. "It would appear that I owe Member Mellifas three apologies. Terafin," he added, bowing as formally as a man could, who held a kicking, struggling child in his arms.

"Master Levec. How long do I have?" The Terafin was cool. Regal.

"I do not know."

If the answer surprised her, she failed to show it.

                              *   *   *

Sigurne came. Torvan led her, and to either side, she had four
House Guards. No, Finch thought, examining them more closely.
Four of the Chosen. She was as grim as the Captain of the guards.

As unflappable as The Terafin herself. "Terafin," she said, as she
executed a formal bow.

"A web," The Terafin said softly. "And a mystery."

Sigurne frowned. "Terafin?"

"Forgive me. I speak but a portion of my thoughts, and they will
do you little good." Her chin tilted, and in the morning light, Finch
could see that her eyes had lost their terrifying glow; they were
brown, the irises so slender they might have been all pupil. "There
is magic at work here."

"Ah."

"But it is not a magic that is familiar to me."

"Terafin."

"And were it not for your aid, it would not have been familiar to
Adam."

Adam had almost ceased to struggle, but Levec wasn't fooled;
he held fast.

"You were not dying."

"I am not a healer," The Terafin replied. "And I cannot say that
with certainty."

"She was." Levec grunted as Adam's elbow struck his chest.
"Adam saw it."

"What did he see?" The question was so soft, so neutral, it
seemed to be barely a question—until one looked at the face of the
woman who ruled the magi.

"A trap, Member Mellifas. A . . . web." Levec closed his eyes as
Adam slumped against him. Finch noticed, for the first time, that although he restrained Adam, no part of their skin was in contact.

"She has the plague," he continued. "But someone wasn't certain
that the plague would be enough to kill her."

"Oh?"

"Something . . . magical . . . was wrapped around her heart. It
was . . . almost alive."

Sigurne frowned. "Alive?"

And the master of the most famous Healing House in the Empire
closed his eyes. "Alive," he said quietly.

She frowned.

Finch was already in motion. Teller came with her because she
used all of her weight in her attempt to break free of his hand.

She flew around Master Levec, and before he could stop her—before he could fully open his eyes—she caught Adam's hands in hers.

He clung, as she expected. But where Levec's hands had been sweaty, his were like Northern ice.

"ATerafin," Ellerson offered, in warning.

She held fast. "He had to kill it," she told him, the words snapping the brittle disapproval as if it were the finest, the thinnest of reeds.

"Yes," Levec said wearily. He did not attempt to warn Finch away. "He had to kill it. With his gift. You see clearly, little one."

She shook her head fiercely. "I see Adam."

"She couldn't hear me," Adam said, speaking for the first time since The Terafin had rejected him. "I could hear her. I could *almost* reach her. But she couldn't hear me. Because it was there. It was in the way."

"It's gone now?"

He swallowed. "Gone."

And she threw her arms around him with a ferocity that would have surprised even Jay, had Jay been there.

"I could not see what he saw," Levec told Sigurne. "I could hold her body here. I could preserve her life. But I could not do what Adam did."

"If you hadn't been there," Adam said, in slow, deliberate Torra, as if Levec were the child, "it wouldn't have mattered. I couldn't do both."

But his words brought no comfort to Levec, and Finch realized that the master of the houses of healing had once again failed one of his charges.

No one blamed him.

No one had to.

CHAPTER THREE

THEY were ordered out of the bedchamber. Only Morretz was allowed to stay.

Adam huddled against Finch, but Levec still held him fast, denying him freedom. She was glad that Levec had come; she could not have born the burden alone. Not because Adam was larger, or stronger, than she—although he was both—but because she couldn't bear to see him in such obvious pain.

He looked like the boy she had seen in a large bed in the rooms of Master Levec on a day that belonged in a different life. She had waited patiently while he had gathered his strength; had waited patiently while Levec had forced what knowledge he *could* force into "that boy's thick skull." She had seen him struggle to master his need and his desire, and she had been proud of him.

Very proud.

But that was gone; what remained was the visceral truth of the evening's work. He was alone again, and terrified.

She had been both in her time.

We shouldn't have brought him here, she thought. But she spoke to herself, and she answered. The Terafin needed him. And Finch had proved herself to *be* ATerafin; she had sacrificed Adam's progress to House Terafin's need.

"Girl," Levec said, "the decision was mine."

She started to answer, but the door opened upon her words, and when she turned to see The Terafin in black, white, and gold, she surrendered all argument.

"Finch. Teller. I think it would be best if you returned to your rooms."

Not a request.

"Master Levec, forgive me, but I fear I require your presence."

He said, "Let me see them to safety, Terafin, and I will join you." Before she could speak, he added, "We both have our responsibilities and our duties."

She nodded. "In the healerie, then. Sigurne?"

"I have spent most of the evening there," the magi said quietly. "We have touched little, but we have made the preparations and begun the delving. I do not wish the careful night's work to be lost to House Guards; if you will have me, I will accompany you."

Just like that, the den was rendered superfluous. Finch watched The Terafin sweep past; Torvan and the Chosen followed in her wake.

"Foolish girl," Levec said.

She glanced up at him, across the awkward bridge of the Empire's greatest healer.

"Yes, I'm talking to you. She values you highly. And she knows what this night will cost you."

"I'm not a child," she said, keeping the obdurate whine out of her voice with great effort. "I know what we've lost."

"You think you know. But you will come to understand the peculiar grace of shock. The Terafin gives you time—and she may not have the luxury of that gift in the future. Accept its wisdom, ATerafin, and tend to your kin."

Sigurne did not speak because The Terafin did not; they walked at a leisurely pace, two women of power who chose to grace the length of the Great Hall with their presence. The servants scurried from one door to another. The Terafin frowned; they were better trained than that.

Amarais was weary. She had never been so weary, she was certain, in all of her life. Her slender wrists she hid beneath the length of full sleeves; more than that, she did not take the time for. But the ring around her finger was loose; the crest slid in toward her palm.

She had girded herself with sword, but it was a strange sword; she took comfort now in the presence of her Chosen, in the presence of Sigurne Mellifas. She was too aware of Morretz to find peace there, and he knew it; he knew almost everything about her.

Almost. Adam knew everything.

As Alowan had.

Knowing everything, Alowan Rowanson had agreed to serve her. He had never taken the name she had to offer; he had never taken the position that was hers to grant. But he had taken the healerie, had made it his own. She thought of the fountains, the plants, the ghost of the man who tended them, watering vase in hand. He loved the plants, he had said, because they demanded nothing.

They demand your care, your time, your attention; even though they are mute, they speak to you.

"Yes," he had said, tipping water with care beneath the broad base of hanging leaves. "But the answer I offer in return is of little consequence. They grow, with or without me."

She had raised a brow at the trickle of water, and he smiled.

"I did not say they grew *well* without me. But I am free to let them grow and wither in their season. They are my responsibility," he added quietly, "but the failure of that responsibility is one I can easily live with.

"I have no dreams of dying plants. I have no nightmares. They exist, they will continue to exist."

Yes, she thought, seeing marble, seeing glass, her shadow cast back and forth like a child's toy. *But they will not love you, and they will not grieve. They do not care who tends them.*

"I have no desire to cause grief, ATerafin. It is a burden of affection. When I go, I would leave as much peace as the plants do."

She was silent.

You see? She could hear his voice so clearly. *Plants are not so complicated. They are not double-edged; they are not even single-edged.*

But in their fashion, they bring beauty into a small life.

Alowan, Alowan, nothing about your life was small.

The Chosen did not speak until they came to the open doors of the healerie. There, they offered their assurances to the Chosen who stood guard, speaking in quiet, measured tones.

It was to The Terafin that the man and woman looked. She knew their names almost as well as she knew her own, but they eluded her. She did not attempt to catch them, to bring them back. Instead she nodded.

They bowed their heads over their grasped pommels, chins almost touching their gorgets. Sigurne, Amarais thought, would take this as a gesture of due respect. But she saw more in it; they granted her privacy by failing to notice her expression as she passed them and stepped across the threshold.

Another funeral, she thought. Another death. The old guard passed away so brutally, deprived of the peace she had brought the House by the expedient of vicious war.

And what had that war wrought? War, she thought. Death. Delayed by years, by decades; delayed by vigilance and cunning. But only delayed, not vanquished. She had been so proud of her achievements, here.

Was she to keep nothing of them before she at last departed?

"Terafin," Sigurne said. Her voice was quiet. Amarais did not mistake that softness for gentleness, for she used the same nuance to shade her own steel.

"Member Mellifas."

The fountain had not been destroyed. The plants had not been trampled or broken. Standing in this alcove, she belonged, for a moment, in the past that had been her glory. She might have stayed there, but duty waited, and she knew, although Adam had not said as much, that she had only a few days in which to see to those duties.

Sleep would claim her. She would lie like the dead, impervious to the men and women she had elevated to power. Trust? Suspicion? They would mean little to her.

Reaching out, she lifted the hanging weight of jade leaf. *Like the plants,* she thought. Someone would bring her water. Someone— she looked at Morretz.

His eyes were fixed upon her still face.

Alowan, she thought, as she let gravity take the succulent, *I understand what you desired.* She let him come to stand at her side; the Chosen did not interfere. Why would they? He had become her shadow in all senses of the word, and she could see the failing of his essence in the fading of her own.

He offered her his arm.

She offered him a frown, and his crooked smile offered her what he did not put into words. He bowed.

For a moment, just a moment, she felt at peace here.

Illusion.

The Chosen drew swords as two men approached her, adorned by the heavy robes—the graceless, fine cloth rumpled and gray— and the pendant of the Order of Knowledge.

They were not young, but they were not Sigurne. They were, she realized, her age, their beards stained by time and labor. Although she had offered Alowan the use of House resources, he had refused them; the rooms were therefore hot and humid, where her own were dry and cool. Not all of the magic the House could afford served a higher purpose.

"Member Mellifas," the stouter of the two men said.

"Member Gervano."

"We have taken the liberty of summoning Allister APorphan."

She frowned, her lips folding into worn and delicate creases. "When?"

"An hour ago," Gervano replied with care.

"The sun?"

"Just risen, Member Mellifas."

She closed her eyes. "He has not yet arrived?"

"He arrived half an hour ago."

She nodded quietly.

"Sigurne?"

"Allister APorphan is the member of the magi with the strongest ties to the Magisterium. But he is older now than he was when he found his particular speciality, and he dislikes morning intensely." Her smile was apologetic. "But I do not hear his voice; I do not hear his cursing."

The Terafin raised a thin brow. "And he is given to cursing when he is summoned?"

"Only if woken," Sigurne replied. "And he sleeps past the dawn whenever he is given the opportunity."

"He is a magi of the First Circle?"

"Indeed."

"Then I imagine he is often afforded such opportunity." She straightened her shoulders. "Member Gervano," she said quietly, "what can you tell me?"

"That three people were murdered here," the man said, as if he were unaware of what those people meant.

She waited.

"The girls were killed first."

"How?"

"Beheaded," he replied quietly. "But some damage was done them before they were killed; they offered resistance."

"They were armed?"

"No, Terafin." He turned to glance over his shoulder. "Timman?"

The beardless man bowed low. "Terafin," he said quietly. "Understand that we have not yet completed our investigation; what we say now we may be forced to retract when more complete knowledge is made available to us. What Member Mellifas says of Member APorphan's temperament is, of course, accurate—but he has not uttered a single syllable of resentment. He has not, in fact, spoken a single word since he crossed the far threshold. We . . . are hesitant . . . to interrupt him. If any member of the Order of Knowledge can unravel the night's events, it is he."

"Understood. But I would hear what you have to say."

"They were not armed. The younger of the two died closest to the arboretum. Her body fell backward."

"Was she fleeing?"

"No. I believe," he said, swallowing, "that she had chosen to stand in the small arch that separates the arboretum from the infirmary."

"The infirmary was not touched?"

"There were no patients in it," he said quietly.

She frowned. Nodded. "The second woman?"

"She died running." His eyes were an odd color; they hovered between green and brown as he spoke, and she could see the flecks of gold that burned there, reflecting the light of the sun that passed through the domed window. "We believe that she sought to give warning to Healer Alowan."

"Show me."

The two spoke to each other, but wordlessly; the whole of their exchange was in their brief glance, their slight hesitation. She waited.

If she had little time, she also had the need to preserve the illusion of more.

"Our apologies, ATerafin," Gervano said at last. "But we ordered the healerie to be sealed. Nothing has been touched or moved."

Timman frowned. "Nothing has been touched or moved," he amended, "since the bodies were discovered. But I believe that the young man who was responsible for reporting this crime to the House authorities did indeed disturb the body of the Healer."

"Where is Captain Arrendas?"

"He is with Member APorphan, Terafin. There is another House Guard as well."

Torvan, she thought. Torvan, and not Alayra. "I am ready," she told them both quietly.

It was even true.

Member APorphan did curse when they passed through the arch that led from the arboretum. Her skirts brushed the marbled floor, and her steps, light and deliberate, drew his ire. He mastered himself, but not quickly; it was clear that he had not recognized her.

Which was reasonable; she had indeed heard of Allister APorphan, but had never had cause to meet him; she would not have known him, but would not have excused his slight easily, had it not been for Sigurne's apologetic description.

Sigurne said nothing without reason.

"My apologies, Member APorphan," she said, when realization intruded upon outrage at the possible disturbance of his work and his jaw slackened. He was an old man. But he had none of Sigurne's outward frailty, and none of Alowan's gentleness. "But I am required by Terafin law to visit the site of a crime committed within my walls. If you desire it, I will leave my guards in the arboretum."

"Leave as many people as you can," he said, trying to ram grace into what was an inherently graceless command.

She nodded. "You will not have objections to the presence of my domicis?"

"I—of course. Of course *not*, Terafin."

"And Member Mellifas?"

"Listens to no one but herself anyway."

"There is no better man for this work," Sigurne said to The Terafin.

Amarais forced herself to smile. It was hard; the body of Lila ATerafin lay, headless, scant feet away. Her head had fallen and rolled; the trail of blood that marked its passage was dry, but it would be the work of many hours to remove the blood from the grouting between the tiles.

She wanted to close the wide, wide eyes, the open mouth. She wanted to tell the girl—and she was that, the newest of Alowan's assistants—that she *had not* failed the House.

And she would, but later. Later, after she had spoken to the parents who had been so proud of their daughter's early adoption into House Terafin. Later, when she at last chose to summon the House to the side of the open grave.

"The blow was clean," Member APorphan said. He was almost a different man; his voice was studied, neutral, but his gaze was not. "She died quickly, and she felt little pain."

"Thank you," she said softly. "Where is Fiona?"

"She managed to make it halfway to the healer's quarters. Come. And forgive me, Terafin; I am a brusque man by nature." Brusque or no, he led her to the second body.

She knelt, taking care to gather the black and white of her skirts; taking care to touch nothing. Fiona's head lay before her; her back, unwounded, lay exposed. Her hands were curved into fists; rigor and its passage had not softened her empty grip.

"She was not injured before she died."

"No. I doubt she saw the blow that killed her."

"Where is Alowan?"

"He is in his chambers."

She rose, and with as much care, she left Fiona behind. She did not hurry. Had no desire to see what must be seen. To acknowledge what must be acknowledged.

The door to Alowan's chamber was open.

The magi must have been watching her; when she turned to speak, he nodded.

"The door was as you see it."

"Did the man who discovered the deaths touch the door?"

"Yes."

"Did he unlock it?"

"No."

"Was it unlocked?"

"Yes, Terafin."

She waited, and he offered her a brief half bow. "Thank you, Terafin," he murmured. Lifting his hands, he gestured and the door swung wide.

The room itself was a disaster. It had not always been a disaster; when she had first opened the healerie for Alowan's use, it had been sparsely furnished; a large room for a man who had no name, and no House title.

It was not large now.

"Nothing was disturbed?"

"By the young man who entered these rooms, yes. By the person who preceded him? Nothing."

"At all?"

He nodded grimly. "You begin to see the difficulty."

She let that pass without comment. "I can no more walk through this room without disturbing its contents than he could," she said quietly.

"I have . . . made allowance . . . for that." He did not tell her to disturb as little as possible. But he glanced at Sigurne, and Sigurne said, "I will wait here, Terafin."

"No," The Terafin said quietly. "You will not."

The magi found his feet fascinating.

But Sigurne said quietly, "I have already passed this way."

"And you saw?"

"I saw enough to summon those members of the Order who are better qualified to handle the investigation than I."

"Ah. Apologies, Sigurne. It has been a long night, and I am not as young as I once was."

"No more are we," Sigurne replied. She turned to Morretz. "You may accompany her."

He was the perfect domicis; he waited for his Lord's permission. She gave it simply by entering the room. Navigating the paper, the dishes, the shards of a shattered planter, took most of her concentration.

But never all of it. "Member APorphan?"

"The planter was not shattered by the young man who passed this way," he said. "Farther in, you will find the corpse of the cat responsible for that bit of destruction. It died before the healer did."

She nodded. Alowan's bedroom door was ajar. It had no lock.

She took a deep breath, waiting as the magi once again pushed a door aside without touching it. As if it were a wooden curtain, she thought, and he a technician responsible for revealing what lay behind it.

But he had not set the stage; he had not written the play. What he knew of the actors in the drama he had discovered only after their exit. She did not want him here.

Still, she had long passed childhood. What she wanted, and what she needed, were now divided by experience, and she accepted the guidance of only the latter. She entered.

The bed was a dark, dark shade of red.

Above it, sheets ran with the same color, and beneath them, hands in repose, the body of Alowan. His head had been placed above his neck, and his eyes had been closed. She wondered if he had wakened; if Fiona's cries had alerted him at all.

This time, the magi did not read her thoughts, or if he did, he offered no answer to the question she did not ask.

Here, finally, lay the man who had known her best. She had taken comfort from that knowledge, for she little trusted herself in the months that had followed the struggle for the succession. Although she had suffered herself to show no outward sign of it, she had come as close to wallowing in self-loathing at the moment of her triumph as she had the day that she had walked away from her grandfather's House.

Alowan had known. He had not visited her in the upper remove; instead he sent a summary message. She could still feel the parchment in her hands, could see the scant, curt words that he had penned himself. She had almost forgotten.

She had come to the healerie alone. Not even Morretz had been allowed to accompany her. Although she had not been young, she had been too mindful of the cost of any public humiliation. The years had taught her much. She would not now dismiss her domicis. Had not.

But then?

She had opened the healerie doors and Alowan had stopped her before she could enter them. He stood beside the spot which the fountain now dominated.

"Your weapons," he had said coolly.

The House Sword. Her dagger. She had raised a brow.

"You will not bring them here." Not a request.

She had concealed all her hesitation, caught a moment by indecision; she was The Terafin; he was not even ATerafin, and he had made it clear to her that he would never become so. Perhaps, she thought then, he had known what she must become to *be* The Terafin. Perhaps he left himself this graceful exit, for divorcing oneself from a powerful House could be unpleasant.

He did not offer her any help; he had given her his command, and he waited to see whether or not she would follow it.

She had owed him so much. It stung, but she bowed, her hands fumbling with the buckle of the emblem by which she intended to guide the House. Removing the dagger was easier.

She left both on the other side of the door and returned to him.

His back was toward her.

"Terafin," he said, when the door clicked shut.

"Alowan."

He turned. "There will never be weapons in the healerie while I govern it. There will never be weapons in the infirmary. I don't care if the Chosen themselves should gather here—they will do so without their swords or their daggers."

His words were clear and clean, his voice was strong. She would not offer her own to him until she could match his tone, and minutes passed while she struggled.

But perhaps her obedience pleased him.

"Terafin," he said, turning. "Forgive the curtness of my summons. Come. This place is . . . cold. Steps echo unpleasantly here, and there is little natural light. With your permission, I would change these things. They are not to my liking."

These words, too, were clear, but they were sweeter; she had not been addled by nervous fear.

"You will stay?"

A pale brow rose. "Did I not say as much?"

"Before the war had been joined in earnest," she replied. "Yes. You said so. But war changes much, and things happen during the course of battle that cannot easily be excused or forgiven." She looked down at her hands as if they belonged to another.

"And you regret these things?"

No witnesses. None but Alowan. "Yes," she said softly. "But it is a pallid regret, for I would do them all again if it brought me to the position I now occupy."

"Would you do more?"

She closed her eyes. "Why did you summon me?"

"To ask you for your permission to build here," he said, serene now. "I am not a warrior. I am not a soldier. I am not a Commander. What is left me of the battlefield is what has always been left a healer: rebuilding. But building is costly, and it is seldom that the lord of a great House turns over the treasury to a man who will never become one of its members."

"It is seldom that a healer gives the gift of life to a dying combatant," she replied. "Were it not for your intervention, I would not be lord."

"I am aware of that." For the first time, a glimmer of humor transformed his somber features. "And you, Amarais, are aware that I *am* a judgmental man. It has always been a failing of mine; a displaced pride."

"Yes—although it is not a trait I consider a failing."

"I will heal for you. I will work here, in the land you grant me, as long as it is *mine*. My law, my rules. I will obey your commands, Terafin, as if you were my patris. But I ask you to consider carefully the cost of the healing that you require."

"The dying?"

"Even so."

She was stunned by the enormity of his gift. Humbled by it. "I thought—"

"Yes," he said quietly. "I know."

"And you can accept me?"

"And no other. I know what you have done in the name of the House throne. I know what you would do to maintain it. But I know, also, that there are things you *will not* do, and it is these boundaries that concern me. You will be The Terafin; you will be the ruler of the most powerful of The Ten. But you will bring a law and a peace to the House by your rule that will silence the accusation of the dead."

"Alowan—"

He smiled. "Amarais," he said quietly. "It is by the rebuilding, in the end, that you will be judged. Trust yourself."

"It is so obvious that I . . . have doubts?"

"It is obvious to no other but myself. We traveled from death together; we were reborn together. Were you a person who could so easily be shaken or changed by your achievements, you would not have achieved. The dead are dead; they are no longer troubled by the means or the manner of their death.

"Let them drive you, if you must—as you must. But let them drive you to a better place."

She bowed to him and he walked over to where she now knelt, and placed his hand gently upon her bent head, as if he were priest and confessor, as if he could, by such simple gesture, grant her absolution.

And he could; she trusted him.

Reaching out, she touched his cheek, unmindful of the magi, the investigation, the room itself. His skin was cold; the flesh that had housed the man would never again be warm.

She could see that the death had been quick; that it must have been painless. And the justice in that? None.

How old she had grown. She did not rail; she did not seek to diminish her sorrow and her rage by outward display. She accepted the fact of his death almost dispassionately, and took comfort from the fact that it *had not hurt*.

Oh, but it had. It did. "Alowan," she said quietly.

The need to be known was a weakness. The need to be understood. She realized that she had not risen above them; she had left behind the need to be loved; had given up all but the practical elements of the need to be acknowledged; had in the end accepted that the need to be admired would be too costly to maintain.

But the need to be *known?*

She thought of Adam. And of Levec.

Then, with something akin to a sigh, she withdrew her hand and turned to examine the body of the cat.

The kitchen lights were flickering. The lamp dominated the table because the shutters to the courtyard had been closed. With a little care and imagination, one could pretend that the den was housed in the dead of night, a time of dream and nightmare.

Adam sat by Finch's side, as close as the separate seats of two large chairs allowed. But he was distracted; his head bobbed between her and the still door, passing over those who sat in between.

Just as well.

Ellerson was absent. He had taken the extraordinary step of requesting a short leave of absence, and Finch had been too numb to do anything but nod. She had before her paper, a quill, an inkwell, and hands that were black and smudged; the words themselves were more solid in intention than in execution.

"How long does she have?" Finch asked at last, setting the quill aside. She spoke Torra, and Angel frowned.

Adam started and then turned to face her. "I don't know," he said, repeating what he had told The Terafin. "Days, if she is like the others."

"How often can you do what you did tonight?"

He closed his eyes. She was suddenly glad of Levec's absence.

"As often as necessary," was his quiet—and surprising—reply. "Kalliaris willing, that won't be often."

"She wants Jewel back."

Finch frowned. "We all want Jay back."

"Then why do you wait? She *is* your Matriarch."

"Jay's not exactly easy to find." Finch heaved a sigh, pushing herself away from the table with the flat of her hands. "And even if she were, it sounds like she's already fighting for her life. I don't know if she'd make it back in time."

"She came to us through the fires," he said, serious now, his expression so earnest, Finch could almost see the flames in his eyes. "Could we build a fire in the courtyard?"

"Only once," she said, a wry smile tugging at her lips.

His frown was subtly wrong. A powerful frown, and a familiar one. "I am serious, Finch."

"So am I. Look, Adam, we *could* get permission to build a fire, and we could build it almost anywhere—but it'd be such an odd request that everyone in the House would know about it."

"So? The Terafin is the Matriarch."

"She is the ruler," Finch said, correcting him gently. "Yes."

"And Jewel is her daughter."

"I'm not sure that word means what it means in Weston. Jay is her—"

"Jewel ATerafin will be . . . ruler . . . when The Terafin dies."

"If you know that, you also know that The Terafin has not announced it; she has *not* made it known. If the fires were built—these fires that drew her to *you* in the South—they would be questioned. We could tell the House Council to stuff themselves—but they'd just watch. If Jay *did* return, they'd all know. And they'd know it was significant."

"But—" His expression shifted. "The House Council. Someone there is responsible for the old man's death."

"Yes."

"And The Terafin's condition."

She frowned. "If we knew that for certain, we'd be ahead of the game. Do *you* know it?"

"She does."

"But she has no proof."

He struggled again, and when he spoke, he spoke in Weston. In clear, flawless Weston. She was shocked. And not a little frightened.

"Then we must have proof." He rose.

"Adam—"

"The House is her family," he said, severe now. "It is the only family that she knows; she has given up all others." A frown—a duality of deep lines—chased themselves across his lips like the play of shadow in lamplight. She tried to follow them, to pin them down, to identify them. At last he said, "Why did she forsake her kin?"

"Maybe her kin didn't need her."

His eyes were wide, but they narrowed; he did not attempt to hide his confusion. "What has need to do with blood?"

Ah. "Everything, in the Empire. Or at least it's supposed to." Her smile was gentle. "These people are *not* my kin," she lifted an arm and swept it in the crowded half circle that contained all of her den.

"And your blood-kin?"

"They abandoned me," she replied unself-consciously.

His face twisted. "But *why?*"

And she realized that she wasn't as unself-conscious as all that. Stiffly, speaking because she heard the profound need to know in words that were not meant to wound, she said, "Damned if I know."

"Mine died," Teller offered.

"Mine left me," Carver said.

Angel shrugged, giving nothing away.

"I left mine," Jester said brightly, "so I guess The Terafin and I have a lot in common."

"Mine are dead," Arann said.

Only Daine was silent. Completely silent. He did not speak a word. His hands were brown with the blood that a cursory washing had not removed; they rested upon the table, as motionless as they had ever been.

"But—but the rest of your family?"

"The rest?"

"Your grandparents. Your aunts. Your uncles."

She shook her head. "I don't know. I didn't know them."

"But—"

"Adam," she told him softly, "this is not the South. I don't know how large your families are there. I don't know how much land they own."

"They own nothing but the road they travel."

"But here, in Averalaan, people are often poor. Or worse. They do things that . . . that they have to. To eat. To live."

"So do we."

She shook her head. "These *are* my kin. They're the only kin I have. The only kin I want."

"But you are ATerafin, yes?"

"Yes—but none of the House members are related by blood. Only by loyalty and allegiance."

He shook his head.

"Rymark is Gabriel's son," Angel said quietly.

"I'd forgotten that."

"It's easy to forget."

"This is why you war," he said at last.

"In the South, there is no war?"

"In the South there is always war. But among families? Almost never."

"And there are no deaths?"

He hesitated, his perfect Weston faltering. Finch was afraid, and not for the first time, of the healer's gift. Afraid for Adam. She touched his arm, and his hand, still until that moment, gripped hers tightly. "There are deaths," he said at last. "The Matriarch is the law; she decides."

"Why?"

"Because. I don't know. If you betray the family, you die. If you abandon the *Voyanne*. If you conspire with the clans against the dictate of the Matriarch. If you kill or injure the children." He shrugged.

"And no one wants to be Matriarch?"

"I wouldn't want to be. I don't think Margret did."

"Oh." She absorbed this. "Many people want to be The Terafin."

"Why?"

"Because they think they'll have power. No. Because they *will* have power."

"But they carry the weight of the family."

Her smile was bitter. "Not if they're like Haerrad, they don't. Or Rymark."

"I don't like Elonne much either," Carver volunteered.

"Whatever."

"Maybe this is why the men don't rule the families. Only the clans."

"Maybe. Men rule here. Sometimes."

"She doesn't want a man to rule. She wants Jewel." He hesitated. "And I want her here as well."

"Why?" Teller spoke softly.

Adam shrank, his slender form folding to lose inches. "Because," he said quietly, "it's the only peace Amarais will have."

Finch closed her eyes. Without sight to distract her, she listened to voice, to movement, the shifting of weight on chairs that creaked beneath it, the scuffle of boots against the floor. "Adam, it's *very important* that you keep this to yourself. Do you understand?"

"Yes."

"Even among us."

He hesitated. And then he said, "Am I your kin, Finch?"

The question forced her eyes open. His were upon her, wide and unblinking. Hunger, there. "Yes," she said softly. "Or you wouldn't be here."

His smile was hesitant, but it was there. "Margret won't like it."

"Does it matter?"

"Of course it matters."

"Well, we won't tell her."

He laughed. "She'll find out. She always does." And then his expression shifted again. "Summon Jewel ATerafin," he said quietly. "Summon her now."

She didn't want to. Because she understood that when Jewel came home, The Terafin was free, at last, to die.

But when she received the summons to the upper remove, she felt her resolve harden. Ellerson bore the writ; Ellerson came with clothing suitable to such an important meeting. She almost told him to put it away, but Teller gravely accepted the domicis' choice, and she followed her den-kin's silent lead.

She left everyone else in the wing. Ellerson, she chose to take with her; Gregori had already armed himself.

"Will you be okay with just one guard?" Carver asked nervously.

"We will have more than one," Ellerson said gravely. "Torvan ATerafin waits without; he has at his side no less than seven men."

All of whom were of more use in a fight, and they all knew it. Carver nodded curtly.

"Watch Adam," she told him. "Watch Daine."

Arann looked at them both, and they nodded. Just as they would have, she thought, if she had been Jay.

Gabriel ATerafin met them in the library, and he looked mildly disconcerted to see them there. They had been waiting a quarter of an hour in an increasingly uncomfortable silence that stacks of books did nothing to break.

Finch looked at the right-kin's face; he looked as if he had gone without sleep for over a week. The chiseled gravity and perfection of his somber expression had at last given way to the roughness beneath, and his hair was almost pure white. She was shocked, and said nothing.

Teller rose immediately and tendered Gabriel ATerafin a perfect bow. That perfection was Ellerson's gift—if daily training and almost military criticism could be called a gift. He had taken to it silently; she had taken to it with a series of bitter complaints. Silence seemed to be more successful.

Gabriel ATerafin gathered his bearing quickly. "ATerafin," he said, returning Teller's bow. "ATerafin."

Finch started to speak, but Ellerson's stiff expression had taken on an edge; she closed her lips over the words, straightening her shoulders.

"You wait to speak with The Terafin?" Gabriel said idly.

Finch nodded; that seemed safe.

"I have word for her as well," he replied.

Morretz chose that moment to join them, as if he had been silently watching from the gallery. "Right-kin," he said, his bow putting Teller's to shame—although how, Finch couldn't quite say. "The Terafin is, at the moment, in meetings with the magi. She sends her apologies, but she is unable to attend you."

Gabriel nodded, but Finch could see frustration break the line of his perfect mouth. He did not, however, leave. "Morretz," he said quietly.

"ATerafin."

"The House is alive with rumor. No one—not even I myself—has been granted leave to visit the healerie, and the fact that the guards beyond its closed doors are *all* of the Chosen has been lost on no one."

"And you fight a rearguard action against the demands of the House Council?"

Gabriel's smile was grim. "I'm an old soldier," he said softly. "It is not the most difficult action that The Terafin has ordered me to undertake."

Morretz nodded, his expression so smooth it gave nothing away.

"Ask her to send me word," the right-kin said, a moment after the silence threatened to become uncomfortable. His gaze slid across Finch and Teller. "Tell her I wish to know what she wishes to be known."

"She has faith in your discretion," Morretz replied. "She has always had faith in your discretion."

This seemed to shore the old man up. "Alowan?"

"He is, as you surmise, dead."

And that seemed to take the steel out of his spine. He did not move, but everything about his posture suggested a stagger. He, too, had taken a blow. No thought left for Finch or Teller now; no suspicion about their presence.

"His assistants?"

"They are dead as well, all save one."

"And that?"

"Daine ATerafin."

Gabriel bowed.

"Confirm the rumors, if you must."

He bowed again.

"And Gabriel?"

"Yes?"

"The House Council will be summoned on the morrow, if The Terafin's investigation permits."

Gabriel looked relieved. It was the last of his face Finch saw as he sought, and exited, the double doors.

"Very good, ATerafin," Ellerson said quietly.

She grimaced. "Don't we trust him?" The words were almost plaintive.

And as such, beneath response.

"You would do best," an entirely different voice replied, "to trust no one."

From behind Morretz, a man emerged, changing the landscape of the library.

Finch worked really hard to stop from cringing. She started to rise, and caught Ellerson's gaze; he gave her no direction at all, damn him.

Teller rose, though. Teller bowed.

And Finch bowed as well, although it was hard—she didn't want to take her eyes from Duvari's chill expression.

He didn't seem to notice. He walked past the table that they had just deserted, and made his way to the doors. Without asking for permission, he locked them. Or at least she thought he locked them; his back was turned to them, and it shielded all sight of his hands.

"Devon," he said, turning.

Devon ATerafin joined them, coming from the same shadows that had hidden Duvari. She had always liked Devon, but in his movement, in his neutral expression, his utter silence, she saw the similarities to Duvari. Gregori ATerafin rose; she had forgotten he was there.

She turned to Ellerson again. His fingers touched the tabletop lightly, and she recognized after a moment the signal for silence, for secrecy. It looked odd, given as it was by his domicis' hands, for it belonged properly among a den of thieves.

Hers.

"That was unfortunate," Devon said, his gaze lingering on the closed door, or perhaps upon the route that Gabriel ATerafin had taken.

"It was. Were the Chosen given no instructions?"

"He *is* the right-kin," Morretz said coolly. "And in as much as there is a steward to the House, it is Gabriel."

"They were to grant no one entrance."

"They are not simple guards," Morretz replied. "As you well know, ATerafin. They chose to grant him entry. They will grant entry to no other members of the House Council unless there is an emergency."

"They granted entrance—obvious entrance—to the two most junior members of the Council, and he noted it."

"He is not in contention for the House throne."

"His son is."

An old argument; Finch could taste the stale embers in the words. She longed to crawl under the table.

This was why Ellerson had been so careful in his choice of clothing, damn him. She wondered what *else* he knew. Was wise enough not to ask him.

"ATerafin," Morretz said. When no one responded, he added, "Finch."

"Me?"

Just the hint of a smile touched his lips, and she was grateful for it; everyone else was cold as steel. Even Devon. Especially Devon.

"And Teller. I apologize for keeping you waiting, but what I said to Gabriel was true. The Terafin speaks at length with the magi. She will see you now."

Duvari left the door. When Finch and Teller moved to join Morretz, the Lord of the Compact fell in behind them like a malignant shadow—the kind that only nightmare produces.

She longed to ask why he was here.

"ATerafin, ATerafin," Morretz continued.

Gregori and Devon nodded. The confusion of surnames did not trouble them; they moved like cats across the room. Like great, big, hunting cats.

Together, they walked. This time, however, Morretz took them to the rooms that Finch recognized as official function rooms; the offices, the meeting rooms, in which The Terafin entertained the most important of her guests.

She did not feel particularly safe with her escort; even Gregori seemed remote and dangerous.

Ellerson's hand touched the small of her back; she had slowed to a crawl without realizing it. Teller offered her his arm, and she took it gratefully. Clumsily, if Ellerson's sudden clearing of throat was any indication.

The doors opened, no hands upon them.

Finch cringed. She had seen enough magic in the last day that she could happily live another decade without witnessing any more of it. Teller glanced at her quietly. She wondered when he had become so much ATerafin that he could weather this so easily; he was, next to Finch, the smallest and the youngest of the people present.

But if he could do it, so could she. They had so much else in common.

The Terafin stood. The desk behind which she occasionally sat was pristine in its emptiness. The table that held refreshments during the meal hours held them now, but they were almost untouched; Sigurne presided over them like an aged aunt. Beside Sigurne was a grim looking man only barely her junior, in Finch's opinion—it was hard to tell at that age.

"Take a seat," The Terafin said. The words were flat, even disturbing, although it took Finch a moment to understand why. They were shorn of manners, of grace, of the subtle perfection that kept her at a distance from those she ruled. Jay might have said them, and in just the same tone.

Finch scurried toward a chair, losing Teller's arm in her haste to obey; if Jay *had* said them, and in that tone, it would have meant there was trouble—and Jay wasn't particularly patient during a crisis. Teller, however, paused for long enough to give The Terafin the bow her rank demanded.

Gregori and Devon bowed as well, and they made themselves comfortable in the sloping wooden chairs. Duvari, however, chose to stand. He always did.

"Member Allister APorphan has concluded his investigation," The Terafin said, without preamble, when all who would sit had been seated.

The unfamiliar man grimaced.

Duvari stepped forward. He was the Kings' man, and there wasn't a noble in Averalaan who didn't know it. There wasn't, Finch thought, a single man or woman of power, no matter how inconsequential their birth, who didn't.

She noted, with some satisfaction, that Allister APorphan must be a man of power; he was distinctly uncomfortable in Duvari's presence.

"I was not aware that the Astari had an interest in House business," he said. Her opinion of him shifted remarkably in that one sentence.

"Your perception is not at issue here," Duvari replied. "You serve best by concentrating on your area of expertise."

"I have served the Kings," the magi relied stiffly.

"Indeed. Your record has been exemplary."

Finch thought he meant it as a compliment; she had heard compliments offered in deadly insult, and there was no malice in Duvari's tone. There was no warmth in it either.

Sigurne Mellifas rose.

Sword fights were less noisy than the clash of glares, but not less definitive.

"Member APorphan," she said quietly, and resumed her seat. "Please."

He nodded, although he was no less unhappy.

"I'm not sure what you've been told, Duvari," he began.

"I am aware of the death of Alowan Rowanson."

Rowanson. Finch had almost never heard his family name before. It sounded familiar; she must have. But she couldn't remember when. He was Alowan, Alowan of the healerie; Alowan not of Terafin.

"And its method?"

"There is only one way to kill a healer of any talent, and Alowan Rowanson has proved himself to be such a man over the years."

Allister APorphan nodded. "And the death of his assistants?"

"Is of some interest to me. They were not healer-born, to the best of my knowledge."

"They were not."

"But they died the death of the healer-born."

The animosity faded; the magi's gaze grew intent. Focused. Age did not fall away from his face; it was there, would always be there. But it no longer seemed to diminish him, in Finch's eyes. "Indeed, and that is strange. It is not actually simple to behead a person. In the case of the younger woman, it's clear that she struggled—but the corpse also makes clear that the deathblow was clean and quickly delivered, in spite of her awareness. Her clothing is not torn, and her body is not otherwise bruised; she lies as she fell. Clearly she was not restrained; clearly, she was not held.

"Nor was the second woman. The healer's death is more simple; he lay abed, sleeping."

"You think that his assassins were not aware of the status of his assistants?"

"I believe that they were not certain if they were dealing with the healer-born or no; they chose prudence in their attack; it is clear they meant to deprive the House of its healers." He paused. "I assume, in this scenario, that there *is* more than one."

Duvari's glance went to The Terafin while Finch attempted to assimilate the words.

The Terafin nodded quietly. "There is one more. But he is ATerafin."

"It is widely known?"

"It is obviously known. Had you asked me a day ago, I would have offered a different answer, however."

"And the assassin—or assassins—were not aware that this . . . other healer . . . was not within the healerie?"

"Either that, or they had no choice. They timed the strike," she added, "in such a way that, had things gone according to their regular schedule, he would have been present."

Duvari frowned. "His absence?"

"House business," she said curtly.

He nodded, as if he expected no less.

"The name of the healer, Terafin?" Duvari asked.

She frowned, and the frown seemed to grow crystals, it was so cold. "Do not waste my time, Duvari. You are already obviously aware of his identity."

Duvari had the grace to dip his head in acknowledgment of her displeasure.

"Had Daine ATerafin arrived earlier, he would now be dead."

"This is true?" Duvari said, turning once again to Allister APorphan.

"The deaths occurred less than an hour before he discovered them."

"How much less?"

Allister APorphan frowned. "It is not always possible to be accurate in our assessments," he replied quietly. "But with your permission, I will ask for the discreet aid of the Judgment-born." He spoke this last to The Terafin.

She was slow to answer. Slow enough that the words sank in; had meaning.

Finch had been a member of the House for at least as long as she had been on the streets of the twenty-fifth holding, and in all that time, she had never seen the Judgment-born at work.

Duvari's frown was significant, but he waited upon The Terafin.

At last, she nodded. "I am reluctant to incur the debt, or the wrath, of the sons of Mandaros," she said quietly.

"I understand, Terafin, and if you request it, I will refrain from doing so; they will, however, be able to offer some answer to your questions; answers that we cannot obtain."

"This is a House affair," Duvari said.

"It is," she replied serenely.

"But if it will not offer offense, I would concur with the magi."

And how often, Finch thought, *does that happen?*

"Who will speak with the sons of Mandaros?" The Terafin asked, after a pause.

After a longer one, Allister APorphan said, "I will." But he, too, seemed reluctant.

Finch hesitated, her gaze bouncing between the men and women who chose to grace the silence with speech. Sigurne Mellifas must have sensed her confusion, for she turned to Finch and smiled briefly.

"Mandaros is the Lord of Judgment," she told her gently.

Finch nodded; this much anyone knew.

"But he is also the guardian of the dead."

She nodded again, glancing at Teller; he was still.

"Do you understand what this means? No, perhaps it is not clear. We know little of the Halls of Mandaros. The dead go there; that much is plain. And they are judged; that, too, is known. But what is less well known is that they are not called to judgment—they choose the moment of their approach. Some go swiftly, either to return to the world or to pass on."

"Where?"

"Some go to the Hells, having made their final choice. Some return here, surrendering all memories of their previous life."

"And the others?"

"Ah. That, the gods—none of them—have ever ventured to say. It vexes the magi, and the Order of Knowledge; it always has." She smiled; clearly some memory had returned to amuse her. "But some of the dead return to these lands, reborn, shorn of the memories of their previous lives, and some do not."

Finch nodded.

"There are times—or so it is said—that the dead themselves are restless; they plead with Mandaros, and he allows it, indulging their whims. If they go on, he might at last seek peace by passing on some part of their message to another god; that god, in turn, will deliver that message to one of his mortal children.

"But most of the dead are no longer concerned with the living; they have done their time. They are left to reflect upon the whole of their life—or their lives—and assess their failures, their successes, their desires. This may take years, and it may take centuries—time is subjective to the dead. Or perhaps to us.

"But Mandaros grants them the peace in which to do this, and it is that peace that we must seek to disturb, for a time."

Finch frowned. "I don't understand."

"He will summon the dead, if the dead remain within his domain."

"If he chooses to heed our request," Allister APorphan added grimly.

"Indeed." Sigurne was still serene. "He is their guardian," she said again. "And they are all children to him; he does not wish to upset them by exposing them again to the responsibilities and cares of the world they have been released from.

"Especially those," she added quietly, "who left violently."

He's not going to be happy, then, she thought, understanding the hesitation of the magi.

Morretz looked up suddenly, and then his gaze swung toward the magi; something close to open disapproval was in his eyes, and around the tight corners of compressed lips.

"My apologies, Terafin," Member APorphan said quietly. "But the circumstances that surround this death—and much else besides—seem . . . unique enough . . . that I thought there was a good chance you would agree to this intrusion upon your affairs."

CHAPTER FOUR

A YOUNG man, dressed as an acolyte of Mandaros, wearing muted gray, the sleeves edged in alternating bands of black and white, followed Morretz through the door; Finch craned her neck to see who else would follow.

No one did.

She turned back to the boy, her eyes widening, and Teller stepped firmly on her foot. As one, the men and women gathered in the room rose; Finch was the only one who hesitated, and that, because Teller had not taken his foot off hers. But she managed.

"Son of Mandaros," The Terafin said gravely, "we are honored by your presence."

The boy bowed, his dark hair curved by gravity in a wave to either side of his slender face. He was, she thought, a few years older than Adam.

Until he rose, and turned to face the room.

She had seen the god-born before, but always at a remove. The Mother's Daughter, the Kings, the High Priests of the various churches—all had eyes that were similar to his. But only in appearance.

His eyes were different. Golden, but so much more than that: gold was cold and heavy, inert, its power in the value that others assessed it. Nothing about his eyes suggested that his power was in the hands of others. Nor was his expression cold; it was lively, alert, the gaze itself penetrating.

As if he could look into you, Finch thought, *and see everything you had ever done, good and bad.*

She had been afraid of that, all her life. But she felt no fear of judgment now, and it gave her the oddest sense of peace.

Duvari was the only man in the room who did not deign to meet the god-born eyes. That brought her no comfort at all; even the hint of smug satisfaction was beyond her.

"Micah," Member APorphan said, bowing low.

"Allister." The boy smiled. Grave, older than his apparent age could possibly account for. He added, "Be seated, please. Of all people, you should know better."

The magi grimaced, and the boy smiled; years fled his face. "Allister found me," he said quietly, looking suddenly at Finch. "I was not born to the temple or the priesthood, and the transition has been an interesting one."

"Where did he find you?" Finch asked.

Teller's foot hit hers again.

The boy's smile deepened. "Not far," he said, "from where you were first found; not far from where you were born."

She could have taken shelter in confusion, but it would have been a lie; she knew what he meant when the words left his lips. Her own opened in a small circle of shock, but she spoke around it.

"I'm sorry," she said quietly. "It's just that I've never seen one of the god-born—in Terafin—who wasn't attended by priests, acolytes, or Kings' Swords. Lots of them."

"Normally, I would be," he replied, with a twist of the lips that made his distaste clear. Finch liked him then. "But there was urgency in the summons, and Allister wanted discretion." He shrugged, the movement slow and lazy. "To be fair, I don't much like being attended. It's not that the priests are bad men—not even that they're difficult. But they insist on pomp and ceremony, and they burn incense in braziers which they insist on lighting just before we leave the temple." His nose wrinkled; he looked fourteen. She thought she saw freckles against the pale backdrop of skin. "It always makes me sneeze."

Teller cleared his throat and looked away.

Finch, unwisely, laughed out loud.

Dark brows rose. "You think that's funny?"

"It makes me want to sneeze, too," she said, containing laughter with effort. "Or it makes my eyes water. It never occurred to me that it would bother the god-born."

"Well, it can't be seen to, of course. It makes talking *really* difficult, though. One day, I was in the Magisterial Hall, and I *could not* speak because I would have sneezed all over the sons of Justice." He laughed, "I think they know."

"Micah," Allister said, speaking sternly. Speaking, Finch thought, as if to a wayward but much loved son.

"Sorry." He shrugged again, but winked broadly at her.

No one seemed to notice. But Teller stepped on her foot for a third time. *I'm going to kick him,* she thought.

"I wouldn't," the young son of Judgment said. "The old man beside you will have a heart attack, and you *know* that will get you in trouble."

She laughed out loud again.

"Micah!"

"Sorry. No, honestly, I meant that one."

The Terafin's expression almost collapsed; Finch caught the shifting line of her mouth with surprise. Realized that she had never once heard The Terafin laugh out loud. And realized as well, that it had been a very long time since she had seen her really smile.

Duvari's expression shifted into something truly grim.

Finch wondered if the amount of mirth in a room full of powerful people had to be a constant. Funny thing, though: when Duvari turned that frown on *her,* her own mirth dried up really quickly.

"Micah is a bit . . . unusual . . . for the priesthood," Allister APorphan said apologetically. "But he really is perfect for the job at hand."

Duvari had the grace not to look openly doubtful, although doubt radiated from him as if it were warmth, and he was a bonfire. A bonfire lit under the feet of people who had done something particularly bad in an imagined barbarian country.

Micah's smile dimpled his face. Finch loved it. "The god is pretty tolerant," he told her. "He doesn't mind lack of formality. Well, from me at any rate."

"He is used to overlooking the faults of the merely mortal," Allister said, aggrieved. "Micah, the woman to your left is *The Terafin.*"

The boy nodded. "I recognize her. I've seen her in the Hall of The Ten, in *Avantari.*"

"This," the magi said severely, "is the *other* reason why he dislikes an escort of priests. They would, were they present, be swarming all over him, like bees to honey."

"Would they sting much?"

Micah nodded. "And they'd buzz a lot, too. Just the other day, Priest AVallin said—"

"*Do not* indulge in your impressions here, Micah. Please."

"Allister," Micah said gravely, "would have made an *excellent* priest. I never understood how he could end up on the Council of the Magi; he's not nearly dotty or obsessive enough."

"*Micah!*"

Finch had thought Allister's reluctance to speak with the god had something to do with the god himself, but seeing his reddened cheeks, she had to wonder.

Micah shrugged once more, as if to exert independence, and then walked over to Allister APorphan and carelessly took the empty chair at his side. "Sorry."

"It is," Allister told Finch, "his most commonly used word. It is *not,* however, his most heartfelt one."

"No. That's reserved for the swear words I'm not allowed to use anymore."

"Me, too!"

That made *him* laugh openly. It was worth Ellerson's pinched expression, too.

"Okay, okay. I'm ready to be serious." And just like that, he was. Finch almost regretted it; he looked old again, austere. "You want me to speak with my father." He looked not to Allister, but to The Terafin.

She nodded.

"Given that it's Allister who summoned me, I'm going to guess that the dead didn't leave voluntarily."

"No one leaves voluntarily, do they?" Finch asked.

"More or less. The old. The very sick. The suicidal, but that's a bit of a different case."

"Really? Why? If life is bad enough that they choose death to end it, don't you think they deserve some sympathy?" She thought of all of the times she had considered it, in the twenty-fifth holding. Most of them had been before Jay, before Teller—but not all. The winters had been brutal, when the snows had come. The hunger—she could remember it clearly.

And his eyes flared, miniature suns, proof that warmth and heat were not, could never be, the same.

"I'll take that as a no," she said, almost stepping back.

"It's a no," he said, voice devoid of humor, although the cadence of the words used did not descend to formality.

"Forgive her, Priest," The Terafin said, with just a hint of a smile. "She is easily influenced, and you are perhaps not the influence that those who shepherd her would have chosen."

"As long as she doesn't say that in my father's hearing," he replied. His eyes became his eyes again, but slowly. "You'll ruin it for sure."

"She will not speak *a word* in your father's presence."

He nodded.

"You mean I have to . . . to be . . . *there?*"

"You've never been Between, have you?"

Finch hesitated a moment. And then she shook her head.

"It's . . . a bit disconcerting. Try to remember that even if it feels like there's nothing beneath your feet, you won't fall. Exactly."

Funny how comforting that wasn't.

"And try not to mind about his voice."

She turned to look at Teller; Teller offered her a lot of profile.

"Duvari," Micah added calmly, "you want to stay?"

As if he were just another man.

Duvari looked very unamused; it was his only answer.

"Suit yourself," Micah said—she had long since given up trying to see him as a priest—with, yes, a shrug. "He bothering you?" he added to Finch.

Finch nearly croaked.

"Micah," Duvari said coldly.

"Well, you bother almost everyone else. But I figure the others can take care of themselves."

"She *is* ATerafin. And a member of the House Council, at that."

Micah whistled, his eyes narrowing. They were still comfortable to look at. "You are?"

She nodded. She expected he knew it very well, but was suddenly uncertain.

"I didn't figure you for a politico."

"I'm—"

"She is, like you," The Terafin told him, "new to the constraints of this particular life, and like you, she has little choice in the matter."

"Fair enough. Hint, though," he added, as he closed lids over those remarkable, dangerous eyes. "Don't piss Duvari off."

"You are."

"Yeah, well. He can't exactly kill me, can he?"

Someone coughed. It wasn't Teller and it wasn't Ellerson, which was good, but it was familiar. It took her a moment to place the voice, and when she did, she swung round to look at Devon. She had almost forgotten he was here.

But he *was* here; the Devon she thought she knew. The one she liked.

For a moment she envied him his distinct ability to *be* two people at once; to live in two different worlds; to serve two different masters.

"Don't," Micah said, which was starting to get a tad annoying. But his voice was kind enough, and she felt—although he didn't say it in so many words—that they had to stick together, orphans of the street, those who lived in the grace of the patriciate without ever quite becoming part of it.

The mists began to roll in.

She thought it was smoke, at first, and almost leaped out of her chair, her eyes wide in terror.

Fire, she knew. And the death it left in its wake was so terribly ugly, so obviously painful, that she was young again. Summer young, autumn young, her life surrounded by, made by, dangerously old buildings.

Teller was by her side, and for the first time since they had entered The Terafin's library, they were siblings, caught in the same memories, the same old fears.

Ellerson rose like sunlight, breaking nightmare. His hands fell upon their shoulders in silence, and when he judged the silence to be inadequate, he said, "Do not fear the mists. And *do not* run from them."

She would have felt better if Micah had spoken, but she saw that he couldn't; his arms were stiff at his sides, and he was trembling. His eyelids fluttered up and down, like window shades gone insane.

"How do you *know* it's safe?"

"I know. That will have to do," he added quietly. "It is not wise to speak of other gods in the presence of one, unless he chooses to speak of them first."

"But—"

"Finch."

Teller had calmed, and Finch found it impossible to hold onto her panic. Ellerson's voice was reasonable, calm, low; it held dispassionate knowledge, delivered, as always, in the calm tones with which he criticized etiquette and clothing.

Sigurne said, "Mind him, both of you. Running in the Between is . . . ill-advised. You do not know who you might run into—but you should know that you will not escape the Between until the gods have finished."

She nodded, and watched as mist ate away at the floor, the walls, and the windows; as it absorbed the limbs of chairs and tables, as it devoured sunlight. The last thing to go was the scent and taste of the ocean, the ever present ocean.

She reached out and caught Teller's hand; he didn't pull away.

"Allister," Micah said. If she hadn't seen his lips move, she wouldn't have recognized his voice. "Be ready. He comes."

But Allister APorphan needed no more warning than the change in Micah's voice. He stood at once, hands fussing with the collars of his robes as if the god were as fussy as the highborn. And maybe he was.

The god was *tall.*

Taller than the ceilings that had also vanished; taller, she thought, than the trees in the Common. Certainly older, although it was hard to tell his age; his features shifted as if they were the surface of a swiftly moving river. A muddy river; she could not see beyond those features, because she kept trying to pin them down.

He—although even that was inaccurate—looked down slowly. When he spoke, his voice matched his face; it was not one thing or the other. It was young and old; it was male and female. No, more than that it was all of those things at once—as if every voice she had ever heard had suddenly been joined together to speak in unison.

She didn't like it.

But she couldn't ignore it either.

"Micah," the god said. "You have been long away from my lands." There was a rich, deep affection in the words.

An affection that she suddenly desired. She was loved, and knew it, but for just a moment, all mortal affection seemed insignificant and flighty.

"It's not," Micah told her, and he turned to face her, his eyes glowing like lamps, but still his own.

She swallowed and nodded, unable to entirely crawl free from the weight of the feeling.

He turned back to the god, who waited as if his time had no meaning. "Sorry," he said.

She almost laughed. But it would have been a wild, fleeting sound, more hysteria than amusement, and she didn't want to share it.

"You apologize too much," the god replied sternly.

"I have a lot to apologize for."

"Let me be the judge of that."

"You always are." Micah's lips curved in a quirky smile. He bowed. "Father," he added. "*Mandaros.*"

She saw Micah as his father made miniature when the name left his mouth.

"Why have you called me?" the god asked serenely.

She expected some smart-ass answer, but it didn't come. Instead, Micah bowed, his hair vanishing into mist. When he rose, that mist trailed about him like a living presence, brushing against his chin, his cheeks, the lids of his flickering eyes.

She *really* didn't like where the thought led, and she stifled it quickly. But she felt it now: the mist was alive.

"Father," Micah said, his voice deepening, "we beg your indulgence."

"As always."

"As always."

"And this time?"

"Three have come to your Halls this last day."

"Many more than three," the god replied. Thunder laced the words. Warning. She couldn't have spoken if she wanted to.

"Of course."

"And of these three?"

"They did not leave peacefully," he replied. He was placid now. "Who were they, in this life?"

Micah turned, at last, to Allister. He lifted a hand, and mist trailed from his fingers like liquid. The magi rose, and without any marked hesitation, he took the young man's hand.

"Father," Micah said. "You know Allister."

"I know him," Mandaros replied. His eyes fell upon the magi, and Finch realized suddenly that *this* was what Allister APorphan had feared. She watched his ashen face; sweat grew in the folds of skin that seemed—to her—too old to shed it. But he did not bow, did not buckle, and did not flee. He weathered the god's regard.

The god nodded and released him; Micah's knuckles were white. "Allister," Mandaros said gravely. "You know that I am the guardian of the dead."

"Mandaros," Allister replied, his voice so thin and shaky in comparison to the god's chorus that Finch could barely hear him.

"You know as well that I am loath to disturb their peace; they have lived in your dim world, they have suffered there, and they have earned what little rest my Halls may grant them."

The magi nodded grimly, as if this were a ritual with which he had become reluctantly familiar.

"Why, then, do you ask my son to disturb them? They have come new from death, and their deaths were not pleasant."

"It is the manner of their killer that disturbs us, Lord. And if we are not to flood your halls with the newly dead, we must know more of their final hours, their final minutes."

"The living have no purchase upon the loyalties of the dead," Mandaros replied. "I may ask, but I *will not* command."

"We ask no more, Lord. I have never asked more."

"No," the god replied, the word echoing. "You have not. I will do this thing, and I will hold you accountable for it when you have at last finished your brief sojourn upon the plane."

"I will pay your price," the old man replied with a pale gravity.

"Do not agree to pay a debt that you do not understand," the god said.

"Yes, Lord."

Mandaros lifted a hand, and the mists rose like curtains, fine and thin. Finch could see through them, but the shifting shape of the god had become more diffuse, and she forced herself to look away. It was that, or go mad.

The mist grew thick in the shadow that the god suddenly cast. It had not been there before, Finch realized, and it was almost not there now; it was subtle, and nothing else about the god was. She was not surprised when the mist gathered momentum and began to

spin beneath his outstretched palms. Tendrils returned, pulling away
from Micah's hands and face until three columns stood, each the
height of a man.

These, the god began to sculpt.

He had no tools; he did not need them.

Here, in the presence of the living, he *made* the dead forms they
might wear. Like garments, she thought, spun fine.

The dead came and cloaked themselves in ghostly raiment, their
features becoming distinct; the points of nose and chin emerging
first, the rounded curve of forehead quick to follow. Eyes came last,
lids closed. She saw limbs, but they seemed insignificant; she drew
breath and held it, waiting for those eyes to open.

They did.

They were shorn of color, shorn of expression, but these things
developed as the god worked, and when he at last lowered his
hands, expression flooded into faces that were blessedly familiar.

Without thinking, Finch started forward.

The god's hand fell like a scythe. "*Do not touch them,*" he said.

She froze, trapped by his gaze, a rabbit waiting for the claws or
jaws of a predator.

"Micah is my son," the god continued, "but he is sadly lacking
in training. I know that he told you little; he comes to the Between
naturally, and he forgets himself when he begins to enter it.

"The dead are dead. Do not touch them; they cannot return, and
I will not have them disturbed by the living."

She did not speak, and after a moment, the storm gentled. "There
are always things left unfinished," he said. "There are always regrets, even in the most blameless of lives."

She nodded, voiceless.

But her eyes went to Alowan's, and Alowan met them with his
own, the artifice of a god giving him the life that the god himself
said was over.

It was suddenly important to Finch that Alowan not be angry;
suddenly important that he know no fear and no further pain.

"I'm sorry," she whispered. "Alowan—"

The girls screamed in unison, catching the name she had spoken
aloud and making of it something to be feared and dreaded: death.

The god touched them gently, a finger upon each of their foreheads. "Peace," he whispered, and bending, he breathed across their
faces.

The breath had substance. She could see it leave his lips. And
when it did, it took warmth with it; there was anger in his eyes.

But none at all in Alowan's.

"Finch?" he said, as if slow to remember her name. That stung. But she nodded hopefully.

"And . . . Teller. Yes," he added softly, to himself. "Teller." Teller nodded, but he had listened; he didn't speak.

"Why are you here? Have you come to the Halls?"

Finch swallowed and shook her head, willing Allister to speak. Allister, the bastard, was silent.

"No," she said, because Alowan clearly expected a reply. "We're here." Lamely she added, "In the Terafin Manse. The—The Terafin is here, too."

"Ah. Amarais." None of the hesitation that had marred her name was present when he spoke The Terafin's. He turned, and his lips folded in a very familiar smile.

But the girls, Finch noted, were silent. Like statues. Like the dead.

"He has walked near the edges of my realm before," Mandaros replied. He did not speak with kindness. "And he has taken the dead from me before I could protect them."

"They are not fond of healers here," Alowan said, with a wry grin.

"We are fond of all who cross our threshold."

"Ah?" Alowan said. "You don't make the passage back any easier."

"We do not deny your nature, or your gift, healer. Be at peace."

Alowan nodded. But he was full of life. The age that had come upon him, growing heavier with time, left him unbowed. "Amarais?"

The Terafin bowed. "Alowan," she said.

Her voice. The sound of her voice. Finch almost raised hands to her ears to block it.

She turned to the girls, and Mandaros lifted a hand. "Not them," he said sternly. "They may speak, if I judge the need is there, but they . . . have only begun their sojourn in my realm. No apology you offer will be heard," he added. "It is up to the living to find their own peace."

She nodded, regal as ever, but slight and shadowed in the presence of the god. "Alowan."

"Amarais. What he does not choose to tell you—and what he does not seek to prevent me from telling you—is that you and I have already met on the edges of his domain; he could no more prevent us from speaking once he summoned me than I could ignore his summons."

She bowed her head. Lifted it slowly. In front of all of these men—and women—of power, she said simply, "I will miss you."

"I know. I would grieve, but it would anger him."

"You seek to protect me even now?"

"Amarais," he said gently, "I never sought to protect you. But I valued what you believed in, and in some fashion, I still value it. My death, you could not prevent. I do not hold you responsible for it. I chose to join you."

She smiled. So much regret, Finch thought, in that smile.

Allister APorphan cleared his throat. The Terafin nodded.

"You were sleeping," she said quietly. "When you died."

"Was I?" He frowned. "No," he said at last. "I did not sleep."

"Did you see who killed you?"

His face clouded. "Yes, Amarais. I saw."

"And the girls?"

"I don't know. I arrived before they did."

Allister APorphan frowned. "That is not possible."

"I am not here to argue possibility with you. I tell you what I know to be fact." He glanced at the girls, and his expression shifted again. Care returned to the lines of his face. Finch couldn't look away, but she tried anyway. There was only so much pain she could bear witness to.

"It was the cat," he said quietly.

Everyone stared.

"The cat is dead," The Terafin said quietly.

"I know. I do not know how, or when, but the . . . cat . . . was host to the demon."

The Terafin closed her eyes.

Allister APorphan said, "Describe what happened."

"The cat . . . died. I knew that it was dying. I . . . am fond of that cat. I thought to heal it, and I realized my mistake far too late for flight. I am an old man, but even were I a young one, I would not have escaped that death."

"But you—"

"I was . . . enspelled. I could not move. He had much to say; demons are particular when they gloat."

Allister said, quietly, "Can you tell Member Mellifas what the creature looked like?"

"Is Sigurne here?"

"Of course, Alowan." She, too, rose. She looked older and frailer than he. "We suspected something, or I would not be." She hesitated. "The creature?"

"Ethereal," he said softly. "Even his arms. They passed through the wall, at one point, and they did no damage there."

She frowned.

"But they did not pass through *me* with the same laudable result." His grin was slight. "It—he—was taller than any man I have ever met, but frayed at the edges, as if he were made of coarse fabric. He had two obvious limbs, and like demon limbs, they were grotesque. Blades," he added quietly. "I believe he could solidify them at will."

She nodded, but she was pale now. The mists seemed to shore her up.

"You do not recognize this creature."

"I am not a demonologist, whatever else may be said about me." He nodded.

"He had no need to open doors," he added, after a moment. "But I believe that he could, had he the desire."

"Thank you, Alowan. That is . . . enough." She looked at Allister APorphan, and nodded.

The magi spoke. "The Terafin's illness . . ."

"Is not natural."

"Ah. You suspected this?"

"Yes. I told her as much. But suspicion and proof are not the same; although I am skilled, and I could heal the damage I could touch, I . . . could not ascertain what caused it. It troubled me."

"We believe you were killed on the eve that she herself was meant to die."

He shrugged.

"They obviously failed."

"You are not the only healer in Averalaan."

"Nor in Terafin."

Silence.

"And one of the other healers was able to break some part of the binding that held her. She is . . . not well. But she is not yet dead."

He nodded again.

"Were you aware of the plague in the holdings?"

"Yes."

"And the similarities to The Terafin's illness?"

"Yes; I spoke with Levec."

"Can you—"

"What I knew, he knows." He lifted a hand. "I have . . . spoken with the girls. They are . . . not yet free of their past. It would not be a kindness to speak with them now.

"But I . . . thought . . . that Amarais might call us. I will tell you what they know."

Allister frowned, but one glance at the god's face—at his multiple, sudden frowns—ended all argument he might have offered.

"They were killed by the same creature that killed me; they were not aware of my death. The creature came through the arboretum. He made himself visible, and known; Lila sought to delay his passage. She perished just beyond the arch."

"We know how the other girl died," Allister said quietly, lifting a hand.

"You seek knowledge," Alowan said, his voice growing thin as the mists surged upward, "but you seek it in the wrong places."

"How so?"

"The plague is not what you think it is. It is physical, but the physical is the symptom, not the cause. Seek the Lord of dreams," he said quietly. "Ask him what the dreamers know."

The Terafin seemed to stiffen a moment, as if something unexpected—and familiar—had suddenly shown itself.

"That," Mandaros said, as Alowan at last fell silent, "is as much as any of the three can offer. Micah."

"Father," Micah said, his voice as thin as Alowan's had been.

"You must learn to husband your power. This will be costly."

"Father," he said again.

The mists began to clear, taking with them the ghosts, the god, and the endless, amorphous landscape.

Micah seemed frail enough that he should have gone with them—but Allister APorphan's arms suddenly reached out to catch him. His curses were too softly spoken to offer offense, but they were there; the boy swooned into his arms and the last of The Terafin's office returned in all of its dim glory.

Even day, Finch thought, was dim in comparison to the gray clouds of the otherworld.

Cacophony erupted. Every voice the room contained seem to begin at once, silence deserting the occupants as the mists did. But where the god's multiple voices had spoken to one purpose in unison, these voices were fractured, fractious things: arguments in the making. Dissonance.

This was only impression. The Terafin was silent, and Morretz offered little speech; he leaned toward her for a moment, and she nodded. That was all.

But Devon, Duvari, and Gregori now conversed, heat transforming their expressions; the magi joined them, and even Sigurne's words were broken by the shards of inexplicable temper.

Teller turned to her; Ellerson caught her shoulder. "Not now, Finch," he said sternly. "Perhaps later. Why did you speak?"

"Did I?"

His lids closed a moment; she thought, were they open, she would see his eyes roll.

The Terafin lifted a hand, and when that gesture failed to bring the silence it obviously commanded, she lifted her voice. "*Enough.*"

Everyone froze.

"What we have heard this eve bears thought and study; there is a lack of quiet for the first, and a lack of resources for the second, that make this room an inappropriate place for either. I am weary, and there are duties to which I must attend."

Sigurne rose at once, and tendered The Terafin a deep bow. "Terafin," she said. "Forgive us. There is much that has been said here that we do not entirely understand. We will repair to the Order, and we will make our report to you before sunset."

"I look forward to it," The Terafin replied quietly. "Duvari. Devon. Gregori."

The three men bowed stiffly.

"You have your duties."

"Terafin."

"Terafin."

Duvari said nothing.

"Finch, Teller," she added quietly, "remain."

They nodded timidly while everyone else made their way to the door.

Micah was last to leave, and he lingered a moment, waiting until he was certain he'd caught Finch's eye. He winked. He might have said something, but Allister APorphan caught him by the shoulder and dragged him out.

"So," Finch said softly, when the door closed on his odd expression, "he's one of the god-born."

"Doesn't seem like the son of a god to me," Teller said quietly. "I liked him."

"Me, too."

* * *

Morretz did not clean; he did not tidy. There were those among the domicis who counted menial tasks among their duties, and when they did, they performed them diligently.

He wished, for a moment, that he had been among them. His duties were different. The day waned.

The Terafin spoke with Teller and Finch, but only briefly; she was not amused by Finch's unfortunate lack of awareness, and she took pains to make this clear. Finch herself retreated into a stricken, youthful silence that was at once endearing and annoying.

So much depended upon them. Finch. Teller. The rest of Jewel ATerafin's den.

The domicis watched them, chastened, as they left the office. It was silent in their wake, as if all life had already fled the room.

Morretz held paper in his hands; it trembled, ink drying. Magic had gone into the making of the ink; magic had gone into the composition of the paper. Even the wax which would seal it when the letters had dried had some component of the mage's gift to strengthen it.

He handled the paper with care. He was one of three people who *could*. Not even the right-kin had been woven into the subtle protection that bound and protected the words; once sealed, the document itself could be opened by only one person, and even then, only after an event of significance occurred.

He would not think about it. Had struggled so long not to think about it, he almost failed.

The Terafin's fine, strong hand had penned what lay within with care; the official words glittered like steel against the fine thickness of paper. And they were steel, of a sort; a weapon as fine as the House Sword.

The Kings could read them, if they were conferred by the hand of the right bearer.

The door swung open. The Terafin stood in the frame it left behind, waiting. Her eyes were red, but he expected that; she had left him suddenly, forbidding him to follow, and these days, there was only one reason that she chose to retreat.

Nor did she stay away for long.

"I have summoned the House Council," she said quietly.

He nodded.

"And I have received, from the hand of a Member of the Magisterium, the writ of permission that we require." She held it aloft as if it shed light. Hand shaking, he took it from her.

Magery, he thought; open use of magic. She had been subtle in obtaining the writ, but it bore her name as signatory. Bore, in fact, her signature.

He said, "Duvari—"

And she stiffened. "Duvari understands," she said quietly, "the cost of his original mandate. Had we dispensed with the demon in the Household, had we even considered the possibility of his—" She shook her head, drawing breath. "I am . . . sorry . . . Morretz. I am not capable of being what I must be."

"Terafin, let me remind you that you spoke against Duvari's request—"

"Let me remind you," she said softly, "that I *am The Terafin*, and more than speech is in my hands. I should have refused what the Kings requested. Instead, I let the demon wander unhindered in my House—"

"He has been watched."

"He has not been watched *enough*. I have lost three House members in one evening. Were it not for accident, were it not for *chance*, I would have lost four, and Terafin would now be without—" She shut her mouth.

He said, "You take too much upon your shoulders, Amarais. There is no certainty that the demon we are aware of was in any way responsible for the deaths."

"There is every indication that he was not," she said coldly. "But we are not wise in demon lore." She looked out the window, and after a moment, she left the door's frame and stood before the wide, flat glass. Beneath her, the grounds of Terafin bloomed in season; gardeners had left them open for the use of the House members. The day dwindled in silence.

And neither he, nor she, knew whether or not she would wake when she at last surrendered to sleep.

"The Mother's Daughter has sent a priest," she told him, her back toward him. "Cormaris' son has come in person. He did not linger, and he did not offer advice."

She was lying. But he let her shelter in the comfort of lie, choosing to feign belief. "When the magi come, send Devon with them; give him the daggers the priests left. He will know what to do with them."

He bowed.

"You know what you must you do."

"Not today, Amarais."

She spun, then, the drape of black and white the only colors that she allowed herself. That and a hint of gold; the colors of Imperial mourning. Grief had power; had he needed proof of that, she stood before him.

"If not today, *when?* We have *no time,* Morretz."

"Tomorrow," he said quietly. His voice shook. He could not contain the shaking, and he had no desire to even make the attempt.

Her expression softened. "Morretz," she said quietly. "There is no other I can trust with this duty. Not even Gabriel."

"There are others—"

She met his eyes and held them. She was his lord. She was the life he had chosen. Still, he looked away.

"Tomorrow," she said at last. "Tomorrow, then. But I will have your word."

It was a blow. He absorbed it, but the pain would never leave him. "Amarais—"

"Or I will send you now."

Swallowing, he gave his word, and the giving wounded them both.

Moonlight vigil. This, this brought him comfort. Not by its existence, for it had become the part of his day that he most hated. But it *was* part of his day. It was part of the routine that The Terafin had built over the preceding months.

The servants were silent, and as night descended, they were less numerous. But candles had been lit upon and down the length of the Great Hall; some blocky and fat, some tall and slender; some in the great candelabras that the wealthy possessed, and some in pewter holders. Wax dripped across the floor, and although it was not sealing wax, it served the same function in a symbolic fashion; she paused before them, and they flickered at the passage of her skirts when she left.

These had been offered for the dead.

For Lila ATerafin, whose parents had been so proud when she had been summoned into The Terafin's presence and offered the Terafin's name. She had been given a silver ring that bore the House crest, and she had almost wept with joy when The Terafin herself had placed it upon her finger. She had been a gentle, quiet girl—one who often seemed nervous with youth's energy, but whose hands could be steady when the bleeding and the injured lay beneath them. She was gone. She would never see babe into the world again; she would never bind wound, or comfort the visitors who made their way to the healerie to visit the patients therein.

There were two small paintings of her face in the Hall of Mirrors. The Terafin bent down and retrieved the smallest of the two; this she brought to her forehead a moment. When she looked up, she did not set the picture down in its resting place; she chose instead to slip it into a generous, hidden pocket.

Morretz said nothing; he held a lamp aloft instead, urging her forward in silence.

But although she went, her progress was slow, for there were other candles, and other pictures.

Fiona ATerafin. She had come to the House as a servant, and had been absorbed into the Household staff. No one had been more surprised than she when Master Alowan had chosen to request her presence in the healerie.

"She is a practical woman," he said. "And if her tongue is a bit sharp, her hands are steady and gentle. Since Amelia has gone, I have missed an aide, and of those offered me, I have found none who would suit me better."

"Fiona requested this transfer?"

"Would that be less offensive to the Mistress of the staff?"

Morretz smiled a moment at the memory. He did not shy from it; memory was all that was left of the dead, and he, like the rest of Terafin, did not wish to dispel its fragile beauty. It eased pain.

She had been transferred, and after two years, the Mistress of the Household staff had forgiven Alowan, hard woman that she was.

Fiona's face could be seen; the Household staff had never forgotten her, and she had lived a good many years longer than young Lila. Some of the paintings and drawings were rough, and some very fine; some were of Fiona in a youth as full with promise as Lila's. Morretz imagined that the House was far less clean and shiny than it had been two short days ago, for hours of labor had gone into the work; he saw the Mistress in evidence here, for such hours would be bought only with her permission.

And she had given it.

In front of one of these, The Terafin paused again, and again she lifted her chosen portrait to forehead. It was not a painting that she had chosen, and not even a colored drawing; it was a dash of charcoal and pencil, a rough assembly of thick and thin lines that seemed intent on capturing not likeness, but motion.

This Fiona held a boy in her arms.

He cringed. Lila had been too young to have children. And Fiona's were not yet old.

Still, he knew the fate of the son and the daughter; he himself had drawn up the documents of legal adoption that *any* new mem-

ber of the House required, regardless of age. They were young
enough that their signatures were not required; they had been given
to Fiona's husband.

And Morretz was suddenly certain that the image itself had been
drawn by the husband, for it was the only one that contained the
children who had been little part of her daily labor.

The Terafin's forehead bore the smudge of charcoal with an odd
and perfect dignity. This offering, too, she took care to slide into a
concealing pocket.

Last, she paused among the candles and pictures that had been
left for Alowan Rowanson. They were less numerous than Fiona's
pictures, and they were unusual—for Alowan had never been
adopted by Terafin; he had always chosen to stand apart. A name, he
had said, meant much, and he could not take a name that he was not,
in the end, certain he could live up to.

He should have taken it; he had died as ATerafin, no matter what
he had been called. How many people in the manse knew his family name? How many, in the end, had cared? How many children
had come to the healerie with scraped knees, seeking a moment of
his time? How many women had come, near the end of their confinement, to nervously ask for his presence at the birth of their as yet
unknown children?

How many had come with illness, with disease, with a terrible
fear of mortality?

Ah. Alowan, as Fiona and Lila, had been loved. Had been
known. Among the candles and the portraits offered, flowers had
been scattered, cut fresh from their stems. Morretz knew that the
gardeners would look the other way at this obvious theft of their
labor, for the flowers were fine indeed, and they could have come
from no other place.

It was a flower that she chose, in Alowan's place, but Morretz
himself carried a silver-framed enclosure which bore the most
canny of his likenesses, for he knew where it would sit.

Terafin had witnessed many deaths. But not even the deaths of
Alea and Corniel had occasioned this outburst of mourning, for the
lords of the House always chose to maintain a distance from those
they ruled. Alowan? None whatsoever.

He had not desired to leave grief in his wake, Morretz thought.
But grief was the natural order; it flowed out of affection and respect, and Alowan's wishes aside, there was no other way to express
it. He decided, at that moment, that he would invite Lila's parents to
visit; that he would offer them sight of this, this grief and this re-

spect. He had no illusions; he did not expect the candles and the pictures to dim their loss.

But he knew it would give them comfort, for any parent would find comfort in knowing that their daughter had come to be so greatly loved in so scant a time.

Amarais cleared the Great Hall and he followed, lantern swinging gently in the silence of Terafin at night. The servants and the guards who patrolled these halls knew the hour of her arrival, and they absented themselves from their duties to give her the privacy in which to grieve.

They shouldn't have.

She was The Terafin, yes, but she was also *of* Terafin, and all who grieved in the end could find solace in the company of others.

Still, they had done what they could; they had chosen to place this testament on a path they knew she must walk, sooner or later, and he knew that it would not be cleared until she gave the order.

Knew that she would not.

The grounds were quiet, now. Starlight and moonlight hovered in the vault of the heavens with a cold indifference; they rose and fell over all atrocities with a similar, distant grace. He did not resent them; he did not resent the tide that was the heartbeat of the city. Instead, he joined Amarais as she made her way to the only shrine of import the grounds contained.

The path was perfectly tended. But here, too, candles were lit; they were finer, encased in glass globes that protected the heart of their small flames, and they rested above cut flowers tied with black and white ribbons. There were no pictures here, no names; the weather, as the moon and stars, was indifferent to grief, and if rain fell, what might have been otherwise offered would be destroyed.

She walked this path as if it had been created for her. She paused from time to time, but she did not touch the flowers that had been cut and gathered; did not touch the ribbons that made clear what their purpose was.

But these led to the Terafin Shrine, and she followed them, unable to escape the outpouring of grief and mourning. It was her company, he thought, for he himself was too much part of her to offer what she needed.

He regretted that.

He paused when he reached the foot of the path that led to the shrine. She walked away from him, dwindling beneath moonlight, and he watched her go.

And then a stranger's voice said, "Do not leave her now."

He turned, the lamp careening, and saw no one.

Heard no other words. He wondered if the days and the nights deprived of sleep or rest had finally taken their toll; magic limned him with orange light. His own; a ward against unknown enemies.

But the words offered in a stranger's voice would not come again, and they offered him what he desired. He left the spot of *his* nightly vigil, as he had done only one other time, and he walked swiftly.

She did not appear to notice that he had joined her.

Or perhaps she expected it. She mounted the steps to the altar, and he followed here, too, the lamp bringing light. The brass eagles had been cleaned, but the oil in their hearts was low.

She placed her palms across the cool, smooth altar stone, and then she withdrew them; she reached into her pockets for what she had taken from the hall, and these she arranged with care; a single, long-stemmed rose, and the portraits of the girls. To these, her domicis added the painting of Alowan, placing it gently behind the others.

"Thank you." She turned to meet his gaze, and her eyes were once again reddened. He wanted to hold her, then. His own desire.

"They were not sacrifices, Terafin."

She did not gaze at Morretz; she knew that the voice was not his. Just as he knew it was not hers.

"Were they not?" Her words were bitter.

"A sacrifice is made with knowledge," the voice replied. No body contained it. No ghostly visage. No familiar face.

As this did not disturb her, Morretz allowed himself to relax, but only barely. Magic coursed through his limbs, his hands, waiting only his invocation.

"Not all sacrifices are made with knowledge," she replied. "Nor with consent. Had my Chosen been taken, I would have grieved. But this is . . . worse. This is wrong."

"All murder is wrong," the voice said, its severity lessened by the gentleness with which the words were delivered. "Terafin," he added after a moment, "I did not kill them."

"You did not save them."

"That has never been my duty," he told her.

And she wilted, like any flower removed from its sustenance. "No," she said quietly. "It was mine."

"You do not see the future, Amarais."

She stiffened. Morretz did not understand why.

"And I sent from you the woman who could. Do you ask yourself what she might have seen, and what she might have prevented?"

The Terafin offered no reply.

And the Terafin spirit expected none. "I ask it, as well. But I do not see the future clearly either. It was not my gift."

Her hands fell in fists against the stone, leaving skin behind as she dragged them away. She had disturbed nothing.

"Your burden is heavy," the Terafin spirit continued. "And I see it more clearly this eve than I have ever seen it. A person can only be asked to endure so much before endurance passes into numbness and indifference."

"And will you ask no more of me?"

"I will ask no more of you," he said softly.

She stood almost stricken by the words; they were offered as gift, and Morretz understood that to her, they were far, far more.

"But of the one who serves you, I ask a greater task."

She stiffened, and then she said, "No."

"It is what you yourself have asked, no more."

"No."

"Morretz," the voice continued, as if her command held no force. "You must summon Jewel ATerafin home."

He bowed, although there was no one to receive this gesture. "I know."

"She is in the South," the Terafin spirit said, "and the war that has transformed that land will finally be fought in earnest. They will desire her presence."

"They?"

"The Commanders," he said. "And the young man who would be Lord of the South. She is almost upon them."

"Where?"

"I do not know if I can tell you, in words. I know because she is of my House. She has sworn her vows, here; she has offered me all that she can. I have accepted what she has offered."

The wind moved; leaves rustled against the bed of fine, shorn grass. The voice took form.

Jewel ATerafin's form.

The Terafin was not surprised by this, although she was grim in her silence. "Amarais," the spirit said, speaking now in a voice that was both familiar and entirely foreign, "I know what you fear."

"I do not fear death."

"Not your own, no. You desire peace," he said. "You desire cer-

tainty. You would leave your House in peace if you could be certain
that what you have built will be protected."

"It can't be," she said flatly.

"Not by you, no. We have our wars to fight, and they shape us;
we take up sword, literal and figurative, and we make our path
through the bodies of our enemies. You have a warrior's heart."

"I am not a warrior."

"You are not *only* a warrior, but it is some part of your gift." He
reached out and touched the painting of Lila ATerafin. His finger's—Jewel's fingers—passed through it. "I cannot offer you
peace," he said, "although I would if it were in my power. But I say
to you that I had trust in my choice when you came to this shrine so
many years ago, and that trust was not misplaced.

"If you cannot trust yourself, and you cannot trust me, trust my
choice."

"I have no other option."

But this Jewel who was not Jewel turned to Morretz and held out
a hand. "You intend to leave Terafin to seek Jewel ATerafin," he said
quietly. "You will take horse, you will ride, you will trade it for a
fresher beast. You will take no one with you; you will rely on magic
and your own knowledge to carry out the task she sets.

"Is this not so?"

Morretz nodded.

"And you have agreed that you will leave on the morrow."

He nodded again.

"If you follow the course you have planned, you will fail the
House," he said quietly.

The Terafin lifted a hand. "And you would council him to abandon his plan?"

"Yes. But not his intent."

"There is no other way," she said softly. "Meralonne APhaniel
might have sought the South with magery, but he is already lost to
us; the resources the magi offer do not include one who can dis-
tance-walk without paying a heavy price. Nor," she added, eyes narrowing, "do the resources that House Terafin can bring to bear."

But he did not acknowledge her. "The choice, domicis, is yours."

Morretz bowed. "I cannot go to a place I have not seen," he said
at last.

"Morretz—"

"Amarais," he said, with quiet dignity.

"I forbid it."

But he did not look at her; for the first time in his life as her domicis, he did not acknowledge an obvious command. "Where is she?"

The Terafin spirit did not falter; he did not speak. But he did not lower the hand he had offered to the domicis.

And Morretz understood, then, why he had been asked to accompany his Lord. He took a deep breath, and he held out his own hand, pausing a moment to set the lamp upon the altar.

The Terafin spirit brought his palm down, and the Terafin Shrine was lit from within by a blinding, incandescent light.

CHAPTER FIVE

26th of Corvil, 427 AA
Terafin Manse, **Averalaan Aramarelas**

THERE are things that keep you going.

Sometimes they're the things you value, or have learned to value; sometimes they're a single unexpected act of kindness in a life made bleak as desert by expected acts of cruelty; sometimes they're the strength that you gain by the simple expedient of survival; of learning to walk—again—of learning to speak—again—of learning to return to the world of people so reluctantly, someone else has spent years coaxing you out of the past.

Sometimes they are none of these things.

And sometimes—sometimes you don't know what they are, but you keep on going.

This was the day the world ended.

But it started out like any other day. Any other miserable day.

Once again the weather was a small act of betrayal. The sun rose through the curtained windows, pink and orange taking the sky that would lighten and deepen in stages. Ellerson was there, clothing in hand, and the clothing he had chosen was the least loved of all Finch's clothing. She did not hide under the covers; she did not attempt to pretend that she didn't know the time. She rose quickly, as if she'd hardly slept at all. Funny, that.

She had been dreaming, if something so terrible could be called dream, and it lingered in her eyes; everything seemed dim in the daylight, as if the world had already begun its transformation into a land of ghosts. The mist was in her eyes, broiling and pulling, its tendrils sporting unexpected teeth.

She was white.

"ATerafin," Ellerson said, bowing deeply. "You must take breakfast with The Terafin this morn."

"Early breakfast?" she asked, before the significance of his words sank in.

"Yes. In her quarters."

She swallowed. "Am I to go alone?"

"No," he said, and when he turned to face her, when he had finished laying out the stiff, perfect dress, she saw his eyes. They were far, far too dark.

"I'll get Adam," she whispered.

"I have taken the liberty of waking him." He drew breath. "And I have taken the liberty of summoning Healer Levec."

Teller was dressed. Angel and Carver were dressed; they had not yet donned full armor, but they had girded themselves—or more likely, judging from the exasperation on his face, Arann had girded them—with swords.

Some glimpse of half-forgotten past intruded: Arann, trying to teach Carver and Angel to fight; Angel, humiliated beyond bearing, with a black eye and a waving dagger, and Jay with a voice loud enough to stop them from doing something they'd regret. They didn't have that temper now, and she held the memory for just a second before she let it go.

Jester was shifting his weight rhythmically from one foot to another; not quite hopping, but not able to contain himself in stillness. Not a good sign.

She fussed with her hair, but it was still hers; still frayed at the ends, and still too short and thin to do anything much with. She pulled it free from her face and shoved it back with clips; they wouldn't hold for long, but they'd past muster.

"Did Morretz—"

"Morretz came," he said quietly, "before sunrise. He did not linger."

Something about the way he said the words matched his eyes, explaining their darkness. She froze. "Ellerson—"

And he shook his head. "He is The Terafin's man," Ellerson told her quietly. "And I am grateful for that; it was the position he needed."

"Do we wait for Levec here?"

"No, ATerafin. Devon and Gregori are here, as escort. They will take you to The Terafin's hall. Do not pause to speak to *anyone*. Do you understand? Do not stop."

She swallowed and nodded. "You're not coming with us?"

"I am," he said quietly. "But I have much to do this day, Finch, that will leave some of my usual duties untended. I apologize," he added gravely. "But I have taught you much these past months, and you must prove that you have been an adept student."

She swallowed. "I—"

"Yes." Just that.

"Ellerson?" She couldn't help it. The word left her lips as she gained the foyer of the den's wing, and it could not be contained. Too much was in it, too much was pressing against her mind. Fear. Something worse than fear. Certainty.

"ATerafin?"

"Where is Morretz?"

26th of Corvil, 427 AA
Annagar, Terrean of Averda,

Jewel woke poorly.

Avandar was by her side when she at last jerked free of sleep; his hand held magestone light, something comforting in the darkness of the pitched tent.

Her back ached, but she'd become used to that. Her arms, however, were stiff; she could not lift them above her shoulders without feeling the sudden limit of muscle. She might have tried, but her hands were shaking.

And beside her, the child Ariel sat, knees curved beneath her delicate chin, the open windows of her unblinking eyes.

"I'm—I had a nightmare," she told the child, in shaking Torra.

Ariel nodded. "Too many nightmares," she said. "The Lady is angry."

"I hope she's not angry at *me*."

"Sometimes it doesn't matter who she's angry at," Ariel replied. More words than she usually spoke.

Jewel wondered why, but she didn't like any easy answer she could come up with.

"ATerafin," Avandar said.

"Don't."

"Jewel, then."

She grimaced. "Sorry." Stood. "Where is the Winter King?"

"In the forest," Avandar replied. "As you'd know if you were thinking."

She rose, shedding sleeping silks. The desert was long behind them, but the nights of Averda were cool. Cold, if one took into account the silence that had descended upon the Lambertans when they had at last chosen to cross the border.

The border, in this case, being a stretch of land that had nothing at all to mark it; nothing that made it clear that it was owned by one lord or another. Certainly the birds and the animals didn't much care; she was certain they'd have fled regardless of whose banner flew in the intermittent wind.

The Lambertans had been prepared for resistance. They had made plans for it. They had sent scouts ahead—although given how much damn noise those horses made, even singly, she wasn't certain how much use they'd be.

But they found nothing.

And that didn't make them any happier.

If she had thought that the men the Lambertan Tyr had come to Damar at the head of were staggering in their numbers, she was to find that this was due to lack of experience on her part; they were joined, on the road, by seven times that number. Avandar told her there were eight thousand men at his command by the time they crossed the border.

He also made it clear that this was not the entirety of the force he could muster, but Jewel wasn't listening; seven thousand men had stood ready and waiting, and they couldn't have mobilized on a day's notice. Or even, she thought, a week's.

Her tent was almost on top of Kallandras', and his in turn bordered that given to the Matriarch of Havalla. The Serra Diora had been offered the privilege of joining the part of the encampment that the Tyr'agnate himself claimed as his own, and she had refused.

It seemed natural enough to Jewel, but it had drawn the breaths out of the cerdan that surrounded the Tyr. Even Ser Alessandro had fallen utterly silent, but his glance had strayed to the Tyr.

The men might have stayed that way, struck dumb by gods only knew what, but the Radann par el'Sol chose that moment to speak, and although his voice was soft, his words were clear.

"She has traveled in the company of strangers since she fled the Tor Leonne," he said, pitching his voice so that it might carry only as far as the Tyr'agnate. "And in so traveling, she has accrued debt.

She does not doubt your ability to keep her in safety, Tyr'agnate, and she casts no aspersion upon your intentions; you are Lamber-tan, and she prizes that name highly.

"But it may be that on the road we travel, she will have no other opportunity to repay the burden of debt she has been given, and she must seek to do so where she can."

Clever man, Jewel thought. All the eyes that had rested upon the perfectly bowed head of the Serra Diora now flickered uneasily over the closed flaps of the tent that contained the Matriarch of Havalla.

"Perhaps she is wise," Ser Mareo said at last. "And certainly she undertakes her task with duty and honor. I will not deny her this re-quest."

The Serra's perfect bow deepened; she did not offer him words. She had given their keeping to the Radann, and he used them well.

Not something that Jewel could have done, but then again, not something she'd ever had to do. She let her hand drop, and when it did, she realized that it had been hovering an inch above her dagger hilt. As if, she thought, with bitter humor, the dagger would be of much use.

"I, too, have accrued such a debt," the Tyr'agnate continued, when all thought he was finished, "and I would not deprive the Ma-triarch of her support or her solace."

He had noticed, then, that the Serra Diora tended the Matriarch. As if she were seraf.

"Radann par el'Sol," he said at last, turning. "Come. We have much to discuss, and the time in which to discuss it lessens with each step we take."

Marakas par el'Sol nodded.

And Jewel realized then that they had been spotted. *Knew* it. She lifted a hand, as if she were in her wing of the Terafin Manse and she wanted to catch someone's attention.

Avandar's frown was brief. Or rather, her glimpse of it was brief; she was certain it was etched there.

"We've been spotted," she said.

The Tyr'agnate raised a brow. "Oh?"

And she remembered just how much he would appreciate North-ern advice. She fell silent.

"How do you know this?" His voice was cold, distant, and dis-tinctly unfriendly.

Better to say nothing, she thought.

A bit late for that, ATerafin.

"You're at war with Callesta," she replied, reasonable now. "And there aren't many roads that lead to it. If you weren't challenged at the crossings, it's probably because of the numbers you travel with. But they have to know."

"Indeed," he said coldly. He turned then. Left.

An hour later, they summoned her anyway.

Food was an interesting thing in the wake of army life. Three days on the wrong side of the border, they had passed through their first town. The Tyr'agnate had gathered his men in the fields outside of the town; the men and women who worked them had vanished. Jewel suspected that they hid in the sparsely spaced buildings that housed their beasts of burden, but she wasn't given permission to check for herself.

In fact, she was given orders to the contrary, and they didn't sit well with her.

"These are not our lands," Avandar said. His words were curt, but he spoke them with force, as if they were of import. They were, of course.

"I never said they were." A child's response. She hated it, and bit her lip; her way of trying to stop more petulant words from following. The lack of sleep had taken its toll, and the dreaming images of nightmare were clearer to her at this moment than any waking memory.

Even the bad ones. She did not want to let Avandar out of her sight. Was aware, in a way that she had not been before Damar, that he had tended her after her nightmares for all of the years of his service; that she had taken it for granted, had even *resented* it.

She did not resent it now.

"They may well be dead."

The words were unwelcome. Worse than unwelcome.

"They're *farmers*," she said, almost spitting.

"They're *serafs*," he replied, mimicking her tone. "Slaves. They are owned by the land, not the other way around."

"What good will killing them do?"

"It will leave the fields untended," he answered, with a calm that she *hated*. "And it will leave the crop ungathered. Had they time, they might also torch the fields.

"In time of war, who do you think the wheat will feed? Not the serafs, Jewel. Just the army. And the army in question has been crossing the Mancorvan border for many bitter years."

She stood. Started to walk away.

A small hand gripped her tunic and held it fast.

Looking down, she saw the wide, wide eyes of Ariel. She tried to smooth the anger from her face, but she wasn't much good at it. The girl cringed.

But she did not let go.

"What is this noise?"

The Havallan Matriarch condescended to leave her tent at that moment. As if, Jewel thought, she'd been waiting. Her pipe was in her hand, and she leaned heavily on a thick, gnarled cane. After a moment, the Serra Diora came to stand by her side, and she offered her fair, pale hands as support.

But she, too, looked troubled.

"The Tyr called Jewel," Ariel told them. Words. More words. Why?

"And she goes to meet with him?"

Ariel shook her head. Stray curls, so reminiscent of Jewel's hair, clung to her forehead; the sun was high. When had the girl's hair gotten so curly? "She wants to walk through the cerdan to . . . to see . . . the serafs."

"Why?"

"She's afraid they're dead."

Yollana shrugged. "They may well be. What of it?"

Avandar's hand joined Ariel's upon Jewel's shirt, but he caught her arm and shook it slightly. She didn't lose the words, but she didn't say them either.

"She wants to save them."

Yollana's eyes narrowed. It wasn't pleasant.

But then again, neither was Jewel's Oma's anger, and she'd been much younger when she'd learned to weather it. "You have a problem with that?"

"You have your duties here," the Matriarch said. "And it's a poor leader who abandons her duty."

"I have a—"

"A greater responsibility?"

Jewel was silent. After a moment, she nodded.

"Then take some comfort, girl child. The Tyr'agnate of Lamberto has crossed the border with men, but he has ordered them *not* to interfere with the village."

"And the serafs?"

"If they were not fool enough to raise hoe against him, they will be safe."

"And their food?"

The Matriarch's smile was grim. "Does it matter whose mouths that food feeds, if it doesn't feed theirs? This is war, you fool, not some pretty noble hunt. One way or another, the serafs in Averda go hungry this year."

"Are they alive?"

The old woman looked at Avandar. "Is she always like this?"

"Always."

"Well. It's a wonder the North has won even a single battle against the South. I don't know if they're alive or not. I only know that you risk more death if you interfere. You are here on sufferance, Northern girl. You may pretend to be of the South, but he will not believe it; you wear that golden ring, and you carry yourself like a—"

"Matriarch?"

"No Matriarch would be this foolish. You had better attend the Tyr, girl. He'll send men, otherwise, and I think your men will cause trouble for us all if they come."

"I don't have any men here." She was genuinely confused.

The Havallan Matriarch spit to one side. One very narrow side; spittle almost hit Jewel's boot. "No. You have the beast. You have the Forest Lord. You have a man who speaks with the voice of the wind. Whose are they, if not yours? *Think.*"

The Winter King's shadow cut the ground at her feet; he knelt there. She knew a command when she saw it, and after a moment, she disentangled her shirt from Ariel's shaking hands, and mounted.

But she wasn't finished yet.

The Tyr'agnate waited. He had clearly been waiting, and he was, just as clearly, unused to the experience. She was aware that, as a woman, she had committed six different crimes by simply arriving in his presence. Luckily, she could take refuge in ignorance; she could only name a few of them.

First, she rode. Second, when she chose to dismount, she did not immediately fall over her face in an attempt to abase herself. Third, she spoke.

"Tyr'agnate," she said quietly. "I have a question to ask you."

His brows rose, as much shock as she had yet seen him show.

His Tyran were better composed, however; they held swords, and they waited his word. Hers seemed irrelevant, and probably would be until he decided otherwise.

"I did not summon you here to answer your questions, ATer-afin," he replied coldly. "Come. You may join us."

Us, she thought. Ser Alessandro. The Radann par el'Sol. Other men that she did not know by name. They stood around a low table, and upon that table lay food that had clearly not come straight from the field. She couldn't name it all, but she didn't much care to try.

Her body, however, betrayed her dignity; her stomach growled. She was aware of her lack of armor, her lack of surcoat, her lack of arms. But the Winter King followed three feet at her back, and he did not pause until she did.

"I want to know what happened to the serafs," she said bluntly.

Avandar, to his credit, had surrendered; he did not speak a word.

The Tyr'agnate seemed genuinely puzzled. "The serafs?"

"The farmers," she amended. "The ones who worked the fields we're busy trampling flat."

He honors you, ATerafin, Avandar told her. *He chooses to ac-knowledge you by speaking, when you have so clearly spoken out of turn. Take care. The indulgence is his to offer, and his to with-draw, and he is not known for indulgence of anything Northern.*

She swallowed. Forced her knees to bend, although it did take effort. "My pardon," she said, striving for something akin to Southern grace. "The serafs are not mine, and the war that you fight is not mine either. But I want to know—I need to know—what happened to them."

"Why?"

Why. Always, always why. "Because," she said simply, "I care."

"Why? Have you ties with Averda that you have not seen fit to disclose?"

She sidestepped the trap. Not neatly. "I don't give a rat's ass about Averda," she snapped. "Or Callesta, if that's what you really mean."

"You have met the Tyr'agnate of Callesta?"

"I've . . . seen him."

The silence could have cut stone. "When?"

"In Averalaan," she said, wishing—and not for the first time—that she had better instincts when it came to politics.

"He had business with your House?"

"No!" She flushed. "No. He had business with the—with Valedan kai di'Leonne."

"And you were witness to this?"

She sighed. "We were *all* witness to it," she said quietly. "All members of import to The Ten Houses. All of the priests of significance in the Churches. All of the heads of the various Guilds. All of the crown princes, the Princess Royale, and the Queens. Even the Kings."

"He spoke to you *all?*"

"No. He spoke to Valedan kai di'Leonne."

"Explain."

She said, "When you tell me what has become of the serafs."

The silence was loud, profound.

She was almost surprised when he chose to break it; she had pushed his patience to the farthest edge of its elasticity, and she didn't want to see what happened when it snapped. "And if you do not like the answer?"

"I'll be bound by my word anyway. Tell me, and I'll tell you what I saw."

He hesitated, and she could see in the thin line of his lips that he was capable of great cruelty. But he was capable of more, she thought, as his eyes studied her face, her lamentable posture, her peasant's hair.

"They live," he said quietly.

She closed her eyes. "Are you going to kill them?"

"That is my business, ATerafin."

She waited.

He understood this waiting, but in spite of this, his expression shifted, the lines of his face changing. "You are a child," he said at last. "And a poorly tutored child at that. You have been indulged. You have been served poorly by those who claim to serve you.

"But I begin to understand your concern, and although I am not bound to tender this answer, I will answer. I have no intention of killing them. They are prisoners; they are safest that way."

She ran a hand across her eye; the sun was in it. That was all.

"Ramiro di'Callesta," he said.

"It's more about Valedan," she countered. "It's really all about him." And she watched his face.

"Tell me the tale, and tell it quickly. We must be ready to move within the hour."

"My lord—The Terafin—was summoned to the Hall of the Kings," she said quietly. "One of the Southern hostages had chosen to petition the Kings, and we were there to bear witness to that petition."

"Such cases are normally heard by all of power in your realm?"

"Only when they involve a foreign monarch." Avandar's thoughts pressed, wordless, upon her. She tried to make her tone less insolent. "Valedan kai di'Leonne came before the Kings. He spoke of the murder of his clan, his kin, and claimed the Tor Leonne for himself, by right of blood."

Mareo's eyes widened again. And then they narrowed. "He was ordered to do this?"

She shook her head. "No."

"And you spoke with him? You ascertained this for yourself?"

"No. I know it the same way I know that we were seen."

"You are of the Voyani," he said quietly. "North or no. Continue."

"The Kings debated his petition. The hostages were to be executed. Not," she added fiercely, "the way the hostages in the Tor Leonne were; not for sport, not for humiliation."

His expression was grim. "It is not a custom of our people," he said at last, grudgingly.

"There doesn't seem to be much of a law against it," she countered.

"Power is our law."

"Well, it's a pretty—"

Avandar caught her arm; she saw that he had chosen to crouch by her side. His face was an inch from hers, but he did not speak. Enough that he had been forced to interfere.

"He claimed that his execution was wrong, that they would be acting against the rightful monarch of the Dominion. And after a time, he was granted a stay of execution. But the others—the other hostages—were to meet their deaths."

"And you had nothing to say against this, who argues for the lowest of serafs?"

"The serafs have no power, no position, no money, no ability to defend themselves," she snapped back. The heat was impossible to dampen.

"Very well. What of the Tyr?"

"Oh, wait. He came during the petition. King Reymalyn said that Valedan could not claim to be Tyr if he had none who would follow him.

"And Ramiro di'Callesta strode into the Hall then. He was not a grand figure; he was new from the road, and if I had to guess, he probably didn't pause to stable his horses either. He entered the

Hall and he walked straight to Valedan, and he offered him his sword and his allegiance."

The silence that followed the words was profound.

"And so he saved the boy's life."

"Yes and no."

"And no?"

"The Kings granted *Valedan* his life, as the wronged monarch. They would not grant him the lives of the rest of the hostages. Valedan said that he spoke for his people; he would not buy his own life at the expense of theirs. He wouldn't desert them. He said he was willing to abide by the decision of the Kings, and he was willing to suffer the fate of the hostages, if that was what our law demanded."

Now, now the Tyran were talking. Their hands remained upon their swords, and they had not so much as shifted in position—but her words had sparked theirs, as if theirs, hidden, were dry, dry brush, and she a small flame.

"The hostages?"

"They lived."

"And the kai Leonne?"

"He lived as well. He might not have, but a—a servant of the Lord of Night tried to kill him before the Kings had made their decision."

If she had thought the Tyran lost to words before, she had been mistaken.

Only the Tyr'agnate was silent, and the full weight of his attention was hers to bear.

"We have heard rumors," he said quietly. "And it will not surprise you that we have had *only* rumors. What contact we have with the North does not usually require conversation." His first smile followed the words, but it wasn't particularly pleasant.

"He almost won the Kings' Challenge," she told him.

He frowned. "Almost? There is seldom an almost in victory, ATerafin."

"He chose to withdraw."

"He was injured?"

"Oh, he was that, all right. But it was more. He—there was another demon."

"It seems the Lord of Night has some respect for the Leonne line, even diminished as it has become."

"It wasn't the demon that caused him to withdraw," she told the Tyr'agnate. "It was Ser Anton di'Guivera."

Just like that, the Tyran fell silent.

She had spoken a legend's name.

"Ser Anton?"

"Ser Anton challenged him to a duel. A Southern duel. The rules of the Kings' Challenge are clear: they forbid any fights that must end in death.

"But the laws of the Kings are also clear: What Ser Anton offered, Ser Valedan was free to accept, if he chose to eliminate himself from the Challenge; neither man is a citizen of the Empire, and within the duel circle, both men claimed the citizenship of the South; they were granted leave to fight."

"Ser Anton did not win?"

"He lost," she said quietly. "But Valedan did not choose to kill him. And Ser Anton offered Valedan his sword, and his life."

"Enough," the Tyr'agnate said, standing. "You will speak no more of this."

She wouldn't. But she knew that the others would.

The Tyr'agnate questioned her. He was calm and deliberate, and she knew from the tone of his questions that he intended to catch her in a lie. She also knew that she was a terrible liar, which was why she had given up trying years ago: lies were complicated.

Truth was often complicated, but at least it was easy to stick with. She told him only what she knew: That they had been sighted. That the Callestans were aware of his presence.

At the end of the hour, he gave her permission to leave, and she managed a rough bow. But she heard the orders he sent to his men, and she knew they'd all be marching for a long, long time this day.

25th of Corvil, 427 AA
Annagar, Terrean of Averda

Kiriel di'Ashaf was restless. The sun was hot, and the heat produced, in her, a languid stupor, a desire to sleep. She fought against it, bringing hand to forehead to wipe it clean of sweat.

There was none. She stared at her dry hand a moment, and then turned her gaze to the glowing orb the Southerners called Lord. She saw only sun, the height of day, and when she at last looked from its visage, the ground was blue. Her eyes recovered slowly; her shadow, as short as it would be this day, was almost shapeless beneath her boots.

Days had passed since the corpses of the Lambertan Tyran had been exhumed. She had spent those days on the march, beneath the bower of old Southern forests, but she was never far from the dead.

The Ospreys had been given the duty of protecting them. As if, she thought, there was anything of value to protect. Better to let them lie as feed for insects and carrion creatures too small to hunt; at least they'd serve a purpose.

Both Northerner and Southerner oft spoke of death as if it were sleep, and these, motionless, decaying, were allowed no rest; they were surrounded by a ring of incense that kept insects at bay, and those insects formed a thin, moving dome above the bodies, waiting their chance.

She killed a few, out of boredom; it staved off the desire for sleep. But the desire was strong.

"Kiriel?"

Auralis AKalakar came to stand beside her, lifting a hand; his nails were still dark with the new-turned earth. He had washed, had bathed, had come clean to the field, and the dirt still clung. Her own hands were as pale as those of Serras. As pale, she thought, looking at them as if they belonged to another, and as unblemished. The bodies of the Ospreys, dark with sun, cracked and blemished with the scars of old wounds and the accidents that occurred during their days of rigorous training, were so unlike hers she could see herself for a moment as they saw her: young. Unmarked.

"I'm . . . tired," she said.

"I noticed. You didn't sleep last night?"

She shrugged. Last night—and any of those that had passed since the destruction of the temple's nave—she had felt no desire for sleep; every sense she possessed, and some that she had almost forgotten she owned, had been alive with the texture, the sound, the silence of night. The moon's face had passed into part shadow, but the silver crescent of light that was moving to nadir was more than enough to see by; night robbed the landscape of nothing.

By contrast, the sun's light made pale all of the greens and the whites of the Callestan fields; it made distant gold, moving at the behest of wind, seem so colorless a light it might as well be silver. The river was loud, but its water was also white, and its moving reflection of all that passed around it, of all it passed through, hurt her vision.

Auralis dragged a cloth across his forehead, and his hair, dripping sweat, now clung to the creases of his forehead. He cursed armor, padding, and surcoat with a careless grunt; she understood his words, and wondered if he would be any more graceful if he stood naked in the scant breeze. Doubted it; she knew him well enough by now.

"We're ready to move," he said quietly.

She nodded. Of course, they had been ready to move for the better part of two hours. If life with the Ospreys had offered its share of mystery and frustration, life with the Kings' army was worse. They moved, gathered, moved, dispersed, moved, and waited.

If she were ever to rule, the first thing she intended to do was dispense with *waiting*. With wasting time. With caution.

Tents lay like flat, short buildings, all of a color against the open fields. Here and there, trees offered shade and boundary, and the Ospreys were quick to claim those positions for their own, fearing no attack in the heart of Callestan territory.

The arguments that such meager shade produced irritated her. Shadow or sun, they were hardly a matter of life or death; they were—they should have been—beneath notice.

"What are we *waiting for*, damn them?" she asked, when the second hour had melted into a third.

"You weren't paying attention to Duarte, were you?"

"I paid as much attention as you did."

He shrugged. "It's a skill."

"What's a skill?"

"Not paying attention. You have to learn how to pick out the important words; gods know there are enough of the other kind."

She snorted. Her hand crossed her forehead again, and again it came back free of sweat. When had she become so used to sweating that its absence worried her?

There had been a time . . .

Auralis was frowning. When she met his eyes, the frown eased, but she saw it lurking there, in his eyes, in his too-watchful nonchalance. She said, "I don't know when it started."

And he knew what she meant. She wondered when that had happened, as well.

"Well, don't make a big deal of it; you'll have the envy of every man and woman in the unit, and as we're—whatever we're called, you know how useful that would be."

She nodded. Tired. The sun was too high.

"I'm really tired," she said at last.

"I know. We're going to move soon, though."

Ah. "I'm sorry—I forgot. Why are we waiting?"

"The Lambertans are on the field," he said quietly. "Or they will be, at the rate they're marching."

"How do we know this?"

"Birds fly." He shrugged. "And mages speak to them. Or something like that."

"How many men?"

"Five thousand if we're lucky."

"And if we aren't?"

"Ten."

She whistled. It was Auralis' whistle.

Almost an hour later, they moved the bodies onto a closed, enchanted wagon. They put rushes and flat boards under the wheels; the ground here was damp, and the foliage had been smeared underfoot. Rain would have been a disaster.

For the others. For her? It would be water, she thought. Like sweat. It wouldn't touch her anymore.

The Serra Alina di'Lamberto was silent.

But she was not still. Although Valedan had ordered her to fulfill her role as a member of the Northern unit that was given responsibility for his safety, he could not, in the end, deprive her of what—or who—she was; she had taken the time that the others used in restless waiting to find flowers in the field and in the lee of the forest. They were simple flowers, paler and smaller than those with which she was accustomed to work, but she was gifted; she made of their stray and wild nature a work of beauty.

These, she placed upon the table that held maps.

And he came to the maps and hesitated a moment, staring at the flowers that she had gathered and arranged in such a pleasing fashion. A smile touched his lips; the Northern Commanders who shadowed his steps seemed unmoved—even annoyed—by her gift.

It pleased her, this small annoyance, this transgression of their sense of sterile, ugly order. And it embarrassed her, to be so pleased by something so petty. Perhaps, she thought, with just a hint of bitterness, she was Lambertan after all.

These men had killed her nephew.

And if ignorance excused them, if ignorance absolved them of malice, it did not change the fact of his death. The nobility of it, senseless though it was.

Ser Baredan di'Navarre, however, offered her the slightest of nods, and Ser Ramiro di'Callesta reached out and gently brushed the falling petal of a wild rose to one side. Its shadow fell across the valleys, like an omen.

Primus Duarte and the magi—the silver-haired, silver-eyed magi who seemed to set them all on edge—spared her a glance, no more.

But it was the silver-haired magi who chose to speak. "They are almost upon the Western valley," he said quietly.

"How far?"

"They have camped outside of the village of Cesanno," he replied, his finger hovering over an impersonal flag on the long, detailed map. The map itself had caused some conflict between the Tyr and the Commanders, but in the end, pragmatism reigned: they could not clearly command their considerable forces with scant knowledge of the terrain, and the maps they had chosen to bring with them were those used by the various merchants of The Ten.

She wondered if the gaining of even that much information had been costly; The Ten, like any high clans of power, did not easily part with any hard-won advantage.

But those maps, and the maps of the Tyr'agnate, were blended in stages by the most skilled of his cartographers; watched in progress by the most skilled of theirs. What emerged was something that neither could have come up with on their own.

She wondered what it meant. But her flowers sat above it, blades and stems skirting the sharp, colored pins that were so frequently jabbed into the surface of paper. When the paper itself was distorted by many such pins, they would begin anew.

She found Cesanno on the map.

"Have they razed the town?"

"No, Tyr'agnate. They have not yet entered it, although they prepare to march."

"And the fields?"

"The fields have been trampled, but even then, trampled with care."

"My people?"

"There have been four deaths that I am aware of. You will understand that a closer count would require more of a risk of discovery than the magi feel is wise at this time. Commanders?"

"I concur," Commander Allen said quietly. His words were seldom offered, and when they were, they were informed with an almost grudging respect for the man he had come to serve. The Tyr'agar. Valedan kai di'Leonne.

In the South, men were men who could take and lead armies;

men were men who could raise and wield sword, and not die upon the edge of the blade.

To Serra Alina, this boy that she had followed in his training, this Northern hybrid with his gentle eyes and his equally gentle silence, his sensitive perception, his slow and even awkward growth, had become a man; his youth did not tell against him in her eyes.

But in theirs, she saw clearly, it would.

She bowed her head as Valedan turned to face her.

"Serra Alina," he said, and then, correcting himself, "Alina."

She lifted her head, brought her hands behind her back, stood as a Northern soldier stands, acknowledging his attention with infinitely more grace. "Tyr'agar."

"What will the kai Lamberto do?"

She could have laughed. Or smiled derisively. She could have said something that would have diminished her brother in the eyes of his enemies. Could have. Would have, once.

But she understood what Valedan understood: Mareo kai di'Lamberto was necessary. Enemy, yes, but not a fool; he was necessary.

And by his actions in Cesanno, he knew it as well.

"He will not raze the village," she said quietly. "But if he encounters the moving forces of Alesso di'Marente, he will burn as he retreats, and he will sue for compensation later."

"Of course," Valedan said, cool now. "And the Tyr'agnate of Callesta?"

"Will accept a reasonable suit for compensation. But the armies of Marente are not so near the Western valleys as they are the Southern." To them, beyond the scope of her delicate arrangement, he now went, like a great bird of prey, his shadow vast.

His shadow did not falter. But it did shift, and his face, when it rose, was much closer to hers than the table should have allowed. The Commanders were silent; they stood in a single line, their chins lowered, their eyes upon the language of cartographers, the plans of generals. They would cede these pins, and those; they would cede those of lesser color. They would move them, call them back, rush them forward—and they would do this as if they were simple metal, simple steel.

They had already decided which villages they could lose, and which they *would,* burning fields that had not yet ripened for harvest, so that they might grant nothing to the pretender.

She had known, of course, that *this* was how wars were fought.

And she had expected to stand as she did stand: dispassionate. Unmoved.

But the mask was just that; it was not unlike a veil, although it exposed her skin to sunlight in a way that would have been costly had she any illusion of a future marriage. She saw death in all of this, and in all of it, saw little chance of life.

"Serra Alina di'Lamberto," Ser Ramiro said, "I have in hand a letter that was written to my wife. It is the last such letter she will send to the front." He took it from the folds of his sash and held it out to her.

"It arrived in haste; it was delivered by foot, and by air. It passed to the Serra Amara by a young girl's hands."

"A seraf?"

"No. Voyani."

"Which family?"

"Arkosa," he said quietly.

She nodded. "Arkosa will gather its forces upon the open road," she said, "and they will stand by your side, or in your stead." She held out a hand, and took what he offered, but she hesitated to open it. "The Serra Amara—"

"The Serra Amara regrets that she must be absent in this time of trial," he said quietly. "But she sent the letter by her most trusted messenger. Alfredo!" The name was a bark.

Alfredo kai di'Callesta exited the tent at the edge of the clearing. He was dressed in the finery of the high clans; his surcoat was bright with the colors of Callesta, and edged in the blue and white of mourning. He came at his father's command, but he halted five feet from the Tyr'agar, and he offered him a perfect bow.

"Tyr'agar," he said.

"I am grateful for your presence," Valedan replied, giving him leave to rise. "And for your sword, kai Callesta. Come. See what we have made of our maps."

She could almost feel the younger man's excitement, although it was contained with care; he was in his father's presence, and there would be no harsher judge of his manners than the Tyr'agnate of Callesta.

"Will the Serra Amara take kindly to such a reading as you offer me? Letters between Serras are often private."

"She sent it to *me*," he said, with the hint of a smile, "And she knew well that I would take much time to interpret it—if I interpreted it correctly at all.

"It is not our custom to have our Serras upon the field of battle;

no more would we summon our children or the less well-trained of our serafs. But you have won some respect in her eyes, Serra Alina; it is to you that she wished this letter to be delivered." He paused. "It was written by Serra Donna en'Lamberto."

She had known, of course.

And she took the letter, standing now in the stead of the Serra Amara. She opened it, and read the first few lines; they were pleasant greetings; they spoke of the fame of the gardens of Callesta, and prayed that those gardens would not be injured by the passage of so many men.

"For if much that is said of the Northerners is not true, it seems true to me that they are men, and men value war more than they value the gardens we must tend."

She looked up; all eyes were upon her. "Must I read aloud?" she said, with just a hint of amusement.

"No," The Tyr'agnate of Callesta said curtly, after a momentary glance at the Tyr'agar.

"She speaks of war," Alina said quietly. "And she speaks of the cost of war."

"The gardens."

"Yes. All the things that we have grown by dint of patience and time."

He nodded.

Ah. She stopped reading. Lifted her head and turned eyes to Valedan, and only Valedan. "Kai Leonne—there is much here that is personal. Would you—"

"If you can," he said quietly.

She swallowed. "You must know that she mentions the death of her kai," she said quietly. "It is not a . . . perfunctory mention. She speaks of his loss, of a woman's loss, of the years in which she tended her gardens and her harem without the sound of his voice; without the need to admonish him for his inability to play well within the delicacy of her trees."

Silence.

"Does this bode ill, Serra Alina? The death of the kai Lamberto has long been the wedge between our Terreans—and more, much more, than that."

"It might bode ill," Serra Alina said quietly, "if not for the words that follow. *But I speak of loss at a great distance, for although it shames me to say this, I will admit now that there are days when I can no longer recall my son's face. I see him as a child, I see him as a babe; I see him as the boy who thought it might be interesting to place an insect on his tongue.*

"As a man? I do not see him. He died before I could see the changes war wrought in him, and the changes that I did see were the changes that any mother sees when her kai returns a hero and lays at last in a solemn grave.

"What you must feel now, with your kai so newly dead, I cannot understand."

The Serra Donna en'Lamberto was gracious, gentle; she allowed the Serra Amara the greater grief.

"I would speak to you of loss. I would speak to you of time, and of its ability to fill that loss. But I would speak false if I did; the loss is always present.

"What you have suffered, you have suffered; I cannot undo it. No more could you give me back my son. But I say to you, Amara the Gentle, that if the loss has governed me, if the anger has blinded me, I govern myself now, and I see clearly.

"It is said that your son was killed by Lamberto. It is said that Lambertan Tyran murdered him without challenge while he rode upon the periphery of Callesta. I will not call you liar; I will not gainsay the truth that you have seen with your own eyes.

"But I will say that this was no plan of my husband's, this death. He is Lambertan, and he is proud; the vengeance he desired was not so simple a thing that it could be achieved in such a dishonorable way.

"I do not know if he will come to your husband; I am no warrior, and it is not of war that he comes to me to speak; when we speak at all, I speak of womanly things, of things that are preserved only in the harem's heart.

"But if he does come, he will come with caution, and if he is received with care, we might at last be free to speak again, who have only had letters behind which to hide the truth of our faces."

Alina looked up. Her eyes were dark, and her expression was so grave she almost bowed her head again. But she had chosen to follow Valedan's orders, and she was dutiful and obedient. She spoke instead.

"The Serra Donna offers peace," she said, her own voice rising slightly at the unexpected boon. "And if we do not ride out against the forces of Lamberto, we might meet them without battle."

She handed the letter back to the Tyr'agar.

"There was more," he said softly.

"Yes. More. She speaks of the Voyani, the Havalla Voyani. They have promised her aid, and they have already delivered on that promise; Ser Mareo di'Lamberto was not in Arral when she chose to pen this letter, and it is clear, from the force of her chosen words, that she undertook this task on her own."

"Then she does not speak for her husband."

"No Serra speaks *for* her husband," Alina said quietly. "Not even the Serra Amara. What they speak of here, what they hope for here—or what Serra Donna does, for I have seen no like letter from the Serra Amara—is something that cannot be held true by the strictures of warriors and men of honor."

"Meaning?"

"She guesses her husband's intent," Alina said quietly. "And she tells us that the Voyani of Havalla are, in this battle, to be trusted as allies. For as long as the war endures."

"Arkosa," Ser Ramiro said softly, "And Havalla. The two greatest of the Four."

"And if Ser Mareo brings his army to war?"

"That is up to you, Ser Ramiro, to decide. But there is one other thing she speaks of."

"The Northerners."

"She does not mention them openly. But she feels it wisest that their support of the Tyr'agar be subtle."

"And this means?" Commander Berriliya said, breaking the flow of their artful Torra with his brusque, commanding Weston.

"That should he come to the army, he must be met by Ser Baredan di'Navarre, Ser Ramiro di'Callesta, and the kai Leonne; if you choose to show your presence, if your men are given better ground or vantage, if it is clear in *any* way that this is your war, he may choose to react in a way that would not be of benefit."

"To the kai Lamberto?"

"Certainly to the kai Lamberto," she said quietly.

Valedan smiled. "And to the kai Leonne."

"That, Tyr'agar, she does not say. She writes your name once, and she writes your title once, and in each case she is hesitant. She does not know you; she has heard rumors that you travel with Ser Anton di'Guivera."

Ser Anton stood in the position that Tyran might occupy. He was a swordmaster, but it had never been his calling to command men. Only their hearts.

"Then we will make ready to move," Ser Ramiro said at last. "And we will make ready to move upon words written by the timorous and the gentle." There was a wry note in the words. "This is not the war I fought more than a decade past, Serra Alina. During that battle, I had the aid of the Lambertan Tyr, and I had the cunning of the General Marente.

"But I did not have command of the armies. And I do not," he added decisively, "have them now. Tyr'agar, your will?"

"We move," Valedan said. "But let us first move the Callestan army; let us leave some ten thousand of the Kings' men to guard the Southern valley under the command of The Berriliya."

Devran bowed formally. The command, Alina thought, was to his liking—but it was difficult to tell. She had become accustomed to Northern expressions in her time in *Avantari*, and had learned to understand that what *was* obvious was obvious.

It was therefore more difficult to read the shuttered face of the Hawk. Had he been Southern born, she might have seen triumph in his studied neutrality—but she had seen just such an expression on his face when he waited for his horse to be brought, and she did not know what this meant.

"The others?"

"If they can, split them. Take one army to stand guard over the Eastern edge of the valleys; take one to stand guard over the West; we will march together until we see the standards of the Tyr'agnate."

"And then?"

"He knows that you are present, Commander Kalakar. He knows, as well, that Commander Allen is here."

"You credit his intelligence."

"Yes. Both kinds." He paused a moment, and after a brief hesitation, he added, "There are stockades around the valleys. The river may carry your supplies some distance, but . . ."

"Rain."

He nodded. "Rain and the rivers. The Tyr'agnate of Averda has generously offered to open his stockades at need; he requests in return that you supply his men where the rivers are the safer form of conveyance."

She nodded quietly, but her glance strayed to Primus Duarte. The Primus did not meet it.

"Member APhaniel?"

"It is with the armies of Marente that we will face the greatest danger," he said softly.

"How so?"

"They travel with the kin." When these words changed only the posture of the Northerners, he added, "The servants of the Lord of Night."

"And they have been on the move," Valedan said quietly. He lifted a pin, a series of pins. "Fire has burned in the villages, but not in the fields. I believe that he approaches with confidence; he desires these lands, and not their scorched remains."

"It is what I would do," Ramiro said quietly. "And what he would have done, years past. We have lost many serafs in those villages, and many clansmen."

The silence was profound.

"With your permission, Tyr'agar, my kai and I will accompany you at the head of the Callestan army."

"Granted."

They passed through Cesanno at the height of day. Jewel felt the sun's unpleasant stickiness upon her exposed neck, but she had no desire to let her hair down to protect her skin; she hated the way hair clung in the heat, and the heat was oppressive.

That and the *smell* of a few thousand men. Although the Tyr was privileged with baths, the men themselves made do with scant river water, and they watered their horses first.

They spoke to those horses; they sequestered them; they rode them across the fields in small bursts. She winced when the weight of their hooves exposed dirt. No rain, she thought, pleading for Kalliaris to smile, even this far from her rightful home.

But the plea was short-lived; it was followed by horns, more horns, their sound cacophonous and distinct.

She turned to Avandar.

Avandar raised a brow. "Even if you do not understand their calls," he said coolly, "the context must make their message plain."

"Humor me."

"The Tyr'agnate has called a halt."

"Why? We've been marching three hours, and he's certainly driven us harder than that."

"Ah. The scouts have returned, ATerafin, and they bear word."

"*Avandar.*"

"The Callestan army has been sighted."

CHAPTER SIX

26th of Corvil, 427 AA
Terrean of Averda

AVERDA was blessed with the valleys, and in its valleys, the widest and clearest of the rivers ran. They bore names; the widest and clearest of these was the Arafeld, but as it branched out, it was given lesser names, and none of these were familiar to strangers.

Against the swell and ebb of those smaller twisted webs, fields had been planted. Avandar identified the odd rows of submerged rice where water was abundant—and it was. Jewel could count the number of mosquito bites growing by dozens as the day progressed; it was the first time in her life she had thought kindly of armor.

But she thought less kindly of the men who wore it. They were not gentle with the serafs who tended the fields, and although the kai Lamberto's words had been very fine, she saw men perish.

Men whose only crime was the defense of their children, their wives. She hated war, had known that she hated it, but was unprepared for the visceral reaction to the casual deaths that it caused as a matter of course.

The Winter King was beneath her for much of this, and only when the camp had been ordered, and the lands for it appropriated with care, had she dared to venture forth. She made no bones about her mission; she took with her the Northern bard and Lord Celleriant, with his blue sword, his blue shield. Avandar followed, and at more of a distance, Ser Alessandro himself; she wasn't sure if he meant to bless her activity with his rank, or he simply didn't trust her. It didn't matter.

It was to the Northern bard that the greatest debt was owed, for where he walked—and at speed—he sang, the lute in his hands as much a part of him as armor and sword were a part of the Southern cerdan. He did not accept Ser Alessandro's offer of horse, not because he couldn't ride—he could, and damn well—but because he did not wish to remind the Lambertan Tyr of his presence.

Of what his presence meant.

Yet on foot, and at a distance, he made his soft-spoken plea in the cadence of song. And the song seemed to quiet fear, or at least to caution those who were so right to feel it.

He did not sing Northern songs, but he did not sing Southern ones; he sang some hybrid bastard of both, born of necessity. He quieted the children before they could flee screaming; he quieted the women to whom they fled, and he asked the men who held hoes and rough swords as they stood planted in the ground before the women and the children they clutched so desperately to remember whose army this was.

The army of Ser Mareo kai di'Lamberto.

That wouldn't have brought Jewel any peace, for Yollana had made clear that the Lambertans had casually razed whole villages in retribution for losses taken at the hands of Callesta. But it somehow brought peace to the serafs. And because they laid down arms, the cerdan of Lamberto were forced to show mercy. Rough mercy, to be sure, but it was more than she had hoped for.

It was all that she could bear.

The cerdan of Lamberto were not unmoved by bard song, even if they little trusted it. They were lulled by the tales of their Tyr's achievements, and warmed by the description of Lambertan honor; their resolve to live up to that fulsome praise grew as the hours passed. Even those prone to cruelty were caged in some fashion, for the Lambertan Tyr did not dismiss what the Northern bard sang so sweetly of, and if he did not, they could not—not in safety.

She would have kissed Kallandras, but he wouldn't stop singing, and besides, it would have been awkward; the Annagarians as a group didn't seem all that keen on public displays of affection.

But she was surprised to see a horse walking alongside the Winter King, for the horses were afraid of him and they usually kept their distance.

She was more surprised to see that she was joined, not by Ser Alessandro kai di'Clemente, but by the Tyr'agnate of Lamberto.

Great, she thought.

The Winter King's chuckle vibrated up to her knees.

"You are truly from the North," Ser Mareo kai di'Lamberto said quietly. "You, and the minstrel."

She nodded, trying very, very hard to be polite.

"Your servant is not Northern."

"My servant?"

His gaze slid, with quiet meaning, to Avandar.

"I . . . don't know where he's from."

"How long has he been in your service?"

"Half my life," she answered promptly.

"And he has never once failed you?"

"Not in the time I've known him."

"Ah. And before?"

"He wasn't my responsibility then."

"A fair answer."

She watched as the last of the serafs were encouraged to return to their homes. Here, there were fewer beasts of burden—and none of them were horses.

"The Tyr'agnate of Callesta will no doubt be grateful for your intervention on behalf of his serafs."

"Would you, if we had entered your lands?"

Cruel smile followed her question, but she saw it as something that did not quite fit his crinkled eyes. "You *are* a child," he said. "And in some fashion, we tolerate much from our children. Yes, ATerafin. Had you interceded in such a fashion for my own people, I would be grateful."

"Even if I'm from the North."

"Even so." His horse kept pace with the Winter King. "But I have not come to offer gratitude."

"No."

"The banners of the Tyr'agnate of Callesta are flying in the fields beyond the rise of the distant hills," he told her, the softness in his voice a mockery of gentleness. "I have sent Tyran over the hills; they have yet to return."

She was tense, then, although perhaps she'd been tense all day and only found another justification for it.

"And when they do?"

"When?"

"If, then."

"Let us say 'when.' When they do, we will ride forth to join them. They will of course send their own Tyran—ah, you see?"

And she did. The hill was like a hump of plain kicked up from beneath, and folded there. Grass and short brush lined it, but the trees that bounded the valley fell away from the rise, as if it had been cleared on purpose. Which, she thought, it probably had.

Because if it hadn't, it would have been much harder to spot the men who now came. They did not come for war, although they came accoutred for it; they carried a flowing banner as they cantered down the incline.

It was a Southern banner, and it was not one she should have recognized, but she recognized one thing about it: It was blue, bright blue, and it glinted with the ferocity of reflected, golden light. "The sun?" she asked hesitantly.

His eyes widened. "You have come ill-prepared for war," he told her, chidingly, "if you do not recognize what you see carried. It is," he added, because he knew she could not make significant what she did not recognize, "the sun ascendant, with a full ten rays. Beneath it, although the folds take its shape, is the crescent sword. To either side, swords as well. But the crescent is the most significant aspect of that flag: It is marked by sun. By the Lord.

"The Tyr'agar is on the field. It is not my desire to take you with me," he continued. "But I feel it prudent."

"Why?"

She realized, belatedly, that there was a reason he accompanied her shorn of Tyran or cerdan; a reason that he left behind even the Radann par el'Sol. She *questioned* him. And he afforded her, in privacy, absolution for her presumption. She could not be judged— nor could he—by words that were not heard.

"Because, ATerafin, you are not the only Northerners upon the field. There will no doubt be others; let them see that you come by my side. Let them make of it what they will."

She shook her head.

"You refuse?"

And shook her head again, much more sharply.

"Ah. A Northern gesture. What does it mean?"

Clearing her throat, she said, "It means that I don't understand your war at all. If you arrived with our heads on pikes, they wouldn't be surprised."

His smile was cruel again.

But he left it at that. Or at least he left the discussion of war behind. His brow relaxed as he looked across at her; although stags were not the equal of horses in most lands, the Winter King was easily as tall in leg and haunch as the finest of the destriers. As tall, she thought, as the great, black horse that Ser Mareo rode.

Seeing the direction of her gaze, he said, "This is Lady's Night. He has been with me for almost eight years; this battle may well be the last."

"An end to war?"

"No; an end to his service. An honorable end." He pulled on the reins, and the stallion lifted its head, coming to a dancing halt.

"I did not expect to find a child among the warriors," he said quietly.

She tried not to bristle; she was old enough that she shouldn't be bothered by a couple of simple words.

"But I see why women are not allowed upon the field in the South. It is not because they cannot fight—clearly, you have shown us, if the Voyani have not, that this is a cultured lie.

"It is because they weaken the resolve; they lift war out of the realm of the sword."

"I don't understand."

"No. No, you don't. Let me say just this, child. My Serra, Serra Donna en'Lamberto, would decry your terrible lack of grace, your lack of manners—but she would find much in you that she would like. Take care; those she likes, she writes to, and she is much at her writing these days. I give you the gift of the serafs," he added.

"They're not yours to give."

"No. But their lives—as any who are not defined by the Courts and the Sword—are mine to take."

In the encampment, the Serra Teresa di'Marano was awake. She had awakened some two days past, and she had not immediately fallen back into her fitful, terrible sleep. But waking was almost worse, for she called a name that she had not spoken aloud in Diora's presence for what seemed a lifetime.

"*Alora!*"

Diora heard everything in the single mention of her mother's name; everything. Terror. Fear. Loss. She knew what it meant, for she had woken from sleep countless times, different names upon her lips. Different losses.

The vulnerability and exposure was the same.

She was unseemly in her haste, but Yollana was a simple taskmaster; she freed Diora at once and let her run.

The skirts that she wore were the silk of gifted sari, and she hated them; they confined her legs, forced her stride into a hobbled echo of what it had been while she walked as Voyani. No matter that they were soft or fine; that they were colored and painted with delicate, feminine blossoms, that they brought her own color to light in a pleasing fashion; they were simply in the way.

She meant to offer her Ona soothing words and sleep, but when she saw her, she froze, for she realized that Serra Teresa di'Marano was, at last, *behind* her expression.

And the expression itself was so hollow Diora almost looked away.

Instead, she knelt upon the rough tent fabric, and took her Ona's head into her folded lap. She stroked wild, dirty hair, and she spoke soothing words.

But the words failed to soothe.

"Na'dio," Serra Teresa said weakly. She lifted trembling hands, catching and crumpling fine silk into permanent creases. "Na'dio, I can hear *nothing*."

Diora closed her eyes. What she might have said, in a harem, surrounded by the peace and tranquillity of carefully arranged flower, pillow, divan, she could not say here: That the Serra Teresa di'Marano was finally free of her curse. That she might, even now, find a man worthy of her, a harem worthy of her.

"Na'tere," she said. She had never called her aunt by that name; it was a child's name, and Serra Teresa had so long left childhood behind the name would have been an insult. At any other time, an insult.

Hands left silk, gripped hers.

"You killed the demon," Diora told her quietly, putting power into the words. "You stopped it with a word. We are alive, Ona Teresa. All of us, alive, because of you."

"I can't hear," the Serra Teresa whispered. Just that, over and over.

It did not occur to Diora to lie to her Ona, because a lifetime of experience had taught her that lies were useless; Ona Teresa heard them all, and understood not only that they *were* lies, but why they had been offered.

Yet this woman could no longer hear the truth beneath the words.

"Ona Teresa," she said again.

And Ona Teresa began to return to the living. She returned in silence; her limbs were thin, and her face gaunt, but it was the shadows around her eyes that were hardest to bear.

We are cursed, Diora thought. *And in the end, like all cursed things, we have learned to love what has almost destroyed us.*

Two days. Two short days.

She gave up her palanquin entirely for the Serra Teresa; she ordered saris to be offered her. They were refused until Ramdan approached; only Ramdan was allowed to touch her, to bathe her, to feed her; only Ramdan was allowed to clothe her.

Because he had almost never spoken. All of the words they had shared had been hers; he had endured in silence, had served in silence, and had lived in silence, and she had come to rely upon that silence for safety.

She relied upon it now.

He offered her an arm, and she took it only until it was clear that cerdan attended them. She released it, then.

"Na'dio," she said, with effort. Her voice, Diora thought. She could not even hear her own voice.

"Serra Teresa."

"The Tyr'agnate?"

"He has left," she said quietly.

"Alone?"

"Not alone. He has taken with him Jewel ATerafin and Kallandras of Senniel; Jewel ATerafin has taken with *her* the great stag, the white warrior, and the man she thinks serves her."

"And no others?"

"Ser Alessandro kai di'Clemente and the Radann par el'Sol." She frowned. "And Jevri el'Sol has also chosen to attend."

"And the Callestan Tyran?"

Even injured, bereaved, *deaf,* she was cunning.

"They bear the banner of the Tyr'agar," Diora replied carefully. "And they travel to either side of the Lambertans."

Teresa swallowed. "Then it is time, Na'dio."

Yollana of Havalla stood with the aid of canes; the pipe that was her habit and her comfort had been tucked out of sight, although scent lingered in the air around her hands, her lips.

"Yes," the Matriarch said. "High time. Girl, be ready. We have no horses, and we must travel quickly, without the benefit of guard."

Diora did not feign ignorance. Instead, she bowed to the Matriarch and rose. Her steps were perfect. Her grace was irreproachable. Where a moment before she had resented the entrapment of sari, she now considered it duty. And armor. She returned to the tent in which she had lived upon this road, and after a moment, Ramdan left the side of the Serra Teresa, and joined her there.

The tent was fine; it was tall and high, as unlike the tents her companions occupied as Callesta was from the village of Cesanno. And in it, a dress, a pale, perfect dress, wrapped in a thick and plain blanket. She reached for the blanket carefully, and Ramdan stepped past her.

She allowed what Serra Teresa allowed; he dressed her, taking care not to catch crystal or pearl in the length of her unbound hair.

It was not done quickly, although she desired speed. Nor did she offer criticism; she waited with the patience of a Serra. He chose her shoes, for these, too, had been preserved; he chose the combs he placed with deliberate care in hair that was far too dusty.

Last, he held out a fan, and she accepted it, her throat heavy with gold, her wrists heavier. These were her known burdens, but they were not the only ones that she must carry.

That last came to her from the tent of the Havallan Matriarch.

"Here," Yollana said gruffly. She handed the Serra Diora a small box, suitable for the lesser jewelry of a middling clanswoman. Its lid, adorned by symbols in an ancient tongue, was closed; Yollana could not open it. Nor, Serra Diora thought, had she tried. "It won't suit what you wear, but it is the reason that you have come this far. Bear it only a mile or two, Serra Diora, and you will have done what you can."

The Serra Diora bowed her head, and with care, she removed the box's simple lid. Within its cramped confines, wrapped in silken blankets, lay the Sun Sword. No eyes but hers had seen it since it had been taken from the Swordhaven; no hands but hers had touched it.

She did not desire to touch it now.

But it was time.

For this, Serra Teresa di'Marano had forsaken the power that had defined her life, preserving theirs. For only this. Could she do less? Diora took the scabbard from the open blankets; she did not gird herself with it; she had never done anything so foolish. But she held it with the same caution she had displayed when the Sun Sword had come, reborn, from the waters of the Tor Leonne.

"Will they allow us to pass?" she asked softly.

Yollana offered her a grim, grim smile. "Oh, yes," she said. "I myself will accompany you. Teresa?"

Serra Teresa nodded. Voiceless. Wordless.

Ramdan finished Diora's grooming with care. Although he did not speak, and did not offer her the comfort of shade and shadow, he stood in the path of the sun's glare, protecting her as he could. He worked in the shadowed light cast by shoulders and back; she bent before him, upon the mat he unfurled at her feet.

When he finished, he stepped back and looked once to the Serra Teresa. She nodded; she had become as silent as the seraf, but she had taken command of grace, of the things that her illness had so nearly destroyed. She was strong, Diora thought; stronger, in the end, than Diora herself. She bore all, could bear all, for the cause that she had chosen.

And that cause? That cause, Diora thought, lifting the Sun Sword and gaining her feet. But she did not name it. There were no Northerners here. There were no Marano cerdan, no Leonne Tyran. There were no fine horses; the destriers of war had been sequestered upon fields that were meant to stop the strained jockeying for position and dominance that not even their riders could entirely restrain.

The hill seemed a great distance away. She began to walk toward it, sword in the palms of her hands. Her hands were cool; Ramdan had powdered them with care. If the sun was not graced by the veil of clouds, the powder would eventually cake with sweat—there were no trees beneath which she might seek shelter.

None needed now. Shelter was for another Serra. Shelter was for a different life.

The road was made and marked by the sharp hooves of the war-horses. It was marked by the banners of the Tyr'agnate, blowing and flapping in the strength of the valley breeze.

She had seldom seen the valleys of Averda, and she understood, as she traversed their outer edge, why they were so highly prized; why the wars were fought at their edges. Here, in the heartland of Averda, lay all that was of value.

She meant to leave them. Or to enter them.

The sword was heavy.

To war, she thought. She took it to war. She remembered the first time she had entered the Swordhaven upon the plateau of the Tor Leonne; the first time she had seen the sword upon its stand, its sheaths—ornate and simple, one for dress and one for battle—beneath it. She remembered the scent of incense, the burnished bronze of the braziers at which incense must be offered if one chose to approach the steps of the haven itself and stand before the greatest of Leonne's gifts.

The greatest of its responsibilities.

And she remembered, more clearly than all of these things, the first time she had ever seen it drawn.

For war, she thought, and she closed her eyes upon the memory, not to deny it, but to contain it.

The kai el'Sol had perished in the flames of a blade that surely had no mercy and no sense; he was a great man, a noble man, a *worthy* man; he had dedicated the whole of his life—and at cost—to the service of the Lord, and his only reward was that death. Ashes.

And out of the ashes, she had lifted the blade. She had wondered, then, if it would burn her as well, but she had been past caring.

Today, she knew that care had returned.

When, she could not say, but she felt that it had begun in the desert, in a land so devoid of native life that all life, all death, were seen clearly and without the trappings that gilded it.

I do not want to die, she thought.

No panic in the words, and no fear. It was a statement of fact; it was a fact that she accepted. She wanted others to die. She wanted—had she the strength—to kill them. But she wanted to survive that act.

And why?

Why, when she had no wives to return to, no child to hug, no cradle song to sing?

Numb, she could not say.

The sun's light was in her eyes; it glinted across the moving folds of river, the still stretches of pond, the stagnant length of distant fields.

It glinted, she thought, across the bent wide leaves of plants, the glimmering sheen of horses as they galloped across their runs. Much that was beautiful was exposed by the light of the sun, the Lord's face.

And here, all was seen.

She felt Yollana to her right; felt Serra Teresa to her left. They walked behind, as if they attended her, the two women who had done so much to define the lives of all those they touched. She drew strength from their presence. More; she drew a sense of family.

The only woman she missed was Margret.

Margret should have been here.

My story will travel to you, even in the Tor Arkosa, she thought. *The bards will sing of me, and you will pare away the pretty words until you have only the truth, and you will know what we have achieved. And then, Margret, my sister, you will be proud of me, of a clanswoman with pale, uncallused hands.*

That, too, strengthened her.

The hill was gentle, the slope gentle; she could walk it without bowing head or shoulders, without robbing herself of the essential grace of a Serra's perfect movements.

Ser Valedan kai di'Leonne had been attended by serafs. The finest of his dress clothes had been presented, and the Serra Alina herself had judged which of these he might wear. To his surprise, she had chosen to discard the most ornate of the surcoats, the richest of the offered robes; they had seen little wear, and they had seen—clearly seen—no combat.

"Mareo is a man of the Court," she said dispassionately, "but he *is* a man. The armor that bears the scar is the one that will speak to him; it will tell him what you yourself cannot gracefully put into words."

She would have counseled him to carry a different sword, for the sword he did carry was known to Lamberto; it was the sword of the kai Callesta, and it bore all the marks of its ancient legacy. The man who wore this sword, the man who raised it, was blood-kin, and sworn to Callestan service.

But she understood that Valedan would not be parted from it; understood, as well, that Ramiro di'Callesta waited in silence upon the gravity of that choice.

As did Baredan di'Navarre and Ser Anton di'Guivera. Ser Andaro di'Corsarro would have served in honor had Valedan chosen to take a simple dagger as weapon; he had become in all things Tyran, the only Tyran who served Valedan kai di'Leonne.

"Serra Alina?"

She nodded as he presented himself.

"He will come?"

"He is coming," she said, and turned to the North.

Valedan nodded.

"Valedan?"

"Alina?"

"The war is decided here. If Lamberto and Callesta do not stand together, you will lose."

He nodded gravely.

"Even with the Northerners, and their vast army, you will lose."

He nodded again. And she knew that he understood all that she did not say.

"Give me leave to retire," she said softly. But she knew what his answer would be.

"I need you there."

"I am of the South, in my brother's eyes. I am not of value," she added bitterly, "but I am of the South. He will see me, in Northern armor, by your side, and he will judge you by my presence."

"Then let him judge the truth; I will not lie to the Tyr'agnate. If he means to offer me his service, he must understand what he offers that service to."

"If he orders me from the field, I am beholden to him; he is my kai."

"And to me?"

"I owe you a debt that I cannot repay, and I repay it poorly by standing thus."

"But you repay it," Valedan said quietly. He met her eyes, and she saw in his expression the face of the boy who had, in the courtyard of the Arannan Halls, in the distance of *Avantari,* asked her to be his wife.

She nodded gravely. She had offered him what warning she could; she knew him well enough now to know that no further offer would move him, and she was far too proud to plead.

A fault, that; it had always been a fault. A woman's strength lay in the way she adopted weakness and used it against the men in her presence—and it was not a weapon, in the end, that she had ever mastered.

"You do not need to carry the sword," he said quietly.

Her smile was slight, but it was there. "The sword is part of Northern armor," she replied, "and if I am to lend the armor the respect that it is due, I will wear it. But do not ask me to draw it; that will be too much humiliation. If you have chosen to be attended by a Serra in such a fashion, you cannot choose to have her fight *for* you."

"It is not for the sword that you are here."

"But it is a matter of swords that defines the ground upon which we stand. Ah, the Tyr'agnate of Callesta waits."

Valedan nodded. He walked out of the pavilion without a backward glance; in that, her lessons had finally taken hold.

As his foot touched the flattened grass, Ser Baredan di'Navarre knelt at his feet.

It had been a long, long time since such perfect formality had been offered Valedan by the General. He met Baredan's eyes. "General," he said quietly, "you almost lost your life in an attempt to preserve mine the first time we met. You did not know, then, what I would become; could not know that I would not be my father."

"But you acted anyway, and I have never forgotten it. Rise," he said. "And even when the Tyr'agnate of Lamberto seeks audience with us, do not bend knee again. A man cannot fight on his knees."

"A man," Baredan replied gravely, rising as he had been bid, "can fight in any position, if he yet draws breath, Tyr'agar."

The Tyr'agnate of Callesta likewise offered him the perfect, full obeisance of liege to lord, but his timing was better; he waited until the men who crested the hills could see, and be seen. When he was certain of their attention, he drew *Bloodhame,* and again dedicated her service to the kai Leonne. In the full glare of the Lord.

This was not a surprise.

What was, was Ser Alfredo. He, too, fell to one knee, and the bend of his back was as perfect as a seraf's. He shook; his hands shook. He did not raise face until he was prepared for any expression that Valedan kai di'Leonne might choose to offer, and he was gratified when he met it full on: Respect.

"I carry your sword, Ser Alfredo," Valedan said. "And a man cannot make a better gift to his liege lord than the Sword of the kai Callesta."

Ah, formality was rigid here; the air was thick with it.

But Ser Alfredo was still young, and he was not—if the cerdan were to be believed—his dead brother's equal. As if to prove the truth of their gossip, he whispered, "I want it back."

Valedan laughed. The laughter caught everyone's attention, and Ser Ramiro's was a bit too sharp.

"You will have it back," the kai Leonne replied, standing tall beneath the banner of his rightful rank. "And I will return it to you as brother. As kin." He bowed again. "Rise," he said softly. "All of you, rise. I will not meet the Tyr'agnate of Mancorvo upon my knees, and I will suffer none of you to do so."

"They come," Ser Anton said quietly.

Ser Andaro had already taken up the position his rank demanded. Tyran. Captain of the oathguards. Valedan's man, until death.

Primus Duarte stood to Valedan's left. He filled the position of Tyran, and this had caused some concern for Alina. But there were no others Valedan trusted, and he had come to value the rough manners, the bickering discussions, of this unit that had once been feared across the Dominion.

Auralis stood guard. Sanderton. Cook. All men he knew.

Alexis was nowhere in sight. Nor was Fiara. None of the women save Kiriel di'Ashaf.

Valedan had wondered aloud if the choice of Kiriel had been a wise one. But he knew that, if there was treachery, she would be necessary. She knew it, too. A change had come upon her slowly since they had arrived in Callesta, and he recognized the full significance of that change now: She did not sweat; her skin did not darken with sun; she no longer tired at night, although the sun seemed to burden her lids. But even in the day, she was alert.

Night, he thought, better suited her.

It worried him.

The only Northerner—for Valedan could not quite think of the Ospreys as Northerners—who had been summoned was the magi, Meralonne APhaniel. He was diffident when he spoke to, or of, the kai Leonne; he was less so when he spoke among the Northern Commanders.

Now, hair swept back in a Northern warrior's braid, he was silent and watchful. He wore no armor, and carried no sword, but he radiated the confidence that comes with certain power.

Callestan Tyran approached; they joined the Tyr'agnate, but although they spoke at length with their lord, in the end they chose to retreat. Fillipo par di'Callesta stood beside his brother; Ser Miko stood to his left.

Ever politic, Ramiro di'Callesta had chosen to surround himself with lesser numbers than Valedan could easily summon. A wise man, Alina had called him. The most dangerous man in the Dominion.

It was true.

The second banner dropped as the horses at last crested the head of the hill: the banner of Callesta. It was not as large as the banner of the Tyr'agar, but it was fine and heavy, weighted against the vagaries of the wind. Ser Ramiro meant to leave no doubt at all in the mind of his enemy.

And his enemy approached with greater numbers, his son, Valedan thought, by his side, and behind him eight of the Tyran. He did not come with a larger party; he traveled with no Widan. But there were two among his party that had about them the look of the Radann, and one wore, openly, the symbol of the sun ascendant, with eight full rays.

They came to parley.

To parley, an army of at least five thousand at their back, beyond the rise of the hill. No, Valedan thought, with a moment's wisdom: More than that. Ten thousand. Fifteen.

At a distance of ten yards, the Lambertan Tyr pulled up his mount, and this, too, was done for effect; the destrier was tall and fine. Sunlight glinted blue across the contours of his muscles; his coat was short and healthy, and his eyes were the size of a man's mailed fist.

He snorted, pawing dirt into airborne clods. But he was not the envoy, merely the conveyance.

Ser Mareo kai di'Lamberto dismounted.

Now, Valedan thought, *we will see.*

Ser Ramiro di'Callesta stood, hands clasped loosely behind his back; Ser Fillipo stood, hand on sword. No weapons were drawn; no horns; silence pervaded everything that the wind did not touch.

But the Lambertan Tyr lifted his hand, a signal. A command.

Valedan knew what he called for.

The dead.

*   *   *

This, then, was the boy.

Ser Mareo kai di'Lamberto did not so much as shake his head. He took the reins of Lady's Night, and led him with care across the trampled ground.

All decision had come upon him in a single night. But he had not yet declared himself, and the questions that arose from that decision were free to trouble him. He saw the flying banner of the sun ascendant, and he knew it; he would have known it had it been used as shroud or adornment. Beneath just such a banner, he had offered his life and his sword to the man who had died such an ignominious death.

He had done so without doubt, for he had followed the custom of his father's people, of his clan, since the dawn of the Leonne age. He had paid the price for this folly, and it was a price that he would never willingly pay again.

Pretty Serra's words aside, he felt the past keenly in the valleys of Averda; it was a grim past. He could do nothing to change it.

But he could do much to give it the force of strength; he could do much to fulfill the oaths of kin.

"Tyr'agnate'?" his kai said.

"Dismount."

Ser Galen kai di'Lamberto was utterly silent. Even his movements were unaccompanied by the presence of sound, as if he did not wish to offer even this much in the presence of his brother's killers.

He was tall now, this boy who had been par; he had fought and killed many Callestan cerdan in the border skirmishes that had defined his entire adult life. He had named his enemies at feasts and victory celebrations, and he almost named them now; Mareo could see the bitter fire in the youthful glare.

A wise man would have left such a son behind.

But Galen was not without grace; not without sense. Twelve years old he had been when Ser Andreas kai di'Lamberto had fallen upon the field. Twelve, when he had at last seen his brother's body home.

He was no longer a youth.

But the startling blue of his eyes was the color of the sky, the Lord's sky.

"Galen," Mareo said quietly. "We do not come for battle."

Galen bowed.

"What you see here, you will remember. Say nothing."

"Tyr'agnate."

Grave, grave man. Had Mareo ever been so grave?

"Do you see the banner of the Tyr'agar?"

Galen nodded.

"Do not dishonor it."

"But he carries it at the behest of the *Northerners*."

"We have discussed this, Galen. I am Lord here, and when you rule, you may decide the fate of the Terrean without my interference. But if you wish to live to rule, you will obey me here."

"Tyr'agnate."

He spoke softly to his son; his Tyran marked the words. What they took from it might harm his son later; he could not say. But what his son might do now would change the course of the future in a way that Mareo could not easily predict.

"And will we offer them peace?" Ser Galen asked, as his father began to walk.

Because he did not know himself, he gave no answer.

Ser Ramiro di'Callesta did not bow. Between equals, a bow was not required.

Because he did not, Ser Mareo di'Lamberto almost refused to bend. But the highest of the banners demanded acknowledgment of one form or another.

The Radann par el'Sol, however, was not likewise encumbered by history; he tendered the sun ascendant its full due. He bowed low, although he offered no word—and Jevri el'Sol followed his lead, dropping full to knees in the sight of the Lord.

"Radann par el'Sol," Ramiro di'Callesta said gravely. "You were not expected upon this road." Suspicion marked his words, but it was quiet; they offered no open accusation.

"I walk in the light of the Lord," Marakas par el'Sol replied gravely. He rose from his bow.

Ser Mareo kai di'Lamberto watched, the unfamiliar weight of indecision holding him still.

"Ser Mareo kai di'Lamberto," Ser Anton di'Guivera said quietly, before he could make such a decision. The Dominion's most famous swordmaster stepped forward, leaving the side of his Tyr, and he offered what the Callestan Tyr considered beneath dignity: a full bow. A respectful one.

"So," Mareo said quietly. "It is true."

"I am here in the service of the Tyr'agar," Ser Anton replied gravely. He bowed a second time, this to Ser Galen kai di'Lamberto.

Galen was silent, absorbing his first exposure to the men who served the Tyr'agar, and not much liking what he saw.

"Ser Anton. It has been many years since you have graced Arral with your presence."

"Many," Ser Anton replied genially, "and I regret my absence. Is your wife well?"

"She is well, but as women do, she frets; war is ever in her mind."

"It is in the minds of all who must wait without power."

"Even so."

"And in the mind of the Tyr'agar?" Ser Galen kai di'Lamberto said sharply.

"He is ready to be judged," was Ser Anton's mild reply.

It was not what either of the Lambertan kais expected.

"Come," Ser Anton said. "Meet him."

Ser Mareo di'Lamberto stepped under the banner of the sun ascendant; he felt no warmth in the flickering golden light. He did not bow. He did not draw sword. Instead, he gained his full height, armor shifting at the joints.

"Ser Valedan kai di'Leonne," he said at last.

The younger man lowered his head a moment in a deep nod.

And Mareo kai di'Lamberto came face-to-face with the Serra Alina di'Lamberto.

He had not recognized her until this moment; she was dressed in the disgraceful armor and surcoat of the Northern Kings.

He had expected to feel rage, but what came instead was something that was almost kin to regret; he could not speak.

And because he could not, she stepped forward, and finding some space in the grass not occupied by the heavy feet of men, she found her knees, folding her back into the perfect grace of the supplicant's posture. It should have been impossible, given what she wore; it was not. She had always been canny.

Thus protected, she spoke. "Tyr'agnate."

"And have you been brought South as a reminder of the capacity in which you serve the North?"

She was beholden to answer. "No, Tyr'agnate."

"No?"

"By the grace of the Kings, by the grace of the Tyr'agar, I have been given my freedom; there are no hostages now within the Imperial Court who do not stay there for reasons of their own safety in the coming war."

"You have lost none of your ability with words, Serra Alina. But if you do not serve in that capacity, why are you upon the field?"

"At the pleasure of the Tyr'agar," she replied. Twice now, she had used the title, but the second time she chose to weight the words with the full edge of her voice. He had always disliked that in a woman.

Especially this one.

"All of the Imperial hostages have offered Ser Valedan kai di'Leonne their swords," she continued. "Even Ser Kyro."

"Perhaps he would not have been so quick to make that offer if he knew what use you would be put to."

"Tyr'agnate."

The boy Tyr moved. "Serra Alina," he said, his voice soft, "rise."

And he looked up and met the eyes of the Tyr'agnate of Mancorvo. Ser Mareo knew youth; he understood all of its guises. Little of that youth now adorned the almost delicate features of the boy who claimed the last of the Leonne blood.

The boy who had given a command to the Serra Alina in the presence of her kai.

Alina did not hesitate. What Mareo had chosen, in subtlety, to deny her, she took for herself. That had always been her way.

"Ser Mareo kai di'Lamberto," Ser Valedan said, his voice just as reasonable, "I am honored by your presence."

Ser Mareo knew what the manners of the Court demanded. But he could not bring himself to offer it. Instead, he said, "And your Northern allies?"

"They guard the borders of the valleys," Ser Valedan replied smoothly. "At my command."

"Yours? And you will tell me that they serve you?"

"They serve my cause," he replied.

"And what, Ser Valedan, *is* that cause?"

Serra Alina di'Lamberto lifted a hand; it was a subtle gesture. A woman's gesture.

From down the steps of the pavilion came serafs; they were fine, and finely trained; too fine, Mareo knew, for Ser Valedan. Callestan? Almost certainly.

They approached with long-necked jugs, and small, perfectly spun cups. These, they filled with sweet water. They offered first to the kai Leonne, and he accepted their gift as his due.

But they offered second to the Lambertan Tyr.

He took the water and gazed into its perfect clarity for a moment;

his shadow hid the sun's light, and none of its striking gold played across the surface of the liquid.

"My cause?" the kai Leonne said, lifting the cup to his lips and drinking. "The Tor Leonne."

"And not the North?"

"I have lived in the North for most of my life," Ser Valedan replied. "As you must know. The Northern customs are not the customs of the South."

"You mean to make no war upon the North?"

"I fight no war that I cannot win," the boy replied. Prudent, that.

"And so you league with them instead, and open up the heartlands of Averda to their passage?"

"I am in their debt," was the even reply. "And the decision of their deployment is in part due to the grace and the wisdom of the kai Callesta; what he will not gainsay, I will not. These lands are his lands; these people are his people. The choice was his, the offer his to make."

"Yet we have heard that the Northern army numbers thirty thousand strong."

Valedan shrugged. Marco watched his face, seeking some sign of acknowledgment, some sign of surprise.

"Their exact numbers are best known to the men who have command of their movements," the boy who would be Tyr said. "And if you have come to seek an alliance, you will in time speak with them."

"Alliance, is it?" The tone was much harsher than he had intended. Much harsher.

"If you seek justice," Valedan continued, "then you seek Southern justice, and you will find it." It should have been a threat. That it was not was also surprising. Much about the boy was.

"But there is a matter of a death between the clan Callesta and the clan Lamberto, kai Lamberto, and I would speak to you of this death before we continue."

Ah. At last. If the boy offered open accusation, Mareo's decision was made for him.

Ser Valedan kai di'Leonne turned to the Callestan Tyr; Ser Ramiro had offered no word, no expression, nothing that could be considered either order or advice. But he nodded. Ser Fillipo par di'Callesta bowed and retreated into the maze of tents.

As they waited for the return of the par Callesta, Ser Valedan kai di'Leonne continued to speak. "I fight Leonne's fight," he said quietly. "Leonne the Founder. Leonne the warrior. He did not struggle for dominance among the clans; he did not lose wife and child for the simple gain of political power. He faced the servants of the Lord of Night, and against such servants, he offered no compromise.

"He might have been Lambertan," the kai Leonne continued. "But if he was not, it is certain that he relied upon the wisdom of the Lambertans during his long fight."

"You know much of our history."

"It is *my* history," the kai Leonne replied, with the first real hint of warmth. That it came from anger made no difference.

"And do you know, as well, the history of the last war fought across our borders?"

"I know it," Valedan replied. The momentary flash was gone from his dark eyes, and subduing the anger had subdued him. He was hooded now; watchful. Steel, Mareo thought, that had been tempered.

He could well believe that *this* boy had stood against the servants of the Lord of Night. Could believe, now, that the Northern woman who was almost a child, had indeed spoken truth.

"I did not take up the title in order to wield its power in the South," he continued. "But rather, to succor my people in the North. I would leave no one of them behind; I would offer no one of them to the justice of Kings, even if that justice is above question."

So that, too, was true.

"You have made a legend of yourself in a short time," he said grudgingly.

"Legends are for the dead," Valedan said. "Or made of them. I am neither legend, nor dead. I seek to avenge my father, and the Serra Antonia, the woman who was my Oma in the harem; I seek to avenge my brothers and sisters—those that I lived with. Those that I will never see again, except in the winds."

"A worthy cause, kai Leonne." He offered the boy that much.

"For these things, the North cares little. But I seek to drive the enemies of the Lord from these lands, and it suits the Northern Empire to join me in that task."

"You are naïve; it is for the Tor Leonne that they have gathered."

The kai Leonne's expression did not change. "Take their measure upon a different field, and you will understand why I believe what I believe," he said at last.

"I will take their measure upon this one," Ser Mareo said. He bowed his head a moment. "Understand," he said softly, "that I loved my kai. He perished at Northern hands. I have lived these ten years and more hearing only his voice in the wind; his voice and my failure. What you want, I understand. Do you ask me to deny my own cause?"

"You would never serve a man who asked you to abandon an honorable cause, Ser Mareo."

The boy surprised him. Here, his blade still untested, he offered wisdom. And although he listened intently, the Tyr'agnate of Mancorvo could not hear the echo of Ramiro di'Callesta in the kai Leonne's words.

Valedan turned and spoke a word to Ser Andaro di'Corsarro. Mareo recognized the man; he was one of the finest of Ser Anton's students. But it was not as student that he stood, and there was a story there, another story. He cursed his own impatience with all things Northern; had he been a more patient man, the Northern woman might have gifted him with the tale.

Ser Andaro bowed. "It may take time, Tyr'agar."

"Take the time."

"Tyr'agar."

Ser Fillipo returned before the Tyran did. He bowed deeply to the Tyr'agar. To his brother, he offered the obeisance required of Tyran, but even in this, there was something strange to the eyes of the Lambertan Tyr: Ser Fillipo tendered genuine respect to the kai Leonne. And Ser Fillipo par di'Callesta was brother to the kai Callesta in all things; he was no fool.

"They are here," Ser Fillipo said quietly.

"Good." Steel was now the whole of the boy's face. Had he seemed young? Age no longer defined him.

What defined him was war. Ser Marco had not expected this from the orphan son of a concubine, the least of concubines that Leonne owned. He regretted the fact that Ramiro di'Callesta had seen the boy's full measure first; regretted his own ignorance.

Wondered what the cost of alleviating that ignorance would be. His son's killers were here. His kai's death. All of his bitter history. Here, he faced truth, the truth that had always been at the heart of Lambertan struggle: pragmatism over honor.

And the choice was not made simpler by the approaching wagon.

It was a farmer's wagon, a seraf's wagon, its wheels tall and slender; the wood, unpainted, had faded in sunlight, and the changing humidity of the Averdan seasons had conspired to crack the wood, to bend its walls. They did not bring food, in this wagon. They did not bring the harvest.

They brought a challenge, he thought.

Nor was he wrong. His sister stiffened; he could see this clearly, even beneath the loose uniform of the North. She was pale—as were all Serras—but this particular paleness seemed to extend from her heart center to engulf everything about her; she knew what waited upon that wagon, and she did not wish to face it again.

Curiosity had never been the worst of his burdens; he felt it now, but more, felt the sharp edge of necessary caution.

"Tyr'agnate," Ser Valedan kai di'Leonne said. There was no youth in his tone; there was fire, cold fire, and grim. "The kai Callesta was murdered within Callesta almost a month ago."

Ser Mareo bowed his head, as if the news was indeed news to him.

"His killers did not escape, but they did not live to see justice done."

Again he nodded.

"We have exhumed their bodies; we have not burned them; we have not released them to the wind."

The cart drew closer, and above it, like a dark cloud, flies, carrion insects. They hovered in a dome, their bodies sliding and skittering across a surface that Lambertan eyes could not see except by tracing the line of their failure.

"We have used Widan arts to preserve them," the kai Leonne said quietly. "Against this meeting and this moment."

"You accuse me of this crime?"

"No, Ser Mareo; if I believed you were the hand behind it, we would not now be upon this plateau; our armies would not be living in tents upon the field. Fires would burn; swords would travel."

The Tyr'agnate nodded.

And the bodies of the dead at last came into view.

Death had taken its toll, and time; the Widan arts were not entirely proof against them. But proof enough. He recognized the men that lay within.

And the kai Leonne saw that glimmer of recognition, as if he expected no less. "They were your men."

"They were my Tyran," Ser Mareo said quietly. "And I would take them from you, if they are offered. They have been much missed."

"The offer is not mine to make," the kai Leonne said. He turned to the Callestan Tyr.

The Callestan Tyr stood apart, hands behind his back, chin lifted against the breeze that drew flies back as parted curtain. "These killed my kai," he said coldly.

Ser Mareo kai di'Lamberto bridled. His anger was not feigned. "Impossible."

"My own Tyran bore witness, from too great a distance to interfere." A challenge there.

A trap. Mareo stepped aside. "I will not question their word," he said softly. "But I know my Tyran as well as you know yours; they are not of my kin, but they serve me. Lamberto does not descend to assassination."

"That was our belief," was the neutral reply. "How, then, do you answer this?"

"I have no answer," Ser Mareo replied. "But I know you well enough, Ser Ramiro; of the games you play, this one would be beneath you."

The Callestan Tyr did not nod. But he did not move.

Instead, the kai Leonne did. "There is mystery here," he said softly. "And we have done much work to unravel it."

"We?"

"Callesta," the boy replied smoothly, "as my vassal. And the Northern mages, as my allies." He turned to the slender, silver-haired man who had stood silent as a banner pole throughout all discussion. "Member APhaniel."

The magi stirred. His gaze shifted, and at that moment, to his annoyance, the Tyr'agnate realized that he was not silent through forbearance; he was lost in thought—as if matters of Tyrs were of little concern to him. The North was cold.

But although it was cold, this winter man, this sword, now offered the perfect Southern bow; his grace, his supple movements, made the Tyr'agnate feel old and ungainly. "Tyr'agnate," he said quietly. "I am Meralonne APhaniel of the Order of Knowledge, and I was sent this distance because of my knowledge of the antiquities.

"These men were dead long before the kai Callesta died," he added smoothly. "Their flesh walked; their swords moved. I do not think they spoke, but our magics are not so complete in that regard."

"How is that possible?"

"It is not Voyani magic, if that is your thought."

It was. And it was an unpleasant thought.

"Whose?"

"The Lord of Night's," Meralonne APhaniel replied. "There are, among his servants, those who can take the flesh and form of the living for some time. The living are absorbed; they die within their bodies. But the creature itself continues to feed, and the body he takes becomes his own."

"There are three," the kai Lamberto said quietly. "And only two of the dead are my Tyran. The third, I do not know."

"Indeed. Three vessels. Such demons as might take human form would be a gift of great significance from the Lord of Night to the General Marente."

"The Lord of Night."

Valedan lifted a hand. "There is almost no need to drive a wedge between the two Northern Terreans," he said quietly. "War has troubled your borders since the end of the battle of the Empire. You have made history with each raid; they have made history in like fashion.

"No man would think that either of you would lay down your arms; that either of you would sit across from an oath medallion, swords raised to that purpose and no other.

"No man," he added, "who was not driven by pragmatism. I have not been long in your company. As you have not taken my measure, I have not taken yours. I have the word of Ser Anton di'Guivera, and I value it highly. It is his opinion that no Lambertan could be brought to countenance such an act, let alone carry it out.

"Yet it would resolve much; the death of one kai for the death of the other."

The boy was young. Or he was shrewd. "It would resolve nothing," the Tyr'agnate said coolly. "Would it, Ser Ramiro?"

"Ser Ramiro di'Callesta has been the most practical of men. He speaks the Northern tongue fluently. He understands the Empire's power, its culture, its ruling class. He has made treaties with the Northern traders—"

"We are aware of those."

"—and he has both defended and enriched the people of his Terrean, from the highest of clans to the lowest of serafs. The damage you have done him in your quest for justice is not—would not have been—enough to guarantee that he at least would not seek to treat for peace or even alliance with the clan Lamberto in the face of the war that you both know is coming.

"But the death of his kai?"

"That would be enough," Ramiro di'Callesta said coldly.

"And now, Ser Mareo, you must decide."

He heard horses, the thunder of hooves at a gallop. They were distant, but they would not remain so.

"To follow you?"

"To offer me your sword," the kai Leonne said, "and your oath. To give into my keeping the lands of Mancorvo. To accept my word as law."

"You ask much for a boy who was raised in the North."

"I ask what the Tyr'agar has always asked."

Ser Mareo di'Lamberto was silent; the horses were loud. He understood that the last of his test was to come, and he bore its arrival with patience. But he turned to his son. "Galen," he said quietly.

His son nodded; he drew closer to the father until they seemed inseparable, waiting upon the flat of the plateau, the banners of their sworn enemy an accusation of the faltering of their long resolve.

"Go," Ser Mareo said quietly. "Crest the hill. Summon the Northerners who wait; I would have them by my side for this . . . display."

"But you—"

"Do you doubt my ability to defend myself?"

Ah, his son was no fool. Although he paled—he was that perceptive—he spoke no further word.

"The kai Callesta will not strike against us here," Mareo offered at last; it was a concession.

Galen's expression was the understated Court expression of skepticism.

"If he strikes against us here, he strikes beneath the banner of the Tyr'agar. You have listened to what the kai Leonne has said. Do you think that the kai Leonne would grant either permission or absolution for that act?"

Galen bowed. And because he was still young, Ser Mareo kai di'Lamberto added, "Ser Anton di'Guivera serves him. And he serves willingly."

Ser Galen di'Lamberto bowed again, and followed his father's orders.

CHAPTER SEVEN

THE Winter King lifted his tined head; Jewel was instantly alert. She had thought to be done with waiting when the Tyr'agnate summoned her up the hill, but was not terribly surprised when she was ordered to wait behind the crest of its slope. Tyran surrounded her, as tense and quiet as she, but without the annoyance that stiffened her shoulders and her jaw. Hurry up, hurry up, hurry up, wait. It was like a child's game, and she resented it.

The waiting was almost done.

She could see a man flanked by a single Tyran atop the hill; he rode quickly, but his horse's legs did not stretch in all out gallop.

"ATerafin," Kallandras said quietly. "We are, I think, required."

But Lord Celleriant had turned in the opposite direction, and he said, "I concur."

It was to the Arianni lord that her gaze was drawn.

"Celleriant?"

"Look," he said quietly.

She did. Her gaze moved down the slope toward the familiar sight of men in a sea of tents. But it halted before it reached those tents, for upon the road made by the passage of heavy hooves, three people stood. They were barred by soldiers; Tyran, she thought, although their backs were toward her and she could not easily see the crest they bore.

ATerafin, Avandar said quietly.

She nodded. "Kallandras, stall." She didn't wait to see what he did; she turned the Winter King around and headed down the road.

What was not always safe for horses was safe for the Winter King; nothing halted his passage when he chose to move with speed. Not water, not mud, not fallen trunk or low-lying branches. Not even, she suspected, a small wall of armed men, glinting in the sunlight.

This last was not tested; the Winter King had not chosen to move in silence, and they heard him come at their backs, parting and turning suddenly to face his charge.

He came up short almost instantly; no momentum disturbed his graceful halt.

"What's going on?" Jewel said in rough Torra.

The Tyran were mute.

"I asked you a question."

The old woman answered. Yollana of Havalla. Tyran, Jewel thought, for sure; the cerdan would have fled the expression on her dark face. "We seek passage," she said quietly.

"To where?"

"To the kai Leonne."

And Jewel's gaze fell upon the Serra Diora and what she carried. She had seen this woman before, in a dream.

In three dreams. *This* woman, in *this* dress, had forced her to abandon House Terafin in crisis. This woman, and the death that waited in her shadows; the war that she carried.

Had they truly been companions upon the *Voyanne?* Jewel

looked at her, gaping, as if she had never encountered her before: The most beautiful mortal woman that she had ever seen. The most dangerous. Had she carried a sword in the vision that had, in the end, driven Jewel from House Terafin? Had she carried *that* sword in the sight granted those who were touched with the seer's talent?

It didn't matter. She carried it now.

And Jewel *knew* that this was the last of her duties upon foreign soil. A simple duty.

"Serra Diora," she said quietly.

The Serra bowed head; she did not drop to ground, did not bend at knee. Had not, Jewel realized, done it in the presence of the Tyran either.

"You," she turned to the Tyran. "Will allow her to pass."

"We have our orders," the oldest of the Tyran said, drawing blade.

She knew what that meant. But she knew that it didn't matter; that she could not *let* it matter. Had she struggled to save lives? Had she decried the terrible casualty with which those lives were taken?

Yes. And she knew that, forced to kill them all, she would continue to do so. But she didn't want to kill them.

Avandar Gallais came to stand by her side. "Serra Diora," he said quietly.

"I don't want them dead," Jewel whispered.

"Ah," Avandar replied. "You surprise me."

She could have slapped him, but it wouldn't have helped her any. She held her hand.

And as she did, another horse came down the slope, this time at a gallop.

The kai Lamberto, Avandar said quietly. *The son.*

She waited until he was beside her.

And then she turned to him and said, "We want what you want, kai Lamberto. But these three, the Matriarch of Havalla, the Serra Diora, and the—the woman who serves the Matriarch, must be free to travel."

No fool, he. He looked long at the three; longest at the sheath in the hands of the youngest and fairest.

"Serra," he said, breathlessness fighting with gravity, "only put down the weapon and the Tyran will allow you free passage."

The Serra Diora met his gaze openly. It was, Jewel realized, a shock to him. But she said nothing.

"Kai Lamberto," Jewel continued, "we have been your allies,

whether or not the full extent of our work here is known to you. But we will see the Serra Diora to her destination."

Lord Celleriant of the Green Deepings drew his sword.

Until that moment, Jewel had thought him at a safe distance; he had followed so silently she had not been aware of his presence.

He would kill them all at a word.

She knew she had but to give it, and they would be dead. Knew that this was why she had come, in the end. Not for the Hunt in the Tor Leonne; not for the Matriarchs, and their terrible duty; not for the rising of the Tor Arkosa in the vast, terrible emptiness of the Sea of Sorrows; not for the Winter King; not for the masks that had almost destroyed the Tor Leonne and signaled the early coming of the god that haunted her nightmares, waking or sleeping.

Just for this: to see a woman and the burden she carried to safety.

The Tyr'agnate's heir hesitated.

"The Radann par el'Sol understood what she carried," Jewel said softly. "And made his oaths to the Matriarch of Arkosa; if you raise sword against her, or against us, he will also be drawn into the fight. We understand honor," she added. "It is not Southern understanding, but we know damn well that the Tyran will fight to the death here upon your command.

"Know that they won't survive. Understand that we can call the winds, and speak with their voice. If we must, we will.

"But we'd really rather not. It is perhaps the worst of the crimes the Lord of Night can commit: to set against each other those who should stand united. Decide," she added softly, aware that she was the wrong person to offer command, and aware as well that she was the only one present who would. "And decide quickly."

His eyes were clear and blue, pale as sky. He dropped hand to sword hilt, and a second later, blade had cleared scabbard.

She waited; the Winter King lowered his tines.

A second, two, and he would be gone.

And so would the war, she thought bitterly.

But he did not strike. The blade was strong and true; it caught sunlight, as if sending a message in fractured light.

"Move aside," he told the Tyran.

"Kai Callesta—"

"*Now.*"

The command was not—quite—his to give. She saw that truth in the faces of the Tyran. But she saw more: indecision. It was a blessing.

But it was not quite enough.

"Would you bring the wrath of Havalla upon the clan?" Ser Galen continued softly. "Would you bring the wrath of legend upon us? We are in the debt of these strangers; will you shame Lamberto in the sight of the Lord?"

"Our oaths," the oldest Tyran said, with a burning dignity.

"Your oaths are to my father. And if you fail them, you will be given the honor of taking your life. Choose," he added, and the anger slid out of his words, leaving his face, his expression, hollow. "Your lives, or the lives of the clan."

The man was silent. After a moment, he turned to the five Tyran who accompanied him. "Let them pass," he said coldly.

Ah, the Winter King said. Just that.

But something about his voice was odd. *Ah, what?*

He takes it upon himself, the Winter King replied.

Takes what? He's been given the command by the heir to the clan — what cost is there?

He owes loyalty to one man, and to that man's orders. So, too, do all the men who serve the Tyr'agnate. They cannot obey the son without disobeying the father, but they understand the cost of their obedience.

But he is the Captain of the Tyran; the Tyran must obey him.

It is his life, and only his life, that ends here.

We're not going to kill him, Jewel snapped. But she was uneasy.

No, Jewel. We will not.

No comfort there.

The Tyran bowed deeply to their Captain, and they parted. The Serra Diora began to walk forward, sword in her arms.

But she, too, paused before the Captain of the Tyran, and for the first time since Jewel had seen her upon the incline, she fell to her knees. She took care to keep the sheath from touching the earth, but took no care with herself; her supine back was perfectly flat.

And then she rose.

Yollana walked with canes; Serra Teresa walked without any aid at all.

What did she say? Jewel asked the Winter King, for she could see, by the expression that graced the Tyran's face, that she had indeed spoken.

She said that she has had the privilege of meeting both the kai el'Sol and the Tyr'agnate. She said that had Leonne had in his service men a tenth as honorable as those who serve Lamberto, Leonne would never have fallen. She begged his forgiveness, Jewel, for what she must do, begged his understanding for the burden that she carries, and the duty that she owes.

And the Tyran found comfort in those words; Jewel could see that clearly.

But she had no like words to offer the man who now stood like a ghostly sentinel, as if he had already passed from this world to the next.

The riders came from beyond the Callestan tents, and Ser Mareo kai di'Lamberto tensed. His hand fell to his blade. He did not draw it. Did not know why.

He recognized the Northern man and the Northern woman who rode horses that had come from weaker Southern stock. There were others; the two did not choose to arrive unattended. But they drew the whole force of his attention.

The whole of his anger.

Ser Valedan kai di'Leonne did not waver. He did not look back to see who approached; it was clear that he expected them. He stared, instead, at the kai Lamberto, his hands behind his back in pale imitation of the kai Callesta's posture.

"The Northern Commanders," he said, when the horses came to a stop.

"There are only two."

"The third protects the Southern edge of the valleys," the kai Leonne replied. "For it is there that we expect to meet the General Marente."

Commander Bruce Allen dismounted. Commander Kalakar followed. Their reins were given to those who attended them, as if horses were merely a matter of conveyance. Mareo waited.

But he saw that they wore Imperial sashes, prominently displayed: black, white, and gold. The Northern colors of mourning. Ramiro kai di'Callesta did not turn; did not otherwise acknowledge their presence.

He stood forward and said, in a clear, loud voice—a voice that wind could not steal, that sun could not scorch, a voice that men would remember, "Did you kill my son?"

And the Tyr'agnate of Mancorvo drew his blade. But his Tyran did not.

"I will give you a man's answer," he said evenly.

Ramiro kai di'Callesta raised *Bloodhame.*

But Ramiro had not sent his son away, and his son's sudden start added the only touch of awkwardness to the moment. Had he been a lesser man, Ser Mareo thought, he would now be dead.

"Ser Alfredo," the kai Leonne said unexpectedly, "*be still.*"

And the youth did still at the brief display of steel in the young man's voice.

Bruce Allen watched the swords as if they were the raising of curtains. As if they presaged finality, the end of something too intense to be rivalry.

Much had been said in Callesta. Much had been witnessed. He glanced at Ellora; she was watching the two men as if she were, indeed, a kestrel, bright-eyed, hunting. She waited to see who would blink.

She was his ally, and one of the most competent men he had ever had the privilege of commanding; she brought to her office what was politely referred to as a common touch. She had made some place for herself in the streets of Callesta simply by being who she was.

But he knew that she would never understand what he was about to do; he did not speak of it. Did not look at her. Instead, he lifted a hand.

That caught her attention; that and the bright blades of the South. "Do not interfere," he told her quietly.

She would have spoken, and that would have been unfortunate. He stepped away from her quickly, stepped away from the small party of Northern soldiers that formed his personal guard.

Stepped, truly, onto Southern soil for the first time, the high-flying banner of the Tyr'agar a shadow above his brow. Blue shadow, glinting with golden light. An odd shroud.

His knees were not as supple as they had once been, but he knew how to kneel; ceremony was a part of his existence, and in *Avantari,* he knelt before the Twin Kings in their ancient Halls. There, Northern gods dwelled behind the golden eyes of their children.

Here, the gods were silent.

As they should be, he thought; men made what they made of all things. In peace. And in war.

His hands were steady as he unbuckled the sword that now rested awkwardly against the ground; it had no curve, no Southern heft, no single edge.

He did not draw it; instead he set it aside upon the trampled grass. He removed his daggers as well, adjusting only the fall of the sash that spoke of death, of sorrow; spreading its black pleats, its clean whites.

And then he lifted his head, clear-eyed, the sun upon his brow.

"Tyr'agnate," he said. "Tyr'agnate."

As one, both men turned at the sound of his voice.

He had faced them upon the fields of a war that their now dead lord had chosen. What he had achieved in that war haunted the breadth of this one. *Old ghosts,* he thought, seeing two proud men. *And never laid to rest.*

Ser Mareo kai di'Lamberto raised a brow; his sword rested in air, unmoving. His arm was that steady.

Everything was a risk. Everything.

"Kai Lamberto."

The Mancorvan Tyr acknowledged the word with his eyes, no more.

"I am the man responsible for the death of your kai."

He spoke in Torra. He spoke slowly. In speaking, he changed the face of the war, and he was aware of the weight of each syllable.

The kai Lamberto said to the kai Callesta, "Is this a Northern game?"

Ser Ramiro kai di'Callesta turned. "It is not a Callestan game," he said quietly. "Not, I think, a game at all." He hesitated; the hesitation was profound.

And then, in the sight of Callestan men, he brought *Bloodhame* to his palm, and drew it across the mound of exposed flesh. Red flowered there; the cut was not shallow. Without expression, he returned the sword to its sheath, and he tendered the kai Lamberto the first bow of the day; a genuine bow.

Respect, between these two.

But that was almost always the way between men of war.

That left Commander Bruce Allen, the Eagle of the Kings' army, upon the field.

"Why do you kneel?" the kai Lamberto said. He, too, spoke slowly, measuring each syllable. But he turned, he took a step, he halved the distance that separated them.

Commander Allen did not rise. Hard, though, to keep hand from his sword; perhaps the hardest thing he had ever done.

"We did not mean to kill your kai," he said. "We meant to preserve him. We did not understand his rank or his position."

Dark brows rose, changing the geography of a powerful man's face. Lending it more than the patina of surprise. Of anger. Words fled; sword trembled, as if the weight of its steel had suddenly returned.

As if it must fall, and soon.

Its shadow darkened grass.

"What game do you play, Northerner?"

"I play no game," Commander Allen replied. "I am the man responsible for the orders given. I am the man responsible for the message sent to your son's Commander." He bowed his head then, exposing the back of his neck. Breeze played against his skin.

"Then rise, Northerner," the kai Lamberto said softly. "Take your sword. Draw it."

"It . . . is not the way, in the North," Commander Allen said quietly.

"It is not the way of Northerners to die fighting? Do Northern men seek to end their lives on their knees?" Insults, all. Deadly insults; Ser Mareo kai di'Lamberto knew it.

The Tyran were silent. Mute. Even the Callestans.

None had foreseen this.

Ellora spoke. She had been given orders, but it was probably too much to expect her to *obey* them; he regretted Devran's absence keenly.

"Your son was a child," she said to the Southern Tyr.

Bruce Allen did not raise his head; he saw her shadow on the grass, and he knew that she had not yet drawn her sword.

The Kai Lamberto's shadow did not change, but his voice did. "He was no child. He lived, he fought, and he died *as a man*."

"We do not send our children to battle. None of our soldiers were as young as he. We could not . . . conceive . . . of his import upon the field." She did not bow. She did not kneel.

The Eagle cursed her silently.

"Then you are a *fool*."

"Yes," she said, as if they spoke of weather, of the contents of a meal.

"Commander Allen," the kai Lamberto said coldly. "You will rise, or you will die as you sit. Decide."

And Bruce Allen raised his head. "I have already made my decision. In the North," he said quietly, "when we are guilty of crime, we accept judgment. We do not struggle against it."

"And you have waited twelve years to make this . . . confession?"

"We have lived twelve years in ignorance," Commander Allen

replied. "And this is—perhaps will be—our only opportunity to alleviate it.

"I—and only I—am responsible for the death of your kai."

"Yours was not the sword that killed him."

"No more was yours the sword that razed Callestan villages upon the Western border, but it is upon your head that all responsibility for such an action must rest. *You* are the Commander of the Lambertans. You are their leader."

The sword rose as Ser Mareo kai di'Lamberto stepped forward. Ellora's sword left her sheath.

"Commander Kalakar," Commander Allen said, speaking now in Weston. "You will *sheathe your sword* and you will *not interfere.* Is that clear?"

"Bruce—"

"That is an *order,* Commander Kalakar. If you do not sheathe your sword *now,* you will be placed under House arrest."

Her eyes were blue, her face pale, her lips a thin white line. He thought she would refuse. And that would be unfortunate.

But she knew he was serious. She forced her hands to fight all instinct. She disarmed herself. "What use is suicide to us now?" she said bitterly.

"We cannot fight this war without Lamberto," he replied evenly. "We cannot fight this war if either the kai Callesta or the kai Lamberto fall here. General Marente is on the field; we will be divided in a way that will destroy us. Or would you have the *Allasakari* upon the Southern throne?"

"Bruce—"

"Enough. Enough, Ellora."

She was silent.

And the Tyr'agnate of Mancorvo said, in heavy, unpleasant Weston, "You will die here."

"Yes," Commander Allen replied.

Valedan kai di'Leonne took a single step forward.

Ser Anton di'Guivera placed an arm upon his shoulder. It was not gentle. "Ser Mareo kai di'Lamberto is not *your* Tyr," Ser Anton said gravely. "No command that you give him will be honored, and if you give a command that is not, you will lose face." His gaze was opaque; it rested upon the Eagle, and it did not waver.

Serra Alina said quietly, her voice for his ears alone, "Ser Anton is right." But there was a muted awe in her words, and they, too, were for Commander Allen.

"Take his measure," Ser Anton said.

But Valedan did not know of whom he spoke: Commander Allen or Ser Mareo kai di'Lamberto.

Jewel ATerafin saw the sword fly.

She had not yet crested the hill, but she *saw* it, and she knew that they were almost come too late. She recognized Commander Allen, although his position, knees bent into flattened grass, was almost beyond comprehension. She recognized, better, the Lambertan Tyr who had so reluctantly allowed her to travel by his side.

"What is he doing?" She turned to Avandar, her eyes round, her face pale.

What she had not put into words, he had nonetheless heard. "Your Eagle *is* the Eagle," he said softly.

"He will die there," she told him, forcing the words out.

"Perhaps. If he faced a lesser man, yes."

"The kai Lamberto has spent his entire life bent on vengeance."

"On justice, ATerafin. Remember that."

Frustrated, angry, she turned to look at the women who trailed behind. *We will arrive too late,* she thought.

She knew that she could not hurry them; the power that would do that was not gifted to her.

But the Serra Diora di'Marano lifted her pale, perfect face, her round, dark eyes a study in neutrality. Without a word, she began to run, legs hampered by the folds of white silk, the glitter of crystal, the soft luminescence of pearl.

This was not the battle he had imagined.

Not the fight he had lived for.

Not the death he had promised Andreas, his long-dead kai.

He did not trust this Northern man. *Warcry* was silent in his hand; silent and heavy.

He spoke its name in the oldest Torra he knew, and he lifted the blade with a cry.

But the man upon his knees did not flinch or blink.

Warcry fell in the stillness.

Its tip, the farthest reach of its perfect edge, grazed pale skin from cheek to jaw. Blood fell. Blood, but not the man who shed it.

Remarkable, he thought. The strength of this man in a posture of helplessness, remarkable. He did not move. He did not acknowledge the wound. It stained his face; the creases worn there by wind and sun almost swallowed red liquid.

At no time did his hands leave his lap, although his sword was an arm's length away.

Warcry rose again. This time, Mareo's hand did not shake.

An accident? he thought, bitter now. *An act of ignorance? You thought my Andreas a* child?

And it fell again, and again it fell short, splitting skin. Offering no death.

Truly, the Eagle was the Lord's.

But who, among the Lord's men, would go silent and unmoving to his death?

A name came to Ser Mareo kai di'Lamberto. It should have been his son's name. It should have been, but it was not. *Na'donna,* he thought.

Blood ran along the curved edge of *Warcry,* clinging to the minute serrations there.

This was the death he had desired, but as he lifted sword for a third time, he knew that he would gain no satisfaction from it.

But his son would. His dead son. His kai.

The sword was high, and not even the sudden strength of a wind that had remained gentle in the Averdan valleys caused it to waver.

The slope of the land shifted suddenly beneath their feet. The grass rose at their backs, and they rose with it, as if the whole of the land was a platform, a simple conveyance.

The Winter King was not fazed; the horse that carried Ser Galen kai di'Lamberto leaped up in fear's sudden prance. Nostrils wide, the horse spoke his fear; his rider's knees clamped tight.

Jewel did not hear what Ser Galen said to his horse, although had she chosen to listen, she would have. Instead, she looked to Avandar Gallais.

About his body, a nimbus of light changed his shape. In its folds, he stood, the green glow robbing his skin of sun's touch, sun's warmth. He raised his hands; the flats of his palms lay above the earth itself, rising as it rose.

She saw birds fly up, and up again, in a sudden panic; heard animals as they bounded from tree to shaking tree; heard the shudder of trees far, far older than she as their roots were pulled up in the shift of earth.

She could not speak for gratitude. She looked to Avandar, and saw that his eyes were closed; she wanted to speak, to offer him something—but those words had never been her words, and she was awkward with them; she let the moment pass.

The Winter King said softly, *He will know.*

She took comfort from that, from only that. "Serra Diora," she said.

But the words were wasted.

The most beautiful woman in the Dominion now stood upon the flat of a hill that overlooked the standard of the Leonne clan. Jewel could see what she saw, but she knew that she would make no sense of it; she knew that the Serra Diora labored under no such ignorance.

The Callestan Tyr's expression shifted. His hand fell to his sword. His Tyran, frozen until that moment in the act of witnessing, moved at once, drawing blades, interposing themselves between their Tyr and what lay beyond the turned back of the kai Lamberto.

Ser Mareo was aware of his Tyran; he heard the voice of steel. His own blade was silent as his eyes narrowed.

"Treachery," he said softly. To his surprise, he felt a profound relief; the speaking of that single word freed him.

But the expression the man at his feet offered caught him again; made of him a captive. There was no triumph in it; no relief. There was nothing at all except the waiting; death had already descended, taking the eyes and most of the awareness. But not all, for the Eagle's gaze had shifted, and his brows rose and fell in muted confusion. Confusion, Mareo thought. Not surprise.

He was already dead. He had accepted this; had offered it cleanly. Not as Southerner, but not as a Northerner.

Finish it, the kai Lamberto thought, weary now. *Finish it, and be done.*

But *Warcry* was heavy. It was the only way in which the sword ever spoke.

His will was divided, and as all things divided, it caused him to turn, to see what had managed to capture the barest part of the attention of the Northern Commander.

And even he was caught.

The crest of the hill now stretched out for a mile, perhaps more. He had ridden up the incline; he knew that it had somehow changed shape.

But he had not felt the changing shape in the bones of his feet; had had no warning of quake, of the breaking of earth.

Mute, he watched.

His kai, Galen, rode *Wind's breath,* and *Wind's breath* was determined to live up to his name; every step he took was a struggle. Ser

Mareo felt a moment's pride at Galen's skill, for the horse *did* step; he rode the crest of hill, giving his will over to his rider.

Beside his kai, a great stag strode across the land, steps sure and light, tines raised feet above the tines of lesser deer. Even at this distance, through the thicket of those antlers, Ser Mareo kai di'Lamberto could see that a woman rode, shorn of saddle, of reins, of stirrup. She did not sit to the side, but her legs were loose, and her face was turned back, her hair a wild thing with a life of its own. She did not fear to fall, he thought.

Were the Northerners so strange? Were they all so haunted by legend, cut by the crossed swords of fate? For this woman, ATerafin by name, had at her right side the quiet, pale man with the silver hair; at her left, the graceful Northern bard.

He had commanded their presence, and he had received it.

That should have been warning enough; it was not.

For beyond his son, beyond these Northerners, he could see three women.

Yollana of Havalla.

The Serra Teresa di'Marano—how was it that he had not recognized her sooner?

And between them, guided, guarded, the Serra Diora di'Marano. The Flower of the Dominion.

He knew what she held.

Anger came and went; he wondered idly if his Tyran now lay dead beneath the sword of the palest of the strangers. *They will pay,* he thought. But he had thought that before, and his sword was falling, falling, blooded only by the barest of scratches.

Around him, Tyran gathered. His own. Callestan.

Among them, in ones and twos, the interlopers, the hated Northerners. Not one among them spoke.

Not even the kai Leonne.

But as the strangers approached, the men—all of them, fell away. As if by some unspoken command, they fell to one side or the other, their allegiance and their vows no containment for their ranks. Here, the sun rising met the sun rising, and the colors of the fields beneath made no difference. There, the sword and the rod, the two crowns, the black and the white, all melted into gold, into the will of the Lord.

At last, only one man stood at their head: the kai Leonne. The boy.

And he stood, his hand upon the hilt of a sword not his own, his face grave, his eyes watchful.

The Serra Diora di'Marano was beautiful. Mareo had forgotten just how beautiful—or perhaps he had never realized it; beauty faded, in memory, and his thoughts were oft given to other pursuits. She was, had been, of the High Court; she was—had been—a prize, a thing to be owned and displayed.

Nothing owned her now. He saw it clearly. She was like a new sword, a tempered sword, a master's sword. Even dressed as she was, in the full, flowing white of the Lord's Consort.

He turned, then. Jevri el'Sol had been forgotten. All had, until this moment.

But Jevri's face was also beautiful, in its fashion. For he had eyes for the Serra alone, and it was clear that the dress she wore had been one of his making. His pride, Ser Mareo thought, and his gift. He had thought them a waste; he had certainly thought them wasted upon the cold and severe Radann.

Marakas par el'Sol was the first to fall to one knee. It was . . . unthinkable. It was almost an insult, for he had bent knee to no one since he had arrived beneath the banner of the Tyr'agar.

But if the kai Leonne understood the depth of the insult offered, he showed no sign of it—and Marco, judging youth for what it was, thought him above such a petty knowledge; he had not blinked. He had not moved. He stood, and had he been any other boy—had he been Ser Alfredo kai di'Callesta, for instance—his jaw would be open, his mouth unhinged, his tongue exposed.

And if he were honest, Galen would have fared no better.

They came now, these three women, and as they did, they walked more slowly. They looked neither to West or East; their eyes were bent upon the South; upon the sun ascendant. Upon the man who was foolish enough, naïve enough, to claim it for his own.

When the stag and the destrier reached the tail end of the men who formed their imperfect, human wall, they halted. *Wind's breath* was calm now, although sweat glistened across his brown coat. Galen dismounted with care, catching reins close to mouth and drawing the great head down.

And the ATerafin woman dismounted, sliding off the bent shoulders of the stag. The stag waited, joining the Tyran.

The Northern woman waited as well, and her men chose to stand by her side.

Three women continued to walk. The Havallan Matriarch made better use of the canes than he would have thought possible, but no one among them would have dared to offer her aid where she did not ask for it.

She did not ask.

The Serra Teresa di'Marano paused only a moment, touching the folds of her niece's white silk. Arranging it as perfectly as she had arranged all else in the courts of her home. She, too, was changed; slender, he thought, even gaunt. Her skin was no longer the white porcelain that was so highly prized among Serras; the sun had finally touched her; the wind had scoured her. Darkness rimmed her eyes, and her hair, dark and long, was scattered with white that the light could not disguise.

But she bore all with dignity, and in silence; her only care was for the Serra Diora di'Marano.

The Serra Diora.

He heard the words "Flower" and "Dominion"; they were whispered by men who had forgotten their tongues.

She held them all, and she held them without intent; her gaze shifted between two things: the sword that she carried and the boy who now waited in the lee of the curling banner.

She passed the outermost of the Tyran, and as she did, they bowed heads, almost to a man. Insult again, Ser Mareo thought, but the words were so foreign they might have been Weston. He felt the gravity of her presence, and he saw, in the perfect fluidity of her stride, the embodiment of duty. The warrior's heart.

Ah, brother, he thought, the word surprisingly sharp. *I better understand your folly. I better understand your death.*

His sword's tip rested against grass, painting it with Northern blood. He lifted it with effort. But he did not lift it to kill; he did not lift it to threaten. He was surprised a moment by the sight of the Commander of the North; his posture seemed part of a different tale.

An instant, he balanced between these two, the life after the death of his kai and the life that began with the arrival of the Flower of the Dominion. And then he held *Warcry* perfectly straight before his heart center, edge exposed; the most formal of the warrior's salutes. This, too, was an insult.

But it was not meant as such, not offered as such.

For he knew that *this* was the reason that Fredero kai el'Sol had chosen his death; this was the cause he had given his life to.

Do you see her, Fredero? Are the winds graceful, this day? Do they drive you to the valleys, and the site of our feuds, that you might witness at last the blossoming of your Flower?

The wind, of course, did not answer.

She did.

She paused four times before she reached the Tyr'agar. Once, before the Radann par el'Sol, once before Ser Alessandro kai di'-Clemente—also forgotten until this moment—once before the kai Lamberto, and once before the kai Callesta.

She did not speak; she did not kneel. But she lifted the sword she held—the blade heavy, too heavy, for her delicate, pale arms—acknowledging them all by that gesture.

Her gaze passed above the Northern Commander.

And then she walked to the kai Leonne, and there, as was her duty, she at last found her knees. She did not struggle with the folds of the dress; did not deign to acknowledge its train, the glittering length of finery that had defined her at the Festival of the Sun. She did not appear to notice the Serra Teresa di'Marano; nor did she acknowledge the Havallan Matriarch.

Her back bent, perfect, supine; her hair, caught in combs of jade and gold, left her slender neck exposed. *Sun witness,* he thought, *but do not touch.*

A foolish thought.

They waited; they breathed as she did, as if they were all of a single body, as if by breathing, by simply living at this moment, and in this space, they asked a question too portentous for words.

And she answered it; she answered them all.

She lifted the Sun Sword, her back still prone, her arms as steady as the finest of Tyran, and she held it out before Valedan kai di'Leonne, taking care that nothing but its shadow touched the ground.

He did not move.

His eyes did, flickering across her raven hair, her ivory skin, the perfect white of her dress. Not even the Sun Sword drew his attention from her; he was transfixed.

Ser Mareo could not keep the grimmest of smiles from turning the corners of his mouth in genuine amusement. The kai Leonne was, indeed, a young man.

Another thought came, and it came to them all: The kai Leonne did not recognize the Sun Sword.

But if he did not, another did; Ser Anton di'Guivera bent a moment and spoke softly to the kai Leonne.

The boy started, and if he had not gaped, this sudden return to life and motion spoke of his youth more clearly than anything else.

Mareo thought he would bow.

And that, he knew, would have been a mistake, for what the Tyran offered, what the Tyr'agnati offered, the Tyr'agar *could not.*

But he caught himself as he bent, and his hands went out; he retrieved the scabbard, taking its weight for his own. The Sun Sword.

The kai Leonne.

The Serra Diora di'Marano looked up as the blade left her hands.
Her palms were exposed a moment, but only a moment; she took a
fan from the folds of silk, and she lifted it to her face, hiding what
they all knew existed behind a mask of modesty.

Ser Valedan kai di'Leonne said, "This is the Sun Sword."

She nodded gravely.

"And you . . . must be . . ."

It was not permission; he had not granted her words. But she
took them anyway, and her voice was so soft it seemed impossible
that her words could carry the length of this short, significant field.

But they did. They traveled, Mareo was certain, a far greater distance than that.

"I am," she said softly, softly, "the Serra Diora en'Leonne."

The kai Leonne met her gaze, the scabbard in his hands. He absorbed the words, but the meaning escaped him; that much was
clear.

It escaped no one else. No one.

The Tyran were not silent; the Northerners were not silent. Only
the Tyr'agnati afforded this woman the respect that was her due. For
the second time, Ser Ramiro di'Callesta drew *Bloodhame*. He lifted
it, as Ser Mareo had done, in a rigid posture of attendance; hilt to
tip, the sword was unwavering, its edge exposed.

They waited.

They waited for some acknowledgment of her name, the name
she had chosen to offer him.

But the boy was Northern bred, if not born. What she said made
little sense to him—and how could it? What, after all, was marriage
in the North? Who among the Northern barbarians could understand
the significance of the word *en'Leonne*?

"Serra Diora," the kai Leonne said, speaking as if only they existed. "You have brought me my crown."

She said nothing. Bereft of burden, bereft now of duty, she was
reduced to the role birth had given her; she waited.

And the kai Leonne took the scabbard firmly in his left hand. He
offered the sword of the Callestan kai to the Callestan kai; Ser Alfredo took it quietly and then stepped back. No blade had significance upon the field except the one.

And the one had yet to be drawn.

The right hand came to hilt.

Breath was taken; wind filled lungs. What would come of it, only the sword would reveal.

Closing his eyes, the kai Leonne drew the Sun Sword.

And the field was bathed in light. Sun's light. More. The kai Leonne held the Sun Sword. He lifted it high—lifted it, Mareo realized, straight up, the hilt above his waist, the tip in air, the edge exposed.

To her. To the Serra Diora.

They waited, and they watched. But the fires did not come; the kai Leonne, son of the least of the Leonne concubines, claimed his birthright in the only way that mattered: the Sword acknowledged him.

And he acknowledged the Serra Diora.

He did not bow. He had no need. Instead, he held out the scabbard, and Ser Anton di'Guivera carefully retrieved it from his hand.

Then he bent again, and he offered the Serra Diora his hand; she took it, and rose as he lifted. But he did not acknowledge her words in any other way. He had taken up the Sword.

But the Flower of the Dominion lay upon the field, a thing of singular beauty.

She did not leave his side; she stood in the shadow he cast; the Lord had begun his decline, and the night would soon hold sway.

He lowered the blade slowly, and the light that had blinded now offered illumination; he was gilded; he was anointed. He turned to the Tyr'agnate of Mancorvo, and the Tyr'agnate met his eyes. The second sword he carried was heavy at his side. He did not draw it; since the night of Damar, he had not suffered it to leave its scabbard.

It was not, in the end, his sword.

And only his sword would do. *Warcry* was not one of the five. But it was Lambertan; it held, in the enduring length of steel and perfect edge, the whole of Lamberto's history.

"Tyr'agnate," the kai Leonne said.

And Ser Mareo kai di'Lamberto bowed to fate, accepting at last what he had thought he might never accept.

He broke the unintentional ranks of this mixed group of men, and he walked, as the Serra had walked, between them. If he did not have her grace, he had more: the right to bear the sun rising, its eight rays distinct.

"Tyr'agar," he said, his voice loud. He buried his sword in the ground before the young Tyr's feet.

There was ceremony, of course; the Leonne clan had always understood the value of ceremony.

But the boy did not. He accepted the whole of the truth the title contained; he offered no questions, he made no demands. Instead, he looked to the only man who remained upon his knees.

The Eagle.

The man who had killed Ser Andreas kai di'Lamberto in a war Ser Valedan's father, the Tyr'agar Markaso kai di'Leonne, had so foolishly, so vainly, chosen.

But the young Tyr'agar made no command, and by this lack of command, Mareo understood that the choice was to be his.

He bowed to his Tyr, and when he rose, he shifted his hold upon *Warcry*. With care, with deliberation, he walked to stand before the Northerner.

And there, in sight of his men, he sheathed his sword.

Only then did Commander Allen rise. He rose slowly, as if his legs were weak. As if, Ser Mareo thought, he had never intended to rise at all. Death hovered above him; death held him.

This was not territory that the kai Lamberto had ever traversed. He watched in silence, and unbidden, the shadow that the Commander cast wavered a moment in the sun's light, and he saw not a Northerner, but a Southerner long lost to the clan Lamberto, and much loved in his bitter absence.

Against the Lord of Night, Fredero kai el'Sol—Fredero *par di'Lamberto*—had made such peace. *Warcry* was silent. And Mareo whispered two names. Two. And bowed his head. Moments passed before he raised it. When he did, he was the Tyr'agnate of Lamberto.

He felt no contempt as the Commander struggled to stiffen his knees, to gain his footing, and hold it. In spite of himself, he offered this most dangerous of his enemies the formal bow of the Tyr'agnate of Lamberto. And more; he offered his hand.

The Commander did not see it. He was alone, a moment, in the unexpected territory of the living.

No insult offered. None taken. Ser Mareo waited until the Northerner looked up. They stood surrounded by Tyran and Northern soldiery, but they stood apart.

"What of your kai?" the Commander asked quietly. His eyes were too bright, Mareo thought. The living was too much, for the moment. But he understood this.

"You have given him death," he replied.

With some struggle, the Eagle said, "But I live."

"You live again," the kai Lamberto said softly. "The death has been offered; you are not who you were."

And he realized, as he said this, that the Northerner did not understand. "You are changed," he said quietly, as if to a child. "You are not the man you were."

And when, at last, the Commander's eyes were less bright, he added, "You will bear the scars."

"All of them," the Northerner said, in Torra. "But in war, there are always scars." He took the hand that Ser Mareo kai di'Lamberto had not withdrawn.

Ser Ramiro kai di'Callesta bowed when the Tyr'agnate of Lamberto released the Eagle's hand. "Kai Lamberto," he said softly, "I bid you welcome to the Terrean of Averda. My home is your home, and my lands are open to you."

"Kai Callesta," the Tyr'agnate said, and he, too, bowed. "I accept the honor you offer, and in return, I offer you welcome to the Terrean of Mancorvo at war's end."

A sharp smile touched the face of the Averdan Tyr. He bowed again, and then turned to gaze upon the unguarded face of the Tyr'agar.

"He has the blood of Leonne," he said to Ser Mareo.

"And the Sword," the kai Lamberto added.

"But he has more than that."

"The armies of the North."

Again, Ramiro offered the edge of his smile. "He has the approval of the Serra Amara en'Callesta, and the respect of my kai. He is not his father's son. Nor his grandfather's. I believe that he is greater than any kai that has graced Leonne in living memory."

"He will have to be," the kai Lamberto said softly.

"What other Leonne could have claimed the allegiance of both Averda and Mancorvo?"

"All of them."

"Ah, yes." Wolf's smile. "But I speak not of ritual, Mareo. I speak not of form. Look at Ser Anton. Look at Serra Alina. Look," he added, with a touch of chagrin, "at the face of my par. The Captain of my Tyran. They serve *him*. Were he not Leonne, I believe they would still be content to serve him. History defines us, but it does not define him; he has chosen a path that history itself could not make.

"We will fight," he added softly, "and the Lord will watch. What we achieve will define the Dominion."

"Then we had best win, Ser Ramiro."

"How could we do otherwise? The Eagle will fly. The Hawk circles the valley in the South, and the Kestrel has been unhooded. Do you recognize the men who serve as the kai Leonne's guard?"

Ser Mareo frowned. "They are of the North."

"They are. And when last they came South—and they came—they carried a black banner."

The kai Lamberto's brows rose. Ramiro took some small satisfaction from the expression. "The Ospreys."

"The same."

"And not the same," the kai Lamberto said quietly. "Time has tempered youth. Even ours."

"Has it clipped their wings?"

"They serve a Southern Tyr. How could it not?"

"They were at home in the South; the only Northern unit that was. Do not discount them."

"I? I discount nothing. But the Ospreys did not hunt in Mancorvo. And perhaps if you can accept their presence here, my own kai will be at peace."

Primus Duarte looked up, then, and met the eyes of three men: The Tyr'agnate of Mancorvo, the Tyr'agnate of Averda, and the Commander of the first of the Northern armies.

He did not speak.

Jewel ATerafin's hand rested against the fur of the Winter King. Her legs felt weak, and her vision blurred. She might have pretended that these were the effects of exhaustion, but she had never been much good at lying to herself. She was afraid.

It was a particular fear.

Avandar Gallais was by her side in an instant, as if he had never left it. As if he never would. Without thinking, she reached for his arm; her hand burned at the contact, but she did not break it.

He raised a dark brow as he gazed down at her face. "ATerafin?"

She shook her head. Her mouth was almost too dry for speech.

"Jewel."

She closed her eyes; the sound of her name echoed in the silence and the red darkness of day.

Jewel.

She was afraid. She didn't say the words.

Why? What do you see? What will happen?

Nothing. I . . . see . . . nothing. It was true. But the nothing was endless, terrible.

Familiar.

Jewel. The Winter King's voice.

No. No. She was *not* a child. She had not been a child since her eleventh year in the hundred holdings. She was *never* going to be a child again.

But this close to fear, age receded like tide; she struggled to hold it, and as she did, things slid in between her trembling grip.

Her mother's death. She hadn't *seen* it; it was almost too big for vision to encompass. But she had known, and had refused to know. Because she had refused it, because she had *been a child,* it had all happened, just as she had feared.

Her father called her name.

But he was dead, too.

No, she thought, breathing, trying to breathe. *No.* And she realized then that what she was fighting was childhood; it had returned in all its barren helplessness. She broke free. She tried to *see.*

She opened her eyes to sunlight. Struggled with silence, struggled to break it.

"Get Celleriant," she said roughly.

Avandar nodded. "He is with the bard."

"I don't care. Get him."

"Jewel—"

"Just *get him.*"

Lord Celleriant of the Green Deepings stood in the sunlight of the Averdan valleys. The trees were silent, stunted, the forests too new to be truly alive. They had been shorn of heart and strength, made tame, a stretch of human wilderness, pathetic and crippled.

Kallandras of Senniel stood by him.

"I fear," Celleriant said softly, "that it is not our fate to stand upon this field together."

Kallandras frowned, but he did not speak. In that, he was like the forest; one could find silence within him, deep as the oldest of seas. Mordanant had offered just such a silence. But Mordanant's life did not fly by in a short span of years; the companionship he offered was eternal.

Celleriant had often found beauty in ephemera. In the short, brief lives of mortals; in their power and the grandeur of their ancient cities; in their deaths, in their ghosts, in the grand tragedy of their brief passage.

He had never found companionship.

He lifted a hand and touched his brother's shoulder, and Kallandras of Senniel covered that hand with his own.

"What do you hear, Kallatin?"

But Kallandras did not answer. Instead, he turned, his face inches from the Lord of the Green Deepings'. "There are things we may not speak of," he said softly. "Not to one another."

Celleriant nodded. If the Arianni could feel chastened, he did.

"Meralonne APhaniel is coming," the bard continued. "Speak with him if you will. You will not have long." He bowed. "I am no part of your history," he added quietly. "And your history does not concern me. We will meet again. We will raise weapons upon another field, a darker one."

"You have sight, little brother?"

"No. Not I. But there is one among us who does."

And she was there. Cloaked in night, in midnight, her hair darker, her eyes violet, her skin traced now with fine, deep lines. Her hood framed her face, and it shuddered there, as if it were a restless hand.

"Kallandras," she said quietly. And then, with the barest of nods, "Lord Celleriant."

Lord Celleriant frowned.

"Evayne."

"I have come with warning," she said quietly.

His pale eyes were dark, as if they reflected her, and only her.

"What warning?"

"Walk with me, Kallandras."

He bowed again, and they left, man and shadow, man and doom. Even Celleriant could sense the power she contained in the faltering flow of robes that had been spun and fashioned by hands that were not mortal. He felt young a moment, and youth ill-suited him, here.

But it came anyway, like mortal season. Like Arianni season.

The man that Kallandras of Senniel had named Meralonne APhaniel stood before him. Where the woman's raiment was living, his was not; he wore mortal weave, mortal medallion. But he, like she, carried about him the tattered grandeur of a different age.

"Lord Celleriant," Meralonne APhaniel said. Smoke wreathed the fine bones of his face, circling gray eyes. The glint of pale hair haloed those features, as hood had haloed hers, as if they were different aspects, in gender, in color, of the same doom. He did not bow. But he lifted a pipe, as if in greeting.

And Lord Celleriant of the Green Deepings bowed.

"You are far from the Court of your Queen," Meralonne APhaniel said.

"And you," Lord Celleriant replied with care, "are far from any Court."

"You will miss the Summer."

"I miss it," Celleriant said quietly. Because it was true, and because the truth could not be hidden here.

"Why are you here?"

"I serve a mortal."

Gray brow rose; pipe drifted earthward. "Which?"

"Jewel ATerafin."

"And her mount is yours?"

"Ah. No, Illaraphaniel. Her mount is her own; Jewel ATerafin wrested him from the Winter Queen."

The pipe fell. Embers left its crude bowl and threatened the flat of trampled grass. Without looking down, Meralonne APhaniel snapped his fingers; ash remained, fire a memory. A cool one.

"The Winter King," he said quietly.

"That is what she calls him."

"And she will ride him home?"

"I do not know where she will ride him. Who I serve, I obey, and obedience does not require knowledge."

"You will find her a different master than any you have served."

"I have served only one."

"Indeed. But you have intrigued with many mortals in your time, and they were not Jewel ATerafin's equal."

"I would have said that they were—to a man—her superior in all ways. But . . ."

The pipe rose; Meralonne APhaniel did not bend to retrieve it, but held out his hand, palm up, in the unfettered sunlight. It came. "But?"

"She stood against the Winter Queen upon the roads of the Stone Deepings," he said. "And although she should not have been there, although I would have said it impossible that she could stand—and live—in the Deepings, she *held* that road. She could have held it until Scarran had passed."

"She would have regretted the holding."

"Indeed. But she is not aware of the cost she might have paid, and had she been, I think she would have held the road regardless."

"Mortals are often unable to appreciate the consequences of their choices," he said quietly. "Until those consequences are upon them."

"She is one such."

"Indeed."

"And you, Illaraphaniel? Why are you here?"

"The war is here, for the moment."

"And your sword?"

"My sword is restless."

"Have you met them, then?"

"Yes."

"They will be here?"

"They are already here. They are hampered," he added quietly. "But you have seen this. If you are here, you have seen it."

Lord Celleriant smiled. The smile was light, and quick; it was without ferocity. "Is it almost time, Illaraphaniel? Are we, then, to bear witness to the End of Days? I remember their beginning. I remember the voices of the old forests. I remember the wilderness, untouched by man, that stretched from the great mountains to the old seas. I remember the full voices of the wild magics, the elemental doom. Will they return?"

"I cannot say," Meralonne replied. "But I am not so weary of life that I seek the End of Days." He lifted empty pipe to lip and grimaced. "I was not blessed with sight," he told the Lord of the Green Deepings. "I am not blessed with it now, if indeed it is a blessing. But I offer you this; it is not advice, for you are above advice; it is not comfort, for the Arianni lords seek no comfort."

Celleriant nodded, waiting. He felt the hilt of sword form in his hand, and knew by its presence that he faced, or feared, threat. Exulted in it.

"Serve her well. Serve her, protect her, and offer her guidance."

The Arianni lord frowned. "I told you, Illaraphaniel, I am hers. I obey."

"If I am not mistaken, you have already begun to form ties to the mortals with whom you travel."

Celleriant's frown deepened. The sword appeared; sunlight did not lessen its fire, its perfect blue light.

"Do not," Meralonne said, "press me. Not here."

With effort, he sheathed the sword.

"I have spoken with Kallandras of Senniel many a time," the magi continued, as if the sword had not appeared and the warning had not been given. "The weapons he now carries were a gift, my gift. I understand him as well as I understand any mortal. I seek no weakness, Lord Celleriant; I seek to exploit nothing that is yours."

"Why are you here?"

"I was sent here by the Kings," the magi replied. "For I am one of the few who dwell within the Empire who can sense the *Kialli* when they approach; one of few who can read their names, if they still own them.

"One of few," he added, with a sharp, cold smile, "who can stand against them, and survive."

A bitter hunger gnawed at Celleriant. He knew, then, that he would be called away, and he wanted to stay.

"The time is coming," Meralonne said quietly, "when you will draw sword and see battle. Do not falter then. But do not leave her side, Lord Celleriant, for it is at her side that much of what must pass, will pass."

"You speak of the Oracle."

"I speak of the Oracle," he agreed, genial now. "But I do not know what Jewel ATerafin will do when the Oracle summons her; she is not of the old world, and the old world does not speak a language that she is willing to learn. Be her translator," he said. It was not a request. It was not even cloaked in the semblance of request. "We will meet again." He bowed. "And if I am not mistaken, you must leave now." And he turned.

Avandar Gallais stood ten feet away, as silent, as perfect, as cast shadow. He nodded to both, his bearing too proud to be humble, too humble to be commanding. But they felt his power.

"Lord Celleriant," he said quietly, "forgive my intrusion. But Jewel ATerafin has need of your presence."

Celleriant bowed to Meralonne APhaniel. "Until we meet," he said softly.

And Meralonne APhaniel nodded.

CHAPTER EIGHT

IT HAPPENED this way, and it seemed—as it must seem to all witnesses of any sudden tragedy, any accident—to happen at once, an act of storm, a strike of lightning without the portentous, distant voice of thunder to mark its passage.

A man appeared upon the plateau.

He could not have appeared without warning; there were mages present whose study, whose speciality, was the detection of such approach. Nor would he have remained unmolested, for those mages were already in motion, the hidden lines of their power, the ancient trajectories of weapons that depended not on hand or arm or shoulder, already traced, already defined.

But his feet hit the ground as if he had fallen a great distance, and his knees buckled instantly beneath the full force of his weight; his shoulders jerked, his spine collapsing slowly beneath a gravity that no one else was subject to. And his robes, strange to the eyes of the Southern clans—as strange as the sunlit bronze of his hair, the color of his eyes—were not so strange to those of the North; Commander Kalakar's brows clenched and gathered, changing the line of her face. Robbing it not of ferocity, but of momentary context.

She lifted a hand, shouted a command; her Weston broke the ranks of mages as if it were spell. Had they not heeded her, they would have heeded the second voice, for it was Meralonne APhaniel's, and the magi were there; they were his to command.

No one had realized just how much that was true until he, too, spoke—and the magi froze. As a man, they froze. He *ran.* He ran to the man upon the ground, his hands upon the gray of robes, his hands upon the shoulders that were locked in a shudder that would never leave him while he lived.

But the man's eyes were open, and in shudder, they had not lost the ability to see, to comprehend what was seen. He spoke. The word crossed only the distance between the two, mage and magi, but it was enough.

Lifting this stranger, this interloper, this newcomer, as if he weighed nothing, Meralonne APhaniel rose, and he shouted across the plateau a single, Northern word.

"ATerafin!"

But it happened that way only at the end, and the beginning was different.

26th of Corvil, 427 AA
Terafin Manse, Averalaan Aramarelas,

Morretz of the Guild of the Domicis stood in the shadows of early morning. He stood by a bed, a bed that should have been empty.

But it was not, and because it was not, he stood guard. It was an empty gesture; the warding spells, the locks, the keys, the sigil banes, even the doors, would do more than he could now do.

But he did not wish to leave her side. Not while she slept.

Truth? No, not all of the truth. He was bitter. The bitterness weighted him, locking his knees; his feet had grown into the wood grain, traveling the length of carpeted plank as if he would never be removed; as if the floor itself would be uprooted before he was at last free of this.

He reached out gently and touched her face. She did not stir. Would not stir, not for him; he could slap her, could strike her, could stab her, and she would not stir. She would bruise, perhaps; bleed certainly. But she would remain at this unfathomable distance.

He spoke her name.

And then, because he could do nothing else, he began to brush her hair. It was long and fine, its color fading at last into the sunset of white and gray that all such colors knew before death. Her skin was not old, but in repose, it was fragile. Her lids were fine and thinly veined, her lashes long and unbent. Her chin had no strength, her lips, none.

But it was her eyes that he missed. That he would miss. She would not wake. And he could not be certain of the waking, now.

Finch and Teller would come.

Adam would come with them. Perhaps Levec, again. He had made contingencies for their arrival; had reluctantly agreed to allow Devon and Gregori ATerafin to pass. Duvari could wait in hell, or at least in the antechamber, although Sigurne, too, was given his permission—*his,* for Amarais was not here to argue—to enter.

He closed his eyes, and his knees finally released him; he bent by her bedside and rested his cheek against the fabric. What he wanted was complicated; he did not touch her again. Because he could not touch her and leave.

Something flared in the center of the room, catching his attention; a ward spoke in a language that none but Morretz would understand. It was his ward; he had bound it with strength, made it impervious.

But he knew what it said, and after a moment, he nodded.

The doors faded, and beyond them, Ellerson waited.

Ellerson.

"Go away," he said quietly. But although the words were exact, the tone was wrong. He was not surprised when Ellerson crossed the threshold. Magic responded to many things.

"They will be here soon," Ellerson said quietly.

"How did you arrive before they did?"

The domicis did not answer. "Will you not reconsider?"

"How?" Morretz shook his head. "It is the last thing she asked of me."

"She did not ask *this*," Ellerson said quietly.

"The Terafin did."

"Not The Terafin you serve."

Ah. The sigils were speaking now. Ellerson was correct; the youngest members of the House Council were upon the lower stairs. They moved with purpose. But they would wait, he thought, until Levec reached the library; those were the instructions he had left.

"You told me," Morretz said softly, "that if I took action after her death, I would be disbarred." He said it without anger; he felt none.

"Yes."

"But you know me. You, of all people, must know. You taught me everything—"

"I taught you everything you were willing to learn," Ellerson said gravely. "But, Morretz, you were a much younger man then. You had not the weight of experience, the gravity of service, to anchor you. You had only loss, your own loss. Anger. Fear. Desire."

"I have only those things now," Morretz said softly. "I want to kill them all."

"I know."

"And you would never approve."

"Does it matter?"

It did. To his surprise, it did. He stood a moment in the shadow cast by the older man, and he accepted the truth. "Yes, Master Ellerson."

"And this is why you pursue this course?" Anger, disapproval. More. Morretz did not know how to evaluate what he heard, and he had lived at Amarais' side for the whole of her tenure as Terafin; he had missed *nothing*.

But the question deserved answer. It deserved his answer. He gazed at The Terafin, at the gray tinge to her skin, the circles around her eyes, her mouth; the blue of her fingers. Only her breath spoke of life, and that life was withering.

"It is not . . . all the reason . . . that I pursue it," he said at last. "I chose to serve her."

"I know."

"You offered me that life of service. You chose her, and when I understood her, I chose to accept what you offered. You knew me well, Master Ellerson. I am not a vain man, but I have been proud of what we have built. Here, in Terafin. And abroad, in the smaller

Houses throughout the Empire. The House is not the House it would have been under the butcher."

"And is that worth what you pay now?"

"No."

"Ah." Ellerson grimaced.

"And yes," Morretz continued, looking at her. He walked away from her, leaving her under Ellerson's watchful glance, and when he returned, he bore a man's cloak, one that had faded with sun and salt, with the passage of years. Magic lay across its many threads— a magic of preservation. Very, very gently he spread it across her. "She was the strongest person I knew," he said quietly. "And she is stronger yet than Jewel ATerafin. But among the House members, there is no other who will preserve what she has built. Who will understand it, without understanding it, who will instinctively seek to make whole what the war will break.

"Jewel is needed," he added quietly. "And it is her presence alone that will give Amarais peace."

"And you?"

"Yes," he said quietly. "Because no other can now do what I can do. Not in time. Not for her." His smile was crooked. "Pride," he said quietly. But it was more than that.

"You will not wait to see her wake?"

"No."

"Why?"

"Because it will pain her, Ellerson. Because it will hurt her. Alea, Courtne, Alayra, Alowan—gone."

"And you?"

"She will know."

"Kindness and cowardice are seldom so intertwined."

The words didn't anger him. "Protect her den," he said quietly, speaking not of Amarais, whose time had almost passed. "And if she asks after me—tell her I will wait for her."

Ellerson bowed. "Pride," he said softly, "has fangs and teeth, Morretz. I was proud of you. I *am* proud of you. If I teach again, I do not think I will find a student who will be your match." His smile changed, although it did not dim. "And I am not certain, if I did, that I could bear it. We are all creatures of emotion, in the end, and our loyalties must therefore be divided.

"Go. I will watch."

"Thank you, Ellerson."

Morretz walked over to the bed table and pulled out the drawer, shallow and almost decorative, that it contained. He pulled from it the scroll that she had written. It glowed as he touched it, and quieted as it recognized his hand. "You will stay?"

"I am in service to the den," Ellerson said quietly. "And I give you my word that I will stay to see it prosper. Or perish."

We build. We build, and we spend a life repairing what is built. Improving it. Struggling with old imperatives and ideals, with the compromises that people force upon them.

If life were art, if life were story, there would be structure to it, purpose to its chaos, an end that was whole, that satisfied. But there would *be* an end, and the end is what struggle defies.

Morretz bowed his head, the thoughts clear.

Did he love her? Had he loved her? Yes. Certainly. Here, in privacy, he had loved her. There, in the public display that was the responsibility of any leader, he had loved her. This truth did not pain him.

But did she know? Could she? She had never spoken, and he— he was domicis. The respect he offered, the advice that she seldom took, were the whole of what he was allowed by position to speak. He had been given leave to comfort her only once, although he had always desired the ability, the permission, to do so.

And he took no comfort from it; it had been costly to them both. Wisdom came late.

Did she know? He would never be certain.

He took breath, and then he took light, blinding himself, forcing his eyes to open, to *see*. The Terafin spirit had never spoken to him before that one eve, and he was grateful for its silence, although he had envied it The Terafin's regard until that moment.

A duty had passed to him, and a gift. He took them both, and he called upon the magic that had been his birthright, the only birthright he had taken from the remains of his village a lifetime ago.

He had not been a warrior then. He had come to Averalaan, determined to make himself so strong that he would never again be unable to protect the things he loved. He had gained power, but the power itself was empty; it was only when he chose to set aside the earlier quest that he had found himself, and that he had found his calling: Amarais Handernesse ATerafin.

And in the end, he acknowledged the fact that the ability to protect the things one loved was never a given; certainty was illusion.

The words of a magi in the Order of Knowledge tickled his

memory, rising above the flotsam and jetsam of others more important.

He acknowledged their truth, accepted them, and cast his final spell.

26th of Corvil, 427 AA
Terrean of Averda, Dominion of Annagar

She flew.

The Winter King carried her before the sound of her name—the only name she possessed that was of import in the North—had fallen into silence. Avandar was not at her side, but Celleriant joined them as they ran, his feet as swift as the feet of the Winter King, his stride unencumbered by the simple impediment of length.

She saw past the gathered bodies of Tyran, swords gleaming; saw past the familiar surcoats of the Kings' men; saw past the Tyrs and the Tors and the horses that were almost their kin.

In fact, she saw only one thing as she rode, and it brought Winter to her in an instant.

Death did that.

She was off the back of the Winter King before he could stop; it was the only time that she felt the impact of ground, the difference between his speed and her lack. He had no time to react to her reaction; she had given him no warning.

Not even the warning of emotion, of the thought that presages words, that hides behind them.

"Morretz!" His name left her so easily it might have been the only word she knew; it came again and again, cadence changing, meaning delivered into only these two syllables.

She heard her name.

She did not look up.

The shadows shifted at her side, at either side; the gleam of boots, the shin splints of armor. Things made inconsequential by the presence of The Terafin's domicis. By his inexplicable, sudden presence.

Meralonne APhaniel held him close, as if he were precious. She had never cared for the magi, but at that moment, she would have given him *anything* he had asked for, for she knew that she couldn't carry Morretz.

Knew it, and held out her arms anyway.

But Meralonne APhaniel shook his head. "He is not yours to

bear," he said quietly. "It is not for that that he has come this distance."

Morretz was awake. Aware. His body was racked now by shudders that broke his words as if they were earth and he were the quake that destroys it. "ATerafin."

She nodded; she hoped to preserve him, somehow. "Don't speak," she said softly, bringing her hands to his lips.

But Meralonne's eyes flashed and her hand fell away, numb, burned by spell.

"You—are s–summoned—home." He struggled a moment, and she saw that he carried something in his shaking hands. A scroll.

A scroll that should have been buckled and creased by the sporadic clenching of fists. It was not. She saw it as a rod, as a thing of power, light like a coruscating rainbow covering the whole of its visible surface.

"The war—"

"The Terafin summons you, ATerafin," Meralonne said quietly.

The voices that she had ignored took shape and form, storm's voice. She looked up to see Commander Allen.

"That is not possible," he said flatly.

She wanted to slap him.

"ATerafin," Meralonne said. "I have, somewhere in this camp, a writ delivered me by the Kings."

She heard the words at a great distance.

Meralonne continued. "It gives me permission to find you and to second your services to the armies under the Command of Commander Allen."

"Jewel."

Kallandras' voice. She did not see him. But she didn't need to.

"He buys you time. He will leave to find the writ. You must not be present when he returns. I am . . . sorry."

He did not speak again. But Meralonne APhaniel turned to Lord Celleriant, and he nodded.

Lord Celleriant stepped forward and held out his arms; Morretz was transferred between them. He didn't seem to notice; he noticed nothing but Jewel.

And Jewel let the rest of the world fall away.

She had felt this helplessness before.

Before, and before, and before, death already written, pain already nestling where memory couldn't dislodge it. "Morretz," she said, grabbing his flailing hand. It was strong; she hadn't expected that. "I will return," she told him. "I swear to you, I will return. I will *be* The Terafin. I will preserve the House."

His eyes watched her. His teeth chattered. She knew that he wouldn't speak again. But she also knew that he listened, and that she had not—yet—said enough.

She swallowed. "I will lose what I must lose," she whispered. "I will pay the price that I *can* pay, and still rule Terafin as it has been ruled. I swear it," she said again. "I was afraid. I *am* afraid. Nothing I've ever done scares me more than this does. But I've been afraid all my life.

"The House will *be* my den. All of it."

And he closed his eyes, then. She turned to Celleriant, although it was pointless, and said, "Don't let him go."

Lord Celleriant nodded gravely.

"Avandar!"

"ATerafin." His voice was inches away.

She spun about and saw that he carried, in his arms, a child. Ariel. She had almost forgotten Ariel.

"We can't take her," she said curtly. "We go to war."

He raised a brow, the expression both familiar and foreign.

They go to war, ATerafin, the Winter King said quietly. *In neither place is she guaranteed either safety or life. Leave her or take her as you desire, but do so in knowledge.*

She made her decision.

Meralonne was gone. Meralonne would return. Commander Allen stood inches from her, his hands only barely by his sides.

"Commander Allen," she said, hating him, hating that she hated him. She bowed, as if in acquiescence.

And then she said, in the silence, *Avandar, take us home.*

26th of Corvil, 427 AA
Terafin Manse, Averalaan Aramarelas

It was harder, the second time.

Finch knew, watching Adam, that it was harder. Levec was pale, slick with sweat, but he cursed softly almost as often as he drew breath; Adam was profoundly still.

Watching him, she knew that she *could not* ask this of him again. Not so soon. She had a moment of panic—one that she did not dare give voice. Adam would go with The Terafin. Adam would leave them. And it would be her fault.

Jay, she thought bitterly. *Jay, damn you, damn you, come home.*

But The Terafin returned instead, her bright, sharp gaze trapped in gray; gray of skin, of lip. If a corpse walked, this is what it might have looked like. Finch turned away as The Terafin rose.

And turned back as Adam fell.

She was there, beside him, her hands upon his back, before she heard Levec's voice. She turned, crouched over his form, and almost snarled, as if the bedroom had resolved itself into the dead end of an alley, and she was alone, again, with the dead.

"Finch," Teller said, speaking loudly. "Don't go there."

And because she knew his voice as well as she knew her own, she came back. But she did not leave Adam. Instead, she said loudly, too loudly, "He can't do this again."

It was The Terafin who answered. She had managed to sit, and she now clutched the folds of an old, gray robe in her arms, pulling it up to her face, dropping her chin and her cheeks into the cloth before letting it slide away. "He won't have to," she said quietly.

"Terafin—I'm—I—"

"No. You're right. He cannot do this again, and if he can, *I* cannot. Levec," she said quietly.

Healer Levec met her gaze. Met it, held it. The sweating grew worse; Finch wondered what it took, to sit there. Hoped she'd never have to find out.

"You must leave me now," she said quietly. "All of you but Sigurne."

When they stood, dumb and mute, she added, "Now. Finch, Teller, you are summoned to the House Council. Be there, and take every guard you are allowed. Devon, Gregori, attend them. Do *not* allow any of the House Guards to be assigned in my absence; let Torvan choose. Let only Torvan choose."

Devon fell to one knee. It was instant, and the gesture was unmistakable in its gravity. "Terafin," he said softly, the word so heavy he might never have spoken another, had he been a different man. But he was Devon ATerafin, Astari. He rose. "Finch," he said quietly. "Teller. Come."

Finch struggled a moment with Adam's weight. Teller came to help her; Levec sat motionless. Finch wasn't certain he could move.

Adam was not dead. Nor was he conscious. Her fingers fluttered at the base of his neck, searching.

"He lives," Levec said, unexpectedly. "He lives, girl. But you are right. He cannot do this again." He bowed to The Terafin. She did not seem to notice.

Devon came to stand beside Finch, and after a moment, she realized that he meant to help them. To carry what neither she nor Teller could. Devon had never seemed a huge man, not to Finch; he was too graceful for that. But he was not small; they were. She accepted his help. Jay wouldn't have. But Jay wasn't here.

Levec followed them out, and only when they had gained the library did Finch realize that Ellerson was nowhere to be seen.

Torvan met them at their wing. It was bristling with House Guards, and she froze a moment at the sight of their naked blades. But as she put names to the faces that hovered above those swords, she relaxed. As much as she could. As much as she would, this day.

"Duvari is waiting," he said quietly.

She nodded. It was all she could do.

He waited in the kitchen. She hated that. *How much does he know about us?* she thought, as she saw the chair he had taken. *How much do we know about him?* As much as she wanted to. More, maybe. But she nodded stiffly and forced herself to glide through the swinging door.

"ATerafin," he said. He nodded. "I have assigned two men to your party. One for yourself and one for Teller ATerafin. You will take them."

"No," she said softly, "I won't."

"You will," he replied. Almost bored, he held out a writ. She let it lie upon the tabletop.

"Why?"

He didn't answer. Everything about him was cold and autocratic; it was impossible to believe that he was not a patris. "The House Council meeting will proceed. Half an hour, ATerafin. I will see you after it is finished."

She nodded because she didn't feel like arguing.

Devon came into the kitchen and paused there; she looked up to see his frown. Was glad she'd looked up; it was gone before her eyes left his face.

"Duvari."

"Devon."

"Is it done?"

"It is," Duvari said quietly. "And it will be costly."

"What? What's done?"

Neither man spoke. She took brief satisfaction in hating them, but it was hollow; what she wanted instead was more complicated. "Devon—Adam is—"

"I will wait here," Duvari said coldly.

It didn't comfort her. Much. But she couldn't imagine a better guardian.

"Go with them. Take these." Duvari held out daggers; they were four in number. "ATerafin?"

She said, in a small voice, in an alley voice, "Is one for me?"

"It is. If you do not need to use it, hold it." He rose. "I will attend your Adam now. Devon."

Devon bowed.

When Duvari had left, Finch said, "Why is he here? Terafin can't call upon the Kings—"

"Yes."

"Or we will be weakened."

"Yes."

"Devon!"

"There is more at work here than you understand, Finch, and it is best that you remain ignorant." Just that. She knew he wouldn't tell her anything else.

She went out into the hall; Teller was waiting for her. "Adam's sleeping," he said first. "Just sleeping. He woke up."

She started toward his room and he caught her upper arm hard. Their eyes met. He didn't look like a boy anymore. First time, she thought, and realized it wasn't true. She wondered what she looked like. She *felt* like the same Finch she had always been.

He let go of her arm when she stilled. "Arann's waiting," he said quietly. "Jester's going to stay here, with Duvari."

"We should take Jester."

Teller shook his head. "Not today, Finch."

"Angel? Carver?"

"They stay, too." His voice shook a little on the last word.

She said, "Why?" Little girl voice. As if all the death and loss had already taken place, in his words.

"Because she told me to leave them," he said, and he nodded in the direction of his room.

Finch took a step.

In the doorway, in blue robes, she saw a woman that she had never forgotten. She paled. "You're not here to help us, are you?"

The woman didn't answer. As if all the words had already been spoken to someone else. But she lifted her hands, and in them, light burned. For a minute, Finch couldn't see the crystal that contained it, it was that bright. "ATerafin," she said quietly. "ATerafin. I have . . . spoken with The Terafin. Go."

She held out a hand; the hand was still limned in light, as if light had texture, like webbing. Finch almost shook her head, but the violet eyes, unblinking, compelled.

She touched the woman's palm. Felt fire lance up her arm, like a dagger. Or worse.

"I am sorry, Finch," she said softly. "But I have given you the gift that I *can* give."

She heard the words, but only distantly; her ears were ringing. When she looked up again, the woman took a step forward and vanished, taking all of the light in the room with her.

Captain Torvan was waiting, Arann by his side. Captain Arrendas was with them, but he did not intend to stay; she saw it in the compressed line of his mouth, the narrowed edge of his dark eyes. His hair was slick, pulled back from his forehead; too short for warrior's braid. But his armor was not as fine as Torvan's, and he carried a shield across his back. So, too, did the men at his side.

"ATerafin," he said, bowing formally. "These four will serve you." He gestured, and from the ranks of what seemed to be dozens and dozens of guards, two women and two men stepped forward. "They are Chosen," he told her grimly. "They will obey no orders but hers."

"Not ours?"

He did not answer. Answer enough. Everything seemed to move at a blinding speed; she could not contain it, could not catch enough of it to make memories that would last. She thought she should be grateful.

Devon and Gregori joined them. "We serve in the capacity of advisers," Devon said softly. "And our companions serve in that stead as well." He nodded briefly, the nod encompassing strangers.

She gazed at these newcomers with both confusion and suspicion.

Two men, she thought. Two strange men, chosen not by Terafin, but by Duvari. They were as cold as Duvari, but older and grimmer. They looked once to Devon, and Devon nodded. "They will stand behind you in the halls," he said quietly. "Mind where they stand. Remember it. If it comes to it, they will tell you what you must do."

"They aren't ATerafin—"

"Finch," Devon said, catching her by her arms. His face was an inch from hers, and his eyes, she saw, were lined with fatigue. "The time for those games is done; it may come again. But not today."

She swallowed. Nodded.

Ellerson joined her. Ellerson, old now, and bent with the weight of the unseen. "ATerafin," he said, his voice blessedly familiar, his own. "ATerafin."

Teller bowed. He shouldn't have; she could see that in the crinkle around Ellerson's eyes. But she held herself erect, as if afraid of falling.

Angel and Carver were waiting at the farthest reach of the wing, at the invisible boundary, and the visible one, that doors provided. Angel hugged her. Carver tousled her hair.

"Hey," Angel said, as she crossed the threshold.

She turned.

"If anything happens, meet us at Duster's old place."

If anything happens. She winced. Duster's old place. A bar in the twenty-fifth holding. "Is it still there?"

Angel's grin was crooked. She took that as a yes.

"Watch out for Jester," she told them both. And then, in a panic, "Where's Daine?"

"He's with Adam. With Duvari. They're as safe as they can be, for now."

"What's going to happen, Angel?"

"Gods know," he said.

And that was that; Ellerson's hand was upon the small of her back as he gently and firmly shoved her through the door.

The manse was spread before her like a map. A living map, with walls, with roof, with paintings and hangings as landmarks, the rise and fall of thought its valleys, its rivers. She did not need to read carefully; she was not the navigator. The Chosen were. Torvan.

He had led them through the manse on their very first day here. He led now. But he did not spare her a backward glance; he did not offer her any sign of encouragement or pity; his gaze went to doors that were open, and doors that were closed; his hand rose and fell, and he stopped, frequently, to study the mound of his palm, as if something new was in the process of being written there.

Magic, she thought.

And she was truly, deeply afraid.

Teller took her hand and met her eyes. She glanced away, but then glanced back; she knew he was apologizing for his early grip. She wanted to cling, but she knew that this was not the time; they were being watched.

Yes, watched; the servants watched. They came in ones and

twos, in their blacks and whites, the colors of mourning for those who had passed. She wondered if they sought justice for Alowan from this Council meeting; wondered if she did.

Realized that her perfect dress was also black and white, that it was edged in gold as fine as The Terafin's dress; that she *was* the face of the House to the servants now. She lifted her chin, squared her shoulders, drew herself up to her full height. But more, she paused where she could to meet the eyes of those who, day in, day out, served House Terafin.

The ones that had bedded Carver and Angel and Jester. The ones that had watched them for all of their years here, quietly encouraging them, striving to ignore the manners of years in the hundred holdings. They were proud of her, she realized; proud of Teller. And she wanted to live up to that, for as long as she could.

The halls passed, the roof seemed so far away it might as well have been sky. Exposed, willing to be exposed, she followed the Chosen until at last she saw the doors of the House Council before them.

Even here, Torvan stopped and lifted his hand.

The guards at the doors crossed swords, barring his way. He spoke to them; he announced the presence of Finch ATerafin and Teller ATerafin. They drew their swords up to center, and he pushed the doors open.

There, in the long, tall hall, she saw The Terafin. By her side, there was an empty space; Morretz had not returned from his mission. Sigurne took up the position to her left; she did not sit. Did not stoop.

Finch thought her eyes were golden then.

They entered the room.

Rymark ATerafin was seated; as was Marrick. Haerrad had not yet arrived, and his seat, beside Elonne, was empty. Finch walked to her chair, and Ellerson pulled it out for her. She sat awkwardly, her legs beneath the unpolished underside of the vast expanse of wood. She wanted to be able to move, if she had to. She wanted to be able to flee. Or hide.

Teller sat beside her. He was stiff and silent. He was, she thought, like she should be, and she tried hard to imitate him.

The Terafin frowned. "Where is Haerrad?" she asked. The annoyance in the question was unmistakable. It should have filled Finch with glee; it did not.

Two of the Chosen rose, as if at command; they left by the doors that swung closed upon their backs. The room was utterly silent. Not even Marrick smiled.

"Gabriel," The Terafin said.

Gabriel nodded, stiff as Teller. Was he afraid? Even Gabriel?

"Let the meeting begin," The Terafin said. "Let it be noted that Haerrad ATerafin was absent from Council at the appointed time."

Gabriel took up pen. He wrote, and it seemed to Finch that the act of writing calmed him. It was normal. It was the only normal thing about this meeting.

The Terafin stood.

Until this moment, everything had happened so damned fast, Finch had been unable to comprehend it all. Now, things froze in place. Minutes might have passed, or hours; The Terafin cast a half-shadow before the latticed windows that let in light. It was long, that shadow; the afternoon sun was slanted toward sea.

Sigurne Mellifas was the other half of her shadow, her bright shadow.

"We have much to discuss," The Terafin said. "The formal investigation into the assassination of Alowan Rowanson has yet to be concluded, but Member Mellifas has come to report the findings of the magi to Council."

A breath crossed the table; several breaths.

Relief, she thought. Relief there.

"But before we discuss Alowan," The Terafin said, and breath ceased, "there is another matter of import to the House which must now be addressed. It will take only a moment of your time."

She stood straight, this slender woman, this personification of Terafin authority. And as she did, the hilt of her sword could be seen, bright in the sunlight, where all else was black and white.

Finch looked at the rest of the table. She saw the faces of the House Council. Gabriel's, white now, jaw rigid, eyes upon the paper that the pen no longer touched; Elonne's, pale and graceful, her expression as cool and collected as it always was; Marrick's, fierce now, freed at last from joviality.

Rymark's.

It was his face she would remember, and she would remember it, she thought, forever.

He smiled.

The room *shuddered*.

The doors, braced against all attack by force of magic as old as the manse, shuddered as well. Glass cracked; lead buckled; the table danced across the floor. The whole of the building seemed to stagger as if at a blow.

Only The Terafin stood unmoved, and she stood taller now. Even Sigurne struggled to maintain her footing.

The Terafin spoke. Some of her words were lost to the distant sound of thunder. Thunder, Finch thought, throat dry. The skies were *so clear.*

"I speak of the House heir," she said, and then, when thunder answered, repeated the words. No one failed to hear them; no one. Even though Elonne now looked to the door, to the guards that lined the room, to the windows that had bowed in the stone of frame, she waited, as they all did.

"For it is time, now, that the heir be chosen, and named."

The manse shuddered again, and this time The Terafin did as well.

Finch rose. Teller rose. No one else. They braced themselves against the table. As the floor's rumble dwindled to stillness, they made their way to The Terafin, Devon's angry words forgotten, his warning part of some other life. She did not acknowledge them; she did not turn to them for aid. But they did not leave her.

And Sigurne Mellifas said, in a soft, quiet voice, "Be ready, children."

Meant for them, Finch thought, without a trace of bitterness. Her hand dropped to her sash; to the awkward, ceremonial dagger that she had tried so hard to conceal there. Teller's did the same.

The doors flew open; wood shattered, splinters flying like ill-aimed arrows. Shadow gathered beneath the peaked frame, consuming it.

Finch had seen demons before. Teller had. But that demon and this one were not the same; they froze.

And the demon spoke.

"Too late, little mortals, too late." His neck was long, like a dragon's, and his wings unfurled forever, cloaking the whole of the room. He lifted talons, and in them, fire swirled like liquid.

So much happened then. Too much happened.

Finch screamed as the fire engulfed her. Screamed as it lapped at floor and carpet, as it sundered table from one end to the other; chairs became ash, collapsing beneath the weight of those they contained.

"Who bears the mark?" the demon roared.

The fire had not burned her. Her hands were glowing with or-

Michelle West

ange light, an orange that was bright and somehow gentle where the flames were not. She thought of Evayne, then. Evayne's gift.

Teller was by her side, and together, they drew their daggers and stood on either side of The Terafin.

Men *moved.* The Chosen came to life; the galleries above were filled with the flight of quarrels. She heard shouting, as if it were dim and distant; saw lightning flare beneath the vaulted ceiling of the dark heavens.

The demon roared; something struck it, burning there, burning white and blue. It rose, wings lifting its bulk as if it were bird.

Sigurne Mellifas shouted a word, a single word, and the creature's black eyes widened; Finch saw the void in them, endless night rimmed by fire. The Hells.

It struggled; Sigurne spoke again, and from her hand, a golden thread emerged, thick as a Southern snake, but supple, free to move. It leaped and it stayed, twining itself around her wrist.

Finch heard a name. It was not a name she could pronounce. It was not a name she would ever recognize again, although it was, at the same time, not one that she would forget; it held a truth so profound that memory could not be shaped to contain it, but could not be forced to release it.

She turned to look at Sigurne; saw that the magi's face had paled completely; her eyes were blue and white, their pupils almost nonexistent. A third time she spoke.

The demon roared, fighting her, it seemed, and only her. It raised and dropped its arms, and she saw swords fly, some still clenched by hands. But the wings were tattered now; sunlight gaped through the wounds Sigurne Mellifas had made simply by speaking.

It was almost enough.

Had the creature been any other, it *would* have been enough. Finch knew it, without knowing how, although later—much later—she would understand.

Roaring, it sprang, shield now across its right arm, sword almost the whole of its left. Slowed, it was not slow.

And when it landed, in the ruins of the table, its blade came down in a single strike.

Just like that, Finch thought. Just like that, the world ended. The Terafin fell.

Sigurne Mellifas stood in the center of the storm, its eye. She did not see the death around her; she saw only the creature.

It turned to face her, and Finch and Teller scattered in that moment, weapons forgotten; no weapons were up to this task, this creature.

But Sigurne did not move; did not attempt to flee. She stood, and the sword came down again.

She spoke the name; the sword *shattered.* The creature's roar cracked glass, tore lead; it was the storm's voice, and Finch had lived with the ocean storms all her life.

They would die here, she thought. They *were* dying, in ones and twos, the men and women who served Terafin, the House. The woman, they would never serve again.

She found her courage, then. Late, she thought, bitterly. Too late for The Terafin. But not too late for Sigurne. Not too late for the den. She twisted the blade about, holding it as a pole arm and not as a dagger, and when the creature's wings fell, like the wings of an angry swan, she struck. Not enough, never enough, but it was all she could do.

The wing caught fire, blue fire; the demon snarled. But gold bound it, gold hampered it, Sigurne stood.

And then the gold grew bright, brighter still. Finch looked up, realized that she had fallen to one knee, as if she could cower behind the table that lay in two pieces.

The doors the creature had deserted were not empty.

Beneath the frame, limned in light, stood two men.

She would have recognized them anywhere. Even if she had never seen them before, she would have recognized them.

For they had eyes of gold, golden light, and one carried a rod, and the other, a sword. The Kings had come to Terafin.

They leaped as one man, with one purpose. The creature turned, or tried; Sigurne had him, and held him fast, binding him somehow. He had no sword, but he needed none; his talons were long and sharp, red with blood even though the blackness seemed to deny all color.

He struck, and they struck; a talon flew, like cast-off dagger, across the room. What it struck, it burned. Roaring in pain and anger, the demon lifted a foot and broke the floor upon which they stood.

Sigurne staggered. Teller fell.

But the Kings sprang up at the moment the floor shuddered, and they landed as it stilled; they were in motion, like heroes, like legends. Gods walked a moment upon the earth, cloaked—but barely—in mortal flesh.

And she crawled as the gods fought; she made her way to the fallen body of The Terafin. She touched shoulder, touched cloth, pulled as hard as she could. Too late, and she knew it, but it was all she could do now.

But The Terafin's eyes were open, and they were not—yet—sightless. She saw Finch. Blood coursed from the corners of her lips as she tried to speak.

Above her, above them both, the storm gathered, the thunder broke, and broke again; lightning struck.

And then, amidst gold, there was blue: blue sword.

The demon's shield shattered.

A man Finch had never seen lifted sword again, and with a great cry, a beautiful ululation, he swung.

The demon's head rolled free of its shoulders.

It came to rest to one side of Finch's feet. She hesitated a moment, and then she gave it a kick, a feeble kick. Its jaws snapped, missing her foot because she wore boots; the soles were sheared clear of their leather moorings.

"Enough," Sigurne said, her voice cracked. "Finch, enough. There is still some work to be done."

And Finch shook her head, shook her body, surrendered volition.

But Teller's hand gripped her shoulder so tightly her arm went numb, and she looked up to see his face, his wide eyes. He lifted his arm, pointing, and she looked up, her arms around The Terafin.

There, in the wreckage of door, upon the back of a great stag with blood-red tines, she saw the answer to her prayers, to her months of prayers.

Jay had arrived.

Too late.

Jewel ATerafin slid off the back of the Winter King. She heard his voice, heard the urgency in it, as if it came from a great distance; as if crossing the threshold between the South and the North had at last freed her.

She raced across the room, trampling the twitching wings of demon, the shards of table, the ashes of chair, until she reached Finch. She stopped there, her face pale, her brown eyes wide and unseeing.

And then she sank to the ground before Finch, and she lowered her head; her unruly hair hid her eyes, but she didn't bother to push it out of the way.

"Terafin," she said softly. "Amarais."

There was no answer; there would never be an answer. But The Terafin's lids fluttered briefly, and her lips turned up in what might have been a smile. It stilled as Jewel bent to touch pale face.

"Jay?"

She looked up. Teller was there. Finch. They were too pale, too quiet, too Northern in dress. They were almost strangers.

But the dead were not so kind.

She reached out and touched the face of The Terafin.

But her eyes were dry. "Teller," she said quietly.

He nodded. As dry-eyed as she, but smaller somehow and infinitely more fragile.

"ATerafin," a voice said. Two voices. Twin voices. She tried to ignore them.

But they spoke again, and this time she heeded what she heard there: the voices of Kings. Her Kings.

She was already upon her knees; it wasn't—it shouldn't have been—hard to turn to face them. But she was anchored to the floor.

She had seen this, seen some part of this, and she had left.

Avandar.

He did not answer. She wondered if he would. She remembered idle conversations with Devon about the limits of magery, and she had asked him—had commanded him—to bear them *all* here.

Without his guidance, she met the gaze of the Justice-born King, and saw his raised sword. Bowed her head, exposing neck, as if acknowledging both crime and failure.

"ATerafin," the Kings said again.

She stood. Tried to remember what to call them. "Your Highness," she said at last, the words foreign, Weston words. "Your Highness."

Her throat was dry. Her shoulders ached. She had taken on burdens that she had promised to carry, and already she was immobile beneath their weight.

Elonne had gained her feet, and Rymark. Marrick lay beneath the table, his arms bleeding. Gabriel rose with the help of his son, his eyes as wide, as shocked, as hers must be.

"We apologize for our intrusion," the Wisdom-born King said. He looked down; the body of the demon had begun its slow unraveling. Shadows lifted, and with it, an age. The Terafin was dead.

"Your Highnesses," Rymark ATerafin said quietly. He bowed.

Elonne bowed as well, but less certainly.

The House, Jewel thought.

"We did not think to find you here, ATerafin," King Cormalyn said.

"I . . . hoped . . . to arrive earlier," she replied faintly. Remembering another meeting, a different time, a different demon. Remembering that the last time she had spoken with the Kings, things had been simple: she had groveled, almost supine, on the level with floor and the foot of two thrones. She swallowed. "There has been . . . fighting . . . in the North Wing."

The Kings nodded gravely.

"And some in the East, I think. I came here; the servants told me that the House Council was in session." She looked down, at the body of The Terafin. Forgot words again, forgot their meaning. Their texture remained, foreign and implacable.

"The Terafin was to announce her heir," someone said.

To Jewel's surprise, it was King Reymalyn.

"She invited us to witness," he continued quietly.

Gabriel ATerafin shook his head, as if waking, and at that, waking poorly. "She did not . . . live . . . to name an heir," he said.

"You were her right-kin, Gabriel ATerafin," King Cormalyn said. He had lowered the rod, and as its light faded, Jewel could see that he wore armor. Not the ceremonial armor in which he led the armies in procession; not the robes in which he presided over the Hall of Wise Council or even the Hall of The Ten. Just armor, scored and dented. As if he were a soldier.

"I was."

"Did she not name her heir to you, before this meeting was called?"

Gabriel shook his head.

The silence was profound.

"Father," Rymark said quietly.

Gabriel turned to his son.

"The truth," he said softly. "The House Council is here, and the Kings bear witness."

As if she watched a play, a drama, some costumed display that was one side of reality, Jewel was audience, mute witness.

Gabriel seemed confused, and only confused, by Rymark ATerafin's words. Rymark turned smoothly to King Cormalyn. "The Terafin spoke with me at length before this meeting," he said softly. "It was not widely known in the House, but her health was failing. The healer, Alowan Rowanson, was able to attend her while he lived, but with his death, her condition declined rapidly.

"We spoke," he continued smoothly. "And at length, she offered me her seal, and the legitimacy of the House Title. I am heir."

Elonne's brows rose, but she did not speak.

Jewel could not.

"Right-kin," King Cormalyn said softly.

Gabriel looked at his son. Jewel saw the lines play across his face, and lodge there like shadows. Like unexpected age.

"She drafted this document," Rymark said quietly. "And signed it." And he pulled, from his robes, a scroll. It was not sealed. "I signed it as well, and she intended to present it to the House Council this day. Did she not draft it with your approval, ATerafin?"

To his father, Jewel thought, and waited.

Gabriel hesitated. Jewel had never seen him so profoundly weakened. She wondered what he would say, if he would speak at all. Wondered just how he would damn himself.

But another voice saved him.

"I contest your claim."

Haerrad ATerafin had arrived. He was injured; blood ran across cheek and forehead, and spread across his chest like a crimson map, the cartography of war. He staggered, reached out, caught the wall in mailed fist. No one came to his side; no one dared to offer help.

Or desired to, Jewel thought bitterly.

"My apologies to the House Council," he said coldly. "I was detained. But not permanently." And he smiled, wolf's smile, his teeth red.

All eyes turned to her, then. All.

She said nothing.

"The House Council has much to discuss," the Wisdom-born King said softly. "And we have much to discuss as well. We will leave you, and repair to *Avantari*. When you have reached your decision," he added, his gaze grazing Jewel's forehead, "we will hold audience in the Hall of The Ten."

So much in those words, and so little. Jewel wondered if Amarais had heard them, in her time, from different Kings, from different sons of gods.

They bowed. They all bowed.

She might have ended it there. Might have. But she *knew* that she would not survive the night if she spoke. She had never been much good at waiting, but she intended to learn. Intended to keep her promise, if it killed her. Even if it didn't, although in some ways that might be harder.

Let the wolves fight among themselves for a night. For a day. For a week. She turned to Finch and Teller.

"Kitchen," she said softly. That was all.

But as they rose, as they turned to follow her, she thought bitterly of the price the Southern war had demanded of her, and of her den.

Morretz was in their wing. Avandar had carried him there, somehow.

Angel and Carver met her—met them all—at the doors, and their eyes rounded in utter silence. Arann followed. He had taken two wounds; they were deep and ugly. But Daine was here. Daine would help him.

The walls of the wing had never seemed so small to her, so confining, as they did now. She tried to smile, but the attempt was more than a failure.

"Where's Ellerson?"

"Ellerson?" Jewel said, repeating the word as if it were foreign.

"Ellerson," Teller said quietly. "He's here. Somewhere."

"Kitchen," she told the others, although she was already leading them into that perfect darkness. She threw the shutters open upon the world outside, thinking to see fire, to see ruins, to see death.

Only the gardens greeted her.

"Tell me." She stood, framed by the window. "Tell me everything."

They gathered around her in ones and twos. She would tell them about the Winter King after they finished. About Lord Celleriant. About the child.

About the gods-cursed war. The Southern war.

Win, she thought, with the force of a growing, mute anger. *Win, or it's all been for nothing.*

CHAPTER NINE

26th of Corvil, 427 AA
Terrean of Averda

SERRA Alina di'Lamberto was utterly silent.

Valedan understood her well enough to know that she skirted the edge between bafflement and annoyance. Neither of these were to his advantage.

It had become almost natural to see her in Northern garb; almost easy to speak to her as if she were an Osprey.

And that, he thought, would be a terrible mistake at the moment. He smiled, but kept the expression to himself. He was learning.

In ones and twos, the Tyran and the Northerners had dispersed, granting him a moment's privacy. He had ordered a tent for the Serra Diora; had offered accommodation to the Havallan Matriarch. Both had been accepted in silence. For the first time since he had come South, he felt that in this dance of manners, in this strange political world of these Southern women, he had misstepped.

But only one would tell him how, and he waited until she was ready to speak.

While he waited, his gaze turned to the Sun Sword. It lay across his sleeping silks, bright in its dark sheath, almost mesmerizing, terrifying. Around his waist he still wore the sword of the kai Callesta, for he was a man of his word; he had vowed that he would draw it in battle, and that battle had not yet come.

Ser Alfredo kai di'Callesta had returned it to his hand, and if there was reluctance in the gesture, Valedan failed to notice it. Deliberately failed to notice it.

But the Sun Sword, he thought. Just that.

The Serra Alina di'Lamberto knelt before his feet, her back exposed, her neck exposed. Sun had darkened her skin, and he knew that this was one of the gravest of sacrifices that he had asked of her. But even that seemed wrong to him, for Mirialyn ACormaris had been bronzed by sun, and strengthened by wind, and neither could diminish her.

This world, he thought. This was a world he did not understand. How was he to rule it?

"Serra Alina," he said at last, giving her anger time to show itself in the perfection of her posture. "Rise. Please."

She did, although she did not leave her knees; she was indeed annoyed; had decided on annoyance. And perhaps this was safest.

"Speak freely," he told her. She knew she could speak her mind at any time; she forced this permission from him, and he gave her what she demanded.

"Tyr'agar," she replied gravely, using the most formal of her tones, the most formal of his titles.

"Serra Alina."

She met, and held, his gaze.

Any act of contrition was beyond him, because he did not understand what he had done that aggrieved her so.

And after a moment—a long, long moment—she sighed.

"Valedan," she said, the accent in her voice shifting as she adopted the Weston tongue. "What do you intend to do with the Serra Diora?"

His brows furrowed, and hers echoed the shape and the contours of confusion. "Alina," he said at last, risking more anger, "I'm sorry, but I don't understand your question."

She closed her eyes.

"I intend to honor her," he said, after a moment of uncomfortable silence. "She brought me the Sun Sword. She brought me . . . my crown."

"Valedan—"

"And I do not intend to keep her here against her will; if I understand the South, she is far from her clan, and the Tyr'agnate of Lamberto owns her clan's allegiance."

"Valedan, did you not understand the significance of what she *said?*"

He thought back, but he could not remember clearly anything that she had said when she knelt at his feet; her face banished words. Her face.

He shook himself a moment, and saw that Alina was staring at him.

"I don't remember what she said," he admitted.

"She called herself Serra Diora *en'Leonne*."

He frowned.

"Valedan," Alina said, rising. "You have been so adept in the games of the South—how is it that you can stand in such perfect ignorance?" Her eyes flashed; she was almost beyond annoyance.

Without pause for thought, he said, "She is the most beautiful woman I have ever seen."

And Alina's expression shifted. After another pause, the anger left her; she looked at him as if he were the one kneeling, he the one supplicant. "I forget myself," she said softly. It was not an apology. "She is the Flower of the Dominion, kai Leonne."

"She is the widow of my half brother, yes?"

"She is that. More than that."

"What was significant, Alina? We might stand here for the rest of the day, and the night, and the next day, and I do not think I could guess."

"After the death of Ser Illara kai di'Leonne, she was returned to her father's clan," Alina said quietly, "as the Serra Diora di'-Marano."

He frowned.

"Must I say it?"

He nodded.

"Have you listened to so little, kai Leonne? Have you understood none of her game? Do you think she came by the Sun Sword easily, that she brought it for no reason?"

His frown deepened; her questions forced him to think.

To think about something other than the Serra Diora's face.

"If Ser Alesso di'Marente could have wielded the Sword you drew, he would *be* the Tyr'agar. None would gainsay him. Think," she said again, beseeching.

"She brought it to me," he said quietly, "because I am the last of the clan Leonne."

"And why, then, should she care? What role is given Serras in such a battle as you prepare to fight?"

He shrugged. "She doesn't like the General Marente."

"No," was the dry reply. "If you could say nothing else, that at least would be self-evident. She does not . . . care for the General."

He frowned a moment; memory came; words drifted by. He reached out to catch them and examine them. "Her father—"

"Yes. Her father, Ser Sendari par di'Marano, is the General's closest adviser. His personal friend."

"And she—"

"Yes. She took the Sun Sword from the Tor Leonne. She came to you as a woman of the clan Leonne."

"But you just said—"

"I told you to *think*," she said, her voice soft.

He did, then. He was silent and still, as if the fountain in the Arannan Halls trickled water before him in the cool Northern night. But he could not say the words that came to him. She saw them anyway; it was seldom that he guarded his expressions from her, and even if he tried, she often discerned the thoughts that lay unspoken.

"Her dress, kai Leonne. What of her dress?"

White, he thought. Perfect, long, almost luminescent in the full rays of the day. Like the dream of a dress. Like its ideal.

"The Lord's Consort," he said faintly.

"Yes. The Lady. But it is more, could be more, than that. She has come to you as bride. What will you do?"

He gestured and she fell silent. After a moment, he said, "I need privacy, Alina. I need to think."

She left, then, but it was clear from her expression that she agreed with at least the second sentence.

* * *

She did not linger by the tent, however. Had she the opportunity, she would have found her own small tent, and she would have shorn herself of Northern armor, Northern surcoat; she would have removed, from the length of her hair, the stigma of Northern braid. She would have taken gold chains, gold bracelets; she would have adorned her hair in jade.

She did none of these things, and it hurt her. But she had her duties.

These did not include her brother.

He had seen her, of course; he had even paused to meet her gaze. But beyond their first words, he had not chosen to speak to her, or of her; he had not requested, by the gestures of clan, her company. And she would not grace him with it otherwise.

Instead, she sought the tent of the Serra Teresa di'Marano.

Was not surprised to find that it also housed the Havallan Matriarch.

She bowed at the opening of the tent, as carefully, as gracefully, as she would have bowed at the gateway to another woman's harem. She eased her shoulders down her back, forced her hands into a limp, feminine stillness, and waited.

The Serra Teresa did not keep her waiting long.

"Serra Alina," she said, rising at once from the side of the old woman. "Please. Enter. The sun is high."

And she did. Sun had blinded her, but as the cool shade and shadow returned clarity to her vision, she gazed wordless upon the face of the Serra Teresa. Upon the most perfect of the Serras in the Court of Arral—perhaps in the Court of the Tor Leonne. The sun had been kind to neither woman.

But it was not of the cruelty of the Lord that she had come to speak; if she had, they might have been there all week, and she knew that they would be required to move, and soon.

"Matriarch," she said, rising. She inclined her head coolly. It was not the first time that she had met Yollana of Havalla, and even the eye patch over withered skin did not lessen the old woman's menace.

"Alina," Yollana of Havalla said. "It has been many years."

"Too many," she replied. But the reply was formulaic; words deprived of the truth of meaning. She did not linger on them. Instead, she turned to the Serra Teresa.

The Serra Teresa said, "Tell me of your Tyr."

She did not speak of Mareo.

"He is as you see him," Alina replied. "The kai Leonne. The Sun Sword accepts this truth; the Tyrs accept it. What more can be said?"

"Much," the Serra Teresa replied, and this was a surprise. It was not the sun alone that had changed the Serra; there was something else about her that had been lost.

"Tell me," Alina countered, "of your niece." As if they were mothers, now, and bartered over the marriage of less significant children.

"She, too, is as you see her."

Détente.

"What will the Tyr'agar do?"

Ah. Alina weighed her words with care, and then discarded them; perhaps Northern garb made, in a fashion, a Northern woman. She could not say, and she did not choose to examine herself too closely. "That was my question as well," she said quietly. "It is to give him time to think that I have chosen to retreat from his tent."

"I told you, Na'tere—he is a boy."

Alina bit back the sharp words that might have followed. Valedan needed no protection here.

"He is older than the Serra Diora," she said quietly, her only offered defense.

"And he has seen less," Yollana said sharply. "Come, Alina, you were always sharp of tongue. What will your boy do?"

After a moment, she said, "I don't know."

The Serra Teresa said, simply, "My niece has made her offer in the only way she can."

"And you do not speak for her?"

"I am not her father. I am not her mother. I have been her companion, and where I can, I have offered advice. But the young are the young, as you must know, and advice is heeded only when convenient."

"What advice, Serra Teresa?"

But the Serra did not answer the question. Instead, she said, "He seems very Northern, to me."

An insult, but delivered quietly, and in measured tones.

"The Serra Diora was promised, by her father, to the Tyr'agnate of Oerta," the Serra Alina ventured at last.

"She was."

"It was said—is said—that she was also highly valued by the General Marente."

"That, too, is true."

"Because of her words at the Festival of the Sun?"

"Because of her words after the death of the kai el'Sol."

It was a place that Alina had struggled not to go; she went now. *Fredero*. A boy, she thought. He had been a boy when last she had understood his thought. A proud boy. A Lambertan. She could clearly remember her father's anger, her mother's mute shock, when he had informed them of his decision to join the Radann.

Even she had not been immune; she had spoken with him, on the outermost edge of the harem, where their early lives still defined them in some fashion.

"Mareo is kai," he had said, his gaze upon the opacity of harem wall, his hands behind his back. "I am par. I am proud of my brother, but it is not my desire to live in his shadow. What else might I do, in honor?"

"To serve as par Lamberto *is* an honor," she said bitterly.

"An honor denied you," he replied. As always, he was perceptive, and his words were chosen with care not to wound. "The Radann are not what they can be, Alina. I will *make* them more."

"And Lamberto will lose you."

"Lamberto will gain," he said softly, "an ally."

"You must disavow all blood, all kin," she answered. "Even I know that. Why, Fredero?"

"Because," he said again, "I am not content to be par, and there is no other path open to one such as I."

And three days later, he was gone. Mareo's anger was not his father's anger; he understood Fredero's desire. Alina thought, although Mareo had never said as much, that he approved of it.

And Fredero kai el'Sol had drawn the Sun Sword before the clansmen of the Dominion—those who had answered the summons of Alesso di'Marente. He had wounded the General by the simple expedient of his unfair, his untimely, death.

Had he done that for the Serra? Had he struck the first blow, that she might land the second?

For she had taken the Sun Sword, and by delivering it to Valedan, she had granted him the legitimacy that his Northern armies, his Northern upbringing, would otherwise deny him.

"He is not of the North," she said at last, but without a trace of defensiveness in the words. "But he is not—quite—of the South. He owns no serafs; he suffers their presence at my request."

"None?"

"He has the serafs granted him by the largesse of Callesta. He . . . is uncomfortable in their presence."

"Why?"

"They are slaves, to him," she said softly. "I have been in the North for over a decade, and I almost understand his reluctance." It was true. But truth, too, followed. "But I am here, now, and to me they are a part of our life; they are a part of the fabric of the clans. I missed their grace," she said, seeing the past, where the present was so prevalent. "I missed their silence, their competence, their ability to serve as the situation required."

"And you, Serra Alina?" Yollana said.

"What of me?"

"You dress as a Northerner. You travel with the army. Surely this counts against him?"

"We spoke of advice," she said, with just a touch of bitter smile. "Some is taken. Mine, in this case, was not."

"Then he values you highly."

She said nothing. Could say nothing.

"And you value him highly."

"He is not my husband," she said sharply.

"No; you have none. The whole of Mancorvo knows this."

"But he made the offer, Matriarch." Unwise, to say the words; they had been a precious secret, a guarded one.

"And you refused him."

"I could not accept what he offered, although in truth, there are times when I regret it."

"Why?"

"Because he will be a fine husband," she said softly.

"Ah, you misunderstand me. And that happens so rarely, I'll assume it was deliberate." Her smile was yellow and weathered, but it lacked no teeth. "Why did you refuse? He intends to be Tyr'agar."

"You answer your own question, Yollana," the Serra Teresa said softly. "It is beneath you."

The Havallan Matriarch, far from being chastened, shrugged. She opened the flap of a weathered bag, and began to stuff her pipe with leaves.

But the Serra Alina said, "It is a fair question; I should not have spoken."

"And the answer, Alina?"

She wished this harsh woman, this sharply perceptive woman, elsewhere. Even hobbled, she was dangerous.

"I am not the wife of a Tyr," she said coldly. "I could offer him wisdom and guidance, and were he any other clansman, that would be enough—but he is *not* any other; he seeks to rule the South. There is only one wife he can claim now."

Serra Teresa said, "You do value him highly."

"Yes."

"Will he claim her?"

She spread her hands out upon her lap, palms exposed. "I do not know. There are questions he will have that no Tyr would ask. Things that will matter to him in a way that they would matter to no other. If he accepts what the Serra Diora has offered, and if the Serra Diora understands what he offers in turn, he will be a husband unlike any she could conceive of."

"If?"

"He is politically adept in matters of the sword," she said quietly. "What you have seen upon the field is his truth. Ser Anton di'Guivera serves him willingly, although he knows him to be blood of the man who ordered his wife's and his son's deaths. Ser Baredan kai di'Navarre serves him completely, although he fusses overmuch— he is like a doting mother, and he is not a man who will take the advice of a woman he does not own; I cannot curb him. Ser Ramiro di'Callesta serves him willingly, and the Serra Amara en'Callesta would offer him all but the lives of her kai if it furthered his cause."

"In truth?"

She nodded quietly. "He has befriended Ser Alfredo, a boy set on hating him; he has made the Black Ospreys his personal guard." She hesitated a moment, and then said, "The Kings sent a writ to the Northern Commanders, Serra Teresa; they are to serve Ser Valedan; they are to accept his orders over their own should there be conflict. They are here as *his* men."

"They do not like it."

"They have not yet had cause to dislike it."

"They will," Yollana said, and something in her tone brought both women up sharply. But she was busy lighting her pipe now, bringing an acridity of something other than her harsh voice to the private, enclosed space.

"If he is canny enough to accomplish this, he is canny indeed. Why then do you hesitate?"

"He is of the North," she said at last, "and he believes in matters of the *heart.*"

Yollana spit. "Will we have a fool as Tyr?" she said, cursing the Lady's blood.

"We have had worse."

"Not in the face of so much danger, Alina. Speak to the boy. Make him see sense."

But the Serra Teresa was absolutely silent.

The Serra Diora was numb.

Her hands lay against the mute strings of her lute, and she could not move to give them voice. Her lap was a spill of white; grass clung to the hems of her train. Ramdan had come, and Ramdan had gone; she had not given him leave to help her undress.

So many losses, she thought, exposing her scarred palm, her obvious imperfection. *So many sacrifices.*

Her arms felt empty. She had given the kai Leonne the Leonne sword. She had thought, while she carried it from the stretch of land around Raverra to the heart of the Sea of Sorrows, that she would be glad to be relieved of its weight, but she better understood now how one's chosen burdens sustained one.

The one, she had surrendered with joy; the ghosts of her wives. They were silent now; the wind did not contain their bitter accusations. She knew that she might see them again, and even if she did not know their faces, even if they were reborn as children, and she an ancient woman, bereft at last of grace and bearing, this certainty filled her with a sense of peace.

But the Sun Sword's absence made her feel frail. It offered no strength and no peace.

He had taken the sword. He had drawn it. The fires had not consumed him.

But he had done nothing, said nothing, else. And she had knelt before him, in the dress of the Lord's Consort, in a field of war, exposed. Witnessed.

Her pride, she thought, and was ashamed. But in the privacy of thought, much truth could be given words. He had looked upon her, and he had not spoken a word; there was nothing there that she could read.

Or rather, nothing that she could understand.

Ramdan entered the tent. He bowed.

She did not look up; she expected her perfect silence to be enough of a command that he might once again leave her in the questionable peace of introspection.

But he stepped past her, and rummaging through the Voyani pack that he carried, he handed her her fan. "Serra Diora," he said, his voice dry and almost devoid of emotion, "the Tyr'agar requests your presence."

                              *   *   *

Valedan waited in his tent.

He was nervous. Not since he had confronted the Kings in their own halls, with the price of his failure the deaths of people he had lived with for almost all of his living memory, had he felt so nervous.

He didn't know why.

And he did, and it made him feel . . . stupid.

He had learned by the side of Mirialyn ACormaris. He had learned at the feet of Serra Alina di'Lamberto. Two more intimidating women could not be found in the Empire. He had survived them; what, about this girl, could be worse?

He had his answer when the flap of the tent was pulled back by her seraf. She stood before him a moment in white, like a vision, something he was almost afraid to look at because of what she might see if he did: a gaping, awkward child. A seraf's child.

Nothing about her was out of place. Not a hair on her head, not a nail on her hand; he could not see her feet for yards of silk, and that silk glittered, crystal and pearl a complement to her skin, the dark cloud of her hair, the pale blush of her mouth.

He shook his head, clearing it. The seraf let the flap fall only when the Serra was within the large tent.

She knelt.

As Alina would have knelt, but more certain in her subservience. More graceful.

There were questions he wanted to ask, and he forgot all of them. Because he couldn't think of what he'd been about to say, he said instead, "I owe you a debt."

Her fan rose. Her eyes crested its painted ridges, but no more. She might be laughing; she might be frowning. The fan knew; he didn't.

After an awkward moment, he added, "For the Sun Sword."

Still she didn't speak; he had the impression that she was evaluating him. That he was already failing.

It was easy to be blunt with Alina. It wasn't always wise, and it wasn't always safe, but it was easy.

This woman—no. But she waited, and he knew enough about the South to know that she would continue to wait, compounding his inability. Squaring his shoulders, he said softly, "You named yourself Serra Diora en'Leonne."

She nodded, then.

"I am the last of the Leonnes," he continued. "And your husband is dead."

She nodded again, watchful.

"But you came in the dress of Consort. Serra Diora," he said, speaking more forcefully, although he could not actually bring himself to use the clan name, "was it your intent to be the Lord's Consort upon this field?"

She lowered her fan. It lay, spread, in her lap.

Like a shield, he thought. Delicate armor.

"Or mine?"

She waited.

"Speak," he said softly, "as freely as you desire. A command, Serra. And a request."

"I will be wife to the Tyr'agar," she said quietly. "By the acclamation of the clansmen who gathered for the Festival of the Sun."

That was her answer. It was the answer that he . . . wanted. And wanting it, he did not trust it.

"Why?"

For a moment she was still, still in a different way than she had been when she abased herself at his feet. He wanted to walk over to her, take her by the hands, and raise her—but he was afraid to touch her. He stood his ground, taking refuge in the title that kept him aloof from so much.

"I do not know why they agreed to hear the plea of a Serra," she began.

"Not that," he said. "I know why they listened. If you spoke, I would, and I would hear little else."

This, this answer was expected. He saw that. But it did not satisfy him.

"Why did you give yourself that name?"

Ah, the silence was infuriating. Perfectly correct. Entirely correct. Brimming with respect.

"Serra Diora," he said quietly, "you have never met me. You have not seen me lift sword. You know that I was born a seraf, the son of a concubine, the half brother of the kai. You must know that Ser Illara did not count us among his kin."

She said nothing.

"And you must know," he added softly, "that I would never have been sent North as a hostage if I had been valued. I would never have been baptized in the waters of the Tor Leonne; I would never have been claimed as full son. I served my father best by my absence." He was surprised at the heat in the words; surprised that he had said them at all. They were not the words he had thought to speak. But they were the truth, and truth was dangerous; once begun, it developed a will of its own.

"I was raised in the North. I wield the Northern bow. I speak Weston as if it were the tongue of my birth. I do not own slaves."

He had surprised her. She let it show—and he was certain that, had she desired otherwise, he would not be aware of it.

"I could never marry a person I owned."

Her brows rose now, perfect arches in the paleness of her complexion. "I am not a seraf," she said quietly.

"And you come to me of your own will?"

Again, again the brows spoke the words she did not.

She said softly, "I did not come bearing the Sun Sword with my father's blessing. He is a man of the Courts, and he has promised me to Ser Eduardo kai di'Garrardi for his part in the war we now face."

"You do not desire the kai Garrardi."

"No," she said. She spoke quietly, but the word rippled, losing some of its perfect composure.

He said, "It has not been long since the death of your husband."

"No."

"I have spoken with Ser Alessandro kai di'Clemente, Serra Diora. He traveled to the Tor Leonne for the Festival of the Sun. He saw you there, as Lord's Consort. He saw you lift the Sun Sword from the waters upon the plateau. He heard the honor you offered your husband. Have you had the time to grieve for his loss?"

She was utterly silent. After a moment, she touched the fan in her lap, closing it with a snap that seemed a type of punctuation to a speech she had not yet offered.

"Tyr'agar," she said quietly.

"Serra Diora."

"I will never have enough time to grieve for what I have lost."

His turn to lose speech.

But she filled his silence, unexpectedly filled it. "What would you have me say? I am a Serra. It was my duty to marry Ser Illara kai di'Leonne. It is my duty to marry now."

"I absolve you of that duty," he said, too quickly.

"And should Ser Anton absolve you of the duties you have taken to the Dominion, would you then set down the Sword and return to the North? For you are of the North," she added coldly. "You are so very Northern."

"Yes," he said mildly. "I am of the North. And I am of the South.

But I will never be all of one or all of the other. Why have you offered yourself in marriage?"

"Because," she said quietly, "it underlines your legitimacy."

He was silent; it was not the answer he expected.

She saw this clearly.

Heard it in every word he said. He took no trouble to hide himself; indeed he took trouble to expose what he was. All weakness, all foibles, he put on display as if they were not a danger. As if she were not.

She had imagined many things on the road—on all of the roads—she had traveled. But this kai Leonne was not among them.

The Tyr'agnati had understood her the moment they saw her upon the plateau; they understood the significance of her dress; they understood the significance of all the weight she bore. All of it. But the kai Leonne?

He played with words, she thought, hating them.

And he didn't.

She could speak freely. He had granted her permission, but men so often did who wanted no such freedom; she had learned to offer men the illusion of honesty with such perfect grace she had almost forgotten that substance lay beneath it. Yet to this man, she could speak the whole of her mind, and fear nothing.

She felt anger, then, and she, too, did not understand its source. She was tired. Weary. She had lost *so much*.

He said, "Did you love Ser Illara?"

In Weston, she thought; the language of bards. He must have spoken in Weston; the words made *no sense* in Torra.

She said, "Did your half sisters love the men they were given to?" And then she realized that he had been a boy when he had been given to the Northern Courts; the answer was beyond him.

He said, "Serra Amara loves Ser Ramiro di'Callesta."

Perhaps she did; the Serra Diora had never been invited to the vast halls of Callesta; had never resided within its harem as guest.

"What of them?" she replied softly. And then, almost against her will, "It is not seemly to speak so openly of such affection. Neither the Serra nor the Tyr'agnate would think it wise."

"Is that why you won't answer?"

In frustration, she said, "I have answered, Tyr'agar."

He said, "You did not love him."

She said, "Nor did you, when you lived in the harem." It was not an accusation. And it was. In the South, it was.

"He would have had us killed," Valedan answered quietly. "When he ascended the throne. When he claimed the Lake."

"Yes," she replied, voice spare and dry. "He was a weak man. In no other fashion could he have felt secure in his title." She paused and then asked, "Could you have learned to love such a man?"

"No."

She lowered herself into full supplicant posture. "Then do not ascribe to a mere Serra a feat that Tyrs could not attain."

"Serra Diora," he said quietly. She listened.

But the words gave her no answer, and no future. *He wanted more,* she thought angrily.

"I loved my wives," she said, without raising her head. "I loved their son. I would have saved him, had my husband lived. I would have done that much.

"But he did not. And with his death, theirs were inevitable. I lived," she added bitterly. Had she thought the dead at peace? Ah, perhaps they were. But she lived. Still lived. "I lived because my father is Ser Sendari di'Marano. Because my aunt is Serra Teresa di'-Marano. I lived because I was useful as incentive to the Tyr'agnate of Oerta.

"Do you not understand why I am here? Do you not understand why I have offered what I have offered?" She rose.

His gaze was mute.

The silence frustrated her curse and her gift.

"They killed *my wives,*" she told him, measuring the words. Using them as if they were weapons. But they were of two edges, like daggers; they cut both ways. "They killed *my son.*"

"You had no children—"

"I *had* a son." Her voice was rising; she let it go; gave it wings. Freedom. "He was a babe in arms. He was a seraf's son, a concubine's son. But he was cursed with the blood of Leonne; a threat. To the General Marente. To Ser Sendari. To the Widan Cortano di'Alexes."

"But the women—"

"Who could be certain that they were not, themselves, with child?"

She knew what he would say next, and she raised her hand, stemming the flow of his words, the pain of them. "Yes," she said, "there were other ways to discern this. But they involve magic, the Lady's rites. They would have taken *time.* The concubines of a dead kai were of no import, no interest, to the man who claimed the Tor."

"Serra—"

"And I did nothing," she said. "I did nothing, then. So that I might do something *now*."

"The Sun Sword," he said softly.

"That," she said quietly, "and more. I am here. The clansmen know me. They will know, if you choose to accept me as wife, that in the eyes of the Lord's Consort, *you* are the only heir worthy of the waters of the Tor."

"I . . . see," he said quietly.

And he did.

She had said too much. Could not believe that she had said so much. Mute, she waited.

"I am your weapon," he told her softly.

"And I am yours," she replied.

"Serra Diora," he said, grave.

She knew he would dismiss her. But she did not know what he would do after; she waited for his words, and when they came, she gathered her skirts as if she were once again a captive in the Tor Leonne, denied the aid and company of serafs.

Three conversations. The first:

An hour later, Ser Anton di'Guivera entered the Tyr'agar's tent.

No one accompanied him, and this was unusual; Ser Andaro di'Corsarro shadowed the weaponsmaster of the late kai Leonne as if they were bound, inseparable. It was not an act of affection.

Valedan looked up when he entered; raised brow when he entered alone. "Ser Anton."

"Tyr'agar." The old man's bow was perfect, and when he rose from it, his expression was grave. He glanced, once, to the Sun Sword, and then looked to the kai Leonne. The Sword was a weapon to Ser Anton, no more; it was to wield weapons that he trained his chosen students.

Even this one. Especially this one.

"Have we received word?"

"None, Tyr'agar. Or none that I am aware of. Commander Berriliya is in the Southernmost tip of the valleys."

"If word traveled—"

"With his Northern magi. Word will travel swiftly, when it comes. Commander Allen expects it; so, too, does Ser Ramiro di'-Callesta. Ser Mareo kai di'Lamberto has repaired to his own tent just beyond the rise of the hill; his men are moving now." He met Valedan's gaze and held it. The boy did not move.

"You have been hours in this tent," he said at last. He did not couch his words in careful tone; he had chosen to speak to Valedan kai di'Leonne as if he were a student. A difficult, talented student. The criticism was deep.

Nor did Valedan kai di'Leonne set rank between them as the armor that it was, in the Southern Courts; he accepted Ser Anton's tone—and intent—as if he stood in a Northern circle, drilling.

"The Serra Diora," he said at last, "has occupied my time and my thought; I would have been of little use among the marshals of war."

The Serra Diora. Yes. "She has been hurt," Ser Anton said quietly.

Valedan met his gaze. "I know," he said at last.

"There are men who would not take her to wife because she has already shared a bed with another."

Valedan's brows rose and fell, darkening the whole of his face. "Ser Anton—"

"My apologies, Tyr'agar." He bowed smoothly. "I speak truth, Southern truth."

"I don't care if she's shared a hundred other beds," he replied.

Ser Anton bowed. It was shallow, and it was brief, but it was there. "They speak of it now," he said softly. "Not even the Tyr'agnati are certain of your position."

"What should I have done?" Valedan said. Anger guided the words, shaping their choice. "Should I have lifted her, as if she were just a Sword? Should I have claimed her, as if she were no more than—"

"What she did, no other Serra has yet done, in the history of the Tor Leonne. It was bold, yes. And by your inaction, you have almost humiliated her."

The boy looked stricken.

Ser Anton understood. "You were raised in the North," he said softly. "And I have seen the North; enough of it to understand your hesitation. The women are strange there. They rule the Houses. They often choose not to marry. Because they *have* choice, their choice is significant.

"But because the Serras have none, hers is more so. Do you not desire her?"

Valedan shook his head, raising hand to hair. It was a youthful gesture, full of hesitation. "Who wouldn't?" he said softly. "Who among us wouldn't? She is—" He shook his head again.

"She is injured, as I was injured," Ser Anton said quietly. "She has lost wife and child, and she seeks vengeance."

"Justice," Valedan said quietly.

Ser Anton's smile was slight. The boy protected her, even now; it had started, and he was young enough not to see it in the word he spoke. "In the South, they are not so different."

"And am I to take her as wife for that reason?"

"No, Tyr'agar. Let me ask, instead, a different question."

"Ask."

"Why did you take my service?"

Valedan's brow rose. "You are Ser Anton di'Guivera," he said at last.

"And what of it?"

"You are—"

"You know the whole of the truth, kai Leonne. You know what I desired, what I was driven to. I am considered a man of honor by those with less knowledge. But children died while I practiced and taught those students who best had a chance of ending your life. Northern children," he added quietly, thinking of Aidan. Feeling again, like a lingering caress, the slap of the young boy's hand.

He would go to Aidan, after he had finished speaking with Valedan. And Aidan, with gravity and enthusiasm, would heal those memories, those self-inflicted wounds.

A gift. Unlooked for. A Northern son.

"I accepted your service," Valedan replied, "for many reasons."

"Indeed. And among those, the legend that attended me. The legend that you yourself believed."

"I still believe it."

Ser Anton shrugged. The answer did not please him.

"She and I are not so different," he said, after a pause. "And the legend that attends her is one of her own making, but it serves the same purpose. As I was known, she is known. She was raised to be the wife of a Tyr," he continued. "And as wife, she will have no peer."

"I—"

"Do not speak to me of Northern love," Ser Anton said coldly. "Unless you wish to be treated as harem child. You do not *love* her now, although you desire her; do not demand that she offer love where you cannot."

"I don't expect—" The words died.

Ser Anton bowed. "She is canny," he said quietly. "She has a warrior's heart. A warrior's scars. She is the Flower of the Dominion, and if she grows in the shelter of the shadows you cast, she will strengthen you. I strengthen you, not by my sword, but by association. I am aware of this; I use it.

"She will do the same in your cause."

"In her own cause," he said quietly.

"Until the war is over, Tyr'agar, they are one and the same."

"And after the war?" Valedan's hands were curved into fists, but they lay at his sides, weaponless. "I intend to win this war," he added. "I intend to survive it. What comes *after?*"

"That is not a warrior's question, kai Leonne, and it is only by being a warrior that you will win the Tor. But if you do not find her pleasing, set her aside. It has been done."

Valedan's smile was bitter. "She is not a sword," he said softly.

"No. She is more. But if you plan to remake the Dominion, you must understand her, for she is a part of its heart."

"She is like no other Serra, Ser Anton. You yourself have said as much."

"She is like no other Serra," he agreed quietly. "But everything she has done today, everything she might do tomorrow, is Southern. It is the essence of who we are."

Valedan said nothing.

"She has been injured," Ser Anton said again, "and she is young; the injuries we take, when young, the losses we suffer, inform us in a way that no others can. You will not find a stronger woman if you search the breadth of the Dominion.

"But you will not find one more vulnerable, in the end, either. She knows what you need," he said quietly. "As I do. She is willing to serve. As I am."

"Must this be done now?" Valedan said quietly. "Can it not wait?"

"There is much that can wait, between the young," Ser Anton replied gravely. "But matters of war have their own imperative.

"Acknowledge her name, kai Leonne."

"And her grief?"

"Trust that in time she will come to you; she is like the hunting hawk, and she has been long in the air."

Three conversations. The second:

The song of bards. The Northern song. The strum of lute, of strings both familiar and foreign.

Serra Diora lifted her head as Kallandras of Senniel entered her tent. She had not expected him, but she seldom did; he was like the wind, the heart of the wind, and he moved in a like fashion. She nodded, regal now.

And he bowed, stilling *Salla's* perfect song.

"Serra Diora," he said quietly.

His voice was flat and perfect; smooth as Northern glass, warm and cold the way gold was warm and cold; a delight to one sense, but heavy in the hand. He seldom exposed himself to anyone with the voice.

But not never. "Kallandras," she said quietly. "Ona Teresa—"

"Yes," he said. "She sent for me. She sent me."

"To speak with me?" Serra Diora said bitterly. "To speak as she no longer can?"

"She is not a fool, Serra Diora; her loss has not addled her. She knows your strength as well as I, perhaps better. I can gild my words, but you can hear beyond them, and I cannot force you to do what you yourself have no desire to do."

"And what does she seek, then?"

"Of you? Nothing. Nothing more than what you have already given."

The Serra frowned. She did not lift hand or lower veil. That much, she granted him.

"She has never lived in the North," Kallandras said quietly. "And I have spent much of my life in its heart. It is of the kai Leonne that I have come to speak."

His words were like the opening of a harem's screen; she could hear something between the syllables. But he was careful, well practiced; she could not easily name what she heard, and because she could not, it had no use.

"He means you no dishonor," Kallandras said, and *Salla* shifted in the lap he made as he sat. "But he treats you as a Northern woman. He treats you as if you were of their Courts, and not the Dominion's."

She said nothing.

But he heard what she did not say.

"He already desires you, Serra Diora. There is nothing you could do that could make that desire stronger."

"Am I become so obvious?" she asked quietly. "Is this the price I pay for passage through the Sea of Sorrows?"

"No," he said softly. "And yes. Judge him, if you must, but understand what it is that you judge."

"A Northerner," she said, contempt beneath the perfect surface of her voice.

"And more," he said quietly. "He fears you, Serra."

Surprise robbed her of words.

But it did not likewise thieve them from Kallandras. "He fears you *because* he desires you. He doesn't know you. He knows that without knowledge, without time, he cannot trust you. He doubts himself; he doubts his desire. He does not wish to wrong you. He is shrewd, for a boy his age; in the North, even more so than in the South. He understands your political value. He understands what you might mean to him, as wife, in the Dominion. He tells himself all of these things, and he believes them because they happen to be true.

"But he believes other things as well. He questions his motives, in this."

"His motives should be clear," she said quietly. "He desires victory."

"Na'dio."

She stilled at the use of the cradle name; he had shifted the whole of the conversation by its use.

"I have seen him, in the North. I have seen him, briefly, here, and I will tell you that he is a man that Fredero kai el'Sol would have valued. He has changed, and he has not changed; he has refused to give up his beliefs, his ideals.

"He could never marry a woman that he must own."

"He told me that," she said faintly.

"You heard the truth in the words."

"He took no trouble to hide himself."

"And yet you are angry."

"I do not understand him, Kallandras." She lifted her fan, examining its pleats, its folded, stiff silk.

"No. It is why I am here. If he accepts you as wife, he must accept what comes with that responsibility: he will be your Lord; you will be *his*. Your life, and your death, his to decide."

"If he is so honorable, what fear is there in that?"

"He fears to have too much power."

"He goes to war for far, far more."

"Yes. And until this moment, he has been able to pretend that what he gains in the winning of that war is the freedom of the Dominion.

"You are not like the Serra Alina di'Lamberto, and she is, of the Southern Serras, his closest confidante."

"I do not . . . know her well. I have heard of her, but she left the Dominion long before I left my father's harem."

"She is clever, wise; Southern and Northern. She will never marry," he added softly. "But it is not of Alina that I have come to speak, and we have little time."

She felt the force of his words as if they were blow. The truth of them, the certainty of them.

"What does he desire of me?"

Kallandras shook his head. "The wrong question," he said quietly. "If you are determined to do what must be done, you must find a way to be both Southern Serra and Northern wife; you must find a way to ease his uncertainty."

"I?"

"He does not trust himself," Kallandras replied, "and because he does not, he does not trust you. I have seen you in the South; I have seen you in the desert; I have seen you atop the towers in the Tor Arkosa.

"You have come as Serra, and you know that role well; it is yours in its entirety. Learn to be other," he said.

"Must I then profess to love him?"

"Na'dio, that is beneath you."

She closed her eyes, accepting the correction as if she were, in truth, Na'dio. "I do not understand what he wants."

"No. But you should; it is not so very different from what you yourself wanted from your wives."

"He is *not* a wife," she said fiercely. Protecting her dead, her loved.

"No. He will never be that. He will never replace your dead. Set that fear aside, Na'dio. Let it go."

After he left, she sat in the quiet of the tent in silence. It was silence she was free to choose; Kallandras had set *Salla* down at her feet. As Adam had done. So many freedoms, she thought bitterly.

Then she shook her head, hands reaching for the lute. She did not play it. She could not. Not yet.

And so the last conversation: the Serra Teresa came to her niece's tent.

She did not speak; not to ask permission to enter, not to greet. She sat almost stiffly, as if a sari no longer suited her, as if her knees were no longer capable of the very fine, very perfect bend that she had lived in for most of her adult life.

She had not intended to come thus to the Tyr'agar's camp; she had intended to wear Voyani clothing and pass, in the end, as one of Yollana's tribe. Ser Mareo kai di'Lamberto had ended that choice, and she had accepted his decision.

No, Diora thought, seeing her aunt's pale face. She had had nothing left with which to fight it. She drifted, as if lost—and she was.

Of all the things that the Serra Diora had expected to face, this was not one: Ona Teresa, bereft, truly bereft, and alone.

She could not speak. She started to, but the voice that she used was not one that could be returned, and she was afraid to remind her aunt of injury and loss.

Dark eyes met dark eyes; Diora understood why Kallandras had come in the Serra's stead. And so she touched the strings of the lute, and after a moment, she began to play it.

But that, too, was wrong.

She lifted it gently, almost reverently, and she reached out to her aunt. Their hands touched as the Serra took the lute from her, mute, tired.

The strings spoke; silk brushed them.

After a moment, so did fingers.

This is how they spoke: the Serra Teresa played, and the Serra Diora, after a moment, recognizing the tune, began to sing.

Cradle song.

"Kiriel?" Auralis, accustomed to the strangeness of Kiriel's moods, had learned to read her sudden silences, her stillnesses. He understood when she was weary, when she was tired, when her thoughts had turned to the kin; he knew when Lord Telakar was near, for the lines of her face shifted, becoming tighter, the angles more acute.

He understood her anger, which was much like his; understood her lack of humor, what the sudden clipped end of her words often meant.

But he had never seen a silence like this one.

She turned from him, turned from Fiara and Alexis, turned from Sanderton; Cook was snoring on his feet, and Duarte was in conversation with Ser Andaro, their tones low and muted.

"Kiriel?"

She didn't answer. That was not unusual. But she began to walk away, and that was. She was, after all, on duty. The bodies of the dead Tyran had yet to be interred, and the Ospreys were given the duty of watching them. As duties went, it was pretty unpleasant; not even magery could mask the smell of days of death and decay.

But it wasn't the type of thing that usually fazed her. Nor did the heat, these days. All of her attention seemed split along the divide of North and South; if she was not gazing distantly into the one, she was concentrating on the other, as if she could hear, from the distance of hundreds of miles, the hooves of Marente cerdan.

Duarte broke off, lifting a hand; Ser Andaro followed his gaze. "Sentrus."

But she did not stop; did not appear to hear him.

His frown, in the open day, was severe.

Auralis shook his head, lifting a hand in turn; his fingers danced a moment in the air, a request.

Duarte's frown deepened. But he nodded.

Auralis left his post and followed. He moved almost silently, and he moved with care; the days when Kiriel could be approached from behind were eroding slowly. She was becoming a stranger, the girl she had first been when she had been thrust upon the Ospreys.

It disquieted them all, but no one acknowledged it; she was still one of their own.

He watched her shadow, lengthened now by the sun's slow dwindling upon the Western horizon. He stayed well out of sword range, and he did not touch his weapons. But he trailed her.

She moved from plateau to tents, and from these—familiar, small, and gathered, to larger ones: the tents of Tyrs and Commanders. He tensed.

A shadow lay across his path; not hers, but one he recognized. Lord Telakar. The demon's smile was cold and unpleasant, but it was not a challenge; he, too, was drawn toward Kiriel di'Ashaf.

"What do you see in her?" the demon lord asked. The words did not mean what they would have had anyone else offered them.

Auralis shrugged. He felt exposed, as he always did when Telakar's gaze fell upon him. After a moment, he said, "Kiriel."

"She is not one of you," the demon said quietly. But he watched, fascinated by something that Auralis did not see.

"She's not one of you, either," Auralis replied, keeping the words steady.

"I have never been foolish enough to claim her. Only one among us has, and he has paid. What do you see, mortal?"

"Kiriel," Auralis replied again. He moved past Telakar, aware of his presence. Aware that he exposed back to follow Kiriel. A choice, that, and he made it with difficulty. He still didn't understand why Kiriel had chosen to let this particular demon live.

But she had, and he wasn't about to argue with her.

She moved from the large tents to the newest ones. She moved slowly now, her steps heavier than he had ever seen them, and she paused, at last, in front of one that he recognized—that any man would have recognized.

The Serra Diora's tent.

The guards to either side of its closed flaps moved to intercept her. He would have shouted a warning, had they been Ospreys. They were Callestan. He held his tongue.

And she dropped hand to sword hilt. It was her only gesture, her only form of conversation.

He cursed silently. They drew swords.

He did not draw his; he was still behind her. But he moved now, and quickly. There were things that Duarte was prepared to overlook; things that Valedan would forgive. The death of Callestan Tyran was not among them.

"Kiriel," he said, closer than he should have been.

She stiffened; her hand was upon the hilt of her blade, and he knew that once it was drawn, the game was over.

But the guards did not stand alone by the tent's side; out of the shadows, a man stepped. Northern man, hair fringed in dark dyes, but unmistakable: A master bard of Senniel College. The most famous of the bards.

Their eyes met, and Kallandras of Senniel College nodded slightly. If Kiriel noticed him, she did nothing to indicate it; her gaze was wholly focused upon the tent.

From beneath its closed flap, Auralis could hear the strings of a lute; the soft and indistinct syllables of a woman's song. He frowned.

The Tyran spoke to Kiriel.

And Kallandras shifted his stance, and spoke to them. His voice was all but silent; Auralis could see his lips move, but he heard nothing leave them; no Weston words, no Torra. Slowly, almost imperceptibly, their swords fell.

They stepped aside; Kiriel did not seem to notice. But she stepped forward, and her hands touched fabric as if it were smooth stone wall. Her palms lay flat against it; he could see her back, and only her back, the wild fall of her hair.

She pushed the flap aside and stood in the door.

He heard the song more clearly.

The words were Annie words, the voices Annie voices. He couldn't pick out meaning from the syllables, and didn't try; the words he knew well enough to recognize weren't likely to be sung by Serras of any clan.

The words faltered; the music did not.

Kiriel stood a moment, exposing her back, and then she stumbled forward, as if struck by something, or as if at last acknowledging the severity of an earlier wound. The flap closed upon her, swallowing her; the sound of song receded.

He started forward, and Kallandras of Senniel moved to intercept him.

"No, Sentrus."

Auralis had managed to crawl his way up to Decarus again—not that it made much difference, since it seldom lasted—but he didn't correct the bard. He chose his words carefully. "She's not dangerous."

Kallandras smiled. "She is," he said. But the words were devoid of argument. "But I think that today Kalliaras smiles. Leave her be, Sentrus. She will harm no one."

"You don't know that," he said softly.

"I do," Kallandras replied. "I know what they sing."

He wanted to ask, but didn't. He shrugged instead and settled in to wait.

CHAPTER TEN

SERRA Diora looked up when the light changed. The Serra Teresa did not; she continued to play the lute in silence, letting its resonant notes—unchanged, in her hearing—form the whole of her speech. If she noticed that Diora's voice, changed too much, had stopped, she gave no sign; music held her.

But music left Diora as she looked, for the first time, upon the face of this dark-haired, pale-skinned stranger, a girl who was neither Southern nor Northern by look, with eyes as dark as the Lady's coldest night, eyes as clear.

She wore armor, this girl, and a sword that rivaled the swords of Tyrs in length; she wore her hair in the Northern warrior's braid, as if she were a soldier. And she was; Diora knew the faint marks upon her surcoat, the sword and rod. But her face was unscarred, unblemished, as devoid of sun's hand and wind's avarice as any Serra of the High Courts.

She was not old. But she looked, in the light, like a girl who had never been young; there was something about her that spoke, in the musical silence, of danger and death. Neither of these were strangers to the Serra Diora, although she had never seen them so openly upon a woman's face. She was transfixed, her voice still, her hands folded in her lap.

The moment broke; the girl met her eyes and hesitance marred danger. Without a word, Serra Diora lifted hand, beckoning; the girl stepped into the tent, enclosing it against intrusion from the outside world.

She said, "The song. The song you sang."

Diora chose the most perfect of her Court faces, inclining her head with care. But she answered the rough question. "Cradle song," she said softly. "A song for evening. Or children."

"It's not—it is not evening," the stranger said, stumbling over the Torra. "It—there are no children here."

"No," Serra Diora said quietly, "it is not evening, and there are no children here." And then she added, softly, "but we have all heard it, and it speaks to that part of us that thought it offered safety."

"There is no safety," the girl said bitterly.

"None," Serra Diora replied, both matching the bitterness and hiding it beneath her perfect face.

The stranger sat awkwardly, crossing her legs as if she were a man. It seemed to surprise her, and Diora was unsure whether that surprise spoke of the awkwardness or the posture. For just a moment, danger and death gave way to youth, the cracks appearing in armor that shifted with movement.

She did not know this girl, but she knew something of her; her voice said much. Too much. *Death. Darkness.* And if that had been all she could hear, things would have gone differently.

But she heard this, too: the child who had heard the cradle song, and who had come across this field of battle to hear it again; it was a hunger.

She asked, softly, "Who are you?"

And the girl answered, "Kiriel. Kiriel di'Ashaf." A Southern name. But Ashaf was no clan's name that Diora knew, and she thought she would know it if it could produce this woman. She inclined her head.

"Among men," she said softly, as if speaking to the child, and only the child, "we do not sing this song. And among men," she continued, "we do not sing without permission. You wear the armor and the sword; must I ask your permission to sing?"

Kiriel di'Ashaf shook her head, and her warrior's braid beat against her neck and back like an instrument. Her eyes were unblinking; she leaned forward, bending at neck, her supple spine curving a moment. She lifted her hands, leaving the hilt of sword, and cupped them with care beneath her chin.

And Diora felt a shock, something akin to recognition, although she recognized nothing. The girl drew, from the folds of hidden shirt, a chain, and on that chain, heavy and pendulous, a stone hung.

It was clear, Diora thought, but not entirely colorless; it seemed to catch light, even ambient light, and it made of what it had captured a pale skein of green, a thing to bewilder the eye.

Kiriel looked up at that moment, brows creasing; her eyes met Diora's. She said, "You see it."

Diora nodded, her hand touching the hollow of her own neck. She brushed aside the dead strands of gold, the adornments that might make her seem—to men—a thing of value; all that lay beneath them was skin, cool and damp to the touch. The Heart of Arkosa hung a moment, like a ghost, around her neck.

"Do not expose that here," she whispered, her eyes widening.

Kiriel said quietly, "It helps me remember the words." As if it had no other significance.

And Diora heard, in her voice, another truth: that it was seldom that Kiriel di'Ashaf took comfort in memory, any memory It shouldn't have mattered to her. She had taken on burdens far greater than the momentary hesitance, the strange wonder and hunger, the unspoken fears, of a soldier.

But she dropped her head and accepted the Lady's truth, in the Lord's time. It did matter. Perhaps because the stranger was not a man, and neither Southern nor Northern. Or perhaps because the hunger she saw was one she could easily appease.

She began to sing, for Serra Teresa had not once ceased to play, her fingers moving across the strings like a lament.

Hands wrapped about the pendant she cradled, Kiriel di'Ashaf began to sing as well.

And her voice almost stilled Diora's. Not because it was good; it was not. It was rough and hesitant, broken, unpolished. It carried the tune because Serra Teresa played; it stumbled over phrases and words as awkwardly as a farming seraf might dance.

But it held, in its depths, a true night: a memory as dark as Diora's. It held grief, and guilt, and a terrible, impossible desire. Shorn of practice, shorn of gift, it might have been her own voice, her own penitent song, that she heard—a mirror.

And so she sang. Cradle song. And when she spoke the child's name, invoking both promise and certainty of its failure, it was not

Ona Teresa's name that came to her lips, and not the name of her
dead wives, her dead son; it was a stranger's name. Na'kiri.

The stranger did not notice.

Because she did not, Diora understood another truth: That she
had heard it sung, and had only heard it sung, to her. In the harem
of Diora's youth, many voices had offered that song. Across the
plains, within the fields, within the quarters of the lowest of clans,
the lowest of serafs, she had heard it sung.

This girl had not; only one voice had offered it, and that voice
was lost. But the song still moved her; perhaps it moved her more.

Diora did not notice when the girl's voice gave way, not at first;
she could not say on what verse the words trailed off. But she knew
the sound of weeping when she heard it; it was contained, and only
barely, in eyes that were now wide and shimmering.

"Na'kiri," she said, speaking softly, as if to a frightened seraf. "I
will teach you the words to the song. You need not rely on any
memory but your own."

And the girl looked up, stiffening, the whole of her face shifting
and shuttering in that moment. She scrabbled to her feet, moving
backward, her hands dropping what they held.

Diora watched as she fled the tent, and she bowed her head a moment before she put power into her voice and continued to sing.

The orb was pulsing in the hollow between her breasts, as if it
were her heart, pulled from chest and laid bare. It was warm and it
was loud, its beat insistent; it was heavy. The song had done this,
she thought.

But she knew it for lie, and took no comfort from it. She could
not touch the pendant, not here. But against her skin, it seemed to
move, to blossom, to grow until it encompassed the whole of her.

The sun's light was hot and the air was damp.

Kiriel di'Ashaf looked up wildly, and met the eyes of Auralis
AKalakar. She saw only his eyes. The return of her vision, the ability to see the colors beneath skin, the colors that were deeper and
brighter than flesh, faltered; she saw him as she had seen him in Averalaan; a man, a puzzling, difficult man.

A friend, she thought, although the word was foreign.

His hand was raised, as if to touch her; he dropped it.

"Kiriel," he said quietly.

She met his gaze and shook her head; the sun would dry the
tears. She could not lift hand to her cheek to brush them away; it
would be acknowledgment of weakness, public acknowledgment.

Her earliest lessons, lost.

"Auralis," she said, but her voice broke, foundering between syllables. Nothing familiar there. Nothing Southern.

"What happened in that tent?" His hand fell to his sword; his face sharpened, his gaze darkened. She understood that this was for her, that it was a gift. But it was a gift that she did not want, and she shook her head gracelessly.

He let it go.

That was what she best liked about him, although she had seldom thought it so clearly: he let it go, as he let all things go. As the Ospreys did: the past was not their country.

But it was hers. The orb spoke in a long dead voice, and other voices joined it, whispers, susurrus of sound that might have contained words if she could take the time to hear them. She looked across the height of the Eastern edge of the Averdan valleys, and she knew them as she had not known them before she had entered the tent; she felt a word take root in her mind, and grow deep, and quick, into memory: Home.

She saw the green of the valleys' trees, the trampled grass, the distant fields, some flooded, some not, and they were familiar to her in a way that they had not been before she had tried to sing Ashaf's favorite song. Could not be. She had lived her life in the blinding, perfect white of the Northern Wastes, in the citadel of the Shining City, the Shining Palace, its two towers long and high, things of stone that no mortal hands had help in fashioning.

She did not desire that place. She did not desire its cold, its constant games, its death.

This one spoke to her instead. *Averda*.

She said, "I recognized the song they were singing." Hadn't intended to say it, but did not attempt to recover the words; they existed. They were free.

He nodded, none of the concern assuaged.

She said, "The Serra Diora is very beautiful."

But even this did not invoke the response she expected; he did not whistle or smile or wink; he did not laugh, or offer her his envy. His eyes devoured her expression.

She shook her head, to escape them.

Recovering was hard, here. Because she knew, as she walked, as she looked at the land that lay beyond Auralis' back, that the memories were *not* hers. They were Ashaf's. Ashaf's, contained by stone, and come slowly to life.

Ashaf had never visited *Callesta*. Ashaf had never seen the Tyr'agnate.

But this stretch of land? She'd seen it, or land like it, and she had loved it: the trees that were older than she could ever hope to be, and the ones that took root in the lee of the older forests; the animals that jumped from branch to branch, and the birds that weathered there, building nests, singing, and dying. She loved the dragonflies, the bright, hard-shelled beetles, the flies that glowed soft in the evening light.

But best of all, Ashaf loved the serafs who toiled in grooves of dirt.

Kiriel looked. She could see them, in the distance, their movements stiff and wary.

Ashaf. Ashaf knew what that wariness meant, and Kiriel knew it because she would not turn away from the memories. They brought the old woman to life, and it was a life that Kiriel so bitterly missed that she clung to it. Like a child.

Like the child she had been, in the towers of stone and ice, in the arms, the shaking, weak arms, of a woman who had never known freedom in Kiriel's life.

Kiriel pressed her hand to her chest, as if it pained her. She dropped slowly to one knee, and felt Auralis' hand upon her shoulder.

"Kiriel!"

Kiriel closed her eyes. The orb was beating, and she recognized the thud-thudding of its noiseless awakening. Wondered how she could not have. It was, beat for beat, the sound that she had heard when Ashaf had at last fallen silent, the song sung, the moment passing, when Kiriel had listened to the heart, caged and cased in frail flesh, that spoke of life.

She had come this far at the side of Valedan kai di'Leonne. Had come under the command of Primus Duarte, as part of the Kalakar House Guards. Had fought, with some glee, some joy, at the side of Auralis AKalakar. Had not even questioned why she had come.

But all of that knowledge was buried beneath the simple sound of heart's beat. What she knew, now, as she listened, what she felt in the moment of tenuous peace, was this: she had come *home,* and she had come home for a reason.

She rose slowly.

Ashaf, she thought, the name causing her only the briefest of pains, *I will protect what you cared for.*

*   *   *

Primus Duarte AKalakar called for Auralis AKalakar hours later, and Auralis sauntered into his tent as if the command itself was only barely worth heeding.

But Duarte saw wariness in the face of his Decarus. He wondered, idly, if Auralis was heading for Sentrus again; he had, of course, forbidden betting pools, but knew who stood to win, and lose, by the count of days.

Auralis snapped a sloppy salute.

Duarte frowned. "Decarus," he said, "as you were."

Auralis dropped his hand to his side. "You wanted to see me?"

"In a manner of speaking."

"Well, I'm here."

Definitely heading for Sentrus. Duarte frowned. And shrugged. He had deliberately chosen the meeting to exclude the Commanders and the Southern Tyran. "I want to talk about Kiriel," he said quietly.

Which was about what Auralis expected. The wariness grew. "I received word, from a source that will remain unnamed, that there was almost an incident today."

Auralis shrugged.

"What happened?"

"Don't know. Wasn't there."

"You spoke for a time with Telakar."

Another shrug. As Duarte himself used the gesture often, he couldn't be offended by it. But he was, of course.

"It can't have escaped your notice that Telakar is now situated within our camp."

"No."

"Good. It shouldn't then escape your notice that because of his presence we are now being watched. Closely."

Auralis shrugged. "You're the Primus," he said. He did not add, *you deal with it,* but he didn't have to.

"Kiriel is part of the Kalakar House Guards," Duarte continued. "And as such, she is tolerated. But there are concerns."

"And those?"

"The South has changed her," Duarte said quietly. He let go of the military bureaucracy then. "Even Alexis has noticed it. She is growing . . . dangerous."

"She's always been dangerous."

"Do you trust her?"

"With my life."

"And with ours?"

Auralis shrugged. "You're the Primus," he said again. "It's your call."

"Why did she not kill the demon?"

"He serves her," Auralis answered. It was his only honest response.

"And she serves us?"

"She's an Osprey."

"The Ospreys don't exist anymore."

Auralis said nothing to that.

And Duarte had no time to challenge the silence; it was broken by Alexis. She walked briskly into the tent, her shoulders a straight, taut line. "Marching orders," she said.

"Now?"

Her nod was slight. Grim. "The Berriliya's magi just sent a message. The scouts have picked up something; we've lost aerial contact."

Duarte nodded, Auralis forgotten. "Marente?"

"On the field," she said. "Or at least that's the Hawk's best guess."

"How many men?"

"Commander Allen didn't volunteer that information."

Duarte nodded and rose. "The bodies?"

"The Lambertan Tyr told us to get rid of them. Properly. It's being taken care of now. When we're finished, and when the Radann are finished, we're to form up behind the kai Leonne." She paused, and then added, "The Eagle's in a foul mood."

"He would be. He lost his seer."

"He can press charges when he gets back."

If he gets back. The words hung a moment, like ghosts. They had been spoken before.

"I hate the valleys," Alexis added. "But they're the heartland of Averda."

"I know." And our dead, he thought, are here. "Decarus, dismissed."

27th of Corvil, 427 AA
Terrean of Averda

Anya hated the cold, when she forgot to protect herself against it. But she wasn't certain, after a few long hours, that the heat was any better.

For *one*, she was not allowed to build herself *anything*. Lord Ishavriel had been very, very strict, and he watched her even now, like a cross parent, his arms folded and his eyes narrowed into slits. *Two*, she was not allowed to *kill* anyone. Even the Southerners who annoyed her so very much. And they did. They watched her as if she were either stupid or crazy, and she hated them almost instantly.

An old memory tickled her; the stories told in the free towns of her youth had encompassed the war with the South. Why exactly were they supposed to be her friends now?

Three: No one would tell her where Lord Isladar was. And she was certain they knew. How could they just misplace him? It annoyed her. Kiriel was supposed to be in the South, she remembered; Isladar had said so. At least she thought it was Isladar.

It was hard to think here. The colors of the Northern Wastes were not so loud, and they did not have the multitude of tastes, the odd smells, that the riot of colors here did. She detested them. She wasn't certain she could bring the snows this far, if she could move them at all, but had been willing to try.

Lord Ishavriel had said curtly that this was magic, and that therefore it was forbidden. He used that word: forbidden. It was a word she didn't like. She explained that it wasn't *real* magic, but he refused to *listen*. She was itchy. There were *bugs* here.

And worse, much worse, there were fields here. Farmers. They huddled in terror. Some of them died. They all made her feel uncomfortable. They reminded her of things she didn't want to be reminded of.

She spoke a moment with the grass, because it whispered and hissed; she told it to be *still* and it was. This was better, but the horses all started to scream and their voices *bothered* her, and she told *them* to stop, and they didn't listen, so she told *them* to be still, and they were, and then Ishavriel came, and he was very, very angry.

And then, worst of all, the annoying Cortano came to speak with them, and he was angry—at her—and the whole of his body was a sheen of color and light that made him hard to look at. When she tried to ignore him, he used magic.

Magic was the only voice that she understood here.

So she spoke *back*.

"She is here too early," Alesso di'Alesso said quietly.

Lord Ishavriel did not mistake the meaning behind the words. He bowed. It was, Alesso knew, costly, and he did not therefore deign to notice the depth of the gesture, the correctness of it. Anya a'-Cooper was mad, had always been mad—but something had changed. It was not easy to determine what, for madness had its own rules, and they were beyond the contemplation of the sane.

But she was wild now, and dangerous.

Six horses were dead. The flats of the plain upon which the rest grazed were dry and withered. She had not killed the men, and for this, he knew, he should be grateful; he struggled to find that grace as Lord Ishavriel rose. Cortano was beside him, and beside himself, although he troubled himself to hide his rage.

"She is here," Lord Ishavriel said, "early." He bowed again. "We will, of course, replace the horses."

It was the wrong thing to say.

Alesso said quietly, "The horses are not so easily replaced. They are not cattle. They are weapons, and they have a history that gold does not erase."

"Horses are bought and sold across the Dominion."

The day was bright. Ser Alesso turned to the Widan, Cortano di'Alexes. "The birds?"

"They have not returned. But I feel it was unwise to dispose of them." The accusation was mild; the meaning was not.

"Agreed," Ser Alesso said smoothly. "But the Lord Ishavriel has given his word that he will consult with us before he undertakes such action in future."

It, too, was a warning.

"The birds were their scouts," Ishavriel said, "as you well know. They were used in the previous war to known effect; we could not afford them here."

"We could. If they had remained in flight, the Northerners would not now be aware that we are ready to move. And we are not—yet—ready. This action does not favor us."

"In what way? Even if we are not ready, their certain knowledge of our numbers and their disposition cannot serve us."

"It served us," he said quietly. "It drew their attention, and held it."

"There are things that must be done that they cannot witness."

"And those?"

Ishavriel's silence was not a comfort. He said, after a pause, "Why are we not ready to move?"

"We wait," Alesso said quietly.

"We wait upon whom?"

"The second army."

Ishavriel frowned.

Alesso glanced at Cortano, and Cortano gave the barest of gestures: No.

"And we continue to wait," he said. "But the second army is not the difficulty that Anya a'Cooper will be if you do not curb her or return her to the Wastes." As he said it, he dropped his hand to the hilt of his sword. It was meant to be a threat; it was perceived as such.

"She is necessary," Ishavriel said, "or we would have left her there."

"What purpose does she serve? She has done more damage today than the Callestans have done."

"Six horses and a field."

"Six horses and a field at the hands of a *woman* wielding the Sword of Knowledge," Cortano snapped. "Of what use is she?"

"She is needed," Ishavriel said, the words weighted with the cold of the Wastes, "to trace the boundaries of the valley."

"Your pardon, Ishavriel, but what purpose does that serve in this war?"

"When we cast this spell," Ishavriel said, "it will prevent the Northerners from retreating. Any who attempts to cross that boundary will perish before his foot lands."

Alesso was silent. Silence was a struggle.

He raised a mailed fist. "Ishavriel," he said coldly, "I have said, from the beginning, that this war is *mine*. You will send Anya a'-Cooper back, or you will take your army of demons into the valleys; I will remain here."

"That would be unfortunate," the kinlord said. His eyes were faintly luminescent in the shadows of a tent protected from eavesdroppers.

"It would," Alesso said mildly. "But it will be done. If I am to rule here, I rule." He did not draw his blade. But it was close; the desire was stronger than any desire had been, except the one that drove him now: the Tor Leonne.

And that desire—barely—eclipsed the desire for blood; he was still.

"Against the Northern armies, General Marente, you cannot win without aid."

"That has yet to be tested."

"The will of the South has been broken once against a lesser force, and the South was united behind its Tyr'agar."

"A lesser leader was responsible for that loss," he replied. "And

I will not have Averda enspelled in such a fashion. It is not to my liking, and it will not be done."

"The barrier will also serve to keep men out," Lord Ishavriel said softly. "You might control the whole of the war in such a fashion."

"Oh?" Dangerous word, that.

"If the Northern armies are not already gathered upon the mainland—if, as you suspect, some portion of their forces are confined to the sea—they, too, will find traversing the borders difficult."

Alesso did not acknowledge the words. Instead, he turned to the Widan. "Your Widan," he said calmly.

Cortano nodded, bowed, and left.

Dangerous, to be without magic in the presence of a kinlord. Alesso smiled.

Ishavriel stood a moment, and then the light in his eyes faded to black. The black was not more of a comfort, but it was familiar. "You risk too much," he said at last, his voice neutral.

"And you," he said, "do not understand what you have risked by bringing her here."

"She is needed."

"We do not require her spell."

Ishavriel paused for a moment, and then said, "She serves another function."

"And that?"

"She is conduit to His power, here. Without it, no more of my kin will arrive in the valleys in time; without it, none will escape detection when the battle is done."

Alesso's smile did not shift or change; it was blade's edge, his self laid bare. No weakness there. He did not, of course, trust the kinlord's words; nor did he believe that they were, in their entirety, lies. He weighed them carefully, as he weighed all else.

A different man might have taken a moment to feel fear; to acknowledge uncertainty. Alesso, none. "Take her elsewhere, Ishavriel. Take her North. Find a town, occupy it, and wait."

Words not to his liking. "I am the Lord's Fist here," he said.

"And I am the General." There would be battle, Alesso thought; two. But they must be fought distinctly, and at a time of his choosing.

The sound of men shouting invaded their stiff silence, and Ishavriel broke gaze first, cursing in a language that Alesso did not—would never—understand.

"Anya," Alesso said quietly.

Ishavriel bared teeth that were too pale and too sharp, but the snarl contained acquiescence. And then he was gone.

But it was not over. Cortano di'Alexes entered the tent minutes after the shouts had died into stillness.

"What has she done now?"

"Moved the forest," Cortano said, his tone entirely neutral.

Alesso grinned. "It is not to our advantage to have her here," he said, but with real humor. "But it is not . . . entirely . . . to our disadvantage. Ishavriel is hampered by her presence." The grin faded, but Alesso's expression lost none of its edge. "What do they plan, Cortano?"

"I am little on the council of their warlords," he replied, a trace of bitterness lacing the words.

"No. But you are powerful; the most powerful of the Widan."

"They have not taken the time to teach me their magics," Cortano said, hands now touching the edge of his beard. "Isladar explained much of the Lord's intention, but not all.

"But Sendari has a few theories. He will be with us in an hour."

"Good. And the rest?"

"They are with him. You will find what they have to say interesting."

Alesso nodded quietly. "The kai Garrardi?"

Cortano grimaced. "His only concern is the Serra Diora."

"That, too, is not to our disadvantage."

"If he continues to be so publicly impolitic, it will not be to our advantage either."

"Jarrani?"

"Occupied with his men. He will hold."

"And his kai?"

Cortano said, softly, "Hectore is, of the kais, the most competent."

"And the least trustworthy?"

"I cannot say. He is not Widan; he is not one of mine."

"No. He serves Jarrani."

Cortano nodded.

"Lamberto?"

"You were correct."

"Ah. It was not unexpected."

"It was not expected; he moved with little warning, and he moved upon our forces in Damar."

Alesso said nothing.

"None of the kin escaped."

"Then there is power, yet, in the lands of men."

"There is . . . power yet. The Widan did not escape the slaughter either."

"But they sent word, and it is enough. The Serra?"

"If Ser Alessandro's words are to be believed, she must now be assumed to be the property of Ser Mareo kai di'Lamberto. At best, she will be returned to the kai Marano. At worst, she will be a pawn to the seraf's son."

The kai Leonne.

Alesso shrugged. This was less to his liking, and Cortano knew it; he did not bother to hide or veil his displeasure in nonchalance. Insulting the intelligence of the Sword's Edge was the act of a fool—or a man so assured of his power that he feared little. Alesso was neither.

But he did not fear to fight; did not fear to die.

"What of the boy, Cortano?"

"No word," Cortano replied.

"And the death of the kai Callesta?"

"The Tyr'agnate of Averda has always been a pragmatic man." He shrugged. "He is no Lambertan, to hold fast to a point of honor when his Terrean is at stake."

"I disagree. He is pragmatic, but he honors his bloodline. It was not his par that was killed, but his kai. An act of war."

"Indeed. But he is not a fool, Alesso. If Ishavriel did not deal with care, then there is—in my opinion—as great a chance that Ser Ramiro recognizes where his enemy lies. If he accuses Mareo kai di'Lamberto, the Lambertan Tyr will deny the accusation. Were he Lorenzan, were he Garrardi, were he . . . Marente . . . his denial would mean nothing."

"But Lamberto?" Cortano spread his hands. "It was a risk, and it was not a plan to my liking."

"Nor to Sendari's." Alesso shrugged.

"But it was done. And if the Lambertan Tyr was in truth in Damar, then he will face a decision; to ally with Callesta in a battle for the North, or to remain within Mancorvo, and watch."

"Your guess?"

"Damar will be costly."

Alesso nodded quietly. "I fear it, as well. The Northern Commanders?"

"Your guess was good; they came by ocean."

"Ah."

"Alesso, I recognize the expression you wear. What concerns you now?"

"The kai Leonne," he said softly.

"He was raised in the North."

"Indeed."

"And he is the son of a seraf, a graceless concubine."

"Indeed. But what information we choose to offer our cerdan, while it serves our purpose, may not be the whole of the truth. How much of this war will be his?"

"How likely is it that the Northerners will cede control of their armies to the Tyr of any Terrean?" Cortano's beard lengthened at the pull of his fingers. "The boy concerns me less than the *Kialli*."

"But our answers—such as they are—are almost here; it is the boy who remains under cloud." He shrugged again, and turned. "Go to meet Sendari; ascertain that Ishavriel—or his mage—is no longer within the camp."

Cortano nodded.

When he was alone, Alesso smiled and closed his eyes.

Sendari di'Marano was troubled and exhausted. Mikalis was tired. The rest of the Widan, Cortano's men, were likewise weary with heat, but they were pale. Sendari had lost some of his taste for war, in this investigation, if he had ever had it.

Cortano met them upon the road, horsed and without escort. Lines of orange, radiant and bright, cut across the fabric of his robes, as if they were part of its weave. They were, Sendari thought. Until the end of the war, they were.

He did not speak as they approached; they slowed their horses to a trot. The sun was in the final half of its ascendancy; soon the Lady would watch them all. Or the Lord of Night would.

It was not a thought that brought comfort to Sendari, but he was still sane. Cortano waited until Sendari drew close, and said one word. "Anya."

Sendari paled.

In silence, he rode the rest of the way into the camp, and in silence, he viewed the dead grass that seemed to stretch half a mile out from the forest's odd line of trees. Ah, the trees, too.

"Cortano—"

"There is no need. The cerdan are speaking with the wind's voice today; word of her will spread. It cannot be contained."

Sendari nodded. He dismounted in the lee of the Tyr'agar's standard, and strode to the tent; the Tyran noted his presence with a nod, their hands upon their swords the formality of gesture, no more. He passed between them, wordless, his hands by his sides empty.

They did not ask him to disarm.

"Alesso."

"Sendari." Alesso stood, arms behind his back. "Cortano has no doubt informed you that Anya a'Cooper is—or was—present?"

Sendari closed his eyes. The road had been long and harsh; the birds of the enemy numerous. He could see them, their eyes preter-naturally—unnaturally—bright in the clear light of day. Could shelter his presence from their notice with ease. An army could not, of course, be shielded in like fashion without an expenditure of power that would be noticed in other ways. Thus, the trade-offs of war.

"What has Ishavriel been doing, Sendari?"

Sendari bowed. It wasn't, strictly speaking, necessary, but it gave him time to compose his expression, to shelter the weariness of the road behind a neutral mask. He reached into his robes, and he pulled out a carefully wrapped bundle. "Do not touch it," he warned, as he set it upon the table.

Alesso nodded.

Sendari set about unwrapping it with care, as if it were a delicate, Northern glass. It was not; it was, to the unpracticed eye, a simple sapling, a tree of pale bark, white roots, few leaves.

It was the leaves that had drawn his attention, although they might otherwise have been missed; they were small. Missed, cer-tainly, by the eyes of the watchful, winged scouts. Missed by the cerdan whose paths did not carry them into the deeper copse of wooded lands, the shadowed veils of Averda's forests.

But by men who sought a sign, some symbol or gesture of magic, no.

Sendari took care to glove his hands. Alesso watched this fastid-ious act of caution with open curiosity; the gloves themselves were not the wear of gardeners, but something thinner, finer.

Only when both hands were thus accoutred did Sendari reach down to lift a leaf. It glittered in the poor tent light, akin to gold or silver, veined with something white.

"Do you recognize the plant?"

Sendari shook his head.

"And the Widan?"

"None of them recognize it. One, who for obvious reasons will remain unnamed, said he wasn't a gardener."

Alesso's expression darkened.

"I think it was meant as humor," Sendari added, humor entirely absent from his own voice. He held the leaf in his open palm, its veins spreading and folding as if they had suddenly found the lines of his, beneath the surface of glove that protected weathered, callused skin.

"This is one sapling," he said softly. "But it was not the only one. If you desire it, we will have the rest removed—but it will be a costly endeavor. They stretch the length of the Terrean's border, for as far as the eye can see. Or rather, for as far as Widan can, who are searching for them."

"They border Averda," Alesso said quietly, no doubt at all in his voice.

Piqued, Sendari said, more sharply than he had intended, "And only Averda?"

Of this, Alesso was less certain. Unwilling to expose his ignorance, he chose not to answer. Sendari understood the silence—but he had had years in which to learn to read the General's silences.

"The cerdan?"

"I am not certain the cerdan would serve you well in this undertaking."

"How so?"

"The tree—and it is a sapling, not a weed—was not easy to uproot. It would not have *been* uprooted were it not for the use of magic, and even this use took time. We were uncertain as to the nature of the magics contained by this plant, and we practiced some caution."

"The roots are short."

"Indeed, they seem so. But they are the color of maggots, and they burrow. Were it not for our own arts, I think they might have sought new rooting in our flesh." He paused a moment, and then said, softly, "I believe they were originally rooted in flesh."

"There was a corpse?"

"Not a full corpse, no. But bones."

"Human."

Sendari nodded grimly. "It is a subtle magic, Alesso. The equal, I would guess, of the masks that were gifted the Tor for the Festival of the Moon."

Alesso's nod was curt. "What is their purpose?"

"We cannot say, with certainty, what their purpose is. But the fact that they border the Terrean is significant."

"Lord Ishavriel implied that there was to be a magic cast around the borders of Averda that would seal it."

Sendari's glance shifted, changing in place. The weariness evaporated, like sweat in sunlight. "What did he say?"

"That Anya a'Cooper was required to build this boundary; that it would kill—instantly—any Northerner who crossed its line."

"I think that it would kill any man who crossed it, if that were indeed its purpose. The *Kialli* are not gifted enough to choose between our blood and the Northerners'; to them, we are all mortal."

"I concur."

"And it would be a costly magic," Sendari added, thoughtful now. "Such a spell might be attempted on a smaller scale. It *is* done, by Widan of Cortano's power. But not by lesser Widan. And not," he added, "across a Terrean."

"And Anya?"

"She is mortal," he said quietly. "I have heard Cortano speak of her. He does not hold her in high regard, but there is no question that he respects her power."

"Her power, old friend, is worthy of respect. The madness behind it is worthy of fear, and I value fear little."

Sendari nodded.

Alesso laughed. "Go," he said, with humor. "Speak to your Widan. Tell them what I have told you, since you will hear nothing else, and think of nothing else, until you have begun to confirm—or reject—the truth of Ishavriel's words."

"I do not doubt their truth," Sendari said, letting the leaf fall. "I doubt, rather, that he has spoken all of the truth. There is a power in the North that could cast, and sustain, such a spell."

Alesso's humor vanished. "The Lord of Night."

Sendari nodded. But he bundled the sapling with care, and retreated.

In silence, Alesso stood, gazing at the empty surface of table. He had expected the *Kialli* to move against them, but had also expected that they would wait until the battle itself had been joined.

It was what he would have done, in their position.

Hard, to deal with enemies so foreign. Not even the Northerners were so alien; they fought, and won or lost by the simple expedient of living or dying.

Yet thinking this, he turned to the North, the whole of his mind now occupied by a single question.

A man's name.

Valedan kai di'Leonne.

27th of Corvil, 427 AA
Terrean of Averda

Kiriel at a distance was both a good thing and a bad thing, and one could have too much of either, Auralis thought. Her mood had infected his, and not subtly: it was like a disease that grew worse, untended and unacknowledged.

The darkness that had slowly been growing seemed to be hemmed in now by something utterly unpredicted. She was enthralled by two things, the scenery and the Serra.

He could understand, on some base level, anyone's interest in the Serra Diora, although two of the Ospreys had been put on latrine duty for speaking her name out loud. Duarte's idea. That they were on duty at all was a testament to the needs of war and camp; Duarte had been less than pleased.

But he had not offered a warning to Kiriel, and Kiriel, when off duty, seemed to drift toward the tent that hid the Serra from things as mundane as sunlight. Sometimes she was allowed to enter, and she disappeared as well. He watched the tent, then, and listened, but whatever was said within its folds was private.

It could not be a matter of war. Could not, or she would speak of it. But this was the first thing that Kiriel had ever done, in Auralis' memory, that had not been dictated by her impulse to fight, to kill, or to survive. If she played a game at all, it was so well concealed that he could not see either rules or conditions of victory; it remained beyond him.

And he found, much to his chagrin, that he missed her.

Of all the Ospreys—or whatever it was they were now—she was most like him.

Men did not carry mirrors.

In the pristine surroundings of the High Courts, serafs served that function, and wives, if they were bold. Upon the fields of war, men did. And with practice, one could read one's reflection in their gazes, the slight shift of their shoulders, the line of their lips, the narrowing of their eyes.

Ser Mareo kai di'Lamberto looked at himself through the face of his son.

Ser Galen was white. White enough that silence attended him; he had momentarily lost the ability to speak. And that, Mareo thought grimly, was wise. He adjusted the fall of dark silk, arranging what he could see with the practiced casualness that spoke of artless care.

It didn't matter. Had he touched nothing, had he left sash undone and wandered out, like an injured man or a drunkard, his son's expression would had been no different.

"Galen," he said quietly.

Galen did not reply. Could not. And Mareo did not choose to leave the tent until he could. Time passed, and with it, some march of miles; the men were ready. Joining the Tyr'agar's armies presented a challenge the like of which no Lambertan Tyr had ever faced.

But it was a challenge that Ser Mareo kai di'Lamberto could not refuse; he therefore approached it with the prudent caution that he approached all else of import in his life, and he adorned that caution with a boldness that had always stymied his enemies, on the field or off.

He tied his sash, and lifting *Warcry* from his table, slid it beneath the gathered silk folds. It was lost a moment to the midnight of blue, the white of sun off water. Not even the glitter of gold thread could draw the eye from those twinned colors, for they represented much.

"Come, Galen," he said. "We have already committed ourselves."

"You cannot wear those colors," his son said at last. He would have said more, but wisdom ruled him, a moment late. "Father."

Ser Mareo simply said, "I am a man who has lost my kai. I understand what that loss means, and I honor it."

"It is because of the Northerners that Andreas is dead!"

"Yes," Mareo agreed. He sought the shelter of no deception with this son, this Lambertan son. "But it is cloth, no more."

"It is more than cloth," Galen said, heat rimming the words, the shell of words. "Join them, if you must, but do not—"

He lifted his hand. "Galen," he said calmly, "would you have me remain in Mancorvo while the war for the Dominion is fought? Or do you imagine that, once the Callestans have perished, Alesso di'-Marente will not then march his armies across our borders?"

"We have discussed this," Galen said curtly. "And I have agreed. For the sake of Mancorvo—for the sake of the Dominion—we will stand beside our enemies. The Lord of Night is the greater threat."

"Indeed," Mareo said, lifting hand to beard. The beard was cropped close, but it had lengthened with the march, and it would lengthen again before the last death. "We have agreed to stand beneath the banner of the Tyr'agar. Do you despise him?"

Silence. Answer enough.

"I do not."

"Because he can wield the Sun Sword?"

"Because Fredero died for just that."

"Fredero chose to abandon the clan," Galen said coldly.

Mareo did not strike him. He would have, had he been any other man. "Fredero chose to lead the Radann," he responded, "and by leading them, he changed them."

"Does it matter? He changed them, but we are still *here*, in the lands of our enemies. Fight by their side, yes. Fight beneath the banner of a Northern pawn, yes. But *this?*"

"We are allies," he said quietly. "And our allies demand a gesture of respect. There is none that can make this statement so clearly as this one." He paused. "There will be death," he added. "We cannot prevent it. But let those deaths be deaths caused by battle against the Lord of Night; let them be fought on the field, and not on the road. We cannot choose a course and cleave to it with half our will, half our heart."

"Let the Callestan Tyr show the same respect for *our* dead! He has long shown no regard for our loss, and our loss—"

"Enough, Galen. Enough. Do you think I have forgotten?"

"It will look that way," Galen said softly, relenting.

"It is a gesture," Mareo said quietly, "of commitment. We have chosen. Respect the choice, or revoke it."

Galen struggled in the silence with the oldest of his hatreds, the greatest of them. After a moment, he bowed, mute, mutinous.

Not a good start.

Ser Ramiro di'Callesta sat astride his destrier, waiting. The Callestan Tyran that he had selected to accompany him were few: Ser Fillipo and Ser Miko. He did not regret the absence of the rest, but he felt it keenly; the Lambertans held this crest of hill, this patch of grass, this edge of forest, and years of instinct struggled against acquiescence. These were Averdan lands.

"Is this wise, Ramiro?"

"No."

His par laughed. It was genuine; he found the situation humorous.

Ramiro raised a dark brow.

Ser Miko might have done likewise, but he was absorbed with the weight of his duty: the safety of his Tyr. Here, surrounded by Lambertans, that duty seemed almost impossible to achieve. The Court struggled with the warrior, and the Court won, but it was close.

"We have chosen our Tyr," Ramiro said, when Fillipo's brief burst of inappropriate laughter subsided. "And we have chosen our enemy. The Lambertans will honor their Tyr'agnate; they will not attack us here." His smile, when offered, was grim. "Or they will pay; the kai Lamberto accepts no slight to his offered word."

"No more does the kai Callesta," Fillipo said stiffly. He was no child now, no youth, but some small part of that early regard for an older brother still informed him. It was seldom that he revealed that much; it appeared that he was nervous, after all.

"Ah, is that said? I hear it seldom from any who are not mine." He shrugged. "Lamberto is known for its honor."

"They are not happy with that honor, Ramiro."

"No more are our own."

"No. But when we take our men into battle, they will hold."

"Then we had best find battle soon, or they will make it," Ser Miko said.

"Indeed."

They waited. The sun crept up the sky by slow degree, and they marked the passage of time by the movement of shadow, the shortening of its length. Heat had already returned to the day; the nights did little to quell it.

The Tyr'agnate of Mancorvo rode into view.

The words that the Tyr'agnate of Averda had prepared deserted him; he gazed across the closing distance in perfect silence.

Ser Mareo kai di'Lamberto had chosen to adopt the formal colors of mourning that graced the Tyr of Callesta and his Tyran; that, in lesser degree, marked all of the Callestan cerdan. But it was not the colors alone that marked the Lambertan Tyr. Nestled in the folds of perfect silk were beads and crystal, sewn in such a way that they invoked the shadow and light of the Callestan crest.

He meant to offer respect for Carelo, and he offered it without ambiguity. A Lambertan gesture.

Ser Ramiro di'Callesta was aware that he had no like gesture to offer; that in fact, he had never offered it. He had never regretted it, although the political cost had been high; he regretted it now.

But regret was not an emotion to offer the Lord.

What was left was simpler. He dismounted.

Fillipo and Miko were forced to dismount as well. But their reluctance—if it existed—passed without notice; Ramiro had eyes for the Tyr'agnate, and only the Tyr'agnate, of Lamberto.

Mareo's horse was stately, calm; an older horse, he thought. It moved with ease through the ranks of Tyran, and stopped feet away from where the Callestan Tyr waited.

Ramiro bowed. He bowed deeply; it was not a bow he could have offered had Valedan been present.

"We are old for change," Mareo said softly, gazing down from the height of Mancorvan horse, and acknowledging, with that gaze, what had been offered. "Kai Callesta."

"Kai Lamberto."

"But we are not old for war; it is what made us, in the end, what we are. We fight this war," he added, pitching his voice so that it carried above the Callestans, reaching the corners of the encampment with ease, "to rid the land of the servants of the Lord of Night. And in the end, *that* is the only fight worthy of our endeavor. It is worthy of the whole of our efforts.

"And when we win this war—and we are men of the Lord; we *will* win—let *that* war define us."

"Ser Mareo," Ramiro said. He rose. Mounted his horse and waited until the Tyr'agnate of Lamberto drew abreast. They were like kin, in the distance; Ser Mareo kai di'Lamberto's colors guaranteed it. Although his face and his standard were unmistakable, no Callestan would note, at a glance, which of the men were Lambertan and which Callestan.

"You have met my Serra," Ramiro said.

"I have had that privilege."

"She would be honored by the honor you pay her son," he continued, quietly. "And she is not a woman who forgets any honor done her sons."

"Women are the keepers of memory," the Lambertan Tyr replied. "My Serra remembers more easily those things which pained her greatly, but she, too, remembers honor offered."

Ramiro nodded gravely, gracefully.

Together, the Tyr'agnati who now served Valedan kai di'Leonne began a slow inspection of the troops of Lamberto. After they had finished, Ramiro thought, they would do likewise over the crest of the hill; they would travel among the Callestans.

Let the Callestans see what the Tyr'agnate offered them. Let them understand, as he did, the measure of the man who had been enemy, and who chose now to be ally.

Ser Anton di'Guivera requested the presence of the Tyr'agar an hour later, and Valedan kai di'Leonne stepped out from his tent into a changed world. He saw the banners of Tyrs, raised high, their colors distinct and unfettered by the dirt of the road, the dust of travel. They were held close, and at a level, as if they were brothers, and the two men who rode beneath them were likewise attired.

Ser Anton bowed his head.

After a moment, Valedan joined him.

"This is a costly gesture for the Tyr'agnate of Mancorvo," he said quietly. "And a fitting one."

"It was necessary," Valedan said softly.

"Oh, indeed, it will help our cause enormously. But what is necessary, kai Leonne, even among men of honor, is not always done. Take his measure here, and understand him well."

"You admire him."

"I have always admired the Lambertans," Ser Anton replied. "But not even I would have dared to suggest the course of action he has chosen for himself. He lost his kai to the Northerners who are now in league with your forces, and the forces of Averda. To the very Northerners who travel with us. This cannot have been undertaken lightly."

Valedan nodded. And, like the student he was, he took his lead from the weaponsmaster of Leonne; he took the measure of the Lambertan Tyr, and wondered idly if a Leonne son raised in the Northern Empire would be able to live up to it.

CHAPTER ELEVEN

THE Serra Diora fascinated Kiriel. Not simply because she was beautiful, for beauty mattered little to Kiriel; in the Northern Wastes, what was beautiful and what was deadly were inseparable.

Here, too, in the South she found that truth. For she could see death in the delicate Serra, could hear it in the cadences of her words. Only the cradle song was devoid of its ice, its distant anger. When she could, she came to sit by the Serra's side over the next two days; it was not often. The army marched, and she marched with it.

But Valedan did not forbid her the tent; if he was curious at all, he did not choose to ask; he accepted what the Serra Diora permitted. And he accepted, Kiriel thought, the odd laws that bound the Ospreys.

It was the Serra who asked questions. About Valedan. About Ser Anton. About life in the inexplicable Northern Court.

On the third day, she asked about Ashaf.

"Kiriel di'Ashaf is a Southern name," she said quietly, her hands stilling the strings of her harp. "But you are not of the South, Kiriel. Why have you chosen a Southern name?"

So many questions in the words. Kiriel was silent beneath their weight; they invoked memory. But memory had blossomed anyway; the crystal at her neck was warm and vibrant with color, with the hint of memory, and it did not sleep.

After a long pause, she said, "Ashaf was my mother." The voice she heard was not her voice; it was thick and foreign, heavy, unfamiliar.

Diora said nothing at all. Kiriel had expected questions. More questions. Anything but what she was offered: cradle song in the quiet of a private tent.

Funny. In the absence of questions, Kiriel found her words. She spoke, first, of Essalieyan. Of Valedan kai di'Leonne. Of Ser Anton. Of Jewel ATerafin. She spoke of The Kalakar, because Diora seemed curious about the women of the North; she spoke of Averalaan, its crowded streets, its salty air, the humid, hot summer; the winter rains.

When these stories were finished, she spoke of the Ospreys. Of Duarte, Primus and sometimes peer, of Alexis, Fiara, Cook, and Sanderton. Last, she talked of Auralis, and even then, Diora did not question her.

It was Kiriel, in the end, who offered questions.

She said, "The men of the South are killers. Jewel ATerafin wasn't. And Valedan kai di'Leonne isn't." She looked at the Serra Diora. "Do you think he will rule, if he can't kill?"

Diora answered, "All war involves death. He will learn."

Kiriel frowned. "I didn't say he couldn't kill. I said he wasn't a killer."

And the Serra nodded quietly. She said, "He's not what I thought he would be."

"What did you think he would be?"

"Different. He is not . . . Northern. And he is too Northern."

"You came here for him."

"I came here," the Serra said quietly, "for myself. We have our duties," she added. "And we fulfill them where we can. My war is with the Lord of Night."

Kiriel stilled. "You mean *Allasakar.*"

"What is that?"

"It is his . . . it is what he is called, in the North."

The Serra's perfect brow rose. "He is named, in the North?"

"He seems to be the only Southern god who *is.* Don't choose him as your enemy," she added quietly.

Something in her voice must have offered warning to Diora, for the Serra stilled—although she almost never seemed to be in motion. "There is no other enemy, Kiriel; there are his allies, there are his servants. Why else do you think the Lambertan Tyr now stands beneath the banner of the kai Leonne? Why do you think the Northern Generals—ah, no, Commanders—traveled South?"

And then, as if she realized that she had asked her first real questions, she asked a last one; a neutral one. "What do they say of the Lord of Night in the North?"

"That he's the Lord of the Hells," Kiriel said softly. "I don't know what the Lord of Night means here."

"Death," Diora said quietly.

"All gods mean death, in the end."

"Why?"

"Because they *don't* die." She was touching her sword as she spoke, and realized it when she followed the Serra's gaze. "Choose a different enemy, Serra Diora."

"There is no other," the Serra said again, allowing ferocity a home in her words. "With his aid, my wives lie dead."

Kiriel frowned. "Your wives? Do women marry, in the South?"

"They marry."

"But not each other?"

Diora frowned. "No."

"Then why do you call them yours?"

"Because they were."

"But—"

"In the South," the Serra said quietly, "the clansmen of means take many wives. It is a show of their wealth, and their power. But men of power are often absent, and they leave their harems in the care of their first wives. Or their oldest wives. It differs from man to man.

"The wives are often friends," she added softly. "And they support their husband, when he requires—or desires—support. Without a husband, they have no protection; if he fails in his duties, if he dies, they are likewise shorn of the little they do have when they hold his name. They bear his children. And those children become the children of the whole harem. Those wives *are* wives to each other."

Kiriel frowned. "I don't understand."

"No. You are not of the South."

"Ashaf was. But she never spoke of her wives."

"If she was not wealthy, she would not have had them."

"She wasn't wealthy," Kiriel said, touching the pendant. Her hands were cold, and it warmed them, beating against the flesh of palms. "In the North—in *my* North—there was no wealth. Power ruled. And rules."

"It is not different here."

"No. The South is less . . . uncomfortable . . . than the Northern Empire. But it is still not like my home."

Diora waited, but Kiriel shifted, signaling an end to this particular conversation. As she rose, she said, "The Lord of Night, if he took to the field, would crush you all without effort. Serra Diora, choose a different enemy."

And then she was gone.

The Tors came to Valedan's banner in ones and twos as his armies traversed the length of the valleys. Ser Ramiro di'Callesta's banner was therefore prominently displayed, and it never fell. It marked the borders of the moving camp; it marked the road; it stood just below the banner of the Tyr'agar, enforcing the legitimacy of the Leonne claim within the heartlands of Averda.

These men came, with men, across the fields, riding down and out of the folds of land which housed serafs, fields, and granaries. Not by accident had this route been chosen, and if Ser Ramiro di'-Callesta was not pleased with the presence of the Commanders here, he did not show it. The stockades that had been constructed for the use of the Tyr's armies were opened to the men and women who commanded the joint forces; the tents were therefore used less often as they progressed.

The Northern Commanders carried much of their supplies with them, and they found the going more difficult, for the Imperial roads were a distant thing in the terrain of the South, and the wheels of the Northern wagons were often not up to the passage of the more un-usual terrain. Mudlands were not uncommon, although the season had been dry; the Southerners were quiet when the Northern con-tingent of the army was forced, by the construction of those wheels, to dally in the marching light.

Valedan was silent as well. He had spent little time in the North

studying the logistics of mobile armies, and the idea that whole villages would rise around granaries and stockades built solely for the
transit of the forces was new to him. He watched, he listened, and
he learned, feeling the weight of his scant years as a failing.

"They will attack the train," Ramiro said, when the Commanders
gathered on the evening of the first day of Henden.

Commander Allen nodded grimly. "We have seen little sign of
their presence thus far."

Ramiro's brow rose. Ser Mareo kai di'Lamberto met his gaze,
held it a moment. "What would you counsel?"

"The supplies should be moved to the stockades," he said. "And
housed there, with Averdan supplies. The Lambertans carry their
food, and it, too, makes them more vulnerable."

"A stockade," Commander Ellora said, "is not without its vulnerability. It is not mobile. Its location is often known."

Ramiro shrugged. "If we are forced to abandon the stockades,
we will not leave them the supplies."

More, he did not offer.

Commander Allen shook his head. A map lay across a table beneath the broad beams of a low ceiling; magelights burned away
the shadows of poor windows, fading sun; their rounded glow lit
the whole of the flat Averdan surface as seen through the eyes and the
inks of cartographers.

This, too, was a risk, for the maps were Averdan.

But it was a time for risk; the time for safety—had it existed—
waned after the passing of the Festival Moon. "It has been too
quiet," Commander Allen said at last. "Since the loss of the border
villages, we have seen little movement from the General and his
forces."

Ser Ramiro lifted hand to chin; he stood a moment in contemplation. "Indeed," he said at last. "It has been quiet. What do you
suspect?"

"I don't. But were I Alesso di'Marente, I would not now sit and
wait unless there were reason for it."

Ser Mareo's eyes narrowed. He had become part of the council
of war, and he accepted the honor and the responsibility of this position—but he did not stand at the side of the Northerners, where it
was possible to avoid them, and he rarely answered questions they
posed.

He looked, now, at the map. "Our forces," he said at last, "are too
concentrated here."

"I concur," Commander Allen replied.

The silence was heavy and uncomfortable.

"Kai Leonne?"

"If we split our forces, and send Commander Allen to the South and West, Commander Kalakar to the South and East, what will happen?"

"If our scouts are correct, we will meet Marente with equal numbers, either to the South, the Southwest or the Southeast."

"And if they are incorrect?"

"They will attack us, and we will find it difficult to hold the line."

They spoke quietly, and they did not speak with condescension, but they clearly expected him to offer no answers. "Commander Allen?"

"He has to have more men than our scouts have counted. The banners of Oerta and Lorenza are clearly marked; the banner of the Tyr'agar is marked as well. The First and Second armies seem to be in place but . . ."

"But?"

"But they are small, to my eye. Did the kai Leonne—the previous kai Leonne—see fit to stand down whole units?"

Ser Ramiro frowned and shook his head.

"The Third army?"

"It is . . . scattered. Individual units will no doubt be on the field, but the Third army was Baredan di'Navarre's, and it is unlikely that Alesso di'Marente could assemble them in a march against Baredan di'Navarre without some justification."

"Even so," Commander Allen said, "the numbers are wrong. What have our scouts missed?"

Meralonne APhaniel shrugged. He was present; he was always present for these meetings. Pipe smoke rose from his lips in an almost insolent haze, and hovered above the magelights.

"We may have missed much," he said without concern. "Birds do not make the best scouts, and the armies of the South do not suffer their presence gladly. We have lost some handful to the Widan."

Baredan, silent to that point, nodded. "They will know. It is a tactic you used to advantage in the previous war. It is not one that they will fail to exploit now."

"And the trains?"

"It was also considered a weakness of the Imperial forces. He will be aware of those. But he will come from the South; the trains are in the North. The valleys provide some protection from attack, and they will continue to do so until the armies are close."

"What else will he be aware of?"

"More," Baredan responded. "It is not unlikely that among the cerdan gathered here, there are spies that serve Marente. It is difficult; the Widan arts are subtle and they are not always easily detected if their sole purpose is to deliver information."

This, too, was true.

"Understand," Baredan added, "that the General Marente has the Sword of Knowledge at his disposal; he has the Sword's Edge as his adviser. Very few of the Tyr'agnate can boast an equal power. The magics used in our skirmishes are often purchased—at some cost—from the Voyani; we do not have many of the Widan at our disposal, and those that we have in times of peace we will seldom suffer to accompany us in times of war."

"That would be a grave disadvantage," Commander Allen said.

"Indeed. It is one of the chief reasons why there has been so little open rebellion against the Tyr'agar. The cost of failure is the clan, and the chance of failure is high. The Sword of Knowledge serves—inasmuch as any man of power serves—the Tyr'agar."

"We have the magi."

Mareo kai di'Lamberto said nothing, but he nodded. "The magi are men. They make the same assumptions—whether warranted or no—that their masters do."

Valedan said, "There must be another army."

Commander Allen looked at the Tyr'agar a moment, and then he nodded. "I concur."

"He cannot use that army in Mancorvo; he owns perhaps the lower fifth of the Terrean, and the use of that army there would be questionable."

"He has used his forces in Mancorvo," Ser Mareo said. "They were not great in numbers, but they had the power of the Widan behind them. The power," he added, "of the Lord of Night."

"Do you think he has a greater force within your borders?"

The Lambertan kai shook his head. "If they are present, they are not on the move, and they have chosen to conceal themselves in all but the one case."

"If they were there—and they might be, as Marente could not depend upon Lamberto for support—they might simply await his orders. He could bring those armies here, to attack the Western flank."

Commander Allen frowned. "He could."

"You think it unlikely?"

"As you said, Tyr'agar, that border is too insecure. The kai Lamberto's men might guard it, and they will not be willing allies."

"Not all of them."

Valedan frowned. "There are only the two Terreans; Mancorvo would seem a more likely Terrean than Averda in which to act in secret."

A silence followed his words, and the Eagle's gaze narrowed; in the light, he looked like a hunting bird with wings suddenly folded, and descent a certainty.

"The ocean," he said.

General Alesso di'Marente looked up.

Sendari stood in the lee of the tent's entrance, his hands clutched around a tube that bore the markings of the Widan. "Word," he said quietly. He bowed; the bow was formal, and it offered Alesso brief warning.

As he entered the tent, Ser Jarrani kai di'Lorenza joined him, and following the kai Lorenza, Ser Eduardo kai di'Garrardi. They bowed.

"Enter," Alesso said. "We have much to discuss."

"Ser Sendari summoned us," Jarrani said.

Sendari handed Alesso the tube; no other hand could break the runes that glowed faintly with captured light. Not in safety.

He took what his Widan offered, and he held it a moment above the map. "The armies," he said.

"Lorenza has been ready to move for the better part of two days."

"Garrardi has likewise been prepared."

"Good." He smiled. "The Second army has now positioned itself. It lies across the delta of the River Arafeld; we own it. No Northerners will join the Callestans after this day, and some great part of their supplies will be seconded for our own use." He broke the sealed tube and pulled out the message that lay there. Reading it took little time; it contained what he expected. What he had, in fact, just stated.

"They will join us; we will make our way to the heart of the valleys. The kai Leonne's banner is there, surrounded by the banner of the Callestan Tyr and those who serve him."

Ser Jarrani frowned. "Lamberto?"

"We must assume, given Damar, that he stands—or will stand—with them."

"His numbers?"

"Not yet clear. They will be, and soon."

"And the Serra Diora?"

Ser Jarrani's frown was brief; it touched his lips and brow, but did not hover.

Alesso smiled. "Yes, Ser Eduardo, we have found your Serra. She is with the armies of the Callestan Tyr, and she will remain there until we retrieve her."

"Good. We will set out today."

"Tomorrow," Alesso contradicted. "The Second army does not move quickly, but it moves; we want to meet it. Without the numbers the army will provide, we will be in a much weaker position."

It was not to the kai Garrardi's liking, but he said nothing.

Alesso took a deeper breath. "We have, however, a more pressing difficulty."

"And that?"

"The Shining Court."

Kiriel knew these valleys.

She had never walked them, but she knew them. She studied their rise and fall, and she watched in a hush of heartbeat and silence.

The Serra Diora had taken the liberty of leaving her tent for the dusk; she would return to it before night had fallen, and the men who now gathered to either side of her would see her there in safety. They did not speak; they did not approach. But they allowed no other to approach her either, and Kiriel thought this precaution a wise one; she could see the men who gathered at the fringes of their party, and their light was often drowned in a darkness that spoke of coming choice. She did not trust them.

But then again, she didn't trust anyone. Or she shouldn't have.

She turned to the Serra Diora. "I'm sorry," she said quietly, meaning the words, "but I missed what you said."

The Serra smiled. "You are a strange warrior, Kiriel di'Ashaf. You are not a Serra, you are not a seraf, you are not cerdan. You can hear the slightest movement of leaf a mile away, but you often miss the word that is spoken scant feet from you."

Kiriel smiled. Could not help but smile. She loved the sound of the Serra's voice, and there was very little that the Serra could slip into that voice that would have met with disapproval. "I often miss words that are spoken if they contain no threat."

"Ah. You would find life in a harem difficult, then."

"I find life difficult," Kiriel said quietly. Her hand fell to the hilt of her sword; it was cold. Stark contrast to the heat of day, the height of sun. She said, "Where are we, Serra?"

"In the Averdan valleys."

"But we have been walking two days now."

"Almost three. The Averdan valleys stretch across most of the length of the Terrean, and they are wider by far than any other valleys of note in the Dominion. They are verdant," she added, "and highly prized; much of the food that feeds the Dominion of Annagar comes from the valleys."

"Then why risk it to armies?"

Serra Diora shook her head slightly, gaze grazing the silent shoulders of the Tyran that were her honor guard. "I am not a soldier," she said quietly. "Not a warrior. It is not a question that I have ever asked. But if I were to make a guess—and it would be, at best, the guess of a Serra who has never gone to war—I would say that they do not willingly risk it; the armies come to the valleys, because there is food here, and armies must be fed. It is difficult to stop them if they have gained the borders of Averda."

They had; the Ospreys all knew it.

"But the valleys afford the army some advantage, if that army holds the heights; they afford the Tyr'agnate of Averda advantage, for he knows the terrain. They house the granaries which feed the army; they hide the roads upon which the army marches." She smiled. "And they speak to the cerdan. They seem to speak to you."

Kiriel nodded. "They do," she said softly. Her hand touched her breast, but she did not speak of what lay beneath armor and surcoat. Nor did the Serra ask.

But the Serra fell silent as Kiriel suddenly turned.

"Kiriel?"

"Men," she said quietly. "Horsed men; some hundreds, I think."

"Where?"

"To the South. They come, now, and with speed."

The Tyran shifted a single glance between themselves, as if it were too hot to hold for long. They were caught, Kiriel realized, with a hint of dark amusement, in an unfortunate predicament; they could not hear the horsemen, they did not doubt her word, and they would lose face if they appeared to take heed of the words of women upon the field of battle.

This much, at least, she had come to understand about the South. She waited.

At last the oldest of the Callestan Tyran, Ser Miko, nodded

grimly. "Serra," he said, bowing to Serra Diora, "it is time for us to return you to your tent."

She nodded at once, for she accepted their word as law, but her gaze lingered a moment upon Kiriel's motionless face. She gathered her skirts slowly, Kiriel thought, taking care to leave no silk upon the trodden undergrowth, the flattened, slender stalks of saplings.

Because she took this time, because she gave the appearance of perfect obedience, the Tyran could say nothing; they were trapped by her delicate grace. The horses that had first caught Kiriel's ear now thundered at a distance; the Tyran looked up, and as one man, they drew their single-edged swords, waiting; the time for flight had passed.

Diora waited as well, behind the line of Tyran; behind Kiriel.

The Northern women were as strange as the demons to the Tyran. They were not in need of protection; did not demand it, and would not accept it.

Kiriel drew her blade last. She shouldn't have, and knew it, but she was filled with a momentary desire to impress the Serra Diora. Stupid, that. Stupid, stupid. But she felt no regret.

The banner came into view, and even in the light of dusk, it was clear: but what it said, Kiriel could not read. She saw the rays of the sun, but she could not count them; she knew that the sun was rising, and not ascendant. Tor, she thought, then, frowning.

Something about the standard itself was familiar. It was dark; blue, she thought, although the fading light made it somewhat darker. She saw the glimmer of gold; light was there, to gild it, light to mark it.

The Serra Diora said, "Valente."

And the word struck Kiriel like a blow. She staggered; the weight of pendant had shifted, dragging at her neck. *Valente.*

"Ashaf," she said softly. "Ashaf kep'Valente."

She had not meant to speak the name aloud. Had not even known that the name existed until it left her lips. But it had. A seraf's name.

Ashaf's name.

She turned and saw that Diora now stared at her. She wanted to deny the truth of the words, but it was late, for that. Ashaf had been a seraf. Ashaf had been a slave.

She had known it on some level; she had thought of Ashaf as a woman who had never known freedom. But this . . . was different.

As if the enormity of that truth were spell, it held her, and the men continued their headlong rush down the road. The horses kicked up clods of dirt, and sent it flying; they were not clean, these great beasts; they were not rested. Foam flecked their muzzles, sweat glistened upon their coats. They had been ridden, and hard, down the length of the valley.

And at their head, the banner of Valente flew.

"Summon the Tyr'agnate," Ser Miko said quietly. His words should have been lost to the hooves of horses; they were mute, to Kiriel's ear. But the order had been heard; two of the Tyran detached themselves from the thin line and ran back toward the building that now housed their Tyr.

She did not watch them go.

Instead, she watched the men approach, her eyes glinting in the dusk. No Lord here, she thought. No Lady. Just men.

And riding at their head, a man she did—and could not—recognize. The gem was blazing now; the hollow in her throat must be a vast cavern of blistered flesh, an empty socket in which a second heart now hung, vast and impenetrable.

She turned to Diora, stricken, and Diora shook her head. And spoke. **"They cannot see it, Kiriel di'Ashaf. They cannot see it unless you draw it. Do not draw it."**

And she realized that what could not be seen had been joined by what could not be heard. Later, she would understand the significance of the gift. Now, comforted, she turned.

She should have left the road. She knew it. Duarte would be angry. Then again, she was Sentrus, the lowest of the low; there wasn't much farther down she could go, and Duarte had shown, time and again, that he did not have the taste for physical cruelty. It was a weakness.

Kiriel had always told him it was a weakness.

The Tor'agar, Ser Danello kai di'Valente, traveled the road, and she stood, ten feet from the Callestan Tyran, waiting.

Some signal passed back among the riding men, like a wave in tall grass. She watched the ripple move, watched the horses slow, and at last, when the Tor'agar was almost upon her, when his banner was at its height, and the dusk had almost given way to the full of the Lady's night, she found her knees.

Kneeling, she waited.

She realized her mistake almost immediately; this was not her natural posture. This was a Southern form, a Southern act of prostration. He would understand it, and he would understand nothing.

But he did stop. The Tyran did not bend before him; it was their right, perhaps their duty, to remain standing. But the Serra Diora knelt, her posture the more perfect of the two, and she, too, waited in the road, without the benefit of seraf, of mat beneath her silks.

He did not speak to them; he spoke above their bent backs, and Kiriel felt both annoyance and relief. They warred with each other, her memories and the memories of the woman who had been like mother, and in the end, she gave the latter their due. She remained as she was.

"The Tor'agar, Ser Danello kai di'Valente, rides to war," a man said. Not the Tor.

"The Tyr'agnate of Averda bids you stop," one of the Tyran replied. Miko, she thought.

"The Tor obeys the Tyr," the man replied. Formulaic, the response, but heavy with meaning. "He has ridden with the men he could muster; he will fight by the Tyr's side, upon the field of his choosing."

Ser Miko said, "The Tyr'agnate serves the Tyr'agar, Ser Valedan kai di'Leonne. It is his banner that controls the field. If you would approach, you must be aware of this."

Now, the men spoke. Their words melded, losing the distinct edge of syllable; like leaves in a windblown tree, they rustled. But it was not yet fall; they did not scatter.

The men held their ground.

The Tor'agar rode forward.

"Where is the kai Leonne, Ser Miko di'Callesta?"

"He is to be found by the side of the Tyrs."

"The Tyrs?"

"The Mancorvan Tyr, Ser Mareo kai di'Lamberto, has joined the Leonne forces; his banner flies beside the Callestan banner; his men are camped beyond the bend in the road."

Again, the men spoke. This time, their voices carried a name, two names. She heard anger, but she did not lift her head; the pendant weighted her neck, holding it in place.

"I would speak with the Tyr'agnate of Averda," Ser Danello said at last. "We will wait his pleasure here, upon the road."

"He has been summoned," Ser Miko replied. "And we will wait with you."

Ser Danello did not speak again for some minutes. And when he did, he spoke not to the Tyran, but to the women who groveled on the ground before his great horse.

In the fading light, Kiriel thought the horse brown; she could not be certain; she could see his hooves, the flashings around his legs, the glimmer of chain—barding?—that overhung his knees. More, she could not see. Did not try.

"Rise."

Her legs moved before she understood that the words were meant for her; for her and the Serra Diora.

The Serra, likewise, rose, unfolding with perfect, unconscious grace. She wore no armor; she made no noise as she unfolded. The same could not be said for Kiriel; the metal against metal sounded wrong to her ears. She knew a moment of fear that was completely foreign, and understood it as Ashaf's.

Yet it was not fear *of* this man; it was a different fear, a subtle one. As if she feared to embarrass him. She did not fear for her life.

She lifted her head last, and she met the grave eyes of the Tor'agar.

His face was familiar. Older, she thought; much older than it should be. His hair was still dark, but time had grayed its edges; in the night, in the warmth of lamplight, lines could be seen around eyes and lips, etched there by sun, by wind. The sands did not come to the valleys, and the kai Valente was of the valleys.

Ashaf had been of the valleys. Kiriel knew it now.

"I do not recognize you," he said quietly, to the Serra Diora.

"I am Serra Diora en'Leonne."

"Ah." He tipped his chin a moment, from the height of a horse that was, indeed, brown. "And your companion?"

"She is of the North, Tor'agar."

His frown was sharper, edged with danger. "The North?"

"The Northern armies are here, under the banner of Leonne."

"Of Leonne, and not Callesta?"

"Callesta is here under the banner of Leonne," she said quietly. "But more than that, I do not know. Forgive me, Tor'agar, for my ignorance."

His brow rose. "That would be little to forgive," he replied at last. "For the Flower of the Dominion was not known for ignorance."

She said nothing, but lowered her gaze until it rested upon the chest of the destrier.

He turned, then, to Kiriel. "And you?" He spoke Torra.

She answered in Torra. "I am Kiriel di'Ashaf."

He frowned. "What did you say?"

"I am Kiriel di'Ashaf."

"That is not . . . a Northern name."

"No, Tor'agar." She bowed her head. Lifted it again, with some struggle. "It is not."

"And the clan, Ashaf, must not be a Southern clan, or a minor one indeed, if it surrenders its women to the Northern armies."

Kiriel said nothing.

"But I knew an Ashaf," he said.

"Ashaf kep'Valente," she replied. His eyes were night eyes now. The moon was bright. Sudden in her rise, in her dominance. Had so much time passed?

"Ashaf kep'Valente," he said quietly. "Ashaf en'Valente. Yes. How come you to know her name?"

Now, now the words were hard and large; they would not leave her throat. She swallowed and they lodged there, painful in the silence.

"She was a seraf in one of my villages."

Kiriel said nothing.

"And wife to my father, before his death. She vanished without trace almost seventeen years ago."

Kiriel nodded. Her mouth was dry. The desert—winter or summer—had descended, taken root within her. Mute, she gazed at his face.

"We searched for her," he continued. "My serafs searched. We found nothing. Rumors of a stranger who had come to visit. Rumors of the presence of the Havallan Voyani." His frown deepened. "For that reason, our relations with the Havallan Voyani have been . . . cold . . . these past two decades.

"Come, Kiriel di'Ashaf. Tell me what you know."

"She is dead," Kiriel replied. "I would have spared her that, but I came late. She is dead."

"And you bear her name."

"It is the only thing of hers that I bear. Her name."

"Why?"

"I came late," she told him. The words burned.

"You choose to honor her."

Honor was too meager, too insignificant a word. Kiriel wanted to say more to this man. Ashaf might have. But Ashaf was gone, and the memory that lingered was not enough—barely—to compel. Silence reigned.

It was broken by the steady clip of hooves. The Tyrs had arrived.

*   *   *

The Tor Danello kai di'Valente was a tall man. His hair was dark, and his beard, dark as well, although silver had worked its way into the fold of his chin. His eyes were set in front of a hawk's nose.

Ashaf had liked this man. But Ashaf had never seen him as a man; even grown, even titled, he had been a boy to her, a harem boy. She had treated his rank with the respect and deference that was its due, and he had publicly accepted—and expected—no less. But Ashaf had always believed that he cared for her.

The truth was there now, in the night of his face. Kiriel could see it; he was angry. Cold.

The Tyr'agnate, Ramiro kai di'Callesta, rode just behind Valedan kai di'Leonne. He dismounted only after the Tyr'agar dismounted, and he did not suffer his banner to be carried to the field. Only the Tyr'agar's banner flew in the growing depths of night, but the lamps marked it clearly, lending warmth to gold.

"Ser Danello," Ramiro di'Callesta said.

"Ser Ramiro." He, too, dismounted; the men at his back followed, their movements stiff but somehow perfect. The ride, she thought, had been both hard and long.

The horses were skittish. They nickered, tossing their reins, their manes like smoke at their backs. The Southerners brought them some calm by the expedient of word and hand, but the calm was superficial.

They were afraid, Kiriel thought, of her.

Valedan raised a brow in her direction, but he did not speak. Not yet. Instead, he turned to the Tor'agar and he nodded.

A minute passed; the Tor'agar's glance shifted from the face of the Callestan Tyr to the boy by his side.

"The Tyr'agar, Ser Valedan kai di'Leonne," Ramiro said. The words were edged; the command in them was clear.

Still, it was a moment before Ser Danello kai di'Valente chose to bend at the knee. His sword remained in its scabbard, and the sword, in the South, was the greater prostration.

Valedan did not acknowledge the slight.

"Ser Danello," Ramiro kai di'Callesta said softly, "we did not expect you here."

"No, Tyr'agnate. We have ridden in haste, with the forces we could muster. We have come to join your banner."

"And your Torrean?"

The hesitation was marked.

"Come, Ser Danello. Join us. We have adjourned our council of war to come to the road, but we have much to discuss."

The kai Valente nodded.

"Sentrus," Valedan said quietly. "See the Serra Diora to her rooms, and after she is safely ensconced, join us." It was not a request.

Kiriel di'Ashaf nodded quietly.

"Na'dio."

Serra Diora looked up. But she looked slowly.

The Havallan Matriarch, bracketed on either side by canes and shadowed by the Serra Teresa, stood in the entranceway of the small room. Silks had been exchanged for Voyani wear; this disquieted Diora, although she did not speak.

The tents suited the Voyani better than the rooms in the stockade, and Yollana had made this clear. She made much clear; the Callestans and the Lambertans found little to agree on, but their dislike of the garrulous old woman was one of the few things that drew them together.

Had it been just an act, a move in a larger game, Serra Diora would have applauded the Matriarch. But she knew better; she had journeyed by her side for too long.

"Matriarch." She rose when the Serra Teresa caught her eye, and came, pliant and obedient, to the Matriarch's side. It fooled no one.

"You spend time with the Northern girl," Yollana said. "Kiriel di'Ashaf."

Diora nodded. It was, after all, what she expected to hear.

But the warning, the witchery, the veiled hint of seer's wisdom, did not follow. Instead, Yollana asked, "What do you think of her?" The old woman was still canny; her words sounded casual, but they were a wall; they let nothing out.

The Serra shrugged delicately, but it was not a delicate motion; it was a defiant one.

"Na'dio," Teresa said quietly.

"She is a Northerner," Diora replied. "And a warrior. We have little in common."

"Aie, you see, Na'tere."

Teresa nodded. "Diora."

"You know she's dangerous," Yollana snapped. No question, there. The Matriarch rummaged a moment in her satchel and came up with a pipe.

"She is dangerous."

"Perhaps you don't know who she is."

"No. I don't."

Yollana snorted. Her single eye rolled a moment in her face, half an expression of frustration. "Be grateful you are not one of mine," she said darkly.

Diora bowed her head.

"Na'dio," the Matriarch continued, after a ring of smoke had escaped her lips and now lingered near her mouth. The desert had not left her cracked, parched lips, and Diora thought it never would; it resided in the whole of her face: Sand, sun, and wind. "You have carried the Heart of Arkosa."

Diora was still.

"What the Heart sees, the heart sees," she said, continuing to breath acrid smoke into the small room. That she knew it annoyed was clear; that she took some satisfaction in it, clearer.

"Does she wear anything unusual?"

"Her sword," Diora said quietly. "It is not natural, and at times, when the sky is darkest, I can almost hear it speak."

This stopped Yollana a moment, and her face seemed to pale. But although she drew a circle across the air, she did not falter. "That is all?"

Diora made no reply.

"Na'dio," Teresa said, her voice wholly devoid of power, but not of command. It was the first time, since the loss, that Diora did not resent it.

"She is not your wife," Yollana said sharply. "She is no man's wife. Do not seek to protect her."

"I could not," Diora replied. "I am Serra. She is soldier."

Teresa drew away from the Matriarch, and entered the room. Without looking back, she said, "Tell her, Yollana."

"Na'tere—"

"Tell her."

"And will you take responsibility for the knowledge?"

"She will," Teresa said quietly. "She understands war. This is the war she has chosen."

And smoke filled the room, the stale breath of ancient dragon, long past the prime of fire. But not of death, Diora thought. Not of danger.

"She calls herself Kiriel di'Ashaf," Yollana said quietly. "And Ashaf is a name I know well."

Her voice was still surface, would never be anything more. But the words were significant. Diora met her eye.

"Almost seventeen years ago," Yollana continued, retreating behind the surface of those words, her shoulders straightening, "I came to the village of Russo, and I spoke with a seraf there. An older woman. An old woman, by your standards.

"She was not lovely, although in her youth she had been; she was concubine to the Tor's father, and she hated the life. The son had some affection for her, and when the father died, he gave her her freedom, and a home in the village of her birth.

"He gave her permission to marry, and she married; she bore children there. None survived."

The beginning of a story. Diora knelt slowly.

"A stranger came to the village of Russo, shortly after the death of her last living child. He . . . offered her a position. I knew what she had been offered," Yollana added, her voice softer now—a younger woman's voice. "I knew that she would leave the Torrean, the Terrean; that she would die in the cold and the white of a distant desert."

"You saw this?"

"Ah, no. But I knew it, Serra Diora. And I knew where it was that she would go.

"We have prepared for this war for the whole of our line's existence. We have watched, and we have waited, and we have lived upon the open road until no other road defines us.

"Where she went, we could not follow. What she would see, we could not see. And what she would learn, we *must* learn. Do you understand, Na'dio?"

And Diora did.

"I gave Ashaf kep'Valente a parting gift. A pendant, I told her. A piece of jewelry that was worn only by the Voyani, and only by their women. She had seen similar pendants in her time, and she accepted this. I gave her some ability to use it. She was told that it was simply a pendant in which to trap memory. A piece of home." Yollana's pipe was an orange glow; ashes ringed the flame. "But you have seen it, haven't you?"

Diora said nothing.

"Na'dio."

"Yes." Diora surrendered the word quietly. "And more. It is Kiriel's. It is the only thing that remains of the woman she thought of as mother. She will not surrender it without a fight, and you will not fight her."

"I may have to."

"Then you will perish, Yollana, and you will leave the war to your daughter."

"I wish to speak with her."

"You may speak," Diora said softly. "But speak with care. Yes, she bears the Heart of Havalla. No, she does not know what she carries. She knows only that it was Ashaf's. She will not surrender it."

"Without it, we will not win this battle."

"And with it? Is there a guarantee of victory?"

Yollana said coldly, "You are not a child, Diora. You know the answer to the question."

"You intend to take it from her. You intend to leave."

"Yes."

"This eve."

"Yes."

Diora shook her head. "She will not surrender it." Her hand, pale and perfect, touched the hollow of her throat, as if seeking the comfort of a similar weight. It was gone, but the ghost of its memory remained. "And even if she could—"

"What Evallen did, I did not do," Yollana replied. "Nor could I, and live. The pendant will not cling to Kiriel; it will leave her. And if I am any judge, it will leave gladly."

"Have care," Diora replied. "Do *you* know who she is, Matriarch?"

"I know who she must be," Yollana replied. "Although I do not know how she came to be here, with the Northerners. It is the Lady's grace." She slumped into her canes. "You value her. I do not understand why, but it is clear that you have chosen to . . . defend her.

"Speak with her. Tell her. Ask of her what must be asked. We will wait."

The kai Valente froze in the doorway, his hand upon the frame.

Ramiro had offered no warning; this was a test, both of courage and resolve. What the kai Valente did here would define him, in Callestan eyes: worthy liege, or less. There were few places upon the paths of war in which Court law ruled; this was one. Here, and beneath the banners of the Tyrs, etiquette was more than a skill; it was an act of survival.

The kai Valente was not like his father. The former Tor'agar had been both cruel and cunning, a man of vast ambition and pragmatic loyalties. Ramiro had admired him—at a safe distance. He had not, however, been surprised when he had died in a riding accident. Serra Amara had privately guessed that he might die peacefully, in his sleep. A harem death.

They were not unknown, although they were rare; Ramiro had

visited the Valente harem, by his father's side, and he privately concurred. He had therefore taken care to cultivate the son, and had found it less difficult than it might have otherwise been, for the wives were fond of the son, and they owed him a loyalty that cruelty and fear could not engender.

And the son had proved to have some of his late mother's cunning; it was different in almost all ways from the father's, but it had served him well. Ser Danello now stood upon the threshold, his Tyr's watchful eyes upon his still face.

After a moment, he drew breath and rose. He did not glance at his Tyr, but instead moved across the almost empty floor to where Ser Mareo kai di'Lamberto stood, watchful in his silence, keen in his appraisal. He wore the midnight of blue, the pale of white; mourning colors. And he wore a sash that made clear who those mourning colors were for.

"Tyr'agnate," the kai Valente said, offering the kai Lamberto the deepest and most formal of bows.

"Tor'agar," Mareo replied. He did not hesitate; he returned the bow, shading it slightly in the direction of superior rank, but offering, in its depth, a real respect. "I have often heard of Ser Danello kai di'Valente, and it has been one of my regrets that he has never tendered his service to Lamberto."

Ramiro lifted a dark brow; Mareo did not condescend to notice.

"It is said—by the Radann—that the clansmen who administer your villages are good men; that the serafs who labor in your fields are both honest and protected. It is also said, again by the Radann, that you have set an example that the Tor'agnate who serve under you have been compelled to live up to.

"In all, Ser Danello, you have been a credit to Callesta for the whole of your reign."

Ser Danello was gifted; he did not show obvious pride or pleasure at the compliment—and he was a man; he must have felt them. Instead, he said, "The Tyr'agnate of Averda has set such a high example to his Tors that we are honor bound to do the same; what comes from above trickles down. Like rain," he said with a smile, "or the fall of water from the heights of the valley's hidden folds." After a moment, he added, "The caliber of the lieges of Lamberto must indeed likewise be high."

Ser Mareo kai di'Lamberto laughed out loud. It was a deep sound, textured with a genuine amusement and a genuine pleasure. The first such laughter that Ramiro kai di'Callesta had yet heard.

Ser Danello kai di'Valente kept answering smile from his face.

"And the Tyr'agar," he said, after the sound had muted, the smile lingering like echo, "must be blessed indeed, for the two best Tyrs of Annagar now serve his banner and his cause.

"Could Valente do otherwise?"

Yet, having spoken, he turned his attention to the Commanders who stood apart in the large room. They were silent; they watched, but they did not interfere.

Ser Mareo kai di'Lamberto stepped back, waiting.

This, too, was a test.

Ser Danello turned to Valedan kai di'Leonne.

Valedan nodded and stepped forward. "Ser Danello kai di'Valente," he said, speaking with perfect Torra accent, "may I introduce you to Commander Bruce Allen, and Commander Ellora AKalakar, of the Imperial army."

Commander Allen stepped forward, and extended a hand. It was a Northern gesture; a purely Northern gesture.

Ser Danello kai di'Valente looked at the hand a moment, and then, taking a breath, stepped forward, extending his own. It was not a Southern greeting, and he performed the politeness awkwardly.

"Verrus Korama AKalakar," Valedan continued, as another Northern stepped forward.

"Yes," Ramiro said quietly. "Rumors are true, in this case. We ride with the Northern armies at our side."

Ser Danello, obviously accomplished with words, took refuge in silence; it was safest.

"You know of Ser Anton di'Guivera," Valedan continued.

Ser Danello nodded as the former Leonne swordmaster stepped forward. "I do," he said, and for an instant, his expression was a youth's expression, shorn of the changes that life makes. "Ser Anton."

"Ser Danello," Anton replied gravely. "We have met seldom; it is rare indeed that bandits have reigned in the Green Valley. Your cerdan are vigilant."

"My cerdan," Ser Danello replied quietly, "live by your example, Ser Anton. What must be done, they do, and for like reason; they protect their kin—and mine—from the losses that the bandits might otherwise cause." He bowed. He held the bow.

"I serve the Tyr'agar, Valedan kai di'Leonne," Ser Anton said. "I serve him willingly, and without reservation. I have traveled by his side since he left the land of the demon Kings; I have seen his sword work, and I have seen his enemies. They are my enemies now."

"You were in the North?"

"For the Kings' Challenge."

"Ah."

"Ser Valedan kai di'Leonne might have won their wreath and their crown," he added quietly, "were it not for his decision to accept a Southern challenge upon that hallowed ground. It is said that few men may choose their masters in the South; power chooses for them.

"In my case what is said is not true; I have made my choice, and I have been honored by its acceptance." He glanced at the Commanders. "What Valedan kai di'Leonne learned in the North, I cannot say; I am not *of* the North. But what is Southern in him the North could not dislodge; there is no weakness there."

Ser Danello bowed.

Ramiro raised a brow, but he did not speak. Ser Anton's words were not refined, and they were not subtle, but it was not for subtlety that the swordmaster was known.

"Why have you ridden in haste, Ser Danello?" Valedan asked.

Ser Danello straightened his shoulders. "We have brought word," he said quietly, "and men."

"The men are welcome; they are known, and they are valuable. But the word, I would hear."

"The forces of the General Marente are in the valleys. They are three days' ride from my borders; they will take the villages. Their forces far outnumber my own."

Valedan glanced at Ramiro, and then he nodded.

Ramiro said heavily, "It was as we expected. Have you emptied the villages?"

"We did not wish to give more warning than our flight would give," he replied. "I have . . . taken some precautions with my city; my harem is scattered and in hiding, my kai is by my side." He bowed his head.

"Commander Allen?" The kai Leonne said quietly.

Commander Allen shook his head. "Commander Berriliya has his men by the delta; they would not arrive in time to halt the progress through the Southern valleys, and if the numbers of the Marente army are in truth as we suspect, we would lose that encounter."

"Then we will surrender the villages," Ramiro replied. His face was smooth as the flat of his blade, and just as cold. "We have been waiting for his movement, but we were . . . uninformed of this turn of events. We will withdraw to the North, and we will wait."

*   *   *

"No!"

As one man, they turned in the silence that single word evoked.

One of the Northerners who served Valedan kai di'Leonne personally stood in the door, her hands bunched in fists, the white of her face as pale as fine ivory. But her eyes were dark; darker than the whole of the Lady's night. They invoked a different night, a hint of their ancient enemy.

Ser Danello's hand had dropped to his sword; Ser Mareo's, likewise. Ramiro was chagrined to note that his own hand had fallen to the hilt of *Bloodhame*. Had there been more to witness it, it might have gone ill.

But Ser Anton did not touch sword; the Commanders did not. And notably, Valedan kai di'Leonne did not; he stood in silence as Kiriel di'Ashaf approached him. Ser Andaro di'Corsarro, still as shadow, stepped up to join his Tyr's side, but he did not draw blade. He waited.

"Sentrus," Valedan said. He spoke in Weston, and by choosing the foreign tongue, emphasized the differences between their two cultures.

She stepped forward as if the rank had no meaning—and it was the slightest of the Northern ranks; it had little.

But Ramiro had seen her fight. He knew how dangerous she could be, when she desired combat. He waited, forcing his hand to his side.

Ser Fillipo, as silent as Ser Andaro had been, joined him—but significantly, he did not touch his weapon. As if the shadow and darkness about the girl could be controlled or caged, as if it represented no threat at all to the Tyr'agar or the men who had, by circumstance and beguilement, chosen to fight under his banner, he stood at ease.

"Tyr'agar," she said. She accented the words in Weston, choosing to follow Valedan's lead.

"Is there a danger here?"

Her hesitation was clumsy and profound. She opened her mouth, her eyes narrowing; Ramiro thought she would lie.

But in the end, Valedan was Valedan, and his command of the Ospreys unique. She said, "Not to the army."

"Then why do you gainsay the Tyr'agnate? He is well versed in the terrain; he will lead us to the best vantage for defense. The villages are his; the Tor'agar of Valente himself does not believe they can be preserved."

She said, lifting a shaking hand until it hovered over her heart's center, "then dismiss me, Tyr'agar. Dismiss me, and I will go South."

"I will not strip myself of your protection," he countered. Ser Ramiro wondered just how much of the conversation Ser Danello understood; few of the Tors had chosen to study Weston.

She hesitated again, and then said, "I have to protect one of those villages. I've sworn to protect it. I've given my oath."

"To who?"

"To the dead," she whispered. For just a moment, her eyes shone clearly, and the night dispersed. "I have fought by your side; I have fought in your service. I have faced the servants of the Lord of Night, and I will face them again at your command.

"But I will not—I cannot—desert those villages."

"Kiriel—"

"And if you must leave them, you must. I'm not a Tor or a Tyr; I'm not a Commander. I'm only barely an Osprey. But—" her hesitation grew.

After a marked silence, she fell to her knees. The gesture was profoundly awkward; Ramiro wondered if she had *ever* bent knee before a greater lord in the North.

"I ask it," she said quietly. "Dismiss me. Let me go South. I will make them pay, and pay dearly, for any damage they do there."

He frowned. "Sentrus, rise."

But she did not. She bowed her head a moment, and then she said, "I cannot leave this place."

Commander Ellora AKalakar stepped forward. "Sentrus." Her voice was harsh and grating; a man's voice, trapped in a woman's throat.

Kiriel did not acknowledge her. And Ramiro knew enough to know that she was of the Kalakar forces.

"Please, Valedan," she whispered.

This, too, shocked the Tyrs and the Tor; they were silent at her boldness.

But the kai Leonne met her gaze and held it for a long, long time, and then he turned to the Averdan Tyr. "We will keep the villages," he said quietly.

Ramiro's brows rose.

"On the morrow, we will move South. Let us build the line of our defense around Valente territories."

Commander Allen said, "Tyr'agar—"

But Valedan shook his head. "I owe her my life," he told them quietly, sliding into Torra. "I owe her that much. She—and she alone—can stand against the most powerful servants of the Lord of Night. I do not understand what ties the Sentrus to Valente, but it is clear that those ties cannot be broken in honor. I will stay," he said again, drawing strength from the words. He turned to the Commanders, to the Tyrs, and said, "See that it is done."

CHAPTER TWELVE

THE TEXTURE of the silence spoke of storm; the wind was howling in the stillness. Ser Danello kai di'Valente stared at the Tyr'agar as if he only suddenly understood the significance of his presence here, among Tyrs, upon the field of war. The Lord's field; the Lord's chosen field.

Valedan said, "Rise, Sentrus."

Kiriel rose.

"Go. Tell the Primus that his presence is required."

She started to speak, saw his face, and saluted instead. No Osprey had ever tendered so exact, so perfect, a salute. She left the room to the Commanders and the Generals, wondering what her absence would mean; she knew enough to know two things: they were shocked, and they did not approve. But she felt something else as well, something strange.

Her hands were shaking. It was not their emotion, but hers, that she had begun to recognize. Memory.

Ashaf.

"Isladar says I'm to trust no one."

Bent with age, hands not yet stiff with cold, though in time they would be, Ashaf's back faced the tower window. It was open, although not even wind could enter, but it was cool. Kiriel did not feel the cold.

"No one but Lord Isladar?"

"No. No one." She paused. "Why did you teach me this word?" She was young. She could not say how young; if she truly shared some part of her heritage with the *Kialli*, perfect memory had nonetheless been denied her. A failing, Isladar had said, of her mortality: the inability to remember.

And a kindness.

She hadn't understood, then, how a flaw could also be a kindness—and kindness was not a word that Isladar often used, so she
hadn't asked him. She understood now. Wondered how much else
she would grow to understand in time. Time was not her friend.

Ashaf turned away from the window, pulling her shawl close. It
was threadbare, the old shawl, something that she had taken from
her home in the distant South, and still cherished. She had been offered much finer, but she had disdained the offer. *Never accept a gift
when you do not know the price you will be asked to pay for it.*

"I taught you the word because it is important to me."

"But Isladar says it is a weakness."

"It is. But so am I, Kiriel."

Kiriel frowned.

"Look at me. I cannot even leave the tower or the least of the kin
will kill me. If the kin fail, the cold will not. And if neither kills me,
because I am hidden here, age will. I am weak."

Kiriel didn't like the words. But she didn't argue with them.

"Because I am weak, I value things that Lord Isladar doesn't understand. Trust," she added quietly, "is one of them. Love is another.
Have you spoken to Lord Isladar of love?"

Kiriel was silent.

"No, then. You should ask him."

"Love isn't trust."

"No."

Silence again. Ashaf looked at Kiriel's face and then reached out
to touch the underside of her chin, tracing the pale white of jaw and
cheek. Only Ashaf did this. Only Ashaf was allowed. Not even Isladar touched her face, although he sometimes lifted her and held
her in his arms. Arms that never shook.

Arms that were never warm.

Understanding gained a foothold in her mind. It was true that she
did not know how old she had been, then, but she knew she had
been old enough. She said, "I trust you." It was half question.

"Yes, Na'kiri. And I trust you."

"Because you are weak?"

It was an honest question. So many of the pointed questions, so
many of the words with their hidden edges, explicable only to people with the age and experience to know they'd been cut, had been
honest. Cruelty would come later, before the end.

"Yes," Ashaf said. "Because I am weak." But her arms tightened.

"But I'm not weak."

"No."

"I won't be weak. Isladar says if I'm weak, I'll die."

Ashaf nodded. "Yes. But if you—who are strong—cannot learn how to be weak, you will never learn to live."

"But, Ashaf, I'm alive."

"There is a difference, Na'kiri, between living and being alive."

"Are you alive?"

She couldn't see Ashaf's face, she could see the window, and beyond it, the utter whiteness of the Northern wastes. The wind seemed to be the whole of the old woman's answer, but after a time, Ashaf said, "Yes."

It sounded like "No."

"We are alone here," she continued. "Ashaf and Na'kiri. Kiriel and her Ashaf. If we do not trust one another, who can we trust?"

"We're not supposed to trust anyone."

Ashaf lifted her off her feet.

"We are not demons," Ashaf told her quietly. "And mortals, people who know life and death, must trust. And love."

"And hate?"

"And hate, too, if it comes to that. Although I hope you never have cause to hate."

"There's no one else to trust." Kiriel told her.

"Not yet, Na'kiri. But I pray to the Lady every night. I pray that you will find someone that you can trust. I pray that you will be someone that someone else can trust."

"But why?"

"Because I do not want you to be alone," Ashaf had said.

"But I'll never be alone. I have you."

Memory stopped.

By force of will, by dint of terror, it stopped.

"Sentrus?"

Kiriel looked around the room. Alexis was there. Fiara. Auralis. And in their center, looking bored and slightly irritable, Primus Duarte.

She offered him the perfect salute. She knew it would do nothing to calm his expression; she'd done it to annoy. Wondered why.

"Kiriel."

"Valedan sent me."

He was alert. The change was instant, tension devouring boredom and leaving the edge of suspicion in his slightly narrowed eyes. He did not trust her. He had never trusted her. But he had given her a home.

She would never understand Duarte AKalakar.

"What does the Tyr'agar want? Does he require my presence?"

She nodded.

"Kiriel," Auralis said. He came to stand beside her as if she needed help. Auralis trusted her. Alexis did not. Fiara didn't care enough either way. Kiriel thought of them all. Cook forced himself to trust her, and he did—mostly. Sanderton trusted her completely, but he was so much younger than she was, than she had ever been. Were these her people, truly hers?

"Valedan says that we will travel to the edge of Valente."

"But the Tor of Valente is here."

She nodded. "He came with his men." And waited.

"And why are we to go to Valente? Are the kin there now?"

"I don't know." But a different answer came on the heels of the first. "No."

"Then—"

"We're going to build our defense around the borders of that Torrean."

Duarte frowned. "Kiriel, are you certain that this is what he said?"

"Yes."

"But . . . the valleys there are not as wide; they are not good ground for cavalry. Not," he added, "as good as the Torrean of Irreno, two days' North."

Auralis was looking at her strangely. After a minute, he said, "Spill it."

His way of asking for information. She had always wondered why—were words like liquid, and she a vessel? Did she tip and drop them, scattering them haphazardly where all could see? But she met his gaze.

"I asked him," she said. Because it was true.

"You . . . asked . . . him."

"Yes."

"When?"

"In the war room."

"That's where, Kiriel. When?"

"Now."

"Why?" She could hear the word as if it were spoken by every Osprey alive. It was sharp with shock and something darker. Suspicion. She frowned, feeling it, knowing that it was the natural order among people of competence and power. She didn't even dislike it.

"Because," she told Auralis, although Duarte had asked, "I am going to Valente."

Duarte opened his mouth. Auralis shut it by the simple gesture of a raised, open hand. "Kiriel, why?"

"Because," she said, offering him more than he could possibly understand. "It was Ashaf's home."

The Tor'agar of Valente was waiting for her when she left.

She knew that he would be, but did not know why; she was prepared to face him. But not to face him alone.

He stood in the darkling night, his hand upon a lamp. His banner was absent; the insignia he bore faded into insignificance at the coming of the Lady's time. No Toran accompanied him, and if Kiriel was not of the South, she understood their import well; a man might sooner set aside his sword than his oathguard.

Yet he stood.

She remembered that she was a woman here, and that women bowed. But she had bowed once, in the dirt of the road; had bowed a second time before Valedan kai di'Leonne. Her knees were stiff with the echoes of an old resentment, and they would not bend a third time.

If he understood her reluctance, he said nothing. But he did not step aside; he did not allow her to pass.

"Ser Danello," she said quietly.

"Kiriel," he replied, inclining his chin gravely. His beard brushed his surcoat before he lifted his eyes again. "I have come to offer my gratitude for your intervention. And to ask you again why you bear the name di'Ashaf."

She said, "Pride." And meant it.

"It is a seraf's name."

She said nothing. The truth still hurt her somehow.

"A seraf," he added softly, "that I valued."

And understood why he had come without Toran.

"I searched for her," he continued, when she offered silence. "For days. For months. She was as mother to me, when I dwelled as child within my father's harem. Even though she suffered. Even then. She did not judge blood by blood; she nurtured, when she could."

"She was like that," Kiriel said softly, remembering.

"When did you last see her?"

"Months ago."

"Was she alive?"

"No."

He did not close his eyes or turn away; the truth pained him, but it did not weaken him. For a moment, she envied him his strength.

She had never thought to envy any mortal that.

"How did she die, Kiriel di'Ashaf?"

"I wasn't there." A lie. But the truth was the harshest of truths, and she could not face it here. "I failed her." This, at least, she could offer.

"And where she lived—and died—were women so burdened with responsibility?"

Memory touched her briefly—a strange memory, a dark one. The heart was glowing in the hollow between her collarbones, its warmth akin to flame. She almost lifted a hand to remove it. Almost.

But the Serra Diora's words were command, here; she endured.

"No," she said softly. "No more were they burdened with responsibility in your father's harem."

His face darkened. "I, too, was young," he said quietly. "And I, too, was . . . absent . . . on those nights. I could not protect his wives. My mothers. Ashaf survived. Many did not."

"She never blamed you."

"She would not, I think, blame you."

"No. No, she wouldn't. But it doesn't matter, does it? She's dead. I'm not."

"And Valente?"

"She loved her village. It was—it was one of the only things she loved. She loved you," Kiriel continued, as the night deepened, her words slow and measured. "And she feared you."

He flinched. "She said that much?"

"She never spoke of her life." Ah. She caught her mistake before she could compound it. But she could not offer lies.

"And yet you know of it."

"She was raised in the South," Kiriel replied. Uneasy, now, understanding part of Ashaf's fear. He was canny. "Men rule here."

"Not all men rule poorly."

"No. She trusted your rule."

"And you?"

"I don't know you."

"But you will fight upon Valente soil."

She nodded quietly. "Her dead are there," she said at last. "Her family."

"Yes. Would she counsel you to face death in order to protect the dead?"

"No."

"No," he said gravely. "That was not her way."

"She loved the living as well."

He nodded again. "I had thought to lose the villages," he said at last. "War in the South is not kind. And in the North? It comes seldom, if I understand the North. The Kings rule all."

"They're not demons," she snapped.

His smile was thin. "No. Or so I have been told. It matters little. Their rule is not contested. Ours is. And has been.

"Did she tell you how I came to be Tor?"

"No."

"Did she tell you why?"

"No."

The heart beat against her skin, and her skin felt fine and thin, something so close to breaking that she wondered at the lack of blood. The pain was there.

He bowed his head. "The killing of kin is a dangerous business," he said at last. There was threat in the words, but it was muted; she did not even reach for the hilt of her sword.

"She was my kin," Kiriel said, defiantly.

"She was not of your blood."

"No. But—I chose—to accept her. She was mine as much as she was yours."

"I do not seek to take from you what you hold," he told her. "But I offer you this." He held out his hand. In it, a small circle made of hardwood lay, unblemished and unadorned.

She frowned.

"It is made for oaths, Kiriel di'Ashaf."

"We make no oaths," she replied stiffly.

"We? In the North, oaths are offered, and oaths taken. All of the soldiers who serve the Kings have sworn them."

His hand did not waver.

Hers did. But it held nothing. He was canny, yes. Sharp-eyed, his steel hidden by softer memories, none of which were hers.

"What oath do you offer? What oath do you ask of me?"

He smiled. It aged him. She had rarely seen a smile have that effect.

"I offer none yet," he replied gravely. He set the medallion upon the ground, and knelt before it. She watched; the light was now silver, a thing of moon and shadow. The stars were bright; clouds, if they existed, existed as memory. Perhaps that would change.

But not now, not yet. Not when it was needed.

The darkness hid nothing from her.

The ring hid nothing.

She saw him for a moment as something more than, less than, he was: gray light, with a hint of white and black edging: a soul who had not yet chosen its final destination.

"It is said," Ser Danello kai di'Valente told her, his hand drawing sword so silently only the glint of steel spoke of its movement, "that men swear oaths to no women." The sword reached the height of his shoulder; he did not rise.

"And it is true, in its fashion." The sword hovered a moment, as if weightless; his eyes met hers as the blade fell.

Edge struck wood. She was silent.

"Therefore no oath that you claim, no boon, will be honored if my clan is dead. And clans have died in wars such as these; I offer no guarantees." He lifted the blade; the medallion clung there until he reached for it. "But against future need, if my clan outlives this battle, I give you this. It bears my mark upon the unscarred surface. If you have need, or desire, make the cross cut and bear it in my name. What you ask, I will grant, and if I am not alive to grant it, my kai will."

She was mute. Her hand seemed to rise of its own accord, her palm exposing itself to the wood that he placed against it.

He rose then, and bowed, accepting her silence at the enormity of his gratitude.

"Where I come from," she said at last, "blood seals all oaths."

"All?" His smile was softer now, worn into his face. "And did you demand that from Ashaf? Or did she make no promises?" When she did not answer, he said, "You loved her. She must have offered you love first, if not in return. I do not know what she would make of you now, dressed in armor, bearing a sword, walking in the company of the Northerners who once devastated our Terrean.

"Yes," he added, "I recognize them. Shorn of their black bird, their cursed banner, I would know them anywhere." He shook his head to clear his eyes of the momentary anger. "I do not know what Ashaf made of me. What I made of her, in the end, was my own choice, my own doing. It is the same with you, Kiriel di'Ashaf.

"I am a vain man. It is not something I would speak of in the Lord's time, for the Lord accepts only one vanity; the Lady knows a multitude, and what she sees she does not speak of in the company of men.

"But of vanity, I will say this: it is my belief that she would shelter no one unworthy. She sheltered me. She sheltered you. I have not asked where you come from. I will not ask now. But I believe in her choice."

"My people killed her," Kiriel said. She could speak softly, but the words were harsh and terrible.

"My father almost killed her," he replied quietly. He bowed. "I have never forgiven him. I have never forgotten."

She kept the medallion.

In the morning, the army began to move.

"Serra Diora."

Diora was quiet. She had been given a task by the Matriarch of Havalla, and she had not yet chosen to perform it. Perhaps, had she, she might have been spared this sudden audience.

She did not hesitate; her shoulders lowered, and she bent gracefully over her lap, covering her knees. Her hair, bound perfectly, caught the sheen of lamplight and held it a moment against perfect black; she was aware of its play, of what it entailed. She could speak, now; she could edge her words with power. Desire, after all, was just another weapon, and in her war, she needed this man.

But she held her gift behind closed lips.

"Please rise," Valdedan said softly. She heard the irritation in the words, although it did not break their surface. He was not so practiced as Ramiro di'Callesta, not so cautious as Yollana or Kallandras. She accepted what he offered. "I am not of the South," he told her.

It surprised.

She lifted her shoulders, her back, and last, her chin, resting her empty hands delicately in her lap. The fan lay closed beside her; the samisen was quiet.

"In the North," he continued quietly, "I was graced by the presence of the Serra Alina di'Lamberto, and she taught me much that I am grateful for now. But I was taught more by the Princess Mirialyn ACormaris. Neither woman chose to hide behind a curtain of deference."

She could have feigned ignorance, but he had come alone, and she, shorn of all but Ramdan, was as isolated as she had been in the Tor Leonne.

But he was not Alesso. Not the kai Garrardi.

She met his gaze. Held it, measuring him. Letting him know that she did so.

All risks were hers, she thought. But thinking it, realized that it was not true.

"You expose too much," she told him, her voice gentling the words.

"I have little to hide."

"There is always something to hide," she said quietly. "From the Lord. Or the Lady."

"It is not their time."

"It will be."

"And it will be ours again; the sun rises and falls."

She hesitated a moment and then said, "You have chosen to take the army to Valente."

His brow rose a fraction, changing the lines of his face.

"Why?"

He smiled. Ruefully, she thought, an expression of surrender. "Because Kiriel asked it."

Her expression did not change, but he had surprised her again. "And what will you tell the General? What will you tell your Tyrs?"

"They know."

"How?"

"She asked it of me in their presence."

"And you granted her request?"

"It is the only thing she has ever asked of me," he replied quietly.

"She is a woman."

"She is. But she is also my guard, and she has saved my life many times."

"You cannot be seen—"

"I have been."

"She is a *woman*," Diora told him again, speaking now as if to a child.

"She is Kiriel. Kiriel di'Ashaf. But I did not come to speak of Kiriel."

Diora raised a hand. Just a hand, but she turned it, palm out, toward his face, covering his lips although he stood just beyond the door, and she, close to the tent's edge.

"You will never hold the Dominion if you are seen to be so weak. Or so indulgent. Have you learned nothing from the fate of the Leonne clan?"

He did not reply.

"Kai Leonne, have you ever killed a man?"

He was silent.

"Have you ever ordered a man's death?"

Silent again. This time, she felt herself being measured. She struggled a moment with words, and lost. "You do not understand that death is the Dominion. The deaths that you order. The deaths that you offer. The deaths that you withhold. You cannot hope to keep what you seek to gain if you do not learn to kill."

"And you, Serra Diora? Have you killed?"

"I am a woman," she told him quietly. "It is not my place to bring—or withhold—death."

"We've had this conversation before."

She fell silent.

He turned away from her. Speaking now to the door, to the freedom of the dusk, he said, "I never get this right. I came to ask you—"

All of his silences bore weight.

She remembered Kallandras' words. But she could not yet live up to them. Her wives. All her wives. She said, "I will never bring you a harem."

"I have no desire for a harem," he replied, too quickly.

"You are the Tyr'agar. You will be judged by the harem you keep; by both its quality and the number of wives you support. Men will offer you their sisters and their daughters, and they are not men that you will be able to easily refuse."

"You have just said—"

"I will not choose wives," she told him quietly.

"Then do not choose them."

She was frustrated by him. He was like a child, a child with power. She wanted to know just how much offense she could offer, but she was wise enough not to test it; let time unfold, and with it, the answers that were certain to come.

"If you are willing," he told her quietly, "I will marry you."

She nodded, graceful as ever. Watchful as ever.

"But in return for this, I will ask of you one thing."

"And that?"

"Never lie to me. Never offer me pretty words, unless they contain truth. Say nothing, if truth is distasteful." He turned to face her again, his hands behind his back. "I do not need a seraf. I do not need a subservient, meek wife."

"What do you think you need, Tyr'agar?"

"A friend," he told her. "A comrade."

"I am not a warrior."

"You are the only other person who has borne the Sun Sword

into battle," he replied evenly. "Even if you did not draw it, you carried its weight. You were its swordhaven."

"And now?"

"Now, I bear it. But it is heavy, Serra Diora. A weight that I did not expect. I know you are capable of carrying it. You have delivered it to me, and I have promised to honor you for your bravery. Marriage is not what I intended," he added softly. "Because I'm not certain how much of an honor such a marriage will be. To you." He blushed as he spoke the two rough words. "If you will serve my cause, serve it; but be the woman who walked the open road at the side of the Voyani. I do not require the white of the Lord's Consort; I do not require the perfection of the Southern Court."

"You do," she said sharply. Speaking as he had commanded her: freely, and without dissembling.

"There will be a hundred other Serras who are skilled in such arts. Not a one of them would have approached the Swordhaven. Not one would have dared what you dared, and even had they, not one other would have succeeded."

She was silent.

"There is not a man in the Dominion who would not gladly take you to wife. And there is one who is willing to give up much for that privilege. You honor me."

She lifted her head. And then, unbidden, she rose. She had expected him to offer these words; they were Court words. But . . . there was nothing of the Court in them. His face was expressive, but so, too, were the faces of the Northern Commanders. She had learned that those expressions were masks, as certainly and completely as the neutrality on which Tyrs prided themselves.

No. It was in his words. He spoke, not as a man, but as—

He raised his hand. Took a step back from her; it was an awkward, graceless step; the back of the tent's flat struck his shoulders as he bent to accommodate the lowest part of the cloth roof.

She stopped, and her cheeks reddened. Her hands fell to her sides; she stood there, almost lost, composing her face.

"I know that you did this for your dead." He looked above her head, to some spot beyond the heavy cloth walls. She heard the movement of horses, the gathering of men, the lowing of horns. Drums beat in the distance: Lambertan drums. "I don't envy them their death," he said. "But I envy them your . . . your dedication."

Storm's warning.

"I would have waited," he added, although he did not meet her gaze. "I wanted to wait."

"For what?"

"For you."

It was not the answer she expected.

"But waiting is a luxury that neither of us has time for." He bowed. "When the dawn rises, and the Lord bears witness, I will take you to wife; I will make truth of the name you offered me when we first met." He turned from her and touched the tent flap, but did not raise it.

"Kai Leonne."

He stopped.

But she lost the words when his eyes met hers, and even after he left, she could not in honesty recall what she had been about to say.

For the first time, she felt something akin to fear as she watched the cloth rustle and settle.

He did not ask permission. That much, he spared her. But he gave her permission, obliquely, to refuse him. In the Lady's hour, she did.

Silently, at first, and alone.

Angrily, as the hour wore on. She did not speak, although her lips moved over the syllables, the unseemly, unfeminine Torra. He was not, she said, a man.

But Adam had not been a *man*.

Treacherous voice, and cool; it was also hers. She bowed her head a moment and lifted hands to cheeks. The Lady did not need open sky to bear witness; she witnessed all, and she offered no comment.

This is what you wanted, she thought. *This is what you labored for. Just this. This.*

No, not all. Was she to surrender the field to a stranger? Was she to give, to him, the death that she desired?

"No."

She looked up too quickly, although she recognized the voice. Kiriel di'Ashaf stood, silent, in her tent. She had heard nothing, no movement of cloth, no clinking of armor, no fall of boot—yet she stood, like shadow, in the scant light. Long shadow, and dark.

Diora did not move.

"We are going to Valente," Kiriel said, when the pause had grown awkward enough that the silence had to be filled.

"I know."

"I will fight there."

As if the army itself were of no consequence. Looking at Kiriel di'Ashaf, Diora felt that it wasn't. The Serra had a dagger, and her hand touched its hilt; light flared around her palm, shining through skin made orange and translucent by its intensity.

Kiriel's brows rose. Her own hand touched the hilt of her sword, although she did not draw it. Not here.

But the dagger *lumina arden* was her enemy, Diora realized. And she recognized it.

"Do you want to marry him?" Rough question; Northern question. Or child's.

Diora chose to see it as the latter, although Kiriel was no child. "I don't know."

"You don't have to. He won't force you."

"No," Diora replied bitterly. "He won't."

"He's not a child," Kiriel said quietly.

"He's not a Southerner."

"No. But it was the Southerners who killed your family. It was the Shining Court that killed mine." She held out a hand; the glove was gone, and the skin that sheltered beneath it was white as a Serra's; perfect and cold. "You have power, Serra Diora."

"Yes." She could have lied.

"He doesn't understand what he faces."

"No."

"But you do. You do, I do. Yollana does."

Diora nodded.

"There will be no witnesses on this field. There will be no civilians. No noncombatants. You have power," she said again. "You can wait."

Diora frowned.

"To marry. If you want. You can wait. He would."

"He cannot wait."

"And you?"

"I cannot go where he goes if I wait." There. It was said.

"If you ask him, he will take you. He will let you travel with the army. Tell him that you will find no safety anywhere else, and he will believe you. You can make him believe you without—" She stopped. "You can."

Diora's smile was grim and bitter. So much bitterness, here. She had thought it scoured clean by sand and wind, but some seedling must have remained by desert's edge, waiting.

"The crown was broken," she said softly, so softly that had she been any other woman, the words would not have carried. "I could not remake it in any other way. I *am* his crown, Kiriel."

"In the South, the Sword will be enough."

"In the South, if he were *of* it, it would. But he is not of the South. He is of the North, and he is tainted by his place in that foreign Court. I am of the South. I carry the weight of his legitimacy for the clansmen to see. They will know me."

"And him?"

"They will know him because I am with him."

Kiriel frowned. She looked down for a moment, and the shadows that lined her face seemed ordinary, robbing the darkness of threat. For this woman, Diora sang the cradle song, again and again, patiently teaching the words by simple repetition.

She said, "I want to help you."

And Diora, hearing truth in the words, was comforted. She had seen much in the short passage of a year; she could accept what she saw here.

"Na'kiri," she said gently, holding out a hand.

Kiriel lifted her face, but the edges had seeped out of the darkness that lurked only in her eyes. Her golden eyes.

Diora schooled her face with care, and with tenderness, and she began to sing softly, aware that she might have no other chance to sing this song again.

Aware that Kiriel also knew it, and had come for just this.

Jevri el'Sol came to her tent before dawn.

She heard him; he made no effort to be silent. Made effort, she knew, not to be; he was seraf trained, and that training would never desert him. But he had been long in the service of the kai el'Sol—if it did not desert him, he had come at last to a point where he could set it aside.

"Honor me," he said softly.

His voice was smooth, but his request was not; it was broken by past history, by all of the other times he had helped another dress.

She hesitated a moment, and then she nodded gracefully to Ramdan. He bowed and left the tent.

"At dawn?" she asked him softly.

But he shook his head. "Before dawn," he replied.

"But—"

"The Tyr'agar wishes the ceremony to be complete before the Lord reigns."

A delicate brow rose, changing the contours of her face.

"No, Serra," he replied, although she had not asked. "I did not ask him why." He shrugged. The will of Tyrs, he seemed to suggest, was not to be questioned.

He walked to the chest at the foot of her small bed, and opened it with care. Folds of white cloth shone as he lifted lamp; crystal and pearl caught light and held it as it passed above their patterned captivity. He set the lamp aside, and the dress fell into shadow, fell into the care of his bent hands, his wrinkled skin disappearing beneath its ivory folds. He lifted the dress from its haven as if it were the Sun Sword itself.

She stood.

"He wishes the time to be his own," Jevri said, unexpectedly. "The Serra Alina was not pleased by this departure."

This elicited a rare smile from the Serra Diora, but she held her peace. "My seraf—"

"Let me," he said again. His fingers traced the beads with care; they were his work. "I am no armorer," he told her, although he did not look away from the dress.

"You are," she replied. "This is my armor, my shield; this is meant for the field I have chosen."

He bowed gravely, gracefully, his chin dipping a moment in gratitude.

He helped her dress. She divested herself of her sleeping silks, her simple robe, and gave herself over to his care.

Our time, she thought, as he worked. She had no mirror, no silvered glass, nothing in which to view his work; his face, his expression, the folds of skin around his eyes and his lips, were the only reflection she was allowed.

But they were reflection enough.

"The Tyr'agnate of Lamberto offers himself in your father's stead," he told her quietly.

She almost nodded. Almost.

But the sun had not risen, and the moon was absent from the sky; the last of night was fading as the Lady chose her veils and surrendered, as they all must, to the coming of the Lord.

She said, "The Lord bears no witness."

"No, Serra."

She had been married once, in full view of the Lord's bright face. Then, she had had her father's wives as her attendants, and her father had waited, grave, fearful, to take her hand while she still belonged to his harem.

"No," she said at last. "It is not the Lord's time. I need no man to stand in my father's stead."

Jevri cl'Sol nodded quietly, as if he had expected no less. "The Tyr'agnate will not be offended," he said quietly. "The ceremony itself is already . . . unconventional."

"Will he always be this difficult?"

Gray brows rose. "He is the Tyr'agar," was the grave reply.

"He is like no Tyr before him."

"No, Serra. And perhaps that will be his strength."

"Or his weakness."

"He is of the North," Jevri said quietly. "And in the North, all weapons of note have two edges."

She said, "Daggers have two edges."

"Yes, Serra. And daggers are women's weapons."

He stood back and examined her with care. "You have no rings," he said quietly.

She shook her head.

"And your combs?"

She nodded. "They are in the drawer at the bottom of the chest."

"Will you bind your hair, Serra?"

She hesitated.

He lifted a hand and retreated from the sanctuary of the tent. She heard voices without; Tyran, she thought, although she did not recognize them.

After a moment, he returned. His hands were covered in pale, pink blossoms. "Jade is cold," he said quietly.

"But the flowers aren't white."

"No, Serra."

She hesitated a moment and then said softly, "Yes. I'll wear them."

"And your hair?"

It fell almost to her knees, like child's hair, but thicker and fuller. She hesitated again, and then said, defiant, "Let it be."

His smile was gentle. "Fredero would have been proud," he told her quietly. "Of you. Of what you have accomplished."

"I am only a Serra."

"And he was only a man."

What serafs see, she thought, no man sees. She bowed. His fingers grazed her forehead like a blessing, and she felt the delicate, cool skin of petals against her brow.

"Come," he told her quietly. "He waits."

"The Tyr'agnate?"

"No. The Tyr'agar."

She rose and followed the servitor out of the tent.

*   *   *

He watched her at a distance made of hill and grass. It was ringed by cerdan, their armor dull in a light that had not yet given way to sun. The color of the sky was turning, but gray clung to its height like a mantle, delicate and wide. *Man's time,* he thought. *Our time.*

He saw the cerdan part at the base of the hill. Held his breath. He was aware of Ser Anton di'Guivera, of Ser Baredan di'Navarre, of Ser Andaro di'Corsarro. Aware, as well, of Primus Duarte and the Ospreys that the Primus had chosen as escort and guard. Much argument had gone into the choosing, and in the end, Alexis and Fiara, hidden much of the time from the cerdan, took up arms and armor with the pride and the disdain that mixed so strangely in the Ospreys. They were joined by Auralis and Cook, by Sanderton and by The Kalakar.

Commander Allen stood apart, watching grimly, his eyes straying to the distant horizon as if he dreaded the rise of the sun.

The Northern bard, Kallandras of Senniel, played his lute wordlessly as the Serra Diora broke through the ranks of the cerdan.

She came alone. He could see the kai Lamberto, but the Tyr'agnate had not chosen to step beyond the ring of men who now bore witness.

He had not expected that.

But he waited, the world falling away from his awareness until she alone occupied it. She grew larger in his vision, her hair flowing from her face down her shoulders and back, a black cloak that rustled at the behest of the breeze. Strong breeze, but gentle; the wind's deceptive voice.

No one escaped the wind, in the South.

And no one was blessed by it.

She walked, attended by two men: Ramdan and a simple Radann. Both were older men, and both were silent, graceful shadows; they added to the slow depth of her movement, and demanded no recognition for themselves.

The clansmen bore witness in silence.

And beyond them, in a lesser silence, the Northern soldiery; she was lovely, quiet, grave: her walk was like the beginning of a story, of a legend.

She came to stand at his side. He wanted to say something— anything—but words had deserted him; they were not his to offer. He met her gaze, and then lowered his; she wore no veil.

Significant, that she wore no veil. Alina had said that she would.

"Serra—" he began awkwardly.

But her gaze, like Alina's, deflected words. He turned as the Radann par el'Sol appeared, as if the earth itself had disgorged him. It was disorienting.

Marakas par el'Sol bowed.

Valedan did not. The skies were not yet clear; clouds brushed the treetops, a different veil. Beneath the gray light, the rays of gold across his chest were dull; the sun was not ascendant, although he claimed it by the right of blood.

"Serra," he said quietly.

"Tyr'agar."

It pained him, the formality that she offered. But he offered her no less. Could offer her no less; his words were broken a moment by her presence. She wore no powder; she wore no color; her hair was the only thing that framed her face, beneath the fragrant blossoms of the valley's tended trees.

He said, "I chose the time."

She inclined her head in silence, and it came to him that silence was the only thing that a Serra was allowed to offer her husband in the presence of his men.

He wanted to send them away, then, but held his hand; they were his witnesses.

"Serra," he said. "Serra Diora."

She lifted her face and turned to him; the Radann par el'Sol said nothing.

"I have no ring to offer you."

"It is not the custom of the South."

"But the gold—"

"Gold is an adornment that the rich offer," she told him coolly. "A pretty chain. A symbol of wealth. Or power."

She wore none.

Needed none. He held out his hand, his empty hand, exposing the mound of his palm.

After a moment, she laid hers across it; it was light and almost weightless.

"This is not the Lord's time," he said quietly.

"No."

"Nor the Lady's. In the South, it is the time of men. But in the North," he added, "it might also be your time; the time in which you might choose your own fate." He was awkward, and knew it; knew as well that in her presence he would never be anything else. Delicate and petite, she made him feel gangly; his height was a crime.

But he did nothing to lessen it, aware of the distant circle of Southern men.

"Do you bring the North with you?"

"Some of it," he said quietly. "Does it still offend?"

Her face was a map. Smooth, contoured, slow to change, to offer change. It lay before him, so close that he might touch it. His hand tightened a moment over hers. This marriage would give him the right.

And he wanted it.

"No," she said at last.

He knew that this was not the ceremony of the South. That it was shorn of finery, shorn of the import that pomp and circumstance lent the marriages of Tyrs. But the battlefield was his home, and he would have no other until he had proved himself its master.

He raised her hand, but did not kiss it.

He wanted to talk to her. He wanted to say something, say anything, that might reveal to her what he felt.

But he couldn't; he wasn't certain himself. She was so distant, so perfect, she could not be owned.

Instead, he turned to the Radann par el'Sol, and said, "Let all men acknowledge the Serra Diora en'Leonne."

Even these words were too quiet.

But the Northern bard began to sing, and his voice carried the whole of the wind, transforming it.

The lay of the Sun Sword unfolded around Valedan, around them both. Leonne the Founder accepted the gift—and the burden—of the Sun Sword; the rulership of a fractured, and fractious people; the enclaves of light in the midst of a land ruled by the Lord of Night.

Her hand was smooth and cool.

Leonne the Founder gathered his warriors in ones and twos, in handfuls from the towns and villages upon which the whole of an empire was fed; they came to his side with hoes and picks, with poor men's spears, and with the swords of blacksmiths long away from the field.

Her fingers bent slightly, pressing themselves into his palm. Her face was expressionless, her lips still.

The clan Leonne, with little power and little influence, had the might of a single sword behind it, but the sword spoke with the sun's voice when the enemy was near, and the enemy that had once seemed invulnerable fell before its perfect, single edge, its unswerving enmity.

Valedan's hand was shaking. He looked up to see the Tyr'agnate of Callesta, the Tyr'agnate of Lamberto. They were formal; they bore witness. He thought that Ser Mareo smiled, but he could not be certain; his eyes were drawn to the Serra, until his nervousness drew them away again.

He found comfort in the lay of the Sun Sword. In the voice of a master bard.

Leonne the Founder made his way to the Radann, and among the lesser servitors, he found his men of honor, and to them, he gifted the lesser swords, the Five, and they joined him, exhorting the free men of the Dominion to his cause against the long shadow, the endless night.

She would be his wife.

She would be his Serra. Impossible to believe it. Impossible, in the face of these witnesses, to understand what it would mean.

And at last, the Sun Sword found its home and haven upon the plateau of the Tor, and the Lady's Lake opened to receive him, and only him, who bore the sword against her enemy.

Valedan and the Serra Diora listened, hands joined and heads bowed, until the song's end.

But the song did not end.

In Torra, in perfect Torra, it continued, speaking of years of troubled peace in the Dominion; of the Tyr'agnati and their quest for power; of the death of the kai Leonne, a man made weak by thin blood. Kallandras' voice rose, and rose again, as he spoke of the coming of Night, of the end of the Festival of the Moon, and of the Sun Sword's secret journey from Swordhaven to the hand of the kai Leonne upon the field of battle. He sang of the bravery of the Serra Diora, the sheath of the Sword's heart, as she traveled the darkest of roads to bring the blade to the only man in the Dominion capable of wielding it.

He sang, again, of the men who toiled in the fields, of their hoes, and their picks, of their crude swords and their bright hearts, their unspoken promises to the man who would, once again, lead them from the depth of the Lord's Night.

And he sang of the joining of these two: the heir and the Serra, the Tyr and the Flower of the Dominion. No man upon the hillock could fail to hear the song.

And no man beyond it, tents folded, packs heavy with supplies and the utensils of life upon the open road, was unmoved.

The song made them part of the unfolding of history; made them instruments of the Lord of Day against the fall of shadow and un-

holy Night. And at their head, and their heart, the man and the
woman, the Tyr and the Serra.

"The Lord comes," Valedan told the Serra Diora quietly.

"The Lord watches," she replied, serene now.

He had given her what she required. And he was aware, that in
the acceptance, she gifted him with what he also required.

But he wanted something different, and it almost hurt.

The Serra Diora en'Leonne returned to her tent, flanked only by
Ser Andaro di'Corsarro. There was no grand pavilion, and no feast,
to mark this rite of passage; there was the rise of sun, a reminder that
much marching light had yet to be lost. It was as different as it could
be from her first marriage.

Ramdan joined her unobtrusively, sliding into the tent in silence
while she knelt. Her back was stiff, and the line of her jaw trembled;
she was home, if this was home, and this—this empty, weathered
place, this folding room, was the whole of her harem.

She had not asked for her aunt, and did not ask after her now; she
was daughter to Marano, but sundered, by her actions, from them.
She knew it. She did not miss them.

Not them, but the wives of her father lingered in memory; their
absence, their sorrowful loss, lingered as well. She had been—she
remembered this so clearly it was not a blessing—so *afraid* to leave
the harem of Sendari par di'Marano.

Death had rid her of fear, as it so often did—but it was not *her*
death, and it was no kindness. Grave, almost implacable, she looked
up to meet Ramdan's eyes.

His were upon her for a fraction of a second too long, and when
he realized it, he bowed.

"Is this marriage, in the North?" she asked him.

He did not answer; nor did she expect him to.

But she knew that her husband was now surrounded by his Generals, his Tyrs, his Northern Commanders; that the war that she had
come to bless by presence alone, now had his sole attention.

It should have pleased her.

"This is marriage," a soft voice said, and she lifted her bowed
head as Ona Teresa entered the tent, "in the South, Na'dio. It is a
marriage that is born of war, and made for war."

No peace in the words. But no breaks either; her aunt had recovered the ability to mask all emotion beneath the sheen of words.
"Do you regret it?"

Diora shook her head, and petals fell across the curve of her cheek. "How?" she asked her Ona. "How could I? This is all I have labored for."

"And now your role here is done?"

The Serra Diora closed her eyes. And opened them to an unchanged world. "I don't know," she said bitterly. "He is not a man."

"And Ser Illara was?" There was scorn in the question; the Serra Teresa did not trouble herself to hide it, although her face was serene and composed.

"I understood Ser Illara," Diora answered.

"And what you understood, you could control."

Words that were spoken only at the heart of a harem, and only between kin. The younger Serra's eyes glittered. "Yes," she said softly. "While he lived. Yes."

"He needed to be controlled," the Serra Teresa said, after long minutes had passed. "But I think Ser Valedan kai di'Leonne is different. You will have freedom here," she added, "and freedom is like the Northern sword: It has two edges. There is safety in the confines of a harem; there are rules that guide and guard all behavior. But the choices are few.

"He will not come to you now. He will wait, I think."

"For what?"

"For the choices you *do* make, Na'dio. He is Northern, yes. But I think that he is not so weak as you fear." She rose. "The Tyrs have gifts to offer you," she said, as she reached the periphery of the tent.

"I have no need of gifts."

"No. You don't. It is not for your sake that those gifts will be offered. And you know this," she added, with a hint of reproval. "You are still the Flower of the Dominion. You have made at least this choice. Honor it."

Serra Diora rose quietly.

CHAPTER THIRTEEN

THE Widan worked.

Not in fields, as laborers do; not in the Court, as serafs do, but rather, in the untended stretches of forest that defined the border between Mancorvo and Averda. Some of the Widan had been sent in haste to the border of Raverra, there to find the small saplings that

seemed to have taken root and grown as quickly as the most perni-
cious of weeds.

Alesso missed the Widan, and agreed reluctantly to their departure—but he did agree; Sendari's pinched face, the perpetual motion of hand in beard, did not allow for argument. Or not productive
argument. They had come far, these two, on trust, and that trust had
not yet outlived its usefulness, if it ever would.

Sendari, however, he would not spare.

The army was therefore lopsided in its travel, and it edged closer
to Mancorvo than Alesso would have liked; too far from the host of
the Second army that now moved along the riverside, destroying the
outposts that had been laid there against Northern need.

The grain, however, he kept. He mentioned this in passing to the
Widan who was in theory his closest adviser, and knew that he
might as well have spoken of the tilling of fields. For Sendari's
reply had been simple:

"Some experiments have been done."

The small trees did not give before the hands of normal men, and
those that attempted to pull them sickened inexplicably and died
within a threeday of their endeavor. It was an apt method of execution, but used sparingly; the trees were numerous, and they were
growing.

Widan Mikalis labored in secret in tents prepared for his use. Of
the Widan, he was the only one who traveled enough that he had
contacted the Voyani, and it was their scant knowledge, their legends and folklore, upon which he built his thesis, testing and destroying as he went. He did not sleep much, and this was wise: the
Tyr'agar waited for the results of his labor.

One thing became certain, with the passing of days: the plants
that were uprooted were not replaced. They left a gap in what appeared to be a line, and although nothing else grew in the hole made
by the sundering of roots from soil, no magic caused them to be reborn.

Sendari di'Sendari worked by the side of the Widan Mikalis, in
a like grim silence. He had applied many things to the saplings that
stood contained by magical barrier, denied soil and water, denied
light or shadow, and the only thing that seemed to move them was
blood.

The type of blood itself did not matter; he could offer fish or
bird, could offer cattle or horse; could even offer human blood. But
he tried that only once, and he found that although the donor never
touched leaf or vine, he, like the others that had, sickened and died.

That was a breakthrough, of sorts. For there was a magic that reached from plant to the man who stood within the ranks of Alesso's cerdan, and with intense effort, and the eyes of Widan trained to the studies of magical vision, that line could be followed, tested, probed.

It could not be severed.

They had tried. Even Cortano had tried.

But the bond that had formed could not be moved or harmed, and in the end, it drew life as certainly as it would have drawn water from soil. If that was what nourished it.

The bones that had been taken from the soil beneath the saplings had been exhumed for study. They were not old, but they were not freshly killed; the magic that had gone into this binding of life and death had been long in the making. Sendari almost envied the mage who had created such a work, for it was clear that he—or they—had much time in which to study, to plan, to *make*.

What was left the Widan of the South, poor cousins? Scant time. No time. The hours of the Lord and the Lady. The passing hours in which the army did not move, and move again, jostling them all and interrupting their necessary privacy with the imperative of a war that was not meant for Widan.

Or not Widan such as he. Not Mikalis.

Cortano's shadow entered the long tent. It was his, had to be his, for no chimes announced his presence, and no guard requested permission for his entry. This domain, given to them for study, was his, be it moving or no. His frown was etched in place.

"We have seen nothing of Ishavriel since he left the encampment," he said.

Sendari cursed. It was—would have been—a shocking breach of etiquette in a different place; here, it was commentary, a blend of breath and sound.

"And the others?"

"The *Kialli* have retreated. Alesso has no desire to summon them back; he feels they will not come without fight, and such a fight—in broad daylight—does not serve his interest when the Sword is on the field."

"It may not serve ours," Sendari snapped. "To have them so hidden. They must know what this means," he added. "And we have found *nothing* of value."

"The dead?"

"Nothing. Not even Mikalis can speak with what is left, and he has some of that art."

Cortano's pale brow rose. "I was not informed of this."

"No. No more does Widan inform a rival of his research. Leave it be, Cortano; if there is time for politics, it is not now."

The Sword's Edge said nothing, and after a moment, Sendari bowed stiffly. It was all the apology he could force himself to offer, and because it was, it was accepted.

"Sword's Edge," Mikalis said, standing, his shoulders cracking as he unfolded them for the first time in hours, "I do not believe that we will unravel this mystery before its time. Our enemies are in the North," he added, "and the soldiery of the Empire lies between. The Imperial magi are noted for their research into the esoteric and the ancient—and there are spies, or so we are constantly told—who view all that we do and deliver some word of it to their masters.

"Can we not make use of these spies? This barrier is not to our liking, and it is certain that it will not be to theirs; let us force their Widan, their magi, to the same task."

"And that?"

"The breaking of the spell," Mikalis replied.

Sendari had never seen a Widan stand so close to death and survive it. But the days had taken their toll, and Mikalis had never been a man of the Courts; if he understood his peril, he was brave indeed.

"Denied," Cortano said softly. Too softly.

"Mikalis is the only man among us who has any hope of unraveling what has been woven," Sendari said.

"Indeed. And he is no closer than when we started."

"No."

"The breaking of the boundary continues, but it is slow, Sendari. The Second army has been ready for three days, and two villages lie in ruins in its wake; the men are not easily contained this close to battle. I have taken Widan across the Southern tip of the valleys, and I have found nothing planted there; the trees do, indeed, seem to lie only upon the borders. I have come to tell you that we will move into Valente within the day."

The wind was cold.

Valedan felt it across his cheeks, his brow, and his hands almost reached for the bow that had been his final gift from the Princess, Mirialyn ACormaris. In such weather as this, he had hunted by her side, learning the pull and the weight of a simple curve of wood, a simple taut string.

"Tyr'agar?"

The Tyr shook his head. His hand fell to his side; the bow was not across his back, and he suddenly missed it. Serra Alina di'Lamberto had been clear: Bows were not valued, and the men who wielded them were seen as cowardly, for they chose not to close in battle. The true test of men.

"Primus?"

Duarte's face was grim. "Commander Allen requests your presence," he said, saluting. Sharp salute. Perfect salute. A harbinger of worse things to come.

Valente's lands were fecund, and his people many. Three villages, each of notable size, lay within his domains. The village of Karra, the village of Russo, and the village of Essla. Above the last village, the Northernmost of the three, smoke wafted windward in great, black clouds.

He was silent a moment; could not find words to speak.

The Tyr'agnate and the Tor'agar were likewise silent, but their silence was both heated and cooled, like a blade being tempered.

"What has happened?" he said. "Is the enemy already within Valente?"

"The General's army moves slowly," Ramiro di'Callesta replied. "If the words of the Northerners are to be believed, it cleaves to Mancorvan borders."

"The words of the Northerners are to be believed," Valedan responded, more curtly than he intended. He turned to Commander Allen. "What has happened?"

"The men are in Essla," he replied. "The Kings' men. And the Tyrs'."

"And no word has arrived at the camp."

They were silent. They looked at each other, and then turned to the Primus.

Valedan closed his eyes. "Kiriel?"

"She is gone."

Valedan took to horse with as much grace as the Callestan Tyr. Upon the field, however, no one matched Mareo kai di'Lamberto. He was silent; although the sun had darkened his skin, what lay beneath was pale. He did not speak; his Tyran spoke in his stead, marshaling those who were fit—and ready—to accompany his banner. The roads into Valente had been well trampled by the kai Valente's men; rain and morning mist had dampened it, and the horses did not

have the full stretch of gallop because of the numbers that now left
the encampment, thundering like storm in the clear sky.

When they were gone, the Serra Diora en'Leonne left her tent.
She wore a sari, but it was simple; the white had been carefully removed and carefully set aside. She did not think she would wear it
again, but had not thought—on the day of the Festival Sun, in a different life—that she would ever have need of it; she therefore kept
it safe.

Valedan kai di'Leonne had not spoken a word to her since they
had parted and the army had moved. He had left cerdan at her tent
and at her disposal, not understanding—never understanding—the
strictures that kept her from speaking to them. Without kinsman—
and she had none—without serafs, and she had only Ramdan, she
was mute in a man's world.

And she, who had loved the grace of her early life, now hated its
confinement. Margret's gift. Margret's curse. She longed for Arkosa
bitterly.

And perhaps because she did, she failed to notice the approach
of Kallandras of Senniel College. He did not come alone.

"Serra," he said, bowing at a formal distance, while her
guards—Valedan's guards—moved to block all sight of her from
him. "Forgive me for my intrusion; forgive me if I presume too
heavily upon my association with your kin."

She lifted fan and nodded, moving so that she might see him
framed by the lifted crescents of Southern sword.

"The Radann par el'Sol is coming," he continued, "and with
him, some of your traveling companions. You have, perhaps, not
heard of the misfortune in Essla."

Her frown was delicate.

She had not heard, of course.

"It is not the duty of a Serra to learn the arts of war. Nor to pay attention to its details, and again, I apologize for my intrusion." He
spoke for the benefit of the cerdan; they were not mollified. They were
Ramiro's men, and if they had accepted the presence of the Northern
army, they did not love Northerners. Kallandras, hair now curled spun
gold, was too pale of feature to come from anywhere else.

But he spoke Torra perfectly, and he knew all the signs and gestures. It made them more suspicious, not less.

She might have cursed their stupidity.

Instead, she nodded.

Marakas par el'Sol came down the rise of the slope. As the
armies approached the Marente forces, she had been moved; the

tents of war were now beyond her vision, and the banners made for men of power could no longer easily be seen. But the sun across the chest of the Radann par el'Sol was as bright as the eye of the Lord. She fell at once to the ground, although her cerdan did not likewise offer their respects; they had been given their orders, and the orders of the Tyr'agar superseded all but the orders of the Radann kai el'-Sol.

"Serra Diora," he said quietly.

"Radann par el'Sol."

"Please rise," he told her.

She did. She heard the urgency in the words, although he did not give any other sign of worry or haste. "I go to Essla," he said. "And with your permission, and the permission of your cerdan, it is my desire that you accompany me."

He might as well have said that he intended her for the slave block and the auctions; the cerdan were rigid with surprise and anger. "The Tyr'agar," the oldest man present spoke, "ordered us to guard her in safety. Essla is *burning*, par el'Sol. It is no place for the Serra."

Marakas bowed, as if agreeing. But he rose a shade too quickly, and his hand was upon his blade. *Verragar*, she thought. She could almost hear its voice.

Could hear it, keening.

Her eyes widened.

"Yes," he told her. "The cerdan are correct. Essla is burning, and many have died there. The fields have not been fired, and some of the serafs survive—but there has been . . . difficulty . . . within its borders."

"And I am needed?" she asked him, and only him.

"It was not my decision," he said. "Nor would it be my advice."

"But you are needed, Na'dio." No one spoke with that voice. No one but Yollana.

She stood, swaying on canes, her face haggard, her single eye dark, and ringed as if she'd been struck.

"Matriarch."

"Bring your lute," she said. "Or your harp, if you still have it. Bring your wit as well, girl. We have need of both."

The cerdan raised sword as the Matriarch approached, but the swords did not fall; she whacked the only man who had spoken sharply across the chest. "We fight the Lord of Night," she said sharply. "Will you bar our way?"

"She is the Serra en'Leonne," he replied. Diora did not envy him.

Yollana lifted her hand sharply; the cane stayed where it was. Everything about the old woman suddenly spoke of power. "She is the only person who dared to bear the Sun Sword to the kai Leonne. The only other person to hold the naked blade."

His eyes widened. "You lie," he said softly. "She lives."

"She did not draw it. She did not attempt to wield it. But it was her hands that lifted it from the waters of the Tor Leonne, and hers that bore it back to land, to its sheath, to the haven.

"She has walked by the side of the Arkosan Voyani, and she is counted as kin by their Matriarch. She has accompanied me upon the secret ways of Havalla, and she is counted kin by *me*. Keep us from our kin at your peril," she continued, her voice losing volume, but not edge.

No, she did not envy the cerdan.

"I will protect her," the par el'Sol said. "I will see her back in safety, or I will perish. I will stand in the stead of the clan Leonne."

The men hesitated, and then the oldest said, "We will accompany you." He offered his life with those words, and at the hand of another Tyr, his death. But the kai Leonne? Diora could not be certain. And because she was not, she could afford to be careless with their lives.

"Take what you need," the Radann par el'Sol said, "but gather it quickly. We have no time."

Essla was on fire.

The fire, dark and black, was heavy with the grease of burning flesh, a pyre's flame. The Radann par el'Sol drew *Verragar,* and in the light, she burned. In daylight, she held the sun's heart.

The cerdan drew swords as well, but their silences were now drawn and tense, things brittle with sudden fear. They were good men; they did not flinch or ward themselves.

The Matriarch of Havalla was under no such compunction; her behavior was above—or beneath—their judgment. Her hands shook and trembled, but they flew across her chest in a pattern that seemed to trace light in the light, drawing it all toward her. Her canes did not fall; they were held in place by the Serra Teresa.

"Aye, Na'dio," Yollana said grimly. "I have poor legs; they will not carry me. The lands will owe a greater debt to Marano than men can know before this day is done."

There was no doubt at all in the words, and the fact that Diora could hear certainty spoke, at last, of the Matriarch's fear. She hobbled, and she hobbled slowly; the cerdan, crawling, could outpace her.

But they did not; they drew around the Serra Diora as if she were, in truth, their lord's banner, their lord's crown.

"What happened?" Diora said, for Kallandras alone.

Kallandras did not turn or stop, but he answered just as cleanly, and just as privately. "The serafs in the village mounted a resistance against the Lambertan cerdan. Or so the Lambertans said."

The Lambertans had no need of, and no history of, lying. She believed it. "And the Lambertans fired the village?"

"It would seem to be meant to appear that way."

She lifted a brow.

"There is not one, among the Lambertans, with that ability—not in so short a time. No, Serra; the Callestans arrived, and with them, the Kings' men."

"They did not set this fire."

"No. It seems that among the serafs were men of power."

Not men, she thought, as she heard the odd inflection of the word. As she gazed, again, upon the flat of *Verragar* unsheathed, and saw the fire that was its edge.

"We may have arrived late, for Valente. The kin were present here."

"And in the villages to the South?"

"We cannot yet say. They will be approached with caution now. But the men are . . . restless."

The pause told her more than words could. She paled.

"Matriarch—"

"Aye, Na'dio." Tired voice. Tired woman. "I will do what I can."

Sanderton was dead.

What remained of his body—and it was little—was barely identifiable. The magi might gather the whole of his remains. No one else would recognize him.

No one but the Ospreys who had been to either side when the fire roared up from the packed dirt beneath his feet in a column, a thing of light and edges.

They weren't Ospreys now.

They weren't anything else.

Auralis roared with anger. Alexis roared as well, her voice higher, its range broken and raw. Fiara had dragged her to safety. She was wild with fury, and she did not consent easily. They all had their pasts.

No safety here.

They had been in this village before. In this village, in a dozen villages like it. Duarte was already gone; the open spaces between burning huts absorbed movement and light, offering scant shadow and little protection, but he took what was offered.

Little, as the Ospreys knew, was better than none. Sanderton could not be saved; could not even be found. Cook almost lost his hand as he grabbed Auralis by the shoulder; he was a big man.

The fire turned toward the largest and friendliest of the unit, reaching out with arms, searing the brows and hair from upturned face.

Living, dying, the Ospreys returned at last to the Annagarian valleys.

Auralis joined Cook and Duarte; lost sight of Alexis and Fiara. He knew magic; had a feel for it that he had developed at some small cost to Kalakar, and some greater to himself. This was magic, yes—but it was not wholly magic.

The fire gained shape and strength, gained height; death gave it a majesty that only battle knows.

Auralis lifted his voice in a cry, a command. "Kiriel!"

She heard him above the falling timber of building, the screams of the living, the wails of those who had not yet—and perhaps would not—acknowledge the death that had already taken them.

She heard swords leave sheaths, again and again; heard the clang of hoe and pick off the flat of breastplate. Clumsy hands, seraf hands; the hands of the dead. She herself was in motion as the fire turned, the only Osprey to hold her ground in the face of its sudden appearance.

Her hand burned; the fire had reached out to touch her face, and she had riven it, tendril from coiling arm, with the shadows, dark and cool, of her sword. And it *was* her sword. She felt it call her name as if her name was a sensation, a caress.

Its name was just beyond the tip of her tongue, and she had no time to discern it, to put into syllables what was felt in the cacophony of everyone else's voice.

But her hand felt the fire. And when she could spare a glance, she saw that the fire was not red, not orange, not the golden white of fire's heart; it was white as the dress of the Lord's Consort, white as the colors of Imperial mourning, white as the snow in the Northern Wastes, and as bright, as painful, as all of these things.

The ring was burning.

She could not remove it; she knew this.

But she could not afford to be without her power here; this was *kinlord* in his full glory, and against such a lord, she had barely prevailed in her past life. She could not see his name.

And without his name, she had nothing.

Nothing but speed, and a sword, and the training that years in the Shining City had given to no mortal living but she.

She swung her blade with a cry as the fire approached, and fire fell like rain against the pocked and blackened dirt. Somewhere, it burned flesh, the remains of a body. It drew no sustenance from the burning; the life had already been taken.

And the kinlord had no time, no leisure to take anything else. This, at least, she could do.

Would do.

Memory was fierce, hot, terrible; memory was savage, gleeful, liberating. She took refuge in the latter. She gave herself to the fight. Name? None.

But hers, she gave him ferociously and gladly, for he took nothing from it, could take nothing from it: she was not dead.

Not yet.

Above the village, and at a distance, Lord Isladar watched. He was not yet at his full strength, and perhaps he would not—in the length of her life—attain it again. No matter. She was Kiriel, and he recognized her. She had finally come this far; only a little farther, just a little farther, and she would again be his.

Movement was quick and brief; if she was diminished—and she was—she was not impoverished. The ring that burned so brightly upon her pale hand could be seen, tracing defiant light against his vision: he knew what she wore. It explained much.

But he smiled.

Another village, he thought.

Another village, and this move, this elaborate stage in the long game, would be complete.

She had been taken by shadow.

Of all the Ospreys, Auralis knew it best: he had seen it before. She was white and black; the tan and sweat of the early days in the hot Southern clime had been absorbed by the battle she now fought.

He felt a hand upon his arm, and turned.

Duarte's gaze was cold. He shook his head; his fingers moved in the air, without the cadence of speech to give them strength.

No matter; the rough gestures were command enough. Auralis was still Decarus for a few brief minutes; he obeyed.

In the distance, the armies were coming. The village lay in the flat of the valley; the road wound between the tall crest of trees. He could hear what he couldn't see. Too much of it.

He shrugged himself free of Duarte, and his hand opened and closed, fingers splaying and returning to palm's center in a fist.

Kiriel was fighting.

Auralis AKalakar mimed the toss of a die, the universal gesture of those who followed Kalliaris and commended themselves, time and again, to her fate. He did not need to draw blade; it was drawn.

Find Alexis, he said, lips moving, breath sparing him the effort of sound which he knew would not reach the Primus' ears.

And then, rank be damned, he was gone.

Valedan kai di'Leonne arrived at the edge of the village that he had given Kiriel oblique leave to preserve. If he regretted the decision, the regret did not touch his expression.

Men poured from either side of the road toward the fight that had consumed the serafs, the village center, the crude founts that were meant for contemplation. There was no temple here; the Radann did not make their home in every holding, and he knew—from his brief conversation with the kai Valente—that the next temple was farther South.

If it existed at all.

Ser Ramiro kai di'Callesta paused at his side. "Tyr'agar," he said. Even at this distance, he was forced to raise his voice to be heard; the orders—Torra and Weston—shouted to and from the commanders of smaller units, broke the syllables.

Lambertan horns were raised, winded, dropped; shields rose and fell. Horses lay among the dead, twitching, their greater girth making them the easiest of the victims to see.

Valedan drew breath. "Andaro."

His Tyran was almost touching him. "Take Ser Anton," Valedan said. "And where you can, preserve the serafs until—"

"The serafs are fighting us!"

"*Until,*" the Tyr'agar continued, his hand upon his sword, his voice steady, even, preternaturally quiet, "we can determine *why* they fight us, and if they fight willingly at all. They are clumsy," he continued.

"They are *serafs!* They can't *be* anything else!"

Valedan's head snapped round. Ser Andaro stepped back. "That was not a request," he said. "Ser Anton!"

Ser Anton di'Guivera was as impassive as steel.

But he turned to his student, assessing him silently in the background of too much noise, too much fear. "Yes," he said at last. Acknowledgment. More.

Valedan kai di'Leonne drew the Sun Sword.

Light erupted in the basin of the valley, in the footpaths that led to the village of Essla.

She cut flame.

Again and again, she cut it, and it fell like liquid—something too sinuous, too destructive, to be blood. But the kinlord, nameless, hidden beneath the perfect armor of the elemental flame, regrouped, burning buildings now in a widening arc.

The serafs who fought in the lee of his shadow died as he needed them; she saw this. Was satisfied by it, in a grim fashion; the deaths were too quick, the pain too brief, to be of much use.

But fire burned tabard, burned cloth; fire danced against the length of her hair, denied easy victory by the darkness that swallowed all light, even his. The armor that she wore was not her own; it was Kalakar armor. It was mortal.

She shrugged it off, chain parting as if it were unnatural liquid, and the shadow consumed it. With it went weight and confinement. She moved freely, now, and with an ease that she had not felt in far too long. The ground melted beneath her feet, and this troubled her; she could not touch it, and finding no purchase, found little to offer her momentum. She was forced to confine her fight to a pattern of her enemy's choosing.

The ring burned flesh.

She fought it.

The horses would not approach Essla. They shied and jumped, and had the cavalry been given ground and plains to gather speed, this would have been fatal.

But Valedan kai di'Leonne was not, had not been, trained to horseback. His feet left stirrups, his hand released bridle. It was a mistake, of a type; the hooves of fearful horses were not a thing to be lightly chanced, and he was among them, as vulnerable as a seraf in spite of the weight of armor behind which he sheltered.

He heard Baredan's booming voice, and ignored it.

The Sun Sword drew him forward, through the thicket of falling legs, the sideswipe of heavy heads. He had almost cleared the horses, passed his men, when he heard the faintest hint of something strange: song.

It did not trouble him long.

He knew the voice of the bard-born minstrel, although the words were indistinct, and he saw almost instantly the effect of the magic that was so feared in the South: the horses stilled. They would not ride forward, but they gathered skittishly as if at a fence, and not at the edge of madness and death.

A gift. A Northern gift.

He entered Essla.

Primus Duarte AKalakar came out of the shadows of the outlying buildings; he offered no salute, no formality, no obeisance.

Valedan asked nothing for a moment, and then he said, "Capture those that can be captured. Kill only those who will not surrender." Knowing, as he said the words, that there was less than half a chance they would be obeyed. Dark smoke lingered in the creases of Northern skin, and in the eyes, fire raged, like a reflection.

He ran then.

The ground was broken with bodies, most charred beyond recognition. Another gift, if unintentional and grim. He found his footing by the way they rested, for the ground was treacherous here, the dirt melted in places as if it had been laid at the heart of a forge.

The Sword was shaking in his hands now; he felt that he was the weapon, and the Sword the master, and he struggled briefly against the thrall of its power.

But he was well trained; he knew that to fight on two fronts against two powerful enemies, was to court instant death. He chose his enemy, and his fight, and gave himself over to the guidance of the Leonne weapon.

Kiriel felt his sudden presence; it caused her pain, an echo of pain. Not even the fire itself had so sharp an edge, so harsh a light.

The kinlord turned, and she struck, but she was not yet close enough to offer death; the kinlord did not even grunt. Not when she hit.

But Valedan kai di'Leonne, limned in a light as pale as her own, caused *pain*. The Sun Sword stripped both fire and flesh from the *Kialli* lord; the armor of enchantment and wild magic peeled back in an instant, and blood boiled.

It was *her* fight. Hers, not his; she had claimed it.

But no, the sword whispered, as she lifted it, as she parried. She had *not* claimed it. The ring had deprived her of that claim because she was blind: she could not see the name. She snarled in rage, and she struck, but even in rage, her training held.

It was not for her own death that she had come to Valente.

She consented to what she could not prevent: allies. Aid. She saw the Sun Sword again, and as it fell, a shadow followed it, something so dim it would have evoked laughter or even contempt in a distant, Northern Court.

Auralis AKalakar.

Auralis' sword.

Dark blade, light blade, and something in between, intersecting for a moment, all motion slowed and refined in this instant. And this is what she remembered, although there was more: fire, flame, blood, the writhing of blue-limned shadow, the roar of a voice ancient as the land itself.

The silence was, as they sometimes said in the North, deafening.

"Kiriel!" Auralis shouted, as if unaware that she could hear him now.

She turned to look at him, and he took a step—only a step—back. Then she turned to face the kai Leonne, and the blade he held. Her own, she put up, but he struggled a moment with his. A long moment.

"Kai Leonne," she said. Her hair was rising on feral wind, her own wind, her power. But she kept her words even. Forced herself, inch by slow inch, to bow to him, to acknowledge his rank, although rank itself meant so little to her.

"Kiriel," he said, struggling, his jaw clenched. Sweat lined his skin, matted his hair; they were like and unlike in their coloring.

She sheathed her sword.

And after a moment, he sheathed his.

Cerdan, she thought, were speaking in their desperate, excited Torra. He had sheathed the blade while the blade still burned. They would look at her. They would know.

"What happened?" His voice.

"The kin were here," she replied, neutral now. "They were waiting."

"They?"

"Two." She shrugged a moment. "Lesser and greater."

"The last?"

"Greater."

"Were they waiting for us?"

"I don't know. They were . . . surprised, I think."

"They were surprised," Auralis said. "I think they moved in after the kai Valente left with his cerdan."

Valedan kai di'Leonne closed his eyes.

"Kiriel," he began, but she rose.

"I'm going South."

Not a question. He hesitated for a moment, and then, grim and silent, he nodded.

The Serra Diora en'Leonne walked quietly into the village of Essla. She had never seen it before, and thought she might never see it whole; it happened. But Kallandras walked by her side, and trailing her, the Matriarch of Havalla. She did not therefore hesitate. If there was fear—and there was—she did not trouble herself to name it; things named had power, or so the stories said.

And she walked in story; legend was no longer a matter of dim history, tarnished by politics and the struggle for acknowledged lineage. She was part of it.

The serafs who now dropped hoe and pick, who dropped wooden poles and staves, who fell at once to knees—or worse, to chest, their arms extended as far as arms could be that were still whole—were not; they were caught by it, trapped by it, broken and killed by it. Their names would never be remembered; they would never be recorded. Perhaps the village might be mentioned, but even that was unlikely; Essla was small and insignificant.

This is the way of the Dominion, she thought.

She had witnessed slaughter before.

She saw it again, gathering force, like storm, in the cerdan of Lamberto and Callesta. The horses were screaming in ones and twos, and the end of those cries marked the end of their lives. To a warrior, a horse is worth far more than a seraf.

To a warrior.

"Serra," Kallandras said, his voice loud enough to draw her attention. Her hand had lifted fan; she had fallen, unconsciously, into the standing posture of a Court Serra, and a Serra of the High Courts had no place in a village like Essla.

But she had come.

"What would you have me do?" she asked him bitterly, in the tongue of bards. "Look; not even the Northerners are at peace. If the vaunted weakness of the Kings' men cannot hold their hand, of what use am I?"

He did not answer.

Did not speak of power. She had power, and he knew it; no one knew it better, save for the Serra Teresa, and the Serra Teresa would never have contemplated interference here. Not even the Matriarch of Havalla was in the mood for mercy; her lips were set and grim as she surveyed the fallen serafs.

Men died as she watched. Some cleanly, and some horribly.

She lifted fan higher, thinking their deaths just; they had fought against their rightful Tor, their rightful Tyr; they had dishonored his banner.

She stood upon the blackened ground; soot clung to the hem of her sari, and it would be there, like bloodstains, for a long while; the road did not lend itself to the washing and care of silk.

Upon the stage of the broken village, the drama unfolded, as if it had been written by a wordsmith with an unfailing eye. One of the serafs, one close to her, was lifted by hair the color of night; a gauntlet caught it, twisting tight as it pulled a woman's face up from the ground.

The old man by her side cried out; he grabbed her arm and struggled to hold her. A foot broke his jaw, caved his nose in, changing the contours of his face. He had already lost teeth; he lost more, choking as he swallowed blood. He would die, she thought.

The girl was dragged from the ground.

She was young, but not so young that she was unaware of her danger, the certainty of her fate; her face was wild with panic, and the dirt that clung to her cheeks and her chin seemed to frame her face, rather than marring it.

Her skin was not white, but it was not dark; she had a worn hat, and the strings of its bindings, loosened, had not yet snapped; they wove round her neck like a thong of leather jewelry. She was a seraf, yes.

She might remain one, if the men vented their anger with care.

Even this, Diora had seen.

She lifted her fan. Her spine was the shape and consistency of the blade of the Leonne sword; she could not be bowed. *The Dominion,* she thought.

She had called the North weak, and it was, and for just a moment she yearned for that weakness.

But it lay exposed as lie, for another hand grabbed the girl's shoulders, and around the girl, upon a field that was not yet strewn with corpses, the Kings' men now wandered, their rods and swords a stark contrast—a meaningless contrast—to the rising sun.

They had lost comrades here.

They intended to exact some vengeance.

She should have closed her eyes.

Should have. Did.

But without vision, her hearing was sharper.

The baby cried.

Kallandras, she thought, bitter now with the sting of betrayal. She did not accuse him; she had withdrawn behind the mask of Serra, and a Serra said nothing to give offense to a man of power.

But she was surprised to find that she had moved before her eyes opened; that she had dropped the painted, perfect fan that protected her face and shielded her both from the vision of others and the ability to see them.

She heard Yollana's harsh, Voyani bark, and ignored it. Ona Teresa did not speak at all.

The stranger, the seraf, the pretty girl with hair twined around steel gauntlet, had clung tight not just to earth, to ground; beneath her slender body she sheltered an infant.

A child.

Kallandras, Diora said again, but to herself, only to herself. She walked quickly. She walked where Serras did not walk, her face set in lines that Serras did not wear, her expression free from control and containment.

Her shadow fell shorter than the shadow of cerdan and soldier. The woman kicked and cried out. One of the cerdan turned to the child.

"Stop."

They froze. They *all* froze.

But if she had exposed herself, she did not care. Had her part not already been played? Had she not given herself in marriage to the kai Leonne? Had she not delivered, to his hand, the only true sign of his legitimacy? Was she, in the end, to be allowed nothing?

"Do not touch the child."

The cerdan could not; he could not move. She wondered what this would cost her later. Wondered without care.

She moved past him, past his drawn sword, past his blackened armor, his bloodied face. Kneeling within reach of the choking old man, she lifted the crying child from his flat cradle of earth. Held him, as she had held only one other child in her life. She did not know if the babe was boy or girl, and she did not, at this moment, care.

The girl was weeping.

"Is the child yours?" Diora asked her softly.

She nodded.

"And your husband?"

She shook her head, mute now.

Dead, Diora thought. To the cerdan, she said, "Let her go." Just that. Shock loosened the spell of her voice, releasing them from its power. They knew her. They all knew her.

But not one of them had ever seen her like this.

She stood as a man might.

"Can you stand?"

The girl nodded. She knew better than to speak.

"Stand, then."

The girl had almost lied; she was graceless, as a seraf of the field might be, stumbling awkwardly as she attempted to find her footing. But she was lovely, as a seraf of the field might also be. Her skin was not powder white, although this could be changed; she was unscarred. Not untouched; the babe was evidence of that. But unscarred. Her eyes were large, and weeping had swollen her lips. Bruising had done the same.

The Serra gentled her voice. "Tell me," she said, as the babe quieted against her. "Tell me what happened."

The girl shook her head, but it was not a refusal. She was afraid.

"**Tell me,**" Diora said again.

"The—the men—came to Essla. While we were in the field. After the Tor had passed through the village."

"Which men?"

"Three men. They—we thought them—" She shook her head. "They ordered us from the field. They killed a dozen. With their hands," she added, turning her face away. "They didn't have swords. Just . . . their hands."

"They gathered the children. The children who could walk." She closed her eyes, then, shuddering. "One of them led them away."

"When?"

"Three days ago."

Diora did not ask where they had gone. They were dead. She knew it.

Wondered why.

"Why did you take up arms against your Tyr?"

The girl's eyes were wide, and the tears now fell freely. The cerdan no longer touched her, but they lingered, and the threat in their presence was obvious.

Diora looked beyond the girl, and she lifted her voice again. "**Do not kill them,**" she said, speaking with *power* to the three disparate forces who roamed the field as if they sought to harvest. **"By the orders of the Tyr'agar, they are not to be touched."**

Oh, she would pay, she thought. She would pay for her work this day. They *could not* disobey her. She had unmanned them all.

She tried to regret it.

But the babe, soot-blackened, was a burden that she could not, would not, surrender. Not to them. Not to Lamberto, Callesta, or Leonne. She wanted to lay him down and swaddle him more tightly; he was that young.

But the boots of the cerdan were careless and swift. For just a moment, she hated them. It was a piercing, terrible hatred, nameless, larger than the whole of her life.

"They . . . made us . . . fight," the girl said, weeping.

"How?"

"I don't know. I don't know, Serra." Her hands were free; she brought them to her face.

She was too old, Diora thought. Too old, although she was not old. She had lived her life in this village, and she was as graceless, as clumsy, as any village seraf. The time to teach, or teach well, had passed; she was roughened by her life here. Spoiled by it.

"Don't let them kill my son," the woman said, lifting her hands as if they were curtains. "Don't let them kill him."

"And you?"

"I don't care." She was terrified, but she swallowed fear as if it were liquid in the desert. She spoke with ferocity, and the ferocity gave her words the patina of truth.

Beneath them, open and completely obvious, was the desire for the words to *be* the truth.

"We are on the field of battle," the Serra Diora said quietly. "There are no wet nurses here. If I spare your child, and you perish, he will follow."

The girl swallowed. "If he lives," she said softly, "there is hope." For herself, she kept none. She knew her crime, and it was twofold: she had lifted arms—a hoe—against the banner of Tor and Tyr. And she was a woman.

"What is your name?"

"Teyla."

"Na'tey," the Serra said softly, "is your father among the living?"

She knew the answer. Yes. But perhaps not for long.

The girl nodded. Turned her glance upon the old man who lay bleeding, his jaw broken.

"And your mother?"

She shook her head.

"Your Ona?"

She shook her head again.

Ah. "Then there is no one to bargain for you."

The words, Diora saw, made little sense to the girl. They made little sense to Diora. But she had spoken them, and she knew why. She held the baby. She rose, her skirts now black and dark with blood.

Kallandras of Senniel College passed her, and stepping between cerdan, frowning at soldier, he offered the old man his hand.

The old man took it, and rose. When he had gained his feet, he fell to his knees, struggling for dignity. Or grace. Her shadow fell upon his bent back.

"What is your name?" She asked.

"Sergio kep'Valente," he told her. He spoke poorly, and with great pain; air hissed and bubbled through the broken cartilage of his nose.

"Thank you." She turned again, speaking now to the cerdan who had so roughly handled the girl. "Please," she said, no plea at all in her tone, "send word to the Tor'agar. Tell him that the Serra Diora en'Leonne has need of his aid."

The cerdan was awkward. He did not bow—nor was bow necessary—but he did obey what was only barely a request. He left.

When he returned, Toran and their Tor'agar accompanied him. The Tor'agar was now mounted, and the hooves of his horse cut dangerously close to the prone serafs. He was not pleased.

She would be surprised if anyone survived this day's work.

"Tor'agar," she said, falling to her knees. Grace was difficult, for the baby was heavier than lute or harp; heavier than samisen. She no longer held fan, and she had no escort, no brothers or uncles behind whom to shelter.

"Serra," he said. "Were you attacked?"

"No, Tor'agar."

His nod was still grim. He did not dismount. Nor, she noticed, did the Toran; they held naked blades, and they surveyed the groveling, silent serafs as if they, too, were harvesters.

But she said, "The Tyr'agar does not wish the serafs destroyed, unless it is your wish."

"The Tyr'agar has not yet spoken of this."

"No," she said softly, daring much. "He has been otherwise occupied. But he has given me leave to speak in his stead. The servants of the Lord of Night appeared in Essla hours after your passage. They took children, in number. They did not expect to see your return."

"Ah."

"The serafs did not choose to attack your banner; they had no cause. Widan art was used here, to force their hands; it is why they were so clumsy.

"It is said—and it is said truly—that you are a worthy Tor; that you are just and merciful."

None of that mercy now gilded his face. His expression was dark and stiff.

"Serafs have no defense against Widan arts," she continued. "And these serafs are victims of such an art. You saw the fire," she added quietly. "And in it, the greater work of the Lord of Night."

His voice gave nothing away; he did not give her words in which to seek purchase. He waited.

She felt his disapproval keenly.

But she had dared the Sea of Sorrows, and that passage had changed her. She drew breath as the infant began to cry again, his voice weak.

"They could not defend themselves; the compulsion was laid upon them, and they obeyed, like puppets. When the fire was guttered, the strings were cut.

"Judge them for their weakness, if it pleases you," she added, "but understand that their crime is not in their disloyalty, but in the weakness that makes them what they are: serafs. Yours."

His eyes were dark and bright. She met them without flinching. Without remembering to look away, to look down, to *be* a Serra.

"Our Tyr," the Tor'agar said at last, "has taken to wife a bold Serra."

"We, serafs, Serras, wives, all serve men of power," she replied. She wanted to stand; the child needed rocking or movement to quiet him, and she could give him neither.

"I will speak to the Tyr'agnate," he said at last. "And to the Tyr'agar." His hands caught the reins of his horse, and its great, dun head rose impatiently.

"Tor'agar," the Serra said quietly.

"Serra Diora."

"I beg your indulgence."

"You have it," he replied, no indulgence whatsoever in the words.

"Sergio kep'Valente has a daughter."

"He has two."

She bowed her head, acknowledging the correction.

"Teyla kep'Valente," the Tor'agar said, looking at the girl. His gaze passed to the injured old man. "Sergio, where is Carla?"

The old man spoke poorly and with great pain. But he answered. And unlike the Serra Diora, he knew his place, and kept it; his gaze never left the ground. "She is dead, Tor'agar."

"When?"

"Three days ago."

"How?"

"When the—the strangers—gathered the children. She tried to save her daughter."

Ser Danello kai di'Valente's frown shifted, changing in texture. "And Teyla's husband?"

"He, too, is dead."

"Ser Danello," Serra Diora said softly. "Your Serra is not present."

"She is not." Nor, his tone implied, should the Serra Diora en'Leonne be.

"She cannot therefore speak with me; she cannot bargain for the price of a seraf."

A dark brow rose. "It has been much rumored, among the Callestan cerdan, that the kai Leonne has little use for serafs," he said coldly.

"He has, indeed, little use for serafs," she replied serenely. Serenity was her mask. Behind it, encased in the cover of words, was the beginning of a bitter turmoil that she could not—would not—allow to interfere. She had only one recourse, if she was to save this child.

And although she should grovel and offer apology to her dead, she did neither. "But the Tyr'agar has need of a harem.

"I would speak with your Serra," Diora continued, "but I fear that I will come late to your harem."

"Speak, then. Speak freely," he added, with just a trace of irony. "But speak briefly; the matters of Serras do not concern their Tors."

She nodded, as if grateful. She was not. "I wish to purchase the seraf Teyla kep'Valente."

"For the Tyr'agar."

"For the Tyr'agar."

He paused. The pause was brief. "Let her be my gift, if he will have her."

She bowed, then, folding herself protectively over the child.

"Give the child to Teyla's father," he added.

Her arms tightened. "There are no wet nurses in the village," she said. It was not necessarily the truth.

His brow rose.

"The child is young," she continued. "And weak. He has little value to you at this time, and he will have none if he is separated from his mother."

"You will not barter with me, Serra. I have seen this done before; it will take hours, and I have minutes at best. I told you, the matters of Serras are beneath my concern; I will not engage in them. If you will, take the child. Your husband will not thank you."

She bowed again. With care. With far less grace than legend gave her; the child was delicate. Or she was. She could not separate the two with ease. Now she sought ground with her gaze, and held it, at last becoming her title.

His horse began to move, taking the tallest of shadows with him before she rose.

The mood of the cerdan had been broken by his appearance. By hers.

Kallandras came to stand by her side as she struggled to her feet. It had been long indeed since she had held a living weight; the Sun Sword was heavier, but more forgiving.

She would not allow Kallandras to help her stand, although he offered his hand. At this moment, she would have refused the aid of her husband, even publicly offered; she wanted the touch of no man.

"Teyla kep'Valente," she said softly, "follow me. You are now Teyla en'Leonne, and you belong to the Tyr'agar, Valedan kai di'Leonne. As does your son."

The girl touched ground with her forehead, an abasement.

Beside her, the old man performed the same courtesy. But he rose before the girl did, and because he rose, Diora could see the tears that mingled freely with blood. He had been foolish, she thought, although she did not judge him unkindly.

He had prayed to the Lady during the hour of the Lord.

And he saw that the Lady had answered.

Valedan kai di'Leonne came to the tent two hours later.

Diora was not yet ready to see him. Teyla en'Leonne was a year younger than the Serra, but her shoulders were broader, her arms widened by the musculature of years spent in the field. Her thighs were wide, her hips generous. The saris that had been given Diora by the Serra Amara en'Callesta—a parting gift, delivered by ser-afs—fit her poorly; they were not long enough.

But they were fine.

Ramdan, Lady guide and bless him, had met them at the tent, and he had taken Teyla into its confines. He did not touch her. But he did not judge her either.

Some serafs of the High Courts were as cool—as cruel—as their masters. They held position that placed them at an odd advantage over the common, but free, cerdan, and they took a pride in that position that made them desire separation from serafs who toiled in menial positions throughout the Dominion.

Had Ramdan been such a man, the Serra Teresa would never have kept him. He was silent, as he always was, but in his silence he offered kindness; all of his movements were gentle and slow. He did not touch the village seraf's face at first; he brought, instead, the sari that his Serra requested, and laid it upon the small cot.

"You must wear this," Diora told the girl. She might have been speaking Weston for all the comprehension the girl showed. "But first, you must bathe."

Even this seemed beyond her understanding. Diora did not frown. She recognized shock when she saw it, and as she could be, she was kind. But she expected Valedan to arrive, and she did not wish to present Teyla to him as a seraf of the field.

To a different Leonne, it would have been the girl's death.

Ramdan brought water and towels, but it was the Serra Diora who sponged the girl clean, removing from her the rough but sturdy clothing of a villager. "You will not need it again," she said softly. "And it will harm my—our—husband if you attire yourself in such a fashion." She had powder, but little of it, and no powder would hide the girl's dark skin; only time would lessen the effects of sun and wind, and they had no time.

"Am I—am I to be—" the girl swallowed.

Diora said inexplicably, "Did you have no wives?"

Teyla looked simply confused. No, of course not. She had a husband, one assigned to her by her overseer. "Your husband—"

She looked away. It came to Diora, then, that the girl had loved him in some fashion. Love, like weeds, grew in the most inhospitable of climes, where so little else of value might be found. She wanted to give Teyla time.

But time, she did not have.

She combed out her hair, and that, too, was difficult; much of it came out with the combs, and much that remained was gnarled and tangled; too curly, too wavy, to be worthy of the High Court. That, she could change, but not here, not in a tent upon the field of battle.

She pulled it tight instead. It pained the girl, but the girl was silent, for Diora had at last surrendered the child to her. She watched the infant suckle against the curve of white breast.

It hurt them both, but for different reasons.

"He is your first child," she said softly.

Teyla looked up and nodded.

"What is his name?"

"Na'diro," Teyla replied, her voice quivering. With fear. With affection. She recognized her mistake the moment the silence grew awkward. "You can name him," she said, the words a terrible rush of sound.

But Diora shook her head softly. Gently. She watched the baby try to find the breast, and the smile she shared with Teyla en'Leonne was a smile that only four other women would have recognized; they were all dead. "The pain passes."

"W–when?"

And Diora smiled. "I . . . I don't know for certain. I saw it only once. But it does pass. He will grow. You will grow."

"You have wives?"

It was not the question she expected. Her hands stilled. The jade in them was hard, but it was warm; she had carried it pressed too tightly to palm.

Ramdan came then, and took the comb from her hands. He pulled Teyla's hair into as straight a line as it would fall, and then he bound it, with pin, with jade, with a hint of gold.

Still, she did not answer.

The sari was wrapped with care around Teyla's arms; Diora again took the child and held it close. It slept, satiated now, the fire and the cries of the dying forgotten.

And before Ramdan had finished, Valedan entered the tent.

He made no noise, offered no warning; he simply appeared. His armor was scarred with the breath of fire, and his weapon hung loose by his side; his gauntlets were black. So, too, were his eyes; they made his skin look as pale as a Serra's—a Northern conceit.

No fault of his.

Diora bowed instantly to ground, and Teyla made haste to do the same, but once again, the babe was between the Serra and her customary grace. Ramdan came to her, but she could not—quite—let go of the burden she had adopted.

"Kai Leonne," she said. Teyla said nothing.

"Rise."

She rose instantly, adopting the face and stance of the obedient wife. It was not meant to please, but it was not meant to annoy; it simply was.

Valedan met her gaze and held it. He did not seem to see the village girl, and he did not seem to notice the baby.

"I cannot stay," he said, formal Torra coming from his dusty lips. "The army must move twenty miles this day. The first column has already left camp. The Callestan Tyr leads it."

She nodded.

"But I wanted to offer you my thanks."

And froze. She met his gaze. There was no amusement in it, and no indulgence; there was no hostility, no subtle sarcasm. She expected none of these things, for she heard only truth.

"My pardon, kai Leonne, but for what?"

His eyes narrowed a moment, judging her. He looked tired. "For the villagers," he said quietly. "The Tor'agar of Valente spoke with me briefly before he gathered his men."

Because he offered her the whole of the truth, she exposed herself utterly. "I did not do that for you."

"No. But you did it in my name, and it was what I would have desired, had I been present." He hesitated for just a moment, and then said, "Because I am Northern, and weak."

And then he was gone.

CHAPTER FOURTEEN

ESSLA was not Ashaf's village.

Kiriel's hand bore the deep indentations of a large crystal; it had drawn blood before she noticed, and the blood seemed to sink into the surface of gem, its cut facets absorbing whole a liquid that should have smeared its face.

Kiriel looked at the pendant, drawing it into the light. She knew what it had been to Ashaf, and because Ashaf had never lied to her, she had believed her. But with time, Kiriel had come to understand—however much she hated the understanding—that Ashaf was, and had been, a simple woman; a slave. What she knew was not all that could be known.

The pendant had grown heavy as they had approached Essla;

heavy and warm. She had felt it beating against the hollow of her throat, the space between her collarbones, as if it were a living thing, and at that, one that threatened sudden growth.

It was nascent now.

It was almost certainly magic.

But it was a magic that she didn't understand. She had seen magic before. She had been trained to know it, to understand, before it came to fruition, what its color entailed.

Not all have the sight, Isladar had said. *You have been gifted with sensitivity. Use it well. It is one of the few gifts you have that will keep you alive.*

Isladar.

Her hand ached.

She let the chain drop and looked up.

The Matriarch of Havalla stood before her, hands on two canes, one eye peering out from a tangle of gray. Like clouds, her hair rested upon her head, tucked in part beneath a frayed square of faded cloth. It might once have been blue.

"Where are you going, Kiriel di'Ashaf?"

"I am going South," Kiriel replied. "South with the Ospreys."

"You are going to the village of Russo," the old woman replied.

Kiriel was on her guard in an instant. There was something about this old woman that was familiar, and something about her that she did not like. "I don't know its name."

"No. You don't. But it is the village in which Ashaf kep'Valente was born; the village from which she was taken, as wife to the Tor'agar, and the village to which she was returned when he died. It is the village in which she was given permission to marry, and the village in which she buried not one, but all, of her children."

Kiriel said nothing.

And the Matriarch, waiting, said nothing.

But youth can know patience when it is gilded by fear, and in the end, Yollana of Havalla poked around in her pouch for her pipe, dropping a cane to do so.

Kiriel did not pick it up.

"Did she not tell you that?"

Again, Kiriel offered silence, but it was a resentful silence. How could this old woman know more about Ashaf than she did? Ashaf was *hers*.

"You don't ask me how I know."

"I don't care."

"No?" The woman's smile was not toothless, although it should have been. Kiriel briefly considered correcting the cosmetic flaw.

"I know it," Yollana told her, pushing leaf into pipe's bowl as if she were simply fidgeting, "because I went there to see her before she left. You were born then. You were young. Too young to remember."

"What does this have to do with me?"

"With you? Nothing. And everything. I have some gift of my own, a hazard of birth and inheritance. In my youth, I was much feared."

She was feared now, Kiriel thought, if she was a Matriarch. The men feared her. The women feared her.

"But in age, I am humbled, as we are all humbled. Age is distant for you, isn't it? But it will not always be so. You have the eyes of the god-born."

Kiriel started. Stopped. "My eyes are brown."

"They are to those without vision. To me, Kiriel di'Ashaf, they are gold, and bright." She finished playing with leaves, and lifted her hand. She did not play the elaborate game of seeking flint or tinder; instead she raised her palm above the pipe's bowl and leaves began to smolder.

It took control, to do that; control or meager power.

"I know who your father is."

Kiriel's hand touched the hilt of her sword; it hummed beneath her fingers. She had removed her gloves after the combat, a habit that had come from months of exposure to heat and the sweat it produced. It was not necessary now. The heat no longer touched her.

But the ring did.

"I came to Ashaf, one of three visitors."

In spite of herself, Kiriel was curious. Isladar had often warned her about the danger of curiosity, and she had seen, for herself, the truth of the warning; he had saved her life many a time.

He was not here.

He would never be here again.

And she *would not* miss him.

"Who were the three?"

"Ah, you've found your tongue."

"Old woman—"

But the pipe smoke curled from her lips, the guttered fire of an ancient dragon. Her smile was unkind, but Kiriel thought her incapable of any other smile. The lines that were worn around her mouth and eyes suited it, and only it.

Ashaf's smile had been different.

"The first was *Kialli,* the enemy."

Isladar, Kiriel thought. She said nothing.

"The second was I, myself."

"And the third?"

"I do not know if you have met her yet, but I would be surprised if you had not. She is called Evayne a'Nolan."

Kiriel closed her eyes.

"Shortly after these visits, Ashaf kep'Valente disappeared. We knew—we three—that she would never return to the Dominion; not alive, and not dead."

The old woman leaned forward then. "And we knew, as well, where she would go." She turned to the North, her pipe falling to her waist as she squinted against the day's light. But she did not name the Shining Palace, the Shining City, or its terrible Lord.

"Our enemies dwell there," the old woman said. "My enemies. I do not yet know if they are yours."

"They are mine."

"So you say. But you are young, and your allegiance is not yet clear to me." Her frown was brief. "You bear the shadow, girl. The Sun Sword wants your death. The Radann par el'Sol will not draw *Verragar* in your presence, at the command and request of the Tyr'agar."

"Blood is not choice," Kiriel said, through clenched teeth.

"Not for us, no. But for the god-born?"

"What do you want, old woman?"

"I gave Ashaf kep'Valente something of mine," the old woman replied, her throat raspy with smoke's sting. "It was a pendant, a stone upon a thick chain, a thing worn by Voyani women, and only Voyani women."

This much, Ashaf had said.

"You have it now."

Kiriel nodded warily.

"But it is not—and cannot—belong to you. It did not *belong* to Ashaf kep'Valente. I sent it North in her care and keeping because I knew that she would go North to where our enemy builds his great fortress, and plans his great war.

"And what she saw, it saw. What she knew—and she was not a foolish woman—it knows. It has returned to us with the tide of war, and it must come, at last, to its owner."

Kiriel said, "I have it now."

"It is not yours," Yollana replied warily. "It is around your neck, but it is heavy; it was not made for one who bears your blood."

"It has never rejected me, old woman. It has never hurt me."

"That is not its power," Yollana replied. "Nor its intent. Does it speak to you, girl?"

She was silent.

"It speaks to me. I hear its whisper."

"Then listen carefully," Kiriel snapped, "because that is all you will have of it."

"Kiriel di'Ashaf, you bear the Heart of Havalla."

The gem flared. Fire ringed her neck, bright, multihued. It was not a physical fire. But it was; the old woman's words had evoked its hidden magic.

"And Havalla has lived too long without its Heart."

"It will have to endure for longer," Kiriel replied. "Much longer. It is *all* that I have left of Ashaf, and I *will not surrender it*. You knew she was going to die." Anger heated the words, and the anger was old, unassailable, ungentled. "You used her. You all used her. But I—"

No. She would not admit that weakness here.

"We are all going to die," Yollana said quietly, losing some of the sharpness of feature that made her age so prominent. She raised a hand to the patch that hid part of her expression, and then let it fall. "And we have sacrificed much to ensure that our deaths aren't pointless.

"Ashaf lived in the North, but she was never at home there. If she were, you would not now be going to Russo, the Green Valley. You would not have insisted on staying in Valente, to your Tyr's detriment.

"I used her. Yes. We all did. But ask yourself, Kiriel: what would Ashaf tell you now, if she were here?"

"To eat more," Kiriel snapped. "And to sleep."

Yollana's frown was instant and sharp. Her tolerance for the defiant young, it seemed, was almost nonexistent.

"If I told her that her pendant was crucial to our efforts in this war, would she have held it? Would she have kept it to herself?"

"It doesn't matter, old woman. She's *dead*. And I don't care about your war."

Kiriel walked away. Yollana lifted a hand, opened her mouth, and then, as the young woman's back grew distant, let the one fall and the other close.

"She loved you, Ashaf," she said, speaking aloud and speaking to herself. With a grim nod, she bent—slowly and with some pain—and retrieved her fallen cane.

It was not what she had come for. It fulfilled none of her desire, and none of her family's need.

But in some strange fashion, it afforded her hope, and hope was in scant supply.

Anya a'Cooper looked up.

The fields were occupied by men and women; the children ran through short, muddy stalks. She remembered fields, in a different place, and they were nothing like this.

Lord Ishavriel had told her not to use her magic.

But the plants were speaking to her. Their colors had loud voices, and even pleasant ones; the wind was discordant, and she lifted a hand to still it at once. It was only in the way.

"I'm bored," she told the kinlord. Her hair had fallen flat with the absence of breeze, and the heat now made it cling to her skin. She *hated* that.

"Be patient, little Anya. We are almost done."

"But the barbarians—"

"Yes. They have caused us some damage. There is a chance that they will weaken the foundations of our spell. And if they do, they have a chance of breaking what we make of that beginning."

She snorted. "Hah. They can't touch *my* magic."

His smile was indulgent. But the shadows about his face, framing his pale skin, were loud and unpleasant. She wanted them to go away. She often did, but the one time she had tried to *make* them leave, he had been very angry.

"We have taken precautions to strengthen the spell's foundation," he told her genially. He wasn't angry now.

"Oh? What precautions? Where?"

"In a village North of here. If you wish, I will explain the theory."

She snorted again. "Oh, theory," she said, with a wave of her hand. "I don't like theory."

"As you wish."

She said, "The people here are frightened."

"Yes. They know that a war is about to be fought in their lands."

Her nose wrinkled. At her age, it looked odd; she had aged much in the time that Ishavriel had held her in his keeping. With age, her power had matured—but it was wild, this power, and unpredictable.

When she had come to the village, the first thing she had done was form a throne for herself from the trunk of a great tree. That itself was bad enough; worse, though, was the fact that she had first caused the tree to *grow*. It lay in the center of the sprawling village, where farmers' stalls ringed it, as if in obeisance.

Those stalls remained conspicuously empty.

The serafs themselves did not speak to either Ishavriel or his mage. He had chosen to come in the vestments of a wealthy clansman, and they had offered him the hospitality of their poor lands. It was difficult to accept only what was offered, but he had learned much in his time with Anya, and one of the most important of the lessons was this: she could not stand the reaving.

Women and children might die at her hand, but only because she was careless; there was no intent or malice in her uncontrolled magic.

But if the kin chose to harvest the stray soul, to take the life, slowly and at leisure, of the helpless, she killed them.

He was not in danger, of course, but he could not afford to offend her. Not yet.

Therefore, the people of this village had been kept safe by her idiosyncrasies. The time for that safety would pass. He could afford the wait; even in mortal reckoning, it would be short.

The horses were slow.

Kiriel thought it was because the roads themselves were fortified by reeds and wood chips; the hard, stone passages of the Empire were nowhere in evidence in the Terrean of Averda.

But if the horses were slow, the men on foot were slower still. Auralis had to call her to heel—his words—half a dozen times.

"Look," he finally said, wiping rivulets of sweat from his forehead and sparing his eyes in the process, "you've *got* to *slow down*."

She stared at him as if he spoke a foreign tongue. A tongue other than Weston. "Why?"

"You're outpacing the horses," he snapped. His chest rose and fell as he swallowed air between the carelessly placed words.

"So?"

"You aren't sweating. You aren't breathing heavily. You're outrunning the horses, and they don't like it."

"They don't like me," she replied, shrugging his hand off.

Except that it clung to her shoulder.

"Yes," he said, his voice quieting. "They don't. For a while, they didn't care. Think, Kiriel. What does it mean?"

That you're afraid, she thought with contempt. It was true. But it was Auralis' fear, and it was for her.

She slowed.

"The cerdan saw the Sun Sword," he said softly. He had no bardic gift; he could not keep his words from lofting on breeze and wind to prying ears. "They talk. This—this run—will make them talk more."

"I'm not afraid of them."

"No. You're not. I won't even tell you you should be. But I will tell you that you're weakening Valedan's position with every step you take."

"He gave me permission."

"Yes. Gods know why, but he did. Kiriel—"

Her eyes were dark. Dark and gold, a combination that spoke of both power and death. Auralis didn't flinch. Any other Osprey would have.

"We don't have time," she said at last.

"I know."

"Then why do you—"

"Time isn't our only enemy."

She started to speak, and he said, "Sanderton is dead because we moved too quickly. We know what we might face, now. We can't afford to walk into another trap."

"It wasn't a trap."

He hesitated. "It doesn't matter if it was a trap in intention or not; in the end, the effect was the same. Meralonne—"

"Don't speak to me about magi."

"All right. I won't. I'll speak to you about Kiriel."

She frowned.

Auralis shook his head. "Fight it," he said softly.

"Fight what?"

He caught the hand that bore the ring, and lifted it aloft. "This," he told her.

"I can't. I can't remove it."

He shook his head in frustration; it was a very familiar gesture— but not from Auralis. "This was made *for* you," he said at last. "If I understand Meralonne APhaniel at all, it was *meant* for you. It came for a reason."

"To weaken me?"

He shook his head. And then he nodded. Caught between these

answers, he was silent for a moment. "It's not a curse," he said at last. "I think—I'd bet—that it was meant to be a gift."

"With your own money?"

He laughed. "Yes, Kiriel, with my own money."

She had slowed; the horses had passed her. The banners were curtained by the fall of heavy branches, the long, long arms of trees that curved groundward in the lee of the path the army followed.

The Ospreys surrounded her now. Valedan kai di'Leonne stood at their center. She bowed as he approached, his horse suddenly restive. It eyed her warily, but it did not shy or jump. She made no move to approach it.

But she remembered that she could, at one point. That the horses of the South had not feared her touch.

"The army will not enter the village of Russo without you," Valedan kai di'Leonne said, looking down, the advantage of height surrendered by the openness of his expression.

She nodded. And then, looking down at the ring upon her hand, she slowly and hesitantly raised her palm to touch the side of his horse.

The horse didn't seem to notice.

Alesso di'Alesso gathered word, and it came from many sources, but in the end, it meant one thing. Time.

He did not smile. Did not allow himself that much expression. He hoarded his energy now, knowing it to be both necessary and precious.

"Send for the Sword's Edge," he told his Tyran. "And send, as well, for the Widan Sendari di'Sendari."

While he waited, he called for sweet water; he banished wine from the tent. Chairs, as well, were moved until they touched the side of canvas; only the table stood as it had been erected.

They came quickly, but they stood like shadows drifting around the heavy poles that anchored the weight of fabric. The energy that he hoarded, they had spent.

Both men bowed; he returned their grace with a nod of his own.

Cortano said, "You've had word."

He nodded. Smiled. "It appears," he said, "that the kai Leonne has chosen to march his forces through Valente." His shadow darkened the map as he leaned across it.

"That puts them a day's march from the body of our forces," Sendari said.

"A day's long march."

"Alesso," Sendari said quietly, "we have not yet broken the riddle of the *Kialli* seedlings."

"I have faith, old friend," he replied, the warning heavy in his voice. "You have never failed me. Do what you must; I will do the same."

He lifted his head. "Cortano."

The Sword's Edge nodded gravely. "You take a risk," he said.

"Men do," he replied. "The Lord's men. Summon the kin," he added. "And tell them that it is time."

Ser Jarrani kai di'Lorenza sat astride *Warfoot*; the banner of Lorenza shadowed his perfect helm. On either side, his sons were likewise mounted, and they gazed into the Northern trees as if they were the thinnest of veils, as if vision itself might part them. The sun was high: the Lord's visage was free from cloud in the azure of his dominion. Swords were unsheathed and they glinted like teeth; the teeth that gave the jaws of the army strength. The war drums were distant; Jarrani could not say with certainty which clan now played their thunder beneath the clear sky. A clan of the plains and valleys; a clan that was not made and broken by the dry winds of the desert.

In the South, no drums were sounded; none were needed. The Lord heard the hearts of men who, in silence, greeted the boldest of opportunities.

Fortunes would be made.

Legend would be written.

The day was theirs.

Eduardo kai di'Garrardi held the banner of Oerta by holding his own, aware of the duality of this existence. *Sword's Blood* was restive, as he himself was, although for different reason. He had been given no word of the Serra on whom his allegiance with Alesso di'Alesso depended. Shaky allegiance.

He had seen land ceded him as the army marched North into Averda, and he had accepted it as his due. It was not what he desired; it had come with neither bloodshed nor battle, and as such, was almost beneath notice. His Tyran knew this well. His Tors? Some knew, some did not. Some knew and chose not to believe. What man, after all, would place the value of a simple Serra above the value of the fertile lands of Averda?

His smile was sharp, contemptuous. For land, for the serafs of the fields, for the inconsequential, his men would surrender much.

Their lives. And what would they gain? Rice? Wheat? Oats to feed beasts of burden?

These, he had.

What he lacked was a wife who was worthy of him.

What he lacked was the Serra Diora di'Marano.

Still, he had played this game poorly. He could not now withdraw his men; the armies of the Tyr'agar—of Alesso *di'Marente*—were not the equal in number or strength of the armies they faced without the men of Oerta behind them.

But Alesso would march, regardless. And if Alesso marched and failed, the Serra Diora would pass from his hands as if she were wind, the wind's voice. In victory, he had his chance. Where else would she go? Where else, but to the side of the last of the Leonnes?

For he knew, although it had not been widely spoken of, that she had taken the Sun Sword.

No other woman would have dared.

He was reduced to trusting the word of the General who had slaughtered the whole of the Leonne clan, save one; reduced to trusting the word of the man who had subverted the Captain of the Leonne Tyran, and then offered him such an ignoble death for his trouble.

It did not sit well with him, but little did. Let him see battle, and he would find his strength again. All things with edges needed honing and sharpening.

The *Kialli* came, when called.

Dogs came in like fashion, but Alesso was no fool; he took a wary satisfaction from their presence, but nothing more. He did not trust them. They did not, of course, trust him. But they circled each other warily, their eyes turned outward, their thoughts inward. The warrior's dance; the dance of alliance. It was his dance, a sword-dance played out over the whole of a battlefield, with an army as his weapon.

Lord Ishavriel came alone. He offered Alesso all due respect in full view of the Tyran and the Tyr'agnati, and when he rose, said simply, "Anya is otherwise occupied, but she will join us when the time is come."

Almost more than could be hoped for.

"The others?"

"They are already among you," he said, showing the hint of teeth in a brief smile.

He was not speaking the whole of the truth, and this was unsettling, but not unexpected.

The Radann kai el'Sol had already pinpointed those of the kin who stood within the ranks of the common cerdan; they were few. Too few. The Radann par el'Sol watched them in a silence that was weighted with an intensity born upon the plateau of the Tor Leonne; they bided their time, but poorly and with ill-concealed enmity. Had that enmity not served his purpose, he would have been ill-pleased; as it was, he allowed the Radann the freedom of the encampment. Their blades sang. Even sheathed, he could hear their call.

But he did not choose to dally in argument here. The men were waiting. The wind held its breath as he took his place upon the plateau, beneath the banner of the sun ascendant. For a banner, it was huge, and it was weighted so that only the strongest of gusts would ripple the perfect gold of its embroidered surface.

The making had been costly and inconvenient. For the first and only time, he found himself missing the previous kai el'Sol. He let it go; the banner was what it was, and it served him as backdrop, a more certain and loyal liege than many of the men gathered here to serve him.

Kiriel di'Ashaf traveled toward the village of Russo.

She walked in the midst of the Ospreys, in formation around the Tyr'agar and his banner. The road had dusted it, paling the azure field upon which the sun rose. No one seemed to notice.

Thoughts were turned, instead, to war, and they were grim thoughts, judging by the expressions of the Ospreys. Sanderton's death had shaken them in some way that she could not fathom. This was war, she thought, and in a war, men died.

Auralis understood her confusion.

Understood it, and was only barely angered by it. Although she did not ask him, he offered the words that, strictly speaking, were forbidden dress guards. The Ospreys had learned much in the South; enough so that they were suitable company for a Northern Commander.

They would never learn enough to be suitable for a Tyr.

"He was the only one," he told her, the shape of his lips belying the movement words necessitated, "that didn't come to us from the gallows. The only one," he added, "that didn't bear the scars of the valleys of Averda."

"And that didn't make him less yours?"

Auralis snorted. It was an honest question, but he had little truck with honesty; the death had bitten him, drawing old blood. Aggravating old wounds.

"It made us a peacetime unit," he replied. "Yes, he was ours. But he was the only part of us that was Kalakar."

An anchor. She thought of the ships in the harbor of Essalieyan's largest city, and realized that she almost missed the taste of salt. "He was a symbol?"

"Yes," Auralis answered, but quietly, quietly. "He still is."

She didn't ask him of what.

She could see it, in the face of Duarte AKalakar, in the hunched shoulders of Alexis AKalakar. Fiara's face was slick with sweat and something other; she did not acknowledge the tears that fell. As if acknowledgment would somehow change their existence. But her hand was upon her sword.

Of the Ospreys, Fiara had been the only one to kill the village serafs. Alexis had reined her in, but it was a struggle. There was a madness about her that nothing but death would dislodge. It didn't matter whose.

But still . . . she walked with the Ospreys. If they had lost Sanderton, they still had one anchor: Valedan kai di'Leonne himself. He was not, and would never be, one of their number.

But he had fought by their rules, and he had failed to betray them; he was as close as an outsider could get.

Kiriel said softly, "Sanderton was not the only one."

Auralis frowned. "Kiriel—" And then he looked at her. He was certain of foot; he did not stumble or lose the rhythm of their march.

"But I'm not Sanderton," she continued, staring ahead, the ring cool upon her hand. "Whatever it was he had, I lack."

Auralis shook his head. But he did not offer pretty words or pretty denial. He said, "Sanderton wasn't one of us."

"But you just said—"

"We counted him, Kiriel. But he was a boy. He had never killed a man before. The only combat he saw, outside of drill—"

"He broke his hand in drill."

"—was against the demon kin. And that's cleaner."

"Clean?" Her brows rose into the line of her hair.

"War doesn't mean the same thing to you as it does to the rest of us."

"What does it mean to me?" The words were sharp. Sharper than she intended, and certainly sharper than she wanted. She stopped speaking.

"Who have you killed?" His hand rested easily upon the hilt of a sword.

She shrugged. "I've faced far greater dangers than even the kin-lord in Essla."

"You've faced demons," he said. "We've faced men."

As if men were somehow the greater threat.

The ground beneath her feet seemed to shift, and she didn't like it. Auralis was . . . her friend. Darker than the rest of the Ospreys. Tormented. And he was placing something between them that made no sense at all to her.

"And we've killed them. Like Fiara killed them. Worse." His face was impassive.

"Because you enjoyed it?"

He shrugged. He was gone now.

"Fiara killed the serafs," she said. She hadn't meant to say even that much.

"Because they attacked us. Because they wore an enemy's mask. Because she had to make someone pay for Sanderton. It's not the same." He shrugged. "Sanderton would have left us if he were forced to do what we did gladly in the last Annie war. He wasn't there; he joined us. He tagged along. We could have killed him, but we couldn't be rid of him in any other way.

"You weren't there when he arrived. He was our joke," he added, although the humor in the jest eluded them both. "We made the most of it. There's not a lot that makes an Osprey laugh, and it usually involves someone else's misery. The hazing he endured would have been enough to send anyone else back to the House. But Sanderton was persistent. He saw us as rebels. He saw us as Kalakar House Guards who somehow managed to stand outside the confines of natural order.

"He was a *fool*. He romanticized us. He thought our inability to parade and dress made us as common as he was. But he wasn't, in the end, like us. He couldn't have done what we did then."

"And now?"

"Men are soldiers," he said quietly, ignoring the intent in the two words. "They do what they have to do to survive. They stop thinking about it. It's easy not to think when someone is trying to kill you. But after—after, you think."

She didn't.

"You think that there's not much that separates them from you. Your unit is your family. Your unit is your friend. That's it. You do what you have to, to survive. You need to eat. You need to drink.

You need to sleep. So do they. The Generals? The Commanders?"
He spit. "They make their plans. They draw their maps. They line
up little markers and flags across their tables.

"Those markers are *us*. And we pay when they fail. We die."

"But you call them Annies."

Duarte's hiss was enough of a warning. She lowered her voice.

He shrugged. "They call us worse. It's part of the game."

"What game?"

"War. Survival."

"And the serafs?"

He shrugged. "Even that."

"The death of the helpless proves nothing."

He laughed. It was as dark a sound as she had heard in months.
"It proves power," he said bitterly. "It proves that we have it, and
they don't." She lost the march as she turned to look at him. For a
moment, the sunlight in her eyes, she could see the colors that
bound him, dark as night, threads of gray turning out from the middle as if struggling toward day. And losing.

"Demons are easy," he said. "They don't need what we need.
Food. Sleep. Shelter. Coin. They aren't *us*. They'll never be us."

"They'll never be you," she said coldly.

He closed his eyes. Even momentarily blind, his footing was
sure and certain. This was his life.

But it wasn't hers. She could feel the other life, biding its time,
coiled beneath the surface of a featureless, plain band.

"They're a gift," he said softly, the darkness leaving his voice.

"A . . . gift."

"Yes. Because when we fight demons, we can pretend, for days
at a time, that we *aren't* demons ourselves."

"I can't," she said, just as softly.

He reached out to touch her shoulder and then let his hand fall
away.

She knew when the distance between Essla and Russo vanished.
The sudden bend in the road carried them through trees, and the
trees were the same for miles. But there was something about their
placement here that struck her, absorbing her attention.

Something warmed her throat, the skin in the hollow between
her collarbones. She did not fight it; this was Ashaf's memory, and
it was as close as she would ever come to Ashaf again.

Sanderton was forgotten.

Ashaf remained. And Ashaf's knowledge lay hoarded within the heart of a gem that the Matriarch of Havalla claimed as her own.

Let her try to take it. Old woman, crippled, one-eyed—what threat did she pose? She had used Ashaf, and Kiriel had no intention of rewarding her.

No intention of depriving herself of this.

"Kiriel?"

She looked up. Auralis' expression had shifted.

"What?"

"Is there something wrong?"

She shook her head. "Not wrong," she answered. "Familiar."

He was on guard before the last syllable was taken by breeze and the rustle of leaves. She did not correct him. He was not part of Ashaf's world.

But the trees here were. The bend in this road. The certain sight of fields beyond the dip in the land that led to the valley's heart. She turned to look down the column of moving men, but she could not see Ser Danello kai di'Valente; his banner was lost in the distance, lost to emerald and jade, to leaves with white edges and yellow hearts.

She had started to move too quickly, and Auralis caught her arm, pulling her back. Had he been any other man, she would have killed him.

She held her hand, but it was difficult; the army was not a part of Ashaf's life, and she was leading them toward it.

Ashaf feared soldiers. She always had.

And Kiriel had not known even that much until this moment, although she could have guessed.

"Kai Leonne," she said.

"Sentrus?"

"Where will the army encamp?"

His smile was brief and strange, as unlike an Osprey's smile as—as Sanderton's had been. "Three miles outside of Russo," he replied. "The trees there have been cleared, but fields have not yet been planted. They will hold us, with difficulty, but they will not require us to take from the village what it does not have. The river runs through both," he added.

She nodded, fighting the urge to throw herself at his feet in gratitude. It was not hers. It was Ashaf's, a seraf's.

"Kiriel?"

She held herself still.

"What does Russo hold for you?"

"My mother was born here," she told him, and then she was silent. The lie left her lips with the desire that it somehow be transmuted into truth. *Like lead,* she thought, *into gold,* thinking of old stories, *Kialli* stories, about the folly of Man.

He did not ask. Instead, he said, "We will take care to make certain that what waited us in Essla does not lie in wait in Russo."

She nodded.

Feeling, as she did, that something was wrong.

It was the tree.

It stood alone in the center of the valley's flat, and it towered above the small huts and houses, denying them the light of the sun. And perhaps, in the South, that denial was a gift.

But her frown drew words from Auralis.

Her name. "Kiriel."

Funny, how often he said her name, how much he could put into the syllables.

"The tree," she said.

"What about it?"

"It wasn't there before."

"When before?"

"Sixteen years ago. Seventeen."

He frowned. "Trees don't grow that much in seventeen years."

"I know." She held up a hand, palm out. It was not mailed or gloved.

Valedan pulled his horse up, and his Tyran—Andaro—lifted a horn to his lips, blowing a single high note into the sound of marching feet, heavy hooves, cracking undergrowth. An army was a sluggish thing; it started and stopped slowly and ponderously.

"Sentrus?"

She shook her head. "Let me go," she said quietly.

"What is wrong?"

"The tree."

He raised a brow. "What of the tree?"

"It wasn't there. It shouldn't be there now."

He frowned. "Take the Ospreys with you."

She shook her head.

"Sentrus—"

Thinking as she did of Fiara, and Fiara's endless anger. "No. Not the Ospreys. You—you may need them." It was a lie. Funny, that she had grown up in the Shining Court and had never learned to lie well.

"Primus?"

Duarte AKalakar's frown was more felt than seen; she did not take her eyes from the tree, although her eyes trailed its length, following the shadows it cast as if they were a map.

"Take Auralis," he said at last. "Sentrus."

She opened her mouth, and then snapped it shut on the words.

Kallandras of Senniel said, from out of nowhere, "I will accompany your Sentrus, kai Leonne. With your permission."

"And I," Meralonne APhaniel added.

She had not seen them approach. Had not even wondered where they had been, and how long they had been listening.

"Done," Valedan said quietly.

It came to Kiriel, before she began her descent into the flat, that Valedan was concerned for *her*. She turned back to look over her shoulder and met his gaze; it was steady.

"I don't understand," she said.

He was too far away to hear the words; she knew this. But in spite of the distance, he nodded, as if the words themselves were superfluous and meaning flowed between them unencumbered.

Kallandras was disconcerting. He made no noise.

His feet did not seem to break undergrowth; his shoulders skirted the underside of low-lying branches. Only his shadow gave evidence that he moved at all, and this was unsettling. Many were the creatures she had met who were capable of this silence.

Meralonne APhaniel did not trouble himself to hide his presence. He strode firmly, clad now in the awkward and cumbersome robes of the magi. Yet she noted that he, too, did not leave much of a trail in his wake; that was left to her, to the girl who did not know how to move without destroying something.

But Ashaf had not known how either. Ashaf, whose feet were light in youth and heavy in age, had come down this path many times, and her feet had left their mark. A season's passage erased it; a small herd of children erased it—but it was there for a moment, evidence that she was real.

Auralis' tread was heavy; heavier than her own. But he did not seem to notice. He accepted the presence of bard and magi as if it were commonplace, and perhaps it was—in the Empire. Here, in the forests and valleys of Averda, it should have been worthy of note.

But he noticed only her. He glanced at her often, as if she were a weather vane, and he could tell the prevailing wind by a glimpse of her expression. And perhaps he could.

Serafs toiled at the edge of the village, in fields that lay sprawled within the basin of the forest above. She did not recognize them.

And she did.

"Kiriel?"

She shook her head and familiarity receded. "The tree," she repeated.

He nodded.

"Stay here," she ordered quietly. "Kallandras. Meralonne. Stay."

The three men looked at each other in silence.

Kallandras asked, "Is this wise?"

She shrugged.

"Kiriel—Duarte said—" Auralis began.

"You can ignore his commands when it suits you," she snapped. "Do it when it suits me."

His brow rose, singly, in a familiar arch. Nothing of Ashaf there, but it was comforting. "If you meet a demon—"

"I'll send it back to the Hells," she said cheerfully.

"You're already up on me."

"This one won't count."

He snorted.

"No one who has money riding on it is watching."

"I have money riding on it."

"Liar."

He laughed. "Go," he said. "We'll wait here for half an hour."

She wasn't invisible. Armor alone guaranteed that. Children pointed to her; her hair was long, but braided, and she was slender enough that distance did not immediately make gender an issue; she was armed, and armored. She wondered if they thought her a young clansman; they did not approach.

In fact they seemed to burrow into the fields until they were unseen; she wondered at that as well. But she did not call out; did not command their presence. She knew how, by now; she had seen it done often.

No, she wanted them gone; wanted them as far from the tree as possible.

It lay at the heart of mystery, and mystery was death.

As she approached the tree, the huts grew closer together, and layers of roof and shingle hinted at their age. There were gardens around the open doorways, and from the open windows, creepers trailed groundward. At this time of day, those huts would be empty of all but the sick or the dying.

She hoped they were empty now.

They lay in shadow.

The tree's shadow.

As she cleared the last of the houses—last and largest—she saw that the tree itself had been twisted in its growth; that the bark had been smoothed away at its base, and the trunk warped and twisted into a shape that nature would never have grown: a chair.

A chair beneath the bowers, a thing that hinted at either majesty or power.

She knew, then.

Breath escaped her in a hiss.

"Anya!"

Echoes were absorbed by the tree.

She called again, and again silence answered.

She did not waste breath a third time; instead she walked to the half-exposed roots that twisted beneath the great branches above, and climbing them, she made her way to the chair.

It was a throne, of course. Made not of stone but of wood, and yet recognizable for all that. Anya had always had a fascination with thrones—but normal chairs wouldn't do; she had seen the work of the Lord, and she desired to mimic it in some fashion, to make the chair part of a whole that involved ground and roof; a single work.

Only Anya could have done this.

And where Anya traveled, Ishavriel also went.

She did not sense him, but the ring might prevent it; she felt its sudden chill upon her finger.

There were many ways to summon Anya a'Cooper, and none of them were precisely safe. Kiriel chose the easiest: she sat upon the throne.

The door to the large house flew open, slamming against mud and wood. It seemed out of place in the village, where few dwellings had such a Northern conceit. It was, of course. Anya was very particular about her privacy.

Minutes passed, and then someone emerged; Kiriel could see the clenched fists exit the door first, followed rapidly by shaking arms and a bowed head.

She folded her arms and gestured, and Kiriel braced herself, watching with interest as Anya disappeared.

And reappeared just to the right of where Kiriel now sat.

She was old, Kiriel thought, with surprise. She hadn't looked so old the last time they had met. But age did not bind or fetter her, and her voice—when it at last emerged from the awkward gape of open lips—was as young as a child's.

"Kiriel!"

Kiriel di'Ashaf smiled and rose at once. "I'm sorry," she said, "but you weren't answering, and I thought it was the easiest way to get your attention."

"Kiriel!"

The younger woman laughed and held out her arms; Anya threw herself into them and tightened her own about Kiriel's slim shoulders.

She pulled back with a frown. "Why are you wearing *that*?"

"That?"

"That sword. I don't *like* it, Kiriel."

"It was a gift," Kiriel replied gravely. "From Lord Isladar and Lord Anduvin."

"Oh."

It was a simple conversation. They had had it many times in the winter of the Northern Wastes. It seemed just as natural beneath the summer sky.

"Ishavriel didn't tell me you'd be here!"

"Is he here?"

Anya's lips twisted in a grimace. "No."

"Where is he?"

And lifted in a smile, a sly one. "He's gone," she said, and giggled.

"Did you send him away?"

"Me? No. He was summoned." She lowered her voice. "We're about to work a great magic here," she said, in the confidential tones of a mad child.

"And he's left to start it?"

The frown again. "I think he's gone to join the barbarians."

"Oh. Well, that seems boring."

"It *is*. It's terribly boring. But it was worse, there. Too many men, and Ishavriel said I wasn't allowed to kill his kinlings."

"Kinlings?"

"Oh, he has them hidden away in the army," she said casually. She slid herself into the seat that Kiriel had vacated, stretching her arms against the length of the rests as if they were cats. "At least, he thinks they're hidden," she added. "But they're not. The men know all about them. Ishavriel thinks men are stupid. They're not. Well, not all of them."

"And the men haven't killed them?"

She shrugged. "Maybe they were leaving them for me." Her eyes brightened. "Or maybe they were leaving them for *you*!"

"That would be nice of them," Kiriel replied. She looked up, and up again; to see the height of the tree, she risked falling. It was a risk worth taking; at this distance, the tree was impressive.

And Anya a'Cooper had never been much of a threat to Kiriel.

"Are you going to join the army, too?"

"Not now," Kiriel said. "At least not that one."

"Why not?"

"Well, it's boring, for one," Kiriel said. "And they don't let women join them, for two."

"They don't?"

"No."

"Oh. But I was there."

Kiriel could imagine just how well that had worked out. "But you're here now."

Anya yawned, exposing yellowed teeth. "But I'm *bored.*"

"Then tell me about this great magic of yours."

"Well, it's not exactly mine," Anya confessed. "But if it weren't for *me,* it wouldn't work. Ishavriel said so."

"That's because Ishavriel doesn't have a tenth of your power."

Anya laughed. "I told him that once. It didn't make him happy. The shadows hissed and burbled for *hours.*"

"Were they rude?"

Anya nodded. "*Very.*"

"Well, then, it's best not to tell him that again. Not yet. Still, he does need you. They all do."

"They do."

"What does the magic do, Anya?"

"Why?"

"Well," Kiriel said, looking out into the village, "this was Ashaf's home."

Anya fell silent. After a moment, she said, "Ashaf's dead." Her voice was flat and heavy—a woman's voice.

It was when she was oldest that she was most fey. But Kiriel wasn't afraid. "Yes," she said, her voice as dark as Anya's.

"Is that why you left me?"

"Yes. I had to leave," she added.

"Why?"

"Because I couldn't kill them all."

Anya nodded. "You should have asked me," she said quietly. "I would have helped you. I *liked* Ashaf. Even if she was afraid of me."

"She was afraid of me, too."

"I know." Anya shook her head. "But she loved you anyway. Do you think she loved me?"

"I'm certain of it," Kiriel said, and reaching out very gently, she placed her hand over Anya's.

"She never sang her song for *me*."

"Because you weren't a baby."

"Oh. But you weren't either."

"No—but she brought me when I was a baby. Remember?"

Anya frowned. Then her expression flipped, turning instantly. "Yes! I remember. You didn't cry too much."

"She sang me the song when I was a baby," Kiriel said. "And then she forgot that I wasn't a baby, and she sang it anyway."

"Do you want me to help you kill them all?"

"Yes, but not now."

"Why not?"

"Because they're in the North."

"Oh, that." Anya's smile grew sly. "They're in the North now, but they won't be in the North for long."

Kiriel's expression didn't shift or change. Nothing about her did. Her hand continued to rest atop Anya's, as if they were sisters, or kin.

"What do you mean, Anya?"

"Well, it's the magic I told you about," she said, her confidence growing.

"What about it?"

"It's supposed to bring them all here."

"*All?*"

"Well, maybe just the important ones."

"When, Anya?"

"When the armies meet. There are more than one," she added. "I remember Marcus used to talk about armies when I was little. Southern armies and Northern ones. It was a story. Mother told me I shouldn't ask him, though. He lost his hand," she added, lowering her voice. "He had a stump."

"He didn't go to a healer?"

"He didn't have money," she said. "And it's more expensive if you wait. That's what my mother said."

"How does this magic work, Anya?" Allowing Anya to speak of her mother or father was perhaps the most dangerous thing that

Kiriel could do. She had learned it, at cost, in the curiosity of her childhood.

Anya wrinkled her nose, or rather, she added depth to the wrinkles that bracketed it. "I don't know. Something about trees. They're only supposed to come *here*. There's a magic that's like a giant door. You know, like the gate."

"That's a big magic."

Anya nodded solemnly. "I helped build the gate," she added.

Kiriel nodded. She did not bother to flatter Anya; flattery was a dangerous game. Anya was mad, but she wasn't stupid.

"Well, this one is different. No snow, for one. And lots of people. And trees. It's hot here," she added, "and I don't like the heat. Where was I? Oh, I remember. It's supposed to work in a big, big space. Bigger than this village. Bigger than The Lord's gate." Her voice got smaller when she mentioned The Lord. It was her version of respect.

"But the Northern Empire will know," Kiriel said. "That's why we wait in the Wastes. Or is The Lord now ready to face the Empire?"

"The Empire won't know!" Anya leaped lightly out of her chair. "There's a barrier," she added. "It can't be crossed by magic." She sidled closer to Kiriel, and added, "It's made of *trees*. And there are so many trees here, who's going to notice a few more?"

"That's very clever."

"I think it's a waste of time. Who cares if they know?"

"The Lord does."

"Oh." She deflated. "Then I guess we'll just have to live with it."

"Anya, who is coming?"

"I don't know. The Lord's Fist, probably. I don't think Isladar will be there, though."

Kiriel said nothing.

"You're sure you didn't know about this already?"

"I wouldn't ask you if I knew."

Anya nodded to herself. Her gaze was caught a moment by the knotwork of roots; Kiriel knew she was listening to their voices.

"But there is another army coming," Kiriel said quietly.

"When?"

"Tomorrow. It will cross through the village."

"This one?"

"This one."

"Should I fight it?"

"Not by yourself," Kiriel told her. "And not here."

"Why?"

"This was Ashaf's home," Kiriel said again. "And I want to protect it for her."

"From the Northern army?"

"From both armies."

"Oh. All right, then. I haven't killed anyone."

"Thank you."

Anya stood up brightly. "Ishavriel said I should stay here."

"You can stay here, if you want."

"Well, I don't want to meet an army," she said, thinking to herself. "Soldiers are always cross. Cross or frightened. Or they kill people. They even kill the women and children. And then, of course, I have to kill *them,* and then *everyone* complains."

"Well, in the South, the women and children aren't valued as highly as the men."

Anya snorted. "They're more important to *me,*" she said, dangerous now.

All of the danger was for others; none for Kiriel. "Why don't you stay here, Anya? If you leave, you'll meet the other army."

"I already *know* that one." She wiped her palms absently against her robes; they were very fine, and entirely out of place. "I think I'll leave. Will you watch my throne?"

"Yes."

"Make sure no one sits in it."

"I won't let anyone sit in it. But I have to ask you a favor," she added.

Anya tilted her head to one side. "What's that?"

"Lord Ishavriel has never liked me," Kiriel said.

"Well, no. He only likes me."

"I know."

"You don't want me to tell him you're here?"

"I think he might have already guessed," Kiriel said quietly. "But he thinks he's so smart. If he hasn't, I'd like it to be a surprise."

Anya sniffed. "He's part of the Lord's Fist," she said, thinking it over. "And *they* won't be happy."

"No, and if they are very unhappy, they will try to kill me. I may have to go away again."

"But I just found you!"

"I know," Kiriel agreed.

"Well, all right then. What should I say?"

"Tell him that the army is coming, and that you didn't want to fuss with them."

"Oh. All right."

"And I'll see you soon. You'll come with the other army?"

"I'll be there. But I won't let them hurt you," she added, reaching out to touch Kiriel's cheek. "And I won't let them hurt Ashaf's home either. Okay?"

"All right."

Anya nodded, and began to walk away. "Oh," she said, turning back.

"Yes?"

"You can sit in my throne if you want. But only you."

CHAPTER FIFTEEN

COMMANDER Bruce Allen had only one question in the hole Meralonne's brief report made in what had been a discussion among the strategic commanders.

"Where is the Sentrus, Kiriel di'Ashaf?"

The mage's silver brow rose over gray eyes, an arch that indicated some measure of independence. He was not, however, a truculent man—for which the other Commander present was grateful. She was also grateful that Devran—The Berriliya to his forces— would meet them on the *other* side of Russo; she had enough of a headache as it was, and his smug, condescending glare would have added to it immeasurably. He was always testy in situations like this one.

Sadly, he wasn't the only one. Bruce Allen swiveled on one foot, and although his glance was not—quite—a glare, its meaning was obvious. "Ellora?"

No rank here. That would have set Devran's teeth on edge, given the number of Annagarians present. Oh, well. Win some, lose some.

"I think the disposition of a single Sentrus insignificant given the weight of the news she sent." Beside her, she could see Verrus Korama wince. She'd give him that; it wasn't exactly a brilliant comeback. Nor did Bruce dignify it with a reply.

"Master Bard," he said stiffly, to Kallandras.

Kallandras of Senniel College executed a perfect bow. He was an artisan with words, but what might have come from his silver tongue was preempted by the boy Tyr.

"I gave her permission to wait within Russo," Valedan said. "Given her sensitivities, and her particular abilities, I thought it might save us the experience of another Essla."

Commander Allen stiffened.

Ellora felt some private sympathy for him, although she also had to struggle to keep a smile from tugging at the corners of her lips. While Bruce had never born the Ospreys the same personal contempt that Devran did, he was aware of their nature.

"I concur," he said, although his tone was completely flat. He was not used to a field that was not within his command. It chafed. It chafed them all.

But the boy had yet to disgrace himself.

That, she could hear Devran say coldly, *is because we have yet to see battle.*

It was true. And much rode on the outcome of this battle. The war.

"But at the same time," Commander Allen continued, leaning back from the map and continuing to enforce the iron discipline he was famed for upon his own expression, "we have only a second-hand source of information."

"It *is* possible," Meralonne APhaniel said, reaching for his pipe without bothering to ask if smoke was welcome, "that she felt a magi was a better judge of the truth of the information she imparted."

The magi were a different problem. Ellora took a step forward and felt Korama's hand upon her shoulder.

"Well, magi," she said, shaking it off, "judge. Is what she spoke of even possible?"

"Who can say, where gods are concerned?"

"We were hoping you could."

He smiled, and embers flared orange in the bowl of his pipe.

To either side, the Tyr'agnati evinced mild distaste for the habit they were now subject to. Pipe smoke seemed a custom of the North; in the South it was considered feminine, in a fashion, for only the Voyani women seemed to cling to it in the Dominion. But they did not otherwise offer offense to the magi.

"In my considered opinion, yes."

"Then the question that has to be asked—and it can't, one assumes, be asked usefully of you—is how many of the kin there are."

Meralonne nodded. "She spoke of the Northern Wastes," he said quietly. "It is not an area that is easily traversable by our geographers. If we take her life as evidence of their prior presence, if we assume that they have been biding their time in the remote isolation of the Wastes for at least sixteen years, the answer is . . . not comforting."

"A hundred? A thousand? Ten thousand?"

"Tens of thousands, I would think. Depending on many factors."

Commander Allen did not blink. Nor did the Tyr'agnati. But they offered silence; Bruce was pragmatic. "Such as?"

Meralonne frowned. Smoke trailed from the corner of his pursed lips, wreathing his face, and lending it the patina of age, of dirt. Ellora had never trusted people who aged gracefully. Then again, if she were perfectly honest, she didn't trust people much, period. It was safer.

"Commander Allen, Commander Kalakar," he said, inclining his head, his expression shifting subtly, "we must speak here of things that are customarily forbidden us in the presence of outsiders."

Ramiro kai di'Callesta raised a dark brow. "We are hardly outsiders in this," he said, but there was a hint of dark amusement in the words.

The Lambertan Tyr showed no such grace.

"It concerns the kin," Meralonne added softly, "and the Empire's last . . . difficulty . . . with the threat they present."

Valedan kai di'Leonne said, "I am aware of some of the history of Averalaan."

"You are aware of the Henden, then, in the year 410?"

He nodded. "It is not something that is often spoken of. Mirialyn told me."

He shrugged. "What she told you is common knowledge."

"Then deliver what is commonly known," Ramiro said quietly.

"Seventeen years ago the demons found a way to reside beneath the city streets. They took many of the Imperial citizens with them, and they . . . killed them. The whole of the city could hear their deaths.

"The Princess rode through the streets of the city, then. She rode with Commander Sivari and the Queen Siodonay, and they rallied their people."

"And the demons?"

"They stopped. They were defeated."

"How?"

He shrugged. "The Kings and the priests of their gods gathered the warrior magi—"

"Mag*es*," Meralonne interjected.

"Mages, then, and they went to the statue of Moorelas. Or Morel of Aston—the scholars argue a lot about his name—and they passed out of sight of all witnesses."

Meralonne raised a brow. But he nodded.

"Commander Allen?"

"The army was not called to serve," he said stiffly. "Not there."

"You did not bear witness to what occurred," Ramiro asked quietly.

"No."

"But you know."

"I read the reports that were filed after. Such as they were." His glare slid off the side of the magi's face. The magi in particular were not known for their love of any paperwork that did not somehow garner the attention of their peers—and peers were defined as other mages.

"And those?"

Commander Allen chose his next words with care. But they seemed casual enough to all listeners, even Ellora, who knew better. "They found a passage into the underground, and they found the demons. They fought them there, and with the aid of envoys from the Western Kingdoms, they managed to avert the destruction of the city."

"How?"

Silence.

"It may be relevant, Commander," Valedan insisted.

"It may be, but it is not a feat that we could repeat," he replied.

"What he does not say," Meralonne continued, picking up the scant, curt threads of a story that had been eviscerated, "is that the demons were there for the sole purpose of summoning their Lord."

"Their Lord?"

"The Lord of Night, as you fashion him in the South. We have another name for him in the North, but I will not invoke it here."

"Wise," Ramiro agreed. The Lambertan Tyr said nothing.

"The forces of the North succeeded. And," Meralonne added, as the embers in the pipe died, "they failed."

"It was not—"

"It was not a complete failure. Had it been, the forces you face now would be forces against which you would stand no chance."

Ser Mareo kai di'Lamberto could be expected to bristle. He did not. His hands remained by his sides, one resting upon the hilt of an ancient sword.

"But the Lord of Night is here."

"The Lord of Night is here," Meralonne agreed.

It was always difficult when the magi were agreeable.

Baredan di'Navarre strode into the tent, accompanied by Ser Anton di'Guivera. He bowed stiffly to the Tyr'agar. "My apologies for our absence, Kai Leonne. Ser Anton was training the newer cerdan," he added, by way of explanation.

Ser Anton, however, seemed to feel no need for apology. In the South, this said much about his worth to the Tyr'agar.

"The Serra Diora?" Valedan said, a shade too quickly.

"Ser Andaro di'Corsarro remains at her side," Baredan replied. This time, a hint of humor showed. Clearly, the Tyran did not think much of his duties.

"Good."

"And, in case you worry, the Matriarch of Havalla has also taken up residence in her tent. If there is a danger to her, it will not come from the men. Not more than once."

Valedan nodded and subsided.

"The Lord of Night is in the Northern Wastes, but in the opinion of the god-born—or rather, their parents—he is much diminished by his entry into this world. He cannot sustain his presence without sacrifice, and in the Northern Wastes, such sacrifices are, out of necessity, rare.

"Without them, he has little power."

"Little power?"

"Relative to the power he once possessed."

"And we therefore have some chance of defeating him."

"Of frustrating his aims in the South, yes. If he comes to the field itself, we will lose."

There was no question at all in the words. Less than none; there was absolute certainty. The pipe was emptied in the silence, and filled once again with noxious leaf.

"Then it seems clear," Commander Allen said, "that he must not come to the South. APhaniel, there are magi scattered throughout the three armies; summon them. I put them at your disposal."

"I do not consider this wise," Meralonne replied. "But give me half, and I will do what I can to unravel this mystery."

Ser Mareo kai di'Lamberto raised his hand then. It was so unusual, everyone turned.

"You will have help, I think," he said quietly.

"Help?"

"Kai Callesta, you have fought by the side of Alesso di'Marente.

As have I. Is he a man who would willingly allow the Lord of Night free passage into domains he considers his own?"

Ramiro di'Callesta shook his head. "But it is clear that the par Marente has chosen to ally himself with the forces of that Lord."

"He would ally himself with the forces of any," the kai Lamberto said quietly, "who could offer him the Dominion. But he would not do so with the expectation that he would rule as a puppet. Others, perhaps. But not the General."

"I concur."

"Then you think this is done without his knowledge?"

"I think it is done without his certain knowledge," Ser Mareo replied, struggling with the odd sounds and syllables of Weston. "But it is done. In the South, we accept this as truth: Allies are enemies who stand beside you, rather than behind you. The ally who stands at your back is either Tyran, or a man with a dagger. But allies have their own plans, and their own goals, not all of which involve your survival."

"And how does he intend to control these allies?"

"That is not clear," Ser Mareo replied. He looked at the Callestan Tyr. The Callestan Tyr did not immediately reply. But at length, he said, "Send your magi. Your mages," he added, before Meralonne could speak. "We have Widan among our ranks, but they are few indeed, and they are not to be trusted."

"In a task of this nature?"

"In almost any task. They are beholden to the Sword's Edge, and the Sword's Edge stands beside the General Marente."

"Can we capture one of the kin?" Commander Allen asked. He was watching Valedan.

Valedan shook his head. "Not capture, no. But there is, within the encampment, one who might better understand their nature."

"And that?"

Meralonne's pale brow rose. "You risk much, Tyr'agar," he said softly.

"Always," was Valedan's serene response. "But I have everything to lose."

Meralonne guttered his pipe with a gesture. "If you will allow me, Tyr'agar," he said, bowing low, his robes flowing around his arms and down to ground.

Valedan nodded. "But, APhaniel, proceed with caution. He is beholden to the Sentrus Kiriel di'Ashaf AKalakar, and everything you say or do reflects upon her."

"I will endeavor to bring him here. Wait," he added. Then, turn-

ing, he nodded to Kallandras of Senniel College. The bard waited a
breath's beat, and then, bowing, joined him.

They did not go to find Lord Telakar. Not precisely. Instead, they
went to the isolated tent which held the Voyani woman. Elena of
Arkosa, Daughter to the Matriarch. She allowed no healer, and no
healer's touch, or so she had said—but they found her in the presence of one healer-born. Ser Laonis di'Caveras, a man who traveled
in silence and anonymity in the van of the kai Leonne. He did not
wear the twin palms of the healer, so prevalent and so revered in the
North, and his beard and hair had been sun-touched in his travels to
his homeland.

He was silent.

The woman in the bed was sleeping.

She had been bandaged, and her wounds bound; days—perhaps
weeks—had passed since she had been quietly inserted into the
army. Valedan kai di'Leonne had given permission for her to travel,
but he had given it reluctantly. It was easy to see why.

Although she had suffered only two wounds, they had been
deep; the possibility that blood loss would kill her had been grave
for the shadowed four days she had clung to life.

In that time, in all that time, the Lord Telakar had remained by
her side, menacing and cold. She was a seraf, although the Voyani
were free, and he was her owner. She had survived the wounds
taken at the hands of said owner, but she had not thrived in the confines of the Callestan domis. The open road, however, did not suit
her either, or so it seemed to the men who now stood in her presence.

Ser Laonis rose instantly as they entered.

Kallandras of Senniel bowed low to the ground. Meralonne did
not. "You will forgive me," he said, his voice cool, "but I am an old
man, and my knees are stiff in this clime."

"Why are you here?" Ser Laonis said, standing, his hand upon
the hilt of his sword. It was awkward to see a healer so armed, as
certain a sign that they dwelled in the South as they had yet seen.

"We have come to visit Elena of Arkosa," Meralonne replied, before Kallandras could speak. "She desired no healer," he added,
"and if I am not mistaken, such desires are instrumental in the continued existence of said healers. She is Voyani."

"In the South, healers rarely heal," Ser Laonis said quietly. "It is
considered unmanning."

"And you are here?"

"I am well versed in arts that are not the Lady's," he replied, with a quiet dignity.

Kallandras recognized him; he had seen him before, within the arena in which the final test of the Kings' Challenge was performed. Had seen him by the side of the kai Leonne, after the battle with Andaro di'Corsarro and the doomed Carlo di'Jevre. "Your pardon," he said, his voice smooth and placating. "I did not expect to find a Northern healer in the South."

"Nor did I, if we are honest," Ser Laonis replied. He tried to smile. It was dismal failure. "She is well, but she will not rise. She will not speak. She eats little."

"You have joined her in her fast?"

Ser Laonis frowned. Some Southern steel ran through him, and this familiarity of question bordered on the offensive. But he did not speak; the truth was plain to see. The South had devoured the comfort of Northern food and peace.

"Why are you here?" he demanded curtly.

"We must speak with Elena of Arkosa," Kallandras replied.

"Why?"

"Because she has shown herself to be of value to Telakar," Meralonne cut in, his voice harsh in spite of its quiet, its calm. "And we have need of him."

"If it is true that you have need of me, Illaraphaniel," Lord Telakar said coldly, "you had best consider with care what you next do."

The magi shrugged. "Lord Telakar," he said, turning, "what a surprise to find you here."

Lord Telakar of the Shining Court stood in the heart of the Tyr'agar's tent. He was not on display, but he might as well have been; Ser Mareo kai di'Lamberto was almost white, an alabaster relief of a severe man.

Nor did Valedan himself seem comfortable in the presence of the kinlord—but Valedan kai di'Leonne openly carried the Sun Sword, and it sang in its sheath; it was not silent.

Lord Telakar frowned at the two men. Frowned, but did not speak. He stood just in front of Meralonne APhaniel, and to one side of Kallandras of Senniel College. Their placement was no accident, although the tent itself encouraged physical proximity by simple expedient of size.

The kinlord bowed briefly. It was not—quite—a gesture of respect. But it was acceptable; no man present demanded the burden of his loyalty or his allegiance.

"Lord Telakar," Meralonne said, "has spent much time in the Shining Court."

"I have," the kinlord said, his voice a thing of desert night. "And I warn you all now that there is a risk in my presence here."

"That risk?"

"If the Lord of Night takes the field, and he is aware of my presence—and he will be—everything I have learned will be his for the taking."

It was a costly admission.

Mareo kai di'Lamberto drew sword. He drew it slowly, but the speed of the gesture made it no less threatening, for the blade was glowing with a light that wavered between blue and white. It cast no shadow, but it demanded that no shadow be cast, and in the room, there was only one.

Lord Telakar raised a brow, and his features shifted subtly, changing the line of his face. He was tall and slender, but the light added hollows to his cheeks and length to his chin, length to his arms and his fingers. The effect was striking.

And uncomfortable.

"We have had word," Meralonne said quietly, "that the Shining Court may indeed present itself in the South."

"Some of its members are already in the South."

"Which?"

"Ishavriel," Lord Telakar said quietly. "The others will follow."

"How many?"

The kinlord frowned. "I am not of the Lord's Fist, Illaraphaniel. I cannot, with accuracy, delineate their plan of battle."

"In Essla, the children were taken from the village. Nothing has been found of them; no bodies, no blood."

Telakar nodded.

"There were thirty-four, in total."

He nodded again.

"To what use will they be put?"

Telakar's eyes narrowed. "Do not play games, Illaraphaniel. You know as well as I that the cost of a great magic is measured in lives."

"The lives of mortals."

"Nothing that is not mortal lives," he said coldly.

"A broad definition of life, Telakar."

"APhaniel," Commander Allen said.

Meralonne's nod was slight, but it was noted.

"The *Kialli* are not, by any definition, alive," Telakar continued. His expression was chill. "Their blood can be used to bind, but even then, only others of their kind. Mortality suggests both beginning and end. Children have a greater potential because the end of their lives, in theory, is distant. We kill," he added, with just the hint of a cold smile, "not simply because we wish to be called evil or depraved; there is motive behind the deaths, and reason."

"You will be judged for it," the kai Lamberto said coldly.

Telakar's laugh was unexpected; it hung in the tent, as if it had a weight beyond the simple texture of sound. "Who will judge us? We are the keepers of the *judged*; we are the tormentors of those who have finally chosen. The ability to be judged—or pardoned—is carried in its entirety by those who are mortal.

"But as to the fate of the children, I do not know."

"We have heard that the kin intend to erect a barrier along the entire Averdan border," Meralonne said quietly.

"Impossible."

"Perhaps. But we have strong reason to believe the groundwork for such a spell has already been laid."

Telakar frowned. "Show me."

Meralonne said nothing. But he turned to the Tyr'agar and lifted silver brow.

"Commander Allen? General Baredan di'Navarre?"

"I do not trust him," Baredan said quietly.

"Nor I," Valedan replied.

"And you are wise," Telakar replied. "But the questions you wish answered cannot be answered without further study. If you wish, I will accompany Meralonne APhaniel. I believe it is your intent to send him West."

"It is the closest border."

"Send us, then. We can travel and return far more quickly than any other."

"APhaniel?"

The magi nodded grimly. "I . . . have no fear of Lord Telakar. His place in the Shining Court has long been an unusual one."

"How so?"

"He has always been fascinated by the creations of Man," he replied. "And it is a bitter fascination."

"He is a *demon*," Mareo said softly.

"He is. But in the last twenty years, kai Lamberto, he has killed far fewer men—or women, or children—than the General Marente."

"The General—"

"The Northern hostages would not agree with what you have not yet said. Do not say it."

"I had no hand in that."

"No. Had you, you would not be here. Give us leave to travel, or forbid it; we will work with what we have."

Commander Bruce Allen rose. "If you vouch for him, APhaniel, the Kings' army will accept the risk. Tyr'agar?"

Valedan nodded.

"Elena."

She heard the word.

She had come, over the course of days, to a wall, and it was a comfortable wall behind which to shelter; a shadow wall. Such a trick had been taught her by Evallen, then the Matriarch of Arkosa; it was meant to protect the secrets of the family from those who would take them by force. She had to know it; she would be Daughter, one day, to Margret.

And she had listened well.

Beyond the wall she built, Ser Laonis di'Caveras sat. His voice was not the blades or fires of torture, but it was just as painful. The spell of defense had not been taught her for this purpose, but it was useful in its fashion, if harder to summon in the absence of physical pain. She had learned how to move around the wall, to position it between them, until his voice was a distant babble.

But in truth, there was little of it. He was a clansman, and talk was for women.

The newcomer was another story.

She had seen him walk the wind, and she knew that she could not ignore him. Even deaf, she would be forced to listen to what he had to say. And she did not want to hear it. She turned away from him.

When she turned back, Ser Laonis was gone. But Kallandras of the North remained, his arms folded across his chest.

"Elena," he said again, softly.

She nodded.

"Has he bound you?"

And frowned. It was not the question she expected. "Bound?" She almost knew what it meant.

"No, then."

She closed her eyes.

"You are not prisoner here," he said quietly. "There are none, among *these* Tyrs, who would be foolish enough to imprison the Daughter of Arkosa."

"I am not the Daughter of Arkosa," she said, forcing the words out. They were stiff, unnatural; they left her only because she was Voyani, and she knew that he would hear a lie if she offered it.

"Margret has not disowned you."

"It doesn't matter." To her ears, her voice was the more distant of the two.

"Does it not? I think that she would differ."

"She has already had to bury kin," she said. She had not witnessed it. Had not been there to lend Margret the strength that understanding—true understanding—offered. But she *knew* it for truth. Nicu was dead. "I would not do that to her. Not me, too."

"You do that now. You do not eat. You do not speak. You barely move. You remain here, at the side of a kinlord."

"I have nowhere else to go," she said bitterly.

"You have grown so helpless that you have forgotten how to fight?"

For the first time in days, she sat up. Her arms were trembling and pale beneath the bronze of desert skin. She hated him. He was ignorant and foreign. He understood *nothing*.

"I led him into Callesta," she said, her voice the edge of whisper, but loud and raw. "Don't you understand? He would have had no way to reach the Tyr; he used *me*. And I let him do it."

"And the alternative?"

She snarled, but the whole of the sound was contained in expression.

"Does it matter?"

"It must," he said softly. "You made the choice. What would have happened, had you refused him?" When she did not answer immediately, he said, "not your death. You would have died, had that been the choice offered you."

It was true. The truth was a bitter salve; it stung, it made the wounds throb.

"You are not Voyani," she said bitterly. "You wouldn't understand."

"He would have killed the cerdan at the gate."

She closed her eyes. "Yes."

"And you saved their lives."

"*Yes*. I saved *their* lives. And what are they? Clansmen. No blood of mine."

He was quiet now. The wind was still.

"The most ancient of our vows," she continued softly. "Broken. And for what? Strangers. Clansmen. Men who prey on us when the harvest is poor; who tolerate us when it suits their wives."

"You have left the *Voyanne*," he said.

She closed her eyes and brought her hands to her face; they trembled.

"But, Elena, so too has Margret."

"She—"

"She has left the *Voyanne*. The open road has finally reached its end. She has finished her voyage, she has brought her people home."

Home.

"It is not my home," she said quietly.

"No."

It surprised her. Enough that she looked at him between the stretch of stiff fingers, the cage of her hands.

"The road still calls you, Elena of Arkosa. In this battle, in this war, the Matriarch of Arkosa has left the field. Some of her people remain in Averda. And you remain. Because you chose."

She started to speak.

"Mercy is unfashionable in the South." He spoke in perfect Torra. "It has always been unfashionable in the South." He lifted his pale face, and turned, his gaze passing through the fabric of tent toward the North. Which North? She could not tell.

"But, unfashionable or no, it has often been offered. In this war, there are many ways to make a false step, and many paths to tread that seem fair and end in darkness."

"I know."

"No," he said quietly, "I do not think you do know. If you did, you would not cower here."

"I—"

"What you chose to do, you did. Do not now sit waiting for the grave to be dug. If you must, dig it; it will give you something to do with your hands. But while you dig, Elena of Arkosa, understand this: Your role here may turn the tide of this battle, and if it does, Arkosa will be safe for some time."

"How much time?"

"I cannot say. Because," he added, seeing her expression as her hands fell away, "I do not know.

"So much, in the end, turns out badly. Good men die and bad men live. Evil occurs and we are powerless to prevent it."

She swallowed.

"But we are not powerless to prevent *all* evil. Think on that. And think, too, on this. It is a Northern saying. An Imperial saying."

"What?"

"There are some shadows that light cannot pierce."

She started to speak, and he held up his hand.

"And in those shadows, we walk blindly, and we make our way in darkness. What we offer, where no light shines, no man sees—but it is offered, and if it is the only illumination that is permitted us, it will do. It will not light the way. It will not destroy the darkness. But in darkness, mercy and compassion are still felt, and still known. What comes of what we offer, the wise do not say. But they say this: Mercy lifts the sightless veil."

"That makes no sense."

"No," he said quietly. "I imagine that it doesn't. Not yet. You chose," he said quietly, "and because you so chose, Lord Telakar is with us."

She closed her eyes.

"Because he is with us, we may survive what is to come.

"If you have left the *Voyanne,* Elena, you have stepped, blind, into a larger world. You have a part to play, and perhaps it is, in the end, a part that only you can."

He bowed.

"Bard—wait—"

"Yes?"

"Who am I?"

His eyes met hers, and she saw them for a moment as if they were not eyes, and not the Northern poets' windows, and what she saw, she turned away from.

But an hour later, she rose, and for the first time since she had silently joined the army, she bowed her head in the darkened tent.

And asked the Lady for a sign.

The border was a day's travel.

If one traveled by foot. By horseback, given the valleys, it was either shorter or longer—but no horse would bear Telakar willingly, and the kinlord was wise enough not to approach beasts made skittish by the hint of his presence.

Instead, they followed the mage roads; the landscape compressed by magic as they stepped forward into forest. It was old forest, but it was not Deep forest. Both knew this instantly.

"Telakar, why are you here?"

"I thought to deliver warning to the Tyr'agnate of Callesta," he replied. His face was white slate, the color of chalk and dust.

"A dangerous game."

Telakar shrugged. "A game," he said softly. "I might ask you the same question, Illaraphaniel."

Meralonne smiled. "I might tender the same answer."

"You have changed."

"It *is* possible. Time runs differently in these lands."

"Time has always troubled the mortals," Telakar replied. "And it has diminished them."

The magi nodded. He lifted his hands in a complicated dance of power, and only when his hands glowed faintly, his palms taking the color of burnished, ancient silver, did he fall silent. "We search," he said.

Telakar nodded. "I admit some curiosity," he said. "I did not lie; I am not among the Lord's Fist, and I am not privy to their councils."

"No?"

"Only Lord Isladar could stand on the edge of that circle, neither one nor the other."

"He is gone now."

"Perhaps."

"I saw him, in the city of the god-born. He is not what he was."

"Who can say with certainty what he was? Or is? He is Isladar. There has never been another like him, in the long history of the Hells."

"Ah."

"Illaraphaniel?"

"You were young, kinlord. Young, when he was old. I think that he has changed little."

Telakar raised a brow. "You have not seen the Hells, magi."

"No. Nor will I."

"As you say." He was quiet for a moment, and then he frowned, his hands dropping to his sides. "Illaraphaniel?"

But the magi had already fallen silent, his eyes narrowing. He moved with purpose between the trees, and bent a moment, hands pressing lightly into the earth beneath his shining palms.

"Blood was shed here," he stated.

Telakar said nothing.

Meralonne moved then, rising on bended knee. His hands traveled, as if they were independent of him, until they came to rest. "There," he said. "Be still."

Telakar was still. Movement had not defined him the way this stillness did; he stood out, a moment, in the arboreal forest. Not even the light seemed to touch him.

Meralonne's eyes closed, lids flickering, lashes touching cheek. His hair brushed cheek as he bent; it moved away as the breeze came, and it did not return.

The earth shifted, breaking slowly as if it were ice thawing. Ground broke beneath their feet, and they rode the movement, bending slightly to absorb it. Small trees cracked; undergrowth slid out of view. The earth disgorged its burden whole: the roots of a sapling, a silver-white tree.

They stared at it, as it lay against the ground, roots exposed.

And then the roots began to move, seeking purchase blindly, maggots infesting the body of the earth.

The living earth. The Old Earth.

Meralonne cursed quietly. "So," he said softly. "This is how it was done. This is why we sensed nothing."

Telakar was silent.

They stood a moment, staring.

"The earth demands its price," Telakar said at last. "And I would have said that there were none among us who could invoke the wild magics. Not here."

"We are far from the Deepings," Meralonne said at last. "Too far. But far or no, she will sense this, and she will not be pleased."

"If the Lord's Fist was wise," Telakar replied, "none of these . . . saplings . . . will be planted along the hidden paths."

"The paths?" Meralonne spit and reached for his pipe. "The paths have shifted, kinlord. The earth is waking, and its movement changes all things. I say again: She will know."

"The Old Earth was proof against the anger of the gods," Telakar said quietly. "And it was the voice of the mortals—and the Arianni—that best invoked its ancient power. The mortals are scattered and diminished; there is not one among them that would do this thing.

"And the Arianni?" Meralonne's voice was cold. A warning.

"Not among the Arianni," he said in response. "But there were those among the *Kialli* who were strongest in the presence of earth. Even if the earth is dormant, it recognizes old rites and sacrifices. The children died here, I think."

Meralonne nodded, but hesitantly. "They must have taken others."

"Indeed. Invoke the earth, Illaraphaniel. Invoke it, while time remains."

Meralonne was grim when he rose; mist curled around his face, wreathing from the flat of pipe's bowl. "I cannot."

"Cannot?"

"Will not, then. To invoke the earth, we must offer, measure for measure, what was offered here. And the dead . . ." He shook his head grimly.

"Surely the mortals will understand the cost—"

"They will see the sacrifices," Meralonne replied curtly, "and they will call us evil."

"They will perish."

"Perhaps." He gestured; the tree was ripped from its loose moorings. "We will take this with us," he said quietly.

"With care."

"With much care. We will burn what is left. If we have time."

"It will not be enough."

"It will have to be," the magi said softly. "But there are other ways."

Telakar was still. "They will be as costly," he said at last. "Not a one of us stood willingly between the wild elements."

Meralonne nodded. "But in the camp, there is at least one who can call the wild wind, and the wind will respond in force." He grimaced. "What is the intent of the barrier, Telakar?"

"I think, if I am not mistaken, it is a gate."

"A gate."

"Mortals are not entirely predictable. The battle would take place in Averda; of that, the Shining Court might be certain. But Averda is large."

"Then the gate will be diffuse."

The kinlord said nothing.

"Come, Telakar. We have scant time."

And nodded.

In the tent, lamps were lit, and bowls of open water and wine offered to the hidden moon. The Tyr'agnati made these supplications with their own hands, and although they were curious, the Commanders said nothing. Commander Allen, at least, knew enough of the South to know that they did not pray.

But what they did, in delicacy and in silence, seemed very close.

Valedan kai di'Leonne aided them, and it seemed strange to the Northern observers that in this act alone, he seemed youthful. He stood upon the field with the Tyrs, and he gave gravity to his rank, a dignity beyond the years he did possess. But here, with wine and water, his hands shook slightly, and his head stayed a moment too long in the bowed position; he glanced from side to side, seeking anchor from the experience of the older men who framed him.

Beyond the bowls, suspended above air by the magics of the magi, the small tree lay, its roots curling in upon itself in a parody of life.

"The choices are all grim," Meralonne said quietly. "I will offer them to you, without judgment or prejudice."

He waited, however, until the Tyr'agnati had finished their ablutions. When they had gathered at the side of the Northern Commanders, he noted the distance between their shoulders had lessened; they stood, in grim silence, as one.

"The magic done here is not a magic that we can hope to reproduce. Not quickly, and perhaps not in time."

"What magic, APhaniel?" Commander Allen's gaze was the eagle's gaze.

"They have made a pact with the Old Earth," he said softly. He met the expected lack of comprehension in their gazes. But lack of understanding did not prevent unease; the tree was twisting in the air, seeking purchase. They had offered it none of their blood, but a rabbit had been killed and brought forward, and the tree had devoured it, burrowing into still warm flesh. What it took, it took sustenance from; it was larger now, and shining palely.

"The Old Earth is a force that understands both life and death. It is not the wind," he added. "Or the fire. The water understands life in its fashion, but it is not a thing of roots." He bowed head to fingers, massaging brow. "These trees exist along the border. They are evenly spaced; they are numerous, but they are not so thick that they might be easily noticed by men who were not looking for their presence.

"They are, of course, magical."

"They are of the Old Earth?"

"The trees? No."

Silence. "They are not of earth, although they may once have sheltered there. Some binding was necessary, and some offer, to ensure that the earth would sustain them."

"Their purpose, APhaniel?"

"They are the pegs that hold the tent," he replied. "They are vessels for magic."

"You can draw upon the magic?"

"I? No. Not I, nor any of my kin."

"Then—"

"They are not meant for our use. And the spell that will invoke them is not one that we can easily untangle in the time left us. We will take them as we find them, Commander Allen. Such reaving has already begun. But I fear that we will not easily remove the threat before the magic is called upon."

"You spoke of options."

"The oldest compact the earth accepts is life, and life's blood. Offer the earth, measure for measure, what was offered for the planting, and the earth will—perhaps—condescend to displace the saplings."

"Measure for measure?" Valedan's voice. Soft voice.

"The children of Essla," Meralonne said quietly. "And others, besides. It is my belief that each tree required one such sacrifice. I cannot, however, be certain; the tree roots break bone and devour much."

"What will come of the magic when it is invoked?"

"As feared," Meralonne replied, his hand straying to pipe but not quite reaching its comfort, "I believe it will create a gate with the power necessary to allow the Lord of the Northern Wastes to step through."

"And if that magic is weakened?"

"I cannot be certain," he said quietly. "But of certainty the god's hand is in this. Not even the magi could create the trees from which this spell is woven. They mimic life too closely."

"The Lord of Night was not a life-giver," Ser Mareo kai di'Lamberto said gravely.

Meralonne said nothing.

"What other options do you offer us, APhaniel?" Valedan's voice. He lifted a hand as Commander Allen stepped forward, and the command in the gesture was as natural as breath.

Meralonne replied, "None as certain."

"And the less certain?"

"The elemental magics are . . . aware of each other. They are not friendly. It is possible—but barely—that the earth's hold might be weakened if other elements were invoked."

"The wind," Valedan said quietly.

"The very wind. And I will say, now, that such an act will cause at least as much destruction—and death—as the sacrifice of a chosen few."

"Where is Lord Telakar?" The Tyr'agnate of Averda asked. He

cast shadow upon the makeshift shrine that stood in the Western edge of the tent, as if protecting it.

"He is elsewhere, but he is still within the encampment."

"And not here."

"It is not wise to have him present for this discussion. He is . . . unusual . . . among his kind, but in the end, when the Lord notices him, he will be slave to his god's whim. What he does not know, with certainty, he cannot betray."

"He told you this?"

"No, Tyr'agnate. And it is little known, even among the magi, for the magi are forbidden the study of the ancient rituals of summoning and control."

"But you know it."

"I know it; I am a master of ancient lore and history. Study is not mastery, however. The *Kialli* are bound to their Lord by means that they did not choose." The silence that settled about him was accentuated by the thin line of pale lips; he would say no more on this subject.

"I will not see children sacrificed," Valedan said.

"You will," Meralonne replied, neutral now. "To the winds."

"The winds, they have faced all their lives."

"Not these winds, kai Leonne."

"And would you counsel us to murder?"

"I would counsel you only to think on what the presence of the Lord of Night—the true presence, and not the shadow of his servants—might mean to these lands. There is no Morel here. The blade that was forged for his use has not been seen in the lands of man since the Sundering, if it still exists at all. And if it does, there is no god, save perhaps one, that would aid you in its retrieval."

"I say again that I will not allow it." He turned, then, to the impassive rigidity of Ser Anton di'Guivera's face.

Ser Anton nodded.

"Kai Callesta?"

Ramiro said nothing.

"Kai Lamberto?"

The Lambertan Tyr also nodded, but his gaze slid sideways, seeking purchase in the face of the Callestan Tyr. He found none.

And as they stood, grim now, Commander Allen said quietly, "Ellora—"

And she shook her head.

"Ellora."

"No. The Ospreys were disbanded." Her voice was cold as night.

Anger dented every word, and hinted at a hundred others, kept in careful check. But barely.

"Commander," Valedan said without raising his voice, "if you attempt this thing, I will see you destroyed."

"You will see the Dominion destroyed, kai Leone, and with it, the Empire."

"There must be reasons why the Lord of Night has not chosen to leave the Northern Wastes. There must be strength in the Empire yet to withstand him."

"There is," Meralonne said softly. "But the golden-eyed are murdered here, at birth; there is no such strength within the South."

"There is," a new voice said. A woman's voice.

The flap of the tent had been pulled to one side, and in it, in the odd light, stood the bowed form of Yollana of Havalla. Beneath her arm, sustaining the greater burden of her weight, the Serra Diora en'Leonne. Even the guards placed at the tent would have had difficulty denying entry to two such women.

"Na'dio."

The Serra Diora lifted her head. Her pale, flawless skin caught light; she seemed the Lady's scion in the shallows of evening.

"What strength, then?" Commander Allen asked quietly, in a voice that was almost shorn of hope, but desired it nonetheless.

"It is buried," Yollana said quietly. She lifted a hand and laid it against her chest. "Here," she said. "And within the Sea of Sorrows."

Diora's gaze was sharp, but she was silent, and she made silence perfection.

"It is time, Na'dio."

"Matriarch," the Serra said. She bowed head to her husband. More than that, she could not do without forsaking the Matriarch, and Valedan did not seem to notice the slight.

Perhaps he would, but later. Meralonne, watching the young man's face, could not be certain.

"What aid can you offer us, Matriarch?" Valedan asked with care. "We are far from the Sea of Sorrows."

"Havalla will stand beneath your banner," she replied. "And Havalla will take what your magi has brought. With," she added, "your permission."

"The tree?"

"If it can be called that, yes. We have not yet reached the end of the *Voyanne*, and while we walk it, there are roads that are open to us that your men cannot travel. Let us do what we can."

"Will it be enough?"

"Who can say?" But her smile was grim and mirthless. "It was, once. The Voyani have long evaded the grasp of the Lord of Night, and here, at last, *I* know why. I do not thank you for the knowledge, kai Leonne. But it brings me a measure of . . . certainty." She gestured then, and light ringed her hand.

As magery went, it was not impressive.

But it was tinged with gold and silver, and it seemed faintly metallic as she made her way—aided, always, by the Serra Diora— toward the offering bowls beyond which hovered their doom.

"Tyr'agar."

"You have my permission, Matriarch," he said quietly. But his gaze was upon his wife's face, her averted profile. His hand seemed to rise of its own accord; it fell with his effort.

She was aware of both, and as she passed him, as he made way for the Matriarch, she met his gaze and held it a moment, tilting her chin up to do so. She did not smile; did not choose to offer either encouragement or comfort; did not seek either from him.

But it was enough, for the time; Valedan kai di'Leonne nodded as he moved aside.

The Matriarch of Havalla said, "Be ready." She spoke to the Serra, and the Serra favored her with the slightest of nods.

"Mage," she said, using the Weston word, "now."

Meralonne APhaniel frowned. But he, too, lifted hands; they rested a moment palm up in the still air, before he turned them groundward.

When they fell, the tree fell into the Matriarch's outstretched hands.

The fire that ringed them flared; gold and silver were lost at once to the immediacy and the danger of white.

This the witnesses had expected.

But what happened next, they had not: The Serra Diora began to sing.

Her lips moved, and her jaw; she fashioned words out of the purity of notes, but Meralonne could not hear them. Nor, he thought, could any man present.

Roots twisted in air, shunning fire and flame; they reached for Yollana's wrists, their tips edged and cunning, twisting like snakes.

Blood flowed where they caressed aged skin, but Yollana's grip did not falter, and the fire did not dim. Instead, it caught crimson, adding its color to the mix.

An offering, Meralonne thought. He bowed his head, but not so completely that he lost sight of the Matriarch of Havalla. The magics of the Voyani Matriarchs were a mystery, and the Order of Knowledge had long desired to examine them.

What gnashing of teeth and tearing of beard would accompany his story, if he survived to tell it in the chaos of the Order's halls? It made him smile to think of it: those bearded, robed men envious as children, and just as open.

And then he forgot that glimpse of normality, for the tree was shuddering now; the roots were still. Branches writhed as the flames penetrated silver bark, sap flowed between the cracks of smooth, flawless tree's skin as wounds broke its surface again and again.

It had no voice but the voice the Serra gave it, and she gave it voice: Meralonne recognized, at last, the song that she sang.

It shocked him into silence.

He pushed his way past the Tyran of Callesta, the Tyran of Lamberto, and they let him pass. He shouldered Commander Kalakar to one side, and ran into the chest of the Eagle, but this, too, he eluded. The Tyr'agnati, surrounding the women like a thin wall, were impassive.

His hand summoned sword—and stopped there.

For the song's last note, attenuated and haunting, now faded into silence, and with that silence came a stillness that was profound.

Roots against her wrist, like adornment, the tree was still.

And it was a thing of silver and white, of golden bud, a thing of diamond leaves, glittering in the lamplight. He shook his head, the magi asserting himself, and when his hair settled, his hand was once again by his side.

The Matriarch of Havalla said, "So." She gazed at the Serra Diora. "You learned much, in the Sea of Sorrows."

But the Serra did not reply. Not with words, and not with the cursed beauty of a song that Meralonne knew he would never, ever forget. She had power. She was bard-born. He had not realized it until this moment. But she was bard-born in a way that no bard had been in his memory; not even Kallandras of Senniel could have done what she had chosen to do this evening.

She did not seem to understand how much she had exposed. Or she did not choose to acknowledge it; her face was so still it was hard to judge. Instead, she lifted a perfect hand and touched the sapling. It was strong, now; straight and tall.

"It is a Winter tree," Meralonne said faintly. "I did not see it; it was so corrupted, so abased . . . I did not know what it was." His gaze fell upon the Serra Diora. "Serra," he said, his voice as cold as the season he had named. "Where did you learn that song?"

She met his gaze. Held it a long moment. And then she said quietly, "I am kin to Arkosa, and I cannot speak of it. Do not ask."

"APhaniel?" Commander Allen's hand was upon his shoulder.

"There is only one place that such a tree grows," the magi continued softly. "This . . ." words failed him.

"What do you mean, APhaniel?"

"It is a sentinel of the Hidden Way," he replied. The Winter touched his face, his voice, the white of his hair. "And it marks a season. They have grown powerful indeed to commit such blasphemy." He shook himself. "But things are clearer now. It is not a gate, Tyr'agar. It is a road. They are attempting to build a road, to twist a path that already exists, to call a *season* into being for their use. They will pay."

CHAPTER SIXTEEN

"WHAT song, Serra?" Valedan's voice was low, even in the confines of the cramped tent.

Teyla kep'Valente looked up in panic, and her arms must have tightened around her dozing child, for the boy began to cry.

The boy. Na'diro. Not her son's name, but a name so like her own it gave her pause.

She had almost asked Teyla to rename him, but had stopped herself; why burden a babe with the name of the dead? She had bowed her head, accepting his life, the responsibility of it already an anchor and a weight.

Teyla had offered her the child, but she had demurred; she was content to watch them, mother and child. She had saved them. They were hers.

And she did not wish to share them with the Tyr'agar of *any* clan.

She met his gaze. The evening's work had tired her immensely, but she could not allow this to show; her pride. Her folly. She knew that she should falter, that she should offer him the weakness that would complement his strength. This much she had been taught, and she had never forgotten it.

But she could not now do what she had learned; the life she had been meant to lead had vanished, and in its wake, she was waking, and she found herself enamored of strength.

"Na'tey," she said gently. "Take our son outside. The Tyran will protect you."

Teyla scrabbled to her feet, ungainly and awkward in her haste to avoid the man who now owned her. But she held the babe with care, and his cries quieted.

Yet Valedan did not notice.

The whole of his attention was focused upon the Serra Diora. He did not see that her silks were almost common, that she did him no service as wife.

He said quietly, "You are bard-born."

And she replied, in Torra, "I do not know what that means."

"You know," he answered. It was almost accusation. "Word has come to me from the cerdan who were in Essla. You used the voice there."

She nodded, then. Shorn at last of the pretense that was to have saved her her aunt's fate, she faced her husband.

"I have seen the voice used," he said calmly. "I do not know your master, or the tenets by which you were taught. I hope—I pray— that you were taught by Northern bards."

"Why?"

"Because I *know* the bards," he replied gravely. "I know what rules govern them; I know what binds them." He shook his head. "I . . . am aware that this gift is not a gift, in the South, and I will speak of it to no other, although I believe it is already beginning to be known. But to you, I must speak. Tonight you sang. I could not hear your song. No one could."

She said, "I heard the tree's voice." Just that.

"And the song?"

"It was the simplest of our songs. The cradle song."

She was surprised when his brows rose and fell; she recognized the play of memory across his open expression. He hid nothing. A flash of old contempt blinded her unexpectedly; she fought it in perfect repose.

"What you sang," he said softly, "is *not* what the magi heard."

"He spoke of it?"

"No. To no one. And if I know him at all, he will not. But he did not hear what you thought you sang, Serra." He paused, turning from her. "And do the other trees speak to you?"

"No."

"And the voices of men?"

"Are the voices of men. It is not for men that the song is sung."

"It was sung for me," he said, surprising her.

"It was sung for you when you lived in the harem," she said. "You were not a man then. You were one of us."

"Must we give up everything that comforts us when we cross that threshold?"

"It is not for me to say. I am—"

"You are Serra Diora," he said quietly. "Serra Diora en'Leonne. If you must hear it, then hear it: You are given leave, always, to speak freely."

"In the company of men?"

"In any company you choose, Serra."

Contempt. "So you have said, and I admit that I have taken you at your word. But you have bidden me to be honest. I do so, now. Do you not understand the cost of your permission?"

"I don't care."

"You should. You are no child, and it is not as child you will be judged."

"I will be judged," he said, lifting his face and staring, for a moment, beyond her shoulder, "by the outcome of this battle. Only that. I am not afraid of your gift."

She heard the North in his voice, and for a moment, she wanted it for her own. But she was of the South; she let the moment pass.

"Tyr'agar," she said, dropping at last to knee, "there is more that I may be called upon to do."

"I know," he replied.

This, too, surprised. "What do you know?"

But he shook his head, and after a moment he left her.

In the darkness, the moon's light passed beneath clouds born by night winds. A cool breeze came from the West, and although it retained no hint of salt, it had touched ocean. Kallandras knew it, not by the dint of romantic belief, but by the answering flicker of light that straddled his finger: the diamond, winking like star, cold and distant.

He waited in shadow. The lamps of the Kings' soldiers were warm and orange in the passage of moon, brighter when the light above was momentarily eclipsed, bronze to its silver.

She came, passing between the patrols that offered the illusion of safety. Her hood was high, its folds almost rigid around the shadows of her face. But he knew the clothing as well as—better perhaps—than he knew the woman. He wondered what age she would be.

Her voice answered: It gave him nothing.

"Kallandras."

Nothing at all. Old, then, and at the peak of her power. He bowed. To the young Evayne, he offered the comfort he was allowed to offer, but to the older woman, he offered nothing. It was all that could be offered, in safety.

"The sword," she said quietly. "The sword that you took from the hand of . . . assassins . . . during the Kings' Challenge."

His nod was slight. "It is here."

"How?"

The bard was silent.

"Very well. Keep your secrets, if you must. But the time has almost come. Pass it on. Let it go to the man who hears its voice most clearly. It will serve no other."

He bowed again.

"Take it to the Green Valley."

"Russo?"

"Yes."

"When?"

"On the morrow." She glanced up. The folds of fabric, dark as midnight, did not shift at all.

"You know of the barrier."

She nodded. Fabric rustled, as if it were one beat out of time with the person who wore it. "I know of it," she said softly. "And I know what you intend. It is why I am here."

He did not ask. He waited.

After a moment, she looked away from the moon, as restless now as she had ever been. "The war is waiting," she said. Distance informed each syllable. But it was a distance he understood.

"How many have died, Evayne?"

"Many." The word was stark, shorn of emotion. She could do that now. Had she spoken the word at a different age, he might have reached out to touch her. Spared that, he was still.

He had never asked her of his own death, although he was certain she had seen it.

"Do not offer sacrifice to the Old Earth."

He raised a pale brow. "It was not," he said softly, "my intent."

But her eyes, darkened by bruise and blood, did not so much as flicker; she was intent on speaking, and only on speaking. What he had to say in turn was not of interest. She was powerful, yes, but she had tested that power severely; he saw this clearly now.

"Do not summon wind," she told him. "Do not call the air."

"We have no other defense against the Old Earth."

"You have," she replied. She reached into the folds of her sleeves, and he could see, resting in the sudden translucence of palm, the seer's crystal. The seer's heart, exposed. But it was exposed to Evayne, and Evayne alone; he saw cloud and light, an echo of the night sky. "You have," she continued, "although you do not know it."

"And will it succeed?"

"It must."

He nodded again.

"The sword," she said. "Take it. And the lute. You are not unarmed here."

"And of Kiriel?"

The hood fell away as she swept it back.

There was blood upon her face, and her left eye was dark and bruised. It would have shocked him, if anything about Evayne could. But she did not seem to feel it, and what she had not acknowledged, he could not.

"Kiriel has her own battle. She is god-born," Evayne added. "And the gods take poorly to interference."

"She is not a god."

"No. But she is the only child living whose parent walks the plane. I cannot see her clearly. I have tried."

"You are not present upon that field."

"Perhaps not."

The answer was subtly wrong.

"You are," he said, a question in the statement.

The tang of broken tree, crushed grass, autumn stalk, rose up from her feet. Time returning.

"The sword," she said; for a third time.

What she spoke of in threes could not be ignored. But it had been a decade or more since he had tried to ignore Evayne a'Nolan. The anger that had sustained even that attempt was gone, guttered at last. There was war. Death. An ending.

His future.

She said, "You are changed, Kallandras."

He bowed.

"Have care. The lord of the Green Deepings *is* of the Deepings, and it will call him, soon or late."

"It will not call him now."

"No. He has come to care for you, in his fashion. It will not be a kindness, to him. To you, I cannot say."

"Now is enough of a concern. The future holds what it holds, if we live to see it."

She let the hood fall, like a scarf, around her neck. "I am weary," she told him. "But I will see this to its end."

He bowed. He was not surprised, when he rose, to find himself alone, the distant beat of feet muted, the orange light of swaying lamp flickering in the breeze.

He wondered, for a moment, where Lord Celleriant was. But just for a moment.

Duty bound him, as it always had, but this time, he offered those bonds no struggle. They were his, and he accepted them.

He looked to Russo, and saw only the path that led, in the darkness of trees and old forest, to its scattered fields. They would be golden, in sunlight, and in sunlight, the promise of their harvest would be golden as well.

Ashaf's memories were strong.

So strong, that they led Kiriel along stray paths in search of the familiar. In many places, only nature tended the footpaths; serafs had been called away upon other duties.

Auralis was her shadow. At night, she barely noticed his presence. He offered her few words, but she accepted his silence gladly. She had nothing else to give him.

Her palms were warm with the weight of the pendant, with its steady, insistent beat. It was comforting, but only when the sun had at last fallen beneath the rim of the horizon did she know why: It was the same sound, measure for measure, that she had felt against the curve of her cheek for the whole of her childhood.

Ashaf's heart. Here.

Her own memories warred with Ashaf's, and won clear for a moment. The cool of night was warm, and the winds silent and gentle, as the Shining City returned. For as far as the eye could see— the internal eye, the child's eye—the world was covered in white, endless and perfect. At sun's height, the glare was harsh and unrelieved, but in moonlight, there was beauty.

She missed it.

It was the only thing about her childhood home that she might return to; Ashaf was gone.

And Ashaf was here.

She took breath; tasted air made strange by the growth of wheat and the burden of animals. It had been hours since she had eaten. Hours since Auralis had eaten, and she thought he noticed it more.

"We'll stop soon," she told him.

"Where?"

She didn't answer. She had become fascinated with the night sounds of insects; they seemed to remain at the same distance, no matter how carefully she chose to approach them. Where her feet trod, there was silence, absolute silence. But beyond it, in a widening circle, the village at night: insect speech and birdcalls, soft throated and tentative, branches heavy with autumn weight not yet shed, the distant trickle of river against rock and bank.

These were Ashaf's. They had no place in the Shining Court.

But if she were honest, she had heard them all before, for Callesta was situated at the Northernmost point of the valley, and she had wandered often beyond its walls.

Still, the experience was not the same. Here, the heart in her hands, all sound seemed blessed. Even the sound of Auralis' boot hitting exposed tree root, and the cursing that followed.

"It's the clouds," he muttered, lifting himself from the ground for the third time.

She noticed them; when they passed before the moon, the shadows darkened, and the texture of the night deepened. But darkness did not rob her of vision. It should have surprised her. In the months since the ring that had dropped from Evayne's hand had been wakened, she had learned to walk with care in the city streets, between the gentle, diminished glow of magelights. Her own toes had not been proof against the rise of dislodged stone or the rise of exposed root.

But here, again, such awkwardness seemed out of place. Heart in hand, she knew these lands. She had walked them before, and if they had changed—and they had—they nonetheless had about them the familiarity of a long loved, long missed place. She wanted to call it home.

But the Winter dwelled within her, and where she saw tree and hill, field and river, she saw also the glittering crust of snow undisturbed by anything but wind and storm for centuries. As if there were two Kiriels.

As if she could separate the part of her that was mortal from the part of her that had been gifted her by her unnamed, and little known, father. That was what Ashaf had desired, in the height of the second tower the Shining Palace boasted: that she be mortal, human, unfettered by all shadow save that cast by light.

No, she thought. *She knew that the shadows within were the only weapon you had.*

Not her voice. Or perhaps hers. It was hard to tell.

It was how you used that darkness. It was that you used it, rather than being used by it, that was important to her. She knew what you were.

She never loved what I was. Child's voice. Adolescent's voice. Small, almost too small, to be her own.

How could she do otherwise? She knew. She always knew.

And thinking it, being told it, she saw herself for a moment as Ashaf had first seen her: Babe in swaddling, held in the arms of Lord Isladar, in the shallows of the Lady's night, her cries silenced by magic, her face red and wrinkled, a newborn's unlovely face.

"Kiriel?"

"Almost there," she told him.

Ashaf kep'Valente had taken that babe in arms. Had seen its golden eyes, had known it for dead, should it remain in the South. She had been unafraid. Or rather, she had known fear, but fear *for* the child. Fear *of* the babe would come much later, and it would come at night, in the cold, when there was nothing left—nothing but the pendant itself—to remind her of where she had lived.

And in between that?

She had touched the pendant. Kiriel could feel the ghost of her hands, the weathered, callused skin of her palms, against the sharp lines and edges of the heavy stone. She touched them, held them, refused to let them go. They led her here.

Here, to a small house made of wood, and girded beneath by stone. In the Shining City, it would have been an outbuilding, something unworthy of note or mention had it existed at all: the Lord valued stone, and ice, the things he might easily shape. Wood such as this was scarce, and it was oft used for burning.

"Here," she whispered to Auralis.

Auralis said nothing.

Seventeen years, it had stood. It did not occur to Kiriel to wonder if it had stood empty for all that time until she approached it, her feet finding the path that led to its single, sliding door, its summer face.

She lifted a hand as she approached, her steps silent. Auralis' were not; they were heavy. But he moved with grace as he shadowed her steps, and he did not ask what she sought. She wouldn't have answered, and he knew it.

When she reached the door, she regretted the lack of light. The ground around the small house was tended; where weeds had overgrown some of the pathways that Ashaf had once walked, they were absent here. Someone had chosen to take up residence in an empty house.

Kiriel wondered how long it had been before they had dared. If they feared to do so at all.

She lifted a hand, touched wood, and then made a fist of her fingers. She knocked once. Twice.

Movement stilled her hand.

Not hers, and not Auralis; he had grown still as he waited. No. Within the house itself, someone was moving. She heard the murmur of voice shorn of distinct syllables. There was some fear in the tone.

And why should there not be? War was coming to the valley. She might be cerdan, or Toran, or far, far worse. Her sword was by her side, but she did not touch it; instead she moved it awkwardly to one side, to better hide its presence.

The ring upon her hand glinted in the moonlight as cloud passed away and veil was lowered. Silver, it looked, and plain—a thing that the poorest of serafs might possess. It was the only thing about her that could speak of servitude, for she once again wore armor, and she could not divest herself of its weight and its strength before whoever now moved gained the door. She did not try.

Instead, she waited, barely breathing. She was not tall, and she made, with the slight stoop of shoulders, as little of the height she did have as she could.

And when the sliding door at last moved, she raised her head, pushing her braid to her back. Her skin was the pale white of the Northern Wastes, and she could not say for certain what color her eyes were; she would know, by the reaction of the person who at last came into view.

A woman.

An older woman.

She wore no silks, but she had draped a blanket around her shoulders, a heavy shawl in this weather. Her eyes were narrow, and her hands were hidden by the far side of the door; Kiriel had no doubt at all that she had chosen to arm herself—but with what, she couldn't say.

Ashaf's memories told her clearly that serafs were not allowed arms.

Told her clearly as well that swords were not the only weapon a man—or woman—could raise, should the need drive them.

"Valla," Kiriel said softly.

The woman frowned. Her eyes narrowed further. Her vision was not good.

"Who is it?" Valla kep'Valente said, layering the words with suspicion.

"I am Kiriel di'Ashaf," the girl replied.

"Di'Ashaf?" The woman frowned, and then her expression slid into something that was between familiar terrains. "Di'Ashaf is not a clan name," she said.

"Ashaf is the only name I care enough to claim," she said. "Ashaf kep'Valente raised me."

Valla's eyes grew wide and round in the moonlight. Kiriel needed no lamp to see them, and she felt, as she stood in this doorway, her feet inches from the threshold, that she would never need one again.

"You know Ashaf?"

"I knew her," Kiriel replied, measuring the words because otherwise they would come out too quickly.

"She's dead, then." The woman's words were flat.

Kiriel nodded. She had said the words before. She did not wish to repeat them, not here.

"And you've come to bear word of her death?"

"No."

"Then why have you come, girl? And why are you dressed that way?" Suspicion again.

It was merited. "I have come a long distance," Kiriel said, with care. "From the North."

"Ashaf lived in the North?"

"The far North," Kiriel replied. "She spoke often of her home. Here," she added. "This village. She spoke of you."

It wasn't true. And it was. We choose our own truths, and we own them, are owned by them. Kiriel wanted to touch the pendant, but she kept her hands by her sides.

"And what did she say?"

"That you were wise, but quick to anger. And that your son would grow up to be a fine man in spite of that."

Valla kep'Valente offered her first smile. It was a mixture of pride and rue. "She would say that." Her smile faltered as she turned to look over her shoulder. "I don't live alone," she told the girl, "and there isn't much room in the house. But come, if you will."

"I have a companion."

"Who is she?"

Kiriel shook her head. "It's a he, and his name is Auralis. He—comes from the North as well. He looks dangerous, but he's—" she took a breath. "I trust him."

"Wait a moment, then. I'll wake my husband."

She could hear the voices so clearly there might not have been a closed door between them.

"Valla, you *never* think!"

"But she said—"

"She said what?"

"She told me what Ashaf said. About me. About our son."

"And so you trust her? The same could be said about *any* mother's son!"

"It is the Lady's hour. If she were a danger—"

"She is wearing *armor.* Think, Valla."

"*If* she were a danger," Valla continued, and Kiriel could almost hear the glare she couldn't see, "How would she have known to come to *this* house and speak of Ashaf? Or have the powerful become *so* powerful they concern themselves with serafs now?"

"With serafs who disappeared, perhaps. Maybe Ashaf was captured. Maybe she went North. Think, Valla," he said, lowering his voice. "The Tor has left these lands with our cerdan. He has returned. There is war here."

"And if she is what she says?"

Silence.

"Ashaf is dead. She said Ashaf is dead. Would someone who feigns friendship not offer a more pleasant lie?"

"We don't know why Ashaf spoke to these strangers," he said at last, after the silence had stretched. "We don't know that she spoke willingly."

"The girl is the right age," Valla replied.

"For what?"

"For Ashaf to have raised."

"Valla—"

"Ashaf raised no evil child. It was not in her."

"And she raised a foreign child? Why?"

"She loved children."

Silence again.

"And she buried all of hers. The Lady was not kind to Ashaf. Except perhaps this once. Will you turn her away?"

Unbidden, old words came to Kiriel—none of them hers.

You will never have to bury her.

And she knew, then, why Ashaf had come to the North. To die.

She almost ran. She turned away from the closed door and collided with Auralis. It was awkward and noisy, and when she gained her footing firmly, the door was open, the single room revealed by this sudden, unexpected gesture.

Valla kep'Valente stood framed by the sliding door, and beside her, an older man with a face as smooth as steel, and just as friendly.

"Kiriel," Valla said quietly. She sent her husband a grim glance, and he remained silent. When Kiriel did not move, Valla stepped fully into the frame and held out her empty hands, palm up. "Kiriel di'Ashaf."

Kiriel turned slowly. Auralis' hands steadied her—or held her fast; she wasn't sure which. Her own hands remained by her sides, although she could not hide the hilt of her sword easily. She had hoped, but it was a vain hope, as so many hopes were in the end.

The man was silent, but at length, he, too, offered her sight of his hands. As if, had he held a weapon, he would be more of a threat. She searched a moment and found his name. Arrego. The crystal was warm as it hung against her hidden breast. She thought of it; thought of how impossible its concealment should be, given its awkward size.

"You are Arrego kep'Valente," she said at last.

He nodded. He was not, Ashaf remembered, a man of many words.

"Kiriel," Valla continued, when she saw that the girl was no longer poised for flight, "why have you come?"

"I came," Kiriel said quietly, "to save the village."

Husband and wife exchanged glances.

"It was Ashaf's home," Kiriel continued, as if speaking, once begun, could not be halted. "And everything she loved was here."

"You were in the North," Valla said, keen now, her eyes seeing many things in the stillness of Kiriel's face.

Kiriel said nothing to that, but after a moment, she turned to Arrego and said, "This place made Ashaf who she was. I wanted to see it."

"Why?" No friendliness in his tone, in his single word. Less in the glare his wife offered him.

"Because I failed to protect her, in the end. And maybe—

maybe—if I can protect the other things she loved, it will be enough."

"You could not fail her," Valla said quietly, her voice stronger than her husband's, and softer at the same time. "You live."

"I was not the daughter she wanted," Kiriel replied.

Valla's smile was almost rueful. "None of us are. The daughters our mothers wanted," she added. "We've our own mind and our own tongues, our own lives. We make the wrong choices because we lack wisdom, and when we have wisdom—ah, then it is almost always too late." Sadness was there, in her eyes. Kiriel knew that Valla's mother was gone.

"You didn't come here alone," Arrego said, folding his arms across his chest.

"No. This is Auralis. He is my—"

"He is a foreign soldier."

She nodded. "He is."

"And he did not force you to travel here?"

"What did he say?" Auralis asked.

"He asked me if I came voluntarily. Or he asked me if you forced me to come here."

Auralis snorted. The easy derision was not devoid of humor. "Tell him—"

"I brought water," Kiriel said, ignoring the rest of Auralis' words. "It's not—it's just water."

The woman's face softened. "Come, then. We will take water with you here, in the Lady's time."

The light was precious. Kiriel knew it, although she had never thought of light that way before. Tallow burned, and wick flickered at the lazy movement of air; very little breeze troubled them as they knelt before an old table. Knees seemed to trouble Arrego, for he shifted often, wincing as he did.

"It's the heat," his wife said. "The humidity is bad for his bones."

Arrego growled. Literally growled, his brows drawing in and down to frame a dour expression. "You make me sound feeble, wife," he said. Bark of a voice, a grizzled bear. Kiriel did not dislike him.

Because Ashaf had not.

"Is Daro still the overseer?"

"Daro? Aye, still. He's older, mind. And he sits a lot while we work." Valla's smile was genuine. "His son is stronger, and takes after his mother."

"Can I meet him?"

"Of course. But not now; he wakes poorly." She smiled. "Now is not the time to visit the village. The darkness makes us all nervous."

"But it's the Lady's time."

"Aye, the Lady's. But the Lord of Night whispers with the wind's voice. We've all heard rumors of Essla."

Kiriel nodded. "This isn't Essla."

"It could be."

"No." She said it harshly. "It will never be Essla. Not while I live. This is Ashaf's home."

"You're a girl," Arrego said. "Not even a woman yet. And if you serve the Lady, I'm a clansman."

"I serve the Tyr'agar," she said serenely.

They were both silent, at that. "The Tyr'agar?"

"Ser Valedan kai di'Leonne."

More silence.

"He comes from the North, but he bears the Sun Sword, and he will fight. Here. No, wait—not here. But a few miles outside of Russo, there are fields that have not been used, and beyond that, the flattest and widest portion of the Valente Torrean."

"That is not the flattest or widest portion of the Averdan valleys," Arrego growled.

Kiriel shrugged. "Do you argue with Tyrs, in Russo? He made his choice. There, there he will lead his army."

"Where is he?"

"Just outside. Of the village. When he calls me, I will join him."

"But he gave you leave to travel here?"

She nodded quietly.

"What kind of man is he?" Valla asked.

Kiriel shrugged. "A man." And then, seeing that the answer was no answer, she added, "I think that Ashaf would have liked him."

Valla nodded quietly.

"But he's a Northerner, isn't he? He brings the Northerners with him."

"He brings Ser Anton di'Guivera with him," Kiriel replied. This was almost rehearsed, and it came easily. "And the Tyr'agnati of both Averda and Lamberto."

Arrego's eyes rounded. "Impossible," he said at last.

But Kiriel smiled bitterly. "They know what they face, and they are willing—barely—to face it together."

"But the kai Callesta—"

"Was killed by the servants of the Lord of Night."

Silence, then. Long silence.

"And the kai Lamberto?"

"I don't know."

Valla poured water into earthenware bowls, bowls as plain and solid as she. Kiriel took one in the palm of cupped hands, and as she did, she saw—for just a moment—a different woman across the table. A younger one, eyes dark as midnight, hair paled by the beginning of a long winter. She did not recognize her, but the name Yollana was a whisper in the silence.

"Valla," she whispered, staring at the surface of the water, her reflection lost to shadow and flickering light.

"Yes, Kiriel?"

Kiriel wanted to speak. But speech here was weakness. She shook her head suddenly and rose. Auralis called her, but she was out of the hut before the last syllable of her name faded.

She ran, but not far.

In the moonlight, she could see the markers—stones, and small offering bowls glinting with liquid in the light. Graves here.

Ashaf's dead.

Kiriel dropped to a knee and bowed her head. It was hard to speak. Hard to think. What had she wanted to say, that she had had to flee?

The footsteps that came at her back were soft, but they were not silent; Valla kep'Valente moved with the sturdy gait of a seraf who felt no need to hide. She came to stand by Kiriel's side, and she also knelt.

They bowed heads together.

"Ashaf's husband," Valla said, when Kiriel did not ask. "And her children. Katrina was her eldest, and the first to die. There, her oldest boy, Mikal. Constance, her daughter, the youngest, the second." She shook her head. "I do not know if she spoke of them to you."

Kiriel shook her head. "Never," she said softly.

Valla was silent. After a moment, she said, "My husband is old and afraid. We have children in Russo, and grandchildren, and war is not kind to serafs.

"If he were less afraid, he would see clearly, but you know the old saying—fear makes sight slanted."

"What would he see, Valla?"

"He would see a young woman who loved our Ashaf."

Kiriel's eyes closed. The darkness behind her lids was a blessing.

"He does not understand why you are here, Kiriel."

"And you do?"

"No. But for me, it is not important."

Kiriel drew breath, and in the silence she weighed her words. They were heavy, and hard to contain, and after a moment, she spoke. "All she had left were her memories. And she thought she would die unknown and unremembered. I—wanted to bring her home. I couldn't."

"But you came, Na'kiri. No, don't speak if speech troubles you. I know what Ashaf would have done, were she here. My husband—" She shook her head. "He means well."

It was the name that was her undoing. Both names. "I am here to prove that I am *worthy* of being her daughter." She bowed her head in the cool night breeze, and after a moment, a woman that she had only just met wrapped an arm around her shoulder.

In the morning, the army passed around the village in two large columns. They did not march through the village, and they did not touch the fields—or the serafs who labored in them—but the serafs were aware of their presence.

Word traveled from tree limb to ground and back; the children, those old enough to evade their mothers' anger or fear, passed word, from mouth to ear, and ear to mouth, like a living chain that existed only in the moment of connection between its links.

Word did not travel perfectly, of course, but urgency gave the children little time to embellish—and indeed, little embellishment was needed. Parents fell silent at once, and grandparents laid down the baskets and sticks, retreating into the imagined safety of the village heart.

But even there, strange things ruled, for the tree towered above them all, casting its long shadow.

And in the tree—sitting to one side of the throne made of bark and wood—was Kiriel.

"He hasn't called you back," Auralis said quietly.

She looked up at the sound of his voice, and she seemed, for a moment, to be a child herself. The frustration and vulnerability that he had seen in the streets of Averalaan were a shadow of what he now saw: he stepped back, lost his footing, and tumbled down the side of a root two feet above the earth.

She waited while he regained his feet, and when she looked at him again, she looked down, her lips tugging at the corners as he exercised the power of Weston cursing.

She had shed her armor within the protective confines of Valla's house, and had donned, instead, the worn shirt and pants that Valla filled. They were too large for her; they made her look waiflike and pale.

She had not chosen to divest herself of her sword, however, and it hung incongruously by her side.

"I can't leave it," she'd told Valla, while Auralis watched.

"We are not allowed such weapons, by law," Valla replied.

"I know. But I can't leave the sword."

"Why?"

"Valla, I only know how to do one thing."

"Ashaf did not teach you that."

"No. But we had no fields," Kiriel said, pulling the shirt over her head, her words muffled as the cloth slid over her lips in heavy folds. "She tried to teach me other things, but this is what I was best at."

Valla clucked, birdlike and severe. "The North must be strange indeed, to have no fields but the smithy."

"It . . . was strange. And cold. But if I could not wield this sword, I would not be able to protect you."

Valla said nothing, but Auralis, watching the lines of her face shift as Kiriel bent, knew what she was thinking: one child cannot save a village, no matter how fine the weapon given her.

Yet she was kind, in a fashion, for she did not speak against the blade again. Instead, she offered Kiriel a waterskin. "Your companion—"

"He has to rejoin the Tyr," Kiriel said.

Auralis raised a brow.

But he, too, chose to be silent. He couldn't leave his armor here. He couldn't set it aside, and even if he could, his Torra was so rusty he might never have learned it at all. He would be either monstrosity or curiosity, and he knew what the serafs of the South were capable of in times of war: he had seen it often.

But he saw no sign of it here, in the Green Valley. A dozen years had passed since the Kings' army had marched, and they had never come this far South.

"Hey," he called.

She looked down at him.

"Take care of yourself. If Valedan needs you, I'll come." He took a step away from the tree; the shadows at his feet shifted.

The villagers looked at him nervously, but they didn't try to stop him. Just in case it entered their heads, he let his hand drop to the hilt of his sword. He couldn't speak more plainly.

"Auralis?"

He looked up.

"Don't kill anyone."

And laughed.

"You're just afraid I'll finally get a chance to beat your numbers," he said. "And I've got money riding on the outcome—I told you that." As if money was everything. He grinned again, renewing the subtle offer of fellowship.

But the Kiriel in seraf's clothing was not his Kiriel; she didn't even crack a smile.

She spoke in Weston, only Weston, creating the illusion of privacy. But her words were stranger's words. "I've never asked you what you did the last time you were here."

"You didn't need to," he said, stark now, camaraderie gone. "You could see it. That first time."

"I can see it now," she replied evenly.

Bad sign. He knew it.

"And I don't care. What you did then. I don't care."

As if she had to convince herself. Not for the first time, he wondered who Ashaf was.

"But here," she continued, speaking slowly and softly, as if to a child, "I do care. These were her people, and they're *mine* now." As she spoke, he saw it: a glimmer of his Kiriel. The ferocity of the fight hadn't left her; she'd just moved it whole into some foreign territory. "I don't want you to kill anyone."

"I'm not in charge, Kiriel," he said, neutral now.

"You're an Osprey. They'll listen to you."

He laughed out loud, startling the villagers; they fled like sparrows, alighting a safe distance away.

"Don't kill anyone," she said again, and this time he heard, mingled with command, some hint of plea.

"Not until the war horns start," he replied. "But after that, all bets are off."

The Ospreys were waiting.

Damn names anyway; they were what they were.

"Where did you leave her?" Alexis asked, as he pulled up through the rows of tenting and the innumerable patrols that passed for the Annie version of military police. She shoved her hands in her pockets and leaned idly against a pole.

Unfortunately, that pole held the banner, and it listed beneath her weight. She cursed, losing her careful composure, and kicked Auralis in the ribs when he started to laugh. It hurt.

It hurt a lot.

Reminder, here. He shrugged. "In the village."

She might have cursed him for a fool, but she was busy cursing the dirt, the pole, and the pretty banners that nobility always used to mark their places. Pissing, in her opinion, would have made more sense.

Or so she said, and often, but she was no one's fool. Fiara took a risk: she moved in to offer help, but she offered it in a dead silence that didn't touch face or move lips. Safest way, that, when Alexis was in this foul a mood.

"What the Hells does she want with that damn village anyway? What's in it?"

"A great, stinking tree with a throne jutting out the West side," he said with a shrug.

That got her attention.

"What did you say?"

"I said—"

"Never mind, I heard what you said. What did you mean?"

"I mean there's a tree there that's about two hundred years old, and it's got a throne growing out of its base. Covered in bark and everything."

"You reported it?"

He shrugged. "I'm bad with the paperwork." And grinned.

She smacked his head—or she would have, but her kick had been all the reminder he needed. He ducked. Winced, too; the ribs were bruised.

"No, I didn't report it. I just got in. They didn't ask me to file at the guard post."

"Talk to Duarte."

He nodded. "What's happened here?"

"Hells if I know. We're not important enough to actually be *told* anything, remember? This is war."

But she glanced at the constant stream of men who moved throughout the camp. It was a long patrol.

"The Kalakar?"

Alexis shrugged. "She's up with the Eagle. The Hawk is out there, by the river delta. He's holding his forces." She spit and stepped back from the pole. The ground here had once been used for farming; it was still soft. Auralis, were he a praying man, would have offered the rain gods—if the South had them—whatever he possessed, short of his life, if they went somewhere else for a week or two.

"It stinks though," Alexis continued, shoving her hands back into her pockets and around the hilt of short sword and dagger. "Of magic."

"What do you mean?"

"The magi called in his crack troops," she snapped curtly, "Which you'd know if you hadn't gone baby-sitting."

"Crack troops?"

"Do you pay attention to *anything* that isn't short, pasty, and mean?"

"Sure. I'll settle for just mean."

Fiara whistled a warning, but he didn't need it; he hit the ground and rolled. Alexis had obviously been practicing behind their backs—she was damned fast.

"Meralonne APhaniel was joined by his warrior magis," Fiara said, as Auralis backed away from the Decarus. "They've been huddled in the big tent for two hours now."

"Magic?"

She nodded grimly. "'Lexis isn't telling. But Duarte has that look on his face."

"Great."

"Could be worse."

"Oh?"

"Could be demons."

He shrugged. "Why don't we go two for two and bet it's magic and demons?"

"You're tempting Kalliaris, you stupid bastard."

"She's tempting me," he shrugged. Rolling on the ground with a sword strapped to your side was decidedly poor planning. "Where are we deployed?"

"We aren't."

"Bullshit."

Fiara shrugged. "The Kalakar spoke to Duarte this morning. He kicked us all out of the tent. Or she did. Doesn't matter. It was a real short meeting."

"She was with the Eagle?"

"Nope. She came on her lonesome."

"And we're not being deployed. Right. She didn't ask us to do—"

"She was interrupted by Valedan," Fiara said. Now that Alexis was still—and gods knew how long that would last—he took the time to really look at Fiara's face.

Didn't much like what he saw there, and wondered why. This was his youth. This, this war, these valleys. She wanted to kill something. She was almost past the point of caring *what*.

"Why?"

Fiara shrugged. "Who knows? He didn't say. And she wasn't telling. But she left in a hurry, and he waited until she was good and gone before he followed. Best guess? I'd say he doesn't approve of the Ospreys."

"Funny way of showing it."

"What's that supposed to mean?"

"We're his Chosen, here," Auralis offered. "We're his Tyran. He hasn't chosen any others."

"He's almost one of us. For an Annie. But push comes to shove, and he'll choose his own. Wait and see."

"Fiara, he already did. He's here because of Kiriel."

She was silent, then. If Kiriel wasn't one of them, she wasn't an Annie either, and they all knew it.

"He doesn't want us killing his Annies," Fiara snapped. Then, tight-fisted, she added, "Sanderton's dead."

He said nothing. Nothing was safest.

But Alexis snap-kicked an inch from the pole.

"What did The Kalakar want?"

Fiara's expression was grim. "Why don't you ask Duarte? The rest of us haven't had shit for luck. And you've got an excuse—you're due to report, aren't you?"

"Yeah." He was. He backed away from Alexis, from Fiara, from Cook's immovable, silent shadow, thinking as he did that it was always the women that had to be watched.

Duarte was in a mood.

Which is to say, he was absolutely silent. Auralis offered him an out: he sauntered into the tent and pulled up a chair, draping himself across its back and folding his arms over the curved wooden height. Didn't even produce a frown.

"It's bad?" he asked.

"It's worse."

"You need us to work?"

Duarte said nothing. Too much of nothing.

"It's Valedan, isn't it?"

Duarte's gaze seemed to focus on Auralis as if that much attention took effort.

"He's not an Annie, at heart. And he's not a soldier." When that didn't merit a comment, Auralis abandoned the chair.

"If I asked you to go out and kill forty children, more or less, could you do it?"

Auralis shrugged. "Maybe."

"And the others?"

"Maybe."

"If you knew it was against orders, *strictly* against orders?"

"Maybe. Why?"

"Because the demons have come up with some complicated magic that scares the shit out of the magi," Duarte replied tersely. "And Member APhaniel seems to think the only way out is to balance their sacrifices with sacrifices of our own."

"For argument's sake, let's say we can't. Then what?"

Duarte shrugged. "We don't know."

"When will we?"

"Best guess?"

Auralis nodded.

"When the spell kills most of us."

The Sentrus hesitated, and then shrugged. "Kiriel's not afraid. Of the demons," he added.

"Kiriel wasn't here."

"I'd bet money—mine even—that she has some idea."

"Kiriel isn't afraid of much," Duarte said, after a pause. "What is she doing?"

"She's trying to blend in with the serafs."

That forced Duarte's brows up toward his hairline. "Is she succeeding?"

"About as well as you'd expect."

"What is she playing at, Auralis?" His voice was low. Intent. Whatever it was Auralis had said—or hadn't said—had caught his full attention.

"Funny thing," he replied, careful now. "I don't think she's playing at much."

"What does she want with the village?"

"To save it."

"To save it?"

"To save it."

"Why?"

He shrugged. "She's spent most of her time with the Ospreys saving Valedan. Maybe she's gone soft. Forty, you said?"

"Forty. Give or take a few."

"And it has to be kids?"

"There's some theory about the power they provide. Potential," he added bitterly. "All those possible years."

"And if we kill them, we break the demons' attack?"

Duarte grimaced. "No guarantees."

Auralis was stiff now. "Cook won't do it," he said at last. "I'm not sure Alexis will, and if she won't, you've got maybe five men, give or take two."

"Get them."

Auralis AKalakar bowed.

CHAPTER SEVENTEEN

THINGS might have gone differently.

Auralis AKalakar left Duarte's tent. In any future, he would have left that tent, and in any future, he would have stood a moment in the safety outside of its flap, gathering his thoughts.

In any future, he might have counted to himself the four or five men he thought capable of doing what Duarte had asked, obliquely, be done—and perhaps had he started to search before thinking, the whole course of a war would have been altered.

But the first name that came to mind was *hers*. Kiriel.

He didn't lie to himself; didn't need to. He had learned, long ago, exactly what he was capable of. How he had lived with it, he didn't know. Had made it a lifetime's work not to care. He could kill those children, if it saved his life. He could do that.

Kiriel could have done it as well.

In the sun of the South, verdant valley on every side crowded by tent and ditch, by countless men, he could see her briefly as she had been: young, alone, ill at ease—and dangerous. Walking death.

Auralis AKalakar had been attracted to death for a long, long time.

But she had changed. Not imperceptibly, as Alexis had—truly, as most of the Ospreys had, eroded by peace—but all at once. He had marked the change because it was both invisible and obvious, obvious to them all. Had he disliked it? Impossible to tell.

She was Kiriel.

But the Kiriel he had first met was not the Kiriel that had chosen to stay in the village of the Green Valley, surrounded by men and women who were not, by law, allowed the use of arms. That Kiriel would have viewed them all with distant contempt.

And this one?

This one had asked him *not* to kill. As if she had known, then, that he would. Or could. She had always understood him.

He shook his head to clear it.

He had been saved from the gallows of the Kings' Justice during the last war by Duarte AKalakar, and he had earned the right to live by the service he had offered the Kalakar mage. His companions waiting the noose had sometimes fared well, and sometimes poorly; not all of the men who were gathered by Duarte were in the end of use. What the hangman could not take, Duarte had, using as example those who could not be used in any other fashion.

He had hated Duarte for it then.

Twelve years. More.

He had faced the shadow of death, accepted it, and made peace: peace had been sundered. And he was—accept it—a coward. The life that was held out in one open hand was not much of a life, but he could not stop himself from grabbing it with both hands. He clung, then.

Now?

Now he had been asked to prove, again, that he was worthy.

And worthy, here and now, meant a very different thing than it did in the streets of Averalaan. Aie, they had all grown soft and complacent. They had *talked* of war, but they had chosen to forget what war *meant*.

And here it was: death.

His, or theirs.

But children?

He had not thought to ask Duarte how much time they had. But he knew it, the way he knew he needed breath or sleep: the men were gathering. Some were drilling, although they did it without the formality of orders; some were marching in the loose patrols the Kings' army always commanded; some were writing letters to the families they had left behind in the Northern capital. He was spared this last: he had no one to write to.

Everything that he valued—if value was a word that he had the right to use—was here.

Here, in these fields, and beyond them.

Kiriel.

Don't kill.

And if the alternative is death, Kiriel?

Don't. Don't kill anyone.

He began to walk. A shadow crossed his path and he looked up, expected to see Alexis. Found Fiara instead.

"Well?" she prodded, falling into step by his side.

"You were right. He's in a mood."

Her dark eyes narrowed, shadow slits. She swore at him, and the near-whisper of the curses added weight and texture to their meaning. "Don't give me that," she said at last. "What did he want?"

Fiara could do it. Sanderton's death had brought her home. It had failed to move Cook, and it had moved Alexis in an unexpected direction—but Fiara was his, if he wanted her. He examined her face; her hair was shorn to skull, a boy's cut; the scar upon her cheek was pronounced. She had taken a wound in the village of Essla. No one had asked from what. It suited her. It underscored everything that she was. He smiled. It was not a pleasant expression.

But something held his tongue.

"Auralis."

He nodded. "Yes," he said, because he wasn't going to be rid of her any other way. "He wanted something."

"I'm in," she told him.

"I'm counting on it."

"Where are you going?"

"To get the others," he replied.

"Which ones?"

"Enough, Fiara. We swing on the arm of the big tree if you don't *shut up*."

She shut up. He liked that, in her.

Of course, she didn't *stay* shut up. "Sanderton's dead."

"I know," he told her curtly. They all knew.

"Let's make it mean something."

As if death ever *meant* something other than food for worms. He wanted to slap her then. To slap her hard. He almost did.

But then he'd have a different fight on his hands, and he wasn't ready for it. The Commanders and their forces frowned on lethal combat among their soldiers.

"Where are you going?"

"To the magi," he said, surprising himself. It was not the answer he expected to hear, because until he spoke the words, they hadn't even been a possibility.

She whistled.

"Uh, where *are* the magi, exactly?"

And laughed. It was a grunt of sound, something dark and forced. She lifted a balled fist and, uncurling fingers, pointed among the twisting row of tents.

He nodded. "Wait for me," he said.

"Where?"

"Back at the tents."

She looked as if she was going to argue, and he braced himself, but in the end she shrugged. "Your funeral," she said. "They're not in a pretty mood."

"No one is."

The tree surprised him.

Well, the guards surprised him as well, but they were Southern, and he suppressed all knowledge of Torra until they were forced to look for translators. He waited, his hands folded behind his back, his expression almost dress perfect.

Meralonne APhaniel appeared between their shoulders.

"To what," he said coldly, "do I owe this interruption?"

"I've come from the village," he replied. "I was told to tell you that there's a large tree growing a throne in its center."

His brows rose. He spoke to the guards and they parted like a curtain; he stepped between them without acknowledging their presence.

Beyond their stiff backs, the world shifted. The tent itself was open to sky, and the light that shone through its ceiling was white and radiant, uninterrupted by grass or cloud.

"Where is your friend?" Meralonne APhaniel asked quietly, when the flap fell between the outside world and the inside one.

"She's still there." He would have said more, but trees were on his mind, and the tree that had taken root in the flattened grass over which the tent had been constructed commanded the whole of his attention. It was pale, like silver, and it glinted as if it were made of the metal. Its leaves glinted as well, heavy and sharp, golden buds. But those buds that had given way to shape and form were the most astonishing, for they seemed, to his jaded eye, to be made of living diamond.

"Don't touch it," Meralonne said curtly, and Auralis' hand fell away. He was unaware of lifting it until that moment.

"I hate magic," he said to no one in particular.

There were other men in the tent. Eight, he thought, although the tent should have been crowded with their number. Magic? It was all over. Subtle and quiet, it informed the interior in a way that not even the medallion of the Order could.

The hair on the back of his neck rose in warning or complaint; he ignored both. "What is it?"

"A tree," Meralonne replied. "And if the tree you spoke of was its kin, you are both blessed and cursed."

"No. The tree I spoke of was . . . a tree. An oak, maybe. Something that looks like it could live here." He paused, "Or West of here, in the impassable woods. The Green Deepings." He paused again. "It's old," he added, looking at the sapling and thinking of the throne.

"But not natural."

"Not unless bark normally takes the shape of a throne with a high back and high arms."

"Is it a large throne?"

The question made as much sense as a slender tree with leaves of gold and diamond. "No. It wouldn't fit me, if I tried to sit in it."

Meralonne nodded. "And it's new?"

"Apparently."

He turned and spoke a name. The syllables were oddly muted, but a man responded anyway. "Gyrrick."

A younger man joined him. He was built like a soldier, not a paunch-ridden old scholar, and he snapped a salute that would have made any Osprey feel uneasy. Even Auralis.

"It's true," the man said. "Sallis has it in his sight."

"Thank you. The other?"

"Three more trees have been uprooted; they'll be here in two hours. Horus asks that you be ready to receive them. But given the length of the border, we won't be able to take them all." He frowned. "Marris asks me to tell you that fire—as you guessed—doesn't burn them. They'll stand, regardless."

Meralonne nodded grimly. "Keep working," he said, and Gyrrick saluted. But his gaze glanced off Auralis' closed expression, and lingered there like suspicion.

Bright boy.

"The army moves tomorrow," Meralonne said, and to Auralis' surprise, it was spoken not to the magi but to him.

He nodded.

"The enemy forces are already in position, if our spies are to be trusted." He paused. "But there is some evidence that their mages— like ours—are otherwise occupied. Perhaps by the same mystery." He nodded at the tree.

But the nod itself was wrong; it contained something akin to reverence. Nothing, certainly, that Auralis was prepared to see. The magi and the army were, at the best of times, like oil and water. And war was the flame.

"You're in contact with their mages?"

Slate-gray eyes narrowed. But the magi chose to treat the question with contempt. *That* was more like it.

"Why are you here, Sentrus?"

"I have a hypothetical question."

"Ah. Ask."

"It's rumored that the enemy has somehow used human sacrifice to build a spell that will be complete when the army marches."

"Rumor is seldom that accurate."

Auralis shrugged. "It is also rumored that, with the right . . . propitiations . . . the spell might be rendered ineffective."

At that, silver brows rose. They reminded him of the slender branches of the tree that stood at the heart of the tent. This close, Auralis could see that the tent was not, in fact, open to air: the whole of the sunlight seemed to emanate from the trunk of the tree, from the heart of its leaves.

"With the right preparations," the magi replied, cautious now. "But such preparations have been expressly forbidden us."

"What would it take?"

"More than you are capable of," he replied.

"Could any of your warrior magi do the trick?"

Brows fell into a sharp line. Answer enough.

"There are perhaps three in the entirety of the camp who could do what must be done; the propitiations of which you speak would be rendered simple murder without one of these three.

"The first would refuse outright. Do not ask her."

As he had no idea who the magi spoke of, Auralis nodded. Easy concession.

"The second might now have difficulties that would not once have constrained him, but asking him would be safe."

"The third?"

"I am the third, Sentrus." The words were like cold steel. They cut. "What do you intend?"

"What I always intend," he replied, as sharply as the magi had. "To survive. This war, or any other war I happen to be part of."

"Choose your side, then." Meralonne's smile was no more reassuring than his frown.

"Already have," he replied. "I'm here."

"Good. You hope to accomplish this on your own?"

"No, sir."

Meralonne nodded. "How many others are willing to take this risk?"

"Enough."

"Bring them, then. Wait until the sun begins to set."

Auralis nodded.

"Ask for me, Sentrus. Speak to no one else of this."

He nodded again. But he did not salute, and before he left, he turned his gaze upon the tree. It seemed, in the space of scant minutes, to have grown. The tent would not contain it for long; the edges of its leaves glittered like readied weapons.

Serra Diora gazed upon the back of her sleeping wife. Her brown arms were curved protectively over the babe that fussed in silence; she would wake when he woke, and if she were lucky, she would sleep again.

A tent was not a harem, but a harem's heart was more than gilt and wood, stone and art. She had broken all promises, to be here, to sit and watch this tableau. She wanted to rise, to press lips against the babe's forehead, to touch his tiny fingers, and press them against her silent lips. But the mother might stir, and she knew what dreams would take form and shape in the minutes before waking; she was not unkind.

The desert had changed her.

Sea of Sorrows, it had opened its bitter, bleak heart, and she had fallen into its depths. She had never learned to swim well. This one clumsiness had been the source of cold, unpleasant amusement among the clan Leonne, and she had born such laughter with the steady grace that lack of choice can foster in the determined.

The scar upon her hand, hidden by the grace and certainty of years in the harem of the High Courts, was white; the writing of experience, the beginning of an end.

But what end?

The sun was bright, but not high; the skies would soon pale into the pink and deep blue that heralded the hour of man. One of two. Beyond it, the Lady lay in wait.

Or the Lord. Of Night, she thought. Her hand, she turned palm down, and she was once again perfect: the Serra Diora en'Leonne.

But of her husband, she knew little. He did not come to her tent again, and the question that he had offered lingered like the refrain of a song that would not—quite—leave. A ghost.

Ah, well. If she was to play host to ghosts, she had experience, and music was a haunting she could be at peace with.

Yet she was not at peace.

She had been ordered to rest, and indeed she had tried to retreat into the folds of sleep; it might be denied her in the evening. The army that they faced did not require day in which to do the worst of their work, and the Lady was—had shown herself to be—powerless in the face of brute force.

But powerless? No. No more than she.

She rose. The sari that she wore was almost confining; it was a poor replacement for the Voyani robes that had been her armor during her sojourn in the desert, although it had cost far, far more. She wondered whose hands had gone into the making.

"Na'dio?"

Ona Teresa knelt in the corner of the tent, her dark hair swept back into simple braid. She, too, wore sari, and Diora knew, looking at her, that she would never be comfortable in silk and gold again. The changes that had been wrought within the Serra Diora were made manifest by the Serra Teresa. All loss, all gain, was there. Her skin was no longer ivory, and the sun had not been kind.

But what was kindness, here?

"Ona Teresa," she said at last, sparing only a backward glance at Teyla and the baby. "I am restless."

She rose.

"You wish your samisen?"

"No."

"The lute?"

"No."

"Then what?"

"The Sen Margret," she replied.

The instant the words left her lips, she regretted them. She had not intended to say them; could not have. The Sen Margret was no part of her life.

"You mean Margret?"

"Yes," she said, but lamely. She knew fear, but it was passing; this woman had not the hearing or the gift left in which to catch the lie.

And yet, bereft of gift, she did. "Na'dio."

"My harp," she said, forcing perfect stillness into the syllables. She offered her aunt a smile, tilting her chin with practiced ease.

The Serra Teresa frowned, but she accepted what she had been offered and rose.

The Sen Margret was long dead. Her voice was silent. The Heart of Arkosa now beat against the breast of another woman, and the Serra Diora would never bear its weight again.

Would never hear its voice, its multitude of voices, would never see the ghosts of its many, many bearers. She was bereft of their guidance, as deaf in her fashion as the Serra Teresa now was.

But she had, in the place of the Heart, memories which came from a life that she had never lived.

She had been Diora.

Then, and now.

No, she had been the *Sen* Diora. Equal in rank to the master she served; equal in any power that birth did not grant her.

She had been sister and servitor to the Sen Margret, and she had seen the Sen Margret do many, many things. She had stood by her side during most of them.

The memories had receded. She thought them—had thought them—gone. Gone with the Heart of Arkosa. Gone with the City that she had desperately desired, foolishly desired, to call her home.

But they were present now, and rising, like tide along the Eastern shore.

She rose before the Serra Teresa returned, bearing the Northern harp. Of the instruments she owned, it was the only one that was not within her tent, and for that reason, it was the one she had requested.

Sunlight, pale and faded, now lapped against the foot of her guarded domicile. But in its dying, it was beautiful, an elegy for the day.

She acknowledged beauty, as all who must struggle to achieve it will, and then she looked beyond it—for she was used to guile and superficial appearance, and she understood both its substance and the imperative of seeing beneath its surface.

The army was slowly coming to life. Lamps and torches were being lit, and the campfires around which men—and Northern women—gathered. Conversation would begin in those groups, and some of it would no doubt carry upon the wind; there was drink here, and the food that the Tyrs could offer those who might not live to eat again.

There were many, many soldiers gathered here. She saw them with two sets of eyes: hers, and the vision of the Sen Diora.

The Sen Diora felt contempt, pity, and a vague fear.

So, she thought.

She listened, then, and heard it: the voice of the wild. Within the heart of the Tyr'agar's camp, gaining in strength and cold majesty, the tree was growing.

Lady, she thought, bowing her head above the sleeping form of this new, strange wife and this new, strange son. *When your time is come, grant me mercy. Protect them.*

She had not thought to utter that prayer for anyone again.

She walked past her guards. They were Tyran, and they hesitated as she brushed between them. It was death, to touch her. It was death, to allow her to be touched by any save the Tyr'agar. She knew it.

"Serra," one man said, his blade reflecting crimson light. She turned and met his gaze. In the Tor Leonne, she would never have been so bold, and she knew that she injured her husband by her lack of grace.

But grace was a thing that time allowed, and only time. "I must go," she said softly.

"The Tyr'agar has not summoned you."

"No."

The men looked to each other. They were not young, and they were not easily intimidated; had men, in numbers, come for her, they might have stood her down by the weight of stares and the scars they bore. Scars spoke, after all, of survival.

And other things, to the Serra. She let the moment drag.

At last, one of the men departed. He did not move with grace, but grace was not necessary; he was Tyran.

She could order him to stand, and he would stand. She had already revealed much of herself to the magi and the men who ruled them.

But she could not—quite—bring herself to this. It was a crime for which she would not be forgiven, and she knew—who better than she?—what happened when Tyran turned against their lords.

Ser Andaro returned by the Tyran's side. The sole Tyran her husband claimed, he looked haggard. She did not like him, but she did not dislike him; she waited.

"Serra Diora," he said, tendering her a nod. "Night will fall shortly. What is it that you require?"

"I am summoned," she told him.

"The Tyr'agar has not summoned you."

"No. But I am called, Ser Andaro, and if I fail to answer the call, there is danger."

What danger could a woman know? She saw the thought cross his features. His eyes narrowed as answers suggested themselves to his superstitious mind, but he was well trained; he did not speak them aloud.

"The Matriarch?" he asked.

It was as good an answer as any. She did not reply, but the expression she built of her lips and eyes implied much.

"The Tyr'agar must be informed," he told her curtly.

"He is much occupied, Ser Andaro, with the coming battle. This is a matter for women. Will you interrupt him with no just cause?"

"He values you," Ser Andaro replied. His dark eyes were narrow now. She had misjudged him; he was no fool. And yet he served as if service was a sacrament. She had seen him by her husband's side, and she knew that his life was not his own, and that he was glad of it.

Hers had never been her own. The last time that fact had brought her joy . . . ah, the time. The time.

"He values me," she said softly, "and you do not understand why."

A dark brow rose. He did not lift his hands to ward himself against the words, but she was not Voyani; she bore the taint of their presence, but her birth was above suspicion. "I have . . . heard rumors," he said at last. His voice was dark.

"Rumors are for women," she told him serenely. "Or for the idle. Or the wind. I am only a Serra," she continued. "Will you not let me pass? The Tyr'agar has given the Matriarch of Havalla free passage of the encampment; there is not a tent to which she is not welcome."

"She is not with you now, Serra."

"No. You are." She drew breath. "If you will not let me pass, accompany me, but do not delay me." It was a command.

And he knew it. She had seldom seen a Tyran's face so rigid, and each time she had, men had died. But he would not kill her. Could not.

"I will accompany you," he said.

She nodded gracefully and swept her sari into her hands, drawing its hem up from the crushed grass, the exposed dirt. Her shadow was long and slender.

He would know, soon enough, that she lied. But she thought that he would have other things to worry about when he did.

The tent was guarded.

But the voice of the tree passed through stiff cloth in disregard of all boundaries.

"Ser Andaro," she asked him, as they walked, "do you hear nothing amiss?"

He did not snort; he frowned. "I hear the men," he answered. "I hear the sound of fire, the sound of argument. I hear nothing unusual."

She said nothing, and after a moment, he surprised her.

"What do you hear, Serra Diora?"

She looked at him, and the face behind the Tyran's mask met hers. She thought, for a moment, that she had misjudged him; there was about him a seriousness that spoke of thought and curiosity. Of loss.

She wondered, then, if there was a reason that he was the sole Tyran that Valedan had chosen. He would be Captain of the oath-guards, if Valedan survived, and as Captain, he would know everything. Everything.

"Song," she answered quietly.

He frowned, his brow furrowing. "I hear Northern song," he said at last, with a shrug. "But it is not a song that is suitable for a Serra."

"It is a song suitable for the battlefield," she replied with just a hint of a smile. "Although I have never understood the comfort taken in something so graceless."

He shrugged. "It is their way," he replied. "It is how they defy death."

"There is comfort in death," she answered, and then they were silent for a few steps.

"Kiriel di'Ashaf has not returned?"

"No, Serra."

It was strange, to speak so openly with a man. "Will she?"

"When the Tyr'agar calls her."

"Ah."

He frowned. "Do you understand this Kiriel, Serra?"

"No more than you; I have seen her little, and you have traveled leagues by her side."

"But she does not come to my tent."

"No." She smiled, but there was no joy or amusement in the expression. "We are both strangers here, and often strangers find comfort in each other's presence."

"You speak her tongue."

"She speaks Torra."

"She speaks Weston as well."

"Yes, I speak Weston. I was taught it by a man who frequented the Tor Leonne. He was also a singer."

"And is it his song that you now hear?"

"No, Ser Andaro. But if it were my choice, it would be."

"Then what song?"

"The song," she said simply, "of living things, shorn from their moorings. Strangers," she added. "It is a lament."

"A lament?"

"For the passage of days," she said softly. "And the end of Summer."

His brows rose. "You are strange," he said softly. "Flower of the Dominion, you have been planted in foreign soil."

"And you, Ser Andaro? Did you not offer your lord your life in the North?"

His smile surprised her. It was as genuine as hers had not — yet—been, but genuine or no, there was pain beneath its surface. Such a smile, he offered her. "I did."

And in return, she offered him honesty, thinking that honesty was like too much wine; it was dangerous, and once begun, it was not easily forsaken. "Have you not yet told our Tyr that he must gather other Tyran?"

"I have, Serra. I have told him many things. As you, no doubt, have also done. Has he listened?"

And the smile she offered was unfettered. They were alone here, and there was a danger. But there was so much danger, this one seemed to pale into insignificance. She glanced up at the sky and saw why: the Lord was gone, and the Lady had not yet taken residence in the heavens. It was their hour. "No. But perhaps he has less reason to trust me than he has to trust you; I am daughter to his enemy, and I have also betrayed my father."

The confession was a known truth, but it was freely offered. She waited.

"He has more reason to trust you," Ser Andaro said quietly, "for I was sent North to kill him."

Her brows did not rise, her expression did not shift. She absorbed his words whole as the gift they were. "You trust him," she said, the last word rising.

"He is worthy of trust." He paused, and then added, "He frustrates all expectation. He is not a Northern man, but he is not entirely of the South; he exists between the two nations, like a nation of his own. He will not come to us; we must come, at last, to his banner, and serve him."

"And you have."

"Yes, Serra Diora. I would have said it was impossible. I would have sworn oath to it, beneath the open sky. But the sun was in my eyes, and it is in my eyes no longer: I see him as he is. Do you?"

She had no answer to offer him. But an answer of sorts was required. She said, "He is a man of power, and I have known powerful men for the whole of my life. He is not those men. I thought him weak."

"He is. But he is one of those rare men who make weakness a strength. He will not be entirely of the South, no matter what we two do or say. But between us, between those who have elected to serve him, we may yet serve the most worthy Tyr that the Dominion has known since the Founder."

She nodded and then turned and began to walk; she walked slowly. The conversation would end, and she found that she wanted it to continue. "He seems reluctant to take wives," she told Ser Andaro. "I have explained our customs, and indeed he seems to understand them."

"Yet you took wife in his name," Andaro said quietly, "and he did not gainsay you."

"No. But he knows that I did it to save her life, and the child's. He knows that she will die if he refuses what I asked in his name. He is of the North."

"He is. He will not have serafs."

"And does he think that by refusing to own them, he will do away with slavery?"

Andaro laughed. "You are much like—" And the laughter ebbed.

She understood why; she heard the bitter edge of loss in the trailing syllable of the last word. "Forgive me," she said, speaking as Serra.

He shook his head. "You have committed no crime. Others might accuse you of weakening the Tyr, but I have come to understand him. You are right, of course. He desires an end to slavery."

"He will have only war if he tries. No," she added, lifting a hand, like a man would, to stem the reply. "I think that change is possible. I would not have, once. But I have crossed the desert." She lifted her hand, then, and exposed the scarred palm.

In the fading light, scar tissue formed a symbol.

"But it must come from within, and it must grow. Even the serafs would fear him, if he were too strange a lord."

"I do not grudge you your honesty," Ser Andaro said. "I was trained for the High Courts, but I am not of them; the women of the low clans are more like the Voyani than any of their men would care to admit."

"But you have no wife."

"No, nor will I. And I will have no need of one. Ser Valedan kai di'Leonne will, and he will need a strong wife."

"And a loving wife?" Her tone was sharper than she had intended. Honesty, it seemed, was a contagion.

But he met her gaze openly, and studied her face, her perfect face, for a moment.

"You think yourself so different," he said at last, and she felt the difference in their ages keenly and unexpectedly.

"Am I not? I am simple—"

"No, spare me this, Serra. We both serve the Tyr'agar, and if we served at the start for our own reasons, in the end, we still serve.

"I do not ask you if you love him; that is a child's question, and a child's game. It is not of concern to me now. But I will tell you that I think that the two of you are not so different. You think him weak, but you exposed your own weakness in Essla. You saved the child. You risked everything *to* save the child.

"So would he have, had he been present. Decry his weakness, if you must. Decry your own while you do. But understand that you have an advantage."

"I am a *woman*," she said softly, as if amazed that she need speak so plainly to a man who served as oathguard. "What advantage do you speak of? My curse? My voice?"

He shook his head, his eyes steady. "You are armed, yes. Rumor is unkind, and it will hurt your husband, and not only does he understand this, but he does not care. When told of your actions upon the field, he said, 'The Northern Kings have no fear of the bardborn, and they are well served. I will be no more cowardly than they.'"

She drew sharp breath.

"No, it is not of that that I speak. You have the advantage because you *are* of the South. What you have taken in weakness, you will know best how to protect in strength. The more you take, the more you will have to lose, and you will fight against that loss with a canniness that the Tyr'agar does not yet possess. Give him that, and he will hold all that he takes on the morrow.

"Give him less, and everything we build will falter at the slightest breeze."

"You are canny," she said softly. "Can you not—"

"I? No. But all that he wants from me, he already has."

"And of me?"

"He wants what men want," he said quietly. "Men of the North. And in time, perhaps, you will give him that. I cannot say. I can only say again, that you are not so different."

"Judge, then," she said. "For we have arrived at the tent of the magi, and we are not alone."

Ser Andaro frowned, and the whole of his posture shifted as he turned to look. The man who had offered her such unexpected kinship was gone. Only the Tyran remained, and his hand was upon his sword; the hilt was an inch from the lip of its scabbard.

In the fading light, exposed to the darkening sky, six men had exited the tent.

And five of them were Northern soldiers.

The sixth man was Meralonne APhaniel.

His hair was silver, a braid that fell down the length of his armored back. Gone were the robes that the Northern magi wore; gone the medallion by which he marked his office. He wore no obvious sword, and carried no shield, but he was marked for war.

He turned as Ser Andaro di'Corsarro approached.

His stillness was the stillness of a warrior when challenge has been offered. But he inclined his head.

"Ser Andaro," he said.

One of the Northerners spoke. His voice was a whisper.

But the Serra Diora heard it as clearly as she would have heard shouting.

"No," she said, speaking as softly and gently as a Serra might, "that would be unwise. Ser Andaro di'Corsarro is Tyran here, and to kill him is to slight the Tyr'agar."

The man cursed. The cursing was louder than the question had been.

"Serra Diora," Meralonne APhaniel said, bowing, his lips turned in a cold little smile. "To what do we owe this honor?"

"To my husband," she replied. "For his command was clear, and it was unequivocal."

"And he sent you?"

"Ah, no," she replied, bowing prettily, her knees too stiff to bend. There were none Southern here to witness her singular lack of grace, or to mark it for the anger that it was. "I was called by something other, and I have responded to it."

"You must have matters to attend to."

"Indeed, magi, I do. So, too, does Ser Andaro."

"That would be unwise."

She smiled. "Then he may remain as my guard." She lifted her head, exposing the white of perfect throat.

And she called a single name, as loudly as she could.

No one heard it.

But Meralonne APhaniel stiffened. "You interfere in something that you do not understand."

"I understand it well," she replied. "You intend to appease the Old Earth."

His pale brows rose.

"How do you know this, Serra?" There was menace in the question. Death. Her own; Ser Andaro's.

But she had heard death before, and it did not cause her to falter; it was only her own. She had longed for it, had planned for it, had cursed it for its lateness in arriving. But the single night of slaughter in the Tor Leonne had deprived her of the fear. She knew that things existed that were far worse than death, and knew, too, that she was strong enough to weather them all.

"I have spoken with the Old Earth," she told him.

He was utterly still.

"What is she saying?" One of the Northerners hissed. A woman.

"That you had best return to your unit. And quickly," the magi replied, in a full, deep Weston.

"*What?*"

"She has summoned the Tyr'agar, and if he arrives and you are present, not even The Kalakar will raise hand to save you."

Valedan kai di'Leonne did not come alone.

Ser Anton di'Guivera and Ser Baredan di'Navarre accompanied him, one to the left and one to the right. They abandoned the stately grace of measured step for the urgency of speed, and arrived in a clatter of heavy steps. Their weapons were drawn, and glinted in moonlight and lamplight.

Only when they approached the Serra Diora and saw her standing, unharmed, in the presence of Ser Andaro did they slow; their weapons remained at bay.

Valedan nodded to his wife. "Serra Diora," he said. He did not ask her why she had summoned him. He seemed to understand that her gift, exposed, was still something that could not be openly acknowledged.

She now bent knees and fell into the full supine posture required of a Serra—any Serra—in the presence of Tyrs. She knew it would not please him, but knew also that it would be noted by the General and the swordmaster. Balancing his anger with their sense of propriety was not a simple task; she did not hold the posture for as long as she would have liked.

But she held it long enough, and when she rose, she accepted the hand that Valedan kai di'Leonne should never have offered.

Hers was shaking. She could not stop it.

But his, firm, could mask what she had no desire to reveal.

He raised her to her feet, and then drew her to his side, displacing the General. It was not wise—it was instinctive. Ser Baredan di'Navarre said nothing, did nothing, to indicate his awareness of the slight.

But perhaps his time in the North gave him cause to excuse much.

"APhaniel," the kai Leonne said quietly. "You are dressed for battle."

"As are you, kai Leonne."

"The magi are not soldiers, by the reckoning of Kings."

"No. We are seconded to the army, but we retain the rights—and the obligations—of citizens. The military does not rule us."

"And the soldiers?"

"There are no soldiers here, kai Leonne."

"Ser Andaro?"

"Five men," Andaro di'Corsarro replied.

"Whose?"

"Yours."

"The Ospreys." It was not a question.

"I did not recognize all of them," Ser Andaro replied cautiously. "But, yes, in my opinion, they were Ospreys."

"Why did they come to you, APhaniel?"

The silence was heavy. Much was woven into its texture, and none of it pleasant.

"Ser Andaro, you will summon Primus Duarte AKalakar. Now."

Andaro saluted. It was the only time his hand left his sword. He skirted Ser Anton di'Guivera as he disappeared into the darkening shadows, the shallows of night.

Diora gazed at Valedan's profile. Had she thought him weak? For a moment the memory was displaced, the past giving way to the present. Very, very few were the men who dared speak in such a way to the Widan.

Perhaps the Northern magi were different.

But what she heard in the voice of *this* magi was power shorn of the need of politics; what informed it, she did not know. Was not certain that she wished to.

Lady, she thought, for the Lady's face now reigned in the night sky.

Meralonne APhaniel continued to stare at her.

Ser Anton noted it. Ser Baredan noted it. If Valedan did, he did not betray it.

"APhaniel," a new voice said.

Kallandras of Senniel College came out of the Southern lee of the tent. He bowed to the Tyr'agar, and then, in turn, to the men who accompanied him.

He saved the lowest, and the most courtly of his obeisances, for the Serra Diora.

She returned his bow with a nod; she could not fall into the supplicant posture again because Valedan's hand was still upon hers.

"Why are you here, Kallandras?" she asked him, her lips hardly moving, her voice pitched in such a way that only he would hear it.

"For the same reason you are, Serra," he replied, **"although I fear that the source for my caution, and the source for yours, are different."**

"And now?"

"We wait."

But waiting was difficult. She looked at the magi and said, "The tree is calling."

He said, voice flat, "I hear nothing." But he did not guard his words; she heard a bitter envy in them.

She would have apologized for her indiscretion, but his expression left no room for nicety. She said, "Then I must be our ears, Member APhaniel."

A silver brow rose. She thought he might refuse her.

But Valedan lifted her hand. "What does it say, Serra? What does it want?"

"It wants its kind," she replied, after a brief hesitation. "It does not . . . speak . . . in words. I do not know if mine are sufficient to express what it says."

"They must be," he told her. "For I, too, am deaf."

"And I," Kallandras told her quietly. "What you hear, I cannot hear."

She might have said more, but Duarte AKalakar came into the clearing. He came alone, and the bow he offered the Tyr'agar spoke volumes: It was perfect.

"Primus," Valedan said, letting Diora's hand fall gently to her side. "The Ospreys appear to have gathered here."

"Have they caused difficulty, Tyr'agar?"

"For you, yes."

The Primus stiffened.

"There were five men," he said. "Or five soldiers. I want them."

Duarte saluted.

"Now."

"My apologies, Tyr'agar, but I don't know who they were."

"Perhaps Meralonne APhaniel will enlighten you."

The magi stifled a yawn.

Diora almost forgot to breathe; she had seldom seen such obvious lack of respect.

But Valedan was above it. "You will not play these games," he said softly to the magi. "You are not a soldier here; you are not under my command. But you are within my domain, within my Dominion. You will answer the question, APhaniel, or you will leave."

"I have only one name," he replied at length, as if the matter bored him. "And it will do you little good; the men were off duty, and they broke no Imperial Law."

"By the grace of the Serra Diora," Valedan replied tightly, "and the presence of my Tyran, they were given no opportunity. Duarte, I will speak with the Ospreys. Now."

Duarte's fist was mild thunder against the stiff line of his chest.

She had never seen Valedan angry.

She had tried to anger him. She had tried to annoy. She had—foolishly, callowly—desired to see this reaction. To know that it was within him.

But the desire and the actuality were grimly different. She would never, she thought, try to displease him again.

Still, she reached out to touch the mailed bend of his elbow, and although the chain robbed him of sensation, he was aware of the slightest of her gestures. He looked down, his neck bending, his stance speaking of the difference in their heights. "Serra?"

"I must stay a while," she said softly. "The tree. If Ser Andaro will bring me an instrument—any instrument—I will sing to it."

"Must you? I would have you by my side when I address the Ospreys."

"They are not Ospreys," Baredan di'Navarre said quietly.

"They *were not* Ospreys," Valedan replied. "And I will clip their wings, or break them, before I hunt them in that fashion. Before I see them hunted in that fashion."

"I will accompany you if you desire it, Tyr'agar," she told him, but her eyes were drawn to the tent.

He shook his head. "You were here for a reason, Serra Diora. Be here. I will return when I am done."

She bowed.

"But if you will not bear witness, let Kallandras of Senniel College bear witness in your stead."

Kallandras bowed. Bowed, and turning to the Serra Diora, offered her the lute that was strapped across his shoulder.

She had played it before, but as it came to her hand she realized that the last time she had touched its strings at night had been during the night that the storm had swept across the Sea of Sorrows at the behest of the flying serpent.

Margret's brother Adam had brought it, awkward as a child, and had offered it into her keeping. He had listened while she played, and he had offered her words that might better explain the sister he loved and respected. She had barely listened then. Her own resentment for the Matriarch of Arkosa had been almost as strong as his affection.

But Margret's brother had borrowed *Salla* from Kallandras, and he had promised to return the lute without delay, and without harm.

Adam had died, that night, to keep his word; she could still see his stiff, bloodless hands in rictus around the neck and the bowl of the lute.

She had not thought to touch it like this again.

She thought of Kiriel di'Ashaf, as if the thought could banish older, darker memories; her hands shook.

But she spoke the lute's name softly as she gentled sound from its perfectly tuned strings. She bowed to the bard, and then she turned to Valedan and said softly, "Thank you."

His eyes rounded; she couldn't bear to watch them and turned away, seeking the entrance of the tent.

But she was disappointed—and why? Foolish, she thought, foolish girl—when he let her go.

*   *   *

The Ospreys gathered. They were not so great in number that they required a vast empty plain upon which to stand—but Valedan chose to address them at a distance from the main body of the encampment. Such a space was not easy to find, but it *was* found.

The Tyr'agnati were not asked to attend, and they were not given oblique leave to do so; The Kalakar was, however, asked to be present, and Commander Bruce Allen was likewise given permission. Permission, in the South, was an order.

Although Valedan had taken much from his time in the South, and had learned much in the training grounds of Callesta, he chose to style himself a Northern leader here; he waited while a platform was erected for his use, and he did use it. He stood, flanked by Ser Anton and the Commanders; Ser Andaro stood by his right, his arms crossing the breadth of his chest.

Beyond them, before them in ragged ranks, stood the Ospreys, that portion of the Kalakar House Guards that had never been much for dress duty. At their head stood Primus Duarte. He was rigid; he stood at attention. Others aped him, but they did so poorly. Were it not for the seriousness of the situation, there might have been humor in it.

"Tyr'agar," Commander Allen said. "The men are ready."

"As ready," Kallandras added softly, for Valedan's ears alone, "as they are capable of being."

Valedan did not smile, and the bard fell silent.

"Commander Kalakar," Valedan said quietly, "you will say nothing while I speak."

She raised a bronze brow, but her lips were a thin line. She knew why she was here. Commander Allen said nothing.

"Primus," Valedan began, lifting his voice, lending it the strength that his years belied. "Is this all of your unit?"

"Sir," the Primus replied, saluting heavily. "Sentrus Kiriel di'Ashaf is absent with your permission. The rest are present."

"Count off," Valedan said quietly.

Duarte accepted the criticism implied by the command, and turning, gave the order. One by one, each Decarus spoke his or her name and rank; those men or women under their command then offered their names and their ranks. Valedan knew them all, and he kept careful count as they spoke.

It took little time; the Ospreys were no more than thirty here. A good number for bodyguards, an insignificant number for the battlefield.

"You are here," Valedan said quietly, "because this evening five of your number were seen in the company of Meralonne APhaniel."

The discipline of the Ospreys, never good, faltered as word spread out in little circles, the eddies of conversation that were, in theory, forbidden.

"I have not asked why they chose to meet with the magi. I will not ask what they hoped to achieve. I will tell you all, instead."

Silence, then. He had their attention.

"Against my orders, my explicit orders, I believe that they intended to neutralize the underpinnings of a spell that we barely understand. The spell was—we are told—built upon the bodies of the newly dead. And it was—we are also told—scaled with the blood of the children of Essla, the village children who were taken some days before our arrival.

"It has been put forward, by the magi, that an equal number of dead might suffice to weaken the spell the servants of the Lord of Night have built."

Words sparked like lightning across the unit. Some were barely audible and some were raucous as crow's song.

"It has been my privilege and my honor to be served by you. Without the Ospreys—by any name—I would not have arrived in safety in the South, and the Dominion would not now be within my grasp." He waited a moment. A heart's beat. Two. "I have never asked about your history. I have not questioned you about your time in the valleys of Averda. I am aware that it was costly. I am aware that, by your actions, the North was given its necessary face of ferocity among the Southern Tyrs.

"What you did, you did in name of a war that you did not ask for and did not begin. I will not judge it. It is past. Is that not the rule among the Ospreys? The past *is* past. The present is what defines you.

"And it has defined you. Until tonight, it has defined you."

Primus Duarte lifted head; his chin was level with the flat, damp ground.

"You gave up your colors to come South. Your unit was stood down, in Northern terms; no Southern term exists for what was done, because no Southern army is formed the way the Northern armies are.

"But you did not, perhaps, understand that you gave up more than that: You surrendered your history. You chose to live in the present.

"I have commended you as men—and women—of honor. I

have argued for you, and for your presence, within my retinue. I have never been disappointed by it, and I *do not intend to be disappointed now.* We are measured by our grace under pressure.

"Do you seek to fail that measure now? Will you shame me in front of the men whose alliance I require?"

As if the question were rhetorical, the Ospreys waited.

Primus Duarte spoke. "We seek, Tyr'agar, what we have sought since we accepted your service. Your survival. No more, no less."

"What survives, when all honor is discarded?" Valedan asked, his voice louder although the words were smooth and unbroken.

"Southern honor?" A woman's voice. Fiara's voice. "You speak of Southern honor here?"

"I speak," Valedan said coldly, thanking her, "of *your* honor. And of mine. It is said that I am not of the South. I accept this accusation as truth. I was born here, but I was given to the North, and the North has made me what I am.

"And what I am is not a murderer. I am no dark god's priest. I am no killer of children. If I survive in such a fashion, why should we fear the Lord of Night? We do his work, and willingly, in order to *survive.* All that we are, all that we must be, we give not on the edge or point of sword or spear, but cravenly, cowardly, hiding behind the banner of 'necessity.' I will not see it done. I would perish here first."

"And what if the rest of us don't want to share your fate?"

"You are free to leave," he replied.

"We're part of the army. Leaving is called desertion."

Valedan turned then to The Kalakar.

Her complexion was pale in the darkness. Her expression was devoid of warmth. But not of certainty.

"The Kalakar will grant you the dispensation. You are Kalakar House Guards. Whether you wear the Kings' symbol or no, you are hers. Tell them," he said softly.

"You are free to leave," she said. "Resign your commission, but speak now if you must. I will protect you from the Kings' Justice and the Kings' wergild against the crime of desertion." The words were taken from her as if by unseen force.

By Valedan kai di'Leonne.

"I say again, that I have been privileged to have you as guards. I will not count as cowards those who now choose to serve elsewhere. But I will kill each and every one of you who seeks to break my edict and *my* law."

"It is the Kings' law," Kallandras of Senniel said. He was the only man on the dais who dared to interrupt the kai Leonne. "And in this fashion, Tyr'agar, you uphold the law of the Kings. They would say no less were they present. They would say, perhaps, more."

"Primus Duarte."

Duarte saluted.

"Poll them. Pay those who will not risk death; retain those who will serve as they have served. But make clear that I mean what I say; the crows will be the only funereal song your dead will hear if they perish by my hand."

To punctuate the words, he drew the Sun Sword. Its edge was flat, but the sheen of it was blue, a hint of the presence of their enemy. "Do you understand me?" he asked softly.

"Kalakar?"

Her nod was bleak. If she was angry, it showed only in that weathered gesture.

"Commander Allen?"

He offered, measure for measure, the same nod. The Ospreys waited, understanding why the Tyr'agnati were not present; the Northern Commanders were being humbled in a fashion that the South would not easily forgive, were it to bear witness.

He waited, and when silence answered him, he said, "Primus Duarte. Your men."

Duarte stepped forward, his rank not enough of a distance between him and the forces he had once shaped. He approached the dais without permission, and once he had reached its wide lip, he stood directly in front of, and beneath, the Commander of the Northern armies.

Valedan kai di'Leonne had, by his words this evening, become in truth what the flimsy weight of signed paper had made him in theory. Boy king.

But not a boy.

"Tyr'agar," he said, and he offered the Tyr a perfect, Northern salute, fist across chest. "We will serve."

"You have not polled your men," Valedan said quietly. "And I will take the service of *none* who will not accept my law."

"They serve," Duarte said quietly.

"They serve you," Valedan replied evenly. "You have served The Kalakar. Serve *me*, Primus, or you may stand down."

Duarte said, "This is not a war like any other."

"I have seen what it will be. But I believe that there are—there must be—other ways to win it. Let us not lose what we struggle to gain." His voice had grown quiet; it carried the distance between himself and Duarte, no more.

The Ospreys strained to hear; they were silent now, which was unusual. He had them.

Duarte bowed stiffly, with just the flicker of glance at his liege lord, at Ellora AKalakar, the woman he had vowed to follow to the Hells and back.

Hell, it seemed, was no longer an option. And what remained was stranger than even the course of the war had been.

"This is not what we came South for," he told the kai Leonne. "You have not asked for our history, and I have not given it to you."

"It is not of interest."

"We are the unit that did what had to be done," Duarte said anyway, "*when* it had to be done."

Valedan nodded grimly. "I have told you what must be done, Primus. I have told you what must *not* be done. You have your legend, and it echoes in the decade between that war and this one. Make your choice."

Choice.

Duarte turned then, to seek Alexis.

Found her. Her face was strained and pale, but there was something in it that he had not seen since they had begun the long march out of Averalaan. An echo of peace, here.

She wanted this. She wanted what Valedan offered.

Was it weakness, then? Was this what she had become?

He bowed head a moment.

"Decarus," he said quietly.

Alexis, no fool, saluted crisply and joined him. She was the first, and the Ospreys watched her like the circling birds of prey whose name they once bore.

"I came through the Averdan valleys once," she told him softly. "I'm not afraid to face them again."

"We faced them on our own terms."

She laughed, low and bitter. "We faced them on their terms," she told him. "And we survived. I'm not afraid to face them on *his*."

"Are you afraid not to, Alexis?"

Her brow rose sharply, defining—redefining—the elegance of her face. Sun had darkened it, and something else now added color as well. He thought she might slap him, which would be an unfortunate display of poor discipline.

But she held her hand steady.

It came to him that Alexis, his Alexis, wanted a clean fight. She wanted to face demons, not men.

Gods, they had aged in the Empire.

"I'm staying," she said simply, but she offered the words to Valedan kai di'Leonne.

Cook came next, shouldering his way through the ranks of the Sentri. His large hands were by his sides, and his sword was an inch away. He looked up at Valedan, and down at Duarte, and then shook his head. No approval there, but Duarte expected none; he had not been among the men Auralis had gathered.

"I'm staying," he said quietly.

And so it went.

One by one they came, all discipline, all codified approach, forgotten. Some glanced briefly at The Kalakar, but most were content to watch Duarte, Alexis, and Valedan.

Valedan did not move. He accepted what they offered as if he had expected no less, and his eyes did not flicker over Fiara's sullen face.

The line dwindled.

Auralis AKalakar was last to make his approach.

CHAPTER EIGHTEEN

KALLANDRAS stiffened as Auralis made his way to the platform. He was last to make this choice, and this was significant, for of the men present, Kallandras had recognized Auralis instantly as one of the five who had joined Meralonne APhaniel. There was something in the gait of the man, something in his carriage, that was ineluctably his own; subterfuge, for Auralis, involved not being seen.

Kallandras himself had no difficulty with the choice that Auralis had made, nor indeed with the one that Meralonne had himself chosen; his years in the labyrinths of the *Kovaschaii* brothers had given him the distance such killing required.

Were it not for the words of Evayne a'Nolan, he might have joined them in a different fashion, forsaking lute and the title of master bard for a time.

But Evayne's words harried him now, in an entirely unexpected way.

The sword by his side—a weapon not his own—was humming. He could hear it clearly. That Valedan or the Commanders could not was obvious, for they did not look up, did not look to him, evinced no obvious curiosity.

He let his hand drop to the sword's hilt; it burned.

The only warning it would now offer him, although he had taken it from its place of dishonor in the hands of a darker brotherhood than his; he had arranged for it to be carried here. He had kept it safe, if the hands of the magi could be said to be safe, and Meralonne APhaniel had done what Kallandras had requested without question.

Still, the master bard felt a twinge of ancient envy as he accepted the truth of the sword's warning: It had chosen its master.

But it was not a master that Kallandras would have foreseen had he been given to games of idle speculation. He gazed upon the set, harsh features of Auralis AKalakar.

Why this man?

Auralis AKalakar bowed. "I will not serve," he said quietly. "I will not remain upon this field, in this capacity."

Valedan kai di'Leonne nodded.

"With your permission, Tyr'agar, I will join Kiriel di'Ashaf in the village of Russo, in the Green Valley."

"If you will not cleave to the laws of my command, you will not be granted that permission," Valedan stated.

Auralis bowed. The bow was brief, and in a fashion, it was genuine. But when he rose, there was an expression on his face that marred it in an unexpected way: he looked young.

And the youth sat uneasily on his face, a testament to horror and a past that could not be escaped.

Valedan kai di'Leonne showed his strength. He did not step back. He did not bend.

Before he could speak, Kallandras of Senniel College did. He stepped forward, stepped past Valedan kai di'Leonne, the movement so graceful and silent that Ser Andaro barely had time to respond to the effrontery.

"Kai Leonne," the bard said, "I ask a boon."

"Ask it," Valedan said, his tone unchanged.

"Grant him what he offers. I fear that his fate and the fate of Kiriel di'Ashaf are entwined, and it may be that his presence by her side will accomplish what his actions here could not."

"If he will not abide by my law——"

"Kiriel di'Ashaf will countenance no killings here. If I am certain of nothing else, I am certain of that."

Auralis looked up at this unexpected ally. Or at least he seemed to. But his eyes did not reach the bard's still face; they hovered instead at his waist. At the hilt of a sword that Kallandras had never drawn, and could no longer carry in safety.

His bronze brow furrowed, drawing in, a single bunched line, a thing kin to metal.

Valedan kai di'Leonne turned his gaze upon Kallandras, and then upon Primus Duarte. "Primus," he said quietly. There was, in Kallandras' hearing, the hint of regret. It was subtle; others would not hear it so clearly, if they heard it at all.

You like this man, Kallandras thought, with some surprise. *You understand the part he might have played, but you are still fond of him.*

"He is one of mine," Valedan said, divining what Kallandras was far too politic to put into words. "As Kiriel is. Between them, they have saved my life—and more—and I am not ungrateful.

"Auralis AKalakar, I charge you to uphold my honor and my law. If you return to Russo, I charge you to do what Kiriel di'Ashaf has chosen to do: defend those who dwell there against the servants of the Lord of Night. No more, and no less.

"I will deprive myself of the two most capable men in your unit if I grant you leave to depart in any other fashion."

Acknowledgment.

Auralis bowed, and the bow was not perfect, but it contained the deceptive strength of Auralis AKalakar; the subtlety of movement, the certainty of it.

He said, so quietly it could be heard only by the men and women immediately surrounding him, "I would have killed you, you know." It was casual, and it was framed by his famous, lazy smile. A smile that had been seen so seldom in the South it reminded them all of better times. The North.

Valedan, remembering their first fight, returned that smile. "I know. And if I had been so easily killed, the Lord would have rendered his judgment."

The smile slid from the face of the Sentrus—when and why he had lost his rank, again, no one but Duarte knew—and he added, serious now, "And I would have died for you."

"I know. I have . . . learned . . . to accept that gift. It is the hardest of the lessons this war has taught me." He paused. "Or perhaps

not. You would kill for me. I accept this. And perhaps we make a
nicety of war that the Southerners have no need of; I accept that you
are here to kill for me.

"I retain the right to choose who, and how."

Auralis said nothing.

"I will not discharge you from service," he added.

"So much for your word."

"I will retain it. Go as my agent, Auralis AKalakar, and return if
war leads you to me."

Auralis bowed again. He started to walk away and then turned
back, as if jerked. His gaze fell upon Kallandras of Senniel, and
Kallandras bowed as well, but to the inevitable.

"Yes," he said, in a voice that only Auralis would ever hear. With
care, he unbuckled the belt that carried the sword's weight. He
leaped lightly off the dais, landing three feet from where Auralis
waited.

"This is yours, AKalakar."

Auralis took the sword.

And the sword flared, golden and orange, in the darkened sky. A
lot of words followed, broken vocal tapestry of human surprise.
None of them were Auralis' words. None, Kallandras'.

"What is it?" Auralis asked, almost whispering.

"Draw the blade, and you will know," Kallandras said. And then,
almost against his will, he added, "But if you are unwilling to bear
it, do not draw it."

"It's a sword," Auralis said, with a lazy shrug.

"You have one."

But it was not *this* sword.

The only fear that Auralis habitually showed involved money—
more specifically the losing of his own—and bets of the same kind.
So his hesitance could not quite be called fear. But he understood
some of the weight of the blade, for he held its scabbard a long time,
staring at it.

It was simple, the scabbard. It was not the sheath that had once
adorned the blade, for sheaths age and wither with time. So, too, the
hilt itself.

The power was in the blade.

"Kallandras?" The Kalakar said sharply.

The bard did not answer. His training as *Kovaschaii* had nothing
to do with his attention; it was the bard that held him now, for he
witnessed some small part of history in the making, and he wished
to record it, to find words that would contain its significance.

Auralis AKalakar drew breath and sword in the same instant, and he stood in its momentary light, transfixed.

The master bard of Senniel College nodded grimly. "It is done," he said. "The choice is made."

But Auralis did not appear to hear him.

He heard, instead, the voice of steel.

Men spoke of sword's song when they sang; they spoke of it when they recited battle lays that had come down the tides of history in the tongues of bards. He had always thought the pretty words vaguely stupid, for the voice of a sword was the simple swing of arm and the ability to *get out of the way*.

But he knew himself as ignorant then.

The blade spoke a single word.

His name. He cried out and his hands tightened of their own accord—for he would have dropped the sword in that instant.

But Kallandras' warning, he realized, had been offered in deadly earnest; the blade did not leave. The hand did not open.

"What is this?" he asked, his voice near to shouting.

Kallandras' face was pale and full, a mirror of the moon's face, and just as distant. "It is an ancient blade," he said quietly. "A Southern blade. How it was made, and why, I do not know; where it was made, and when, I do not know.

"I have seen three like it in my life, and you are the only man who has ever been called to wield it who did not serve—" He fell silent. The words were dragged back into the perfect line of full lips, and Auralis knew they would stay there.

"Take it," Kallandras said quietly, "and make your peace with its voice, if you can; if you can't—" Again, he drew upon the strength of silence, but the warning that was not spoken was made manifest by the blade itself.

"Kai Leonne," the master bard said, "I must leave you now. There is work that I must do, for the Serra Diora has been untended here, and I believe that it is my duty to aid her."

Valedan frowned. "The sword is not one of the Five," he said at last.

"It is not one of the Five," Kallandras agreed gravely. "It was not meant to serve in the war against the Lord of Night. What it can—or cannot—do is decided in its entirety by its wielder."

Auralis heard the words as if they were spoken behind glass. The wind that swept the clearing did not touch him.

The blade did. It was old.

And it knew his name.

He could not flee that knowledge, but he was Auralis AKalakar; the whole of his life had been made by the decision to flee, and he fled now, as he could, his stride wide and decisive.

But it only carried him so far.

The village of Russo was distant, and the sky had shed the last of the day; night's light was stark and silver, and it made the landscape a thing of black and gray.

Permission, he thought.

He had seen The Kalakar's face, and he didn't envy Duarte. Or the kai Leone. The only good thing to come of the assembly was the absence of the Hawk.

Auralis had no doubt whatsoever that the Hawk would learn of what had happened, and it was partly to spare himself the arrogant judgment of The Berriliya that he had chosen to take his leave.

But only partly.

He had been willing to kill. Children, if necessary. That was truth. He had also known how to find the few who would follow him in that *necessary* task. They were gone now; he'd left them to dry in the wind, a better fate than hanging there.

Would you have enjoyed it? The question hung in silence, and he broke the silence with his grinding step.

Did it matter? If the death was ordained, if the death was ordered, what difference did a little pleasure make?

He laughed grimly. All the difference in the world. The world was full of hypocrites.

A root caught the underside of his boot; the path had seemed well lit, but it—like so much that seemed clear—hid its little treacheries. He righted himself; a stumble in the dark could be costly.

Turning, he gazed at the torches and the moving lamps that heralded the presence of the military guards.

Why the Hells had he said he would go to Russo? What was there for him, after all? The children that he had intended to steal?

The thought was bitter. Ugly.

All his truths were.

The usual avenues of retreat were closed to him; he had no drink, no tavern in which to start a brawl, no fool to challenge to a forbidden duel. He had a sword. Two swords. How Southern.

And in the distance, waiting, Kiriel di'Ashaf.

* * *

It took him an hour to reach the village, if he were being generous. He had journeyed by moonlight before, and he had learned—in a halfhearted fashion—to mark time by the moon's passage through the night sky. But he wasn't a sailor; he knew that the timing could be off by as much as an hour.

Night had fallen, and in a seraf's village, night meant sleep. Tallow was expensive, and the hours in which work was best done were the Lord's; the Lady's time was marked at the very beginning, and the very end, of her tenure; sleep was given to her keeping, and such safety as any rule of the South might vouchsafe its slaves.

He had seen nighttime villages before.

He had watched them burn.

But this one held no such consuming fire; he approached it carelessly.

She met him at its edge, in the last bend of road before the village opened up in the flat of the valley. He might have missed her; she didn't choose to stand sentinel in the middle of the footpath, but stood instead at its edge, hemmed in by trees that were taller, and wider, than she.

But something about her presence cause the hair on the back of his neck to rise, and his hand was on his sword hilt before recognition caught up with it: she was *Kiriel*.

And she was armed.

"Hey," he said, but softly. He had stopped well away from her. Instinct gave him enough room in which to leap. Or draw sword.

"You're alone."

He nodded.

She listened anyway, and only when she was satisfied that it was the truth did she lower her sword.

"Why are you here?" she asked coolly.

"Valedan sent me."

"Why?"

He shrugged. After a moment, he said, "There's a spell around Averda."

"I know."

"It was secured with blood."

She said nothing.

"It might be weakened the same way."

And the blade came up. He did not move a muscle. Not even the ones that framed his lips. He waited.

In the night, eyes sensitized to shades of gray, he saw that the sword was darker than she was. She held her ground, waiting as well.

Time passed.

"You can trust Valedan," Auralis told her at last, the bitterness a flat inflection that informed his words.

"And not you?"

"You know me, Kiriel. You've always known me."

She nodded. "I can see your colors," she whispered. "They're darker now."

"Can you see your own?"

"No. Never."

He shrugged. "Kill me?"

"I should."

He nodded. The hair on his neck flattened slowly and he took his hand from his sword.

She swung then.

His feet were like roots; they kept him still. But barely. Barely. The tip of the blade touched the underside of his chin, and he could hear its whisper in the darkness. His name. The whole of his name.

He forced himself to meet her eyes, his gaze following the length of the blade, the hand that held the hilt, the arm that held the weapon steady, the shoulder that was level to the rise of the path. The pale face, the golden eyes that skin framed.

She could kill him now. Without pause.

But not, he saw clearly, without regret.

"What will the spell do, Kiriel?"

She shrugged. Carefully, her left shoulder carrying most of the motion. "Does it matter?"

"It does to me."

"I don't know. Maybe bring the *Kialli*. Maybe bring the Lord."

"And you think you can face them all?"

Her silence was answer enough. "Why?"

"Why not? I've nowhere else to go."

He spit. "You've got plenty of places to go. You can leave Averda. You can return to the Empire. You can head to the free towns or the Western Kingdoms. You can travel South. Nothing keeps you here but memory."

She cut him then. "I don't want to run away from my memories."

And he shrugged. There wasn't anything she could say to him now that he hadn't said himself, and if the words were old, if the years had dimmed them or hidden them, he'd never managed to bury them entirely. "I'm good at running," he said at last.

"Then keep running," she told him curtly.

He stood before her, and he was aware that he had come, at last, to a threshold. It had been a long time since he had had the leisure to examine death. Fear was primal, instinctive—a reaction, something that thought couldn't fight, that resolve couldn't overcome.

This was not yet fear.

"Don't much feel like running."

"You came here."

He shrugged again. It was his most common gesture, after all. "I thought you could use some help."

"Did you?"

"No."

Her smile was unexpected. She lowered her sword. "I don't understand you," she told him, as she sheathed the blade. It struggled against the sheathing. Some compact had been broken here, and he thought she might pay for it later.

Or that someone else might.

Whatever. It wasn't him.

Something like relief left a bitter taste in his mouth. "Don't you sleep here?"

"I slept."

"When?"

"During the day."

He nodded. "I didn't."

"Too bad."

"When will they come, Kiriel?"

"Not until the armies meet."

"And when will the armies meet?"

Yes, her eyes were golden; brighter by far than the moon and the cold distance of starlight. "Not tomorrow," she told him. "And not the day after."

"We're set to march tomorrow."

"You won't."

"Well, I won't, no. But the army—"

She shrugged. "It'll rain," she told him quietly. "The rain will flood the delta. The Hawk'll come late."

"But the General Alesso di'Marente—"

"He's missing a third of his forces as well. They'll have a harder time of it."

He frowned.

"They're crossing well traveled ground. They've got more horses. The mud will slow them down."

"And you know this how?"

"I had a visitor."

"Human?"

"More or less."

"Old friend?"

She spit. "Maybe. Maybe not."

"Who, Kiriel?"

Her smile was cool. "Doesn't matter. She's never been wrong."

"What else did she tell you?"

"That I might want to watch the roads tonight," Kiriel replied.

"Did she tell you how you're supposed to defend the Green Valley?"

"No. But she wouldn't—that's my problem, not hers."

"And her problem?"

Kiriel shrugged. "I don't know. I don't really care."

"You still staying with the old couple?"

"Not tonight."

"Tonight?"

"I'm staying here."

He rolled his eyes. "I don't think I'm being followed," he said quietly.

"You'd be wrong," Kiriel replied.

Auralis frowned. His hand found the hilt of his sword again, and he stepped off the road. "Mind if I join you?"

She shrugged.

"Mind if I smoke?"

And frowned. "Yes. But that's never stopped you before." She took a breath, held it, and let it go. "Was Alexis with you?"

He could have pretended ignorance, but there wasn't much point. "No. She might have been, twelve years ago. But she's changed. They've all changed."

The line of Kiriel's shoulders shifted; to other eyes, it might have seemed that she relaxed.

"Fiara," Kiriel said, after a minute. "Lindon. Leslie."

He nodded.

"Who else?"

"You figure it out."

She shrugged. "I'll kill them," she said, as if she was talking about drill.

"I know."

"Meralonne?"

"Yes."

"Kallandras?"

"No."

She nodded at each terse reply. He had thought, in the city of Averalaan, that she seemed young. Tonight she seemed ancient, as out of place on the footpath as the tree in the tent of the magi.

"If it makes any difference," he told her, as he stuffed leaves into the bowl of his shaking pipe, "I'm sorry."

"It shouldn't," she said, after a pause and a glare, "but it does. You promised."

"I didn't promise to die."

"Not to me."

The pipe fell. He cursed, bent, retrieving both it and the scattered leaves.

She swore. "Where is he?"

"Where is who?"

"Meralonne."

"These were the Firstborn," Meralonne said quietly. His hands hovered an inch above the sheen of silver bark; hovered, but did not touch.

"Not these," Diora whispered. What he would not do, she now did; her fingers caressed the tree's slender trunk. She heard, at her back, the intake of his breath, sharp as sword, but he offered her no warning. "This is young."

"It is new," he said quietly. "But it is not young."

She hesitated a moment, and then said, "I don't understand."

"No. You wouldn't."

"Shall I ask, then?"

"Ask. If you receive an answer, you will pay for it."

"Bold mage," she whispered. She was not afraid of him. As she had not been afraid of the Sun Sword. "How did they hope to use these trees?"

"Did you not understand what you saw?"

"No. I saw Yollana of the Havalla Voyani touch it, and I saw it revealed."

"You saw more, Serra. I am not a simple cerdan. I am not a Tyr or a Tor. You sang, and it heard your song."

She said, "I sang a cradle song, APhaniel. I did not lie."

"And why that song?"

"It is a song that is sung to the newborn," she replied.

"To the newborn," he answered, smoke streaming from his lips, "of the South. But this is not of the South. It is not something that you can cradle in the crook of your arms. What comfort can it take from your words?"

"Ask it," she answered, with just a hint of superiority. She regretted the display almost instantly. If he was not an obvious threat, if his power was not yet feared, it was still power.

"It was in pain," she told the magi. "And it was fearful. The newborn often are. But they are easily comforted, and perhaps that is why we offer them comfort; we take strength by showing strength."

"It is an illusion," he replied. "I know of your song. Should I tell you what it says?"

She shook her head. "What it says is not as important as how it is said. Or sung." Her palms lay flat against the tree, as if she could discern the beating of its heart. "And you, APhaniel, could never sing it, no matter how long you studied, how well you learned."

His silver brow rose, but although he was proud, he did not demur.

She had won some small ground here. "What was done to it?"

"It was a seedling that was rooted in flesh," he replied. "It took life there, and it grew. It sought the same when it was uprooted, mistaking it for earth. It is a mistake . . . that is not, could never be, natural.

"The Matriarch of Havalla returned to it the sense of its home," he added quietly. "The earth holds it now, but the earth is weak and silent."

"And flesh was not?"

He did not answer her, and after a moment, she said, "No."

"You know much," he told her. The pipe smoke was nearer now, pungent. "More, I think, than even the Matriarch of Havalla."

"How would that be possible?"

"I do not know. It is, I admit, of curiosity to me. And it would be of interest to my brethren in the Order."

"Where did this sapling come from?"

"From the borders of Averda."

She shook her head. "Before that, APhaniel."

"You know."

And she did. The Sen Diora did. She stood a moment, and the weight of ceremonial headdress, of garments foreign and stiff, bore her down. Shadows and memory. She could see them clearly reflected in the smooth, curved surface against which her hand seemed suddenly small.

"How?" she asked softly.

"It is Summer," Meralonne said. His voice was soft, so soft that she could not hear the break in the words. "And the Winter King is dead. The trees should know the turn of seasons."

"They should shed their brittle leaves."

"Ah. Indeed, Serra Diora. They should. But they are Winter trees, and they have been caught in a Winter that stands outside of natural season."

"Natural?"

"Nature has many guises. The wild roads retain much that the mortal realms have forgotten." He bowed his head; she saw this as she turned, although she could not quite release the tree.

"Where the trees stand," he told her softly, "so the road follows. It is slender, and it is not easily traversed. No mortal could follow its thread."

"It was not built for mortals."

"No."

She said quietly, "Arianne."

And he lifted a hand. "Do not speak that name," he told her.

"The tree does."

"Does it?"

"I . . . think so."

"She will not come."

"What will?"

"I think you know, Serra. I do not know how. But I think you know."

She nodded. Although they were not her memories, they existed for her, stronger than story, weaker than experience.

"You went into the desert."

"Yes."

"What did you find there?"

"The Tor Arkosa," she said quietly.

He was silent. But the silence did not last. "It was coming anyway," he said. "The End of Days."

But she did not flinch; did not pause. Instead a smile touched her lips, revealing steel in their curve. She was Southern. "So we—so they thought, when the Lord of Night buried the City. The End of Days." She shook her head. "But the days are here, and they are long."

He did not argue with her. "Serra—"

Because she did not give him the chance. "What governs immortals does not govern us. We are diminished, but we exist." She let her hand fall, at last, from the tree. "When?" she asked him.

"I do not know. Even rooted in flesh, the trees need sustenance."

"Will they kill?"

"They have been spread in a thin line for as far as the magi have traveled," he said wearily. "I do not know how. But if they are awakened, and that line is crossed, if they are . . . called . . . they will kill. They will do it blindly, and they will be forever stunted, forever scarred and tainted, but they will take what they feel they need."

"The earth," she said quietly.

"Yes, Serra Diora. In their natural environment, they are rooted not in the mortal ground, but in the Old Earth. Its voice sustains them, there; they speak the long dialogue of the ages. It is quiet here."

"It is quiet." She drew silk from her shoulders and wrapped it about her face. "I will come with you," she told him, "when the time is right."

"And will you know?"

"I don't know. You will."

Wordless, he pulled the pipe from his mouth. Bowed to her. "You are like the old Men, come again."

"The Sen," she told him quietly.

He stiffened.

"The Sen in the Sanctum. The seers."

"Serra—"

But she lifted a hand, and he fell silent. Command. Once, command had been a gift, granted her by the Sen Margret.

"What will you tell the Tyr'agar?"

"The truth."

He guttered smoldering leaf. "I think it is time," he told her quietly. "Let us walk a while, Lady. The moon is high and her face is clear."

Auralis should have been surprised when Meralonne APhaniel came slowly around the bend in the footpath, but he wasn't. He was, however, surprised at his choice of companion, and he whistled in spite of himself.

Kiriel hit him.

The magi, however, did not seem prepared to encounter Kiriel di'Ashaf, and he stiffened.

It made Auralis feel slightly better.

"Magi," Kiriel said, her hand on her sword.

"Sentrus," the magi replied, bending stiffly at the waist. He wore the robes of his office; the darker clothing that he had chosen for a different night's work might lie beneath the folds of long cloth; it was hard to tell. He frowned. "Sentrus," he added, seeing Auralis AKalakar.

Auralis shrugged. It was the Osprey version of a salute when there were no significant officers present.

"Serra," Kiriel added. "You keep strange company."

"And you," Diora said, smiling softly. Of the three, she felt no fear of Kiriel di'Ashaf, and her comfort showed. She walked past Meralonne, and offered Kiriel both of her slender, white hands. Kiriel hesitated for just a moment, and then surrendered sword to take them. They stood like two young girls, meeting in secret.

Meralonne drew his pipe, and settled back against the trunk of a leaning tree. His expression, lit by orange flame, was hooded and cautious, but he offered no obvious threat.

"We did not expect to find you—either of you—here."

"You knew I was in Russo," Kiriel told him.

"You are not in the village at the moment."

She shrugged, her gesture as respectful as Auralis' had been. "I thought you might be coming."

"Did you?"

Her eyes were golden in the darkness. But if the Serra Diora noted their change of color, she said nothing, did nothing. Her hands had captured, and held, Kiriel's, and not for something as cosmetic as demon eyes would she release them.

She was a strange Southerner.

"You are powerful here," Meralonne said at last.

Kiriel said nothing. To him. But to Diora she said, "Have you come to see the Green Valley?"

Diora smiled. "I have never seen it. But I do not know if it would welcome strangers in its sleep; serafs seldom do."

Kiriel nodded. She released the Serra's hands, but hers rested by her sides, as if her sword was either forgotten or no longer necessary. "There are still things to see," she said at last.

Turning to the magi, she added, "You are welcome here if you come in peace. But come to take anything of value from the village, and I will kill you." No doubt at all in her voice that she could do it.

And because there wasn't, Auralis didn't doubt it either.

Meralonne's brows rose a fraction. "You would not find it easy," he said at last.

"No. But easy doesn't matter."

He nodded. Glanced at Auralis. "You knew." He spoke to Kiriel.

"I guessed."

"You were told."

She smiled. "Maybe. Have you come to gather sacrifices?"

"No, Kiriel di'Ashaf. It may surprise you, but I do not relish the idea of killing the young." He glanced at the Serra Diora. "And it may be that in my haste, I overlooked other options."

The Serra said nothing.

"Or it may be," another voice said quietly, "that you were wary of the risk."

They turned as one.

The road was full of billowing cloth, dark as night, and of it.

Meralonne gestured; his pipe guttered. Moonlight reigned.

"I should have guessed," he said quietly. "Your hand was in this."

"Not mine, not from the start," Evayne a'Nolan replied. "But I have always observed." She raised hand to lower her hood, and Auralis AKalakar froze.

No one noticed. Not Kiriel, not the mage. But the Serra Diora glanced at him a moment, as if caught by his silence—as if she could hear silences as well as he knew she could hear what was given voice.

He had never much liked the bard-born.

But truth: he had not, for a long time, liked anyone much. He had made a family of the Ospreys because, like them, he had been saved from his past at the whim of Duarte AKalakar. But he had become attached to Kiriel di'Ashaf, and in the moonlight, he knew that it was an attachment he couldn't afford.

That it was too late to avoid the cost.

"APhaniel," Evayne a'Nolan said. Her hair was black, dusted with strands of white that had always perched there, framing her face with a hint of Winter in the darkness.

His bow was not friendly. "It has been long since I have seen you so . . . well."

She smiled. "You mean young," she replied. "And I am not, by the age of man, reckoned to be young. I am not—yet—old."

Kiriel said nothing.

"Yes, Kiriel," she said, divining the words that lay in the stilted silence, "I know you. I have seen you before, in the Shining City, and in the streets of Averalaan. I am not so young that this is the first time I have met you." She nodded almost gently and lifted a ringed hand.

Bands bound it: three. They fit her fingers oddly; Auralis

thought them loose. They were costly; jeweled, intricate, complex pieces. Almost art. He eyed them at a distance, calculating their worth.

A soldier's calculation, and probably low.

The Serra said, "And me?"

And Evayne a'Nolan closed her eyes. "You are much changed, Serra," she said at last, her hands disappearing into the folds of her robe. "And little time has passed since last we met." She looked away, as if meeting the Serra's steady glance was painful.

"You told me to wait," Kiriel said.

"Did I?"

Silence.

"My apologies, Kiriel. I have not—yet—spoken those words. But you have heard them, and my presence here is proof of their truth."

"What am I waiting for?"

Evayne's eyes, violet, were bright. Too bright.

"For Meralonne," she said at last. "And for the Serra Diora en'Leonne." The last was said with a lift of tone. A question.

The Serra did not speak.

Auralis did not speak. But his silence was no shield. Evayne turned to him and inclined her head.

"I know you as well," she said quietly. "But you are much aged."

"I'm still alive," he replied quietly. He could speak in no other way. Seeing her had taken the strength from his voice, the years from his memory.

The first time was alive, bright, terrible. The worst of his past.

"You know her?" Kiriel asked.

His shrug was stiff, unnatural. "I know her," he said at last. "She saved my life once."

Bitterly, Kiriel said, "She saved mine as well."

"And mine," the Serra Diora said.

Not one of them spoke with gratitude, but they looked at each other differently, weighing and measuring.

"She has not yet saved my life," Meralonne APhaniel said, coming in a fashion to their rescue, "and I am not therefore in her debt." The last word was heavy with irony. What he knew, he did not speak.

But Evayne had the grace to flinch. "You have not grown less cruel with time," she told the magi quietly.

He shrugged. "I have," he said. "You do not remember the years that I taught you, if you can say that."

"I am mortal."

"So you have said. An odd mortal, who travels through time with such apparent ease. Why have you come?"

She said, "In truth?" And the crystal shard was in her hands, like silvered glass. "The time is short, APhaniel, and I would not tell you all of my tale were it long. Accept it."

"I have."

She lifted a brow, but no more; clearly she hadn't come to argue. "Kiriel."

Kiriel met her gaze warily, and almost against his will, Auralis drew closer to her unguarded side. "What?"

"The Serra Diora will stand upon the battlefield when it is finally joined."

Her frown was tense, skittish. Young. "She won't."

"She will."

Before Kiriel could answer, Serra Diora raised a hand and touched her arm. "Kiriel," she said quietly.

"Valedan won't let you!"

But the Serra Diora shook her head. "You do not understand the nature of the woman before you," she said, "but I do." She bowed then, and bowed low. "She does not command me; she does not seek to give me orders. She merely tells me what *is* and what *will be*."

Evayne's brows rose, and the crystal in her hand glowed brightly.

"I know what that cost you," the Serra continued. "And I understand the price you pay to bear it thus."

"You did not, when last we met."

"No. And I would have cursed you. Or killed you. I cannot yet, with grace, thank you for my life." She smiled, and the smile did not reach her eyes. But neither did the anger. "Can you tell me when?"

"In three days, Serra."

"The army will not move on the morrow?"

"The rains will come."

"The skies are clear."

"The treachery of nature," Evayne replied. "Or its boon."

"And until then?"

"You are free to do as you will."

"Then I will stay here," she replied. "In the Green Valley. I will see the home of Ashaf."

Kiriel said nothing at all. But there was something about her stillness that Auralis did not recognize, and by the time he did, Evayne was gone.

"APhaniel." Kiriel turned to him.

"It appears that I am here merely as escort," he said coldly.

"You choose," Serra Diora told him, her voice cool, "and you are known by your choice. She sees," she added quietly, although Evayne was no longer among them, "and she speaks of it as she can. The seers are not always . . ." She shook her head.

"Sane? No, Serra, they are not. But Evayne a'Nolan has clearer sight than any born in this age, and she has not yet been driven to the edge of madness by her visions. She is not—"

"She is not Sen," Diora replied serenely.

Auralis frowned. But he was unwilling to expose ignorance to the magi.

"You are wise, Serra," Meralonne told her. "For one who has already suffered her grace."

At this, Serra Diora stiffened and paled.

"She does not choose to speak of all she sees," he added, with just a hint of an unpleasant smile. "Does she?"

Kiriel moved so quickly Auralis barely had time to touch his sword's hilt.

But Meralonne APhaniel was not there; he leaped up, and up, and when he at last came to rest, it was far above the ground upon the swaying limb of tree.

For just a minute, Auralis thought she'd bring the damn tree *down*.

But the Serra had recovered the poise for which she was legend, and she touched Kiriel's shoulder delicately.

"He speaks only truth," she whispered.

"He meant to wound you," Kiriel said, her chin tilted up, her eyes unblinking.

"Truth does," the Serra said. "But it is a curious weapon; it cannot wound without my consent."

Auralis felt a pang at the softness of her voice, and for the first time—the only time—he wondered what Kiriel saw when she looked at the Serra. What she saw beneath perfect skin, what she saw beneath almost perfect composure.

"Magi," the Serra said quietly, "I will be in the Green Valley. When you have need of me."

She turned, but she did not release Kiriel's shoulder, and Kiriel stood a moment, tense as pulled bowstring.

Yet in the end, she chose to come away with the Serra; to leave her anger and the imperative of it, at the foot of the tree. He didn't understand the significance of it, but Auralis AKalakar understood that it *was* significant.

Intimate.

He waited while they walked, and when they were far too distant for words to travel, he glanced up.

The magi was smoking his pipe.

"Do you know what she is?" he asked Auralis.

"Yeah. Pissed off."

Meralonne surprised him. He chuckled. "Well, AKalakar. The evening's work is done. If it is not the work that we agreed upon, it is of interest nonetheless. Will you stay here?"

"I'm not going back."

"Good." He leaped groundward, and the tree shed his weight as if he were breeze; the leaves rustled, but the branch did not spring upward at the sudden lack of weight. Magi. He hated them.

"I have been blind." Meralonne unfolded, his knees stiffening, his robes a whisper of cloth against the ground. "This spell, this barrier, this making—it is for her. For your Kiriel di'Ashaf."

"She had nothing to do with it," Auralis snapped.

"No. She probably doesn't understand what *was* done. She is remarkably ignorant for a child of her parentage."

Auralis wanted to ask. He didn't.

"We fight two wars here," the magi continued. "We can afford to lose neither, but they are not the same. You came here to fight one."

Auralis shrugged. "I came here because I was given orders."

"And yet you are also one of Evayne's pawns. I would not have guessed it," he added, and he turned, his silver eyes too bright in the moonlight.

Auralis took a step back, and then held his ground. Had he faced any other man, he would have slugged him.

"What price will you pay for her interference, I wonder?"

"What price have you paid, Magi?"

"I told you: she did not save my life."

Auralis shrugged. "I think I've already paid."

But the magi's eyes narrowed as he stared at Auralis AKalakar, and Auralis felt as exposed beneath silver gaze as he once had beneath Kiriel's. He said nothing, turning.

Something caught his gaze.

Something slender and delicate, gleaming in the moonlight. Gold.

He had bent, knees in crouch, before he recognized the metal. The serafs of the South weren't rich, but their lords were, and he had done his share of scavenging in the aftermath of a fight. It was second nature, now.

Meralonne said nothing at all. That should have been his first clue.

But greed was greed, as much a part of Auralis AKalakar as the need for breath or sleep. His hand curled round something cool and hard, and he brought it up to his eyes.

It was a ring.

He whistled as he lifted it. It was a heavy ring. The gold was worked in bands, three bands, that snaked around each other like braided hair. And in their thick strands, caught and held by the artistry of its maker, was a ruby the size of his knuckle.

He tossed it up in the air and caught it with practiced ease. "Not bad for a night's work." He turned his smirk upon the magi and froze.

Meralonne APhaniel seemed taller and straighter than he had ever seemed. His hair, fine and white, was unbound, and it dropped the length of his chest, blending with cumbersome robe. Like snow, he thought. Like the crest of Evayne's white hair.

"What are you staring at?"

Meralonne said nothing. Did nothing. The pipe that had been smoldering was gone from his hands, as if it were parlor trick or illusion.

"Finders keepers," Auralis snapped. But he was ill at ease.

"Oh, indeed, AKalakar. I would not take what you have in your hand if you offered it and the course of the war depended upon that offer." He bowed. "It has been an evening of revelation."

Auralis shrugged again, but the movement was forced. Defiant, he slipped the ring over a finger. His forefinger, his shield hand.

He should have been surprised when it fit. Or when it didn't. It was tight when he tried to remove it.

He cursed. Just what he needed: a woman's ring. He could hear what Alexis would say. It didn't take a lot of imagination. He twisted the band, pulled, and then cursed again.

But the magi said nothing.

And it wasn't Alexis alone who would be the problem; half of the Ospreys would be sharpening their daggers with an eye to his finger, or worse, waiting like vultures for the chance to retrieve it from the battlefield. Greed made poor backups.

"There is no point in struggling with the ring," Meralonne APhaniel said softly. "It will not come off."

Auralis froze.

The hair on the back of his neck came up and his eyes widened as he stared at the ruby.

"Yes," the magi said. "You have seen something of its kind before."

"Kiriel's ring."

"Kiriel's ring," Meralonne agreed. "What do you hear, AKalakar?"

"A really annoying magi."

At that, the magi smiled. "As you say." He offered Auralis a bow. "Go. Keep an eye on the Sentrus. If I am not mistaken, she'll need you."

He laughed. "She'd better not," he said bitterly. And then, remembering where he was, and with who, he added, "She's the only Osprey who can outfight me."

It was lame, damn lame.

But it was all he had. He turned on heel quickly, clutching his ringed hand in a fist.

Wondering why he had slipped the damn thing on in the first place. Wondering if the ring *could* be cut off. Kiriel had tried, with hers. And she had a better sword.

"Illaraphaniel, you are cruel."

Meralonne watched Auralis disappear, as Kiriel and the Serra Diora had done before him. "You say that to me?"

"I say it without judgment," Lord Telakar replied. "Indeed, I find it refreshing. The Lords of men in this paltry battle are far too well behaved."

Meralonne gestured and the pipe fell into his cupped palm.

Telakar glanced at its bowl. "You've cracked it," he said with a shrug.

"I can make another."

"Will you?"

Silver brow arched in reply.

"Forgive me. I was simply curious."

"You are never simply curious, Lord Telakar. You have traveled far from the encampment."

The kinlord's smile was sharper and whiter than the magi's. "I was bored."

"It was a failing of yours."

"It still is."

"And your companion?"

"Have a care, Illaraphaniel. There are many ways to relieve boredom."

"Not all of which are fatal." But this was banter. The pipe was, indeed, cracked.

"Did you know?"

"That the ring would go to Auralis AKalakar? No. How much did you hear?"

"Not all; the blue-robed witch was present, and she is . . . unpleasant, even at a distance."

"At this age, she is tolerant."

"We have met her," Telakar replied. "There is nothing about her that is not bent or bowed by power."

"No."

"But she has survived much."

"Yes."

"Come, Illaraphaniel. You have witnessed history, this eve."

"History is largely a matter of the past."

Telakar raised a brow. In the moonlight, they might have been kin. "History is a matter of significance; the insignificant are buried beneath its weight, like corpses beneath the dirt."

Meralonne nodded gravely. "Come," he said at last, straightening the clenched line of his shoulders and adding height to his posture. "You are correct. I have much to think on, and much to discuss with my servitors."

"And with me?"

"You are already a threat, Telakar. I do not doubt your intent, but intent is like so much that is mortal; it is easily waived."

Lord Telakar began to speak, then fell silent. "I must return," he said at length. "But I thank you for this; it is a gift to one such as I."

CHAPTER NINETEEN

ELENA Tamaraan stood in the moonlight.
Dirt clung to her knees, and the ache of old wounds made her ribs throb. But of the wounds that Telakar had made, there was no sign; her body did not seem to acknowledge they had ever existed. Ser Laonis di'Caveras, the healer who was mad enough, brave enough, to serve Valedan kai di'Leonne, had taken them whole.

Ah, and thinking about the healer offered a deeper, darker ache. She wondered what he was doing. Knew: he was in his tent, writing a letter to his wife—his wife, safe for the moment in the Northern city, *Averalaan Aramarelas*. He missed her greatly. She would, he knew, have difficulty reading what he wrote; his words would be simple, the writing lacking the elegance expected of a clansman. But he would choose them with greater care.

She envied this woman, this Lissa. Envied her and felt an echo of the same love, the same protectiveness; his gift, to her. Exposure of his vulnerability.

Adam, she thought. *Is this what you will suffer? Is this what your gift will cost, again and again?* For she knew Adam as well as she knew any Arkosan child, and she knew that the ability to refuse need was not in him. Not yet.

And if he never learned it?

Margret. Lady be merciful. Lady.

She lifted the third of the offering bowls, and with care, she emptied it into the furrow she had dug in the ground.

Her hands did not shake until the liquid began to spill, and she steadied them by force of will. Someone else's will. She could hear Evallen's harsh, grating voice—a storm, a childhood harbinger of displeasure. But she could hold that displeasure at bay if she performed her duties perfectly.

Margret, alas, had never managed to comprehend this simple truth. It would have saved her some humiliation.

"It is quaint, this custom," a familiar voice said.

She did not drop the bowl; did not tilt it; the blood fell evenly and perfectly, as the wine and sweet water had done before it.

"But there is no power in it."

She finished, and when the last of the bowls was empty, she set it against the ground. She would gather it soon, along with its companions, for the ground here was traversed frequently by the Northern soldiery.

"What is its meaning?"

"It's an offering," she said, kneeling now.

"It is not a sacrifice."

"No."

"To whom is this offered? Who requires your blood?"

"The Lady," she said simply.

"Ah."

She thought he might leave her. Since the healer had been shorn from her side, Lord Telakar had existed as shadow, a distant threat. He spoke seldom, if at all, and although she had once opened eyes to the glint of light off his fingers—odd light, the kind thrown by blade's edge—he had not touched her.

She had the sense that he watched while she slept. But she could not bring herself to ask it, not of the healer who sometimes visited, nor the men who watched over her with wary contempt. But when she woke, he slowly retreated.

Not this eve. "Which Lady?"

She shook her head. Her hair was tightly gathered, tightly bound; none of her kin would have recognized her. She had traded severity for the wildness of her youth.

"Elena," Lord Telakar said. "Are you finished here?"

She nodded.

"Then look at me."

And rose. Short of sitting astride a horse, she would never be of a height with the kinlord.

"You have made a decision," he said. His words touched her; his hands remained by his sides.

"Yes."

"And that is why you perform this rite?"

"Yes." Almost against her will, she added, "Do you have no rituals or observances?"

"In the Hells?"

She shied away from the word.

"They are my home."

"They are a Northern conceit," she told him quietly. And then, because he stood before her without touching her or threatening her, added, "That was our belief."

"It is not yours now."

"I don't know. We have always been taught that the dead howl with the wind's voice."

"The dead howl," he said, his smile cold.

She shrugged.

"What decision, Elena?"

"Does it matter?"

"For a small while, yes."

"What do you mean, a small while?"

His smile was cold, and it was unkind. But his lips were thin, and his eyes narrow almost by nature; she did not think he was capable of a smile that was not unkind. "You live so short a span of years," he said.

"And you will be here all that time?"

"No."

"How long, then?"

"As long," he said, the texture of his voice changing, "as The Lord allows it."

"Did you lie to them, then?"

"Them?"

"The Tyr'agar. The Northerners. The kai Callesta."

"What do you mean, Elena Tamaraan?" He was lazy, as if he played a game.

But the taunt was a test, and she knew it; she passed with ease. All of the obvious tests in her early life had been passed that way. Evallen was not cruel. At least not to one not her daughter.

"Does the Lord of Night know you're here?"

"No. He has not turned his attention toward me, and if he is given no cause, he will not. The spell that is being woven at the edges of the Terrean will consume the whole of his thought; only if I threaten it will he notice, and even then, it will not be obvious that it is I unless he extends some part of his power."

"Why do you serve him if you dislike him?"

"Do I, Elena?"

She frowned, but the expression was almost formal. "I am not a fool, Lord Telakar. You do not trouble to hide it. When you speak of him, your eyes narrow and your voice grows cold. Colder," she added.

"Very well. You are at least that observant; I will not deny it. Think, though, Elena Tamaraan, Elena of Arkosa—if I revered my Lord, and I wished your trust, what little of it you might grudgingly offer, would I not then respond to his name and its use in exactly that fashion? Not so open as to be noted by all and sundry, and yet not so careful that I cannot be read by one such as you, who cannot comprehend the subtleties of the Shining Court."

She frowned again, and this time it was a more natural expression. But she kept the curses to herself, struggling to tame her tongue. Not for her kin would she have made the attempt, not even for Margret. She bowed her head a moment, and then shook it. "You . . . have cause . . . to hate him," she said at last. She met his gaze.

He nodded, as if she had performed a simple trick particularly well. "What does dislike—or like—have to do with service?" His eyes were entirely black. Not even the sky above was so colorless when the Lady's face was veiled. "Ask your serafs—"

"We do not keep serafs."

"Ask your kin, then. Ask your cousin. Service is service, Elena, and if it is not always tendered willingly, where men of Power rule, it *is* tendered.

"You will die in Averda," he added quietly. "If you are here at all."

"Can we leave the Terrean?"

He gazed a moment at the unveiled face of the Lady. "No," he said at last. "Not now. If we walk, you will die. If we . . . travel in other ways, this close to the spell's heart, we will be noticed—and you will also die."

"Does it matter?"

"Don't you know?"

She shook her head. "I don't understand you," she said at last. "They fear you." She nodded toward the Northern tents, and then, after a pause, the significant Southern ones.

"They are wise."

"Telakar—this spell. Tell me what you know of it."

"You would be better served by the old woman. The Matriarch of Havalla."

"I do not know if she would speak to me without cursing me," Elena replied starkly.

"She will speak with you." His menace was elegant.

"No, not that way. You do not know Yollana."

"I understand mortal suspicion. You are mine," he added quietly, "and she will wonder why. She will speak with you to satisfy her own curiosity."

"And after it is satisfied?"

He shrugged. "She will not harm you." She heard what he did not say, and it brought her no comfort.

But the Lady's offering had. Kallandras of the North was wise, and he had shown her the Lady's road. She hesitated a moment, and then, quietly, she offered Lord Telakar her hand.

Was surprised when he took it.

"It will rain," she told him, trying not to stare at his hand. "Tomorrow."

"And tonight?"

"Take me to see them."

He bowed. But he did not release her hand.

The clouds were thin and fine. They would gather; the wind did not hurry them, and they did not disperse. She gazed a moment at the Lady's face, and tried to discern her expression. It was foolish; the Lady had only one, and it was full of a distant sadness.

"Do not touch the sapling," Telakar snapped, his voice as sharp as the memory of his hands. The reality belied that memory. Although they were cold and smooth, they were simple hands.

She nodded. The tree was thin and slender, and although it was pale, there was something about it that spoke of darkness. Something.

Sometimes, when her instinct was that certain, she could hone it, using it like a shovel to dig away the ignorance until little bits of truth could be seen, enticing and confusing in their lack of cohesion. She had been born with the stronger blood; Margret had always said so.

She closed her eyes, whispering the words Evallen, then Matriarch of the Arkosan Voyani, had taught her.

These words will gather the strands of your vision, she had said, her hand hovering to one side of Elena's face, as if by simple slap she could embed her advice. *They will hone it, if there is aught to see.*

Elena had tended to be attentive whenever Evallen raised her hand in that particular fashion. It meant she was *almost* serious.

Serious was reserved for real crimes, and real punishments. Elena had always wondered what would become of Margret when she was forced to face either.

And she still did.

Nicu, she thought bitterly, *how did you die?* She didn't try to divine the answer. She wasn't certain which answer she wanted to hear.

Some Northern idiot had once said, *The truth will free you.* She thought she could remember a time when she even believed it.

"Elena?"

She shook her head; Telakar's voice was not the voice she wanted to hear.

But her kin, like the sight, were beyond her. All she could see, beneath the heights of old forest growth that stretched out in layers of deepening night, was the slender sapling. After a few more minutes, she shook her head in frustration. But the words that would once have followed, she kept to herself.

"Do you know what it is?" he asked her quietly.

She shook her head and turned full to face him. "What are *you*?"

A dark brow rose.

"I am *Kialli*," he replied.

"But what does that *mean*?"

"I serve the Lord of Night." There was an edge to the smile he offered. It was a familiar edge.

"Don't treat me like a child," she snapped.

He did not react with anger. He did not react in any way she could have predicted. He lifted a hand and almost—almost—touched her face. "How, then, am I to treat you? When I was your age—and I was, even I—I was a child. And when I was far beyond your span of years, they counted me child still."

"Treat me," she said quietly, "like myself."

"Who are you, then?"

"Elena."

"Of Arkosa?"

"Just Elena." She shrugged. "I'm trying to discover who I should be. I'm not who I thought I was."

"Ah." He lifted finger to chin, caught by her words. She could see them reflected in his eyes, as if they were solid.

"Are you?"

"Am I what, Elena?"

"Who you thought you were."

"I have seldom questioned what I am."

She laughed bitterly. "Lucky you."

"Luck. It is a mortal conceit."

"So much is."

If he caught the irony in the words, he failed to acknowledge it.

"I will answer your question," he said at last, "if you will answer it of yourself."

"I told you—I don't know who I am. I'm Elena."

"Then I must confess that I am Telakar. I am called Lord Telakar by those whose power is beneath mine; I am called Telakar by those who are stronger, unless they wish my willing service."

His expression made clear how often that had happened. "The kinlords seldom trust volition."

"Well, we don't have much choice."

"No." His eyes were dark. She wondered if they had always contained that darkness.

Asked.

His brow rose, framing shadow, lending it a human face. "No," he said at last. "They were not always as you see them now."

"And you?"

"No. I am . . . not as I was. To your eyes, to the eyes of those born without power or mortal talent, I might seem the same. But I am changed."

"How?"

"You are bold, this eve. I am not certain I approve."

She forced her shoulders to be still; the shrug that she would have offered anyone else wasn't safe. She *knew* it.

"But I will answer, Elena." He lifted his head, and his hair fell around his shoulders like a cloak. It was pale, long, fine; it reflected moonlight as if it were armor. "I am dead."

"I've seen a lot of death," she said, choosing her tone with care, although the words were her own. "You don't . . . seem dead."

"No. It confounds us all, at one time or another." He cupped his palms in the air, as if to catch it. "You do not understand what life is," he said at last. "And perhaps it is best that way."

But the wind now pulled at his hair, and it touched *nothing* else. Before she could speak, fire grew in his palms, as if it were sapling, or flower, unfolding in petals that trembled and fought against the sudden breeze.

"I will not whisper water's name," he told her, and his words were almost gentle. "For you are right. The storm waits. There is a time for everything."

"And earth?"

"The earth is the harshest of the elements," he said quietly. "The oldest, the slowest to waken. But wake it, and it lingers. All life belongs, in the end, to the Old Earth." He paused a moment, and then added, "and it hears us. It hears the echo of what we once were, and it knows that we have forsaken it.

"It is, like the wild magics, a jealous thing: it will not forgive. It never forgets. But it sleeps."

"The earth," Elena said quietly, "protected the Tor Arkosa."

"It swallowed the Tor Arkosa," he replied. "And all of the Cities of Man. Some few survived, beneath its weight. Some very few." The fire guttered. "I hear its voice." His own held both wonder and loss.

"Why do you speak of before and after?"

Dark eyes rounded. She had surprised him.

"I forget," he said, as if it was a new discovery. "I have spoken with the human Court in the distant North, but they guard their tongues and their knowledge with care. You are not their equal.

"But you are not their pawn."

She waited. Around the moon's face, the clouds were thick enough that they shone.

"There was a war," he told her, his eyes shining with the captured light. "There was always war. Between the wild magics. Between the Firstborn. Between the gods. How mortals came to be, we do not know—nor do we understand fully how they survived; they live so briefly, they learn so little. And yet, they created the Cities, and the Cities flourished. What you have wakened will never be their equal. But the shadows of the Cities are still a thing of wonder, to those of us who remember their glory.

"We do not know—we who serve—how it came to pass, but during that age, when Men's rule of the Cities had finally crumbled, and the desert was birthed in their wake, a sword was forged by the gods and the men who served them, and it was given to Moorelas of Aston. It was not given to him alone," he added, "and perhaps this is something your legends do not record."

"None of our legends speak of this man," she said softly. "But . . . we have heard his name. In song. In Northern song. Who else was given such a sword?"

"You mistake me, Elena, or perhaps I am not clear. There was only *one* such sword. It is not like your Sun Sword; it is not like the Five that sleep in the hands of your Radann. It is a thing unto itself, and it lives, and dreams, and sleeps; it requires sustenance, and it has a will that cannot be mastered."

"How do you know this?"

He shook his head. "I will not tell of it," he said. "For there are secrets which The Lord himself seeks to unwind, and he will hear its name upon the wind."

She nodded. The air from the North was cold and sudden.

"We must come away from the sapling," he told her. "For it, too, listens."

She stared at the tree. Bent toward it, leaving her hands by her sides. It carried a scent that she thought she should know, something bitter and woody, something damp and sweet. It lingered in nose and on lip.

"It's trapped," she said softly.

His brow rose. His gaze sharpened. "You have some power," he said at last, an accusation.

But she spared him no glance. "Can we not free it?"

"Not by fire," he said. "Nor by water or wind. No, Elena. Do not touch it. If it can be released, it is not by you or I. Come."

He offered her his hand, and she took it.

They walked away, into the quiet of the forest, its paths hidden. But although she could not see well, he did not let her stumble or fall; he was her guide.

"The sword was given to three hands," Telakar continued. "And two men, it destroyed utterly. The third was Moorelas. He accepted its weight, and he made his peace with its demands. In his hands, it came to life, and the gods knew then that they had created not The Lord's bane, but *godslayer.* If they could, they might have undone what they had helped create, but there was one among their number who argued against it, and in the end, his voice held sway."

"These are Northern gods."

"Elena, these *are* the gods. The Lord, the Lady—they are some echo, some memory, of the truth. You have your own truth, you Voyani, but even it is bent beyond recognition."

She listened, and found only truth in his words. It should have upset her. It did. But she gazed up, to where the moon now tinted cloud, and she drew a deep breath. The forest was in her lungs, and the night, and a sense of freedom made her dizzy.

Freedom here, a demon's hand in hers, her whole life surrendered to the unknown.

"The Northern gods," she said at last.

"Yes. They were not Firstborn, although they were here when the First wakened. We do not know what they were; we know what they are, and what they are has changed, slowly and subtly, with the passage of time. With the taint of their offspring."

"Which god? Which god spoke for . . . for us?" she asked, in a small voice.

"He is nameless," Telakar replied. "Men called him Mystery, or Destiny, but it is not a true name. Names have power."

"Ours?"

"Perhaps even yours. We do not mention the man of the North in the presence of our Lord."

"So Moorelas took the *godslayer*. But he did not kill the God."

"No."

"Why?"

"He is long dead, Elena. And we—*Kialli* or *Arianni*—are not privileged to speak with the dead. Men could, in the past. Some exist who can speak with them now, if they dare Mandaros' wrath."

"Mandaros?"

"The Lord of Judgment. He presides over the spirits of the newly dead. He weighs them, and when they are ready, he chooses the time and place in which they will return, unaware, to the mortal world."

"Return?"

His smile was thin. "Not as I have, no. They are born. They age. They die. They live at Time's whim."

"But—but why?"

"Why?"

"Why are they sent back?" She wondered then what other lives she had lived, if his words were true. And they were true; she could not doubt it. She had that much gift.

"Because they have not yet Chosen, Elena. The choice is a long, slow choice, and each life unravels it or furthers it. Those who come, in the end, to the Hells, have spent lifetimes achieving the state of that particular grace."

"Mandaros knows what happened when Moorelas failed to kill the Lord of Night."

"Perhaps. Perhaps not."

"You don't know either."

"No. I was not present. None of us were. But the Lord of Night was injured. He bled. His power was greatly diminished and his City was broken; the earth was wakened that day, and it was many days before it slept."

"And then?"

"The gods made peace. Or truce. My Lord was given the choice of death or dominion, and he chose dominion. He rules the Hells," Telakar continued bitterly. "And we chose to follow him there."

"Why?"

"I hope, for your sake, that you never have cause to meet him," the kinlord replied. "And I pity you, because even if you do, you will never understand the answer to your question, although you will receive it. He is beautiful, Elena. He is The Lord."

She was silent. Many, many words came to the edge of her lips, but she bit them, hard, and they chose to retreat.

"You went with him."

"We went."

"And what did you do in the Hells?"

"What we still do. We guard the dead."

"But you said—"

"The dead are not dead, in the Hells. We call you mortal, and you are, but there is, in each of you, some hint of the immortal. You do not know it. You cannot see it. You will never touch it or hold it. But it is there, and all of us who have never been subject to the whim of age and death can see it clearly."

"Even in me?"

He laughed. The sound was low and rich, and it built, like the storm that gathered above. She did not ask again.

"How can you be here, then? Are you here and there?"

"No, Elena. I am here."

"But you said—"

"Names have power," he told her quietly. "And when power is mingled with the name, we are given some measure of freedom. We are forced to the plane, and the plane judges us by the power that we have gathered. We struggle against its pull, and if we are strong, our will prevails."

"And if you aren't strong enough?"

"We have no choice in the form we bear."

"What do you look like in Hell?"

"In the Hells?" He laughed again. "I have not the words to answer your question. I do not think it has been asked often."

He was lying.

"But you said you were dead."

"To the plane, I am. I can kill," he said. "But I cannot create life. I am like the desert; I cannot even sustain it."

Her brows rose. She did stumble, then, and he righted her, his hand steady and cold. "Did you have children?"

"You misunderstand me," he said quietly. "There were children, as you reckon them, but they were few indeed, and not by simple coupling were they brought into being. But when I walked the world, when I was *of* it, I could speak with the trees, and the birds that littered them; I could understand the horses that rode across the Southern plains; I could stop a dragon in flight if I raised my voice in song. I could—when careful—speak a language that cats might pretend to ignore." His smile was strange. "They shun me now." And gone.

She said, "You didn't know." And knew it was true.

His eyes were sharp, narrow. She did not expect him to answer her. But he said, "No. I did not know. I learned quickly that there were limitations to my presence here. The forest falls silent when I walk it. The birds become still; I can hear their labored breath, the sudden speed of their hearts; I can smell their fear. This, I could not avoid knowing. But there were other losses that I did not foresee; other losses that I did not understand. Not until the night that I almost killed you." His grip tightened; she was silent, although she thought her bones might splinter within its sudden pressure.

"Why that one?"

"Mortals do not know us," he said quietly. "Men do not distinguish us from themselves, if we are powerful enough to bear form similar to theirs. If we are not, and we still wield power, we veil ourselves in their sight. We might speak with them in any guise, and our words are *their* words. Language is no barrier."

"The fire comes at my call," he whispered. "And the water. The wind howls for me. With will, I can move the earth; I can speak to it, and it will condescend to listen. But I bear a taint, and it listens in anger; there is no gift offered, and none accepted, between us. Those who have been here longer than I do not seem to notice the ways in which we are diminished."

"Because they're powerful."

"Yes," he said, voice remote. "Because they are *powerful*." The word was like a curse.

She slowed, and he slowed; it was either that or drag her. "Why are you telling me this?"

"Because I wish to understand you," he told her. No lie there.

"Then shouldn't you be asking the questions?"

"Ah. You misunderstand me, Elena. Understanding is not information. If I wished information, it would be mine; there is not a thing that you know that I could not take from you, given time. And time, I have.

"But understanding is different. It is shaped by experience, and it is not shaped in isolation. What will you do with what I tell you?"

"I . . . don't know."

"No. Nor do I. Do you begin to see how it works? I answer your questions because I will see, in the end, what you make of my answers." He reached out then and touched the side of her face. His palm was like stone, but it was smooth, flat stone, an artisan's likeness of a hand.

She did not pull away.

"What does The Lord want?"

"What he has always wanted," Telakar said.

"Power?"

"Dominion. Over all things. Mortal and immortal. This is a game, Elena. The gods play it at a distance. We are all reavers. Those who choose to walk in darkness come, in the end, to darkness; they are ours."

"And the others?"

"I cannot say. I am a denizen of the Hells, and it is the Hells that I understand. But perhaps The Lord knows. I do not know. He knows this much: That those that choose to walk in light walk away from us; they are lost to us. If The Lord rules the whole of the world, then in time—and we have time—all souls will walk in darkness. All. In this life, or in the next, or in the lives to follow, they will work their way toward him. No soul is proof against change, and he will claim them." He lifted his face as the first of the rain began to fall, and he stared for a long, long time at the darkening veil of clouds.

"Come," he said at last, and the tone of the word made her look not to him, but to the skies.

She was, of a sudden, afraid.

And he knew it.

He could sense all her fear; all of it. There was not one part of it that she could keep to herself, keep hidden as all fear *must* be. Exposed, she stood, and she might have stayed long, but he caught her in his arms and drew her rigid body against his chest. Her back touched layers of cloth as if they were his skin; cold skin.

"Elena," he said quietly. "We must return to your people."

"My people," she began bitterly, "are long away from here." And then she stopped.

Because she remembered the Sea of Sorrows.

"Yes," she whispered. Just that. She gave herself into his keeping, and to her great shame, felt the edges of her fear begin to fray.

It rained. Before Elena returned to the tent that was home, the rain was a steady murmur of water against the leaves and branches of the forest. But the forest provided no cover when she reached the edge of the encampment. Lamps, covered glass, held flame that struggled and hissed against the encroachment of falling drops, and the army itself seemed sodden.

Where the grass and the undergrowth had been worn away by the passage of too many feet, water traced paths in the dirt, small rivulets that trickled down into the floor of the valley. Such earth would not long bear the weight of horsed riders.

The tents were oiled, and they shed water, but the water continued to fall.

Bruce Allen sat in the tent that served as his command center; it was deserted. His guards weathered the elements in perfect silence; he cursed the same elements with far less grace.

The magi, Gyrrick, entered the tent, dripping. His hair, darker with water's weight, was pulled back in a warrior's braid—something that ill-suited a magi, in the Commander's opinion. As did his perfectly executed bow.

It was not, of course, a salute; the magi were not here as soldiers. But it was as close to a salute as the magi ever came. No, it was *better*.

"Member Gyrrick," Commander Allen said, rising.

"I have word," Gyrrick said gravely, "from The Berriliya."

"Commander Berriliya."

"Forgive me. Commander Berriliya."

"And that?"

"The rains have hit the delta hard, and the army has been forced to pull back. Two of the wagons are mired in mud, and some of the supplies have been lost; the river has risen."

"And the men?"

"He did not mention the men."

No. Devran wouldn't.

"They are in position," Gyrrick continued, "but they will not be able to move any notable distance if the rain continues. The scouts have seen some evidence of the General Marente's forces."

"Where?"

"Near the delta."

Impossible. But the word didn't leave his lips, because this was a war, and he had learned, with bitter regret, that nothing was impossible.

He cursed.

"He awaits your orders with interest."

"Those were his words?"

"They were the words of the mage who transmitted the message."

"Ah. Tell him—tell the mage—that the army is to wait in position." He rose.

Serra Alina di'Lamberto rose as well, in a tent not far from the Commander's. Her knees felt the damp with the sudden cold; the storm came from the North. It reminded her, for just a moment, of

Averalaan Aramarelas, and if she closed her eyes, she could see the color of gray tinged with green and the edges of charcoal and black, as the sky lay across the wild sea.

Boats in harbor were not safe during such storms.

"Valedan."

He met her eyes.

"The Serra Diora has not returned."

And said *nothing*.

Alina found his silence difficult. But she found much about him difficult. He had retreated to a place that was neither Northern nor Southern; she was uncertain how best to reach him.

"And the rain grows worse. The winds—"

The tent's walls buckled, but the moorings held.

He nodded grimly. His hands were behind his back, and he wore the dirt-stained armor of a Northerner. Southern armor waited him, in fine, burnished plates, its wide legs and wide arms ceremonial. He had yet to don it.

"Where is she, kai Leonne?"

"In truth, Serra Alina, I do not know."

Her brows rose and fell in a sharp line.

The small dwelling that Valla kep'Valente called home became crowded. Kiriel di'Ashaf entered when Valla pulled the screen wide, and behind her—behind her, in silks far too fine for a village—a young woman whom Valla did not recognize. Would not recognize, even if she suspected her identity.

Still, she fell to knees that ached with the weather, and she bowed her head to the flat, worn boards, making haste to bid her enter.

Her husband was far more gracious with the Serra than he had been with Kiriel di'Ashaf; he, too, offered her his obeisance, and if he was slower to bend, it was due to age and stiffness.

The Serra simply said, "Please, do not bow to me within your own domis; I am the visitor here. I am the one who seeks shelter."

Her voice was soft and pleasant; it belied the storm and the intent of the storm, creating in Valla the momentary sensation of peace. She lifted her head, her eyes wide, and touched her forehead with her palm, as if seeking fever.

The Serra smiled.

The smile would have broken hearts, young and old, for miles.

"Kiriel," the Serra said, "will you not introduce us?"

"Oh, sorry. Valla, this is Diora. Diora, this is Valla. And that is her husband, Arrego."

Valla's breath slowed to a halt. Had Kiriel been her daughter, she would have cheerfully strangled her. As it was, the temptation was strong.

But the Serra was gracious; she did not notice the brusque and entirely inappropriate use of her name. She merely knelt and offered Valla and her husband the proper bow of a visitor to a domis.

The thunder roared in the silence of Valla's shock.

The Serra frowned. "Kiriel?" she asked.

Kiriel di'Ashaf looked up, as if the roof had been pulled back from the four walls that upheld it. And it might yet be, thought Valla grimly, pulling her shawl tightly around her shaking shoulders. When had the winds gotten so fierce?

Aie, it was good that the season was done.

Good for war, she added bitterly, and for death.

"Please, Serra," Valla said, rising a little too eagerly. "We are not wealthy, but we are not without hospitality to offer. If you are tired from your journey, there are mats upon which you might sleep, and if you are thirsty, we have sweet water and wine."

"And bread," Arrego said unexpectedly.

The Serra bowed again. "I have no like gift to offer for my intrusion," she said almost meekly. "And I have not traveled far. I am honored by your offer of shelter, but I will not intrude further if I am to offer so little in return."

Kiriel's smile was a girl's smile. It surprised Valla. "Ask her to sing for you," she said. "She has the most beautiful voice I've ever heard."

The Serra's gaze swiveled gently, but Kiriel didn't meet it. She seemed guileless, like a child. Were it not for her pale skin, her odd eyes, she might have been a village girl on the verge of womanhood.

But in truth the village clothing suited her poorly. Valla did not ask her when she had chosen to forsake it for armor. And she did not ask why.

"Kiriel," the Serra said, "the hour is late. Valla and her husband were sleeping before we arrived; it is best to let them return to their sleep."

"But they wanted to meet you."

Child indeed, and a terribly poor liar, as most children were.

"And they have," she replied sweetly. "In the Lady's time. But on the morrow, in the Lord's, they have duties to which they must attend, and sleep is a gift."

Something about her words changed the expression on Kiriel's face; the child was lost instantly. Valla felt a pang. She shouldn't have. But she thought of Ashaf constantly now, and she knew that this girl, this woman, this stranger, was the last of Ashaf's children. The only one to survive.

She felt that connection most keenly when the girl was buried beneath the warrior. She couldn't say why.

"Arrego," she said to her husband. "Come. The Serra is right. We need our sleep, for the morning."

His brows fell, but he offered his silence. Silences were often cursed in this house—*it's like arguing with stone*—but she felt it as a gift this eve. She took his hand and led him to the farthest corner of the room.

From its shadows, she watched.

"Kiriel," Diora said, in a voice that passed no farther than Kiriel di'Ashaf's ears.

Kiriel nodded.

"Do you hear it?" Diora's hands were shaking. She stilled them by placing them in her folded lap, palms down.

"I hear it," Kiriel replied. She could not speak as Diora did, but she lowered her voice.

"The war starts early," the Serra said bitterly. "And it starts poorly for us."

The storm's voice was keening now. Loud.

She had heard its like only once before, and she had thought never to hear it again. The desert lands were the distant lands of story, of the magic that lies on the borders between life and death. But the Green Valley was not those lands.

"What should we do?"

Kiriel said nothing. But her hand fell to the hilt of her sword, and it remained there.

Meralonne APhaniel stood in the storm's edge.

His hair swirled around his slender face, and his eyes, silver, were edged in a light that would have made the Southerners circle themselves and glance away. The wind's voice? He heard it.

He heard it all.

He lifted his hands, and water streamed through the cracks of his fingers, clinging to cloth. Thus did the banners fare, which spoke the ranks of their lords; they were sodden now, and only the gale would make them fly.

But they fluttered like dying birds.

"APhaniel."

He did not turn; he did not lower his arms or his face. Lightning brightened the sky, lifting the shade of night a moment. Thunder followed, rumbling like the breaking of the earth.

"Kallandras. You are out in the storm," he said, seeking moonlight.

"As are you, APhaniel. But you seem . . . drier."

The magi shrugged. Water shifted in the changing folds of cloth his movement made. And then he heard familiar voices, and he did turn.

The bard was armed.

The weapons that he carried in left and right hand were blades with high guards; assassin's weapons. The Lady's weapons, and she, forgotten god, except by the chosen few.

But they were hers in shape and form only. They spoke in a voice Meralonne recognized. They spoke in a language he understood.

"Can you hear them?" he asked.

Thunder answered.

But so did Kallandras of Senniel College. "I hear little else," he whispered.

"But not nothing."

"No," he replied gravely. "Not nothing."

"The storm," Kallandras said, when Meralonne's silence lengthened.

"Yes," the magi said grimly. "It is not entirely natural."

"It was."

"It was." Silver brow arched. "You cannot fight the storm with those."

"Not the storm. But I find the weapons surprisingly versatile." He bowed slightly. "And I thank you for them."

"They were never mine."

"They were in your keeping."

"As was the sword you delivered to the Kalakar House Guard." He smiled; the rain passed over his face without touching it. "But I was not willing—I was not able—to pay the price your weapons demanded. I feared to use them." He shrugged. "And in truth, they are better suited to you."

"Now."

"Now is all that is required."

Kallandras bowed. The winds grew. "Have they called the wild water?"

Nothing about this man could surprise Meralonne. "I don't know."

"But the wind," Kallandras said.

"Yes. The wind drives the rain's fall."

"Who summons it?"

"I believe we shall find out," the magi replied. "Come. The Commanders wait. The Tyr'agnati wait with them."

"Indeed. It was to summon you that I was sent."

"The Eagle is not gracious about the waste of his time; have care, Kallandras."

The bard smiled. "The bards, like the magi, serve the Kings; they are not soldiers."

"In this war, there are no civilians."

Lord Telakar stood in the corner of Valedan's hall. And it was a hall, if a hastily constructed one. A gift of the kai Valente. He, too, waited, but he waited without apparent fear.

Valedan kai di'Leonne glanced once at the *Kialli* lord. But he did not speak to him, or otherwise acknowledge his presence. Instead, he nodded curtly to the Averdan Tyr and the Lambertan Tyr, stepping past their Tyran and into the heart of the hall.

"Kai Leonne," General Baredan di'Navarre said quietly. "Telakar of the North has come with word from Russo."

Valedan's eyes narrowed slightly. The rain had flattened his hair to the rounded contours of his skull; it was impossible to look dignified in such a circumstance.

But he almost managed.

Commander Allen and Commander Kalakar entered the hall. They, too, stood without benefit of serafs, and they made their way across the long carpet that was meant to absorb the water they shed. It squelched beneath their heels.

"The rain," Commander Allen said, "is bad. Tyr'agnate, will it continue?"

The Tyr'agnate met the Commander's gaze. "Averda seldom sees storms of this magnitude," he said quietly. "And seldom at this time of year. I cannot with certainty predict its course." His gaze sought Telakar and remained there a moment longer than necessary.

Meralonne APhaniel and Kallandras of Senniel College entered next. The Lambertan Tyran stiffened instantly at the sight of the bard. A bad sign. Worse, still, was the fact that Kallandras did not deign to notice. He was armed, but not for war. He made a statement. Even in the North, he would have been noted. But in the South? The weapons he carried changed everything.

Ser Anton di'Guivera coughed.

"Commander Berriliya is detained," Commander Allen said curtly. He handed Valedan a broken tube. Valedan accepted it wordlessly, but he did not open it.

"The storm?" he asked.

"It hit the delta first."

"Then it traveled in a circle," Ser Mareo kai di'Lamberto said, voice flat.

"Storms are not swords," Meralonne APhaniel replied in perfect Torra.

"This one is," the kai Lamberto replied. "We will not move while the rain persists. And after?" He shrugged. "We will not have any advantage from our horsed men."

"Our soldiers won't be that much faster," Commander Kalakar said. "If the rain doesn't stop, we'll be mired in mud."

"Marente's Widan can't control the weather," Commander Allen said. But it was not a definitive statement. He looked to the magi.

Meralonne APhaniel shrugged. "If they can," he said quietly, "they control it poorly. Member Sallis says that it extends the entire length of the valley—and beyond it."

"How far beyond?"

"Far enough," the magi replied, "to encompass the whole of their army."

The Eagle seemed to relax. "Then we both lose time."

"Yes," Meralonne said, and the edge in the words caused the Commander's shoulders to stiffen again. "We lose time."

"Speak, APhaniel," Valedan told him. He stood above the splayed surface of a map, but he did not yet approach it; the ink would smear and blotch if water fell upon the carefully drawn lines.

"It is my guess, Tyr'agar," he said, offering Valedan a bow that he would never have tendered the Commanders, "that the enemy in the far North knows that we know of his plan. There was some danger in uprooting those saplings."

"How?" Alesso di'Alesso's voice was curt and sharp.

"This is a magic beyond the Widan," Sendari said, his own voice carefully modulated. Neutrality granted no safety, but it was dignified. No one knew better the import of dignity. "And such magics are tampered with at unknown cost."

If there was criticism in the words, it went unheeded.

"Cortano."

"Widan Mikalis has studied the tree," he told his Tyr. "And the four that we brought him as well. He has spent much power in his attempts to understand their meaning and their nature."

"And he has failed."

Cortano's brows drew down; water followed the curve of his nose. "He is hampered by our enmity with the Voyani," the Sword's Edge said, after a pause. The criticism was plain. But Cortano di'Alexes was powerful enough—necessary enough—to take that risk.

"It is not their spell."

"No. Of that, at least, Mikalis is certain."

"And the rain?"

"The rain. Yes, Tyr'agar, the rain is the heart of the matter. We assumed it to be of natural origin. This assumption is not yet proved false."

"It is a convenient disaster."

"For us, no. But it does not serve the Northerners in good stead; it does not aid Callesta. Some part of their force, as you know, is bounded by the river; they will not move, now, if they are wise. But we can ascertain—at some cost—that the armies of the North are well within the storm's boundaries."

"We have made a half day's march," Alesso said grimly. "And we have lost a horse to the rain."

"We have lost at least four," Sendari said quietly.

Alesso's expression might have seared the desert sands. "This is a game, then."

The Widan exchanged a careful glance.

It was Cortano, again, who spoke. "We believe . . . that our enemies . . . may also have discovered the saplings."

"And they have had better luck ascertaining their purpose than the Sword of Knowledge?"

"That we cannot say. What we can say is this: The storm's course is not natural. The winds hem it in on both Northern and Southern fronts, compressing it."

"Is the Court capable of this?"

"The mortal Court? No."

"Any of the Court."

Cortano exhaled. "I believe," he said, with caution and with obvious regret, "that there are some among their number who are capable of just such an action. But it is costly," he added.

"It will not end the war."

"No."

"But it will slow it."

"Yes."

He raised a hand, twisting it until the edge fell into silence. "The trees."

"Indeed, Tyr'agar. If the Northerners have somehow damaged the spell that has been laid here, some delay may be required."

Alesso was grim.

It was a grimness that Sendari recognized. The tent was his cage, and it was too small a cage to contain him for long. He paced alongside the long, flat table upon which his most valued possession lay: the work of the cartographers.

When he stopped, they waited, watching the slow lift of his chin.

"It tells us something," he said at last, and this time the anger was buried by the momentum of thought.

"Tyr'agar?"

But Sendari knew. They had been friends for a long time. His hands ceased their wet trek through his long beard as he inclined his head.

"The spell that is dependent upon those trees is intended for the battle, and only the battle."

Widan Cortano di'Alexes said little.

Sendari said, "I must speak with Mikalis."

"Wait a moment," Alesso said quietly.

The Widan nodded, but he was weary. Of waiting. Of war.

"Old friend." It was not a plea.

"Yes," Sendari said, his breath leaving him with the word. "They take much strength from death. Ours, our enemy's—to the *Kialli* we are all simply mortal."

"If we are not the cause for such a delaying action, we may benefit from it."

A dark brow rose. Two.

Alesso smiled. "The Northern mages are learned, or so it is said; the Widan do not treat with them."

"We are considered rogue," Cortano said dryly. "By their law, it means our destruction."

"Let it rain, then; we cannot stop the rain. But when the rains end, we will wait. Give the Northerners time to spend their knowledge. Give them time to unmake what we ourselves have not even begun to understand. I will not fight a war on two fronts."

"Ser Eduardo kai di'Garrardi will be most annoyed," Cortano observed, with a smile as unpleasant as any he offered.

Alesso's smile deepened. "We must take what we can when it is offered. Sendari, return to Mikalis, but order a seraf to summon the Tyr'agnati. I will inform them of the obvious."

Sendari bowed. He knew that Mikalis slept poorly, if at all, and also knew that although the storm raged, he had succumbed, again, to exhaustion. It would be a miracle if he survived.

And men in the South did not look for the miraculous.

"Tyr'agar."

CHAPTER TWENTY

MERALONNE APhaniel and Kallandras of Senniel College were almost dry when they were at last given leave to depart. "APhaniel?"

Meralonne was silent. He stepped into the rains as if their current could be navigated. But he had heard the bard, and after a moment, he said, "Only a few of the magi gathered here can take to the skies."

Kallandras nodded. "It is not known to be a common skill, even among the First Circle."

"They are not First Circle magis."

The bard nodded. He offered the conversation—such as it was—no resistance. The momentary lull that the hall provided was gone; the storm remained.

And upon his finger, the ring was warming. It would not be long, he thought, before heat gave way to fire; he would be marked by the night's work. Meralonne's voice was not the only voice he heard.

"Will you take this risk?" The magi's hood rolled down his shoulders.

Kallandras nodded quietly. "It is one among many," he said casually.

"You have risked the storm before."

Kallandras nodded.

Meralonne did not ask. They stood a moment, and lightning played across their pale features, casting them in white light, bleeding color from their clothing.

Thunder answered.

"If you are found," Meralonne said at last, "they will know what it means."

"And what will it mean, APhaniel?"

"That we know."

"Do they not already suspect this?"

"They must suspect it," the magi replied. "But destruction and knowledge are not necessarily the same, even in the minds of the *Kialli*. Perhaps especially in the minds of the *Kialli*."

Lord Isladar weathered the storm in perfect silence. He had learned, with time, to build this silence into everything he did; the forest life did not retreat from his presence, the birds did not cease their chattering cries when he moved beneath their nests. No other kinlord had yet achieved this truce with the mortal world, and he doubted that any would. It required not only patience—which the *Kialli* did have—but also a willingness to accept a complete lack of power.

He moved. The rain fell, and he caught it a moment in his cupped palms; it was water. Simple water. That was good.

He could not sense Kiriel.

But he knew she was present. The village held her.

He had not expected that the Serra Diora, who had so confounded the expectations of the Shining Court, would wait with her. So many things that mortals did were unpredicted, unpredictable.

Strangest of all was Kiriel. She had made friends. Not allies, as the *Kialli* did, but friends. He wondered if they would impede his work, or if they would in the end be its crucible. But he knew that Kiriel could not take her position if they hampered her.

He wondered, idly, if the time had come.

But the storm answered with its wordless thunder: Not yet. Not yet.

He lifted his face to the skies; the bower of sodden trees hung low, offering him a glimpse of roiling gray. Beyond it, he could hear the wind's howl.

He spoke a name.

After a moment, he spoke it again, adding force and the majesty of tattered power to the single word. Now, the forest would be aware of his presence, and the life within it would desert him in a widening circle, as it did for all of his kind.

He shrugged.

The Swordsmith appeared.

"Anduvin," he said, and bowed. He lifted a hand as if in greeting.

The Swordsmith drew his weapon.

The forest was lit from within by the blue light that glowed along its edge. It was an old weapon, and although it had been altered by the Swordsmith's return to the plane, it was still recognizably his.

"Isladar."

"Who rides the wind?"

Anduvin's slender face was perfectly still. Water did not touch it. After a moment, he said "Nugratz."

"And his kin?"

"His kin. Only his."

"They are far from the North."

"Yes, and they are not pleased to be here; it is early, and they are without support."

"They do not fear the mortals."

"The mortals? No. But the Summer has been invoked, Isladar. Even you must have felt its touch."

Isladar nodded. "Illaraphaniel is here," he said, after a long moment.

"He is. But of all the magi present, he would not be the one to invoke it."

"Then who?"

"The Voyani," Anduvin said quietly.

"They are with the army?"

Anduvin shrugged. "If you can call this pathetic gathering an army, then yes. They must be."

"In number?"

"They are mortal, Isladar. Their study was not my study."

"Ah, I forget myself."

Anduvin's expression made clear his lack of belief. It brought a smile to the kinlord's face.

"Will She come?"

Anduvin shook his head. "The road that they seek to build is weak," he said quietly, "and it is a Winter Road. I do not know what happened," he added, and the yearning for knowledge informed the bleak words, "but the seasons have turned. She rules the Summer Court now; she is the Summer Queen."

Isladar said, "So."

"Yes. There is no guard upon the Winter Road. Who wrought this, wrought in cunning." He reached out and his sword scored the bark of a new tree.

Blue fire flared and burned a hair's breadth from the wood without harming the wood itself.

"Can you destroy them?" Isladar asked, glancing now at the silver sapling, the young tree.

"No."

"Have you tried?"

"Yes."

"Ah."

"And you, kinlord?"

"I have not tried. They remind me of my youth," he added softly, "and even twisted, they are beautiful. I do not seek to destroy what scant beauty exists in these impoverished lands."

Anduvin laughed. "You have made the study of mortals your calling for the millennia. Surely you find no beauty there?"

"I don't know, Swordsmith. You have seen my only student. Judge for yourself."

The silence was cold. The rain should have frozen in its fall, landing like snow or hail upon the forest floor. But it fell; the discussion of two, even these two, did not trouble it.

"She does not know what you did," Anduvin said.

"You have said this before."

"Yes."

"And to another."

"Yes."

"Will you tell her?"

Anduvin's laugh was bitter. "No. You saw to that."

Lord Isladar nodded. "Where is she?"

"Can you not sense her?"

"I . . . hoard my power. This close to Kiriel, if I sense her, she will know that I watch."

"And is the game not yet finished?" Anduvin sheathed his sword. It rippled a moment, as if it, too, were falling groundward by the storm's command, and then it was gone. But Isladar felt its presence, and its message was clear.

"Not yet," he said softly. He did not lift hand to touch the tree. "The road is stronger."

"It is night," Anduvin offered.

"Indeed. But it is not in the night that the army will come." He did not speak of either the Marente forces, or the Leonne. To Lord Anduvin, they were beneath consideration.

"It should be."

"It should," he said agreeably. "But what test would that offer?"

"She is not your student, Isladar."

"She will never be anything else. Seek the wind, Swordsmith."

"To what end?"

"You will know," Isladar replied gravely.

"I seek no battle here."

"You will find battle regardless."

"When?"

"The study of the Lady's Court was not my specialty."

"No." He paused. Drew breath. "It was mine." He reached out then, and planted his palm against the bark. The contact made him shudder. After a moment, he withdrew. "She will know of this," he said quietly.

"She will know."

"The Lord's Fist risk too much."

"They have no choice, in this. Their hand has been forced. The Tor Arkosa has risen; how long can it be before the other four seek the skies?"

"The Lord defeated the Cities once, when mankind was at its height. How much of a challenge can they pose when Man has fallen so low?" But his hands caressed the moving air, and after a moment, eyes closed, he said, "Three days."

"Three days. And will the rain fall for the whole of that time?"

Anduvin shrugged. "Whether it falls or no, the trees take root as they must. They will reach the peak of their power in three days."

"And the earth?"

Anduvin's frown sharpened. "Isladar."

The *Kialli* lord nodded genially.

"Do not risk The Lord's wrath."

"It is no longer The Lord's wrath that I fear," he said quietly. "And the Lord's Fist has never concerned me."

"It should."

"Once, perhaps once, it might have." He shrugged. "Three days, then. Will you seek Nugratz now?"

Anduvin lifted a hand.

Isladar's smile shifted, and his eyes grew dark. If he was without power, none among the *Kialli* would have known it. "What do you hear, Swordsmith?"

"A challenge," he replied. "Can you not hear it yourself?"

Isladar said nothing, but his gaze turned toward the North.

"It seems," Anduvin said, his voice distant, his eyes wide, "that the Queen of the Hells is waking."

Isladar stared at the face of the Swordsmith. As if he were a thing of steel, as if he had been forged in his own bellows, he seemed to reflect light; his eyes burned.

Kiriel, he thought.

Mortals were difficult. So much that they did was done without deliberation, without planning; so much that they touched, they destroyed or altered beyond recognition.

She had come, at last, to this village, to the home of Ashaf kep'-Valente. He had planned for this, but only for this; the ties that bound Kiriel to the others were ties that he could not have foreseen. The mortal seer. The Serra with her inexplicable beauty, her delicate, invisible defiance. The Northern soldier, with his twisted, dark strands of soul.

How much would she offer for them?

"A challenge?" he said at last, his voice soft.

Anduvin nodded.

Too early, Isladar thought. But although his slender fingers curved into fists, he said nothing at all.

Lord Telakar twisted suddenly in the confines of the hall. Every eye was instantly upon him. He dropped to one knee, and if the position suited him poorly, he adopted it nonetheless. "Tyr'agar," he said, in perfect, modulated Torra.

Valedan kai di'Leonne looked up from the maps and the conversation that circled them without end. He frowned. "Telakar. Speak."

"Your mages," the demon lord said.

"They are not mine."

"They serve your armies, Tyr'agar."

Valedan nodded. His gaze narrowed, his expression hardening until he looked at last at home among these veterans of earlier battles. "What of the magi?"

"Member APhaniel has the power of flight." The kinlord's voice was neutral.

Commander Allen frowned. "Does he?"

"He does. Perhaps some of his servitors have it as well."

"What of it?"

"Summon them, if you can."

Valedan lifted a hand. Ser Andaro di'Corsarro was at his side before it fell. They spoke a moment, and Ser Andaro bowed and walked past Telakar; the kinlord felt his shadow. Saw his soul, burning like torchlight in the Lord's Night.

"To what purpose, Telakar?"

"Kiriel di'Ashaf," Lord Telakar said uneasily, "calls me. I must go to her side."

"And the magi?"

"They, too, must now be watchful. She has—" He glanced at the stony face of the Lambertan Tyr. Fell silent.

Ser Andaro di'Corsarro returned quickly. "Tyr'agar," he said, bowing low. "Meralonne APhaniel is not in his tent."

"Where is he?" Commander Allen's voice was sharp.

"Member Gyrrick does not know."

Sharper, though, when he cursed. "Damn the Order," he said, as if the words were a command to some unseen deity. "Where has he gone?"

The kinlord shrugged and stood. "He has gone where I must go," he told the Tyr'agar, rising. "I serve Kiriel di'Ashaf and she has made a challenge."

"A challenge? In Russo?"

"Not in the Green Valley, kai Valente. But above it."

"Above it?" Commander Allen turned to The Kalakar; she shook her head. Her adjutant left; the door to the hall swung wide as he ran. He lacked the grace of the Southern Tyran, but not the determination.

Primus Duarte returned in the lee of Verrus Korama. They were wet. Wet was a state that would be common in the days to follow. If they survived them.

The Primus saluted The Kalakar; they stared at each other and Telakar was aware that some brief, spare conversation occurred in the movement of their hands. He watched idly, seeing the gestures, memorizing them. They might be useful at a later date.

"Primus Duarte, can Kiriel fly?"

Duarte's brows rose. Whatever he had expected from the strategic command post, it was not this.

"Fly, Commander?"

"Fly. Like the magi fly."

"No."

"You're certain?"

"With Kiriel, it's impossible to be certain. But I've never seen her do it, and I've seen her in a lot of fights where flight might have been useful. In a strategic way," he added. "Kiriel's not much for fleeing combat."

The Kalakar nodded to Lord Telakar, and Lord Telakar rose. For just a moment his impatience frayed his perfect control; shadows eddied at his feet, and his hair flew in the wind of his power.

He struggled to contain it.

Succeeded.

"Why do you ask?" the Primus said, although he shifted away from Lord Telakar.

"It seems—to her servant," The Kalakar added, the word forced even to Telakar's ear, "that she has offered a challenge to—to what? The storm?"

"Those who ride it," Telakar said grimly.

"Let her challenge them," Commander Allen said, with a grim humor. "Who knows? She may even succeed."

"She may," Telakar said gravely. "With your permission, Tyr'agar, I would join her now."

Valedan nodded.

The Lambertan Tyr spoke softly; the Callestan Tyr waited. But Valedan said clearly, "I trust *her*."

They might have argued. But although they were uneasy—and everyone was, in this suddenly small room—they did not offer argument.

Auralis AKalakar *felt* her. Hearing came later, when he was halfway across the sloping hills that bounded the Green Valley. His sword was in his hand and his shield was no longer a shell across his back; it girded his arm. He seldom fought with shield, but in the darkness he did not trust the smaller dagger that graced his left hand.

He did not run flat out; the moon was obscured and the rain made the hill's growth treacherous. His footing was not as sure as Kiriel's when visibility was poor, and he made an effort to be cautious.

But when he heard her roar, he froze.

He had heard her before, just this loud. He had thought, then, that she must be demon-born, for dragons—if they existed—would have possessed that voice. He hadn't heard it for a long time.

Not since—

The ring.

He drew a deep, wet breath, cursing the rain; he lifted his shield above his head as if it were an umbrella. His eyes were wet, but squinting in the darkness, he began to lengthen his stride. Fear rode him.

But for her, or of her, he couldn't say.

He just knew that he ran *for* her, and that that should count for something.

* * *

The Serra Diora en'Leonne stood by her side. The rain made her hair heavy, but the combs that had been placed there with such precision by Ramdan clung stubbornly. Her silks were damp and weighty with water. Not for the first time, and certainly not for the last, she missed the Voyani robes.

But the obvious shelter of the small seraf's home was not yet hers. She waited at the side of Kiriel di'Ashaf, trembling, and not from the cold.

She could *hear* what Kiriel said. Not in words; the words were beyond her comprehension. But her gift gave them shape and form, and she resonated with their force. Once, once before, she had flown into the eye of a storm such as this one. But she had flown strapped to the deck of a flying vessel, *lumina arden* in her hand. She had seen the Serpent's vast pinions bend as it rode the winds, commanding them.

There had been no Kiriel di'Ashaf at that battle.

And had there been, she would have felt no comfort; she felt none now.

She lifted a hand, but she could not bring herself to touch Kiriel. She could not see, in the woman by her side, the girl for whom she had sung the cradle song.

But if she could not touch and she could not see, she was not without weapons. She spoke.

"Kiriel."

And Kiriel turned. Her eyes were shining now, golden with warmth and the blood of a Northern god. Which god? Ah, it was the wrong question.

"You must seek shelter," Kiriel said, forcing the whole of her great voice into words too thin to contain it. Kiriel was not born with the voice, but she didn't need it; the words held the force of command.

And Diora was driven back by them.

She stumbled, righting herself with a grace that she owed to years of training. As she did, lightning took the sky, and in its brief flash, she saw Auralis AKalakar, running toward them.

"Kiriel!" His voice was not as smooth as Diora's, but it was stronger.

Kiriel looked toward him, and her eyes narrowed, shedding none of their light. She waited while he ran.

Or rather, she waited. The storm was stronger now. The house rattled, its boards pulled by wind. Diora lost her footing again, and this time, she let the wind force her to her knees.

She had lived so much of her life that way.

Auralis AKalakar reached Kiriel's side. He lowered the shield and stared at her.

Kiriel stared back, and the astonished annoyance in her face was an odd comfort. "*Why* are you here?"

"Gods know," he said, adding a string of foreign words to the statement. Kallandras had never seen fit to teach these particular ones, and the Serra was grateful for the oversight. She could imagine what they meant, however.

"What in the Hells are you doing?" He shook the shield at her, as if it were his fist.

Kiriel laughed.

Like the roar itself, the laughter made the Serra tremble; it was huge, loud, twin to the voice of thunder. "Funny you should ask that."

His glance fell to her hand.

Kiriel's fell as well, and then she lifted the hand in a fist.

"Not tonight," she said, exultant.

He cursed again, but quietly. "Kiriel—you could wake the dead with that voice. Don't—"

"Don't?" Just that.

Auralis took a step back.

"You can't fly," he said quietly.

She laughed. "Can't I?"

"Damn you, then. *I* can't."

"Watch the Serra," Kiriel told him. She gazed up, and smiled. "And wait. We may not have to fly."

The wind replied.

And the Serra Diora spoke again, but this time, she made herself *heard*.

"Kiriel, the Green Valley is not the desert, but you will make it one; the winds will destroy the village."

She knew. She had seen them before.

Kiriel turned slowly. Her hair had pulled itself free from the Northern braid that bound it, and strands of it rose, impervious to water, dancing now to a wind of her own making. The storm did not touch it.

Ashaf kep'Valente, Diora thought, as she bowed into the wind, her fingers sinking into drenched earth, *I regret that I will never meet you. You must have seen this. You must have known.*

And you sang to her. You loved her.

"I will protect this village," Kiriel said, and Diora heard the darkness in her voice. She had heard it before from other lips, and it touched her the same way. She was afraid.

She rode the fear.

In the South all faces were masks. Kiriel, unadorned, wore one, but she had several. Diora did not doubt this by force of will alone. The girl who had come to sit by her side in the tent, the girl who had asked, in a child's voice, for her song, was as real as the demon that stood in her place. She had heard both truths, and she accepted them.

But it was hard to cling to the one when the other raged. *All storms,* she thought. Her own hair fell across her face, Serra's dignity lost to the wilderness of the wind's howl.

The air changed.

At Kiriel's side stood Lord Telakar. He was taller than she, and his eyes were the color of night; the Serra could see them through wind and rain as clearly as she could see Kiriel. Auralis AKalakar was a blur.

Lord Telakar lost height as he bowed to Kiriel.

"Lady," he said, and his voice carried above the rumble of thunder, "what is your command?"

Kiriel did not look away from Diora.

And Diora could not look away from Kiriel. The wind hushed a moment, and the silence was as unnatural as the woman before her.

"Come, Telakar," another voice said.

Diora did not turn. She didn't need to. She could hear, in this new voice, the same velvet, the same death, that graced Telakar's. She was afraid now.

But Kiriel's eyes were still golden.

"Is it not clear what she desires?"

Kiriel looked away.

And because she did, Diora could.

Beside Lord Telakar, in armor that was pale as sunlit water, stood a man at least as tall. His hair was pale, and his sword was blue; blue and red.

"Anduvin?" Kiriel said.

The stranger bowed. "Kiriel."

"Why are you here?"

"You called, Lady," he replied. "And, as Telakar, I heard the summons. Lord Nugratz rides the storm."

The name meant something to Kiriel. Her face paled, her eyes brightened, her hair spread like dark wings. She said, "Only Nugratz?"

"And his kin."

"He knows I'm here."

"Any of the kin will now know you are present," Anduvin replied. He raised arm, and shield came to it, from nowhere that the Serra could see.

But Kiriel hesitated. It was the first hesitation, and Diora regretted—briefly—her words. Among creatures such as these, hesitation and death were kin. She knew it; she heard it in their voices.

"Peace, Na'dio."

She closed her eyes then.

"Kallandras."

"Yes. I am here."

The wind dwindled. She lost her fear of its voice the moment she heard his. **"I do not understand,"** she told him, lifting her head. **"The servants of the Lord of Night gather here, but they wait upon Kiriel di'Ashaf."**

"I do not understand it either, but trust your gift, Serra. Do they mean her harm?"

"No."

"She has her role to play, Na'dio. What she is, and what she will be, are not yet, I think, decided."

"And what will decide it in the end?"

He gave no answer.

"Kiriel," she said softly. She put no power into the word.

Kiriel looked at her anyway, hesitating again. Then she bent, and extended a hand.

Diora took it. Hers was wet and chill; Kiriel's was warm.

"Swordsmith," Kiriel said quietly.

The creature that answered to the name Anduvin bowed.

"Can you stand against Nugratz?"

"Upon the ground?"

"Anywhere."

His smile was slight and deadly. It was the whole of his answer. "Telakar."

Lord Telakar bowed. When he rose, he, too, wielded sword. It had come from nowhere. "Lady," he said. "Your command?"

Her hand shook. Diora felt it. But she did not mistake the tremor for fear.

"Bring him down."

And he smiled softly.

But Anduvin frowned a moment. "We are not alone here," he said at last.

Kiriel looked up, but she did not surrender Diora's hand. They were joined.

"There," Anduvin said quietly, lifting a hand and pointing into the clouds above. "Can you see him?"

Kiriel shook her head. "Who?"

"Illaraphaniel," Anduvin said. His voice was different. Diora heard something in it that she could not name.

"He is with the army," Kiriel said distantly.

"He is upon the field, Lady."

She did not gainsay him again. "Join him."

"As you command."

The winds bore him aloft.

"Telakar," Kiriel said, without turning.

She had the whole of his attention.

"This village is of import to me. If it is destroyed, you will all perish."

Diora could see, above Kiriel's stiff shoulder, the sudden smile that adorned the creature's lips. Cold smile, but not entirely malicious.

"Lady," he said, bowing, "you play a dangerous game. Do you understand the risk you take?"

She spun, then, pulling Diora up with her.

But before she could act or speak, he lifted a hand. "Peace," he said. "You have already acknowledged my weakness, and I serve your interests here. I speak of risk," he added, "because I know it better than any who now call the Hells their home."

She let him go.

And when he, too, had been taken by wind, when the clouds enveloped him, when his hair, white and pale, spread like wings, she turned to the Serra. "Come," she said brusquely. "You will freeze here."

"And me?" Auralis AKalakar said.

Kiriel shrugged.

He cursed, his Weston fluent and welcome. Only when she heard it did Diora realize that neither of the demons had spoken in a language she knew.

* * *

Isladar smiled. The storm passed around him, as if afraid to leave
its mark.

Not yet, he thought, and nodded.

But he was not immune to the challenge that she had sounded,
and he struggled against its pull; the *Kialli* were abroad, and they
shed their mortal guise as they summoned elemental air.

He longed, for a moment, to do the same.

Odd. He had thought himself beyond such games.

But perhaps he would never be beyond them now; she was in his
blood, and what she knew, he knew.

One day, he would stand revealed in just such a fashion before
her.

But not this eve.

She was coming into her power, but she did not yet understand
what that power meant.

He watched the skies; saw the clouds lurch and shift, disinte-
grating into patches of night. Mortal time was a miracle, a hurried,
graceless affair. And now so much depended on it.

If she took the mantle at the wrong moment, all of his effort
ended in failure; if she failed to take it at all, failure was his as well.
Between these two certainties, his game resided.

He was content.

But his sword had come to hand, and when he saw its gleaming
edge, he lost the smile that sustained him and bore shadow instead
as his burden.

There were no more lessons to recall.

Kallandras of Senniel College gave himself over to the restless,
angry wind. It became his voice, and when he lifted it, he rose. He
was not so graceful as Meralonne APhaniel, and in truth, Meralonne, one of the earliest of his allies, was not whom he wished to
stand beside.

But if no specific memory drove him to the heights, the sum of
those memories kept him there; he knew what he had to do, and if
the circumstances were not of his choosing, it signified little.

He watched the magi rise and, nudging the elemental air, he
joined him.

Evayne had warned them all not to summon the wind; not to call
it against the earth. The earth was not yet wakened. But he could not
be certain it would not be; the howling was a physical sensation.

He could not see clearly in the dark of the night sky, but he had learned to fight in the darkness, and what vision denied, hearing granted.

The *Kialli* were there, and they were coming in number to where Meralonne APhaniel now brandished his sword like lightning. Kallandras' blades were dark.

But they desired this battle; they woke and they pulled at his hands.

Best to be master here; the only other choice was death. He held them tight. But he heard their humming, their ancient, deadly voices all but silent: they knew the names of their enemies.

He wondered if the *Kialli* would see, in the blades, a like weakness.

Lord Ishavriel, shorn of shield, had taken the time to remake the limb he had lost to the kai Callesta. He did not speak of it; of all the things that had happened in his short time upon the mortal plane, it was the most humiliating. Not even the antics of the crazed, unpredictable Anya came close, for hers at least were predicated entirely upon her power; it was the power itself that had driven her into insanity.

The kai Callesta was simply and entirely mortal. No hint of greater talent graced him; he was a man.

And his sword, as far as Ishavriel knew, was a man's sword. It should not have left its mark. It should never have been able to sever limb, to shatter shield.

Had the world changed?

Perhaps. Perhaps so.

When The Lord had ruled the mortal world, the kinlords were not ordered to skulk, to hide in human guise, to restrain their power and sublimate their desire.

He had been weakened, and weakness was the only sin the Hells did not forgive.

He accepted its bitter truth. The spell, anchored by Anya, and guided by The Lord, was almost—*almost*—in place, and when it was done, when it was at last invoked, there would be an end to weakness, an end to hiding, an end to an existence in the vast Northern Wastes.

But it was a bitter spell.

He looked up, the taste of its magic fouling the air that he did not require. The skies were dark; the rain swept in at an angle that was close to even with the plain. The horses were sodden, sullen, and even enraged. Their masters were stalled; the rain seeped into the earth, turning its rich, thick browns into the mud that they found so difficult to traverse.

They were weighted by gravity, by their own mortality.

But they were not, it seemed, without allies.

For in the South of Averda, he heard *her* cry.

He raised his own magic against it, seeing red tint the shadows of night. Within the encampment, the *Kialli* best suited to mortal form were waking, their magic straining against the compulsion set upon them by Ishavriel's binding.

Her voice was strong.

Stronger than he had yet heard it, and he had heard her scream the night that the Shining Court had been sundered by the ferocity of her unexpected, inexplicable, attack.

He might have killed her then; he had certainly planned no less than her death. But she had killed what could be killed, destroying the flat of the great stone table in the Hall of Sorrows before she fled the Northern Wastes.

They searched for her. For days. For weeks.

The Lord confirmed her survival, her existence, but not until Etridian's failure in the city of the cursed offspring of the distant gods had the Lord's Fist known for certain.

And it appeared that she had traveled the leagues between that city and this place.

He smiled, but the smile was grim and empty. He could not, in safety, ascend to the skies; he could not dance in the storm that raged above. He could not give his servants leave to do so without compromising them, if they had not already done so on their own.

She was wild, and they responded with a wildness of their own; they wanted the contest. They wanted the kill.

So, too, Lord Ishavriel, but for different reasons.

She had *called* them, and if she was unaware of the force of her demand, he was not: it was there, and growing.

And Ishavriel of the Shining Court, Ishavriel of the Lord's Fist, Ishavriel, ruler of the demesnes of the Hells in their grim and perfect glory, had no intention of allowing her to reach the apex of her power. He knew what it meant; they all did.

And he would perish before he bowed to a mortal, even one in whose veins The Lord's blood also flowed.

Two more nights, he thought.

But he wondered, as he thought it, if Lord Nugratz was up to the task set him.

It mattered little; he could not now flee in safety to the Shining Court; the cost was too great. Etridian and Assarak were already occupied; of the Fist, only Alcrax might deign to come South so soon—for he had suffered much in her night of slaughter; the lieutenants lost to her sword were in great measure his.

He frowned.

He had only one source of power within the Dominion; one source of magic that might withstand the night's reaving. But Anya a'Cooper was not so easily directed or controlled, and she had always had a weakness for Kiriel.

Kiriel did not accept the towels Valla offered; she barely noticed the older woman.

Diora, however, was grateful—and gracious; she did what Kiriel could not. The roof shuddered now, and she lifted her head, lowering the towels as she looked up. Water dripped down the perfect line of her face, landing in her lap and blending with the deep hue of wet silk.

Arrego was awake.

Diora wondered if there existed any seraf in the Green Valley who was not; the storm would uproot trees.

"Kiriel," Valla said, but her voice shook on the last syllable, dying as the girl turned to face her.

The Serra rose. "Valla kep'Valente," she said, her voice both kind and formal, "the storm is not of the Lady's making. Be at peace, as you can, but leave Kiriel di'Ashaf; she must think." She laced the words with command and comfort, and Valla nodded, but the worry that lined her face, adding weight and texture to the wrinkles and crevices age and sun had put there, did not disperse. It was anchored to the storm.

"Arrego kep'Valente," Diora continued, "where is the village overseer to be found?"

"In the village center," Arrego replied. More words than he had offered anyone this eve.

"It's not safe to travel," Valla added, in case this was not obvious.

Diora nodded.

Lifted her voice again, speaking to the wind's heart.

"Kallandras."

She did not know where he was, but he heard her.

"Diora."

"The wind will destroy the dwellings," she told him. **"And much of the valley. Can it not be stilled?"**

He did not answer.

She offered him her silent apology, wondering if he faced Serpent, demon, or both in the storm's heart.

But Kiriel touched her shoulder.

"I will go," she said quietly.

Her eyes were so bright, Diora almost looked away. Almost. But they were not demon eyes, and the darkness had been shorn from her voice. She met the gaze and held it.

But she did not argue.

Auralis AKalakar, dripping and sodden, rose from his place in the corner. "I'll go with her," he said.

"No you won't."

"Stop me."

Kiriel frowned. "Auralis—"

"I won't stay here," he told her grimly, "if you won't."

"I can't stay." She lifted a hand, then, and reaching out, she touched the shuddering planks that girded the walls. *Old wood,* Diora thought. But it had existed in this place for at least as long as Kiriel had lived—longer, she thought.

And beneath Kiriel's hands, it stilled. The wood itself seemed to lose the brittleness that the storm had invoked; the howl of the wind became a thing of sound and not sensation.

Auralis frowned. And then his bronze brows, dark with water, lifted a moment in question. Not—quite—in wonder; wonder was an expression that would never sit easily upon his face; he had swallowed age, and it had devoured that part of him.

That much, the Serra could tell from his voice alone.

"Kiriel—"

But Kiriel shook her head. Her hair was damp and wet, a mess of dark strands that clung, unconfined, to her armor. She stroked the wood, and then stared at her pale fingers. When she lifted her hand, it shook.

"The ring?" Auralis asked. He knew what she had done. They all knew.

"I . . . I don't know."

"Arrego!" Valla slapped her husband's shoulder.

She needn't have; he was already rising. He did not join Kiriel and Auralis, but instead walked opposite them, as far as the confines of the small building allowed.

There, he, too, raised his hands. They were not her hands; they were gnarled and knotted, his knuckles like old, exposed tree roots, his hands dark and red with labor. They curled in fists; he struck the walls, rapping them as if they were instruments.

Then he walked to the room's center and clambered up onto the flat of the table; he reached up with both palms, for he was not a short man, and placed them against the roof. He stood there but a moment, and then he closed his eyes.

"Let her go," he told them all, although he did not look at Kiriel.

"Arrego—" his wife began.

He spun, slow and ponderous, as if he had never been capable of speed. But his expression silenced his wife.

"We have no lantern," she said, bowing to the inevitable, her face pale with shame. "You will have to go in the darkness."

"There isn't a lantern in the Terrean," Kiriel replied, "that would withstand these rains." And she met Valla's eyes.

Valla looked away, her hands trembling in front of her breasts, her fingers dancing circles in the air.

And Diora knew that the gold of Kiriel's eyes was no hidden gift, no hidden light: they could see it. They could *all* see it.

"Valla," the Serra said, her voice weighted with the desire— foolish, useless, but entirely her own—to protect Kiriel di'Ashaf, "the sun's light also shines."

"The Lord has no mercy," Valla said woodenly, struggling with fear. "And no pity."

"The Lord came to the first Leonne," Diora countered. "At a time when the Lord of Night sought dominion over these lands."

But her words had no effect. Valla kep'Valente had already made her choice.

She was old, graceless, unlovely.

And she was none of these things. She turned to the Serra and said, "She is Ashaf's daughter." Just that, and the words were too grim, but they were firm. Final.

"And her father?" Diora said softly. A test. Perhaps an unkind one.

"In the South, to those of us who work the fields and tend the valleys," the seraf replied, the commitment growing both wings and roots, "the child is known by the mother, and often only the mother. There are always wars," she added bitterly, "and men are unkind; they take what they desire, and what they leave behind, they leave. Should we judge the child by their actions?" She shook her head. "We are all serafs," she said. "We have all had sisters or daughters or mothers who have suffered.

"By the mother," she added. "We judge."

And Kiriel di'Ashaf's face, the face that had been bone dry in the fall of rain, was glistening in the nighttime hut.

"Ashaf knew what you were," Valla said, turning to Kiriel. She bridged the distance between them with words, and only words. But sometimes words were enough. "She must have known what you were.

"But she did not abandon you to the care of your father. What she could not do, I will not do: we loved your mother, and she would have had no gift from us but this one, if she could have asked it."

Arrego said, gruff now, "Shut up, wife, and let her go. The Green Valley needs her."

And Kiriel di'Ashaf fled.

Serra Diora en'Leonne watched her go. As the screen opened — and it seemed to Diora that it sat more heavily in its groove than it had when they had first arrived — the winds howled in fury; the storm had grown worse, and branches now flew in its folds.

She lifted her voice against the storm's voice, and she offered what Valla kep'Valente offered: a gift to a child. A song.

Lord Nugratz was the only member of the Lord's Fist who abjured human form. He had the power to take it, but it was not to his liking, and he had forced, from earth, the gift of flight. His wing membranes stretched across pinions the length of a small dragon's as he rode the storm. Beneath them, buoying him, the wind whirled in fury, but it did his bidding: he was kinlord.

His weapon was in his hand. His sword. The shield he had not yet summoned, for it was cumbersome, and in truth, he liked little the aerial struggle. The wind demanded its due.

And although he had intended to give it some part of the forest and the whole of the village, he knew, now, that he could not sacrifice his hold yet: the Lord's whelp had cried out a challenge that the whole of the valleys, from the foothills to the deserts, must have heard.

She was waiting.

He watched for her, tingling, fire in his eyes.

The first of his enemies rose through the roil of clouds, arms extended, wind leashed in the same fashion that he had leashed it.

But he did not face Kiriel.

He faced, instead, Lord Telakar.

The kinlord bowed, his face grim, his eyes dark. Blue light shrouded his shadow, and red light limned it.

"Lord Nugratz," he said, his voice a volley. "You attack the holdings of my Lord. Retreat, and spare yourself humiliation."

Lord Nugratz laughed, his voice deep and full, the fluting of a great bird of prey.

But he did not speak; instead he folded his wings and began his sharp and sudden descent.

Kiriel struggled against the storm; the rains were almost horizontal. Branches battered her, clanging off her raised arms; she had lifted them instinctively to protect her eyes.

Behind her, she heard the distinctive sound of sword leaving scabbard. It should have served as warning, but it was, instead, a comfort.

An idiotic one. She turned, speaking into the wind and not against it.

"*What* are you doing?" she shouted.

Auralis AKalakar, armed, lowered the shield that protected his face from the worst of the rain. In reply, he struck a branch as it flew past; it landed and rolled in two pieces, each taking flight as the winds continued.

She frowned, seeing the sword.

It wasn't his.

And it was. She could almost see his name against the flat of the luminescent blade.

"You're an idiot!" she shouted.

He laughed. Struck another branch. He intended to battle his way across the village to the tree that its center harbored.

So did she, but she hadn't meant to do it so literally.

Her eyes narrowed as she looked at his hand. Upon his third finger, glowing brightly, she could see the square facets of a ruby. She looked at her own fingers, at the unmarked, unadorned band that nestled against her skin.

And she knew.

She thought of Evayne, then. She had wondered why Evayne had come to them on the nighttime path. Had thought that it concerned Meralonne APhaniel because so much magic, so much history, did. Clenching her hand in a fist, she raised it.

"Follow me!" she shouted.

He laughed, and she could see the darkness in him straining for freedom.

Not this life, she thought. *Not this one, and not the next. But soon, Auralis.*

He ran into her; she had stopped her desperate, lurching walk.

"What?" he shouted. The wind tore his word away, but she heard it before it was lost.

"If I went to the Hells," she asked him, uncaring now about the volume, "would you follow me?"

"Why not?" His laugh was unfettered. "They can't be any worse than this!"

She nodded. "Remember that!" And began to walk once more. Her hair did not rise, and her power did not demand it; the rain struck her skin with the wind's fury. The water was cool, but she needed it. It reminded her of everything that she was.

The tree at the village's center had lost branches, and the branches were a danger. But even a storm such as this could not threaten its roots; they were deep and planted well within the confines of the sheltering earth.

But so, Kiriel thought, were the dead.

Ashaf's dead.

All of Russo's.

She did not want to add to them; let time do it. Let war do it. Let famine or pestilence or plague do it.

But let them do it some other night. She had traveled all the way from the Northern Wastes with no clear mission, no real purpose— or so she had thought. Until she had come to the Averdan valleys. And now she understood.

If she could do this, she could do anything.

If she could do this, then Ashaf had not failed.

She knew deserts. She knew, now, what their opposite was. Life was complicated, and ugly, and painful; it was also haunting, and beautiful, and brief.

She wanted this. Just this.

But she wanted it more than she had ever wanted *anything*. Anything except for Ashaf's life back, and that was denied her, would always be denied her.

But Ashaf would have given her life for this, and if Kiriel could save Russo, she could tell herself that Ashaf had. It was better than the truth.

No, she thought, as her hair laid itself against her eyes in thick strands, it would *be* the truth. Truths are made, and unmade, unmade and made, by those who seek them.

She forgot about the battle that raged above, even though she had demanded it.

Instead, she struggled to reach the next house.

When she did, she was unaware of time; she only knew that there was so little *of* it. She reached out and grabbed the shaking walls; they were thinner than the walls of Ashaf's home, and closer to breaking.

Her palms felt the wood as she pressed against it, diverting the falling water as if she were a rock that stood in its path.

"Kiriel?" Auralis shouted in her ear. "What in the Hells are you doing?"

"Nothing in the Hells," she snapped back, although she was half certain he wouldn't hear it.

The wood was not alive.

But it was. She could feel its span, the beginning and end of the old, cut beams; the joins that made it a home. They rested in her palms, and the winds sought to unmake it.

Damn the winds.

She forced the wood to straighten, as if it were under her command and she could lend it dignity and power by the simple force of will.

She couldn't, not by will, and nothing about it was simple except the imperative.

Kiriel di'Ashaf made the house whole. She made it strong. She offered it a rebirth, if such a thing could be offered to the cobbled together corpses of many trees.

And as she did this, lightning played across the sky, sheet lightning, a flash of illumination. In its intermittent light she stared at the backs of her hands, seeing at last in their active repose the other side of the medallion that had been the only evidence of her birth mother's existence.

Ashaf had been the mother she desired.

But she had always had two.

CHAPTER TWENTY-ONE

TELAKAR'S dance was brief and graceful; Nugratz chose power to make his statement. The winds howled beside him, like the face of a jagged cliff, and he traced them, falling, his plummet controlled by the shadows of the Lord of Night.

But his wings came up short, tearing him out of the dive, as he screeched a wingspan above the second blade. This he recognized, not by vision, for he moved too quickly to look, but by something more visceral.

The shock shored him up.

In the roiling of the wind, he called his servants, and they came.

"Anduvin!" he roared.

And the Swordsmith replied; he cut *wind* with the edge of his blade, his cursed blade. The wind could move faster than the eye could see, but the wind had no need of sight; it could not move faster than *that* blade's edge, and in its fashion, it bled, its trail an awkward gash across the path of flight. Nugratz' flight.

It changed the face of the battle.

Lord Nugratz would pay for this. The wind would demand its price, exact its toll. Small cost, but the battle had hardly been joined; the kinlord could measure the whole of the night's work in the single figure of the Swordsmith. He did not like the accounting.

"What Telakar offered," Lord Anduvin said, "I, too, will offer. But I offer it less willingly."

The Swordsmith.

Here.

It was almost beyond belief.

"Do you have any idea of what you *do*?" Nugratz yelled, his wings gathering wind in their upward stretch.

Anduvin offered no answer. Telakar was likewise silent.

"The Lord will confine you in the Hells for eternity!"

It was Telakar who replied. He laughed. "And what would that signify?" he said, in a voice so smooth it should not have carried over the breaking beat of thunder. "To confine us, he would have to be in the Hells, and of them—and he has returned to the mortal realm; he will never again surrender what he has worked so hard to gain."

Nugratz was silent for a moment, and when he spoke, he was graceless. "I will see you destroyed."

Telakar shrugged. "And you differ from the rest of our kin in what fashion, brother?" His blade rose.

When it fell, it missed the limb of the demon that appeared to his right. But only barely.

"The Hells will have a Queen in the absence of our Lord," Telakar continued. "And who will argue with her? She will rule the whole of the realm; there is not a demesne within the Hells that will not know her for what she is."

"She will *never* live to rule."

"You failed to kill her when she was a mortal babe; she is much,

much more than that now. How will you succeed when she has grown in power?"

The second demon came, and the third; the sky was littered with their presence. They were not without power, but they were not Lord Nugratz; in his Court, he suffered no equals.

In silence, in the bond of blood, they asked his will, struggling against its imperative at the same moment. And in like silence, he bade them kill.

But they attacked Anduvin first.

She stopped at each building she could see, and although the storm still raged, she felt its darkness lift. Some ancient power gave strength to her vision, and if it was shadow, if it was *his,* she did not question it and did not deny it. What she needed, she took.

Behind her every step of the way was Auralis AKalakar, and if he had thought to slay demons this night, he bore in patience this unexpected change of plans.

But she heard his voice as she walked; heard it as she stopped to give strength to the structures that defined the village, that protected those who were so weak and so defenseless even the least of Hells' creatures could have ended their lives with glee.

He asked *how*. He asked *what she was doing*. He asked if she understood what price she would have to pay. And she ignored it all, brushing it aside as if it were of no more significance than hair or the water that persisted in its fall.

But she did not send him away; she did not tell him to *shut up*; she did not anger at the incessant flow of his words. They were part of him, and this was a battle that she only barely understood.

He had never failed her.

Even in his uncertainty, in his darkness, in his pale, inexplicable cruelty, he had hovered by her side or at her back. Why she wanted him there, she didn't know; the Ospreys themselves sometimes questioned it.

The buildings shuddered.

The wind was worse than restless; it was angry.

Yes, angry: she could hear its voice. Not well enough to understand the flow of its ancient, terrible words—and perhaps she would never understand it. But words were superfluous. Something had changed in the skies above the Green Valley.

Lord Anduvin understood the attack.

He smiled. The kin were slow; their struggle for freedom—impossible freedom—informed every move they made.

What was the first rule of the Hells?

Ask a kinlord, and the answer would be: Power rules.

Ask an imp, and the answer would differ. Survive.

These were no imps. The imperative of survival at any cost had long been buried by centuries of power, and it was slow to surface. In some, it would never surface at all.

And while he severed limb from shoulder, while he cut blades from wrist and chest, where blades bristled like spines, he stopped a moment to cut the wind; to force it to feel the edge of the only blade he had ever made that could injure the oldest of the magics.

The only blade but one.

She came at last to the largest of the houses, and here she paused. It was made not of wood, but of stone, and clay adorned it, colored and dyed in such a way as to declare its occupant of Valente, and not owned by it. The rain had not yet dislodged what lay there, perhaps because it was tended. In the Lady's night, the colors were almost indistinct.

She hesitated here.

Auralis caught her shoulders as they sagged; her knees were stiff. The cold—for it *was* cold—had slowly taken hold of her limbs.

"Kiriel," he shouted. His voice was loud, but it would be; his lips were practically in her ear. "Do you have any idea what in the Hells you're doing?"

She shrugged herself free.

No.

She even understood the question.

But because she didn't answer, he persisted. "Look, I know you're using magic. Even Cook would be able to see that. I've never seen you use magic like *this*."

She wasn't sure if he meant the act itself or the fact that the magic was not somehow involved with, part of, combat. All of her gifts were shadow-born, and she knew their limits. Had known, she corrected herself, as she clenched fist and the ring caught momentary light.

But this, this was different.

"Look, you idiot," he said, shaking her, his lips leaving her ear. "Every magic has its price. You use more than you can, and *you* pay. Have you never listened to a mage?"

She shook her head. "Don't like mages," she told him. It was less than she had meant to say.

He swore. A lot. Then her feet left the ground as he lifted her. "You're cold. Do you know what that means?"

It's cold? She mouthed the words at him.

"Very funny."

But she did understand him.

In the Shining Palace, in the Towers, she had never felt cold, and the cold could kill, and did. She had played with one of the beasts of Hell, at the tower steps, and he had bathed her in the fire of his breath, hiding his fangs only in the presence of Isladar, but she had never burned.

In the streets of *Averalaan Aramarelas*, she had learned, after the ring had been awakened, to feel the heat. But the cold had eluded her; she had never wintered there, and she had been told the winter, in most years, was too mild to be worthy of the name.

She felt it now.

The ring?

She meant to ask Auralis if it *was* cold, but she couldn't; she couldn't reach his face. Could not, in fact, *see* it. She could hear the steady drone of his swearing, though, and that was impressive.

He carried her up to the massive doors—real doors, not sliding, Southern contrivances—and he kicked them. Hard. After a moment, he kicked them again, but this time with the flat of his foot.

Light, unlike the white, brief flashes that troubled the skies, appeared like a crack in the darkness; it flickered, orange and red, as it grew.

Auralis AKalakar swore beneath his breath.

"Kiriel, now would be a *good time* to stand up."

She felt the ground beneath her feet again, or beneath the soles of her boots. She remembered a time when boots were first offered her, and she disdained to wear them. Winter, there. White, white memory. White and black, the colors of Imperial mourning.

She looked up abruptly, memory fleeing as Auralis tilted her face toward the light. With her hair. She'd get him for it. Later.

She saw a lamp.

Heard a voice. Just one.

But she saw what Auralis had seen, and she frowned, forcing vision to surrender something that made sense.

It was a quarrel. With a crossbow all around it.

And behind it, hands holding its weight steady, was a man with long hair, hair that had once been black. He must have been expecting trouble, because it was gathered and knotted; she could see it spill from the top of his head, and it looked ridiculous.

But probably not as ridiculous as it would have unbound.

"Daro," she said.

His eyes narrowed. His finger tightened.

She realized that it was *not* a good time to have eyes that were the wrong color, and she knew they were the wrong color.

Her hands were shaking. Yes, it was cold. It was, in Alexis' words, *bloody* cold.

She had been a coward, and she repented of it, as was often the case with cowards, too late. She had avoided Daro di'Valente, although she was certain that he had seen her from a distance. Valla had introduced her to almost everyone else; as the village overseer, he couldn't avoid seeing them, grouped around the base of Anya's tree.

"Why are you here?" He asked it of her, but his eyes never left Auralis.

Auralis replied in very bad Torra. He might as well have spoken in Weston; the language marked him anyway. Everything about him was of the North. Except for the new sword, and he was too smart to draw it.

But Daro di'Valente didn't shoot. That told her something.

Ashaf kep'Valente told her the rest.

"Daro," she said, catching the words that Ashaf had asked, and letting them spill from her lips before she could understand the whole of their import, "do you love this village?"

His eyes narrowed further.

And then his brows rose.

Anyone might have asked him the question that she now asked; the question that Ashaf had asked on her last day in the Green Valley. Anyone; he had been the overseer of the village since his father's death, and in many ways, it *was* his.

But Kiriel thought that no one else had then vanished from sight, never to be seen again.

He said, never lowering the weapon, "It is my responsibility."

Ashaf's memories had not prepared her for the weight and the gravity of those words. They carried, she thought, a form of majesty. Shorn of finery, of ceremony, of sword and rod, it was nonetheless something she recognized.

He had aged, since he had last answered that question. His hair was paler, and his face more lined. She wondered what time had taken from him, since Isladar had taken Ashaf.

But she said, "And you understand responsibility well. This is a village unlike any village in the Dominion, and it was made by the Tor'agar and by you. Give me your word, in the presence of the Lord, that you will guard it when I am gone."

He stared at her. His eyes met hers, and it was Kiriel who was forced to look away.

He said succinctly, "The Lord does not hold sway now. It is the Lady's time."

And she said, "And men don't swear oaths to women, anyway. Not oaths that *count*. If the Lord of Night is not to hold sway over everything that you have built and loved . . ." and she found that she could not continue. It wasn't the cold—although dammit, it was cold—it was Daro. And Ashaf. Her own loss she had lived with for what seemed a lifetime.

But not until this moment had she countenanced other losses. Ashaf was *hers*. Had been hers.

She surrendered the weight of that burden in the moment she met his eyes again.

It hurt to speak, because she couldn't speak quietly, not here.

"Let us in," she said, trying to make it sound like a request. "We can't speak here."

He hesitated, although his hand was still and calm. After a moment, he backed away from the door—slowly—the crossbow still readied, still a threat.

But he let her in. Or rather, he let them in; Auralis picked her up and carried her across the threshold.

Daro did not close the door. The storm still wailed, but it was contained by the frame and lessened by the length of the hall.

"Speak, " he said. Not a request.

Weary now, shuddering a moment with cold, she forced her lips to move. It was easier than she had thought it would be; there was a warmth at the base of her throat that stilled her.

"Yes," she told him, "I'm golden-eyed."

"You were not, yesterday."

"No."

The crossbow waited.

"And maybe I'm even demon-born."

"Are you?"

She wanted to shrug. But she understood who he was now, and she held on to the knowledge. Ashaf's knowledge. "But Ashaf found me. You know—knew—her. She couldn't hurt a field mouse. She trapped them and let them loose."

He said nothing. It wasn't the encouragement she wanted. But she seldom got what she wanted, and at least the lack proved good for something. She continued.

"She couldn't kill me. Knowing the laws, knowing what Ser Danello would have said, she couldn't kill *me*. Will you do it for her?" She didn't expect an answer, and she didn't get one. "She raised me, instead."

"Impossible."

"If she could have killed," Kiriel told him starkly, "she would have been a widow within a week of her marriage. Death didn't frighten her then."

His eyes rounded slightly, and he nodded.

Did the quarrel dip? Even a little?

"She served the Lady," Kiriel added quietly. "And she died a long way from the only home she loved."

"Why are you here?"

"Because this *is* the only home she loved," Kiriel said bitterly. "And because I—think—I can protect it."

"From what?"

"Don't you know?" she asked him. Auralis did not set her down, although she motioned for him to do so. She was dripping; could see the light reflected in the pools at his feet .

"I know what you are," he told her coldly.

"So did she. But she—I think she had some hope for what I might *also* be."

"You come with a Northern soldier."

"The Tor'agar comes with the Northern army," she told him in return.

He did not argue. He had at least this much knowledge.

"Why are you here?" he asked her again.

"Because," she said irritably, "Auralis carried me."

It was not the answer he expected.

"His Torra is poor," she added, choosing a different set of words than the ones which would have come naturally. "But he guards the Tyr'agar."

It wasn't what she wanted to say. But she had no control over where the conversation drifted. It was cold, even here.

"She needs help," Auralis said, each word distinct, each word foreign.

"I loved Ashaf," Kiriel continued, dogged now. Determined. "I loved her more than you can possibly know. I would have brought her here, but I failed her, and she died. She believed that the winds contain the dead. I don't know if it's true here; it isn't, in the North.

"But if the winds contain the dead, and she watches, then she'll know that I listened. To her. To everything she said.

"And maybe she'll forgive me."

He said, "I should kill you."

And when he did, Kiriel knew he wouldn't. Words were perverse.

"What did he say?" Auralis asked. "Tell him that I've got a sword and he doesn't have time to reload."

"No."

"Kiriel—"

"No. And if he shoots me, you walk away."

"If he shoots you, you won't be in a position to dictate." He shook her. But he held her.

Daro spoke only after Auralis had stopped. "But you come to me, speaking words that I have spent the long month dreading. I cannot protect the village from the storm," he added.

The crossbow fell slowly as he lowered his hand. It aged him.

"But maybe you can, demon kin. Maybe you have the power to do what I cannot. That would be her way, to turn the enemy against itself by gentle arts. Yes, you are right. Had she been capable of killing, she would have been a widow within a week. She never spoke to me of her time as wife to the Tor'agar, but . . . his son did. If you are not demon, if you did not reave this information from her, then she must have trusted you. She was rarely wrong," he added. "But you are young. I see that you think she erred.

"Let me tell you what you would know, had you been raised among us. Had she killed the Tor'agar, she would have died. Even if the heir rejoiced, even if he approved, he would have had no choice: a wife does not kill her husband. She would have had her freedom, in some fashion, and perhaps that would have been a kindness to her. Instead, she chose to endure the father's cruelty so that she might love the father's son, and raise him to be a *man*. She made, of a monster's offspring, a Tor'agar without rival. When he gave her back to us, we were afraid. But we understood his mercy, in time—and we understood her gift.

"He was sorely distressed when she vanished."

Ser Daro removed the quarrel and then fired the disarmed weapon. "The Havallans came a month ago," he added quietly.

"Without their Matriarch. They offered their usual veiled advice; I thought it a threat.

"But now I see that they spoke of you. Kiriel di'Ashaf. Daughter of the dead."

His wife joined them when Daro raised his voice. She was close by, and Kiriel saw, with surprise, that she was also armed. But her hands were not steady as they carried the crossbow, and if she didn't disarm it, she'd lose a foot.

Daro knew; he disarmed it. But he moved slowly, almost gently, as he did. He asked her a question; it didn't carry the length of the hall.

But she answered with a nod.

"Come, Kiriel di'Ashaf," he said. "You have met the rest of the village. Meet my family."

She was shuddering. She had surrendered to the cold, and her only defense against it was the hand she raised. In it, she gripped the pendant, the only proof of Ashaf's existence left her.

Her hand stilled.

He didn't seem to notice. Sliding an arm around the shoulders of the solidly built woman, he pulled her to his side. Her hair was darker than his, but her face was lined, and there were circles beneath her eyes that spoke of sleepless nights.

Kiriel recognized them; she had seen them before on Ashaf's face.

"This is Nora en'Valente, my wife. My daughter sleeps, and my son is in the far wing, with his wife."

"You had two daughters," she said.

His lips thinned a moment, and then his shoulders relaxed. "Yes," he said quietly. "I had two."

Kiriel bowed her head.

"Ashaf was as close to a healer as our village could afford," he continued, sparing her nothing. But the accusation was slight. "Who is your companion?"

"Auralis," she replied.

"What?" Auralis snapped.

"I'm answering a question. Your Torra isn't *that* bad."

"He is no friend to us," Daro said evenly. "If I am any judge of men."

"He's my friend," Kiriel replied as firmly as she could. "And I *am* an able judge."

"Kiriel," Auralis said. "Tell him you need to rest."

But she shrugged him off, turning her shoulder, with difficulty, away from his chest.

"What did the Havallans tell you?" she asked him.

He shook his head. "The Voyani guard their words," he replied.

"They might," Kiriel replied, "but their Matriarch was with us. She travels with the Tyr'agar. And the Tor'agar."

His brows lifted.

His wife stepped out of his shadow and walked across the length of hall that separated them. It seemed a long way to come, in Kiriel's opinion; the walls seemed oddly curved.

The woman's face was heavy, but it was not as grim as Daro's. Not even when she frowned, as she did now. She lifted an aged hand, a callused one, and touched Kiriel's forehead.

Then she hissed and turned.

"You might as well shoot her," she said to her husband. "What were you thinking? She's burning."

"She's demon kin," her husband replied. "And they are not like us."

"Daro di'Valente!"

"Perhaps I will repent of my introduction," he told Kiriel, but something about his tone had shifted from the beginning of the sentence to its end.

"You," Nora en'Valente said, poking Auralis' mailed breast with a blunt finger. "Why are you standing there like a half-wit?"

"What did she say?"

Kiriel shook her head. "I told him to stand there," she said. She hesitated, and then added, "He brought me here. I was . . . afraid to come."

"And no wonder," Nora replied. For just a moment the lines of her face hardened, and her eyes, in the dim light, seemed black. Black and white.

"Your eyes," she added quietly.

"I know."

"Have you decided, husband?"

"Obviously."

"Then the child must be offered a bed. She needs a place to sleep." Her expression relaxed. "I guess even demons fear the storm with cause."

He hesitated.

"Daro."

And then bowed slightly to his wife. "Very well, Nora. But she is not as weak as she looks."

"No. But she is as sick as she feels, to my hand. The night's work may be done for you if you don't move."

He moved, gesturing for Auralis to follow.

Auralis shifted his grip on Kiriel and stumbled forward; his steps were loud.

Nora walked beside him; the hall was wide enough to accommodate them both. She said nothing, but every so often she touched Kiriel's face and neck.

Kiriel had never liked being touched, but this felt so natural she barely noticed it. A weakness. She knew it.

But she thought, as she was carried, that she needed to redefine weakness, to better understand its danger, and its strength—if indeed such strength existed beyond the realm of fancy and hope.

Daro's lamp bobbed as he walked, and in the end, he opened one screen after another, as if he were a seraf, and not the lord of the domis. Kiriel was aware of the water that followed them in a wet trail, but she was mute.

The room that opened at last was large and empty; it was also quiet. She said, "I don't hear the storm."

"Listen for long enough," Daro replied, "and you will. But this room is not bounded by the outer walls, and it will protect you best."

"I'm not the one who needs protection." She started to sit up, and Auralis cursed the redistribution of her weight. She was not large, had never been large, but neither was she weightless or light.

Nora was at her side, her hands pressing into the rounded curve of shoulder joint. She frowned. "Your armor," she said at last. "Will you take it off?"

Kiriel nodded mutely.

"Good. You two, leave."

Daro's brow rose. "Wife," he began.

But she shook her head. "Not now," she said, her voice firm. "I do not embarrass you in front of our people; there are only strangers here, and they do not know our customs."

It wasn't entirely true. But it was close enough.

Auralis might not understand the words, but he understood the finger that pointed firmly toward the screen. He hesitated. "Kiriel?"

She smiled.

He nodded and set her down on the Southern mats. "I'll be outside the door," he said.

But she had turned toward Nora di'Valente, and, prone, she raised her arms. As if it were that easy to shed the weight of armor. As if she could leave it in the hands of a seraf.

*   *   *

"I don't mind the wind," she told Nora. She wasn't sure when; the light had dimmed, and Nora was pressing a cold cloth to her forehead.

Nora's nod was gentle, and it said nothing.

"I don't," Kiriel continued. "I've always heard it. My room was open to the wastes, and the winds always howled."

The older woman nodded again. Her face was there, briefly, in lamplight, and gone again. But Kiriel could hear the steady rhythm of her breath, no matter what the light did.

It helped.

She was cold.

"I've never done that before," she said.

"Done what, child?"

But Kiriel couldn't make sense of the question. Cold, yes. Why was it that she had never appreciated the cold when she lived in it?

She closed her eyes, thinking of snow. Of ice. Of towers that rose against setting and rising sun, against the moon's full face, against the star-strewn night, and against the bright, bleak azure of the cloudless day.

At the height of the towers, her home. With Ashaf.

And at the base, the hound, the three-headed dog.

Falloran. His breath was a plume of fire; he seldom chose to use all of his heads at once. She had seen him do it, though. He didn't like Isladar.

It hadn't occurred to her to wonder why he liked her.

She missed him.

She had grown up, and away, from both his breath and the jaws he carefully hooded when he snapped at her arm in play; grown out of his huge shadow, the wall of his large, heavy body, the first armor she had been offered that she couldn't wear.

What had she done instead?

She'd learned how to fight. She'd learned how to kill. She'd learned to appreciate the power her father held over all of his kin-lords, his creatures.

But she wished Falloran were here, now. He might breathe warmth back into her.

Of course, he might just kill her instead; he was of the Hells, after all.

*   *   *

"She wants her dog," Nora said quietly, as she left the room for the fourth time.

Daro looked up. The storm knocked at the doors, driving branches and small stones into the heavy wood. The village would pay for this night.

"Her *dog?*"

Nora nodded. She was weary.

"Why don't you sleep," Daro said, the offer implicit in his words.

She shook her head. "I've done this before."

A moment of pain passed between them, shared, and lessened in some way by the sharing. Loss did that; it strengthened or it weakened, but it never quite left you the same. "You were younger," he said gently.

But he knew, as he touched her face, that she had to see this to its end. The one great failure in their lives had started with hope and desperation, and it had ended with a grim, bitter silence that even tears were not allowed to pierce. Those had come later.

Failure had never weakened resolve; it was as if, each time they faced this threat, they walked the same path; as if, by succeeding here, they argued, at a growing distance, with death.

"There are things you don't forget," she replied. "The body doesn't forget them either. Why don't you sleep?"

He offered his gentle surrender, and she moved past him, to wring out warm cloths, and to drench them again in cold water.

"I don't understand what ails her," she told her husband when she returned. "She has no rash, her breathing isn't labored, she bears no wounds, no infection that I can find. But she has the cold fever, and I fear that it will rise before the dawn."

He said, "She will survive."

"How are you so certain, husband?"

"The Havallans," he replied grimly.

"They spoke of this girl?"

He said instead, "You've seen her, Nora. You've listened to her. Does she sound like a demon to you?"

Nora shook her head. "But it is said that demons are cunning and appear without guile."

"It is said."

"You fear her."

"Yes," Daro said grimly. "But I fear the Tor'agar as well. Perhaps she will be Ashaf's, in the end. Perhaps the words she spoke will be true enough."

"For what?" Nora's voice was quiet.

Daro understood what that quiet meant. He offered her a weary smile. Vulnerability often disarmed his wife. But this eve, the girl's vulnerability outweighed his.

"They warned me of the storm," he said quietly. "The Voyani did. They would not stay within the village, or within the Green Valley itself. They warned me to watch the serafs and to protect the children that might be used against us," he added. "But they said they had further word to carry, and that it would not wait."

"They spoke of Essla," Nora said.

"I think, yes, they must have had some glimpse of Essla's fate."

"And how are we to protect ourselves against such a fate?"

He rose and paced the hall in a tight circle. The foreigner still sat, back against the wall, his blade resting between his shins, its hilt across his shoulder. But he also snored loudly.

"I did not think to ask them," he said at last with just a hint of dark humor.

"When was this, husband?"

He shrugged. "The Lady has hidden herself at least once since their passage. They did not come in daylight," he added. "Nora—"

She nodded. "I heard her speak," she told her husband. "And I have no doubt at all that she knew Ashaf. And that she loved her."

"And does the North produce dutiful daughters?"

"I do not know, husband. But I know that Ashaf was of the South, and some part of the South must cling to the child. I will trust her."

"We are meant to," he said darkly. "And it may be that the child trusts herself. But so, too, does the young bearer of plague."

"Daro, what did the Voyani tell you?"

He shook his head, his eyes resting upon the closed screen, as if by force of will he could see beyond the opaque paper. "They told me to be wary of the daughter of the dead," he said quietly. "They said that Russo would stand in her shadow, and if the shadow was too strong, it would be the first of the villages to fall—but not the last."

She reached for his hand, although she looked to the room. "They did not say," she said, before she left him, "that she was the daughter of *our* dead. She is one of us, whether or not we accept it; the village already has."

Meralonne APhaniel knew the Swordsmith at once.

He saw his name, thin and translucent, like a banner above the endless field. Night did not diminish it, and time did not tarnish it. He smiled, but the smile was bitter.

The first time he had laid eyes on Kiriel di'Ashaf, he had counseled the Kings to kill her. She had disarmed that desire, with time, but it returned now, unexpected and strong. *Has she grown in power to such an extent?* he thought. *Does she command you, Anduvin?*

The fear was sudden and sharp. Although he had spent much of the last twenty years anticipating the war to come, none of his careful plans, none of his extrapolations, had encompassed her existence.

Not even in his youth would he have guessed that she could be born and survive the birthing.

Ah, the wind was wailing. Its fury was second to its pain; what the Swordsmith brought to bear changed the whole of its awareness. The Swordsmith was the enemy, here, but he was not the only one.

Telakar also claimed his place in the sky, and the magi could see, drifting upward in a lazy, cautious spiral, the only mortal who had fought this way in millennia: Kallandras of Senniel College.

The Lady marked him this eve.

Meralonne bowed. He had taken time to observe, but the time for observation had ended abruptly.

Lord Nugratz called his name, and he felt it: the Challenge of the *Kialli*. He gave himself over to battle, and his sword fell like lightning against the damp, swirling clouds.

Kinlord, kinlord, and Illaraphaniel.

Nugratz called fire, for fire was his element, and fire came. It did not rest easy in the height of sky, for there was little to burn.

But in Nugratz' experience, that made the fire keen, and its voice and desire were driven by desperation. For if there was little to burn, it made the burning necessary.

He let it go, and it took form and shape, growing wings that gave off enough heat on which to rise.

His pinions flexed and stretched; the cold did not trouble them, but the lack of the air on which they might rise had. He would not dive now; he could not give in to frenzy. He was of the Lord's Fist, and he had not gained his position by surrender.

Not even to himself.

Kallandras knew the moment the fire was summoned. He had enough time to change the direction of his awkward flight before he felt it burn, and he saw a Serpent rise, water steaming into nothing against the folds of its translucent skin.

It was not careful; it devoured, whole, the lesser servants of Nugratz—and he sacrificed them; they were pawns.

But Kallandras had no desire to feed the flame, and the sudden scream of the wind told him clearly why Nugratz had summoned the fire.

It was hard to fight on two fronts.

And everyone whose flight now depended on air was forced to do just that. The wind desired combat with the fire—and only the fire. Every other imperative was beneath its contempt.

The *Kialli* did not seem to notice, and Meralonne APhaniel was high enough in the storm that the bard could no longer see him.

He weighed his choices carefully, and then, with regret, he sheathed the blades. They struggled—as wind did—in his hands, and he bent them to his will; they went, unblooded and unsatisfied, to their casings.

To the wind he gave voice, but first he asked it to return him groundward; he could not control it on two fronts.

Let the others deal with the demons.

He threw back his head, exposing throat, and he sang the wind up, the words a benediction and a grace. The diamond that was the heart of Myrddion's ring grew white, too bright to gaze at long. And it burned. The scars that lay beneath its bands had healed, but he knew that this night they would blister and bleed again, if he was lucky.

If he was unlucky, he would lose the use of the hand.

But he chose to test luck; he summoned the air in its full force, and it came. To him.

Look, he told it, his voice dwarfed by its howl. *Look well. Your enemy has gained the sky; will you surrender your demesne to his dominion?*

And the wind answered, cooling the hand now hot to the touch: It roared and rose.

He imagined that he could see wings in the way that the fall of water shifted; that he could see a long neck, a great and terrible serpent's head, a tail that lashed out and destroyed what it could reach.

But it was simple bardic fancy; the wind needed no form. That was a conceit of lesser elements.

The *Kialli* were thrown across the length of the village in all directions by the impact of wild air and wild fire. Swords that had been raised now foundered, shorn of moorings; had they been mortal swords, they would have fallen.

But they were made *of* the lords that wielded them, and not to such a simple shock were they lost.

Nugratz, free now of the need to contain the wind, had the advantage. He turned, circling, and he came down, his talons shifting as he drifted.

He struck Anduvin in the back, and he felt armor give, and the flesh beneath it. But it was not a killing blow; Anduvin had the wind again, and it offered no resistance; he was driven back from the death that Nugratz threatened, and he found his feet just above the height of the great tree that alone still spoke of the village below.

Fire had blackened its bowers, and the leaves had been shorn from branches, but it was firmly rooted; it did not bend or bow; it did not break.

He touched the branches, and he heard their protest; knew again what he was, and what he was not.

But he spoke a name the tree understood, and if it was spoken in a voice heavy with taint and death, it had power. The tree bore his weight.

It served as his anchor; the wind clamored for freedom; the fire was too strong.

Nugratz would tire before the fire did.

But not, perhaps, before the Swordsmith, wed to the form he had chosen. He bled, and something about the wound was comforting.

Telakar took Nugratz from above, damaging his wings. The sword's arc was wild; the footing in the skies was treacherous as quicksand, and it waited to devour—or dislodge—the unwary.

Those like Nugratz who had wings now had the advantage, but they lacked power. Telakar reminded them of this, to their cost.

But the scent of smoking branches was almost overpowering; the winds were so strong they bore all else away. He banked, the wind too wild, and he, too, found some stability in the branches of the tree; branches that were already dying high above the ground that sustained them.

He let the wind go; let it seek the fire that was its natural enemy. One of three: those who sought to tease it by the hint of command were now beneath its notice.

What the others could not do, Meralonne did.

The tree heard his voice, and it understood the whole of his command. But he was not Telakar, not Anduvin; what he remembered, the great tree remembered. It rose, gaining substance and weight, its trunk widening in the storm.

Branches that were blackened and unadorned stiffened and straightened like thorns or spikes; they could not be navigated with ease by the winged, for they grew too close.

He had thought to use a different power this eve, but this was just: the pure tree, the untainted tree, was a fitting weapon against those who had taken the seeds of Winter and planted them during Summer's height.

The *Kialli* died in numbers, their bodies dissolving like ash in the winds.

And Nugratz, falling, cut the magi's shoulder from joint to blade, exposing everything that lay above it: muscle, vein, flesh. The armor that he had chosen was not proof against the shadow, and it smoked like dry branches.

The sword, he called back, absorbing its power before it could fall; to lose the sword was death, either here or later, and he had no desire to die.

Not when the end seemed so close.

But the tree stiffened, and the limbs that had served as stakes bent again into a more natural shape.

He could not reach the wound; not to staunch the flow of blood. It mingled and fell groundward, heavy with water. He wondered what color it would be before the damp ground swallowed it.

And he smiled.

The Old Earth slept.

Very little touched it or disturbed it.

But not nothing. Above it, the air and the fire joined in battle, and their voices were loud. They were not—quite—enough to wake it from its slumber. But blood fell in their wake, and it was a blood that had been tasted and tested before; it had the authority of the ages in the certainty of its fall.

Death?

No.

The ground shook as the earth stirred.

Kiriel di'Ashaf rose. The cold had not left her; the fires had not banked. But beneath her feet she felt the storm, and its voice sent her out the doors.

She barely remembered to open them. They were not the doors of her youth; they slid, instead of swinging, and they were almost silent.

She tripped over Auralis, and her weight woke him.

"Kiriel?"

Daro di'Valente and his wife looked up from their perch on the stairs. Low stairs, and flat, they were seldom seen in Southern homes. Funny thing, to think that now.

She shook as she walked.

Her feet left the ground.

"Where do you think you're going?" Auralis said, lips to her ear. Without the storm to drown them out, the words were loud.

But not so loud as the grumbling beneath her feet.

"Out," she told him.

Nora en'Valente rose as well. "Kiriel," she said softly. "The storm still rages." She reached out, and her exhalation was almost sibilant. "You must return to your room. You are not well."

But Kiriel shook her head fiercely. "I have to go," she said to the old woman. "You built this house on stone."

The words made no sense to Nora en'Valente; this much was clear. She turned to her husband.

Ser Daro di'Valente said, "The ground is shaking, wife. Can you not feel it?"

"What of it?"

He shook his head, and when he stood, he pushed his wife gently but firmly to one side. "Come, Kiriel. If you dare the storm, I will go with you."

Kiriel shook her head. "Not you," she said.

"There is no one else."

"Send Auralis."

"Auralis? Ah, the Northerner." Daro looked up, beyond her shoulder, and then back to her face. "What must you do?"

She said, "I don't know. But—I have to go."

He nodded. His wife's outraged squeak was all of her reply; something about his expression stifled what would have certainly followed. But as he led Kiriel back down the hall to the door, he said, "When you have finished, return. There will be a place for you here."

Nugratz tried, and failed, to have the tree destroyed.

What attention the fire would spare him—and it did, but so grudgingly now, the attempt to communicate put him at risk—

was paltry; a tendril of flame leaped from the edge of its wing to the tree's trunk.

It should have been enough.

Not even Illaraphaniel would dare to wake water here, in the presence of fire and air.

But the tree did not burn.

And as fire touched it, something shimmered around the whole of its girth.

Lightning struck the fire's heart.

He roared in fury, for he recognized the signature behind that sudden defense: Anya a'Cooper. She had somehow granted this tree her protection.

He had not the power to bring the spell down.

Not and fight.

Perhaps not at all.

The earth rose slowly.

Meralonne APhaniel felt its rumble reach up from the tree's roots to its heights.

From the recesses of a theater made of bare branches against the backdrop of elemental roar, the Swordsmith spoke. "Illaraphaniel."

Meralonne's smile was grim. "Nugratz has grown in power," he said.

"Or you have weakened," Anduvin replied. "You feel the loss of your shield, here."

The magi shrugged. It was foolish and painful, but it was not without reason. The wound would take time to close; let it be useful while it still bled.

Lord Telakar spoke as well. "We are hampered by form. But not by wit. Illaraphaniel, are you certain of the wisdom of your action?"

"I am certain that it is unwise."

"Ah."

"But necessary."

"You seek to uproot the saplings," Anduvin said.

Meralonne's brows rose. Even here, even damped by the endless fall of twisting rain, that much could clearly be seen. He did not reply.

Telakar said, "The village will be destroyed."

"The village is not at the border of the Terrean." He did not otherwise disagree. Gray eyes met dark ones; knowledge passed between them.

"What is a Terrean?" Anduvin asked. "To the earth, what is a Terrean?"

"It is the land bounded by the Winter trees," Meralonne replied.
"It is a land bounded by their voices. What we cannot hear, it will
hear. What we cannot stop, it can."

"If it so chooses, Illaraphaniel."

"If it so chooses."

"And if it does not?"

The magi shrugged. Blood fell.

He listened for the last of the voices.

Unexpectedly, Telakar said, "Kiriel will know."

The words disarmed him a moment; they made little sense. But
as the wind gathered itself, it released the edges of storm, and the
rain's fall gentled. He saw where Lord Telakar looked.

And shrugged. "It is a village," he said softly. "Once. What we
lose, if the earth does not heed us—"

And Telakar said, "No."

She cleared the stone frame and the storm's voice was hushed.
Spinning, she turned to look back, but Daro di'Valente was there,
and the building that he called home had not suddenly shifted in
place. She was in Russo. The Green Valley still waited.

Her feet were cold. Her arms shook.

She reached for the pendant and held it aloft. The winds did not
touch it. The rains did not fall upon its exposed facets. Its light was
steady and warm.

She whispered Ashaf's name, but the pendant was silent. Ashaf
had no memory of this, and no advice could be found in the memories she had hoarded. Only fear, and Kiriel knew that fear would
teach her nothing.

But she did not set the pendant aside.

Failure was measured by the memories it contained. And it contained, in some fashion, the whole of the valley.

She bent, and her fingers slid uselessly off the folded lip of wet
leather. She had not donned her armor, and she regretted it; cloth,
made heavy by rain, clung to her, impeding movement.

"Auralis," she whispered.

He stared at her as if she were mad.

But he understood what she asked of him, and after a moment,
he complied. He helped her remove the only things that protected
her feet.

She set feet against the earth, and found it unexpectedly warm.

It was no comfort.

*   *   *

"No?"

"No."

Meralonne gripped branches in his hands. Nugratz was waiting, but the tree, where Meralonne touched it, confounded the reach of his wings. He could fold them and join his sundered brethren among its tines, or he could wait.

He chose, for the moment, to wait.

Costly moment.

"And how will you stop me, Lord Telakar? The earth will not bear your touch for long; do you think it will listen to your words?"

"You did not hear her command," Telakar said quietly. "We are to preserve the village. It is the only thing that drives her."

"This village?"

"Just this. Go West," he said. "Or East. Go North or South. But do not call the earth here. What it demands as price for parley, she will not pay."

"And you?"

Lord Telakar bowed. There was reluctant menace in the elegance of the gesture.

"She does not understand the cost of failure," the magi said coldly. "You do."

"We measure failure in different ways, Illaraphaniel. The Lord is not present upon this field. *She* is. And she is Queen here."

The word, the single word, numbed his hands.

"Queen?" he asked.

"Queen of the Hells," Telakar replied, his words gentled by regret, his expression sharpened.

CHAPTER TWENTY-TWO

RAGGED Queen, and cold, unaware of the honor conferred on her, she stood upon the flat of the valley. Above her, the tree's branches kept time with the wind that had inexplicably gentled.

She did not know where its ferocity lay, although she thought she could hear its voice. She only knew that the rains fell straight, a beaded, continuous curtain from sky to earth.

And it was to earth that she went, as if she were already dead. Her feet found it first, and her toes sank into the dirt dislodged by the rivulets that had begun to worry the short roots of the weeds it harbored.

Her knees met it next as she stumbled, partly by accident and partly by design. They sank an inch, and then stayed, shoring her up.

Auralis, boots heavy, breath mist, was by her side. Still by her side. He carried his shield, but his sword was sheathed; she could see him so clearly he might have been the only other person alive.

But she could see him by the light the ring on his hand gave off; it was deeper than the flames of the lantern Daro held.

Daro had not closed the door. He was judge here, and witness.

"Auralis—"

But his eyes were narrowed; the ring had also caught his attention, and held the whole of it now.

He lowered his hand, his left hand; the shield, he held with his right. But the rain was an afterthought. "Kiriel."

She nodded. Her hands found the earth next, her palms flat, her fingers splayed wide to support the rest of her weight. The pendant hung loose, hovering above the wet, wet ground. She watched the path it traced, and willed herself to retrieve it; her hands, mired in mud, disobeyed.

Auralis looked up. And up. She could see his Adam's apple rise and fall as he swallowed; his throat was exposed. She had never seen it so clearly before; it was almost white. "I can see the fire," he whispered.

She couldn't. She saw the ruby instead.

He said, "I can hear its voice." And then, after a moment, added, "It's pissed off."

"Maybe," she told him, her elbows bending, "it doesn't like the rain." It was the last thing she said before her chest hit the ground with a wet slap.

She lay across it like a meager blanket, threadbare, inadequate. The rain had blended with so many things the cloying scent of earth was sweet. If she opened her mouth, she could taste it, but she feared to do so.

For she felt the edges of the pendant against her, and they were sharp and hard. Warmth had fled, and with it, silence; she could *hear* voices.

She could almost understand them, and it frightened her.

Never show fear.

Isladar's voice. She hated it, but she could feel the lines of her face conforming to the oldest of his commands, the first of his lessons. As if the pendant had eyes. As if it could see.

None of the voices were Ashaf's.

They were harsher than Ashaf's had ever been, even in anger. They were older. They were shorn of mercy.

But not of wisdom.

Daughter, they said.

She shook her head. Her cheeks tore wide-leafed plants free of their moorings, and they clung to her pale skin like a mask.

The earth moved beneath her.

As if she were already a corpse, it *moved.* She wanted to shout. She wanted to call Auralis. But more than either, she wanted to keep her lips closed, because if she swallowed dirt, the earth would be inside her.

Instead, she was inside it. It swallowed, and she fell.

"Too late," Meralonne APhaniel said.

Telakar leaped.

The magi leaped as well, but lightly, his footing sure. Nugratz cast a shadow in the fire's light, and it fell as a warning to them all.

Anduvin was still. His sword flared briefly in the night sky, and then it was gone. "Telakar!" he shouted.

Lord Telakar turned.

"He is correct."

Lord Telakar stiffened.

"There is nothing we can do now but wait."

Yet even as he spoke, the fire turned, the wide wings of its flames banking. As if it heard the earth's voice, from the distance of the heights, it began to descend.

Nugratz roared in fury.

But the power in his voice only slowed the flames he had summoned. And the wind harried it, shearing its plumes as if they were flight feathers.

Kallandras turned. His feet felt the movement of earth, but it was not the earth that concerned him.

Across the width of Russo, he saw the flash of ruby light; it encompassed the whole of his vision, lending the landscape its august, reddened glow.

The storm did not diminish it; instead, its outer edges were lit in a fine mist that spread outward, bleeding at last into night gray.

He gazed at his hand, and saw that the light that flared upon the bands of Myrddion's ring now pulsed, as if waiting.

And he knew, then, that he was not alone.

He looked up, and saw that the fire—and therefore the battle—was descending through the clouds, and he turned and ran, his footing sure, his step light enough that a moment's rain washed all existence of its presence away.

Auralis stared at the ground.

Kiriel was gone. He had turned his face skyward for just a moment. Just one. But that had been enough.

"Kiriel!"

The thunder was louder than the word, but it did not linger; his cry reverberated in the sudden stillness. He bent with care, dislodging his feet from the too soft earth.

There, he thought, his palm flat. She had been there.

Or there.

The rain hissed.

He straightened, turned, and froze.

The light had descended from the heights, and it hovered a tree's span above Russo; it was red, orange, yellow; its heart was blue.

And it had taken the shape of a Serpent, a legend that now roared, evaporating water as it fell. He swore. That came easily to him. But although his hand found the hilt of his sword, he did not draw it.

Beneath the fire, he saw a lone figure making its way across the terrain as if chased by the demons that they had not found within the village.

"AKalakar!"

He knew the voice. Didn't much like it, but he knew it. And as he had no way to respond, he waited while the figure drew closer. Kallandras of Senniel College, master bard, was dressed in dark clothing; the night should have hidden him.

But fire exposed what the night held close.

Fire turned to follow him as he ran.

An instant before flame gouted in breath from a Serpent's jaw, he shouted a single word.

And he felt *pain* as the ring tightened about his finger.

Flame fell, but it fell just short of its target.

Kallandras rolled across the wet ground, came up on his feet, and continued to sprint. He had made his choice; had called upon his reserves; nothing less than death would stop him.

But he felt the wind's anger as he ran; felt its sudden descent.

The fire would hold sway for only a moment longer; it would be pulled apart by the storm he had summoned.

Or not.

What had Meralonne said? The wild magics. The wild magics. Fire to burn, water to drown, earth to bury—and air? He could not remember. It was his element. He was part of its voice. Hard, now, to separate the two. But necessary.

He had had decades in which to practice.

And Auralis AKalakar had minutes.

It came to him slowly as the pain subsided that the fire could understand him. Or that he could understand the fire. *The ring*, he thought, wild now. His ringless hand clawed at it, trying to separate its bands from his skin. But he had no more luck, now that he had some knowledge of its purpose, than he had had in ignorance; the ring held fast.

He slammed his hand against the ground, and it hit the inner curve of his shield. He'd dropped it. He didn't remember when.

The fire spoke, and all of the cold that had seeped in slowly with water and night wind disappeared in its lambent heat.

But although he could understand the sense of its voice, he could not force what he heard into words. Something to be grateful for. Later.

Fire shrieked in fury, and he felt the wind press against its mighty wings; flames, small and inconsequential, were sheared from its bulk, and they fell.

Where they fell, they burned.

He had seen magefire once in his life. No, more than once—but it had all been contained in the Averdan valleys. He cursed them. Cursed the Annies. Cursed the kin.

But cursing, hating them, delighting a moment in the sudden flare of thatch on roof, the sudden incineration of the flatland weeds, he struggled to find a voice like the fire's—because he knew that only that voice would be heeded.

How?

Magic, gods. He hated magic. *Hated* it.

He asked the fire what in the Hells it was doing. It was not a command.

But the fire heeded the question with a snarl and a hiss of smoking water. Fighting. Fighting to gain dominion of the things it most hated: the air. The earth.

Air? If the fire had been an Osprey, he would have questioned its sanity. But the fire fought, and as it did, he could see—in the absence of flame—that the air did indeed offer combat.

Beneath his feet, the ground trembled.

Not here! he shouted. Trees caught flame, were adorned by its glow as his hand was adorned by the ring. But they blackened and twisted, and the fire that had destroyed them began to crawl across the land.

It was *wet.*

Fire couldn't burn wet wood. Lord knows he'd learned that the hard way, and he'd only ever tried new wood.

You're too damn impatient, boy, his father said.

He froze.

Too damn impatient. You want a fire? Find a dead tree. You've done nothing good with that ax today.

Da?

But the voice was silent. Memory.

And in the wake of that memory, worse ones would follow. He needed a drink. He needed sleep. He needed a fight.

A fight?

Aic, his hand burned.

Kallandras of Senniel College peeled away in layers. What lay exposed was both older and younger.

For the man had been a young man, and the young man, a boy. The boy had often asked questions of anyone who would sit still for long enough to hear them. The old. The sick. His father.

The young boy had learned, quickly, that there were some things that were *never* questioned. And the young man had been too angry to expose what the boy had never completely surrendered: curiosity.

He was neither boy nor young man now.

Nor was he *Kovaschaii,* although he could hear the names of his brothers—the men who would have been his brothers—if he listened. They joined his song, when he was too weak to distance himself.

Tonight, he could not afford weakness.

He forced them away.

Not bard, here. Not assassin.

But men were defined, in his experience, by what they *did.*

In the South, he had been offered life by a stranger in the streets of the Tor Leonne. He had been desperate, hunted, and in need of shelter. He had accepted the offer, and had found a home in

Melesnea, the labyrinths of the *Kovaschaii.* Later, in the streets of *Averalaan Aramarelas,* he had been offered a room in the vast halls of Senniel, and this, too, he had accepted, too numbed by loss and grief to question.

And in the desert, he had been offered what he most craved: A brother in arms. Lord Celleriant. Yet even that, he had accepted.

Tonight, for the first time in decades, he asked the gods *why.*

Why Auralis AKalakar?

Why a man whose allegiance to life was so slender he tested it again and again in the meanest of city streets?

Kallandras had not often spoken with the Osprey, but as he had been taught in so many of his lives, he had listened. Only in Kiriel di'Ashaf could he hear a more certain death.

Asking questions of the gods had never been satisfactory; it was less so now. He ran as the fire spread across the boundaries of the forest.

Kiriel forgotten, Auralis *ran.*

Not away from the fire, but toward it. His sword slapped his thighs, and he almost threw it away in disgust; it was either that or draw it.

Something forced him to hold his hand, some instinct that was older than the memory that had bitten him. He obeyed because to argue meant to stop, and to stop meant death.

Why do you care?

No.

Why do you care now? You ran once. You broke every oath you valued, every oath you made, to run.

Shut up. Shut up shut up shut up.

The fire raged, but he had swallowed it; it burned him from within. And that was fine with Auralis AKalakar, bronze godling of the Ospreys.

He reached the first of the burning homes.

Heard the screams of the people, waking from slumber into nightmare, and from nightmare into painful death.

These are Kiriel's people.

These are Callestan people.

These are the men and women who would have hunted you down and made carrion fodder of you and your men with pitchforks and crude spears.

Why do you care?

It almost worked.

But struggling from the lee of the fire came a small girl. Not a woman, and not a girl old enough to be to his jaded taste; she was prepubescent, her body slim as sapling, dark with sun.

Her eyes were wide, and her hair was tousled; her face was black with smoke.

And in her arms, coughing and howling, she dragged a younger child. He could not tell, in the dim light, if that child was girl or boy.

She looked up as she saw him, and she raised her voice in what should have been a scream. This, too, he had seen. In a dozen villages. In a different life.

His sword.

His sword was in its sheath.

He could draw it and end this now. He'd done it before.

But she babbled at him. Her voice was ragged with plea. He could not understand her words.

No.

That was a lie.

He *could not* understand Torra.

But whatever it was she spoke, he heard it clearly.

"My mother and father—my sister—my brothers—" She lifted an arm, and the squirming child bit the hand that still clung to its shoulder.

In fire's light, he saw blood.

But although she winced, she did not let go.

"Please—please—help them!"

Help?

"Don't you know what I am?" he shouted. But he had no shield, and his sword was nascent. He grabbed her roughly by the shoulder and lifted his hand.

He meant to strike her.

Cartanis' oath, he meant to.

But instead, he clipped her on the ear, and the brother's eyes widened in shock; he went still.

"Get him out!" he yelled. "Take him—take him to Daro. *Now.*"

As if he were bard-born and wielded voice as a weapon, she obeyed, leaving him before the stage of the burning house. As if she had understood his Weston. As if she could speak it.

No, that was wrong. The ring was wrong. The fact that the girl still *lived*—all wrong.

He had lit just such a fire before.

Fiara had stood by his side. Alexis had stood at his back. He had had oil in his hands, and in his nostrils, and all the words that his father—or mother—might have said to guide him had died that night; they had never had words with which to encompass the act.

Later, he had done other damage.

It rode him now.

We won the war for them, he thought. *What we did—it won the war. We proved that we were men enough—*

Lies, of course. All of it. Lies.

Someone had cared enough to make it truth.

Someone had arranged for an ambush in the Averdan valleys. Someone had neatly cut off the Ospreys on three sides, and swords had come down like scythes in the press of their bodies, their sudden grim panic.

Truth?

He had meant to die that day.

Of the Ospreys present, he alone had lifted voice in a wild, wild laugh. He had drawn his sword, and had tossed aside his shield; he had lifted a dagger in his shield hand and he had leaped into the nearest flank of cerdan.

Death would have been a mercy. Because there was no way he could run; nowhere he could run to. All that was left him was to stand and face it.

And he had faced it, and he had lost. He had survived.

Facing the fire, and all that it spoke of, he knew that death would have been a mercy. And of course, mercy was to be denied him always. Mercy was *earned*.

From inside the hut, he heard a choking wail. He heard a scream. A shout, a panicked older voice. Man's voice.

He had set this fire.

Gods curse him.

Gods curse them.

The screens had been shoved aside a crack by the girl in her flight. She'd been smart. Or close enough to the doors to flee.

Auralis did not fear death. But he wasn't fond of pain. And fire was a painful death.

He had no wet cloth with which to gird his mouth and lips; nothing to protect his lungs.

Clay and dirt and stone had been mixed in a poor man's jumble; it was the wood that gave first. But wood held up the ceiling—or it had—and the thatched flat had listed badly in the center.

Auralis AKalakar grimaced, and drawing breath, he lifted his foot and planted it through the screen.

*　*　*

The ground was shaking now.

Kallandras leaped from foothold to foothold, wondering when the earth would open. He felt what the wind felt, and he knew that he should be running in any other direction.

The wind offered him safety.

He could not afford to take it.

He could see Auralis AKalakar's back, made dark by the light before it. He saw the Osprey kick the screen; saw the screen shatter.

"Not that way!"

But Auralis was gone.

The war with the Annies did not drive him.

He had come to it, bitter and full of self-loathing, and it had embraced him. He had almost found a brief home for himself on the gallows before the Ospreys had unfurled their wings and offered him flight.

He should have refused them; he knew what they were. They had come to the gallows, same as Auralis, and their reasons made them just as suspect.

He had never thought to like them. He had never thought that they would become family; men—and women—like that were just as likely to murder their kin as fight for them. Probably had.

But something had driven him *to* the war.

And he had embraced that war, sinking into the darkness of innumerable acts as if to acknowledge with each the truth that he had discovered about himself.

Where was that truth now?

The truth? It had changed the day that Sanderton had been given the colors. He just hadn't seen it clearly.

He kicked down walls and they splintered, centers shattering like coated glass; the fire had weakened them.

Why it hadn't destroyed them utterly, he wasn't certain; he had seen what the flames had done to the trees, and it was quick and ugly.

He found the man and his wife first. They were huddled—like mindless fools—in the farthest corner from the flames. He felt a contempt that words couldn't embrace, and he almost left them. Almost.

But he saw that the man's arms held the woman tight; that she was struggling against him, her voice raised in a piercing, terrible shriek.

It stopped when she saw him, framed by the shattered door.

"Get up," he said roughly. He had said it before.

And he had followed its obedience with a brutal death. With tens of such deaths, daring smoke and flame.

"Get up!"

He kicked the mats aside and walked toward them.

The woman stilled. The man rose. Seraf, he, muscled by years in the field with no excess to fatten him. His skin was dark, but his face was pale; it was an odd combination.

"Your daughter is outside with your son," he said. It was not what he'd intended to say. "She needs you. Both of you. The boy is mad. *Go.*"

The man hesitated; he didn't trust Auralis.

Which meant he wasn't stupid.

"Go," Auralis said, "or die here."

The woman said, "My children—"

"There are three. Here. I'll find them. But you'll get in the way, and you'll kill them if you do. Your choice."

She grabbed the blanket at her feet. Drew it about her as if it were armor. Her arm shook as she caught her husband's hand. But she had made her choice.

He left them.

Kallandras called the wind, and it fought him.

He was prepared for it, and he paid, abstracting pain.

He set the air upon the roof of the nearest house, and it savaged the flames rooted there.

In bardic voice, he called the inhabitants out.

He had just enough time to do that before the fire descended again.

Auralis found the children in a room that was being devoured by flame. They were huddled, as their parents had been, in the room's corner—but they had cause; the door was gone, and the walls were on fire. He felt the heat, and he lifted an arm to his face to protect himself.

Drawing breath, he charged through the flames.

They didn't burn.

The flames didn't. Memory did.

Three children. Younger than the girl and the boy who had struggled their way to such dubious safety. A boy of maybe five looked up. He had thrown his body across the others, for all the good it would do; his hair was long and sweat had matted it to his forehead. A girl of three lay beneath him, and beside her, a child who might—with luck—be able to walk a few unsteady steps.

Packed like rats in the hundred holdings, their dark eyes reflected fire light.

But they saw him.

The boy was coughing.

The girl was crying, and the child beside her was unconscious.

But they lived; that was enough. He approached them with less contempt than he had their parents.

"Boy," he said, to the oldest.

The child nodded, eyes wide.

"The fire will kill you all if you don't do exactly what I tell you to do."

The boy nodded again. But when he rose, he caught his siblings in either hand, and only when he tried to lift the youngest did his expression shift into panic.

They didn't have time. A beam dropped at Auralis' back; he heard it crackle as fire at last consumed it. No time.

No safety.

Reaching down, he lifted the two younger children. To the boy, he said, "hold on to my leg. Stand on my foot. No matter what you hear or see— No, wait. Close your eyes. Hold my leg, boy, and close your eyes."

The boy swallowed.

But he wrapped his arms—his tiny, reedlike arms—around Auralis' thigh, stepped onto the flat of his upper foot, and clenched his shaking fists. His eyes closed; his lashes, dark and curled like a girl's, trembled.

Auralis AKalakar, burdened in a way he had never thought to be burdened again, walked through the fire.

For a second time, the fire failed to touch him.

Kallandras accepted the inevitable.

He could not impede fire's progress if he wished to save the whole of the village; the wind, fighting him, could not also fight the element that would, if it touched the ground, incinerate everything that stood in its path for as far as the eye could see.

He had saved what he could.

He left the rest to the gods, and let the wind go.

They were waiting for Auralis.

Mother and father. The girl and boy had obeyed his command; they were nowhere to be seen.

He handed the two children to the father; to the mother, he gave the oldest of the boys. He had to struggle to unlock the child's hands; lack of blood had twisted his fingers into a vise.

The mother fell to her knees when her son was given to her. Her eyes were wet with the tears that she had refused to shed; even now, she held them back.

It was almost too much for him. He had played a game, here. He had pretended to be a hero.

But he failed, again, to end it. "Go to Daro," he said.

"But you—"

He turned toward the other homes. Three more were burning. They were farther away, and he thought, with luck, he might reach them in time.

But Kalliaris was a poor Lady; always had been.

As he watched, a roof collapsed.

He set off at a run; the village serafs whose lives he had just saved were already just another part of his history.

And beneath the earth, Kiriel di'Ashaf was waking.

The roof had collapsed. No one had left the building. It was too much to hope that he could be of aid here.

Hope? The word was a sneer. His sneer.

Shut up, he said wearily.

Flamed gouted from beneath the sliding door, and he lifted his foot. Saw the flames lap leather, pulling at it. Playing.

The ring hurt his hand.

He snarled and slammed his fist into the wall; it buckled, but did not give.

No, he said to the fire. *Not these.*

Realized that he had been saying those words the entire time he had walked through the burning home.

If he stopped saying them, the ring would stop hurting; they were twined, and not in a pleasant way. But he was used to pain, and he grunted as if in pleasure.

He walked through the fire.

And although the fire was hot, he felt its heat at a distance.

He found the four people who lived here, and in twos, he dragged them out. As long as he held them, the fire veered; it lapped above and around them, but it couldn't grab hold.

Daro di'Valente stood in the storm.

He saw the fire, and more, he saw the Northerner enter the homes that were burning at the storm's eye. His wife was busy; in ones and twos, the villagers who had been rescued from certain death made his home theirs; Nora tended them, opening up the halls that were kept for the Tor and his men.

The Tor'agar would not have grudged her her choice. Ser Daro did not. He spared it thought, but only a little; his attention was split between the fires and the search.

But although he looked, he could not see where Kiriel di'Ashaf had gone.

The Ospreys had razed a village.

It came to him clearly, as clearly as the fire. They had burned it, slowly, to the ground. The people who had escaped death by fire had not escaped them, and although fire was a terrible death, Auralis was not certain that they had been better off.

He held a wailing babe in his arms, and the temptation to drop it was strong.

But he also held the mother close. Her arm was broken; a beam had struck her, pinning her. She bled, and her eyes were wide with shock; he was amazed that she could move at all.

But the imperative of her child—her only child—kept her going; he thought such a force might animate the dead, if the dead could hear.

What would Fiara say, if she could see him now?

Had he not gone to her to tell her that the evening's work meant the death of children exactly as young as this one?

And she could do it.

He had seen her do it.

He had done it himself.

He stumbled; the woman's strength shored him up. He cursed her, and she understood everything he said, but she kept him moving.

She should have been afraid of him.

He wanted her fear.

But something else had intruded upon the life he had built, and it was breaking him; he had stepped into the fire, had been baptized by it. What he would be when he emerged, he couldn't say.

But he intended to emerge.

The wind battered the fire, and the flames that had made their progress through rain drenched thatch banked as the element turned its attention to its ancient enemy.

Kallandras whispered a benediction to the wind. It was an offering, and because the battle was so close, the wind accepted it.

But the bard's hand bled.

The earth shook again.

The last house.

Auralis stepped into it as if it were a bonfire.

It was. But he knew what he would find: its inhabitants, surrounded by flame, but as yet unharmed. Because he commanded it. Because he desired it.

Where had that desire been, a dozen years past?

He had found it, in glimpses, with the Ospreys. He had used what little of it there was to save Valedan kai di'Leonne, a boy he had thought to despise.

Had been ambushed by it, time and again, in the company of Kiriel di'Ashaf.

But he had never given thought to the lives of strangers. Not since he had fled his home had he done so.

It hurt, to come into it again in such an unexpected fashion.

You wanted a fight.

Yes, I wanted a fight. But not this one.

He gathered these serafs in ones and twos, his arms bearing the whole of their weight. They were heavy, but they were not as heavy as Kiriel had been, and he carried them because—

Kiriel.

He carried the people out. They were unconscious, and the rain failed to wake them. He wondered if anything would. He stood, cursing them, the water billowing from his face and shoulders in a cloud that sizzled.

And a man spoke.

"Leave them with me," he said softly.

Auralis looked up and saw fire. It was contained beneath the safe curve of glass, sheltered from wind and the rain, but it burned. Slept. He could wake it with a word.

"Leave them," Ser Daro di'Valente said, the words now slow and distinct, as if he spoke to a child.

Auralis didn't tell him that he understood.

Instead, he handed the last of his burdens to the man who would bear them all; the man's arms tightened as if the child were his own.

"Where is Kiriel?" Auralis said.

If Ser Daro di'Valente was surprised at the clarity of the question, he did not show it; his face was pressed into the child's, his fingers at its neck.

But he answered. "I do not know. She fell," he added. "And the earth swallowed her."

Auralis nodded grimly. He started to walk, and the village headman called him.

He stopped, but he did not turn back.

"Thank you, Northerner."

"Don't," Auralis said sharply. "Save your thanks for her. She needs them. I don't." *And I don't want them,* he added silently.

But he was no longer certain that that was the truth, and he hated himself for it.

He left Ser Daro at a run, and his feet fell heavily, the mud lapping at his ankles. He cursed as he pulled them out; cursed as he put them down; he made a litany that accompanied his movements like a dirge.

The earth spoke.

She heard it. She could not move at all, either to attack or defend herself; the earth surrounded her. Here, water was taken at need, but the fire and the wind were abjured; the earth needed neither to live.

And she needed both.

Who calls me?

Not me.

If she could have, she would have trapped the words. But the earth had a majesty that she had seen only in one other thing in her life, and she had no strength with which to defy it.

Not when she lay in its presence, prone as if obeisance were her natural posture.

Blood has been offered.

Blood has been accepted.

Who calls me?

She said, *I don't know. I can't see anything but you.*

And the earth trembled, moving her limbs. She thought they would break with the sudden pressure.

But, daughter, I hear your voice.

She said, her lips clenched shut against invasion, *I hear yours. I hear theirs. I have summoned nothing.*

The price has not been paid.

She understood this. Understood it not in words, and not by the instinct which had kept her alive in any battle she had chosen, but by something older.

By blood.

But the offer has been made. What do you seek?

There was nothing comforting in the voice. After a moment, her legs bent toward her chest; the earth had folded again. She felt herself held in its great hand, exposed and examined.

You are god-born, it said.

She could not nod. But she said, *I am.*

Have all the gods returned?

The voice, old, held its first hint of anger.

Only one.

The silence, broken by the movement of earth, continued. The earth did not speak quickly. But it spoke. She would remember its voice when all other voices had faded. Even Ashaf's. Even hers.

She thought of Ashaf then.

Thought that Ashaf's dead were all here, in the hand of the earth, and that they were loved in spite of it.

What do you wish, Daughter of Darkness? I have accepted the gift of your father. I have taken the seedlings into my body, and I have made them a part of my flesh.

She said, *Uproot them.*

And earth said, **Pay the price, and I will accede. Their presence is not to my liking.**

What price? she asked. But she knew, or thought she knew.

Each seed was given me in the lifeblood of a mortal. Give me a life for each seed.

She would have. She would have made the offer gladly.

Instead she said, *Not all mortals are equal.*

Clever child.

I hear the fire's voice. I hear the wind. I will end them now.

She could hear neither. But she surged up and the ground moved, and she understood what this meant. The village was rising, or some part of the earth beneath it. And she was certain that the village itself would not survive.

Ashaf's loved were here.

She did not want to join them.

She had promised that she would not add to them.

But she had no shadow, here, and she did not dare to call it. The cold was in her bones, and the earth had done nothing to warm it.

She said, *No.*

No?

No. I will not pay that price.

The earth's rumble was its laughter. It almost killed her.

You are of the darkness. Why will you preserve this village? In whose name will you sacrifice it?

I will never sacrifice it, she said. Her palms were flat and exposed, and she tried to stretch her fingers out to their full length. It was hard. It was as hard a task as any that Isladar had ever set her.

What she had done with the houses of the village, she now attempted with the body of the earth.

In the heights of the great tree, Meralonne APhaniel frowned.

Anduvin, Swordsmith, was the more sensitive of the two *Kialli* lords. "Illaraphaniel?"

"The earth is waking," the magi said softly. "But it does not speak to me."

Anduvin's silver brows rose. "Then to whom?" he asked softly. "There is no other present who has the ability or the knowledge to invoke the Old Earth."

"Not safely," Telakar added bitterly.

Bitterness was no part of Anduvin. He watched and he listened.

"There was no other," the magi said at last. His lips were thinned in frown; whatever it was he heard, the kinlords could not hear, but he did not take the trouble to hide his displeasure.

Nugratz crowed a challenge from the heights.

They could not meet it in safety. The wind and the fire warred beneath them; to summon the one was to strengthen the other.

Nugratz knew it.

He called them by their ancient names, but he did not call them by their hidden ones. And because he could not, they waited.

"It is an odd Queen," Meralonne said coldly, "who has never sat upon the throne."

And Anduvin's brow lifted further; his hair played against his back like a fine, silver cape. He bowed. "She has never taken the throne," he agreed. But the words were as much a challenge as Nugratz' call.

"Then she is not—yet—your lord."

"There are many bindings by which a lord is known," Anduvin replied gravely. "And you have knowledge of several."

"She was not aware," Meralonne said.

"And now, Illaraphaniel?"

But the magi shook his head grimly. "I do not know, Anduvin. What your Lord intended by fathering this one is a mystery to me."

"It is a mystery to all, save perhaps Lord Isladar, and Lord Isladar parts with none of his secrets."

"They are," Telakar added, "the only possession he values."

"He is either canny beyond belief, or foolish beyond belief."

"The two are often similar."

But Meralonne shifted his hold upon the branches of the tree. "I fear, Swordsmith, that I must leave you to your musings."

And without another word, he began to descend. He did not offer his back to Nugratz again; where he moved, the tree moved as well, forming a wall of branches, like the grounded pikes used against the open charge of cavalry.

"Illaraphaniel!"

"I must speak with the earth," the magi said. "And you, I fear, must speak with Nugratz." But he paused and added, "Lord Nugratz is no longer uncontested in his control of his element; there is another voice that speaks to the fire, and it may contest his mastery. Make of this what you will."

The earth stilled.

As the houses had done, it ceased its tremble. She was caught in it, and the lack of movement in the darkness almost undid her.

But what she had begun was begun; no simple fear could end it.

And what had she done?

She said, *Swallow the fire.* She said, *Trap the air.* She said, *Do as you will with them, but do it without destroying those who live upon your surface.*

And what gift am I offered for this task?

But she continued, speaking as if the voice of earth had not reached her, did not reverberate through her prone body. If she had had to use her lips, to force air between them, to shape it with tongue and teeth, no words would have escaped her at all.

I will make you whole.

She felt surprise gather, like storm, slow and ponderous. She felt amusement, the amusement an adult gives a child when the child is indulged.

Almost gently, the earth said, **You are of the darkness, child. Do you not understand what this means? Your blood does not heal; it burns; it fans the flames; it frees the air and wakes the water to drown and destroy. Even I—**

And then there was silence, deep and long.

She thought she would suffocate.

She knew she should have, by now. But the earth had not yet finished with her, and the earth knew—who better?—that the dead did not listen.

What is this?

She could feel its body beneath the flat of her hands. She could feel the roots that pierced its surface; could tell, by their order or their chaotic jumble, which plants those must be. She could measure their length, following their descent as they traveled.

Some, like the great tree, traveled for miles; it had found purchase in the heart of the Old Earth, and when the ground was broken, it would remain.

But others, like the dormant seeds that had been scattered in wobbly rows by mortal hand, would be dislodged whole, their pattern broken and shattered.

Press farther—and she did—and the edge of the village was clear, for the trees bounded it on all sides; they did not encroach upon the cleared lands.

And the lands that were cleared were not of interest to the earth; there was nothing in them that could speak with its voice over the passage of years.

No, she thought. Not nothing.

The dead were here.

They had been laid in troughs and furrows, very near the surface; the digging that had been done in the earth was akin to the scratches the forest inflicted upon those who passed through its thick growth.

But this was the *South*. And if the Southerners lived in ignorance, if they denied the existence of the true gods, and made instead an empty religion that spoke of Lord and Lady, they cleaved to ways older by far than the Empire's enlightened rituals.

They made their offerings.

Daily, weekly, by moontide, they made them.

Sweet water. Wine. And, where the supplicant was not too squeamish, blood.

It was the blood she felt, as wet and new across the distant stretch of fertile land as it had been when it first fell.

Ashaf was old and Ashaf was obedient; Ashaf was diligent. For every birth and every death, she offered the three libations.

And the earth had received them all.

She said, *A price has been paid you.*

The earth's voice was silent.

She said, *For every death suffered by those who live upon your surface, unwary and unheeding, mute and deaf, a price has been paid.*

They made no request of me, the earth said quietly, **and they**

made no offering. But its movement was nonexistent now; she had the whole of its attention.

They made their offerings, she said. *And their offerings were accepted. You protect the fallen. You protect the dead.*

It was not life's blood that was offered.

But it was. She wanted to tell the earth that the whole of Ashaf's life could be traced by the offerings the old woman had made, knees pressed into the unyielding ground, head bowed, neck bent while sun beat down upon her darkening skin.

But she did not offer the earth Ashaf's story. What truth it contained was delicate, and beyond the element's comprehension.

Instead, she said, **It is not the only time that you have guarded things buried.**

And her voice was not her own.

The pendant spoke through her.

"Na'tere," Yollana said quietly.

The Serra Teresa di'Marano looked up. In her lap, a samisen sat mute; she could play it, but she could not accompany it.

Had she been asked to surrender her curse in exchange for Alora's life, she would have done it without thought. Had she been told that she would grieve at its passing, she would have offered the contempt of her silence.

And she would have been wrong. She struggled daily with the inability to hear; it scarred her, shadowing her face. Age had descended, and she had not the power to lift it again.

"Matriarch," she said, a lifetime of grace forcing the response from her still lips.

"We must go to the Green Valley. We must go to Russo."

The rain still fell. The Serra looked up, to where the tarpaulin moved like slack drumskin at water's hand. "Is that wise?" she asked.

Yollana shook her head. "But wisdom and necessity make poor bedfellows, or so it is said."

"In Marano, it is said that wisdom and necessity dance the sword-dance."

Yollana shrugged. "That is not said by the Havallans." She lifted her pouch from the ground and fastened it around her middle, checking for the pipe that the rain would render useless. Habit.

Fear.

She rose. "We must go to Russo."

And Teresa rose as well. "Shall I tell the Tyr'agar?"

"Tell him, if you must; let the wind tell him if you can forgo the customs of your people. We have tarried long."

It was not the first time that the Serra Teresa had seen fear grace the Matriarch's face. But it was the only time that it lingered, weakening her determination.

Making of it something very like desperation.

For the sake of the Dominion, Yollana of Havalla had surrendered both heart and vision; Teresa had surrendered only the talent that had marred the whole of her life.

Grief would have given her the strength to refuse any other companion. Shame, in the presence of Yollana, was stronger.

She bowed to the Matriarch, and then retrieved the old woman's canes from their resting place in her shadow, although she thought they would be of little use; the ground was wet enough that they would sink if weight rested upon their flattened tops.

The earth was silent.

After a moment, it said, **I know you.**

Kiriel struggled to find her own voice. But that voice was lost to the stretch of the earth, to the intricate dance of roots that were changing, constantly, with the passage of time. She could, she found, trace their upward rise; could mark the instant that root gave way to bark, to trunk, to branches that depended upon the soil below, no matter what height they attained.

We know you, Kiriel replied, in a voice that was not her voice. She felt it, though, as if it came from her heart's center. **Daughter,** it whispered.

Gods had a voice such as this.

Old and young. Wise and fey. Feckless and reckless. Terrified and determined. But all of these voices were women's voices; if men were contained in the multitude, they were silent.

This is not your place, the earth said to her. Through her.

No, eldest, it is not. Not ours. It was never meant to be ours. But we are the sum of our voices, and our voices have grown over the centuries.

Not all of our voices bear the blood.

As if the earth could make sense of gibberish—and Kiriel couldn't—it rumbled. But its motion was gentle now; a caress and not the making of a fist.

You paid the greatest of prices, it said. **Greater than the gods paid.**

The whole of your City resides within my heart. You taught

me to speak with the voice of Man. Not since the Firstborn have
I been granted such a gift. Will you take the cost of that now?

No.

She wanted to scream a different answer.

The roots twisted in her hands, and the earth growled.

She let them go as if they were fire and she had left her hand in
it too long.

You have taught her your gift.

No, eldest. Her gift is no part of us. It is in her blood.

Her blood is dark.

Yes. Dark, but also mortal.

She cannot grant life.

No.

What does she do?

The voices were silent. Kiriel wanted to ask them if it was her
turn yet, but she knew this was childish.

And felt very much a child.

Daughter, the pendant said softly. **Daughter of the dead. We
have the attention of the eldest. It is our gift.**

She was wary of gifts. Weary of them. *And what will I pay?* she
asked.

You know the price.

She did.

**You have made the village yours, inasmuch as a village is
ever owned. We have given you that time. We have given you
the memories that we deem wise. It is time, daughter. You have
born the Heart of Havalla, and you are a part of us now; but we
must come at last to our kin. Let her bear the greater burden.**

Kiriel said, *Tell me what I must do.*

And the voices, almost as one, laughed. It was not a gentle laugh,
but neither was it unkind; it simply was. As the earth was.

Speak with the eldest, a single voice said. **Speak only. Do not
offer it your life, for it will accept what is offered, and you are
needed elsewhere. But speak, child. You have touched the earth,
and you know it now.**

And then, to the Old Earth, the voices said, **She is mortal.**

She is god-born.

Yes, eldest. But her mother was not. And she has—against all
hope or ancient wisdom—something of her mother in her. She
cannot heal. She is her father's daughter. But she can make
strong what must stand in battle, and she chooses to define her
own war.

Can you not see her?

The earth moved again. Kiriel felt herself rise.

No, the earth said quietly. **But I can feel her. She touches the trees. She attempts to wake the seedlings the mortals reave. She . . .**

Yes, they said, as one. **And she cannot do it; you live. You live yet.**

The price, the earth whispered.

It will be paid.

Child of Darkness, what is your name?

Kiriel, Kiriel answered. *Kiriel di'Ashaf.*

I will protect your dead. For the offerings made. For the gift you have attempted, in ignorance, to give me. I hear you, Daughter of Darkness. I hear your voice, and it is not unpleasant.

The fire?

Let me take the fire, and the wind. They are weak here.

Can you take them without destroying the village?

I cannot see the village.

I can.

Show me.

She did. She could trace the foundations of buildings in the surface of the earth. She did not know them all, but Ashaf had, and those that were unfamiliar to Ashaf were few. Kiriel found them all, traversing the earth's surface as if it were her skin.

Child, the earth said, as she spoke in this silent movement, this motionless travel. **Why is your face wet?**

She couldn't shake her head. She couldn't deny what the earth felt. She said, *It's just a river. It's not important. Can you feel my home?*

Yes.

Then save it, she whispered. *For the dead. The living cannot give you anything if you destroy them.*

They can give me their life's blood.

She was silent.

And after a moment, the earth sighed. **I would talk with you,** it said, **but you would not survive it; you would age and die. Go, then. Go.**

And the seedlings?

Your enemies have paid the price, the earth said, and the ground hardened around her.

She did not ask again.

* * *

Meralonne was halfway down the tree when Kiriel di'Ashaf rose from the ground.

The earth disgorged her whole, and not even mud clung to her clothing; she was pale, but she found her footing.

She had to; the earth continued to rise around her in a ring. She could be seen from above, and he had the vantage; she could not be seen by anything that lived in the village.

It had been a long, long time since he had seen the earth wake in majesty. Longer still since he had stood at its center, and he felt a bitter envy; he would not reach the ground in time, for he dared not call the wind. Not now. The fire's voice was strong.

He wondered if Kiriel would survive.

Had his answer a moment later, as another pillar rose like a great arm. It was followed, minutes later, by limbs formed of root and rock and stone.

But he could see the pattern to its upheaval; the houses of the village remained where they had been planted. No tremor broke them, no shift disturbed their repose.

The fire screeched and roared; the wind was sibilant. But they were not the equal of the enemy that now joined their fray; they were contained and confined by the power of those who had summoned them.

The earth was unleashed.

No voice drove it; no command hampered it.

He felt its presence clearly.

Kiriel di'Ashaf drove hands through the barriers that contained her, and the barriers—to the surprise of the magi—gave instantly as she did.

She stepped through them.

"DARO!"

He was there. Or rather, a man was, and he turned instantly at the sound of the word on her lips.

Sight made keen by the flippant use of paltry magery saw brows rise as the girl who had destroyed the sacrificial fall of magi blood ran toward him.

"GET THEM INSIDE! GET THEM ALL INSIDE!"

He did not hesitate.

He carried a woman in his arms, and Kiriel's voice did not disturb her. Nor did his, but he lifted it and shouted in clear Torra.

Kiriel ran, her legs wobbly, her face white as Northern snow.

Caught a child in her arms, as she moved. The weight slowed her. But not enough.

The earth was aware of her, Meralonne thought. It would not destroy her, if it had not already done so.

Together, Kiriel di'Ashaf and the man she had called Daro ran toward the only stone house in the village, dragging behind them the bedraggled serafs that the fire had almost killed.

CHAPTER TWENTY-THREE

IN THE stone halls of Daro di'Valente, Kiriel's knees collapsed. She fell over the child she had somehow managed to carry; their bodies hit the ground with a dull thud. But the child did not waken, and Kiriel forced only a hand to rise. This she placed against the exposed surface of his darkened neck.

When she felt the pulse beneath her fingers, she let go. Of everything.

She could hear Daro's voice clearly. He could say what she could not: Is everyone here? Is anyone missing?

In ones and twos, other voices answered him. Some were cracked and broken by coughing spasms; others were heavy with fear or tears. One or two children were wailing, and the sound was comforting; they were healthy.

Hands touched her arms. She was pulled from the ground, but not forced to stand; instead she was lifted and carried.

She recognized the armor her cheek rested against.

Auralis.

He said nothing. Nothing at all.

But after a moment, Daro di'Valente came to them as they stood in the lee of the door. It was still raining, but the wind no longer howled.

"Kiriel," Daro said quietly. And then, after a moment, "Northerner."

You have to tell them, she said. *You have to tell them to stay inside.*

Except that no sound left her lips. Her throat was raw with screaming.

"Kiriel?" Auralis' lips, pressed—as they had been for much of this long, long eve—against her ear.

She reached up for his face, but her hands wouldn't obey even that simple command.

"Leave her, AKalakar," said a voice she recognized. She felt Auralis' arms stiffen. "She has kept her promise." She felt another hand touch her brow, and she wanted to pull away.

As if he knew it, the hand retreated. "Kiriel di'Ashaf," the bard said softly, "what must I tell the villagers?"

Daro di'Valente said, "Tell them to stay inside."

She would have wept, but that, too, was beyond her.

"If you can," he added. "Tell them to stay inside no matter what they see or hear."

Had she told him this?

She couldn't remember.

"And, Northerner. Carry her back to her room. Tend her; there is water there, and towels. Nora makes broth now; if she will drink it, feed it to her.

"Keep her warm," he added.

"She's already burning."

But the village overseer was gone.

Kallandras lifted his voice in song.

Curled about the familiar, Southern words, was command: he bid the serafs sleep. There was not one among their number who had the power to disobey him, but it was costly, perhaps too costly. He had used much of his power this eve, and he did not wish to lie as Kiriel did, in the shadowed halls of Valente.

But he knew what she had not said; he had heard it clearly. Those born to the voice, those trained to its use, could.

And he heard more, although this was no gift of magic; he heard the heavy fall of Auralis AKalakar's boots; he heard the slide of screens, as the man struggled with both her weight and the simple mechanism. He heard a seraf offer aid, and he heard the soldier refuse it. But if the refusal was curt and abrupt, it was not unkind.

He heard more: another voice, lost in the distance, singing in harmony with his own.

Diora.

He had almost forgotten the Serra.

But she had forgotten nothing, and her voice, of the two, was the stronger. He surrendered the melody to it, choosing the subtleties of harmony for his own, and together they gentled command as it swept across the village.

But Meralonne APhaniel did not sleep.

He heard the words, and the song, and the gift they offered, and he rejected them quietly. He did not fear the earth, although it moved and twisted.

As if the pillars that had formed were the foundations of ancient ruins, he walked among them, speaking softly. Occasionally he laid a hand against their moving surface, but when he did, he fell silent; the earth was not his, this eve.

Not his.

He was bitterly disappointed, but there were none to witness it.

Had the earth taken the village, the pathway would be uprooted, and the Terrean purified. If he could have offered the earth what lay between its deliberate mounds, he would have—but he knew enough, by touch, to hold his peace.

Whatever Kiriel di'Ashaf had done beneath its vast surface would remain a mystery to him. The effects, however, were clear: nothing that stood was destroyed. Not the homes, pathetic and weak as they were. Not even those the fire had destroyed. Not the fields, where seeds had been planted and lay in wait, gestating beneath earth's shallow surface.

Not, he thought, *the dead.*

There was, as Evayne had promised, power here to withstand the armies of *Allasakar.* It was a power that defied comprehension and knowledge, and he was a learned man; the Order of Knowledge had left its long mark in the workings of his mind.

He looked up; he could not see Telakar; could not see Anduvin.

Nor, he thought, was Nugratz in the air. If the battle had not been won, it had not been lost; the storm was no longer hemmed in by the wind.

Not even Nugratz would have dared that much; the earth's voice was stronger than thunder.

Only the gods had had the power to summon the whole of the element, and even for gods, it was costly; they were not masters of the wild magics, but distant kin.

He wondered if *Allasakar* would know of the evening's work. Or care. What the god desired, he maintained: the trees were growing.

He bowed his head a moment and then straightened his shoulders. It was time, now, to leave this field; another field waited. And another.

But he lingered a moment, feeling in the ancient presence of the awakened earth the whole of his youth, and its yearning.

Yollana of Havalla came upon the village of Russo from the rounded height of the pathway. She stopped; the trees that had stood at its outermost edge were gone, washed away in sooty rivulets. The Serra Teresa, ever attentive, stopped instantly.

"Na'tere," the old woman said.

"Matriarch."

"My canes."

"The ground is—"

"My canes."

The Serra removed them from the sash that bound them to her back. Without another word, she handed them to Yollana, and Yollana took them. "Look carefully, Na'tere. See what must be seen. Remember it."

Serra Teresa di'Marano looked down at the flats of the valley. At what had *been* flats. Mounds of dirt had risen between the houses that stood across its length and breadth. Pillars of stone stood beneath the vault of the heavens, as if upholding the sky.

Only the tree at the village center was taller, and it looked, to her eye, as if its heights had been sheared and clipped.

She drew the circle across her breast, and then stopped, for Yollana had not lifted hand to do the same. "Matriarch," she said, the word a question.

"No, Na'tere," the Matriarch replied, lingering over the name as if it brought comfort, "It is not Voyani magic. Not one of the Matriarchs could have done this on their own, save perhaps the first." She frowned. "And it is best if you look and fail to listen."

Teresa surprised herself; she smiled. And not even the strange landscape that had been—that still, against all belief, *was*—a village, dimmed that smile. "Where do we go, Matriarch? Shall I follow?"

"Aye, follow. And pick me up if I stumble."

It was not stumbling that Teresa feared. But as they descended the gentle slope, she realized that the rains had not softened the earth; it did not give beneath the rounded points of Yollana's canes.

"What has happened here?"

Yollana shrugged. It was habit; her expression was as unguarded as Teresa had yet seen it, and wonder lurked in the expression the folds of her skin made. "The rains will stop," she said at last.

They were already much diminished.

The two women made their way around the pillars of earth. Yollana stopped only once, and when she did, she barked an order to the Serra, but the Serra heeded it by instinct: she touched nothing.

"There was a path once," Yollana said curtly.

"You know this village?"

"Averda is home to Arkosa," the Matriarch replied curtly. After a pause, she added, "But, yes, I know it."

Her footing was certain. But of the path she had mentioned, no hint remained; the whole of the earth had been remade, here. No weeds grew, although they would, given time; the scent of new earth was profound and powerful, and it promised life.

"There are lights in the distance, near the tree," Teresa said after they had walked for some time.

Yollana cursed her vision, or her lack of vision. It was her way of offering thanks. "Take me there," she said. She was so graceless, so lacking in shame.

And this, too, invoked a smile. "Matriarch," Teresa said.

"Na'tere," Yollana snapped, "not even my grandchildren were foolish enough to humor me."

Teresa placed a hand in the crook of the Matriarch's elbow; the old woman refused—by gesture alone—to surrender her canes. They progressed slowly, but they did make progress, and at last they came to the stone home of the village overseer.

"The home of the man who claims responsibility for the village in the absence of the Tor'agar. Ser Daro di'Valente," Yollana said, as if she could hear the question that Teresa did not ask. "Aie, Na'tere, the pillars here will stand for lifetimes, mark my words."

"He is awake," Teresa said. "The doors are open. Lights burn in all of the windows."

The Matriarch spit. "Waste of tallow," she said.

"It is lamplight, Matriarch."

"Even worse. Come."

"Is he expecting you?"

"Hardly. But he will not turn me away. Even with this," she added, rapping her eye patch, "he'll know who I am."

They entered the hall. It was crowded; silks and blankets colored the gray of stone and the pale, smooth honey of exposed wood. People slept here; some were aged, and some too young to walk. They did not stir as Yollana passed them by, although her cane rapped against the wood with the authority of power.

Yollana passed over them all, as if they were part of the floor. She walked the length of the hall, and then paused a moment to catch her breath. It was darker here; the lights that flickered seemed to enhance the shadows.

But Teresa felt the Lady's presence; she did not fear the darkness. "Come," she said, after it became clear that Yollana could not walk any farther. She took the canes; Yollana's hands gripped them firmly. This time, Teresa insisted; she pulled.

If Yollana was devoid of grace or courtesy, she still valued dignity; she let them go. Her expression was sour as old wine, and it made Teresa smile for a third time.

"A few years on the open road and you'll look your age," the Matriarch said, almost pertly.

"Yollana, come. You have led us this far; what is there to fear?"

But as she nudged the old woman around the corner, she had her answer: two men.

One, she half-recognized: he was Northern, and he often shadowed Kiriel di'Ashaf when she came to Diora's tent. The other was Southern; his eyes were lined with a night that would never leave his face, and his hair, pale and streaked, had been wound round itself in a knot. Its length was coarse and wild, but it fell down his neck and across his back: a man's knot.

It was the Southerner who rose. He lifted the light in his weathered hands, and as it swung across his chest, orange flickered beneath his chin. A beard graced that chin, lending it the appearance of strength.

He wore no uniform, no crest, no symbol; his shirt was a nightshirt, and it was rumpled and stained with soot and dirt. And sweat, she thought. Night took away its color, damping it, denying it.

"Ser Daro," Yollana said.

And Daro di'Valente bowed low. By this alone, Teresa knew he recognized Yollana of the Havalla Voyani.

The Northerner rose as well. His hand fell with practiced ease to the hilt of his sheathed sword—his way of stating, clearly, that he recognized her as well.

"Your daughters came," the Southerner said quietly.

"This eve?"

"Ah, no, Matriarch. They came when the moon was last waning; they left before the night had passed."

She nodded grimly. "And they carried word?"

"Do you not know?"

"I know what they should have done," Yollana replied. It was evasion. No gift was needed to understand that. But Teresa wondered what she would have been able to hear, were she not deaf.

"But the ways of children are not the ways of their parents. You have children; you have seen this."

He did not smile, but the straight line of his shoulders bowed slightly. "They offered warning," he said quietly. "Have you come to offer another?"

"The night has offered all that it can," Yollana replied. Then, fishing around in her wet, leather satchel, she drew her pipe.

It seemed to take hours to line it with weed, for half the weed was damp and she had to choose the leaves with care. It took just as long to light it.

During the whole of this ritual, no word was spoken.

"Kiriel di'Ashaf is here," she said, smoke leaving her lips with the words. Both lingered.

Daro looked to the Northerner, but his face was silent and shuttered; it gave nothing away.

His hand, however, tightened.

Auralis, Teresa thought. Her thoughts were as muddied as the earth in the land outside of this village. Auralis AKalakar.

"Kiriel di'Ashaf is here," Daro agreed. But he moved slightly, until he stood shoulder to shoulder with Auralis AKalakar. As if the North and the South had never fought a war; as if they were not in the process of waging one now.

Yollana's brow rose.

"I have not come to threaten her," she said, speaking around the stem of her pipe. "Merely to speak."

"She is not awake, Matriarch. She sleeps."

Something about the cast of the man's expression made Teresa step forward. It was done without thought, without care; it was done, however, with perfect, fluid grace.

She heard Yollana lean suddenly against the wall, and regretted the movement instantly. Or tried to.

"She sleeps?"

Again the men exchanged glances.

"She sleeps," Daro said, more firmly. His arms were now across his chest, and they formed as much of a barrier as any wise man offered to a Matriarch.

"So," Yollana said.

"Ser Daro," Serra Teresa said, and she offered him obeisance.

His brows rose; of all the things he had expected, she was not one. But he saw, now, that she wore silk, and not the heavy linen of the Voyani; saw that she dressed in sari, and not the traveling garb of the road.

He said, "I am in her debt." Just that.

But it was warning enough.

"The Matriarch does not intend to threaten her," Teresa replied. "And it may be that she can be of aid. Her sleep is not natural, is it?"

The silence stretched out, broken by the inhalation and exhalation of pipe smoke.

He said, "Serra, I do not know you. You are not of the North; you are not Kiriel's companion."

"I am the Serra Teresa di'Marano," Teresa replied, "and I have served the Lady for the whole of my life." Had she power, she would have inflected the words in such a way that truth carried.

But she was not, she found, without that skill anyway.

"No," Ser Daro replied at last, uneasily. "She has the fevers. She burns."

"Let us see her, Ser Daro. Come, if you will; bring her Northern guard, if you will. We will take nothing from her; we will offer her no harm."

It was a request, and it was so sweetly offered that his reply seemed coarse and common.

It was. He nodded, and the Northerner frowned—but although his hand did not leave his sword, he stepped aside.

As if he were seraf, he pulled the screen back. He did it poorly; the screen made enough noise that the Serra winced.

"It is dark," she said softly.

"She wanted the darkness," Ser Daro replied. But he lifted the lamp as he followed Yollana of Havalla into the wide, empty room.

The Serra walked to the side of the mats upon which the young girl lay. She touched her forehead gently with the flat of her hand and then with its back. Her expression shifted; she reached for the towels and the bucket that lay upon the floor, and without another word, she began to sponge the girl's face.

"My wife would tend her," Ser Daro said, showing his first uncertainty, "but the house—as you no doubt saw—is full this eve."

"I will tend her," Teresa said gently. "For now. Has she spoken at all?"

Ser Daro nodded.

"And what has she said?"

"I don't know, Serra. She doesn't speak Torra." He hesitated, and then added, "And she doesn't speak the Northern tongue either."

"What ails her, Na'tere?"

But Teresa would not say. She had seen it before.

And she knew that death courted her.

"Na'tere." Sharper word. Harsh with command.

Teresa considered the silence briefly. In the soft light of lamp, the girl looked like a child; her expression was unguarded, and her skin, pale and soft, was untouched by sunlight.

By any light.

"Widan fevers," she said at last.

Yollana cursed. Even Daro's brows rose when she continued to do so.

"Yollana," Teresa said at last.

The Matriarch levered herself to the ground. "We'll wait," she said stonily.

"Ask for silks," Teresa said quietly. "For if you wait here, it will not be for a short time."

But Yollana shook her head.

"And you, Serra?"

"I have slept," Teresa lied. She knew that the lie was transparent, but Ser Daro did not argue. "I do not know Kiriel di'Ashaf well," she added quietly, as the cloth continued its passage over her face.

"You know her, though?"

"I have seen her many times," the Serra replied.

"Where?"

"She is—was—a soldier in the Northern army."

"Ah."

"And the Matriarch chose to travel with that army."

It was never wise to ask questions of a Matriarch; it was almost as unwise to ask questions about one. Ser Daro was old enough to be wise. "What did you think of this one?" he asked instead, indicating Kiriel by the brief dip of beard.

"She frightens many," Teresa said. She spoke as if words were simple containers for truth. "And she is highly prized by Ser Valedan kai di'Leonne."

Ser Daro's brows rose.

"But she is also prized by Ser Danello kai di'Valente," she continued softly. "For when it came time for the army to choose its standing ground, she asked the Tyr'agar to travel South of Russo."

Daro was silent, waiting.

She rewarded his wait, her hands wringing a hot towel dry. "She wished to preserve this village, and he honored her: he acceded to her request. It is not a request that Ser Danello would have dared to make."

"Did Ser Danello mean to abandon us?"

"What is abandonment in war?" Soft question.

Ser Daro looked at the motionless face of Kiriel di'Ashaf. He said, at last, "She is golden-eyed."

Teresa dipped the towel into the cool water, and wrung it dry again.

"She is a child," she told the overseer. "She came to the tent of my niece many times when the army stopped, and each time, she asked my niece to sing the cradle song."

His brows rose.

"And my niece sang. It quieted them both." She paused and then said, "Ashaf sang it to her, in the North."

Ser Daro closed his eyes. "Can a demon child be cradled, Serra? Can a girl not past the cradle song truly stand against the Lord of Night?"

"I cannot answer the question you ask," Serra Teresa said, her hands once again pressed against the forehead of the unconscious girl, a thin towel separating their skin. "I am but a Serra, and war is a man's game. Even this war."

"She is no man."

"No, Ser Daro, she is not."

"But she wears armor. She bears sword. She—"

"She is still a child, for all that. One day, she will sing the cradle song, instead of asking that it be sung for her. Is that not our way?"

"Aye," he said, his voice gruff. "I was afraid of her."

"And now?"

"You see how it is," he replied, as if Yollana were not in the room. He motioned to Auralis AKalakar. "I think, had she not come to Russo, we would have perished."

"If she had not come," Yollana interrupted, her voice dark and severe, "the village might never have known threat. Only the storm."

"The storm brings war," Ser Daro replied sharply. "And all war is a threat to serafs."

"And will you harbor a daughter of demons?" Yollana demanded. She did not rise. Had she, she could not have been more menacing.

Ser Daro's hesitation spoke loudly.

But not as loudly as his word. "Yes," he said. Just that.

Auralis AKalakar knelt by the Serra's side. He, too, ignored Yollana, but Teresa thought that this was simple ignorance; he was of the North, after all.

"Will she make it?" he asked, in Weston.

"If you mean, will she survive, I cannot answer," Teresa replied.

"She has the mage fevers."

"That is not what we call them in the South, but yes. I did not know—"

"No one did."

"Why does she suffer, AKalakar?"

"Damned if I know." He shrugged, restless, confined. "She fixed a bunch of houses."

"How?"

He shrugged. "She touched them. I don't know."

"Just that?"

"And she—" He shook his head. "The earth," he said, after a pause. "She came from the earth. It swallowed her. It spit her out."

Yollana coughed. Loudly.

"You will not speak of this," she said.

"The whole village saw it," he countered, shrugging.

"They will not speak of it."

"They're people," he said. "They'll talk."

"Matriarch—" Teresa began.

"It's not possible," the Matriarch said flatly. "Not for her."

"Then who?"

Yollana closed her eyes.

In the morning, the rain stopped.

The Serra Diora di'Marano slid the screens wide and stepped out into the pale light. Sleep, a gift she had offered, had eluded her, but she bore its lack with a grace that only death would shake.

It was not yet the Lord's time. It was past the Lady's.

She closed the door behind her; it was heavy, but it was also silent. Valla and her husband still slept.

"Serra Diora," Kallandras said.

She bowed. "Kallandras."

And looked beyond his familiar face to the changed landscape of the Green Valley. Pillars rose into the sky, their roughened stone wrapped round with vines and roots. Dirt clung to those roots; she thought the plants themselves would wither, exposed to day.

But she stared at them as she spoke. "Why that song, Kallandras?"

"The cradle song? It is a song that quiets fear," he replied.

She said, "You do not guard your voice with care, this morn."

"Ah, an oversight, Serra."

Her smile was soft. "A gift, rather."

As was his. He wore sleep's lack with as much grace as she, but with more experience. She looked at him then. His clothing was darkened in places, but it bore no blood. "The rain," she said softly.

"It has moved on. Perhaps it will fall in the desert, where water is needed."

"Where is Kiriel?"

"She sleeps," he said quietly. "In the home of Ser Daro di'Valente."

Diora bowed her head a moment. The song, she thought, and she lifted her hands to her lips; she had no fan with which to offer the benediction. Instead, she took three shallow bowls from the rough leather pouch that interrupted the folds of her sari.

"Will you make the offerings with me, Kallandras?"

"I? I fear that I have little to offer the Lady."

"Then accompany me; I have much."

"You will make the offerings?"

She nodded quietly.

"You are Serra Diora en'Leonne," he said gravely. "And the Serra of the Tyr does not bear the scars of ablution."

"He does not see scars," she said quietly. "But he understands gratitude. He will forgive me the imperfection, I think." She lifted her hand and looked at the white line across its palm. It trailed down, almost to the wrist. She had so feared the taking of it, in the desert.

Where had that fear gone?

Kallandras echoed her bow, and when she left the flat steps of the small domis, he fell in beside her, shortening his stride.

It seemed to the naked eye that no stone had been left unturned, but the eye was careless; here and there, there were patches of grass and the feckless autumn flowers that grew in the wild made them more than green. The Serra came to such a patch and stopped; there were stones that had been laid against the earth that marked this place. She asked, "Have all the graves been left undisturbed?"

And he raised a pale brow. After a moment, he replied, "Yes."

He could have offered a different answer. He knew the village no better than she. She knelt with care; she had no seraf, and no mat to protect the silks that she wore. But she could not do what must be done standing.

From the satchel, she withdrew a silver spade. It was tarnished and scratched, but it had been cleaned, and it shone with the yellow warmth of age that new silver does not possess. She dug a short furrow in the dirt; her pale hands were marked by the task, and her nails darkened.

As she worked, she said, "I have seen so much in the last year."

"You have walked a path given to few," Kallandras replied. She saw his shadow, its lines blurred and softened by the thinning clouds.

"I was so angry when I left the Tor Leonne." The second furrow took shape beside the first. She almost hated to dig here; what there was of the grass and the village greenery should be revered, not disturbed.

But other reverences intruded.

Kallandras said nothing.

"But I would not have learned what I learned had I stayed." She paused. "Had I stayed," she added softly, "with my wives. I might have been safe. I might be dead. I would never have witnessed a miracle."

"And is this a miracle, Serra?"

The third furrow. She placed her hand between the first two, measuring their distance with precision and a critical eye.

"All of it," she told him quietly. "You have seen far more than I, Kallandras of Senniel College. The Northern cities must flourish with the song of the bards to guide them."

He said, "The bards and I have little in common. We sing," he added quietly, "at the command of the powerful."

"Are you owned?"

"We are all owned by something."

"And you, Kallandras? What owns you?"

"Duty," he said. She heard more in the single word than she had heard in his voice in a lifetime.

Looking up, she said, "You do not owe me this."

And meeting her gaze without blinking, he said, "No, Serra. I don't."

But the texture of his words did not change; there was life in them; a man's life, and a man's experience. She heard a profound, distant loss that spoke to her of her own. She finished digging and set the spade to one side.

"Are we all marked by loss?" she asked him then.

"You hear as I do, Serra; you must judge."

"I would rather not," she told him gently. "I have spent much of my life judging. Can one both judge and live?"

He laughed. It was a gentle sound. An unfamiliar one. "One cannot live *without* judgment. But, no, I understand your meaning. I have met those who have suffered no great loss."

"Are they children?"

"Not all," he said quietly. "In my youth, I resented them bitterly. I loathed their ignorance."

It was true. It was all true. She should have been disquieted, but she was too immersed in the wonder of this moment's vulnerability.

"But now they seem—to me—to be like Northern glass sculptures; one can see through them, yes, and one knows that it is likely they will shatter, or be shattered, by some experience that has not yet befallen them. But while they are untouched by our misery and our duty, they provide faith and a strange beauty. And if I could, I would preserve their ignorance."

She nodded, as if keeping time with the rhythm of his words. From the sagging folds of cracked leather, she pulled a crystal bottle. She placed it upon the ground. Beside it, she placed a wineskin, and beside that, a dagger.

Then she took the three bowls and laid them, one each, at the base of the three furrows.

"I wish Ramdan were here," she said.

"If you summoned him, Serra, he would come."

"Yes. And he will. But he will not be here *now*." Her smile was pained. "He is the Lady's seraf, Kallandras. He has served my Ona and myself as if we were the very Lady. If he has ever resented his life, he has never shown it; he does not speak of freedom or captivity.

"But he is captive."

"Free him," Kallandras said quietly.

"I think that would break his heart."

"You might be surprised, Serra Diora. But then again, so might I; the ways of the South have grown strange to me with the passage of years." He bowed a moment. "I remember when I first heard your voice."

She looked up. The crystal stopper of the aged bottle rested in her palm. "When was that?"

"At the Festival of the Moon," he said quietly. "Before the last war."

"Ah. The night you came to us. To save Lissa."

"No, Serra; it was before that. During the day, when the Tyr'agar and his formidable wife enjoined the children to sing. You were there, among them."

She poured the water carefully into the first bowl. No drop fell upon the earth; the desert had taught her to hoard water when it passed into her hands, and she wondered if she would ever forget its lesson.

"And you were such a child," he continued softly. "Unmarked by loss. I heard the power in your voice, even then, and I thought of what you might be, with training."

"And so you trained me." She set the bottle aside and lifted the wineskin.

"I? No, Serra Diora."

She looked up.

"What I did was too meager, too scant, to be training. What you have learned, you have learned on your own." His smile was gentle. Everything about him, in this hour before day, was. "I watched you grow," he added quietly.

She poured wine in equal measure to water; the wind was completely absent. "Have I finished, then?"

"Ah, no, Serra. Nor will you, for some time. But if I could see you learn one lesson, it would be this."

She lifted the dagger last. It was Arkosan, and it was hers; of all her possessions, save perhaps the samisen, it was the one she treasured most. But as she unsheathed it, she drew a sharp breath and held it; the dagger's edge rested above her unblemished skin.

What Kallandras had said was truth: The Serras of the High Courts did not bear the scars of ablution. It was left to their scrafs.

She wanted this, but she feared it.

"What lesson?" she asked, and her voice was not entirely steady.

"You believe—you have always believed—that you could kill without compunction."

"I am of the South," she said softly. "I am of the High Courts. It is said by the Voyani that death is the only thing we know."

"To know death is not the same as to cause it," he replied gravely. "But there will come a time when your resolve will be tested."

"I would have killed—" She fell silent, thinking of Nicu of the Arkosa Voyani. Margret's cousin. There were some things she could not speak of. Not to Margret. And if not to her, not to anyone.

"Would have is not the same," he said. "You will be tested, and only then will you know, for certain, if what you believe is true."

"And the lesson?" she whispered, as the knife at last pierced skin.

Blood dripped onto her silks. She frowned as she passed her arm over the third of the bowls, gritting her teeth; the cool morning air had a bite that she had been unaware of until this moment.

"That you discover that you are not, in fact, a killer."

And what she heard in his voice might have stopped her blood from running. She met his eyes, and knew that the time for vulnerability was passing; the Lord would wake, soon, and he would become a different man.

"You are," she said at last. "And you do not regret it."

"I am," he nodded. But of regret, he did not speak. "Valedan kai di'Leonne is not his father."

It was an odd thing to say. She watched blood drip freely into the last of the bowls; it took longer than either water or wine had, and she wondered if the cut she had barely been able to make was too small.

But Kallandras knelt by her side, and with a brief grunt, tore a strip of whole cloth from the edge of his shirt. "Your wrist," he said.

She offered it, and he bound it.

"He will have to kill," she said, staring at the rough bandage and the blood that seeped up through its weave.

"Yes, Serra. He will have to kill. Does this make you happy?"

Had any other asked, the words would have carried either accusation or disdain. But neither marred his voice.

She said, "I don't know."

"Good. It is not the answer you would have given on the eve of your marriage."

She shook her head. "No," she said quietly. "But he—" And then her eyes widened. "My wife."

"Your wife is not his wife, not yet. Perhaps not ever. He knows what she lost, Serra. He knows what *you* lost. He is afraid to become a carrion creature."

"He fears too much."

Kallandras laughed. "If kindness is fear, then, yes, he fears too much."

But she thought, as he spoke, of Ser Alessandro kai di'Clemente. A man who had married his brother's wife, had promised to accept a son not his own as heir. He had not seemed a gentle man; Diora was certain that, had the battle failed, she would now be his gift to Marente, a sign of his new loyalties.

"Will Valedan kai di'Leonne learn to love Teyla?" she asked softly. Her wrist was throbbing, and conversation had robbed the sky of its neutral gray. Before Kallandras could speak again, she lifted the first of the offering bowls. It was heavy in her hands, for the wound had made them clumsy. Perhaps she had cut too deep.

But she had been hampered by far worse pain than this. As if she had been raised to the offerings, she emptied the bowl perfectly from the top of the furrow to its messy edge.

"What is love, Na'dio?"

Love is what I felt for my wives, she said. Except that the words did not come. She laid the empty bowl down, and lifted, in turn, the second. Wine, for the Lady's repose.

"In time, he will learn to love her," Kallandras continued, as if the words that were silent were clear as the rising sun. "In time, Serra Diora, he will learn to love you."

"According to some, he already does."

"Ah, but you are no child, Na'dio. You know that love and desire are not the same; they are not even sides of the same coin. He desired you the moment he laid eyes on you, and that was your intent. It is what you were raised to do; invoke desire, retain mystery, hold on to a man of power."

"But love? Love is different."

"He does not love me."

"But he has already begun, Serra."

"When?"

"The day you returned from Essla. He knew of what you had done. All of it. And he knew that it would be costly. Believe that the Serra Alina di'Lamberto has offered him the harshest words of advice that a Serra may offer. He knows that his first concubine should be a woman of worth, from a notable family; he knows that, instead, you have given him the lowest and least graceful of serafs—one who has already born a son, proof of her use by another man.

"He does not see this clearly. He sees instead what you did to save a helpless woman and her babe. And he carries the memory with him now."

She set the second bowl down; her hands trembled. "And is love, then, a collusion of weaknesses?"

"If it is weakness that leads you to make your choice, then, yes, Serra Diora. Do you think less of him, for his silence?"

The third bowl. The last. She lifted it. "I—"

Her own blood jeweled the ceramic curve. It was Valla's bowl, and it was rough and inelegant. But it was made to offer, no more and no less.

She turned to Kallandras, hating the passage of time, the constant loss of moments of intimacy. The bowl shook now, and it was the last and most important of the offerings; she had already erred by allowing her blood to touch the unturned earth. "No," she said starkly. "I think no less of him." And bowed her head.

"I do not know what husband you dreamed of, when you resided with the wives of your father," he said gently. He reached out and cupped the back of her hands in the palms of his; she felt calluses there; a gift and burden of strings.

"I do not know if you dreamed of husband at all."

With his hands to steady hers, she made the last ablution.

She said, "I am afraid of him."

He said gently, "I know."

When the Serra Alina di'Lamberto at last found Valedan kai di'Leonne, the Lord was in the sky, and the sky was pink and pale, the veils of the evening storm lingering around its face.

She had words to speak, advice to offer; the Commanders were gathering, and it was the desire of Ser Anton di'Guivera that the Tyr'agar be present whenever the Northerners met in number. It was also the desire of Baredan di'Navarre, of Ramiro di'Callesta, and, yes, curse him, of her brother, the Tyr'agnate of Mancorvo.

But the words that she had prepared—for she was canny with words, and spoke seldom without knowing how to weight them and when to use them to best advantage—failed to come.

For Valedan stood outside the Serra Diora's tent, treading across wet ground in a varied, awkward circle, mud causing his feet to cling.

It was not his pacing that surprised her, for she had seen him pace many a time, and if the mud made the action unwise, it mattered little.

No, it was the child he held in his arms. His unmailed, exposed arms. His dark hair fell around the sides of his face, hiding the perfect height of his cheekbones, the rigid strength of his jaw. His neck was bent, and he seemed to be speaking.

The child was crying.

"Valedan?" she said, when she could speak at all.

He looked up, and she saw that his eyes were dark with lack of sleep. So, too, the eyes of all the men who had chosen command— or had had it thrust upon them—in the war. But she thought that this lack was different, and the words he next spoke proved her instinct true.

"The baby won't sleep," he said.

"The baby," she said sharply, "is not your concern."

"Teyla is tired," he replied. "And in shock. She needs to sleep. She is almost—"

"She is almost *what?*"

He knew the tone, but it startled him; he lifted his head. And winced. "She needs sleep," he said, lame even to her ears. "And I told her I would watch the baby. But he started to cry half an hour ago, and I can't do anything to make him stop."

Alina's brows had almost disappeared. She wore Northern clothing, and her skin had darkened with sun, but the darkness was absent; she was pale. She marched over to the tent entrance and thrust the fabric to one side.

"Valedan," she said without preamble. "Inside, please."

He hesitated a moment, and then he nodded. But he held the infant with care as he walked, and he walked slowly.

"Did Ser Andaro not tell you—"

"Ser Andaro said that it was unwise," Valedan replied. "But the child—"

"She is a seraf, Valedan."

"She is my wife," he said, with the first heat of the morning.

Oh, to be married to a man such as this. Alina was torn between envy and pity, both for the Serra Diora. Anger, however, was also present.

"The child cries because it is hungry. As you've not the ability to feed it, I suggest that you—"

But Teyla en'Leonne was already rising. Her silks were in disarray, and her expression was a battlefield expression. It silenced Alina, where Valedan himself could not.

But Valedan smiled gently. "He's all right, Na'tey," he told the woman. "But we think he's hungry."

She looked at Alina, and she shrank back, the arms that she had half lifted falling woodenly to her sides.

The girl was *stupid*. She did not even understand that Valedan kai di'Leonne could *not* be seen by his men carrying a seraf's child while war waited.

Alina wanted to say this. But there was death in the girl's face; death, loss, the muteness that accompanies both. The Serra hovered a moment between the visceral desire to slap sense into her, and the equally strong desire to comfort her.

In the end, she did neither.

Valedan knelt carefully; his boots had already dirtied the tent's floor. He gave the child to Teyla en'Leonne and rose. "I'm sorry," he said—which blackened Alina's mood further, "but the Commanders have no doubt gathered. I will try to—"

"I will send someone to aid you," Alina said coldly to the girl.

Teyla nodded, and this time her arms did bend to take her child's weight.

"Serra Alina?" Valedan said quietly.

She nodded and preceded him out of the tent, her hands almost in fists.

"You cannot do this," she told him, when the tent was once again secure.

He shrugged.

"Valedan—you are not in the North. You will never again be in the North. The child—"

He said coolly, "Had we not failed Essla, the child would not be in my keeping. Would not, in fact, be my son. Had we arrived in time, had we been prepared for the magery and boldness of the enemy, Teyla kep'Valente would have a husband who would do what I have done. This is my responsibility because I have failed in the greater responsibility, and I will not deny it."

"Not even Ser Ramiro, in time of peace, would do as you have done. Do you not understand? The harem is guarded and private for a *reason*." She drew breath; she saw that the arguments she offered had found no purchase. "If you have enemies here—and you do, kai Leonne, even if they have not yet realized it—they will now know that you value that child. Do you understand?

"They will know, and they will make plans, in future, to use that child against you. You endanger *him* by your display, and if you do not care about yourself, think of him. Think of what it might mean."

This silenced him.

After a moment, she said, "We have had no word from Russo."

Valedan said, "I sent Andaro."

"That was unwise. You have no other Tyran; you force the Tyr'agnate to disarm themselves entirely in the presence of the Northern Commanders."

"I—" He started to speak. Stopped. "Alina."

And she surrendered. "It will not always be this difficult," she told him. "And in Ser Andaro's stead, you will have Ser Anton; his name alone is worth the presence of a dozen Tyran."

He nodded, but his attention had drifted.

To a man who offered him a deep bow, and held it. The grounds were wet, and mud was already more than a danger; he had not prostrated himself.

And he was seraf; such prostration was necessary.

Valedan, of course, took no notice of the breach of protocol. In the North, it would signify nothing.

Alina recognized the old man; he was the Serra Diora's, and his bow—if not entirely correct—was perfect.

She had never heard him speak.

"Tyr'agar," he said.

"Rise," Valedan replied.

Ramdan rose. "If you would trust me with this task, I would be honored."

"With—" Valedan's brows rose. He hesitated.

The old man said, "It has been my privilege to serve the Serras of the clan Marano."

The seraf knew, Alina thought. He knew that Valedan disapproved of serafs. Of slavery, as it was called in the North. She understood then why Ramdan had not assumed the subservient posture; he offered Valedan what Valedan required.

"Yes," Valedan said, before the silence grew awkward. "But—"

"I am called Ramdan."

"Ramdan. The Serra Diora values the woman and her child. I would keep them as safe—and as happy—as I can until her return."

Alina could have wept with frustration.

But the seraf was calm, almost placid, in the face of the monumental ignorance Valedan showed; it was as if no slight had been offered. And it had.

"I understand," the seraf said. Words, she thought, that he would not have had to say had he been seraf to any other master.

Valedan hesitated, and Alina swore, in silence, that if he said another word, she would disgrace herself. But in the end he offered a nod, no more, and he made his retreat.

"The Commanders," he said as she followed.

CHAPTER TWENTY-FOUR

DEVRAN looked up.

The sky had shed, in his estimation, tons of water, and the river was nigh impassable. Although the sun showed through the thinning clouds, it would be some time before he felt dry. If, he thought, with a nod to age, ever. Still, he allowed his men some time to celebrate the passage of the storm; Ellora was not here to see this slight loosening of discipline.

"Commander?"

He turned. Sedgewick stood, arms neatly pressed to his sides; a model soldier. A model adjutant. He smiled. "Well," he said. "It looks like the magi were off in their predictions."

"Thank Cormaris for that," Verrus Sedgewick said.

He had lost a number of horses, and some of the supplies had been washed into the river; boxes that were not meant to weather rain had fallen, no doubt, to the riverbed. Retrieval was impossible.

"Let's hope that the Callestan stockades merit their reputation," he said grimly. "Report."

"We have word from Commander Allen. The storm seems to have abated in the North."

He nodded. "The troops?"

"They'll move. But at a third their former speed."

A third was better than nothing.

"Orders?"

"We are ordered to stand our ground," Sedgewick said, with just a hint of relief.

Devran frowned. But he nodded. "Our reply?"

"The river is too swollen to ford. The bridges have been washed out five miles to either side of the encampment. We can press ahead, but we'll have to follow the Southward bend in the river."

"Fair enough." Devran rose.

"We lost one boat," he said quietly.

"To the rain?"

"Lightning."

One was better than he'd hoped for. "Tell them we wait."

Sedgewick nodded and retreated. Devran disliked the magis on principle; Sedgewick was practical. He viewed them as instruments of war; no more and no less. But they were necessary instruments; he treated them with caution and respect.

It was hard for Devran to do the same; they certainly showed little respect for the army.

Or they had. He was thoughtful, this morn. There was little else to be. Three of his magis were exactly what he expected; fractious, prone to argument among themselves when not actively arguing with Devran. But two were . . . like soldiers.

He had often wished that the Order of Knowledge knew how to produce men of discipline; he tested the wisdom of that wish and found it wanting.

Sedgewick returned after half an hour. "Commander," he said, bowing. Not exactly a promising sign.

"What news?"

"The army is camped South of the Torrean of Valente."

"South?"

Sedgewick nodded.

"Why South?"

"The Tyr'agar chose the standing ground," was the cautious reply.

Devran said nothing. His jaw tensed, but he betrayed no other obvious sign of displeasure.

"It is not the optimal place for cavalry," Sedgewick offered.

"And we have it."

"So do they, and in greater numbers. Perhaps the decision was not as unwise as it appears on the surface."

"Commander Allen said that?"

"Commander Allen said nothing."

"And Commander Kalakar?"

"Notably silent."

"Any other news?"

"The Lambertans and the Callestans have not yet descended to open warfare among the rank and file."

"How surprising."

"There is one other piece of information."

"Good or bad?"

"Both, sir. The enemy appears to have placed the foundations of a spell along the borders of Averda."

"The *entire* border?"

"Yes, sir."

"What the hell does foundation mean?"

"Trees, sir."

Devran shrugged. "There's nothing we can do about them; we're not near the border."

"No, sir."

"What, Sedgewick?"

"There's nothing that the army seems to be able to do about them either, sir. The trees, as far as I could tell from the magi, appear to . . . eat people. Sir."

Devran rose abruptly. He disliked the magi, but he disliked ignorance more.

In Russo, the sun rose.

And as it rose, it burned away the last vestiges of cloud; no hint of storm remained in the sky. But beneath the sky, the pillars rose as testament to the evening.

The village serafs rose; they clustered around Nora en'Valente as she bustled about the stone halls of the domis. Food had been made, with the help of the able-bodied women who had managed to shake off the nightmare of storm, fire, and wind. They were bruised, and their eyes were darkened by circles and new lines, but they had not suffered from the fires.

If losing home and everything in it did not count as suffering. They talked among themselves, but quietly, and their talk did not cause their work to suffer; it was their own they fed, after all.

Children slept in the hall, but as they began to wake in ones and twos, their cries could be heard in the long kitchen, and Nora gave permission for their mothers to leave. She was not unkind, and she was also practical. No woman here could quite believe that the night had passed without death. They waited, as they worked, for the price that would be demanded of them.

Let them see their young, she thought. Let them hold their sons and daughters. Let them offer comfort, if comfort would be taken. She knew what the shadow of death did, and she did not wish it upon any of them; they were almost all younger than she.

The dining hall was vast, but it was occupied by what seemed the whole of the village. It was; the villagers who woke to this strange new world came in ones and twos to the home of Daro di'Valente, carrying their hats in their hands, the tools of the field all but forgotten.

He bid them enter, and he bid them welcome; he answered their questions as patiently as he could. But he was stretched thin by the evening's work; for Daro, it had not yet ended.

Kiriel di'Ashaf did not wake.

Nora was proud of her husband. That was the truth. She had seen him in the long, silent hall, pacing and fetching water; she had seen him in the kitchens during the height of the Lady's time, thickening broth and cooling it while he waited.

She had seen him leave the manor in the hour between the Lady's time and the Lord's, and she knew that he had taken the offering bowls with him when he went. She knew, also, what he prayed for in the silence of the broken village.

He had not asked for her company. By this, she knew he was supplicant, and he was a man, with a man's pride. He had no desire to be seen on his knees.

But she had waited for his return, and she had offered him warm wine and cold bread, and the ample strength of her arms.

"Shall I tend her, husband?"

He shook his head. "The Matriarch of Havalla is there."

It was explanation enough. Although they traded with the Voyani when the harvest was good, the serafs had no love for them, and not a little suspicion.

And the last time the Matriarch of Havalla had left them, Ashaf kep'Valente had also disappeared. Daro di'Valente was a wise man; he had never leveled open accusation against the Havallans. But their welcome, in the decade and more that followed, had been scant and cold.

After the morning meal had been served—and the morning encompassed the hours at the Lord's height, for those who had come from homes that were gutted woke latest and with great hunger—Valla kep'Valente came with a visitor.

With two.

Nora en'Valente saw their shadows in the hall, but she might have ignored them had they not been followed by a spreading wave of utter silence. Serafs—hers—were not silent except in the face of death.

Not like this.

She wiped her hands clean on her aprons—if clean was a word that could dignify their state—and made her way past her son and his wife.

"Na'kallos," she said sternly, when he rose to accompany her.

He reddened. He was newly married, barely out of his boyhood, and he resented the use of that name.

His wife, however, smiled.

"Sara," she said, "tend to my troublesome son. And you, Kallos, tend to *your* son."

"But Sara—"

"Whose house are you in?"

"Father's."

She boxed his ears.

Sara stifled a laugh; the gesture had no force behind it but affection.

Kallos was not yet a man like his father. But Nora thought, given time, he would be.

Lady, give him time.

Give time.

He did not sit. The women of the village tended him as if he already were Daro, but she let them; he was uneasy, and some reminder of his role wouldn't hurt.

She walked out and saw that Valla had taken to her knees, pressing her head into the flat, smooth wood. A bad sign.

"Valla—what are you . . ." Her words died. For at Valla's side, in perfect obeisance, was a young woman she had never seen.

She wore silk sari, and if the sari was not clean—and it wasn't; it was bloodied, and dirt clung to its hem—it was far, far too fine for village wear.

But Nora was no fool; she gathered her words with care.

"Please accept my apologies, Serra," she said, hiding her hands behind her back. "Ser Daro has not been informed of your arrival."

But he would be, she thought. The hall had slowly emptied, and only the children too young to know better now clung to its walls, staring at the stranger with eyes that would tear from lack of blinking.

"Serra," the young woman replied, easing her pose and lifting her perfect back, "no apologies are necessary. Valla kep'Valente offered me the hospitality of her home, and sheltered me from the storm. But I came to Valla's home with a companion, and she has not returned; I have been told that I might find her within."

"A companion?" Nora's gaze was as blank as her mind, but only for a moment. "Do you speak of Kiriel di'Ashaf?"

The young Serra nodded gravely. Perfectly.

Nora felt old and ugly. Or rather, she should have. But something about this young woman's steady, clear regard denied such feeling; it offered respect. More.

"Yes," Nora said quietly. "She is here. Ser Daro tends her."

The Serra rose, and as she did, Valla rose as well. Or tried to; her legs were older and they had cramped in the uncomfortable posture of the seraf; it was seldom called upon.

But before Nora could move, the Serra did; she offered Valla kep'Valente her perfect, pale hand.

And Valla took it without question.

Who are you, Nora thought, trying not to stare. *Who are you, Serra?*

When Valla had gained her feet, she answered the question that Nora had been too wise to ask. "Serra Nora en'Valente," she said, using a formal title that was almost never called for, "this is the Serra Diora en'Leonne."

Daro looked up as movement caught the corner of his eyes. His lids were heavy and his legs ached. His arm, bandaged, ached as well; it had been many, many years since he had made the offerings to the Lady.

He could count them. He could count the months and days as

well, and with a little thought, the hours: She had failed to spare his daughter. He had never asked for anything from her after he had laid his child in her grave, as if the granting of a lesser gift would insult both his memory of his daughter and her loss.

He had thought he never would.

He knew that there was no balance. No justice. He knew that the Lady did not count the death of his daughter against the whole of the village—but he thought that, had she, he would not have been able to cede the child, and he wondered at the bitter gift of her mercy.

In the South there was no greater harm done to a parent than to ask him to choose between his children.

Humbled now, he rose, and as he did, he saw that his wife walked beside a stranger.

A beautiful stranger. A Serra. Her movement defined grace, and her steps were almost silent beside the heavier tread of his wife.

He waited, and when she knew that she had the whole of his attention, she knelt. This, too, she did with perfect grace.

At a loss for words, he said, "Rise," and watched her unfold. It was almost inconceivable that a woman like this could spend so much time on her knees that the posture looked as if it had been designed solely for her use. But the High Courts were strange places.

"Ser Daro," she said, and offered him the prettiest of bows. "Forgive my intrusion."

"You honor us," he told her, meaning it. And then, he added, "Have you come to see Kiriel?"

He could not have said why he asked, for Kiriel di'Ashaf and this Serra had almost nothing but youth in common.

But her smile was reward—for his guess, and for the whole of his night's work. "Yes," she said quietly. "If you will allow it."

"Daro," Nora added, her voice almost grating, "this is Serra Diora en'Leonne."

As the name penetrated his exhaustion, he froze.

But she was already beside him, and her hands were upon the closed screens. "No," he said, without thinking. "Let me—"

"It is a Serra's work," she said sweetly. "Or a seraf's."

The screen slid so quietly he would have said it hadn't opened at all. Obdurate wood, he thought, that complained whenever he touched it. But he did not grudge her the silence.

She stood in the doorway, and after a moment, he heard her say, "Ona Teresa."

The dark-haired woman looked up. Her smile was kin to the

Serra's; harder perhaps, but experience often had that effect. "Serra Diora."

She stepped into the room. After a minute hesitation, Ser Daro followed. Not even the great pillars seemed as strange, as awe-inspiring, as the Serra Diora en'Leonne. Men called her the Flower of the Dominion, and he cursed the paucity of their poetry.

She walked to the mats that lay pressed against the far side of the room. "It is dark here," she said quietly. "And peaceful." She knelt beside the woman she had named aunt, and she took the towels out of her hand. "Sleep," she told her.

"Ha," the Matriarch of Havalla barked.

The Serra Diora turned, and bowed low. It should have been awkward. "Matriarch," she said.

"If she sleeps for you, girl, I'll be offended. I've told her to sleep—"

"On the hour, every hour, for the past eight," the Serra Teresa said dryly. "The Voyani have, it seems, a perfect sense of time, even when they cannot see the shadows the Lord casts."

But she moved aside while Diora took the bucket and the bowl that lay, full, in her lap.

"Widan fever?" she asked.

"Widan fever."

"How long has it run?"

"The whole of the night."

"And she has not been woken?"

"We have tried, Na'dio. But, no, she sleeps."

"Father was taken by the fever three times," the Serra replied gently. "I am aware of what they require."

"Then perhaps I will rest."

The Matriarch snorted.

"Ser Daro," the Serra asked, "where is the other Northerner?"

"Eating."

She nodded.

And then, smiling softly, her hands full of towel, she began to sing.

She could have sung in the silence of her gift. She should have.

But her song was a different form of gift, and she offered it now to two women: the one who slept, and the one who had raised her.

Serra Teresa was silent.

"Ona Teresa," she said, as the first stanza died into stillness, "will you not accompany me?"

"I have no samisen," the Serra replied, wooden now. Cold.

"Nor have I." She met her aunt's gaze and held it. "But I would wake Kiriel, if I can. Help me."

It was almost a request.

The Serra Teresa di'Marano, who had done nothing graceless in a life spent in her niece's company, now spread her empty hands. It was the only argument she offered, and it was gently rejected.

Diora began to sing again, taking the melody, and after a pause, the Serra Teresa joined her.

She began the harmony with a hesitance that marred the song; it was as if she was a child again, and awkward. But Diora extended the note, changing the beat of the song. Waiting. It was a simple song, and open to the embroidery of the ambitious.

And Serra Teresa di'Marano was known for the quality of her song. Her voice grew stronger, and deeper, as the notes played out, accompanied by the words that children kept long after they had grown.

What she had lost—ah, what she had lost—had occupied the whole of her thought; what remained had seemed almost ghostly, a thing a step away from death. But she heard Na'dio's voice, and she heard her own, and they blended perfectly.

Na'kiri, they sang, young woman, and older one. Shorn of audience—for Ser Daro and the Matriarch were in some ways silent participants—they found a footing that they had established many, many years past, and the path was still strong.

It was left to Diora to wake the sleeper; Teresa had no power with which to do it.

No power but the song itself.

And she was not certain, afterward, which of the two carried more weight, for pale lids began to flicker as if in dream, and dark lashes trembled in the shadows of the windowless room. Yollana covered the lantern. They sang in darkness.

And it was a song that was sung in darkness, the Lady's song, some part of the edge of her hem, the fall of night.

Kiriel di'Ashaf's lips turned up in a smile; the skin cracked and bled, but she did not notice the pain. Her eyes widened, and in the room's scant light, they were still the color of gold.

But gold did not seem so threatening, here.

The storm had passed. The wind had been silenced, the fire guttered.

The girl murmured a single word. A name.

Ashaf.

The women did not lose the thread of their song, and if they felt—for a moment—that the song itself offered the comfort of a lie, they also knew that in the South, all comfort *was* a lie.

A lie that belief tainted while it was sung.

Diora sponged her face gently.

"Na'kiri," she said when the last refrain had dwindled into silence.

Kiriel said, "Ashaf's not here."

"No."

"Diora?"

"I am here."

"I can't see."

"It is dark, Kiriel. The Matriarch said you asked for darkness. Shall we lift it?"

Kiriel nodded. Her face, felt beneath the cool membrane of damp cotton, was hot; the water dried too quickly. She lifted a hand, and caught Diora's in it, and as Yollana lifted silks from the lamp, unwinding them layer by layer, the Serra saw a glint of simple band around Kiriel di'Ashaf's finger. She thought it glowed faintly; she did not ask why.

Instead, she lifted the cooled bowl of broth. "You must eat," she said.

But Kiriel frowned, turning her head in the direction of the Serra's lap. "I smell blood," she said softly.

Diora nodded quietly. "It is mine," she told the girl.

Kiriel snapped upward, then, throwing silks aside, her hand groping at her waist for a sword that lay just above the hard pillow at the mat's edge.

"No, Na'kiri," Diora said quickly. "I was not wounded. I was not attacked. It is—I—" She shook her head, and her smile was almost awkward. She lifted her arm and pulled the folds of sari aside; beneath them, the bandage caught light. It was stiff with dried blood.

"What happened?"

"I made the offerings," she said quietly.

"The—" Eyes widened, and then narrowed. "Oh. Why?"

Fever spoke.

Diora answered it gently. "For the village," she said. "And for you. Ashaf would have done it, had she been here."

"She would never have let you do it," Kiriel said solemnly. "Not you."

"Why not?"

"Because you're a Serra. A Serra of the high clans. She said—she says—" The girl fell silent, brow furrowed in heated confusion.

"Yes," Diora said quietly. "It is true. In the South, we are judged by perfection, and the smallest imperfection is the greatest loss."

"But you—"

"You brought me a husband," the Serra continued, "who does not understand these rules. And I am unkind enough to take advantage of them." She bent then, and kissed Kiriel's forehead.

Kiriel slid slowly back to the mats, and let Diora rearrange the silks. "Are we safe?" she asked.

Golden-eyed. Wide-eyed. Young.

"Yes. Safe. But you must drink this."

Kiriel nodded. She drifted in and out of wakefulness, and Diora gently fed her what she could swallow.

"My wife," Ser Daro said, speaking quietly, "knows herbs. She has tended fevers—"

"She is needed, Ser Daro," Diora replied. "And not one of us can replace her, save perhaps you; the villagers do not know us, and they will not trust us."

"They will do what you tell them, Serra."

"Yes, but that is fear, Ser Daro. And fear is not what they require."

But Ser Daro shook his head, half in wonder and half in surprise. "They will fear your name," he told her gently. "Because it is a name they know. They will fear to offend the husband whose name you bear. But you? If they fear you at first, they will let it go; it will not bind them."

"Fear is a way of life, for a seraf," Diora replied, serene now.

"Yes," he said, nodding.

"And for a Serra," she continued.

"Yes. But a Serra does not bear the scars of ablution." He bowed to her then.

"Will it aid my husband in any way?"

"It will aid him," Daro replied. He was quiet, serious, and not without grace. "For his story will become your story, and you will come to us after the salvation of Russo."

She would have stayed, but Kiriel, drifting, had heard every word that had passed between them. She caught Diora's hand again, and held it in hers. "Ashaf," she said, lips bleeding again. It was a request.

It was all the request she could make.

Serra Diora en'Leonne rose. "Yes, Kiriel. I will do what she

would have done, if you will mind the Serra Teresa. Eat. Drink.
Sleep."

"Ser Daro," she added quietly. "The sari I wear is . . . poor. If
your wife or daughter—"

He said, "They will know, Serra. And nothing of this village is
fine enough, in the end, for a legend."

"I am only Serra—"

"And Ashaf was only seraf."

She had no reply to offer. Instead she rinsed her hands in the
bucket, and offered the cloth to the Serra Teresa. "Sing," she said
quietly, "when it is necessary; it will quiet her."

And so the Serra Diora en'Leonne traversed the halls of Daro
di'Valente. She shadowed Nora, and when Nora became comfortable with her presence—and this happened subtly—she left her,
tending to the women and the children. Speaking softly and with ad-
miration, to the men. Treating them all as serafs—as cherished
serafs, obedient serafs, honored serafs.

The cradle song, she sang several times, and when she did, in-
fants quieted, their blue eyes turned toward her face as if it was the
whole of their world. Mothers watched her, and some, emboldened
by her gentle grace, joined their rough voices with hers. They were
not the Serra Teresa, but the imperative of love and fear gave their
song a truth and a heart that touched the Serra deeply.

She had never learned to cook; she had learned to arrange food
with care and artistry, and this she did, to Nora's consternation. But
Nora could see the steel beneath her quiet expression, and she did
not gainsay her; instead she muttered something about diamonds
and swine.

She did not leave the halls until Ser Daro summoned her, and
when she joined him, he said, "Kiriel is awake. She is asking for
you."

Nodding, she kissed the brow of a sleeping boy—a boy too old
to be coddled—and withdrew.

"Yollana." Kiriel's voice was raw.

The Matriarch lifted an eyelid as if it weighed more than she did.
"Aye, Kiriel. I'm here."

"Is Ashaf in the pendant?"

"No."

"But her memories—the things she loved—"

"Yes, child." Child. It was not a word that she had ever thought to use. Not for this one. But she did not regret it, and her voice did not harden. That took effort. "Yes, all the things she loved, she imprinted upon the pendant."

"And the other things? The things she hated."

Yollana said, after a considerable pause, "All of them."

Kiriel lapsed into silence, but her hands rose to cup something at the base of her collarbones. Yollana could see it clearly. Teresa could not.

"I was angry," Kiriel said softly.

Yollana wasn't certain if the confession was meant as apology. "I know anger, girl," she said, falling into the rougher cadence of a Matriarch. "Anger is like a Northern sword. It has two edges. The one, hone and temper. Keep it sharp. Keep it ready.

"But the other? Let it go. If it does not prey on you, if it does not ride you, if you have the strength, let it go." She paused, groping for her pipe. That was her song and her comfort; no one sang cradle song for a Matriarch.

"How am I supposed to know the difference?"

"One cuts your enemies," Yollana said, speaking now as if to a daughter. Her daughter. "It makes them pay for their crimes. It stills the demands of mercy and pity. It serves justice, or what we make of it."

"And the other?"

"It cuts *you*, child. It makes you bleed. It blinds you, it changes the world in your vision until the only thing that matters is your vision."

"Ashaf was afraid of you."

"Aye, girl," the Matriarch said bitterly. "And with cause."

But Kiriel said, "Everyone is afraid of me."

"Not everyone."

The silence that followed the simple truth was enormous.

"You are."

"Yes, girl, I am. You hold the fate of my family in those hands, and you always have."

"Is fear like a Northern sword, too?"

"Yes." She was surprised at the question, and let it show; she put the dried leaves aside. "But for fear, you need both edges."

"I was taught never to show fear."

"You were taught well, then, and not by Ashaf." It was a shrewd question.

"Not by Ashaf," Kiriel agreed. Her hands cupped and tightened. Yollana thought they would bleed.

And blood was not offered to that pendant. But she made no move to stop the girl; she had earned this.

"Fear," the Matriarch said, to quiet her own, "has two faces. The first is the fear that is aimed at you. It falls like a sword's blow, flies like an arrow. It will be offered you by people you hope never to frighten, and when you see it, you will be changed by it. You will never forget it.

"But it has its uses. In the South, men rule by fear."

"I am not of the South, and I am not a man."

"No. You are of the North, and you are more than man."

Silence.

"The second is the fear you yourself feel. To hide it is more than wise; it is life. Hide it well. But do not ignore it; do not become numb to its imperative. What anger cannot give you, fear can. Do not act in fear, but act on it."

"Did you like Ashaf?"

"Yes, Kiriel. I admired her. I hurt her, but I admired her."

"Why?"

"Because she was all the things I'm not. Can never be. I didn't envy her. But I saw it clearly." So many words, now. Too many words.

But Yollana knew that she offered them not because of any magical compulsion, and she refused to silence herself.

"I would have spared her," Yollana said quietly. "I would have spared my kin, if mercy had any part to play in my life. It didn't. And if I had to do it again, I would." She shook her head. "No one can be spared. Not even me."

Kiriel nodded. "They told me," she said softly.

"Who?" The word was too sharp.

"The Matriarchs," Kiriel said, sleep ladening the words and blunting their edge. She clasped the Heart of Havalla in her hands, pressing tight, holding on. There were tears in her eyes, and they were lit from beneath by lambent sun. Yollana was not moved; the sun made deserts, after all.

And then those pale hands relaxed. "I'm afraid," she said, in the smallest of voices. A child's voice.

Yollana was immune to it.

"You will remember Ashaf," she said, understanding the fear. "You will remember her because you will see her here, in every face in Russo."

Kiriel said, "Help me."

And Yollana reached for her canes.

The Serra Teresa, silent as statue throughout the whole of their conversation, was silent now, but she rose with perfect grace, and placed the canes within Yollana's reach. Her expression was a mask, a Serra's mask, and if there was accusation in the brief brush of glances, it was fleeting.

She did not offer aid to the Matriarch. Because, Yollana thought, she couldn't. She knew.

"Will they remember her?" Kiriel asked quietly.

"Yes, Kiriel di'Ashaf. The Matriarchs will remember her. And I will remember her when I join them." It was a vow. A promise.

Kiriel waited while Yollana arranged her knees. It took a while; they were swollen with the damp of the passing evening, and they caused her much pain. The pipe weed numbed it, but she had denied herself its use. A reminder that pain, like anger or fear, had its edges.

Her hands shook. With age. That's what she told herself.

This was Kiriel's homecoming, but it was Yollana's as well. Together, they lifted the chain that held the Heart of Havalla, and together, old hands touching younger ones, they lifted the Heart.

And then, the young hands fell away, inch by inch, and the old ones remained. They lifted the single stranded chain, and with care, placed it over the Matriarch's head.

The stone flared in the darkness, in greeting.

Kiriel di'Ashaf closed her eyes.

But her lashes were wet, and they shone.

"Na'tere," Yollana said quietly. "Will you stay?"

Teresa said nothing.

The Matriarch rose. And although she rose with care, there was a new strength in the legs that bore her. "Yes," she said softly, speaking to herself. Speaking to the Serra.

She took a hesitant step. Followed it with a firmer one. But her brow was creased in concentration. There was no pleasure in her.

"I must join my daughters," she told the Serra. "They will be waiting for me."

"In Mancorvo?"

"No." Her smile was a network of wrinkles, and the lines around her lips stretched in such a way that the expression almost seemed a frown.

"You will stay in Averda."

"Aye, Na'tere, I will stay in Averda. The borders are closed to us; not even the Deepings will grant me another passage." She shuddered a moment, and she reached up to touch the patch that covered her eye.

"Too late," she said, again speaking to herself. The hand fell away.

"But there is much now, that I must speak of, and the old have a habit of speaking to themselves. I must leave you, if you will not accompany me." She shook her head again.

"Lyserra and Corrona will not come. Even if called, they will not come."

"Arkosa?" Teresa asked softly.

"No, Na'tere. The Arkosans have left the *Voyanne*. If Margret can offer aid, she will. But the form of that aid, and its timing, is Arkosan, and a mystery to me."

She shook her head a moment, and raised hand to her single eye, as if to clear it of sleep. And then she smiled again. Turning, she bowed to Kiriel di'Ashaf.

"Ashaf's daughter," she said softly.

Kiriel opened her eyes. She was a child, in this room, and she wanted what a motherless child wanted.

"I will learn not to fear you. It will not come easily, but lessons seldom do; the Matriarchs of Havalla are stubborn and they cling to tradition. You must stay here. This is where the story began, and it is where its end will be writ."

"What end, Matriarch?" the Serra Teresa asked.

"Na'tere, if I could tell you that, I would be a far greater Matriarch than even the first." She bowed. "Now come. I have seen that you will be my companion for some time yet. But not forever, Na'tere. There is no home for you in the South."

The Serra Teresa said nothing.

But she looked to the door, and it slid open.

Serra Diora en'Leonne stood upon the threshold.

"Na'dio," the Serra Teresa said gently, "it is time. We must leave now."

"I know." She walked over to where Kiriel lay, and she knelt there, pressing her hand to forehead. "Let me say my good-byes."

The Serra Teresa lowered her head. "You might remain here," she said at last.

"I . . . cannot remain," her niece replied. "I have done what I can do in the village; the Tyr'agar waits for me. But, Ona Teresa, if you could wait outside a moment?"

Teresa glanced at the expressionless face of the Matriarch. It was seldom without expression. At last she gave her assent.

But Diora did not see it. "The fever," she said quietly, touching Kiriel di'Ashaf's brow.

Kiriel said, "What fever?"

Diora shook her head gently.

The Matriarch nodded grimly; the Serra Teresa, gracefully.

They left the room to two motherless daughters.

They marked the lack of rain in silence.

Valedan watched them. Ser Ramiro kai di'Callesta. Ser Mareo kai di'Lamberto. Ser Alessandro kai di'Clemente, and the Radann par el'Sol, Ser Danello kai di'Valente, Ser Anton di'Guivera. Ser Baredan di'Navarre. They stood as Southerners, stiff and tall, but not so stiff as to offer offense. It was a skill, he thought, that he himself had yet to master.

The Northerners carried themselves in a different fashion. And they marked the barriers between themselves and the Southern Tyrs. He wondered if that were conscious. On the part of Commander Bruce Allen, he thought it might be. With Ellora AKalakar, it was impossible to tell. Duarte AKalakar stood alone, in silence, his face impassive and grim. He deferred, in some fashion, to Southern dictate; Alexis was not by his side. Valedan had no doubt that he would pay for it later.

But they would all pay.

Meralonne APhaniel attended them, accompanied by Member Gyrrick of the Order of Knowledge. He was dressed in the robes of the Order, but they hung loose on his shoulders, as if they fit him poorly. It was a sudden shift. The war had changed him. No clearer sign existed than the presence of Lord Telakar, for Lord Telakar stood beside Gyrrick, as if he, too, attended the magi of the First Circle.

Kallandras of Senniel College stood in their wake.

They were silent.

Valedan said, "The rains have stopped."

Kallandras nodded.

The Commanders exchanged a glance; it contained a brief question, but no certain knowledge of the answer. They looked to the magi, their expressions similar: they trusted him only to a certain extent. And the presence of Lord Telakar defined that extent.

"There are three sides to this war," Valedan said quietly. "And it seems—to me—that the most dangerous faction is undeclared."

Marakas par el'Sol coughed briefly.

But Commander Allen nodded, lifting a hand to the back of his neck almost wearily. "The rains do not suit Alesso di'Marente. They will not suit the cavalry. Not," he added, "as well as the flats of the valley suit him." There was open criticism in the comment.

Valedan nodded. "Understood," he replied. "Can we take no advantage from the valley's height?"

"The magi can," Meralonne said, speaking to Valedan and only to Valedan. "But not with precision. We can harry the forces of the Marente cavalry, but when the armies meet, our forces will suffer if we are not precise—and if we are, we will be of no more use than archers." He did not need to add that they were outnumbered by the Northern bowmen.

The Southerners frowned, although Ser Alessandro was carefully neutral.

"You know the General," Valedan said to the two Tyrs. "If we sue for peace, or for a brief cessation of hostility—"

Ramiro di'Callesta smiled. It was not a pleasant expression, but it was answer enough. "We sue for peace," he said, "with your life."

"But if the plans of the demons do not suit him—"

"They are his allies," Ser Alessandro said sharply.

"They work against him here."

"Allies are often unpredictable. He will have some understanding of their weaknesses."

"But no control."

"Not enough, apparently." The Southern Tyr shrugged. "Peace will ensue upon either your death or his. What he has claimed for himself is what you claim, no more and no less."

Valedan nodded. "APhaniel," he said quietly.

Meralonne bowed.

"It seems to me that the demons hope to gain some advantage from the battle itself."

"Indeed."

"If battle cannot be avoided, how do we undermine an advantage that we don't understand?"

"We have a better understanding," Meralonne answered cautiously.

Lord Telakar laughed. "Tell him, Illaraphaniel. Tell him, while there is time."

Meralonne's frown was not the frown of a magi. It seemed to carry the cold of the Northern Wastes within its momentary folds.

Telakar's laughter diminished, but the echo of it lingered in his smile.

To the men gathered there, Meralonne said, "A kinlord rode the storm."

Commander Allen nodded quietly. "As we suspected."

"The rains themselves were not . . . unnatural. But they were gathered, and the winds that moved them kept them here, compressed, above your chosen battlefield."

"And the demon was destroyed?"

"No, Tyr'agar."

"But the rains have stopped."

"Yes."

"How, then?"

"Some forces are older than the demons," he said quietly. "And the demons fear to anger them."

"The winds," the kai Callesta said quietly.

Meralonne raised a silver brow. "The winds," he said, nodding. And then, after a pause, he added, "And the fires."

"In the rain?"

"If you travel to the village of Russo, you will see evidence of its passage. Rain does not trouble the elemental fire."

"What evidence? Speak plainly, APhaniel."

"The forests have been . . . cleared for a mile to the South."

"Cleared?"

"They are ash," he explained.

"And the demons feared the fire?"

"No, Tyr'agar," Telakar replied. Meralonne did not turn; did not acknowledge the spoken words. "The demons called the fire."

"What do they fear, then?"

"The earth," he responded. "It is in the earth that the saplings are planted. They do not belong here. They do not belong in the Deepings that gird Mancorvo. They exist in the forests of the Hidden Way, and they exist in only one season.

"Travel to Russo, and you will see evidence of the earth's awakening. It is a much changed place."

Ser Danello stiffened. "Changed?" he asked softly. There was threat in the word.

"The village itself stands," Telakar replied. "But the landscape has shifted, and not in your lifetime will it change again, unless the earth truly rises."

The Tor'agar bowed to Valedan kai di'Leonne, but Valedan shook his head, denying the request. This was Southern. To speak openly was to engender an obligation; to refuse it was to engender hostility.

"But you can end this," Telakar continued.

"How?"

"Kill Kiriel di'Ashaf."

"I will not believe that she threatened the village," Valedan said flatly.

The first words were left to him.

Duarte, about to speak, subsided.

"Not by intent, no," Telakar said. "I will grant you that."

"Easy enough to grant," Meralonne said sharply. "It costs you nothing."

Telakar shrugged. "I give you advice, Tyr'agar."

"You serve her."

"Yes."

"It is clear that the service of the *Kialli* is treacherous on all sides."

Telakar's smile did not dim. "Indeed. We are what we are."

"Why her death?"

"It is a precaution," Telakar said, his voice lazy.

Meralonne explained, "He serves her, and the *Kialli* are not content to *serve*."

"He speaks a truth," Telakar replied, unfazed. "But not the whole of the truth."

"And you?"

"I do not know the whole of the truth. I guess, now. The kinlord that ruled the storm was one of the Five, and he is not without importance or power."

"He would also be well pleased by her death," Meralonne said.

"Yes." Telakar glanced at the magi's profile. "So would all of the kin."

"Why?"

"Because she is the daughter of the Lord of Night," Telakar replied.

The silence was thick and sudden. What gathered within was not.

Meralonne said quietly, "Telakar."

But the Tyr'agnate of Lamberto spoke. "Tyr'agar," he asked, "is this true?"

Valedan, as surprised as the others, said nothing.

And Meralonne APhaniel said, "It is true."

Pandemonium then.

*   *   *

Yollana of Havalla drew close to the long tent. She would have known where it lay had the night been at its darkest; she could see the magic that spread across its boundaries. It glowed.

The pendant gave her that, heightening her awareness. But she was not without talent of her own.

"Na'tere," she said quietly.

"Matriarch?"

"I think it best that you return to my tent."

Serra Teresa di'Marano hesitated a moment, and Yollana recognized the hesitation; she had seen it many times, and had taken advantage of it. No one disobeyed a Matriarch without paying the price.

But she had not given an order, and the Serra understood that by Voyani custom, she had been offered a choice. She weighed it carefully.

Good girl, Yollana thought. But she *knew* what the Serra's choice would be.

"I will accompany you."

And she accepted it. Na'tere was not her daughter; would never be her daughter. She did not have the blood. But she had given much in Havalla's cause, and the Havallans were mindful of the debts they accrued.

"Very well. But do not speak, Na'tere."

"It would do little good if I did," the Serra replied, with just a trace of bitterness.

"Give me my canes," the Matriarch said.

The Serra complied without question, although she knew that they were now simple adornments.

Together they approached the tent.

The guards chosen were a blend of Northern soldiery and Southern Tyran. The Southerners gave way without pause; the Northerners attempted to interfere.

She would have cursed them, had she the time.

Instead, she lifted a cane and pointed it, as if it were a crossbow. She spoke in sharp, slow Torra, as if to the ignorant, or children, and it was clear that they understood her words. "I am the Matriarch of Havalla. I have information that the Tyr requires. Delay me at your peril."

Well, it was clear that they understood the gist of the words, at any rate. They parted slowly, and only after one of their number had disappeared into the tent.

Light gleamed off drawn sword, and it was a sharp, harsh light. A contrast to the night and the room in which Kiriel di'Ashaf lay.

The Lord's time, she thought.

When the man returned, she was given leave to enter.

The Northerners did not fear her. Not yet. A pity.

But she forgot this lingering resentment as she entered the tent itself, for sound erupted around her like Widan fire. If words could carry heat, they would have all been scorched.

But she understood what was said, even if her Weston was poor. They spoke of Kiriel di'Ashaf.

"I don't care," Ellora AKalakar said coldly. "She is one of *mine*. She has committed no crime; she is on leave with *permission*. I don't care if she *is* the daughter of the Enemy. She's *not* the enemy."

"Did you know this?" The Tyr'agnate of Callesta demanded, speaking in Weston as well. His voice was cold. Funny, that a land which saw so little cold could produce such ice.

"I didn't ask," Ellora replied. "She gave the House her oath, and *I* accepted it. What she does, I will take responsibility for—"

"You may be dead," Ramiro kai di'Callesta replied. "And there are some risks that are too great to be claimed as the responsibility of a single Commander."

"So you counsel us to take the word of a *demon*?"

"I counsel nothing," he replied.

"Bullshit."

"Ellora," Bruce Allen said, grabbing her shoulder in one hand. It was his sword hand. "By the Kings' writ, the choice is Valedan's— and Southern law takes precedence. We *will* abide by their decision."

Yollana of Havalla lifted a cane and brought it down, hard, upon the surface of the room's water table. It did not crack, but the shock of sound reverberated, breaking the heated argument.

"Tyr'agar," she said, with what wouldn't have passed for a bow among even the Northerners.

The Tyr'agar nodded. He understood her worth here.

"I have returned from Russo, and it appears that I have done so in good time."

"You were in the valley?"

The contempt that the question might have elicited had it been offered by any other was lost in the intricate lines of age. Yollana leaned heavily upon the single cane that still touched the ground, accentuating her vulnerability.

Ramiro kai di'Callesta was instantly on his guard.

But Ser Mareo kai di'Lamberto was not. He said, "Matriarch."
And she nodded.

"Your daughter came to my domis with word, and we traveled.
What word do you now bring?"

Yollana was not raised to the High Courts, and she had the Voyani dislike of them. But she knew some of their arts, and she employed them now. She veiled the truth. "Kiriel di'Ashaf saved the village of Russo from both fire and wind." She paused, and then added, "And from the earth that would otherwise have buried it whole."

Valedan lifted his head, and his shoulders slumped as he let go of the tension she saw in the youthful lines of his face. Oh, to have that face again—a face without lines to mark it; a face that could move, with ease, from anger to joy, and leave no echo of the former in the passage.

"Why do you speak, then, of her death?"

"She is the daughter of the Lord of Night," Ser Mareo said. The words were flat; he might have been speaking of the rain. Or the wind. Or the sun. Of the things, Yollana realized, over which he had no control.

A wise man, she thought. But she had always thought it.

"Ah," the Matriarch said quietly. "So. Now you know."

And the Lambertan brows rose a moment. But he did not ask her what she knew, and he did not ask her how. She blessed the South that had formed him.

What he did not ask, the Northerners did not ask.

And Yollana of Havalla said, in a deceptively weary voice, "Among the Voyani, the only blood that counts is the mother's."

"And who, Matriarch, is the mother of whom you speak?" Ser Mareo asked. *Who would bear the seed of the Lord of Night?* She heard the question.

And chose to deflect it. "I do not know," she told him. It was true. "But I know this: She was raised by Ashaf kep'Valente."

"Then that was no lie?" Ser Danello kai di'Valente asked.

"No. It was truth, and it was a profound truth. It is, by her choice, the only truth she values, and the only one she willingly claims."

This, too, was true. If Ser Mareo kai di'Lamberto was wise, he was also canny. He would know a lie. She did not offer one.

"She saved the village, and she pays the price. When I left her, she was struggling with the Widan fevers, and I am not certain that she will survive them."

Ser Mareo's eyes narrowed. But he did not press her.

"She is not a mage," Meralonne APhaniel said flatly.

"She is not," Yollana said agreeably.

The Tyr'agnati exchanged a single glance.

At last, Ramiro kai di'Callesta said, "We have been counseled to kill her."

The old woman's brows rose and fell in a single motion. "Why?"

But she knew the answer. Knew it fully in a way that no one else could. For Ashaf kep'Valente had known it as well.

She did not wait for a response, "She bears the taint of her father. I think we have all seen this. But she also bears the mother's blood, and there is strength in it."

"What strength?"

"I . . . do not understand it." Yollana let her irritation show. Ignorance *was* galling. But it was also useful. "And I think that she herself did not, before last night. I will be honest. I did not go to Russo to be of aid to Kiriel di'Ashaf. I went to retrieve something of value to my people, a gift given to Ashaf kep'Valente before she departed these lands.

"But I saw, in Russo, some proof that Ashaf kep'Valente also had a gift to give to the lands of her birth. Destroy her, and you destroy that gift."

"What gift, then?" Ser Mareo said softly.

Lord Telakar, restive, spoke then. "Weakness." There was contempt in the word, and more.

"I believe that she will be, in the end, all that stands between our people—and yours, Tyr'agar—and the armies of the Lord of Night."

CHAPTER TWENTY-FIVE

"ALESSO di'Marente may choose to move," Ramiro di'Callesta said. "But he will have more horsemen than we now possess, and the mud will make travel costly."

"If he has not destroyed the stockades or the villages that supply them, he will have some leeway," Commander Allen said.

Ramiro nodded.

The magi and the Matriarch had withdrawn from the tent in silence. Matters of mundane war were of interest when there were no other emergencies to concern them, but the thin line of sapling trees still surrounded the Terrean. They had waited Valedan's dismissal, and they had waited with infinite grace, given their ranks.

Valedan watched as the two men spoke, exchanging opinions. They had not yet agreed upon a course of action; nor had they looked to Valedan for advice. He was content to wait.

For although he was neither magi nor Matriarch, the significance of the trees weighed heavily upon him. The trees and Kiriel di'Ashaf. Had he a choice, he would have sued for parley, if peace was not possible. But neither of the Tyrs thought this prudent, and he was hampered by ignorance. By what was viewed as weakness.

He could not approach General Alesso di'Marente from a position of weakness, and to offer such a truce showed that he valued the Terrean of Averda too highly. Alina would have said as much, had she chosen to speak at all.

But he was so accustomed to her manner of speech and thought that he heard it anyway.

He stared at the map. At the width of the valley. There were three places in which horsed men might easily maneuver, and he had chosen one of them. It was to no one's liking, save perhaps the Tor'agar of Valente, and for that reason, the Tor'agar absented himself from discussion. But not from observation.

But the Commanders seemed unconcerned. "If they have superior numbers," Commander Allen said quietly, "our scouts have given no indication of it. We may make some use of the landscape for our own cavalry."

Ramiro frowned. "They have the whole of two armies," he said quietly, "and the forces of Oerta and Lorenza. If they do not outnumber us, neither do we have the advantage. The Callestan forces have gathered in full strength, but we do not have all of the Lambertans at our disposal, and if the Matriarch is correct, they will not arrive before the borders are . . . closed."

"We know the lands."

Ramiro nodded grimly; he looked once at the Tor'agar of Valente. Ser Danello nodded.

"We wait here," he said at last. "Let us make use of the valley's height."

But Commander Allen grimaced. "The valley is too wide to arm the heights in a meaningful fashion."

"Perhaps we can force them into a tighter formation; let us make the edges of the valley too costly to travel."

As Ellora AKalakar exited the tent, she turned to one of the soldiers. He saluted, and she spoke briefly. Too briefly to be clearly heard.

He nodded and departed, and she turned to her adjutant. "Korama," she said quietly.

He nodded as well. "Commander Allen?"

She shook her head, and he, too, departed.

She was left alone a moment, and she gazed out into the sea of tents, thinking about the Averdan valleys. About the Ospreys, wings clipped. So few had survived.

And in the end, she was not to fly them; not to hunt them. Not to wage war in clear and Southern terms. It should have been more to her liking, but she saw the cost; no smart man rested easy in the presence of so much magical potential.

And were it not for the Southerners, they would not be so hampered. She cursed them all genially. She was not a particularly religious woman, but then again, in the North one didn't have to be; the gods were within reach.

Here?

The Lord. The Lady. The superstitions that surrounded the Lord of Night. And the only obvious god-born child, the daughter of the greatest threat.

She watched the shadows lengthen, inch by inch. The sun had passed its height. The ground was drying, but slowly, and the passing of patrols across its damp surface had worn furrows there.

What would horses do?

She didn't ask; she knew.

Korama returned and she followed him.

They made their way to a tent, one among many. But it was larger, and at the moment, it was all but empty.

When the armies met at last, or shortly before, it would be full, and pallets would surround it. Ellora bowed as she entered. It was not a military bow.

And it was returned by a matronly woman and the two men who served her. "Kalakar," the woman said.

"Merilee," she replied.

"The storm has passed."

"The storm," Ellora said bitterly, "has barely started. Have the mages come?"

"Not yet."

She grimaced, but held her peace; the woman and her two companions were not ballast here. They served the army in their own way, and if it was not always comprehensible, it was still service.

"There is a risk in what we seek to do," she said quietly.

"I know." The woman smiled. "Frederik, Edmond, your services are not required for the moment."

Frederik bowed, but Edmond frowned. "Merilee—"

"If anything goes wrong, it is best that you are not present; in the end, if you are to be of service here, you must be trusted."

"As much as the Southerners trust the healer-born," Edmond said curtly. He was tall, and he seemed a tad on the young side. But then again, most of the men here did.

"They trust the healer-born," Merilee replied. "It is the god-born who are not welcome here."

"Should we then give in to their ignorance?"

"By command of the Kings, yes."

"Merilee—"

"What I bring to the infirmary is of far less value than what you can," she replied calmly. Ellora privately thought she undervalued herself; she had experience and the gravity that comes with that experience, and she would not founder.

Ellora cleared her throat, and the words that Edmond gathered abated. "Healer," she said quietly. "You are here in service to the priest, and she has requested your absence. I will be present. She will not come to harm."

He could have argued.

He almost did. But in the end, he chose to be prudent. Good man.

Frederik led him out by the arm, however, not trusting the permanence of this state.

Ellora and Korama relaxed. As much as they ever did in the field. "The Callestans are not a threat," The Kalakar said. "But the Lambertans cleave to the old ways."

"And perhaps there is wisdom to be found in them," Merilee replied. Which was just like her.

"There is never much wisdom in a lie," Ellora said, with a shrug.

"Ah, but there is, Kalakar. At the very least, a lie lets you know what someone else wants you to think, and that is a truth of a kind." She paused, and looked at last to the South, although she could see nothing but unadorned tenting and pegs. "This is not a land that loved the gods."

Meralonne APhaniel walked into the tent and held up a hand before Ellora could protest; behind him walked the Matriarch of Havalla, and beside her, the Serra Diora en'Leonne.

"They know," he said curtly.

If she could have done it safely, she would have strangled him. But First Circle magis—especially in circumstances where violence could occur—were protected in ways that normal people couldn't easily detect.

She expected Korama to bow; he bowed with a grace that could almost match the Southerners, when he chose to. But he withheld the gesture, instead offering the Matriarch a stern nod.

Her brows rose, and her lips were tugged by the faint hint of a smile. "You watch," she said to Korama.

He nodded. "It is possibly the best way to learn."

"If you survive it."

"As you say, Matriarch."

"What we do here," Ellora said quietly, "we do against the wishes of the Tyrs."

"Which is to say, they don't know. Or you think they don't," the old woman said. "But I, too, am here to watch, Verrus Korama."

His brows rose slightly.

Her smile deepened. "And, if possible, to learn."

"And the Serra?" Ellora said grimly.

"She is here," Meralonne replied, "at her request. She has . . . keen hearing."

"And more, or so I'm told."

He shrugged. "She offered me a choice: she could follow, or she could depart."

"And you chose the former because?"

"Her destination, I'm afraid, would not be to your advantage."

Ellora frowned. She assessed this beautiful stranger as if seeing her for the first time. But in the end, she nodded. The Serra's peaceful expression gave nothing away—and it wouldn't. "Merilee," she said curtly.

But Merilee crossed the tent, and came to stand before the Matriarch of Havalla. "I have heard of you," she said.

"Anything good?"

"It depends."

"Ah."

"And, Serra," she added softly, and this time she did offer a bow, albeit a Northern one. "We have all heard of you. Of what you did in Essla."

Diora lowered her head.

"You are welcome in this tent at any time you choose to visit."

And raised it again, her eyes almost wide. It was as much expression as she'd yet shown. "It is true, then," she said at last. "That you have no fear, in the North."

Merilee's laugh was low and deep. "No," she said. "If that is said of us, it is definitely not true. But we have no fear of you."

"It is said that you have healers here."

"They are occupied elsewhere at the moment, but if you come at another time, you will meet them. Frederik is older, and he has seen battle before; Edmond is younger. I ask, in advance, that you forgive Edmond his youth; it makes him rash and quick to anger."

"He is a man," she said, as if that excused all. Or at least explained it.

"No, Serra. He is a boy."

"And what is a man in the North, then?"

"I think you know," she replied. "Member APhaniel?"

He nodded gracefully. But he did not move or gesture. It was as much an active display of his ability as he had yet shown.

"Kalakar?"

Ellora nodded. "Let us speak," she said quietly, "with the Mother."

The Serra Diora watched.

She was aware of each person in the tent. Even if sight had been denied her, she would have been aware of where they stood; their breathing was audible in the silence. Yollana of the Havalla Voyani took a seat on the nearest cot. Her hands played with the flap of her pouch, but she did not draw pipe.

She was the only other person in the tent who was nervous; her breath came a little too quickly.

But The Kalakar and her adjutant were calm and relaxed, and the woman who held their attention was happy. Truly happy, Diora thought, in wonder.

She was not young, and she had never—in Diora's estimation—been beautiful. But what she had been denied in feature, she had in presence alone: Had she spoken, Diora would have listened to no other in the room. Not even Kallandras, had he been present.

Her smile was deep and almost constant, and although she faced the grimmest of wartime duties, she did it with the same contentment with which Diora's father's wives had prepared their rooms; this *was* her place.

You would have saved my father's wife, she thought quietly. And if she had, the whole of the Serra Diora's life might be different.

And where would she be, when the war came to Annagar? Not here, surely not here.

Yollana cursed sharply, the word ending in mid-syllable.

Diora looked down, then. The ground had disappeared beneath her; mist had rolled in, but from where, and when, she couldn't say. It was not a cold mist, and it was not a wet one; it seemed to exist for the eyes alone.

She looked up again, and she saw—with some surprise—that Merilee's eyes shone golden in the odd light. It had not dimmed; indeed, the mist seemed vaguely luminescent. But she had seen eyes of exactly that color only once in her life, and recently.

So, she thought. It was true.

She did not move or speak. If it had been appropriate, she would have knelt. So much of significance had happened while she did. It was the only natural way that a Serra could witness power; by being apart from it. This felt wrong.

But that was the South speaking, or perhaps the High Courts. She had not come to beg.

Only to learn.

When the mist had risen to her waist, she looked to Yollana. Yollana rose, her eyes hooded, her lips thin. Her hands were balled in fists by her pouch, but she did not speak again.

And Merilee said, "Mother." Just that.

A word denied Diora for the whole of her life.

Her breath quickened and her hands rose, as if the word were something solid that she could catch and hold.

The Northern Commander bowed her head; it was as much a gesture of respect as Diora had seen her show, and it made the Serra uneasy. The Verrus by her side also bowed his head, but Meralonne APhaniel simply waited. He had grown taller, or so it seemed to Diora; the mists seemed to well at his feet, giving him a wide berth.

The tent could no longer be seen.

Diora wondered, if she walked in these mists, if she would be able to touch the absent walls, or if she had left the lands that the army occupied. She did not ask.

She might have, but something answered Merilee.

And the voice that she heard was so unlike any that she had ever heard before that she was almost numb at the force of it.

"Daughter," it said. The mists rose, then, as if summoned; they trailed like streams of vapor in the wind. But the wind was silent, and it moved nothing else; not even the hair of the men and women who watched.

If a village spoke as a single man, it might speak in an echo of this voice. If every man and woman gathered beneath the Lord's face were to speak so, they might come closer—but perhaps not. She could hear the oldest of voices, and the youngest, the deep baritones of a man and the fluting, sweet heights of a woman given to song; she could feel in each, something that she was afraid to name.

"Mother," Merilee said.

"You are far from home," the Mother said, speaking as quietly as such a multitude might do.

"Far," Merilee agreed. "But not so far that you cannot hear my voice."

"I would hear your voice in the Halls of Mandaros, should you choose to call me there," was the soft reply. "Why have you called?" And the mists rolled away.

Standing before them—and above them at the same time—was a woman. She was not old, but neither was she young, and she was at once beautiful and plain. She was not slender, had never been slender; she was far too solid for that. She bore a basket upon her right arm, and in her left hand, a scythe. Above her flew small, bright-winged birds with silent voices; they were lovely, and harmless.

None of the Lady was in her, for the Lady was cool and distant. And the Lady did not smile.

"Illaraphaniel," the god said, inclining her head.

The Northern magi bowed.

"You are well."

"I am."

The god frowned slightly. "Daughter," she said, "where are you?"

"I am in the lands of the South," Merilee replied gravely.

"You are not in the lands of the Winter Queen? You do not walk the Winter Road?"

"No, Mother."

The god bent down to touch the ground at her feet, and after a moment she rose; the frown grew troubled. "It is Summer in the Court of that Queen," she said at last. "And it is nigh Winter here. What has happened?"

"The seedlings of the Winter have been taken," Meralonne APhaniel replied, "by the Lord of the Hells."

"Impossible."

"They have been planted," he continued, as if speaking with a god was no more significant than speaking with Tyrs, "in the blood of the living."

She was silent.

"If the saplings bloom here," she said at last, "it will be difficult for the Summer Queen; there will be no Summer King."

Merilee's eyes widened.

But the silver eyes of the magi did not. He waited.

"My brother has grown canny," the god said at last. "For I see that you are correct, Illaraphaniel." Her eyes narrowed.

"I would see the land cleansed," he said quietly. "Of the taint of these saplings."

"So, too, would I—but that is not within my power. The Hidden Ways are still of your world, and I have little jurisdiction there."

The Northern Commander now lifted her head, and the Mother gazed at her; the frown deepened. "Ellora," she said gravely, "do not seek to undo what has been done."

The Commander paled, but she held the god's gaze. It was more than Diora could have done. "We must," she said evenly, "if we are not to lose more lives."

"There are some things that cannot be justified in such a fashion, warlord. Not even if the justification seems fair."

"I note that you do not counsel the magi in a similar fashion."

"He is what he is," the god replied, "and beholden to the laws that govern his kind. You are not. For better or worse, you have a range of choices that he seeks only at his peril."

"And those?"

The god's frown deepened. It was the whole of the answer she offered.

"Mother," Merilee said softly, "I do not know what has been attempted. I know only that we stand upon a field of battle in the shadow of your enemy's magics. We do not understand their purpose."

The god was silent.

After a moment, she turned to Yollana of Havalla. That surprised the Serra; indeed, it seemed to surprise the Matriarch.

"Yollana," the god said quietly. "You carry the answers."

"I have not yet had time—"

"You mistake my meaning. The answers that can be found will be found in the history of your line, and only there."

"Are the gods not all knowing?"

The Mother's smile was dry. An older woman's smile. It made Yollana seem . . . young. Awkward.

But she said, "I have heard that the Tor Arkosa has risen."

And this time, it was not Yollana who spoke.

Diora did. "The Tor Arkosa?" she said. "Can you know that, in the North?"

"I know," the Mother said quietly, "what my children know. But it *is* known, in the North. I cannot say how widely." She looked at them all, and then said, "And I cannot say in the end what part the Tor Arkosa has to play; if I am not mistaken, it will not be in *this* war."

"It is said," Diora told the god, "that the Cities stood in defiance of the gods themselves."

"It is true," the god replied.

Diora wondered if gods deigned to lie.

"And it is true, as well," the god added, "that in the Cities of Man, voices were raised that could be heard by the eldest." Her gaze was keen and bright, and for a moment, it was the only thing that Diora could see. "Yes, Daughter," she said, lifting the scythe. "Even yours."

Merilee bowed. "Mother," she said quietly, "if you can, tell us what is meant by this spell."

"I do not know," the Mother said quietly. "But I know this: the Winter has never been friend to man." She paused, and then added, "and this, too, Daughter: that the blood of the living has always had strength to those of us who could use it in safety."

Merilee bowed.

The god returned that bow with the most patient of smiles.

"I think that the Winter Road has been invoked—or will be," the Mother said. "And I think, as well, that it is not the greatest threat." She lifted the basket. "Yollana of Havalla, your kin were not my kin. But perhaps the time has come when you will shed the worst of your history and its burdens.

"I cannot command you," she added, "nor can I compel. And the gods of the North do not beg."

She lifted a hand in farewell, and when she waved, the mists rolled back so suddenly they might never have existed at all.

But the tent looked cold and harsh in the light of day.

And the Northerners, tired and disappointed. "Korama," the Commander said curtly. "This was not all we hoped for."

"Commander," Korama nodded. "Merilee, we thank you for your time. If—"

But Yollana of Havalla lifted a hand. "It was," she said bitterly, "what I expected. The gods were ever a disappointment—or a

threat—to my people." She lifted the flap of her satchel and withdrew her pipe. "I will speak," she said heavily. "But I must have
time, now, to consider my words."

The Commander snorted.

The Matriarch frowned, the pipe halfway to her cracked lips.

They were, Diora thought, both frightening in their fashion, and
both accustomed to command and the respect that came with it.

But she looked to Yollana, and she offered Yollana a perfect bow.
"Matriarch," she said, as if the Commander no longer existed. "Let
us withdraw. The Northerners must speak among themselves."

And you, Diora thought, with just a hint of pity, *must speak to
your dead.*

For she knew what the god spoke of; she had seen it in Arkosa,
and she would never forget.

"I have never asked what occurred within the depths of Arkosa,"
the Matriarch said. She sat in the center of her tent. To her left, she
had placed a small dagger; to her right, a small cup. The dagger was
sheathed, its blade hidden. The cup, however, stood in plain sight; it
was old.

Old enough that the Serra Diora could not read what was written
around its rim, although the letter forms were clear.

She had seen this writing before.

"Aye," Yollana said quietly. "What you see, you see. You must
have offered your blood to the Heart of Arkosa," she added.

Diora said nothing, but thought, *I offered my life to it.*

No, not hers. Not *this* life.

"Good girl," Yollana said, when the silence had grown in length.
"You do not speak of what you saw. Do not speak of this."

"I will leave," Diora said quietly.

"If you leave, you must send the Serra Teresa. This is not something, in the end, that I can do alone."

"Your daughters—"

"They are in Averda," Yollana said, but the words were distant.
"Yes," she added, when she saw the look of surprise cross Diora's
face. "But they are not near, and we cannot wait upon their arrival.
If they arrive at all, it will be to a carrion feast; they are not within
two days' travel of here, unless they steal horses and ride."

"And you cannot call them."

The old woman's smile was bitter. "If I could, Serra, I would.
But, no, I am granted at least that mercy. I *cannot* call them. Not

even your voice could reach them." She drew a deep breath. "Decide, Na'dio. I will abide by your decision."

But the Serra Diora knelt in front of the Matriarch of Havalla. "What you will spare your daughters," she said quietly, "I will spare my aunt."

"She will not think it a kindness," the Matriarch replied gravely.

"No. But she would tender a similar reply." Diora hesitated, and then said, "I know, Matriarch. She does not."

"No," Yollana said quietly. "She does not. You remind me."

"I offer no advice to the Havallans," Diora replied serenely. "And the Havallans offer no advice to the clans."

"Ah, Na'dio," the old woman said, lifting the dagger. "If only you had been born to the Voyani."

"I have been born," Diora replied, as the dagger left the sheath, "to Annagar, and perhaps in this war we will see the end of older ones."

"There is no end to war, girl." The blade bit her pale skin. Blood welled, but Diora had already lifted cup to catch it.

And Diora said softly, "To end the wars, the Cities fell."

"Then they fell without reason."

But Diora shook her head. "What would you have me do, Matriarch?"

Yollana's lips thinned. "Be graceless and clumsy, just once."

Diora smiled. "And what purpose would that serve?" She set the cup in Yollana's hand; the blood had not yet dried, and it spread in a smear beneath the rim of ancient writing; bone-colored ceramic adorned by a dark, dark red. The cup was wider than it had first appeared, the words brighter.

She had never participated in any of the Havallan mysteries. But she lifted *lumina arden* from her sash, and she unsheathed it. It shone.

Yollana's brows rose. Their eyes met, and the Matriarch nodded.

With a slight grimace, Diora turned her scarred palm toward the dagger's light. They met, flesh and steel, in an act as old as the desert. She bled. Yollana's hands were less steady than Diora's, but they were just as quick; no blood was wasted.

"Why blood?" she asked softly.

The Matriarch's face froze. When it relaxed, the old woman said, "I don't know. Perhaps because it is the water of life."

"Water is the water of life," the Serra replied. She was almost reckless. "Without it, we perish."

"Aye, there's truth in that." Yollana shrugged. "But the young think of truth as a single, flat thing, immutable and unchanging. The old know that truth is like the Heart of Havalla: it has many sides, many facets, and yet each is a part of the whole."

She set the cup down.

The tent seemed darker, but Diora realized that it was the cup that was brighter; the words that rimmed it now seemed to move, as if they were in the process of being written. Or rewritten.

Yollana lifted the chain that held the Heart of Havalla. Her hands shook, and although her face gave nothing away, Diora knew why: it had been many, many years since it had rested about her throat, and she was hesitant to part with it.

But she did, and more: she slowly set it into the cup.

The Heart of Arkosa had required no such price for its knowledge. Diora wondered, for the first time, how different the histories of each Voyani family were. But she did not ask; instead she watched as the Heart slowly sank.

Blood did not touch it; blood did not cling. The Heart was bright and clear, as if it were a diamond catching the Lord's gaze. She frowned. It *was* clearer now; color, if it had that, faded.

And after a moment, so did its shape, the whole of its size. In alarm, she looked up, but Yollana's gaze was both intent and calm; if the Heart was dissolving, it had obviously dissolved before without harm.

Only when it was gone did Diora notice that the blood had gone with it. And when she did, she became aware, as if for the first time, that some part of that blood was hers.

"Aye," Yollana said quietly. "And it will know you, now." The words were stark.

"Matriarch—"

"Are you frightened, girl?"

"No," she replied. "I am honored."

Gray brows rose, like rusty blades. The whole of Yollana's eyes were dark. "Then you are a fool," she said.

"I am," Diora replied gravely. "Fool enough to raise the Sun Sword from the waters of the Tor Leonne."

"Hush," Yollana said. "And bear witness. *Listen.* If I do not survive, you must do two things. Bear word of what is said, and bear the Heart of Havalla to my daughters."

"And if I do not survive?"

Yollana said, "Don't be clever, girl." She sounded distracted.

She was, Diora realized. A woman now stood to her left, and another to her right. They were armored in breastplates so fine and so adorned with imagery they seemed to be sculpted from metal; nothing so glorious could be worn in open battle. It would almost be a crime.

Both were far paler in complexion than Yollana—or any of the Voyani; but the woman to the left had raven's hair, hair as dark as Diora's, and the woman to the right had hair the brown-red of dried blood. They were Sen, she thought.

"Daughter," the woman to the Matriarch's left said, in a voice that made the coldest of Yollana's threats seem friendly.

Yollana winced. "Matriarch," she replied.

"Daughter," the woman said again to the Serra, and then, frowning, looked *at* Diora. But the frown withered as she watched it, and the face fell again into its cold, clear lines. The Sen Margret had never looked so grim.

But the Sen Margret had done much to merit such an appearance, and the Serra Diora knew better than to place much faith in looks. She was steady now; her knees were beneath her, and her hand—her unblooded hand—was in her lap. She took care, even here, not to bloody her sari; she had lost one already.

"It has been long since we heard your voice," the woman said at last. "Why do you call us now? Why do you call us to speak outside of the confines of the Heart of Havalla?"

"The enemy," Yollana said quietly.

The woman to the right spoke for the first time, and only when she heard this second voice did Diora realize that she could hear *nothing* but the words themselves. The tones they were offered in were clear, but came at a great remove. She wondered if this was what Ona Teresa heard now, in every word she listened to.

"We have many," the woman on the right said. Her eyes were as dark as Yollana's. "Speak plainly, if you must speak."

"The Lord of Night," Yollana replied.

They were silent, then; they glanced *through* each other, as if unaware that they did not exist in isolation. "What," the woman to the left said, "of *Allaskar?*"

And Diora lifted a hand, her fingers tracing a circle in the air before her chest. "Do not," she said, before she could stop herself, "speak his name here."

"There are none here to hear it, if we speak it," the woman replied. "And we must speak, Daughter."

Yollana looked grim. The interruption was costly.

"We are far from the desert," the living Matriarch said. "And we are far from the roads that we roam. But the Lord of Night has taken the seedlings of the Winter trees, and he has placed them around the borders of these lands."

The woman on the left raised a hand. It was not mailed, but it should have been. "Winter trees?" she asked softly.

Yollana replied with a phrase that Diora did not understand. And realized that she would have, had she been wearing the Heart of Arkosa.

But the woman, the eldest, did not seem to suffer from the same inability. Her face, already pale, paled further. As if the dead could. "When?" she said starkly.

"We do not know. But I have seen the trees," the Matriarch replied. "And I have liberated one."

"You?"

Yollana's silence was heavy with annoyance. It comforted Diora. "How many, Daughter?"

"We do not know."

"How were they taken? How were they planted? Does Arianne now work in concert with her enemy?"

Yollana shook her head. "They were planted in the blood of mortals, and they were twisted by the growth. They are not without their power, but that power is also twisted."

"Was the whole of the harvest taken," the woman on the right asked.

Diora wished, for just a moment, to know their names. It passed.

Yollana actually rolled her eyes. Curtly, she said, "Be aware that we have almost no time. I have lived *neither* of your lives, and if I understand your words, it is either an artifact of your blessing or your curse."

The woman on the left smiled slightly. "Daughter," she said, "you have learned much since your youth. What is the question?"

"Sen Savanion asks if the whole of the harvest was taken."

The woman's eyes rounded.

"The enemy, too, has learned much," she said at last. "The Hidden Ways are weaker now than they have ever been." She turned her face, and a perfect profile gazed away, to East or West, Diora was no longer certain. "The time is coming, Daughter."

"Matriarch," Yollana replied, smoothing the annoyance from her face. "What must we do? We cannot destroy the trees in time."

"You must *not* destroy the trees," Savanion said. "For if you do, the Summer Court cannot be convened, and the Summer King cannot be chosen. Those trees must be planted," she added quietly, "In memory of the Winter King, and in preparation for his return. But they must be planted in the ceremony of renewal; they must be planted at the marriage of the High Queen and her Summer King."

"Why?"

"They prepare for the return of the Winter King."

Yollana's irritation showed. Summer, or Winter—a Northern word—were not part of her history; Diora saw the ignorance writ plainly and enfolded by growing anger.

Savanion saw it as well.

"Understand that Arianne is of the Firstborn; she is governed by the seasons of this world. If she acknowledges no Winter King, she cannot acknowledge the Summer King, and if she takes no consort in the Summer, she will be barren. The seasons, for the Court, will not turn; time will not pass. Do you understand?

"The planting of the Winter trees marks the change of the season. If Arianne is trapped between the seasons, her Court will have no purchase in the mortal realm."

"Understood," Yollana replied, grave now. "But I have seen this Arianne; we have all seen her hunt. I think that it would not be counted a loss should she lose all ability to call it."

"Then you are foolish, Daughter, and you have forgotten much of your history. If the Lord of Night is upon the plane, you *must* have the Summer Queen; she is his natural enemy. So, too, is the Winter Queen. The trees are essential.

"If they are planted here, if they are taken and twisted by old blood magic, she will not be able to gather them."

Yollana nodded again. "They are planted here," she said, as if history lessons were over. "But they are used in a fashion that we do not understand."

The woman to the left nodded, and again, Diora glimpsed her perfect profile. If ghosts indeed appeared as they had in the moments before their death, this one had not died bent or withered by age. She was strong now.

"As you suspect, Daughter, the trees form a branch of the Hidden Way. It can be used by the *Allasiani*. It can be followed from there to here, if they are near a crossroad."

"Then we will face an army?"

"It is likely," the woman replied. But her face was creased in frown or thought; the two were intertwined, as if the thought was unpleasant.

"The army is not yet here."

"I would guess that the trees have not yet achieved their stable growth."

"And when they do? We have reason to suspect that the enemy waits upon the meeting of *our* armies."

"What armies, Daughter?"

"The forces of the two men who claim the rulership of these lands."

"Only two?"

"Only two are needed, in a war."

"The lands have grown strange, Daughter. I had almost . . . forgotten."

Savanion said quietly, "Yollana, the trees—you said they were rooted in blood?"

"It seems clear."

"How many?"

"We don't know." She paused, and then said, "Some thirty or forty children were taken not a week past from the village of Essla."

But Savanion frowned more deeply. "A week is not enough time," she said softly, "for the trees to take root. The children were taken for some other purpose."

"To appease the earth," the Matriarch replied quietly. "The Old Earth."

The two women fell silent; it was the elder who broke that silence. "Yes," she said distantly. "We heard its voice. Offer it an equal sacrifice, and it will loose its hold; it does not approve of the changes made to the trees themselves. It can hear their voices."

"What do their voices say?"

But the woman shook her head. And Savanion shook hers, her braid flying. It looked almost as if she'd been struck.

"Think," she said quietly. "And tell the eldest to think, and with care. I did not reside, in my life, in the Tor Havalla. I was not present for the acts of allegiance offered the gods there. Nor was I present for the acts of purification. I know of them; I learned of them from her."

"You tell her to think," Yollana snapped. But she drew a deeper breath. "Sen Kalias," she said quietly, speaking the name of the second woman for the first time, "Savanion bids you recall your time in the Tor Havalla." •

"To what purpose?" The voice had cooled. The face had frozen. Whatever had passed there, it haunted her, and it brought her no comfort.

"She speaks of acts of allegiance and acts of purification," Yollana said hesitantly.

And the Sen Kalias stilled. She raised a hand, palm out, as if testing the wind. "Daughter," she said at last. "You must carry us to the field. Lay the Heart against the earth. Bring the dagger; leave all else safe."

"The field?"

"The meeting place of armies," she replied. "Now."

"We are upon it," Yollana replied. She lifted the chain; nothing weighed it down. But that was illusion, must be illusion, for Diora could almost feel the thud of the Heart against the tenting.

With care, and with marked hesitation, she set it against the flat ground. It lay where it had been placed, glowing faintly. Everything about its light was wrong.

"So," the Sen Kalias said, after a long pause. "Tell Savanion that she is wise. Cursed, but wise. There are two magics here, Daughter. The magics that warp the trees were set *to* warp them. They have fed upon the living and the dying, and they have known no other life.

"But the magics that gird the field are different. An old rite has been performed here."

"What rite?"

"The beginning," the Sen Kalias said, "of an act of purification so profound we would not have considered it possible in the Tor Havalla."

"Between the seedlings' voice and the power of the earth, they have built an altar of the land. It is *his* altar; the blood that is spilled upon it will strengthen his chosen Champion. In a history these lands have long forgotten, one such Champion would have been . . . me."

"And not the Lord of Night?"

"If he chooses to traverse these lands himself, then yes, it will strengthen him. But if he had made such a choice, such a magic would be unnecessary and costly. No, Daughter. There is another vessel."

Yollana looked up.

The Serra Diora was pale.

Both women bowed, the one in respect and weariness, the other in fear.

"If we destroy the vessel?" Yollana asked, voice deceptively soft.

"The power is meaningless."

She nodded.

But Diora said, "Does the vessel have no will, Sen Kalias?"

The eldest shuddered and turned her face away, into shadow. "Will?" she said, though the word could barely be heard.

"Choice. If the power is there, but she does not choose to use it—"

"You have never felt the power of his shadow," the woman said. Her voice was shaking. "You have never known majesty, who have not seen it."

"Yet you left him."

"Yes, I left him. And the echoes of that loss destroyed me. Had he known—had he known what we planned behind the safety of our walls—we would not be here now. There would be no Heart, and no Havallans.

"His power devours," she said quietly. "That is the common truth, and it *is* true. But what is forgotten, conveniently or by necessity, is *also* true. We welcome the devouring. We give ourselves to it gladly." She turned to look upon Yollana of Havalla, and said, almost gently, "ask Savanion how I died."

Yollana shook her head, mute in the face of knowledge that was taking form and shape behind the walls of her eyes.

"Ask her, Daughter."

"No."

"Then I will tell you. She killed me."

Yollana closed her eyes.

"She was right to do so," the Sen Kalias continued. "I know that four families survived the long fall. But in our past, my determination did not carry me beyond the blasted plain. I knew what we faced. I knew what was necessary. I *loved* my daughters and my sons; my grandchildren; the people whom I had chosen to take with me when I made my escape.

"But loving them, in the end, was not enough; it was too mortal a force. Too weak. I bent, and I bowed. Savanion *was* my daughter, the best of my children. The strongest, the swiftest, the quickest to judge.

"She is also the only one who survived. Think on this, Daughters. For I hear what you do not say: You know the vessel, and you hold it in affection.

"So, too, did my children." She raised a hand and placed it upon Yollana's shoulders, and the Matriarch went pale. Diora had thought, until that moment, that the two were ghosts. But she understood, as Yollana's eyes rolled back, exposing their whites, why the Matriarch had spoken of her possible death.

"When you speak of armies," the Sen Kalias said, her grip

tightening, "you speak of tens of thousands of lives. Boys, men in their prime, the horses upon which they ride. All. Had I attempted such a feat, I would have been destroyed by the gift. Do you understand? Not one of us could have sheltered the whole of his grim harvest; not one of us could have survived to use the gift.

"Savanion was Havallan. Do not be less, Yollana."

She lifted the hand. Glimmering in the dark of the tent, her fingers were red with blood.

Diora rose as the ghosts vanished.

"Matriarch," she said, and reached out to touch the old woman. Yollana slumped forward, heavy now, into the Serra's arms.

Diora caught her, holding the whole of her weight. She spoke again, to no effect. But the third time, she weighted the word with the force of command, and Yollana's eye shifted as white once again gave way to brown. It teared.

"So," the Matriarch said. "I am still alive." She did not sound particularly happy about her fate.

"And I," the Serra added.

"And now you know."

But Diora said, "That the ancestors of the Voyani served the Lord of Night? I already knew, Yollana. Margret knows as well."

"Aye. I had almost forgotten; she had never made that trek as Matriarch before. It is a bitter homecoming."

"You cannot kill Kiriel di'Ashaf."

"According to the Heart of my people," the old woman replied, "I have no choice."

"The Heart of your people—the Hearts of all of the Voyani— were made by grim and terrible women; women whose lives and power were predicated upon the sacrifice of the helpless."

"And the powerful," Yollana said softly.

Diora shook her and then withdrew. "And the powerful," she said, thinking of the Sen Diora. Thinking of Sen Margret's foolish son. "But Kiriel is different."

"How, Na'dio? Give me hope, and I may be foolish enough to take it. *How?*"

"She is the Daughter of Darkness," Diora replied, hating the words. "And even so, she has never sacrificed the living in return for the gift of power."

"And you know this?"

"Yes," the Serra replied starkly. "Because, had she, I would have heard it in her voice. She *has* killed. Of that, I am certain. But . . ."

"But?"

"Ashaf kep'Valente," Diora said quietly. "Ashaf would never have accepted it."

"You place too much faith in the dead."

"I am not the one to invoke them."

"Ha!" Yollana's laugh was grim and brief. "You are wasted in the life you have been given," she said.

"I might have thought so once," the Serra said, and she offered a wan smile. "But that is past. I am Serra Diora en'Leonne, and that is all I wish to be."

"You will not speak of this."

"No. And the men of the South will be far too wise to ask. But the Northerners? They wait, Yollana. What will you tell them?"

"What I always do," the Matriarch said, rising slowly, her knees wobbling. "As much of the truth as suits me."

Diora said, "And how much is that?"

Yollana's eyes narrowed. "Do not think it, Na'dio. I am old, but I am difficult to kill."

"So, too, was the Sen Kalias."

"She was maddened. I am not."

"No, Matriarch. You are not." Diora bowed, and the hand that had gracefully retrieved the dagger now slid it into its customary place in the folds of her sash. "But I have seen Kiriel di'Ashaf."

"And you are willing to take that risk?"

"I am. I would not have been, once. But I have seen the Tor Arkosa, and I have spoken with the Sen adept of the Tor Havalla. What they did, they did in another time, but it both marked them and made them what they *were*. I know what the Cities were like," she added softly. "And the best of ours are a shadow of their glory.

"We do not have the ghosts that linger like gargoyles upon the heights of buildings too tall to construct; we do not have the wealth of information, the art and the music, that made the Cities so beautiful.

"But neither do we have the Lord of Night. We are not what they were."

She added quietly, "You will learn of Kiriel di'Ashaf from the Heart of Havalla."

Yollana's brows dovetailed. "Speak clearly, Serra."

"You will come to know Ashaf kep'Valente," the Serra replied, serene now, her hands by her sides, "and the life she lived. You will almost certainly learn of her death."

"She held a living Heart."

"So, too, did I. And if I held yours," she continued quietly, "I would tease the memories of Ashaf kep'Valente free of their encasement now. Ask Ashaf kep'Valente—if she has voice—about her daughter. Ask her about her time in the North.

"It is why you sent the Heart with her, is it not? To see what she saw, and to make use of it in the war to come?

"Make a different use of it now."

"Did you not hear the Sen Kalias? Not even she could stand against the—"

"I heard her. But she was tainted by his power and the desire for it. Kiriel is not."

"She understood his power," Yollana said quietly.

"Perhaps Kiriel will. Perhaps she never will. But the words that you spoke to the Commanders when they discussed her death were *true*. They are not less true now."

"And you see this, Na'dio?"

"No, Matriarch. I heard it then. I hear it now."

Yollana lifted the empty cup and shoved it, without ceremony, into her satchel. "Then we have an impossible task. We are forbidden to destroy the trees—if they *can* be destroyed, and we are forbidden to destroy the Lord's vessel—if she *can* be destroyed.

"How, then, Serra Diora, are we to win this war? Say that you are a Serra and that wars are the concern of men, and I will slap you."

But the Serra Diora said instead, "The war that is fought without is their war. But the war within? That is the province of Serras. It is all we have been given leave to know."

"Clever child."

"This is not a matter of armies."

"But it is, Serra. There are three. Marente. Leonne. And his."

Ser Andaro di'Corsarro was waiting for her when she left the tent. She bowed deeply, and he returned that obeisance with a nod. "I arrived late in Russo," he said at last.

"You were in Russo?"

"The Tyr'agar commanded it."

She nodded. She should have known, but she was immersed in the shadows of Havalla, and it would take some time to emerge.

"I should also tell you that your seraf has offered to serve the

Tyr's new wife. She is troubled, and sleeps poorly, and her child—it appears—does not sleep at all."

Diora nodded gracefully; all of her surprise was hidden.

"I must return to the village," she said softly.

Ser Andaro folded arms across his chest. "*This* time, Serra, you will return in my presence."

"Does the Tyr not need you here?"

He said, "I saw Russo."

And she nodded.

"Why must you return?"

Because, she thought, *I do not trust Yollana.*

And if we attack Kiriel di'Ashaf, will we not drive her to the arms of the father she has never acknowledged? But she did not speak the words.

When Ser Andaro saw that she would say nothing, he made a request. "Speak to Valedan, Serra Diora."

"I will speak with my husband, if the Northerners and the Tyr'agnati do not command the whole of his attention." She started to walk away, and then turned to face Ser Andaro di'Corsarro.

She bowed.

"Serra," he stated, "if you played some part in the salvation of that village, you are either blessed by the Lady or favored by the Lord. If a bow is offered, it should be offered by me."

"And in the end, that would not serve our Tyr," she said with a brief smile. "When I met him, when he did not accept what was offered, I saw the things he was not, and I bitterly regretted them.

"But in Russo, and in this encampment, I have come to understand *all* that he is not. I cannot say with certainty that I know what he is. But I will learn, in time."

"He is a worthy lord," Ser Andaro said quietly.

"Yes," she responded softly.

Valedan kai di'Leonne was in the tent when she entered it. And she stopped there, her body blocking the sunlight, as she saw his profile. He held the babe in his arms while Teyla slept.

And Ramdan, seraf, held the silks in which the baby should be swaddled. She watched them both in silence, seeing in their unguarded expressions something she rarely saw in either man or seraf. She almost left, then, but Valedan looked up, and their eyes met. To withdraw would have been awkward.

But to stay was awkward as well; there are some things which should not be witnessed.

No, she thought, relaxing her shoulders. There are some things which *must* be witnessed.

But the kai Leonne blinked. "Serra Diora?" he said. He sounded like a boy. At that, a boy caught in an unfortunate act. She wanted to smile.

She did.

"Ramdan," Valedan said, his voice rising on the second syllable. But the seraf's face was shuttered once again, and for the first time in her life, Diora regretted his perfect composure—and she envied Valedan, for he had been gifted, a moment, with the old man's vulnerability.

Ramdan took the child and retreated.

And the Serra Diora, whose work it should have been, stood, arms empty, in front of her husband. She met his gaze. "Thank you," she said.

It was not what he had expected; his brows rose and his cheeks colored. But he composed himself as much as his heightened color allowed, and he let his hands fall.

"I have been absent," she said quietly. "But I see that I have not been missed."

He did not grope for words he did not have. Instead, he waited.

"And I am grateful," she told him gently. "I have been in the village of Russo; I returned with the Matriarch of Havalla, but I think that I am needed in the Green Valley."

"And not here?"

"I trust you here," she replied. It was not as difficult an admission as it might once have been.

"What happened in Russo?"

"Yollana spoke of it at the meeting of the Commanders and the Tyr'agnati," she told him. "And what she said was truth—but it is not so visceral a truth as seeing the village itself. The earth has moved, and although it is quiet now, it has changed the face of the valley.

"But I think that Kiriel di'Ashaf saved the village; I quieted it. I . . . helped."

He did not ask her how. Instead, he said, "Thank you."

And she smiled. "I am Southern," she told him gently, gazing now at the sleeping face of this new, this strange, wife. "And I had not realized until now how difficult that must be for you.

"But you have the Serra Alina, and I am certain she has told you just how difficult you must be for the rest of us."

His smile was genuine. "Frequently."

She hesitated and then said, "I believe that there is some chance that you may be called upon to kill Kiriel. It is why I must go."

His brows rose and his expression shifted. What remained was a warrior's mask. She did not know how to react to it; seeing it upon his face was oddly unsettling.

"I have already said that I will not see her destroyed."

"Valedan, we now understand what the whole of the spell around Averda is meant to do."

His brows rose.

"And when you do, you may regret that decision. No, do not ask me how I know. I may not answer in safety. And, no," she added gently, "do not seek to protect me against my vows of silence. Let me tell you what can be told, and let me go."

He nodded.

"The spell is twofold. The first, as Meralonne APhaniel discerned, is a twisting of ancient paths. They are not paths that we can travel in safety. But the older . . . creatures . . . can. They will not be bound by the conventions of magic in their travel, and an army might move, in speed, to the cradle of Averda.

"But it is the second half of the spell which is more difficult. The armies—yours and the General Marente's—are meant to meet in battle, and the dead that fall upon the field will be consecrated to the Lord of Night. He derives power from their pain and their death in some fashion."

"The demons do," Valedan said.

She nodded. "But he is not, it is thought, to be upon the field; the power that is taken from the battle will be conferred upon his chosen."

"Kiriel."

She lifted a brow.

"It is Kiriel?"

And nodded.

"Does she know?"

And blessed him, in the safety of silence.

"No."

He did not ask if she was certain. She thought, then, that she would never understand him.

"Why does the Lord of the Hells think she will serve him?"

"I don't know."

"Does it concern you?"

She hesitated, and then nodded.

"But not enough that you would see her dead."

"Not enough. No. But I would be present if she is called," she said quietly.

He looked at her carefully, and then said, "I've seen her. When she was . . . his daughter."

Diora waited.

"She was terrifying. And beautiful. She was death."

"And you will not see her destroyed?"

"No. She became what she was to save my life. And she has saved it many times. I owe her this."

"You know that in the South a man is not beholden to a woman."

He nodded.

"You know that he makes no oath to a woman, and that he honors no oath made."

He nodded again. "But this oath is not made to Kiriel di'Ashaf," he said quietly. "And it is not made to the Serra Diora. It is made to *me.*"

She smiled softly. "You are learning," she told him.

"I want to learn more," he said, and reaching out, he caught her hand. She hadn't realized that he had moved close enough to do so. "I want you to survive this."

And looking at the sleeping woman and the baby who now lay in Ramdan's steady arms, she said quietly, "So do I."

It was her gift.

"Will you take Andaro with you?"

"He has been commanded to guard me; unless you order otherwise, I have little choice." But she smiled, and the smile robbed the words of their sting. "He is not . . . like other Tyran. He is quick to judge, and he is quiet; he sees much."

"You approve of him."

"Yes," she told him, tightening her slender fingers around his. Aware that she should have disavowed the importance of her approval.

"He lost much, in the North."

"And I lost much in the South," she countered. "But perhaps it must be this way: you will gather the mourning and the bereaved, and they will find something in you to believe in. Something less harsh than the Lord's glare and the howl of the empty wind."

He did not blush. But he lifted her hand halfway to his lips. Then he froze.

No, she thought, she would never understand him. But given what she had come to understand in her life, perhaps this was a blessing.

"I will send word from Russo," she told him.

He released her hand slowly, and then he offered her a deliberate bow.

CHAPTER TWENTY-SIX

SER DARO di'Valente was waiting for her.

Or he seemed to be waiting; he stood in the lee of one of the great pillars that had risen in the shade cast by the blending of afternoon sun and the thick bowers of the great tree.

He looked up only when she was almost upon him.

The presence of a man dressed in Leonne colors made him stiffen, robbing him of the easy lack of grace that the serafs knew. As if he had expected no less.

He bowed to the Tyran, and Ser Andaro di'Corsarro bowed deeply. "You are Ser Daro di'Valente," he said.

The bow deepened.

"My lord is much beholden to you," Ser Andaro said, speaking in the grave, measured tones of the High Courts.

Ser Daro rose slowly and looked beyond Ser Andaro. It was clumsy, but he did not seem to realize it.

"There are no other Tyran?" he asked at last.

"I need only one," the Serra replied, speaking for the first time. "The threat that you have faced here could not be answered by a dozen such men."

"The men who serve the Tyr'agar," Ser Daro began gallantly, "are—"

"Not men who could overcome the earth itself, Ser Daro," Ser Andaro replied. His smile was slight. "I take no offense where none is offered; the Serra Diora en'Leonne speaks simple truth." He gazed at the pillar, and after a moment, reached out and placed a mailed palm against the stone.

"You must serve a truly worthy lord," Ser Daro said, after Ser Andaro at last lowered his hand.

"I serve Valedan kai di'Leonne," Ser Andaro replied. "And if there is only one man in the South who might be called worthy, it is the kai Leonne." But he stepped out of the pillar's shadow as he spoke, and again he offered his quiet smile. "But there are many who are worthy. It is said that the quality of the ruler is judged by the quality of those he rules, and if this is true, Ser Danello kai di'-Valente must be among them."

Where a woman might have blushed or lowered her face, Ser Daro seemed to grow several inches; his chest rose, and his chin rose with it.

"We have come to see Kiriel di'Ashaf," Andaro continued.

"I had hoped as much."

"She is awake?" Diora asked softly.

"She woke an hour ago, Serra, and she asked for you."

Something must have shown on her face, for he added, "And you have come in time. We did not know when you would return," he added, too politic to say *if.* "But come with me, and I will take you to her." He started to walk, and she joined him, Ser Andaro by her side. But he stopped and turned to her, facing her directly, his great body too close to meet the demands of etiquette. By this, if nothing else, he showed his heritage; the low courts were his home.

"The Northerner, Auralis AKalakar, is exhausted. He sleeps against the wall, wrapped around his sword, as if he fears the coming of an army."

"An army will come," she said quietly.

"Aye, perhaps it will. It is too quiet today. There are no birds. But lack of sleep makes a poor cerdan. Or *soldier,*" he added, using the Northern word.

"If I can convince him to sleep, I will," she told Ser Daro gravely. "He is of the North. Among his compatriots are women who have taken to the sword as easily as he himself has done; he will take no offense."

"Ha."

She smiled. "I will *offer* no offense," she conceded. "What he takes, of course, will be of his own choosing."

"He could not be offended by you, Serra," the villager said, his words tinged with awe.

And at what? Her sari. Her title. Her distance. Her courtly mimicry of perfection. She felt oddly humbled by his regard, and unworthy of it.

But she kept it. She waited with perfect patience while he turned and walked toward the open doors of his stone domis, and when he was two steps ahead, she followed. Ser Andaro began to walk as well, his steps flat and perfect over the uneven, dimpled ground.

Auralis woke as they entered the hall, and lifted his unshaven face. He did not normally wear a beard, which made the lack of razor notable; the whole of his jaw was shadowed by growth. By dirt, by sweat, by lack of sunlight.

He rose quickly, his hand upon his sword hilt, but he did not draw the weapon. Which was good, she thought, as she looked to her left. Ser Andaro di'Corsarro was likewise attached to his weapon's hilt. Men.

"Auralis AKalakar," she said.

"Daro," Auralis snapped. "Why is the Tyran here?"

Ser Daro's iron brow lifted in shock, and fell in resignation. He turned a side glance upon both of his guests, and when neither showed even a trace of annoyance, he muttered, "Does no one in the North understand courtesy?"

"Courtesy in the North," Auralis snapped, irritable now, "doesn't come armed and armored." But his shoulders sagged as he leaned against the wall, bracing himself there.

"We have come to see Kiriel," Diora said quietly.

"With him?"

"He is one guard," she replied. "And I am wife to the Tyr'agar. Do the Queens travel unescorted in your vaunted cities?"

"How the Hells should I know?"

Which meant "no." She, like Valedan, was learning.

"His Torra has greatly improved," Ser Daro told her. "When he uses it."

"It is probably good that he does not use it more often, then," she replied, her tone and the texture of her voice light and youthful.

Ser Daro laughed.

Auralis frowned. "I understood that."

"The Northerners value truth above all else," the Serra said gravely. "And in truth, they find no offense. Or so we of the South have been told."

He snorted. "By who?"

And she smiled again. "Will you let us pass, AKalakar? We have traveled from the encampment just for this purpose."

"Whatever. Yes," he added. "Go ahead. She doesn't want to see me anyway."

"Maybe she would," Ser Andaro di'Corsarro said, in perfect but accented Weston, "if you washed and shaved."

Bronze brows, mired in dirt, rose, disappearing beneath the disheveled line of hair that had escaped the Northern braid. There was much of it.

"What's that supposed to mean?"

"That we can smell you from where we stand," Ser Andaro replied.

Ser Daro looked at his feet, at the floor beneath it, at the walls to his right. At anything, in fact, but the face of Auralis AKalakar.

After a pause that was just a little too long, Auralis AKalakar said something that was a physical impossibility. "All right," he snarled. "I'll clean up."

Diora wondered if he would make it as far as clean water. He listed as he walked.

But dirt and lack of sleep were not likely to kill him, and as he moved aside, she stepped forward quickly, to spare Daro di'Valente the embarrassment of opening the screens.

They slid wide, and just before she entered the room, she said to Andaro, "That was almost . . . rude."

He laughed. "It was Northern," he told her, shaking his head from side to side in amusement. "And it was understood."

He did not comment on her choice of words; did not point out that they were, in Southern terms, at least as bold as his had been. She wondered, then, if the North was such a strong place that it could taint even those who had not lived many years in its shadow.

She found it an oddly comforting thought.

"Kiriel."

Kiriel di'Ashaf looked up as Serra Diora en'Leonne entered the room. Her eyes widened, but she did not speak.

Diora took her place by the girl's side, and she reached for the towels and the basin of cool water.

But Kiriel shook her head mutely. "It makes me feel clammy," she said.

Frowning, the Serra placed the back of her hand against Kiriel's forehead. She pulled it back in surprise. "Ser Daro," she said, lifting her voice without raising it.

Ser Daro di'Valente was not far from the door. He stuck his head into the room. "Serra?"

"The fever," she said softly, and with just a trace of hesitation, "has broken."

His face cracked in a smile. He looked younger, and he also looked a great deal more tired.

"Have we been gone so long?" she asked. "Is the hour so late?"

"It is midafternoon, Serra."

She shook her head again. Lowering her voice, she said, "You are very strong, Kiriel."

"I don't feel strong."

No, the Serra thought. She looked at the Northern face, and thought something amiss; it was only when Kiriel blinked that she realized what it was. The girl's eyes were once again brown.

"Have you eaten?"

Kiriel hesitated. "No."

"You must eat, Na'kiri." The name fell from Diora's lips as if it were the only natural name to use. And in this place, it was.

Kiriel's chin reached toward her chest; had she been standing, she would have looked like a much younger woman. But the evasion didn't work well while she was prone.

"If you like, I will go to the kitchen."

"No!"

Diora smiled. "I am tended by serafs," she said quietly. "But I am nonetheless not without skill."

"I don't want you to go."

"Then I will stay." Diora turned to look at Ser Daro, who lingered like an absurd puppet, his shoulders and neck stretching over the room's threshold. "If the Serra Nora en'Valente has time," she requested, "and she can be spared—"

"I'll get food," he said. He vanished.

She lifted Kiriel's hand, holding it gently between her palms. "You saved the village," she told her.

"Everyone?"

"Everyone. If there has been a death, Ser Daro has not spoken of it. Nor have the serafs, and serafs are open with their grief. It appeases the winds," she added.

But Kiriel did not seem content.

Diora knew why. The Heart of Havalla no longer offered her the company of the dead. She did not speak of Havalla, or its Heart, or the dead.

She did not speak at all. Instead, with a brief pang of regret for lack of instrumental accompaniment, she sang.

If the fever had broken, and it had, Kiriel was still weak. She slept fitfully, her lids closing slowly and opening suddenly, her gaze wild. Diora sat quietly by her side, and when Kiriel woke, she spoke softly, easing her return to the world.

The Serra's father, Sendari par di'Marano, had never been like this. Even racked by fever, he had been Widan, and he obeyed the law of the South: he showed no weakness.

Kiriel seemed to be *only* weakness, as if the strength had been shorn from her by the voice of the wind, the fire, and the earth. She spoke of Ashaf, but in the half sentences of those who are not aware that they speak at all. Listening carefully, Diora could not piece together a narrative that made sense.

Nor did she need to. She had no greater need for meaning than this: to sit by the side of a child, in a darkened room. To answer, with patience, the sudden questions that erupted in panic. *Where is my sword? Where is Falloran? Where is Ashaf?*

They were not a child's questions, but they were asked in as young a voice as Kiriel had yet revealed. Diora did not lie, and she did not seek to gain advantage or comfort from Kiriel's unexpected vulnerability; instead she rose to retrieve Kiriel's sword, and she explained gently that she did not know where Falloran was. She also told Kiriel that Ashaf was waiting for her in the Halls of Mandaros.

It would have had no meaning in the South, and she was not certain what meaning it would have for Kiriel, but it seemed to have some, for she was comforted, and lapsed into the half sleep that had emerged from her Widan fever.

But when the sun at last fell, Kiriel woke fully and sat up. The room was now dark. "Diora?" she called.

"I am here, Na'kiri."

"The Lord of Night is gathering power," Kiriel said.

"We know."

"You can light a lantern, if you need one," Kiriel told her.

"You wanted the dark," Diora replied. "The fire disturbed you. Even contained."

"Oh."

"Can you see me?"

"Yes. It's quiet."

"Yes. The storm has stopped. There has been no rain, this day."

"Oh."

"The village is much changed. But the tree is still standing at its heart."

"It's Anya's tree."

"Anya?"

Silence.

Diora let the silence spread, like a blanket.

"I think they need Anya," Kiriel said after a while. "If you met her, you would understand."

This time, Diora asked no question.

"She's broken," Kiriel continued. "She's older than you are. Older than I am. But she isn't. She's like a child." She paused and then said, "She's the most powerful mage in the Shining Court. She's the most powerful mage in the world. And she likes thrones. She calls them big chairs, most of the time. If you let her build them, she's happy."

Diora absorbed the words. "Kiriel—the tree—when you said it was Anya's—"

"Yes," was the stark reply. "She grew it. It wasn't there when Ashaf lived here."

They were silent a moment, and then the Serra said, "Can you speak with this Anya?"

And with a touch of pride, Kiriel answered, "Better than anyone else can. We're friends. Sort of."

"Could you find her?"

"Yes." But Kiriel shook her head. "She's dangerous, Serra. She doesn't *mean* to be, but she kills when she isn't thinking. Ashaf was afraid of her, and she liked Ashaf. If she were in the village, she would kill."

"By accident?"

Kiriel nodded. "She doesn't understand. She doesn't really think she's that strong. She—" She shook her head. "I might be able to find her. But not like this; I wouldn't survive it."

"She wouldn't harm you?"

"No. She wouldn't. But she won't be alone." Kiriel reached for the cold bread at the bed's side and tore it almost fitfully into smaller pieces, none of which she brought to her mouth. "But they'll need her there, when they try to cast the whole spell, and I might be able to reach her then."

"Kiriel—"

"What?"

Diora hesitated. After a moment, she braced herself in the shadows, finding comfort. It was empty comfort; she knew that Kiriel could see what she herself couldn't. "We know what the spell is supposed to do."

Kiriel was completely silent. Completely. The quiet rhythm of her breath vanished as she waited.

How best to tell her, without alarming her? How best to tell her without driving her from the village?

"It is a road," she said slowly, "that is meant to bring The Lord's servants from . . . from wherever it is they now reside. They can travel quickly, and without paying the cost of that travel."

"How many?"

"Enough. More than enough." Diora hesitated. It was marked.

"There's more," Kiriel said quietly. The whole tenor of her voice had changed. "What are you afraid of?"

Northern, Diora thought her. Cold and brusque as the Northerners were. She swallowed her Southern words and her Southern hesitation, and she said, "There are two parts to the spell."

"And the second?"

"We—think—it is meant for you."

"It's supposed to stop *me?*"

Silence.

"Serra Diora, what *is* it supposed to do?"

"Empower you," she replied starkly.

"Empower? I don't understand." Absolute truth, in those words. But Kiriel di'Ashaf had never been adept at hiding the truth beneath the surface of words; she had worn the Heart of Havalla, but she was no Matriarch.

"Nor do I. But . . . when the armies meet, they will fight and they will kill."

Kiriel snorted. "They're *armies.*"

"Those that die will bleed, and their blood will somehow be consecrated in the service of the Lord of Night; they will be his sacrifices, even if it is not the hand of his priests that spill the blood."

Kiriel said, "I don't understand."

"I understand it little, myself."

"How is this supposed to work?"

"I don't know. Although we are rumored to sacrifice our young in the South, such practices are older than legend. Not even the children speak of them."

"Why do you think this has anything to do with me?"

"Because it is felt—"

"By whom, damn it?"

"It is felt," Diora continued, using the words deliberately, as if they were blunt instruments, "that the power thus gathered must be contained in a living vessel. You," she added.

"Why me?"

"Because you are his daughter, and it is thought that no other could contain the whole of the gathered power."

Kiriel rose, agitated. Diora could hear wayward steps; Kiriel walked to the screen and retreated several times. "I have to leave," she said at last. "If I leave—"

The Serra closed her eyes. It brought comfort. Kiriel's words did not. She had hoped that the girl would offer some denial, some plausible reason why that power would not be a threat.

"Na'kiri," she said softly, when the steps had faded. "If you leave, there will be no one to face the army."

"I can't face an entire army," Kiriel whispered.

"Three," Diora replied. "But you won't face them alone."

"You don't understand—"

"I understand only what I saw the night of the storm," the Serra replied gravely. "The demons," she added. "You . . . called." She knew that Kiriel could see her expression. "They came."

"You don't understand," Kiriel replied, weary. "Telakar has always had a weakness for mortals."

"And the other?"

Kiriel shook her head. "He made my sword," she said curtly. "He armed me." She did not tell the whole of the story; it was hinted at only in the shadows that gathered at the edges of hard words.

"Kiriel," Diora said, forcing herself to choose a less gentle name. "The *storm* heard you. Something in its heart answered."

After a moment, Kiriel said, "Yollana told you."

Diora said nothing.

"She must have. She . . . knows a lot. She knows more than you know."

"She is the Matriarch of Havalla."

"Did she send you?"

"No."

"Does she know you're here?"

"I don't know."

"Did she tell you to kill me?"

That surprised Diora. She was silent.

"Because if I were her, that's what I would have done." No resentment lingered in the words; none. They were cool and thoughtful.

"If she had, I would be under no obligation to obey her," Diora replied carefully.

Light flooded into the room as Kiriel swung the screen open. She said, "You don't know what he's like," as she turned back, shadowed by the harshness of the outer world. "You've never seen him."

"I . . . know a little . . . of what he can be like," Diora told Kiriel. "I, too, carried a Voyani Heart."

"You don't know what his power is like," Kiriel continued, as if Diora hadn't spoken at all. "I'm not sure I do. But if you're right, I want to be somewhere else."

"And if I'm right about the army?" Diora asked.

And Auralis AKalakar said distinctly, "The Hells with the army."

Kiriel turned in a single motion. Her hand reached for a sword that wasn't there, and it froze.

He was weaponless. "Kiriel," he said.

He had, Diora saw, cleaned up. His face, now that it had been scrubbed, was pale. He reached for her, and then, seeing the face that was turned away from the Serra, lowered his hand.

Diora rose. "AKalakar," she said, offering him a scant Northern bow. She needn't have; he didn't notice. It was hard to offer insult to the Northerners without being blunt.

"You haven't seen her," he said. "When she's standing in shadow."

"Yes," she countered, "I *have*."

And he fell silent, although she had put no power into the words.

"She came to Russo. She carried—" She shook herself, and the words fell away. "She promised to save the village."

"She saved the damn village," he snapped.

"For what?"

"They aren't her responsibility." Guttural words. Angry words. The anger made the Serra take two steps back, into the darkened room. He made an effort to hide himself, but the effort, like so much of his self-control, was poor. What she heard in the four words almost silenced her.

Almost.

But she had been born with the curse of voice, born with its gift. In such a battle, she was better armed than he. "That is not your decision, AKalakar."

"She's already made her decision!"

"No. She's voiced her fear. It is not the same."

He took a step past Kiriel. The girl's back was frozen, as was she. He took another step, and then a third, and the Serra Diora forced herself to stand her ground.

But when he lifted a hand, she lifted both of hers.

And Kiriel di'Ashaf caught his arm and sent him flying.

"Don't," she said, her voice stiff and unnatural.

He rolled against the mats that had been her bed for almost two days. Found his feet with ease that spoke of practice.

"Never do that again."

"She doesn't care about you," Auralis said harshly.

Diora did not deny the accusation. She met Kiriel's gaze and held it, and after a moment, she said, "I once let everyone I promised to protect die." She did not dare put power into the words; she could barely say them at all.

But she thought that she was doomed to return to this, again and again, no matter how far past it she thought she had come.

Kiriel's eyes were wide and dark. Dark and wide. Diora thought she could see her reflection in them. She did not like what she saw, but she had faced it before. Would face it again.

"Why?" Kiriel asked.

"Because," Diora said bitterly, "Evayne a'Nolan told me that if I tried *anything*, I would perish. She told me that my death would count for nothing; nothing at all." Her throat was dry. "And she told me that if I chose to live, the *only* thing that would be left me would be revenge."

"And was it enough?" Kiriel whispered.

Diora said, "I don't know yet. I have not finished." But her hands were shaking, and her lips also trembled. She lifted her eyes, and only her eyes; the weight of tears threatened her perfect face, and she would not shed them here.

And as Kiriel watched, Diora said, "No." And bowed her head. "No, Kiriel di'Ashaf. No, Na'kiri. It is not enough. If I could, I would go back. If I could, I would *try*. And if I died—" She turned away.

"You were afraid," Auralis said, harsh now. "You didn't want to *die*—"

If she had been standing beside him, he would be dead. Her hand was upon the hilt of *lumina arden*, and it burned.

But another hand touched hers, and she met the eyes of Kiriel di'Ashaf, and her grip slackened.

Kiriel said, "I'll stay." It was a whisper.

Auralis said, "Kiriel—can't you see what she's *doing*?"

And Kiriel said, "Yes. I do. She's trying to prevent me from making the same mistake."

Diora closed her eyes.

"Surviving is not a mistake!"

"I am not the Serra Diora," Kiriel said, her voice still barely above a whisper. "Look at her, Auralis. *Look at her.*"

Auralis, in silence, obeyed.

But what she saw, he could not see; that much was clear.

"I didn't know that Ashaf would die," she told Diora, although she spoke to Auralis as well. "If I had known—" She swallowed. "And I would go back, if I could. It haunts me, Auralis. The dead I couldn't save.

"This is all for her. For Ashaf. If I leave—" she shook her head. "I won't be able to be like the Serra Diora. I *can't* be like the Serra Diora. I would, if I could." She let go of Diora's hand slowly, and turned to face her Northern companion. "But I think . . . I would be . . . like you."

Auralis' eyes widened, and without another word, he leaped past them both and vanished into the hall.

"That was . . . unkind," Diora said quietly.

"He was unkind," Kiriel replied.

"Yes. He was."

Kiriel turned away. "It was true," she said, offering the most meager of defenses.

"Truth is a harsh weapon."

"You could have said it."

"Yes."

"You didn't."

"No."

"Why?"

"What purpose would it serve? Wounded, he is careless."

"He's careless anyway." But she looked now at the gaping door. "You can't see him," she added softly. "You don't know what he's like."

"I can hear him," Diora said. "And if we speak truth, it is true that he is concerned for you. I think he would die for you."

"He would die on a whim in a dangerous bar," Kiriel snapped.

"Yes," Diora agreed. "But if that is true, it doesn't lessen the other truths." She bowed her head.

"He meant to hurt you."

"Yes. And he did," she added quietly. "But he hasn't said anything that I have not thought."

"Then why don't you—"

"Because I am not always certain that he doesn't speak the truth," she replied. "I did what I did, Na'kiri, and I live with it. But it is seldom indeed that we are offered the ability to do something for one reason, and one alone; there are many. Always."

"Why did you save that girl?" Kiriel asked softly.

"Teyla?"

"The villager. The seraf."

Diora spread her hands wide, looking at them as if they would give her answers. In the end, they were just hands. "I don't know. I think—I think I wanted her child." It shamed her to say it, but she offered that shame to Kiriel because she had so little else to offer.

"Like Ashaf wanted me?"

And Kiriel, as always, surprised. Diora lifted a face that was nothing at all like the face of Ashaf kep'Valente, and after a moment she said, "Yes."

Seeing, in the stark, sharp lines of the young woman's face the utter truth of the syllable.

It was enough. Kiriel shrugged and said, "I'd better go after him."

Diora said quietly, "Take your sword."

"He won't try to kill me."

"No. Not you."

Kiriel cursed under her breath, foreign words. Diora smiled hesitantly.

"What?"

"When this is over, Na'kiri, you will have to tell me what those words mean."

"You don't know them?"

"I was never taught them. It was not Weston that would be suitable for a Serra."

Kiriel laughed. But she bent and picked up the sword, and it seemed to lend strength and weight to her slender arms.

She had risen from the fever whole.

Diora was both grateful and frightened, and the emotions, two halves of a single truth, silenced her. But she left the room with Kiriel and they parted only when they reached the end of the hall.

Kallandras of Senniel College was waiting for her.

She saw him as Kiriel left the open doors of the domis, and she lifted a brow in question.

He bowed, Northern bow, a supple bend of waist. "Serra Diora," he said softly, "that was deftly done."

"You heard?"

"I heard some of it," he replied with care.

"You have not returned to the army."

"I am not beholden to the army," he replied. "But to Senniel College. I serve the Kings at the command of the bardmaster, and the bardmaster is not here."

"Will you go back?"

"I will," he said, and his tone stilled all movement. "When you return. When Kiriel does. But not before."

"Whose work do we do here, Kallandras?"

"Does it matter?"

Did it? She shrugged. It was Northern, but she lent the movement a lifetime of grace. A short lifetime.

"When this is over," she said, as if it would be, as if they would be standing and whole at its end, "what will you do?"

"I? I will return to Senniel College," he replied gravely, "and I will make my report."

"To who?"

"To the bardmaster."

"Who is he?"

Kallandras smiled. "*She* is Solran Marten."

"She must be powerful," Diora said.

"She was not born with the voice," he replied gravely.

Diora was silent. After a moment, she commented, "The North must be a strange place, Kallandras. And Senniel College must be stranger. How is it that you are ruled by a woman of little power?"

"I did not say she was without power; I merely said she was without the gift that binds us."

"But the bards—"

"They are all moved by the intricacies of song and the desire for an audience," he said with a smile. "But they are not all, nor have they ever been, bard-born. Solran is capable, and she is cunning; she was chosen by Sioban Glassen, the woman who found me."

"In the South—"

"The Dominion is not a kind land. When bards are sent from the North, they are sent with that knowledge in mind. Some handful have come who do not have the voice, but they are never sent alone."

"You came alone." She thought of the first time she had met him.

"I did not come to sing," he told her quietly.

"But you sang."

"Yes, Serra Diora. I sang." He lifted *Salla* and offered her to the Serra. "The former bardmaster, Sioban Glassen, often said that she could send me to the Hells and I would find my way back."

Diora said, "She was a wise woman."

"She is a wise woman."

"But you said that—"

"That Solran is bardmaster now? It is true."

"And Sioban still lives?"

"She lives."

"I wish I could see your home," she told him, pensive.

"It would not live up to your expectations, I fear."

"Perhaps not. But I think I would find freedom there."

"Find it here, Serra," he said gently. "It is waiting, now."

She took the lute from his hands. But she did not play it. Instead, she reached out and caught his wrist.

His pale brow rose; she had surprised him.

"When you go," she said, the words quick and almost graceless, "take her with you."

He could have pretended to misunderstand her. She had, in the tumble of carelessly chosen words, given him that leeway.

But he reached out with his free hand and touched her cheek. "I did not intend to leave her behind." He brushed strands of her hair from her eyes. "The Serra Teresa has suffered much here; lost much that she had to lose. She will not find it again, and perhaps she will mourn its passing; I cannot say. But if she is willing, she will find a home in Senniel College."

He stepped away. "Come, Serra. Kiriel di'Ashaf is occupied, and there is much of Russo to see."

"I have seen it."

"I have not," he smiled. "But I would be honored by your company."

"I—"

"Take the time that is offered you, Na'dio. When the war comes, you will need it."

"And what does Kallandras of Senniel College need?" she asked him gently.

He laughed. "A song," he said, "from the most famous voice in the Dominion."

For Ona Teresa, she could offer these thanks. She almost knelt, but he raised a brow, and she straightened her knees. "The Green Valley," she said.

"Yes. Preserve the memory for your children."

Kiriel found Auralis at the outskirts of Russo. It wasn't hard; he stood in the ashes of what had once been the forest's edge, his back toward her, his armor glinting in the clear light of the moon. His sword was free of scabbard, but it hung by his side like a crippled arm.

She could see him so clearly she almost stopped in wonder, but it was a dark wonder; he was on the edge. The shadows and the pale strands of light that they hoarded spoke the spirit language that demons knew instinctively. Even Kiriel. Pain strengthened darkness. It was food, of a type, for the soul, and if it lasted for long enough, so did its scar.

She understood him; understood the edge he walked. It was, almost step for step, her own.

"Auralis," she said, when she stood ten feet from his back. She did not dare—not yet—to move closer.

He offered no answer. But he did not turn and he did not flee. It was almost an invitation.

She was not beguiled; wariness clung to her, and she held it. He was not himself, this eve.

Or perhaps he *was* himself.

"Auralis."

"What?" He lifted his head, and his braid dipped lower between his shoulder blades. In the night, it was silvered bronze. His skin was almost darker.

"Come back," she said quietly.

He turned, then, spinning so quickly she was grateful that she had kept her distance. His blade traced a circle at waist height—his waist. Eyes shining, he looked like a cunning madman. She had seen this before.

But not in Russo. Not in Ashaf's land.

"To *what*?" he asked her. He lifted his free arm, his shield arm; the shield was nowhere in sight. "I did this," he told her, as his hand encompassed ash and the emptiness of the forest.

"The fires did," she whispered. But she heard some implacable knowledge in his voice, and her gaze was caught by the jeweled ring upon his hand. Evayne's ring.

No, she thought, her hand becoming fist, the band she wore almost rising above her knuckle. It was his, now. Gift or curse, it was his.

What he saw in her face, she didn't know, but it seemed to calm him. Funny, that; in the home of her youth she had never learned to offer comfort. But she had taken it, and perhaps the taking had changed her.

She said, "Who died?"

His brows rose. With it, his voice came, wafting upward on an almost gentle breeze. It was not a kind laugh; it was as wild, as feck-less, as he.

"Who didn't?" he whispered. He looked past her; the whole of Russo lay at her back, taking what sleep it could in the strangeness of its changed geography, its new face.

"You didn't," she told him firmly.

He spit and turned away. "Do you know what I did while you struggled, Kiriel?"

She waited.

"I saved them. *I* saved *them.*"

A hundred words rushed to her lips, and she bit them back; she knew, instinctively, how to wound him. But bereft of cruelty, she found she had little to offer. And she had no desire, now, for cruelty.

No; that was a lie. It was almost *all* of her desire—but she rode it, struggling against its imperative. Knowing, for a clear moment, that she could.

She knew what he felt. All of the deaths she had offered her own dead had done nothing to ease her pain. Nothing to expiate her guilt. But the lives she had saved reminded her, in ways that death could not, of all of her loss.

She lived with it.

The alternative was worse.

She said, "I can't judge you. I, of all people, can't judge."

"Why not?" He spun again, like a drunk man, his footing uncer-tain. "You can see what they can't. You know. You've always known."

"Yes," she told him quietly. "But knowing it didn't change any-thing."

His fist rose skyward. She waited.

And when he lowered it, shaking, she crossed the distance that separated them. Her hand was on her blade; she did not draw it. Could not; not here.

Liar, she thought. "It did," she told him softly. "It changed every-thing. I wasn't afraid of you. You were the only person in the Os-preys I understood.

"You were like me."

He laughed again. "Like *you?*" The words were meant to wound. And because they were, they didn't.

"Like me," she said again.

"Then why are you here, Kiriel? Why will you stay in Russo? Why won't you flee?"

"You stayed," she told him, still speaking softly. It took effort.

"I—"

"During the last war. You stayed."

He was silent. She had not meant to hurt him, but the words caused pain. He said, "I want the fire."

She said, "I know."

"Will you stop me?"

She shook her head. "You won't call it."

"I can *hear* it."

"That's just you."

His brows rose, changing the contours of his face. He said, "I want to die."

"Yes. And you don't." She lifted her free hand, in offering. "So do I."

"And you'll risk that, here?"

"I'll risk more," she told him quietly. Russo at her back, reminding her, she said, "I'll risk failure. And failure, here, isn't death. Not mine."

"Why do you live?"

"It's what I know," she told him. "It's all I know. If I live, I can fight. If I die . . ." she shrugged. "I'm not certain I'll be any more peaceful. Come back, Auralis."

"Why?"

"Because I don't want to face this war without you."

That stopped him a moment.

And then he roared and his sword crested the line of his shoulder as he brought it to bear.

Had she been a different person, she might have offered him her trust, but her hand was already in motion, in an arc that was, measure for measure, the one he had chosen; her sword met his, and the clash of the blades lit a spark across the sky; lightning without storm.

No; lightning without rain.

The storm was within them.

Diora looked up.

Kallandras touched her shoulder gently. "Serra," he said.

"I saw—"

"Yes."

"I hear swords."

He nodded quietly. "Let them talk," he told her.

"The swords?"

"Their bearers."

She said, "If we sing—"

"We will, Serra. But not yet; for those two, the night has not come, and they will accept no comfort and no peace."

Her hands, pale and perfect, palms hidden, curved. They did not become fists. "Kallandras—"

He reached out and pressed a finger to her lips, and the touch of his callused skin was a shock. "They were chosen for a reason, Serra Diora."

"Chosen?"

But his smile was firm, and it yielded nothing.

She didn't have time to think.

But thought was an anchor; it slowed her hands, diminished her reflexes, took from her the strength she had learned in her youth. The strength that had kept her, time and again, from death.

She ducked; Auralis' sword moved the air above her head, its edge shearing the ends of her hair. That close.

She felt shadow take her vision; she could not see him clearly. What she saw was simple: foe. Threat.

It was a blessed simplicity.

What was less simple: the voices of the blades. Her own she knew, but his was new to her. It tasted of sun and light; its whisper was the crackle of flame.

But she had stood in the wake of Falloran's breath, as a child, and she had taken no harm; fire was warmth, and warmth was something that she had never needed.

She parried and swung, kicking at his legs.

He leaped above her foot, and when he landed, she was at his side. He was fast; she had meant to catch him from behind.

Edge met edge and steel slid in two different directions.

"How will it end?" the Serra asked.

Kallandras said, "In the end? The way it always does. With death."

"Kallandras—"

He shook his head.

He spared her nothing.

She had seen him fight before. Had observed him, even while standing by his side. That was her way; that was her gift. What was offered on the edge of life and death became a visceral part of her knowledge; everything else was work.

Fire danced at the edges of her vision, singeing the ground that had already been charred. She felt its heat, and it was unlike the fire that Falloran had offered; it almost burned.

She drew shadow as shield, wielding it; it met flame, and where they touched, the air sizzled in complaint.

He was fast. Faster than he had ever been before.

And she met that speed with speed of her own; with ferocity and desire and—yes—pain.

He drew first blood.

But first blood did not stop him.

And if she were not already damned, she would be before she let him draw blood again.

"It is discourse," Kallandras said, as the blades sang in the distance.

"Are they trying to kill each other?"

"Does it matter?"

"To me, yes."

"A good answer, Serra. I do not know. But it is speech, to them; they have not our gift with words. This is their conversation, give and take; this is cleaner than the words they might use, now."

She said, "You would not let them come to harm."

And his smile, slight, gave her nothing to hold on to.

She drew second blood.

She could almost taste it. Had he slowed for even a second, she would have.

But he noticed the wound no more than she had noticed hers; it was slight.

They circled each other like blade dancers, swords welded to hand, extensions of their limbs. They did not speak; they had no need of words. The fury that drove Auralis had deprived her of distance and calm.

She wanted to kill him.

"I bear the scars of my earliest lessons," Kallandras told the Serra Diora. *Salla* lay in her lap, in silence; she could not bring herself to pluck the strings. Instead, she listened to the clash of blades as if they were instruments; as if they were a song that she could learn.

"We all bear scars."

"Mine are cleaner," he said quietly. "Yours are hidden."

She looked at her palm; touched the arm that she had cut in order to make the ablutions. Hidden? No.

But she thought she understood his meaning; they were scars that she had chosen to bear, and she had come to them without pain. Almost without pain.

They reminded her of many things.

"You begin to understand," he said.

She had not spoken; what he saw, he saw. The gift that they shared gave him nothing.

But perhaps it was not his only gift.

The trees loomed above them as they covered the landscape. By unspoken consent, they did not carry their fight to the village; they struggled over a bed of ash, and beneath the bowers of trees that were scarred by proximity to fire. Scarred, but not gutted.

One misstep, and it would be over.

One slip of blade, one slow parry.

She had to move quickly; she had to dance out of the greater reach, the greater momentum. He knew it; he had driven her to the shadowed bower of old growth by the ferocity of his attack.

But she was not bowed; she was not defeated. What he offered, she offered in her turn: strength and purpose.

And what purpose?

One false step. Just one.

But she could not bring herself to make it.

"Did you never dream of a wife?" Diora asked him quietly.

"I? I seldom dreamed, Serra."

"You were not always what you are now."

"No."

"And you are of the South."

His pale brow rose, but he did not deny it. "Once," he said. "Perhaps once. Before the death of my family." He shrugged. "It is not what I dream of now."

"What do you dream of, Kallandras?"

"Song," he whispered.

And the blades sang.

The night air was cold, and the moon was bright.

Darkness trailed the edge of her sword; she needed it to see by.

Fire brightened his.

End it, the blade whispered.

The first voice that was not hers beneath the evening sky.

She ignored it.

Had to; Auralis was upon her again, his frenzy unabated. She met him, leaping above the low arc his blade traced. Leaping, now, above his head, the breadth of his shoulders. His skin was glistening with sweat; hers was pale and dry.

Almost, almost; she sliced back, and for the first time since blade had left sheath, she heard him curse.

But there was no pain in the grunt. He had fallen and rolled to the right of her.

She brought the sword down; dirt flew as it rose.

He was beyond her.

For just a moment, beyond her.

She followed, taking the sword in both hands.

He cut her arm from wrist to elbow, and she grunted in surprise. Even that was brief; she was on the move again.

Damn him, anyway.

Kallandras stood. He lifted a hand, and swept it across the sky, as if in farewell or greeting.

And the winds came, gathering speed and voice; the trees broke beneath the weight of its syllables, scattering branches and leaves.

Fire consumed them; shadow devoured them.

But the combatants were driven apart, and when the winds died—and they died as suddenly as they had begun—they were once again separated.

Auralis AKalakar lifted a hand to his brow. "I win," he said. He raised the sword, and it seemed for a moment that he struggled with its weight.

But he sheathed it.

She said nothing. Hers was a night blade. It drank moonlight.

The madness was gone.

But the blades remained. She sheathed her sword slowly, and lifted a bleeding arm to her brow.

"You'll pay for that," she told him.

He shrugged. "Make me."

And she laughed. Her shoulders relaxed; she let the weight of her body return to her.

They stood a moment in silence, and then Auralis said, "Sorry." It was a curt two syllables, and it lacked conviction.

But it was a start. "I'm not."

Bronze brows rose. "You could have died."

She shrugged. "So what else is new?" She caught her hair and pulled it back, containing it. So much of it had shed the braids that bound the Northern soldiery. She couldn't say when.

He shrugged as well. "Nothing much."

They waited, the slope above them lined with trees. "You're really staying?"

"I'm staying."

"Why?"

"Clean fight," she said.

"What the hell?"

"You said it yourself. This is a clean fight. All the choices are clear."

His brows rose higher. It was almost funny.

"The demons, remember?"

"Oh." Pause. "Yeah."

"I know what you were," she added quietly. "But you're changing."

"Into what?"

She shrugged. "You choose."

"I'm not much for sane choices," he said. He glanced at her arm, and this time, his expression did sag. "Let me—"

"Don't even think it." She looked at the blood that was already drying. "This would have been nothing, where I grew up."

"It would have meant more, where I did."

"Neither of us live there anymore."

"Where?"

"Where we grew up."

"You haven't."

"Haven't what?"

"Grown up."

She swore at him. Loudly.

He lifted a hand in surrender. "I didn't say *I* had."

And she laughed. She walked over to his side and touched his shoulder lightly, and together they met the gaze of the winter moon.

And Kallandras of Senniel College said, "Now, Serra."

The Serra Diora en'Leonne began to play the lute.

"I don't want you to die."

"I don't want to die."

"Kiriel, leave. With me. Just leave this place." But he said it by rote. He knew what she would say.

"I'm not afraid of demons, Auralis."

"Neither am I anymore. It's me I'm afraid of."

She nodded. "Maybe I need that fear. Maybe it feeds me."

"I don't love you," he told her, his gaze drifting groundward.

"Does it matter?"

He said nothing. But after a moment, he shook his head. "I'll stay."

"Thanks."

"Not for you."

"Doesn't matter."

His nod was curt. "When will they get here?"

"I don't know." But she gazed at the Western trees, and the hair on the back of her neck stood slowly. "Soon."

She turned away and started to walk.

"Kiriel?"

"What?" She didn't look back. Didn't need to.

"Thanks."

CHAPTER TWENTY-SEVEN

THE rains had stopped. Across the length of the valley, men stepped out beneath the clear face of the regnant moon, and they made pilgrimages, sometimes traversing miles, to the Lady's hidden shrines.

The army carried no such shrine with them. On either side. But on both, such observances were now offered by the men of the South. They were offered in silence, and sometimes in secrecy, for men of the South did not bespeak the Lady openly when they sought favor from the Lord.

Superstition.

But more. Alesso knew the value—and the truth—of superstition; it guided the army, and it strengthened or weakened them.

Them. For a moment, he was alone.

The moon was high, and her face was already veiled; she gazed across the whole of her lands with a peaceful certainty that did not seem—at this remove—shaken.

He knew; he stood by the quiet body of the moving river and stared at it, as if it were a lake.

As if, in truth, it were *the* Lake.

The isolation passed; the moment did not.

In the darkness, in this darkness, only one man dared to join him. But he waited for that man to arrive, as patient as he had always been.

It was a burning patience, and not a quiet one.

"Alesso."

"Sendari." He looked up, for he stood upon the bank's incline, his feet sinking slightly into ground that had not yet grown firm.

Sendari, beard silvered in moonlight, looked like a much older man. But so, Alesso thought, did he; he knew the truth although the water moved too swiftly to offer him a glimpse of his nighttime reflection. So much change, in so little time.

Little? A decade had passed. Another moved over them now, slow and inevitable.

"Did the Northerners stop the rain?" he asked softly.

Sendari framed no reply, but after a moment, he lifted the edge of his Widan's robes and descended the incline. When he stood by the side of his oldest friend, he said, "We believe it is so."

"The men are spoiling for battle," Alesso said. He placed his hands behind his back, clear now of hilt, and turned. "Have we lost, old friend?"

The words haunted him. But they had to be said, and there was only one time to offer them. Here and now. There would be no other.

"She has taken the Sun Sword to the kai Leonne," Sendari replied.

Alesso did not ask who he spoke of. Tone alone conveyed all that was necessary. After a moment, the man who had claimed the Tor Leonne as his own nodded. Where else would she take the sword?

"Has he drawn it?"

"He has."

"And it did not consume him."

"No, Tyr'agar."

Alesso lifted a hand. "Not here," he said quietly.

"Alesso—"

"Not here."

Sendari drifted closer. Beneath the weight of Widan robe and Widan duties, Alesso could see the ghost of the hesitant, slender man who had once given up the possibility of power for the sake of a wife.

Nothing had moved Alesso to do likewise.

"The *Kialli*?"

"They have not returned." Sendari grimaced. "Cortano is certain he knows of at least five within your ranks, but there are others."

"And when will they return?"

"Cortano does not say," Sendari replied, hesitating.

"Speak plainly."

"But he fears that their return will presage a different battle."

"Have we been outmaneuvered?"

"I have never been a military man, Alesso. I cannot, with certainty, answer your question."

"Answer it without certainty, then. Without fear."

"I think that there is no question I will answer upon this field that does not bear the taint of fear," the Widan replied. He frowned as his glance was at last born down by weight and uncertainty to fall upon the bowls that lay at Alesso's feet.

His peppered brows rose, and Alesso laughed. "Is that not why you came, Sendari?"

"I have always made my peace with the Lady," the Widan replied, almost primly.

"And there is much peace to make," Alesso replied. "But the gods of the South, Lord and Lady, have little care for the whiles or whims of those who traverse their lands."

"The Lady is capable of mercy," Sendari said.

"Is she?"

"The mercy of the South."

Death, then. Alesso nodded. "I thought to wait," he said, "until the Northerners had time to do whatever it was they felt necessary."

"And now?"

The bowls were empty. But blood pooled in the last, and it was his.

"And now, old friend, it is time to turn the tide of this war." He bent and stacked the bowls almost carelessly. It was illusion; he did not chip or break them. "It was our war," he added.

"It is not yet lost," Sendari offered. But there was more question in the words than statement.

"Cortano?"

"He will stay the course."

"And the Widan?"

"They are restless, Alesso. In this, in the trees, in the storm's voice, they see portents. None of them are to their liking."

"And yours?"

"I have . . . little to lose," Sendari replied.

"And I," Alesso said agreeably. "It seems the *Kialli* make even poorer allies than the Tyrs."

Sendari nodded. "They do not understand the dance."

"Perhaps they do not need to. Think of it, Sendari: eternity and power. Certainty. There is freedom in it."

"But they bow," Sendari replied darkly. "And they bow to a different Lord."

"He is not our Lord," Alesso said.

"No."

"And he will never be our Lord."

"No."

"I thought to use them," Alesso said, staring up now at the face of the moon. "I thought that I understood their need for power. I was wrong," he added, and these words were as costly as the others had been, as difficult to say. "There is a lesson in this: Never trust the enemy that you do not understand."

"In the South, we trust seldom."

"Aye, old friend. And at cost." He turned away from the moon's face, but the silver brightness lingered in his vision, an echo of the sun's harsh light.

"What will you do?"

"I? I will do what I have always done," Alesso said, with a sudden, fleet grin.

"And that, Alesso?"

"Wait," Alesso replied. "And fight."

"I will be here."

"I never doubted it. Of all the men who stand beside me now, you are the only one of whom that is true. Come, old friend. There is wine here, and the shadows in which to drink it in peace. On the morrow, there is much to do."

The sun shone. Clouds faded in its heat, and the blue of sky remained, gathering color in the fold of its boundless height. The ground dried, and grass that had not been trampled unfolded slowly. Across the length of the Averdan valleys, the storm was forgotten.

And across the breadth, men moved, gaining height as they scaled the hills and the short, sharp heights. They carried bows and long poles with hooked blades; they carried tents and torches, the crude beginning of flame; they wore armor that glinted harshly, scattering light against the high bower of trees. As they found the heights, they spread, receding into the tree line; mirrors evoked the light that no longer touched them.

Crude work, that, but it would do.

Valedan watched.

"Tyr'agar," Commander Allen said as he came to stand in his shadow.

The Tyr'agar had never felt so unworthy of the title; he accepted it with a nod.

"The men are in place."

"In the right place?"

"That remains to be seen." The Eagle's smile was a thinning of lips, but there was nothing subtle about the expression. The rain had passed, and with it, any hesitance on the part of the Commanders.

"Commander Berriliya bids me offer his thanks for the storm's end," he said.

Valedan said nothing, but his hand fell upon the hilt of the Sun Sword. He had drawn it only once since the day that it had been given him; instead he had relied upon the Callestan blade. He had promised to draw it in battle, and he intended to honor that oath. But he found the weight of two blades cumbersome.

"Will they come?" he said, when the Commander's silence had grown too heavy.

"Who?" Commander Allen asked. "The General Marente or the demons?"

"The General," Valedan replied softly.

"He'll come. Whether he extends himself this far remains to be seen; he understands war in the valleys."

Valedan nodded. "And the demons?"

"They'll come, too." The man's face was a steel mask; it showed no hint of fear or uncertainty.

"What will stand against them?"

Commander Allen smiled grimly. "You'll see."

Alesso di'Marente sent his troops up, to either side of the flat expanse the cavalry depended on. His men climbed the sloping hills, creating new paths across the older ones. He watched them go.

When the forest had swallowed them, he gave a curt command; his Tyran bore it upon the swiftest of his horses. The Widan could send word without the need for travel, but Alesso di'Marente knew better than to depend upon the Widan in battle; he had already paid the price for that folly once, even if the choice had not been his.

And the Widan would be needed elsewhere.

"Is this wise?" Sendari asked.

Alesso said nothing. They stood in a tense but companionable silence as the cavalry began to travel in a slender wedge down the valley's length. The ground there was soft, and often treacherous; pools gathered, depriving the earth of solidity beneath the feet of war-horses. Even his own.

"Wise?" he said, when the banners of the clan Garrardi appeared, and the Tyran bearing those same colors brought their horses to bear until they stood in a single line. He waited a moment, and then turned to face the man known as his closest adviser.

If Tyrs valued advisers at all. No others held such a public position, no others were held in such obvious, such open regard. But even such a man might offer no overt criticism. He met Sendari's gaze and held it.

What Ser Sendari saw there was not made clear; the silence extended. At last the adviser chose to speak.

"Ser Eduardo kai di'Garrardi is not famous for his self-discipline."

"He chose his position upon the field," Alesso said mildly, satisfied. "And he stands behind my army."

"He stands almost at the forefront of your forces," Sendari replied, his voice as mild, the words sharper. "And his banner is of a height with yours."

Alesso shrugged. "It is not higher," he said at last.

For which they could be thankful. Sendari was not in a mood to offer praise to the clan Garrardi.

"You have driven yourself," Alesso said.

"With cause."

"With cause, old friend. But the storm is gone, and it will not return before we have the answer to our long question."

"The storm," Sendari replied, "is held in abeyance. But we will see its full force yet, and we will cry for simple rain."

"The *Kialli,*" Alesso said.

"The *Kialli.*"

"What have you discovered?"

"Nothing of import," Sendari said wearily.

Alesso grimaced. "The kai Garrardi is reluctant to accept my advice. We can delay the march; indeed, it seems wise." He looked

skyward. "But it will be costly." He looked back at the Widan.
"Cortano said that the rains ended early."

"So, too, did Mikalis."

"Then perhaps we will take advantage of this."

The advantage of the ignorant.

"Our spies?"

Sendari shook his head. "The Leonne army lies within the valley. It has not moved."

"And Ishavriel?"

"He has not returned."

Alesso nodded. "Then we will change our plan, old friend. Accept it."

"What plan, then, Tyr'agar?"

"We ride," Alesso said softly, "to war. Will you travel with the Widan?"

"I will travel at the side of the only Tyr I have ever been willing to serve," Sendari said. His hand fell to the hilt of a sword that he had drawn only once in years.

Alesso nodded. He turned and spoke a few sharp words to his Tyran.

To Tyran that he would never fully trust; it was at the hands of the Tyran that the last Tyr'agar had fallen, and if Alesso di'Marente had not been a man who could live above the vagaries of ill judgment, this at least could still be said: he learned well from the errors of others.

He stood a moment, his gaze encompassing the valley, and the valley encompassing his gaze. They were one, here, which was fitting: it had started in the Averdan valleys, and it would end here, one way or the other.

The Lord was high; the skies were his.

And Alesso di'Marente, Alesso di'Alesso, had always been the Lord's man. His hand fell upon the hilt of *Terra Fuerre,* and he smiled.

Valedan kai di'Leonne gazed at the moving folds of the same river as grain was removed from a low-lying barge.

"How long," he asked quietly, "do we have?"

The Commander Ellora Kalakar was tight-lipped and pale. But she still used the economy of a shrug to save her from words. "We have assumed that the rain was not meant to kill us," she said, when the kai Leonne failed to accept the gesture. "And we know that the rains did not stop at their whim. If the rains were meant to fall for at least another day, we can assume that we're a day and a half ahead of whatever it is they intend."

She had to be careful. Was careful. But it was wearying. The whole of her focus was upon the distant movement of troops; many of them were hers.

"We need the mages," she added quietly.

Valedan's nod was no comfort. But it underscored his youth and his inexperience; upon the field of battle, there was no such thing as perfect communication—but without the mages, there was truly no such thing as communication at all. The Annagarians accepted the lack without comment; they had other ways of fighting.

"Meralonne APhaniel says that the mages will be ready when the enemy is sighted."

"We need them in position," Ellora snapped. She fell silent when the Tyran and Toran shifted uncomfortably at the range her woman's voice traveled. She could be heard for miles if the wind wasn't against her.

There were, at the disposal of the Kings' armies, a handful of the bards; they wore the colors of their colleges and mingled, catching phrases in colorful Torra that they would no doubt attempt to translate into equally colorful Weston. Battle songs were all about color.

The substance would be found in other places.

Still, the bards were less acceptable to the military than the mages; she had never quite understood why, but admitted to herself that this was probably because she was easily beguiled; the bards knew how to work a room.

Even a walless, windowless one. The valleys.

"Where will they come from?" Valedan asked.

Ellora said, curt now, "We can't say with certainty. If—as has been surmised—they intend to invoke the passage of the hidden roads, they'll come from the border." The kai Leonne did not tell her how useless this response was; he didn't have to.

Ser Anton di'Guivera lifted his head. "The Western border," he said.

She concurred. It was closest, and if they were to travel in number, if they were to meet the armies that waited upon the plateau, it would be from the West that they would arrive.

If they were human. If distances mattered. If food and supplies were an issue.

But Meralonne APhaniel—useless in all other ways—had assured them that they weren't. And so their forces and their scouts were scattered and spread too damn thin. She didn't like it.

But then again, there was little about this war that she *did* like. Being under the command of a youth irritated her; had Commander Allen been less steady in his open allegiance, she would have run with the frustration and made it a tool.

But Bruce knew her well; too well. She was certain it was why he'd chosen to send Devran South. Devran was a man who could live in the narrow confines of the law; Ellora was a woman who embraced what was useful and discarded the rest. And there was an awful lot that was useless this time out.

"The forces of the General Marente are on the move," Ser Anton said, when the silence had been broken by the call of horns—and their answer.

Valedan nodded. "The ground?"

"Muddy," Ser Anton replied. "But not impassable. We will see them within the next day, if they progress with any speed."

The kai Leonne nodded again. But it was not the Marente forces that he now feared. Those, he could understand; the kai Callosta and the kai Lamberto had spent much time delineating the clans that were for and against him. The whole of the battle would turn on those shaky allegiances, but removed from the viscerality of war, he saw it as an act of politics.

The *Kialli* were more than that, and less.

He had seen the Ospreys face demons; he had seen them win. Every time.

But he had never seen demons in number upon the field. He could not imagine them now.

And the failure rested poorly upon his shoulders.

Ellora could see this with ease; it governed her thoughts as well. The rest of the Annagarians acted as if it was of little import; it frustrated her.

But she had had the rule of Kalakar for almost ten years, and if she had taken it reluctantly, it had changed her nonetheless. She could wait.

Korama appeared at her shoulder and stood there, respectfully tendering the dozen or so bows demanded by the mere presence of so many high clans.

When he finished and rose, he said, "The magi are waiting."

She nodded curtly.

* * *

"They will come from the West," Meralonne APhaniel said quietly.

"You said that they didn't—"

"We have broken the storm," he replied. "And we now move at our own speed, not theirs. Whatever they do, they must now do in haste. And magic is governed by its own imperative."

"Will they botch their spell?"

His brow rose in an arch that spoke of arrogance. Comforting in its familiarity, it was also annoying. He failed to answer the question. Bastard. But answer enough.

"Speed will be of the essence," he said, when he again had her attention. "Therefore they will choose the swiftest route."

"If the road travels like a road."

"It does not," he said gravely. "And this is the only gift that the magi can grant you, Commander. I do not know why Valedan kai di'Leonne felt it wise to choose this particular arena, but I will say this much: he chose well. The old roads are weaker here than they would be by the sea."

She didn't waste breath asking how he knew this.

"With some effort, we can narrow the gap that the road will take—but we cannot control the road itself, and we have no method of denying passage to those who travel upon it."

"At this point, APhaniel, the only thing we give a damn about is numbers. How many?"

The silver brow was pointed in its fall.

"They are not a mortal army." His hand fell to the bowl of his pipe, the way lesser men's fell to sword or horn. She preferred the sword or the horn, but she kept her preferences to herself. "Their strength will not be determined by numbers."

"The morale of the men who face them will."

Meralonne APhaniel shook his head. "You are wrong," he said curtly, "and we have little time for it. The demons that grace the General's army have almost certainly been chosen for their ability to adopt a mortal guise."

"Oh?"

"If the kai Leonne is weakened by his obvious ties to the North, the General will be devastated by any obvious ties to the Lord of Night. As he still leads a considerable force, it is clear—must be clear, even to you—that knowledge of the nature of his allies has not yet reached the men who serve him."

"They have been hampered," he added, face wreathed in the smoky scent of burning leaf, "but they will be unhampered when they arrive." He blew lazy rings in the still air of the tent. "The creatures that arrive in the flats will not bear a marked resemblance to the men you expect to stand and fight."

"You've never understood my men," she told the magi. "They'll fight."

"Perhaps," the magi conceded. "But there is an irony here. It *is* those who can adopt mortal guise who will present the greatest danger; the kin who cannot do so have a lesser power."

"And your men?"

"They have faced demons before. They have experience that the Annagarians lack. And power," he added. His eyes were faintly luminescent in the shadows of the tent.

"Your warriors."

"Mine," he said. "But if they serve me in that capacity, they will not be available for your use. Decide, Kalakar."

"Where?" she asked him.

"They will form the apex of a triangle. Here."

"And the armies?"

"If battle has already been joined, they will be ignored; our enemy and our part—is upon the Western heights of the valley."

Commander Allen was not happy.

Not for the first time, he cursed the absence of the Terafin girl.

Ellora was more philosophical. "We won the first war without a seer," she said with a shrug. "And seers often speak in riddles; they barely understand what they can pull from the land of what-if."

He said nothing. But he studied the maps for a while. "The magi," he said at last.

"We have the message cylinders," she reminded him. "And the men are drilled in horn calls, if it comes to that."

"We keep at least three mages," the Eagle said.

"Probably more. But the ones he'll leave are the fractious ones."

"We're used to that. And the Tyrs are not accustomed to Widan upon the field; they have their own methods of gathering information."

"You trust them?"

"For this war, yes."

Couldn't ask for more, really.

"And Devran?"

Commander Allen frowned. Fighting a war on two fronts necessitated a shift in plans. But the initial plan had been sound, in Ellora's opinion.

"He has his mages," the Commander replied. His tone was thoughtful and distant; he had not yet reached a decision. "I don't want him on the field," he said at last.

"And you don't want him behind the General's forces."

Bruce Allen nodded, and moved a small flag. "If we fail here," he said at last, "I want him to move North in haste. The forces arrayed against us are not seafaring forces; he can return to the ships and head back to the Empire with word of what has passed."

"They'll have word," she said quietly.

"The magi are our first line," Commander Allen replied, equally quiet. "They may be in contact with other members of the Council, and they may not. But if the Kings are prepared for war, they will still want some part of an army with which to fight it." He stepped back from the table.

Yollana of the Havalla Voyani was not accustomed to waiting, and she waited poorly. But she did wait, her cracked lips clamped around pipe stem, her feet drumming the beat of her impatience against the soft ground that lay in the shadow of the Lambertan banners. Those banners were weighted, and the wind was slight; they barely moved. But they glinted; gold was worked into the edge of the sword that lay beneath the rising sun, and gold rose as well from the sun's face.

Between the curve of Southern blade, upon a green field that stretched from edge to edge, was a stallion. The pride of Mancorvo, their horses.

This one wore ceremonial barding, and a mask of steel, and he traveled between silver swords. Silver, she thought. Moon color. She wondered if the ancient choice had been made deliberately.

Ser Galen kai di'Lamberto came to stand before her, and he offered her the lowest of bows. Although it was crisp and flawless, it was also informal; no bow was offered, after all, to women upon the field for any reason other than courtesy.

But the Lambertans had always been courteous.

"Matriarch," Ser Galen said. "The Tyr'agnate will see you now, and he wishes to extend his apologies for the length of time you have been kept waiting. He is conversing with the Serra Alina di'Lamberto."

His polished youth did not give way to expression, but she chuckled anyway. She knew both the Tyr and the sister, and she did not envy them the conversation; she imagined that it consisted mostly of forceful silence and barely hidden anger.

"He offers water," the young kai said, "and wine, if you will have either."

She shook her head. She'd had enough of water and wine in this dismal place; they led to blood, and blood led to vision and dream. But she remembered to thank him for his offer.

He led her into the tent, between the rows of Tyran who guarded its entrance. They did not bow—nor could they, and see to their duties—but they offered her the formal dip of their heads as she passed them. She recognized them all, and hoarded that knowledge for future use. It was good to have the Heart of Havalla in her possession again.

The Tyr'agnate looked up as she entered, and the Serra Alina, dressed as a Northern soldier, fell slowly to her knees. The prostration did not suit her attire; she wore the Kings' colors, and their deep blue, their straight, two-edged sword, their equally simple rod, was at odds with everything else in the tent.

Even, Yollana thought, with the Serra herself. She made noise as she bent; she wore mail beneath that foreign surcoat. And her hair, gracelessly braided, was pulled severely from the contours of her face.

Yollana did not bid her rise; it was not her province. And if she was Matriarch—and she was—she was not yet so foolish with power that she was willing to slight the Lambertan Tyr. Not over something trivial.

"Serra Alina," Ser Mareo kai di'Lamberto said, "you are no doubt familiar with the Havallan Matriarch."

Alina rose. Her gaze traveled between the brother to whom she owed her obedience and the Matriarch. "Yes," she said softly. "Yollana."

"Alina," the Matriarch said. "The North has changed you."

Alina's smile was supple and thin, but it was genuine. "It has, Matriarch."

"How much?"

"Enough."

"Aye, enough that you dress like a man."

A slender, dark brow rose. "I carry no sword," she said quietly.

"Ah, that's what's missing." Yollana carried no sword; had she, she would have been forced to surrender it before being granted her audience—and she did not wish to follow that path to its unfortunate conclusion; Matriarchs surrendered *nothing* to anyone but the Lady.

And sometimes not even then.

"Tyr'agnate," Yollana said, turning from the sister.

"Matriarch."

"Forgive me for intruding."

"We are finished," he said stiffly. The temper, she thought, was all on one side. It almost made her smile.

"I see that the Tyr'agar has begun his preparations for the visit of the General."

The kai Lamberto's nod was noncommittal, but it did not invite further observation.

Too bad. "The Northern magi are being deployed to the West of the valley."

He shrugged, but she saw by the slight rise of silvered brow that she had given him information that he did not yet possess. Be careful, she told herself, wanting her pipe.

She settled, instead, for the balls of her canes, leaning into them as if they were needed. Theater, she thought, but it was a grim play.

"The Havalla Voyani will serve you in the coming battle."

At that, his brows did rise, and he did nothing to anchor them to the otherwise still lines of his face.

"My daughters are not yet here, but they walk the borders between your lands and the lands of Averda, and they have sent word: the borders are not yet closed."

"How long, Matriarch?"

She pretended to misunderstand him. He was not fooled, of course, but he allowed it; it was the only courtesy that she could afford to offer.

"How long do we have until the borders are closed?"

"Two days," she told him. He did not ask how she knew, and in this, he was Southern. The Northerners asked so many questions it was almost impossible to fit *answers* between them.

"Not enough time, then."

"Not for the gathering of men, no." She paused, and then added, "But some of your Tors will be with us before the sun sets."

"Which clans?"

"Dagarro," she replied firmly, "Saranis and Haela."

"Then we are further in your debt."

"There are no debts," she replied starkly. "You fight what *must* be fought, and we aid as we can. We are not an army," she added, "and we will never be one. But we are not without our skills."

She waited for his response; he gave it slowly. A nod.

But when she had it, she removed her satchel. "I have a gift to offer," she told him as she unbuckled its cracked, familiar flap.

He was alert and watchful.

So, too, was the Serra Alina.

She drew from her weathered bag a tarnished, silver clasp. It was—or had once been—ornamental; it was meant to be worn upon cloaks.

He wore gold. But he did not hesitate; he removed his cloak, revealing the colors of his clan as he did. Not for Mareo kai di'Lamberto the dust and dirt of the open road; he was the color of the sun across the open plains. But his horse was unfettered by barding or shoe; it ran free.

The Serra Alina took the cloak, and with care, she removed the gold clasp. He allowed this; it was scraf's work, and in the Dominion, there was often little difference between women and serafs; both served.

But so, she thought, before annoyance could gain a foothold, did the kai Lamberto. She passed the clasp to the Serra, and the Serra took it with care; she placed it firmly upon either side of the cloak's height.

While she worked, Yollana drew a second item from her satchel. A small, chipped bowl. Writing rimmed it in a circle, but the words were faint, and she doubted that the kai Lamberto would be able to read what was written there. It was pale, like fired clay, but yellowed, like bone that has long forgotten the feel of clinging flesh. It was not large.

The third thing she offered was a silver horn.

It, too, was tarnished; it bore the weight of unkind years. More, it bore history.

He accepted the two gifts, the bowl in the cup of his right palm, the horn in the cup of his left. His hands were large and callused; the hands of a swordmaster.

The Serra Alina lifted the cloak, and her brother allowed her to place it upon his shoulders; she straightened its fall and then stepped back, a critical eye upon its hem. It was a simple cloak, a brown-gray that could sustain the illusion of cleanliness, no matter how much travel it saw.

"I can offer you no like gift," he said quietly; he lifted his hands and closed the clasp. It was utterly silent.

She snorted. "I hope not," she said, and meant it.

They waited. Had she been in Amar, she would have kept them waiting a little longer; very few of the Voyani disliked an audience when they were given to acts of generosity—and even fewer were given an audience of such gravity and power.

But she had other things to attend to, and she put the meager pleasure aside.

"The clasp," she said, "will grant you some protection against the servants of the Lord of Night. It is not—as you can plainly see—armor; what little armor we have, we will not have time to unearth."

He nodded.

"It will grant you more, however, when the Lord's light falters. All who serve you will see you should you choose to be seen.

"Choose otherwise, and they will overlook your presence, as if you were the least of your cerdan."

"And the enemy?"

"They will be fooled in a like fashion." She bowed her head. "It is old, kai Lamberto, and it has seen much use. Guard it with care; use it with wisdom."

He nodded.

"The bowl," she continued, "is older. It will serve you in this fashion, should you choose to pay its price. Water will flow from it in abundance, should water be required. Wine will be purified, should you choose to place it in the bowl." She hesitated, and then continued. "But if you choose the third ablution—and it must come from you, kai Lamberto—it will offer you more. While the blood is warm, you will have the perfect mirror; it will seem wider and longer than the bowl itself. If you have the will, you will see yourself in it. If you have more, you will see, beyond your own image, the field of battle shorn of artifice. Where there is magic, you will see either golden light, or the utter absence of light. Where there are servants of the Lord of Night, you will see their true form." She hesitated again.

"Matriarch?"

"And if you see these creatures, and you do not flinch or turn, it will grant you a single gift."

"What gift?"

But she shook her head. "You will be able to use it only once, and if you are not strong enough, you will see only what I have spoken of, no more."

"And if I am, Matriarch?"

"You will see names," she said quietly.

He was utterly still.

"Call those names, and those who bear them will be forced to answer your summons."

"The hidden name," he said quietly.

"Yes." It was a stark word. "But what answers will not be bound to you, and not beholden to you." Her gaze fell to the sword at his side. "And it will come for you, no matter who or what stands in its way. Let no other hand touch the bowl," she added. "Let no other blood mingle with yours; you have a weapon which might serve you in good stead, should you be able to invoke the greatest of the bowl's magics."

He slid the bowl into the folds of his sash, and she realized again that he was not a small man.

"The third gift," she said, gazing at the horn that remained in his hand, "is also invoked by blood. Sound that horn, and it will be heard."

He nodded. "Matriarch. You will always be welcome in my lands."

She said, so quietly that he had to strain to catch the words, "We will not be in your lands much longer, kai Lamberto. But while we are, and as long as we have been, they are *our* lands as well; they have been home to the *Voyanne* for longer than your line. We have taken much, and we have offered what we can in return; this will pay all debts."

She bowed to the Serra Alina. "Come, Serra," she said. "We must visit the Tyr'agnate of Callesta; the Arkosa Voyani will not venture into Averda now, and it is upon Averdan soil that we stand. We will be in no man's debt."

The Serra Alina offered a graceful obeisance to her brother; it was so perfect, so utterly Southern, that it could only be meant to annoy.

Ser Ramiro di'Callesta met the Matriarch with a silent gravity that was shorn of Lambertan humility. Greater difference could not be found between these two men, although the clans could bicker for days over their merits.

"Matriarch," he said, the caution evident in the smooth lines of his near expressionless face.

"Tyr'agnate," she replied, her voice cracking on the last syllable.

"The army comes?" he asked her calmly.

"Soon." She handed her canes to the Serra Alina, missing the edgeless grace of Na'tere's company; the discussion with the Tyr'agnate of Lamberto had left Serra Alina sour.

Not that it showed in any obvious way, but the beak of her nose was more pronounced. She was a bird of prey, fettered here by gender. Yollana felt no envy for her.

"It has come to my ears, Tyr'agnate," the Matriarch said, when she had tendered a bow and it had been accepted, "that you have done damage to one of the kinlords."

His brow rose, but he did not offer comment.

"I do not know how," she continued, "but I commend you. You live."

He still waited. She found it irritating. She had never been a woman to fill the silences, no matter how awkward they became.

But he was not Lambertan; she reminded herself of this, although she knew it well.

"I have come to offer you the blessing of the Havalla Voyani, Tyr'agnate. We are aware that were it not for you, no war would be fought upon these fields; we are aware that you will bear the brunt of the losses, this day. You have been cursed for your affiliation with the North. Aye, you have," she said, with a dark smile, "even by me."

"And now, Matriarch?"

"And now, Tyr'agnate, those who dare to do so might even call you wise. You traveled at the side of Baredan di'Navarre, and you took from the North the only man who could wield the Sun Sword; you brought him here, kept him safe, and offered him the obedience and the loyalty that his line has not earned from your family.

"We are in your debt," she said abruptly.

He offered her the first of his smiles; it was shallow and thin, but it indicated that he saw much. "The Voyani dislike debt."

"As much as the next clan."

"Then I discharge all debt," he said. As if it were in his power to do so. Her eyes narrowed as she met his; his did not blink or flinch. Very little unnerved this man. He met her approval.

"How so?" she asked, with genuine curiosity.

"I did not deliver the Tyr'agar to these lands for your sake, Matriarch. Nor for the sake of Arkosa, nor any of the other Voyani clans. I did not do this at the behest of the General Baredan di'Navarre; nor did I choose it for the benefit of my people. I certainly did not do it for Lambertans.

"General Alesso di'Marente had already chosen the Tyrs he would favor and the Tyrs he would supplant; the only way to wage this war was at the side of the kai Leonne. I do not intend to lose."

She nodded; he had told her nothing that she had not already surmised. "It is true," she said, appraising, "but it does not lessen our debt. The Averdan valleys have been home to much war and much loss, and where the Lambertans chose to wall themselves up within *Amar,* you have chosen a more prudent course."

His brow rose, and his lips bent again.

"But you will follow the Tyr'agar, should he emerge from this battle whole," she continued. "And in the end, whether it was your intent or no, the lands will change. This is a war that must be fought."

"Men fight," he said quietly.

"Aye, and the Havalla Voyani would fight as well, if they could in safety cross the borders of your Terrean." She bowed her head. She wanted her pipe. "Therefore let me give you what they can no longer use."

He stilled, then, and his hand left the hilt of his sword. She recognized its scabbard, and she nodded quietly. "*Bloodhame,*" she said, as if calling it.

He raised a brow.

"Your sword is known, kai Callesta."

"But it is not one of the Five."

"It is not."

"And against the demons?"

"You have already shown what damage a Southern sword can do, wielded with will," she replied. Her hands delved a moment in the lighter folds of her satchel; the leather was cracked and worn, and its hue was now a pale, mottled brown. She could not say what shade it had once been; it didn't matter.

"If you will entrust me a moment with your blade," she said, the question unasked. She marked his hesitation.

"It is my clan's blade," he replied, with some hesitance. "And be it of lesser significance or no, I will wield it."

She snorted. "Of course. You are the Tyr'agnate. It is Callestan."

He studied the ruined lines of her face a moment, and then he nodded. He drew the blade.

It shone in the diminished light of his tent.

She reached out almost imperiously and he handed her the sword; she marked his hesitation, and appreciated it. She knew *Bloodhame's* legend and its demand, and she grimaced. So much blood shed, and no battle yet joined. Ah well, so be it. She caught the edge in her palm and grunted, paying its price.

He said nothing, but he was surprised.

She said, "What I offer you is as old an heirloom as the Voyani possess upon the open road." And as she spoke, she opened her left palm. In it, glinting light was fractured by the facets of a large gem. She whispered a word in the still confines of this artificial room.

The gem began to gather light in the center of its heart.

"It adorns the pommel," she told him.

"I fear you will find few craftsmen who will—"

She lifted a hand, demanding silence. "Bear witness," she said.

"It is said that the Voyani hoard their secrets; to be called to witness them is to place oneself in the hands of their Matriarch."

"Aye," she said softly. And she placed the gem above the unadorned hilt. The claws around its ancient setting reached out as if they were alive, and they burrowed themselves into the wood and leather grip.

She spoke another word, older than the gem itself, and the light was expelled.

When it was done, she held out the sword.

He took it.

"The name of the sword cannot now be changed," she said, with some regret, "nor would I ask it. But wield this, and the enemy will have cause for regret. It is not a weapon of the Lord," she added, "but it is wielded by a man of the Lord. Do not falter, and it will not falter."

She held out her hand, and the Serra Alina bound it, taking strips of cloth from the satchel.

"Who made this, Matriarch?" He gazed at it with care.

"Men," she said softly.

"Men?"

"In the times before our history," she told him, "when the word 'man' meant something that even the *Kialli* feared. The sword will not leave your hand, once drawn, until you sheathe it, or until you are dead. If you are summoned to unexpected battle, and the sword is across the camp, call it and it will come."

He sheathed *Bloodhame*; she had paid the blood price.

"And when the battle is over, Matriarch?"

She laughed. "It is yours, now, Tyr'agnate. For as long as the blade lasts, it is yours. The power to remove it from its chosen blade has long since been lost; we would have to steal the sword and labor many weeks to reclaim it." She lifted a hand. "And we are not so unwise as that; we understand what is symbol and what is more than symbol. We would sooner take your life than your blade.

"It is a gift. But it is a gift that will best serve our cause in your hands."

He nodded.

"I will not be in your debt, kai Callesta."

"You have never been in our debt," he replied evenly.

"Fight well," she continued. "Win. Do what the Havalla Voyani cannot do."

"And that?"

"Wage this war," she told him.

"I have already said that we are committed," he replied.

"When you made your commitment," she replied starkly, "you did not know the army that you would face."

"Does it matter?"

"No, kai Callesta. To men of honor, it signifies nothing."

His dark brow rose; she had surprised him. "That is not a . . . word that is often applied to Callesta."

"I have wandered these lands in my youth," she said quietly, "and in the past decade, after the disaster of the last Leonne war. If it is not given you by those who do not dwell within your boundaries, if it is granted reluctantly behind your back by those who serve you as your lieges, it is granted far more readily by the serafs whose existence is tied to Averdan soil.

"Earn it," she added severely.

He laughed. And then he tendered her the bow he had withheld.

"One more," she said to the Serra Alina, as she left his tent.

The Serra nodded.

"Where is the kai Leonne?"

And smiled. "He is with the Northerners," she said.

"Good."

Valedan kai di'Leonne stood by the side of Ser Anton di'Guivera. His sole Tyran was nowhere in sight. The two Commanders had been carried by the vagaries of duty to other places; the Tyr stood alone.

Even the Tor'agars did not trouble him; they could not easily stand in his presence in the absence of their Tyrs. She understood this well, and she approached him with the bent back and shaky walk of a half-crippled old woman.

But he was quick to notice her, and quick to offer her the depth of his bow; as unlike both Lambertan Tyr and Callestan Tyr as a man could be who hoped to lead both.

His strength remained untested. It was her greatest regret.

"Matriarch," he said.

Ser Anton did not step aside, but he did not step forward. He did not trust her.

Which was fair; she trusted his legend, but she saw the man behind it clearly.

"Tyr'agar."

"Have you come with word of the village?"

"I am not a messenger, Tyr'agar." She looked pointedly at her leg. "And it would be a poor Tyr indeed who tried to force speed from these legs."

Valedan smiled. "It would be a poor Tyr who judged any Voyani Matriarch by her appearance," he said gravely.

Ser Anton afforded the boy a smile.

It was more than she was willing to do.

"In two days," she told him severely, "you will be tested. Are you ready?"

He nodded.

She almost believed him.

"The Havalla Voyani cannot take to this field," she told them both, the swordmaster and the Tyr. "But if they could be here, they would. We serve in other ways," she added.

"You have served in many," he replied, and for just a moment she wondered what his wife had chanced to tell him.

She nodded. "We fight the same enemy, and alliances have been built on far shakier ground."

He nodded, waiting. After a moment, he said, "Will you sit?"

"I would appreciate it."

He nodded to Ser Anton, and they retreated from the gentle ridge. A tent had been made for him here; he entered it and retrieved a wooden bench from its side. The weight bowed him, but not for long; he had youth, and youth was elastic.

"Serra Alina," the Tyr'agar said. "You were missed."

The Serra Alina offered him an expression that the Matriarch could not—quite—read. *So,* she thought, *you build your odd alliances. You have her heart, boy. If her brother had half your wisdom, he would tend it himself.*

"I will not speak of gifts here," she said, as she took the seat he offered. The Serra Alina brought sweet water in shallow bowls. "But I have come to offer you advice, if you will have it."

He stood before her, and she was aware of his height; he had not the width of an older man, but that would come in time.

"General Alesso di'Marente *is* the Lord's man," she said severely.

"And I?"

"You are the Lady's," she answered.

Ser Anton's frown was loud enough to be felt.

"Listen," she said, her eyes flickering to the older man before coming to rest again upon Valedan kai di'Leonne's face. "In the Cities that once occupied the Sea of Sorrows, there were no Lord and no Lady; there were gods, and the gods had the names that the Northerners give them now."

Ser Anton was rigid.

"It is a painful truth, but it is truth." She closed her eyes. "And in those Cities, the Lord of Night was one of many gods, and he found welcome among those of power.

"My kin were estranged from him. My kin," she added gently, "opposed him. But it was costly. We could not stand as you stand now, even at the height of our power. We knew too much."

"And it is an act of ignorance that leads us to war?" Ser Anton snapped.

"Glorious ignorance," she said, without pause. "You want justice, boy. You are young enough that you might find it, and young enough that you might not see the cost of its purchase."

Valedan was silent, but his gaze held hers, measuring it.

"You carry the Sun Sword, and it is an ancient sword."

"It was given the clan Leonne by the Lord," Ser Anton said severely.

"Aye, perhaps it was. But *which* Lord, Ser Anton?"

"The Lord of Day," he said. He would not be moved.

She shrugged. "It was meant for one purpose, and one alone: To destroy the servants of the Lord of Night."

He nodded.

"It has not been called upon for generations. Its legend is weak; it lies fallow.

"You seek to make a legend in this battle, a new legend. I do not discount it. But I will say this again: The General is the Lord's man."

"The Lord of Night," Ser Anton said.

"No, Ser Anton. The Lord. What has he done that others have not done, in our history? Little. He follows the rules made for those who seek power. The Lord of Day will not judge him and find him wanting. He seeks to leave a legacy; he seeks to elevate his family."

"He has done the one; the other he will never do."

"No," she said. "If we have victory here, perhaps not. But he was made from the Dominion; it is inseparable from all that he is."

Ser Anton's lips were almost white. But he did not strike women; certainly not Voyani women.

"You, kai Leonne, were born to a concubine."

Valedan did not stiffen; he seemed to take no offense at her words.

"And you were taken from the harem, through the streets of the Tor Leonne; you were given to the Northerners as a concession to 'peace.' They raised you," she said softly. "What have you learned?"

He answered, "It has taken a lifetime to learn it; will you have me speak of a life in a few words?"

She clapped her callused hands. "Good, good!" she said, with a harsh laugh. "No, I would not have you speak of it at all. But I say this: You are not the Lord's."

"By your own words, I cannot be the Lady's; she is not a Northern god."

"No. But in *this* land, she is, by default, *all* that the Lord is not. I say again, you are hers. Trust your instinct, kai Leonne. And when that fails you, trust what you know." She lifted the water bowl to her cracked lips.

"Ser Alesso has come this far alone. You would never have made it to these fields without the allies that you have chosen. But you have chosen wisely; and what you have taken, you will keep. Understand this; it is your gift."

She reached into her satchel for the last time.

And she handed him a piece of worn cloth; it was rolled like Northern parchment, and tied with cracked leather thongs. "This is the whole of my gift to you," she said quietly. "Do not open it, and do not read it here."

"When, then, shall I do so?"

"If you are lucky, never. But if you are not, you will know the moment. We have killed the golden-eyed and hunted those who are born with the gift of voice; we cannot undo the harm done by these two acts.

"But we can assuage it in a small fashion. This will allow you to speak, once, as the bard-born do. No matter what distance separates you, no matter what battle, the people you choose to so bless will hear your words, and those words will be known as yours.

"It will work only once," she added softly, "and it has no power to compel."

She rose. "I will leave you now," she said. "But I will linger here, like shadow or ghost; this is my battle as well."

"You honor us," he told her. He meant it.

Against her will, she found herself liking him. It added a depth of pain to the coming battle, and brought her no comfort.

She said, "I owe a debt of pain to the General."

"I know it."

"But I have born pain in my time. We are Voyani, and in the end, we are governed by the practical. Do not forget what I have said this day."

He nodded, and she knew that he hoarded the words.

"Serra Alina," she said quietly, "I am finished. I will leave you with the Tyr that you have come from the North to serve."

CHAPTER TWENTY-EIGHT

THE DAY passed slowly.

For a moment, Lord Ishavriel could feel the sun inching toward the horizon. Day was not a threat to the *Kialli*, all legend to the contrary; but night was writ in ancient laws of natural order, and the road that waited could not be traversed with ease while the sun held sway in the open sky.

This, he thought, as he watched the slow lengthening of shadows, *is mortal time.* And he, *Kialli,* kinlord, was not bound by such trivialities—or should not have been. Yet he waited, as they waited, and the time seemed, in his judgment, to be the same time.

At a distance—a great distance—he could see the men who served the General Alesso di'Marente, a mortal who had confounded the subtle demands of The Lord. Those men now lined the valley, from the flat of its long floor, to its heights. Those heights were gentle; they had not the craggy treachery of the mountain passes to the North—but they caused their difficulty; the rain had softened the earth, and only the roots of the trees served their purpose; they were deep and not easily dislodged.

Horses had been taken from the lowlands, but not in great number, and their purpose was simple burden; the men in their oddly styled armor did not mount or ride.

At his side, Anya a'Cooper fidgeted.

It was a human word and a human activity; there was no grandeur in it; nothing that hinted at the power that resided beneath the wriggling lines of a face constantly in motion. She hopped and jumped and dug a trench in the ground with her toes, filling it with leaves and the odd branch she could find. She was, he thought, although he was a poor judge, a child.

There were no children in the Hells.

"Patience," he said softly. Where she was concerned, his voice was always gentle.

"But it's been *days,*" she whined.

"And it will end soon, Anya."

"How?"

He said nothing. But she was bored. And boredom, where Anya was concerned, was a dangerous state. "You will know," he told her.

"But how will I know?"

"I will tell you."

She gazed at the trees with a barely concealed longing, and he shook his head. "If you cause another such tree to grow," he said, "it will uproot its brethren."

"You're just worried about the silver trees."

His eyes narrowed.

"What trees, Anya?"

"The silver ones," she said impatiently. "You know. The special ones."

But they were not silver; not to his eyes. Not to the eyes of the other mortals. He was surprised, again, by her power. And he had had many years in which to grow accustomed to its depth.

"The tree roots will not dislodge the special ones," he said quietly. "Very little can."

"Then why can't I grow one? Just one?"

"Because it will be seen," he said.

"But why does it matter? You said it's too late for them to do anything about it anyway!"

"Because if they can see the tree, they will know where you are."

She shrugged. Her smile was feral. "So?"

"They will come," he continued. "And we will be forced to kill them."

She shrugged again.

"But if we do not kill them all, they will return; and although you are powerful, Anya, you are not proof against the whole of an army."

"Liar," she said.

He stiffened.

"You just don't want them to die *here.*"

Oh, she was canny in her insanity. Too canny. He did not however correct her; he had learned, in the earliest of their years together, that that could be costly. She was direct, and in her fashion, she was honest; she hated to be lied to.

The litany of reasons for that hatred—a small catalog of pathetic little wrongs done her as a child by other children—was not one he willingly invoked. It never changed, and it produced the most irritating of her attributes: angry tears.

"Yes," he said at last, "not here. It will signify nothing. We will have wasted much power and effort, and The Lord will be displeased."

She quieted at the mention of *Allasakar's* title. His name, Ishavriel did not invoke; it frightened her.

And Anya frightened was more of a danger than Anya bored.

"How *many* days?"

Patience was something that all of the *Kialli* possessed, but not in abundance.

Not for the first time, Ishavriel wondered how it was that Kiriel had survived her childhood in the Wastes. But he did not go so far as to admire her mentor.

Instead, restless, he walked the long, thin line that the trees strengthened as they grew. He reached out, his fingers falling short of the first stunted bud, the first twisted branch.

"Not many," he said softly, and with some satisfaction. "Not many at all, Anya. The road is growing stronger as we speak."

Yollana of the Havalla Voyani now made her last pilgrimage in isolation. She did not call the Serra Teresa and she did not trouble herself with the numerous cerdan who marched in their imprecise lines along the valley floor. Nor did they trouble her; she did not wish to be seen.

She cast a shadow, but the shadow itself was lost to the long squares of tenting.

One more, she thought, and then she might take her momentary rest. She had no desire to return to her tent; the shadows there had not yet diminished and the wind that might drive them more quickly from the camp did not exist in any place but the Sea of Sorrows.

But it was shadows that she sought, and she found them; the height of the sun did not disperse their strength.

The tent itself was not remarkable; it was larger than the Northern tents, but not larger than the tenting that housed the Southern cavalrymen. She stopped at the sealed flap and drew herself up to her full height, setting the canes to one side.

Then she entered.

"Elena Tamaraan," she said quietly.

And Elena, once Daughter to the Arkosans, looked up. As did her companion.

The Heart knew him.

And he knew her by its presence, although he did not know it; it lay hidden to the eyes of those who served the Lord of Night.

"Matriarch," Elena said, and rose. She offered a bow made clumsy in comparison to the bows the high clansmen had offered. But it was a good Voyani bow, and it spoke of instant respect.

"I have come to speak with you," the Matriarch said. "And I will speak with you alone."

Her companion raised a flawless brow; he was close enough to the Arkosan woman that he could lift a hand and touch her shoulder. His hand did rise, but he met Yollana's one-eyed gaze and it froze there.

"Old woman," he said coldly. "Do not interfere in matters that you do not understand."

"I understand much that you have forgotten," she replied.

"I am *Kialli*," he said, and his voice managed the impossible feat of being colder. "I am defined by my ability to remember."

"You are defined," she said curtly, "by an ancient, foolish choice. No more and no less. This is not your Lord's Court; this is *mine,* and I say again, that I will speak with Elena Tamaraan *alone.*"

She lifted a hand to the Heart that hung, invisible, in the hollow of her throat.

It was a threat.

It was perceived as a threat.

"I have suffered your presence," the Matriarch said, "because the Tyr'agar wills it. But he is not present, and were I to make my plea for privacy, he would not gainsay me. You may leave," she added, "or you may stay. But if you stay, you face the wrath of the ancients."

"So," Lord Telakar said, "there is truth in the old fears; you maintain some part of your power."

"Decide."

His gaze traveled Elena's face; Elena was frozen in place. But her fear—and it was clearly there—was not easily read; it could have meant many things.

Yollana saw them all. It was a costly clarity.

At length, the servant of the Lord of Night bowed. "Do not harm her," he said softly.

She laughed bitterly. "What harm can I do her that she has not already done herself?"

Elena Tamaraan flinched. She said nothing, however; she was Voyani enough—barely—to understand the command in the Matriarch's request. Even if Yollana was not her Matriarch.

Lord Telakar did not choose to leave by the tent's flap; he raised arms, crossed them, and allowed the shadow to take him.

It was cold indeed when the shadow lifted. The breath of the two women hung in the air like fine mist.

Elena dropped at once to her knees.

But Yollana remained standing.

"Yes," she said, when Elena raised her face, "I have recovered the Heart of Havalla."

Elena lifted her hands and made a gesture that crossed her chest; it was involuntary—a warding. A useless one.

"I am not—" she began, but Yollana raised a hand and she fell silent.

"I have spent this day dispensing with the past," she told the younger woman. "Trinkets that I have carried against this day since the time I first placed the Heart in a stranger's hands have now left Havalla forever. I have offered advice, but advice is like rain; it falls, and what it causes to grow, I have no control over."

This was her way of saying that she was weary. That she was in an ill humor was obvious.

"I was born with the Lady's gift," she said, "but it was a poor gift. My visions were not strong, and they did not come at my command; to invoke them was—and is—costly." As she spoke, she took a dagger from her sash. She unsheathed it in perfect silence.

"But you, Elena Tamaraan, were born with the same gift."

Elena said nothing.

"And the Lady's gift has never been given without price. Pay it now."

Elena lifted a hand.

Yollana's blade sliced the palm open, and she bled.

"I cannot give you advice," the Matriarch said. She opened her left palm, and with an ease that spoke of too much practice, she sliced through callused skin. "Any advice I might have given can no longer be heeded."

Elena lifted the palm where blood pooled, and Yollana placed her own against it; blood mingled in a ceremony as old as the *Voy-anne*.

"Blood of my blood," she said quietly, her fingers locking around Elena's.

And Elena murmured, "Blood of Havalla."

Yollana said, "I offer you a gift. I offer it freely, and without en-mity." She knelt then, and set the dagger aside. With her free hand, she reached for the chain that held the Heart, and pulled the Heart from its cage of safety.

"Look, Daughter," she said quietly. "Do not tell me what you see; do not tell anyone. But look, and take from the depths of our Heart the knowledge and wisdom that it will offer."

Elena's eyes widened; the brown of iris was lost to the black of pupil. Yollana could see the reflection of the Heart's light in her eyes. She could see, as well, that Elena, born to Arkosa, was cau-tious; she did not lift hands; did not touch the cut facets that con-tained Havalla's history.

Yollana did not trouble herself to look away; she waited while the light grew bright and the cold in the tent receded.

Elena whispered a single word; it was lost, a movement of lip shorn of breath.

But when she said it, Yollana released the chain that held the Heart; it fell, once again, into the concealing safety of Voyani cloth. "Do you understand?" she asked, as softly as a Matriarch could.

Elena shook her head; tears rimmed her open eyes; she had not once blinked.

"No more do I," the old woman said. She rose. "You have cho-sen your road, Elena; but it has also chosen you. Do not fail us."

She left without looking back.

Auralis, never comfortable with praise—either the giving or receiving of it—was in a great deal of discomfort for about five minutes of the morning. After that, while he stood in something akin to stunned silence, Ser Daro di'Valente came and ushered the village serafs from the long hall.

Kiriel snickered.

Auralis frowned. "What the Hells was that about?"

"You *did* save their lives," she said pointedly, as she knelt to one side of the table. Auralis cursed the lack of both height—the table's—and chairs, and then knelt as well. But he stared at the empty hall for a while before he condescended to eat.

"You saved them," he said, around a mouthful of something that was like mush, but warm and spicy. "They're not throwing themselves at *your* feet."

"I'm a woman," she replied.

He said something crude, sliding back into the bitter certainty of self. She raised a dark brow, but shrugged. Then she rose, and he turned to see why; the Serra Diora had entered the dining hall. She bowed in a pretty and utterly un-Northern fashion—although he recognized the exquisite motion belatedly as she sat.

Kallandras of Senniel College joined her; he nodded gracefully to both Kiriel and Auralis. "Where is Ser Daro?"

"He's eaten," Kiriel said. "Quickly. He apologizes for his absence."

"And Ser Andaro?"

"He is with Ser Daro," Kiriel replied. She set her bowl down. "They woke early and they have been traveling through the village."

"Preparing," Serra Diora said, a question in the single word.

Kiriel nodded.

"Will the battle come this far North?"

"If we lose," Kiriel replied. She reached for the water and stopped as her hand brushed the Serra's. The Serra colored.

"My duty," she said gently.

"Not here," Kiriel told her firmly.

"I am the Serra, Kiriel di'Ashaf. You are the warrior. We each have our duties."

"It's just water," Kiriel said.

Diora's smile was disarming, but there was a shadow that inhabited her eyes. "I have journeyed in the Sea of Sorrows," she told the Northern girl, "and I do not think that I will ever see water in the same way."

"Even after the rains?"

"Even so. There was rain in the desert."

"Kiriel," Kallandras said, "what news?" It was meant to distract, and after a moment, Kiriel let her hand fall back to her lap. The ring caught the light, its flat curve stretched round her finger. It seemed loose.

The Serra Diora poured water into the cups; she did not waste a drop.

But Kiriel thought, watching her, the desert had not done this: it was part of her.

"Where will they go if the armies come?" Kiriel asked.

The Serra Diora was quiet. "They will stay in the village," she said.

"And fight?"

"Even so. They are not cerdan," she added, "but they are not without weapons."

"And the children?"

"There is no place for the children to go. They can flee, but they will not reach the next village on their own; the road is not easily followed without a guide, and there is not one among them who has left the village."

"Auralis—"

"There are no children in the Northern Wastes, are there?"

She shook her head. "There was one," she added, after a pause. "But she left."

"Where did she go?"

Such simple words. She ate quietly and slowly, but she did not look at her companions again.

The wind told a tale.

It swept leaves from the branches of fallen trees; bowed stalks of wildflowers and shadowed, slender plants; it changed the fall of hair against face and nape of bent neck. Dancing, always dancing, it whispered; the sun did not still it, and the heat did not diminish it.

Throughout the Green Valley, the serafs labored. They tended the fields, as they often did in the aftermath of too much rain—but their thoughts were elsewhere.

The children who were many years from the threshold of such worries now played their games of hide-and-seek around the trunks of the great pillars that adorned the village; they called them stone trees, and their elders did not demur or offer any corrections; they had no words for what had happened, and wished to discover none.

What was spoken had strength.

Even here, among the least of the people of the Dominion. Perhaps especially here.

The oldest of the women tended the children, as was often done; the oldest of the men supervised the work in the new fields.

But their gazes were drawn South, again and again, the rhythm of their daily progress shattered. Although the sky was clear and unfettered by cloud, the storm was in the air, and it spoke with the wind's voice.

They knew that voice; as the years deepened loss and made joy a prized rarity, they had come to accept that what begins, ends. Children, caught in the eternity of youth, had yet to leave it; they had no understanding of age, and wisdom was as foreign as the Northerners who lived with Ser Daro.

But fear, the guardians knew, would change nothing.

So they offered their young the only shelter that they understood: ignorance.

They could not, however, enter that shelter themselves. Soldiers in their own way, they stood guard, fierce sentinels, aware of how much they might lose, and aware, keenly aware, that there was little that they could do against what gathered.

"But there must be *something* we can do."

Auralis looked down at the top of Kiriel's head. She was pacing. He'd seen caged cats that looked more comfortable.

"There is," he said, shrugging. "But not yet."

"We can't just sit here like trapped rats," she snapped. "We've so little time—we can't just waste it!"

Kallandras looked at Kiriel, and then lifted his glance; Auralis met it. Neither man spoke.

"Serra Diora—"

"Na'kiri," the Serra said quietly, "we are but five. A hundred years would not suffice to build the citadel that would keep these serafs safe, and we have days at best. Could we build it even given the scant time, we could not man it."

"But we have—we have power—between us. All of us. We have—"

"We have," Kallandras told her, "But so, too, does the army What they cannot stop, we cannot stop."

"How can you just sit there and say that?"

"You could have," Auralis said, the words coming from a dark place. "When we met, you could have, Kiriel."

"Yes," she said bitterly, "because when we met, I wouldn't have *cared*." She felt no shame; he saw that clearly. She was not like him in that.

"So now you care," he said, more sharply than he intended. "And what difference does it make?"

She was white. Her eyes were the color of night.

He should be careful. Knew it. "I'll tell you. It hurts you more. That's it."

"AKalakar," Kallandras began, lifting a hand.

"And you know what? They don't need *your* pain. They'll lose more in this war than you will. Even if we win."

"If we win, they'll be alive—"

"If we win, yes, they'll be alive. And as long as the growing season is good, they might not starve. The stockades are either empty or *burning*, Kiriel. The granaries are being emptied. Where do you think the replacements will come from?"

"AKalakar."

"When the Tyr'agar retreated from Averda, before the Northern armies advanced, he razed whole villages," Auralis added grimly. "So that we couldn't make use of them. If the Tyr'agar is forced to retreat—"

"He'll never do it."

"Then he's a fool. Because leaving the villages standing will only feed his enemy, and he can't afford that. He'll take what he can, but he won't leave much behind. And you know what? Serafs don't travel with armies."

Her hands were fists now.

"If we win, if we force the General to retreat—ignoring the *demons*—he'll do the same. He won't take this village, but if he hasn't already done it, he'll strip the rest. And the only difference between those villages and this one is—"

"Ashaf," Kiriel said starkly.

"She's already dead," Auralis snapped. "She doesn't care."

Kiriel hit him.

She moved fast, but it didn't matter; he wouldn't have ducked.

Her armor made more noise than anything else in the room, and it left when she did. At a run.

"That was unnecessary, AKalakar."

He shrugged, rubbing his jaw. All things considered, he was lucky it wasn't broken. "Yeah."

"She is young," Kallandras continued, staring at the open screens. "And the young bring much to a war."

But the Serra Diora rose as the bard spoke. "AKalakar," she said quietly, using the Northern title, "you cannot save her from pain."

"I don't give a shit about her pain," he snarled.

"I wasn't talking about her pain," the Serra replied. "She is what she is, but she does not seek to take advantage of yours."

He really hated the South then. "Do you know what I did in the last war?" It was a whisper. It was a threat.

"I know," she replied calmly.

That stopped him.

"It is in your voice, AKalakar. You have not learned to hide it." She turned to Kallandras. "I will find her."

"I think it unwise, Serra."

"Seen in this way, all war is unwise—but some wars must be fought."

She left the room to the two men.

Only when she was gone did Kallandras speak again. "I know what you think to do, AKalakar. But it is costly, and if you push her too hard, she will feel only frenzy; love will give way to panic, and panic, to the possibility of failure."

Auralis' laugh was ugly and wild.

"You want a companion," the bard continued. "You want someone who has been scarred as you've been scarred. Feed her fear, and you might build what you desire."

"And you, bard? What do you want?"

"An end to the threat of the Shining Court," Kallandras said serenely.

Auralis snorted.

"Death is death," Kallandras continued.

"Easy for you to say. Have you ever been afraid?"

"Of many things," the bard replied. His burnished hair was dark in the room, and the faint hint of silver edged his curls. He was not a young man; not even as young as he looked.

"But I am not unlike you, in this place: I do not fear the deaths that I cannot prevent.

"But I do not wish to engender fear."

"I want her to *know*—"

"If it brings you comfort, AKalakar, lie. But lie quietly, and keep the words to yourself."

Auralis thought about hitting the bard.

But something in the bard, at this moment, spoke of death. It was the first time he had seen it so clearly, and it shaded all of his memories, changing the shape of his knowledge. Knowledge was malleable.

"I don't want her to die."

"No," Kallandras said. "Death would be too easy, and it was denied you."

Against that, Auralis had nothing to say.

She's a girl, he thought bitterly. *Just a girl. She doesn't know what she's facing. She'll learn. She'll understand it.*

And when she does, bard, I'll be there. Not you. Not the Serra. Me.

And what would he say?

Shame stained the anger and the viscerality of the unspoken words.

The children caught her.

She was afraid of them; they were small and weak and easily broken. She saw them as their smaller fingers found purchase in the rough face of the pillars; as their shaking arms and nimble toes found holds that supported their negligible weight. They shouted taunts and gleeful boasts as they gained height; they were lords of great fortresses, and above the common serafs.

In the lee of the pillars, cast-off sandals disappeared into grass and uncut shrubs in ones and twos. She wanted to tell them to *climb down,* but she didn't want to scare them, and she realized that although she had the words, she didn't know how to use them; not to speak with these running, wild, irrepressible creatures.

She had never been such a child.

But it was children like these that Ashaf had loved: helpless and unaware of the cost of such helplessness.

As she watched, two boys fought for supremacy of the height they had managed to gain. Their blows were openhanded and without force, but their grip was lessened by the freeing of their hands, and at last, one child fell.

She watched him drop, and heard his howl a full minute after he'd hit the ground.

She didn't know what to do.

But she moved anyway, and came to stand by the boy's side. He had his leg clutched in his hands—his left leg. She looked at it; it was not at an odd angle, but it was definitely changing in color.

She bent to pick him up; he was crying now, and tears had changed the complexion of his face.

All this from a fall of such small height. She shook her head in wonder and then bent and lifted him; he weighed nothing. Less, she thought, than her sword.

"Na'kiri."

She turned; the child's voice had quieted, but tears still mired his face, blending with dirt that was not, until water touched it, inseparable from the rest of his skin.

"Serra—I didn't hurt him. He fell."

The Serra's smile was enough to make her freeze. And blush. She didn't know why.

"You would never hurt a child," Diora said. "But children are not so wise. You," she ordered the young boy who had won his place at the pillar's height. "You will come down and you will go and get the Oma. Now."

The boy's angry face wavered between fear and disobedience, but in the end, the tone of her language and voice made clear that she was Important and therefore not to be ignored.

"And," the Serra added, "you will apologize before you leave."

"But he *started* it!"

"He did not injure you," she replied. "And it doesn't matter who started it; you will apologize for the pain you've caused and then you will get the Oma."

The boy clambered down; his feet sank into the earth, crushing white flowers between his small, splayed toes. "Sorry," he mumbled.

Sincerity was lacking.

But clearly the mumbled word was enough; the Serra nodded and he left at a run.

"He won't come back," Kiriel said.

Diora smiled. "He'll come," she contradicted serenely.

"Why?"

"Because if he doesn't go to the Oma first, he will have to let *us* tell her what happened; this way, he can plead his case without our intervention."

"Where should I take this one?"

"If he is not too heavy, hold him," the Serra replied gently. "He is not afraid of you," she added, "and he is in pain. I don't think the foot is broken, but he looks as if he landed on the ankle; it may be some time before he walks without pain again."

She reached out and gently brushed dirty hair from the boy's face. Kiriel watched; her own hands were bound around his body, but even if they had been free, she wouldn't have dared to touch him.

"You are a brave boy," the Serra said softly. "To scale such a height. But you are not very smart."

He swallowed and nodded.

She reached out and took his hand in hers. "I'm Diora," she told him.

"Serra Diora," he said.

"Yes."

"Am I in trouble?"

"I don't know. Is your Oma very strict?"

He made a face, and tears started again; answer enough.

"Did she tell you not to play here?" Kiriel said. It was the first question she had asked.

He nodded.

And she thought of the price she would have paid for such disobedience. She could remember, clearly, the first time she had deliberately disobeyed Isladar.

It was the last time.

She had almost died.

And yet, when he had come to her rescue, he had held her, his arms longer and wider than hers were now; he had tucked her beneath his chin and rested its point upon her hair. His words were cool and distant, but they were not unkind; they were his.

And she had felt so safe then, all fear of death had receded.

She almost dropped the boy, remembering it.

If Isladar were here, she thought, *if he were here and he chose, he could save the village.*

Treacherous thought. He could—but he wouldn't.

He had never raised a hand to save any life but hers.

And that had made her special. She hated it now; it burned. But it was the truth. It had made her *special.* And she had wanted that, as a child the age of the child she now held.

Ashaf had been kind to everyone—among the human Court; the demons approached her at their peril. She had been kind to Anya, and Anya had terrified her. She would be kind to the least of serafs—to children like these.

Truth? Kiriel had desired Isladar's affection *because* it was unique.

She thought to hate children now.

But the boy in her arms could not be hated. He could barely be reasoned with. He was what he was.

And she, too, had been what she had been. Ashaf had understood half of it. Isladar had understood the rest.

The children returned—it appeared that the young girls were not content to let the miscreant tell his story uninterrupted—their hands clutching the wide skirts of a bent old woman.

Bent, Kiriel thought, as Southern swords were—curved, but in such a way as to hold an edge. Her face was broken by wrinkles; her brow creased permanently, her eyes crinkled at corners, her lips creased in the same way.

But she stopped, extricating herself from the small hands of children as she saw the Serra Diora. She bent, and she would have fallen to knees—but age prevented her from moving quickly enough.

"No," the Serra Diora said, "do not offer me obeisance. I am—"

"You are the wife to the Tyr'agar," the old woman said firmly. "And the children should know how to behave in your presence."

"Ah, but they'll learn," the Serra said.

The old woman's expression changed. "Aye," she said, but she stopped her slow fold. "That they will. Where's Na'van?"

"I have him," Kiriel said. "I think there's something wrong with his foot."

"It couldn't be his head," the old woman snapped. "Too thick."

The boy didn't speak.

"Well, Na'van, what did I tell you?"

He mumbled something.

"Let's take you up to the house, then. You'll have to stay off the foot—but at least you'll be easier to keep an eye on."

After she had left the boy, Kiriel was silent.

"Na'kiri?"

She shook her head. "Is it stupid?" she asked at last.

"To want to save them all? No, Na'kiri. It is many things, but it is not stupid." She used the Weston word.

"But it terrifies me," Kiriel whispered. Hearing, again, Isladar's cold voice. *Never show fear. Not even to me.*

"Fear of failure is always terrifying," the Serra responded. "But it is the fear that defines you. There are many—the General among them—who know no such fear. It is because of the lack of fear that he wars now."

"But fear can be used. Against you. Against me."

"Yes, Na'kiri. But without the fear, there is no joy. You pay for the one with the other, at times like this, and you pray that there will never *be* times like this."

"But you aren't afraid."

The Serra's face was pale in the full light of the sun; she wore a large brimmed hat that hid her face in shadow, and the shadows served to heighten her loss of color. "Is that how I am seen?" she asked softly.

Kiriel di'Ashaf looked back at her, the whole of her attention held by the sudden stillness of the Serra's expression.

"It is because you are Northern," she said at last. "In the South, fear is understood differently."

"In the far North," Kiriel said, "we show no fear at all."

"Because you don't feel it?"

Kiriel's thought was almost as loud as her words. She shook her head, half-shamed. "Yes," she replied. "Because we don't feel it."

"In the South, we feel it," the Serra said. "We feel it, but we do not show it."

"Why?"

"It is a weapon. It can be used against us. Where there is fear, there is leverage."

"And what if—"

"And if the worst that we fear comes to pass, we hide loss," the Serra continued. "Because it is the only way in which we can frustrate our enemies. And because," she added quietly, "if our enemies realize no gain from their actions, we have vain hope that they will choose a different method of attack in the future."

"But if the worst has come to pass, they've already done all the harm they can."

"To us," Diora said. "But there are always others, Na'kiri. I am one among many, and other stories have yet to be told, their endings mired in uncertainty."

She lifted her perfect hands; they shook. "We do not understand each other," she said, exposing her palms to the open air as if asking for something from the cloudless sky. Her hands remained empty. "But we try. It is enough, to try."

"Tell that to the villagers," Kiriel said bitterly.

"They know it, Na'kiri. They are of the South; they are not of the North. There are no certainties here, but in the South, we cling to hope."

She touched Kiriel's upturned face, and her hand became an anchor; the pacing stopped. "Everything that you can do, you will do. Expect more from yourself, and perhaps you will not be able to do even that."

"Serra Diora—"

"I will fight," the Serra said. "But not with Sword, and not with shadow. They are not my strengths." She smiled as she spoke, and the smile itself was calming. "Auralis AKalakar is afraid of failure."

"Why?"

"He has failed," the Serra replied gently. "He tells himself that he did everything he could do."

"But he—"

"He does not believe it."

"And you?" Kiriel said, the wildness of confusion giving way to the edge of her sudden perception.

Diora shook her head. "No," she said quietly.

"But you're not like him."

"No, Na'kiri. But I am not a warrior. I am not a Northerner. I am accustomed to cages with little room."

She might have said more, but Kiriel's eyes widened, and as they did, the brown bled out of them like a thin layer of dark tears. Gold remained.

It was unsettling.

"Serra," she said, bowing a little too quickly. "I have to—I—"

Diora bowed and let her hand drop away from pale cheek. "I will return to the domis," she said, turning.

But not turning quickly enough to miss the sudden appearance of a stranger. She did not want to hear his voice; she knew it would contain only darkness and death.

"Kiriel." Lord Anduvin bowed. His shadow cut across the village floor, the edges of ground broken by the rise of the Old Earth now falling in upon themselves in a parody of healing. The Southern warmth fled; the sun remained, as piercing in its clarity as it had been when it lay upon the frozen white of the Northern Wastes.

She saw him in the harsh light, and for a moment, she was twelve again, and the sword in her hands a gift that she coveted. He was, as all of Isladar's odd allies, a misfit in the Shining Court; he reeked of power, but he did not dally in the games that were meant to gain it.

He was old, older than the mountains; something that existed in the same way that the Shining Palace did.

And she? She was aging.

Childhood passed as she raised hand to her eyes, to shield it from light. "Lord Anduvin." She lowered the hand; it fell to the hilt of a sword that she would never return and never surrender. She heard its whisper and its warning.

"The *Kialli* have left the Shining City."

"When?"

"In the moonlight, Kiriel."

She raised face to the open sky. Something about his words felt wrong; they were wrapped in shadow and velvet. *Like lies,* she thought. "It is too early. The road is not yet wide enough to bear them."

A dark brow rose; he bowed again. "It is early," he said. "But the *Kialli* are not bound by the dictate of time; that is your gift and your curse. They move in haste."

"Because of the storm."

"Because of the voice of the Old Earth. It is waking now, beneath your feet, and you have done what the eldest could not: you have gained its ear. They do not know how. And because they are uncertain, they take the risk of the road.

"They travel in lesser number."

"That's all we gained?" The words were a whisper; a thought interrupted by sound.

"You gained much, Daughter of Darkness. The Lord himself spoke your name in a voice that sundered the mountain peaks. He is angry."

"Will he come?"

"No."

She breathed again.

His gaze swept across the village. She knew that what he saw, he committed to memory—and she didn't like it. "This place," he asked, "is it worth the risk you take?"

Velvet voice. Powerful voice. She felt at home here. Turning, she began to walk, and he fell in beside her, as if the movement was command. She allowed it.

Together they approached the exposed roots of the largest tree in the valley. "Anya's tree," she told him.

His grimace of distaste followed the use of the name.

"She is here, somewhere, in the valley."

"She is Ishavriel's," he replied.

"She is her own. Ishavriel cannot hold her."

"And you, Kiriel di'Ashaf?"

Kiriel laughed. "I have never tried to own her. She is Anya. On a whim, she plays with time. On a whim, she speaks the language of the trees, and the trees grow and shift at her command. This is her throne," she added.

"Do not rely on Anya a'Cooper."

"Funny. If I were in the mood to give advice, I would say the same thing. She is wild, and dangerous.

"Where is Isladar?"

Lord Anduvin did not reply.

"The road does not travel through the Deepings," he said instead. Kiriel shrugged.

"But the forests of this place now echo with the spirit of the Deepings; they bear some of its power, even at this distance. The road has opened, Kiriel di'Ashaf. Prepare yourself."

She nodded. "And you, Lord Anduvin?"

"While the Lord remains in the North, I will abide here."

"I don't trust you."

His smile was a perfect *Kialli* smile. Watching its edges, she felt a sudden longing for the simplicity of the Court.

She turned away. "They cannot travel in day."

He did not answer.

"Lord Anduvin."

"You are growing in power," he told her slowly. "And in knowledge. But I fear the knowledge is not given you by the mortals with whom you keep company; what you know, you know by instinct and blood. Your blood is strong, Kiriel."

"I am god-born," she replied with a shrug.

"Yes. The first of the god-born in millennia to be born to a god *upon* the plane. You and he are part of the same world.

"If the mortals are wise, they will kill you."

"They won't even try."

His smile grew sharper. "A pity," he said softly.

"Why?"

"You understand so little. I am the Swordsmith, Kiriel, and you bear the last blade that I will ever forge." He paused, his eyes the blue of midnight. "It was made by the dead and even I cannot say with certainty what it will do."

"By the dead?"

"That is all we are." His bow was low. "And among our number, there are those of us who have become resigned to serving the living."

She looked up to meet his face; it was perfect. No lines marred it, no scars, no imperfections. She wondered what he had been before he had descended to the Hells, and he smiled.

"You will never know," he told her. "You cannot see the difference between the living and the dead; you serve the dead, and they drive you."

"We're supposed to do *what*?"

Duarte AKalakar was just this side of losing all patience. Not a comfortable place to be. The encampment was like a cage, bounded on all sides by the damnable trees and the ridges of the valley's height. Memories hemmed him in, but those memories involved motion, planning, death.

"Which word was unclear, AKalakar?" he said coldly.

Fiara glowered. Of the Ospreys, she had taken Auralis' defection personally. Or rather, she deigned to show it.

Alexis was not happier, but she was smoother, more polished, in her defiance. The best of the Ospreys, he thought. He had always thought it. But she was all edge today, and colder for it.

"The Primus," Alexis said, using his title as a wedge, a means of separating them, "said we were to start daytime shifts. We *sleep,*" she added quietly. "Now. We run a skeletal watch while the day holds."

"So that we can do what? Travel by night?"

Duarte said little; he trusted Alexis at the moment far more than he trusted himself.

Fiara turned back to her mail; the rain had done its damage, and the cleaning it required appeared to capture the whole of her attention. Green was scraped from the places where chain links clung together; the valleys were humid.

Beside her, Cook labored in a like fashion, and the ghost of Sanderton sat between them, keeping them company.

"The order of battle," Duarte said, after they had worked for some time, "has been set. My people will accompany the Tyr'agar's banner when he takes to the field. It is our job to see that the banner is safe."

"And Valedan?"

"He comes with the territory," Alexis snapped. "He falls, and there's pretty much no point in the rest of it; we might as well pack up our things and go home."

"What about the Annies?"

As there were no Annagarian cerdan present, Duarte let the comment pass. He had come to the point where choosing his fights would be critical.

"Ser Andaro appears to have left the encampment; he is responsible for the safety of the Serra Diora. Ser Anton will stand by the Tyr'agar."

"And the other two?"

"They have their forces, and their instructions," the Primus said. "And we are not privy to them."

Fiara spit.

"Sentrus," he said mildly, "that was not a request. If you have problems sleeping during the day, don't sleep. But you had better be fit for active duty when we're called."

Cook rolled his mail into a noisy clatter of steel rings. He put away the small chisel and the oiled cloth used for cleaning, pausing to lift a waterskin to his lips. Duarte was fairly certain it no longer contained water.

But he rose and offered Duarte a grim salute. "Fiara," he said.

"What?"

"They're coming."

"Who?"

"The cleaning fairies," he snapped. "With dust brooms and pans."

She cursed his ancestry, but she also put aside her mail. Duarte watched them retreat. The General Alesso di'Marente would not attempt to attack the encampment by night, but it was not for the General that such preparations had been made.

The magi were behind this.

But ignoring the magi when so much hung in the balance was never wise.

"Alexis?"

"They'll sleep," she told him. "You should."

"And you?"

She shrugged. "I'll be ready for duty."

"Will you—"

"I'll be ready," she said, stepping back as he raised a hand. As if, he thought regretfully, the gesture was meant as a blow. Or received as one.

She shook her head, turning the moment with an earthy smile. It was all she was ready to give him.

"The cerdan are not happy," Ser Jarrani said quietly.

It had to be said quietly; the flats of the gentle plateau were occupied by men of differing ranks.

Alesso was grim.

"I am not concerned with their happiness," he replied stiffly. "I am only concerned with their obedience. I require men who are well rested. The move through the valley at night will be difficult and we cannot afford to have men fall asleep in the saddle."

"That is not the issue, Alesso," Ser Jarrani replied. His hair gleamed blue-black in the early light. Age had been swept up and gathered carefully, and the pale grays had been hidden by the style of the knot. "They are the Lord's men; the move through the Lady's territory does not suit them. They rely on the Lord's judgment; they will not be at their best if we rely upon the cover of night in which to begin our attack."

Ser Eduardo kai di'Garrardi shrugged. "If they are truly the Lord's men," he said, with barely concealed contempt, "they will fight. They will accept the conditions that victory requires, no more, no less. Or do they intend to fight to *lose?*"

The Tyr'agnate of Sorgassa stiffened; Alesso would have done the same had he been the Lorenzan kai. Had he the time, he would have allowed the discussion to continue.

"Kai el'Sol," the Tyr'agar said, turning to the utterly silent Radann.

It had been days since Alesso had summoned the kai el'Sol, and they had passed in such a way that he could almost forget the man's presence.

Until such a moment as this. Peder kai el'Sol was not the man who had plotted the death of Fredero kai el'Sol. The Festival of the Moon had changed him. The fires that had singed all adult hair from his face were gone, but his hair was composed of short, dark bristles. No warrior's knot would grace his head again, in this battle or any other.

"Kai el'Sol," Alesso said, when Peder did not answer. "What is the Lord's will?"

Samadar par el'Sol stood by Peder's left side; Samiel par el'Sol by his right. The former had taken all of the strength of age, shedding its weakness; he was like the great trees that towered above them as they made their passage through the valley. Samiel, younger, was quicker to move, but not quicker to speak; his eyes were dark, his skin bronze. But they were par to Peder's kai; if they intended to replace him, they did not intend it to be done in *this* war. A pity.

He needed the Radann, and they were no longer his to command; the sword he had held, almost invisible, above Fredero kai el'Sol was blunted.

Ah, well. It was of little significance. They were the Lord's men, all.

It was why they were present.

Still, if he did not have the weight of threat behind him, he had the advantage of mutual enemy. Peder kai el'Sol knew of the machinations of the *Kialli*, and he knew that they represented the Lord of Night. He understood, as well, that they were allies that Alesso di'Marente had now chosen to discard.

It was a prudent choice.

It was a regrettable one.

But Lord Ishavriel had not returned to the encampment, and Alesso was certain he would not. If Assarak or Etridian came, they would not come to kneel or to offer their services; of this he was certain.

Why had he thought to contain them?

He could no longer remember.

The certainty of his own naïveté was the grimmest thing he faced in the coming of the day. Nothing excused it.

They needed me, he thought. *But I proved too costly, too quickly.*

No. Just too perceptive. They would have integrated some number of their own among his troops—as agreed—but in the end, it would have taken control of his army from his hands.

He saw that now. They were not concerned with replacing the Leonne clan; they were not concerned with an ally upon the plateau of the Tor Leonne. It was only the armies of the North that concerned them—and Baredan di'Navarre, winds take him forever, had managed to bring both the seraf's get *and* the Imperial forces across the Averdan borders.

It was the presence of the Northern armies that had changed the role of the *Kialli*; they had always intended to start a war with the North, and had assumed that the South must be united behind an ally in order to do so.

That, that had been a gift unlooked for.

Bitter gift.

"Kai el'Sol."

"Tyr'agar," Peder kai el'Sol replied, tendering him the perfect bow. "Tyr'agnate, Tyr'agnate," he added. "We are the Lord's men. But there is truth in the words of the kai Garrardi. Our enemy will not seek the fields of day; they will seek darkness and shadow."

"We do not fight the armies of the Lord of Night," Eduardo said grimly.

Alesso tensed.

"We do," Peder kai el'Sol replied. "And in greater number, I fear, than we have yet imagined."

"You seek to tell us that the pretender is allied with the Lord of Night?"

Peder said nothing.

Eduardo laughed. "Tell the cerdan," he said, all etiquette forgotten. "Tell them loudly; tell them clearly. They may believe you. They may forget that the Sun Sword—and its line—was made for one purpose, and one alone: to defeat the servants of that Lord.

"But we are not simple cerdan; we are not the low clans, kai el'Sol."

"I do not speak of the Leonne chattel," Peder replied. "He is beneath consequence to any save those of you who desire a clear line to the crown and the Lake."

"And how, then, will these so-called forces come upon us?"

"In the night," Peder said, the roots of the words deeper than the simple roots of the forest. The certainty in them was unmarred.

"And why now?"

"Did you not hear the voice of the storm, kai Garrardi? Did your Widan not tell you of its significance?"

It was meant as an insult; it was. The kai Garrardi kept no Widan in his service; he did not trust them. He rarely trusted a man he was not certain he could kill cleanly should the need arise.

Ser Jarrani kai di'Lorenza lifted a hand. "My Widan spoke little of the storm, kai el'Sol. But they have been troubled by reports of strange happenings along the border, and they remember the Festival of the Moon."

The kai el'Sol nodded. "If we do not take what rest we can in the Lord's time, we will not have the strength we require for battle. Tell your men this: that the Lord judges *battle*. He will lend them strength, and they will hoard it; it is the Lord's foes we face."

Ser Jarrani nodded. But his expression as he met the kai el'Sol's eyes was thoughtful. "It will be as you say, kai el'Sol. But the army would benefit from the presence of the Radann; if you speak with the voice of the Lord, now is the time to raise that voice."

Peder kai el'Sol touched the hilt of his sword lightly as he offered the Tyr'agnate a perfect bow. He did not, of course, draw the blade; nor need he. Its name was known.

What was not known was where the blade of Fredero kai el'Sol now rested.

"It is as we feared." Simonson handed his Commander a pair of dice. Commander Allen cupped them in his hands, closed his eyes, and tossed them. They left his hands as thousands of dice had done in his youth, and rolled to a stop. They were weighted; a one and a six sat faceup on the table. He nodded, gathered them, and passed them back to Simonson. "Take them to Korama."

Simonson nodded grimly. He was not a man who approved of dice.

But he understood the value of these.

They were not magical. If found, they would be a pair of weighted dice, and gods knew that they could be found in the pockets of fully half the men on the field.

But they carried their message.

Alesso di'Marente's army was on the move.

And it moved at night.

He did not, of course, feel a need to bring dice to any table that the Tyr'agar graced, but he would carry the message. The army was a night's march from the encampment. One day's grace was all that was left them before the battle was finally joined.

Commander Allen stepped out of his tent and into the warmth of Averdan day. The air was damp, but he found himself missing the constant taste of salt in the air; the water here was too clean, too thin, too caged. There was no seawall by which to stand, and no vast expanse of unconquered water over which to gaze; no waves the length of a city to count.

But the army was here.

Devran, he thought, missing the Hawk greatly.

But Devran Berriliya was already wending his way down the river to the delta, and from there, he would take to the ships that lay waiting.

This was not the war the Commander had envisioned in the relative safety of *Averalaan Aramarelas.* But almost no war was. Reality made its own demands.

CHAPTER TWENTY-NINE

O F THE magi gathered in the Averdan valleys, only Meralonne APhaniel could sense the slight shift of the ground beneath his feet that spoke of the hidden path. He felt it as heartbeat, as pulse, and if it was erratic and wild, it would not remain so.

Gyrrick waited by his side.

He could wait.

"APhaniel?"

But not forever. "What?"

"There is some concern," Gyrrick said. "You have been standing upon the heights for a full two hours; you have not moved."

Two hours?

Aye, two hours. And were it not for the interruption, he might still be standing when the road at last opened, disgorging their enemies.

"There is something . . . wrong," he said quietly.

Gyrrick's dark brow rose. It was as close to humor as the warrior came.

"Something walks the old ways," Meralonne said quietly. "Something strange."

"The . . . the god?"

"No, Gyrrick. Were it the god, you would all feel his presence."

Gyrrick relaxed. In a fashion. "The demons, we expect. What else could follow?"

Meaning what could be worse. Meralonne shut his eyes. The answers to that question, he had no doubt, were coming.

"Illaraphaniel."

Meralonne lifted his head. He was weary. It was not a new sensation, but he had learned over the years how best to quiet it. This close to the opening road, his lessons dimmed, receding at last into inaccessibility. His pipe was in his hand, and smoke wreathed his arm without touching his lips; the scent was comforting.

In his youth, he had never touched pipes, except to play them. It was his youth he remembered now, and it was ferocious in its intensity.

Light limned his face as his gaze rose; blue light. His sword hovered within his reach, and it took effort not to reach for it.

All of this, the kinlord saw and understood. He did not approach, but neither did he retreat; he did nothing to further invoke the rage of battle.

Wise, Meralonne thought, asserting himself. "Telakar."

"The old road grows stronger," Telakar said. "I hear its song, Illaraphaniel. It is twisted and grim, but it is unmistakable."

Meralonne nodded. Ash came out of flame, and flame died unobserved in its earthen bowl. "We have this night," he said, "and the greater part of tomorrow."

"If that."

"Just that," he replied, piqued.

"I would remain," the kinlord said, perfectly still, his arms by his sides, "but I think it unwise."

"Where will you go?"

"To Kiriel di'Ashaf."

"Ah. To the darkness-born." He nodded, placed the flat of his hands against the earth, and rose against the stark silhouette of many branches. "Does she know?"

"I do not know."

"Will you tell her?"

"I? Not even I am that treacherous, Illaraphaniel."

"But you will fight for her."

"I will fight," Lord Telakar replied, daring a nod.

"And your mortal?"

"I will not leave her."

The magi nodded again; nothing said so far surprised him. "Why have you come?"

"With warning," Telakar said quietly.

"What warning?"

"The Firstborn will come with the host."

Meralonne frowned. "Who, Telakar?" His voice was thin and cold. Blade came to his hand, and the kinlord watched its glittering edge. That he could prevent his own sword from appearing said much.

Telakar was silent.

"Not Calliastra," Meralonne said, to himself. "And of the First-born, she is the only one who might obey the call of the Lord of Night."

"Not Calliastra," Telakar nodded. "I speak not of the get of the gods, Illaraphaniel, but of the eldest."

Meralonne APhaniel closed his eyes.

"You begin to see," Telakar said. "There is still time to flee this place. You will not triumph here."

"The Beasts," Meralonne said softly.

"Yes. They slumbered long in the Northern Wastes, and he woke them. They are his now; they have forgotten much. They hunger, but the shadow holds them fast, and in the North there is little living that demands their attention."

"They still slumber, if they are content to serve."

"Perhaps. But who will bear responsibility for their waking, Il-laraphaniel? You?"

The magi shook his head slowly. "When did you know?"

"When you should have," Telakar replied, and it seemed, for a moment, that he trembled. "I heard their voices. I heard their steps."

Meralonne nodded. "I will not be in your debt, Telakar."

"You are not in my debt. When the army comes, I will be forced to fight at the behest of one Lord or the other." There was bitterness in the words, but it was old. "She holds the key," he added softly.

Meralonne lifted a hand. "I must travel," he said.

"You cannot."

"No?"

"Try, Illaraphaniel. Try to step upon the road."

Meralonne APhaniel rose. He leaped from the rounded heights

to the valley floor, his tunic billowing as he landed; he made no sound.

When he turned back to the peak of the tree-crested hills, Telakar was gone.

Evayne a'Nolan was waiting for him in the depths of the valley. Her face was bruised and bloodied, and her fingers splinted. But her cloak was whole, and it swirled around her body with a wind that did not move anything else.

"Meralonne," she said, her lips cracked and bleeding. Speech was painful.

"You know," he said. The accusation was plain; he had no time for subtlety.

"I have come from a different field," she answered, and he saw that her hair was paler than it had been; she was no longer young. "And I must leave in haste."

"The Beasts will walk the hidden path," he said.

She nodded.

"How, then, are we to have any hope of victory here?"

"The Beasts are of the plane," she replied carefully. "And they live; they have always lived. The kinlords do not. What they hold, they hold tenuously."

"We cannot unleash them, Evayne. What the *Kialli* could not do, they could."

"So, too, could the earth, or the wind, or the fire; so could the water, if it ran through the fields."

"I would see old battles fought again," he countered, "but there are few upon the field who could survive them. The elements will not come."

"They will come," she said quietly.

"Why are you here, Evayne?" Weariness, in the spoken words. He could shed it in all save that.

"She will forget. Remind her."

He started to speak, lifted a hand, lunged forward—and passed through her. She was gone.

And when she had completely disappeared, he offered a bitter smile. "Of what, Evayne?"

One night.

* * *

Ser Anton di'Guivera excused himself for a few precious hours. He did not claim these for sleep; if sleep restored him, it brought him no comfort.

Ah, he was old, to think of comfort in the lee of battle. But it was the Lady's time. He drew his blade a moment in moonlight and torchlight, and the flash of its length was noted by the watchful men who patrolled. He was, in truth, impressed by the discipline of the Kings' armies. Or perhaps of their Commanders.

But all of this was a moment's thought; the drawing of the blade had been an invitation.

And it was answered, as it so often was, by Aidan. Aidan, the youngest of the men who attended Ser Valedan—and perhaps, of all of them, the one who had most earned the right *to* attend him. White-haired, skin now dark, having passed from red into patched flakes and then beyond, the boy appeared.

"Ser Anton?" His eyes reflected the sword—but they often did, even when the sword was in its sheath. He was, Ser Anton thought belatedly, of an age with the current kai Callesta—but they were different in every other way. Aidan did not yearn for death or battle. To him, the sword was not so much weapon as art. It was a mistake, of course. But Ser Anton treasured it.

"Aidan," he said, with a brief nod.

To Aidan, he had given what he had never had the opportunity to give a son: a sword. It was not a fine one; it had been taken from the Callestan armories. But it *was* a sword. Aidan would value it in a way that would strike the Southerners as Southern. It touched Ser Anton di'Guivera in a different way.

"Where is your sword?"

Aidan's pale brows rose, and then his mouth opened in a rounded "O." The man who could be the harshest of taskmasters frowned, but it was a slight frown. Too much indulgence, he thought. But he had come solely for indulgence's sake, and the frown did not linger. Neither did Aidan; he was gone. When he returned, he bore the weapon.

It was long for his reach. But Ser Anton desired no child's weapon for this child; it would have been an insult. It would not have been perceived as such by Aidan—but the gift, in the end, was entirely Anton's.

"Can I draw it?"

"You cannot use it in its scabbard," the older man said with a smile.

.The boy drew the weapon. And he drew it with surprising grace. Delightful grace.

"War is coming," Ser Anton told him.

Aidan's face paled slightly, but his chin rose. "Will it be like . . . Essla?"

"No," Ser Anton said quietly. "There are no serafs upon *this* field. It will be worse."

"And better."

"And better," Ser Anton agreed gravely. "The kai Leonne has been much occupied since we crossed the border. But occupied or no, Aidan, he values your presence here."

"He didn't want me to come."

"No. But in the end, the choice was his to make, and you *are* here. You will carry his banner," Ser Anton added quietly. "Others will be there to insure that it stands, but the hands that hold it steady, the hands that place it, will be yours. He honors you."

"You're telling me not to die," Aidan said, gravity marking both words and expression. His shadow skirted the folds of tenting, dwarfing him. The fire was high.

Ser Anton nodded quietly. "If the war takes you, it takes you. You die not as a boy, but as a *man*. But, yes, your death will hurt the kai Leonne in a way that few others can."

"You're going to teach me to fight?"

"In a single evening?" Ser Anton's laugh was genuine.

Aidan's frown was genuine as well. He had a boy's sense of dignity, and a boy's desire to *be* a force to be reckoned with. This, too, was precious to Ser Anton di'Guivera.

"I start," Ser Anton said, "as I mean to continue. I do not know if you will be the last of my students; you are old to learn. But you *can* learn; you've both the eye and the heart for it. And if you are not to be the last of my students," he added quietly, "you will perhaps be the first that I have taken in years without—" He let the words die.

But Aidan knew. "I like Valedan," he told Ser Anton, speaking the name, shorn of title, as if Valedan kai di'Leonne were kin. "I think he'll make a good Tyr."

"I, too, think he will make a good Tyr."

"He changes people," Aidan continued, the blade in his hand shaking slightly.

"Yes, Aidan. Even old men such as I have become. That is his gift. He is no Widan; he is not god-born; he has no Northern talent. He was not raised to rule, and because he was not, he discovers what ruling means in ways that I could not have conceived of when I first went North."

To kill him.

Aidan said nothing.

"Keep an old man company," Ser Anton said. "And," he added, with a critical eye, "hold your sword like *this*."

"She does not sleep," Ser Andaro said quietly.

The Serra Diora gazed beyond his shoulder; Kiriel di'Ashaf was standing in the lee of the great tree. Crackle of firelight spoke, orange glow illuminating her still face, her wide eyes. They were burning, at a distance.

Fire and shadow.

"No," the Serra replied. "In the night, she does not sleep." She forced a sweetness into her voice, and said, "but you are awake, Ser Andaro."

He started to answer, and then paused. "Do not," he said softly, "play the game of Courts with me. Not in this village. You must feel it, if you are here."

"I am here," she replied evenly, "because Kiriel is here."

"And what can you offer her?"

"Song," she replied. She lifted her samisen, as if the instrument were either vindication or accusation. But the strings were still; her hands did not give them voice.

"And the Northerners?"

"They are on the other side of the tree," she responded. "They keep watch."

Ser Andaro shivered. The night was cool. "They waste sleep," he said at last. "Nothing could enter this village without her notice."

He did not speak of the color of her eyes; no one did. But he marked them. Was marked by them.

In the day, she was almost normal, but as the last of the sun's light faded, she changed. She seemed taller somehow, and far more forbidding; at this distance it was hard to tell whether or not she intended to be protector to this village or overlord. There was no softness in her.

"We have little time," the Serra said quietly. "Will you not return to the kai Leonne?"

"He ordered me to watch over you," Ser Andaro replied. It was reply enough.

She thanked her husband in silence.

Found that the single word, *husband,* had changed in tone and meaning since she had first crossed the valley, the Sun Sword exposed to the clansmen.

Moon's face was high and clear, and in its light, the villagers—awake and watchful—now paid their frenzied respect to The Lady. The blood that had not been shed during the storm and the upheaval that followed was spilled now; wine was offered, along with the water that was so abundant. Even the children were allowed the night's grace in which to enjoin the Lady; the youngest were held in firm hands, the oldest were brought to heel by sharp words. They could not stand in silence; she could hear their short cries, their brief, fluting laughter, the thudding of their multiple steps.

Could also hear what followed: the voices of their Omas, raised in grim dignity. She smiled, but it was a tenuous expression.

The taint of fear was strong.

Where Ser Daro di'Valente walked, it lessened; he had the loyalty of the Valente serafs. That and their affection. But he could not be in all places at once, and the rounds he had chosen were arduous.

There were dogs upon the footpaths, but they did not lift their voices; they growled instead.

Kiriel di'Ashaf was in their midst.

"Come, Ser Andaro," Diora said. "I will sing, soon, but before I do, I will also pay my respects to the Lady. Will you join me?"

He nodded.

In the hollows just North of the great tree, standing stones marked the entrance of the Lady's domain: small patch of ground, tended and watered, with flowers that bloomed only at night in its center. Bowls had been carved of stone, but they were meant as decoration and reminder; no one used them. No one had the strength to lift them and upend their contents when the time had come.

She knelt here, setting her instrument to one side.

Lady, she thought, as she bent forehead into the earth, *I am come to you, new and whole. We fight in your name. We fight in your cause.*

But even in silence, she could not continue. The gods of the South were cold and distant, and they answered few prayers. And the gods of the North had no place here. Still, the obeisance would be marked, as it always was, by men of power; it would be noted. She was perfect.

Ser Andaro was less so, but not by much, and in truth, less was expected of him: he was the Lord's.

But when the hair on the nape of her neck rose, she rose as well, and turned.

Kiriel stood at her back.

She could not imagine that she had sung cradle song for this woman; she could not imagine that *anyone* would dare.

And Kiriel knew.

"Even you," she whispered, almost in disdain. She did not hide what lay beneath the surface of the words; if night transformed her, it lent her no guile.

"Yes, Na'kiri," she said, forcing the name from her lips. "I am afraid."

"Of me."

"Of you. But I also feared my father, and my aunt; I feared the Matriarch of Arkosa and the Matriarch of Havalla; I feared the kai el'Sol, who gave his life to give me voice. No man, no woman, is all of a season; no man or woman does not swallow the storm and speak with the wind's voice at some time in their life. Fear is a part of me; I have never been without it."

This seemed to quiet the gathering darkness.

"The darkness is part of what you are, and I fear it; only a fool would not."

"And do you speak with the storm's voice?" the young woman asked, vulnerability shading into danger.

"Often," Diora replied, her voice a whisper.

Kiriel lifted a hand, and the ring upon it was a band of light. Brighter than moonlight, whiter than pale fire, it curved round her finger.

An oath ring, Diora thought.

But whose?

Valedan kept watch with the Serra Alina. Ser Anton di'Guivera had, moments ago, returned in silence; Valedan did not ask him where he had gone, or why. Baredan di'Navarre was among the cerdan, although he would return in time. The Tyrs were with their Tyran; the Tors with their Toran. Time slowed; the moon seemed to hang suspended and frozen in the sky. Against its deep blue, the Ospreys were movement and shadow.

"I am sorry," Valedan said quietly, "for bringing you to Averda."

The Serra's smile was soft, even indulgent. "I am not," she told him, lifting a hand to his shoulder, unmindful of Ser Anton.

"You are in danger here," he replied.

"We are all in danger. Here, or there, we depend on this battle. I have never been good at waiting," she added.

His smile was slight, but genuine; it lifted the age from his face.

"I remember," he said. "You wielded dagger against an assassin. For me."

"It was either that or scream."

"My mother chose the latter."

Alina was politic; Valedan's smile deepened. He saw his mother as the Serra saw her, but he saw, as well, the woman who had, in her fashion, loved him; she had never been strong. "We value strength," he said softly.

"It defines us."

"More than our weakness?"

"No. Not more."

He nodded. "Telakar is gone."

She raised a dark brow.

"The Sun Sword is quiet."

"Perhaps that is why he chose to leave."

The thought gave Valedan pause. "I do not understand the demons."

"They probably don't understand you. If it were not blasphemy to say it, I would tell you that the demons have much in common with the clans of the High Courts; they value power, and they seek it."

"They also value terror and pain," Ser Anton's words intruded.

"There are those among the Tyrs who can be said to do the same without lie." Cool voice, sharp as sword's edge. She was awake, here; alive in a way that she had not been since she had parted from the Princess Royale. The moonlight nested within the darkness of her eyes.

"It cannot be said of all," Ser Anton responded.

Alina's shrug was eloquent. Valedan did not seek to silence her, although he felt Ser Anton's growing annoyance.

"Ser Alesso di'Marente is the Lord's man," she countered, the words an accusation. "And it is his actions that have brought us to this place."

Ser Anton said nothing; there was nothing that could be said. And words or no, he did not take to a field in which he was not certain of victory when he had the choice.

"Alina."

"It is the Lady's time," she said, her tone conveying the whole of the apology she would offer. Meager offerings, Valedan thought, but it amused him.

"How is Teyla?" she asked.

"Sleeping," Valedan said, lowering his voice. As if his words could disturb her hundreds of yards away. "She found it difficult to sleep during the day."

He was aware of the smallness of his words. Aware that he should find better ones, or grander ones, to offer. He did not speak of the baby; Alina did not ask. But he thought of him; thought of the strange wife the Serra Diora had brought him; thought of the comfort of the cold North in the spring, and the beat of waves against the seawall.

Alina did not regret her absence from *Averalaan Aramarelas*. But Valedan missed the city. If he could have chosen a place in which to spend his last night, it would be that one, and he would spend it in the quiet of the courtyard of the Arannan Halls, beside the statue of the blindfolded boy. *Justice.*

Choice, however, had brought him here.

"Yes," he said, although no one had asked. "I'm ready."

Sendari par di'Marano made his peace with the Lady.

No fine stones adorned the grounds upon which he knelt, but the trees grew in their place, and he thought them a more fitting monument to her strength. Moonlight, cut by branches, seemed to enfold him. In the distance, he heard the river's voice; closer, the movement of restive cerdan. No other sound broke the carefully cultivated illusion of privacy.

For the first time in months, he whispered his daughter's name.

She was lost to him.

But she had been lost the moment they had chosen to take the Tor, and she had told him the truth in countless ways. Feminine ways. He had chosen not to listen.

He listened now. She had taken the Sun Sword. She had—if *Kialli* reports, half-gleaned and grudgingly offered, were true—crossed the Sea of Sorrows. It was said that no man emerged unchanged from the endless desert, but the Serra Diora was not a man. *Na'dio.*

The face of the moon was round, her light soft: full circle. He bent his head and stared a moment at the scars upon the backs of his hands; they were pale white webbing, and they could be read by those who had the experience to do so. He read them now, as if he were a Voyani charlatan, offering cheap fortune in exchange for coin.

His hands shook and curved as he set them down upon the flat ground; he made offering to the Lady, and it was not an offering that any but he and his estranged child might understand: He placed a small mask upon the uneven earth. A Moon mask, a mask for the Festival.

Na'dio had desired it, a decade past, and he had paid for it. Had his wives been present, they would have chided him for his public indulgence of a daughter; it was for that reason that he had chosen to leave them all behind. He had wanted that moment of intimacy, that moment in which he might be all things, and grant all things, to a cherished child.

She had returned the mask to him on the night of the last Festival Moon they would share. And he offered it to the Lady, who might understand the offering better than he; his heart, like her light, was cut by wild growth, and he did not understand how to read what crept through the strands of darkness.

He made no prayer.

He asked nothing.

But when he rose, he left the burden behind. Of the dead, he did not speak—or think—and perhaps this was as much a blessing as he could hope to ask for.

Across the breadth of the camp, there was a scattering of song, the hurried move of informal dance, the sounds of something that might be celebration.

Ellora AKalakar listened as she stood in the lee of the fire. Orange light was reflected in the blue of eyes, and it added color to the curve of cheekbones, white to the trail of old scar. Her pale hair had been pulled back in a thin warrior's knot, and the quartered circle shone upon her shoulder as she moved.

She denied them nothing.

Devran would not have approved, but Devran's men were quit of battle; they would cross the river and return to the sea. All of their old arguments, as familiar as her sword and her name, would be left unfinished, the threads dangling, the tapestry of their bitter rivalry unvisited, incomplete.

She regretted that.

It took the element of home from her, and made the whole of the valleys the terrain of strangers.

It was in the Averdan valleys that she had grown to fill her rank, rewarding the confidence of a younger Commander Allen; it was in Averda that Devran ABerrilya had done the same. When that war had ended—at the table, as wars usually did—both she and Devran had returned to the Houses that had given them their adult names, to find a different war waiting.

Hers had been simpler, in the end; if she had not consciously planned to take power, she had made power a part of her lexicon, and coming new from the field of slaughter had given her strength and stomach for bloodshed.

For Devran, it had been different. It always was.

She had never asked him—it was House business, after all— how his own ascension had been achieved; it was a quiet affair. That the dead were in evidence before it was over could not be questioned; that much, Kalakar Intelligence could offer.

But he had been soldier first and foremost, and it was with a grim resignation that he had taken the House name and the House seat; he had never rested easily upon the throne in the Hall of The Ten.

She wondered what changes she might return to, if she survived. Wondered—as she was wont to on the eve before battle—how many of the dead would bear her name; how many she would recognize when the field itself had ceased to move, and only the flight of carrion birds punctuated the stillness.

The soldiers were younger now than they had been. Younger, fresher, untested by the border skirmishes that characterized so much of her time in the Kings' army. They had not lived for months in rotation among villagers who regarded them with such ambivalence; they had not learned that the townspeople of the largest of the holdings both dreaded and desired their presence; they had not yet been called upon to kill.

Well, she thought, as Primus Duarte crossed the invisible perimeter her guards traced, *not all of them.*

Primus Duarte was alone.

He had taken the time—or someone had—to polish what little brass he wore, but his boots were cracked and stained. His hair, short, was no warrior's conceit, and his eyes were too dark. She wondered if he'd been drinking. The rest of the Ospreys were.

But he had rank to keep him company.

"Kalakar."

She nodded. "You're dry," she said, with a wry smile.

"The Southerners make poor camp followers. Wine, where it can be had, is in great demand—it seems that the Lady requires it."

"And the Tyr'agar?"

Duarte shrugged. "His guards are posted. Ser Anton di'Guivera is with him."

She nodded again.

"Commander Allen is with the magi."

That caused a brow to arch. "And the magi aren't gibbering?"

"Not yet."

"Then it can't be serious." She locked her fingers behind her back, and gazed toward the West. Moon rose across the rise of the valley, silvering flat grass and bent tent. Stars glittered, the constellations lost to her. Although she had spent some time in the grand boats of the fleet, she had never learned the linguistic subtleties that governed the men who lived—and moved—at sea; they were strange and bright. Not her problem.

"This is not the same war," the Primus said.

She knew what he meant. Flippancy gathered words, but she bit them back; now was not the time.

"You've spent time with the magi this eve."

He shrugged. "I am familiar with the rules that govern the Order."

"Not familiar enough to follow them," she chuckled.

"If I were, I would never have been given the Ospreys."

No. He wouldn't have. She studied his face. "You've had your wings clipped."

He nodded.

"Do you regret it?"

"Not yet." He shrugged. "Do you?"

She laughed. "I don't know yet. This is not the same war. It's—"

"Cleaner?"

"Cleaner," she agreed. "Korama?"

"No word from the Verrus."

"Good. Let's hope it stays that way."

The better part of the Northern contingent lay between the Tyr'agnati and the Southern valley. There, the men were less rowdy. They watched for an army they understood.

Here? She could almost cut the tension.

"On the other hand, there's nothing clean about death."

"The medics are sleeping."

She snorted. "They didn't get their orders?"

"They got them."

"And?"

"The Mother's—the healer, Merilee, decided that sleep was the better option." He grimaced. "Edmond is young enough to want to join the Kings' men in their revelry. Frederik is barely able to contain him."

The Kalakar snorted. "Let him," she said curtly. "Best that he sees them when they're truly alive; he'll see enough of them as corpses."

"Merilee thinks that more will be corpses if he lacks attention. She doesn't trust Southern wine."

"Devran chose her," Ellora replied with a shrug. "How's Auralis?"

Duarte shook his head.

"Tomorrow," Alesso di'Alesso said quietly to the two Tyr'agnati, "we will cross the last stretch of open valley. The trees are close to the river for three hours; we cannot move quickly there."

Eduardo nodded. For once, his attention was upon the map; the Serra had not—yet—been mentioned.

Eduardo kai di'Garrardi had not been long in the valleys during the last war; his memory of the geography was dim.

Ah, the maps. They were flat; their lines spoke of reality in the captured half-truths of men whose minds were given solely to this endeavor. He had spent much time observing them, and he had learned much; he knew that this passage would take more time than the Tyr'agnati assumed.

And if it did not, Alesso had made plans. He did not intend to engage his enemy while the sun remained in the sky. The lamp was growing brighter; oil encased by glass did not dwindle at the barest touch of breeze.

Ser Jarrani kai di'Lorenza looked thoughtfully at the man whose fortune had been made among the bitter ruins of the last kai Leonne's war.

He was older.

But he held his peace.

And the Widan Cortano di'Alexes rose. "The Widan, Tyr'agar, are at your disposal."

"Good. I want them to watch the valley heights. As we approach the Callestan forces—" always Callestan, never Leonne, "we will no doubt meet resistance there."

But not too great a resistance, he thought. He did not pray; he planned.

The Widan Cortano di'Alexes was not cerdan; his life was not a military life. But he understood the art of war instinctively. Had he been without talent, he would have been a swordmaster of some renown; he had chosen the path of power, and it had wound its way toward Averda, always Averda.

He felt the night, and the unexpected dampness of the river, and he cursed them both in perfectly composed silence. Around him, the Widan gathered. They were respectful, and they were nervous.

As well they should be.

Time had grown short as he aged; he acknowledged its passing with a bitter regret. Of all the things he had desired from his association with the Shining Court, the one he had most coveted was this: freedom from time's constraints. Immortality.

He was not to achieve it, and it galled him.

But he was the Lord's man.

"Come," he told the Widan. He had chosen them with care; they were scions of power, the most valuable of his students. Not for these the scholarly, slow undertakings of Widan Mikalis; they were men who wielded fire and lightning with ease. They bore the scars of their testing with a certain grim pride, their faces adorned by the lattice of their success.

Two among them, he thought, desired the title Cortano had held as his own for decades. This battle might give them that. And it might give them death. They were afraid of neither.

"In the morning," he told them, "we will begin the cleansing of the army."

Ramiro di'Callesta stood by the side of his kai. Ser Alfredo was silent. His shoulders were still slender; they marked him, even on horseback, as a youth.

But he carried his sword as a man does, and he awaited the orders of his Tyr with exquisite and certain grace. Amara would have been both proud and terrified to see him this way.

Ramiro was neither.

"The Tyran," he told his son, "will obey you if I fall upon the field. They will obey no other."

"The kai Leonne—"

"The kai Leonne understands this, and accepts it. The Northerners will accept it as well; they have no choice."

His black hair gleaming in a perfect knot, Alfredo nodded. It brought the Tyr'agnate no comfort; he knew that his son could not conceive of the death of his father.

No more had Ramiro believed it possible, in the last war. But possible or no, death had come, and in its wake, he had taken the title of Callesta, and he had held it.

"While I am alive," he continued, "they obey me. And while I am alive, Ser Alfredo, *you* obey me. If I order you to flee, you *will* flee. If I order a retreat, you will retreat."

His son nodded again, with just a hint of impatience.

First battle, Ramiro thought wearily. And he desired it, this boy who was so unlike his father.

"Will the kai Leonne return my sword before the battle begins?"

"No."

Ser Alfredo nodded grimly. "The Sun Sword—"

"Is the Leonne sword. But he swore an oath to Callesta, and he will fulfill it."

"If he—"

Ramiro raised a hand. Amara's pride in her son would falter at this point, for impatience drove his tongue, and she had seldom found this acceptable.

"Alfredo. Will you impugn your liege lord?"

"No, Tyr'agnate."

"Then trust him, and do not ask me this question again."

"Tyr'agnate."

Ramiro turned back to honing the edge of his blade. It was sharp, and the work was minimal, but it brought him a certain peace; it was an act that had been undertaken before battle by every Tyr before him, and it made him a part of the continuity of the line. *Bloodhame* was older than Callesta.

But the boy had not yet finished.

"If he draws the wrong sword, will it not be costly?"

The stone slowed its movement across steel as the Callestan Tyr looked up. "What would you have of me, Alfredo?"

"Free him from his oath."

"He is a man," Ramiro replied, as if that was the end of an unwanted conversation. But he considered his son as he spoke. The boy wanted his sword; that much was clear. It was the sword that would make him a man, at least in his own estimation—but Ramiro had learned, at cost, that the visions of youth were so brilliant in their intensity, one always risked blindness.

And yet, he thought, it was not just that desire which moved his son. He had come, in some fashion, to respect the young kai Leonne, and he understood the danger.

"He made his oath to you," Alfredo said, when he saw his father would not speak. "You have the power to—"

The sword fell. "He is a *man*, not a boy. The oath that he made was not made to me, nor was it made at my demand. He bears its weight, and there is only one honorable way to be relieved of its burden."

"Then let me join his men," Alfredo said.

Ah.

"I will take the sword from his hands after it has drawn blood. I will make it my own."

"That permission is not mine to grant."

"Give me permission to make the request, Tyr'agnate."

Ramiro looked long at his son. Time made strangers of kin, but the blood ties were still there. He assessed both the request and the likelihood that denying it would result in the boy's death; between fathers and sons, fights were chosen with care, and the father could not afford to enter a battle that he might lose. Not when he faced his sole living heir.

"And what of the Callestans," he asked softly. "What of our people? If I fall, they have you, and only you."

"You won't fall."

The certainty was not a comfort. Amara would have gentled him, and she would—in that act—have anchored him in the responsibilities he was as yet too young to bear.

Young? He was the age of Ser Mareo kai di'Lamberto's dead son. Ser Andreas. Amara would not forget it, were she here. It would haunt her. She would be terrified of the symmetry.

Ramiro kai di'Callesta was no Serra. "If you must," he said.

Alfredo was gone before he retrieved *Bloodhame*.

Ser Mareo kai di'Lamberto was likewise occupied. *Warcry* was unsheathed, and it glittered in lamplight like the waters of the Lake on a still day. He was reflected in its surface, in the obvious way; he was reflected in its edge in a way that eyes could not perceive.

Ghosts stood at his shoulder, watching the progress of stone along blade's edge. He heard their whispers, and he had no way to still them.

Duty was a cold comfort, but it was still a comfort. He clung to it, who clung to honor above all else. His living son came quietly into the tent, and stood, casting a shadow at his father's feet. He did not speak until Ser Mareo kai di'Lamberto lifted his face.

"The Matriarch of Havalla waits," he said grimly.

There was anger between them, yet, and a life. But enough; he stood and said, "The Matriarch can wait a moment."

Galen's expression—the first that was not shuttered and angry—was almost reward enough. But it was not enough. Ser Mareo kai di'Lamberto set his sword down and rose. He caught his son's shoulders in either hand, and was surprised for a moment at their sudden width, their unexpected height—as if heart could not measure what eye could see.

"Tell me," he said, eyes unblinking, "that you want his head, and I will take it."

"You *didn't* take it!"

"I am ruler," he said coldly. "And my duty to the line is my duty to the land."

"Then why now?" Galen shook himself free. "Why will you kill him now?"

"Because," Mareo kai di'Lamberto replied, "my duty to the line resides in *you*. Tomorrow evening, there will be battle here. Can you not feel it?"

Galen said nothing.

"And tomorrow evening, there will be death. Mine, perhaps. Yours, perhaps. Theirs."

Galen kai di'Lamberto assessed his father from a distance of inches. He could not free his expression from anger; it dwelt there, as it had done since the death of Andreas. The Lamberto kin had always been close.

"Fredero died," Mareo said quietly, "to send the Sun Sword—with warning—to the boy who now wields it. He paid. He is gone."

"Andreas died."

"Aye, and for nothing." He said it bitterly, acknowledging at last the truth of too many foreign words. "Killed, in the end, by a Leonne's wayward orders."

"Killed by the Northerners."

"They were the sword," he said. "But when we kill the man, we allow the sword's history to pass on."

"Tyr'agnate—"

"Do not," the father said to the son, "use title against me. Not here. Not now. I have made my offer, and I will abide by it. Make your decision."

Galen kai di'Lamberto took a step back, his hand upon sword hilt. This man, this father, he did not know.

Ser Mareo kai di'Lamberto waited.

"If you kill the Northern Commander now," Galen said, after a pause, "what will happen?"

"I will almost certainly pay the price for his death."

"And the Lambertan Tyran will exact the same price from any who choose to inflict it."

"Aye, that too."

"And the Tyr'agar?"

"He will not interfere."

Galen frowned. "The Callestans—"

"Galen."

"The Northerners will not fight for the man who allowed their Commander's death."

"They are not of the South; they are not constrained by the same honor that binds us. You cannot know that."

"They are men," Galen said, but hesitantly. "And I *can* know that, Father. They come with swords. They wait to fight."

"And die."

"No man plans to die."

"No single man, no."

Galen kai di'Lamberto said nothing. "They came to claim the Dominion for the kai Leonne."

Mareo nodded.

"But you believe he is not theirs."

"What I believe is not at issue, Ser Galen. What you believe is."

"Let me kill him," Galen requested at last.

"No."

"What difference will it make?"

"You know well what difference it will make," Ser Mareo said quietly. "I have offered one kai in service to the Leonnes. I will never willingly surrender another."

"And I am to surrender you?"

"Or the war," the Tyr'agnate said.

Galen's brow rose.

"Yes," his father said quietly, hands falling to his sides. "We may have one or the other, with honor; we may not have both. Which will you choose?"

Galen said, after a long pause, "The Lord of Night."

And Ser Mareo kai di'Lamberto nodded, as if the answer had never been in doubt.

"Leave your anger here," he instructed. "Between kin, such anger is best served by harem walls, and the harem is long past both of us. Andreas, were he here, would not demand his vengeance at the cost of all else he held dear; he would cleave to the oldest of our vows."

"Protect our people."

"With our lives. I will offer the Tyr'agar my sword on the morrow," Mareo kai di'Lamberto said quietly.

Ser Galen said nothing, but the silence was comfortable.

"That is," Ser Mareo kai di'Lamberto added, "if I have not unduly offended the Matriarch of Havalla."

She smiled. She actually smiled.

"Tyr'agnate," she said, nodding. "Kai Lamberto." She held a single tube in the palm of her weathered hand. "I have come with what word I can deliver to you. There has been fighting in *Arral*."

Both men were suddenly pale.

"It has gone well," she added, any desire to discomfort them lost, "although only one of my daughters is now within your citadel. My younger daughter came; she rode hard. She arrived at the borders in time.

"And she sent message to me, but it was not, in the end, for me."

"What word?"

"Your Serra is well," Yollana said. She was capable of mercy when she so chose. "And it is she who writes to you. I did not think to see you again before the battle, but I could not leave without delivering her letter.

"She has offered my daughters—and my people—the shelter of Amar in your name."

Ser Mareo nodded quietly. Only in dealings with the Voyani would his Serra have been so bold, so forward—but men did not treat with the Voyani. He felt a quiet pride; his wife, his Serra, was capable of donning many masks, and each of them strengthened him. "The one has accepted her offer; the other is too far upon the road."

"And your people?"

"They are no fools. Where Nadia goes, they will follow. There is no safety in isolation," she added. "And the *Voyanne* is very, very isolated." Her lips folded up in good humor. "We are defined by our enemies. In times of great peace and plenty, we bicker among ourselves—and we kill, when the passions take us. But there is seldom such a time. In times of hardship, we might war with the other Voyani, and in times of great hardship, we war at last with the clansmen. In the first case, we are simply ourselves: Yollana, Nadia, Varya. In the second, we rise above that; we become *Havallan*. And in the third, we become *Voyani*.

"But now, Ser Mareo, we are simply *men*. The differences between your clan and my family have been rendered meaningless by the presence of the Lord of Night."

"A dark maker of peace," he said, with just the hint of a smile.

"Dark indeed. And perhaps if we were all wise, we would cling

to the illusion that we are *all* brethren." But she shook her head, her
habitual cynicism asserting itself. "In a generation, if we are given
that time, this will be story and legend. We will take no lasting lessons from it."

She handed the tube to the kai Lamberto, and she bowed.

"Matriarch," Mareo kai di'Lamberto said, his palm curled protectively around what she had handed him, "you dislike debt. All
people of honor must. But it is by our debts, in the end, that we will
be remembered."

"Aye," she added, with the faint hint of an approving smile, "by
our debts and how we discharge them."

And as she left, she thought that, had men like Ser Mareo kai
di'Lamberto ruled the Cities of Man, they might never have fallen
at all.

The Radann par el'Sol was quiet. He had been quiet a long time;
the silence nestled within his throat, caged there, captive to will. But
by his side, *Verragar* was likewise silent. It would not last.

He rose, restive, the night sky a mockery of the Lady's time.

He bowed a moment to the South.

The Serra Diora en'Leonne had passed from his care. The
Tyr'agar, he had judged, and he did not find him wanting. All of
his duties had been discharged save this final one: the war itself.
He should have been at peace.

But peace eluded him.

He remembered his dead. His wife, his son, the plague that had
ended their lives while he toiled under the banner of an almost forgotten Tor, in a war that made no sense.

This war was a gift, he thought, forcing himself to see truth in
the words as the echoes of loss passed through him like cold, night
wind. But he had long passed the age in which war promised salvation or peace; long passed the age in which he need prove himself
by some act of prowess in battle.

He had seen war won, and war lost.

He had never fought a battle in which the war itself would decide the fate of every citizen of two nations. The kai Leonne had
gifted them with a worthy enemy.

But it was not the worth of the enemy he doubted.

Lady, he thought, bitter now. *I bear the Lord's weapon, but I am
still your man.*

He missed Samadar and Samiel; they traveled at the side of the new kai el'Sol. The man who had been given the Radann because he was adept at subterfuge.

They were his peers; they were his worthy rivals; they were his army. He waited for them, in the dark of the camp.

Ser Fillipo par di'Callesta stood watch. He did not sleep; none of the Tyran did. The tent of the Tyr'agnate of Callesta lay at their backs, and before them the smaller tents of less significant men stretched out like a diminutive city, a holding shorn of the grace of architecture, planning, and history.

But there was money here, if one knew how to look, and the symmetry of the tents, the flickering of torch and the contained fire of lamp, spoke of a singular power.

Upon the backs of those nameless men, Northern and Southern, lay the weight of Averda. If they faltered, Averda fell, and lands that had been graced by Callestan rule for centuries would at last fall to carrion creatures.

And they had faltered seldom in the heat of the valley. Four of the Callestan cerdan were dead, and their corpses prominently displayed, for their actions among the Lambertan troops; some like number of Lambertans—two, he thought, with a grimace, shedding evasion—were likewise dead.

The Northerners, with their poorer sense of history, had yet to follow like insults with death.

But after the deaths, no others had chosen to offer themselves as bad example; they judged the mood of their respective Tyrs, and they held their peace.

Ser Marco kai di'Lamberto lived up to his reputation. Even the Callestans were impressed with his steely silence; his ability to weather the presence of the Northern army that had been the death of his kai. *For this,* they whispered, when they thought no one of import listened, *for this war, he is willing to surrender some part of blood debt. For us. For Averda.* They knew the honor he did them.

So, too, did Ramiro, and he repaid it with ferocity. The dead cerdan had been stripped of swords; their swords lay broken. They would be denied burial. They would be denied the Lady's ablutions.

This was as harsh as Fillipo had yet seen him.

But the Tyr'agar himself had yet to command the death of a single cerdan, and the behavior of the Callestans and Lambertans who had been called from their homes in the villages was an exquisite embarrassment to the two Tyrs whose banners they served. Fillipo knew, with a bitterness that long years did not diminish, that Ser

Valedan's father had carelessly commanded the deaths of dozens for far less reason; he had been a man with overweening vanity, and he saw insult to that vanity in many, many things. Not so Valedan.

Ser Valedan kai di'Leonne had yet to do a single thing that would dim the respect that Fillipo offered him.

Let the son heal the damage the father had done.

He smiled as he thought it; in silence, he could think many things. The boy who had walked the length of the Arannan Halls on behalf of the Annagarian hostages had given way slowly to the man who now waited for dawn. He had shown grace, then—although he had had little choice.

But he had done more, in the presence of the Twin Kings themselves: He had bound his fate, and his life, to the lives of the hostages he claimed as his people. He was not adept at politics; he meant what he said.

Markaso kai di'Leonne would have done no such thing. What, after all, were the lives of useless hostages compared to his own?

Valedan had wed politics to responsibility. Only death would sunder that marriage.

The blood of the Leonne clan ran almost true in Valedan kai di'Leonne. All trace of the father and the mother seemed to be obliterated in their sole offspring. Fillipo smiled again.

"What amuses you, Fillipo?"

The Captain of the oathguards turned and offered his brother a grave bow. It was a familiar one. He did not answer, however.

Serra Alina and the Princess Royale had mothered the boy, and two such women were fierce indeed. Valedan was their only living legacy, for they had been denied marriage and children.

But what a legacy, in the end.

"Time," Fillipo said quietly.

"It passes," Ramiro replied. "You are thinking of the kai Leonne."

Fillipo nodded. "And of the North," he added. "The kai Leonne was born in the South, but he was tempered across the border. We have seen him tested," he added, softening the implied criticism in the words.

"Aye. Has he been tested enough?"

"He has not yet broken."

"No. And I believe that he will not be broken."

Fillipo nodded. "He is not what I expected."

"Nor I. Perhaps Baredan di'Navarre had some hint of what the future held when he first came to me in Callesta; I cannot say."

"Do you regret your decision, brother?"

"No. Not one of them. Regret is for the old and the useless." His smile was sharp.

"And for the wives of our enemies," Fillipo added, finishing the phrase.

"For them, yes. Baredan is with his men."

"Some part of them. I am not comfortable with their presence."

"No man is comfortable in the presence of those whose oaths are not given to him."

Fillipo nodded. "On the morrow," he said softly.

"You feel it."

"Yes."

Baredan di'Navarre stood shoulder to shoulder with his oldest friend. Halvero kai di'Ferro smiled, and the expression evoked past history: his lips bore the scars of an old battle wound; it had been taken in the valley.

The journey had not been kind.

"The Third army," he said quietly, "would have followed you."

Baredan nodded. It was a simple truth.

"They do not serve under Alesso di'Marente now; they are scattered across the Southern Terreans, those that survive."

He nodded again.

"The kai Leonne, Baredan?"

"You have not seen him," Baredan said. It was not a question.

"No. I seldom ask a question when I know the answer. But you have seen him."

"I have. And I have given him my sword."

"You would," Halvero snorted. "He is the last of the bloodline. Is he Alesso di'Marente's match?"

"He is," Baredan replied with a curt nod. "And more."

"He is young."

"Yes."

"And he spends too much time with his women."

"Yes."

Halvero laughed. "You don't approve."

"I approve *of* him," Baredan said, with just a trace of annoyance. "He is not his father's son."

"Good."

"Halvero, that your tongue has not yet been cut from your mouth is a miracle."

"Aye." Halvero tendered a bow. "It is good to see you too, old friend. Will we fight on the morrow?"

Baredan nodded uneasily. "In darkness," he said at last.

"I will tell my men."

The Serra Teresa di'Marano also made the ablutions. All of them. Yollana of Havalla no longer seemed to require physical support, and she was much occupied, this eve. It left Teresa time.

And silence, too much silence. She thought of her brothers. Adano had arrived that morn. He did not seek her out, and she wondered if any had thought to inform him of her presence. Wondered what she would tell him, if he summoned her to serve, as she had served for the whole of her life.

All of that life led to this. She examined sweet water with a Serra's critical eye. She had broken the only weapon she had been certain of wielding, and when she thought of it, the water trembled.

Still, she was here. Here, in the Averdan valleys, surrounded by Northerners, and the forces of both Callesta and Lamberto. The latter was not a sight she would have ever thought she might witness again, in her life. She wanted to hear what they felt; wanted to delve beneath the surfaces of their words for the meaning that waited beneath them.

The loss was profound. It was said that when men lost limbs, they could still feel their presence. So it was with the Serra. But as with such men, that feeling did not give her the ability to truly hear.

Na'dio, she thought. She gazed at the Lady's face. At the Festival of the Moon so long ago, she had tried to kill Kallandras of Senniel College for the sake of her niece. It had started then. She had not understood it, but that was the beginning.

And this, she thought, pouring wine, the end.

Lady, she thought, as she bowed her head to ground, *be graceful. Do not take from my almost-daughter what I gave up in desperation.*

Kallandras of Senniel College stood quietly, lute cradled in his arms. He touched *Salla's* strings, and drew melancholy from their vibrations; he did not join it to his voice. His voice had too much power, here.

He wore black, now, and against his thighs, the weapons that had been a gift of Meralonne APhaniel trembled. So, too, did the ring of Myrddion. It was restless. The earth, he thought, ill at ease. It slept, but it was no longer deaf; no longer distant.

What would wake it, here?

He wondered, briefly, what Lord Celleriant was doing. No answer was offered him. But he felt certain that the Arianni lord was alive in the distant North.

He prepared himself for battle and for death. His silence slid into the grace of meditation, the summoning and hoarding of reserves of strength that only the *Kovaschaii* possessed. Here, at last, he invoked the lessons taught him by the Lady's brotherhood, and as he did, he set Salla aside.

He would take her to the Serra Diora again. In time.

But now? Even silent, she was a greater part of the man he had become than he would have willingly admitted. Adam, and Adam's foolish sacrifice, had forced him to acknowledge that truth. The boy was gone, but the scar of the lesson—like so many other scars from lessons far less graceful, and far more deadly in intent—was new and ugly.

Kallandras of Senniel.

Kallatin of the Brotherhood.

Upon this field, and upon any he would take hereafter, he was both; the former was no longer something donned to disguise the latter. A gift, he thought, and a bitter one—but he found comfort in accepting the truth.

There would be deaths, here. But he thought the battle would come from the West, beyond the folds of these altered valleys, and perhaps Kiriel di'Ashaf would have what she desired most: the safety of the serafs that Ashaf kep'Valente had loved while she lived.

Stranger things happened.

Auralis AKalakar joined Kiriel di'Ashaf by the side of the great tree.

He saw, instantly, the shadows that infused her; her hair had escaped braid and flew across her slender shoulders like a great cape. He felt the hair on his own neck rise in salute, but he held his ground, offering her the edge of his smile.

"You're awake," she said, and the words were alive with a texture and tone that almost made him step back. But this was simple death, and in the end, he had always walked *toward* it. The ring that bound his hand couldn't change that. The serafs whose lives he had saved did not diminish the desire.

"Can you see me?" he asked her, as if idly curious.

"Yes," she said curtly.

He shrugged.

"They fear me," she added, sweeping an arm wide. Shadow seemed to fall from her hand as if it were grain.

"I guess they aren't as stupid as they look."

"Why don't you?" She turned to look at him, and her expression was, for an instant, the same expression that he had seen in Averalaan. Vulnerable and dangerous.

"You only promise death," he said with a shrug. "Mine. Or theirs. I don't care a lot about either."

She said, "Who did you fail, Auralis?"

And he flinched. He shouldn't have. Not here, not in front of the creature she now was. But he knew that she'd see it anyway, and he was almost beyond caring. He shook his head. "It doesn't matter," he said bitterly. "I failed. She's dead." His hand was a fist, and the glow of ruby against his skin was bright and painful.

"You hate demons."

He shrugged.

Her smile was cruel. And it was not. She was both of the people he had known, and in his way, he treasured each.

And she knew it, and took some comfort from it. Her eyes were gold, and bright, much like the ruby. "Not tonight," she said again. "And not in daylight. You should sleep, if you can."

"And you?"

"I don't tire," she replied. "I can go three days without sleep, although I need it eventually."

He didn't doubt her. And he knew that the battle wouldn't last even that long. The knowledge was there, in her face. He shrugged, his version of a salute, and he sat down by her feet, drawing his wineskin from his side. He offered it to her, knowing that he wouldn't actually have to share; she refused him with a snort.

So he drank, as he often did, alone. It was the worst way to drink.

It was the only way here.

Dawn descended on them all.

CHAPTER THIRTY

B UT DAWN was short. The Lord's time, the bright of sun mingling with the crimson and azure of its rise, was not so clear a thing as the cerdan had expected. They waited, but the skies were tinged with a darkness that the rising sun failed to alleviate.

In an hour, it would become clear to all who dwelled, however temporarily, in the valleys, that that darkness would not now lift. It was not of the Lady; she was, in the end, a part of the South, and she knew her place.

Her power did not inform the skies; did not drive the clouds from their folds; did not deny the sun its due. This dawn, this pale imitation of all mornings before it, was the first of the heralds of the coming army.

All saw it. All understood what it presaged. The colors of the Tyran, the colors of the Toran, the colors of the Kings, could not divide them; they could not assign this false dawn to anything other than the Lord of Night.

So they counted the hours. They spent them, as if they were allowed this last day, and only this one. Some slept; there are always men to be found who can sleep through any circumstance, perhaps even their own deaths.

But many did not.

Men wrote to their wives, or to their children, or both, although they knew the letters themselves would never leave the valley in time.

In the North, it was custom to carry such final letters; death became the messenger, after the battle was done and the bodies counted. It was for this reason—or so it was rumored among the Southern cerdan—that the Northerners did not leave their dead to lie. The last debt accrued by service to the Kings—the Northern name for Tyr, and strange Tyrs, who could *share* a crown—was paid in one way, and one alone: the final words were taken to those who might take comfort from them.

And if the North and the South were separated by gods, by culture, by appearance, the South in this instance learned that there were some customs to be admired, even if they came from the North; those who could speak in the tongue of the demon kings spoke; those who could speak Torra, even rough trade Torra, answered. In the scant hours, the Southerners learned what the Northern writing was meant to accomplish, and many men chose to follow their odd example, asking their brothers-in-arms to take, from their dead bodies if they were unlucky, the words they had written.

The Callestan Tyr chose to encourage his men by setting the example they would follow. But he did not do this out of sentiment; he was ever the practical man.

No; if they wrote to those that they loved, it strengthened them. They were reminded, in the writing, of the things that they *must* have victory to protect. Reminded, as well, that anything less than victory meant the deaths of their kin.

The Lambertan Tyr, suspicious of all things Northern, did not choose to follow this example, but he did not seek to prevent his men from so doing. Because he was practical in his fashion, and it cost little.

But his lips compressed in a thin line as the Northern archers began to form up. Archery was not a *man's* talent.

The waiting was hard.

Kiriel di'Ashaf looked up; Lord Telakar and Elena Tamaraan stood in the lee of her shadow. Even at dawn, it was strong. The sleepiness that day had engendered for weeks now was gone; she was awake, and feral with the desire for battle. Any battle.

"Kiriel di'Ashaf," Lord Telakar said, using her chosen title. "I have come to serve."

The Voyani woman said nothing, but she seldom did. She kept a careful distance between herself and Kiriel; it was almost as great a distance as she kept between herself and Lord Telakar.

"I would have you leave," Kiriel replied, but without cruelty. "You will not be my servant if the Lord's voice is heard upon this field."

"Even if it is not heard," he conceded, "the Lord's power is great, and his reach is long. He might bend his thought to us, and we will be forced to obey him."

"I won't," she said curtly, her hand upon the sword that Anduvin had given her. Costly gift.

"No," he said genially. "You are of the living, and he has, over you, the power of a father over a daughter. No more."

"In the South," Elena said, speaking quietly for the first time, "that is a great power."

"Tell that to the Serra Diora," Kiriel replied.

"I would," Telakar smiled, "but I fear that she would hear little of what I said. She is . . . sensitive to *Kialli* voice. She does not linger when we arrive."

Kiriel shrugged. "She's not without power."

"No. She is not. Will you use her?"

Kiriel shook her head. "No more than I can use any of them. They are not my servants; they are not my lieges. They are," she said, with the first hint of a sharp smile, "as I am: they choose their own fate."

"The Northern laws demand some fealty."

"Yes—but the Southern laws have no rules for women upon the field of battle."

"She is here."

"She's driven to this field. She may help us in ways that you don't see."

"I see little," Lord Telakar replied. "But I feel it: the ways are open. I fear that Anya a'Cooper will finally find something to occupy her."

He bowed to her then. He bowed low.

Elena frowned slightly.

"Elena Tamaraan," he said. He offered the Voyani woman a hand—and it *was* an offer, to Kiriel's surprise. Cold, imperious, it nonetheless left the choice to her.

She did not take his hand, and he withdrew it slowly, his eyes narrowing.

"You have met Kiriel di'Ashaf," he continued, shorn of her hand. "But you have never been formally introduced. She is my Lord," he added, watching the swarthy complexion of Voyani features. Watching red hair in the scant, dark dawn. "And she is my Queen."

Elena frowned. Kiriel realized, belatedly, that the word Queen had no counterpart in the South. Sometimes it was incorrectly translated as Serra. Elena made that translation silently, and just as silently rejected it.

"What," she said, after a long pause, "is a Queen?"

"A Tyr," Telakar replied. "The Tyr'agar."

"Who is she?"

But he did not reply, and Kiriel felt no need to; her eyes were drawn to, held by, the Western horizon.

Ishavriel was in a *bad* mood.

Anya fidgeted. She was used to his bad moods, but she wasn't allowed to retreat into the solace of her chambers beneath the grand halls of the Shining Palace. Drab, dark trees were the whole of her shelter, and she hated them. But she hated the flats of the valleys more: they were too open. She would not rest or sleep beneath the open sky.

There were no bunnies here.

And no fireflies.

If there were flowers, wildflowers, he'd crushed them all beneath his feet. She *hated* that. But he *was* angry, and she tried to be careful.

Tried, very hard, not to be *bored.*

He was concentrating. She could hear it. Could taste it; it was a bitter, metallic mood. Her fingertips were blue as she rested them against the bark of tree, brushed them against the velvet of leaf. Her ears tickled her. Wind. She raised a hand to still it, and then thought the better of it.

But when Lord Ishavriel raised his voice in a thunderous roar, she lifted her hands to her ears and screamed at him. She wasn't certain exactly what she said—it was safest that way.

But the trees caught fire *anyway.*

He grabbed her hands, and his hands caught fire. But his hands, unlike the trees, didn't burn.

"Anya," he said, speaking in his booming voice.

She shook her hands free, and he let her.

"You're *angry,*" she whined. "I don't *like* it when you're angry. Why are you angry?"

"The Southern barbarians," he said curtly.

"What about them?"

Peder kai el'Sol raised *Saval.* She burned. And where she fell, golden fire traced an arc in the darkness of dawn. Samadar was by his side; Samiel before him.

The demons they fought sloughed human visage and the encumbrance of human form when they saw the swords unleashed. They called swords of red flame in reply, and shields of red came as well. The wind roared with the strength of their voices.

And replied with the strength of the Radann.

All around them, in a widening circle, the cerdan of indeterminate loyalties fled. Some paused long enough to draw swords, but the swords were scant protection against the truth: there were demons within the valley. Demons within the encampment.

Peder was glad of their absence. The battle itself could not—like the battles fought in the Tor Leonne—be contained by roof or wall; the demons unfolded, gaining height and width; armored links broke, and the sound, brief and instant, was like the sound of a thousand small gongs.

He had no like music to offer. Instead he offered tabard; the sun was consumed, and the rays made rivulets of gold in the heat of demon fire. He surrendered that much to them, but no more: the only regalia he needed, the only regalia he desired, he wielded.

Saval's voice was vicious and sweet to the ear; it was not a keening, nothing so slight. He swung, parrying flame; the feel of metal against metal seemed incongruous.

Samiel, youngest of the Radann, was also the fastest. And Samiel's blade, *Arral,* spoke to *Saval.* So, too, did *Mordagar,* the blade of Samadar par el'Sol, oldest of the Radann.

But they were weakened by the absence of *Verragar* this morn; three to the demon's five. He fought.

From a distance, Ser Alesso di'Alesso watched. His silence was that of grim fascination, and he shared it with two men: Sendari and Cortano.

"Should we lend them aid?" Cortano asked. The Widan had prepared for just such an eventuality.

Alesso shook his head. "We will wait."

"If there are others, they may flee."

Alesso nodded again. "And they will carry word of our . . . treachery . . . to Lord Ishavriel." His shrug said much.

"Lord Ishavriel is no doubt aware of it as we speak."

"No doubt."

"What orders were given the Radann?"

Alesso laughed. "Orders? I am Tyr'agar," he said coldly. "The kai el'Sol is my equal in rank. I gave no orders."

Cortano's frown was cool.

It was left to Ser Sendari to reply. "He asked—and it was a request, Sword's Edge—that the battle be timed as the army prepared to march. It will cause some small delay."

"Small?" Cortano did not snort. Did not need to.

"Some hours," he added quietly.

"This battle will not last hours."

"No. Not the battle. But we already begin to see the reaction; it will be some time before the cerdan are drawn back into their ranks, and the march will be slowed."

"Is this wise, Sendari?"

"It is not wise," he replied. "But perhaps necessary. If our estimates of the storm's intended length are accurate, we will have need of time. To march now is to reach the field early."

"Early?"

Sendari was quiet. After a long pause, he said, "Mikalis feels . . . uneasy."

Boredom fled, and with it, irritation. "What does he say?"

"That there is . . . a magic at work. To the North and the West.

He cannot discern its nature," he added, "but the skills he learned in his time with the Voyani imply much."

"Be plain, Widan."

"These are not the only demons the Radann will face," Sendari replied, acquiescing. "But this is perhaps the only battle they will have the luxury of choosing."

"When will it be done?"

Alesso's eyes narrowed. "There are three demons," he said. "Three left standing. I do not think it will be long now." His hand fell to his sword.

Sendari di'Sendari reached out and placed a palm upon his Tyr's shoulder.

Alesso smiled ruefully. "No, old friend," he replied, acknowledging what Sendari had not said. "I am the Lord's man, and it is not to my liking to leave such a battle in the hands of others."

He made use of the chaos.

He made use of the time. With a bitter regret, and a deep satisfaction, he extended it, although the valleys and the shadows of overhanging trees waited them all like a promise.

Perhaps he still had hope; the Lord was at his height. But it was a poor, feeble height. The cerdan knew, of course; the whisper of their words—and the arguments those words invoked, with increasing frequency and volume—could not be contained; the wind carried them all.

It is just cloud, the foolish and the obdurate said. But they were young men, given over to the pride of their rationality and their sensibility; they were learned, educated, refined. Not for them, the worship of the Lady, not yet the quiet vigils of night's heart. They would learn, Alesso thought. As he had, they would learn.

But when had that learning begun in earnest?

And to what end?

His mind was now clear. His vision, clearer, although the haze and the unnatural gloom of this dawn, this growing day, seemed to impoverish the sight.

Sun still glinted off the curve of unsheathed blade; sun still adorned and traced the finery of the sun ascendant, and he basked a moment beneath the cold, cold glimmer of its adorning rays. He, Alesso di'Alesso. The only piece of armor he had forgone was his helm; he wanted men to see his face and to know it.

He bitterly regretted his lack of sons.

But on a day such as this, there was little time for regret. He stood, his hands upon the hilt of his blade, his legs planted firmly apart. A dais had been built for his use, and he mounted it to better stand apart from his men.

"Men of Annagar," he said, when as much silence as could be gathered now filled the valley for miles. He waited as Sendari worked his Widan art, to better amplify the words. Cortano di'Alexes had offered that service, but Alesso desired no one but Sendari by his side.

The slight was lost on none.

But the dawn—the lack of true dawn—had drawn together men who played at deadly politics in time of peace; there was no peace here. Would be none.

When he had their attention, he gestured, and men mounted the stairs.

They were not Tyrs. They were not Tyran. They were not in any way that mattered, *his*. But at least one man claimed the right to bear the sun ascendant, and that man stepped to the platform and stood shoulder to shoulder with the man called Tyr'agar in this Southern fold of the Green Valley.

Peder kai el'Sol stood. He wore new robes, and none of these bore the symbol of his rank; none would. The men who could weave such finery had been left in the cities, and they could not now be summoned.

No matter: Peder was known. And the sword he carried, naked as *Terra Fuerre,* was known as well. His face was not a man's face; it was shorn of beard and brow, of *hair.* His eyes were dark, wide, their edges likewise shorn of lash. But he was no babe, no newborn; he stood, and he cast the Lord's shadow.

"Would you speak," Alesso said softly to the kai el'Sol. It was a genuine offer; a genuine gesture of respect.

Had Peder a brow, it would have risen. He did not. "What would you have me say, Tyr'agar?" The question was cold. Night was cold. And day, now. Alesso wondered if warmth would ever return.

Cherished the ice.

"I would have you speak, if you desire speech," he replied, almost grudging. "I have faced the demons in my time," he added, "but never so openly. You have earned your title here."

"I earned it," Peder replied gravely, "upon the plateau, in the rites of Fire."

"The men gathered here see no such rites, kai el'Sol." No irony inflected the title. None at all. But envy? Alesso could not be certain. "And what they have witnessed today binds them to you. If they have followed me into the valleys, they will follow *you* now."

It was a costly admission.

And Alesso was certain that he would pay the price for it—but he was the Lord's man.

Peder kai el'Sol surprised him, then. His gaze was dark and measured as it met and held the Tyr's. No lesser man, save perhaps Eduardo kai di'Garrardi, would have dared such open inspection— and had he, it would have been for different reason.

"Tyr'agar," the Radann kai el'Sol said. He tendered Alesso di'Alesso a perfect bow. A liege's bow. And he did this in the face of the whole of the gathered armies.

"Why?" Alesso asked him, aware that Sendari would allow the syllable to carry no farther than the platform.

The kai el'Sol rose. "I have judged you, Tyr'agar."

"No man judges the Tyr."

"All men must, who have chosen to follow him. Had things gone differently, I would have served you at the head of my order. If we speak of treachery—and we cannot—yours is no less than my own. We are *both* the Lord's men." He rose. "I see that now. The sun was in my eyes, and if it was in *my* eyes, Tyr'agar, than it was a bright, bright sun, a blinding light."

"You are not blind," the Tyr'agar lowered his blade a fraction.

"No. And I would have said, until this moment, that you would remain so. But I understand now the timing of our endeavor. I understand what you seek."

"Do not speak of this," Alesso told him, threat beneath the pleasant words.

"I will not, if you do not. It is your choice, and we are . . . equals in the eyes of the Lord. I have not seen the Leonne boy. But I know what he bears. What he must bear."

Alesso was cold, the silence grimmer.

"And there is only one way in which you will wrest it from him—but if you can, you will *be* all that you have desired."

"And of the past?"

"It is the past," Peder kai el'Sol said, matching the grimness of offered words, as if such a duel were his métier. "And it has long been said, by those who choose to idle away their hours and strength in study and philosophy, that the victor writes and rewrites all history." He stepped back, joining Samadar par el'Sol and Samiel par el'Sol.

Leaving Alesso in command of the dais. Of the armies.

"Men of Annagar," he said again, and his words filled the air like storm's voice. "You have seen the Radann in your midst. You have—as I—heard the voices of their weapons. Let me name them now: *Saval, Arral, Mordagar.* Not since the Lord gifted those swords to the Radann have they sung so loud, and with such need.

"The creatures that joined our number took the guise of cerdan, of men of the Lord. But the Radann's blades are wakeful, now, and watchful; the simple guises of men have been taken from the demons, and the demons have been sent, in flame and fire, to the charnel winds.

"Not at my command, did such creatures walk. Not at the command of Raverra, of Sorgassa, of Oerta. Not for our cause did they linger here, waiting the moment in which they might best strike.

"But they *were* here, and they *are* our enemies; of all the foes we face, the most powerful and the least worthy.

"We have come for war, and war demands our presence and the whole of our attention. If these, enemies of our Lord, are arrayed with the enemies we have taken the field against, we *will know.* And we will have victory."

His words banished fear, allowing none. The cerdan who had fled the fight the Radann had chosen were loudest among the voices that were now raised in approbation, in wild support. He had them all.

"You have seen the dawn. You have seen the gray of night cling to it. But the Lord is still visible in the open sky, and if he is embattled, he is no less our Lord. Raise arms!" he shouted. "And remember our ancient vows. Against foes of even this power, we were victorious once: Do not forget our history. This land is *our* land, and we will never surrender it to the Lord of Night!

"Ready yourselves. We ride upon the hour." He saluted them then. And the fact that the salute was theater, that it was drama, did not deprive it of truth.

Anya was tingly.

She *hated* that. But Lord Ishavriel was now quiet, and she was grateful that the anger had gone away. It meant that she could complain.

And she did.

"It is too soon," Ishavriel told her, brushing aside her plaintive words as if they were spiderwebs. "But we will have no more time than this if our work is not to be undone." He turned to her and smiled, lifting his hands. But although he framed her face, he did not touch her.

He was careful.

"Anya," he said gravely, which was the tone of voice she best liked, "the Lord has great need of you now. You, and only you, can do what must be done."

"What?" she asked, all attention, the tinglies running up and down her spine and swirling around the insides of her ears. "What can I do?" She jumped up and down on the tips of her toes.

"You have cast spells before," he continued, bowing his head to better reach her ears. "And they have always impressed our Lord with their power. You are the only mortal—the only member of the Shining Court—who has tampered with the Shining Palace and escaped his wrath. You have your throne, and not even I can claim one so grand."

This also pleased her; she preened. "What spells should I cast?"

He shook his head. "It is not to cast them that we need you. The words are bothersome," he added, "and are easily said by those of lesser power."

She shrugged.

"We need you here, as we needed you in the North: You are the power which held the gateways open, anchoring them."

"But *demons* came through," she said. Her eyes were wide now, and the skies were the color of moving water, dark with storm. She could feel it, taste it; she couldn't spit it out. Anya did not—and had *never*—liked demons.

And she didn't like the forests here; she didn't like the grasslands. She didn't like the trees, their great bodies shunted aside by the simple act of making a clearing in which they might better stand.

He caught her, then—not by touch, but by the velvet of his voice.

"Do not think of that now," he whispered. "I am beside you. Who has dared threaten you while I stood by your side?"

She shook her head.

"And who, little Anya, has been able to harm you *at all* since I gave you the gift of magery? Not one. Not a single demon, and many have tried."

She wanted to cling to his words. She tried.

But the worst of the memories came upon her like the turn of the skies, the change between day and night: She bit her lip, and the taste of her blood was a sound, a name that she had not uttered aloud for a long, long time.

Devlin.

To her left and right, the great trees that had not been cleared were consumed in sudden flame; it burned hot enough that she felt it across both sides of her face. She lifted her hands to shield her eyes, and heard Lord Ishavriel cursing.

He left me. He left me here.

"He did not leave you here, Anya—you were far to the North, beyond the mountains. And had he never left, you would not have come to me, and you would have remained weak and helpless forever."

Another tree burned.

Another. The flames were hot. They lapped against her feet, destroying the undergrowth. Destroying the clearing, the memory, the hideous sense of herself as something helpless and insignificant. And unloved.

Kiriel di'Ashaf lifted her head.

Lord Telakar had already turned his gaze toward the West, and Elena Tamaraan watched them both, their faces suddenly impassive.

It did not bring her comfort. It did not bring her fear.

Instead, it gave her a moment's silence in which to acknowledge the profound lack of light. No night, this. But no dawn either.

The serafs in the village were praying. Foolish, she thought, almost spitting upon their distant, bent backs. Foolish to pray in the Lord's time.

But another part of her, the hidden child, the youth that she had grown away from but could never entirely discard, spoke different words.

It is not *the Lord's time. Look. Elena. Look at the tinge of the sky. Look at the Lord's face. When, in the reign of the Lord, have the skies been this gray, this dark?*

It is not night. It is not even the Lord of Night's time. It is our *time. Man's time. The hour of man has been extended.*

Auralis AKalakar looked balefully toward her. His sword was sheathed, his shield strapped against his broad back in the style so common to the Northern soldiery. His hair was drawn back in a braid, and it was almost a pity; in this odd light, he was attractive. A man.

"What?" he said, as if her passing glance was an intrusion or a demand. At a different time, it might have been an offer; she was put off by his lack of fine manners, or of any manners, really.

"I am thinking," she told him, uncertain why, "that the color of the sky is not so foreboding as all that."

He spit, but he often did that. She was long enough away from the desert that the gesture did not disturb or disgust her. Let him waste his water here; there was water in plenty. "This isn't natural."

"No. But natural or no, perhaps our enemies do not understand its import to us."

"To you," he said curtly. As if he were brewing for a fight. He was ceasing, moment by moment, to be attractive at all.

She shrugged, the Voyani equivalent of his spit. "To us," she agreed, as if his words were almost beneath notice. "But it is to us that the battle comes. And the sky is the color of the hour between the Lady's time and the Lord's. It is said—in the South—that that hour is man's time, when all things that are said and done may be attributed to us, no more.

"I think, if the day grows no darker, we will be blessed by this."

By little else, though.

Lord Telakar's eyes had closed; his long and perfect lashes formed crescents beneath the thin white of his lids. He was tall; too tall. His height seemed to constantly shift, as if form was not certain. But it was not his height that she found disturbing; it was his expression. His lips were turned up faintly in a hint of smile.

She had seen a similar trance upon those who had taken the wild herbs that brought either peace or insanity.

But she had not thought to see it on his face.

Had not thought to see it upon Kiriel di'Ashaf's. On her, the expression was not one of sensuous delight; it was one of darkness, of cruelty, of dominion. And of, yes, the pleasure that these things afforded the cold and the cruel. Elena knew clansmen. She knew the damage that men with just such an expression did; understood the warped and twisted pleasure they received from invoking the price of their power. She had no doubt—although this was the first time since she had joined the army that she had thought of it—that such lords also existed in the North. They existed where all men were.

But so, too, did they seem to exist where women were, and this was more profoundly disturbing. Of the Matriarchs, those women who held the absolute power of life and death over those who took their names, she could not think of one who could find such a pleasure, and hold to it. The closest thing she had seen was a distant, grim satisfaction, and it did not speak of another's pain in the same intimate way.

If Auralis noticed, he said nothing. Instead, after a shrug that was meant as warning, and at that an it's-your-death warning, he walked away.

That was the sign and the signal she should have followed, for he was clearly Kiriel's companion, and if one such as Kiriel could claim to have friends, he was also that. But he was a man, and she was—had been—a Matriarch's Daughter; what was possible for her was different.

She strode to Telakar's side and reaching out, she slapped his face. She then jumped away as fast as her legs would carry her.

The slap had the desired effect; his eyes widened, first in anger and then in something less pleasant. But he saw her, where a moment ago he had seen . . . something else.

She had no doubt that he would slap her in return, but he did not move; did not otherwise change position. He stood to the right of Kiriel di'Ashaf, the woman he claimed as lord, and his gaze grazed her face.

His smile was cold.

"Elena," he said, although he did not look at her.

"What?"

"That was . . . unwise."

She shrugged. She knew that distance was no safety, but she also knew that the presence of Kiriel di'Ashaf was. Or it had been.

"Why do you take such a foolish risk?" he asked, his focus still upon the younger woman's pale face.

"Because," she snarled, "I don't like whatever it is you're thinking."

"Thinking?" He laughed. His laughter was almost worse than the expression had been. Almost.

In a very different tone of voice, he spoke to Kiriel. "Lady," he said quietly.

She did not move.

"You feel it."

"I . . . feel it," she whispered. And her eyes did open, her face turning. She shuddered, closing them. "I feel it," she said again, and her voice was different.

"Why did Anya a'Cooper come to the Court?" Lord Telakar asked.

"Ishavriel brought her."

"You witnessed this?"

"I wasn't born," Kiriel said softly. "But I was told. When I asked." She shuddered again, as if shaking herself free. But of what, Elena could not be certain. "She . . . is in pain."

"Ishavriel is careless, then. If he injures her—"

"He is not injuring her," Kiriel replied, cold now, her hand by the hilt of her sword. She took a step forward, and Lord Telakar placed a hand upon her shoulder. It was meant to restrain her.

He almost lost it.

Her blade was out of its sheath, its hidden sheath, almost before the last of his fingers had curved round her collarbone. He leaped away, much more gracefully than Elena had done, and Elena realized that his gesture and her slap were kin in a way she did not quite understand.

But Telakar took no offense at the sight of the blade, and he did not likewise draw his weapon. He did not touch her again.

"If you kill her," he told his lord, "the spell will be much diminished. Will you kill her, Kiriel?"

Kiriel's silence was answer. But it was not the whole of her answer. "She was mad," she said softly. "I did not realize how much of the madness was born of pain. He does not hurt her," she added, eyes narrowing, "and you know this, Telakar. You . . . feel the reaving more clearly than I ever could."

"Yet you feel it, this dawn."

"I feel it."

"Do you know where she is?"

"No. But if she does not quiet, I can find her."

"Shall I?"

"No. No; if you can stand against Ishavriel, you can stand—but I do not think you can defeat him, and if you cannot, I will lose you." And then she smiled. "They do not understand Anya."

"Lord Isladar did."

Kiriel was utterly still. After a moment, her blade resting dangerously in the air, she said, "You will never speak that name in my presence again." And her voice was cold, cold night. None of the Lady was in it.

"Kiriel," Elena asked, "who is this Anya of whom you speak? Is she demon?"

Kiriel shook her head. "We do not feel the pain of the kin," she told the Arkosan Voyani. "It is only the damned that wail so loudly, and only the mortals that make the long choice."

We.

Elena met Telakar's appraising gaze.

*   *   *

It took two hours to calm her. It was time that Ishavriel did not have. But to kill her was to end the game, and to end it far too early. She had two roles to play, both crucial. He waited as she rode out the storm, trying to bend her memories and her thoughts into a shape more to his liking.

But she was wild, and willful; what she had taken during the darkest night had changed her in a way that no one of them could have foreseen. Damaged vessel, she had been called, and she was— but the damage was glorious and powerful. She shone. He wanted to kill her, for the first time in decades, not because she was so enraging, but because she was *still* so vulnerable, so open to pain. The desire was criminal, a self-indulgence beyond compare.

But he could wait. There would be others, after this battle was fought; others, when the Dominion was once again subject to the whim of the Lord of Night and his servants.

Still, he had to tread carefully; far more carefully this eve than he had in many. He could not now approach her by guile; he could not appeal to her vanity, to the childlike pleasure she took from praise. He could wait; he could wait out the storm. And he did.

When it was done, he began.

The trees, the warped and defiled seedlings of Arianne's Winter, were so poorly named in this era of gray and lifeless forests. They were bright; he could see them all if he bent his power to the task. He did so now, and although they could not be moved, he could trace the lines of their growing power.

They were thin, like strands of silk or slender chains of what had once been gold. He gathered these in ones and twos. He felt them— what denizen of this plane could not, who had once known the seasons and their passage?—and he twined them together. It did not take power, but it took precision. He had both.

After a while, Anya jogged his elbow, touched his sleeve. He was used to this interruption, for if she seldom let another touch her, she often touched when she wanted attention.

"What are you doing?" she whispered. Her voice was thin and shaky. An old voice. The words did it no justice.

"Weaving," he told her gently.

"What are you weaving?"

"The threads of the trees," he answered. "The special trees."

"Oh. Why?"

"Because we must gather them all."

"Can I help?"

"No, Anya. The power that you have is too significant. Even the lesser *Kialli* could do as I now do."

She watched. In the lull, she lost track of the memories that had tormented her, and he, the desire to increase them. She was, for a moment, his student, his only student; she watched his work.

"They don't want to be gathered," she said unexpectedly.

He nodded. She saw much, had always seen much. It was a mistake to assume her simplicity was stupidity or ignorance.

"Are you sure we should be doing this?"

"I am sure."

"What will happen when you finish?"

"I will need your help," he replied, utterly neutral now, "to bind them. It is . . . not unlike weaving a cloak," he added. "But if the threads pull loose, there is no fabric with which to work. Watch, little Anya. Watch and learn. If you can do this, you will be a mage without parallel."

"What's a parallel?"

Lord Anduvin came an hour later.

Auralis AKalakar had returned, probably because he'd seen him. He didn't like this man. No, not man. And because he was a Northerner, he could not hide his distaste and suspicion; he wore them as plainly as he bore shield.

"I've got word," he said to no one in particular.

Kiriel looked back. "From the camp?"

He nodded.

"What do they say?"

"The magi are in position. The armies are ready."

She nodded.

"Will they come here, Kiriel, or will they come to the valleys?"

She shook her head and turned to Lord Anduvin. "Why are you here?" she asked. The question was quiet, but there was no softness in it.

"You called me," he replied, just as quietly. Just as softly.

"I didn't."

He did not gainsay her. Instead, he smiled and turned his gaze to the skies. "The road," he said. "It is a threat, Kiriel. I heard what Lord Telakar suggested, and it is a good suggestion. Kill the mage in Ishavriel's keep, and the road will fray; it will trap some hundreds of the kin, and the Arianni will hunt them."

"They will not," Lord Telakar interjected, gazing at Lord Anduvin's proud, cold face with the hint of cruel smile.

"No?"

"Unless the Lord was careless, they cannot. The Winter seedlings have been planted here; they have not been planted by her hand. She is trapped upon Summer roads, and if she readies the whole of her host, she will still have no egress here.

"This is a mortal battle," he added.

Lord Anduvin frowned. "This?" He gestured, his hands taking in the columns that stretched for miles across the village of Russo, as if upholding the sky. Or denying it. "Mortal?"

Telakar gave grudging assent to the correction. "Yet the battle itself is in their hands, Lord Anduvin."

"Illaraphaniel will take the field."

"He serves them," Lord Telakar replied quietly.

"Impossible."

"I have spent some time in the mortal encampment. What is impossible to Illaraphaniel? He has seen the passing of the ages. Perhaps not even one such as he is immune to the change that mortals know."

Anduvin said nothing, but his disbelief was there; Elena could almost taste it. She did not like this lord; no more than she liked Lord Telakar. But she found him less threatening, although she could not say why; words had never been her gift.

"I know that you wish to see the Summer Queen," Telakar added. "But it is not upon this field that you are destined to meet again, if ever."

And Elena said, without thought, "You will meet her again."

Lord Anduvin turned to her then, as if seeing her for the first time. "You see this, mortal?"

She shrugged. It was her only defense.

But Telakar's brows rose. "She sees truly, but she has no control," he replied at last. "She has not walked the paths of the Firstborn; she bears her heart within her. But this is perhaps the first time that I have seen her gift used."

Lord Anduvin bowed. To Elena.

And Elena met his gaze, was held by it for a moment too long; she could not look away.

The standard was *heavy*. Aidan hadn't expected that. It didn't look heavy when it lay exposed upon the pole, for the pole was long and slender. But lift it from its hole in the earth, and the truth was different. He looked, in panic, at Ser Anton di'Guivera.

Ser Anton nodded, as if he had no doubt at all about Aidan's ability to carry the banner. His smile was warm; it was almost a father's smile.

And that gave Aidan strength. He could not disappoint Ser Anton di'Guivera. He could not disappoint Ser Valedan kai di'Leonne. All eyes were upon him—he felt them keenly, as if they were hornets, darting to and fro a hair's breadth from his ruddy skin.

"Aidan," Valedan said, smiling openly, where Ser Anton was guarded. "You wear a sword."

Aidan's smile was as unfettered. But he blushed. Luckily, he'd spent so much time in the Southern sun, it wasn't obvious. At least he hoped it wasn't.

"Ser Anton has offered you the use of his horse," Valedan continued.

The sudden gap between cerdan and soldier's words made his hands tremble. "I can't—I can't ride," he mumbled. Although he'd been raised in Averalaan, he learned quickly; he knew that this would make him look *weak*.

But it wasn't contempt that he saw in the faces of the cerdan when he finally found the courage to face them. Ser Ramiro kai di'Callesta tendered him a *perfect* bow. And he didn't have to.

He probably shouldn't have. The standard dipped in Aidan's hands, but it was the only way he let his surprise show. Determined, he bore it aloft, and the winds caught its folds, as if it were a sail.

"You come from afar," Ser Ramiro said quietly. "And your customs are not our customs. But I was witness to your bravery on the day of the Kings' Challenge, and I will say that I think the kai Leonne has chosen well. I believe that Ser Anton di'Guivera intends to ride with you."

Ser Anton nodded gravely.

"And my kai, Ser Alfredo, has also been given leave to travel by the side of the standard-bearer. It is a singular honor, Aidan."

He felt shorter and shorter as the minutes went by.

"Valedan?" he asked at last.

It was, of course, the wrong thing to say. But Valedan didn't notice, and because he didn't, no one else appeared to.

Ser Mareo kai di'Lamberto also smiled. There was a brightness to the eyes of this man that made Aidan want to return the smile; a friendliness and an approval that did not seem confined by Southern manners and speech.

"You have ridden with Ser Anton di'Guivera before," he said, speaking in slow, clear Weston.

A whisper went up among the cerdan. But it was a quiet hush, a thing more felt than heard.

Aidan glanced at Ser Anton di'Guivera, and Ser Anton nodded.

"I approve," he continued. So, too, the whispers. "You are slight in build, but you are determined, and you bear both Ser Anton and the Tyr'agar a great loyalty. It is by such things, in the South, that men are known. And made. The Lord is watching," he added, and his smile deepened. "And Lamberto watches as well.

"All men who take to this field will look for the standard you bear." The smile still informed some part of his expression, although his words were now grave. And they were still wholly Weston.

"You bear the Southern sword, and not the Northern one. And if you are forced to draw it, you will draw it well. But it is not your role. You hold the hearts of our men—all of our men—in your hands; the standard must not fall.

"Can you bear its weight, Northern boy?"

"Forever," Aidan whispered.

The kai Lamberto nodded. "Bear it well." And he, too, bowed.

It took Aidan a moment to understand that they bowed not to him, but to the standard itself. But the realization didn't dim the pride he felt, because they'd entrusted it to *him*.

Ser Andaro di'Corsarro waited outside of closed screens. He had not been allowed to venture inside the room he now guarded; indeed, he had almost been chased from the hall by the wife of Ser Daro di'Valente. Almost. But the Serra Diora's quiet voice had spared him that indignity.

Her appearance, when the doors were at last drawn wide, did *not*. He almost gaped—and in a man of his breeding, such a breach of etiquette would have shamed him for the duration of his life. It was a close thing.

She wore the rough shirt and leggings of a *seraf*. Gone all sign of silk, and gone the bangles and necklaces of gold that had adorned her perfect throat. Even her hair, matchless, blue-black of raven's extended wing, was caught in a simple, single braid that fell between her shoulder blades. She wore boots—and heavy boots at that, boots encrusted with old mud and scratches taken by undergrowth and the scrub near the field's edge; she bore a faded waterskin and another pouch that dangled from a wide, boy's belt.

He would not have known her at all, until she moved—but the clothing did not deprive her of the grace of the High Courts.

"Ser Andaro," she said, raising a single brow. As if, he thought, she asked permission.

"Serra Diora." He lifted his head to look above her—her height at least had not been altered—and met the eyes of the Serra Nora en'Valente. The older woman's lips were pursed in a thin line.

"It wasn't *my* idea," she said, the common tones of her speech laden with both annoyance and worry. "It was entirely her own."

"Serra Diora—why do you choose to attire yourself in this fashion?"

"I will take my place," she replied sweetly, "at the side of Kiriel di'Ashaf." And her hand fell to the pommel of a dagger, as if it were sword.

"I confess that I do not understand Kiriel di'Ashaf," he replied, striving for and finding grace. "But I do not believe that she would approve."

"Approve?" Her voice cooled slightly, but only slightly. "Perhaps not. But she is of the North, and she knows that she cannot command me to do otherwise."

"Leave her be," Serra Nora said bluntly. "Kiriel di'Ashaf hears her voice," she added, after an awkward pause. "And I think she needs to hear it. Or will." She made the sign of the circle across her breast.

CHAPTER THIRTY-ONE

MERALONNE APhaniel sent Member Tipurne from the Western front. As she was one of the few women present, and at that, one of the coldest and least friendly of the magi, she took very little pleasure in the order.

"Tipurne," he said, "you know why you were sent to the South."

She snorted in derision. Beside her, Member Gyrrick began his long glower. It would last, she thought, for the rest of the war. However long or short that might be. But Gyrrick commanded some respect, and she forced herself to be polite.

Member APhaniel was not put out by this. It was said—and perhaps said truly—that he had more tolerance for the women than the men, although if that were true, there should be *more* women. The halls of the Order of Knowledge were not without them.

"It is not to my liking," she said at last, "to be sent to *play at games* with the soldiery when I can best serve here." She held out a palm; in it, flat and oblong, lay a shining metal oval.

Meralonne's turn to snort, and his pale brows folded in the middle. "That is not the greatest of your powers," he told her quietly. "And we have almost finished here." He frowned; he had not yet drawn pipe and set it to lip. "Go. You have the greatest facility with illusion; use it."

She grimaced. But she nodded.

"You know what we face."

"Forbidden arts," she said bleakly.

"The casting and sustaining of illusion is not forbidden art."

"The creatures you wish me to create in such a fashion *are*."

His laugh, low and rich, filled the heights. Magi near and far stopped a moment in their planting to gaze backward at the man who commanded their loyalty. "This is something that we should have done immediately," Meralonne told her.

"We did not know, then, what the enemy intended," she snapped.

"We . . . suspected . . . we might see them, and in force. You've studied the reports, AMaryan. You know what to do."

She nodded, and retreated.

Valedan kai di'Leonne was waiting. General Baredan di'Navarre, with a single companion, shadowed him. Ser Anton di'Guivera. At their sides, Ser Ramiro di'Callesta, Ser Marco di'Lamberto, Ser Alessandro di'Clemente and—what was his name? Ser Danello, the kai of Valente. Other Tors, with names even less familiar, also waited, and among them, scattered like the beginnings of a mob, their Tyran and Toran.

But Tipurne had, as well, the audience of the North: the two Commanders, their adjutants, their chosen guards. Primus Duarte AKalakar, a man she both knew and half admired; his Decarus, Alexis.

It was a very, very crowded plain.

"I am sorry to waste your time," she said, her voice miming apology, her expression miming boredom. Neither were exactly true. "But we have been much occupied. This should have been done sooner. But that's the army for you—everything is either done in haste or at great, great leisure." She nodded to the Tyr'agar, trying to remember her scattered Torra. She failed. Torra was not one of the languages she had chosen to study in her tenure in the halls of the Order. She had studied, instead, old languages: Old Weston,

Old Torra, things that might be written on fragments of clay hoarded by the earth at the burial sites of ancient temples, buried villages.

It mattered little. Meralonne APhaniel was correct: of the magi present, she was the one with the greatest gift in the creation and sustaining of illusion.

"What you will see," she said, "when the enemy breaks through the Western barrier, will in no way be human—and that is to your benefit. The kin that can take human form are among the most powerful of their kind—and no army is composed of just the powerful." She hesitated, as if she would say more, but after a moment, she shrugged pale hair from the contours of her angular face. No warrior's braid for Tipurne AMaryan; no surcoat of sword and rod. She wore, instead, the medallion of the Order of Knowledge, its quartered circle proclaiming the presence of the elements. It was the kindest way she had of making it clear what the cost of touching her might be.

But in spite of the stories she had heard of army life, no one had been foolish enough to try.

She asked for room.

Received it. Commander Allen watched her with narrowed eyes.

"With your permission, Tyr'agar, I will use the magic of the Order of Knowledge. It is our intent to grant knowledge, and the ghost of familiarity, to the men you have gathered here."

He nodded. The woman by his side whispered something that Tipurne couldn't be bothered to magnify.

She had chosen—or rather, had had chosen for her—the dais upon which Valedan kai di'Leonne was meant to make public address; she stood upon a platform that made more of her height than she would have liked. Although there were, among the Order of Knowledge—as among any gathering of individuals—those whose flamboyance naturally sought an audience, Tipurne had never been among their number. She'd never really cared much one way or the other what people she didn't know—and to be honest, didn't care to—thought of her ability.

But as she drew breath and raised her arms—which would have brought a frown from APhaniel, who decried the more dramatic and obvious use of focal movements as a crutch for the weak of will— she realized, with grim surprise, that she *did* care. That she had to. The magi were few in number, and the tone and demeanor of Meralonne APhaniel made wordlessly clear that he expected they would be far, far fewer before dawn came.

If it ever did, again.

So she lifted her arms, raising their rounded curve until her palms were flattened against the thin movement of breeze in the crowded valley. "This is *not* real," she told the men, in her best teaching voice. "It may look real; if it doesn't, I'll have my membership revoked. But do not react to what you see by drawing sword and storming the dais; we are in no danger yet from what I will show you."

She waited, and after a moment, Ser Ramiro di'Callesta took her Weston words and transformed them into fluid Torra.

When he had finished, he offered her a curt nod; it was just shy of an order.

- She shrugged.

"But we will be, and it is essential that you, leaders all, understand what it is that you may face." She paused, and her expression was the pained face of an academic to whom so much is still mysterious and unknown. "It is not *all* you will face. We have taken these images from the various encounters with demons that the Order has come to study over the last two decades, and we are aware that our information is entirely incomplete. It will, however, have to do."

Clouds formed between her hands, dense and thick with colors that she, mage-trained and -born, could see. She could not be certain how many of the men below would see those clouds; she knew that they would see what coalesced from them.

And the first of these, taller than she by two feet, and wider in girth than two men, was covered in spikes, his arms adorned by blades instead of hands. His mouth was wider than her face, and he smiled as she unfolded his moving image, displaying a row of dagger-long teeth.

She heard the momentary silence that followed his inception, and was again impressed by the quality of the Southern guards; they made no sound. Not a single man drew blade.

But she thought they gestured, as if warding themselves against evil.

The pale, lightless sun inched its way toward the heights as she worked; she felt the power leave her, and knew that she would come close to reaching her limit before she was done.

Alesso di'Alesso led his men, inasmuch as Southern Generals *led*. Some hundreds were arrayed before him, the chosen few, the men of the First army that had once served under the banner of the weak and willful Markaso kai di'Leonne.

But it was only a few hundred, men horsed; the body of the army trailed behind. Supplies, in the crested wagons that housed them, were cozened away in the middle of the column, and the wheels were often mired in the soft ground. He had called a halt no less than three times. But his men were good; they offered no word and no gesture that would have hinted at impatience.

And perhaps, he thought, they did not feel it.

As the body of the army marched North, even the sound of song—and the cerdan often sang—faded. Bright, the Lord's face, but it could not diminish the gray of hanging sky—a gray made by no clouds. The sky itself was clear. But in its ashen folds, stars were hinted at, the Lady's veil. The presence of the demons had added a gravity and an urgency to their travel that dimmed their music.

To Alesso's surprise, he found that he missed it.

But for himself, he felt no qualms now; no compunctions. And regret? Ah, regret. It was his truest shadow.

The Radann rode by his side, displaced only by Sendari di'Sendari. The Widan's robes, and the Widan's horse, did nothing to lessen the grim majesty of the Lord's warriors. But Alesso was well aware that had Sendari been offered choice, he would travel with the Widan, under the command of Cortano di'Alexes. A man whose testing had scarred him. Had almost, if Alesso's scant information were true, destroyed him.

That which does not destroy us, he thought, with a grim smile. He had been tested, in a less formal fashion; the fields still bore the mark of his earlier passage. The valleys, he thought, would remember him—both then and now.

But how?

He gave the signal when the wheelwrights had finished their labor, and the army began to move again, lurching into sluggish motion. A column of men did not stop or start quickly.

He counted on that. The sun was now past its height, and he knew—as perhaps only the Lord's truest men could—that the battle that defined him waited for the fall of night.

It would be no Lady's night. The Lord of Night would seek dominion over skies, and if this grim and dreary day were any indication, he would find it. But he would have no more than that; Alesso would cede him nothing.

A messenger rode up to the Radann, and passed them a tube, falling back at once to better give them the illusion, the necessary illusion, of privacy. The tube itself was inspected with care by no less than the kai el'Sol, but it was not his name that glowed within the carved seals, and he passed it without hesitation to the Tyr'agar.

*   *   *

The Tyr'agar cracked the scroll, and pulled from it a single rolled piece of parchment. He opened it, and blinked three times, his eyes adjusting to the folding and twisted movement of dancing ink. He spoke his name, and it stilled, but he knew the movement would continue shortly.

"General?" Peder kai el'Sol said quietly.

Alesso nodded grimly, but with some mirth. "As expected," he said. "We will lengthen our line as we pass into the valleys; the heights are guarded against us by Northern bowmen."

"We have bowmen of our own," Sendari said quietly. "Will you not call them forth?"

Alesso shook his head. "Not yet, old friend. We would sacrifice them before they have a chance to show their worth."

"And the Northern Widan?"

"Their disposition is not as clear. What is clear is this: the kai Lamberto and the kai Callesta are upon the field, and they stand together."

Even this, he now expected.

"But word is strange," he added quietly. "And I believe your Widan Mikalis is underappreciated.

"Why do you say this, Alesso?"

The least formal of his titles. The most welcome, here. In the end—and he admitted it now, in silence—the title that he had given his life to bearing would come to him in only one way.

And in the end, this pleased him in a fashion.

"The main body of the army does not face to the South; although the heights are guarded against us, the greater weight of men are spread to the Western side of the valley. And the army," he added, "the standard of the Leonne Tyr, now faces the West as well."

"They expect no danger from the South."

"They are fools," he said with a shrug. "But indeed, they seem to judge the greater danger to be the Western one."

"And is it not?" Peder kai el'Sol asked coolly.

"It is." The Tyr'agar's reply was equally cool, but it carried respect; he had seen a glimmer of recognition or understanding in the kai el'Sol's eyes, and he no longer sought the comfort of lie or illusion. Politics were decided, in the end, by *this:* battle. He was comfortable now. Although he wielded *Terra Fuerre,* he did so with a stern pride.

Not by the gift of the gods, not even the gift of the Lord himself, would he make his name now. He would stand as a man, surrounded by men, and if the Lord willed it, he would die as one.

A better death than he had granted many.

But then again, so few merited such an opportunity.

"We will arrive," Alesso said quietly, "when the Night has fallen."

"And will our men march through the night?" Peder kai el'Sol asked.

"They have marched through the night unaware until this moment," Alesso replied. "And they will continue. You will know, kai el'Sol, when the time is right. And I release you and your pars from my command in that minute. Give me warning, if you have time or thought for it—but give me no more than that."

Peder kai el'Sol inclined his head, accepting the gift Alesso offered: freedom. And a promise to take no insult from what, in lesser circumstances, would certainly guarantee it otherwise.

"You thought to take the title of Radann kai el'Sol from Fredero kai di'Lamberto," Alesso continued softly. He had not intended to say so much, but he felt that the color of sky made the day the time of man.

Peder kai el'Sol glanced away. It was a brief flicker of eye; his head did not move or otherwise acknowledge the brief flinch. Alesso could be cruel. Had been, when it had suited a larger purpose.

But he found, this day, this coming day, that he could be generous as well. If kindness was beyond his understanding or his grasp—and it was, he did not lie to himself or take for himself an accolade that he could not live up to—respect was not.

It was this that he offered the kai el'Sol.

"I do not understand what passed between the former kai and yourself, but I have seen a truth that has eluded me in a similar quest."

"And that, kai Alesso?"

The first time that Peder had chosen that particular form of address.

"You have become, in fact, the kai el'Sol. Were Fredero here, he would have no regrets."

For a long moment, Peder kai el'Sol said nothing. But the texture of his silence offered Alesso many things. Gratitude, which he expected. Humility, which he had not.

"Win this war," Peder kai el'Sol said at last, and not quietly, "and you will be, in all things, the Lord's.

Alesso smiled. "Nothing less will suffice. Sendari, come."

*   *   *

Meralonne APhaniel troubled himself to offer obeisance to the
Tyr'agar. He did this openly, and in sight of Commanders Allen and
Kalakar, and if they were irritated by a display of open respect that
they knew they would never receive, it did not show.

"I am come from the West," the magi said, when given leave to
rise, "and with brief word; it is to the West that I will return when it
is given."

"And that word, APhaniel?"

"The Western heights of the valley are not safe for man or beast,"
he replied. "Those that have taken up positions there have marked
them well; they will not advance, no matter what they encounter. If
the battle forces us to retreat, the only safety now lies in the valleys."

"Now, Anya," Ishavriel said. His voice was heavy with power,
and she heard it not as a single thing. She didn't like it.

But she obeyed Ishavriel's wordless command, for when he
lifted his hand, she dropped her own into it, and felt his fingers curl
around hers. "Grant me the use of your power," he said softly. It was
not a request, but it was disguised as one. She wasn't stupid; she
knew the difference.

But she saw what he held, and in spite of her growing annoyance, she was curious; his hand—the hand that did not touch
hers—was bright and shiny, all gold and silver. The black shadows,
the blue light, that marked almost all of his power were entirely absent.

And his hands were *warm*. Hers had gotten cold; it was too dark
here, and she didn't like it.

She nodded, as the threads seemed to pull themselves taut in his
hands. "What do I do?" she asked, almost timid. As she had been
when he had first begun to train her gift.

"What you must," he said quietly. "Bind them, Anya. Make them
strong."

She could do that, she thought. But she wasn't certain how.

"How are the Western heights secured?" Commander Allen
asked.

"The ground," Meralonne replied coolly, "has been planted
with . . . metal seeds. No horse, no mount, no heavy creature can
pass across it without . . . causing those seeds to bloom. We will
have warning of their coming," he added, "and we will damage and

harry them for as long as we are able to contain their forward guard." He hesitated, and the sight was rare enough that no one filled the unexpected silence.

"We will not, I fear, be able to contain it for long." He turned to face the Tyrs and the Tors, and he said, "If you have not offered warning to your men, do so now: the Lord of Night's host will bear little in common with the forces you thought to meet when you traveled to Averda.

"They will not be silent," he added gravely. "They will not be human. But they can still be dispatched to the Hells that birthed them."

Ser Ramiro kai di'Callesta and Ser Mareo kai di'Lamberto nodded. "With your permission, Tyr'agar," the Callestan Tyr said, speaking first as was his wont, "we will retire to join our forces. What the magi says is wise: without warning, they may break." He paused a moment, and then said, "We thank you, APhaniel, for the gift of your magi. She has shown us much, and given us much to contemplate."

"Did she tell you," he said, "that it is those who appear *most* mortal who are the most dangerous of your foes?"

The kai Callesta nodded.

"Good. While your men hold their ground against creatures birthed only in nightmare, it is up to you to find those who command them. In a sea of strangeness, they will bear mortal form—or rather, form closest to that of mortals. They will be compelling and beautiful in their fashion, and they will wield a great deal of power.

"If you can, kill them. Their deaths will loose the bindings that contain their kin."

"And is such a loss an advantage to our forces?"

Meralonne's shrug was economical. "The kin were created," he said, "to be the guardians and the wardens of the Hells. In the South, you speak of winds; it is not the voice of the wind you need fear here. But in the North, we speak of the Hells, and it is the Hells that have opened their mouths, disgorging the demons you face.

"The Hells inform the whole of their desire. They feel pain, any pain, and it brings them pleasure. If they are confined, if they are trapped, they will not pause to savor it; they will move forward blindly, pulled against their nature, to grant only death.

"But if they are freed, they will slow."

"And cause pain?"

"A great deal of it," Meralonne APhaniel replied softly. "I am sorry," he added. "But in the end, if the pain is great, it will also slow the losses you will take."

"And how," Ser Mareo kai di'Lamberto said grimly, "are we to gain victory on such a field?"

"Do not ask me," Meralonne APhaniel replied, equally grave. "Ask, instead, the kai Leonne; it is his bloodline that last faced the servants of the Lord of Night, and it is his line that in the end destroyed their hold upon the Dominion."

Valedan kai di'Leonne lifted his shoulders. He glanced once at the Serra Alina di'Lamberto, and once at Ser Anton di'Guivera. Neither moved, and for just a moment, his indecision marked him as a youth.

At such a time, it was not an auspicious mark.

But when he turned to Duarte AKalakar, the older man bowed; he held the bow for a long time.

"AKalakar," Valedan kai di'Leonne said. "Join me upon the dais."

As if Primus Duarte bore no House name, and therefore no other loyalty, he nodded. They mounted the stairs abreast, for the stairs were wide enough to allow three men easy egress, and only when they reached the height of flat slats did they separate. Valedan took a step forward; Duarte stayed his ground.

In Torra, Valedan began. He let his hand touch the hilt of the kai Callesta's sword, and he surveyed the Tyrs and their Tors in a grim, measured silence.

"It is a fair question, kai Lamberto," he said at length. "And it deserves a fair reply.

"The man by my side is known as Primus Duarte AKalakar. Many of you have seen him; you have seldom heard him speak. You know—or many of you do—that he captains the guards I have chosen as my personal escort.

"Some few of you know that he came to the Green Valley before, in a different war. He made his name there, but it is not the name by which I have introduced him."

He had them all, and knew it. Knew as well that he must proceed with caution, for he was in the heart of the South: upon the battlefield, with the war less than a day away.

"But he was known to you all, in his time, although you did not see him: He was the Captain of the Black Ospreys."

The swords that had not left sheath for the display of the mageborn's illusions now rested beneath hands that were almost reflexive in their motion. One or two harsh words accompanied those

gestures, but they were given by leaders and not the men who followed.

Lesser leaders. The Tyr'agnati were silent.

"They were given the unenviable task of preserving my life in
the Northern capital," he continued, when he saw that swords would
not be drawn. "And the men and women who survived the slaughter in the Averdan valleys worked at his command.

"They wielded no magical swords; they wielded no magical fire.
I have seen, in the flesh, the creatures that Member Tipurne showed
us. They are worse in every possible way than her illusion can capture; they exist, not in fancy, but in fact.

"And against these creatures, time and again, the men and
women who were once the Black Ospreys, and who are now simply
a part of the Kings' armies, have *always* triumphed.

"What Member Tipurne told us was true: the loss of an arm or a
limb seldom slows them, although it does enrage them. But the loss
of head, while it does not entirely destroy them, slows them enough
that they can be easily dispatched.

"We faced single demons, not an army. But the men *and women*
under the command of Primus Duarte are not an army either; they
were winnowed, in Averda, and they are few."

"How will we have victory?" he said, raising his voice. He drew
the sword from its scabbard and held it aloft in the poor, gray light.
"By the dint of will," he continued. "And by the use of blades such
as these.

"The Black Ospreys were feared in the South. In the North they
were held in contempt."

Commander Kalakar coughed. Loudly.

"But in the South, they were understood; they were considered
strong enough to fight a real war. They did not, in the end, win that
war on their own. But they were known for their ferocity—as *you*
were known for yours.

"How will we win?" he cried out.

The Tyran and the Toran drew their blades, and this time, their
lords did not gainsay them.

"This way," Valedan said, when the sound of their swords had
died, like metallic cry, into stillness. "And only this: we fight as
men."

"How many of the Ospreys were lost in these fights?" the kai
Lamberto asked, his gaze sliding across the clearing to the shuttered
profile of Ramiro kai di'Callesta.

"None," Valedan replied. "None, until the village of Essla."

The Southern Tyr nodded. "Kai Leonne," he said, both grim and loud, "we will do no less."

When the men had left, Serra Alina di'Lamberto approached the dais. She saw what they did not see, for she knew Valedan well. But she did not demean him by noticing it. Instead, she said, "That was well done, kai Leonne."

"Was it?"

"You have pricked their honor," she said with a slight smile. "And have given them much to prove. And you have invoked the prowess of the only enemies they cared to acknowledge in the valleys in order to do this."

He turned to Primus Duarte. "Thank you, AKalakar."

Duarte's smile was thinner than Alina's, but it was genuine. His eyes glanced off the face of The Kalakar, but she did not choose to speak. "You did not mention Kiriel," he said quietly.

Valedan's shrug was almost Northern. "No," he said. "But I did not draw the Sun Sword." It was true; he held the blade of the kai Callesta, and it was cold, a thing of metal. No god's touch graced its edge. But history informed it.

"Will the men hold?" Duarte asked softly.

"I don't know."

"Will you?"

Valedan nodded quietly. He looked young again. Felt it, as he had not done since his first isolated walk through the halls of *Avantari,* the palace of Kings.

Ser Anton di'Guivera, silent until this moment, said, "If you hold, kai Leonne, they will hold. You are not your father. Your place in battle will be at the heart of the fighting, and not its rear. They will see your standard," he added, turning a smile at Aidan, "and they will know that while you are on the field, they cannot fail."

"Why?" he asked softly, as if he did not know the answer.

Ser Anton allowed him this illusion. "Because you are indeed the last of the Leonnes. You bear the Sun Sword."

Ser Alfredo kai di'Callesta, the lone Callestan upon the thinning field, glanced up at Valedan. The dais gave both their ages and their heights a disparity that level ground could not. "He bears the sword of my brother," he said quietly.

"Aye," Ser Anton agreed, rough word. "He does. But if you are to travel with him, Ser Alfredo, he will not bear it long. Just long enough."

Ser Alfredo nodded. His youthful intensity allowed for no fear. "I will take it from your hands when you have satisfied your oath."

Valedan looked down. "The Commanders have assured me," he replied quietly, "that in battle, such a transfer of weapon is not easy—and sometimes not even possible."

Alfredo's brown eyes widened.

"Ride at my side," Valedan continued. "If you are anywhere else, I cannot in safety pass into your hands what I have held in my keeping."

For just a moment, Alfredo looked as if he might speak.

But although his father was no longer present, and therefore no longer a witness to the conversation, some hint of his father's pride forced him to hold his silence. It stretched. He was young. "You *must* wield the Sun Sword," he said at last, and he was earnest in a way that not even Valedan kai di'Leonne could be. "It is said that the light of the Sun Sword could be seen by all of the men who chose to serve Leonne against the forces of the Lord of Night.

"You were raised in the North," he continued. "And I would not have said—" He shook his head. Hair covered his eyes for a moment. "I am not so good at words as my father. I am better with words than my brother. Than my brother was," he added, the truth of his loss still blurring the lines between the past and the present. "But while you carry that sword, while you bear its weight, you *are* my kin, and I will speak freely."

Serra Alina di'Lamberto said, in as gentle a voice as she could, "The Serra Amara would counsel you against it, were she here."

It slowed him, but it did not stop him. They watched as he labored over his choice of words—for he spoke in Weston. Weston gave him the safety of the foreign; words of import in a foreign language had less weight and less impact than words spoken in the mother tongue. It also offered the advantage of presumed ignorance for any offense.

"You were wronged," he said slowly. "The North was not your home. The Sun Sword was given to the first Leonne because he was the only man in the Dominion who could wield it. Others tried, and the Sword judged them, and their lines failed. Only Leonne was willing to pay the price of bearing that blade."

"What price does the Sword demand?" Valedan asked, as if the awkward words commanded the whole of his attention.

"Honor," Ser Alfredo said simply. "Duty. Enmity to the Lord of Night that supersedes all other rivalries. The ability to risk land, and clan, and home. To risk *all*."

"It is to save those things that I will wield the Sword," Valedan replied.

Ser Alfredo nodded, as if he saw no contradiction in the words Valedan spoke and the words he replied to.

"I do not think that Markaso kai di'Leonne could have wielded that Sword in this battle."

"He could draw it."

"Yes. For display. For pride. But wield it?" Alfredo shook his head. "You should have been raised in the South, in the Dominion."

"But had he," Ser Anton di'Guivera said, sanguine now, "there would be *no* Leonne to wield the Sword. Be at peace, Ser Alfredo." To Valedan, he said, "As you know, kai Leonne, the Sun Sword is said to contain the heart of the Lord's face: when the darkness is at its height, it will be illumination and guide to those who follow Leonne."

Valedan was quiet for a moment. "Let us hope," he told them all, "that there is truth in legend." He raised his head. "Look," he added softly, lifting hand. "The sun is near the horizon now; it can be seen only above the shortest of the trees that line the valley."

Anya a'Cooper now touched the threads that Lord Ishavriel held. They spoke to her in voices that screamed in pain and terror, and she withdrew her hand as if burned. Lord Ishavriel, watching the sun, and aware of it as she was not, did not move. Nor did he give voice to the impatience he felt. It was not the time.

Not yet.

He could feel the ancient ways as if the gathered lives of trees were an instrument; he could hear their song, their shattered, shattering cries, and he took strength from them. But he did not show it; not to Anya. Especially not to Anya.

She rode out the storm of those voices, and after some minutes had passed, she once again touched his hand. This time she was cautious. Her curiosity was greater than her fear.

She looked at the lines he had gathered, and saw that they stretched from him to a point that her eyes, her lesser vision, could not perceive. In the distance, they were spread thin, like spider's web. She wondered if they would break.

Wondered, if they did not, what might crawl across their length, seeking her as she held them.

Again, she pulled her hand free, and again, Lord Ishavriel allowed it. He had begun early for just this reason; Anya a'Cooper could not be commanded by anyone save the Lord, and perhaps not even reliably by he. But Lord Ishavriel heard what she did not say; saw what she could not see. Her power was brighter than she was; brighter even than the twisting threads of a soul that he could not claim for lifetimes yet.

The time would come. If not this life, and not the next, and not the life after, it would come. He would recognize her, although she would bear no living memory of him, and he would both cherish and destroy what he found. His nature. His nature, now; he was a creature of the Hells. Not even *Kiallinan* changed that.

The threads began to tremble. He frowned.

Several of the trees had been lost. They had not planned for that, although they had taken more than they needed.

Yollana of the Havalla Voyani was herself busy this eve. And her labor, unsupervised by the magi who tended the heights, would have met with their disapproval, for she was drawn—Serra Teresa by her side—to the tent which housed the sole tree that she had been allowed to touch.

Others were there, crippled and stunted, their roots white as maggots, and wriggling, denied purchase in flesh or earth by the binding spells of the Northern magis. But they had voices; she could hear them.

Could hear them more clearly, now that the Heart of Havalla hung low about her neck. She had missed its weight in the sixteen years that it had been absent from her family. In desperate exhaustion, she cursed herself for a fool.

"Yollana," Teresa said.

The Matriarch grunted, and Teresa placed her hands beneath the pits of the older woman's arms, shoring her up. Yollana had not dispensed with the canes; she found them useful. Age and infirmity were a pleasant mask behind which to view the busy intersection between the Northern and Southern warriors.

But they were not entirely lies. She lifted a hand to the patch she wore; what the Heart had granted her legs, it would never grant her eye. She had paid, as she had prophesied, the price that she had bargained for, her hands red with the blood of kin, her family's sword by her side. No Matriarch, no matter how ancient, would alleviate the honor of that debt.

But she cursed them roundly anyway.

"Aye, aye, Na'tere," she said gruffly. "I am not asleep and I am not entirely feeble."

"What must you do here?"

"The one," she said, lifting hand to the tree that now grew leaves *through* the canopy of stiff tenting, "We must leave. But the others, the other three, we must take."

Teresa looked dubious.

Because, deprived of voice, she was not deprived of wisdom. "I think that will be difficult."

"Of course it will be difficult," Yollana snapped. "It is part of *my* life, and my life has never been easy."

"Is it even possible?" Teresa asked, relenting with the grace that defined her.

"Not yet. But it will be."

"And when it is," the Serra asked, "what purpose will these trees serve?"

"One at least must survive," Yollana replied. "This one . . . I think it will not." She hesitated, looking up at the slender tree whose brilliant edged leaves had so easily severed cloth. The gift was strong; it rode her. "The servants of the Lord of Night will see it, and know it for what it is; if they can reach it, they will destroy it utterly."

"And the others?"

"Two," she told her, "we will plant. The third we will carry."

"How?"

Yollana's smile was crooked. "Your niece traveled with the Sun Sword, Na'tere. You must know how. We will preserve this last tree, against future need, in the same way."

Teresa hesitated, but only for a moment.

"What?" The old woman demanded.

"You will bear a debt to Arkosa," she said quietly.

"Aye. But it is not the greatest of the debts I bear, and I am content to undertake it. Margret is young. She has not seen what we have seen upon this field. But were she standing here now, she would do as I do; she would do no less."

Teresa did not ask. Instead, she helped the Matriarch to reach the smallest of the saplings.

"*Do not touch it,*" Yollana barked.

It was a waste of breath; the Serra would no more touch those trees than she would touch clansmen.

Yollana began to speak. The words were old, and as they left her lips, they were joined at last by the sounds of dim and distant voices: her dead kin, the Mothers who had kept Havalla safe in the wilderness and isolation of the *Voyanne* for the whole of their journey.

It was almost done. Almost. And that was a good thing; Yollana was weary. Too weary to observe the formality of offering Teresa threat should she ever speak about what she now witnessed to anyone else.

And it was a formality. Teresa had become, in truth, sister to the Matriarch, who had none. For just a moment, Yollana envied the terrible Northern Houses, The Ten—for they were free to abjure all ties of blood, and to take for themselves a new family and a new name that meant just as much. There was no such freedom in the South.

"My pipe, Na'tere."

Teresa nodded, and taking one hand from its base of support beneath Yollana's arms, she opened the flap of her satchel. Many were the things it contained; far too many for its obvious size, its meager depth. But even this did not seem to discomfit the Serra Teresa.

"I lost my eye," the old woman said, as Teresa fished the pipe from the worn leather folds, shunting aside ointment and unguent, dagger and dried herb, brush and sticks that were meant to burn when the danger was highest. "And you, Na'tere, your hearing. Yours was the cleaner loss—and because of it, you feel it more deeply. There is *no* justice in the South."

"Only the justice we make," the Serra replied, and if her voice shook, Yollana could hear no sign of it. "But if we fail to even make the attempt, we might as well be lambs to the slaughter."

"I have often thought of Serras as lambs," the old woman said quietly. "Ashaf kep'Valente," she added, as if the name had power. "A beautiful girl. A foolish one."

"And now?"

"Lambs have fangs," the old woman replied, with the bare hint of a smile.

"So, too, old women who cannot walk without canes."

"Let us see. Take those sticks as well, and take them carefully."

"Are they heartwood?"

"Of a type," Yollana replied. And then, after a pause, "Yes. Older, and meant for other work—but they were cut and tended by no hands but Havallan hands."

Yollana lit her pipe while the Serra retrieved the slender pieces of wood. They were smooth; the roughness of cut branch was nowhere in evidence. She gave them into Yollana's keeping, and Yollana muttered a curse. "We should have brought your niece," she said, adding to the liberal curse a smattering of rude trade.

"She is occupied, Yollana; I do not think she will come in time."

"Aye, she won't."

"Then let us do what we can."

Yollana nodded again, and as fire blazed in the bowl of her pipe, she lifted a stick to catch the small leap of flame.

The stick was alight, and began to burn—but it burned with a golden light that held all of the sun's color, and none of its ability to blind. Nodding, Yollana made her way to the most stunted of the small plants.

There she stopped and began to curse. This time, it was of the Northern magi that she spoke.

"This will be costly," she said, through gritted teeth. "But we will bear the cost." She extended the burning stick as far as the magical barriers would allow her to reach; her hands seemed to stop as if they had hit glass, but the stick was bound by no such law.

"What do you offer?" Teresa whispered.

Yollana should not have answered. But she chose to. "Summer," she said quietly.

"But were not these trees called Winter trees?"

"Yes, and they are. But such trees as these are planted in the Summer; always in the Summer. There are Summer trees," she added, "and they are planted, always, in the Winter." She shuddered as she spoke. "The planting of those trees is far less gentle, and far more costly."

"Why must they cross the seasons?"

"Because the—because their Lady is part of both seasons; they are a part of her. These are not mortal seasons, Na'tere," she added. "But some of that knowledge remains to those of us who live outside of their whim."

The wriggling of those spare and ugly roots became frenzied, but something in their groping, blind movement had changed.

"Do you think to . . . summon the Lady?"

"No, Na'tere. If I did, the Heart would kill me. We . . . were not friends. We are not. But we abide, in some fashion, by those seasons. The longest day," she added softly, "and the longest night."

The roots extended, thinning slowly, as if pulled. But they were pulled to the flame supported by the dwindling, slender stick. An inch, another, and they touched: flame and white wood.

And what the white wood touched, it donned; flame leaped, changing not in shade but in magnitude. The whole of the tent was lit by the glow, and Teresa dropped to the ground, shielding her eyes.

Yollana, however, had the protection of her many, many Mothers: she watched. Neither woman cried out.

White withered; silver gained in sheen. The slender sticks of twisted wood seemed to shudder and lengthen as the Summer took root in the heart of Winter. Buds appeared along that unnatural, perfect bark, and they began to unfurl in leaves of gold. Sharp leaves, glinting like knife's edge—but unalloyed in their beauty.

Yollana's stick was guttered, and she dropped it.

"The next two," she said wearily, and Teresa rose at the implied command.

The breaking of the Northern bindings was not so difficult a thing as it should have had been; they had been specifically tailored to contain what no longer existed. When the last of the saplings had been purified by Summer's flame, Yollana gathered them all in her arms as if they were children.

"We will be seen," she said with a grimace.

"But not stopped."

"No, Na'tere. No one will stop me. Nor will they stop you. Take this," she added, selecting a tree with leaves hard as diamond and just as beautiful, "and find your seraf. He will know what has happened to the box that carried the Sun Sword from the Tor Arkosa. Do not let him touch the tree; you should not yourself bear its weight, but time is its own master, and makes its own necessity.

"When he opens the box, place this one sapling inside it, and close it again. Do not speak—" She stopped herself and smiled. "Hurry."

"Where will you be?"

Yollana grimaced. "I will be in the encampment at as great a distance as I can be from this one tree." Her sleeves chafed her arm as she gestured, the saplings almost tumbling from her hand. "And I will mark that distance; I will plant one tree there, and another at the apex of a triangle."

"Why?"

"Because," the Matriarch replied, in a tone of voice that indicated just how much she enjoyed being questioned. "It is all that we can do, now."

Teresa bowed and left. She drew her cloak across the bundle she carried as if it were a babe, and if the sharp, new leaves cut her skin, she made no protest.

*   *   *

Speak, Yollana said softly, in the oldest tongue, and in silence. But she cradled the trees as she did, and the Heart burned bright between her fallen breasts. *Speak to your brethren. Speak to the Old Earth. Speak, and speak as loudly as you can.*

She dug a small hole in the earth, and although the cerdan watched her, and whispered among themselves, they did not attempt to stop her. The word *Voyani* hung in the air, accompanied by the word *Matriarch.* Although they did not shield their eyes or otherwise flee as any sensible men would, they did not draw near.

It made her proud, a moment, to be among Southerners.

She placed the first of the saplings to one side, and grimaced in distaste as she drew a dagger. What had been offered once to these saplings, she could not offer again. But she knew that some element of the living was necessary, and she paid the price demanded.

Or would have, but as the dagger drew close to her hand it flared with a bright, bright light, and she cried out, her fingers singed.

In the darkness of this unending dusk, she turned to see Meralonne APhaniel. His eyes were the silver of the bark's reflected light, and his expression, the cold of the Northern Wastes.

But he was no fool; he did not ask her what she intended or what she attempted. Instead, he gestured, and the dagger that had fallen flew up from the ground and into his hand as if it belonged there. It was a Voyani knife; he held it for no more than a second and let it fall again.

"Matriarch," he said coldly. "You interfere in things that you do not understand."

She laughed. "You bear the medallion of the most interfering of the Northern guilds," she said with a snort. She did not rise.

"I bear many burdens," he said. "And you cost me time. It is time I do not have."

"Yet you are here, Northerner. What would you have of me?"

He shook his head. "You freed them."

And she nodded hers. "I do not understand why you did not."

"No," he replied coldly. "And if you are very lucky, you never will. But I understand some part of what you attempt." He drew a dagger from his own belt, and it glittered strangely, as different from her own weapon as they were from each other.

He cut his palm, and into the small hole she had dug, his blood fell. It was red, and it flowed quickly.

"Now," he told her. "Plant the tree."

She was not accustomed to orders. Or not, at least, to receiving them. But she did as bid, and the ground closed, like a slow mouth, around its slender girth.

"You have another," he said quietly.

She nodded.

"Then come, old mother. I will aid you once more. We have, as I said, little time."

She rose, ignoring his hand, and as she did, she saw that the planted tree was now the color of moonlight, Lady's face; that its leaves were the color of sunlight; that there was no way that this could be seen and not be recognized. Even as she backed away, leaves of gold were unfurling, and branches, bursting from what had once been silver nubs, reached toward the skies.

Word filtered quickly, passing among the cerdan to the Northern soldiers, and from them to the healers; it passed from the lowest of the sentruses to the highest of Commanders.

Even the Tyrs, positioned now across the valley's flats, looked back to see the glow of silver and gold, and they were heartened by it: there was a cold beauty there that did not speak of the Lord of Night.

But night heard, anyway, and it began its long fall as if there would never be another dawn.

The weave grew brighter—and darker—in the hands of the *Kialli* lord. Dancing among its many threads, paler, smaller fingers moved. Anya had found her rhythm, and she worked the threads, power flowing from her hands, syllables from her lips. Her eyes were closed.

Seen this way, she did not resemble the child that she had been, years ago; nor did she resemble the mortals who were gathered in ones and twos as sacrifices and anchors to The Lord. She had power. He could almost taste it.

But here and there she would stop a moment, frowning.

At last, she said, "You haven't caught them all."

Before he could speak—if he intended speech at all—her hands were flying, as if across a mortal loom; she caught something between her fingers, something bright and slender, and she crowed in delight, the depth of her voice at odds with the expression.

These things, these new things, she added to the tapestry, and only when she had finished did he realize what she had done.

"Anya!" he cried, but she could no longer hear his voice; he recognized the walls of her madness, and knew that the sounds of his words would break against them, and that her mind would make of their shards something entirely different.

But he hid his anger.

What was done, was done.

And although there was contaminate in the weave, the weave was *strong*. Strong enough, he thought, to survive the unfettered threads of purified Winter trees. Wide enough, he thought, to be the bridge that joined the Northern Wastes and the Southern valleys. Bright enough, dark enough, to call The Lord's host from the depths of mortal winter and draw them here.

CHAPTER THIRTY-TWO

T HUNDER.
Loud, rumbling, a thing more felt than heard, it rolled across the valleys, sundering syllables, the sound of marching men, the clopping of restless hooves, the crackle of wood in night fires that were large and evenly spaced.

But where, in storm, thunder was punctuated by the brief flash of white lightning in the regnant sky, this was delivered in fire: red fire, a brief sunset in the West.

And joined to it, enhanced by it, the roars of night creatures: the Beasts of the Lord of Night.

Kiriel di'Ashaf turned to face the West. Her hair broke free of the clasp that held it in its practical braid; this was nothing new. But as her hair rose, it framed her face like the closed pinions of dark wings, lending white skin the gravity of a shadow that had never had anything to do with cast light.

She drew her sword; it came free of scabbard and rested in her slender hands as if it weighed nothing. It was part of her; as natural to her arm as the hand that held it ready.

By her side, the two demon lords stood. They did not yet draw weapons; they did not adorn themselves with shields. But they tested the night wind, and the night wind answered; as she, they gained shape and shadow. Auralis thought them dark angels, night angels, and he realized that they held his gaze because they were *beautiful*.

But beauty had never ruled his life.

He drew his sword as well, and it came to hand with a whisper. He could not hear its words over the din of the thunder that came, again and again, in the distance, slowly drawing closer. But what he could not hear, he felt, for his hand was burning, and the heat of flame warmed him.

He need never fear fire again.

Kallandras of Senniel College came to stand by his side. "Do not," he said softly, his voice clear and cold above the distant din, "listen to its voice, AKalakar. There is only one master: You or the ring. Choose."

Auralis smiled. Or rather, his lips lifted; his eyes did not waver from the dark line of trees.

"Where, Kiriel?" the bard asked.

She listened a moment, as if struggling to translate his words. And when she spoke, she spoke in a tongue that Auralis didn't understand. But he recognized it. Found that if he desired it, he could repeat the syllables, could form them. He didn't try.

The bard, however, understood. "We are three miles from the encampment," he said, offering Weston in reply. "Three miles. Where will we be needed?"

She turned toward the village, to the East. The children had been gathered in ones and twos, and they had been granted the safety of Ser Daro's domis—but his domis, while large, was not capable of containing the entire populace. The old remained in their homes, biding their time in silence and prayer. And the men? They readied their spears, their hoes, the axes which were better turned to wood than flesh; they donned the scant pieces of armor they had gained while scavenging across the fields of an earlier war.

At one time, it might have angered Auralis. But it was clear that the serafs recognized no national boundaries; here and there, they wore the flat plates of Southern cerdan, the leather splints of Northern soldier; they owned nothing that marked them as men of either army. Perhaps, he thought, they were men of both: they were unprepared in every way for the battle that approached, but they waited, silent now.

Ser Daro was among them. And beside him, faded and worn, the curling banner of Valente. It was not finely crafted, nor finely made; it was not weighted by chain, and therefore slid in any direction the wind desired. But even here, symbols had weight.

Perhaps especially here.

The Ospreys had been crippled here.

The Ospreys had died.

But it was not the blood of these slaves that would still the sword's voice; it was not their blood that would ease Auralis and give him the momentary illusion of peace. The fear the serafs felt meant nothing to him—less than nothing. He had long ago given over fear of death.

"Not here," Kiriel said at last. "They will not be here."

"Then we should move to join the army," Kallandras told her, speaking as gently as he might to a child. Or a wounded, wild beast.

Elena Tamaraan raised a hand to her brow, squinting into the flash of red light. She was gray; the hair that framed her face ill suited her pallor. Her lips were stiff and silent, her hands shaking. She had no sword. But the serafs had given her a dagger—that much, they were allowed to offer her—and she had accepted that gift with a silent and determined obeisance that told them all she was in their debt.

The Voyani paid their debts.

But Auralis knew, as the serafs who were comforted did not, that Elena Tamaraan no longer counted herself Voyani. Her gaze slid off the great tree that stood at the village center, passed over the pillars that had grown in the night of storms, and at last came to rest upon the face of Lord Telakar.

As if aware of that regard, he turned night eyes upon her. "Elena," he said softly.

"There is a danger," she said, and her voice shook.

"There is always a danger," he replied, with an elegant shrug.

"To Kiriel," she whispered, although her eyes did not leave his face. He spoke in Torra, and she answered in Torra, but the conversation itself felt foreign in an unexpected way: it was private.

Telakar nodded. "And the village?" he asked, his voice as soft as it always was. As deceptive.

She shook her head. "I—I don't know."

"If she loses the village," Telakar replied, "the danger will be greater. I do not think it wise."

But Lord Anduvin snarled. Such a sound, from a man who seemed to define poise, was almost shocking. "Lady," he said to Kiriel, "loose us, and we will go."

She shook her head. "They are coming," she said, her voice her own, but deeper and slower. "But they are not coming to Russo. Can you hear them, Anduvin?"

Anduvin bowed his head. "I . . . hear them . . . Lady."

"The Beasts have ridden to war."

The *Kialli* lords bowed their heads.

"The flames of the magi annoy them," she continued, as if unaware of the respect offered. "And they have no riders."

"The kin, Lady?"

She shrugged. "Some will be lost. But not enough. The road—" Her hair rose, and with it her face, as if something unseen touched her chin. "Isladar is here."

Neither kinlord spoke.

Auralis realized, belatedly, that she had forbidden them to use the name.

"In Russo?" It was Elena who asked.

She shook her head. "Upon the valley's heights."

"He did not come with the army."

Kiriel shook her head. "I think he has always been here." Speaking to her past, to something that Auralis couldn't see. Didn't want to see. "I will go to the armies," she added.

Just that.

But as she began to walk, two people ran from Ser Daro's domis, circling the pillars that divided the village. Auralis recognized the man, but the boy was a stranger.

Until she approached.

Kiriel di'Ashaf turned to face Ser Andaro di'Corsarro and the Serra Diora en'Leonne, and her face lost some of its ice as her brows rose. "Serra?" she said at last, as if the word made little sense.

Serra Diora offered a Northern bow. Or what was, in form, a Northern bow. The South gave it a supple grace. "Kiriel," she said, the syllables formal, her expression serene and remote. "I will go with you."

"No."

A dark brow rose. Diora's brow. "No?" she said softly.

"No. I want you here. I want you in . . . Russo."

"Why, Na'kiri?"

If the childish diminutive annoyed Kiriel—and even Auralis had to admit it didn't suit her—she gave no sign. "You have no sword," she said coldly. "You have never fought in battle. You have never faced—"

"I have faced the kin," the Serra replied. Before Kiriel could frame a reply, the Serra dropped hand to the dagger sequestered in her sash. This, she drew.

It shone with Summer's light.

Both of the kinlords frowned, but they did not speak.

"No," Kiriel said again, but her tone was familiar to Auralis, and the word she used was Torra.

Diora smiled sweetly. A harem smile. "You are not my husband," she told Kiriel, and with a shock, Auralis realized that they were of an age, this darkness-born girl and the Flower of the Dominion. "And if you can offer command to Lord Telakar and Lord Anduvin, you cannot likewise offer command to me.

"You are a woman, Na'kiri, and this is the heart of the South."

Kiriel's turn to snarl, and the sound was disturbingly like the sound Lord Anduvin had offered. She lifted her blade, and almost in reflex, Auralis lifted his.

But Kallandras of Senniel College stepped between the two women, and he carried the twin blades of his choice. He did not lift them in threat, but they were no pretty decorations, and if his face was as placid as the Serra's, it was also colder.

"What she states as truth *is* true, Kiriel di'Ashaf."

"You will follow," Kiriel snapped at Kallandras. "We have no need of *her*."

Kallandras lifted his right hand, and Kiriel's sword struck; both blades held. But only their sword arms had moved.

"Lady," Lord Anduvin said. "She is one mortal, no more and no less. Will you not—"

And her blade flew again.

Lord Anduvin flew past it, leaping into air some ten feet above where she stood. But he landed on his feet and fell to one knee. It did not suit him. And it did.

"Serra," Kiriel said.

And the Serra Diora, who had faced Tyrs and worse, met her gaze, unblinking.

"Tell her," Kallandras told Kiriel. "Tell her the truth."

The Serra lifted a hand, a gentle, weaponless hand, motioning Kallandras to silence.

But if his words had been spoken without power—and it seemed to Auralis that they had—they meant something to Kiriel.

"*Not her,*" she snarled.

Elena Tamaraan stepped forward, and Lord Telakar moved in that instant from Kiriel's side, his hands gripping the Voyani woman's shoulders. He spoke softly, bending his lips to her ear; what passed between them did not reach Auralis.

Thunder replied in the silence.

"Lady," Lord Telakar told her, "if we do not quit this place soon, we will arrive after The Lord's forces."

The Serra Diora said quietly, "You need not worry for me."

And Kiriel di'Ashaf had had enough. "I won't be able to do anything *else*," she snapped.

"There is no safety in this village," the Serra replied, serene in the face of Kiriel's growing agitation. "If you fall, or if you falter, we will *all* die. Should I then wait here with the helpless?"

"You *are* helpless!"

"No, Na'kiri, I am not."

"You haven't fought—"

"I have. In ways that you can understand, and in ways that you *cannot*, I *have*. If you fall, Kiriel, who will offer you comfort? Who will sing for you?"

"I *won't* fall! *You* will! And I—"

"And you will remember," Kallandras said, daring much, "what it is that you fight *for*. I understand your hesitance, Kiriel di'Ashaf. Believe that it is kin to my own. But no one of us has the right to order the Serra to remain. You can leave her here, but you will leave her to make her way to that field alone; she will not stay behind."

Ser Andaro di'Corsarro said *nothing*. His hand was upon the hilt of his sword, but he had not drawn it; he knew that this was not his battle. But it couldn't have been easy to accept it; his hand trembled.

"I know what we face," the Serra continued. "And I know what we risk."

Kiriel *roared*.

Even the kinlords stepped back at the sound of her fury.

But the Serra did not.

And when that roar had died into thunder, distant and red, Kiriel turned her back upon the Serra with a distinctly Northern curse. Auralis almost laughed. But there was, about the Serra, a dignity that did not allow for it, not even from a Northern soldier. And Auralis was not usually respectful of anyone's dignity.

She headed for the forest path, and the kinlords followed. But Kallandras paused a moment. "Serra Diora," he said gravely, "you risk much."

The Serra nodded. "But I have lost much," she added.

"So, too, has Kiriel, and she fears to lose more."

Diora nodded. "It is why I go, Kallandras."

"I know."

Meralonne APhaniel looked up. The magi were gathered around him; they stood in the forefront of the gathered army, near the

Leonne banner. "Kiriel di'Ashaf," he said, to the kai Leonne, and only to the kai, "is coming."

Valedan nodded, as if he expected no less.

"And I fear that she is in poor humor."

"Will she arrive before they do?"

Thunder answered. And with it, nearer now, the cracking of ancient trees.

The magi looked at the men who stood around him. They were not all of the Northern mages, and they were attired as soldiers; gone were the robes and the medallions that made them obvious representatives of the Order of Knowledge. "The relays?" Meralonne asked.

"They are set," one of the armed men replied. "Tonial has them in hand, and she won't let go."

"And Tipurne?"

"She is with the healers," the man replied.

"Good. Ready yourselves as you can. They come."

Member Gyrrick of the Order of Knowledge bowed to Meralonne APhaniel. It was not, quite, a Northern bow; nor was it Southern. But it was a gesture of fealty and respect; none could mistake it for anything else.

He rose quickly, and he said a single word to the men who now gathered in loose formation around the magi. He drew a bow. From the folds of this night, this dark and final statement, he drew a weapon made of light, one not seen or felt until the moment it appeared.

Ripples of quiet conversation reached out in a gathering circle, as if the bow were a rock dropped into the still surface of a pond.

"It seems, Member APhaniel," Ser Anton di'Guivera said, eyes cold and keen as blade's edge, "that there is knowledge in the North."

"And in the South," Meralonne replied, deflecting all criticism. "And in men." He smiled. Lifted an arm in a grand sweep. As he did, his robes shimmered in the darkness, and the whole of his cloth was transformed, in that instant, into something akin to Northern armor. But it was light, its chain links new as if it had never seen battle.

And no one seeing it believed that was possible.

"Gyrrick," he said, dispensing with even the minimal formality the Order's members offered each other. "Send the signal."

Gyrrick lifted his bow, and taking an arrow, pulled its glowing string.

A trail of summer light cut the evening sky, arcing above the army, and above the solid shadows of distant, high trees.

It was seen.

Like a falling star, it grazed the night sky, and all of those who now looked toward the open valley plains marked its passage, its mute words.

Alesso di'Alesso watched as it fell. He rode now; there would be no more stops, no more fallen wheels, no more hesitation. The reins did not shake in his hands, although he held them too tight.

He shouted out curt orders, and Sendari di'Sendari let them pass before he brought his horse to bear. "Alesso," he asked, as the riders began to form up in a wider line, "is this wise?" He looked now to the shrouded heights.

"I think, old friend, that we do not have the luxury of time. What the heights hold, they hold; but I am certain our enemies will now be occupied with the struggle that comes from the West." He hesitated, and Sendari marked the hesitation. "Yes," he said, gleaning the question the Widan did not ask, "I heard it. The roaring. Night has fallen here."

He lifted horn to his lips and winded it.

And at his back, in the distance that he did not even pause to glance at, others answered its long cry.

War would cleanse them all.

Meralonne APhaniel saluted the Commanders crisply. "Commander Allen," he said, and after a moment's surprise, Valedan realized that it was an oblique request.

Commander Allen nodded. "Send word of their numbers if you can," he added, but there was little command in the words; it was almost as if the whole of the night now illuminated his dark vision. The days of waiting, the days of discovery, the mysteries as yet unsolved, had been a weight that he had born in silence. Hard to see it as weight until he lifted his shoulders, shedding it. He turned to the magi by his side—not a warrior, Valedan thought, and not a man used to the rigors of the field—and said something that did not carry.

But the man replied, and Commander Allen's brow rose a fraction. He turned a quick glance to Ellora. Where Commander Allen was quiet and resolute in his purpose, she was now practical; she was in motion, her arms punctuating her commands. Her adjutant absorbed them all in deferential silence.

Primus Duarte AKalakar, mounted, nodded to the Tyr'agar. "Kai Leonne," he said. "We wait."

It was true. Absent were Kiriel di'Ashaf and Auralis AKalakar—but all of the others bore arms; some bore shields. Only Duarte chose to ride, and this was awkward.

"We do not," Meralonne APhaniel said quietly, "wait for long." He lifted his head, and his hair frayed, loosing itself in a single snap from the leather thongs that bound it. He lifted his arms as if to catch air and hoard it, and as he did, he rose.

The light of the trees that the Havallan Matriarch planted *were* the moon's light, here; her face was denied the Southerners. Even veiled, it was nowhere to be seen. Nowhere but in the silver, gleaming bark.

And in Meralonne APhaniel.

The winds swept him up, and up again; with him went Gyrrick of the Order, and a handful of the magi whose names Valedan did not know. He regretted the lack of knowledge now. He had a bitter desire, a visceral need, to *know* the names of every single man and woman who would fall in battle.

As if names had power.

Birds rose from their harbor of tree and nest, flying toward the East without pause. No carrion birds, these; they were small, the creatures of the forest, insect eaters, mouse hunters. They fled fire, Valedan thought, seeing the glimmer of red light take distant trees.

But it was a comfortable lie, and it ended when the trees on the Western heights exploded, splinters and branches falling ground-ward toward the waiting cerdan.

Meralonne APhaniel's hands clenched in fists, and from them, lightning flashed, blackening what was already black to the naked eye. Ash and cinder reached the upturned faces of the waiting cerdan, and Valedan saw that if the men had flinched, they had not given ground.

Nor would they; Ser Mareo kai di'Lamberto was among them, and they bore his clan's colors.

Horns sounded, cacophony not harmony, and through the opening torn from sundered trunks that were older than the oldest man upon the fields of battle, the army of the Lord of Night at last revealed itself.

Lord Ishavriel turned to Anya a'Cooper. Her face was slack, her eyes dark and round; her hands were in play, in constant, dancing motion—a thing of unexpected beauty. Power, in the Hells, was seldom delicate. Only upon the mortal plains were such small marvels preserved. He tested the weave; saw where its power and containment lay.

In Anya, and only in Anya.

"You have done well," he told her, meaning the words as he seldom did.

She did not hear him, and perhaps this was just as well. The ground shook beneath his feet; the passage had not opened near them, but he could feel its growing presence. Could feel the clean, crisp bite of Northern air as the Wastes were at last revealed. Snowdrifts caught trees, transforming their season, and ending it. Leaves froze; undergrowth died in the sudden encroachment of ice.

Yes, she had done well.

"Hold it," he told her, as gently as he could.

He had cast his spells to protect her from the knowledge of the presence of demons; he had disguised the whole of their voices, the shadowed glimpse of their distant movements. She hated the kin, and he well knew why; he had used it against her—against them—times beyond number.

She looked up as he spoke again, her pale face flushed, her eyes dark. He commanded her; she was caught in the throes of her power, and she did not, as she so often did, choose to fight him. Instead, she allowed him to bind the strands to her, chaining them to her wrists, like filigree. Even this, she weathered; the power she held did not dim. He stood in awe of her a moment, for she was mortal. She was as great a mage as the mortal world could know, and were it not for his artistry, his bending of her tale, she would now be dead.

But he had preserved her against this moment, and while her power was at its height, unadorned by the savagery of her gleeful childishness, he called her to join the battle.

"We are needed, Anya," he said, although he knew she would take sense, rather than syllables, from the words. "There is still work that only you can do; the fires of the enemy await us, and you must quench them; you must contain them. We must meet upon the plain, and only the plain."

She nodded, obedient.

And when he began to walk, she followed, docile now, her power still sustaining the road. They would need it for some time yet.

Gyrrick's arrows struck the kin that the forest disgorged. They were not the only arrows to fly; not the only arrows to fall. But they were the only arrows to cause the damage they caused; the kin screamed in pain and rage, tumbling down the incline of the ravine.

Meralonne APhaniel, by his side, drew sword. It was blue, bright, a thing of power. This, Gyrrick had seen, and this he had expected.

But the edge of the blade was silver and gold, and it shone like contained forge; he had seen the sword a dozen times, but never like this.

And the man who held it? The same. Silver and gold, a thing of precious metal, devoid not of beauty, but of the messy compromise of life. The winds transformed his hair, the shadows bleached his face of all touch, all trace, of toil beneath the Southern sun. In the shadows, he was reborn, and he was strong.

Strong, Gyrrick thought, with a moment of panic, *and wild.*

"Yes," Meralonne said, as the wind took his words, "wild, Gyrrick. Look not to me; look instead to the forces of our enemy, and only our enemy. The winds will sustain you, if you do not falter."

And if I do? But he knew the answer, and he did not diminish himself by asking the question. Trust and obedience had brought him this far, and *this* was where he was meant to be. By the side of Meralonne APhaniel, above the glinting armor, the flat leather, the raised spears and swords of men.

The kin surged into the valley, leaping above their fallen as if the fallen had no meaning.

The heights were not held against them. But the plains? The skies? Meralonne laughed.

And above the dark crest of trees, laughter answered. Lord Nugratz came first to the field, and with him, winged and barbed, the blood-bound that he had not surrendered to the storm. They carried red swords, red shields; they spoke in tongues of lambent flame.

No lesser creatures these. But they were not bound by form and face that had once been *Allasiani.* They looked for enemies not among the men who stood beneath them; they found Meralonne APhaniel, who meant to hold the heights against their passage.

Like a vengeful cloud, they trailed shadow, and the shadows fell; night. Night's fall.

But they came not in ones and twos; they came in greater number than they had come since the sundering of the world and the Hells, and they howled the song of the charnel winds, gliding above it, their black wings extended from tip to tip like thin folds of ebony.

Meralonne gestured and the rest of the warrior magi rose, leaving the purchase of ground. Some two or three of them drew weapons, kin to Gyrrick's in a fashion; golden in light and color, but different in form. Sword, spear, poleax—weapons of fight, not flight.

Gyrrick drew bowstring and let arrows fly, and where they struck, wings opened, gaping, and flight faltered. But he could not shoot quickly enough to stem the tide of an approaching army.

Nor did he expect to.

But not all of the magi were under the command of Meralonne APhaniel, and when those that could be summoned to join him had left the ground, Commander Allen turned. "Ready the crossbows," he said.

They nodded, tripping over their robes in their haste. He almost felt sorry for them; they were faced, for the first time, with the demons whose study was forbidden them, and they gaped not in fear, but in a greedy desperation. What they learned here, they would write *papers* about, and they would gain prestige among their own for their part in the battle. If they survived.

And it seemed, to Commander Allen, that the fear of losing the sliver of knowledge allowed them was far, far greater than any mere fear of death; that was too ordinary for the magi.

They readied their weapons, and as they did, the folds of enchantment that kept them concealed at last fell away. Standing as tall as two men, bound by wooden poles that were bolstered by blacksmith steel, were the weapons of siege.

The Southerners were well away.

Magestones glowed along the heft of huge quarrels. No hands touched them; magic guided them to their place, and magic pulled the strings that would lend them the force of travel. He had read about these, but he had seldom seen them used.

Let theory meet practice, he thought. But he didn't pray.

He turned and lifted a hand; a young man in bardic gray joined him. "Well, Hasu," he said, with the hint of a smile.

The bard nodded. He carried a sword; if he had a lute, it was hidden somewhere in the bowels of the camp. He bore shield as well, and the sign of Senniel College adorned it. Morniel was represented as well; Attariel and Linden had also fielded bards at the request of the army. Those men, stationed among the soldiers, and ranked in a similar fashion, now readied their weapons.

"Commander Kalakar bids you prepare," Hasu said, pulling iron-gray strands of hair from his eyes. "Her men are in position now, but they would fight the injured and the wounded. The demons have not yet cleared wide passage from the heights, but the trees are—"

His words were lost; trees were once again uprooted and laid low. Claws flashed blue, the only light that adorned the kin who did not arm themselves with red swords, and in the wake of their passage, destruction.

He had seen it, of course; they had all seen it. But even had he not, he would have evinced no surprise. None was needed, and surprise was not his ally here.

The crossbows shuddered; their braces shuddered as well, hopping backward as the quarrels flew.

The creatures that poured out of the gap absorbed the whole of the shaft, and some fell back, screaming. But not enough, he thought grimly. He did not count.

Ser Mareo kai di'Lamberto drew *Balagar,* and *Balagar* keened. It was wordless, but battle cries often were. Beneath him, his destrier shuddered with the weight and pull of the blade; the sword was no longer content to wait. Here, Mareo thought, ancient battles were being fought anew, and the sword was like a young warrior, trained only for this moment.

But so, too, the men he had brought from Amar and his surrounding Torreans, and as them, he held it in check. Lady's Night was old; although he was steady, he could not climb the sloping ravine.

No time left in which to do it. Although the body of the moving army, the shadowed black of forms that only nightmare birthed, were riven by something that flew from the heart of the Northern forces, they were not destroyed; they regrouped, and they came, at last, to the fields.

And Ser Mareo kai di'Lamberto came to understand—and quickly—why it was that the Northerners had chosen not to go horsed to battle.

Kiriel di'Ashaf froze on the road. She could hear—they could all hear—the crack of sundered timber, the heavy fall of ancient trees. But more than that: she could hear the roar of the *Kialli* as they were at last unleashed.

Only once had she heard such cruel cries in unison, and the memory of that single event pulled her lips from her teeth in something that only the *Kialli* would call a smile. She could *see* in the darkness. The night and the desertion of moonlight did not blind her, as it might have once. The ring on her hand burned bright a moment, but its power was a paltry thing; she thought, if she desired it, she might at last pull its dead weight from her finger and have done.

But she pulled, instead, the blade of the Swordsmith, and she began to run.

Kallandras of Senniel College paced her—which surprised her. Lord Anduvin and Lord Telakar did the same, which did not. They were bright, things red and dark, their shields and swords girding them. But no, she thought, sparing Anduvin a glance: his shield, as he, was different.

Behind them, struggling to keep up, Elena, Auralis, the Serra Diora, and Ser Andaro di'Corsarro. She cursed them all, careless, certain that her words would travel. But she forced herself to slow, to shorten her stride. It was not without effort. Not without cost.

But as she forced herself to slow, to give weight to the Serra's presence, she felt again the presence of the only other creature in the Shining Court that she had once trusted. Isladar. She looked for him, as only she could, and she could not see him—but she knew he was waiting. To the East. To the East, and not the West, where the greater threat lay.

Greater threat? She almost spit, the fury rising suddenly and unexpectedly. What *harm* had the rest of the *Kialli* done her? They had been her training ground, her proving ground. Even in great numbers, they had failed in their only goal, where she was concerned: she was still alive. Swords? She had fought with them. Had sundered shield.

Memory was treacherous here, but she gave in to it: felt the hard, smooth length of the table in the Shattered Halls; saw again the looks of outrage and surprise offered her by the lesser kin, and saw it dissolve as she took them, one by one.

Her gift, to Ashaf, who had feared and hated what they represented. Her gift to Ashaf, whom she could grant no other gift of value. Even freedom was beyond her.

"Kiriel," Lord Anduvin said, divining the direction of her thought, the whole of her inward intent. "They are gone; they are of no concern."

He stood before her, stiff and unmoving, and she realized only then that she had ceased to run at all.

"Isladar is here!" she roared. The whole of her pain was contained in his name. That, and more.

Anduvin's face was frozen in *Kialli* mask, but his eyes—his eyes were strange. The light in them, the texture of his gaze, both of these were somehow wrong.

And she realized that more than that was wrong: she could sense Anduvin as clearly as she could sense Isladar. More so, because he was close.

He saw the knowledge come to her face, and the shock of it follow, and as only the helpless can, he paused.

Lord Telakar said, "Does she still not understand, Lord Anduvin?"

The ground shuddered.

Only the mortals buckled, and Kiriel was not among them.

"She does not know," Lord Anduvin replied, with no obvious reluctance.

But she did. At that moment, she *did*. "You—you—" She shook her head as shock gave way to knowledge, and knowledge to shock, in a cascade of conflicting emotions.

"Yes," he said, nodding, his hand upon his sword. "To save his life." And he lifted the hand that had rested upon the blade—the sharp, demanding blade—that he had crafted and honed upon his return to the plane. She could see a red-gold light, contained like fire, in the shape of a wound upon his perfectly smooth palm.

"You're blood-bound. To *me*."

"Yes," he said again, as if the information wearied him, no more. The humiliation, the groveling fear, were entirely absent.

Lord Telakar's eyes widened. "To save his life?"

"Lord Isladar's life," she said bitterly, marveling and afraid.

"And Lord Isladar?" Telakar asked.

"To save hers," Anduvin replied, although no power compelled the answer. "To save hers, Telakar, he, too, is bound. She could have taken the sword, but she would not pay its price." If it angered him, no anger informed his words; he was strange, still, unbowed in his captivity.

"But—" she began, as if she could not absorb what she knew for truth.

"The binding is not so obvious," Telakar said. "It is there, but it is infinitely subtle. Only by your presence at her side have I marked it—and even I—" He fell silent beneath the weight of the Swordsmith's shuttered gaze.

"If you call him," Anduvin said evenly, "he will come."

"I *don't want him*," she cried. And there was both truth and lie in the words, but there was also something deeper: pain. They heard it, these two, and she knew that she exposed the whole of her weakness to them.

But if it fed them, they had the grace not to show it.

"Lady," Lord Anduvin said, looking now to the South and the West, "what would you have of Lord Isladar?"

"*I don't know,*" she cried out.

"And of me?"

She shook her head again. "It's not possible—it shouldn't be possible—I'm *not Kialli*!"

"No," Lord Telakar replied, eyes sharp and keen as new blade. "But you bear some of the power of The Lord's mantle, Kiriel. Did you not understand the significance of the last investiture? Did you not mark what it meant to the kin? Do you not understand why, time and again, we have tried to kill you, and only you, among all of the mortal Court?"

She shook her head wildly.

"He has gifted you with some part of the only thing that allows him the rulership of the Hells. He cannot take it back; could he, I think he would." He lifted his gaze. "You have the gift of command, mortal. And with it, the ability to take what only the *Kialli* can take from each other. It does not make you one of us—but it marks you.

"Call Isladar, and he will come."

She shook her head again, and her blade flew in a wide, wild arc. Anduvin was already beyond it, and Telakar's blade rose to deflect the end of its motion.

"Come, Daughter of Darkness. You are needed upon the field."

She looked to Anduvin, then. "I don't want this," she told him, cold now, the shaking gone from the words.

He laughed, and if his expression had been cold and remote, his laughter was not. "You could not have refused it, then," he replied, "and you would not have, had you the chance. You are mortal, so very mortal. You fought him, Kiriel, but you did not wish his death.

"And because you did not, you have taken what we would never have otherwise surrendered. Come," he said again. "The armies have met. Can you not feel it?"

And the worst of it was, she could.

The Tyrs surrendered their horses.

And because they did, while the light of the trees still shone, their men might do the same. They did not look back to see where the horses fled, and indeed, the flight was thunderous. Instead, they waited, almost unmanned, as the enemy at last burst free of fire and wood and death.

What the Northern magi had shown them with her strange power had been almost intimidating; they had displayed no sign of horror then, and offered none now. But they witnessed, singly and together, the truth of Northern words and Northern claim.

The sword of the Radann kai el'Sol blazed in Lambertan hands; Mareo raised it high, and it seemed that sun's light had descended at last, breaking and scattering the shadows of night that clung to trampled growth. But if it was sun's light, it offered no color, no warmth.

Above his brow, both bane and blessing, Northern arrows flew. That, and more. Steady now, he waited, feeling the sudden bite of night wind.

Ser Ramiro kai di'Callesta took up *Bloodhame*. In a battle upon fields such as this, he had earned the right to wield her. But he felt the odd patina of Voyani magics as if it were unfamiliar weight, and for a moment he regretted his acceptance of Havallan largesse. But only for a moment; if the weapon had been changed, so, too, had the rules of war.

Ser Fillipo cried out and lifted a hand, not in warning, but in surprise; Ramiro followed his par's mute direction and saw that the Northern mages—some two thirds of their scattered number—had coalesced above them, like living cloud. They shed light, casting it upon upturned faces and shuttered helm, and they passed above the main body of the gathered army in the folds of the wind. From their hands, strange arrows flew, and bolts of fire adorned the distant thunder. He saw them for a moment as Northern angels, harbingers of battle; he could hear their war cries, although he could not glean meaning from the syllables.

But the shadows that now burst at last from the valley heights split, sundered by the call of two different battles. Some part of the darkness took to the air, and as it did, the shadows became distinct. Wings unfurled, and red swords appeared, hoarding light; blue halo, like to blade's edge, gilded the servants of the Lord of Night.

But distinct from those servants and the Northern magi stood one man, his hair flowing about him like silver raiment. Meralonne APhaniel.

Ramiro kai di'Callesta had been graced once by the presence of that Northerner in the streets of Callesta, and he found that memory was indeed a dim recollection.

From the heights of the skies, second blood was drawn, and it was dark, a thing of ash that scattered upon the winds. The wind carried demon cries across the whole of the valley's flat—but the cries were not human; not mortal. No dismay marked them, and no pain; even fury seemed absent.

Visceral, beautiful, haunting, he heard *desire*. And he understood, in a way that he had never understood it, that these creatures were *made* for, made by, war. It defined them in a way that it did not define the men and women of the Dominion; made of the ambitions of the lesser mortals—and he felt, as he watched the trailing arc of airborne blades, that he was, indeed, a lesser creature—a shadow thing, pitiful in its attempt at mimicry.

These are your enemies, kai Leonne, he thought, humbled for just a moment. But not longer; not longer. Human cries drew his attention from that lofty arena as the demons landed at last among the cerdan.

Lord Anduvin paused.

Because he paused, Kiriel realized that she had stumbled. She righted herself slowly, as if the land beneath her feet were changing, as if it offered no certain purchase for Northern boots made thin by previous battles, previous marches.

"Kiriel," he said.

She shook her head. Shook her head as her hair rose, glimmering with faint, blue light. Her sword rose as well, and she saw it more clearly than she could see trees. More clearly than she could see Telakar or any of her other companions save Anduvin.

"So," Anduvin said softly. Just that.

But Lord Telakar touched her shoulder, and she felt the iron of his grip as both threat and anchor. "Kiriel di'Ashaf," he said gravely, choosing the name with care, "we *must* run."

She did not gainsay him.

Instead, she turned a backward glance upon Kallandras of Senniel College. "Take care of them," she told him roughly.

He did not acknowledge her words, nor did she give him time; she *ran*.

Dying was not done in silence; it was not done with dignity.

And it was not done at a distance, but Ellora AKalakar felt herself freeze as the first human cries reached her ears. By her side, Korama waited, and he was virtually motionless; the armor he wore hid all trace of the rise and fall of chest, the motion that spoke of life.

Instead, he offered her what he seldom did: steel and ice, things both hard and cold. Korama, the most graceful Verrus that her House had ever produced gave her, as always, what she needed. She had seen battles last hours; seen them last days, tidy formations of men slowed by terrain and the cunning of their Commanders. She thought, for a moment, that this might last *minutes,* and the blood left her face, until she, too, stood like steel and ice.

Valedan was not by her side.

And neither were the Ospreys. She cursed the lack of light, the lack of vision, the sensitivity that darkness lent hearing. But her hand fell to her horn, and she lifted it to her lips, winding it. That, she could do.

Lord Ishavriel stepped over the dust left by shards of magical steel. He did not tarry, but he did pause a moment to touch the earth; to feel the path beneath his fingers. It was not whole, and this surprised him. Arianne?

No. No; if she were here, he would know it. His blood-bound kin were among The Lord's forces, and they did not strain against him.

Anya a'Cooper walked at his side. He was careful; when she came too close to Northern trap, he gentled the fall of her step, cushioning it so that her weight and her presence might pass unfelt above death. She was proof against much, but she was careless. Had always been careless.

"Anya," he said, when she stopped.

She shook her head, her shoulders curling inward. "The ground is screaming," she whispered.

His brow rose a fraction.

"And it's the wrong color. It's the wrong taste."

He could not afford her madness here.

Could not afford to quench it; it came with her power, and he had need of that power.

"The ground will not hurt you," he told her.

But she was no fool. Her eyes narrowed, and her hands became fists; the splayed weave of road rippled as she pulled away from a touch that should have been invisible, unfelt.

Not for the first time, he regretted the fact that the living could not be bound. Not with strength, not with power, and not with certainty. They could be killed. They could be tormented—with ease—for an eternity. But they could not in their entirety be owned.

"Anya." No impatience marred her name.

"I don't want to walk here," she whispered. "The ground will eat my feet."

"I stand on it," he replied, gesturing.

She snorted. "It doesn't care about *your* feet. You're dead."

So much wisdom in madness.

"I will carry you, Anya."

Her hesitation was profound. "You'll drop me."

"I am not mortal. You weigh little."

"You'll leave me," she said, her voice lowering and breaking against the syllables. Incongruous voice, child's voice, something not broken by the cold of the Northern Wastes.

He teased the fear as delicately as he knew how. But not with words; she was now standing at the very edge of the abyss, and he could not afford to push her in. It might consume him; her pain was bright, intense. The decades hadn't tarnished it.

"I will not leave you. Did I not protect you when we first met? Did I not carry you from mortal lands in just such a fashion? Did I not teach you how to kill the demons, so that you never need fear them again?"

It was a kinlord's truth: the surface of the words unimpeachable, the substance decayed. A lie.

But she was still a child, would always be a child. Lies could comfort her, here.

"Yes," she said, gripping the folds of cloth and shadow in her free hand. "You did all that." But she was not satisfied. "Why did you do that?"

"Because you are special, Anya." The words were like an incantation to her, a spell of momentary binding. He used them sparingly for that reason. "Because you are special, and because I knew that I would need you." He could not afford to speak the words slowly, but he did; he lost the time.

Because to lose control would be to lose so much more.

He waited, thinking that she would speak now of *love*. It amused him, at times, to hear her sniveling; to hear her speak the words.

All of Anya's love, all the love that he could see, was centered in, anchored by, need. A ferocious child, this one. An eternal child.

"Anya," he said, allowing urgency into the name. "If we do not go, *now*, to the field, The Lord will be angry."

She shrank, folding her spine into an ugly curve. It would be so easy to snap it. So easy.

"If The Lord is angry," he continued, "he will not be angry with *you;* he is never truly angered by you."

She spoke into his chest, and he nodded, allowing his chin to grace her head, her unruly, mortal hair. "Yes, he was angry about your chair. You placed it by the gate, Anya. And he did not kill you.

"But if we fail to arrive, if we fail to meet the army, he will kill me. And if I am dead, who will protect you?"

She quieted. It was payment for the humiliation of speaking the words, but it was only barely payment enough. Words such as these were costly to the *Kialli*.

But anger did not prevent motion; he walked quickly, her weight negligible. The kin were upon the road, but it was a narrow road; he navigated it with caution, anchoring himself to the sleeping earth of the valley's height.

Surrounded by the creatures she hated and feared, she was born at last to the edge of broken, splintered trees. There, she lifted her face, her lashes a single, wet clump.

He set her down, but he did not release her. The time for that might come, this eve—but it might not.

He drew his sword, and only his sword. His shield was gone, a costly reminder that even insects could sting. But the insects were gathered, now, and they gathered according to the plan of The Lord. They would pay. If not in this life, than in their next; in time, as planned, all lives would come to *Allasakar,* and in time, all souls to the Hells.

The magi manned their great crossbows; Commander Allen watched in grim silence. He waited, and his silence did not speak to, or of, patience.

Simonson came to him quietly. "The magelights were planted." At another time, the words might have been a shout; that they were barely heard said much.

But they carried the small distance between mouth and ear. The magestones had been planted, but they did not give off light—not at this distance. And he had seen their light. He bowed his head a moment.

And raised it, when light seared vision, causing him to use his hand to cover his eyes.

"Simonson?"

Simonson didn't answer.

But after a moment of blinking, he didn't need to. Commander Allen could see the crescent of something too bright to be sword, and in the ferocity of its glow, he could see the sun rising, eight distinct rays beneath the silvered embroidery of a horse upon an open field. A war-horse. The fields of Mancorvo.

Ser Alfredo waited. He was silent. He could not have found the words to speak had he desired to do so. But he was not paralyzed; he looked to the man at his side. Not his father, and not his father's Tyran; they were distant now, surrendered to night and the poverty of vision.

He held a sword. It was a cerdan's sword, a poor man's sword, but it steadied him.

As did the banner of the Tyr'agar: the symbol of the clan Leonne.

You must draw the Sun Sword, he thought, but he did not speak the words aloud; they were too much akin to prayer, and men did not pray. He was determined to be a man, upon this field. But his armor was cold, and it was heavy; it was too new. He knew that he stood, untested, by the side of a man who was also untested, and he felt his father's presence solely by absence.

The absence of cunning, of patience, of endurance. The absence of wisdom.

A hand touched his shoulder. He felt it by weight; the padded shoulder splints of his armor pressed into his collarbone.

He looked up to see the pale face of Valedan kai di'Leonne.

And he felt himself nod. Felt the pressure leave him. The Northern guard had arrayed itself before the kai Leonne like a wall of shields. A shield wall. His father had spoken of this formation before, but he had never seen it from the inside.

His Weston was not the equal of his father's; it was not the equal of his dead brother's. The words were loud, but so, too, the crash and clamor of a battle that wended its way, like slow arrow, toward them all.

He caught two names: Auralis. Kiriel.

No answers there.

She staggered again.

The night clouded vision, and lifted it; she looked up and saw the faintly glowing eyes of the kinlords who were her escort.

Saw Lord Telakar stop, eyes narrowing, hand upon drawn blade. Saw the trees in sharp relief against no moon, no light; saw the crest of the valley, the crushed fronds and burning wood that marked the passage of the armies through the heights.

But more; she saw more. Beyond the trees, as if the trees were transparent, she could see the flames of distant lives: the souls of the mortals. She had never seen them so brightly, so clearly, as she did this eve.

She opened her mouth to speak, and she roared.

In the distance, something answered.

And in the night just beyond her, she saw Kallandras of Senniel College take to the skies, shedding the weight of steps. With him went the Serra Diora—bright light, beautiful light—and her Tyran; with him, the Matriarch of Arkosa's heir. She wanted to call them back, but her voice, loosed, could not form words.

Not the words she wanted.

The words that came were harsh and guttural. But they were also beautiful, for power informed every syllable. Like a song. Like a song that would set the yearning for all other songs, at last, to rest.

She had chased peace across the continent, and across two empires, by any name, with a fervor born of ignorance; it had been an impossible goal. How might she pursue it now, listening to the unexpected wealth of its promise?

Without thought, she gathered shadow; it came, shrouding hands and arms, armoring legs, thighs, chest. She leaped, and the shadows shored her up, until she, too, had crested the meager line of standing trees.

Beyond her, moving through the armies as if they were the thinnest of veils a Serra might raise, she saw the kin, the kinlords, the *Kialli*. And she knew their names.

CHAPTER THIRTY-THREE

YOLLANA of Havalla was the oldest of the Voyani Matriarchs, and the most powerful. If an overweening arrogance informed her opinion, it was a delusion shared by the other Matriarchs, none of whom were present upon the field. Maria. Elsarre. Margret.

Aiee, she almost missed them. The Matriarchs, as the Cities that had been their first homes, stood alone. They were warped by their isolation, twisted by it, hurt by it, and in the end, entirely informed by it. It made them what they were.

But only Yollana of Havalla had had to walk this road.

Even Evallen had been spared the worst of it: the deliberate murder of kin. No execution, that; it was a darkness from which the Matriarch of Havalla would never emerge. And it was a darkness that she did not wish to will her children. Or her grandchildren, not that either of her daughters had been responsible enough yet to *have* them.

There was no silence here; a dry chuckle—a host of dry chuckles—accompanied this shrewish observation. Gallows humor, it was called in the North. In the South? Many things, but diffuse.

There is no light here, she thought.

And then, seeing *Balagar* unsheathed, she winced. No woman's light.

But in truth, she had more in common with the Tyrs on this field than she had with the women they sheltered or hid; she bore the responsibility of her family, as they bore the responsibility of their clans, and they would send many of those clansmen to their deaths this eve.

But not in darkness, she thought.

Her hands gripped the sharpest edges of the Heart of Havalla, pressing into them as if they could draw blood. And they did; scant offering, but necessary.

Wield us thus, an old voice said, *and they will know.*

Aye, she replied, bitter and determined, *they will know. But they must know. This is not their land; they left it, and willingly.*

Not so willingly, Na'yolla. Not so willingly as that.

They chose.

So, too, did the first Matriarch of Havalla.

Aye, her voice was there, strongest and coldest: the most isolated of the dead.

I was strong enough to deny him, Daughter, that woman said, unnamed in this bitter place. *But not forever. I have much in common with the* Kialli.

He betrayed you.

He betrayed them, she replied, remote, no quiver at all in the words. *And still they serve.*

You did not serve.

Because I died.

Branches flew over the tips of drawn blades; leaves were sundered. Men screamed in rage and pain, their cries mingling; she could discern no individuals at all, and in a fashion, this was mercy.

But she could see—gift and curse—that their blood made the

field slick; the earth drank it slowly, and found in the dying some power. This, she had been warned to expect.

And she had seen war before; she had been Matriarch during the last Tyr's folly. She and her kin had come like carrion through deserted villages, taking—as they had always taken—what they needed. Pitying the serafs whose lives were bound to land, and only land; whose feet did not know the freedom of the *Voyanne*.

But it was illusory freedom at best; a freedom given to children and to those who did not hold true power.

She surrendered it as she lifted the Heart above her bowed, silvered head. No rain fell, but water adorned her. She lifted her chin, and spoke words that the din swallowed. They did not ease pain; they did not prevent death; they did not grant freedom to those who now struggled against the armies of the Lord of Night.

But they granted something else: vision.

She called for Summer, and anchored in the heart of Winter trees, it came.

Darkness.

Darkness, sound, storm without rain or lightning. Thunder, like an ancient dialect, resounded in ear, as if it had a magic and a life of its own.

Valedan waited a heart's beat, and then he swung the sword in his hands; it came to rest, blade tip above the lip of an ancient sheath. A war sheath; no pretty gold to give grace or beauty to its form; nothing to make of it a lord's sword. Pomp, circumstance, all of these things forgotten in the imperative of survival.

He sheathed the blade.

Ser Alfredo, by his side, tensed, but he did not speak; did not question his Tyr.

Of all men present, he would not: he understood what the sheathing of the blade meant, and he honored it in an entirely Southern fashion. With his silence.

But he did not bow head, or neck, or back; he did not bend knee. Instead, he lifted his sword, the sword given to pars and Tyran. To men whose swords served the living Tyr while life remained them.

Before them, in a loose grouping that would have shamed Tyran, the Ospreys. Their blades were readied; the only thing that they showed Ser Alfredo or Ser Valedan were their backs. Northern backs, all, the colors of the Kings muted by night's fall, the language—hoarse, harsh, unenviable—denied them by the clamor of sword and scream.

But if their feet remained planted, their hands moved, weaving, bouncing in air. He recognized it as conversation, something given to the mute in place of tongue and lip.

"Valedan!" one man cried.

And Valedan kai di'Leonne bent forward, into his knees, his hand upon the hilt of crescent blade, his eyes narrowing. Too much darkness, here; even the torchlight was swallowed by it.

Father, Alfredo thought. He could not see the Callestan standard. He could barely see the Tyr'agar's. But the latter drew his eye, and beneath it, proud and silent, Ser Anton di'Guivera and the young standard-bearer. The best of the South, Alfredo thought, and the most naïve of the North. Is this what Valedan was?

And then thought shifted, breaking, changing; the ground spewed dirt in a dry, loud cough that ended with flame and limb. Red light trailed across the air, like caress, like limb, and beneath its glow, the demons were suddenly there.

The Sun Sword, Alfredo thought. He wanted to say it. For the second time in his life, and only the second, he cursed Southern honor, Southern vow; he cursed the dead, and he cursed the living. He cursed wildly, almost blindly—because it was better than praying. Men did not pray.

Men did *not* pray.

And the Ospreys were *men.* They had been called Northern demons by any cerdan who cared to speak their name; they were hated, but they were feared, and it was a good fear.

He saw it now: they did not hesitate. They did not falter. Only one of them stood his ground, and he, the Captain, Primus Duarte. His hands were wide, splayed, flat—but the weakness that lack of sword should have meant meant nothing to him.

Truly Northern, he *shouted,* and his men, his *women,* leaped, some to the right, some to the left, and some forward, their harsh Weston alive with the sound of steel.

But they were not numerous, these Ospreys; they were not Tyran. They did not cleave to the side of the Tyr'agar. Only two men did: Ser Anton and Ser Alfredo. And Ser Anton had drawn blade, but his attention was now wholly taken with the horse he rode and the boy he protected.

Old man. Proud and fierce.

The young hands gripped banner's pole and held it aloft.

To the left and right, the Ospreys danced, and the center thinned: it was to the center that the red sword came, seeking egress.

Seeking, Ser Alfredo knew, the kai Leonne. Boy Tyr, he had

been called. And boy Tyr, he was. He stood, hand upon blade, knees bent, shoulders perfectly still.

The demons roared; some in pain and some in triumph. Ospreys fell to talons, but none to sword; they bled but they did not—not yet—falter; their line was no Northern line; it was flexible, contorted, a thing in motion. Like whip. Or chain. If their line was broken, and it was, it was not destroyed. To the left and the right, Ser Alfredo saw them lunge and parry; saw blood adorn their faces, in the brief, short glow of torches. Some of those torches fell, and they were guttered instantly by the feet of the servants of the Lord of Night.

But in the pause of extinguished light, the Ospreys were not flightless.

Nightmare fell to their swords, their plain, their *Northern* swords. Alfredo had heard rumors: more, had heard the claim of Ser Valedan kai di'Leonne. Had he believed it?

Maybe.

But that belief and this, this act of witnessing, were different in ways that words, Torra or Weston, could not, could *never* describe. His own sword swung wide as the shadows seeped over torchlight, extinguishing it.

Death, he thought, wild now, a boy.

Death.

But instead, light came.

She saw it all: for just a moment, she saw it all: the whole of the field, alive with the Summer's glow. The demons paused a moment, drawing collective breath, and the Heart of Havalla beat loud in her hands.

This will not last.

No. It wouldn't. But it was all she could do, and she had always done everything within her power.

And in the light, sky still dark, sword still red, Valedan kai di'Leonne moved. As the demon with sword and shield came down to one side of the banner, he lowered his head, tensed his shoulders, and then drew blade. It was fast—it was almost too fast to *see*.

The creature *roared,* and Ser Alfredo flinched; the sound itself was like the cry of a living warrior, but this enemy seemed, in darkness, to be without form or shape. Still he did not step back, and his sword did not waver.

Carelo, Alfredo thought, his kai's name come unbidden and unlooked for. *Do you see?*

As if gaining the pride and the approval of a dead man might
somehow turn the face of battle.

And perhaps it would. Ser Alfredo had seen Valedan kai
di'Leonne use exactly this stance, this move, before. In the fields
outside of Callesta. In the fields of the Green Valley. Beneath the
watchful and critical eyes of Tyrs, before the hesitant but growing
respect of cerdan, he had executed just such a *perfect* maneuver.

But it had never been like this. Never.

The red sword toppled. The arm that held it gouted black liquid,
and where it fell, it burned.

But there was so little *to* burn in this place, the growth crushed
by so many feet, so many hooves, the soil still damp from the tor-
rential rains.

The kai's sword circled again, and again its edge was so fast Ser
Alfredo could barely follow it.

But this time the creature was prepared. If he had no sword with
which to parry, he had shield, and the shield held. Would have to
hold; the creature was a head and a half taller than the kai Leonne,
and the demon was twice—at least twice—his width.

With a cry, Alfredo launched himself forward, taking cold,
nameless steel and giving it a brief taste of history. He heard a shout
given the syllables and textures of a name; he did not falter.

He heard screams as well, but they were beneath him now; he
had found his feet, had found his courage, had given it flight. He
found words, and he offered them; but they were names, and only
names.

Carelo's name. Callesta's name.

Boy became man, as blood fell.

Much of it was his own. But it fell without pain, for a moment;
without cost. For the edge of his sword was black in the pale, pale
gold of muted sun: he had made his mark.

Would have died in the making of it, were it not for the voice of
the wind.

But the wind's voice—a howl, a thing of rage and fury—was
not like the roar of demons: it offered form and substance. It offered
life.

Something heavy fell at the back of the large demon, beyond the
reach of his shield. It was not graceful; the wind did not allow for

grace; it seemed instead to shed the weight it carried roughly, as if glad to be relieved of the burden.

A sword caught golden light, containing it: it was not a Northern sword, yet it was not Southern. It seemed to glow a moment, and when it moved, it traced a path across the air. It traced a word: Ser Alfredo saw it clearly, although he did not understand its full import.

Remordan.

"Get out of the way, you *fool!*" Northern voice. Southern words. They made little sense. But the blow that followed them—from a foot, he thought—made more; Ser Alfredo kai di'Callesta flew across the ground, rolling awkwardly.

An inch from where he had been standing, ebon hand was buried in broken ground. But only the hand; it was sheared from the limb by the arc of the blade.

Auralis AKalakar had returned to the Ospreys.

There was death here.

Death, at last and always, among the kin. Had he feared fire?

No. In truth, even before the donning of the ring, the tongues of flame spoke no threatening language, filled him with no horror. History did, and it was history he fled, his blade as wild, his cuts as frenzied, as they had been over a decade past, in the Green Valley.

Then, he had faced Callestans, intent upon the destruction of the Black Ospreys. Now?

A *clean* fight.

He roared, his words caught and taken by wind, his blade's edge leaving a trail of body parts in its wake. Some of these he recognized as they fell in the orange glow: arms, legs, fingers. Some, he did not. Lack of familiarity did not discourage him. Nothing did.

He heard Alexis' sharp voice; heard Fiara's whoop of victory and recognition. He heard Duarte, piercing and clean, and saw the trail of the Primus' magic across the whole of the slender space that had become his tableau, his circle. No rules constrained him in this particular circle; there was only one imperative.

And he warred with it, this foreign blade singing death and denying him his own. Without pause for thought, his voice joined the Ospreys, becoming a part of the chaos that he had defined as life over the past decade.

As if he were in the basin in The Kalakar fields, as if he were in drill, he raised his own, forcing breath to rise above the din of sword and scream, the movement of men. The Ospreys had no standard here; none save that of the Tyr'agar.

But having chosen to protect that standard, he stood in its lee, leaping above the arms of fell creatures, and seeing in their darkness, a mirror of his own. So easy, to give in to the darkness.

So easy to choose life, to choose cowardice.

But the flight of his earliest years he now denied. He could do that much. He could do more. Had done more, in villages like Essla and Russo, in a war that had nothing, in the end, to do with soldiery or supremacy.

Had he ceded that battle?

Aye.

He had *saved* the villagers Kiriel had come to protect. He had let them call him hero in their broken Weston, their awkward syllables, an attempt to bridge the gap between cultures, the distance between murderer and soldier.

Too great a distance.

Far too great.

Wild laughter trailed from his lips like blood; he coughed. He fought.

Thinking, again and always, that there was an ending here if he had the courage to face it.

The wind swept Kallandras to the heights of a different battle. Air was no less battlefield than the flat earth below; the horses did not mar it, and only the powerful could attain it. But the powerful had gathered.

Meralonne APhaniel was a wild, white light that shone, cold as moon in desert, his sword dancing in the lattice of its own afterimage. In its rise and fall, Kallandras could almost discern the ten-pointed star that the *Kovaschaii* first learned to dance in the labyrinths below the Southern cities, and he fell into step at the side of the magi, his weapons raised. They reflected no light; acknowledged none. Nor did he require it, but as it burned in the heart of the field below, he found comfort in its presence.

It was a comfort denied him by the wind's voice, the wind's imperative. The Old Earth did not sleep beneath him, and his hold was therefore as weak as it had ever been. Leashed, the wind obeyed him—but barely, barely. The cost of power was writ in the struggle to control what he had summoned; to control both it, and the impulse of blades that were made from the heart of demons. His own, he thought, seeing again the taking of their shapes when he had first accepted them from the hands of Meralonne APhaniel. His own, and the Lord of Night's.

Even in thought, he did not name him here.

He took pinions in the wind's fold, snapping them. He took limbs, and in the taking, wounds. He had seldom worn armor; when he had, it was disguise and impediment. Here, his shirt split as claw rent it, and the thin layer of flesh broke as well.

But he felt no pain.

He summoned the power of the *Kovaschaii*, and with it, bore the cost of the summoning: his brothers' voices, all.

They were aware of him, as they had not been in years. Aware of his battle, his location; aware of the foes he had chosen to face. Had chosen to kill, and not by the command of the Lady. Not by her order did he fight them; not by the command of the elders. Nothing marked him but the earliest of his vows, the earliest of his lives. But these were scar enough.

The contempt of his brothers, their silent anger, weapons.

He bore them.

He fought *for* them, although they did not know it, could never acknowledge its truth. He opened his lips in song, and song came: he sang of death, and the kin heard this imperative and no more; they were like maddened creatures.

And maddened, they lost all caution.

Elena and Telakar arrived at the field's edge, and the *Kialli* lord froze.

She, aware of the least of his movements, could not help but be aware of their absence. Her gift, meager, unused, preserved her life: she leaped to the side and rolled as his hand bisected the air that she had, seconds ago, occupied. It buried itself in the side of a tree, falling inches beneath bark.

He had that much control.

She *knew* that he had done it on purpose. To give her *time*. She took advantage of the gift, her own propelling her forward, her knees rolling up to chest as she pushed herself along the ground, away from the shadows that no light cast.

"Telakar!" she cried.

He swung again, both hands now, and again he bisected tree; great branches shuddered above her, as something far older than she shed dead branches in a crash and tumble that spoke of the forest's age.

"*Run,*" he said.

Command. His voice did not shake; no more did his hands as he withdrew them from scored, standing trunk. He stumbled toward her, and she saw that he fought compulsion here, in the lee of the battle.

It was not a compulsion that she had considered when she had fled Russo at his side. Not a compulsion that she had feared, and she *had* cause to fear him.

The Lord of Night was not upon the field.

Could not be.

But his will was present, and it commanded obedience and death. Had Telakar warned her of this? Yes. A dozen times, his quiet voice laced with threat or promise.

And Elena Tamaraan, who had owned nothing living in her life—for she disdained horses—hesitated for just a moment as he stood framed by trees and the red fire of battle beyond his turned back. She leaped to one side as he moved, almost dissolving and re-forming, his crossing of distance was such a blur. Her mouth was dry.

Her memory was vivid.

She met his eyes, and it was almost the last thing she did: they were devoid of death, of the desire for death, of even the desire to cause pain. She was held by them, by fear, by wavering determination.

Just long enough to bleed.

But not to die.

"Telakar!" she cried, as if reason was something that was left them.

Branches *shattered*. Her feet slid across damp undergrowth, crushed leaves, slender stems. Her shoulders took them up, and her hair caught them as she rose; she was mired in the forest carpet, some part of it.

He would kill her.

She knew he would kill her. But she also knew that he did not desire her death. The lack of desire made her hesitate again, and this time, her arm was gashed from shoulder to elbow; she could afford no more mistakes.

But she had seen no slavery in her life that was kin to this. He was powerful. Worse, she had given him her life, and had almost lost it as a result: had she time to *think,* she might have hated him enough that slavery, the loss of will, seemed a just retribution for his untold sins.

She dodged again, and she was aware that his movements,

graceful and deadly, were also slow and deliberate. Aware, as she watched him, that even this much was costly.

And aware, last, that she could change it all by the simple expedience of using the gift of Havalla.

But she was afraid. Not of death; the fear of that was almost too visceral to be felt. All of her response was instinctive, a shadowy offshoot of the bloodline of the Matriarch of Arkosa. Of the Matriarch of *any* line. With its use, its instinctive, its immediate use, she might continue to live.

Not forever.

She had desired to be no man's master. Had barely, she thought, if ever, been able to master herself.

"Telakar!" she shouted.

He shook his head. If he could speak at all—and she thought he must be able to—he denied her the comfort of words. Because that comfort was entirely illusory, and it would end in only one way.

There was a moment between decision and surrender, and it came in pain. The pain itself was clean, the wound shallow. She had time to draw breath, time to keep moving; had she been older, had she lived the cloistered life of a clanswoman, perhaps she would have died regardless.

Instead, she spoke a name. His name.

He froze.

The saying of the name was more awkward than she could have imagined; syllables struggled against her lip and tongue, as if seeking freedom. She lost some of them; had to struggle to catch them before they spilled beyond her grasp. She had to pull at them, pull them in, make sense of their discordance. He was *Telakar,* but the saying of his name, in the end, was almost beyond her. Years ago, she had heard—sitting in the comfort of an adult lap that memory did not name—that demons had *names,* that those names were *true,* and that they, decrying all things truthful, could be bound by them.

She had wondered, as a child, why demons were a threat. Just speak their name, she had thought. Because to her, then, names were known. The names of her mother, her Ona, her cousins; the names of her uncles, her enemies, her rivals. What power could there really be in a name?

As so often happened as she stumbled through adulthood from the wilds of that youth, she repented of her ignorance and her smug, arrogant certainty. She knew, now, why names were no small thing.

Knew that most men could not *say* what had to be said, even given everything that knowledge required.

Yollana of Havalla had revealed the scant syllables that might, in the end, bind this lord of demons. And Elena spoke them, struggled to speak them, as if her tongue was thick with fever or dry with desert thirst. They did not grant her knowledge.

But the struggle granted her a dim understanding of power.

Lord Telakar of the *Kialli* did not waver. His arm was frozen in the sweeping arc that might end in death or dismemberment, and his eyes were cold. Night cold. Desert night.

Aye, she spoke his name; felt her awareness of him grow until she could barely separate the knowledge of him from the knowledge, unconscious and unquestioned, of herself. She lifted an arm, and mirroring her, he lifted his—as if all will had been removed from him, and he remained a puppet, no more.

She rose; the ground was an unwelcome bed, and beyond its prickly repose, the sound of dying was a distant accompaniment. But it was not her death, and not his.

What can I do with this? she thought, rubbing her chin; feeling the warmth of blood and pain from wrist to elbow. She tore a strip from the edge of her shirt, as she had done in the aftermath of countless skirmishes before, and bound the wound.

Still, he waited, frozen.

"I'm sorry," she said. No power in the words, but she still had to struggle to offer them.

"Why?" he asked. His lips moved; his arm did not.

"Because, I—" She lowered her arm slowly, and his at last fell away. He stood as he often stood in the nightscape, a creature of shadow, a symptom of fear. "Why?" she asked.

The question was permission, of a type.

He nodded carefully. "Better," he told her, as if she were still his captive, still his unwilling student.

"Better?" Bitter word. "How?"

"The Lord," he replied softly, "is bound in some fashion by his covenant." He approached her slowly now. "And I, in turn, by my own. I am sorry," he added, reaching out, the edge of sharp fingers brushing the awkward dressing she had made for her arm. "I did not wish to harm you."

"You had no choice."

"No," he replied. "None at all."

But he had moved slowly. Deliberately. She remembered.

"And because I have your name, you still have no choice."

"None," he replied, just as still, just as distant. "What will you do with the power you have been granted, Elena Tamaraan?"

She shook her head. "I don't know. How long does it last?"

"Until I die," he replied, as if speaking of something insignificant. "Or until you do."

"I can't release you?"

"Not in safety, Elena." His frown was a marked gesture of his disapproval. "You know this," he added, and he turned, framed by broken trees, toward the battle that raged in the distance.

"And if I release you before then?"

"You will die."

"But I—"

"Yes," he said coldly. "You did not desire this power. You did not ask for it." He made the words an accusation. Fair enough; they were. She was still that child, the warmth of distant lap a thing to be yearned for, the comfort of strange stories an artifact of campfire and the space peace left in the evening sky.

"Did you know?" she whispered.

"That The Lord would find me? That he would bend me to his will?" Telakar laughed. The laughter, like the lord, was wild and dark. Beautiful, but full of something that might have been despair had it touched his features at all. "I have never been free," he told her.

"Before you left—"

"Before I died?"

She fell silent. But the clash of arms, the cries of the dead, were louder now. As if the battle moved toward them both, drawn to the heights by the captive presence of Lord Telakar.

"Not even then, little one. Perhaps especially not then."

"I could—"

He slapped her.

Or he would have; his hands stopped an inch from her face, and then traced the line of her jaw in a cold caress. She shivered.

"Yes," he said, with the first hint of smile, no matter how bitter. "There is a danger in mastery. The kinlords are subtle in captivity, and they are prone to seek what freedom they can from the unwary."

She swallowed and shook her head, removing herself from easy reach. Wanting, instead, to remain by his side, in his shadow.

"I knew," he added. "But I had hoped—" His silence was powerful.

"Hoped what?"

She saw him struggle, and realized that he fought against her. Against the question that she laid upon him, unthinking, like a compulsion. She would have taken it back, and he saw that hesitance and that revulsion in her features.

Smiled, as if to dim them both. "That Kiriel di'Ashaf might indeed prove true to her birth," he replied. "She has the ability to command us all, if she gathers the power and bends it to her will."

Elena shook her head. But she knew that he spoke no lie. *Knew* it.

"But she—"

"Yes," he said, word shaded with gentle regret. For her, he thought. For Elena Tamaraan, forsworn. "I thought to spare you this."

"Then you did know."

"I know that the Matriarchs are born of lines that had vision beyond your comprehension. If any could deliver me into your hands, it would be that old woman."

"And you let her live."

"I had that choice, yes."

"Why?"

"Because, Elena Tamaraan, I had no desire to kill you. Even now—"

"You do want to kill me." Sharp as shock, that knowledge.

"Yes. Of course. But it is not the only thing I desire."

"Why do you want my death?"

"You hold my name, little one."

"But—" knowledge, blossoming from the seeds of his silences. "The Lord of Night holds your name."

"Yes."

She could not ask the next question. Did not have to.

He laughed. "You see, and if your vision is poor and blunted, it is still cunning. Yes, Elena. No one of my kind is content with captivity. We accept with grace what we cannot change; we accept with grace what we cannot defeat. It is the rule of the Hells."

"Power."

"Indeed." He turned his face away from the battlefield.

"Why do your names hold such power?" she asked, unwilling to look away. "Ours don't."

He laughed. "No. Yours never have."

"But yours—"

And laughter died. He faced her, as he had faced her when she had first awakened, and even secure in the knowledge of her power, of his name, she took a step back.

"We are not like the gods, Elena Tamaraan. But we are kin to them: the Firstborn. Our names have always held some power; the power of intimacy; the power to invoke presence even at a distance. It has been costly. Our greatest of vows were once made on the strength of our names and our blood, where we were strong, and upon the strength of the names of those we chose to serve, where we were not strong enough."

She said, "But that changed."

"For us? Yes, Elena. It changed."

"How?"

"You know so little history," he replied. He did not wish to answer her question. "And perhaps that is wisest. But if you ask this, I will answer; I will not use guile to bewitch you." It was, his tone implied, beneath his dignity.

She hesitated, and then she nodded.

"The Lord's mantle bound us, by name," he replied. "It was the only way in which we could travel, or so he said; the only protection afforded our identity."

"He lied to you?"

"Oh, no, he did not lie. He was a god," Telakar replied bitterly. "He *is* a god."

"But he—"

"We did not understand the mantle; it was a gift, of sorts, from the gods whose will he was forced to accept. But we came to understand its purpose and its use when we left this place, and when we stood at last before him, the strongest of our number realized that we could not stand *beside* him. We could stand in his shadow; we could serve at his whim. Only at his whim, should he desire it.

"Half of our number perished, in a fashion."

"In a fashion?"

"What is death, in the Hells?" He shrugged. "They understood what they had become—how *little* they had become—and they chose to challenge him. He let the names go, and they fled to the charnel winds, the breath of the Hells."

"And the rest of you?"

Telakar shrugged. "Of what use, in the long game, is destruction? We sheltered our memory. We held onto our names. We served. And we discovered, in time, that the names held a vastly different power, even upon the plane, than they had once held.

"Slave to those names, some handful of our number returned. I do not know how," he added. "I do not know why. But what the mantle granted The Lord was not absolute. He is not present; *you* are. And you are of this plane.

"But the god—"

"Do not forget it," he added, with an intensity that had made the rest of his words seem careless, casual. "You are of this world. And although he is powerful, vastly more powerful than you or your kin will ever be, he is not.

"But we tarry," he added, "and there is a cost."

"What cost?"

"Kiriel di'Ashaf," he replied. "You should have killed her."

"You knew I couldn't."

"I knew you wouldn't," he agreed. He held out a hand. "We must go, Elena. Either to the field, or away."

"Why?"

"Because, of the kinlords, there are only two—or three—who can now stand at the side of the darkness-born Queen."

"Why do you call her that?"

"Why do you think?"

She shook her head.

"She was born for one reason, and one alone. I do not understand how she survived," he added quietly. "She was Isladar's, from start to finish; some part of his game. Some part of his plan.

"But she was meant to be Queen of the Hells," he added, and again she realized that her question was a compulsion that he could not ignore. So much power, in a name, in the holding of a name. "The Lord has no desire to return to the Hells; nor can he now ignore what he accepted as his demesne long ages ago.

"She can't rule," Elena said, uncertainty becoming certainty as her gift washed over the words. "She's mortal."

"She is that," Telakar replied. "She will never be anything else. But . . . there are ways. In theory, there are ways. And I have no doubt that what she faces in the Hells, should she ever live to reach them, should she stand at the foot of the ebon hall, and walk its length to the throne there, will make our first rebellion against our Lord look insignificant and weak by comparison."

"You think she'll fail."

He said nothing.

He could say nothing. It wasn't a question, and the question in the words was not, in the end, a question she desired an answer to. Truth, to the Voyani, had consequences. The holding of secrets. The owning of them.

What price could she be asked to pay, if she held too much of them? But she could not stop herself from asking. It was both her nature and the nature of her gift; she *knew* that he thought Kiriel di'Ashaf would, as The Lord before her, succeed. "Then why didn't you kill her?"

"Because," he said, with a smile that showed teeth, a glimmer of light in the night sky, "she is only mortal. And to serve a weak Lord presents opportunities to those of us who still seek the long freedom."

All truth. All of it.

She took the hand that he had not moved; his fingers curled around her shaking palm, folding lifeline into invisibility beneath the flawless curve of his ebon skin.

But it was not all of the truth.

"Yes," she said, shaking slightly.

He did not ask her what she had chosen; he knew. He caught her in his arms, and the forest disappeared.

The magi had fire in their arsenal. It was one of the oldest of their magics, and it had been tried and tested on many fields, perfected with an eye to effect, as if death were the simple result of academic calculation, and not the desired end.

It mattered little to Commander Allen; to see the magi work in concert was . . . disconcerting. But he had learned to expect only what they could offer, and he was impressed in spite of himself.

Impressed until the moment the slender, quiet woman whose name escaped him began to shout in something approaching terror. He had enough time to throw himself into the prescribed boundaries of their domain upon the field, no more.

The enemy proved that it, too, had mastery of fire.

Those outside of the boundaries of protection withered and died like scorched grass. This close, he could smell their charred flesh; could reach out to touch what remained of their bodies.

He did neither. Instead, he turned to the magi and shouted, "Can you hold?"

She didn't answer with words, but fire lapped at invisible canopy, seeking purchase there. It descended slowly, inch by inch, a falling veil. But it did descend.

And in falling, the sky knew a different color.

Sendari di'Sendari sat astride his mount at the side of his oldest friend. The color of their horses seemed, in the odd night, to be of a kind; they might have been brothers, descended from the same stallion, the same mare.

But the hint, the promise, of day blossomed between the distant tops of trees, lending color to their coats and manes, and lending urgency to this almost funereal march. The weariness of ignorance had been a burden these many days, and it vexed him—but the sudden change in the dark hue of sky washed exhaustion away. It left something less pleasant in its wake: fire. Widan fire.

Almost instinctively, he looked to his hands, to the white webs that scarred their backs, the regalia of his first true encounter with the anger of the Widan Cortano di'Alexes.

It was to that man, Sword's Edge, that his second glance strayed, and it was held there.

"Sword's Edge," Alesso snapped, granting the respect of title, but little else.

At this distance, Sendari could feel the heat of flames he could not—quite—see.

He knew that to do so was impossible. Knew it, but could not look away from the pale face of Ser Cortano.

"We are here," the Sword's Edge said sharply, wearily. "The battle is less than a mile away. Will you join it now, Alesso?"

"If I join it, what will I see?" the General asked, shorn of the title he had taken for himself, and left only the truth of the title he had earned in the valleys. It suited him better, Sendari thought. The whole of this battle, the changing contours of its geography, the shift in the games and the politics of necessity—all of these were more natural to him, in the end, than the charade of his short time upon the plateau.

Lord's man. Truly.

"What you must," Cortano said, tight-lipped. "But I must warn you now, Ser Alesso di'Alesso, that Anya a'Cooper is, in all probability, upon that field."

"Why?"

"Because the fire has only a single signature," Cortano replied, speaking more of the truth about the Widan's gift than was his wont in the presence of those who were not Widan-designate or adept. "And it consumes the air above the valleys with the strength of her name."

Alesso wheeled. Peder kai el'Sol was almost upon him, and their horses jostled for position in the uneasy dark of unnatural night. "Kai el'Sol." Much more was granted Peder kai el'Sol than had been granted the Sword's Edge, although only the informal title had been offered to either.

The kai el'Sol drew *Saval*.

She shone so brightly in the scant light that had Alesso been any other man he would have shielded his vision from the sight of her.

Sendari did. Cortano did.

But Alesso grew taller in the saddle, and the hand that did not bind reins now gripped the haft of *Terra Fuerre*. The earth's fire. The fire of man.

"Go," he said. "I release you from the army, and from my command. Do what must be done."

The kai el'Sol did not tender a bow; upon horseback, because it was awkward, it was not required. But he lifted the sword, and in a moment, two other men joined him: Samadar and Samiel. The oldest and the youngest of the Radann par el'Sol.

They drew their blades in unison, and the fire that lit the distant sky paled into insignificance as the three were joined. Their beardless faces, their dark eyes, seemed to mark them at last as kin; the blood that ran beneath the pale surface of skin meant less than the swords—and the duties incumbent upon their wielders.

"We will meet, upon that field," Alesso told Peder kai el'Sol. "I will bring the army there."

"And under whose banner will you fight, Tyr'agar?"

"My own," Alesso said, with a predator's grin. "And only my own."

The banner of the sun ascendant. The banner of Tyrs.

Peder nodded. But before the light took his eyes entirely, he said softly, "What of the kai Garrardi?"

"He is a fool," Alesso replied, "but he *is* a man."

Auralis AKalakar's presence brought them a moment of peace.

And to call such carnage peace? Valedan kai di'Leonne shook his head. Wind swept his hair; warrior's knot held true, but only for the moment.

He had thought to hate death, to hate loss, to bear in full the responsibility for each one that occurred in sight of his banner. But the deaths were so quick, so brutal, so senseless that they seemed a thing of dream, of nightmare—something so entirely beyond his control he could but witness.

Ser Alfredo kai di'Callesta came to stand by his side. The younger man was bleeding; his shoulder was red, his armor rent. But it was a clean wound, and it did not bow him; did not cause him to pale. He bowed to the Tyr'agar, even here, upon this field, where so much death waited the unwary.

Valedan caught him by the shoulder—the uninjured shoulder—and forced him up, denying him obeisance. He could not do so in words; they carried poorly upon the field. *How did orders travel?* he thought, as the noises that shock kept at bay at last gained their true strength.

"Callesta bears witness," Alfredo said firmly, loudly, trusting the strength of his voice in a way that Valedan did not. "You have fulfilled your oath." And he held out his hand.

His hand.

Valedan looked at him a full moment before discerning his intent, and then he shook himself, gaining at last his full height. "Your sword, kai Callesta," he said. If the words did not carry, Alfredo betrayed nothing.

"She has never been drawn in such a battle," the young kai said. He took her hilt from Valedan's hand.

"If we are strong," Valedan replied, his hand falling to the hilt of his other sword as if drawn there at last by the weight of history unfolding, "she will never be drawn in like fashion again."

"Aye," Alfredo replied, and then with a weary grin that was beyond his years, added, "or if we are weak."

Valedan kai di'Leonne drew the Sun Sword upon the field.

And as one, demon voices fell silent across the length and breadth of the valley. Not even the sword of the kai el'Sol had commanded the whole of their attention.

Valedan began to move forward, to move away from the banner Ser Anton and Aidan protected—they were still alive, thank whatever gods now watched and guided them all—guarded. He spared them that glance, no more, but was rewarded for his effort by the minimal nod of Ser Anton di'Guivera.

And then he had no more time. In ones and twos, he gathered the Ospreys by the simple expedient of motion; they followed in the wake of the Sun Sword, his cerdan. No; more than that: his very Northern, very unruly Tyran. Bound to him, by choice and by distant command, they coalesced, and their eyes were dark and shining.

Even Auralis AKalakar joined him.

"The fires," Duarte said, speaking not as Primus but as mage. And he lifted a hand. To the West, to the whole of the West, one flank of the demon army was bathed in an orange glow.

And before them, flesh consumed as armor melted away in rivulets and screams, the Northern army. Commander Allen had chosen that position; Valedan wondered what he thought of it now, if he had time to think at all.

If Duarte feared the noise and clamor of battle, he did not show it. Instead, he gestured and his words became clear, each syllable sharp enough to cut.

"There is a mage among them," he told the kai Leonne. "And only one, of significance. The fire that rains upon the Southern half of *our* army belongs, in its entirety, to that one."

"How can you know this?"

"I can see it," he said coldly. "The kin are our enemies here," he added, "but the mage will do more damage before the hour is out than the demons have done since they arrived."

Valedan nodded. He gave a command, and unhorsed, the Ospreys followed as he began to run.

Ser Mareo kai di'Lamberto was not deaf, although he might wish it; he was not blind. When the flames lit up the Southern edge of the valley, he bit back a cry as deep—as awed—as the cries that were now raised by his men. Fear was contained, wordless, in the sound that rose above the distant din. He had no time to address it. And no choice but to do so.

The momentary lapse in Lambertan concentration was costly; the demons that enfolded them on all sides made headway through their number, for it was clear that they had expected the sudden onset of Widan flame.

Matriarch, he thought grimly. Through the fire's height, vision distorted, he could see nothing clearly. *Matriarch. The debt that we will owe if we succeed here will change the face of the Dominion.* From the folds of his cloak, he drew the silvered, ancient horn that she had given him with as much grace as Voyani gifted any clansman.

He lifted it to his mouth, touched its rim, and felt warmth against his skin; it was an unexpected heat. He drew breath; the warmth spread across his lips, his cheeks, his brow; swept across his knotted hair, his narrowed eyes, fell down the line of his stiff spine. Aie, he wanted a horse beneath him, now. He needed that visibility.

But no; she had seen even that much.

He winded the horn in the long notes of the clan Lamberto, and for a moment, the horn was all sound in the valley; nothing disturbed the clarity, the perfect tune, of its notes. He was not given speech; that would be sundered by the fighting that occurred in every direction.

But this, this horn, the voice of Lamberto—it was heard. And where it was heard, he saw that his men fell silent, their features turned cold and grim. Soldiers' expressions, all.

He let the horn fall to his side again, and lifted his empty hand; this he ran across the clasp that held the Voyani cloak in place. It was tarnished, but it was strong; no movement dislodged it. Not even the searching play of fingers.

He found what he sought; the pin bit his finger, drawing blood. It should have been a minor wound, but this was a foreign magic, a foreign offering; he felt the pain of it clearly, as if it were poison insect's sting. Too small a pain to be acknowledged; too small a hurt to be truly considered costly.

He noticed no change. But he had chosen to place his trust in the gifts of the Havallan Matriarch; she had not promised that he would see himself.

She had promised, instead, that the men he commanded would see him, and know him.

The Northerners were beyond him; the fires that consumed their line, eating away at their best-laid defenses, their long plans, also beyond him. Even had his own men not been beset, it would have been thus; he therefore offered them the barest of nods. The respect of a Southern Tyr.

Then he turned his full attention upon the demons that he faced. They were not legion; the Lambertans had superiority of numbers. But the Lambertans were *men,* and they tired; they needed light to see by, and in its lack, they faltered. The shadows which obscured the true form of the creatures that now took slow command over the Western flank of the valley brought no comfort, for in that darkness, imagination made grimmer the details that the eye could not readily perceive.

Yet it was clear to Mareo kai di'Lamberto that if these creatures were not men, they still labored under a leader. They withdrew and regrouped, and they focused their attacks, hiding concert of effort in savagery and bestiality.

And so, girded by Tyran and the folds of his darkened banner, he withdrew the last of the Havallan gifts: the bowl. Hard to perform such ablutions as it required here; the ground itself seemed to shift beneath his feet, echoing the blows of the enemy.

He offered the bowl no water, no wine; he had no time to experiment. Instead, with a grimace, he opened the mound of his palm with the edge of *Balagar.* Blood fell. Not enough of it, he thought grimly, but it was his own.

He waited.

CHAPTER THIRTY-FOUR

FROM the heights of the valley, Lord Ishavriel descended, Anya in his arms. She was already beyond him; one hand trapped the silver webs of road and held them fast; the other summoned flame. And it was a flame that was almost kin to the elemental fire, with a single notable difference: it was entirely within her control.

She had always been impressive. He could admit that, in the absence of her whining chatter, her annoying disobedience. What power she had—and she had much—was nowhere near spent; she did not so much as shiver as he leaped.

His roar stilled the kin before him, forcing them to stand in a thin line; flames lapped at their limbs, their pinions, and he whispered, head bent now to Anya's ear, in order to preserve them. She had never liked the kin, and this truth brought a memory that made him smile.

She would have hated the smile, had she seen it; had she not been caught entirely by the thrall of magic, she would have sensed its presence, and he would have lost what tenuous control he now exerted.

But dark-haired, older, she was still a child, and caught in the play of discovery; the power felt good.

Or so he surmised, for her own lips turned up in a gleeful smile, a smile that spoke of enchantment.

She raised both hands, and he caught the one that held the path, gently lowering it. "Not yet," he whispered, for the road was still walked. "Not yet, little Anya. Soon." She lowered the hand he had cupped with such care, and raised instead the other on high.

"The trees," he whispered. "They are not ours, Anya; they belong to the Winter Queen, the Wild Hunt. Consume them first."

Her eyes widened; he saw the curve of lash almost touch her brow. Everything with Anya was a gamble.

"But they're pretty," she said at last. "And they have such lovely voices."

"They are death," he whispered. "As all pretty things are. Think of Lady Sariyel, Anya. Think of The Lord. Beauty, in things of this nature, speaks only of *power,* and if the power is not yours, it is not your friend."

Still she hesitated, and he saw the strands in her hand begin their warp and twist as they struggled to entrap the three that stood, unbowed and unshadowed by blood and sacrifice.

They would weaken the road, he thought. And then realized that they already had.

He had power enough to destroy the trees—but to do so would be to give over the subtlety that bound them, master and mage; he could not take that risk. Not yet. He spoke again, his voice soft, his hands still. It was best, with Anya, to take care. No quick motion. No unwanted touch. No pain, no reminder of pain.

"Anya," he told her softly, "The Lord would be proud of you if you could do this one thing. He might even let you change the dragons that skirt the balconies of the Shining Palace."

"Could I make scales?"

"Scales," he said agreeably. "And more."

She hesitated a moment, and then she closed her hand in a sudden fist.

Tongues of flame leaped from the front, shot over the heads of men, the banners of men, the insipid contraptions made by their lesser mages. They touched the trees, and the trees began to burn.

And to scream.

Yollana of Havalla sagged at last into the ground. The weight of the Heart bore her down; she thought she might drop it upon the field, and forced her shaking arms to bend so that it rested against her chest. To lose it here would be to lose all; it would make a lie of every necessary cruelty that had scarred her, twisted her, come close to breaking her.

And she could break here.

It was almost, *almost* done.

But she was not, as she expected to be, alone. And for company, she had no mothers, no grandmothers, no Matriarchs; their voices had fallen silent as they, too, fled the dying of the Winter trees. The coming, at last, of the whole of Night.

"No," a voice said quietly, as if discerning her thought. And then, gently, it added, "You spoke aloud, Matriarch."

"Na'tere."

"Yes."

"Why you?"

But the Serra Teresa, broken and crippled in a way that Yollana understood, bent her slender arms and encircled the older woman's shoulders. It was the whole of her answer in this place.

She began to carry the old woman's weight, as if Yollana's legs were still crippled and still incapable of supporting it. Yollana allowed this. She couldn't say why.

And Teresa, curse her, would never ask.

"Where is your niece?"

"Truly?"

The old woman nodded.

"I do not know. And if I have had no cause to be thankful for my loss, I am almost thankful now. She is where she is, and beyond us."

"She could speak to you."

"Ah. Yes, Matriarch, she could. But I think her thought is given to other things."

"To what?"

"There is more than the comfort of an Ona at stake," Na'tere replied, chiding. No voice chided a Matriarch. No voice chided Yollana, even before she had been called upon to take up the weight of the family.

"But I think," she added, as if aware of her breach of etiquette, "that the trees . . . exact their price. I can . . . almost hear them, Yollana." She shuddered.

Above the valley, Kallandras of Senniel College could hear them as well. But the winds did not turn; the flames were not elemental, and they could not be torn from their moorings by as simple a thing as force.

He had heard worse things, in his life.

He had endured worse things. But something about the dying was beautiful, and this—more than anything he had witnessed this eve—was profoundly disturbing. In their agony, the trees still clung to the Oldest of Roads, the Highest of Seasons, and although he could not understand the language they spoke in their passing, he felt it as something above him, beyond him: a canto, some fragment of a poem written by a master bard the likes of which Senniel would never see.

He had no desire to remember it, but he would. Further proof, if it were necessary, that the taint of bardic life, the need to hide within the walls of Senniel, had long since ceased to be superficial.

*   *   *

And at a distance, no safety guaranteed them, Ser Andaro di'-Corsarro and Serra Diora en'Leonne watched. His hand was upon her arm, and her arm was tense; she had but to open mouth, speak with her gift, and he would release her.

But she would damage him. Better, she knew, to take *lumina arden* in hand and wound him, drawing blood, than to use her gift against him. She grabbed the dagger's hilt.

He caught her other hand.

"My wife—" she said, her voice low. So much in the words. So much. She could see where the armies were. She could see less clearly where the camp beyond them lay: the healers' tents, the tents of the Tyr. She could not, in this darkness, make out the tent in which she had left a woman and a baby, and it was only for that that she searched.

Ser Andaro knew. Although he did not loosen his grip, he said, "They are safe."

"The line is breaking!" she shouted, losing all composure. "We have time—"

But it was a lie. Even she knew it was a lie.

"You cannot face the whole of the army, Serra Diora. And if you are upon the field, it will break him."

"He will not know."

Ser Andaro shook his head again. "Wait," he counseled her softly.

And another voice said, cold as night, as *this* night, "He is, of course, correct."

He released her hands in a single motion, his own hand falling to his sword.

Red light replied as another blade was drawn.

But the Serra Diora drew no weapon. Instead, she lifted her chin, straightened her shoulders, and turned to face Lord Isladar of the *Kialli*.

He did not wear the guise of seraf on this, their second meeting. But even at their first, she had not been beguiled by the appearance of servitude. How could she, and be who she was? She had donned it herself many times, and often when it suited her.

But not, she thought, always.

Although the night was dark, the red glow of demon sword lit the underside of Lord Isladar's face, marking him as a man of power. No serafs wielded swords, and certainly no swords like this.

But beyond the glow of sword, she saw that he wore a simple

robe—a seraf's robe, perhaps. Or perhaps not; in the dark, it was hard to determine the quality of the weave of cloth.

If it were cloth; it seemed to her eye that it moved against the wind.

"There may be a role for you yet, Serra Diora," the kinlord continued, inclining his head. Nothing else about him stirred; his sword did not move. "But if you perish in the fields below, you will never fulfill it."

"Serra," Ser Andaro said coldly. "Move away."

A man's command. In the darkness, she shook her head. It was small comfort that he couldn't see the gesture; the creature could. "He does not mean us harm," she said quietly.

She could see Andaro's back, and only his back, and no new rigidity offered a glimpse into any surprise her words might have caused. But after a long pause, he asked, "How can you be certain?"

"We met once before, upon the plateau," she replied. "He did not kill me then."

"Nor do I intend to kill you now," Isladar added. "But I do not intend to perish here either."

"You do not join your allies."

He laughed. It was a brief burst of sound, and it was laced with something akin to bitterness. "You little understand the Hells, if you can use that term so baldly, little Serra.

"But, no, I am not among the servants of the Lord of Night."

"You are of them."

"We are kin, yes. But forgive us the use of the term; in the South, kin are valued. In the Hells, less so."

She hesitated for just a moment, and then said, "Kiriel."

And his dark brows rose. "You are too perceptive," he replied at last, and something about his voice changed. The threat that had been absent gathered beneath the sheen of his dark words.

But before he could lift sword, she turned away: she could hear the voices of the dying trees. And it seemed to her, when she turned back, eyes wide, that he could as well; he was bound again, still as statue. Cold monument with burning sword, he marked the place in which he stood.

"So," he said. "You hear them."

She nodded. "And you."

"Hear what?" Ser Andaro di'Corsarro snapped. Man's voice again, but thinner than demon's, and far less musical than the dying.

She shook her head. "There was a tree in the encampment."

"More, I think, than one," Isladar corrected her softly.

She listened a moment, and then nodded. "More," she agreed. "But not for long. What do you wait for?"

"I? I wait for Kiriel, as you surmised." He lifted his head, then. Took care, she realized, not to move his sword; not to offer threat to which Ser Andaro might respond. "She is coming," he added.

And he smiled.

Night, in that smile.

"She is not a servant of the Lord of Night," she told him quietly.

"Not yet," he whispered.

"Not ever."

He laughed. "I raised her," he said at last. He sheathed his sword; shadows took him, but they were dense enough that she could tell where he stood. "And you have known her a handful of days."

"Mortal days," she replied, daring much. And then, daring more, she added, "And you were not the only hand to raise her; not the only voice to influence her."

"I could not be. Had I, we would not be here. The Northern Wastes would have been her only home."

"What do you want of Kiriel?"

"I? What any parent wants."

Truth, in the words, but lie as well. Again, she knew no surprise; she had offered both, and just as artfully, in her time.

"Look," he said. "She is there."

He lifted an arm.

Through the trees that should have obscured her from sight, Kiriel di'Ashaf rose.

She did not call wind.

Had she, it would not have come. She had learned this truth time and again by the side of Lord Isladar of the *Kialli*. And she had accepted it then. Now?

Now, it seemed, it did not matter. She had no need of wind; no need of elemental power. Her own buoyed her. Her hair flew about her back like vast, spidery wings, and she felt—truly felt—the presence of the elemental air that she could not summon and could not control, as a thing beneath her.

Kallandras, she thought.

But she did not look for him. Instead, she looked down—as The Lord himself oft chose to do—and saw the movement of armies, as if each were a single, sluggish body.

Her senses were sharp here; no rain fell, no cloud moved, no fire distorted her vision. And fire did burn, but it was distant, a part of the vast game that unfolded beneath her feet.

Beneath the soles of boots that had been gifted her by the Ospreys, by the stern and sour man who served as quartermaster. Thin-soled, they encumbered her, but she did not cast them off.

She had no fear of the quartermaster here. But they were *hers*.

She could not remember why she had come.

And because she could not, Lord Anduvin, lofting upon steps made of air, chose to speak. "Kiriel."

She could have silenced him with a gesture. With less; she not only saw his name, but *held* it.

Instead, she turned to meet his gaze, her arms outstretched as if daring him—daring any of the kin—to strike. "*Anduvin.*"

And when she spoke his name, she heard her voice. Heard it, felt in it a majesty that she had not heard since she had fled the Shining Palace.

She smiled. Threw back her head, exposing the pale line of throat, the unscarred expanse of skin that need never be scarred again.

Power was offered her. She had been raised in a place as close to the Hells as possible, so that she might understand its value. She took it in, closing her eyes. Savoring the moment. Realizing, as she did, that it was not offered *her*. What she sheltered, she did not—entirely—own.

A trap.

She could have cried out. When she was younger, she *would* have. But she was here, upon the field of battle, and she could not afford to display weakness.

Show no fear, Kiriel.

Isladar's voice. Here. Always, always here.

If she could not give voice to fear, she could vent rage, and she did; her voice was the dragon's roar, and carried for miles.

Lord Isladar's frown marred his perfect features.

The Serra Diora saw this because she had looked away; Ser Andaro had not. What he saw in Kiriel, she could not, would not, see. But what she saw in Isladar made as little sense. He was . . . annoyed.

Disappointed.

She recognized the expression because she had seen it often as a child upon the faces of the harem wives, and less often across her father's features.

Kiriel, she thought, fear abating although she could not then—
or ever—say why. She turned her gaze to the battlefield below,
hoarding her own gift against future need.

Against present need.

When the last of his blood had fallen into the rune-rimmed bowl,
the lord of Mancorvo bowed his head. Wind ran across the plain in
a howl that carried voices and caused torchlight to flatten; he lifted
one hand to shield the contents of this last of Havalla's gifts.

But it was unnecessary; even as his hand rose in an awkward,
cracked shield, he saw that the blood had stilled, its surface inexplicably peaceful in the din of the unnatural night. It did not seem red
to him, and this was a boon; instead, it was ebony, and it seemed—
to his eyes—to be without end, its depths unmeasured.

Light, he had expected; some flash or sparkle that might announce magic's presence. The trees were guttered now, their light
extinguished; what little light there was was contained by fire, and
only fire, and the flames did not extend this far.

He could ill afford the time, but he bent both head and will to the
flat surface of his own blood; he saw night in its depths, and he continued to gaze.

As eyes adjusted themselves slowly to a change in brightness, to
a loss of light, he found that as he gazed therein, he could make out
the shadowy figure of a man. He dropped the hand that had served
as crooked shield to the bowl's rounded curve. This was almost a
mistake; his vision made of the bowl something much larger than
his hands felt, and were it not for the strength of his grip, the bowl
might have fallen.

But he corrected this error in judgment, determined that no others should occur. His gaze intent, the shadow took shape and form,
and he recognized it at last: the kai Lamberto. He, himself.

But he was taller than silvered mirror made him out to be; taller,
prouder, darker. Light lay furled like fist between his collarbones,
and light burned bright at his side, sheathed for a moment. He recognized *Balagar.* He recognized, second, the Voyani clasp that
bound his cloak. He could not see the bowl, and he thought that the
vision was marred, but he looked now, to either side, as the field of
vision moved.

He saw, first, his son. Clearer than his father, and far less shadowed, his youth denoted by the roundness of his eyes, the paleness
of his skin, he raised sword, raised voice—the words flew past, as
unintelligible as if they were foreign.

He had the terrible urge to grab them, to hold on to them, to force sense out of them—they were battlefield words, and possibly the last he would utter, and this chance made them precious. But he had not ruled Mancorvo for decades to be felled by a whim that a Serra would have better understood; he let them fly.

He had more to look upon; more that he must see—but in truth, nothing more precious. He understood, at the last, why Yollana had spoken with hesitance of strength; had dared—in his presence, to imply that he might use the greatest of this artifact's power *if* he were strong enough. And he forgave her, then, for the clarity of her cursed vision. He was strong enough.

Barely.

Grimmer now than he had thought possible, he cast his gaze wider, struggling with memory. Struggling to cast it off, at last. The death of his kai, upon this field, or one like it. The death of his oldest son.

And this, too, he accomplished, and it was easier by far than he expected. The Northern Commander had paid the price, in spirit, that his son's death demanded; the Kai Callesta, old enemy and older ally, had paid in honor what his Serra would have demanded

All of them, for this moment: he gazed into the widening depth of strange, dark mirror, past the moving form of his son's blade. He saw the shoulders and backs of men he recognized: Tyran, his men. He could not see their faces, and knew why. They were turned outward in a grim vigilance that death, or his command, would end.

He knew which of the two it was likely to be.

But they would die as men. And they would die fighting, at last, the only true enemy.

Beyond them, beyond their readied swords, cerdan less exalted, wielded their weapons. They fought in a grim silence, and as they could, they fought in formation. The bodies of the creatures did not deter them; their stretched, great jaws, their folding pinions, the blades where fingers or hands might have been had they been men, all of these were less important than the standard of Lamberto.

I would have you all as Tyran, he thought.

It humbled him, a moment.

But it did not stop his gaze from moving into the depths of shadow. Shadow had texture, it had shade. In some parts of the demon army, it was thin as beads of black mist, a curtain through which flesh was glimpsed. In others, it was dense as morning in the lowlands; too thick to pierce.

But the mirror gifted him with a vision that was not quite mortal; he saw beyond it anyway. Saw, as if at growing distance, that all of these creatures desired nothing more to kill; that they were held in place, and to their task, by the hand of a General.

It was to that General that his eyes moved last, dragged by Voyani magic and by his own desire. There, surrounded by creatures that walked on two legs and had nothing else in common with man, he saw a *man*. Or so he appeared; he was tall indeed, and slender, although he radiated the confidence and certainty of power. His hair was dark, and flowing; it crossed his shoulders like the trunks of multiple serpents, never resting, never ceasing its endless play.

His skin was pale, and his eyes the color of the Night itself. But his teeth were white, and they glimmered in the folds of his distorted smile.

Across the meniscus of blood, their eyes met.

And as they did, Ser Mareo kai di'Lamberto spoke a name. A single name.

Alcrax.

The creature froze, the smile breaking against the rocks of those two syllables.

Ser Mareo kai di'Lamberto lifted his head. He emptied the bowl of its contents and stashed it within the folds of his cloak. Then he drew *Balagar,* and heard her wild keening; it was a match for his own.

He raised his voice and shouted the name across the fields of battle.

And the shadows began to part; they roared in greeting and in rage.

Alcrax, the general of this force, threw his arms wide, casting aside his servitors as if they were useless dolls. They flew into each other, blades clanging, wings folding, teeth snapping in anger or fear—at a distance, it was hard to differentiate the two.

"Who dares?" Lord Alcrax cried in fury.

Ser Mareo kai di'Lamberto smiled grimly. "I dare!" he cried back, and the sword of the kai el'Sol swallowed shadow, destroying it.

The demon made his way toward the kai Lamberto, and the kai Lamberto—more careful with the men whose service defined his rank—moved to meet him. The Tyran paused a moment, but only a moment; they made a space in their rank for his passage, closing it at his back. They became his shadow, armed, armored, bearing with pride and determination all the colors of the field: the green of plain, the white of horse, the gold of sun and crescent sword, and across these, the blue and white of death in the Dominion.

He lifted the Havallan horn to his lips and it sang the words that would not carry; his cerdan began to withdraw, to regroup, retreating before the demons they faced, but leaving no obvious purchase in their defense. All this, on foot, deprived of the horses that were Mancorvan strength.

Songs might be written, if any survived to tell this tale. But if they did not, the wind would carry it anyway, for they would *all* ride in its currents, seeking the farthest reaches of the Terrean with the wail of the dead.

The ground broke in front of his feet. Dirt sprayed up, like liquid, falling in patches across the swathe of his cloak. A grave opened before him, ten feet across, like a maw, a thing meant to snap shut, devouring him.

He sprang across the chasm, and *Balagar* bore his weight. *Balagar* chose the field.

Red light flared as Lord Alcrax joined the fray, drawing red sword and red shield. Both burned, as *Balagar* burned, but with a different light.

Marakas par el'Sol heard *Balagar's* voice. He had taken his position within the ranks of the army, and he had joined in the first defense against the servants of the Lord of Night.

But he had not expected to hear other voices, kin to his own, lifted in open cries of war.

He turned his back upon the fighting, the arc of *Verragar* clearing the space between demon neck and shoulder, and he saw the forms of horsed riders. Horsed, here, upon this mad field.

But clearer than that, he saw *Saval*, unsheathed; saw *Arral*, saw *Mordagar.* And he knew that the par el'Sol, unlooked for, had arrived. He had no clear way of telling the Northern watch that these men were friends.

But perhaps the Northern watch understood instinctively what he understood: that weapons of golden light, drawn by men on horseback, were not weapons of the enemy.

He could not say. Had he been asked, he would have sworn that the Northern Commanders would have halted their passage, pausing to question them, wasting the minutes in which lives were lost, were being lost even as he paused.

It was not the first time he would have been wrong. Not the first time that he would have been humbled.

Yet it was not humility that weighed him down; it was something else. Hope, a thing unlooked for.

Peder kai el'Sol had come, and with his arrival, the Hand of God was complete.

They came first to Marakas, and Peder kai el'Sol bid him climb. "The horses will not stand upon the field!" he cried.

Peder's grin was brief and fierce; there was nothing courtly in it. "While we bear the blades," he shouted, "they fear no shadow and no kin. Come, par el'Sol. Come, brother. *Balagar* has taken the field, and we are needed."

He did not wait to be asked again. Instead, he took the hand offered, and grabbing it, leaped from the trampled, bloodied ground to the less familiar height of horseback. He had not been born to the High Courts; not as Peder, Samiel, or Samadar had. The horse was not his home, would never be—he was an indifferent rider, at best, and his mastery of such beasts was only barely sufficient.

But it bore him, and he caused the kai el'Sol no embarrassment, no hindrance. He held fast, clamping knees, his hand upon the hilt of *Verragar.*

In the distance that was fast diminishing, he saw two things clearly: Ser Mareo kai di'Lamberto and Lord Alcrax of the Lord's Fist.

He did not even wonder that he knew the name; he knew it because *Balagar's* wielder knew it, and that was enough.

And he understood, at last, why Jevri el'Sol had taken *Balagar;* understood fully why Peder had, in subterfuge, allowed it. It was meant for Lambertan hands, and if not Fredero, if not Fredero kai el'Sol, there was only one other who might wield it with both ferocity and perfect purity: Mareo kai di'Lamberto.

He wielded it now, and it fell like lightning. Thunder and flame followed as the demon's shield was borne up, deflecting blade's heavy flight. The cloak that the kai Lamberto wore was clumsy and cumbersome; red light tore it away, casting it, flapping, across the field like an injured, dying bird.

A bird of prey.

The horses raced through the gaps in the ranks of cerdan; they reared up as they reached the backs of Tyran, the closed circle so common to Northern drill.

"Give us leave to pass," Marakas par el'Sol commanded them, wielding *Verragar* like a brand. "We have come to the aid of Lamberto, and we will not leave his side until the battle is done."

What the Northerners failed to do, what the Southerners failed to do, the Lambertan Tyran did not: they lifted sword against the war-horses that waited, pawing ground.

Brave men, all. Lambertan to the core. The kai el'Sol raised *Saval*, and he said, "I swear by the Lord's Light that we come as allies, and only allies; that we have no enemy but one upon this field." He drew his hand across the blade; he had no oath medallion to offer, and they had none to bind with.

Blood was the older binding. It was less favored, because its passage could not be captured and contained, and in the end, upon such a field as this, blood was simply blood; the least of the cerdan and the greatest of Tyrs reduced to flesh and liquid.

The captain of the Tyran, nameless, faceless beneath the lowered tines of helm, nodded gravely. "I will take responsibility for your passage," he said, voice grim. "Go. Go now."

They did not dally. The Tyran moved as one, parting like curtains, steel curtains, and the horses galloped through the scant opening, blades passing inches from their underbellies.

They came at last to the side of the Tyr'agnate of Lamberto, and their swords burned brighter, and brighter still, as the Five at last shone in one place. There were demons here, in number; they gathered just beyond their lord, dark mirrors to the Tyran.

But they moved when they saw the naked blades of the Lord of Day; they drew weapons, where they had them, and raised talons and bladed hands, where they did not. They cried out, bestial roars meant to invoke fear in those simply mortal.

But the fires of the Lord burned away all fear; made of it something as consequential as falling ash. The blades responded, driving the men, and the men, at last, gave themselves over to the Hand of God, becoming his sole force upon the field.

Valedan led. He was *fast*.

Fast enough that Auralis, and only Auralis, could pace him. His chosen guards—his, although they had never said the words, and would never say them—fell behind, and Duarte's curse was loud. It was not long; he hoarded breath, hoarded power. The years, twelve, thirteen, had slipped past him. The training in the yards of Kalakar had ill prepared him for the carnage.

At his side, feet lighter and surer than his, Alexis, his Decarus, his. Beyond her, to the right, Fiara. Cook was just ahead. The Kalakar? Behind them. Beyond them. He wondered if she would come to them when they at last reached the narrow pass, the obvious trap; wondered if she would lead her forces, against the will of two Commanders, to preserve what was left of the men he had gathered and trained.

Old scars ached in the damp. Some were visible; most were not. He had no more time than that to ponder their existence; he ran.

By his side, in silence, a stranger ran, and it took him a moment to recognize the youthful face of the kai Callesta. Ser Alfredo, injured, would not be left behind.

And perhaps this was wise. Duarte made a place for this Southerner, by the simple expedient of raised palm at the right moment. He was Primus here; the Ospreys accepted what he accepted.

Nor did he seek to command Ser Ramiro kai di'Callesta's only living son. Even now, the formality of the South was writ upon the young boy's face, and the Northern Primus could not bring himself to break it.

The Ospreys grouped together for moments at a time, when the enemy was thick enough that the Sun Sword and the blade Auralis wielded were not—quite—enough to send them scattering. Here and there, creatures rose, tall as the ceilings in The Kalakar Manse; they spoke with tongues of flame, and wielded it, eyes darker than night, and recognizable only by this fact.

Duarte wondered if the Ospreys were struck by their baroque and twisted beauty; if they were humbled in some fashion by the revelation of creatures born of time and a nature that was both hidden and near-scoured from the world.

Could wonder that, as he paused to cast his warding spells, his scant protections. He had not drawn blade, and would not; it was not in the length of steel that his expertise—such as it was—lay.

But he faltered. Aye, he faltered. When Fiara was struck, he shuddered; when Cook roared back, sword lost, hands upon his face, he froze. But Alexis kept him moving; Alexis, dagger, steel, cold as any battle that he had ever joined.

What she did not do, he would not; not here.

Valedan was beyond them.

But he had halted his headlong rush. The Sun Sword was before him, like a lance; it cut the night on all sides, granting the clearest of vision to those in his wake. Sun's light, bright enough to sear.

Bright enough to burn, although its flame was golden.

Beyond him, the wall of moving fire was not; it was red, and it flickered with hints of blue and white. Ash lay beneath it, and the dead were consumed there, armor and claw melting into rivulets, a molten testament to the power of the mage they faced.

And where, Duarte thought in desperation, was he? Where was the mage?

He moved his way past Alexis, past the other Ospreys who, wounded, were still able to stand their ground. Grim, silent, their hands as mute as their lips, they allowed him passage.

And he saw, as he reached the side of the kai Leonne, that the boy—no, the man—had not paused in fear. He had turned, instead, to Auralis AKalakar, and Auralis AKalakar lifted a hand.

Mage-gift made clear to Duarte what might never have been clear otherwise, and even so, it was a dim flicker, a hint of something bound to Auralis' lifted fist. Red as flame, thin as whisper, it curled round his finger, moving, always moving, as if to escape detection.

"Auralis!"

The Sentrus turned. The madness of battle was not upon him; his face was still and calm. As still, Duarte amended, as Auralis ever was.

"Duarte!" Alexis shouted.

He turned to her.

She lifted an arm—it was bleeding, he saw, but it did not tremble or shake—and pointed.

The line, half Northern, half Southern, had been sundered. The demons were forming up in a wedge between the ranks—cerdan? Soldiers?—of the fallen, and they drove forward toward the camp itself.

Toward the healers' tents, toward the serafs who attended their Tyrs and Tors, toward those who, drawn to the field, were not quite part of it.

He shook his head grimly, knowing that they would be circled, soon; that the forces that fought would be cut off on either side.

Lightning flashed from the height of sky, breaking ground—and demon—in its fall. But not enough of either to truly stop them; they halted, they slowed, but they moved.

The magi were still alive.

All of them.

He turned to Auralis again, and saw the Sentrus lower his sword. It was deliberate gesture, a command.

As it fell, the flames that burned before them fell as well, inch by inch, flickering and struggling.

"Kai Leonne," Auralis shouted. Everything was a shout, now.

Valedan nodded.

The flames suddenly banked in a stretch perhaps twenty yards in length; enough to allow them all passage into the body of the enemy. Enough to allow them retreat, if he could continue to hold the flames back.

Later, Duarte thought. Later, he would ask how this had been done. He had never been one of the magi; had he, he would never have joined Kalakar. But the restless bite of sudden curiosity stung anyway, a reminder of the things he might have been, had he been capable of patience, of other choices. A different life.

Lightning spoke in the distance.

Or not.

Valedan raised the Sun Sword high as the first of the demons came through. The creature stumbled, and the top half of his body fell forward, the bottom half screeching to a stop, as if they were, sundered, still capable of independent motion.

Demon blood, even in the glow of flame, seemed black as tar. But it did not cling to the edge of the blade; only to the young man who wielded it.

Merilee ran sticky hands through her hair. It was a gesture of habit, and it pulled free more hair than it displaced, for her hair was tightly bound gray. Her face might have been severe had she been any other woman, but in the dim lights encased in glass, she was granted the semblance of warmth. Her eyes were brown, but this was costly, and she knew that soon she would have to choose between her own safety and theirs.

She looked at her feet. Everywhere that the flaps of canvas bordered, men were lined up in rows, as if they were already dead. Some clutched injured limbs, some cradled internal organs, some cried out in pain and terror, the voice of youth. No, she thought, wincing. The voice of childhood. The heights of adulthood that so many young men had scaled in such a desperate rush to meet glory were high indeed, and far beyond their reach now.

They wanted their mothers. Or their fathers.

And she, Daughter of the Mother, was not immune to their pleas.

She knew by touch which of these men she could save, and which she could not, and it was to the latter that she lent the least understood of the Mother's gifts: death. Death in a peaceful place: her arms.

Frederik was old enough to understand this; Edmond was too young and too rash. For that reason, it was Edmond's task to assemble and manage the medics who had come with the Imperial armies. She was not surprised to see that among their number, the ruddier complexion of the South had intermingled, bringing their wounded and their already dead.

There should have been more, and she knew it.

Could hear, from the din of the wind and the crackle of falling timber, the height of flame, the screams, that the battle went swiftly, and not in their favor; too many obvious dead lay beneath the feet of the enemy, and none were foolish enough to risk lives to bring those bodies here.

Or none, she thought, with pain, were successful in the folly of that attempt. She understood battle; she understood that the best— and the worst—that a man had to offer was offered *here;* this was their crucible, and what they did here would define the whole of their lives, long or short.

She could not judge them. Brave or cowardly, they were, to her, all children. Her Mother's children, some sundered by the atrocity of the Southern custom of killing the god-born at birth, and some beholden to her in the fashion of the North.

She eased the head of a Southern man from her lap, closing his eyes gently. Bent her head a moment, touching her lips with the tips of cracked fingers, dirty nails. She wanted peace. In the truest sense, she *wanted* peace. But the only peace granted her now would be personal, and she made of it what she could, bespeaking the god whose blood ran in her veins.

This will be my last battle, Mother. Let me not fail you. Let me grant, to these most lost of your children, a hint of your blessing.

So she moved, and although time seemed to pass slowly, she knew this as an artifact of her power. She spent a minute or two with each of the dying, no more. With the living, she spent less time; enough to tell Frederik what was wrong, and what might be done to alleviate the worst of the threat. Alleviating the worst of the pain would come later, if there was one.

We have your stories, she continued, praying in silence. *We know of the servants of the Lord of Night. We know of his kin. But, Mother, forgive this poorest of students; forgive me my lack of imagination, my lack of understanding. What the stories gave us could never encompass this.*

She wiped her brow with a sleeve already too damp and rose again; although the sun was gone from the sky, it was still humid here, still damp and hot. Good weather for infection, she thought grimly, steering herself back to the world of the living.

But when she attempted to ease the shoulders and head of the last dying man from her lap, she was surprised when hands joined her and helped relieve her of this burden. They were dark hands, and they were ringed with gold; the hands of a clansman.

Danger, in that.

But she could not find danger in it, not one that was worse than the enemy they faced. Weary, she lifted her eyes and met the eyes of a stranger.

"Forgive my intrusion," he said, in perfect but accented Weston. "I . . . traveled here with the Tyr'agar, but I am not a warrior. The field is not my place."

"You are a physician?" she asked in Weston. She was too weary to practice her Torra in this place; she saved that effort for the injured.

"I am," he said, bowing. Southern bow, crisp and fluid. His palms, as he exposed them, were red. "I thought to join you, here. I know the work you do."

She thought to chide Frederik or Edmond. Smaller tents had been set up to accommodate those who now came in greater number, and in those tents, the Southerners might safely serve. But not in this one.

"Forgive my lack of grace," she replied, wiping her hands on her undyed apron. "But I—"

"I am Ser Laonis di'Caveras," he said, lifting a hand and forestalling the words she wasn't certain she could offer. "And in your lands, had I wished it, I could have worn the twin palms."

Her eyes widened.

"Yes," he replied, lowering his eyes. "I am of the healer-born. And I thought I might ease your burden."

"Frederik and Edmond come from the houses of healing," she said faintly.

"They are two men," he replied. "And you yourself, the third. Let me aid you, Serra."

She did not correct him. Instead, she frowned. "In the South, it is said that men do not heal."

"I do not count the South as my home," he replied, with just a hint of Southern pride to belie the certain truth of his words. "And my wife is in the North, waiting for me. I could not face her again if I hid in my tent, waiting."

She hesitated for a moment, and then, careful to avoid his outstretched hands, she nodded. "Do not," she told him severely, "attempt to call the dead back. We do not have the time, and we do not have the power. If Mandaros claims them—or the wind, as you call it—you must let them go."

He looked as if he might speak, and she gentled her voice, remembering that she spoke, in the end, to a man. "If you do, you will be all but spent, unless you are of greater power than either Frederik or Edmond. There are injuries here that *will* take the lives of men, but they are not immediately dangerous; it is those that you must tend. Kill infection, where you find it," she added. "Heal arteries. But even then, do not attempt to replace the blood lost; not yet. If there is time for it, it must wait."

The grimness had returned to her words before she finished; so much for gentle. "There is a reason that healers do not often choose the field of battle as their home," she said quietly. "Can you do this?"

His smile was odd in the scant light. "In the South," he said softly, "healers do not heal."

"Impossible."

"No, Serra. It is not. But it is not a comfortable life; in the North, I have found a home more to my liking. But of the healers in your care, I will find it easiest to follow your commands. It is for this reason that I dared your tent."

She nodded, then, and moved on. Afraid now of what he might see. Afraid, and grateful for the fear. Any healer, of any power, was a blessing—and any blessing offered must be accepted.

Aie, it was *hot* here.

Even with Ser Laonis aiding her, his Weston so clear she could hear it above the groans and the quiet pleas of the injured, she was *tired*. This would, this must be her last battle. She was not yet fifty years of age, but for the god-born, that was significant; the blood of the god burned in her, and with it, much of the mortal.

Not yet, she told herself, meaning it. *Not yet,* she told Mandaros, meaning it even more.

A cold cloth touched her brow, and she looked up, thinking to see Ser Laonis. But no; he was across the wide tent, his hands upon the chest of a wounded Northern soldier.

The hands that held the cold compress against her forehead were woman's hands, young hands. She blinked and focused.

The woman knelt. She would have abased herself, but she wore a sling, and in it, a sleeping infant. To bend too far would wake him, and she had chosen practicality.

"Who are you?" Merliee said, the gentleness unforced.

"Teyla," the woman answered quietly. She glanced nervously around her, at the dead, at the dying. All men. All. The Northern women were in a different tent, in Frederik's care.

"You can't stay here," the priestess said quietly, her gaze falling with a guilty delight upon the untouched face of sleeping child. She reached out in spite of herself, and let her dirty fingers play a moment across the soft, soft skin of new life. "Where is your husband?"

"He is on the field," Teyla replied, slowly pushing strands of raven hair from her cheeks, her dark, round eyes.

"He would not approve of your presence here. Go back to your tent."

"He . . . would approve, I think," Teyla said. Hesitance marred the words; she was not certain. But before Merilee could speak again, she added, "You accepted the aid of Ser Laonis. I am not a healer. I have no gift." She held out her hands, and to Merilee's surprise, they were calloused and dark. "But I have strength. I have worked the fields for most of my life. I can carry water, and I can carry *you* if need be. I cannot sit idle while the world—" she bit back the words.

"Your child—"

"He will not remember what he sees, if he wakes. And if he wakes, and he cries, they will hear his voice, and it will remind them. Of why they fought. Of why they are here. I am only a concubine," she added, and Merilee realized for the first time that they were both speaking in Torra, and that Torra had come effortlessly to her. "I am not the Serra. Please, let me do this."

Ser Laonis di'Caveras approached. "Serra," he said, speaking to Merilee above the slightly bowed head of the supplicant concubine.

"What?"

"She is Teyla en'Leonne."

Merilee's eyes widened.

"And I think that she is correct; the kai Leonne would be gratified if you would accept what aid she can offer. If you truly feel that she has no place here—if you feel that she will be in your way—then send her out, and she will leave without further comment." He gazed upon the blue-black head, bowed but not bent to ground, and his lips turned up in a slight smile. "She is his second wife. If you did not hear of her, I will not tell the whole of the tale, but I will say this: the Serra Diora en'Leonne chose better, braver, than she knew when she chose this wife."

Teyla did not move.

But Merilee was moved anyway. "Yes," she said, giving in to exhaustion. "It would be nice to have another woman present. Stay, then."

Edmond's head appeared between the flaps of the distant wall. "Merilee," he said, his face almost gray. "More incoming."

She nodded, squaring her shoulders. "Come, then," she said. "And help me move the dead. We will need the room."

"Aye, you will," a third voice said, and Edmond squawked in irritation as he was shoved to one side and collided with canvas.

The Matriarch of Havalla, accompanied by a woman who looked vaguely familiar to Merilee, pushed her way into the tent. "And I, too, have come to offer what aid I can. You do not know the Voyani," she added, "but Ser Laonis does. I am Matriarch, and I have some skill with herb-lore and medicine."

"I know that Voyani gift is costly." Ser Laonis had risen, and the hands he held before him were clenched in tightening fists. Both the words and the expression behind them were dark.

The old woman's laugh was a harsh bark. "More costly than *this?*" she said, stabbing the air with her pipe.

He fell silent.

Merilee, however, rose like a wrathful dragon. "The first rule of the tent," she said, to the only woman present older than she. "There will be *no smoking* here."

"Unless," Edmond added, having regained his feet and some of his shattered composure, "you're on fire. And you will be, if you don't put that out."

They might have laughed, but it was nervous laughter, and it was guttered entirely by the next man to enter the tent. His robes, the pale, undyed linens so common to those who came to the Mother's service, were red with blood—but they knew by sight that none of it was his.

Eyes wild, Frederik ran straight to Merilee, as if she were the only thing of relevance the tent, long and full, now contained. His knees crumpled, and the whole of his weight shifted to ground before her.

Merilee, Mother's Daughter, reached out and touched his bent head with the palms of both hands. "Frederik," she said, voice as gentle as the Mother's. As commanding. He lifted his face; it was inches from hers. His eyes were wide. "The line," he said.

She closed her eyes briefly.

Opened them and looked across the tent to the suddenly watchful Matriarch of Havalla. The older woman lifted her head; her lips twisted, pulling at the network of lines that sun and wind had etched there. "Aye," she said at last. "The line has broken."

"The demons—" Frederik said, grasping words as if they were air and he, suffocating. "They're coming *here*."

Merilee rose; left him in her shadow. She closed her eyes and pressed her hands into them. She was so tired.

"Mother's Daughter," Frederik whispered, so terrified that she hadn't the strength to correct or berate him, "what must we do?"

"What we are doing," she told him firmly.

"But the demons—"

"If they come, they come, Frederik. But if we flee, we do their work for them." She looked out upon the injured, in their neat and terrible rows. "The Commanders have not yet signaled a retreat; we cannot do less than they do."

"If we die here, we can never help them."

"No," she replied gently, always gently. "Edmond."

Edmond, younger and brasher, nodded. He came to Frederik's side, and placing his hands beneath the older man's arms, levered him up, forcing his feet to take his weight. "They can't move," he said.

And Frederik swallowed air and more, meeting Edmond's eyes. Meeting, Merilee thought, Edmond's untarnished idealism, his naïveté, his utter belief.

The Matriarch made her way to the swinging tent flaps. She pursed lips again as the woman who accompanied her sought to join her once more. "No, Na'tere," she said firmly. "You are needed here."

"But you—"

"I can do very, very little," the older woman replied. "And it may be that I can do nothing. But I will see this for myself." She lifted hand to her throat, closed her eyes, and nodded. "It is important," she added softly, and with just a hint of obvious regret. "To bear witness. To claim history, and not the story that follows it. It is all of the legacy that is valued, by Havalla."

Merilee nodded. "Matriarch," she said quietly.

"Not you," the Matriarch replied.

"I did not intend to leave the tent."

"Nor did I, when I first arrived." She bowed. It was not graceful, but it was somehow perfect—a gesture of respect between those who have reached the age of wisdom.

She walked slowly out of the tent, and she cast her small spells, sharpening her senses. Not hearing; there was enough of that, and the screams of the dying were no more pleasant heard clearly than they were at a distance. But sight, smell, the instinct that had guided her throughout a cursed and difficult life—these she called. They came.

And she saw for herself the truth of the words that she had hoped to doubt: the demons had indeed broken the line that stood between the heights of the Western valley and the flat of its center ground. Men to either side attempted to contain them, to hinder them, to pick away at their number; the demons were not many. Dozens, Yollana thought critically. Had they been men, they would have evoked no fear.

But they were not men, and had never been men. She lifted an empty pipe to her lips and bit its stem. *For this,* she thought bitterly. But she remembered the price that Evallen had paid, and she accepted her place here.

Death was easier, after all, than so much of her life had been. There was peace in that thought. Her hands might never again be forced to wield sword or dagger against her own kin, her own blood; might never be called upon to mete out justice and judgment necessitated by life upon the *Voyanne*. It would be up to her daughters, should they find the Heart quickly, and her daughters were old enough—just—to do that much.

Old enough, she thought bitterly, to pay the price that the Tor Havalla would demand of them—whatever that price might be. She lifted her hand to the patch that covered an empty socket, remembering.

And then she heard it: from beyond the tents, to the South and East, horns were lowing.

Reserves, she thought. But this made no sense; the Tyrs would not hold their own in reserve against such a force as they had expected, and the Commanders? She thought them wise enough to leave no men to protect the camp itself.

But the horn's voice rose, and it was almost stately in its perfect cadence. Southern horns, she thought. She was no clansman; she did not know whose calls played out against the backdrop of so much death, so much fire.

Turning from the West to the East, her gray brows rising in surprise, she did as she had intended: she bore witness.

But when the Northern horns answered the Southern call, she shook her head and retreated. The tent absorbed her for a moment; the smells of the dying and those who would, with luck, struggle once again toward life, assaulted her.

"Healer," she said, for she could think of no other title that she could safely offer Merilee of the North. Merilee with her golden eyes hidden behind a thinning patina of magic.

Merilee, pale, looked up from the stomach of an injured soldier. "Matriarch?"

"The line has broken," the Matriarch told her, reaching into her satchel and drawing out forbidden leaves. Not even the young man attempted to stop her. "But help comes from the East; I do not think that the demons will reach us yet. You were wise."

"What help?" Serra Teresa asked.

Yollana frowned. "I do not, in truth, know, Na'tere."

"And you will watch?"

"No. I will help here. Where there are armies, and men with swords, there is little for me to do."

And there were.

CHAPTER THIRTY-FIVE

THE GENERAL Alesso di'Marente stood a moment upon ground that he had not traversed in a decade. He stood beneath the banner of Tyrs, indeed, the banner of *the* Tyr. But it was night, and the night that had fallen across this valley denied the golden embroidery, the jeweled visage, of the resplendent sun. He felt no anger at the loss of the image; no anger, in the end, at the loss—the momentary loss—of the name he had earned for himself by choices old and new.

From the East, he had ordered his men to halt; they were restless, and they were afraid. He felt both keenly. In the South, there was only one response to fear, only one antidote, and his command denied them that. His horse was restive, and he could see—in the light cast by the five swords of the Radann—that the cerdan and Tyran fought side by side with their Northern counterparts: unhorsed, almost to a man.

But unhorsed, they could not reach their goal in time.

He longed to cry out the name *Marente* in a voice that not even the winds could deny—but he had forsaken that name. Had forsaken the title of General. For this.

He closed his eyes for just a moment, and accepted the weight of responsibility. It had been a dangerous game from the start, and he had played it with the consummate skill of a high clansman. It had not been enough—but he had not yet lost.

And he had made his choice, by the edge of the river, after the storm had left the open skies and his Widan had scattered to their tents in their fruitless pursuit of the answers he had demanded.

Now, answers came to this: he drew *Terra Fuerre.*

He could not address his men in any way but with horn, and he did so. They saw what he saw. Even had he desired to make peace with the *Kialli*—and he desired no such thing—it would have been beyond his skill: they were here in number, the servants of the Lord of Night revealed. And the clans would never willingly, or knowingly, serve such creatures.

Not again.

Ser Sendari was by his side, but the horse upon which he rode was so skittish most of his attention was absorbed in the handling of the beast. Most, but not all.

"So," Alesso said, loudly enough that the words carried.

Sendari nodded. He drew not sword but hands, and he held them across his chest like a shield; they were the whole of his effective weapons.

"Sword's Edge?"

"With pleasure," Cortano di' Alexes replied. "Ride, Alesso, and we will follow. We are not the Northern *magi,*" he added, with unconcealed contempt. "We were trained for war."

They drove their horses down the path that led to the valley, and to death. They rode almost as one, horses beginning their long struggle to escape the shadows cast by the Lord of Night.

But before they had reached the flats, they heard another unit, another small army, and it, too, came from the East. Alesso did not recognize the call. He turned to look; trees girded vision, protecting what the ears could hear from sight.

But he knew that the calls were Northern, and he cursed. "They will mistake us," he called to Cortano.

"They will not," Cortano replied evenly, hearing the command that Alesso did not offer in words. He, as Sendari before him, lifted hands. They danced, the fingers nimble and swift.

Devran of House Berriliya, The Berriliya, sat astride Shade. The horse was not yet wild with fear; he was steady, a destrier without parallel in the Northern army. But his ears were flat, and he was tensing for flight.

Devran was not a completely vain man; he had vanity, but he had adopted it in the cause of the Kings' army, and only in that cause. He gauged the miles between his unit, at half its strength, and the broken line. It was hard to make out, at this remove, who manned the break in that line, but he could tell, by the defensive formation he could barely see, that at least some half of it was Northern. Commander Allen's men. Or The Kalakar's.

He grimaced.

"Commander?" Sedgewick said.

"Tell the cavalry to dismount," he responded.

Sedgewick nodded.

"And tell the magi—"

But the words were lost to wind, and in the folds of that wind, another voice spoke.

"Commander Berriliya," it said, and he recognized the voice of the most famous—certainly the most dangerous—bard that Senniel College had ever produced.

He had no like way of responding; he lifted a hand and his men were instantly still.

"We thought you in the North. You travel with half your men; half at least must have gone ahead. But you are needed here; I think that Commander Allen will forgive your misinterpretation of his orders.

"There are men who approach from the South. They are not ours, but they are not—I believe—our enemies. If they attempt to stand and fight, fight; if they press ahead—as it appears they intend—to where the demons have broken our line, follow them. They have chosen to chance horseback."

They were Southern, then.

Devran smiled. It was a cold smile, but it was genuine. He had no fear whatever of Commander Allen's response to his presence. No, it was Ellora he wished to avoid—for this, this decision, this rash choice, was entirely in character for *her.* And had their positions been reversed, he would have reviled her for it, when the time and the circumstances allowed.

Ah, humility. Even at his age, and with his experience, it was an unwelcome novelty.

"Sound the advance," he told Sedgewick, climbing at last from the back of his horse. "We will find passage more quickly if we do not depend on horseback."

*   *   *

Baredan di'Navarre was injured in more ways than one. His sword arm ached; he had taken a wound that had pierced his armor, and he still bled. But the losses that he had suffered were not measured in his blood; not even measured in the deaths of the men he had chosen, been chosen, to lead.

No, they were in the breaking of the line.

Beside him, uninjured, her sword red and obviously chipped, the Commander Ellora Kalakar was shouting orders. Some half of her forces stood beside his, and the North and the South clashed in style, if not in intent. She could not gain the ground they had lost, but she was determined to lose no more of it.

And the proof of that determination was cut in the bodies that lay, Northern and Southern, beyond their feet. She was grim and fell, as much a man as any he had met upon the field of battle. He had never thought to see her so close; he had believed that the armies might somehow be cleanly sundered. Or that the Northerners might fight at a safe distance from those under their command.

But she had come when the fighting had grown too intense, and she had brought with her the men and women who served as her personal guard.

He had heard the rumors, more than a decade past, that the Black Ospreys reported to a woman. He had barely believed them then, and even when he had seen the truth for himself, he almost failed to countenance it. But he would never make that mistake again.

She cursed loudly, like a soldier, and he was grateful for his lack of knowledge of Weston; he was certain that the words themselves would be obscene, especially coming from the lips of a woman.

But when he heard the first horns, he froze, and she, cutting the foot from the legs of a demon that seemed almost horse, turned to see where his glance had strayed.

To horses.

To men. To a banner that was dark in the night, indiscernible from almost all other banners upon the field. It didn't matter. He knew the horn calls—who better? And he knew that they did not come from Valedan kai di'Leonne.

Alesso di'Marente was upon the field.

At last, and late. But to whom did he now ride?

Lord's man. Lord's man, and proud of it.

In the dark of a moonlit sky, he had first planted the seeds of his rebellion, and he had nurtured them as all men of the high clans must: with caution, with stealth, with grace. He had chosen allies from among his many enemies; his friends were measured by the stature that he himself had attained by the simple expedient of skill.

And truth? He had one. One man.

"Sendari!" he shouted, naming him.

Sendari could barely answer; his horse was too wild with fear. Sendari had never been more than passingly capable on horseback—the challenge of this field and that mount was beyond him. The horse broke stride again and again, his hooves falling awkwardly among the bodies that girded earth.

"Sendari, retreat!"

He had no desire to lose the Widan.

But the Widan pulled up on the reins, forcing his knees to clamp tight. His horse followed where Alesso's led, but barely; there was no way that Sendari could swing sword from his saddle. No way that he could lift hands to manipulate the finest and most subtle of his gifts.

His beard was wild, white and black; it splayed flat against the drifting folds of robe, obscuring the cold gold and rubies that lay pinned to chest: his symbol of office.

That much, Alesso could clearly see. Had he been a different man, he might have paused to play witness; he was the Lord's Man. He drove into the spreading wedge of the demon formation, and he laughed as his sword fell.

The demons fell back before the onslaught, but only for a moment; they regrouped around the tallest of their number. And he *was* tall; eight feet or more from head to foot. He was almost human in semblance, but his skin was ebony, and his jaw was elongated, a beast's jaw. He roared, the sound broken in guttural syllables, like language.

Alesso had enough time—and only enough—to dismount; the reins slid from his fingers as he leaped toward ground.

Talons followed his fall, passing an inch beyond his exposed back. It was the only time that he would expose his back this eve. He gained footing quickly; had time to see his horse pierced by demon hand. A costly sacrifice, but necessary. Its momentum carried it into the creatures, and its screams seemed to hold them a moment in thrall.

Long enough.

Alesso di'Alesso, Alesso di'Marente—what was in a name? He was himself, and only himself, and he had come this far for battle.

Demon arm fell again, and again, moving far too swiftly; he parried, parried again, and found himself slow the third time.

But the blow that would have taken his shoulder did not connect; instead he heard the clang of blade against moving stone, and he took advantage of this unexpected aid: he drove his sword up, and up again, toward the underside of the creature's jaw.

It was not clean. Blood gouted down like warm rain, and shadow troubled his eyes. He heard the creature's breath, felt its movements; its steps were not light when they fell.

But more than that, he felt the presence of another man, and when he jerked his sword forward—and free—he caught a glimpse of a familiar face.

And he laughed again.

"Baredan," he said, his voice raised in shout, the subtleties of tone eluding him.

Baredan di'Navarre cursed him genially. Cursed him, and shouted orders to the men who followed.

They did not hesitate, although the orders did not come from Alesso himself; instead they drew back, their line forming a rough semicircle, a wall against the demon's moving wedge. A second line.

A better line.

"Where is your boy Tyr now?" Alesso shouted. Was he dead? It would turn the tide of the game he had played for half of his life. But the thought did not bring him peace; it filled his mouth with the barely discerned taste of rust and ashes.

Baredan di'Navarre tendered the only reply allowed him: he fought for his life.

Devran's men flowed into the valley, wending their way through the standing tents that defined the martial healerie that all Northern units knew. Some handful of his men departed to join the struggling medics; the others joined their leader. They did not move in silence; there was no point.

Instead, they sang. They carried no Southern drums, no Northern harps; they had no training, and they had no sense of key. They forced the tune from the words by dint of will, and if the tune was broken and lost in places, the words themselves were not. They drifted across the valley, a victory song, a gesture of Northern certainty.

A prayer.

They joined the Southern cerdan who now fought beneath unilluminated banner. They carried their own, and it was likewise dark. But it had meaning, even in the darkness, and they would not set it aside. It was their anchor. A reminder, if need be, of what they were willing to die for.

Gold, and a promise. To the Kings.

To The Berriliya.

"I told them," Isladar said quietly, and with some satisfaction. It did not reach his expression, and it barely broke the surface of his words, but the Serra Diora was an adept. She heard what was there.

And she did not understand it.

Know your enemy, her father had often told her. He had said it in his gentle voice, as if it were a blessing or a child's name, but she had been touched—at almost all ages—by the gravity of his intonation, and she had never forgotten the words.

But this enemy, she thought, she would never truly know. He was death; malice informed his voice, broke his words, shifting them in place. She heard shadow even in the breath he drew to speak.

And because she did, she gave voice to nothing. But she felt what she did not speak of; she was Serra. Teyla and her son were safe for the moment, behind the newly formed line.

"Whose men?" she asked.

"Alesso di'Marente's," Lord Isladar replied, as if the information were inconsequential.

She bowed her head a moment. She had sworn to kill him. She had vowed it, speaking to wind with the wind's coldest voice. But seeing him, seeing what his presence meant to the camp, she was frozen. Hatred provided no heat. Nor did old losses; the threat of new loss dimmed them.

She could barely believe he was here.

And because she did not, she spoke his name. Just his name, but she put power into the word. It was the caress of steel, the hint of threat. But the substance behind it? She did not linger there.

Lord Isladar gazed skyward again, but Diora did not choose to follow his gaze; instead she looked to the farthest point South at which the armies were engaged. At the fires that still burned.

At the brilliant glow of the Sun Sword, whose lay she had sung as both weapon and elegy, in a distant sunset, at the end of a festival.

Leonne the Founder had never been real to her. He was part of the song, of course, and because of it, he had power—but it was mythic power, akin to the whispered name of the Lady in moonlit night.

Valedan kai di'Leonne had none of that power. But she was held
by his presence, mesmerized by it; she forced herself to breathe as
the passage of his blade slowed, and finally stilled.

The wall of fire had broken.

The demons waited.

Auralis could see.

In the light of the sword Valedan wielded, he could observe. The
demons. Their shadow. And beyond them, above them, their Lord
and Commander. He gestured with his sword and fire flared along
its blade from tip to hilt. No fear of fire moved him; he smiled. Forgetting, for an instant, that what could observe could be observed.

Valedan kai di'Leonne, seeing the blade's direction, nodded. He
had only to cut through the hundred demons that stood in the open
gap, and he would have his victory over this danger.

Even a life lived with little sarcasm gave force to his raised brow.

But Auralis was not content to be second to any man, even one
he professed to serve. The sword that he had taken from the hands
of the Senniel bard dragged him forward, and he followed, mad
now, memory riding him. Kindling for rage, for hate.

Old memory.

Older than the village memory. Older than the memories of his
days in the South, when the Ospreys had been fledglings, brought to
hand by Primus Duarte. Older, even, than the memory of his first kill.

His first flight.

Flight. He had come to the Kings' army with a different sword,
and a fine horse. The horse, he had lost in the South. The sword, he
had broken. But he had made a name for himself in his attempt to
flee. And what, in the end, had he fled from?

Only himself. Always himself.

The presence of demons drove him as it always did. Kiriel was
not by his side, and he missed her viscerally; she made of battle a
game, and if it was deadly, it was one of the few pleasures that made
him feel truly alive.

He would do without her here. He cut through the demons that
stood their ground as if they were simple men. They raised arms
against him—real arms, things of sinew and foreign bone. They
raised claws, and some raised awkward shields—all of these, he
discarded by the simple expedient of blade and gravity.

But when he heard the scream, he froze, and were it not for the
presence of Valedan kai di'Leonne, he would have died.

Because he *must be* a demon. He had not realized it until the mo-

ment the scream took shape and form, until it forced itself into the
form of syllables, old ones. His name.

His true name.

"DEVLIN!"

Lord Ishavriel looked down in sudden shock.

Of all things he had expected—and he had expected much, even
the cursed swords that had been forged for just such a battle—this
was not among them.

Oh, he recognized the name. He had heard it often when Anya
a'Cooper had first become a denizen of the Shining Palace, a weak
little mortal under his care and protection. He had heard it while she
wept, and when she whined; he had heard it while she cursed, honing the terrible loss and the certainty of betrayal into something he
could, at last, make use of.

But he had not heard it like this, and he knew what he heard:
recognition.

His arms tightened around her, as if by so doing he could pull her
back from the abyss of knowledge.

But he was late, and far too weakened, to accomplish that task.

The fires faltered at once, banking. The strands of path that clung
to her wrist now shuddered and bucked as she pulled her hand free
from their weave.

"Anya!" he shouted, drawing power, pulling shadow, in his attempt to bind her.

He had done it before, but not often; it was costly, and he was on
the field of battle. But even had he chosen to weaken himself utterly,
he knew that he would fail here: she was a mad, wild child, and she
was beyond him. He could kill her. But he could not pull the strings
that he had always used. Their existence had depended on the death
of that boy, and that death was clearly a lie.

Instead, he attempted to gather what she unconsciously discarded: the threads of the old road. They would fray in his hands; so
much of the power that they depended on was hers.

But he could hold them, he thought, for long enough. He could
hear the steps of the lumbering Beasts, and he knew that they were
almost upon the field.

"DEVLIN!"

He had left her to die.

He had fled, bleeding from a wound so insignificant he would
not notice it now.

Even when he had found the courage to return to the place of his betrayal, to search through the tall grass and shredded tenting for some sign of her body, he had been so certain of her death, his abject failure.

He could not move. Someone stepped in to his left; Valedan held his right. His sword was heavy, far too heavy to lift; it was dragged to earth as he stood before her. Not penitent; that was beyond him.

He opened his lips, and nothing escaped. No apology, no question, no plea. He met her eyes across the distance that demons made, and what he saw in her face—her aged face, still familiar with the passage of decades—made him take his first step.

He should have wondered, then, why he could see her at all; the demons were still enshrouded in shadow, and she was a great distance away. *Remordan,* the sword keened. A word. An old Weston word. A promise and a burden.

He could see her. He could see the fall of her nut-brown hair, the width of her brown eyes, the pale light of her skin. Trees were her backdrop, a dark fence that rose against sky, surrounding them both. Whatever separated them now was simple color, the contorted flat of a stage.

The ring flared around his finger; it was the only warning she gave him.

The whole of the wall of fire banked and guttered, disappearing in that instant from view. But he felt the flames as they were gathered, shrouded in night, and he knew where they would erupt.

He lifted his shield hand; it was empty. He raised it palm up, but whether in command or plea, he could not say.

Instead he found the strength to speak a single word, and it was the same strength that had driven her, although the word was a whisper, choked of breath.

"*Anya.*"

Fire erupted around him.

She screamed a thousand things. The taste of metal was in her mouth, and it ran along the length of her outstretched arms, pulling all of her hair until it stood on end.

She had summoned the fire. She had called it down on him. It had killed far greater, far more powerful creatures. But Devlin?

No!

He stood. He stood there. She could see him clearly as the flames went from red to orange, from orange to white; could see his feet planted above ground that was slowly melting and screaming all the while.

She *hated* him. He had left her to *die*. She would *kill* him. He would *burn*. Magic? She had magic, now. She had *power*, and she would make him pay. Finally, finally, after all this time, she would make him pay.

Oh, she was screaming. Her eyes were all twisted; she couldn't see. There were demons in the way, and she wanted them *gone*, because she hated them, too—hated them almost as much as she hated Devlin.

Because if it weren't for them, she would be with him now, and they would be free, and they would be *happy*—

But, *no*. She couldn't think of that. She couldn't. He had left her. He had run.

It was her turn now. Hers.

Oh, but the demons irritated her. They were in the way. They were trying to kill her Devlin, and no one could do that. No one but Anya.

So she killed them first.

Valedan did not understand. He had time to spring away from Auralis; time to leap back, into the outstretched wing of Osprey guards. Their numbers had been winnowed, but their ferocity remained, and if they were as shocked as he, they showed none of their surprise. They closed ranks.

Even here, they closed ranks.

But they closed them around him.

Duarte was by his side. He tapped Valedan on the shoulder, his fingers dancing stiffly in the silent Osprey tongue. It was the only way to speak, here; the roar of fire was deafening.

And the silence of the man the flames could not consume, silencing.

That one there. Kill.

Not elegant, these movements; grace was absent from this tongueless tongue. But Valedan nodded. His expression conveyed the whole of his surprise: *She* was the mage?

Duarte's grim nod was the only reply he needed.

The Sun Sword was forged in fire; all blades were. But the fire that had tempered its edge was hotter by far than the fire that failed to destroy Auralis AKalakar as he stood, white and motionless, a beacon upon the field.

Valedan grimaced, bracing himself to charge. He did not sheathe the blade; although the stance suited single armed combat, it was not one that would keep him alive here. He let his sword arm guide him.

And it was his sword arm that Auralis grabbed. The whole of his mailed hand formed a fist around Valedan's wrist.

"No," he insisted, and his voice echoed. "Not her."

"She's the mage," Valedan shouted. But he did not attempt to pull free. The demons were already dying, and he was not Auralis, not Kiriel; he didn't care by whose hand. What he had to prove, here, could not be proved by the simple expedient of killing.

"Not her," Auralis repeated, and he swung his sword round.

The silence was profound, and it was fleeting.

Duarte AKalakar stepped forward, touching both of their shoulders with the tips of his fingers. They were bathed in orange light.

Valedan looked to the Primus; Auralis had eyes for her, and only for her.

"The fire wall is broken," Duarte said, speaking in his natural voice. "Sentrus?"

"Not her," he said, for a third time. Drawing breath, he added, "I'll deal with her."

The wilderness of his rage had drained from his face, his body; he was almost preternaturally still.

"Not alone," Valedan told him.

But Auralis shook his head, bronze braid batting the shield across his back. Northern braid. Northern man. "Alone," he said, and he began to walk.

Valedan turned to Duarte, and Duarte gestured: *Let him go.* Just that.

"He's an Osprey—"

"There are no Ospreys," the Primus said. Where once Duarte's statement might have been laced with bitterness, Valedan heard nothing at all in the neutrality of his careful words. Nothing but truth. "Look," he added softly.

The demons were fleeing.

In flight, they took their shadow with them, as if it were ragged cloak; they were beggars now. If there was a Commander of note behind them, he had absented himself from the fray.

"Come, kai Leonne. We are far from the heart of the battle, and we have done what we came to do."

*   *   *

Alexis gathered the Ospreys—despite Duarte's words, they *were* only that to Valedan, always that—and they began their careful retreat. If the fires that had killed fully a quarter of Commander Allen's men had been banked, and the demons directly behind the moving shield of flame dispersed or destroyed, the threat was far from over.

Valedan brought the Sun Sword to bear.

"She'll kill him if she can," he told Duarte.

"Yes. I think you're right."

No permission at all in those words.

"Alexis—" Valedan began.

But her lips were a tight, thin line, and her expression denied utterly any ability to interfere with Auralis' choice. Defeated, he acquiesced.

And turning, he caught sight of the heart of the distant field. He was frozen a moment by what he saw there.

"Valedan?"

The banner of the Tyr'agar. The banner of the sun ascendant. He knew that the banner he saw was not in Aidan's hands, not in Ser Anton's; it was too distant. "Primus."

"Kai Leonne?"

"Ser Alesso di'Marente is upon the field."

Duarte swore.

"If I see truly, he does not fight *us*."

"He cannot—"

"He can," Valedan replied. "By Southern law, by Southern ideal, he *can*."

"If victory here is seen to be his—"

Valedan's smile was cold and slight. He understood Duarte's fear; it was almost his own. "If we have no victory here, the politics of the High Courts, North or South, mean nothing. And if I guess correctly, he is not . . . unwelcome.

"I see the banners of Oerta and Sorgassa upon the field," he added.

"You cannot afford to let him live."

"No," Valedan agreed. He reached into the pouch that he carried by his side; it was small and held little of value. From it, he drew the gift of the Matriarch of Havalla.

"Kai Leonne?"

"A moment, Primus." He drew it out in shaking hands. He had come this far. The Ospreys protected him as he stood, a scrap of ancient cloth in his left hand, the Sun Sword in his right.

He drew breath. *Only once,* she had said. He could use the gift only once.

And if this were the wrong time? If this moment was not *the* moment? He felt young, here, amidst the chaos and the unpredictability of the field. Young, uncertain, unconfident. All things he could no longer afford to be. He missed Serra Alina; he missed Mirialyn ACormaris, the Princess Royale of the Northern Court. It would never be his home again.

But he carried it within him, seeing those who had fallen, and seeing, more clearly, those who had not yet died.

"Valedan?" Primus Duarte said gently.

Valedan nodded, squaring slender shoulders. He unfurled the cloth, and saw that it was glowing in his hands. Hesitation was hidden; he drew the edge of the Sun Sword across his palm, and let the cloth absorb the blood that welled there.

The light grew. It was contained by script, letters swirling in light, and of it. He saw them clearly for a moment as they absorbed some small part of his life's blood, and he knew that to linger in indecision was to lose the moment; he had already decided.

Lifting voice, trusting the Matriarch of Havalla, he began to speak. He could not say, clearly, whether his words were in Weston or Torra; they were his, and that was all that concerned him.

Across the fields of Averda, across the narrow folds of the Green Valley, men looked up at the sound of words. Those who knew Valedan kai di'Leonne recognized his voice at once, and if they were few, they counted.

Ser Baredan di'Navarre, his arm almost numb with the loss of blood, his brow grazed by claw, his eyes narrowed and weary; Commander Ellora AKalakar, her blade swinging, her feet planted above the fallen who lay closest to the demons that were now once again encircled; Commander Allen, sword still sheathed, the magi trembling at his feet in the uncontrollable rage of fevers that signaled their exit from the fray, and perhaps from the world; Commander Devran Berriliya, at the head of the unit that now joined the Southerners in their desperate attempt to reorder the line of battle.

Kallandras of Senniel College heard the words, and they reverberated through him, attuned as he was to all use of the gift. He did not pause to listen; he had no need. Listening was as natural to the bard as drawing breath, and he had need of both. The ring on his hand scorched his finger with its fervor, its wild rage; on the fields below, in the Southmost corner, someone had called the elemental flame, and it had come. He knew who. He fought.

Meralonne APhaniel, beside him, sword glowing with cold blue light, demons ringing him, pinions folding and stretching as they attempted to gain height or lose it in their awkward dance with the bard-called wind, seemed impervious to what was said.

Serra Alina di'Lamberto, sitting at the side of the injured, in a tent meant for women, and only women, lifted her head a moment. Not in wonder, for she was beyond it; the injured had absorbed all emotion, all horror, all hope. But she took some distant comfort, because it meant that Valedan was still alive. And as she listened, she smiled, because she knew that he was also almost wise enough.

Ser Andaro di'Corsarro, at the side of the Serra Diora en'Leonne, and the Serra herself, likewise listened, and in silence; they had not yet left the heights.

Aidan and Ser Anton, banner still held high, the younger with eyes wide and dark, the older with eyes narrowed and weary. He had drawn his sword, and he had killed, but he had not—yet—left horseback, or the side of the child that he had grown, in some unwise fashion, to honor.

Across the valley they raised their heads, and they were joined by the thousands, the tens of thousands, who had never personally heard the voice of the boy Tyr.

"I am Ser Valedan kai di'Leonne. I am the last of my line. Some say that the line has diminished, and I will not argue the point; I am here, and the Sun Sword with me. The Lord is absent from the open skies, and the Lady is hidden. It is therefore men, and only men, who will judge the truth of those words. This is *our* time.

"We have come here by the long road, and the harshest one. We have come because we desire power and dominion over the lands that we have held, or hope to hold. We have played the games of the Courts, high and low; we have intrigued with those who were once our enemies. We have traveled under different banners, and many have sworn their allegiance to one or the other, leaving their families and their fields in the light that must shine beyond this darkness.

"We are one force here. Divided by ambition, by desire, by politics, informed by Southern custom—we are always, and only, one people. The Lord of Night will never hold sway while we draw breath.

"Victory is ours to take. Let us take it. Let us remember the cost of the taking.

"And when we have had our victory, as Leonne the Founder had his, then we will decide the fate of our Country and our people. I am the last of the Leonne clan. If I fall, the man who can wield the Sun Sword will be the Tyr'agar; none will gainsay him.

"But there are two banners upon the field. One I command. One is commanded by Alesso di'Marente, the greatest of our Generals, the Lord's man.

"I challenge him to combat beneath the watchful eyes of the Lord of Day. Before you all, we will fight, and when the fight is over, one—and only one—man will lay claim to the Sun Sword, to the Tor, and to the legacy left by all who fight the Lord of Night."

Alesso di'Marente laughed as *Terra Fuerre* came to a sudden halt. He was wounded; he had not chosen the safety of the second line for his own. But he paused a moment in the lull between demon's fall and demon's rise, to lift the horn at his side.

To tender the boy, the last of the Leonnes, the only answer he *could* tender.

To have come this far, he thought, as the note died too quickly into silence, as his breath once again became attuned to the rise and fall of his sword. He should have tendered the challenge himself, years ago.

He felt no shame, and little regret; Lord's man, indeed.

They followed, who fought at his side. Northerner, Southerner; the lines blended. Thus were the words of the last of the Leonnes given strength and made true.

You are not your father's son, he thought, and he thought it without rancor or bitterness. *And I will meet you at last upon a field of our choosing.*

Ser Alfredo kai di'Callesta ran hand across his brow. The warrior's knot that had gleamed with such perfection at the start of the battle was dull now with ash and blood, but it held. As did Ser Alfredo. He had desired this: battle. War. Glory.

And glory was his, for the taking.

But it was bitter, to take it thus: only living son of the kai Callesta. His brother's voice was lost to him, and he accepted the loss; Ser Valedan kai di'Leonne had proved true to his word, and he had sworn oaths to Callesta. If blood defined family—and it did, in the South—oaths defined men.

When I am Tyr, he thought—and it was the first time the thought had come to him, anywhere—*I will be your man, and you will be my liege lord. There will be no other.*

But he did not bow; he did not offer Valedan his sword. Not in the traditional way. What was left was battle, for if they now traversed the terrain that the Generals would have called theirs, it was not without demons; they could fly, and they did not seem to need rest.

Ser Alfredo was weary.

But what the demons did not demand, he could not surrender to.

Father, he thought. He looked at the men who surrounded him now—Ospreys all—and he gave over the last of his childhood.

Ramiro kai di'Callesta thought of his son.

His dead son, voice raised on high, the wind's ferocity informing its syllables, its accusation. He had failed Carelo, and his son had died.

At the hands of creatures such as *these.*

Bloodhame burned with a light she had never shown; not for the first of her long lineage of wielders; not for the strongest. She was not as bright as the Sun Sword, but she was bright enough that a legion of torches would not have offered her light.

She cast shadows as she flew, his shoulder behind her heft, her familiar weight. Her edge glinted, like tears caught by sunlight; he should have been blinded by her.

But he was not.

Nor were his Tyran.

They had come to fight on the Northern flank of the demon army, and they had not yet been moved. He was aware that the servants of the Lord of Night had chosen to concentrate the brunt of their attack upon the central body of the army, but only peripherally; if he slowed to consider his position, he would now lie dead.

As Miko did, harem brother, the closest of his kin save Fillipo and the son who now stood at the side of the kai Leonne. Did he live?

The question burned him, scarring him as the blade did not. The banner of Callesta flew at an awkward tilt. He was aware of it as it listed; it had been planted in the ground by the Tyran who now struggled to ensure that it did not fall or falter.

They had paid the price for their protection of that necessary, deaf piece of cloth. He would lose more before this ended—if it ever did.

But he had listened to the words of the kai Leonne, and he was almost satisfied. Alesso di'Marente was upon the field. Not by his side—never that, again—but there, his confidence and his canniness once again brought to bear against foes upon Averdan soil.

"Fillipo!" he cried.

He could see his par in the light the sword cast.

Could see that he bled, that his movements were slowed now; awkward. He was far away. Almost too far.

But Ramiro was the wolf of Callesta, and the only thing that stood between his par and him were the dwindling number of the demons that served the Lord of Night. He let loose a battle cry that seemed to freeze the demons for a moment as he began to carve his way—to literally carve his way—to Fillipo's side.

Lord Ishavriel recognized the blade that the human carried. He had not seen it in centuries. Had never thought to see it again.

And he realized, with bitterness and a certain black humor, that in his crafting of Anya a'Cooper, maddened with pain and loss and fear, he had also crafted, with little thought and less intention, a man who could finally wield *that* blade.

He let the stands of twisted trees go, at last. He had the power to hoard their gathering for a little while longer, but to do that was to risk his own destruction; he was granted some part of The Lord's power, but it was dwindling.

And he knew why. He looked up, and to the North, and he could see in the distance the cursed and hated figure of Kiriel di'Ashaf. Lord's daughter. Their enemy.

Anyone of power and consequence must know that she was upon the field, or above it. He knew, and it burned him.

But he was not yet finished.

He turned to face the mortal who had managed to wreak such havoc; saw fire follow in his steps.

Not here, he thought, and his smile deepened. He held Anya a'Cooper for just a moment longer, arms around her shoulders as she raved in a fury that seemed endless. As endless as the power she wielded.

He let the mortal cross the distance that separated them, counting his steps by the fall of the blood-bound kin that served Ishavriel and only Ishavriel.

And when he was close enough, Ishavriel smiled. "She is not

yours," he said, lending the words both gravity and power. "And she will never be yours."

Auralis looked up at the words, as if seeing the demon lord for the first time. "Let her go," he said softly.

"Let her go? If she desires it, I will do so. But you have no right to command me. You fled in terror, like a child. She trusted you," he added, with a cold, cold smile that was hidden from Anya because she faced this man. "She *loved* you."

"Anya—he's a *demon,* don't you see?"

Fire rained down on him. The injured that had not had time or strength to flee were ashes in a second. But Auralis survived, shielded by a growing, different flame.

"You discarded her," the demon continued, "when it suited you.

"But *I* preserved her. I saved her from a slow and terrible death, because I saw what she could be. What she has become. What could you offer her?" he added, and the contempt in his voice made Auralis AKalakar flinch. "You are nothing here. A man with a bauble of a sword who has already proved false to any oath of value. Who would have you?"

"*Let her go!*" He could not keep the pain from his voice. Could no longer hide it behind rage or hatred. At last, he had come to the place in which he had no defenses. Both the wild fire and the sword that he bore seemed insignificant; they did not change the truth of the demon's words. They did not change what he was. What he had known, for so long, he *truly* was.

He looked at Anya's face, at the open rage and hatred in her expression. Kin to his?

He wanted her comfort. He despised himself for it, but it was true: he wanted absolution for his crimes. "Anya?"

She spit.

It hurt him. He was young again, in this fell place. He did not know how to summon his age; all of the calluses built by years of hiding, of lying, of pretending, had been torn away, and he was bleeding profusely.

"She will kill you," the demon said coldly.

Auralis laughed bitterly. "Probably."

"I will not release you from your service to that blade so easily," the demon replied. "Look long. I saved her, when you fled. I offered her strength, where you treasured weakness. *Anya.*"

Anya's eyes snapped open.

"If you want her, hunt. She will certainly hunt you, if you survive."

"Anya!"

She screamed his name again, her hands in fists, her body shaking.

He could almost reach her. Almost.

And then what? He had skirted the edge of death for so long, it looked like peace.

Peace, of course, was to be denied him. Shadow and light filled the clearing, the small space upon which Anya had stood.

When it lifted, she was gone.

"ANYA!"

He sank slowly to his knees, halfway up the incline that led to the trees—to what was left of the trees—that rimmed the valley. The air was acrid; he could smell ash, fire, and a hint of blood. The tail end of the demon army had stood here, devouring by the slow movement of *her* flames any and all who stood in their way.

He had saved lives, by coming here.

He had saved so many lives.

Funny, how little he believed it as he bent his head in the darkness.

CHAPTER THIRTY-SIX

KIRIEL felt his pain so clearly it was like a slap in the face. Buoyed by shadow, wild with it, she looked down through strands of drifting, swirling hair. Auralis AKalakar was almost prone to ground, his knees to chest, his sword all but discarded by his side.

She felt . . . contempt.

Auralis had been, of the Ospreys, the closest to her. She knew, as she watched him, that close was very, very distant. He had fled in fear. She? She had fled for other reasons. The home that had been denied her had been denied by her *choice*. She had not forsaken it; she had rejected it.

Beneath her feet, other pain reached her, but none so clear. Not even the pain of the dying, with their sudden confusion, their loss of focus and direction. Oh, she felt them. She felt them all, like tiny waves lapping against a great, vast cliff.

She was that cliff.

They could not break her.

But the tide, such as it was, had risen, and it would not recede while she stood thus.

She was uncertain that she even wanted it *to* recede.

Fiara was dead. Cook, below her small feet, was dying, blinded by the strike of one of the lesser kin. He stumbled, roaring, across the ground, and she watched his awkward gait, waiting for the moment that it would take him, at last, to the death he had barely avoided.

Alexis was injured.

Valedan, injured.

She could not sense Duarte, but she knew that he felt the loss of the handful of men and women who still served his nameless unit. They had once been proud and fierce, in the South, but the North had at last clipped their wings; they were no more birds of prey than the cerdan and the soldiery that listed against the force of The Lord's kin.

Oh, they fought. She watched, able to make them out in ones and twos, their line stretched and thin, the dead growing in number as the living succumbed to the greater power.

This, *this,* was the law of the South. Power ruled.

And there were none upon that field that were more powerful than she.

Wind teased her hair and she lifted her chin.

Across from her, in the folds of the angry element, Lord Nugratz fought. He was pressed, but not yet threatened; Kallandras and Meralonne APhaniel held him back, hemming him in. Denying him, by the simple play of weapons and the complicated weave of ancient magic, the ground, and the victims that should have been his.

She could feel his rage: He was one of the Lord's Fist, and unaccustomed to loss. The only loss of significance that he had taken yet was at her hands.

At her hands, and the hands of those who served *her.* Who called her, fully and finally, the Queen of the Hells.

She lifted a hand, and her sword came; she was not aware that she had sheathed it until that moment. "Anduvin," she said.

Suspended in air, as she was, he executed a graceful bow. "Lord," he said, without pause and without struggle. He accepted what the *Kialli* themselves had long fought against: the truth of her title. The legitimacy of her reign.

"Telakar."

The sky remained as it was.

"*Telakar.*"

Lord Telakar turned to Elena of the Arkosa Voyani. No, she amended, but without the bitterness and shame that had so scarred her demeanor, Elena Tamaraan. Elena alone.

"Telakar?" His name was like a caress. She was afraid to speak it aloud, and when she did, she knew why. She owned him, now— but ownership was complicated; it did not exist in a single direction. Binding, she was bound.

It should have felt wrong.

"Elena," he said, bowing slightly. She was covered in cuts and scrapes, and she bled from wounds that would probably scar without treatment, although they would not threaten her life. Taken, all, at his hands, she let them go. She had seen worse. Had done worse.

"What is wrong?"

"You cannot hear her?"

She shook her head. "Hear who?"

"Kiriel," he replied softly. "My Lord."

"No." She shuddered. "And I'm not sure I want to."

"Ah. You traveled some leagues in her shadow, Elena, and you did not think to fear her."

"She was different then."

"You are gifted," he replied. "She *was* different. She was like the sleeping dragon." He gazed skyward, through the vast canopy of night trees. The darkness was no impediment to his vision, although it still marred hers. "Now she has begun to wake."

"Is that bad?"

He laughed. "What do you think?"

"It's bad."

He nodded. "She calls me," he added quietly.

"Do you want to go? Do you think you should?"

And his smile was thin. "You do not understand what you have invoked, do you, little Voyani?"

"Your name," she began.

"Yes. My name." He lifted an arm. "And if you desired it, you might force from me any manner of servitude by the simple expedient of will. Do you not desire it, Elena? It will grant you a measure of power that you have *never* known."

"Don't," she said sharply.

"Do not?"

"Don't test me."

He laughed. "It would not have been considered a test, when the Cities of Man ruled the heart of what is now desert. And I would never have been so taken, at that time."

She would have denied that his words were true, but she felt the truth in them viscerally. "Then why?" she asked him.

"Because," he chided her, "I would have killed you otherwise, and with just as little choice. I chose my master," he added. "Then and now."

"Do you want to go?"

"To her?"

She nodded.

"I . . . do not think it wise," he said, after a pause. He reached out and snapped a branch that seemed to be in his way. It was as thick as her leg. "But if I do not go, she will know, and she may fight for me."

"She did not bind you."

"No, clever girl, she did not. You can hold me a while against her dictate; the law of the Hells has granted you the greater power."

"Why?"

"Because this is *your* home."

Elena shook her head, caught once again by the gift that had been denied her cousin for the whole of their adult life together. "This is *her* home," she said softly. "She was born of the world."

Telakar's eyes widened slightly. "So," he said, the syllable sharp.

"Telakar?"

"I begin to understand Isladar now," he said, no pleasure at all in the words. Not even the dark pleasure that so often spoke of malice. "I will not go to her," he added, "unless you command it. I will not go until I have no other choice." He paused, and then said, "But if you do not command it, she may well kill you."

"Can she?"

"Not with ease," he replied. "Not while I exist."

It was enough. She reached out suddenly and caught his arm. It was hard and cold, as unlike the limb of the tree he had casually snapped as stone was.

"She is waking," he said again, and he turned his face to the West, "and your time is short."

"But we're *winning*," she replied. She looked down at the forces upon the field. "The fires are gone," she added softly. "And the line holds once again."

"For now. But she is a vessel, and the power that the dead give her has grown beyond your simple measure." He stilled a moment, and then said, "Can you not hear it?"

"Hear what?"

"The footfalls," he replied, "of the Beast."

It had come. One of two, it had come. The path sundering and fraying beneath its great weight, the fall of its ancient steps, it had journeyed from the barren white of the Northern Wastes, leaving at last the courtyard in which it slumbered.

Its brother was gone; the road had not held the course for long enough that they were both granted passage.

But alone it was more than enough. Feet against the earth, the Old Earth, it woke things ancient, and was in turn wakened by them. Lifting its lumbering, ancient head, it snapped its great jaws, and between the rows of its long teeth, the kin died, leaving dust in their wake.

The earth woke as it walked. The Beast felt the waking and it roared in angry greeting.

Across the field, demons and mortals, twined in deadly combat, froze as the Beast roared. The kin fled it, leaving their victims as they sought safety to either the North or the South; it leaped from the heights with a nimbleness that should have been denied something of its size.

Valedan kai di'Leonne looked up. He had almost arrived at the second banner of the Tyr'agar upon the field; his own followed at a safe distance.

"Duarte," he said, rank forgotten.

Primus Duarte, hands in motion, was as frozen as he.

"What . . . is that?"

Duarte shook his head. "I do not know," he said. And Valedan heard death, at last, in the Primus Duarte's words.

Meralonne APhaniel closed his eyes briefly; Nugratz banked. They executed the penultimate step in a dance that must end in death, and they parted a moment, as if they were only the opening act for what was, in the end, the heart of the play.

The kinlord circled wide, their confrontation all but forgotten.

"You have failed," he cried, in his low grating voice, his bird's voice. "The Beasts have come."

"The Beast," Meralonne replied. "There is only one."

"One is enough. In this place, in these lands, one is more than enough."

"He cannot fly," Meralonne shouted, but Nugratz was circling higher, above the reach of the wind's currents.

"APhaniel," Kallandras cried out, interrupting their conversation. "Whose voice do I hear?"

And weary, Meralonne replied, "The voice of one of the eldest," he replied. "The get of the wild gods."

"Wild gods?"

"Even the gods knew youth," the magi said, words carried by wind to where Kallandras now stood, arms wide, weapons girding both hands. "And in their youth, they were not as they are now; time, distance, and the influence of man have changed them. He is as he was, trapped upon the plane when the Covenant between the gods and man was first put into motion," Meralonne added. "And he is of this world."

"He is a danger to us."

"He is a danger to the world," Meralonne replied, "and he is a force beyond either of us, Kallandras." Weariness informed his expression, his posture; age settled upon his features, as it so seldom did. "We are not, I fear, up to this task." He gazed skyward, at the dwindling figures of Nugratz and his followers.

Turning to the magi who also adorned the skies, he said, "Scatter. But do not touch the ground where the Beast touches it, or it will devour you whole."

"Magi—" Gyrrick began. He was wounded in several places, and the bow that was his first show of strength was chipped.

"No," the magi replied, stern now. "You may indeed hit him with your weapons," he added, "but it will serve only to enrage him and draw his attention. He speaks with the voice of the plains," he added, "and the earth itself will wake when he commands it; there is not a place upon the earth, in the water, or in the air, which will then protect you. Do not draw his attention."

"I fear," Kallandras said, fist forming round the complicated band that girded his thumb, burning there, "that your warning comes late, APhaniel." He pointed, and they looked as if he had used the power gifted him at his birth. Power of bards, of words, of command, although he had used none.

Kiriel di'Ashaf, recognizable only by the armor she wore, began her slow descent from the skies.

She had ridden the Beast before.

Once, when she was six. Once when she was twelve. And once, ah, once, when she was older. The first time, she had been frightened, not of the Beast, but of the Lord who had ridden by her side, on the back of his brother. The tines that ringed the great creature's back were spaced evenly in such a way that the careful and the wary could find seating between them, but it was not comfortable; never that. Although the Beasts responded to the will of The Lord—as all creatures did who lived in the Northern Wastes—they were slow creatures, plodding, deadly only when their stretch of jaws snapped unexpectedly.

Lord Isladar had said they sensed fear, and she, naïve then, had shown and felt none. None save that reserved for the god that the others called her father.

Ashaf had never come to see her ride the Beasts, although she may have watched from the safety of the tower window that was their one vulnerability.

But witness or no, Kiriel had ridden upon the back of the Beast, and she knew as she descended that *this* was her throne. And there was no better, upon the field of battle.

Shadows bore her, enfolding her like cloud. She could see through them, could see around them, could see by them, for their darkness was, to her eyes, a type of light, a beacon. The Beast was not as slow as it had been during any of the three processions; it raised its great head, snuffling at air as if air itself were foreign, a threat.

But she showed no fear; felt none.

Instead, she spoke its name, and her voice was the dragon's voice, a quiet roar, a thing that could not be forced to contain something as simple as syllable.

She felt the kin upon the fields.

She felt their names as if their names were wildflowers or weeds, slender and easily plucked. She pulled them all as Anduvin descended by her side. He fell short of the beast's back, trusting her control. Or perhaps he had no choice; she could not easily say. His name was brighter than the others because it was already hers; the others, she must gather.

Something nagged at her.

Something unwelcome. She lifted a hand to swat it away—and

saw the one place in which shadow did not reign: her finger. The ring burned there, brightly. It caused her no pain; it was, she thought, with a grim satisfaction, incapable of causing her pain.

She almost touched it; she thought that she might—at last— be free of its constraint.

But the nagging something that she had thought might be the ring returned, struggling to capture her attention, and as the great Beast began to move through the line of the kin that were fast becoming *hers,* she heard it clearly: Someone was singing.

And she knew the song.

It was not enough. The Serra Diora lifted voice, and after a moment, another joined hers, adding deft harmony, an underpinning to the melody that carried by voice alone. The Beast, however, continued to move, and as he did, the armies fell silent. He was huge; like a small building that seemed in the process of being constructed. All of the night seemed diminished in his presence; his jaws glittered as teeth revealed themselves, a wall of starlight. Of death.

Yollana's warning made flesh.

Diora bent her head and started to truly sing.

But a hand touched her open lips, and the hand was cold as the rumor of a Northern ice she had never seen. She was astonished; she was not accustomed to touch, and fell silent.

The demon had moved so quickly, Ser Andaro had no time to react.

"You waste your power," he said. There was no doubt at all in the words.

"I have not yet begun," she replied, the heat in the words unseemly for a Serra of her import. For *any* Serra.

"Do not sing yet," he told her with power, the words as much a command as any she could utter. "The earth is rising. Can you not see it?"

She shook her head, to be free of the ice of his fingers. He withdrew, assured for a moment of her compliance.

"Kiriel was born for this," he told them both, Ser Andaro now armed, his sword's edge an inch from the kinlord's hand. It did not fall, and Diora was glad of it; she knew what waited if Ser Andaro truly challenged Lord Isladar.

"No," Diora said firmly. "She was *not.*"

He laughed. It was not kind. "You were barely born, Serra. How can you judge what the intent of her creation was?"

"She is living. She has choice."

"So, too, did the men who were your distant kin," he answered, remote now. "And they chose their deaths long before they accepted the fact. The ground was consecrated, and the sacrifices have been taken. Can you truly not see her in her glory? She is almost akin to . . . the gods."

"What you knew of her—what you know of her—is not all that she is."

"No. But in this moment, it is enough. Do not waste your song, Serra. If there is moment for you to sing again, you will know. And if there is not, it will count for little. This is her crucible. It is here that she will be tested, and she will emerge from that test, and her emergence will be the answer to a long question."

"You live forever," Diora replied. "How long can a single life be?"

"The question was asked long, long before she was born. She is marked by it. She wears the beginning upon her hand."

The singing was gone, as suddenly as it had begun.

But she heard its echoes, as if it were moonlight given voice, the natural consequence of night's fall. The tines of the Beast were sharp as she gripped them; sharp enough to cut. But they cut leather, not flesh; she did not bleed. She knew enough, remembered enough, to know how unsafe that was.

The Beast's jaw snapped. Demons fled, leaping to one side or the other; the battlefield was no longer divided to the West and East; it was to the North and South that the armies now stood.

All save one, and it waited the death that she offered.

She called the kin out, and they came. They came from the heights, cursing her all the while, and she reveled in their fury, their uncontained hatred. She was mortal; they were eternal. But it was in her hands that The Lord's power resided, and from her shoulders, at last, that her father's mantle flowed.

She could see, trapped by flesh, all of the colors that the living never know: the details of the soul, the etchings of a life, another chapter in a long tale, writ there in grays and silvers, in blacks and pale, pale whites. She was struck by their beauty. Death would not extinguish them. But death would drive them from her hands; she could not hold them.

Not yet, a voice whispered. *Not yet, but soon.*

Her father's voice.

Father, a word she had always feared. But she thought it now, although it did not cross her lips.

When? she asked. But she did not ask it loudly, and the ripples of power that ran through her body made her giddy enough that the lack of answer did not trouble her.

Make this land yours, he whispered.

Yes.

Yes, she thought. If it had been hers—if it had truly been hers from the start—then Ashaf would never have left her.

Would never have been able to leave her; her soul would have been captive, cherished, and honored, for all of eternity.

The next time, Kiriel would be ready, because Ashaf would return; Ashaf's soul would walk this world again. That was immutable; the law of Mandaros. The law, as well, of the Hells, but the Hells surrendered nothing, in the end, that had chosen to join it. Nothing.

Valedan saw the Beast as he reached the banner of the Tyr'agar. It was almost all he could see; it filled the whole of his vision, like nightmare. Sleep, the natural context of such visions, was well beyond him. The Sun Sword lit the field like a beacon, and the creature made its way toward that light. It would extinguish the blade, he thought, and he shuddered. But he did not lower it; did not let go.

"General!" he shouted.

Alesso di'Marente, bloodied and unbowed, turned a fierce grin in his direction. "So," he shouted back. "The last of the Leonnes has come, wielding the Sun Sword. This is your crown, boy."

Valedan nodded. "It will be," he said, meaning it.

"Will you stand in the wake of the creature?"

"Will you?"

Terra Fuerre was dull and flat, runnels black with demon blood. Answer enough: He lifted it.

They were enemies. They could be nothing else.

But the enemy of an enemy could be an ally, and they faced each other briefly before turning their attention to the enemy that rode the Beast's back.

Only Valedan knew her name, and he did not call it aloud.

Maybe Ashaf's soul was already here.

Kiriel searched the encampment. Would she know it, if she saw it again? She had seen it every day of her living memory: its soft gray a contrast to the harsh, hard lines of black that informed most of the human Court.

Yet here it was not so unique.

Where would it be, should it return? Where would she be? *Not here,* Kiriel thought, and found comfort. She would go to Russo. Certainly, to Russo.

The village that Kiriel had vowed to protect.

The Beast reared, almost dislodging her. She cursed, tightening her grip upon its spiny ridge. *Show no weakness.* Her earliest lesson.

And Ashaf had been her weakness. In the Court.

Here.

No. No, she thought. Not here. She drew her sword. Not here. Ashaf *was not here.*

The Beast roared again, rearing. She knew that to fall was death; it challenged her as it had never challenged her before. But before, she had ridden by the side of her father, and nothing that lived in the Wastes openly challenged the Lord of Night. Not even the First-born, slumbering in the cold of a courtyard beneath the open moon.

"Take the mantle," Anduvin said. She looked to the side and saw him; he walked upon air. "Take it, Child of Darkness, or discard it; you cannot have both."

"Have what?" she shouted, her fingers slipping. She adjusted their hold, cursing.

"Daughter of Darkness," he intoned, "you will be Queen of the Hells, or you will be nothing. Decide."

Had she not already decided? Did she not now command the vast portion of what remained of this army?

He said, "There is no place in the Hells for souls such as Ashaf's. You will never have her again."

And *she* roared, Beast's voice her own, fury guiding the sound. Anduvin flew back, flew far indeed from view; she was aware of him because she owned his name.

Had she the time, she would have made him pay for his interference.

"You will keep her," he said, and she could hear every word, as if distance was simple illusion, "only when you have darkened her. When she has passed through this world, time and again, and the subtlety of her weakness has been destroyed. You will have what remains, Kiriel *di'Ashaf.* But you will not have what she *was.* Accept it, and you will rule all."

She caught the Beast firmly in hand, shadows binding its head, forcing it down. And as she did, she looked ahead to where the tents lay almost exposed.

Between them, tents and Beast, were gathered hundreds of men. At their head, two, one she recognized and one she did not.

"Destroy them," Anduvin said, his voice carefully neutral, "and you will own these lands. What happens after is up to you."

She nodded grimly.

She knew what the serafs suffered at the hands of the clans. She could do this. She could—

A roar interrupted her litany. It was not the roar of the creature she rode; it was higher, thinner. And it was very, very close. She had time to turn. Time to raise her sword.

Time to see the three heads of Falloran, the demon that had guarded the steps of her tower for the whole of her memory. He was limned in fire; fire gouted from his three jaws, and fire lit his six eyes. His paws were splayed wide, but the great claws that nestled there were encased in his flesh; he had not extended them.

Memory.

He did not extend them. He did not bare his teeth at her, although he exposed them. She froze as he leaped, and her blade swung up in an arc that would have ended his existence had she not forced it down again, a few inches lower.

Even those few inches were not enough; Falloran yelped as it struck him full in the thigh of his foreleg. But momentum carried him anyway, and his weight bore her aloft, and away, at last, from the back of the great Beast.

His fire did not burn her; it never had. It danced along the strands of her hair, clinging there, feeding on the shadows she had gathered.

No, she thought. Not shadows. Lives. But the lives held nothing of value; they were already spent, and what they contained was beyond her.

The weight of his paws bore her back; they had always done that. She could feel the walls of the tower at her back, the ghost of them some part of her childhood. She could hear his growl, his roar, and his whine; the three heads speaking at once. He had never had words. She had asked Isladar once why he did not speak, and Isladar had replied.

"He has forgotten what he once was, and he is at peace because of it. He serves," he added. "He will *never* rule."

"No one will," she had answered defensively. "You all serve the Lord of Night."

Isladar had not replied. She should have known that this was significant; all of his silences were. But she was young, then.

Young a moment, now, as Falloran bore her to ground. He did not lick her face; he was not a dog, although his form implied some kinship with those brief and mortal beasts. But his jaws chattered, and the noise that came from his open mouths was a noise full of accusation and anger. He was jealous.

Jealous.

She had deserted him, at the foot of those stairs, and he had waited there for her return. Had waited in silence, had waited in anger, biding his time.

He had hated Lord Isladar. Had always hated him.

He had never hated Ashaf. Ashaf had feared him, and this fear had drawn his hunger time and again—for no matter what Kiriel told Ashaf, Ashaf had never been able to master the fear. But it was not fear of Falloran, not precisely; had it been, Ashaf would never have survived.

No, it was fear *for* Kiriel.

For what she was. For what she might become.

Kiriel cried out in pain as Falloran lunged. His teeth clipped her skin, and she bled. But had he desired her death, he would have done more.

He did not.

"Get off me, you big oaf!"

He barked. Really barked. Had he a tail, he might have wagged it, and that would have been a crime against the dignity and power of his form. She swatted him with her free hand, and he cried out in pain, cringing back.

The ring was burning.

Inexplicably burning. She felt its sudden presence, its sudden heat. Nor was she the only one.

The great Beast roared and turned, its jaws a vast cavern, its breath a furnace. What Falloran could not do, it could, and Kiriel was almost beneath it.

She cried out, bringing her sword up awkwardly, power forgotten. And Falloran turned, leaping in a single swirl of motion, his middle head fixed upon the underside of the great Beast's jaw.

She cried out again, and this time, she exposed fear without thought. Had to: she could not give name to what she feared.

But the whole of her army faltered as she did.

The ring, she thought in desperation. She should have removed it when she had the chance. She lost sight of the souls of the living; lost sight of the names of the kin. She saw only the Beast, the two beasts, and she was caught a moment as the three jaws of the smaller one snapped at the greater.

Cried out again, in fury, as the great Beast threw up its head, dislodging what clung there. As long jaws snapped shut, crunching bone.

Falloran was truly of the Hells. He did not cry out in pain.

But Kiriel did.

He likes me, she told Isladar, placing her small hands—were they ever that small, truly?—between Falloran's open jaws.

He does not 'like' you, Kiriel. He is bound. Blood-bound. He serves you because he has no choice. If you unleashed him, he would eat your hand. You are foolish.

No, she replied, obstinate child's voice young and high to her adult ears. *He does. He likes me. He doesn't like you.*

He would not. I bound him.

She listened to Isladar in almost all things; his gravity and his certainty carried much weight. But in this, she was certain he was wrong.

Oh, she had been foolish then. She could believe that demons could love. Even her. Especially her. She had trusted Isladar.

She rose from the ground, sword in hand, and she turned it at last upon the Beast that had born her in her isolated moment of triumph.

And all the while, the ring burned, searing her vision, blinding her fully, cutting her off from the power that she could almost grasp. What she had taken was hers; she was to be denied more.

It was not enough.

The Beast's jaws did not open, and she heard, again, the terrible crunch of bones. Falloran would die here. He would die; he would become ash, and the winds would scatter him.

But she had been right. All along.

Her blade swept along the right side of the great Beast's head, taking its eye.

That caught its attention, and she realized, as he dropped Falloran, that she *did not want* his attention. She called the kin, but they did not answer.

Or rather, not all of them did. Lord Anduvin was by her side in that instant, and his blade shone, red and silver, in the night sky.

"Kiriel!" he shouted.

"Take him away!" she shouted back.

His blade pierced the side of the great Beast, like a gnat. It did just as much damage.

"Take him—" Anduvin paused. He gazed at her fully for the first time since she had ascended into the open sky. "Daughter of Darkness," he said.

"Do it!"

She could command him. He was hers.

But he was not hers in the way that Falloran was. Not hers in the way that Ashaf had been.

Her vision blurred as she raised sword again, her feet finding purchase against ground, and only ground. But the ground rumbled, speaking through thinned leather to the soles of her feet, and she realized then that the earth was awake, and that it was listening.

All this for a dog.

For a dog, for a pet, for something that would gladly eat every child in the village of Russo. But Ashaf had never hated Falloran.

She turned wildly, risking death to face Valedan kai di'Leonne. To face him, seeing only the surface: his face, his watchful expression.

The ring burned.

It was the only way she knew it was speaking.

Time froze. Her blade froze; Anduvin froze. Even Falloran, jaws clenched tight to capture all sound, all possibility of sound, was frozen.

She cast her glance across the field, and she saw Valedan, as she had last seen him, Sword burning gold in the grim night. He waited the approach of the Beast; she saw that now.

And he waited without fear.

No, she thought, frowning, as his expression was at last fully revealed. He was not without fear. But there was no accusation in the glance that had met hers; she knew because it was frozen in place.

The kai Leonne, almost Osprey, almost Tyr, had chosen to trust her. And in the face of the truth, he proved himself a *fool*. He trusted her still.

By his side, a man she did not know gazed upon her as well. His expression was schooled, hard as steel, and his eyes were shining brightly. No light girded his weapon, but his weapon was not without strength; she could see the scattered ash at his feet that spoke of the remnants of the kin.

No trust in his face, but why should there be? He was kin to her, she realized; not to Valedan. He lived for the battle. It defined him.

For the whole of her life, it had defined her.

Ah, the ring. She raised it, her hands moving slowly through air made viscous by spell. The whole of her life? No. Not quite.

In Averalaan, she had learned to live without war. She had *hated* it. She had hated the weakness that came with the ring. Had hated the heat, the cold, the humidity; had hated the way her skin seared when the sun was bright, sweated when the day was hot.

But she had learned to live with it.

And she realized that in living with the lack of power, she had gained something else. The Ospreys had ceased to fear her.

It was *so wrong*. Fear had always fed her. She was kin to the Lord of Darkness, and fear was like food. Fear, pain, grief— the dark complexity of human emotion.

She had never felt what she saw in Valedan's face now in the same way. She had never felt it so viscerally as she did other things, and when she had stood upon the verge of adulthood, she had at last given up belief in them.

So it was not as an adult that she stood now, upon this field.

Ashaf had feared her. Ashaf had been hurt by her. Ashaf had grieved for her. All of these things were harsh and sharp; she clung to them.

But Ashaf had offered her song, in spite of these things. And there had been no falsity in the offer.

I loved Ashaf.

Yes. But Ashaf had never truly loved her. Would have hated her, to see her now. Ashaf had denied the darkness, and by so doing, had denied the truth.

Daughter of Darkness.

She had Anduvin, and Anduvin at least she never need fear losing. If he did not love her—and he never would—he could not *leave* her. He could not, should she bend her mind to it, do anything at all without her leave. She could turn from Ashaf now. Could face the memories, could separate them from pain and guilt, could let them go.

But she didn't want to.

What Ashaf felt, complicated, old, was only half of the story; what Kiriel felt, then and now, was the other half. She lifted her hands, one empty, and one wrapped around her sword. One cleaved to darkness and power, and the other? The other was an open palm. Half of two palms.

The symbol of her mother, her birth-mother, in the distant Northern Wastes.

Ashaf, she whispered, *I can never be the daughter you desired. I can never, ever be that.*

But I can be more than the daughter you feared. I have friends, now. I have a place here. I have come to preserve your village. I have done what you could not do.

The ring burned bright, upon her open hand. She held it aloft, hearing its voice, wordless and calm. It spread until she was a silver light, like a ghost, that wavered on the edge of vision, half-glimpsed, half-desired, half-feared.

Yes, the ring seemed to say. You *are* the daughter of the Lord of Night. But you are also the daughter of a healer, and the daughter of a kinlord; you are the daughter of a seraf. You can be any of these things, or you can be none: choose.

She lifted her head. Stared across the field to the heights of the East.

There, she saw him at last, as he stood bearing witness in silence: Lord Isladar.

What did you want of me? she asked him, although her lips did not move. Nor did he. *I understand what Ashaf wanted, Isladar. What did you want?*

As always, with the difficult questions, there was no answer. But as always, she had no courage to ask him the only question she desired be answered.

She turned at last to the Beast, to Falloran, to Anduvin. Raising her sword, she grasped at the power of the dead and the dying, at the sacrifices consecrated to the Lord of Night, and given for her use. Her eyes grew dark, and the light left her slowly, eclipsed at last by night.

With a roar, she moved, and time began again.

She struck the Beast.

Her sword pierced its hide. Its blood was dark, and it ran slowly, as if the frozen wastes still resided in the Beast's heart.

The names of the kin fled her, hovering at the edge of her awareness; the battlefield was no longer hers to command. Could not be, if she wished to move forward. The past was immutable, unchanging; the present was visceral. The future? If she had one, it was *hers*.

And she would decide where it led her, step by step.

I am mortal, she thought.

I am weak.

But it was not weakness that came to her as she lifted sword again; not weakness that she relied on as she drove her blade forward with the whole of her gathered strength.

The Beast could not be faced with *love*. Could not be faced with the pathetic desires that informed the whole of Ashaf's life. It could not, she realized, be faced at all.

The earth erupted in a crown at its feet.

She danced across its broken surface.

Choosing, always choosing, caught in the act and remade by each blow of the sword.

Lord Isladar bowed his head.

Bowed his shoulders, as if in acknowledgment of either defeat or a greater victory.

"I fear I must leave you, Serra Diora," he said quietly. "She has chosen the subtle road."

The Serra Diora lifted a brow, her gaze sharper than it would have been had he truly been a man. "Subtle?" she asked softly. Kiriel, in her frenzy, was the antithesis of the word.

"She has not chosen the power of either birth or mantle," he replied. "Had she, you would know; she would not fight this battle in this fashion. The names of the kin would be hers to take, to reave; she would have an echo of the power of the Lord of Night. But such an echo destroyed Cities in the time of Man."

"You will not stay to help her?"

"Against the Firstborn, in my current state, I can be burden or goad; I cannot deliver her from the danger she faces." He paused, and then added, "No one of my kin could, and there is not another who would even consider it.

"She is much hated, by the *Kialli*."

"Why?"

"Everything is," he replied, his lips twisting in a barbed smile. Death there. But not hers.

"She has made friends, in the North. And in the South as well, if I do not mistake you. I am not mortal, but I have studied mortals in my time. You care for her. It is a weakness." The contempt in the word held her fast; there was no affection in it. But there was a distant satisfaction, and it, of all things, made the Serra shudder. "But mortals have, in the past, made strength of such weaknesses that even the Arianni can envy.

"I must go," he added again, although his gaze touched the field. "If she wakes, if she realizes—" He shook his head. "I will not tell you what to sing again; you will live in a cage all your life, and your song is your only freedom." The words cut.

They were meant to. She knew that he knew of her gift.

He whispered a name, and it fled his lips, carrying only to the Serra Diora's ears.

She would have been stunned by what she heard there; it would have taken her minutes—hours—to assimilate it all. But another voice was louder still, and it demanded the whole of her attention.

The Beast was roaring.

And the earth, beneath its great paws, was screaming at last in rage and fury.

But she recognized its voice.

Recognized it, although it was distorted. No slow timbre, here; no waking curiosity.

The ground cracked. The valley sundered. Men were lost to the sudden cliffs that opened beneath their feet, dizzying in their depths, their darkness a force of nature.

And men were found again, by the howling fury of elemental wind. They rose like puppets or dolls, shorn of the threads and strings that might give them a semblance of life—but they rose; the earth followed, snapping stone and dirt rising in the shape of great jaws.

The shadow of the Beast.

Demons fled.

Men fled.

Only Kiriel di'Ashaf and the Beast remained, surrounded now by rocks, their battle defined by geography, wild and ancient.

And Serra Diora en'Leonne whispered a name as well.

"Valedan."

He could not answer. But she knew that he could hear her, and if she could offer him no more than a word, it was the right one.

"Protect my wife. Protect my child." Something she had never asked of any man. But he was not the Lord's man. Not the Lady's. The North defined him, and for the first time she was unalloyed in her respect for its legacy.

"Kallandras, I am on the Eastern plateau. Summon me."

Bold now. Reckless. She stepped out, and the air caught her, struggling against the flat of her feet.

Ser Andaro di'Corsarro cried out; she silenced him with a gesture. But she hoarded her words and her song, smiling as gently as only a Serra might. Hoping that he would see, and be comforted.

The air buoyed her up, and up again; the height was astonishing. For just a moment, the cage of which Isladar spoke had been opened, and she was free to fly. It was an awkward flight.

The demons who were not anchored to earth circled the air above her. She thought they might come for her.

Closed her eyes, because she needed the peace of ignorance in which to form and shape song.

She called the earth, as the Beast did.

But her demand was different.

In the Tor Arkosa, she had offered her song to the earth.

In the Tor Arkosa, it had answered.

Dwarfed by its voice, she had found hers, and she found it was strong.

All of this, she remembered.

And she remembered as well, what the Old Earth had replied.

It has been a long time, Daughter, since a mortal offered me their song.

I know you now. The rivers know you, that have slept beneath my surface. The land will know you as you pass above it. There will be life, yours and mine, within this cradle.

I take your gift instead of your blood. Bind yourself to the path you have chosen, and when that path has been traveled, when that burden has become, at last, too heavy, I will carry you.

I will sing.

The wind carried her above the heart of Kiriel di'Ashaf's battle. No demons joined the Serra Diora, but Valedan kai di'Leonne, her husband, now dared the broken rock, the new gap in earth, his sword singeing vision. He would not reach her in time; the earth prevented his passage with a blind will.

There was only one way to do what must be done.

And the wind fought against it.

She fell twice, stumbling, graceless as a village seraf. Each time she righted herself, singing a benediction to the wind, enjoining a harmony to the command in Kallandras' voice. The bard did not ask what she intended, and she did not offer explanation; they were of a mind, for just this moment.

He knew where he must place her.

She knew where she must go.

Rocks were gathered in the storm; dirt clung to her face, her hair, her hands. Branches, dry and brittle, tore the village seraf garb as if it were fine silk, scratched her skin, destroyed the perfect shell behind which any Serra must dwell.

Even in the storms above the Sea of Sorrows, she had been conscious of the loss.

But she was wild now; she, too, had chosen. What matter a few scars, a few wounds? The Beast would destroy the Averdan valleys in his rage, and only Kiriel stood between him and that destruction.

And she was losing.

Wind bore the Serra Diora above the small circle defined by the sharp ridges of newly broken rock, and when she had come at last to cast odd shadows, strewn with debris, above their moving bodies, the wind reluctantly banked, and she dropped.

Her knees bent awkwardly; her hands fell through the surface of the earth. Above her, sword's passage keened with a voice as dire as the wind's; she lost cloth to it, and the blade was slowed.

Had she been Northern, she would have cursed.

But words were her only weapons; she dared not use them so carelessly.

Not here.

"Diora, no!" Kiriel cried.

Diora sang.

But she did not sing cradle song; she did not sing the lay of the Sun Sword. Either would have been appropriate. Neither would have moved the earth.

She was not the woman who had bespoken the Old Earth in the Tor Arkosa; not the woman who had, by her song, evoked life in the desert's heart. Something had begun to change, even then.

She prayed that the earth would recognize her now, as it had in the Tor Arkosa. Prayed that it would offer her the peace it had promised.

Was she weary?

Oh, yes. The burden she had borne—the Sun Sword—was now in the hands of the only man fit to wield it. She had sworn, at the height of the Festival Sun, to face the Lord of Night, and she knew, now, with certainty, that this was as far as she could go: the Lord of Night was a god, and she was mortal.

She was ready to accept that word.

Beyond the spikes of stone, the spikes of flesh, the slender length of moving, dark steel, she saw new fissures appear in the earth's surface. Demons were agile; men, weighed down by armor, less so.

These fell, and the wind could not preserve them.

Because the wind fought the earth. Wilderness, here, and no place for mortals in it.

But the earth had promised her peace. And song.

"I am here," she sang. **"I have come, at last, to find the peace you offered."**

There was no peace in the breaking of its surface. No peace at all in the jaws of the Beast, in the claws that broke the earth and remade it.

She reached into the folds of her sari and drew *lumina arden*.

Against the Beast, it was no weapon. Against Kiriel di'Ashaf, no weapon either. And demons? There were none, now. Not one of them dared to face the Beast.

She plunged the dagger into her wrist, cutting vein.

Blood gushed toward the earth as she sang its name.

And its name was not confined by syllables; it was not an easy song. It was long, and made of seasons: planting, growth, harvest. She sang of desert, of hidden water, of the Cities that waited beneath its fallow surface. She sang of gods.

And she sang, again, of herself.

Who are you?

I am Diora. She sang of Teyla, of the miracle in Essla, of the babe who was not yet her son. She sang of fear, because it was almost all she felt.

But it was not all.

Above her, before her, Kiriel di'Ashaf planted her feet. "Diora!" she screamed, and the word made no sense. "Run!"

There was nowhere to run.

The Beast roared. The earth roared.

But it also began to sing. Rough song, the beat of war drums, the beat of death. But it was song, and Diora held it fast, pinning it with her own. Power fled her, blood fled almost as quickly.

She was dizzy with the lack of both.

There are always two voices, she told the earth, and she looked at the bleeding back of Kiriel di'Ashaf as she sang. **There are always two paths.**

She felt her throat; it was raw. Only once had it been this raw, and then, after the passage of hours in the dim lights of the harem's birthing room.

Here, minutes had passed.

Kiriel was wild with anger.

But it was a different anger, and it was bounded, in all ways, by sudden fear. She had thought to fight—and die—alone. She had not feared it.

The Serra's presence destroyed that fragile peace, that blessed certainty. She could not protect the Serra. She could not protect her song.

But she could die trying.

* * *

The earth stilled. The fissures stilled. This valley, as Russo, was altered, would be irrevocably altered, by the evening.

The roar of the Beast was louder now, but it did not reverberate throughout the landscape. And because it did not, Diora heard the changing tenor of earth's voice. Old Earth.

Her last cradle.

She could not stand. Had she wanted to, she would have failed; the earth held her hands fast, and it would not let go. But it had held more of her than hands; she did not struggle against it.

She struggled, instead, against lack of consciousness. She had cut too deeply in her desperation.

The deaths of the armies will be consecrated. They are sacrifices. She is their vessel.

Heard Yollana's grim voice, grimmer warning.

Will this give you power, Kiriel? And then, softer, *Will you take it?*

CHAPTER THIRTY-SEVEN

K IRIEL *knew.*

Imbued by shadow, she was tainted by knowledge; she could hear both the voice of the earth and the voice of the Serra, blending slowly into one thing: death.

Not even the Beast offered that death. Great and ancient, scion of the eldest and the wildest, it had not aged, it had not changed. Whole civilizations had climbed their way out of the devastation wrought by the wars of men and gods, and those had crumbled while the Beast slept.

The Old Earth was not its master. She understood this now: it was parent, it was kin. The Beast, great lumbering death, was some part of its ancient, elemental fury given form and flesh, given leave to traverse the world above.

The wind came to her aid, at last; the earth was spellbound by the dying song of the Serra Diora en'Leonne.

Or so she thought; she still fought, and the Beast, no less vicious for the lack of Old Earth, fought as well, bleeding.

Kiriel bled. But neither of the combatants offered to the Old

Earth what the Serra Diora had blindly, instinctively offered; there was no willing sacrifice here. There was contest for survival. This, Kiriel understood. It was her haven.

Shadow sword broke skin; claws rent armor. Kiriel leaped past the fleet snap of roving jaw. This creature was not a god—but she realized that it was kin to gods.

And so was she.

Teeth glinted in moonlight.

Moonlight. It silvered her blade, and she realized only then that the fog of night had lifted; that the Lady watched, again, from her domain in the Southern sky.

Silence fell.

It was a terrible silence.

Kiriel filled it with a roar, and the Beast joined her; there was no beauty and no grace in their duet, a counterpoint to the fading song of earth and its mortal burden.

But she felt the shift of ground beneath her feet, and she leaped up, caught a moment in the folds of wind, as the great stone circle began to close.

It closed slowly. But the Beast was no airborne creature, and it seemed cumbersome now, weighted to earth. It roared and pawed ground, and the stone cracked at the force of its blow. Cracked, but did not give way.

Slow, the embrace of the earth.

She wondered if it were final.

Lowering her sword, she paid her tribute to this creature, wondering if it, of the two, had born her to the Court of the Lord of Night, in the Shining City that stood at the height of the Northern Wastes.

It struggled a long time against the earth, its cries fading. Kiriel, who had heard the voice of the earth, had been touched and cradled by it, understood for the first time the depth of the Old Earth's power.

And the cost.

Her sword found sheath almost blindly; she was not certain that she *had* sheathed it, for she remembered the distinct motion of tossing it to one side. She snarled in fury as the wind pulled her high, and she struggled out of its grip, to land at last upon the diminishing, broken crown.

Because while she would allow the earth to swallow the great Beast whole, it could *not* have the Serra.

Kiriel had shadow here; some small amount of the power that the dying had granted her still remained. She used it now.

Darkness-born, the Old Earth whispered. **I have kept our bargain. Go, now, and you will be spared.**

No, she told the Old Earth. **You made no bargain with me. Inter the Beast; you cannot have the Serra.**

She came to me, the Old Earth replied, peaceful now, but harboring, always, the terrible threat of anger beneath the placid voice. **And I, too, have vows to keep.**

The voice was wrong. The words, wrong.

Too mortal, she thought, and wondered why.

She will come to you in time, she countered. **In a short time. But she is not yet finished here.**

Daughter of Darkness, the Old Earth said, rumbling beneath her feet. **Leave us.**

Kiriel caught Diora's shoulders and held them fast. She could see neither the Serra's hands nor feet, but she didn't need to. She had found her purchase here.

Let her go, some treacherous part of her mind whispered. *She has served her purpose. You have kept your vows. The village is safe. The army is scattered. Leave her to the earth, or risk its wrath.*

The Serra offered her no aid; she was limp and heavy beneath Kiriel's hands. But Kiriel's hands were strong.

You cannot have her. You have heard her song; it is enough. I decide.

Then decide, Kiriel told the earth quietly. She, too, was sinking. She shook the Serra; the Serra did not respond.

Did you come here for *this*? she wanted to cry out. She even opened her mouth, but the dragon's roar was gone, and what came out was squalor, pathos, weakness.

Song. Broken song, shorn of the power of the Serra's voice, the Serra's perfect pitch, but song nonetheless.

The Serra Diora's gift.

Ashaf's gift.

Cradle song, wrapped in the shadows of a night that was passing, syllable by syllable, above them all.

She could barely hear it.

But Kallandras of Senniel could, and did; she heard his sweet, deep voice join hers, enjoining what she had not realized, until that moment, was a plea. He came across the ground, passing with ease above the fissures and cracks that had been laid there by the Beast.

Wind did not follow, and wind did not join him; he came alone, and unarmed.

She saw him when he was almost upon her, and she closed her eyes as he joined her, his hands gentling the fall of the Serra's dark hair.

He did not speak, but his song was rich and resonant; it offered what Kiriel could not.

And it passed from cradle song to something wordless; she felt her throat constrict at what she heard, although it was not meant for her. A gift, she thought. She could look at him, but only after moments had passed and the song had taken root.

He was a man. An older man. His hair, fine, was pale; his skin, pale as well. He was tall and graceful, his height diminished by his posture: he was supplicant here. But he, too, did not choose to let go of the Serra Diora.

She heard the isolation in him, then; knew that he was alone. But knew, as well, that she was not. He was not her friend, and with the passage of battle, she could not quite call him ally. But he was here.

"Are you keeping score?" another voice said, and this time she did look up, and her grip almost failed her for the first time.

Auralis stood in the moonlight, sword in hand. He was dark with sweat and dirt, where Kallandras seemed clean and perfect, and his lips were twisted in the bitter echo of what might have been a smile upon a different face.

Was, she thought, a smile.

She could not see more of him than his expression, his weapon, his armor. His soul—the colors dark and muted—was once again invisible to the naked eye. Or to hers.

But he was different. She saw that clearly.

He sheathed his blade. "She's stuck," he said, with a small shrug. But stuck or no, he lent Kiriel his strength.

She wanted to weep.

Could not have said why, and would never have given in to the urge.

"Kiriel," he added, as he knelt by her side.

She swallowed and nodded.

"Anya was here," he told her. As if—as if he had to tell *someone*.

"You're an Osprey," she managed at last. "You don't have to talk about your past if you don't want to. Those are Duarte's rules." She froze as the name passed her lips. "Duarte—"

Auralis shook his head. "I don't know."

"Alexis?"

And shook his head again. "I don't know. The field is different. It's like the village."

"The tents?"

This time, he smiled. Nodded. And she felt oddly comforted.

Kallandras sang his song of isolation, desolation; Auralis struggled with his in awkward silence. And Kiriel, caught between them, felt hers no less keenly.

But they stood here, together; they worked together, each in his or her fashion. Neither of these men was Ashaf; she could not turn to them blindly; she could not seek comfort that they did not, could never, offer. But she was older, and found solace in simple presence.

And when Valedan kai di'Leonne scrabbled up the side of sinking rock, she smiled blindly at him.

"Kai Leonne," she whispered, her throat raw. "We have your Serra."

Meralonne APhaniel came last.

He walked, as Kallandras had done, indifferent to the lands beneath his feet. His cloak was whole, his sword sheathed; he held a pipe in his hands, as if he were caught in the middle of an evening stroll.

"You do not understand the Old Earth," he told them all quietly.

No one acknowledged his words.

And he expected no acknowledgment. He heaved a weary sigh. "But I do. Kai Leonne," he added softly, "if you have a healer present, call him; if he is not waiting, all struggle here will be in vain. She is only barely living, if she still lives." His eyes were bright as sword's edge, a silver like moonlight, but colder.

He did not touch the Serra; instead he bent and placed his palms against the earth itself. His lips moved over a smile, and lingered there, but he did not speak; what passed between the magi and the earth, no one would know.

But when he rose, the Serra Diora rose as well, pulled free at last from her moorings. She was limp, her eyes closed, her face bruised and pale.

Valedan hovered above her like an anxious wife.

"Kai Leonne," Kallandras said, with gravity, "now is not the time."

"She is my wife—"

"She is *only* a wife. You are—you desire to be—Tyr'agar. Find the healer," he added, with meaning. "But do not expose yourself further. The men are watching."

"The men are scattered—"

"They watch," Kallandras replied. End of argument.

Valedan was stiff. He inclined his head, the Sun Sword loose by his side. Turning, he began to make his way toward the tents that had, miraculously, survived. They were not unscathed; they listed upon the shallow rise of ground beneath their pegs. But they were whole, for the moment.

He took three steps, turned, and then turned again, wordless.

"You should have let him stay," Kiriel said, when he had passed beyond them.

"You, of all people, understand why he could not."

She turned then, as if seeing the banner of the Tyr'agar for the first time. Seeing *both* of them.

"Why?" she asked, her hands upon the Serra. Auralis, largest of all present, cradled the Serra Diora against his chest. Gently, as if she were a child, all past hurts forgiven.

The bard's gaze assessed her, calculating and intense. After a moment, he shook his head. "My pardon, Kiriel di'Ashaf," he said, and bowed, declining her challenge. Or rather, accepting with peculiar grace—in a man of power—his loss. "Accept that it is so; you may choose to stay in the South, or to make your way North. Valedan has no such choice, and because he does not, he must create the illusion of distance."

They made their way toward the tent, and they were stopped only once.

By a stranger. An old man, with a long, pale beard.

He did not speak. He lifted a hand, and it swayed in the air, marked by a strange hesitation.

"Who are you?" Kiriel asked, her hand falling to blade.

He shook his head.

Kallandras of Senniel College tendered him a perfect Southern bow, but it was to Kiriel he spoke. "He is Sendari di'Sendari. Her father."

The man said nothing. Nothing at all. But he turned and walked away, his shoulders bowed by a weight that Kiriel sensed and did not understand.

"She's still alive!" she shouted, suddenly.

He paused. His back stiffened. But he made his way to the side of a stranger, and he remained there.

*   *   *

Ser Laonis di'Caveras was exhausted.

But when Valedan kai di'Leonne entered the tent, pale and grim, his eyes just a shade too wide, the older man rose, hiding his weariness behind a perfectly schooled Southern expression.

The other men and women in the tent—the Northerners—failed to notice what his presence asked of them. Ser Laonis di'Caveras did not. He tendered his respects, as liege to lord. And when he did, those men of the South who were not too injured to be unconscious attempted to rise, to do the same.

Valedan lifted a hand, and his gesture—perfect, imperious—ordered them, wordlessly, to rest.

"Ser Valedan," Laonis said quietly.

"I need a healer," Valedan replied.

Laonis was no fool. "Your injuries—"

"No. Not for me."

Ser Laonis closed his eyes. "For who, Tyr'agar?"

"For the Serra Diora en'Leonne," Valedan replied.

Laonis closed his eyes. He was *so* tired. His hands ached as he pressed their flats against tent flooring and forced himself to his feet.

Once, over a decade past, he had been summoned to heal the dying wife of a clansman. He had railed against fate; he had dared the anger of the Northern bard who wielded the wind, and he had, in the end, acquiesced.

That dying wife was now *his* wife, and she waited for him in the safety of Averalaan. He had feared to be unmanned, then; he remembered the fear now as if it belonged to a different man.

And perhaps it did; men changed, with time.

I will trust you, kai Leonne.

But Merilee rose and interposed herself—with no subtlety at all—between the two men. "Kai Leonne," she said, the strength of her matron's voice impressive, even to Laonis' ear. "Let me go."

"Not you," Valedan replied quietly.

"Ser Laonis has been busy here, and he is almost exhausted. The risk is too great."

"The risk," Ser Laonis replied, with a hint of Southern arrogance and impatience, "is mine to take." He could not bring himself to use her unadorned, Northern name.

She frowned. It was a mother's frown.

And he shook his head. "You are of the North," he said, giving emphasis to the words, and to the knowledge that lay behind them.

"Mother's Daughter," he added, when she did not budge, "you are necessary here."

And she heard what he could not say in the presence of so many clansmen. *You are demon-eyed, and it is demons that we have fought this eve. You cannot expose yourself here. And you cannot do what must be done without exposure.*

"That risk," she replied, with a severe dignity, "is *mine* to take."

"The Tyr'agar rules the field," he replied evenly, some part of his mind annoyed at this conversation with a woman, and the other part engaged by it, comfortable with it. The North had changed him. But it was not the North, not the Empire, which contained them both, and the rules of the Dominion were reasserting themselves in the lull. "And it is the Tyr'agar who has commanded my presence. I will go."

She seemed as if she might argue further, but Valedan put his hand upon her shoulder; he was a full head taller than she, slender with youth, and impatient with it. "I need a healer," he said.

She bowed, then, and let Ser Laonis pass. "Do not attempt more than you can achieve," she told him severely.

As if he were a child.

But then again, to the priestesses of the Mother, all men, all women, were children. He took no offense.

But he took water with him, and it was scarce. "Where is she?"

"She is coming," Valedan replied, and he edged his way out of the confined space of the tent.

"Kai Leonne!" And stopped there, blocking egress. He looked up at the sound of a woman's voice, and then looked down to see Teyla, his first concubine, kneeling between the rows of the injured. She was damp with sweat, and burdened with sleeping child; her hands were entwined around pale cloth. He frowned.

"Teyla, why are you here?"

"They needed help," she replied with a rough dignity. "May I attend you?"

He hesitated. And then he nodded.

She rose, babe in sling across her shoulder, and she, too, followed him as he made his way out, to the night sky.

It had changed. Ser Laonis looked up at the face of the silver moon, and he smiled; he drew breath, felt gentle breeze across his upturned cheeks, answer to the prayers he was Southern enough not to make.

Yes, he thought. *I will see to this wife. I will pay penance now for all that I failed to do in my youth.*

He followed where Valedan led.

*   *   *

Auralis was almost upon the first tent when Valedan returned to them. He recognized both the healer and the woman who followed, trailing at a respectful distance behind the men.

But the Serra Diora had not stirred. Had anyone thought to ask him, he would have told them she was dead.

Let the healer do it, instead. Let the healer have that grim duty; he was done with darkness for the eve. Injured, arms bleeding, chest aching, he was done.

He was numb now.

Yollana looked up at the Serra Teresa as the tent emptied.

The Serra said nothing.

"Na'tere," she began.

But Teresa shook her head stiffly, her fingers clenching too tightly around the fingers of an injured man.

"Na'tere—"

"No," she told Yollana.

"You are not needed here."

"I need to be here," Teresa replied. "Here, or someplace like it. We fight, here, but without sword, and without the power that the men have. It is a better fight."

"Na'dio—"

"She is in his hands now." Serene, that voice. Serene and perfectly composed.

"You're afraid," Yollana snapped. She could not be gentle, although she attempted it.

"Of what, Matriarch?"

The Matriarch of Havalla snorted at the use of her title. "Of what we all fear. Loss. Death."

"She is no child," Teresa replied softly. "I made my vows. As I could, I have kept them. But if she is injured, here, it is because she so chose. And if I am not wrong, Yollana, she chose well." Dark hair obscured her face as she bowed it, hiding expression. "Her husband is a good man. He is not a Southern man; he will do what I could not do."

"And that?"

"He will bring her back from death," the Serra replied, "or he will surrender her with grace."

Yollana, humbled, nodded. "Aye," she said, reaching for the pipe that so evoked the wrath of Merilee. She stopped herself from putting its stem to her lips, but it was a struggle. A pipe was wanted here.

Old friends, they waited in silence. But the silence was disturbed by the cries of men in broken Torra, and they resumed the duties they had chosen for themselves.

Auralis set the Serra Diora down, and as he did, the last man to join them came into view, gliding silently across the stretch of rippled land. He did not speak a word; it was not his place. Old, serene, unbent by his considerable age, he tendered the kai Leonne utter obeisance.

Uncomfortable with it, Valedan bid him rise, and the seraf did as he was ordered; obedience came naturally to him.

He unrolled a short mat; it was a mat that women used for kneeling, in the South. Auralis recognized it for what it was, and had it not been for the perfect dignity of the seraf who held it, he would have laughed out loud—and there was no kindness in that mirth.

Kiriel touched his arm, and the laugh, such as it was, guttered instantly. She watched him for a while, as the seraf took over the care of the Serra. And then she pulled him back. Not so far back that she could not see what might unfold, but far enough that their words would not easily travel.

She said, "You knew Anya."

Not the words he expected. He nodded, guarding the past that she had so rarely asked about. Osprey rules, here.

"And she knew you."

He nodded again, and this time, meeting her eyes, her golden, bright eyes, he said, "I knew her."

"She wanted to kill you," Kiriel told him.

He flinched.

"And she didn't want you dead."

And raised his brows.

"I saw her," Kiriel said, an answer to the question he did not ask. "And I know Anya."

"How?"

"She was there. Where I grew up." In the past that he, too, had rarely asked about. "She was mortal, but she lived in the demon Court. They feared her. She is not . . . sane." She said the last cautiously.

"How did she come to be there?" Each word heavy with the unsaid. Words could only contain so much.

"I wasn't alive then. But I was told that Lord Ishavriel brought her, frightened and insane. She stopped being afraid," Kiriel added. "But she never became sane. She hunted the demons when he let her."

"They hunted her?"

"Only the stupid ones." Kiriel shrugged. "And there are a lot less of those now. But she spoke to me. I . . . liked her. She wasn't afraid of me." She shrugged again, and then her shoulders stilled. "She spoke, once, of a man. He betrayed her."

Auralis nodded. "I did."

"It hurt her."

"I know." He hesitated, and then he offered her the only thing he could: honesty. "It hurt me. I don't know, Kiriel. I don't know what I'll do." Before she could ask.

Kiriel nodded. "If it weren't for you, they would have taken the Southern flank."

Auralis grimaced.

"Did Evayne know?"

And frowned. "She saved my life," he said at last. "And I hated her for it."

"That's pretty common." Kiriel's smile was odd; lopsided. Devoid of malice. "She saved mine, as well."

"What did it cost you?"

"I don't know yet. Maybe nothing."

His laugh was grim and feral. "It will."

And she nodded. "I know."

Together they turned. The healer now knelt by the side of the Serra Diora.

"She's not injured," Kiriel said softly. "I don't know if he can—"

But Auralis shook his head, lifting a hand and almost pressing it to her lips. He didn't. But it hovered an inch beyond them, shaking. "I'm sure I'm winning," he finally said.

"Winning?"

"I lost track of the number of demons I killed."

Her brows rose, and then she laughed. It was loud, but it was full of genuine humor. "You fudge the numbers all the time," she said. "I'll have to ask someone honest."

"Then you'll have to find someone who was never an Osprey."

"No, I won't. Alexis was betting on me." Her laughter dwindled. "Where is Alexis?"

Duarte AKalakar knelt in the dirt. He carried sheathed sword, and little else of value. But he held Alexis.

Her breath rattled. Her lips were red, and blood trickled from their corners. Eyes wide, too wide, in the stillness of her face. "We did it," she told him softly, seeing something beyond him.

He said nothing for a long moment. He could think of nothing to say.

"Make her give us back our colors," she said, when it became clear that he wouldn't speak.

"No one makes The Kalakar do anything," he replied, stroking her hair, her blade thin face.

"This wasn't really our fight." She coughed. Wheezing breath, rattling breath, accompanied the shallow rise of her chest. He bent his head over hers, and he kissed her forehead gently. Could not bring himself to kiss her lips.

"The . . . others?"

"Fiara is dead," he told her. "And waiting for you in the Halls."

"Cook?"

"We found him. He's lost an eye. His temper is still intact." He paused, and then added, "He killed the demon that—"

She coughed again.

He gathered her close, and held her, just held her. Healers were distant; he did not rise to summon one. If one could be found, he would have to be able to fly across the fissure that separated them from the camp.

Fly, he thought, as Valedan had done.

Ser Alfredo stood at a respectful distance, waiting. The Ospreys—those who had survived—guarded him carefully, but they did so with half their hearts; the other half, he knew, were with Alexis.

But only for a moment.

"It was good," she told him, her eyes now completely wide. "Even in this darkness, it was better than the last time. Go home. Retire."

He said nothing.

"Duarte?"

"I'm here."

"I can't see you."

"I'm here, Alexis."

"Good." She coughed again; last cough. He knew. "Don't let the carrion eaters get me."

"Never."

She was half of his life. He closed his eyes, pressing his face to hers, wanting to kiss her. Afraid that the last thing he would have, if he did, was the memory of the taste of her blood.

"Is The Kalakar going to come for us this time?"

"Always."

She said nothing else.

"She's lost blood," Ser Laonis said, his hands never leaving the Serra's face. "It is the loss of blood that has almost killed her."

"Where?"

"Where, kai Leonne?"

"Where has she lost blood *from?*"

Ser Laonis di'Caveras was no Voyani. Although the Serra's face bore multiple bruises and scratches, none of these were remotely life-threatening. He had cast the lightest of touches across her face, and set it out about her like a net; a healer's net. He could discern no open wound. This troubled him.

"Can you—"

"Yes."

"I will be forever in your debt," Valedan began. He did not hear the doubt in the healer's voice, or if he did, he chose not to acknowledge it.

Ser Laonis shook his head. He would have raised a hand, but he needed the contact with her cold skin. She was almost beyond him. In the North, healers existed with a greater power, but they, too, were beyond him.

"I will call her back."

"Will she come?"

His smile was gentle. "If she can hear me, she will come. She has a husband," he added softly. "And a wife. A child."

"I'm not sure the husband means much," he said, looking very much his age. Ser Laonis almost pitied him. His contact with the Serra gave lie to the words that Valedan offered, but it was a subtle lie; he was not certain if she herself was aware of how important he had become in so short a time. She was injured, as so many men and women were; the scars were internal, invisible in all ways.

But if she did not openly value husband, she valued her wives. There was pain there, and loss—but there was also hope. He looked at Teyla, brown-skinned, common girl, a field seraf. Hesitated for just a moment, and then said, "If you can, give me your child."

Teyla did not hesitate. She was pale and trembling, and her eyes were woman's eyes, wide with fear and unshed tears. She fumbled

a moment with her sling, and unknotted it. With care, she held out
the sleeping child.

Missing his mother's warmth, he stirred.

Valedan caught the child in his hands. "What should I do?" he
asked anxiously.

"Place the child in her arms."

Valedan hesitated, looking at her limp, still arms. "She can't—"
And then he swallowed and did as Ser Laonis ordered.

The fact that it *was* an order escaped him; it did not escape Ser
Laonis. *You are not of the South,* he thought, not for the first time.
But you will do.

The child began to cry.

Help me, he thought, to the infant. *If she will not listen to my
voice, she may well listen to yours.*

He had touched her long enough, and probed deeply enough,
that he understood this much of the Serra Diora en'Leonne. He was
afraid to know more.

He had always been afraid to know more, but he had not lied; the
decade in the North had changed him. Fear was present, but it was
no longer his master.

Trembling, he closed his eyes upon the cries of an infant, and he
began to search in the darkness at the edge of death for the Serra
Diora.

"Aidan," Ser Anton said quietly. "We must move."

Aidan said nothing. Nothing at all. His sword was in his hand,
and its weight now made the slender arm tremble.

"You did well," Ser Anton continued softly, as if speaking to a
wild creature. "The banner did not fall."

"That was . . . that was you," Aidan whispered.

"No, Aidan. The banner was not given to me; it was not in my
care. You are not as strong as many of the Southern cerdan, but you
held it aloft. Come. We must go to Valedan, now."

"Where is he?"

"He is in the center of the valley."

"Across the gap?"

"Across the gap," Anton nodded. "It is not wide; the horse can
leap it."

"But we—"

"We must carry the banner to him," Ser Anton said again. He
lifted his gaze, and studied moonlight for a moment; it was a blessing. The Lady's time had come.

"There is another banner, and it is kin to this one. We must join it," he told the boy, with gentle pride. "And make Valedan's claim known."

"What other banner?"

"The banner," Ser Anton told him, "of the Tyr'agar."

"I—I don't understand."

"No," Ser Anton said. But he had heard the horn of Ser Alesso di'Marente, and he knew it well. Aidan could not be expected to. "It is your last duty. Fulfill it, and you will have done more in the cause of the kai Leonne than even his Ospreys."

In the darkness, she heard a voice.

A man's voice. She had done with men. Mist enclosed her; cold mist. But it offered her no threat. She could hear voices as it rose, and the voices, distant, were welcome. Familiar voices, all.

She could not speak, not yet; but her gift made her hearing acute.

Faida.

Deirdre.

Ruatha.

Ruatha, the wildest, the strongest, the angriest of her wives.

They were not close. But after a moment, she found the strength to approach them. It was hard; she was bound by fear. If this was death, the winds did not howl, but the silence brought her no peace.

Do you forgive me? she asked, wordless. Had she the power to compel answer, she would have used it. But power was denied her here. Wherever here was.

There is nothing to forgive. Deirdre's voice. It would be. Deirdre held no grudges.

There is nothing to forgive, another voice said, an older voice, gentle with wisdom and hidden experience. Selina. Selina en'Leonne, the cast-off wife of her husband's father. Her first husband. *The winds do not howl here, Na'dio. Come. We are waiting.*

Diora.

Man's voice, stranger's voice. She shook her head.

Na'dani is waiting, Faida said quietly. Her voice was nearer. But of the babe, she heard nothing. Perhaps he slept. They had each spent sleepless nights, praying to the Lady for just such a common miracle: sleep. A moment's peace.

I can't hear him, she told Faida.

Silence then.

Ruatha?

The only voice she wanted to hear. She reached out for it as the mist grew stronger.

Ruatha did not answer.

Aie, it hurt, that silence. But Ruatha had always used silence as a weapon; she had other weapons as well, but none so sharp, so bitter. The silence had been so long. Silence of grave, of guilt, of loss.

Diora!

The stranger's voice angered her. She wanted it to go away. But she had no strength to compel. She had just enough strength to deny it, that was all. Move forward, she thought. Forward.

Had she thought the winds silent? She was wrong. They began to howl, and although they were weak and distant, they drove all other voices away. She wanted to cry out, she who almost never cried, but she was numb with fear. With cold.

Ruatha!

No one answered. Not even Deirdre.

She began to struggle.

Ser Laonis di'Caveras looked up blindly.

His face was twisted with foreign emotion; expressions that had never been his crossed his features, transforming mouth, eye, and brow. His lips worked in silence, but his shaking hands did not lift. He was the Serra Diora, but some small part of his mind, given to the healer's gift, was his own, and he knew that if he lifted hands, she would slip past him.

And that it would be a mercy.

This was the South; all mercy was in the hands of the Tyr'agar. And *this* Tyr might have let her go, if he could hear what Ser Laonis could hear.

The babe was wailing now.

She heard him.

She heard the babe's sudden cry, the weak pull of air across small lungs, the inescapable imperative of his demands. Her throat tightened. Her hands tightened. She had wanted this, but she knew that if she accepted it, the other voices would be lost to her.

Knew it, and yet—

Her arms tightened, shuddering, contracting as if they belonged to someone else.

Diora.

And she heard the voice again, but this time, she *listened*. Man's voice, yes, but it was gentle with things Northern, things distant; it was not a young voice, but age had not hardened or cracked it. There was a promise, in that voice, of something that she had almost given up the desire for.

Peace. Love. Companionship.

Diora, he said again. *Come home.* It was a plea.

If it had been a command—if anyone had dared to command her here—she would have been safe. But pleas were their own imperative, and she had never hardened heart enough to ignore them. She had endured them, once, and that endurance had shattered her. She could feel the seams of self stretching as she hesitated this second time.

But the baby *was* wailing. He was hungry.

She could not feed him, but she could take him to his mother. *Deirdre.*

No. Not Deirdre.

The ability to lie to others had been her strength; she had never turned it inward. No, she thought, testing the statement. She had never knowingly turned it inward. This child's cry was *not* her child's.

But it could be.

She closed eyes that were not open.

Diora, the voice said again, softer now.

She waited, and realized that it was growing distant.

That it would leave her, here, in the darkness, with only silence as companion. She reached out, wild with inexplicable fear, and she felt something catch her in insubstantial arms.

She let it; her own were full.

He broke away from her with a cry, his arms trembling with shock. By his side, Teyla en'Leonne knelt, and her arms, shaking only slightly less than his own, formed a shelter around his back. She was whispering a name in his ear, and it took him a moment to recognize it: Laonis. His own.

He caught her forearms in his hands, and he was not gentle; he could not be, and grip them.

"Ser Laonis?" Valedan said.

Laonis di'Caveras shook his head. His grip tightened, and the smaller woman held him fast, allowing him to rise. "She will wake," he said, shuddering. "Soon. She will wake." He shook his head. "I cannot be here, kai Leonne."

Valedan nodded. "Will she—"

"She will be whole," he said, but his eyes were shadowed and dark. He turned away from all witnesses, and began to make his way, at last, toward the tents and their meager safety.

And as he did, the Serra Diora en'Leonne opened her eyes to the moonlit sky of a quiet field. She struggled a moment to sit, and her hands jerked, as if she would reach out for the vanishing healer. But they did not move, because the baby was in her arms, and he demanded both care and attention.

He demanded silence, when she could put the whole of this new, this fresh loss, into her voice. It was not the worst loss she had suffered; she gave him what he needed as her eyes adjusted to this different night.

She met the eyes of the kai Leonne, and she blinked. "Valedan," she said, her voice cracking over the simple syllables.

"Diora," he whispered. "I thought—"

"Where is Teyla?"

"She is here. Or she will be. She—"

"The baby needs her," the Serra whispered. But her arms tightened.

The young Tyr'agar reached out to touch her face. But his hands fell short; he crouched before her, in silence, seeing accusation and loss upon her fine features.

"I'm sorry," he whispered.

She shook her head, returning to the world and its imperatives. "Do not," she said, voice still rough, "say that here."

But he denied her; he spoke again. "I'm sorry. But I—" He shook his head, his eyes sliding away from hers. Honesty, it seemed, was painful.

And it was Northern. "I don't think I can do this without you."

She should have hated him.

Instead, she remembered, more quickly than he, what she was. The Serra Diora en'Leonne. The flower of the Dominion. She took strength from knowledge, and if it was a brittle strength, it was also a familiar one.

"Kai Leonne," she said, voice a mere thread of sound. "Take your son."

He did not hesitate. He caught the babe in his arms, but his gaze did not leave her face.

She hesitated again, and then said, softly, "Thank you." It was, to her surprise, not wholly a lie.

His brows rose. He looked so young to her eye, although he was almost of an age with the man who had married her beneath the watchful gaze of the Lord's men in a different life.

"My wife," she whispered. "My son."

She looked up, then, and saw across the field another banner, another man. Her expression hardened. "So," she said. She rose slowly; if Ser Laonis would have been of a mind to forbid it, he could not. He was gone. "It is not yet over."

Standing in the moonlight beneath the banner of the sun ascendant was Alesso di'Marente. And by his side, bowed by age and knowledge, Sendari di'Marano. Her father and his General, the architects of her loss.

"Take the Dominion," she told her husband, feeling the embers of a bitter anger, an old vow.

And then, because she was Serra, she bowed her head, hiding war beneath her lowered gaze.

Ramdan was at her side in that instant. She offered him a surprised smile, a pained one. What he saw in that smile, he would never speak of, and he offered no like expression in return. Instead, as perfect seraf, he interposed himself between his Serra and her husband, shielding her properly from the public gaze of men.

His hand, she took, when it was offered.

And leaning heavily against him, she rose. Thus hidden, she let her expression fall into natural lines, and she closed her long, perfect lashes, becoming aware of her body. Her arms ached. She glanced at them; her clothing was torn and her limbs were scratched and bruised.

She could not be perfect here. But she did not desire perfection. All she desired was peace.

Leaning on him, as she had always done, she made her way from the field, extracting a strange dignity from her graceless, painful movements.

Aware, as she was always aware, that she was watched.

CHAPTER THIRTY-EIGHT

BEFORE the dawn, the hour of man approached, the sky shedding midnight hue, moon, stars. There was no silence. Men moved across the transformed landscape, gathering their injured and their dead. Voices were raised in howls, lowered in whispers; men moved to carry those who would not be willingly parted from horse or kin. The river's movement had changed, its bed broken; water was gathered and fires rebuilt. Tents were moved, where it was possible, and song was raised and broken, raised and broken, across the intermingled camp.

Everywhere to the naked eye, blue and white sprang up; black and white joined it: the colors of mourning. Carrion birds—crows, in the North—began to circle in the skies above, and they were denied their feast, again and again, by the watchful hands of men. But there were many, many dead.

Ramiro kai di'Callesta was not among them. The gem that had been gifted his clan by the Matriarch of Havalla was of a piece with *Bloodhame;* its claws had vanished into the working of its simple hilt, and it would not be parted from it. A small price to pay.

Ser Alfredo kai di'Callesta was waiting for him. Had been waiting the better part of an hour. Ramiro had personally seen to his Tyran; those that could be moved, or could move, he escorted to the tents of the Northern healers, and those that could not—ah, they were harder. He closed their eyes. He offered the Lady's ablutions, while she reigned.

It had been a gamble, he thought, as he knelt by Miko's side, his Tyran a strong ring around him. And as all gambles, a costly one. The valleys would be scarred by this war. He wondered how many serafs he would lose to starvation in the following year, or two.

But across the wet ground, foliage bloomed, gray in the early morn. An answer, of sorts.

"Fillipo."

Ser Fillipo par di'Callesta nodded. His arm was broken, and it hung awkwardly by his side; he had suffered a physician to tend it, but only briefly. His sword was in its scabbard, and he could not draw it, he had been told, for some weeks. If ever.

"Ramiro," his par answered quietly. "You won."

Ramiro nodded. "Baredan?"

But Fillipo shook his head.

"The Kalakar?"

"She is with the Ospreys," Fillipo said, neutral now.

"Ah. And Commander Allen?"

"He is with the Hawk. They have exchanged words; the cerdan remarked upon the heat of the syllables, but they did not understand the details."

Ramiro offered a smile, the first. It was stern, but not without amusement. "The Northerners have their own customs. I believe that the Hawk was to return to the Northern capital."

"It is better for us that he did not."

"Aye. But perhaps they are Southern in at least one respect: form must be followed."

"Will he survive it?" Ser Kallos asked quietly. He bent on cane, his foot sheared off at the ankle.

"I think he will," Fillipo replied. Here, in the hour between the Lady's night and the Lord's dawn, the form of which they had spoken was forsaken. "The North is not so harsh as the South in that single regard."

"But it is not as weak as some would have us believe," Ser Kallos said.

"It has never been weak," Ramiro replied. "But it has always been different."

"I see the banner of the Lambertan Tyr," Fillipo added. "He seeks audience, kai Callesta."

"I will grant it." He turned to his son. His son was wounded, and would bear scars from those wounds; his skin was pale and his eyes too round. He looked his age, and seeing that age, Ramiro felt his own.

But he smiled, wolf's smile, all edge. "So, Alfredo," he said softly. "You have seen your first true battle."

Ser Alfredo kai di'Callesta fell to one knee before his Tyr. He bowed his head, exposing the unruly knot on the dome of his head.

And Fillipo frowned. "The banners of the Tyr'agnati are gathering," he said to his brother. "Lorenza and Garrardi are also present here."

"Do they stand by the side of General Marente?"

"No."

"Then we will meet, we four," Ramiro replied. He stood slowly, granting this last respect to his fallen.

Ser Jarrani kai di'Lorenza tendered the first bow offered among the four men. He was unhorsed; they all were. And his guards numbered four; four Tyran. It was the minimal number of such guards that a man of his stature could use. An offering, of sorts. Truce.

Their weapons were chipped and their armor soiled or torn. They had seen fighting, within the valley's fold. Hard fighting, and their losses, although they had joined the battle late, had been great.

The bow was held longer than necessary, but he did not wait for permission to rise; only one man could grant that, and that man?

Undecided.

Ser Eduardo di'Garrardi, true to his own particular form, bowed to no man; he offered instead the casual nod of equals. "Kai Callesta," he said, and then, acknowledging Ser Alfredo, "Kai Callesta."

Ser Alfredo was not his father's equal; he stiffened. But he did not speak; Alfredo had seldom had Carelo's heat or impulsive tongue.

"Kai Garrardi," Ramiro said, offering exactly the same measure of respect. "You were late to the field, but not unwelcome." To Ser Jarrani, however, he offered full bow.

"It was well-played, Ser Ramiro," Ser Jarrani said quietly. His own kai and par stood by his side, stiff. Injured. No one would escape this battle unscathed.

"It was not my battle," Ser Ramiro replied cautiously. "Not my battle alone." And he turned to the distant banner of the Tyr'agar; the one guarded, still, by Ser Anton di'Guivera and the young Northern boy.

"No. The Northerners played their part. They are diminished here."

"They are under the command of Valedan kai di'Leonne," Ramiro replied, choosing to use the clan's name, and not the title. The title, Valedan had set aside, and it had yet to be taken.

By one man or the other.

Mareo kai di'Lamberto came last. He was colder than either of the newcomers, and far more formal. But Ser Jarrani offered him a perfect bow, the grace of the High Courts, and Mareo kai di'Lamberto was forced to return it. It must have galled him.

It did not show upon his face, however.

"Ser Galen," Ser Jarrani said, speaking to the Tyr Lamberto's only son. "Your father fought well."

Proving himself Lambertan to the core, Ser Galen replied, "He did not fight alone." And his gaze turned to the North, where the Radann gathered. They, too, were injured, but their injuries were adornments; they were unbowed.

"So," Ser Jarrani said quietly. "To whom do we bow, this day?"

"It has not yet been decided," Ser Mareo kai di'Lamberto said. "But the hour of man draws to a close; it will be decided soon."

"And what is the desirable outcome?"

Mareo kai di'Lamberto raised a brow. "The Lord's will," he replied, his hand resting upon the hilt of *Balagar.* "The Lord will judge."

"Perhaps the Lord has already judged," Ser Ramiro added.

*   *   *

Alina fussed.

Valedan would have bid her be still, but it would have done no good, and he owed her this much; he was almost dutiful in his attention to her words. Which galled her, of course, and set her off in a different direction.

Ser Andaro di'Corsarro waited just within the mouth of the tent, upon his knees. It was a smaller tent; the larger had been lost, its center poles buckled and cracked by the twisting of the earth beneath its pegs.

"Andaro," Valedan said, forcing all irritation from his words, "Get up." Or all irritation that could be forced from them.

Ser Andaro bowed, and after a moment, he gained his footing. But he did so with a pained, almost apologetic grace that ill suited his position.

"You did not fail me," Valedan continued, as Alina pulled at his hair with her long, harem combs. It was a special kind of torture.

"You sent me to protect the Serra," Ser Andaro replied, his words flat. "I was not by her side—"

"You would have died, had you been," was Valedan's curt reply. "She chose," he added.

Ser Andaro raised brow.

"She chose. Were it not for her—" But he could not speak the words. They had no place in this tent, not while Alina was present.

"You must take Tyran," Alina told him, setting his hair into a perfect knot.

"I have all of the Tyran I need."

She frowned. It was the least Serra-like frown that either of the men had seen this eve.

"For now," Valedan added quickly.

"The Radann kai el'Sol is waiting, Valedan," she said. "And I have not heard that he is a particularly patient man."

"He will witness?"

"He will."

Valedan nodded. He touched the hilt of the Sun Sword, and then let his hand fall away. "Must it be this sword?"

Alina said nothing.

Ser Andaro drew his own blade, and offered it to the kai Leonne. "All men have seen the proof of your claim in your ability to wield the Sword," he said.

"It is for the Sword that we will fight," Valedan replied.

"It is for the Tor Leonne," Andaro countered. But he held out his blade, and Valedan took it, bowing. "Which blade will you wield?" The kai Leonne asked the man who would be Captain of his oath-guards.

Ser Andaro grimaced. "Not that one."

And was rewarded by Valedan's laugh.

Kiriel di'Ashaf stood by the side of Auralis AKalakar. Her armor was useless now, and her boots, useless as well. She had not yet made her report, and as no one demanded it, she was left to her own devices.

Auralis said, "You rode that Beast."

"Three times," she said. And then added quietly, "Four."

Lord Anduvin came out of the shadows; shadows seemed to naturally grow where he stood. For this reason, among many, Kiriel had chosen to station herself at the greatest remove possible from the encampment.

He bowed.

"Falloran?" she asked him softly, without much hope.

"He is waiting," Anduvin replied.

Her brows rose. "He isn't—"

"He is still here, Kiriel. He is injured; he cannot move." The Swordsmith raised gauntlet, and she saw the marks of the three jaws along its edge. "Nor will he be moved, I fear, by any but you. The mortals have come," he added.

She snarled. Auralis grabbed her wrist, shaking his head.

"He is not as we are," Anduvin continued, when it became clear that Kiriel would not respond. "He cannot cloak his presence or his identity. What he has become is all that he is." He paused, and then said again, "He is waiting for you."

She gripped the haft of her blade in one hand. "I'll go."

Auralis, his own hand never far from his blade, surprised her. "Do you mind if I follow?"

As if it were her choice. She offered him an Osprey's answer: she shrugged. He fell in beside her, his step heavy.

"You weren't injured?"

His turn to shrug. Whole conversations could be conducted that way.

"Why don't you go back to the Ospreys?"

Auralis shook his head. "They're gone," he whispered.

"What do you mean?"

"Alexis is dead. Fiara is dead." His shrug was different. An inability to offer words.

"Duarte?"

"He's still Primus."

She said nothing, following in Anduvin's wake. "A healer?"

"Not in time," he said at last. "And I'm not sure she would have been grateful, had one been there."

"Why?"

He rolled his eyes. "I wouldn't be," he said at last.

"Why not?"

"Kiriel—"

"I mean it, Auralis."

"I know."

It was Anduvin who answered. "Healers are invasive," he told her quietly. "You should know this."

She shrugged. "I've never—"

"No. You haven't. But it is, in my limited experience, true. They know too much, when the healing is deep. They *have* to know it. And there are many who would prefer death to the knowledge they gain."

She paused, because Anduvin had stopped. He gestured, and the shadows crept slowly away from the small basin of earth they occupied.

Beneath them, hidden—as much as he could be—from the sight of men, lay Falloran. His hind legs were crushed. But he lifted himself by his forepaws, and his heads, half-lolling, reached for Kiriel's outstretched hand.

She touched the middle head, and fire lapped round her wrist like a tongue. It did not burn. Still, after all this time, it did not burn.

"Falloran," she whispered. "Will you not return to the Hells?"

He whined. Like a dog. Anduvin's gaze was a study in neutrality; what lay beneath it was contempt. But he cloaked it for Kiriel's sake. Or perhaps for his own.

"And you, Anduvin," she added softly. "Will you not return?"

"I cannot," he replied, with dignity. "You hold my name."

"I can release it," she offered.

"You can."

When she said nothing, he added, "You would not, if you were truly The Lord's daughter." It was meant as goad.

But she smiled. "I am," she said. "But that's not all I am." She held out her other hand, and Falloran dropped the underside of a jaw into her palm.

"You hold my sword," he said at last. "My last sword."

"I will never return it."

"No. You cannot. And I am content, for the moment, to reside where it resides." He lifted his face to the North. "This battle is won, Daughter of Darkness. But there will be others."

"And you want to see them?"

"I want to see the final one," he whispered.

"Why?"

"Because Arianne will be there," he replied. He did not attempt to lie, and she wondered briefly what she would have done if he had. She had never expected truth from the kin before.

She shook her head. "I will keep your name." She knelt; Falloran, lying upon the ground, was taller than she.

"You should have kept them all," he said softly.

"There was only one way to do that," she answered, as honest as he. "And I can't."

"Can't?"

Almost as honest. "Won't. Not now. Not yet."

She reached out and placed her palm against Falloran's face. One of his faces.

"What are you doing, Kiriel?" Auralis asked. She was aware of his presence, and aware, also, that he hadn't drawn his sword.

"I don't know."

But she did. She felt a warmth in her palms, and it was almost familiar. She lifted her hand, and Falloran whined. Anduvin said something; it was distant.

She heard it anyway.

You have your father's blood. But your mother's gift is there, in part. It was almost a blessing.

In the hour before dawn, she lent what remained of her odd power to Falloran. He was not alive. Not in the sense that she was.

But she knew, by instinct, that her gift was not for the living; her father's blood denied her that. It did not deny her everything.

As she had strengthened huts across Russo, she now rebuilt Falloran, holding his shape and form in memory. Early memories.

She could not have saved Ashaf in such a fashion. She could not have saved any of the Ospreys; could not heal Auralis. If she had friends, they were bound, as she was, by the injuries they received.

But she could heal Falloran, and for now, that was enough.

Ser Alesso di'Marente was attended by only one man: Ser Sendari di'Marano. Having accepted the kai Leonne's challenge, he could ask for no other. But he did not trouble himself with serafs either; his tent was sparse and empty. Gone were the maps that had been his private joy; gone were the plans, the alliances, that had brought them all to the Green Valley once more. It was in the valleys, he thought, that all men of worth were tested in *this* generation.

Sendari looked out of the tent flap, forgoing dignity. "The Tyr'agnati gather," he said, as he returned to the privacy of the enclosed space.

Alesso nodded quietly. "Old friend," he said.

Sendari lifted a hand. But he smiled wearily. "It is almost the Lord's time."

"Almost." Alesso lifted *Terra Fuerre* and girded himself with its strap. "And we will have our answer when the time is come. Do you have regrets, Sendari?"

"No life is complete without regret," the Widan replied. "Regret is the product of wisdom."

Alesso laughed. "I have no regrets."

"None?"

"Perhaps one."

"And that?"

"The kai Garrardi."

Sendari shook his head, fingering his beard. "It would have gained you nothing," he said.

"Which is why he still lives."

"If you take the Tor—"

"If?"

"When," Sendari corrected himself. "What then?"

Alesso shrugged. "We will see," he said at last.

"And my daughter?"

But the General shook his head. "I see her clearly now."

"And I. You are not worried."

"No, old friend." It was true. The Lord's gaze would fall upon them all soon. And Alesso knew himself, at last, as the Lord's man. The Lord valued strength above all else.

Ser Anton di'Guivera smiled briefly as Aidan nodded off. The boy would sleep for minutes at a time, jerking himself awake as he listed to one side or the other, his hand still clutched tight around the banner's pole. His skin was red. The lack of sunlight, however ill it had seemed, had been too short to allow him much peace; the Southern Sun, without the protection of a hat or veil, which Aidan would never consent to wear, was far too bright.

Ser Anton granted him, in silence, what shadows he could. He was subtle, and Aidan was young.

"I will wake you," Ser Anton said, when Aidan started from sleep for the tenth time.

"I don't want to miss the fight," Aidan replied, stretching as if to shake off exhaustion.

And he would, Ser Anton thought. But not before blades were drawn. "You did well, Aidan."

"I did nothing."

"You killed no demons," Ser Anton agreed. "But that was not your task in this battle."

"But—"

"A soldier or a cerdan of worth follows the orders given him. He does not resent them. He does not question them. You fulfilled your duty. Be at peace."

"But—"

Ser Anton relented. "This will not be your only war, boy. Perhaps in another you will find the glory you seek." *Perhaps,* he added silently, *never.* And found himself, as the minutes fled, wishing it were true. He had dreamed of glory in his youth, but the dreams were tarnished and faded by reality. Aidan's eyes, darkened and wide, held horror and respect; the cost was too distant.

But Ser Anton knew that women and children would now be without husbands across the Dominion, and he knew what that meant. He bowed head a moment in thanks for their future suffering.

The Serra Teresa di'Marano was robed as Voyani. She did not disdain silks, but neither would she wear them. Yollana permitted her this subterfuge. And she permitted it in a privacy that brooked no questions from any of lesser rank or wisdom than a Matriarch.

"Na'tere," she said quietly, stuffing leaves into her pipe, "you will not sleep."

The Serra did not answer. Instead, she watched the tent of Alesso di'Marente. Watched as it opened, revealing at last the architect of their mutual sorrows, their mutual risk. He had made allies of them all, and if that had not been his intent, it was a gift, of sorts. The only gift that one could take from the battle in the valleys.

The earth took the rest.

She had labored in the paling sky by the side of cerdan and healers, helping to set the dead to rest. The bodies should have been burned, but the Serra Diora would not allow it, and the only time she spoke clearly was to deny them the expedient of the fire.

"Give them to the earth," she said, her voice clear as morning bell.

"Why?" Yollana barked, testy.

"Because the earth will cradle them now," was the only reply the Serra offered.

And Valedan kai di'Leonne had concurred.

He had stepped down, in some fashion; he had made a challenge that the whole of the armies—on either side of a divide that had become meaningless—had heard, and by so doing, he had surrendered title to combat.

But those who served him, served him still.

Baredan di'Navarre was no longer among them. Valedan had listened to the story of his death in a quiet, grim silence, and then he had given his orders: Baredan di'Navarre was to be preserved by Widan arts until their return to the Tor Leonne; there, he was to be granted burial among the most valued of the Leonne servitors.

He had earned it, if he cared.

His men did, and in the end, it was the living for whom the kai Leonne cared. He was a canny young man, and his heart was far too vulnerable. Yollana, smoking, mused in silence.

And then the second man stepped from the tent, and she turned to the Serra Teresa.

The Serra whispered a word. A name.

"So," Yollana said, with just a trace of pity. More than that would anger Teresa, although the anger would never show. The years of life in the High Courts could not be scoured clean by months of walking the *Voyanne,* and those months were coming, now, to a close.

"You should learn to smoke," she told the Serra.

The Serra said nothing.

But after a moment, to Yollana's surprise, she rose. "Matriarch," she said, bowing low. "Please excuse my absence. I will be but a moment."

Yollana nodded, pipe in hand, smoke wreathing her face. The sun's light was bright, this day; bright enough to cause squint, even in the early morn. Eyes could become accustomed to any kind of darkness.

Serra Teresa di'Marano walked quietly across the wide expanse of open ground. She skirted the edge of the banners that crowded the most accessible part of the field, seeking to avoid the gaze of men of power. Robed thus, she was not beneath notice; the Voyani seldom were, and they did not approach clansmen of significance.

But Sendari seemed to expect her.

He halted his slow, processional step when they caught sight of one another, and he turned a moment, whispering something to Alesso di'Marente. The General shrugged.

When she reached him, she bowed. It was not a Serra's bow, but neither was it Voyani; it was too graceful and too deliberate for that.

"Serra Teresa," he said gravely, inclining his head. "You come strangely attired."

She nodded as well. "And you," she added softly. "Come in Widan robes. Once, I would have said that they suited you ill, but perhaps we have both grown into our clothing."

"The Serra Diora?"

"She is well."

He nodded again, so stiff now, so terribly formal. She wanted to pity him. She wanted to slap him. Caught between these two primal urges, she did neither.

"The hour of man is almost gone," she said at last.

"And the hour of the Lord approaches."

She nodded. It was difficult. She had said her good-byes, as had he. But she learned anew that there was no finality in words, even hers. Perhaps especially hers, now.

His gaze narrowed. "You are not well?" he asked at last, hesitating over the foreign terrain of the awkward syllables. Stepping with a care that he had never previously shown.

"I am as well as I will ever be," she replied, denying him nothing.

"You—"

But she lifted a hand, forestalling him. In this, she was so different, he fell silent. She saw wariness in him, then, and she knew that they had always fenced with words; words had been their weapon of choice, and they had been cruelly used.

"Serra," he said, seeing her naked fingers. "The oath ring—"

She shook her head. "It is gone, Sendari."

He bowed his head.

"Yes," Teresa said softly, "even I."

"Why?"

"Because the dead are dead," she said quietly. "And the living should—should have—commanded our attention and our care. What might we have built, between us, had we ever acknowledged that truth?"

He was not comfortable with her words, the more so because they were shorn of the cool Court malice that she so often hid behind.

"We built," he said at last, and heavily.

"Not us," she replied.

"No," he said, arguing with little force. "We did." And he gazed across the distance that separated the two tents of the contenders. "You have met the boy, yes?"

"I have met the kai Leonne."

"And you found him?"

"Different," she said quietly. "He is not Ser Illara kai di'Leonne. He will never be that man. But he has taken the Serra Diora to wife, and if he survives this, it is my belief that she will, in the end, find some happiness."

His brows rose. "She will be happy?"

And Teresa nodded.

"Does he know—"

"He was raised in the North," she replied, serene now, all turmoil in her eyes, and only her eyes. "He knows. And he honors her for it. He does not fear her."

"Then he is an unusual man."

Teresa nodded again. "He is young enough to care greatly for honor," she added. "And Na'dio will have more power by his side than she would have ever held in any other circumstance."

His smile was bitter, but it was also genuine. "Are we then so horrible, in the South?"

"No. We are what we are. But she is young, and he is young; what they make of the Dominion, we cannot make." She bowed again. "You were my brother," she told him, holding that bow. "And of all the clan Marano, the only one to understand me."

"Have you spoken with Adano?"

She shook her head. And he knew, then, that she would not.

"He worried for you."

She nodded. "Yes. But he did not understand me, and he will understand less what I have chosen to become. She is our daughter," she added, surrendering at last the one thing of value that she had withheld. "And it is time that she left the harem."

"Teresa—"

"And I, too," she added, "am far past the age where the harem can confine me. Go in peace. I think we will speak one last time."

He laughed. It was quiet and dry. "Peace?" he said softly. "I think it unlikely. Look: the kai Leonne comes."

Kallandras of Senniel College held *Salla* in his injured arms. His hands ached; his fingers had been blistered by the force of the angry wind. He had contained it, but barely; Auralis AKalakar had summoned fire, unconscious of its cost, and the fire had come. But the waking of the earth had been worse.

Hard to imagine that they were all silent now; fires banked, wind stilled, earth quiet. Hard, as well, to imagine that dawn could come out of the shadows of that night. But he was bard, and Senniel-trained, and the lays that had been consigned to memory in his earliest years by the seawall were stranger still.

His fingers danced upon lute strings, stopping them almost as quickly. Words blended with the music he called forth and sent away; he was composing in silence the lay of this battle. But the end had not yet been writ.

He gazed at Ser Alesso di'Marente: he was a tall man, with dark hair and broad shoulders; his skin was darkened by sun and toughened by wind. If the Lady graced him at all, there was no sign of her softness in his features; he was the Lord's man. Once, that would have had a different meaning.

His gaze drifted from the General to the young kai Leonne; to Valedan. His hair was also dark, night black, with hints of blue to mark its depth. To Kallandras' trained eye, he was the taller of the two, but he was still slender with youth. The muscles of an older man did not inform him, yet.

And he carried, by his side, a simple sword. Kallandras nodded quietly.

Valedan strode past the waiting Tyr'agnati, and stopped a moment to acknowledge them; they nodded in return, offering no words, no encouragement.

He turned to Ser Anton di'Guivera, and to the boy who stood in the older man's shadow. This time, he smiled.

"Ser Anton," he said, with gravity. "Aidan."

Aidan nodded, and the banner bobbed with the movement. It evoked a smile from all four of the watching Tyrs. Aidan was young. The fact that two of these smiling men would have happily killed him did not diminish their momentary amusement. They were Southern.

Valedan turned as Ser Alesso di'Marente approached. And he tendered the General a respectful bow; a bow between equals.

Ser Alesso di'Marente offered him the same, measure for measure.

"What rules, kai Leonne?" Ser Alesso asked casually.

"Southern rules," Valedan replied, and turned again to Ser Anton di'Guivera.

Ser Anton di'Guivera said simply, "To the death."

And Kallandras touched lute strings again, hearing the song in the stark words. He could capture it, but later.

The two men took up position; twenty yards separated them. Twenty years. Armor, as well; Valedan wore the simple chain hauberk of the Northerners, and although Kallandras suspected Alina had attempted to dissuade him from its use, he had obviously made his choice.

He sought to make a statement here.

But he wasted time, Kallandras thought, and it was a pity. There was only one statement that he could make that would be of value to the men who now watched.

The bard's gaze shifted. Beyond the Tyr'agnati, their Tyran were now at attention, and beyond the Tyran, the watchful eyes of the flight: Eagle, Hawk, and Kestrel. Their role here was at an end, but they witnessed what unfolded in a silence that would have done the Tyrs proud. Their adjutants stood as Tyran; their soldiers, as cerdan. All of them, bound by Valedan's challenge, and the unexpected generosity of it.

The test of men, Kallandras mused.

How is worth in a man judged?

Steel song.

The ghostly clash of blades in the meeting of eyes. Ser Anton di'Guivera lifted a hand; it dropped like a sword, and they were both free to move.

But neither did. They stood as they had chosen to stand, assessing each other. They did not speak; words, here, were superfluous. But there was respect in the silence and the concentrated regard they offered one another. They stood astride two generations.

Valedan kai di'Leonne moved first, but he did not draw his sword; instead, he bent into his knees, his hand slowly moving to his side to catch the hilt of his blade.

Ser Alesso di'Marente watched.

The Serra Diora stood behind Ser Andaro di'Corsarro. She was far too close to the combat, and Ser Andaro had done what he could to dissuade her.

But he was aware that she was both strong enough to stay her ground and fragile enough to fear it, and he saw no purpose in adding to her anxiety. Valedan had given his tacit permission for her presence by his refusal to acknowledge it.

And Ser Andaro di'Corsarro served Valedan kai di'Leonne until death ended that service, one way or the other. "Serra," he said quietly. He held the Sun Sword.

She opened her palms, and after a moment, he offered her what she had born in secret for so long: the blade's weight. It was sheathed, and it was sheathed for war. But neither she nor he attempted to draw or wield it. She tensed to take the blade's weight, but she did not otherwise speak.

Flower of the Dominion, he thought. And what a strange flower she had become: steel, strong and straight as Valedan, a warrior with the Lady's heart. He knew what she had done, and why she had almost perished. He honored it.

"I brought you a sword," she said, surprising him.

"Where?"

She blushed. It was unexpected. "I am wearing it," she told him quietly. "Beneath the cloak. Take it, Ser Andaro. I do not think you will find use for it, this day."

He smiled. And he did what she had asked: he unbuckled the sword belt from its low position around her slender hips, aware as he did that this action flouted every convention of the High Courts.

"You do not suspect Ser Alesso of treachery?"

"He is the Lord's man," she replied evenly. "And capable of all manner of treachery. But here? Beneath the Lord's gaze, he will fight. It is all that is left him. It is all, I think, that he now desires."

Andaro hesitated, and then he nodded. "I concur."

Together, they watched.

Ser Alesso's sword left his scabbard.

Valedan's did not. They watched each other warily as the sun crept skyward and the shadows shortened. Alesso's sword came up; he held it out, before him, at right angles to his chest.

If he had expected the boy to be rash, he repented of the expectation, tossing it aside. The first move in this long game had been his; the first move in its end would be his as well.

Valedan waited, silent.

And then movement started; Ser Alesso approached and Ser Valedan shifted his weight, moving, his blade still sheathed.

The attack came suddenly; the slow, stately closing of distance resolved itself into a ferocious, almost blinding strike.

Valedan's sword left its sheath in that moment, and steel spoke. Steel sang.

"Will we serve the General, if he wins?" Ser Alfredo kai di'Callesta asked his uncle quietly.

Ser Fillipo par di'Callesta said nothing. The silence was significant. The Tyr'agnate failed to hear the graceless question. It was warning enough, for Ser Alfredo; it would not have been, for his kai.

But he felt closer to his dead kai than he did to his father or his uncle at this moment. His hand would not be levered from the hilt of the sword that Valedan kai di'Leonne had—as he had vowed—lifted first in the battle. The kai Leonne had chosen honor over power, and nothing that Ser Alfredo said, nothing that Ramiro kai di'Callesta said, would have altered that choice.

He was almost Lambertan, Ser Alfredo thought, with a flash of rue, some hint of the wisdom that might come if he survived. He watched as Valedan deflected the first strike. Watched as Ser Alesso pressed him, using his momentum, his greater weight, as leverage.

Valedan danced.

Swords sang.

He noticed, as he looked away—he couldn't help it—that Ser Fillipo's hand was also on his sword.

And it came to Alfredo, as he watched and also shied away from watching, that perhaps the words of the Serra Amara might have stilled Valedan; that if she had spoken to him, he might have set aside *this* sword at the onset of battle, forgoing his oath.

He did not understand the kai Leonne. But he was beginning to, and the understanding brought no contempt with it. Ser Alfredo had been his mother's comfort; Ser Carelo had been his mother's worry.

She would have been ill pleased indeed to hear the question he had asked. He pressed lips into a thin line. She would have watched, she would have born witness. He could do no less.

When two men of worth meet in battle, it is said that there are two outcomes: One swift, and the other slow. It was not the first that was given to these two; Alesso di'Marente was denied an early victory by the speed of Valedan's defense. He did not meet the General head on; he was always slightly to one side of the force of the attack. Weight did not favor him.

But time did; he was the younger of the two.

The less experienced.

Alesso feinted.

Valedan managed to recover his parry, but the tip of *Terra Fuerre's* edge grazed his arm; first blood.

Whispers rose, muted instantly by the dim glare of those born to the High Courts. First blood, second blood, third—these mattered little.

Second blood, however, was also the General's.

"Did you train him?" Aidan asked softly.

"Alesso di'Marente?"

The pale head bobbed.

"No, Aidan."

"You trained Valedan."

"No. I guided him; I honed his edge. But what these two bring to their battle was in them before I met them; they are the Lord's men."

And Aidan said, "Which Lord?"

"Judge," Ser Anton replied quietly, "by the outcome."

Aidan was quiet a moment, listening to the song of the sword; the sudden pause in the clash of steel that spoke of a momentary separation. "He's good."

"Yes, Aidan."

The sun rose slowly. Minutes passed. Each one was long, longer by far than the minutes that had passed while the sun crested the horizon at its leisure.

Third blood was also the General's, and the whisper that rose at this could not be quelled. Valedan's forehead was grazed by edge, and the wound left was deep enough to be instantly visible.

But Valedan himself did not seem to notice the injury. He could not sheathe his sword now; his favorite stance was lost him. Footwork was not, nor was the supple stretch of arm, the curve of spine, the quick bob of head that saved his nose.

Beyond them, the only boundary drawn, were the twin banners of the Tyr'agar, the golden embroidery of sun ascendant catching sun's light and blazing with it. Wind was scant; the banners did not move. They were weighted, and they were held with purpose.

No easy victory here.

The Serra Diora did not once look away.

Ser Andaro was aware of this because he did. He glanced, with every connecting blow, at her perfect, pale features, at her utter composure. The Sun Sword was in her arms, and cradled there like an infant; she did not once deign to notice its weight.

She noted only the fight, the flight, the attacks, and her expression did not shift or change. She did not seem to blink.

And why should she? Her fate was wed to Valedan's; the outcome of this battle was the outcome of the war. He had heard rumors of the Serra Diora in the encampment. Had heard that she had drawn the Sun Sword from the waters of the Tor Leonne, garbed in the white of the Lord's Consort at the height of the Festival Sun.

He believed it all.

A whisper rose, a hush, drawn breath, and he turned immediately to see what had happened.

What she did not offer, he did: A smile. Valedan had finally drawn blood.

Kiriel di'Ashaf heard the play of swords across the silent valley, and she lifted her head. Auralis, back toward her, had lifted a hand to his eyes, shading vision from the glower of sun's light in a valley half-stripped of the trees that once provided shade. Whole trunks lay across the ruptured ground, some blackened beyond recognition, some cracked and twisted, great roots exposed.

"Valedan's fighting," he said, without looking back.

She nodded, her hand on Falloran's middle head. She had once asked Isladar why she couldn't just grow extra arms; the other demons could.

She forced herself not to remember his answer. The hand that rested against the brow of Falloran's middle head was comfort enough. He had risen, and his eyes seemed, to Kiriel, to be more intelligent, his expression—if he could be said to have one—more cunning.

"Will you bite my hand now?" she asked, pushing against his skull.

The left head snapped in the air, a hair's breadth from her exposed arm.

"Kiriel? Will you watch?"

She shrugged. "I can't see. They're too far away."

Auralis snorted. Turning, he reached for her arms—and then leaped back as Falloran attempted to rip out his throat.

She smacked Falloran sharply, and spoke three curt words.

"He is not bound to you," Lord Anduvin told her gently. "Not in that fashion. He owes you no obedience."

"He was bound to Isladar," she said.

"Yes."

"But Isladar isn't here."

"No."

"Then he can damn well listen to me."

Falloran whined.

"I want to see them fight," she said, glaring at him in mock annoyance. "And I can't. I can't go anywhere near the army while you look like *that*."

"Kiriel—"

"I *know* what he's capable of," she snapped, cutting Anduvin off. "Isladar chose him as the Tower guardian for a *reason*."

Anduvin raised a brow. "He is comfortable with his form; it was the form that he was given by the plain when he was first summoned."

"Yes. But it isn't a form he needs to wear. He has some choice."

"Kiriel—"

"And I want him to choose a different form."

But she didn't; not really. This form was wed to her earliest memories, and it was some part of her childhood joy and travail.

Falloran began to whine, but he bowed all three heads, and after a moment, he began to change. It was neither pretty nor slow; his flesh seemed to bubble and shudder as he made the effort to conceal two of his heads.

Anduvin's brow rose in surprise.

"He's mine," she said defensively. "And I want to keep him with me. But I can't—not while he looks like a—"

"Like the kin?"

She nodded.

His skin changed as well; ebony gave way to something that hinted at brown, and the hard shell of something akin to chitin gave way, at last, to a sleek, black fur. He had four legs. He had a tail. He had an enormous jaw. A single jaw.

He was also the size of a small pony.

She shrugged; it was the best he could do. "Come," she told him, almost apologetically.

And he followed as she began to walk. Auralis, dubious, fell in step by her side, and Falloran's growl traveled half the length of the valley, but he did not attempt to kill the Osprey again.

As they approached the Tyrs, Auralis bowed to her. "I have to go," he said softly. "I see Duarte."

She nodded.

"I'll come to get you."

And nodded again. She could see Valedan kai di'Leonne now. She could see his enemy.

Both men bled. No single wound had yet stopped them, but the cumulative wounds had slowed them; they were cautious now, and the speed of their movements was hampered by that caution. They sought openings, and where none existed, they sought to make them.

Ser Anton di'Guivera watched, grim and silent. He called no time, ordered no halt; he did not berate form or its lack. It was the first time that he had presided over Valedan's combats in silence.

Endurance would decide much. But if Alesso was the older of the two, he did not flag. The sky was clear, and the Lord's face, harsh. The humidity of the valley made armor uncomfortable.

They were sweating, in the sunlight. Shining with it.

Ser Mareo kai di'Lamberto folded arms across his chest as he watched. *Balagar* hung by his side, and beneath *Balagar,* the sword of his clan. Both were sheathed. Both remained so.

Ser Galen kai di'Lamberto was likewise encumbered by silence. But his breath matched the movements of the combatants.

His father had served a weak Tyr before.

But he knew, watching Valedan and Ser Alesso par di'Marente, that no Lambertan would serve the General. Not in this life. What the others—what even Valedan himself—were willing to forgive, Ser Mareo alone was not.

This was Lambertan truth. The death of a kai? The death of kin? Yes. In the end, even that could be forgiven for the greater good. But service to the Lord of Night? Never.

And Ser Galen knew what such defiance would cost Lamberto, in the end.

Kai Leonne, he thought grimly. *Win this fight.*

"Well?" Commander Allen asked.

Devran did not reply. Ellora shrugged, but the shrug was a mask; she was as tense as any of them.

"He's good," Commander Allen said, when neither of his companions replied.

Ellora did not turn. But she said angrily, "We could have skipped the war, if it was to be settled like *this.*"

Thinking, he knew, of all of her dead. And of the Ospreys, chief among them, clipped, wingless, blind. He lifted a hand and touched her shoulder. But he did not speak again.

Twenty minutes.

Twenty-one. Both men were breathing heavily now, and the weight of their swords had become substantial as the minutes wore on. Blood changed the shade of steel, dimming the sun's reflection across the length of slender surface. They moved slowly.

But with care. The entire weight of the Dominion, the entire weight of the desires that had changed the face of the Green Valley, was born by these two.

They exchanged no words. They did not descend into mockery; they did not attempt to goad. They had eyes, in the end, for each other, and only each other; even the Tyrs and their weighty banners had fallen away, into the shadows beyond the banners that each man fought for the right to claim.

Valedan swung low; Alesso swung high.

Their swords did not meet, but Valedan, leaning forward into the strike, felt the edge of blade pass just above him.

Alesso felt the edge across his knee.

He did not buckle, but he grunted. The first significant wound had been taken.

How is worth in a man judged?

Not, surely, by this. Not by steel. Not by the simple strength of arms, devoid of armies, of wisdom, of anything but the earliest of reflexes.

And yet, Kallandras thought, grave and graceful as he watched, this was still the only fight that mattered to the Southerners. And because it was, it was also the only fight of significance to the Northerners as well.

The Northerners had gathered; they were subtle about it, perhaps because they were compelled to watch and bear witness. But they knew that if Ser Alesso di'Marente emerged victorious here, their position would be, at best, tricky.

Ramiro kai di'Callesta had proved himself to be a stalwart ally; he had not hesitated once since they had crossed the border, inexplicable and wild, that separated two nations.

But he was a political man, and in the end, the Commanders did not trust him. Nor, Kallandras thought, were they entirely foolish.

"Well, Kallandras?"

"Member APhaniel," he replied, not looking away from the fight.

"It is almost done," the magi continued. Across the distance that separated them—and judging from voice, it was little—smoke wafted. The crisp sound of curling, dry leaf was almost as loud as distant breath.

"It is almost over," Kallandras offered, by way of reply.

"Aye, it is. For now."

And after the first significant wound, the second. Valedan's arm was cut to the bone. It was not his sword arm, but in the South, men might use both to greater advantage.

He could not afford another such blow.

But he had not chosen to take the one that hampered him. Grimacing, he wished he could wipe his brow.

"Strength, Valedan," a voice whispered, as he swayed.

He knew the voice well. But the tone was unfamiliar, and he almost closed his eyes to savor the strangeness. Almost. But that was death, and he had not come all this way to die.

He had come all this way, he thought bitterly, to kill.

But the killing of demons had come easily to him, perhaps because he had wielded the Sun Sword; perhaps because he could see no shadow of himself in the creatures he had faced.

Alesso di'Marente did not give him pause to dwell on this; he came in, at an angle, and Valedan gave himself over to the fight. To the simple imperative of survival.

All fights are risks. Some are chosen, and some are given without choice or consent.

There is triage, the hell of the healer-born; there is the decision to lose scouts in an attempt to track the movement of an enemy, or the presence of one. There is the loss of whole units, strategic losses all.

And none of them, in the end, taken by Valedan.

When Alesso di'Marente closed, Valedan made his choice. It was a desperate choice, but he accepted it; he did not move to parry; he moved, instead, strategically.

He offered Alesso an opening, and he shifted to the side at the last moment, seeking not to dodge, but to accept, on his terms, what was offered. He took the whole of *Terra Fuerre* through his left shoulder. Too close to the heart for comfort.

He cried out, let himself cry out, in pain. Pain reminded him of life, and he was still alive.

His right shoulder, his right arm, wounded but still whole, moved. He clenched muscles to contain what must surely follow as the Marente blade moved an inch through his flesh, drawing blood, shearing muscle.

Alesso di'Marente smiled for the first time.

And Valedan surprised him by returning that feral grin. He drove his own sword up. It was not elegant. It was not graceful. It was not, in the end, a strike worthy of Ser Anton, or one of Ser Anton's students. It was messy, bloody, painful.

And it was victory, if victory in the end could be reduced to a sword whose hilt jutted prominently beneath the momentarily exposed jaw of a tired man.

CHAPTER THIRTY-NINE

SER ANTON di'Guivera lifted a hand. "The Lord," he intoned, "has judged." His voice carried; the silence of the valley was broken by breeze and breath.

But after his words had died into stillness, no man seemed willing to interrupt the quiet.

Even Aidan was speechless.

They swayed together, the one man dead, the other bleeding, caught by the swords that they had wielded in grim mimicry of dance.

No one came to offer them aid or support. None dared. The Tyr'agar was upon the field, and it was death to acknowledge any weakness on his part. Had been death, for as long as the Leonnes ruled the Dominion.

Ser Andaro di'Corsarro and Serra Diora en'Leonne understood the man they had sworn oaths to. But they understood, better than he, the imperatives of the office that had taken the oath. They looked first to each other, and then away, ashamed of the impulse that made them want to move.

And then, the Serra Diora smiled. It was a High Court smile. She was dressed in the finest of silks that a battlefield allowed, the bright blues of wealth at odds with the muted night shades of mourning. She wore no veil. An oversight.

"Ser Andaro," she said quietly.

He raised a brow. He even raised a hand, but it fell again almost as quickly as it had risen. He looked away, as if by not seeing her, he could prevent any others from witnessing.

Cradling the Sun Sword in her arms, she began to traverse the field. She walked like a Serra. She walked like *the* Serra, the Serra Diora. But instead of skirting the edge of the Tyr'agnati's banners, she approached them. Bold now, arms full.

She did not speak.

They did not speak. Ser Eduardo kai di'Garrardi looked full upon her face, his eyes unblinking and slightly narrowed. She failed to acknowledge him. He opened his mouth, and Ser Jarrani kai di'Lorenza lifted a hand. It was almost an open insult.

But the man who had offered insult so casually to all offices seemed not to notice the insult offered him. He subsided.

She did not kneel to them, although she should have. That, and more. But she could not do so gracefully while she carried the Sun Sword, and she made her choice: she placed its imperative over theirs, and she bowed instead, holding the Sun Sword at the full reach of her arms until she could touch its sheath with her forehead.

It was a challenge.

But it was a woman's challenge.

No man there knew how to accept it, and they let it be. When she knew for certain that they would, she rose, and turned once again to face the two men, one living, one dead, who formed the Lord's tableau.

Valedan had not spoken a word. But he had not crumpled, either. "**Kai Leonne**," she said, her back to the men who might have witnessed the movement of her lips, "**be strong**."

He coughed.

And she continued to walk toward him, neither slowing nor gaining speed. She had chosen to take a risk, and now adorned it in the manners and nuances of the familiar. So, too, Alesso di'Marente, when he had taken the Tor Leonne.

She made her way to her husband, and when she stood close enough to see the blood running from the sword that still pierced his chest, she finally knelt, raising her arms, her hands flat beneath the weight of the Sun Sword. Flower of the Dominion, and crown, she waited.

But it was difficult; her arms were beginning to shake, and she knew she couldn't conceal their motion forever.

"**Valedan**," she said, speaking privately.

He coughed again, and she felt a moment of sharp, harsh anger. It was wed to fear; she could not separate them.

"**Do not show weakness here,**" she snapped, showing, for the first time that day, weakness of her own. "**This is what you wanted. This is what you came South for. You have achieved what you vowed to achieve—you cannot falter now.**" She did not know what her voice told him. But it told him something.

He turned only his face. The blade of the man who would become the Dominion's most famous General was still buried in his chest, just beneath his shoulder, and she saw that he supported the whole of Alesso di'Marente's weight.

She could not rise.

Not yet.

"**Valedan,**" she said, changing the tone of her voice, smoothing from it the unseemly, terrified anger. "**You must be seen to speak. You must be seen to command. I cannot rise, and I cannot help you, if you cannot do that much.**"

But he was mute. He met her gaze, and he held it; she was close enough to see the unnatural white of his features. Serra white, she thought him, and beautiful, his eyes dark and wide, his lashes long. Blood had congealed across his face, in stark contrast to his pallor.

She had despised him, when they had first met. And she had feared him. Feared the Northern influence, the weakness that demanded reciprocity.

She feared a different weakness now. Her own. She set the Sun Sword in her lap and waited, dutiful wife.

But Valedan did not speak, and in the end, he might never have moved had it not been for the quiet intrusion of a man that she had almost forgotten.

Ser Sendari di'Marano, bent a moment beneath the lie of Alesso di'Marente's proud banner, now straightened his shoulders. His fingers left his beard, and the weariness was banished from his stride as he approached the two men.

Eyes wide, she watched him, thinking suddenly that Valedan could not let him live. It was not a welcome thought; she had bid him good-bye so many times that she had thought herself beyond all ability to be moved by him.

Wondered if she would ever truly know herself.

He did not turn to her. Did not acknowledge her at all. But he bowed to the Tyr'agar regnant, and his voice did not falter as he used a familiar title.

"Tyr'agar."

Valedan said nothing.

"Alesso di'Marente will have no friends," her father continued softly.

"And no need . . . for them," the kai Leonne said. His first words.

She knew why he had spoken. His voice was soft, almost broken, but he found the strength to speak, not to soothe her anger, but to address in some fashion this stranger's pain. His words, unadorned, were not harsh, and what she heard in them made her close her eyes for the first time.

"This is the South," the Widan replied, pulling at his robes, rolling his ungainly sleeves up to his elbows and exposing the scars he had taken in his attempt to gain his title so many years past. "And he has need of one. Will you allow me the honor?"

Valedan nodded.

And Ser Sendari di'Marano put his remaining strength into what he did next: he caught Alesso's shoulders, sliding his hands beneath slack arms, and he took the whole of the General's weight upon himself. Valedan let go of his sword, and reaching up with both of his hands, he forced Alesso di'Marente, at last, to surrender his. They parted slowly, *Terra Fuerre* still sheathed in Valedan's chest.

Alesso di'Marente's body crumpled as Sendari lowered it to the ground and knelt beside it in the harsh glare of sunlight.

Valedan staggered slightly, but he did not join the two men. Instead, he grasped the hilt of his enemy's sword. Grimacing, he pulled it free.

Blood welled from the wound.

"The Lord has judged," he said softly, swaying.

"The Lord has judged," Sendari agreed. He placed his hands over Alesso's open eyes, and gently closed their lids.

"Where is Ser Andaro?" Valedan asked, turning at last to the kneeling Serra Diora.

"He waits," she replied. "For you."

"Then tell him to come to me," he told her. "I hold his sword, and I cannot take the Sun Sword unless I drop it."

She knew, by his tone, that he wouldn't. And knew, by his tone, that he meant for her to use her gift.

She hesitated for a moment, and then she whispered Ser Andaro's name, cloaking it in the privacy that only those born to the voice could invoke.

He came. He was not beholden to the Tyrs, to the Commanders, or to the man who adjudicated the fight by the simple expedient of announcing its end. He did not walk with the quiet, public dignity of the Serra; he barely walked at all, his feet clipping the ground as he traversed the distance with unseemly haste.

And he did not seem to notice that she had summoned him.

Instead, he made his way to her side, and he knelt there, upon one knee instead of two. "Tyr'agar," he said, as he had said once before, while the men of the South—the men of significance—bore witness.

"Take your sword," Valedan told him, forgoing, as well, the airs of the Court. "It is heavy, and I cannot hold it much longer."

"It is not as heavy," Ser Andaro replied, rising immediately, "as the sword you *will* bear."

Valedan's brief smile segued into another grimace; he was in pain. "No," he said. "It's not. Serra?"

She rose as well, and offered him the Sun Sword, as she, too, had offered it once before: in public, beneath the watchful gazes of men of power.

In both of these actions, the difference was profound.

He took it from her, and he staggered as he moved, righting himself by force of will. He was not perfect. But he was conscious, and he was alive.

It would have to do, for now.

Taking a deep breath, and forcing himself not to cough, he drew the blade from its scabbard and held it high.

When he did—and only then—noise erupted in the valley. Horns were raised and winded, voices raised above them. The Northerners beat their shields as if they were instruments, not of war, but of approbation.

Ser Valedan kai di'Leonne began to walk toward the banner held by his Northern standard-bearer. He moved deliberately, his steps traced by the fall of his blood. At a respectful distance, Ser Andaro followed.

The Serra Diora followed as well. Her voice did not join the voices of men; she was silent. But her palms ached, and her arms still shook; she was ashamed. Because she knew that she wanted to catch him, should he falter, and knew that she *could not*. He took steps like a child, faltering, teetering. First steps, steps denied her own son by a man who now lay dead.

She turned suddenly, and saw that her father's eyes were upon her. His face was like a mask: a Festival mask. Everything within it stood revealed in the stark, harsh light of day.

He had never been the Lord's man. He had been his wife's husband, and his sister's brother. He had been, for some time, her beloved father. He had been par, first to Adano, and later, in all but blood, to Ser Alesso di'Marente. All steps taken, all roads, had wound their way to this field.

She wanted to shout at him. She would have, could she think of anything to say. But words were denied her. She felt no triumph; only a curious numbness that settled heavily about her shoulders like a mantle.

"Kai Leonne," she said, lifting her voice, her natural voice.

He stopped. Executed a clumsy turn, so that he might face her.

"This man," she told him, while the Tyrs watched, "is my father."

And Ser Sendari di'Marano closed his eyes.

A healer was called.

Ser Laonis di'Caveras came, exhausted, as pale as Valedan beneath the Lord's gaze. By his side, or perhaps just behind him, came the two Northerners, both men, who worked in the medical tents. They spoke; Valedan could not quite catch their words. Not without effort.

Ser Laonis was clearly irritated. He lifted his hands, one after another, swatting their words away as if they were flies.

They subsided as Northerners do: with no grace at all. But they let him pass beyond their reach, and Valedan saw, from the grim set of their now closed jaws, that it was costly.

"Tyr'agar," Ser Laonis said, bending, falling slowly to one knee.

"Ser Laonis," Valedan replied. He held out a hand, and Ser Laonis rose instantly. "I think perhaps—"

"No."

"You have already—"

"No."

Ser Laonis, it seemed, had also spent too much time in the North. The kai Leonne hesitated a moment, and then, as Ser Laonis engulfed his hand, he asked a single question.

"Why?"

What Ser Laonis might have said in reply was lost.

Men made way, at last, for the Radann.

Ser Peder kai el'Sol bent full to ground. It was not required. It was not, in fact, seemly. But thus offered, his obeisance gave weight and strength to Valedan's claim, if it were needed. He did not speak.

The par el'Sol joined him: Samiel, Samadar, and Marakas. They offered freely what Peder kai el'Sol offered first: their genuine respect.

He bid them all rise, and they did—but slowly, allowing distant cerdan to understand the full measure of their silent pledge.

Marakas par el'Sol stepped forward, but it was not to Ser Valedan kai di'Leonne that he spoke; that was Peder's right, and he did not appear to envy it. "Ser Laonis," he said, bowing.

"Radann par el'Sol," Ser Laonis replied, tendering a deeper bow.

"With your permission, I will tend to the Tyr'agar's wounds."

What he had not granted the Northern healers, he granted the par el'Sol—but only barely. This close, the open light of day underscored the pallid color of skin, the faint trembling of exhaustion.

The Serra Diora en'Leonne almost reached for him, and, as if seeing her, truly seeing her, for the first time, his eyes rounded. His hand rose of its own accord, but it fell with his effort.

He turned, with equal effort, to Valedan, and when Valedan nodded gravely, he surrendered.

And the Serra Diora en'Leonne understood the whole of his need, the whole of his intent; how could she not? She had traversed a dark road at his behest, and she had followed him, at last, into the land of the living. He *honored* her husband.

His eyes, ringed dark, fell upon her face again, and he smiled as if he could hear her thought; as if it were almost a child's thought. "You honor him, Serra," he said gravely.

To the Radann par el'Sol, in a louder voice, he said, "You have my permission."

Marakas par el'Sol smiled. The smile had an edge, but all things Southern did. "You have healed the Tyr'agar before," he said quietly.

Ser Laonis raised brow. But after a moment, he nodded.

"You honor him." Marakas spoke when it was clear that Ser Laonis would not. "I do not know if he knows how much."

"He knows," Ser Laonis whispered. But he retreated.

Marakas par el'Sol took the Tyr'agar's hand in his. "Well fought," he said.

"Was it?" The reply was weary. Quiet.

"You know the role the General played in this battle."

Valedan nodded. "But I know, as well, that had he not arrived, we might not be standing here. In the end, he proved himself the Lord's man, and the Lord values power."

"Not above all else," Marakas replied, resolute.

"No?"

"No."

And Valedan smiled. He felt warmth in his palm, and he knew, then, that Marakas par el'Sol was healer-born. "Good," he said. "Power without responsibility—"

"You speak like a Lambertan," Marakas said. "But you bleed like a normal man." He frowned. "You—"

Valedan shook his head. "Let us repair to my tent. We have much to discuss, the Radann and I."

Peder kai el'Sol nodded, and the Radann formed up around the Tyr'agar, as if they were his Tyran. Thus had Leonne the Founder walked, centuries past, although Valedan did not know it.

He would never return to the North.

He had known it, the moment he crossed the border into Averda, but the knowledge had been distant. Theoretical. Something that could be faced if, and only if, he won.

The reality was visceral, and to his great surprise considering the alternative, deeply unpleasant.

He would never see Mirialyn ACormaris again, and he wanted—as a child might—her approval for all that he had done. She had given him the use of his first sword, training him while the Southerners pretended not to notice. She had given him the bow that he had vowed to use; he had not touched it. Could not.

And she had given him the legacy of her birth: wisdom.

But it was not the wisdom that he would most miss; he had that, in the form of the Serra Alina di'Lamberto, and in the form of the Serra Diora en'Leonne. No; he would miss the *peace*. The long moments of mutual silence that brooked no words, the quiet sense of both solitude and companionship. He would miss the Arannan Halls, and he would miss the courtyard in which his journeys to the South had truly begun.

Serafs did not come to his tent, but he had already accepted that they would; that Ramdan would serve his wife for the remainder of his life; that men, women, and children would be considered rich and worthy gifts between the Tyrs who would pledge their allegiance to his clan and his clan itself.

He wanted to change that.

Was beginning to see that changing something that he did not truly understand would be more difficult than winning the war.

"Tyr'agar."

He turned. "Kai el'Sol."

They were alone in the tent. Marakas par el'Sol had healed the wound, and after he had finished, he had dropped to one knee in a long, slow silence that made Valedan uncomfortable. But he did not speak, not even to ask permission to withdraw.

Samadar and Samiel left by his side.

The two men in the Dominion who were granted the right to wear the sun ascendant now faced each other as equals.

And Valedan found that he had little to say.

But Peder kai el'Sol was not perturbed. "My apologies, Tyr'agar," he said quietly.

"No apologies are necessary here."

"It is a . . . habit of speech."

He lied. Valedan accepted it. He wanted the Serra Alina's presence, and it would not be granted him while the kai el'Sol remained in the tent. She was still dressed as a Northerner, after all; a warrior and not a Serra.

"You will be crowned," Peder kai el'Sol told him, "in the waters of the Tor Leonne."

Valedan nodded.

"Bear the Sword to the Swordhaven," the kai el'Sol continued, "and we will watch it, as we have always watched it."

It was his sword now. He nodded again.

"I will leave you to contemplate your future. You are not the man your father was," he added, as he made his way to the outer wall of the tent.

"So I've been told."

Peder kai el'Sol hesitated for just a moment, his hand against canvas. Then he offered an almost bitter smile. "You are young," he said softly. "But not untested. You have Leonne blood in your veins, and it is strong. Nothing you have done since you have returned to the lands of your birth should give you cause for regret."

It surprised Valedan. It was almost like a confession. But in surprise, Valedan found his grace. "There are so many dead," he said.

"Yes."

"You regret them."

"I regret some of them," Peder kai el'Sol replied. "I regret, most, that the hand that wielded *Balagar*—that *could* wield *Balagar*— was never mine."

"What will you do?"

"The kai Lamberto will offer me the sword," he replied, with a shrug.

"And will you accept it?"

"The South is governed by its customs," the kai el'Sol replied.

And then, with another slight shrug, he added, "I do not know. I wanted the right to bear that sword. I planned for it. I played politics for it. I killed for it. It was costly."

Valedan looked down at the simple scabbard that held the Sun Sword, and he winced.

"No, kai Leonne," Peder said, denying him. "What you desired and what I desired were not, in the end, the same."

"And now?"

"Now? I have seen what we face. I will not forget it. And in time, kai Leonne, I hope to prove myself worthy of *Balagar*. Until I am certain of that worthiness, I will not wield her, even if I accept her return, and the Hand of God will number four."

Valedan nodded. "You served the General."

"We served our own purposes, he and I," Peder said heavily. "But, yes, that was my beginning."

"A Northerner of my acquaintance has often said that the beginning is just that: it is the end that is of note."

"Do not seek kindness in the South," Peder replied, but without heat. "Do not offer it openly; it will compromise your rule." But he offered a smile. "As I can, kai Leonne, and as you allow it, I will guide you."

"As I can," Valedan countered, "I will accept guidance."

They parted then, and after a long pause, the tent's flap moved, and the Serra Alina entered. She was pale, silent, shorn of grace; her eyes were dark with exhaustion. But she smiled when she saw his expression.

"Tyr'agar," she said gravely.

He lifted a hand, shaking his head.

She nodded, and closed the distance between them until she stood inches from him. There, she lifted both of her hands and cupped his face. "You've grown so tall," she said, as if she were an Ona.

He said, his voice giving lie to her words, "Did I do well?"

And she nodded. Her hands remained as support for his face when he bent slowly into them; her thumbs stroked his cheeks as if he were a child in the harem's heart, and at that, a child in need of comfort.

"Mirialyn would be proud of what you achieved," she told him, as he closed his eyes.

"I will never see her again."

"She does not often leave the city," Alina replied.

"She never truly leaves it."

"No."

Silence, for a moment. "Will she come, do you think?"

"I do not know, Valedan. But . . . I think that if you ask it, she will journey here."

"If you ask it," he amended.

He could not see her smile, but he could hear it in the texture of her voice. He knew that it was not unalloyed. "Perhaps."

"Will you?"

"I will ask her," Alina replied, speaking gently, always gently. "But I will not begin to write until you are asleep. Sleep, Valedan. No one will expect you to hold audience immediately."

He said, "the dead—"

And her hands tightened, although they were still soft. She wanted to sing to him, but he was married to a woman whose voice was held in awe throughout the Dominion; she could not bring herself to offer him less. Ah, vanity.

"Northern boy," she whispered, with the open affection that she had showed him only in the Empire.

His lashes separated, and their eyes met.

"It is in the North," she told him softly, "that when men of power retreat from their victories they see only the losses. Only in the North that the taint of loss is stronger than the euphoria of victory itself.

"I was afraid, for you, because of this. I was wrong. You are Valedan, you are the kai Leonne, and you are the Tyr'agar."

"You're not going to lecture me about my weakness?"

"How can I?"

"Don't tell me that you are only a Serra."

"I *am* only a Serra," she said, but with a fierce smile. "And your wife is only a Serra." But she drew his head down, and their foreheads touched. "She holds you in high regard," she added softly.

His eyes widened, and she thought him young, unbearably young, and vulnerable. "She is the only wife that you could have taken, to my regret. But she will be your staunchest ally, and she will be where I can never be."

She kissed him then. "Sleep, Valedan. I will keep the wolves at bay."

Harem child. And when he woke, he would leave the harem behind, at last. She offered him now what she could, because she knew that he did not understand this completely.

How could he, when she had not seen it clearly for herself until this moment?

When the Lady's face was bright above the valley's heights, he woke.

Lamplight burned in the quiet of the tent, and the Serra Alina sat beside the closed door, as she had promised. She had, however, changed; she wore a sari, and if it was simple, it was costly. It was the color of night blue, and white trimmed its edges, lending it both light and gravity.

He blinked slowly and sat up. She rose, then, and offered him sweet water, no wine.

But he shook his head. "The Lady's time," he told her.

"Yes."

"I will offer the ablutions."

She raised brow, but she did not gainsay him. He wondered, then, if she ever would again, and found himself missing the sharp edge of her tongue.

She said, "Marakas par el'Sol has revealed too much."

And he smiled. "I think that you will find that the Radann were shaped and formed by the hand of a Lambertan."

"So was I," she replied sharply.

He stilled, and his smile faded. "If I asked it, would your brother send you to my court?"

She was surprised by the question. At least he thought she was; her silence was longer and deeper than usual. "I do not know," she said at last. "He has taken your measure here, and it may be that he would be willing to flout some convention if you asked it. But I think he would prefer that you had other advisers."

"The advisers that I have had," he said, with youthful dignity, "were obviously all that I required."

"For this? Yes. But to rule?" She shook her head. "The whole of the Dominion will hear of you. But what they hear, and what they choose to believe, I cannot say. I think he would be glad not to have to take me home," she added, "and I think that the time of the Southern hostages is coming quickly to an end. I am not sure that all of them will be thankful."

He waited while she readied herself. Her skin was darker than it had been, but she looked, in all things, like a Serra to his eyes.

"Where is the Serra Diora?"

"She is with the healers."

"Ah."

"Should I send for her, Valedan?"

He hesitated, and Alina nodded, leaving the tent.

When she returned, the Serra was with her. Her sari was crumpled; silk did not weather the travails of the healing tent well, and she had taken no time to safeguard it. But she met his gaze, and she spoke. "You have been with the Radann par el'Sol," she said quietly.

His brow rose.

"I know what he is capable of. But few indeed are the men who would allow him free use of that gift."

"I would."

"I know. You are not afraid of your doubts."

He shook his head.

"You will perform the Lady's ablutions."

And raised a brow again.

She smiled, and she offered him a very Northern bow. Northern at least in form; it was too supple, otherwise. "May I join you?"

"Always."

Together they left the tent.

Jevri el'Sol stood beside Ser Mareo kai di'Lamberto. The torches had been lit, and along the edge of the valleys, the drums of the plains had been prepared. They beat now, hands across stretched skins evoking the beat of a thousand Southern hearts.

"Well, Jevri," the kai Lamberto said, as the Tyr'agar and his Serra came into view. "What will you do now?"

"I?" The old servitor frowned. His hands were curved at his sides; humidity, Mareo observed, made them ache. "I will return to the Radann," he replied.

"And not to Lamberto?"

The old man shook his head. "I have few years of useful service left, and those years would bring no honor to Lamberto. I am not graceful now, Mareo. I am not capable of the artistry required by the Serras of the High Courts, and I am not—I have never been—fit seraf for the men. It was not my duty, and in the end, it was not my calling."

"And what do you hope for? You brought me *Balagar*. You brought me word of Fredero. My mother set you one task, and one alone, when she gave you your freedom, and you never once wavered from it. You honored her. You would find honor in my household for that alone."

"I did not honor the Serra, kai Lamberto." The older man smiled, but it was tinged with pain. "I honored her son. I did not know, for certain, what Fredero would become, when I left harem service. I did not know that he would survive his early years in the Radann. When he spoke to me of his need to rule them, I wondered if the act of taking the title of kai el'Sol would forever alter his intentions."

This seemed to annoy the Tyr. His frown was slight, but it was clear and easily read.

Jevri, however, had no fear. "I have seen many men change, over the years. When they are young, they are governed by passion and the desire for either honor or glory; they are moved by their beliefs, and they act on them. But action itself is difficult and requires compromise; I have seen those same men discard beliefs after testing them, until at last they are much like the men they despised. I do not judge them," he added.

"Then you are not Lambertan."

"No, I was never so blessed. Enough, for me, to serve a Lambertan. I thought my service would end in your house," he added, his voice dropping, his gaze following the Tyr'agar's procession.

No, Ser Mareo realized, not the Tyr'agar's. The Serra's.

"But the Lady has not seen fit to summon me. Not even from this field, when she has taken so many others who were younger than I. And so," he said quietly, "I will continue to serve."

"Who?"

"I will serve the kai el'Sol."

Ser Mareo's frown deepened.

"He is not the man he was, kai Lamberto. But more significant, he is the man, in the end, whom Fredero chose. He is not yet Fredero's equal, and there is every reason to believe that he will never be. But I also have reason to believe that he will attempt to become so, and it is a struggle that I can best serve by my presence."

"You want to make dresses for the Serra Diora en'Leonne," Mareo replied, with just a hint of a cold smile.

Jevri was far too old to blush. "Yes," he replied, serene now. "I do."

Ser Anton di'Guivera was waiting, and he joined Valedan in silence, walking behind him and carrying a torch upon a long pole. Behind Ser Anton, Ser Andaro also walked, carrying a sword. And behind them both, the remaining Ospreys formed up, wordless and expressionless. But they carried the Tyr'agar's banner.

Valedan had not planned it this way, but he did nothing to gainsay it. They had come to offer their respects to the dead, and they were willing, this time, to leave their dead in the valleys that had been their birthplace. Nothing would stop them, however, short of his command, and he did not choose to give it.

Their numbers had been winnowed. Gone was Fiara, grim and merciless; gone, Alexis, the sharp-tongued den mother who had herded them from one extreme to another. Gone, in Essla, Sanderton, the first casualty of the battle.

No, he thought, almost ashamed, not the first. But the first personal loss. It was human nature to value most the people that one knew best; it was lack of imagination to think that the other losses were insignificant. Across the Dominion, grief would spread in a widening circle as word of death traveled by horse and foot to the farthest reaches of the Terreans.

He hoped that pride might somehow lessen the loss; pride in what those deaths had, in the end, achieved. But did it lessen his? He grimaced, and turned to the Serra a moment, seeking the certainty of her beauty, her flawless poise.

The moon was silver-bright, as bright, in her fashion, as the Lord. But her light was cool; no swords were drawn beneath her open face. Daggers were, however; they were brought for his use. For the Serra Diora's.

Primus Duarte came up through the ranks to join him. He offered Valedan a sharp salute, and Valedan acknowledged. "Duarte," he said, voice low.

Duarte nodded. He was pale, in the moonlight. But dry-eyed. Aware that he stood in the South.

"Will you return to the North?"

The Primus' brows rose, and Valedan hesitated. It was not a question that he had intended to ask.

"There is a home for you and your men," Valedan continued, committed now. "If you will serve me, I will take your service, and you will live upon the plateau in the Tor Leonne."

"We are not men of the High Courts."

"Neither am I."

"You will have to be."

Valedan shrugged. Osprey expression. "I need Tyran," he said, after a pause. "And I can think of no others so worthy of that title."

"We are not Tyran, kai Leonne."

"What are you, then?"

Duarte's shoulders folded. "Ospreys," he said, at last. "And long from the hunt."

"The company is no longer called that—in the North."

Duarte said nothing.

"But in the South, that is how it is known, and how you would be known." He hesitated, and then added, "You would wear my colors, as you wore Kalakar colors; you would wear Osprey colors as well."

"We would be known as your men," Duarte said bleakly. "And that is the antithesis of what the Ospreys *were*."

"You will be seen," Valedan continued quietly, turning from him toward the flat, standing stones that had been erected in this spot, beneath the bowers of the few trees left standing upon the Western heights. "And I will not lie; I will be under constant scrutiny from those who consider me too weak to hold the title—or too Northern. If the Ospreys are seen to serve me, it will add to the respect they grant me."

"The respect of strangers."

"Indeed. And that," Valedan added softly, "is almost all of the Dominion. Do not decide now. Speak to the others. Take whatever time you need."

Serra Diora en'Leonne knelt first, upon the mats provided her by Ramdan. He had come out of nowhere, as he so often did, to lay them before her knees. He took her fan from her hands and held it with as much care as she had ever carried the Sun Sword.

Valedan knelt by her side, upon both knees.

She did not correct him, and he did not look to her for guidance. Instead, he turned his face to the height of the stone, and then, gaze skirting above it, to the height of a moon framed by thinned woods.

Three bowls were given them by Ramdan; three bowls were placed before them by the Serra, in a perfect row. Her hands were steady.

Water was brought, and wine. These Valedan took up with care and precision, pouring them as he had often seen Alina do.

But when the Serra Diora drew her dagger, he covered her hand with his. "Let me," he said softly.

"I have made these ablutions before," she replied, her voice just as soft.

"It is for the clan Leonne that these men and women died," he countered.

Her face grave, her expression completely smooth, she said, "And it is through *me*, kai Leonne, that the clan will continue."

"I will not ask you to shed more blood in my cause."

"You did not ask me to shed the blood I did."

"You had little choice if you were to—"

"Enough." Ser Anton's voice towered above them, although it, too, was deceptively quiet. "This is a discussion that is meant for the harem."

"It *is* the Lady's time," Valedan told him, without shifting his glance.

"Even the Lady has some dignity," Ser Anton said. His expression was the expression of the swordmaster, not the liege. "If you truly desire this, kai Leonne, command her, and she will obey."

Valedan frowned.

"But if you do not desire it enough to make a command, then accept her choice with grace. She is steel; she will not be bent easily by simple discourse, and the men are watching."

When Valedan did not lift his hand, Ser Anton's frown deepened a moment, and then he shook his head. "Make the offer," he told them. "Both of you. She is right; through her, your clan will continue, and the child that she bears will bear both your blood and hers. The Lady will accept what you honor her by offering."

Valedan nodded. But in a whisper, he added, "Me first."

And she surprised him; she smiled. She handed him her odd, ornate dagger, and he took it. His hands shook; hers didn't. Steel, Ser Anton had said.

He made the first cut, and it was too shallow; the second was perfect. He bled into the bowl, and was surprised when she, too, bled; she had taken the dagger from his hands, but when, he couldn't say.

When the bowl was as full as the first two she began to pull her wrist away, but he caught her hand in his, and he pressed the cuts together.

Then he released her, and together they bowed in mute appreciation for what they had accomplished here; they did not pray, because in the South, the Lady entertained no prayer.

But as they rose, music began to play—not the music of the drums that now beat in loud, sonorous tones, but rather the music of the lute: Kallandras of Senniel College had begun to sing, in the darkness of the Lady's time, the lay of the Sun Sword.

Valedan recognized it; Diora recognized it. But when it came to its natural end, they were both gratified: the words continued. History unfolded, slowly, before them, waiting upon their choices, their decisions.

Theirs were not the only ablutions offered that eve.
But the other was offered in isolation.

Ser Sendari di'Marano had neither the grace of his daughter nor the promise of her new husband; he had only memory, and much of it was bitter. His hands shook as he placed the bowls; his hands shook as he placed the water and wine before them.

No standing stones adorned the place that he had chosen, but one stone marked it clearly, nestled as it was above a bed of new-turned earth. He had worked almost without stop for the whole of the day, and he had suffered no other men to join him in his task.

Ser Mikalis had offered. Of the memories that haunted him, this was one of the few that were pleasant. Ser Mikalis, ruffled scholar, had come with shovel, his back bent by exhaustion and his face tinged with sorrow.

"Sendari," he had said.

But Sendari shook his head. "No, Mikalis," he replied. "Do not taint yourself here."

"And will you be left to do this on your own?"

"I will."

"Where is Cortano?"

"If he is wise, he has already departed for the Tor," Sendari replied evenly. "And if he is not? He is with the Tyrs. He is a man of power; he surrounds himself, always, with like-minded men. It does not matter to him if they claim power by sword or by sword's edge."

"The Tyr'agar will not allow him to live?"

"The Tyr'agar will decide that for himself; to remove the Sword's Edge would be costly, and he has paid a high price for his work here." He paused, and then added, "He will not seek to destroy the Tyrs who served Alesso di'Marente; he seems, at a distance, that wise."

"You are poorly repaid for your service."

"And you," Sendari replied. He shovelled dirt to one side, stopping a moment to wipe his brow. "But I tell you again: do not taint yourself in this fashion."

"Sendari—"

"We chose," Ser Sendari replied, with a serenity that he did not feel. "And we will be known for our choices. Will you have your name joined to ours in such a fashion? You deserve far more. Go home, Mikalis. Study. Learn. If I am not mistaken, what the Tyr'agar demands from the Widan will grant you the leisure and freedom in which to do both."

"And you, Sendari? What will become of you?"

Sendari shook his head. He could have answered the question, but had he, Mikalis would never have left.

But he had, in the end, and his gait as he walked away was slow; he was burdened in all ways by defeat.

I will miss you, Sendari thought, kneeling now, the night air cool.

In the end, however, he had not finished his digging alone. A stranger joined him.

His sister. She had taken the shovel from his sweating, shaking hands, and she had set it to one side, offering him water from an ungainly waterskin she had perched upon her hips. She looked like a Voyani woman, but she served him like a Serra. Her shoulders were straighter than his, if shorter, and they were still strong; she dug for some time while he drank sweet water, watching her in silence while she buried what remained of a giddy dream. A young man's foolish dream.

When she was tired, and she did tire, he rose and took the shovel again. "Why?" he asked her as he worked, not daring to look at her face.

"I know what you plan, Sendari."

"And you have come to aid me?" Harsh words.

"No. Nor have I come to argue. I heard Na'dio's words," she added.

He stopped all motion, staring at the earth. After a moment, he said, "She called me father."

"Yes."

"She introduced me to the Tyr'agar."

"Yes. It was unexpected. Unfortunate."

He nodded grimly. "It was both of those things. But I do not regret it."

"No. Nor will she, although she will grieve, I think."

"For the man who murdered her wives?"

"For that man, no. But we are not all one thing, not all the other; we live in the Lord's time and we dream in the Lady's. We know both Sun and Moon. It is not the Sun's dazzle that will blind her," she added. "But nor will she forget the Moon's silver. You were graced, by her, in your time." She rose. "The Matriarch of Havalla waits for me, and she does not wait patiently." She gathered up her waterskin and began to walk away.

"Teresa."

"Sendari?"

"Thank you."

She said nothing else for a moment, and then, at last, she relented. "Alora loved you," she whispered.

Alesso. The silent earth did not answer.

Alora. Neither did the dead.

Na'dio. And the living? They were at least as distant. *Will you truly find happiness?*

He offered water, spilling it sloppily, although he tried his best to be precise. He offered wine, drinking none of it, although he desired its heat and warmth.

Last, he drew dagger, and he held the flat of its silver edge against his wrist for a long, long time.

Three ablutions for an honored friend.

For a lost sister.

For a daughter.

The blade bit deep; he caught it in his bleeding hand, and rested red edge against his other wrist. This, too, he cut. Blood poured into the bowl that awaited it, and when it was full—and it filled quickly—he upended it against the mound that contained his friend.

But the blood continued to pour; his wrists stung. He lay back against that grave, his head touching the simple stone marker that adorned it.

He could see the moon, and only the moon, in the height of the sky. And he remembered, as he watched her silent face, another moon, another festival, another man and his cherished daughter.

The darkness closed in slowly; the distant sound of drums beat as if for him, and him alone. The breeze was quiet and still, and this worried him; if there was no wind, what would come to lift him, at last, from the burden of life?

But he bled regardless; did nothing at all to staunch the flow of that bleeding.

Wondered if anyone would offer him what he had offered the General Alesso di'Marente. Wondered, in the end, if it mattered.

He whispered their names while he could, but at last, he had no strength for that, and he closed his eyes, feeling the cold of night, of the last night, as it bore down upon him.

EPILOGUE

SHE CAME upon him in the moonlight, at the farthest edge of the Lady's time. Ser Andaro di'Corsarro was by her side, and they had exchanged many words as they walked. Nor were they Serra's words; they were political words. They spoke, between them, of things necessary for the survival of Valedan kai di'Leonne.

Ser Andaro accepted this from her; from another woman, he would have expected silence, the honor of silence. But to him, she was the Sun Sword's true sheath; she had born it, and more, in the cause of the clan Leonne. Would bear it again, without hesitation or regret, should the need arise. He knew this; she knew that he knew. They were comfortable in the roles that they had both chosen and failed to anticipate before the actions of the General Alesso di'-Marente had forever changed their lives.

Serra Diora had seen to her wife and her son; she had spoken only briefly with her husband. They were all exhausted, in their fashion, and sleep claimed them. All but the Serra Diora herself.

She was restless in the silence of a night punctuated by the movement of cerdan feet. And because she was restless, she rose at last, seeking solace beneath the face of the silver moon.

Ser Andaro had been waiting for her. She had not asked him why; she had simply started to walk, and he had followed. Had she the courage to reveal herself, she would have asked him where the tent of Ser Laonis di'Caveras lay; she did not. But she understood, that night, that weakness was given the healed in two ways, and she was not certain that she would summon a healer again—not for herself. She had suffered enough loss that this bitter echo made her weary.

The moon was low, and its silver had given way to some hint of the dawn that would follow; the sky was clear for miles. They had walked the distance to the forest's edge upon the valley floor; had walked past the standing stones and the offering bowls that both she and her husband had blessed with their mingled blood.

And they continued to walk until they came, at last, to a single grave.

Ser Andaro di'Corsarro stopped. "Serra Diora," he said, bowing slightly, and turning, at the same time, away from the grave. "I will wait for you by the Lady's shrine."

His steps receded; she did not once turn to watch him leave. But she knew that he offered her a gift by his absence, because she was his responsibility, and in no other circumstance would it be safe to leave her alone.

But here? Now? She thanked him numbly, and in silence. Oh, the grave.

She knew what lay across it, and she *could* know it, now: she was alone. She said nothing, but her knees bent slowly, as if they were no part of her, until they rested above the new-turned earth. No plants ringed it, no grass, no wild growth; they would come, in time.

But no one, she thought, would come for Ser Sendari di'Marano. He had chosen to stand by the side of Ser Alesso di'Marente, even in death.

She knew he was dead before she touched him, but she had to touch him anyway; her hands cupped his cold, cold face. His eyes were closed; a mercy. She almost didn't recognize it as such, for she was not accustomed to mercy from the Dominion.

She was no longer a child, and she wore no mask. But the whole of her face fell into unfamiliar lines as she offered him an expression he would have known best in the harem's heart, when he had been a younger man, and she, his unmarried, cherished daughter.

The bowls that he had brought lay empty, discarded. But they were not without use. She straightened her shoulders and glanced again at the Lady's face, as if seeking permission. Or absolution.

She could not bury him; not by herself, and not in time.

But she could offer him, in the end, what he had offered the General who had been friend and kin. She gathered the bowls, no seraf's hand to sustain her, and she drew *lumina arden* from its sheath.

Were her eyes dry? She did not know. Did not care. She poured water, and scant wine, and she opened veins once more, seeking not the Lady's blessing, and not the Lord's, but rather the earth's. She spoke softly, and she adorned her words with power.

"Let my father rest where I could not," she told the Old Earth. It offered no answer, and perhaps this was best; she knew that Meralonne APhaniel would have been angered by her momentary presumption, by the risk she took. Some things were best left to sleep.

"Cradle him. Let him know peace. Harbor him from the wind, and the wind's howl."

The earth and the air were ancient enemies, and they surrendered nothing to each other.

And the Serra Diora? In the end, she surrendered everything—but only as she could: in privacy. In darkness.

Three weeks after the battle ended, there was a dinner. The men of the North broke bread and drank wine with the men of the South; they sang and swore and insulted each other with great good humor.

The Tyr'agnati, however, were invited to join the Tyr'agnate of Callesta within his domis, and they did not refuse; they could not, with grace, although they were eager to be gone.

But Ser Mareo kai di'Lamberto came late.

He was granted the hospitality of Callesta, and he accepted it with silent grace—in the presence of his Serra. She had come, in haste, to meet him, and she had brought him word of his own fair city, but her expression did not soften until the moment she set eyes upon her son.

Her living son.

She did not embarrass Ser Galen by hugging him; did not approach him in an unseemly way. But he was conscious of the tears that she shed behind the screen of her very proper veil, and that was embarrassment enough.

Ser Mareo kai di'Lamberto gave her time to compose herself, and his Tyran greeted her almost shyly. It was very, very seldom that the Serra Donna chose to chance the roads; she was at home in the Court of Amar.

But she had much desired this journey, although she would never have been so crass as to request it, he knew. Their years of marriage, the understanding gained by decades of familiarity, served them both well. He had sent word by the swiftest of methods possible, and she had followed it.

In truth, it was not an indulgence he offered for her sake alone, for he greatly desired the steady peace of her presence.

What she had not done, he did; he lifted her by her hands and embraced her in front of the whole of his gathered forces. "Na'donna," he whispered.

Her smile was slender, and it was informed by some anxiety; he withdrew, allowing her the distance that was appropriate for their stations. But he withdrew with some regret, and knew she was aware of it.

"The Northerners?"

"You will see them for yourself. The Commanders," he added, "will leave on the morrow with their men."

"They will not stay to see the kai Leone crowned?"

"They are concerned," he replied carefully.

"The battle was not decisive, then." The shadows crossed her features; he could hear it in her tone.

"It was decisive enough," he told her, smiling cautiously. "But, yes, they fear that it is not yet over. They have spoken much, and openly; they feel that the servants of the Lord of Night desired war with the North for a reason, and they are anxious to return to the Empire with their armies. They have spent much blood defending our homeland," he added softly.

"Let us hope it is not at the cost of their own."

He nodded, aware that this hope, this wish, would never have been his before this battle had come to pass. "Come, Na'donna. We have received an invitation. We are to dine in the halls of the Tyr'agnate of Callesta, at the grace of his wife."

She was like a child, he thought, like the child he had married. He had been young himself, then, and as the young are wont to be, ignorant of his own foibles.

But it was Na'donna's captive youth, her unchanging ability to show true delight, that he had best loved, then and now. He surrendered himself to her keeping.

The Serra Amara en'Callesta was waiting for them when they arrived. They passed, Tyr, Serra, and kai, through the ranks of brightly burnished armor worn in pride by the diminished ranks of Callestan Tyran, and Ser Mareo stopped before each man to offer a genuine nod of respect.

They did not deny him his weapons; they offered him no questions, even those that were a matter of course between the Tyran of a man and a visitor of significance and power.

By this lack, they honored him. If he was pleased, he did not show it. His Serra, however, did. Had they been one iota less formal, she might have paused to ask them their names, the names of their wives, the names of their children, if they had any.

And he would have let her, but he knew by the position of the dwindling sun that they were already tardy. He took her arm in his, an open gesture of trust in return for the trust the Tyran offered him, and he led her through their ranks, his son following in their wake.

When they reached the first of the interior halls, he stopped. The screens—and they were screens, their opaque cells painted in delicate swirls of navy and white, and adorned by golden writing— were closed.

Serafs came out of the small rooms to either side of the doors as his footsteps stilled, and he allowed them to kneel before the screens. Their hands were certain and silent; they slid the screens apart to grant him entry.

But he did not enter immediately, for framed by the now open doors sat the Serra Amara en'Callesta, and her wives. In the laps of the youngest were children, their hair oiled and pulled back, bound by gold and jade. Their eyes were wide, but they were silent, as well-behaved as harem children could be.

Ramiro's sons and daughters.

What the Serra Donna en'Lamberto could not do, he now did; he bent on one knee, not in obeisance, but rather to bring his gaze to a level with these children.

"You will be Tyran, one day," he said to a young boy.

The boy's eyes glinted with sudden pleasure, and he pushed himself up from his mother's lap. She almost brought her arms up to contain him, but let them fall away as she met the Tyr's brief gaze.

"I will!" he said, his excited Torra accented by youth. He was younger than he seemed, and the solemnity of the occasion was shattered by his cheerful burble. "I want to be Captain of the oath-guards!"

He almost spoke, then, to correct the child. In Callesta, the pars served as Captains.

But in Callesta, as in Lamberto, there *were* no pars.

"It is a worthy goal," he said. "For I have seen your kai fight."

"Really?"

"Have you not heard?"

"They won't talk of war in the harem," he said, his full lips turning down at the corners.

"Then I will tell you only this, lest I risk the wrath of your mothers."

Serra Donna drew closer; it was her only way of giving warning.

"He fought well. He fought the servants of the Lord of Night, and he emerged victorious. He wields a sword that killed demons," he added, "and he stood by the side of the Tyr'agar, in the light of the Sun Sword. He will be a fine Tyr, in his time, and you will be a fine oathguard." He rose, then. "But I will be a poor guest indeed if I tarry here any longer."

"You could never be a poor guest, Ser Mareo kai di'Lamberto," the Serra Amara said, speaking for the first time. She seemed well pleased by his chosen words, and she met his gaze through the gauze of veil. "Is that the Serra Donna?"

"It is indeed." He gathered his wife's hand in his, and drew her gently forward. "Although she has not spoken of it openly, she has greatly desired to see Callesta again, in time of peace."

"And I have greatly desired to have her as guest," the Serra Amara replied.

"Rise," he told them all.

They did as he bid.

"Accept my apologies for the quality of my gardens," the Serra Amara said, speaking to them both, although her gaze fell upon the Serra Donna en'Lamberto. "We have been much prepared for war, and I fear that the tread of cerdan feet have been unkind."

"The same is true of Amar," the Serra Donna replied quickly. "But both gardens will grow again, and more quickly. There is no war between us." She reached out with both of her hands, and the Serra Amara caught them; they stood a moment, as if they were cousins in a familiar harem.

"If that is true," the Serra Amara said gracefully, "it is due in part to the intervention of your husband, and to the choice he made upon the field."

"No," Ser Mareo replied. "It is due almost in full to the harmless letters that pass with such speed between any two Serras."

The Serra Amara was surprised by the generosity of his words; she offered him a deep bow. Would have offered more, but his Donna tightened her grip on the Serra Amara's hands, obliquely denying her the ability to fold to ground once more.

"We have been long from your fair city," the Serra Donna said, "and we have forgotten how gracious your hospitality is. I feel as if we are at home," she added.

"I hope that you will be, Serra Donna, Ser Mareo. Come; the guests are waiting in the long hall, and I was given permission to lead you there myself."

Ramiro kai di'Callesta waited upon the last of the Tyrs in a rare good humor. Ser Eduardo kai di'Garrardi had already offered reparations for damage done to the villages nearest Raverra; he had accepted the offer with more grace than it had been given. He could.

His Tyr had won.

Ser Jarrani kai di'Lorenza had taken the time to engage the Northern Commanders in a discourse about the theories of war and its strategies, and if the Northerners were stiff and clumsy, they were educated enough to join that conversation with some heat. Even The Kalakar. Perhaps especially that woman. She had been silent for most of the evening, and fell silent frequently during the debate.

She was, he thought, a woman. Hard to know it for certain except in rare moments like these; the dead haunted her features. The scars she had taken upon the field were new; they were livid and ugly, crossing the bridge of her broad nose. But beneath them, white and faded, were older scars. All of them had been taken in the Averdan valleys. But he treasured the new ones.

Valedan kai di'Leonne was diffident; he greeted the Tyrs who had served the dead General with perfect formality and grace. By his side, the Serra Diora en'Leonne stood, lilies in her hair. Gone was the bright blue of her sari; she had been given other colors: midnight blue and white, with chains of gold to bind them.

But seeing her thus, in mourning, Ramiro thought of life, not death, of gain, not loss. She was very, very beautiful.

Ser Mareo kai di'Lamberto came into the hall and everyone paused to watch him. But he came at the side of the Serra Amara en'Callesta, and they walked slowly, absorbed in conversation.

Although she wore a veil, it was not a wall; Ramiro could almost see her expression, although her words were properly soft, and did not carry the distance.

She was happy to have the kai Lamberto here. Happy to have the company of his Serra. Proud, he thought, of her role in a war that was never meant for Serras. He denied her nothing.

When she at last led the kai Lamberto and his son to their seats, she reserved a place by her side for his wife.

Peace, Ramiro thought, and he allowed himself a genuine smile. It did not falter when his son rose and joined the kai Leonne; his son, bright-eyed and eager, youthful, honest—was too much like the kai Leonne in temperament, this eve.

But it would be good for Callesta, to have such ties in the Tor Leonne. More than that he did not acknowledge.

Valedan bid the Commanders farewell in the morning, before night had fully left the skies.

Commander Berriliya was polite; Commander Allen was friendly. Commander Kalakar was angry, but that was her way.

"You will not stay?" he asked again.

"No," Commander Allen answered. "What we came to achieve, we achieved. If I am not mistaken, we achieved more than that— but none of us are comfortable with the armies so far from Averalaan." His gaze grazed the face of the Berriliya, who did not appear to notice. "You will be crowned," he added, "but that, too, is formality; the Tyr'agnati have pledged their allegiance to you. Lesser men will follow, unless they wish to invoke the wrath of their lords."

"I could not have come this far without you."

"No," Ellora said. "You couldn't."

Commander Allen cleared his throat.

She glowered at him, remarkable woman. "It appears that Primus Duarte has tendered his resignation. Were you aware of this?"

"Have you accepted it?"

Her eyes narrowed. "You knew."

"No, Kalakar, I did not. But I had hopes. You created the Ospreys," he added softly, "for a different war. They are not what they were."

"They are half what they were," she answered.

"In numbers, yes."

"Take care of them," she snapped, as her horse was brought to her.

Valedan nodded.

Kiriel di'Ashaf stood alone among the towering pillars that punctuated the new geography of Russo. Before her feet were old graves, old markers, and beyond them, a small hut. A home, she thought. Ashaf's home.

But it was Ashaf's no longer, and Ashaf would have been happy to know that Valla and Arrego now dwelled within it, offering it both purpose and the bustle of life. She did not need the Heart of Havalla to tell her that.

But she missed the certainty of its contained memories; she had surrendered them all, as promised, to the Havallan Matriarch, a woman she would *never* like. A woman, she knew, that Ashaf had feared.

Although she had been seen upon the back of the great, wild Beast, none of the Tyran and none of the cerdan who served the kai Callesta sought to deny Kiriel her freedom.

It was not what she would have done had their positions been reversed.

She lifted her head to the North, and the breeze stirred her hair; it was a natural breeze; there was no power in it.

But the shadows of power remained, troubling her features. The

names of the kin were scattered now. She had told Lord Anduvin
that she could not hold them.

She had lied.

She wondered if he knew it.

He did not come to the village, perhaps because he knew that she
did not want him there. She wanted no demons there; none save she
herself. He had vanished, as was his way, and he would come to her
side if she called. Or if war did. This was the South, after all, and
peace was rare.

But not less prized for its rarity.

She would never bring Ashaf home. Ashaf's body lay in the cold
of the Northern Wastes, if it had not been destroyed by the lesser
kin.

But if she had not brought Ashaf home, she had done what she
had in Ashaf's name; it was enough. Would have to be enough.

"Kiriel," a voice said, and she stiffened.

But she rose, leaving graves behind, and leaving, for the moment, the memories that had driven her.

In the sun's light, Lord Isladar stood, his arms by his sides, his
head bowed slightly—a gesture that accentuated the differences in
their height, no more. He was pale, she thought, but otherwise unchanged.

No matter how much she changed, he would remain as he had
always been: an enigma.

Her hand fell to her sword, her unnamed blade. Her fingers
tightened around its hilt, for she had chosen to wear it openly, as if
it were just another sword, another Northern sword.

But its voice was loud, in the presence of Lord Isladar, and it
spoke of many desires. All hers.

She looked away, to Ashaf's home.

"You came here," she said softly.

"With you," he replied, just as softly, the cold of *Kialli* voice diminished in the warmth of Southern light.

"And you took Ashaf from the village."

He said nothing.

"You killed her."

She thought he might smile, and she knew, if he did, she would
kill him. But when she dared glance at his face, it was impassive, as
untouched as the white of the Northern Wastes that had been their
home.

"Yes," he said, when he had her attention, and was certain of it.
"I killed her."

The sword left its sheath in that moment. Left it, keening, as she swung it round, her knees bending a moment to absorb the force of the blow.

He stood a hair's breadth from its outer reach; she had but to move, and she would have him.

But she found that she could not. "I have your name," she said. It was meant as an insult.

But it came out, instead, as something far more revealing.

His frown was the beginning of his answer; it was a frown that she knew perhaps better than she knew any other of his expressions. *Show no weakness.*

He did not speak the words aloud. "No," he said. "The time for lessons has passed; we are no longer master and student, and the world, this world, is a different one."

"Is this what you wanted?" she whispered.

He spread his hands wide. It was the whole of his answer.

It was not good *enough.* She could force him to answer. She knew it. Alone of all the names that had fled her grasp when she had made her decision, his and Anduvin's remained.

But she did not offer Isladar the freedom of the Hells. Or the freedom of death.

"I am already dead," he said quietly, divining—as he had often done—her thoughts.

She turned away, sheathing her blade with difficulty. "Why are you here?" she asked him, weary now. Wary.

"You called me," he told her. His voice was almost gentle.

"I did *not* call you," she replied. The words were a whisper shorn of force, of strength.

"You did, Kiriel," he replied, "else I would be away from this place. It is . . . not to my liking."

"Falloran is here," she said.

He raised a brow, and then nodded. "I saw him. He has forgotten everything that he ever knew."

"He liked me," she told him.

"Are you so certain, Kiriel? He is *mine,* and I release nothing that is mine. Even if you hold my name, you do not alter that truth. Perhaps, in the end, I did not desire your death, and he knew it. I set him one task, and one only: to be your guardian."

"Release him, then," she said, almost reckless.

His smile was cold. "To what end?"

"I want to know," she whispered.

"Kiriel," he told her quietly, "Falloran is not mortal. He is not living. What does not know life, knows little change."

"You changed," she whispered, for she felt it as truth. "When you made your choice. When you followed your Lord to the Hells."

"I died," he shrugged. "In any fashion that matters. And change such as death, even we know." His voice grew colder. "You are not a child," he told her, as if he were once again her master, in a distant, cold place. "You know better than to look for affection among the kin. You have found your people; be content with that."

She was not content.

"You can end it," he told her, almost genial. "With a word. With the sword that you would not truly claim. Lift it; if you desire it, I will not move."

Desire was such a terrible thing. It betrayed everything. She remembered Anduvin's words.

"And if you will not destroy me, let me leave; I will never be far from you, now."

"You killed Ashaf," she whispered. "*Why?*" It was not the question she wanted to ask, but it was close enough.

"To hurt you," he replied. "And to free you."

"This *isn't* freedom!" And she swept a hand across the graves, the small house.

"But it is, Kiriel. You have made your choice, and it is not a choice given to one such as I. Not even one such as I."

"You made yours."

"Yes," he said softly. "When we returned to the Wastes, with your Ashaf, mine had already been made." He paused, and then added, "It was made long before your birth. And it is made, again and again, while I still exist."

"You wanted me to take your name," she said suddenly.

He was silent.

"You wanted *me* to hold it, because if I didn't, The Lord would."

His smile was slight, and it held approval. "You begin to see," he told her.

It was more than she would bear. "What do you want from me?" she asked him, shorn now of anger, although anger remained.

"No more than you have already done. You have made a choice. I was not certain which choice it would be, and either would have suited me."

She hated him, then. And knew that the hate came from a place that was so twined with the need to be loved it burned. "Go," she told him, turning again.

"I will go," he replied. "But I will return. Because, Kiriel, you will call me back, again and again, until we are once more upon the field of battle."

"The battle is over."

"Ah, yes. But war is made of many, and this is but the first. Go where you will go; in the end, you will return to the Shining Palace, the Shining City; the Northern Wastes birthed you, and they are within you."

She wanted to ask him then. *Did you ever love me?*

Wanted to, but didn't. Because she knew what his answer would be, and she was not yet ready to hear it.

But when he had gone, she made her way to Valla's home, and she knocked upon the door so softly she might have been a penitent.

The door opened quickly, and Valla kep'Valente offered her a weary smile. "Na'kiri," she said, pushing the solid screens wide. "Enter. We have water, for the while, and some food."

And Kiriel, thinking of Ashaf and Isladar, thinking of the dead woman whose gift she bore in some fashion, bowed her head to hide the golden tint of her eyes. She let Valla kep'Valente touch her in a way that she would never have let Isladar touch her.

No, she thought, as she took a step across the threshold; that wasn't true. She let Valla touch her because she wanted to be held. Even by Isladar. Perhaps, in the end, only by Isladar.

But she had not come to the village for Isladar, and, ultimately, she had not come for the comfort that Valla could offer, although she had both.

It was upon Ser Danello kai di'Valente that she waited, and he did not disappoint her; in the aftermath of battle and much loss, he came.

He had made no formal appointment with her; indeed, that was all but impossible in the lee of battle's loss. But he knew—how could he not—where she must be, and so he came, with two Toran and his destrier.

She understood that he honored her, for he left the Tyran by the graves that Ashaf had labored over for much of her life, and he came to the home of Valla kep'Valente, where he knocked upon the sliding door and waited, as if he were just another weary traveller.

Kiriel knew it was the Tor'agar by the sudden stillness in Valla. Before Valla had fallen fully to ground, Kiriel had risen from her place by low table. She reached into a pocket, and from it, pulled the flat circle of a half-marked oath medallion. This she carried to him in open palm.

He saw what she held, and he nodded, pulling away from the door, and from the easy hearing of his serafs.

"I am in your debt," he said, when no one could hear it but Kiriel di'Ashaf. "What would you have of me, Kiriel di'Ashaf?"

She shook her head. "For myself?"

"At all."

And she stared at the surface of the medallion. After a moment, she set it almost hesitantly against the ground and drew her blade.

He lifted his hand; gauntlets flashed in the light, a warning and a command to the Toran who had accompanied him.

She made the second cut, accompanying the first. And then she lifted the medallion with care.

"I cannot bring her home," she said softly, staring not at the man, but at the oath that he could not, legally, offer her. "But I want to make sure that she is *never* forgotten."

He waited in silence.

"Name this village," she said quietly. "Let it bear her name, while Valente rules."

And he smiled, although she caught it only when she looked up. "Done," he said softly.

She bowed her head. "She saved this village," she told him quietly.

"In you," he replied.

And in the growing light of day, Lord Isladar was content to watch. He had lied, of course. She had not even tried to detect it.

But he expected no more from Kiriel, Kiriel di'Ashaf.

She had been raised to desire power. This, her blood ensured. But she had been raised, as well, to desire other things.

Things beyond Lord Isladar of the *Kialli*.

He whispered her name, and held his hands up, palm out, as if in surrender.

And when she did not reply, he smiled.

He was beautiful, then.

Tor Leonne, Terrean of Raverra

Auralis swore in two different languages; his Torra had improved greatly over the passage of weeks. At least, sometimes it had.

Today, he understood about as much as he ever had, and he was grateful for it. The ring that adorned his finger, like a woman's piece of expensive jewellery, was cool and still.

The seraf at whom he had sworn knelt at once to the mats of this uncomfortable, thin-walled room, her hair cascading around bent shoulders like a black sheet. He almost stepped on her.

"I swear," he said through gritted teeth, "I will *never* get used to these damn serafs. They're always underfoot."

Kiriel laughed. It was rare enough that he almost considered cursing the seraf some more; the laughter broke the shadows that haunted her face.

She had fought a battle that was kin to his own, and she had emerged as whole as he had. But she was not the same Kiriel that she had been. He had seen her.

And some part of his mind still whispered the word *goddess* when he glanced at her face, her golden eyes. She hid them as she could, but the battle had taken something out of her; they would change color, as if at a trick of the light, without any predictability.

The seraf, however, seemed immune to the sudden change of hue.

In the corner of the room which they shouldn't, by any known Southern law, share, her huge dog lifted its head, growling. It was the only thing he ever offered Auralis AKalakar. Auralis swore at him in Weston.

He knew damn well that given a choice, the dog would rip out his throat—if he stopped at that. Kiriel kept him on a figurative leash.

"You look like a . . . Southerner," Kiriel told him.

"It's the damn armor," he snapped. "It's like wearing shingles."

She laughed again, making the armor *almost* worthwhile. "It's light," she offered.

"The first two layers are." He cursed again, and loudly. "Armor should be something a man can put on by himself!"

The seraf rose, but she did not seem overly troubled. Auralis wondered if she were deaf. Or stupid. She was certainly gorgeous.

But he felt no desire for her at all. No desire for anyone anymore.

"You're thinking of Anya again."

He nodded. Closed his eyes. "All right," he said, snarling. "You can help."

The seraf bowed her head and began to strap things together behind his back.

"She's still alive," he said.

Kiriel nodded. "She's almost impossible to kill. The demons hate her. And they fear her. It's always been like that."

"Is that why you were friends?"

Kiriel shrugged. "Maybe. They certainly hated me. Didn't fear me as much, though." Her smile was dark. "Not then."

"And now?"

She shrugged, her expression once again taking on the darkness. But her words were safe enough. "Stop talking and hurry up. I still have to get dressed."

"I'm going to have words with Valedan when this is over," he snapped. "We can't defend a thimble dressed like this."

She laughed. At him. It didn't sting him now.

Only Anya did.

And it wasn't Anya's day. Not yet. But it would be. He vowed it, quietly—as quietly as he knew how. When this was over, he would find Anya again, and he would somehow fix things.

"I'll go," she told him, studying the lines of his face. "I'll go with you when you leave."

"You can see me, can't you?"

She nodded quietly. "You look . . . different. Maybe you won't be coming to the Hells as quickly as we thought."

He didn't ask who *we* was. He didn't much care. But he didn't accept her offer either. After all, there might be only one way to fix things, and Kiriel had proved, time and again, that she didn't want his death.

Unless, he grimaced, she caused it.

Serra Diora en'Leonne stood beside Teyla en'Leonne. "Well?" she asked.

Teyla, her skin still far too dark for a proper clansman's harem, smiled. She smiled often, in the harem's heart. Her voice was rough—but it had gentled over the weeks. Had had to. Her son was very sensitive to the rise and fall of her voice, and she had learned to speak softly, no matter what she might say.

"You look perfect, Na'dio!"

The Serra smiled. "Jevri?"

The Radann, however, was frowning, pins ringing the compressed line of his weathered lips. He took one of these and altered the fall of the sari that she wore. White caught the spill of sun's light; the screens were open to a courtyard that only the wives of the Tyr'agar could see.

"Not perfect," he said, speaking around his instruments. "But you will be." He was not a young man; he had never been young. And he was now without the grace that still informed Ramdan's movements. But he was not without skill, and not without passion: the silks that she wore attested to this.

"And the kai Leonne?"

"He is not my responsibility."

She smiled. "He wears your robes." It was true.

"He does," Teyla added, "and his mother is very proud of him."

Diora offered her wife a brief smile; it was one of mutual suffering. The Serra Marlena had both a well-meaning heart and a fragile disposition; she was surrounded at all times by the things she professed to adore, but these changed daily, and she was quick to point out her unhappiness the second it occurred.

"Is it the North?" Teyla asked softly, although with Jevri present, she shouldn't have.

Still, they were in the harem for some moments yet, and Diora could not bring herself to scold. Not today. "No," she said firmly. "It is not the North. The Serra Marlena was beautiful in her youth."

Teyla had the grace—won with difficulty—not to look skeptical.

Serafs came to the screen during the fitting, and Ramdan attended them; he came with their words and left with her instructions. The Tor Leonne was vast, and she had had scant weeks in which to make it as beautiful as she could. She gazed a moment at her scarred hand, her scarred wrist, and she smiled.

"Jevri," she said gently, as she caught the shortening shadows the stones in the garden now cast, "there will be other dresses."

The old man pursed his lips together, changing the shape of a row of pins; it was his version of a practical frown. "But *this* dress is important, Serra Diora."

"They are *all* important," she said.

And he surrendered with as much grace as she could expect. "Then I suppose I will attend the Tyr'agar."

She laughed at the wealth of regret in those words. He did not attempt to disguise it. She wondered idly if he knew of her gift, but she would never ask; he was Radann, yes, but he had been trained and raised as seraf in the Halls of Lamberto. What he knew, he would never use to betray her.

He was the final gift of Ser Fredero kai el'Sol, although she had not realized it at the time. Of all the gifts he had given her, she would keep him longest, and treasure him the most.

She summoned Ramdan, and he came, exquisite and unbent. "Have the Northerners arrived?"

"They arrived three days ago," he replied, pulling at long strands of her hair. It was as close as he had ever come to teasing her, and she glanced up quickly as if to catch the lingering hint of smile on his lips. It was, of course, absent. But the weeks had changed Ramdan. The babe had changed him. Teyla had, because she was still not used to the delicate behavior demanded of her by the High Courts. Had he been a different seraf, he would have held Teyla in contempt for her lack of refinement. But had he been that man, he would never have been the Serra Teresa's. Never, Diora thought, have been hers. It was a weakness, but she had begun to understand that some weaknesses could also be strengths. Northern blade; two edges.

Instead, he had taken Teyla under his wing—it was a Northern phrase, and one she often found amusing, given that the most familiar Northern bird, to the Southerners, was the Osprey—and he had bidden her ask them any question that came to mind.

He answered them all with perfect patience; this Diora expected. But he answered them, as well, with indulgent affection, and this, she had not.

"Teyla," Diora called softly. "Na'diro is awake."

Teyla turned instantly, and made her way from the dressing room.

When she had gone, Diora turned to Ramdan. "Well?" she asked him.

He smiled. "She is younger than she first appeared," he said. "And she is not the wife that the Serra Teresa would have chosen for you. But she has come far from the fields of Essla."

More words than he often spoke in a day. She allowed him to pin her hair in place, to add gold and jade to its height.

"Will he ever take her as wife?"

Ramdan's smile deepened. "I do not know, Serra. He is not of the South." Only in the harem could such words be uttered. "And he is still uncomfortable with her station."

She nodded. "He has grown to accept yours."

"He does that, not for my sake, but for yours."

She lifted a brow.

"He understands continuity. He does not," he added, "understand me. He does not understand service, although he serves in a fashion. Do not expect too much of him."

"Do not," she replied, "expect too little." More words, she thought. "Ramdan?"

"Serra?"

"Do you miss her?"

He hesitated. The perfect seraf existed as an extension of his master. The perfect seraf was above desire, regret, even opinion.

But so, too, the perfect Serra.

"Yes," he said at last.

"I miss her," Diora told him. "I would have offered her a home in the Tor Leonne."

"She would not take it," he replied.

"No. Would you go with her, if you could?"

His hands froze. She was offering him a measure of freedom, and it was easily within her power to do so.

"I would," he said at last, "if it would ease her. But she leaves you here, and in the end, it is to a life I know." His gaze traveled slowly to the hanging that separated this room from the baby's room. "Perhaps we are all weak in a fashion," he said at last, and heavily. "We seek to stay where we have the power to do what must be done."

She smiled, then. "If you wanted to travel with her, she would take you."

"I am the Lady's man," he said softly. Almost too softly. "And where she goes, I would have no place. I might remind her of the past—and perhaps that would be unkind. She, too, has changed."

"Too much to remain here."

He did not answer.

But it was answer enough. "Will she come?"

"I do not know, Serra. But I think that she will."

Only one of the Matriarchs had made her way to the Tor Leonne: Yollana of Havalla. And Yollana was the *only* Matriarch who would. The others?

Elena bowed her head. She had seen the Tor Arkosa rise, and she knew where the others must be. Let them survive, she thought—and it was a rare thought; there was often enmity between the Voyani families. But there had been enmity between the Callestans and the Lambertans as well, and it was—now—a simple part of a complex history.

Elena wondered if she should be glad. She was numb, instead, and a little relieved. Treacherous, that.

Lord Telakar stood by her side, casting a shorter shadow as the sun crept toward its height. "Telakar?"

"Elena."

"What will you do now?"

"While you live?"

"While I live."

He shrugged. It was economical and cool; there was little about the demon lord that would ever speak of warmth. "You have my name," he said at last. "And while you live, I am bound by it."

She laughed. It was an unfettered sound, but it bounced in the empty space that surrounded the Western Fount of Contemplation. Here, so close to the moment of Valedan's crowning, the fount was empty. Brass gleamed in the clear light of day; clouds were swept across the sky as if they were dust. They did not cling or linger.

"That perhaps is not the question you meant to ask," he said at last.

"No?"

His smile was sliver thin. "You meant, of course, to ask what *you* will do."

She nodded. He knew her well enough. But she flinched when his hand touched her face, and sensing this, he withdrew it.

"I have left the *Voyanne*," she told him, reaching down to touch the surface of the fountain's still water. "And I am not certain, now, where it leads. I—"

"Yes. You kept me from the battle."

"But I didn't join it either."

"Did you not?" His smile. She looked away.

"I think I will go to Arkosa."

"I would accompany you there, if you would have me."

"Why?"

"Because it houses much that I remember," he said softly. "And I have always been known for that weakness."

"But if I die—"

"Yes." His voice cooled. "If you die, anything I learn of that city will be used against those who survive. It is a risk, Elena."

"I'm not sure it's my risk to take."

"Perhaps. Perhaps not. But I will say this: the Lord of Night has not yet finished."

"He doesn't have to worry about time. He's like you. He lives forever."

"He is not like me," Telakar replied, and water should have frozen at the shift in his tone. "He lives." He hesitated, and then added, "But much of his plans depended upon Kiriel di'Ashaf, and I do not know if he has abandoned them. If he has not, then you will be safe enough; she is mortal, and she will age and die. He has the span of her years, and no more; I do not think that the opportunity to create another like her will exist again.

"Isladar has left the Shining City, and she was Isladar's creation."

Elena's shoulders slumped. After a moment, she cupped the water in her shaking hands, and drew it to her face. "I would like to go home," she whispered. "I want to see Margret."

"You are afraid of that meeting."

"Yes. But—there's no other way to get past the fear than to have it."

He smiled. "You are strange, Elena. You are guided, as mortals are, by fear—but you are guided in a different direction." He lifted his head. "They are gathering in the Tor Leonne," he told her.

"How do you know that?"

"Meralonne APhaniel is there."

She did not ask again; instead she rose. "Then let's watch," she told him. "We can leave after."

Kallandras of Senniel College was present, and as a representative of the justly famous Senniel College. He wore Court clothing, and if the Court was Northern, he was still not out of place; his silks were pale blues and cream, edged in gold. His hair was also gold, and it fell to his shoulders; dark edges had been surrendered to a barber's whim.

He carried *Salla* in his arms, as he had the first time he had ventured, as bard, to the Tor Leonne. She was silent.

"APhaniel," he said, bowing.

Meralonne APhaniel, adorned by pipe and the formal robes of the Order of Knowledge, inclined his head. "It will be a fine day," he said, gazing sunward. "You will sing?"

Kallandras nodded. "I have been given that honor."

"Good."

"And you?"

"I, of course, will watch." Meralonne lit his pipe. "It is over, for the moment," he added, "and I am old enough to take refuge in peace for as long as it lasts."

"And when the ceremony is over?"

"I will return to Averalaan. You?"

Kallandras nodded. "But it will be strange, I think."

"You miss Celleriant."

The bard offered nothing in reply, and the magi smiled. "Be wary, Kallandras."

"I? I have very little left to lose."

"Do not seek to find more. He serves the White Lady," he added softly. "And it is his death to do otherwise."

But Kallandras offered the magi an intent smile, and then his fingers returned to *Salla,* and he coaxed from her a wordless tune. It was not simple, and Kallandras found some difficulty in its playing; enough so that he lost, for a moment, the perfect placidity of Court expression, the neutrality of benevolent smile. His brows folded in concentration, his eyes closed.

The lute's notes could not carry as far as his voice, but they carried far enough, and when he had finished, he opened his eyes to bright sunlight, bright shadow, and he bent to the ground to retrieve the pipe that Meralonne APhaniel had let drop from open palms.

"He will not thank you," the magi whispered, as he took the pipe from Kallandras. But the words held no hint of warning, no hint of knowledge; they were shorn of almost everything that defined him in *Averalaan Aramarelas.*

Nor did he ask where Kallandras had learned the wordless song; it was a Summer song, and he did not give voice to the lyrics.

The Southerners gathered by the waters of the Tor Leonne; the breeze was calm, and the Lake seemed a vast mirror behind which clear water lay. Across its surface, lilies had been laid, although they were not yet in bloom; they were a green promise of the unknown future.

Banners lined the pathways, hidden and open, and the trees were adorned by paper lanterns, things of bright color that echoed the flower beds. Gold glinted along the path that led to the Lake from the gates; silver glinted along the paths that led there from the plateau. The Tor Leonne rose above the waters, viewing platforms open for the use of Valedan's concubines. He had only one, and she had chosen to remain ensconced by the most public reaches of the private harem, although Diora had offered her a place of honor beside the Lake itself.

"You won't be there."

"I will."

Teyla shook her head. "You'll be with him. And he needs you. Diro needs me," she added shyly, and with some pain. "And if our husband is never to be a perfect Tyr, he must be seen to be perfect today."

Diora felt proud of her sole wife. She had learned so much in so short a time. "Shall I leave Ramdan with you?"

Teyla shook her head again. "Take him; he will be hurt if another seraf attends you there."

Or perhaps she was simply perceptive. The Serra Diora bowed, and then impulsively kissed her wife's forehead and cheeks. She bent over Na'diro, and kissed his cheeks as well; he grabbed at the strands of gold that adorned her pale throat, and they had to work to extract them.

But it was pleasant work.

Ser Andaro di'Corsarro came for her, and she almost failed to recognize him; the transition to the Tor Leonne had changed him. His armor was ceremonial and perfect; his hair was dark and perfect, his face still and almost peaceful. He was watchful, yes, but his hand did not cling to the hilt of his sword.

"Serra Diora," he said, "the Tyrs are waiting."

"Will you not attend the kai Leonne?"

"I would," Ser Andaro replied, but without heat, "if he had given me leave to do so. But Ser Anton di'Guivera is by his side."

She heard the pain that the name always caused him, but it was lessened. Both Ser Andaro and Ser Anton di'Guivera had emerged whole from the battle that had shaped the Dominion, and if they were not friends, Ser Andaro no longer labored under his bitter enmity.

As if he could hear her thoughts, he shook his head. "We have all lost much to be here."

"I asked my husband about your history," she told him, as she accepted his offered hand and rose, leaving her wife behind. "And he would not answer."

"Ah."

"Do not misjudge him," she added softly, musically, her voice the perfect voice, her smile the perfect smile. "He does not seek to protect you; he seeks to give you the opportunity to decide for yourself what others know of you."

"Even you."

"Perhaps especially me."

He shook his head. "I have heard of you," he told her, as he had once before. "And I know what you lost here. We have all suffered, and we have all triumphed."

"And our dead?"

His smile was not hers; it was stiff and formal. "It is the Lord's time," he said.

She nodded. But she continued to speak as they walked along

paths shadowed by the tallest trees in the city. "My dead are buried here."

"Are our dead ever truly buried?" He shook his head. "My dead are buried in the North." And he whispered a name. She heard it, but she did not ask. Instead, she said, "Can you accept the Ospreys as Tyran?"

"I am not certain that the Ospreys can accept themselves as Tyran," he replied, and this time his smile was genuine. "They take much comfort in fighting, and little in anything else. But they, too, have buried their dead. Perhaps it is time to let the dead rest," he added.

She nodded, and her hand tightened; it surprised him.

"I don't know where, on the plateau, my wives are buried."

His brows rose.

"But perhaps it is better that way; they are part of this place now. They might be anywhere I walk, anywhere I choose to rest, any place in which I choose to labor."

He nodded as they reached the open path on the Western side of the Lake. They ceased their conversation and their musing, and she looked to where the Tyrs gathered.

Lamberto, she saw first, and she thought she would always see that clan this way. Ser Mareo kai di'Lamberto and his kai, Ser Galen, were dressed in ceremonial armor; it was armor that they had not worn in all her years in the Tor Leonne, and she knew that they honored Valedan kai di'Leonne. The Serra Donna wore gold and white, and her wives were similarly garbed.

But they were not alone; intermingled with the Lambertan harem were the wives of Ser Ramiro kai di'Callesta. He, too, wore full ceremonial dress, although Ser Alfredo had chosen to wear the armor in which he had first proved himself worthy of his title: it was dented, but it had been cleaned and polished.

Ser Jarrani kai di'Lorenza was with his two sons, the only Tyr to be so blessed. Neither had fallen in battle. They were carefully attired in the colors of their clan, and they were surrounded by their Tyran.

And Ser Eduardo kai di'Garrardi stood alone. His Tyran were present, but he kept them at a distance, and when his gaze fell upon her, it lingered. She did not meet it; not yet. Perhaps one day.

Her gaze swept the length of the Lake; it was crowded with Tors and their banners. Silent, she named them all, taking careful note of the men she did not see. She would need that information, for later; Valedan would require it.

Ser Andaro paused a moment, and the Serra Diora looked away from the Tyr'agnati. She saw who had drawn his attention, and she offered a simple nod to the Matriarch of Havalla. She was accompanied by men dressed in the rough clothing of the Voyani; it brought a bitter longing to the Serra, one that she could ill afford. She looked away.

Ser Andaro led her to the platform that rode above the water; it had been erected for this day, and it would be dismantled at its end. It was adorned with flowers, and with the colors of the sun ascendant, but it was otherwise simple.

Ramdan was waiting for her. He bowed as her feet touched the wooden slats, and he laid out a mat upon which she might kneel.

She had knelt for the Leonnes before, even when she had been one of them. Memory intruded, strengthened by the familiar feel of wooden slats beneath her legs, the scent of new lilies, the presence of so many men beneath the banners of the sun ascendant. She remembered that she had been made to kneel, obeisant, for hours, unspoken punishment for her father's refusal to immediately accept the generous offer of the clan Leonne for her hand.

Oh, it stung. Not the patience. Not the waiting. But the reasons for it. Her head was bowed, protected; her eyes, she closed against the sudden sting of sunlight. But no, not today. This was not a day for lies.

Father. She had waited for him so many times, as a child, an indulged harem daughter. She had loved him, then.

Now? Now she felt his loss as keenly as she had feared to for all of those countless hours, those times spent hiding and waiting in his chambers, against the wishes of his wives.

His wives.

The thought twisted the paths of memory, freeing her from the new-turned grave, the newly dead; she glanced up, and saw them, although the waters of the Tor glimmered, separating them. She could make out the bent form of Alana en'Marano. Dressed in shades of midnight and white, she was the only one who dared to openly mourn his passing; not even Diora did so, here.

She felt a moment's anger; Ser Adano would have discarded them. Alana was, indeed, too old to find use; Illana and Illia were younger, and Illia was still graceful, still beautiful.

But they were tainted by their husband's treachery. Thus, she thought with scorn—a private scorn that would never be allowed to surface beyond the reach of the harem's walls—did a man seek to appease the Tyr'agar. The kai Leonne.

No one would speak for the wives. No one, she thought bitterly, would speak for the Serra Fiona en'Marano, the youngest, the legitimate wife; no one would speak for the brother she had—perhaps unfairly—so disliked. Ser Artano di'Marano.

He was *so much* like his uncle. So much like Adano, liege lord of the kai Lamberto. And Artano, bitter and bereaved, would say nothing either. He was a boy, but he was old enough to understand what the loss of the war meant for him. For his mother.

There was no one who would speak for them, now, when Ser Adano kai di'Marano had not.

No one but the Serra Diora.

But Alana did not meet her gaze, across the still waters of the Tor Leonne. Or if she did, her eyes were too distant.

Diora's wrists throbbed in the heat. She bowed her head again, and did not seek to catch the gaze of the women who had been like mothers to her; of the wife who had resented the hold Diora had had over her father's heart. Who had resented, and with cause, the fact that Diora had never valued it as highly as the Serra Fiona herself had done.

But without the Serra Fiona's momentary grace, the Serra Diora might never have understood the whole of the danger the Tor Leonne faced with the coming of the Festival Moon. If the Serra Diora had betrayed her father, the Serra Fiona's crime was worse.

But necessary, so bitterly necessary.

She curled fingers in her lap, waiting.

She knew when Valedan approached the plateau; the silence changed in timbre. She did not lift her head; did not turn to watch him; she listened instead.

And in another life, she would have been mortified; the Ospreys were *talking*. Even here, they could not be the dress guards that the kai Leonne required; they bickered among themselves like harem children.

But that life was gone; in this one, she almost smiled. Valedan had taken his first risk in appointing them, and they had taken theirs in accepting what he offered. They would never rest easy with such a large audience. But they had proved themselves in times of far greater threat than this; no slaughter, no easy death, waited would-be assassins, unless it was their own. She was content.

The Radann came from their temple; they were the last men to place feet upon the shores, and they, unlike the Ospreys, were perfect. They wore armor, not robes, and they carried their swords openly. But they carried another as well: the Sun Sword. The sheath they had retrieved from the Swordhaven was fine indeed; it was meant for display.

So many men had died so that the Sword might at last return to the plateau. And one man had died so that the Sword might be free to leave it. Fredero kai el'Sol. Lambertan.

Her husband joined her. He did not kneel; he was scion of the Lord's chosen. He took the Sun Sword from the hands of the kai el'Sol, bowing before either it or the man who held it; not even Diora was certain which.

And then he rose in silence, and she lifted her face; their eyes met through the gauze of veil.

He drew the sword, and the plateau erupted in the cheers of a thousand men. More, she thought, for women's voices, fluting and delicate, were also raised to gentle the sound.

"The Tyr'agar," Peder kai el'Sol said, in a voice that carried above the loud cries of approval. "Ser Valedan kai di'Leonne."

This was the dawn of a new age; in it, men might find favor who had found none with the father. They came in ones and twos, some hiding that eagerness, and some slave to it. She watched them all as the hours passed, her knees bent, her back straight.

And when they had come, when they had drawn swords and offered them, upon one knee, to the man who now claimed the Dominion, she smiled. Lilies in her hair, upon her breath, water reflecting sunlight; she was the Flower of the Dominion and many were the men who offered her their regard. Many, she knew, were the men who remembered her proud words, her proud plea, made as she stood in the waters of the Lake, the Sun Sword in shaking hands.

If the Lady was kind, she would never bear that burden again. But she would bear others.

The kai Lamberto and the kai Callesta came last to the platform, and they lingered longest; they had earned that right.

"You are welcome in the Tor," Valedan told them both gravely. "And while my bloodline holds it, you will always be welcome." He paused, and then added, "I have taken Ser Baredan's kai into my service. He is not yet the equal of his father. But he survived, when he was hunted; he is resourceful. In time, I will give him all that his father held."

Ser Mareo kai di'Lamberto inclined his head in open approval. Ser Ramiro kai di'Callesta grew silent. "He was your man," he said at last. "In all but title, yours."

"Title, in the South, is important; he served best by retaining the title of General. He will be buried with honor here; the winds will not devour him."

They bowed formally before him.

"You will join me after the ceremony," Valedan told them both.

They nodded again; the invitations had been accepted before they had set out from their respective cities. But this was the first of his orders as the anointed Tyr'agar, and it was a pleasant order indeed.

Valedan turned, then, to the Serra Diora, and he offered her his hand. She rose slowly and gracefully, unfolding to gain her full height.

"You are troubled, Serra Diora," Mareo kai di'Lamberto said.

The boldness of the words surprised her. But she did not deny them. Could not. She could see the dead kai el'Sol as a ghost in this man's face.

Valedan turned far too quickly to look at her, his face showing open concern. "Diora?" He spoke too quickly as well. She would have to do something about that—but it could wait. Upon the platform, for perhaps the first time, the Tyr'agar was surrounded not just by his allies, but by his friends. Time and generations would change that, if the South bred true.

She turned to Valedan and said, "My father's wives."

The men were silent then.

"Your father's wives? What of them?"

"They are here," she told him quietly. "They lived upon the plateau for a short time."

"What of them?"

"They have no home," she told him, "but the home you choose to give them." Measuring him now.

He caught her hand in his; the pommel of the Sun Sword grazed her skin. "Give them any home you desire," he told her quietly.

She said, "It will weaken you." Just that.

"You are the Southern steel here," he replied.

"You have proved yourself—"

"I have been tempered in the North. And in the North, strength is not measured by the disposition of widows." He said this in a louder tone; it carried beyond the platform.

"Ser Andaro?" she said quietly.

The Tyran bowed to his lord, but when he rose, he faced her. "Serra."

"If it pleases my husband, summon my father's wives. Bring

them here. I would speak with them again." She hesitated, and then said to Valedan, "It will weaken you because they were the wives of one of your enemies. Those who might be your enemies in the future—Tyrs and Tors all—will see what you do here, and they will know that their actions will have no cost."

"The women did not raise swords against me," he replied, cool now.

"I have a brother," she told him firmly. "And he at least—"

"Was he upon the field?"

"No."

"The men of the Tyr'agnati of both Oerta and Sorgassa were. They fought against me. They harbored the kin. By their actions, serafs and the men who served the kai Callesta, and through him, me, were killed in the Southern villages of Averda. But they are free men; they are not now corpses or carrion fodder."

"They have no names," she whispered. She was afraid.

"They have names," he answered. "And if I do not know them, their wives do. Their sons and daughters. Diora, don't—"

She lifted her hand, delicately, gracefully, seeking an end to his words

He offered it.

"She is correct," Ramiro kai di'Callesta said.

"As is he," Mareo kai di'Lamberto added.

But she did not look at him again; instead she followed Ser Andaro di'Corsarro with her gaze, and only her gaze. She saw Alana rise; saw Illana and Illia join her immediately. Saw, too, that the Serra Fiona hesitated openly, her arms around her son.

Artano di'Marano. *I hated you,* she thought, feeling nothing at all. *You hated me.*

She could not see him well enough to know what he felt now. But she saw that he pulled himself slowly from his mother's arms, and straightened his shoulders. He wore a sword. She held her breath a moment, terrified that he would draw it.

But he bowed instead, and he led them—he led them—to Ser Andaro di'Corsarro. They did not speak long, although she thought words were exchanged.

They came, in a single line, toward the platform upon which she stood. Between them, Valedan, the kai Callesta, the kai Lamberto, their sons. Ringing these men, the Ospreys, curiosity openly displayed across their proud Northern features.

And when they stood before the Ospreys, the Serra Diora could no longer remain still. She walked past her husband, deftly turning

to the side to avoid colliding with the Tyrs, and made her way past
the Ospreys. Past Auralis AKalakar, past Kiriel, past the one-eyed
Cook and their leader, Primus Duarte.

She bowed formally to Ser Andaro di'Corsarro, but he had already stepped aside, his mission complete.

And then she walked to Alana en'Marano, and lifting her arms,
she stood a moment.

Alana's face was wreathed in lines, and her hair was almost
white. She had aged greatly in the last few months.

"Na'dio," she said, her voice breaking. She opened arms that
were far more substantial, and she enfolded Diora in them, whispering the harem name, over and over, into her daughter's ear.

Diora disentangled herself, and moved then to Illana and Illia.
Each of Sendari's wives, each of them her mothers, offered her the
warmth of embrace and harem name, and if they shook at all, she
did not acknowledge it.

But they did not beg; they did not plead.

Last, she came to the Serra Fiona en'Marano. She could not
openly thank Fiona for anything she had done; to do so would be to
dishonor her. What wife, after all, worked against her husband's
will? What wife would bring word of his plans to the daughter who
had openly defied him?

But the Serra Fiona was not so careful, not so stoic, as the older
wives. Diora had often thought her vain and foolish, and perhaps it
was once true. She was shorn of vanity now. Shorn of power.

She was shorn, as well, of son; she could not cling to him here.
Not with hands. But she said, as she briefly embraced Diora, "He is
your brother." It was as much a plea as she dared to make—indeed,
it was more than she should have dared, had she any sense of caution.

And the Serra Diora turned, at last, to Artano. He was twelve, almost a man. But he was a boy, and he was Fiona's son; his looks had
never favored his father.

"Our father died upon the field," she said quietly.

"Alone?"

She nodded. Even when he flinched, she was still. "I found him.
He spared us all the public humiliation of his execution."

"And his burial?" Alana asked, the words edged with sorrow and
certainty.

But the Serra Diora smiled. "I anointed him with blood of his
enemy," she said, and her smile was laden with pain and guilt. "And

I offered the full ablutions in the Lady's time. We laid him to rest beside the body of the General he served."

Alana closed her eyes.

So many scars, if one knew where to look, or how.

"He died as Sendari di'Sendari," Valedan said.

Diora was surprised, but did not show it. He had come upon them in silence, hiding his height and the weight of the sword he now bore. And he could, she thought, where other men of power could not. He did not fear dignity; he did not fear its loss. He spoke from the heart, always; she heard what his words offered without ever once resorting to the gift that had been her curse.

Serra Fiona looked up at him wildly, and the hands that clasped Diora's tightened visibly. But Diora's tightened as well, in warning, and the Serra Fiona was silent.

"And you, Artano kai di'Sendari," Valedan said, turning to the only man left the newly anointed clan of Sendari, "what will you now do?"

"He fought you," Artano said quietly, granting nothing.

Oh, he was Adano's kin. Marano's son. But he would never again bear the name. The stripping of the name, the creation of a newborn, possibly stillborn clan, was a gift to the honor and history of Marano. And a gift, as well, to the kai Lamberto, who valued Ser Adano kai di'Marano in spite of his brother's choice.

"He chose his death," Valedan replied evenly. Politic now.

Alana turned away, understanding immediately the words that he offered.

Artano frowned.

"I would never lie to you," Diora said severely, speaking as older sister to a troublesome younger brother. "The kai Leonne did *not* kill him." Artano, never the most subtle of children, needed to hear the words. She looked at his face; at his flawless, unscarred skin. At the confusion that lay beneath the surface of his determination.

"Had my husband ordered his death," she said with gravity and, to her surprise, affection, "I would never have been given leave to offer the ablutions."

"*You* truly offered them?"

"There was no other," she said quietly. Her wrists were hidden by sleeves of silk.

"He loved you best anyway," the boy replied, overtaking, at last, the man.

"He sought to start a clan," she countered, choosing how best to use truth. "And it was not for my sake; no woman rules a clan. Had he no sons, it wouldn't have mattered."

And the man closed his eyes. Twelve, she thought. But she remembered herself at that age. "What will you do, Artano?"

She had despised him his envy, and his weakness. He had wanted his father's approval and his father's affection, and Sendari had been—she could admit it now, with his death—a poor father for a boy such as Artano. Artano was the Lord's, even if he was not yet a man.

She did not despise him now. Faced with death—and by clansmen's standards, an unpleasant death—he still stood by his singular honor, his whole desire the preservation of any debt he owed his dead. But what he said next surprised her.

"What will become of my mothers?"

"They are my mothers as well," she told him. "And if it pleases you, kai Sendari," and it hurt her, to say the name, "they might reside upon the plateau, in honor."

"Na'dio—" Alana began. But she met her daughter's face and fell silent, ashamed of her outburst. As she should be.

Artano hesitated, and then he turned to look at his mother. Diora looked away. Moments passed; the silence was broken by the awkward sound of a sword leaving its sheath. If he was Adano's kin, he was still Sendari's son; he had little skill with the blade, even for his age. "I—I will—" He held out the sword.

But he had to say the words.

"Artano," the Serra Fiona said.

"I will serve the kai Leonne." And he offered his sword to Valedan. "I will serve any man who offers my mother the protection of his name and his clan."

Valedan took the proffered sword; it was shaking in Artano's hand, the weight too heavy in all possible ways. "You are my Serra's kin," he told Artano gravely. "Her closest kin. She is my family," he added, "and I will not kill *my* own. I will take what you offer. But I will place upon it one condition."

The boy paled.

"You will offer your sword to Ser Anton di'Guivera, and he will see it trained to use. The sword, in my Court, is no idle decoration. Gain his approval," he added severely, "gain his trust, and you will serve me best."

Artano's eyes widened. Not for one such as he a swordmaster of such renown. The Serra Fiona's son hesitated for another moment, and then he turned, not to Valedan but to the Serra Diora. "Na'dio," he said, his voice breaking.

She smiled, willing him not to cry.

Promising herself that when he did, she would fail to remember it.

But he *was* a child now; it was only as a man that he had faced death with such grim acceptance, and he came from that acceptance weary and confused. The burden that he had taken upon his slender shoulders now tumbled from them as they bent, and he reached for her, as he had not done since he was four years of age.

Hate was a slippery word. It was not hate she felt as she enfolded him in her delicate, perfect arms. "He would have been proud of you, Artano. You are the first of your line."

"So, Na'tere," Yollana said quietly. "You *are* here."

The Serra Teresa looked up from her perch. The Lady's stones, pale gray in the sunlight, were her walls and her hiding place; they had no fount, but they boasted water and peace. "Matriarch," she said smoothly.

"Your niece is either brave or foolish," the Matriarch said. "That will be costly, in future."

"You see this?"

"As well as you do."

Teresa shook her head.

"Will you not greet her?"

"No. I am not here."

"And where, then, are you?"

"She is," another voice said softly, "on the open road." Kallandras of Senniel College stepped out from behind the standing stones of the Lady's statuary.

"And where will it lead her, bard?"

"To the North, Matriarch. To the North, where the bards live." He bowed to the Serra Teresa, and she met his gaze blankly. "If," he added, "she will consent to the journey." He held out his hand.

She hesitated.

"There is no home for you here," he told her gently. "And there was no home for me, when I went North. But Senniel College opened its doors and its history to one such as I; to you, Serra Teresa, it might offer more."

"I have no gift," she said stiffly.

"Not as you did, no. But the woman who commands us all was born without the voice, and I think she will find much in you of in-

terest. There is no finer hand with samisen in the South, and few
finer with the Northern lute. You are canny, and you bear responsibility as if it were a sari; it is natural to you. Will you come North,
Serra Teresa?"

She closed her eyes. And then she held out her hand, and he took
it.

He led her to the plateau, and there, he began to play. She hesitated as he sang, and then, with a hunger and a fear that she had not
yet admitted existed, she joined him, adding a hesitant harmony to
the perfection of his melody.

He raised his voice, daring her to follow; she raised hers, taking
his challenge. Finding in it a peace and a pleasure that had eluded
her. She no longer sang in public. But this once, this once she desired that right, and she took what he offered.

And Diora heard the closing strains of the almost informal
crowning: She lifted her head and looked to where the musicians
now stood. One hand played the lute, and only one, but the two
voices that rose above its flying notes were perfect, and she saw that
Ona Teresa was caught by the bard's rendition of the lay of the Sun
Sword. She wanted to join them, but she did not want to break the
delicate mood that had taken the Serra Teresa, and so she listened,
bore witness, and bowed her pretty head.

When the music died, they were gone.

But she remembered their song.

After the meal—and it was hours in length, and broken by
laughter and too much wine—she retreated to her harem. Afraid, as
she walked, of old ghosts, old whispers. Afraid of the dead.

But the living greeted her instead: Teyla en'Leonne and the smiling, wide-awake Diro. She hugged them both.

And then, she bid them leave her, and she found at last the room
in which her dead son had first found life. She sank to the ground
there, her hands flat upon mats that had been cleansed of blood.

If she cried, there were none to witness it.

Ser Valedan kai di'Leonne waited until the last of his guests had
left. And then he waited longer, while the serafs hovered above a
table that needed clearing. He nodded, to give them leave to tend
their duties, but still they waited, and he knew they would wait until
he left.

But he did not leave until a familiar woman entered the hall. She smiled, and she bowed her bronze-haired head. "Kai Leonne," she said, half formally. And then, when he did not answer, "Valedan."

"Mirialyn," he whispered. "I did not see you upon the plateau."

"I was there," she replied. "And I saw you." Her smile was gentle. "There is no courtyard here. There is no statue, no fountain, and little privacy. But what you make of the Tor will make the Arannan Halls seem the lesser place, in the end.

"The statue was called Justice," she added softly. "It was meant as an indictment. But meaning is the province of the living, and the hands that made that statue have long since ceased to make. We cannot hunt here," she added quietly. "But we can plan. I have seen Alina," she added. "And she has told me much.

"Can you be happy here?"

He hesitated, and then nodded.

"Then be happy, Valedan. Do what you must, and do as you can. We will watch, from the North. And if you are again besieged by the forces you faced in the valley, we will come."

"Will you?"

Mirialyn's smile was sad. "The city is my home. It is there that the whole of my power resides."

He shook his head. "It resides where you are. Granddaughter of Wisdom," he said softly, "what wisdom do you have to offer me?"

She shook her head. "None. And pride seems misplaced, but I am proud of what you have achieved, and of what, if I am not mistaken, you intend to achieve. Move slowly," she added, "and understand the people whose lives you will change."

He nodded. "It's . . . hard," he said. "I thought I could come here and end slavery by edict."

"Slavery knows many forms."

"I know."

She did not hug him, and she did not approach. But after a time, she said, "Hunt sometimes. Take the bow into the forests. Remember what we learned there of patience and watchfulness."

He bowed to her, to the Princess Royale of the Northern Court. He was happy to see her, but the happiness was tinged by regret.

"And go to your wife," she added. "She is a wild creature, and a dangerous one, but you have already touched her."

"I haven't—"

"In any way that matters, you have. She is young, Valedan. You are young. When you approach age and wisdom, you must learn to do so together."

He nodded, hating to lose this private moment.

But in the end, as he had so often done, he obeyed her gentle order.

No serafs were in the room; only the Serra Diora herself, and she sat, lap perfectly folded, head bowed, her back toward the fine hanging that served as either curtain or door. She could not be unaware of his presence. But he wished she could be; he was afraid to disturb her.

"Diora?" he said, when minutes had passed and she had failed to either rise or turn.

"Faida," she whispered. "Deirdre. Ruatha. We saved a child, over the course of a long night. The first time I used my gift, in front of my wives. The first risk I took."

"It wasn't the only risk."

"No," she said. He approached her perfect back, but still, he did not touch her. "You loved them. You trusted them. I am not blind," he added. "Although I do not understand it. In the North, marriage is more confined."

"In the North, women choose who they marry, and why; they choose not to marry at all, if they rule."

He nodded. And then, taking the first of his own risks, he reached out and placed a shaking hand upon her shoulder. He thought she would stiffen. He was right. But the stiffness melted into shudder and was gone. She lifted a smooth hand and placed it upon his, anchoring herself.

"I do not know that I love you," she told him.

"I know."

"But I do not know that I do not."

He said nothing.

"I failed those I loved. Always. I failed them in life, and in death—but in death, it doesn't matter, does it?"

"You failed them," he said quietly. "But your quest, in the end, saved many, many more. Have those lives no meaning to you?"

"None," she said coldly.

He shook his head, and she turned at his movement. "Had they no meaning, you would have left Teyla to die in Essla."

"I . . . couldn't. I would have—but she carried a child. I am not the wife you think I am," she added bitterly. "I am weaker now than I was. I would have let her die without a word. I watched the slaughter of the Northern hostages, and I did not lift voice or finger to aid them."

He closed his eyes. "You will never have to bear witness to such an event again," he said, with the force of vow.

"Men do not make oaths to women in the South."

"I am not of the South," he replied, "and my oaths are mine to make, and mine to uphold. I am willing to wait," he added.

"And if the waiting comes to no end?"

"I will take Teyla's son as my own."

Her brows rose. "You can't," she said flatly.

"The clan is in your hands, Serra Diora. And we are young yet. Perhaps you will find me a wife who will bear *my* sons."

"And could you take her," she said, lifting perfect jaw, exposing perfect throat, "when you could not even accept me?"

His eyes rounded. "I accepted you," he said. "As wife, in front of all of my clansmen."

"But it was not what you wanted."

"No," he said gravely. "It was not. It was not what you wanted either."

"I wanted it," she told him, honest now. The harem enclosed them. "I wanted it because through you I might achieve a vengeance I could never achieve on my own."

"And your enemies are dead."

She rose then. "Do you have no anger in you?"

He was silent.

"Do you have no pride?"

Silent again.

She lifted a hand too quickly, and he thought she might strike him; he caught her wrist as the hand drew close.

"I have pride," he said softly, her fingers inches from his lips. "I am proud of you. Of what you dared to do in Essla. Not for me, the icy steel of Serras who care nothing for the living. Not for me a strength that is determined only by the ability to see horror without flinching."

She was surprised, and she pulled her hand; he did not release it. They were standing so close their breath mingled.

It was hard to force himself to release her hand, but he did. She drew it slowly to her side.

"Do not," she said, when she saw he would speak, "speak to me of beauty. It is only another form of armor."

"It is more than that," he replied. "You are beautiful now, but not in the way you imagine. It is not the sari, it is not the gold, it is not the lilies that mark you. It is Teyla and Diro. It is your father's wives, wives whom no one else would have spoken for. It is your brother. It is the other wives whom you will bring here, in the end, to quell the sounds of your loss.

"I will wait," he told her quietly, meaning it, "forever, if I must."

"You are so very Northern," she said.

She had spoken those words before, and only those words, but these ones were bereft of ice; they were informed, instead, by a hesitant wonder. She touched his face, and he stepped back.

"I'm not—" he began.

But she caught his hand instead, and she pulled him gently to the curtains that lay at the Eastern remove of the room. Pushing them aside, she drew him into the chamber of the Tyr. It was the largest room in the harem's heart, and it was finely appointed; she had seen to this herself.

And in it, in a corner, was a familiar fountain.

His eyes rose in wonder.

"A gift," she told him. "From the Princess Royale."

The blindfolded boy. The statue named Justice.

He almost stumbled as he moved toward it, but he reached its stone rim, its flat base.

"She thought you would value it more than any others who might see it in the future," Diora said.

"I do."

"Why?"

"He taught me much, that boy. He was the angry cry of a former seraf. He was a part of the history of the man who carved him with such artistry and such sorrow. He is a reminder to me of things I must never forget."

She hesitated for another moment, and then she said, "Might I stay here?"

His jaw opened slightly in surprise. And he trembled. He could not stop himself.

"I can sleep elsewhere," he said at last. But it was hard.

She shook her head. "Stay with me," she said softly.

"Diora—"

"I cannot be wife to you yet. I was never truly wife to Ser Illara, although I shared his bed. I do not understand you, and I do not . . ." She shook her head. "No," she said, her eyes wide and soft, "I do trust you. But I do not know what that means for my wife and her son. I understood my role and my power in the war. I understood my value.

"What do they mean now?"

He put an awkward arm around her shoulder. She stiffened and then relaxed.

"It means," he told her, pulling her at last into his arms, "that I will wait forever. I will accept what you give me, and if it is only the advice of a woman who sees the Dominion clearly, it will be enough."

She bowed her head into his chest, and he held her.

And in the morning, she lay in his arms, her sari undisturbed, her cheek upon his chest. He could not sleep, but he could not disturb her sleep; she seemed young to him for the first time.

"This is what we will build, step by step," he whispered, although he knew that she slept. And he tightened his arms around her, precious burden, and he accepted that the future was not his to see, and not his to control, except in this. "You will never lose another wife. You will never lose me."

But her eyes fluttered open; she did not withdraw; she stayed against him, relaxing slowly, her breath a harmony to his silence.

In time, she would bear him children. In time, she would bring him wives. In time. For now, this was enough.

The sun set across the waters of the Tor Leonne.

Serafs toiled, but briefly, as the lamps were guttered; the guests and the witnesses had left the Lakeside, although their voices could be heard across the plateau. For three days, they would reside here, and they would drink the wine and water for which the Tor Leonne was so justly famed.

And then they would return to their Terreans, and they would plot, speaking of their losses, of the hope of future gain; a gift and a bane.

Evayne a'Nolan watched in silence, and in momentary wonder. She was not young, and she lifted her ringless hand to her hood, settling it around her neck. It was seldom that she was given moments of peace; this one was to be treasured. The path had brought her here.

And it would take her elsewhere.

As a girl, she had walked its confines, hating it; there was no hatred of it left; time had whittled it away, leaving only necessity.

Or perhaps her own gathering of power had done that; she could not say. She was not the equal of Anya a'Cooper, but she was, she thought, with a wry grimace, sane.

She wondered if that were an advantage. Her hands touched the curling, silver edges of the lone gift she had taken from the village that had once been her home, a lifetime ago. A flower, a lily of the valley, captured in delicate, etched folds, it hung upon a sturdy chain. Made for her by a man whose first calling had been war, it was her sole treasure.

Her hands shook as she lowered them; she bowed her head a moment. There was peace here.

But for Evayne, it would not last.

"So," a familiar voice said. An old woman's voice.

Evayne turned to face the Matriarch of Havalla.

"Yollana," she said, nodding.

"Have you come for this?" the Matriarch asked softly. In her hands, she held a wooden box. It was finely carved, but it was simple, and it seemed small in her hands.

Moonlight darkened the patch that covered the older woman's eye.

And Evayne was bitterly aware that even in this, she had not truly been granted peace; she had come, as always, for a reason. "Yes," she said, recognizing at last the box that Yollana bore. "I will take it."

"Have you seen it, then?"

"Not yet," she replied. "This is the first time that I have held it. But I saw the fields of Valente, and I know what it is that you harbor. It is not safe, with you," she added.

"No," Yollana replied. She dredged a pipe from the folds of her pouch and filled it. "But I've seen the Winter Lady. Will it be safe with her?"

"As safe as it can be anywhere. This tree will be the start of Summer, if it can be delivered in safety to the Summer Court."

"And you will bear it."

"I . . . do not know."

Yollana raised a brow.

"I am often the bearer of news," Evayne said, schooling her voice with care. "But I seldom choose my tasks. If I can see it in safety to that Court, I will; I have already paid the price of passage."

But of that price, Yollana did not ask. Instead, she gave the box to the seer, and she turned to the task of burning leaves.

"Will I see you again?"

"You will see me again before the end," Evayne replied, remembering.

The Matriarch cursed her. But it was a genial curse; inasmuch as she could be, Yollana of Havalla was peaceful.

Ah, peace. Denied her still by the future that unfolded in all directions, broken and fractured by the path that carried her from one time to another.

Evayne drew breath, and as her shoulders stiffened, she took a step forward.

The Tor Leonne vanished; she stood a moment in the clean, empty white of the Northern Wastes. The Northern winds were cold and bitter, and she watched in silence the twin towers of the Shining City.

MICHELLE WEST

The *Sun Sword* Novels

"Intriguing"—*Locus*
"Compelling"—*Romantic Times*

Tad Williams

THE WAR OF THE FLOWERS

"A masterpiece of fairytale worldbuilding."
—*Locus*

"Williams's imagination is boundless."
—*Publishers Weekly*
(Starred Review)

"A great introduction to an accomplished
and ambitious fantasist."
—*San Francisco Chronicle*

"An addictive world ... masterfully plays
with the tropes and traditions of
generations of fantasy writers."
—*Salon*

"A very elaborate and fully realized setting
for adventure, intrigue, and more
than an occasional chill."
—*Science Fiction Chronicle*

0-7564-0135-6

To Order Call: 1-800-788-6262

DAW 45

Tanya Huff

The Finest in Fantasy

DAW 21